SHATTER ME

TAHEREH MAFI

First published in USA in 2011 by HarperCollins Children's Books
First published in Great Britain in 2018
by Electric Monkey, part of Farshore

An imprint of HarperCollins*Publishers*
1 London Bridge Street, London SE1 9GF

farshore.co.uk

2 4 6 8 10 9 7 5 3 1

HarperCollins*Publishers*
1st Floor, Watermarque Building,
Ringsend Road, Dublin 4, Ireland

Published by arrangement with HarperCollins Children's Books, a division
of HarperCollins Publishers, New York, New York, USA

Text copyright © 2011 Tahereh Mafi

The moral rights of the author have been asserted

ISBN 978 1 4052 9175 0

YOUNG ADULT

Printed and bound in India by Thomson Press India Ltd

A CIP catalogue record for this title is available from the British Library

Typeset by Avon DataSet Ltd, Bidford on Avon, Warwickshire

Stay safe online. Any website addresses listed in this book are correct at the
time of going to print. However, Farshore is not responsible for content hosted
by third parties. Please be aware that online content can be subject to change
and websites can contain content that is unsuitable for children.
We advise that all children are supervised when using the internet.

MIX
Paper
FSC FSC™ C010615

This book is produced from independently certified FSC™ paper
to ensure responsible forest management.

Dear Reader:

The strikethroughs in the Shatter Me books are intentional. The writing in this series is occasionally as erratic as its main character, and serves as a visual representation of the chaos in Juliette's mind. The repetition, the hyperbolic language, the obsession with numbers—these are not errors on the page. As our heroine grows and evolves, so too does the prose, and as she finds her voice, the strikethroughs disappear, the language softens, the repetition dissolves, and the numerals ease into written words. This is, ultimately, a story of change. Thank you so much for reading.

ALSO BY TAHEREH MAFI

SHATTER ME SERIES:

Shatter Me

Unravel Me

Ignite Me

RESTORE ME SERIES:

Restore Me

Two roads diverged in a wood, and I—
I took the one less traveled by,
and that has made all the difference.

—ROBERT FROST, "The Road Not Taken"

ONE

I've been locked up for 264 days.

I have nothing but a small notebook and a broken pen and the numbers in my head to keep me company. 1 window. 4 walls. 144 square feet of space. 26 letters in an alphabet I haven't spoken in 264 days of isolation.

6,336 hours since I've touched another human being.

"You're getting a ~~cellmate~~ roommate," they said to me.

"~~We hope you rot to death in this place~~ For good behavior," they said to me.

"~~Another psycho just like you~~ No more isolation," they said to me.

They are the minions of The Reestablishment. The initiative that was supposed to help our dying society. The same people who pulled me out of my parents' home and locked me in an asylum for something outside of my control. No one cares that I didn't know what I was capable of. That I didn't know what I was doing.

I have no idea where I am.

I only know that I was transported by someone in a white van who drove 6 hours and 37 minutes to get me here. I know I was handcuffed to my seat. I know I was strapped to my chair. ~~I know my parents never bothered to~~

~~say good-bye.~~ I know I didn't cry as I was taken away.

I know the sky falls down every day.

The sun drops into the ocean and splashes browns and reds and yellows and oranges into the world outside my window. A million leaves from a hundred different branches dip in the wind, fluttering with the false promise of flight. The gust catches their withered wings only to force them downward, forgotten, left to be trampled by the soldiers stationed just below.

There aren't as many trees as there were before, is what the scientists say. They say our world used to be green. Our clouds used to be white. Our sun was always the right kind of light. But I have very faint memories of that world. I don't remember much from before. The only existence I know now is the one I was given. An echo of what used to be.

I press my palm to the small pane of glass and feel the cold clasp my hand in a familiar embrace. We are both alone, both existing as the absence of something else.

I grab my nearly useless pen with the very little ink I've learned to ration each day and stare at it. Change my mind. Abandon the effort it takes to write things down. Having a cellmate might be okay. Talking to a real human being might make things easier. I practice using my voice, shaping my lips around the familiar words unfamiliar to my mouth. I practice all day.

I'm surprised I remember how to speak.

I sit up on the cloth-covered springs I'm forced to sleep on. I wait. I rock back and forth and wait.

I wait too long and fall asleep.

My eyes open to 2 eyes 2 lips 2 ears 2 eyebrows.

I stifle my scream my urgency to run the crippling horror gripping my limbs.

"You're a b-b-b-b—"

"And you're a girl." He cocks an eyebrow. He leans away from my face. He grins but he's not smiling and I want to cry, my eyes desperate, terrified, darting toward the door I'd tried to open so many times I'd lost count. They locked me up with a boy. A boy.

Dear God.

They're trying to kill me.

They've done it on purpose.

To torture me, to torment me, to keep me from sleeping through the night ever again. His arms are tatted up, half sleeves to his elbows. His eyebrow is missing a ring they must've confiscated. Dark blue eyes dark brown hair sharp jawline strong lean frame. ~~Gorgeous~~ Dangerous. Terrifying. Horrible.

He laughs and I fall off my bed and scuttle into the corner.

He sizes up the meager pillow on the spare bed they shoved into the empty space this morning, the skimpy mattress and threadbare blanket hardly big enough to support his upper half. He glances at my bed. Glances at his bed.

Shoves them both together with one hand. Uses his foot to push the two metal frames to his side of the room. Stretches out across the two mattresses, grabbing my pillow to fluff up under his neck. I've begun to shake.

3

I bite my lip and try to bury myself in the dark corner.

He's stolen my bed my blanket my pillow.

I have nothing but the floor.

I will have nothing but the floor.

I will never fight back because I'm too petrified too paralyzed too paranoid.

"So you're—what? Insane? Is that why you're here?"

~~I'm not insane.~~

He props himself up enough to see my face. He laughs again. "I'm not going to hurt you."

~~I want to believe him.~~ I don't believe him.

"What's your name?" he asks.

~~None of your business. What's your name?~~

I hear his irritated exhalation of breath. I hear him turn over on the bed that used to be half mine. I stay awake all night. My knees curled up to my chin, my arms wrapped tight around my small frame, my long brown hair the only curtain between us.

I will not sleep.

I cannot sleep.

I cannot hear those screams again.

TWO

It smells like rain in the morning.

The room is heavy with the scent of wet stone, upturned soil; the air is dank and earthy. I take a deep breath and tiptoe to the window only to press my nose against the cool surface. Feel my breath fog up the glass. Close my eyes to the sound of a soft pitter-patter rushing through the wind. Raindrops are my only reminder that clouds have a heartbeat. That I have one, too.

I always wonder about raindrops.

I wonder about how they're always falling down, forgetting their parachutes as they tumble out of the sky toward an uncertain end. It's like someone is emptying their pockets over the earth and doesn't seem to care where the contents fall, doesn't seem to care that the raindrops burst when they hit the ground, that they shatter when they fall to the floor, that people curse the days the drops dare to tap on their doors.

I am a raindrop.

~~My parents emptied their pockets of me and left me to evaporate on a concrete slab.~~

The window tells me we're not far from the mountains and definitely near the water, but everything is near the water these days. I just don't know which side we're on. Which direction we're facing. I squint up at the early morning light. Someone picked up the sun and pinned it to the sky again, but every day it hangs a little lower than the day before. It's like a negligent parent who only knows one half of who you are. It never sees how its absence changes people. How different we are in the dark.

A sudden rustle means my cellmate is awake.

I spin around like I've been caught stealing food again. That only happened once and my parents didn't believe me when I said it wasn't for me. I said I was just trying to save the stray cats living around the corner but they didn't think I was human enough to care about a cat. Not me. Not ~~something~~ someone like me. But then, they never believed anything I said. That's exactly why I'm here.

Cellmate is studying me.

He fell asleep fully clothed. He's wearing a navy blue T-shirt and khaki cargo pants tucked into shin-high black boots.

I'm wearing dead cotton on my limbs and a blush of roses on my face.

His eyes scan my silhouette and the slow motion makes my heart race. I catch the rose petals as they fall from my cheeks, as they float around my body, as they cover me in something that feels like the absence of courage.

Stop looking at me, is what I want to say.

Stop touching me with your eyes and keep your hands to your sides and please and please and please—

"What's your name?" The tilt of his head cracks gravity in half.

I'm suspended in the moment. I blink and bottle my breaths.

~~He reminds me of someone I used to know.~~

"Why are you here?" I ask the cracks in the concrete wall. 14 cracks in 4 walls. The floor, the ceiling: all the same slab of stone. The pathetically constructed bed frames: built from old water pipes. The small square of a window: too thick to shatter. My hope is exhausted. My eyes are unfocused and aching. My finger is tracing a lazy path across the cold floor.

I'm sitting on the ground where it smells like ice and metal and dirt. Cellmate sits across from me, his legs folded underneath him, his boots just a little too shiny for this place.

"You're afraid of me." His voice has no shape.

"I'm afraid you're wrong."

I might be lying, but that's none of his business.

He snorts and the sound echoes in the dead air between us. I don't lift my head. My throat is tight with something familiar to me, something I've learned to swallow.

2 knocks at the door startle my emotions back into place.

He's upright in an instant.

"No one is there," I tell him. "It's just our breakfast." 264 breakfasts and I still don't know what it's made of. It smells like too many chemicals; an amorphous lump always delivered in extremes. Sometimes too sweet, sometimes too salty, always disgusting. Most of the time I'm too starved to notice the difference.

He hesitates for only an instant before edging toward the door. He slides open a small slot and peers through to a world that no longer exists.

"Shit!" He practically flings the tray through the opening, pausing only to slap his palm against his shirt. "Shit, *shit.*" He curls his fingers into a tight fist and clenches his jaw. He's burned his hand. I would've warned him if he would've listened.

"You should wait at least three minutes before touching the tray," I tell the wall. I don't look at the scars gracing my small hands, at the burn marks no one could've taught me to avoid. "I think they do it on purpose," I add quietly.

"Oh, so you're talking to me today?" He's angry. His eyes flash before he looks away and I realize he's more embarrassed than anything else. He's a tough guy. Too tough to make stupid mistakes in front of a girl. Too tough to show pain.

I press my lips together and stare out the small square of glass they call a window. There aren't many animals left, but I've heard stories of birds that fly. Maybe one day I'll get to see one. The stories are so wildly woven these days there's very little to believe, but I've heard more than one person say they've actually seen a flying bird within the past few years. So I watch the window.

There will be a bird today. It will be white with streaks

of gold like a crown atop its head. It will fly. There will be a bird today. It will be white with streaks of gold like a crown atop its head. It will fly. There will be a—

His hand.

On me.

2 tips

of 2 fingers graze my cloth-covered shoulder for less than a second and every muscle every tendon in my body is fraught with tension that clenches my spine. I don't move. I don't breathe. Maybe if I don't move, this feeling will last forever.

~~No one has touched me in 264 days.~~

Sometimes I think the loneliness inside of me is going to explode through my skin and sometimes I'm not sure if crying or screaming or laughing through the hysteria will solve anything at all. Sometimes I'm so desperate to touch to be touched *to feel* that I'm almost certain I'm going to fall off a cliff in an alternate universe where no one will ever be able to find me.

It doesn't seem impossible.

I've been screaming for years and no one has ever heard me.

"Aren't you hungry?" His voice is lower now, a little worried now.

~~I've been starving for 264 days.~~ "No." I turn and I shouldn't but I do and he's staring at me. Studying me. His lips are only barely parted, his limbs limp at his side, his lashes blinking back confusion.

9

Something punches me in the stomach.

His eyes. Something about his eyes.

~~It's not him not him not him not him not him~~.

I close the world away. Lock it up. Turn the key so tight.

"Hey—"

My eyes break open. 2 shattered windows filling my mouth with glass.

"What is it?"

~~Nothing~~.

I focus on the window between me and my freedom. I want to smash this concrete world into oblivion. I want to be bigger, better, stronger.

~~I want to be *angry angry angry*~~.

I want to be the bird that flies away.

"What are you writing?" Cellmate speaks again.

~~These words are vomit~~.

~~This shaky pen is my oesophagus~~.

~~This sheet of paper is my porcelain bowl~~.

"Why won't you answer me?" He's too close too close too close.

No one is ever close enough.

My eyes are focused on the window and the promise of what could be. The promise of something grander, something greater, some reason for the madness building in my bones, some explanation for my inability to do anything without ruining everything. There will be a bird. It will be white with streaks of gold like a crown atop its head. It will fly. There will be a bird. It will be—

"Hey—"

"You can't touch me," I whisper. I'm lying, is what I don't tell him. He can touch me, is what I'll never tell him. Please touch me, is what I want to tell him.

But things happen when people touch me. Strange things. Bad things.

Dead things.

I can't remember the warmth of any kind of embrace. My arms ache from the inescapable ice of isolation. My own mother couldn't hold me in her arms. My father couldn't warm my frozen hands. I live in a world of nothing.

Hello.

World.

You will forget me.

Knock knock.

Cellmate jumps to his feet.

It's time to shower.

THREE

The door opens to an abyss.

There's no color, no light, no promise of anything but horror on the other side. No words. No direction. Just an open door that means the same thing every time.

Cellmate has questions.

"What the hell?" He looks from me to the illusion of escape. "They're letting us out?"

~~They'll never let us out.~~ "It's time to shower."

"Shower?"

"We don't have much time," I tell him. "We have to hurry."

"Wait, what?" He reaches for my arm but I pull away. "But there's no light—we can't even see where we're going—"

"Quickly." I focus my eyes on the floor. "Take the hem of my shirt."

"What are you talking about—"

An alarm sounds in the distance. A buzzing hums closer by the second. Soon the entire cell is vibrating with the warning and the door is slipping back into place. I grab his shirt and pull him into the blackness beside me. "Don't. Say. Anything."

"Bu—"

"Nothing," I hiss. ~~It's a home, a center for troubled youth,~~ ~~for neglected children from broken families, a safe house~~ ~~for the psychologically disturbed.~~ It's a prison. They feed us nothing and our eyes never see each other except in the rare bursts of light that steal their way through cracks of glass they pretend are windows. Nights are punctured by screams and heaving sobs, wails and tortured cries, the sounds of flesh and bone breaking by force or choice I'll never know. I spent the first 3 months in the company of my own stench. No one ever told me where the bathrooms and showers were located. No one ever told me how the system worked. No one speaks to you unless they're delivering bad news. No one touches you ever at all. Boys and girls never find each other.

Never but yesterday.

It can't be coincidence.

My eyes begin to readjust in the artificial night. My fingers feel their way down the rough corridors, and Cellmate doesn't say a word. I'm almost proud of him. He's nearly a foot taller than me, his body hard and solid with the muscle and strength of someone close to my age. The world has not yet broken him.

"Wha—"

I tug on his shirt to keep him from speaking. We've not yet cleared the corridors. I feel oddly protective of him, this person who could probably break me with 2 fingers. He doesn't realize how his ignorance makes him vulnerable. He doesn't realize that they might kill him for no reason at all.

I've decided not to be afraid of him. I've decided his actions are more immature than genuinely threatening. ~~He looks so familiar so familiar so familiar to me.~~ I once knew a boy with the same blue eyes and my memories won't let me hate him.

Perhaps I'd like a friend.

6 more feet until the wall goes from rough to smooth and then we make a right. 2 feet of empty space before we reach a wooden door with a broken handle and a handful of splinters. 3 heartbeats to make certain we're alone. 1 foot forward to edge the door inward. 1 soft creak and the crack widens to reveal nothing but what I imagine this space to look like. "This way," I whisper.

I push him toward the row of showers and scavenge the floor for any bits of soap lodged in the drain. I find 2 pieces, one twice as big as the other. "Open your hand," I tell the darkness. "It's slimy. But don't drop it. There isn't much soap and we got lucky today."

He says nothing for a few seconds and I begin to worry.

"Are you still there?" I wonder if this was the trap. If this was the plan. If perhaps he was sent to kill me under the cover of darkness in this small space. I never really knew what they were going to do to me in the asylum, I never knew if they thought locking me up would be good enough but I always thought they might kill me. It always seemed like a viable option.

I can't say I wouldn't deserve it.

But I'm in here for something I never meant to do and no one seems to care that it was an accident.

~~My parents never tried to help me.~~

I hear no showers running and my heart stops. This particular room is rarely full, but there are usually others, if only 1 or 2. I've come to realize that the asylum's residents are either legitimately insane and can't find their way to the showers, or they simply don't care.

I swallow hard.

"What's your name?" he says. I can feel him breathing much closer than he was before. My heart is racing and I don't know why but I can't control it. "Why won't you tell me your name?"

"Is your hand open?"

He inches forward and I'm almost scared to breathe. His fingers graze the starchy fabric of the only outfit I'll ever own and I manage to exhale. As long as he's not touching my skin. As long as he's not touching my skin. As long as he's not touching my skin. This seems to be the secret.

My thin T-shirt has been washed in the harsh water of this building so many times it feels like a burlap sack against my skin. I drop the bigger piece of soap into his hand and tiptoe backward. "I'm going to turn the shower on for you," I explain, anxious not to raise my voice lest others should hear me.

"What do I do with my clothes?" His body is still too close to mine.

I blink in the blackness. "You have to take them off."

He laughs, amused. "No, I know. I meant what do I do with them while I shower?"

"Try not to get them wet."

He takes a deep breath. "How much time do we have?"

"Two minutes."

"Jesus, why didn't you say somethi—"

I turn on his shower at the same time I turn on my own and his complaints drown under the broken bullets of the barely functioning spigots.

My movements are mechanical. I've done this so many times I've already memorized the most efficient methods of scrubbing, rinsing, and rationing soap for my body as well as my hair. There are no towels, so the trick is trying not to soak any part of your body with too much water. If you do you'll never dry properly and you'll spend the next week nearly dying of pneumonia. I would know.

In exactly 90 seconds I've wrung my hair and I'm slipping back into my tattered outfit. My tennis shoes are the only things I own that are still in fairly good condition. We don't do much walking around here.

Cellmate follows suit almost immediately. I'm pleased he learns quickly.

"Take the hem of my shirt," I instruct him. "We have to hurry."

His fingers skim the small of my back and I have to bite

16

my lip to stifle the intensity. No one ever puts their hands anywhere near my body.

When we're finally trapped in the familiar 4 walls of claustrophobia, Cellmate won't stop staring at me.

I curl into myself in the corner. He still has my bed, my blanket, my pillow. I forgive him his ignorance, but perhaps it's too soon to be friends. Perhaps I was too hasty in helping him. Perhaps he really is only here to make me miserable. But if I don't stay warm I will get sick. My hair is too wet and the blanket I usually wrap it in is still on his side of the room. Maybe I'm still afraid of him.

I breathe in too sharply, look up too quickly in the dull light of the day. Cellmate has draped 2 blankets over my shoulders.

1 mine.

1 his.

"I'm sorry I'm such an asshole," he whispers to the wall. He doesn't touch me and I'm ~~disappointed~~ happy he doesn't. ~~I wish he would.~~ He shouldn't. No one should ever touch me.

"I'm Adam," he says slowly. He backs away from me until he's cleared the room. He uses one hand to push my bed frame back to my side of the space.

Adam.

Such a nice name. Cellmate has a nice name.

It's a name I've always liked but I can't remember why.

I waste no time climbing onto the barely concealed springs of my mattress and I'm so exhausted I can hardly feel the metal coils threatening to puncture my skin. I haven't slept in more than 24 hours. *Adam is a nice name* is the only thing I can think of before exhaustion cripples my body.

FOUR

I am not insane. I am not insane. I am not insane. I am not insane.
I am not insane. I am not insane. I am not insane. I am not insane.
I am not insane. I am not insane. I am not insane. I am not insane.
I am not insane. I am not insane. I am not insane. I am not insane.
I am not insane. I am not insane. I am not insane. I am not insane.
I am not insane. I am not insane. I am not insane. I am not insane.
I am not insane. I am not insane. I am not insane. I am not insane.
I am not insane. I am not insane. I am not insane. I am not insane.
I am not insane. I am not insane. I am not insane. I am not insane.
I am not insane. I am not insane. I am not insane. I am not insane.
I am not insane. I am not insane. I am not insane. I am not insane.
I am not insane. I am not insane. I am not insane. I am not insane.
I am not insane. I am not insane. I am not insane. I am not insane.
I am not insane. I am not insane. I am not insane. I am not insane.
I am not insane. I am not insane. I am not insane. I am not insane.
I am not insane. I am not insane. I am not insane. I am not insane.
I am not insane. I am not insane. I am not insane. I am not insane.
I am not insane. I am not insane. I am not insane. I am not insane.
I am not insane. I am not insane. I am not insane. I am not insane.
I am not insane. I am not insane. I am not insane. I am not insane.

Horror rips my eyelids open.

My body is drenched in a cold sweat, my brain swimming in unforgotten waves of pain. My eyes settle on circles of black that dissolve in the darkness. I have no idea how long I've slept. I have no idea if I've scared my cellmate with my dreams. Sometimes I scream out loud.

Adam is staring at me.

I'm breathing hard and I manage to heave myself upright. I pull the blankets closer to my body only to realize I've stolen his only means for warmth. It never even occurred to me that he might be freezing as much as I am. I'm shivering in place but his body is unflinching in the night, his silhouette a strong form against the backdrop of black. ~~I have no idea what to say.~~ There's nothing to say.

"The screams never stop in this place, do they?"

~~The screams are only the beginning.~~ "No," I whisper. A faint blush flushes my face and I'm happy it's too dark for him to notice. He must have heard my cries.

Sometimes I wish I never had to sleep. Sometimes I think that if I stay very, very still, if I never move at all, things will change. I think if I freeze myself I can freeze the pain. Sometimes I won't move for hours. I will not move an inch.

If time stands still nothing can go wrong.

"Are you okay?" His voice is concerned. I study the furrow buried in his brow, the tension in his jaw. This same person who stole my bed and my blanket is the same one who went without tonight. So cocky and careless so few hours ago; so careful and quiet right now. It scares me that this place could've broken him so quickly. I wonder what he heard while I was sleeping.

I wish I could save him from the horror.

Something shatters; a tortured cry sounds in the distance. These rooms are buried deep in concrete, walls thicker than the floors and ceilings combined to keep sounds from escaping too far. If I can hear the agony it must be insurmountable. Every night there are sounds I don't hear. Every night I wonder if I'm next.

"You're not insane."

My eyes snap up. His head is cocked, his eyes focused and clear despite the shroud that envelops us. He takes a deep breath. "I thought everyone in here was insane," he continues. "I thought they'd locked me up with a psycho."

I take a sharp hit of oxygen. "Funny. So did I."

1

2

3 seconds pass.

He cracks a grin so wide, so amused, so refreshingly sincere it's like a clap of thunder through my body. Something pricks at my eyes. I haven't seen a smile in 265 days.

Adam is on his feet.

I offer him his blanket.

He takes it only to wrap it more tightly around my body and something is suddenly constricting in my chest. My lungs are skewered and strung together and I've just decided not to move for an eternity when he speaks.

"What's wrong?"

~~My parents stopped touching me when I was old enough~~

to crawl. ~~Teachers made me work alone so I wouldn't hurt~~ ~~the other children. I've never had a friend. I've never known~~ ~~the comfort of a mother's hug. I've never felt the tenderness~~ ~~of a father's kiss. I'm not insane.~~ "Nothing."

5 more seconds. "Can I sit next to you?"

~~That would be wonderful.~~ "No." I'm staring at the wall again.

He clenches and unclenches his jaw. He runs a hand through his hair and I realize for the first time that he's not wearing a shirt. It's so dark in this room I can only catch his curves and contours; the moon is allowed only a small window to light this space but I watch as the muscles in his arms tighten with every movement. Every inch of his body is raw with power, every surface somehow luminous in the darkness. In 17 years I've never seen anything like him. In 17 years I've never talked to a boy my own age. ~~Because I'm a monster.~~

I close my eyes.

I hear the creak of his bed, the groan of the springs as he sits down. I unstitch my eyes and study the floor. "You must be freezing."

"No." A strong sigh. "I'm actually burning up."

I'm on my feet so quickly the blankets fall to the floor. "Are you sick?" My eyes scan his face for signs of a fever but I don't dare inch closer. "Do you feel dizzy? Do your joints hurt?" I try to remember my own symptoms. I was chained to my bed by my own body for 1 week. I could do nothing more than crawl to the door and fall face-first into my food.

I don't even know how I survived.

"What's your name?"

He's asked the same question 3 times already. "You might be sick," is all I can say.

"I'm not sick. I'm just hot. I don't usually sleep with my clothes on."

Butterflies catch fire in my stomach. I don't know where to look.

A deep breath. "I was a jerk yesterday. I treated you like crap and I'm sorry. I shouldn't have done that."

I meet his gaze.

His eyes are the perfect shade of cobalt, blue like a blossoming bruise, clear and deep and decided. He's been thinking about this all night.

"Okay."

"So why won't you tell me your name?" He leans forward and I freeze.

I thaw.

"Juliette," I whisper. "My name is Juliette."

His lips soften into a smile. He repeats my name like the word amuses him. Entertains him. Delights him.

~~In 17 years no one has said my name like that.~~

FIVE

I don't know when it started.

I don't know why it started.

I don't know anything about anything except for the screaming.

My mother screaming when she realized she could no longer touch me. My father screaming when he realized what I'd done to my mother. My parents screaming when they'd lock me in my room and tell me I should be grateful. For their food. For their humane treatment of this thing that could not possibly be their child. For the yardstick they used to measure the distance I needed to keep away.

I ruined their lives, is what they said to me.

I stole their happiness. Destroyed my mother's hope for ever having children again.

Couldn't I see what I'd done, is what they'd ask me. Couldn't I see that I'd ruined everything.

I tried so hard to fix what I'd ruined. I tried every single day to be what they wanted. I tried all the time to be better but I never really knew how.

I only know now that the scientists are wrong.

The world is flat.

I know because I was tossed right off the edge and I've been trying to hold on for 17 years. I've been trying to climb back up for 17 years but it's nearly impossible to beat gravity when no one is willing to give you a hand.

When no one wants to risk touching you.

It's snowing today.

The concrete is icy and stiffer than usual, but I prefer these freezing temperatures to the stifling humidity of summer days. Summer is like a slow-cooker bringing everything in the world to a boil 1 degree at a time. I hate the heat and the sticky, sweaty mess left behind. I hate the sun, too preoccupied with itself to notice the infinite hours we spend in its presence. The sun is an arrogant thing, always leaving the world behind when it tires of us.

The moon is a loyal companion.

It never leaves. It's always there, watching, steadfast, knowing us in our light and dark moments, changing forever just as we do. Every day it's a different version of itself. Sometimes weak and wan, sometimes strong and full of light. The moon understands what it means to be human.

Uncertain. Alone. Cratered by imperfections.

I stare out the window for so long I forget myself. I hold out my hand to catch a snowflake and my fist closes around the icy air. Empty.

I want to put this fist attached to my wrist right through the window.

Just to feel something.

Just to feel human.

"What time is it?"

His voice pulls me back down to a world I keep trying to forget. "I don't know," I tell him. I have no idea what time it is. I have no idea which day of the week it is, what month we're in, or even if there's a specific season we're supposed to be in.

We don't really have seasons anymore.

The animals are dying, birds don't fly, crops are hard to come by, flowers almost don't exist. The weather is unreliable. Sometimes our winter days hit 92 degrees. Sometimes it snows for no reason at all. We can't grow enough food anymore, we can't sustain enough vegetation for the animals anymore, and we can't feed the people what they need. Our population was dying off at an alarming rate before The Reestablishment took over and they promised us they had a solution. Animals were so desperate for food they were willing to eat anything and people were so desperate for food they were willing to eat poisoned animals. We were killing ourselves by trying to stay alive. The weather, the plants, the animals, and our human survival are all inextricably linked. The natural elements were at war with one another because we abused our ecosystem. Abused our atmosphere. Abused our animals. Abused our fellow man.

The Reestablishment promised they would fix things. But even though human health has found a modicum of relief under the new regime, more people have died at the end of a loaded gun than from an empty stomach. It's progressively getting worse.

"Juliette?"

My head snaps up.

His eyes are wary, worried, analyzing me.

I look away.

He clears his throat. "So, uh, they only feed us once a day?"

His question sends both our eyes toward the small slot in the door.

I curl my knees to my chest and balance my bones on the mattress. If I hold myself very, very still, I can almost ignore the metal digging into my skin. "There's no system to the food," I tell him. My finger traces a new pattern down the rough material of the blanket. "There's usually something in the morning, but there are no guarantees for anything else. Sometimes . . . we get lucky." I glance out the window. Pinks and reds filter into the room and I know it's the start of a new beginning. The start of the same end. Another day.

~~Maybe I will die today.~~

Maybe a bird will fly today.

"So that's it? They open the door once a day for people to do their business and maybe if we're *lucky* they feed us? That's it?"

The bird will be white with streaks of gold like a crown atop its head. It will fly. "That's it."

"There's no . . . group therapy?" He almost laughs.

"Until you arrived, I hadn't spoken a single word in two hundred sixty-four days."

27

His silence says so much. I can almost reach out and touch the guilt growing on his shoulders. "How long are you in for?" he finally asks.

~~Forever.~~ "I don't know." A mechanical sound creaks/groans/cranks in the distance. My life is 4 walls of missed opportunities poured into concrete molds.

"What about your family?" There's a serious sorrow in his voice, almost like he already knows the answer to that question.

~~Here is what I know about my parents: I have no idea where they are.~~ "Why are you here?" I talk to my fingers to avoid his gaze. I've studied my hands so thoroughly I know exactly where each bump cut and bruise has ravaged my skin. Small hands. Slim fingers. I curl them into a fist and release them to lose the tension. He still hasn't responded.

I look up.

"I'm not insane," is all he says.

"That's what we all say." I cock my head only to shake it a fraction of an inch. I bite my lip. My eyes can't help but steal glances out the window.

"Why do you keep looking outside?"

I don't mind his questions, I really don't. It's just strange to have someone to talk to. It's strange to have to move my lips to form words necessary to explain my actions. No one has cared for so long. No one's watched me closely enough to wonder why I stare out a window. No one has ever treated me like an equal. Then again, he doesn't know

~~I'm a monster~~ my secret. I wonder how long this will last before he's running for his life.

I've forgotten to answer and he's still studying me.

I tuck a piece of hair behind my ear only to change my mind. "Why do you stare so much?"

His eyes are careful, curious. "I figured the only reason they would lock me up with a girl was because you were crazy. I thought they were trying to torture me by putting me in the same space as a psychopath. I thought you were my punishment."

"That's why you stole my bed." To exert power. To stake a claim. To fight first.

He looks away. Clasps and unclasps his hands before rubbing the back of his neck. "Why'd you help me? How'd you know I wouldn't hurt you?"

I count my fingers to make sure they're still there. "I didn't."

"You didn't help me or you didn't know if I'd hurt you?"

"Adam." My lips curve around the shape of his name. I'm surprised to discover how much I love the easy, familiar way the sound rolls off my tongue.

He's sitting almost as still as I am. "Yeah?"

"What's it like?" I ask, each word quieter than the one before. "Outside?" ~~In the real world.~~ "Is it worse?"

It takes him a few heartbeats to answer. "Honestly? I'm not sure if it's better to be in here or out there."

I wait for his lips to part; I wait for him to explain. And then I try to pay attention as his words bounce around

29

in the haze of my head, fogging my senses, clouding my concentration.

Did you know it was an international movement? Adam asks me.

No I did not, I tell him. I do not tell him I was dragged from my home 3 years ago. I do not tell him that I was dragged away exactly 7 years after The Reestablishment began to preach and 4 months after they took control of everything. I do not tell him how little I know of our new world.

Adam says The Reestablishment had its hands in every country, ready for the moment to bring its leaders into a position of control. He says the inhabitable land left in the world has been divided into 3,333 sectors and each space is now controlled by a different Person of Power.

Did you know they lied to us? Adam asks me.

Did you know that The Reestablishment said someone had to take control, that someone had to save society, that someone had to restore the peace? Did you know that they said killing all the voices of opposition was the only way to find peace?

Did you know this? is what Adam asks me.

And this is where I nod. This is where I say yes.

This is the part I remember: The anger. The riots. The rage.

My eyes close in an effort to block out the bad memories, but the effort backfires. Protests. Rallies. Screams for survival. I see women and children starving to death, homes destroyed and buried in rubble, the countryside a burnt landscape, its only fruit the rotting flesh of casualties.

I see dead dead dead red and burgundy and maroon and the richest shade of your mother's favorite lipstick all smeared into the earth.

So much everything all the things dead.

The Reestablishment is struggling to maintain its hold over the people, Adam says. He says The Reestablishment is struggling to fight a war against the rebels who will not acquiesce to this new regime. The Reestablishment is struggling to root itself as a new form of government across all international societies.

And then I wonder what has happened to the people I used to see every day. What's become of their homes, their parents, their children. I wonder how many of them have been buried in the ground.

How many of them were murdered.

"They're destroying everything," Adam says, and his voice is suddenly solemn. "All the books, every artifact, every remnant of human history. They're saying it's the only way to fix things. They say we need to start fresh. They say we can't make the same mistakes of previous generations."

2

knocks

at the door and we're both on our feet, abruptly startled back into this bleak world.

Adam raises an eyebrow at me. "Breakfast?"

"Wait three minutes," I remind him. We're so good at masking our hunger until the knocks at the door cripple our dignity.

They starve us on purpose.

"Yeah." His lips are set in a soft smile. "I wouldn't want to burn myself." The air shifts as he steps forward.

I am a statue.

"I still don't understand," he says, so quietly. "Why are you here?"

"Why do you ask so many questions?"

He leaves less than a foot of space between us and I'm 10 inches away from spontaneous combustion. "Your eyes are so deep." He tilts his head. "So calm. I want to know what you're thinking."

"You shouldn't." My voice falters. "You don't even know me."

He laughs and the action gives life to the light in his eyes. "I don't know you."

"No."

He shakes his head. Sits on his bed. "Right. Of course not."

"What?"

"You're right." His breath catches. "Maybe I am insane."

I take 2 steps backward. "Maybe you are."

He's smiling again and I'd like to take a picture. I'd like to stare at the curve of his lips for the rest of my life. "I'm not, you know."

"But you won't tell me why you're here," I challenge.

"And neither will you."

I fall to my knees and tug the tray through the slot. Something unidentifiable is steaming in 2 tin cups. Adam folds himself onto the floor across from me.

"Breakfast," I say as I push his portion forward.

SIX

1 word, 2 lips, 3 4 5 fingers form 1 fist.

1 corner, 2 parents, 3 4 5 reasons to hide.

1 child, 2 eyes, 3 4 17 years of fear.

A broken broomstick, a pair of wild faces, angry whispers, locks on my door.

Look at me, is what I wanted to say to you. Talk to me every once in a while. Find me a cure for these tears, I'd really like to exhale for the first time in my life.

It's been 2 weeks.

2 weeks of the same routine, 2 weeks of nothing but routine. 2 weeks with the cellmate ~~who has come too close to touching me~~ who does not touch me. Adam is adapting to the system. He never complains, he never volunteers too much information, he continues to ask too many questions.

He's nice to me.

I sit by the window and watch the rain and the leaves and the snow collide. They take turns dancing in the wind, performing choreographed routines for unsuspecting masses. The soldiers stomp stomp stomp through the rain, crushing leaves and fallen snow under their feet. Their hands are wrapped in gloves wrapped around guns that could put a bullet through a million possibilities. They don't bother to be bothered by the beauty that falls from the sky. They don't understand the freedom in feeling the universe on their skin. They don't care.

I wish I could stuff my mouth full of raindrops and fill my pockets full of snow. I wish I could trace the veins in a fallen leaf and feel the wind pinch my nose.

Instead, I ignore the desperation sticking my fingers together and watch for the bird I've only seen in my dreams. Birds used to fly, is what the stories say. Before the ozone layer deteriorated, before the pollutants mutated the creatures into something ~~horrible~~ different. They say the weather wasn't always so unpredictable. They say there were birds who used to soar through the skies like planes.

It seems strange that a small animal could achieve anything as complex as human engineering, but the possibility is too enticing to ignore. I've dreamt about the same bird flying through the same sky for exactly 10 years. White with streaks of gold like a crown atop its head.

It's the only dream I have that gives me peace.

"What are you writing?"

I squint up at his strong stature, the easy grin on his face. I don't know how he manages to smile in spite of everything. I wonder if he can hold on to that shape, that special curve of the mouth that changes lives. I wonder how he'll feel in 1 month and I shudder at the thought.

I don't want him to end up like me.

Empty.

"Hey—" He grabs the blanket off my bed and crouches next to me, wasting no time wrapping the thin cloth around my thinner shoulders. "You okay?"

I try to smile. "Thank you for the blanket."

He sits down next to me and leans against the wall. His shoulders are so close too close ~~never close enough~~. His body heat does more for me than the blanket ever will. Something in my joints aches with an acute yearning, a desperate need I've never been able to fulfill. My bones are begging for something I cannot allow.

~~Touch me~~.

He glances at the little notebook tucked in my hand, at the broken pen clutched in my fist. I know he's staring at me.

"Are you writing a book?"

"No."

"Maybe you should."

I turn to meet his eyes and regret it immediately. There are less than 3 inches between us and I can't move because my body only knows how to freeze. Every muscle every movement tightens, every vertebra in my spinal column is a block of ice. I'm holding my breath and my eyes are wide, locked, caught in the intensity of his gaze. I can't look away. I don't know how to retreat.

Oh.

God.

His eyes.

I've been lying to myself, determined to deny the impossible.

I know him I know him I know him I know him

The boy ~~who does not remember~~ me I used to know.

"They're going to destroy the English language," he says, his voice careful, quiet.

I fight to catch my breath.

"They want to re-create everything," he continues. "They want to redesign everything. They want to destroy anything that could've been the reason for our problems. They think we need a new, universal language." He drops his voice. Drops his eyes. "They want to destroy everything. Every language in history."

"No." My breath hitches. Spots cloud my vision.

"I know."

"No." This I did not know.

He looks up. "It's good that you're writing things down. One day what you're doing will be illegal."

I've begun to shake. My body is suddenly fighting a maelstrom of emotions, my brain plagued by the world I'm losing and pained by this boy who does not remember me. The pen stumbles its way to the floor and I'm gripping the blanket so hard I'm afraid it's going to tear. I never thought it would get this bad. I never thought The Reestablishment would take things so far. They're incinerating culture, the beauty of diversity. The new citizens of our world will be reduced to nothing but numbers, easily interchangeable, easily removable, easily destroyed for disobedience.

We have lost our humanity.

I wrap the blanket around my shoulders but the tremors won't stop. I'm horrified by my lack of self-control. I can't make myself still.

His hand is suddenly on my back.

His touch is scorching my skin through the layers of fabric and I'm caught, so desperate ~~so desperate so desperate~~ to be close so desperate to be far away. I don't know how to move away from him. ~~I don't want to move away from him.~~

I don't want him to be afraid of me.

"Hey." His voice is soft so soft so soft. He pulls my swaddled figure close to his chest and his heat melts the icicles propping me up from the inside out and I thaw I thaw I thaw, my eyes fluttering fast until they fall closed, until silent tears are streaming down my face and I've decided the only thing I want to freeze is his frame holding mine. "It's okay," he whispers. "You'll be okay."

Truth is a jealous, vicious mistress that never ever sleeps, is what I don't tell him. I'll never be okay.

It takes every broken filament in my being to pull away from him. I do it because I have to. ~~Because it's for his own good.~~ The blanket catches my foot and I nearly fall before Adam reaches out to me again. "Juliette—"

"You can't t-touch me." My breathing is shallow and hard to swallow, my fingers shaking so fast I clench them into a fist. "You can't touch me. You can't." My eyes are trained on the door.

He's on his feet. "Why not?"

"You just can't," I whisper to the walls.

"I don't understand—why won't you talk to me? You sit in the corner all day and write in your book and look at everything but my face. You have so much to say to a piece of paper but I'm standing right here and you don't even acknowledge me. Juliette, *please*—" He reaches for my arm and I turn away. "Why won't you at least *look* at me? I'm not going to hurt you—"

~~You don't remember me. You don't remember that we went to the same school for 7 years.~~

You don't remember me.

"You don't know me." My voice is even, flat; my limbs numb, amputated. "We've shared one space for two weeks and you think you know me but you don't know anything about me. Maybe I *am* crazy."

"You're not," he says through clenched teeth. "You *know* you're not."

"Then maybe it's you," I say carefully, slowly. "Because one of us is."

"That's not true—"

"Tell me why you're here, Adam. What are you doing in an insane asylum if you don't belong here?"

"I've been asking you the same question since I got here."

"Maybe you ask too many questions."

I hear his hard exhalation of breath. He laughs a bitter laugh. "We're practically the only two people who are *alive* in this place and you want to shut me out, too?"

I close my eyes and focus on breathing. "You can talk to me. Just don't touch me."

"Maybe I want to touch you."

I'm tempted by recklessness, desperate for what I can never have. I turn my back on him but I can't keep the lies from spilling out of my lips. "Maybe I don't want you to."

He makes a harsh sound. "I disgust you that much?"

I spin around, so caught off guard by his words I forget myself. He's staring at me, his face hard, his jaw set, his fingers flexing by his sides. His eyes are 2 buckets of rainwater: deep, fresh, clear.

Hurt.

"You don't know what you're talking about."

"You can't just answer a simple question, can you?" he says. He shakes his head and turns to the wall.

My face is cast in a neutral mold, my arms and legs filled with plaster. I feel nothing. I am nothing. I am empty of everything I will never move. I'm staring at a small crack near my shoe. I will stare at it forever.

The blankets fall to the floor. The world fades out of focus, my ears outsource every sound to another dimension. My eyes close, my thoughts drift, my memories kick me in the heart.

I know him.

I've tried so hard to stop thinking about him.
I've tried so hard to forget his face.

I've tried so hard to get those blue blue blue eyes out of my head but I know him I know him I know him it's been 3 years since I last saw him.

I could never forget Adam.

But he's already forgotten me.

SEVEN

I remember televisions and fireplaces and porcelain sinks. I remember movie tickets and parking lots and SUVs. I remember hair salons and holidays and window shutters and dandelions and the smell of freshly paved driveways. I remember toothpaste commercials and ladies in high heels and old men in business suits. I remember mailmen and libraries and boy bands and balloons and Christmas trees.

I remember being 10 years old when we couldn't ignore the food shortages anymore and things got so expensive no one could afford to live.

Adam is not speaking to me.

Maybe it's for the best. Maybe there was no point hoping he and I could be friends, maybe it's better he thinks I don't like him than that I like him too much. He's hiding a lot of something that might be pain, but his secrets scare me. He won't tell me why he's here. Though I don't tell him much, either.

~~And yet and yet and yet.~~

Last night the memory of his arms around me was enough to scare away the screams. The warmth of a kind embrace, the strength of firm hands holding all of my pieces together, the relief and release of so many years' loneliness. This gift he's given me I can't repay.

Touching Juliette is nearly impossible.

I'll never forget the horror in my mother's eyes, the torture in my father's face, the fear etched in their expressions. Their child ~~was~~ is a monster. Possessed by the devil. Cursed by darkness. Unholy. An abomination. Drugs, tests, medical solutions failed. Psychological cross-examinations failed.

She is a walking weapon in society, is what the teachers said. *We've never seen anything like it,* is what the doctors said. *She should be removed from your home,* is what the police officers said.

~~No problem at all, is what my parents said.~~ I was 14 years old when they finally got rid of me. When they stood back and watched as I was dragged away for a murder I didn't know I could commit.

Maybe the world is safer with me locked in a cell. Maybe Adam is safer if he hates me. He's sitting in the corner with his fists in his face.

I never wanted to hurt him.

I never wanted to hurt the only person who never wanted to hurt me.

The door crashes open and 5 people swarm into the room, rifles pointed at our chests.

Adam is on his feet and I'm made of stone. I've forgotten to inhale. I haven't seen so many people in so long I'm momentarily stupefied. I should be screaming.

"HANDS UP, FEET APART, MOUTHS SHUT. DON'T MOVE AND WE WON'T SHOOT YOU."

I'm still frozen in place. I should move, I should lift my arms, I should spread my feet, I should remember to breathe.

The one barking orders slams the butt of his gun into my back and my knees crack as they hit the floor. I finally taste oxygen and a side of blood. I think Adam is yelling but there is an acute agony ripping through my body unlike anything I've experienced before. I'm immobilized.

"What don't you understand about keeping your mouth SHUT?" I squint sideways to see the barrel of the gun 2 inches away from Adam's face.

"GET UP." A steel-toed boot kicks me in the ribs, fast, hard, hollow. "I said GET UP." Harder, faster, stronger, another boot in my gut. I can't even cry out.

~~Get up, Juliette. Get up. If you don't, they'll shoot Adam.~~

I heave myself up to my knees and fall back on the wall behind me, stumbling forward to catch my balance. Lifting my hands is more torture than I knew I could endure. My skin is a sieve, punctured by pins and needles of pain. They've finally come to kill me.

That's why they put Adam in my cell.

Because I'm leaving. Adam is here because I'm leaving, because they forgot to kill me on time, because my moments are over, because my 17 years were too many for this world. They're going to kill me.

I always wondered how it would happen. ~~I wonder if this~~

~~will make my parents happy.~~

Someone is laughing. "Well aren't you a little shit?"

I don't even know if they're talking to me. I can hardly focus on keeping my arms upright.

"She's not even crying," someone adds.

The walls are beginning to bleed into the ceiling. I wonder how long I can hold my breath. I can't distinguish words I can't understand the sounds I'm hearing the blood is rushing through my head and my lips are 2 blocks of concrete I can't crack open. There's a gun in my back and I'm tripping forward. The floors are falling up. My feet are dragging in a direction I can't decipher.

I hope they kill me soon.

EIGHT

It takes me 2 days to open my eyes.

There's a tin of water and a tin of food set off to the side and I inhale the cold contents with trembling hands, a dull ache creaking through my bones. Nothing seems to be broken, but one glance under my shirt proves the pain was real. The bruises are discolored blossoms of blue and yellow, torture to touch and slow to heal.

Adam is nowhere.

I am alone in a block of solitude, 4 walls no more than 10 feet in every direction, the only air creeping in through a small slot in the door. I've just begun to terrorize myself with my imagination when the heavy metal door slams open. A guard with 2 rifles strung across his chest looks me up and down.

"Get up."

This time I don't hesitate.

I hope Adam, at least, is safe. I hope he doesn't come to the same end I do.

"Follow me." The guard's voice is thick and deep, his gray eyes unreadable. He looks about 25 years old, blond hair cropped close to the crown, shirtsleeves rolled up to his shoulders, military tattoos snaking up his forearms just like Adam's.

Oh.

God.

No.

Adam steps into the doorway beside the blond and gestures with his weapon toward a narrow hallway. "Move."

~~Adam is pointing a gun at my chest.~~

~~Adam is pointing a gun at my chest.~~

Adam is pointing a gun at my chest.

His eyes are foreign to me, glassy and distant, far, far away.

I am nothing but novocaine. I am numb, a world of nothing, all feeling and emotion gone forever.

I am a whisper that never was.

Adam is a soldier. ~~Adam wants me to die.~~

I stare at him openly now, every sensation amputated.

Death would be a welcome release from these earthly joys I've known.

I don't know how long I've been walking before another blow to my back cripples me. I blink against the brightness of light I haven't seen in so long. My eyes begin to tear and I'm squinting against the fluorescent bulbs illuminating the large space. I can hardly see anything.

"Juliette Ferrars." A voice detonates my name. There's a heavy boot pressed into my back and I can't lift my head to distinguish who's speaking to me. "Weston, dim the lights and release her. I want to see her face." The command is cool and strong like steel, dangerously calm, effortlessly powerful.

The brightness is reduced to a level I'm able to tolerate. The imprint of a boot is stamped into my back but no longer settled on my skin. I lift my head and look up.

I'm immediately struck by his youth. He can't be much older than me.

It's obvious he's in charge of something, though I have no idea what. His skin is flawless, unblemished, his jawline sharp and strong. His eyes are the palest shade of emerald I've ever seen.

He's beautiful.

His crooked smile is calculated evil.

He's sitting on what he imagines to be a throne but is nothing more than a folding chair at the front of an empty room. His suit is perfectly pressed, his blond hair expertly combed, his soldiers the ideal bodyguards.

I hate him.

"You're so stubborn." His green eyes are almost translucent. "You never want to cooperate. You wouldn't even play nice with your cellmate."

I flinch without intending to. The burn of betrayal blushes up my neck.

Green Eyes looks unexpectedly amused and I'm suddenly mortified. "Well isn't that interesting." He snaps his fingers. "Kent, would you step forward, please."

My heart stops beating when Adam comes into view. ~~Kent. His name is Adam Kent.~~

Adam flanks Green Eyes in an instant, but only offers a curt nod of his head as a salute. Perhaps the leader isn't

47

nearly as important as he thinks.

"Sir," he says.

I should've known.

I'd heard rumors of soldiers living among the public in secret, reporting to the authorities if things seemed suspicious. Every day people disappeared. No one ever came back.

Though I still can't understand why Adam was sent to spy on me.

"It seems you made quite an impression on her."

I squint closer at the man in the chair only to realize his suit has been adorned with tiny colored patches. Military mementos. His last name is etched into the lapel: Warner.

Adam says nothing. He doesn't look in my direction. His body is erect, 6 feet of ~~gorgeous~~ lean muscle, his profile strong and steady. The same arms that held my body are now holsters for lethal weapons.

"You have nothing to say about that?" Warner glances at Adam only to tilt his head in my direction, his eyes dancing in the light, clearly entertained.

Adam clenches his jaw. "Sir."

"Of course." Warner is suddenly bored. "Why should I expect you to have something to say?"

"Are you going to kill me?" The words escape my lips before I have a chance to think them through and someone's gun slams into my spine all over again. I fall with a broken whimper, wheezing into the filthy floor.

"That wasn't necessary, Roland. I suppose I'd be

wondering the same thing if I were in her position." A pause. "Juliette?"

I manage to lift my head.

"I have a proposition for you."

NINE

I'm not sure I'm hearing him correctly.

"You have something I want." Warner is still staring at me.

"I don't understand," I tell him.

He takes a deep breath and stands up to pace the length of the room. Adam has not yet been dismissed. "You are kind of a pet project of mine. I've studied your records for a very long time."

"What?"

"We're in the middle of a *war*," he says a little impatiently. "Maybe you can put the pieces together."

"I don't—"

"I know your secret, Juliette. I know why you're in here. Your entire life is documented in hospital records, complaints to authorities, messy lawsuits, public demands to have you locked up." His pause gives me enough time to choke on the horror caught in my throat. "I'd been considering it for a long time, but I wanted to make sure you weren't *actually* psychotic. Isolation wasn't exactly a good indicator, though you did fend for yourself quite well." He offers me a smile that says I should be grateful for his praise. "I sent Kent to stay with you as a final precaution.

I wanted to make sure you weren't volatile, that you were capable of basic human interaction and communication. I must say I'm quite pleased with the results.

"Kent, it seems, played his part a little too excellently. He is a fine soldier. One of the best, in fact." Warner spares him a glance before smiling at me. "But don't worry, he doesn't know what you're capable of. Not yet, anyway."

I claw at the panic, I swallow the agony, I beg myself not to look in his direction but I fail ~~I fail I fail~~. Adam meets my eyes in the same split second I meet his but he looks away so quickly I'm not sure if I imagined it.

~~I am a monster.~~

"I'm not as cruel as you think," Warner continues, a musical lilt in his voice. "If you're so fond of his company I can make this"—he gestures between myself and Adam—"a permanent assignment."

"No," I breathe.

Warner curves his lips into a careless grin. "Oh yes. But be careful, pretty girl. If you do something . . . *bad* . . . he'll have to shoot you."

Adam doesn't react to anything Warner says.

He is doing a job.

I am a number, a mission, an easily replaceable object; I am not even a memory in his mind.

I didn't expect his betrayal to bury me so deep.

"If you accept my offer," Warner interrupts my thoughts, "you will live like I do. You will be one of *us*, and not one of *them*. Your life will change forever."

"And if I do not accept?" I ask.

Warner looks genuinely disappointed. His hands are clasped together in dismay. "You don't really have a choice. If you stand by my side you will be rewarded." He presses his lips together. "But if you choose to disobey? Well . . . I think you look rather lovely with all your body parts intact, don't you?"

I'm breathing so hard my frame is shaking. "You want me to torture people for you?"

His face breaks into a brilliant smile. "That would be wonderful."

I don't have time to form a response before he turns to Adam. "Show her what she's missing, would you?"

Adam answers a beat too late. "Sir?"

"That is an order, soldier." Warner's eyes are trained on me, his lips twitching with suppressed amusement. "I'd like to break this one. She's a little too feisty for her own good."

"You can't touch me," I spit through clenched teeth.

"Wrong," he singsongs. He tosses Adam a pair of black gloves. "You're going to need these," he says with a conspiratorial whisper.

"You're a monster." My voice is too even, my body filled with a sudden rage. "Why don't you just *kill* me?"

"That, my dear, would be a waste." He steps forward and I realize his hands are sheathed in white leather gloves. He tips my chin up with one finger. "Besides, it'd be a shame to lose such a pretty face."

I try to snap my neck away from him but the same steel-toed boot slams into my spine and Warner catches my face in his grip. I suppress a scream. "Don't struggle, love. You'll only make things more difficult for yourself."

"I hope you rot in hell."

Warner flexes his jaw. He holds up a hand to stop someone from shooting me, kicking me in the spleen, cracking my skull open, I have no idea. "You're a fighter for the wrong team." He stands up straight. "But we can change that. Kent," he calls. "Don't let her out of your sight. She's your charge now."

"Yes, sir."

TEN

Adam puts on the gloves but he doesn't touch me. "Let her up, Roland. I'll take it from here."

The boot disappears. I struggle to my feet and stare at nothing. I won't think about the horror that awaits me. Someone kicks in the backs of my knees and I nearly stumble to the ground. "Get *going*," a voice growls from behind. I look up and realize Adam is already walking away. I'm supposed to be following him.

Only once we're back in the familiar blindness of the asylum hallways does he stop walking.

"Juliette."

I don't answer him.

"Take my hand," he says.

"I will never. Not ever."

A heavy sigh. I feel him shift in the darkness and soon his body is too close to mine. His hand is on my lower back and he's guiding me through the corridors toward an unknown destination.

The distance we're walking is much longer than I expected. When Adam finally speaks I suspect we're close to the end. "We're going to go outside," he says near my ear and I'm almost too distracted by the feel of his voice to understand the significance of what he's saying. "I just thought you should know."

An audible intake of breath is my only response. I haven't been outside in almost a year. I'm painfully excited but I haven't felt natural light on my skin in so long I don't know if I'll be able to handle it. I have no choice.

The air hits me first.

Our atmosphere has little to boast of, but after so many months in a concrete corner even the wasted oxygen of our dying Earth tastes like heaven. I can't inhale fast enough. I fill my lungs with the feeling; I step into the slight breeze and clutch a fistful of wind as it weaves its way through my fingers.

Bliss unlike anything I've ever known.

The air is crisp and cool. A refreshing bath of tangible nothing that stings my eyes and snaps at my skin. The sun is high today, blinding as it reflects the small patches of snow keeping the earth frozen. My eyes are pressed down by the weight of the bright light and I can't see through more than two slits, but the warm rays wash over my body like a jacket fitted to my form, like the hug of something greater than a human. I could stand still in this moment forever. For one infinite second I feel free.

Adam's touch shocks me back to reality. I nearly jump out of my skin and he catches my waist. I have to beg my bones to stop shaking. "Are you okay?" His eyes surprise me. They're the same ones I remember, blue and bottomless like the deepest part of the ocean. His hands are ~~gentle so gentle~~ around me.

"I don't want you to touch me," I lie.

55

"You don't have a choice." He won't look at me.

"I always have a choice."

He runs a hand through his hair and swallows the nothing in his throat. "Follow me."

We're in a blank space, an empty acre filled with dead leaves and dying trees taking small sips from melted snow in the soil. The landscape has been ravaged by war and neglect and it's still the most beautiful thing I've seen in so long. The stomping soldiers stop to watch as Adam opens a car door for me.

It's not a car. It's a tank.

I stare at the massive metal body and attempt to climb my way up the side when Adam is suddenly behind me. He hoists me up by the waist and I gasp as he settles me into the seat.

Soon we're driving in silence and I have no idea where we're headed.

I'm staring out the window at everything.

I'm eating and drinking and absorbing every infinitesimal detail in the debris, in the skyline, in the abandoned homes and broken pieces of metal and glass sprinkled in the scenery. The world looks naked, stripped of vegetation and warmth. There are no street signs, no stop signs; there is no need for either. There is no public transportation. Everyone knows that cars are now manufactured by only one company and sold at a ridiculous rate.

Very few people are allowed a means of escape.

~~My parents~~ The general population has been distributed across what's left of the country. Industrial buildings form the spine of the landscape: tall, rectangular metal boxes stuffed full of machinery. Machinery intended to strengthen the army, to strengthen The Reestablishment, to destroy mass quantities of human civilization.

Carbon/Tar/Steel

Gray/Black/Silver

Smoky colors smudged into the skyline, dripping into the slush that used to be snow. Trash is heaped in haphazard piles everywhere, patches of yellowed grass peeking out from under the devastation.

Traditional homes of our old world have been abandoned, windows shattered, roofs collapsing, red and green and blue paint scrubbed into muted shades to better match our bright future. Now I see the compounds carelessly constructed on the ravaged land and I begin to remember. I remember how these were supposed to be temporary. I remember the few months before I was locked up when they'd begun building them. These small, cold quarters would suffice just until they figured out all the details of this new plan, is what The Reestablishment had said. Just until everyone was subdued. Just until people stopped protesting and realized that this change was *good* for them, *good* for their children, *good* for their future.

I remember there were rules.

No more dangerous imaginations, no more prescription medications. A new generation comprised of only healthy individuals would sustain us. The sick must be locked away. The old must be discarded. The troubled must be given up to the asylums. Only the strong should survive.

Yes.

Of course.

No more stupid languages and stupid stories and stupid paintings placed above stupid mantels. No more Christmas, no more Hanukkah, no more Ramadan and Diwali. No talk of religion, of belief, of personal convictions. Personal convictions were what nearly killed us all, is what they said.

Convictions priorities preferences prejudices and ideologies divided us. Deluded us. Destroyed us.

Selfish needs, wants, and desires needed to be obliterated. Greed, overindulgence, and gluttony had to be expunged from human behavior. The solution was in self-control, in minimalism, in sparse living conditions; one simple language and a brand-new dictionary filled with words everyone would understand.

These things would save us, save our children, save the human race, is what they said.

Reestablish Equality. Reestablish Humanity. Reestablish Hope, Healing, and Happiness.

SAVE US!

JOIN US!

REESTABLISH SOCIETY!

The posters are still plastered on the walls.

The wind whips their tattered remains, but the signs are determinedly fixed, flapping against the steel and concrete structures they're stuck to. Some are still pasted to poles sprung right out of the ground, loudspeakers now affixed at the very top. Loudspeakers that alert the people, no doubt, to the imminent dangers that surround them.

But the world is eerily quiet.

Pedestrians pass by, ambling along in the cold, frigid weather to do factory work and find food for their families. Hope in this world bleeds out of the barrel of a gun.

No one really cares for the concept anymore.

People used to want hope. They wanted to think things could get better. They wanted to believe they could go back to worrying about gossip and holiday vacations and going to parties on Saturday nights, so The Reestablishment promised a future too perfect to be possible and society was too desperate to disbelieve. They never realized they were signing away their souls to a group planning on taking advantage of their ignorance. Their fear.

Most civilians are too petrified to protest but there are others who are stronger. There are others who are waiting for the right moment. There are others who have already begun to fight back.

I hope it's not too late to fight back.

I study every quivering branch, every imposing soldier, every window I can count. My eyes are 2 professional pickpockets, stealing everything to store away in my mind.

I lose track of the minutes we trample over.

We pull up to a structure 10 times larger than the asylum and suspiciously central to civilization. From the outside it looks like a bland building, inconspicuous in every way but its size, gray steel slabs comprising 4 flat walls, windows cracked and slammed into the 15 stories. It's bleak and bears no marking, no insignia, no proof of its true identity.

Political headquarters camouflaged among the masses.

The inside of the tank is a convoluted mess of buttons and levers I'm at a loss to operate, and Adam is opening my door before I have a chance to identify the pieces. His hands are in place around my waist and my feet are now firmly on the ground but my heart is pounding so fast I'm certain he can hear it. He hasn't let go of me.

I look up.

His eyes are tight, his forehead pinched, his lips ~~his lips his lips~~ are 2 pieces of frustration forged together.

I step back. He drops his gaze. Turns away. He inhales and 5 fingers on one hand form a fickle fist. "This way." He nods toward the building.

I follow him inside.

ELEVEN

I'm so prepared for unimaginable horror that the reality is almost worse.

Dirty money is dripping from the walls, a year's supply of food wasted on marble floors, hundreds of thousands of dollars in medical aid poured into fancy furniture and Persian rugs. I feel the artificial heat pouring in through air vents and think of children screaming for clean water. I squint through crystal chandeliers and hear mothers begging for mercy. I see a superficial world existing in the midst of a terrorizing reality and I can't move.

I can't breathe.

So many people must've died to sustain this luxury. So many people had to lose their homes and their children and their last 5 dollars in the bank for promises promises promises so many promises to save them from themselves. They *promised* us—The Reestablishment promised us hope for a better future. They said they would fix things, they said they would help us get back to the world we knew— the world with movie dates and spring weddings and baby showers. They said they would give us back our homes, our health, our sustainable future.

But they stole everything.

They took everything. ~~My life. My future. My sanity.~~ My ~~freedom.~~

They filled our world with weapons aimed at our foreheads and smiled as they shot 16 candles right through our future. They killed those strong enough to fight back and locked up the freaks who failed to live up to their utopian expectations. ~~People like me.~~

Here is proof of their corruption.

My skin is cold-sweat, my fingers trembling with disgust, my legs unable to withstand ~~the waste the waste the waste~~ the selfish waste in these 4 walls. I'm seeing red everywhere. The blood of bodies spattered against the windows, spilled across the carpets, dripping from the chandeliers.

"Juliette—"

I break.

I'm on my knees, my body cracking from the pain I've swallowed so many times, heaving with sobs I can no longer suppress, my dignity dissolving in my tears, the agony of this past week ripping my skin to shreds.

I can't ever breathe.

I can't catch the oxygen around me and I'm dry-heaving into my shirt and I hear voices and see faces I don't recognize, wisps of words wicked away by confusion, thoughts scrambled so many times I don't know if I'm even conscious anymore.

I don't know if I've officially lost my mind.

I'm in the air. I'm a bag of feathers in his arms and he's

breaking through soldiers crowding around for a glimpse of the commotion and for a moment I don't want to care that I shouldn't want this so much. I want to forget that I'm supposed to hate him, that he betrayed me, that he's working for the same people who are trying to destroy the very little that's left of humanity and my face is buried in the soft material of his shirt and my cheek is pressed against his chest and he smells like strength and courage and the world drowning in rain. I don't want him to ~~ever ever ever~~ ever let go of my body. I wish I could touch his skin, I wish there were no barriers between us.

Reality slaps me in the face.

Mortification muddles my brain, desperate humiliation clouds my judgment; red paints my face, bleeds through my skin. I clutch at his shirt.

"You can kill me," I tell him. "You have guns—" I'm wriggling out of his grip and he tightens his hold around my body. His face shows no emotion but a sudden strain in his jaw, an unmistakable tension in his arms. "You can just *kill me*—"

"Juliette," he says. *"Please."*

I'm numb again. Powerless all over again. Melting from within, life seeping out of my limbs.

We're standing in front of a door.

Adam takes a key card and swipes it against a black pane of glass fitted into the small space beside the handle, and the stainless steel door slides out of place. We step inside.

We're all alone in a new room.

"Please ~~don't let go of me~~ put me down," I tell him.

There's a queen-size bed in the middle of the space, lush carpet gracing the floors, an armoire flush against the wall, light fixtures glittering from the ceiling. The beauty is so tainted I can't stand the sight of it. Adam gentles me onto the soft mattress and takes a small step backward.

"You'll be staying here for a while, I think," is all he says.

I squeeze my eyes shut. I don't want to think about the inevitable torture awaiting me. "Please," I tell him. "I'd like to be left alone."

A deep sigh. "That's not exactly an option."

"What do you mean?" I spin around.

"I have to watch you, Juliette." He says my name like a whisper. "Warner wants you to understand what he's offering you, but you're still considered . . . a threat. He's made you my assignment. I can't leave."

"You have to live with me?"

"I live in the barracks on the opposite end of this building. With the other soldiers. But, yeah." He clears his throat. He's not looking at me. "I'll be moving in."

There's an ache in the pit of my stomach that's gnawing on my nerves. I want to hate him and judge him and scream forever but I'm failing because all I see is an 8-year-old boy who doesn't remember that he used to be the kindest person I ever knew.

I don't want to believe this is happening.

I close my eyes and curl my head into my knees.

"You have to get dressed," he says after a moment.

I pop my head up. I blink at him like I can't understand what he's saying. "I am dressed."

He clears his throat again but tries to be quiet about it. "There's a bathroom through here." He points. I see a door connected to the room and I'm suddenly curious. I've heard stories about people with bathrooms in their bedrooms. I guess they're not exactly *in* the bedroom, but they're close enough. I slip off the bed and follow his finger. As soon as I open the door he resumes speaking. "You can shower and change in here. The bathroom . . . it's the only place there are no cameras," he adds, his voice trailing off.

There are cameras in my room.

Of course.

"You can find clothes in there." He nods to the armoire. He suddenly looks uncomfortable.

"And you can't leave?" I ask.

He rubs his forehead and sits down on the bed. He sighs. "You have to get ready. Warner will be expecting you for dinner."

"*Dinner?*" My eyes are the size of the moon.

Adam looks grim. "Yeah."

"He's not going to hurt me?" I'm ashamed at the relief in my voice, at the unexpected tension I've released, at the fear I didn't know I was harboring. "He's going to give me *dinner?*" I'm starving my stomach is a tortured pit of starvation I'm so hungry so hungry so hungry I can't even imagine what

65

real food must taste like.

Adam's face is inscrutable again. "You should hurry. I can show you how everything works."

I don't have time to protest before he's in the bathroom and I've followed him inside. The door is still open and he's standing in the middle of the small space with his back to me and I can't understand why. "I already know how to use the bathroom," I tell him. ~~I used to live in a regular home.~~ ~~I used to have a family.~~

He turns around very, very slowly and I begin to panic. He finally lifts his head but his eyes are darting in every direction. When he looks at me his eyes narrow; his forehead is tight. His right hand curls into a fist and his left hand lifts one finger to his lips. He's telling me to be quiet.

I knew something was coming but I didn't know it'd be Adam. I didn't think he'd be the one to hurt me, to torture me. I don't even realize I'm crying until I hear the whimper and feel the silent tears stream down my face and I'm ~~ashamed so ashamed~~ so ashamed of my weakness but a part of me doesn't care. I'm tempted to beg, to ask for mercy, to steal his gun and shoot myself first.

He seems to register my sudden hysteria because his eyes snap open and his mouth falls to the floor. "No, God, Juliette—I'm not—" He swears under his breath. He pumps his fist against his forehead and turns away, sighing heavily, pacing the length of the small space. He swears again.

He walks out the door and doesn't look back.

TWELVE

5 full minutes under piping hot water, 2 bars of soap both smelling of lavender, a bottle of shampoo meant only for my hair, and the touch of soft, plush towels I dare to wrap around my body and I begin to understand.

They want me to forget.

They think they can wash away my memories, my loyalties, my priorities with a few hot meals and a room with a view. They think I am so easily purchased.

Warner doesn't seem to understand that I grew up with nothing and I didn't hate it. I didn't want the clothes or the perfect shoes or the expensive anything. I didn't want to be draped in silk. All I ever wanted was to reach out and touch another human being not just with my hands but with my heart. I saw the world and its lack of compassion, its harsh, grating judgment, and its cold, resentful eyes. I saw it all around me.

I had so much time to listen.

To look.

To study people and places and possibilities. All I had to do was open my eyes. All I had to do was open a book—to see the stories bleeding from page to page. To see the memories etched onto paper.

I spent my life folded between the pages of books.

In the absence of human relationships I formed bonds with paper characters. I lived love and loss through stories threaded in history; I experienced adolescence by association. My world is one interwoven web of words, stringing limb to limb, bone to sinew, thoughts and images all together. I am a being comprised of letters, a character created by sentences, a figment of imagination formed through fiction.

They want to delete every point of punctuation in my life from this earth and I don't think I can let that happen.

I slip back into my old clothes and tiptoe into the bedroom only to find it abandoned. Adam is gone even though he said he would stay. I don't understand him I don't understand his actions I don't understand my disappointment. I wish I didn't love the freshness of my skin, the feel of being perfectly clean after so long; I don't understand why I still haven't looked in the mirror, why I'm afraid of what I'll see, why I'm not sure if I'll recognize the face that might stare back at me.

I open the armoire.

It's bursting with dresses and shoes and shirts and pants and clothing of every kind, colors so vivid they hurt my eyes, material I've only ever heard of, the kind I'm almost afraid to touch. The sizes are perfect too perfect.

They've been waiting for me.

I've been neglected abandoned ostracized and dragged from my home. I've been poked prodded tested and thrown in a cell. I've been studied. I've been starved. I've been tempted with friendship only to be left betrayed and trapped into this nightmare I'm expected to be grateful for. My parents. My teachers. Adam. Warner. The Reestablishment. I am expendable to all of them.

They think I'm a doll they can dress up and twist into prostration.

But they're wrong.

"Warner is waiting for you."

I spin around and fall back against the armoire, slamming it closed in the craze of panic clutching my heart. I steady myself and fold away my fear when I see Adam standing at the door. His mouth moves for a moment but he says nothing. Eventually he steps forward so forward until he's close enough to touch.

He reaches past me to reopen the door hiding the things I'm embarrassed to know exist. "These are all for you," he says without looking at me, his fingers touching the hem of a purple dress, a rich plum color good enough to eat.

"I already have clothes." My hands smooth out the wrinkles in my dirty, ragged outfit.

He finally decides to look at me, but when he does his eyebrows trip, his eyes blink and freeze, his lips part in surprise. I wonder if I've washed off a new face for myself and I flush, hoping he's not disgusted by what he might see. I don't know why I care.

He drops his gaze. Takes a deep breath. "I'll be waiting outside."

~~I stare at the purple dress with Adam's fingerprints~~

I study the inside of the armoire for only a moment before I abandon it. I comb anxious fingers through my wet hair and steel myself.

I am no one's property.

And I don't care what Warner wants me to look like.

I step outside and Adam stares at me for a second. He rubs the back of his neck and says nothing. He shakes his head. He starts walking. He doesn't touch me and I shouldn't notice but I do. I have no idea what to expect I have no idea what my life will be like in this new place and I'm being nailed in the stomach by every exquisite embellishment, every lavish accessory, every superfluous painting, molding, lighting, coloring of this building. I hope the whole thing catches fire.

I follow Adam down a long carpeted corridor to an elevator made entirely of glass. He swipes the same key card he used to open my door and we step inside. I didn't even realize we'd taken an elevator to get up this many floors. I realize I must've made a horrible scene when I arrived and I'm almost happy.

I hope I disappoint Warner in every possible way.

The dining room is big enough to feed thousands of orphans. Instead, there are 7 banquet tables stretched across the room, blue silk spilling across the tabletops, crystal vases bursting with orchids and stargazer lilies, glass bowls filled with gardenias. ~~It's enchanting~~. I wonder where they got the flowers from. They must not be real. I don't know how they could be real. I haven't seen real flowers in years.

Warner is positioned at the table directly in the middle, seated at the head. As soon as he sees ~~me~~ Adam he stands up. The entire room stands in turn.

I realize almost immediately that there are empty seats on either side of him and I don't intend to stop moving but I do. I take quick inventory of the attendees and can't count any other women.

Adam brushes the small of my back with 3 fingertips and I'm startled out of my skin. I hurry forward and Warner beams at me. He pulls out the chair on his left and gestures for me to sit down. I do.

I try not to look at Adam as he sits across from me.

"You know . . . there are clothes in your armoire." Warner sits down beside me; the room reseats itself and resumes a steady stream of chatter. He's turned almost entirely in my direction but somehow the only presence I'm aware of is directly across from me. I focus on the empty plate 2 inches from my fingers. I drop my hands in my lap. "And you don't have to wear those dirty tennis shoes anymore," Warner continues, stealing another glance before pouring something into my cup. It looks like water.

~~I'm so thirsty I could inhale a waterfall.~~

I hate his smile.

Hate looks just like everybody else until it smiles. Until it spins around and lies with lips and teeth carved into the semblance of something too passive to punch.

"Juliette?"

71

I inhale too quickly. A stifled cough is ballooning in my throat.

His glassy green eyes glint in my direction.

"Are you not hungry?" Words dipped in sugar. His gloved hand touches my wrist and I nearly sprain it in my haste to distance myself from him.

~~I could eat every person in this room.~~ "No, thank you."

He licks his bottom lip into a smile. "Don't confuse stupidity for bravery, love. I know you haven't eaten anything in days."

Something in my patience snaps. "I'd really rather die than eat your food and listen to you call me *love*," I tell him.

Adam drops his fork.

Warner spares him a swift glance and when he looks my way again his eyes have hardened. He holds my gaze for a few infinitely long seconds before he pulls a gun out of his jacket pocket. He fires.

The entire room screams to a stop.

I turn my head very, very slowly to follow the direction of Warner's gun only to see he's shot some kind of meat right through the bone. The platter of food is slightly steaming across the room, the meal heaped less than a foot away from the guests. He shot it without even looking. He could've killed someone.

It takes all of my energy to remain very, very still.

Warner drops the gun on my plate. The silence gives it space to clatter around the universe and back. "Choose your words very wisely, Juliette. One word from me and your life here won't be so easy."

I blink.

Adam pushes a plate of food in front of me; the strength of his gaze is like a white-hot poker pressed against my skin. I look up and he cocks his head the tiniest millimeter. His eyes are saying *Please*.

I pick up my fork.

Warner doesn't miss a thing. He clears his throat a little too loudly. He laughs with no humor as he cuts into the meat on his plate. "Do I have to get Kent to do all my work for me?"

"Excuse me?"

"It seems he's the only one you'll listen to." His tone is breezy but his jaw is unmistakably set. He turns to Adam. "I'm surprised you didn't tell her to change her clothes like I asked you to."

Adam sits up straighter. "I did, sir."

"I like my clothes," I tell him. I'd like to punch you in the eye, is what I don't tell him.

Warner's smile slides back into place. "No one asked what *you* like, love. Now eat. I need you to look your best when you stand beside me."

THIRTEEN

Warner insists on accompanying me to my room.

After dinner Adam disappeared with a few of the other soldiers. He disappeared without a word or glance in my direction and I don't have any idea what to anticipate. At least I have nothing to lose but my life.

"I don't want you to hate me," Warner says as we make our way toward the elevator. "I'm only your enemy if you want me to be."

"We will always be enemies," I say. "I will never be what you want me to be."

Warner sighs as he presses the button for the elevator. "I really think you'll change your mind." He glances at me with a small smile. A shame, really, that such striking looks should be wasted on such a miserable human being. "You and I, Juliette—together? We could be unstoppable."

I will not look at him though I feel his gaze touching every inch of my body. "No, thank you."

We're in the elevator. The world is whooshing past us and the walls of glass make us a spectacle to every person on every floor. There are no secrets in this building.

He touches my elbow and I pull away. "You might reconsider," he says softly.

"How did you figure it out?" The elevator dings open

but I'm not moving. I finally turn to face him because I can't contain my curiosity. I study his hands, so carefully sheathed in leather, his sleeves thick and crisp and long. Even his collar is high and regal. He's dressed impeccably from head to toe and covered everywhere except his face. Even if I wanted to touch him I'm not sure I'd be able to. He's protecting himself.

From me.

"Perhaps a conversation for tomorrow night?" He cocks a brow and offers me his arm. I pretend not to notice it as we walk off the elevator and down the hall. "Maybe you could wear something nice."

"What's your first name?" I ask him.

We're standing in front of my door.

He stops. Surprised. Lifts his chin almost imperceptibly. Focuses his eyes on my face until I begin to regret my question. "You want to know my name."

I don't do it on purpose, but my eyes narrow just a bit. "Warner is your last name, isn't it?"

He almost smiles. "You want to know my name."

"I didn't realize it was a secret."

He steps forward. His lips twitch. His eyes fall, his lips draw in a tight breath. He drops a gloved finger down the apple of my cheek. "I'll tell you mine if you tell me yours," he whispers, too close to my neck.

I inch backward. Swallow hard. "You already know my name."

He's not looking at my eyes. "You're right. I should rephrase that. What I meant to say was I'll tell you mine if you show me yours."

"What?" I'm breathing too fast too suddenly.

He begins to pull off his gloves and I begin to panic. "Show me what you can do."

My jaw is too tight and my teeth have begun to ache. "I won't touch you."

"That's all right." He tugs off the other glove. "I don't actually need your help."

"No—"

"Don't worry." He grins. "I'm sure it won't hurt *you* at all."

"No," I gasp. "No, I won't—I can't—"

"Fine," Warner snaps. "That's fine. You don't want to hurt me. I'm so utterly flattered." He almost rolls his eyes. Looks down the hall. Spots a soldier. Beckons him over. "Jenkins?"

Jenkins is swift for his size and he's at my side in a second.

"Sir." He bows his head an inch even though he's clearly Warner's senior. He can't be more than 27; stocky, sturdy, packed with bulk. He spares me a sidelong glance. His brown eyes are warmer than I'd expect them to be.

"I'm going to need you to accompany Ms. Ferrars back downstairs. But be warned: she's incredibly uncooperative and will try to break free from your grip." He smiles too slowly. "No matter what she says or does, soldier, you cannot let go of her. Are we clear?"

Jenkins' eyes widen; his nostrils flare, his fingers flex at his sides. He nods.

Jenkins is not an idiot.

76

I start running.

I'm bolting down the hallway and running past a series of stunned soldiers too scared to stop me. I don't know what I'm doing, why I think I can run, where I think I could possibly go. I'm straining to reach the elevator if only because I think it will buy me time. I don't know what else to do.

Warner's commands are bouncing off the walls and exploding in my eardrums. He doesn't need to chase me. He's getting others to do the work for him.

Soldiers are lining up before me.

Beside me.

Behind me.

I can't breathe.

I'm spinning in a circle of my own stupidity, panicked, petrified by the thought of what I'm going to do to Jenkins against my will. What he will do to me against his will. What will happen to both of us despite our best intentions.

"Seize her," Warner says softly. His voice is the only sound in the room.

Jenkins steps forward.

My eyes are flooding and I squeeze them shut. I pry them open. I blink back at the crowd and spot a familiar face. Adam is staring at me, horrified.

Jenkins offers me his hand.

My bones begin to buckle, snapping in synchronicity with the beats of my heart. I crumble to the floor, folding into myself like a flimsy crepe. My arms are so painfully bare in this ragged T-shirt.

"Don't—" I hold up a tentative hand, pleading with my eyes, staring into the face of this innocent man. "Please don't—" My voice breaks. "You don't want to touch me—"

"I never said I did." Jenkins's voice is deep and steady, full of regret. Jenkins who has no gloves, no protection, no preparation, no possible defense.

"That was a direct order, soldier," Warner barks, trains a gun at his back.

Jenkins grabs my arms.

NO NO NO

I gasp.

My blood is surging through my veins, rushing through my body like a raging river, waves of heat lapping against my bones. I can hear his anguish, I can feel the power pouring out of his body, I can hear his heart beating in my ear and my head is spinning with the rush of adrenaline fortifying my being.

I feel alive.

I wish it hurt me. I wish it maimed me. I wish it repulsed me. I wish I hated the potent force wrapping itself around my skeleton.

But I don't. My skin is pulsing with someone else's life and I don't hate it.

I hate myself for enjoying it.

I enjoy the way it feels to be brimming with more life and hope and human power than I knew I was capable of. His pain gives me a pleasure I never asked for.

And he's not letting go.

But he's not letting go because he can't. Because I have to be the one to break the connection. Because the agony incapacitates him. Because he's caught in my snares.

Because I am a Venus flytrap.

And I am lethal.

I fall on my back and kick at his chest, willing him away from me, willing his weight off of my small frame, his limp body collapsed against my own. I'm suddenly screaming and struggling to see past the sheet of tears obscuring my vision; I'm hiccupping, hysterical, horrified by the frozen look on this man's face, his paralyzed lips wheezing.

I break free and stumble backward. The sea of soldiers parts behind me. Every face is etched in astonishment and pure, unadulterated fear. Jenkins is lying on the floor and no one dares approach him.

"Somebody help him!" I scream. "Somebody *help* him! He needs a doctor—he needs to be taken—he needs—he—oh God—what have I done—"

"Juliette—"

"DON'T TOUCH ME—DON'T YOU DARE TOUCH ME—"

Warner's gloves are back in place and he's trying to hold me together, he's trying to smooth back my hair, he's trying to wipe away my tears and I want to murder him.

"Juliette, you need to calm down—"

"HELP HIM!" I cry, falling to my knees, my eyes glued to the figure lying on the floor. The other soldiers are finally creeping closer, cautious as though he might be contagious.

"Please—you have to help him! *Please*—"

"Kent, Curtis, Soledad—*take care of this*." Warner shouts to his men before scooping me up into his arms.

I'm still kicking when the world goes black.

FOURTEEN

The ceiling is fading in and out of focus.

My head is heavy, my vision is blurry, my heart is strained. There is a distinct flavor of panic lodged somewhere underneath my tongue and I'm fighting to remember where it came from. I try to sit up and can't understand why I was lying down.

Someone's hands are on my shoulders.

"How are you feeling?" Warner is peering down at me.

Suddenly Jenkins' face is swimming in my consciousness and I'm swinging my fists and screaming for Warner to get away from me and struggling to wriggle out of his grip but he just smiles. Laughs a little. Gentles my hands down beside my torso.

"Well, at least you're awake," he sighs. "You had me worried for a moment."

I try to control my trembling limbs. "Get your hands away from me."

He waves sheathed fingers in front of my face. "I'm all covered up. Don't worry."

"I *hate* you."

"So much passion." He laughs again. He looks so calm, so genuinely amused. He stares at me with eyes softer than

I expected them to be.

I turn away.

He stands up. Takes a short breath. "Here," he says, reaching for a tray on a small table. "I brought you food."

I take advantage of the moment to sit up and look around. I'm lying on a bed draped in damask golds and burgundies the darkest shade of blood. The floor is covered in thick, rich carpet. It's warm in this room. It's the same size as the one I occupy, its furniture standard enough: bed, armoire, side tables, chandelier glittering from the ceiling. The only difference is there's an extra door in this room and there's a candle burning quietly on a small table in the corner. I haven't seen fire in so many years I've lost count. I have to stifle an impulse to reach out and touch the flame.

I prop myself up against the pillows and try to pretend I'm not comfortable. "Where am I?"

Warner turns around holding a plate with bread and cheese on it. His other hand is gripping a glass of water. He looks around the room as if seeing it for the first time. "This is my bedroom."

If my head weren't splitting into pieces I'd be tempted to run. "Take me to my own room. I don't want to be here."

"And yet, here you are." He sits at the foot of the bed, a few feet away. Pushes the plate in front of me. "Are you thirsty?"

I don't know if it's because I can't think straight or if it's because I'm genuinely confused, but I'm struggling to reconcile Warner's polarizing personalities. Here he is, offering me a glass of water after he forced me to torture someone. I lift my hands and study my fingers as if I've never seen them before. "I don't understand."

He cocks his head, inspecting me as though I might've seriously injured myself. "I only asked if you were thirsty. That shouldn't be difficult to understand." A pause. "Drink this."

I take the glass. Stare at it. Stare at him. Stare at the walls.

I must be insane.

Warner sighs. "I'm not sure, but I think you fainted. And I think you should probably eat something, though I'm not entirely sure about that, either." He pauses. "You've probably had too much exertion your first day here. My mistake."

"Why are you being nice to me?"

The surprise on his face surprises me even more. "Because I care about you," he says simply.

"You *care* about me?" The numbness in my body is beginning to dissipate. My blood pressure is rising and anger is making its way to the forefront of my mind. "I almost killed Jenkins because of you!"

"You didn't kill—"

"Your soldiers beat me! You keep me here like a prisoner! You threaten me! You threaten to kill me! You give me no freedom and you say you *care* about me?" I nearly throw the glass of water at his face. "You are a *monster*!"

Warner turns away so I'm staring at his profile. He clasps his hands. Changes his mind. Touches his lips. "I am only trying to help you."

"Liar."

He seems to consider that. Nods, just once. "Yes. Most of the time, yes."

"I don't want to be here. I don't want to be your experiment. Let me go."

"No." He stands up. "I'm afraid I can't do that."

"Why not?"

"Because I can't. I just—" He tugs at his fingers. Clears his throat. His eyes search the ceiling for a brief moment. "Because I need you."

"You need me to kill people!"

He doesn't answer right away. He walks to the candle. Pulls off a glove. Tickles the flame with his bare fingers. "You know, I am very capable of killing people on my own, Juliette. I'm actually very good at it."

"That's disgusting."

He shrugs. "How else do you think someone my age is able to control so many soldiers? Why else would my father allow me to take charge of an entire sector?"

"Your *father*?" I sit up, suddenly curious in spite of myself.

He ignores my question. "The mechanics of fear are simple enough. People are intimidated by me, so they listen when I speak." He waves a hand. "Empty threats are worth very little these days."

I squeeze my eyes shut. "So you kill people for power."

"As do you."

"How *dare* you—"

He laughs, loud. "You're free to lie to yourself, if it makes you feel better."

"I am not lying—"

"Why did it take you so long to break your connection with Jenkins?"

My mouth freezes in place.

"Why didn't you fight back right away? Why did you allow him to touch you for as long as he did?"

My hands have begun to shake and I grip them, hard. "You don't know anything about me."

"And yet you claim to know me so well."

I clench my jaw, not trusting myself to speak.

"At least I'm honest," he adds.

"You just agreed you're a liar!"

He raises his eyebrows. "At least I'm honest about being a liar."

I slam the glass of water on the side table. Drop my head in my hands. Take a steadying breath. "Well," I rasp, "why do you need me, then? If you're such an excellent murderer?"

A smile flickers and fades across his face. "One day I'll introduce you to the answer to that question."

I try to protest but he stops me with one hand. Picks up a piece of bread from the plate. Holds it under my nose. "You hardly ate anything at dinner. That can't possibly be healthy."

I don't move.

He drops the bread on the plate and drops the plate beside the water. Turns to me. Studies my eyes with such intensity I'm momentarily disarmed. There are so many things I want to say and scream but somehow I've forgotten all about the words waiting patiently in my mouth. I can't make myself look away.

"Eat something." His eyes abandon me. "Then go to sleep. I'll be back for you in the morning."

"Why can't I sleep in my own room?"

He gets to his feet. Dusts off his pants for no real reason. "Because I want you to stay here."

"But why?"

He barks out a laugh. "So many questions."

"Well if you'd give me a straight answer—"

"Good night, Juliette."

"Are you going to let me go?" I ask, this time quietly, this time timidly.

"No." He takes 6 steps into the corner with the candle. "And I won't promise to make things easier for you, either." There is no regret, no remorse, no sympathy in his voice. He could be talking about the weather.

"You could be lying."

"Yes, I could be." He nods, as if to himself. Blows out the candle.

And disappears.

*

I try to fight it
I try to stay awake
I try to find my head but I can't.

I collapse from sheer exhaustion.

FIFTEEN

Why don't you just kill yourself? someone at school asked me once.

I think it was the kind of question intended to be cruel, but it was the first time I'd ever contemplated the possibility. I didn't know what to say. Maybe I was crazy to consider it, but I'd always hoped that if I were a good enough girl, if I did everything right, if I said the right things or said nothing at all—I thought my parents would change their minds. I thought they would finally listen when I tried to talk. I thought they would give me a chance. I thought they might finally love me.

I always had that ~~stupid~~ hope.

"Good morning."

My eyes snap open with a start. I've never been a heavy sleeper.

Warner is staring at me, sitting at the foot of his own bed in a fresh suit and perfectly polished boots. Everything about him is meticulous. Pristine. His breath is cool and fresh in the crisp morning air. I can feel it on my face.

It takes me a moment to realize I'm tangled in the same sheets Warner himself has slept in. My face is suddenly on fire and I'm fumbling to free myself. I nearly fall off the bed.

I don't acknowledge him.

"Did you sleep well?" he asks.

I look up. His eyes are such a strange shade of green: bright, crystal clear, piercing in the most alarming way. His hair is thick, the richest slice of gold; his frame is lean and unassuming, but his grip is effortlessly strong. I notice for the first time that he wears a jade ring on his left pinkie finger.

He catches me staring and stands up. Slips his gloves on and clasps his hands behind his back.

"It's time for you to go back to your room."

I blink. Nod. Stand up and nearly fall down. I catch myself on the side of the bed and try to steady my dizzying head. I hear Warner sigh.

"You didn't eat the food I left for you last night."

I grab the water with trembling hands and force myself to eat some of the bread. My body has gotten so used to hunger I don't know how to recognize it anymore.

Warner leads me out the door once I find my footing. I'm still clutching a piece of cheese in my hand.

I nearly drop it when I step outside.

There are even more soldiers here than there are on my floor. Each is equipped with at least 4 different kinds of guns, some slung around their necks, some strapped to their belts. All of them betray a look of terror when they see my face. It flashes in and out of their features so quickly I might've missed it, but it's obvious enough: everyone grips their weapons a little tighter as I walk by.

Warner seems pleased.

"Their fear will work in your favor," he whispers in my ear.

"I never wanted them to be afraid of me."

"You should." He stops. His eyes are calling me an idiot. "If they don't fear you, they will hunt you."

"People hunt things they fear all the time."

"At least now they know what they're up against." He resumes walking down the hall, but my feet are stitched into the ground. Realization is ice-cold water and it's dripping down my back.

"You made me do that—what I did—to Jenkins? On *purpose*?"

Warner is already 3 steps ahead but I can see the smile on his face. "Everything I do is done on purpose."

"You wanted to make a spectacle out of me."

"I was trying to protect you."

"From your own soldiers?" I'm running to catch up to him now, burning with indignation. "At the expense of a man's *life*—"

"Get inside." Warner has reached the elevator. He's holding the doors open for me.

I follow him.

He presses the right buttons.

The doors close.

I turn to speak.

He corners me.

I'm backed into the far edge of this glass receptacle and I'm suddenly nervous. His hands are holding my arms and his lips are dangerously close to my face. His gaze is locked into mine, his eyes flashing; dangerous. He says one word: "Yes."

It takes me a moment to find my voice. "Yes, what?"

"Yes, from my own soldiers. Yes, at the expense of one man's life." He tenses his jaw. Speaks through his teeth. "There is very little you understand about my world, Juliette."

"I'm trying to understand—"

"No you're not," he snaps. His eyelashes are like individual threads of spun gold lit on fire. I almost want to touch them. "You don't understand that power and control can slip from your grasp at any moment and even when you think you're most prepared. These two things are not easy to earn. They are even harder to retain." I try to speak and he cuts me off. "You think I don't know how many of my own soldiers hate me? You think I don't know that they'd like to see me fall? You think there aren't others who would love to have the position I work so hard to have—"

"Don't *flatter* yourself—"

He closes the last few inches between us and my words fall to the floor. I can't breathe. The tension in his entire body is so intense it's nearly palpable and I think my muscles have begun to freeze. "You are naive," he says to me, his voice harsh, low, a grating whisper against my skin. "You don't realize that you're a threat to everyone in this building. They have every reason to harm you. You don't see that I am trying to help you—"

"By hurting me!" I explode. "By hurting others!"

His laugh is cold, mirthless. He backs away from me, disgusted. The elevator slides open but he doesn't step outside. I can see my door from here. "Go back to your room. Wash up. Change. There are dresses in your armoire."

"I don't like dresses."

"I don't think you like seeing *that*, either," he says with a tilt of his head. I follow his gaze to see a hulking shadow across from my door. I turn to him for an explanation but he says nothing. He's suddenly composed, his features wiped clean of emotion. He takes my hand, squeezes my fingers, says, "I'll be back for you in exactly one hour," and closes the elevator doors before I have a chance to protest. I begin to wonder if it's coincidence that the one person most unafraid to touch me is a monster himself.

I step forward and dare to peer closer at the soldier standing in the dark.

Adam.

Oh Adam.

Adam who now knows exactly what I'm capable of.

My heart is exploding in my chest. I feel as though every fist in the world has decided to punch me in the stomach. I shouldn't care so much, but I do.

He'll hate me forever now. He won't even look at me.

I wait for him to open my door but he doesn't move.

"Adam?" I venture, tentative. "I need your key card."

I watch him swallow hard and take a tiny breath and immediately I sense something is wrong. I move closer and a quick, stiff shake of his head tells me not to. ~~I do not touch people I do not get close to people I am a monster.~~ He doesn't want me near him. Of course he doesn't.

He opens my door with immense difficulty and I realize someone's hurt him where I can't see it. Warner's words come back to me and I recognize his airy good-bye as a warning. A warning that severs every nerve in my body.

Adam will be punished for my mistakes. For my disobedience.

I step through the door and glance back at Adam one last time, unable to feel any kind of triumph in his pain. Despite everything he's done I don't know if I'm capable of hating him. Not Adam. Not the boy I used to know.

"The purple dress," he says, his voice broken and a little breathy like it hurts to inhale. I have to wring my hands to keep from running to him. "Wear the purple dress." He coughs. "Juliette."

I will be the perfect mannequin.

SIXTEEN

As soon as I'm in the room I open the armoire and yank the purple dress off the hanger before I remember I'm being watched. *The cameras.* I wonder if Adam was punished for telling me about the cameras, too. I wonder if he's taken any other risks with me. I wonder why he would.

I touch the stiff, modern material of the plum dress and my fingers find their way to the hem, just as Adam's did yesterday. I can't help but wonder why he likes this dress so much. Why it has to be this one. Why I even have to wear a dress.

I am not a doll.

My hand comes to rest on the small wooden shelf beneath the hanging clothes and an unfamiliar texture brushes my skin. It's rough and foreign but familiar at the same time. I step closer to the armoire and hide between the doors. My fingers feel their way around the surface.

My notebook.

He saved my notebook. ~~Adam saved the only thing I own.~~

I grab the purple dress and tuck the notebook into its folds before stealing away to the bathroom.

~~The bathroom where there are no cameras.~~

~~The bathroom where there are no cameras.~~

~~The bathroom where there are no cameras.~~

He was trying to tell me, I realize. Before, in the bathroom. He was trying to tell me something and I was so scared I scared him away.

I scared him away.

I close the door behind me and my hands are shaking as I unfurl the familiar papers bound together by old glue. I flip through the pages to make sure they're all there and my eyes land on my most recent entry. At the very bottom there is a shift. A new sentence not written in my handwriting.

A new sentence that must've come from him.

It's not what you think.

I stand perfectly still.

Every inch of my skin is taut, fraught with feeling and the pressure is building in my chest, pounding louder and faster and harder, overcompensating for my stillness. I do not tremble when I'm frozen in time. I train my breaths to come slower, I count things that do not exist, I make up numbers I do not have, I pretend time is a broken hourglass bleeding seconds through sand. I dare to believe.

I dare to hope Adam is trying to reach out to me. I'm crazy enough to consider the possibility.

I rip the page out of the small notebook and clutch it close.

I hide the notebook in a pocket of the purple dress. The pocket Adam must've slipped it into. The pocket it must've fallen out of. ~~The pocket of the purple dress. The pocket of the purple dress~~.

Hope is a pocket of possibility.

I'm holding it in my hand.

Warner is not late.

He doesn't knock, either.

I'm slipping on my shoes when he walks in without a single word, without even an effort to make his presence known. His eyes are falling all over me. My jaw tightens on its own.

"You hurt him," I find myself saying.

"You shouldn't care," he says with a tilt of his head, gesturing to my dress. "But it's obvious you do."

I zip my lips and pray my hands aren't shaking too much. I don't know where Adam is. I don't know how badly he's hurt. I don't know what Warner will do, how far he'll go in the pursuit of what he wants but the prospect of Adam in pain is like a cold hand clutching my oesophagus. If Adam is trying to help me it could cost him his life.

I touch the piece of paper tucked into my pocket.

Breathe.

Warner's eyes are on my window.

Breathe.

"It's time to go," he says.

Breathe.

"Where are we going?"

He doesn't answer.

We step out the door. I look around. The hallway is abandoned; empty. "Where is ~~Adam~~ everyone . . . ?"

"I really like that dress," Warner says as he slips an arm around my waist. I jerk away but he pulls me along, guiding me toward the elevator. "The fit is spectacular. It helps distract me from all your questions."

"Your poor mother."

Warner almost trips over his own feet. His eyes are wide; alarmed. He stops a few feet short of our goal. Spins around. "What do you mean?"

The look on his face: the unguarded strain, the flinching terror, the sudden apprehension in his features.

I was trying to make a joke, is what I don't say to him. I feel sorry for your poor mother, is what I was going to say to him, that she has to deal with such a miserable, pathetic son. But I don't say any of it.

He grabs my hands, focuses my eyes. "What do you mean?" he insists.

"N-nothing," I stammer. "I didn't—it was just a joke—"

Warner drops my hands like they've burned him. He looks away. Charges toward the elevator and doesn't wait for me to catch up.

I wonder what he's not telling me.

Only once we've gone down several floors and are making our way down an unfamiliar hall toward an unfamiliar exit does he finally look at me. He offers me 4 words.

"Welcome to your future."

SEVENTEEN

I'm swimming in sunlight.

Warner is holding open a door that leads directly outside and I'm so unprepared for the experience I can hardly see straight. He grips my elbow to steady my path and I glance back at him.

"We're going outside." I say it because I have to say it out loud. Because the outside world is a treat I'm so seldom offered. Because I don't know if Warner is trying to be nice again. I look from him to what looks like a concrete courtyard and back to him again. "What are we doing outside?"

"We have some business to take care of." He tugs me toward the center of this new universe and I'm breaking away from him, reaching out to touch the sky like I'm hoping it will remember me. The clouds are gray like they've always been, but they're sparse and unassuming. The sun is high high high, lounging against a backdrop propping up its rays and redirecting its warmth in our general direction. I stand on tiptoe and try to touch it. The wind folds itself into my arms and smiles against my skin. Cool, silky-smooth air braids a soft breeze through my hair. This square courtyard could be my ballroom.

I want to dance with the elements.

Warner grabs my hand. I turn around.

He's smiling.

"This," he says, gesturing to the cold gray world under our feet, "this makes you happy?"

I look around. I realize the courtyard is not quite a roof, but somewhere between two buildings. I edge toward the ledge and can see dead land and naked trees and scattered compounds stretching on for miles. "Cold air smells so clean," I tell him. "Fresh. Brand-new. It's the most wonderful smell in the world."

His eyes look amused, troubled, interested, and confused all at once. He shakes his head. Pats down his jacket and reaches for an inside pocket. He pulls out a gun with a gold hilt that glints in the sunlight.

I pull in a sharp breath.

He inspects the gun in a way I wouldn't understand, presumably to check whether or not it's ready to fire. He slips it into his hand, his finger poised directly over the trigger. He turns and finally reads the expression on my face.

He almost laughs. "Don't worry. It's not for you."

"Why do you have a gun?" I swallow, hard, my arms tight across my chest. "What are we doing up here?"

Warner slips the gun back into his pocket and walks to the opposite end of the ledge. He motions for me to follow him. I creep closer. Follow his eyes. Peer over the barrier.

Every soldier in the building is standing not 15 feet below.

I distinguish almost 50 lines, each perfectly straight,

perfectly spaced, so many soldiers standing single file I lose count. ~~I wonder if Adam is in the crowd. I wonder if he can see me.~~

~~I wonder what he thinks of me now.~~

The soldiers are standing in a square space almost identical to the one Warner and I occupy, but they're one organized mass of black: black pants, black shirts, shin-high black boots; not a single gun in sight. Each is standing with his left fist pressed to his heart. Frozen in place.

Black and gray

and

black and gray

and

black and gray

and

bleak.

Suddenly I'm acutely aware of my impractical outfit. Suddenly the wind is too callous, too cold as it slices its way through the crowd. I shiver and it has nothing to do with the temperature. I look for Warner but he has already taken his place at the edge of the courtyard; it's obvious he's done this many times before. He pulls a small square of perforated metal out of his pocket and presses it to his lips; when he speaks, his voice carries over the crowd like it's been amplified.

"Sector 45."

One word. One number.

The entire group shifts: left fists released, dropped to

their sides; right fists planted in place on their chests. They are an oiled machine, working in perfect collaboration with one another. If I weren't so apprehensive I think I'd be impressed.

"We have two matters to deal with this morning." Warner's voice penetrates the atmosphere: crisp, clear, unbearably confident. "The first is standing by my side."

Thousands of eyes snap up in my direction. I feel myself flinch.

"Juliette, come here, please." 2 fingers bend in 2 places to beckon me forward.

I inch into view.

Warner slips his arm around me. I cringe. The crowd starts. My heart careens out of control. I'm afraid to back away from him. His gun is too close to my body.

The soldiers seem stunned that Warner is willing to touch me.

"Jenkins, would you step forward, please?"

My fingers are running a marathon down my thigh. I can't stand still. I can't calm the palpitations crashing my nervous system. Jenkins steps out of line; I spot him immediately.

He's okay.

Dear God.

He's okay.

"Jenkins had the pleasure of meeting Juliette just last night," he continues. The tension among the men is very nearly tangible. No one, it seems, knows where this speech is headed. And no one, it seems, hasn't already heard Jenkins' story. My story. "I hope you'll all greet her with the same sort of kindness," Warner adds. "She will be with us for some time, and will be a very valuable asset to our efforts. The Reestablishment welcomes her. I welcome her. You should welcome her."

The soldiers drop their fists all at once, all at exactly the same time.

They shift as one, 5 steps backward, 5 steps forward, 5 steps standing in place. They raise their left arms high and curl their fingers into a fist.

And fall on one knee.

I run to the edge, desperate to get a closer look at such a strangely choreographed routine. I've never seen anything like it.

Warner makes them stay like that, bent like that, fists raised in the air like that. He doesn't speak for at least 30 seconds. And then he does.

"Good."

The soldiers rise and rest their right fists on their chests again.

"The second matter at hand is even more pleasant than the first," Warner continues, though he seems to take no pleasure in saying it. "Delalieu has a report for us."

He spends an eternity simply staring at the soldiers, letting his few words marinate in their minds. Letting their own imaginations drive them insane. Letting the guilty among them tremble in anguish.

Warner says nothing for so long.

No one moves for so long.

I begin to fear for my life despite his earlier reassurances. I begin to wonder if perhaps I am the guilty one. If perhaps the gun in his pocket is meant for me. I finally dare to turn in his direction. He glances at me for the first time and I have no idea how to read him.

"Delalieu," he says, still looking at me. "You may step forward."

A thin, balding sort of man in a slightly more decorated outfit steps out from the very front of the fifth line. He doesn't look entirely stable. He ducks his head an inch. His voice warbles when he speaks. "Sir."

Warner finally unshackles my eyes and nods, almost imperceptibly, in the balding man's direction.

Delalieu recites: "We have a charge against Private 45B-76423. Fletcher, Seamus."

The soldiers are all frozen in line, frozen in relief, in fear, in anxiety. Nothing moves. Nothing breathes. Even the wind is afraid to make a sound.

"Fletcher." One word from Warner and several hundred necks snap in the same direction.

Fletcher steps out of line.

Ginger hair. Ginger freckles. Lips almost artificially red. His face is blank of every possible emotion.

I've never been more afraid for a stranger in my life.

Delalieu speaks again. "Private Fletcher was found on unregulated grounds, fraternizing with civilians believed to be rebel party members. He had stolen food and supplies from storage units dedicated to Sector 45 citizens. It is not known whether he betrayed sensitive information."

Warner levels his gaze at the gingerbread man. "Do you deny these accusations, soldier?"

Fletcher's nostrils flare. His jaw tenses. His voice cracks when he speaks. "No, sir."

Warner nods. Takes a breath.

And shoots him in the forehead.

EIGHTEEN

No one moves.

Fletcher's face is etched in permanent horror as he crumbles to the ground. I'm so struck by the impossibility of it all that I can't decide whether or not I'm dreaming.

Fletcher's limbs are bent at odd angles on the cold, concrete floor. Blood is pooling around him and still no one moves. No one says a single word. No one betrays a single look of fear.

I keep touching my lips to see if my screams have escaped.

Warner tucks his gun back into his jacket pocket. "Sector 45, you are dismissed."

Every soldier falls on one knee.

Warner slips the metal amplification device back into his suit and has to yank me free from the spot where I'm glued to the ground. I feel nauseous, delirious, incapable of holding myself upright. I keep trying to speak but the words are sticking to my tongue. I'm suddenly sweating and suddenly freezing and suddenly so sick I see spots clouding my vision.

Warner is trying to get me through the door. "You really must eat more," he says to me.

I am gaping with my eyes, gaping with my mouth, gaping wide open because I feel holes everywhere, punched into the terrain of my body.

"You killed him," I manage to whisper. "You just killed him—"

"You're very astute."

"Why did you *kill him* why would you *kill him* how could you *do* something like that—"

"Keep your eyes open, Juliette. Now's not the time to fall asleep."

I grab his shirt. I stop him before he gets inside. A gust of wind slaps me across the face and I'm suddenly in control of my senses. I push him hard, slamming his back up against the door. "You disgust me." I stare hard into his crystal-cold eyes. "You *disgust* me—"

He twists me around, pinning me against the door where I just held him. He cups my face in his gloved hands, holding my eyes in place. The same hands he just used to kill a man.

I'm trapped.

Transfixed.

Slightly terrified.

His thumb brushes my cheek.

"Life is a bleak place," he whispers. "Sometimes you have to learn how to shoot first."

Warner follows me into my room.

"You should probably sleep," he says to me. It's the first time he's spoken since we left the rooftop. "I'll have food sent up to your room, but other than that I'll make sure you're not disturbed."

"Where is Adam? ~~Is he safe? Is he healthy? Are you going to hurt him?~~"

Warner flinches before finding his composure. "Why do you care?"

~~I've cared about Adam Kent since I was in third grade.~~ "Isn't he supposed to be watching me? Because he's not here. Does that mean you're going to kill him, too?" I'm feeling stupid. I'm feeling brave because I'm feeling stupid. My words wear no parachutes as they fall out of my mouth.

"I only kill people if I need to."

"Generous."

"More than most."

I laugh a sad laugh, sharing it with only myself.

"You can have the rest of the day to yourself. Our real work will begin tomorrow. Adam will bring you to me." He holds my eyes. Suppresses a smile. "In the meantime, try not to kill anyone."

"You and I," I tell him, anger coursing through my veins, "you and I are not the same—"

"You don't really believe that."

"You think you can compare my—my *disease*—with your insanity—"

"*Disease?*" He steps forward, abruptly impassioned. "You think you have a *disease*? You have a gift! You have an extraordinary ability that you don't care to understand! Your *potential*—"

"I have no potential!"

107

"You're wrong." He's glaring at me. There's no other way to describe it. I could almost say he hates me in this moment. Hates me for hating myself.

"Well you're the murderer," I tell him. "So you must be right."

His smile is laced with dynamite. "Go to sleep."

"Go to hell."

He works his jaw. Walks to the door. "I'm working on it."

NINETEEN

The darkness is choking me.

My dreams are bloody and bleeding and blood is bleeding all over my mind and I can't sleep anymore. The only dreams that ever used to give me peace are gone and I don't know how to get them back. I don't know how to find the white bird. I don't know if it will ever fly by. All I know is that now when I close my eyes I see nothing but devastation. Fletcher is being shot over and over and over again and Jenkins is dying in my arms and Warner is shooting Adam in the head and the wind is singing outside my window but it's high-pitched and off-key and I don't have the heart to tell it to stop.

I'm freezing through my clothes.

The bed under my back is too soft, too comfortable. It reminds me too much of sleeping in Warner's room and I can't stand it. I'm afraid to slip under these covers.

I can't help but wonder if Adam is okay, if he'll ever come back, if Warner is going to keep hurting him whenever I disobey. I really shouldn't care so much.

Adam's message in my notebook might just be a part of Warner's plan to drive me insane.

I crawl onto the hard floor and check my fist for the

crumpled piece of paper I've been clutching for 2 days. It's the only hope I have left and I don't even know if it's real.

I'm running out of options.

"What are you doing here?"

I bite down on a scream and stumble up, over, and sideways, nearly slamming into Adam where he's lying on the floor next to me. I didn't even see him.

"Juliette?" He doesn't move an inch. His gaze is fixed on me: calm, unflappable; 2 buckets of river water at midnight.

"I couldn't sleep up there."

He doesn't ask me why. He pulls himself up and coughs back a grunt and I remember how he's been hurt. I wonder what kind of pain he's in. I don't ask questions as he grabs a pillow and the blanket off my bed. He puts the pillow on the floor. "Lie down," is all he says to me.

They're just 2 words and I don't know why I'm blushing. I lie down despite the sirens spinning in my blood and rest my head on the pillow. He drapes the blanket over my body. I let him do it. I watch as his arms curve and flex in the shadow of night, the glint of the moon peeking in through the window, illuminating his figure in its glow. He lies down on the floor leaving only a few feet of space between us. He requires no blanket. He uses no pillow. He still sleeps without a shirt on and I've realized I'll probably never exhale in his presence.

"You don't need to scream anymore," he whispers.

I curl my fingers around the possibility of Adam in my hand and sleep more soundly than I have in my life.

My eyes are 2 windows cracked open by the chaos in this world.

A cool breeze startles my skin and I sit up, rub the sleep from my eyes, and realize Adam is no longer beside me. I blink and crawl back up to the bed, where I replace the pillow and the blanket.

I glance at the door and wonder what's waiting for me on the other side.

I glance at the window and wonder if I'll ever see a bird fly by.

I glance at the clock on the wall and wonder what it means to be living according to numbers again. I wonder what 6:30 in the morning means in this building.

I decide to wash my face. The idea exhilarates me and I'm a little ashamed.

I open the bathroom door and catch Adam's reflection in the mirror. His fast hands pull his shirt down before I have a chance to latch on to details but I saw enough to see what I couldn't see in the darkness.

He's covered in bruises.

My legs feel broken. I don't know how to help him. I wish I could help him.

"I'm sorry," he says quickly. "I didn't know you were awake." He tugs on the bottom of his shirt like it's not long enough to pretend I'm blind.

I nod at nothing at all. I look at the tile under my feet. I don't know what to say.

"Juliette." His face is a forest of emotion. He shakes his head. "I'm sorry," he says, so quietly I'm certain I imagined it. "It's not . . ." He clenches his jaw and runs a nervous hand through his hair. "All of this—it's not—"

I open my palm to him. The paper is a crumpled wad of possibility. "I know."

Relief washes over his face and suddenly his eyes are the only reassurance I need. Adam did not betray me. I don't know why or how or what or anything at all except that he is still my friend.

He is still standing right in front of me and he doesn't want me to die.

I step forward and close the door.

I open my mouth to speak.

"No!" His lips move but make no sound. I realize in the absence of cameras there might still be microphones in the bathroom. Adam looks around and back and forth and everywhere.

He stops looking.

The shower is made of marbled glass and he's pulling the door open before I have any idea what's happening. He flips the spray on at full power and the sound of water is rushing through, rumbling through the room, muffling everything as it thunders into the emptiness around us. The mirror is already fogging up on account of the steam and just as I think I'm beginning to understand his plan he pulls me into his arms and lifts me into the shower.

My screams are vapor, wisps of gasps I can't grasp.

Hot water is puddling in my clothes. It's pelting my hair and pouring down my neck but all I feel are his hands around my waist. I want to cry out for all the wrong reasons.

His eyes pin me in place. Rivulets of water snake their way down his face and his hands hold me up against the wall.

His lips his lips his lips his lips his lips

My eyes are fighting not to flutter

My legs have won the right to tremble

My skin is scorched everywhere he's not touching me.

His lips are so close to my ear I'm water and nothing and everything and melting into a wanting so desperate it burns as I swallow it down.

"I can touch you," he says, and I wonder why there are hummingbirds in my heart. "I didn't understand until the other night," he murmurs, and I'm too drunk to digest the weight of anything but his body hovering so close to mine.

"Juliette—" His body presses closer and I realize I'm paying attention to nothing but the dandelions blowing wishes in my lungs. My eyes snap open and he licks his bottom lip for the smallest second and something in my brain bursts to life.

I gasp. I gasp. I gasp. "What are you *doing*—"

"Juliette, *please*—" His voice is anxious and he glances behind him like he's not sure we're alone. "The other night—" He presses his lips together. He closes his eyes

113

and I marvel at the drop drop drops of hot water caught in his eyelashes like pearls forged from pain. His fingers inch up the sides of my body like he's struggling to keep them in one place, like he's struggling not to touch me everywhere everywhere everywhere and his eyes are drinking in the 63 inches of my frame and I'm so I'm so I'm so

caught.

"I finally get it now," he says into my ear. "I know— I know why Warner wants you."

"Then why are you here?" I whisper. "Why . . ." 1, 2 attempts at inhalation. "Why are you touching me?"

"Because I *can*." He almost cracks a smile and I almost sprout a pair of wings. "I already have."

"What?" I blink, suddenly sobered. "What do you mean?"

"That first night in the cell," he sighs. He looks down. "You were screaming in your sleep."

I wait.

I wait.

I wait forever.

"I touched your face." He speaks into the shape of my ear. "Your hand. I brushed the length of your arm. . . ." He pulls back and his eyes rest at my shoulder, trail down to my elbow, land on my wrist. I'm suspended in disbelief. "I didn't know how to wake you up. You wouldn't wake up. So I sat back and watched you. I waited for you to stop screaming."

"That's. Not. Possible." 3 words are all I manage.

But his hands become arms around my waist his lips become a cheek pressed against my cheek and his body is flush against mine, his skin touching me touching me touching me and he's not screaming he's not dying he's not running away from me and I'm crying

I'm choking

I'm shaking shuddering splintering into teardrops

and he's holding me the way no one has ever held me before.

Like he wants me.

"I'm going to get you out of here," he says, and his mouth is moving against my hair and his hands are traveling to my arms and I'm leaning back and he's looking into my eyes and I must be dreaming.

"Why—why do you—I don't—" I'm shaking my head and shaking because this can't be happening and shaking off the tears glued to my face. This can't be real.

His eyes gentle, his smile unhinges my joints, and I wish I had the courage to touch him. "I have to go," he says. "You have to be dressed and downstairs by eight o'clock."

I'm drowning in his eyes and I don't know what to say.

He peels off his shirt and I don't know where to look.

I catch myself on the glass panel and press my eyes shut and blink when something flutters too close. His fingers are a moment from my face.

"You don't have to look away," he says. He says it with a smile the size of Jupiter.

I peek up at his features, at the crooked grin I want to savor, at the color in his eyes I'd use to paint a million pictures. I follow the line of his jaw down his neck to the peak of his collarbone; I memorize his arms, the perfection of his torso. The bird on his chest.

The bird on his chest.

A tattoo.

A white bird with streaks of gold like a crown atop its head. It's flying.

"Adam," I try to tell him. "Adam," I try to choke out. "Adam," I try to say so many times and fail.

I try to find his eyes only to realize he's been watching me study him. The pieces of his face are pressed into lines of emotion so deep I wonder what I must look like to him. He touches 2 fingers to my chin, tilts my face up just enough and I'm a live wire in water. "I'll find a way to talk to you," he says, and his hands are reeling me in and my face is pressed against his chest and the world is suddenly brighter, bigger, beautiful. The world suddenly means something to me, the possibility of humanity means something to me, the entire universe stops in place and spins in the other direction and I'm the bird.

I'm the bird and I'm flying away.

TWENTY

It's 8:00 in the morning and I'm wearing a dress the color of dead forests and old tin cans.

The fit is tighter than anything I've worn in my life, the cut modern and angular, almost haphazard; the material is stiff and thick but somehow breathable. I stare at my legs and wonder that I own a pair.

I feel more exposed than I ever have in my life.

For 17 years I've trained myself to cover every inch of exposed skin and Warner is forcing me to peel the layers away. I can only assume he's doing it on purpose. My body is a carnivorous flower, a poisonous houseplant, a loaded gun with a million triggers and he's more than ready to fire.

Touch me and suffer the consequences. There have never been exceptions to this rule.

Never but Adam.

He left me standing sopping wet in the shower, soaking up a torrential downpour of hot tears. I watched through the blurred glass as he dried himself off and slipped into his standard uniform.

I watched as he slipped away, wondering every moment why why why

Why can he touch me?

Why would he help me?

~~Does he remember me?~~

My skin is still steaming.

Hope is hugging me, holding me in its arms, wiping away my tears and telling me that today and tomorrow and two days from now I will be just fine and I'm so delirious I actually dare to believe it.

I am sitting in a blue room.

The walls are wallpapered in cloth the color of a perfect summer sky, the floor tucked into a carpet 2 inches thick, the entire room empty but for 2 velvet chairs punched out of a constellation. Every varying hue is like a bruise, like a beautiful mistake, like a reminder of what they did to Adam ~~because of me~~.

"You look lovely."

Warner whisks into the room like he treads air for a living. He's accompanied by no one.

My eyes involuntarily peek down at my tennis shoes and I wonder if I've broken any rules by avoiding the stilts in my closet I'm sure are not for feet. I look up and he's standing right in front of me.

"Green is a great color on you," he says with a stupid smile. "It really brings out the color of your eyes."

"What color are my eyes?" I ask the wall.

He laughs. "You're not serious."

"How old are you?"

He stops laughing. "You care to know?"

"I'm curious."

He takes the seat beside me. "I won't answer your questions if you won't look at me when I speak to you."

"You want me to torture people against my will. You want me to be a weapon in your war. You want me to become a monster for you." I pause. "Looking at you makes me sick."

"You're far more stubborn than I thought you'd be."

"I'm wearing your dress. I ate your food. I'm here." I lift my eyes to look at him and he's already staring straight at me.

"You did none of that for me," he says quietly.

I nearly laugh out loud. "Why would I?"

His eyes are fighting his lips for the right to speak. I look away.

"What are we doing in this room?"

"Ah." He takes a deep breath. "Breakfast. Then I give you your schedule."

He presses a button on the arm of his chair and almost instantly, carts and trays are wheeled into the room by men and women who are clearly not soldiers. Their faces are hard and cracked and too thin to be healthy.

It breaks my heart.

"I usually eat alone," Warner continues. "But I figured you and I should be more thoroughly acquainted. Especially since we'll be spending so much time together."

The ~~servants~~ ~~maids~~ people-who-are-not-soldiers leave and Warner offers me something on a dish.

"I'm not hungry."

"This is not an option."

I look up.

"You are not allowed to starve yourself to death," he says. "You don't eat enough and I need you to be healthy. You are not allowed to commit suicide. You are not allowed to harm yourself. You are too valuable to me."

"I am not your *toy*," I nearly spit.

He drops his plate onto the rolling cart and I'm surprised it doesn't shatter into pieces. He clears his throat and I might actually be scared. "This process would be so much easier if you would just cooperate.

"The world is disgusted by you," he says, his lips twitching with humor. "Everyone you've ever known has hated you. Run from you. Abandoned you. Your own parents gave up on you and *volunteered* your existence to be given up to the authorities. They were so desperate to get rid of you, to make you someone else's problem, to convince themselves the abomination they raised was not, in fact, their child."

My face has been slapped by a hundred hands.

"And yet—" He laughs openly now. "You insist on making *me* the bad guy." He meets my eyes. "I am trying to *help* you. I'm giving you an opportunity no one would ever offer you. I'm willing to treat you as an equal. I'm willing to give you everything you could ever want, and above all else, I can put power in your hands. I can make them suffer for what they did to you." He pauses. "You and I are not as different as you might hope."

"You and I are not as similar as you might hope," I snap.

He smiles so wide I'm not sure how to react. "I'm nineteen, by the way."

"Excuse me?"

"I'm nineteen years old," he clarifies. "I'm a fairly impressive specimen for my age, I know."

I pick up my spoon and poke at the edible matter on my plate. I don't know what food really is anymore. "I have no respect for you."

"You will change your mind," he says easily. "Now hurry up and eat. We have a lot of work to do."

TWENTY-ONE

Killing time isn't as difficult as it sounds.

I can shoot a hundred numbers through the chest and watch them bleed decimal points in the palm of my hand. I can rip the numbers off a clock and watch the hour hand tick tick tick its final tock just before I fall asleep. I can suffocate seconds just by holding my breath. I've been murdering minutes for hours and no one seems to mind.

It's been one week since I've spoken a word to Adam.

I turned to him once. Opened my mouth just once but never had a chance to say anything before Warner intercepted me. "You are not allowed to speak to the soldiers," he said. "If you have questions, you can find *me*. I am the only person you need to concern yourself with while you're here."

Possessive is not a strong enough word for Warner.

He escorts me everywhere. Talks to me too much. My schedule consists of meetings with Warner and eating with Warner and listening to Warner. If he is busy, I am sent to my room. If he is free, he finds me. He tells me about the books they've destroyed. The artifacts they're preparing to burn. The ideas he has for a new world and how I'll be a great help to him just as soon as I'm ready. Just as soon as I realize how much I want *this*, how much I want *him*, how much I want this new, glorious, powerful life. He is waiting for me to harness my *potential*. He tells me how grateful I should be for his patience. His kindness. His willingness to understand that this transition must be difficult.

I cannot look at Adam. I cannot speak to him. He sleeps in my room but I never see him. He breathes so close to my body but does not part his lips in my direction. He does not follow me into the bathroom. He does not leave secret messages in my notebook.

I'm beginning to wonder if I imagined everything he said to me.

I need to know if something has changed. I need to know if I'm crazy for holding on to this hope blossoming in my heart and I need to know what Adam's message meant but every day that he treats me like a stranger is another day I begin to doubt myself.

I need to talk to him but I can't.

Because now Warner is watching me.

The cameras are watching everything.

"I want you to take the cameras out of my room."

Warner stops chewing the food/garbage/breakfast/nonsense in his mouth. He swallows carefully before leaning back and looking me in the eye. "Absolutely not."

"If you treat me like a prisoner," I tell him, "I'm going to act like one. I don't like to be watched."

"You can't be trusted on your own." He picks up his spoon again.

"Every breath I take is monitored. There are guards stationed in five-foot intervals in all the hallways. I don't even have access to my own room," I protest. "Cameras aren't going to make a difference."

A strange kind of amusement dances on his lips. "You're not exactly stable, you know. You're liable to kill someone."

"No." I grip my fingers. "No—I wouldn't—I didn't kill Jenkins—"

"I'm not talking about Jenkins."

He won't stop looking at me. Smiling at me. Torturing me with his eyes.

This is me, screaming silently into my fist.

"That was an accident." The words tumble out of my mouth so quietly, so quickly I don't know if I've actually spoken or if I'm still sitting here or if I'm 14 years old all over again all over again all over again and I'm diving into a pool of memories I never ever ever ever ever

I can't seem to forget.

I saw her at the grocery store. Her legs were standing crossed at the ankles, her child was on a leash she thought he thought was a backpack. She thought he was too dumb/ too young/too immature to understand that the rope tying him to her wrist was a device designed to trap him in her uninterested circle of self-sympathy. She's too young to have a kid, to have these responsibilities, to be buried by a child who has needs that don't accommodate her own. Her life is so incredibly unbearable so immensely multifaceted too glamorous for the leashed legacy of her loins to understand.

Children are not stupid, was what I wanted to tell her.

I wanted to tell her that his seventh scream didn't mean he was trying to be obnoxious, that her fourteenth admonishment in the form of brat/you're such a brat/you're embarrassing me you little brat/don't make me tell Daddy you were being a brat was uncalled for. I didn't mean to watch but I couldn't help myself. His 3-year-old face puckered in pain, his little hands tried to undo the chains she'd strapped across his chest and she tugged so hard he fell down and cried and she told him he deserved it.

I wanted to ask her why she would do that.

I wanted to ask her so many questions but I didn't because we don't talk to people anymore because saying something would be stranger than saying nothing to a stranger. He fell to the floor and writhed around until I'd dropped everything in my hands and every feature on my face.

I'm so sorry, is what I never said to her son.

I thought my hands were helping

I thought my heart was helping

I thought so many things

I never

never

never

never

never thought

"You killed a little boy."

*

125

I'm nailed into my velvet chair by a million memories and haunted by a horror my bare hands created. I am unwanted for good reason. My hands can kill people. My hands can destroy everything.

I should not be allowed to live.

"I want," I gasp, "I want you to get rid of the cameras. Get rid of them or I will die fighting you for the right."

"Finally." Warner stands up and claps his hands together as if to congratulate himself. "I was wondering when you'd wake up. I've been waiting for the fire I know must be eating away at you every single day. You're buried in hatred, aren't you? Anger? Frustration? Itching to do *something*? To be *someone*?"

"No."

"Of course you are. You're just like me."

"I hate you more than you will ever understand."

"We're going to make an excellent team."

"We are *nothing*. You are *nothing* to me—"

"I know what you want." He leans in, lowers his voice. "I know what your little heart has always longed for. I can give you the acceptance you seek. I can be your *friend*."

I freeze. Falter.

"I know *everything* about you, love." He grins. "I've wanted you for a very long time. I've waited forever for you to be ready. I'm not going to let you go so easily."

"I don't want to be a monster," I say, perhaps more for my sake than his.

"Don't fight what you're born to be." He grasps my

shoulders. "Stop letting everyone else tell you what's wrong and right. Stake a claim! You cower when you could conquer. You have so much more power than you're aware of and quite frankly I'm"—he shakes his head—"fascinated."

"I am not your *freak*," I snap. "I will not *perform* for you."

"I'm not afraid of you, my dear," he says softly. "I'm absolutely enchanted."

"Either you get rid of the cameras or I will find and break every single one of them." I'm a liar. I'm lying through my teeth but I'm angry and desperate and horrified. Warner wants to morph me into an animal who preys on the weak. On the innocent.

If he wants me to fight for him, he's going to have to fight me first.

A slow smile spreads across his face. He touches gloved fingers to my cheek and tilts my head up, catching my chin in his grip when I flinch away. "You're absolutely delicious when you're angry."

"Too bad my taste is poisonous for your palate." I'm vibrating in disgust from head to toe.

"That detail makes this game so much more appealing."

"You're sick, you're so *sick*—"

He laughs and releases my chin. His eyes draw a lazy trail down the length of my body and I feel the sudden urge to rupture his spleen. "If I get rid of your cameras, what will you do for me?" His eyes are wicked.

"Nothing."

He shakes his head. "That won't do. I might agree to

your proposition if you agree to a condition."

I clench my jaw. "What do you want?"

The smile is bigger than before. "That is a dangerous question."

"What is your *condition*?" I clarify, impatient.

"Touch me."

"What?" My gasp is so loud it catches in my throat.

"I want to know exactly what you're capable of." His voice is steady, his eyebrows taut, tense.

"I won't do it again!" I explode. "You saw what you made me do to Jenkins—"

"Screw Jenkins," he spits. "I want you to touch *me*— I want to feel it *myself*—"

"No." I shake my head so hard it makes me dizzy. "No. Never. You're crazy—I won't—"

"You will, actually."

"I will NOT—"

"You will have to . . . *work* . . . at one point or another," he says, making an effort to moderate his voice. "Even if you were to forgo my condition, you are here for a reason, Juliette. I convinced my father that you would be an asset to The Reestablishment. That you'd be able to restrain any rebels we—"

"You mean *torture*—"

"Yes." He smiles. "Forgive me, I mean torture. You will be able to help us torture anyone we capture." A pause. "Inflicting pain, you see, is an incredibly efficient method of getting information out of anyone. And with you?" He glances at my hands. "Well, it's cheap. Fast. Effective."

He smiles wider. "And as long as we keep you alive, you'll be good for at least a few decades. It's very fortunate that you're not battery-operated."

"You—*you*—"

"You should be thanking me. I saved you from that sick hole of an asylum—I brought you into a position of power. I've given you everything you could possibly need to be comfortable." He levels his gaze at me. "Now I need you to focus. I need you to relinquish your hopes of living like everyone else. You are *not* normal. You never have been, and you never will be. Embrace who you *are*."

"I am not—I'm not—I'm—"

"A murderer?"

"NO—"

"An instrument of torture?"

"STOP—"

"You're lying to yourself."

I'm ready to destroy him.

He cocks his head. "You've been on the edge of insanity your entire life, haven't you? So many people called you crazy you actually started to believe it. You wondered if they were right. You wondered if you could fix it. You thought if you could just try a little harder, be a little better, smarter, nicer—you thought the world would change its mind about you. You blamed yourself for everything."

My bottom lip trembles without my permission. I can hardly control the tension in my jaw.

~~I don't want to tell him he's right.~~

"You've suppressed all your rage and resentment because

you wanted to be loved," he says, no longer smiling. "Maybe I understand you, Juliette. Maybe you should trust me. Maybe you should accept the fact that you've tried to be someone you're not for so long and that no matter what you did, those bastards were never happy. They were never satisfied. They never gave a damn, did they?" He looks at me and for a moment he seems almost human. For a moment I want to believe him. For a moment I want to sit on the floor and cry out the ocean lodged in my throat.

"It's time you stopped pretending," he says, so softly. "Juliette—" He takes my face in his gloved hands, so unexpectedly gentle. "You don't have to be nice anymore. You can destroy all of them. You can take them down and own this whole world—"

"But I don't want to destroy anyone," I tell him. "I don't want to *hurt* people—"

"They *deserve* it!" He turns away, frustrated. "How could you not want to retaliate? How could you not want to *fight back*—"

I stand up slowly, shaking with anger. "You think I don't have a heart? You think I don't *feel*? You think that because I *can* inflict pain, that I should? You're just like everyone else. You think I'm a monster just like everyone else. You don't understand me at all—"

"Juliette—"

"No."

I don't want this. I don't want his life.

I don't want to be anything for anyone but myself.

I want to make my own choices and I've never wanted to be a monster. My words are slow and steady when I speak. "I value human life a lot more than you do, Warner."

He opens his mouth to speak before he stops. Laughs out loud and shakes his head.

Smiles at me.

"What?" I ask before I can stop myself.

"You just said my name." He grins even wider. "You've never addressed me directly before. That must mean I'm making progress with you."

"I just told you I don't—"

He cuts me off. "I'm not worried about your moral dilemmas. You're just stalling for time because you're in denial. Don't worry," he says. "You'll get over it. I can wait a little longer."

"I'm not in *denial*—"

"Of course you are. You don't know it yet, Juliette, but you are a very bad girl," he says, clutching his heart. "Just my type."

This conversation is impossible.

"There is a soldier *living* in my room." I'm breathing hard. "If you want me to be here, you need to get rid of the cameras."

Warner's eyes darken for just an instant. "Where *is* your soldier, anyway?"

"I wouldn't know." I hope to God I'm not blushing. "You assigned him to me."

"Yes." He looks thoughtful. "I like watching you squirm.

131

He makes you uncomfortable, doesn't he?"

I think about Adam's hands on my body and his lips so close to mine and the scent of his skin and suddenly my heart is pounding. "Yes." *God.* "Yes. He makes me very . . . uncomfortable."

"Do you know why I chose him?" Warner asks, and I'm stunned.

Adam was *chosen.*

Of course he was. He wasn't just any soldier sent to my cell. Warner does nothing without reason. He must know Adam and I have a history. He is more cruel and calculative than I gave him credit for.

"No." Inhale. "I don't know why." Exhale. I can't forget to breathe.

"He volunteered," Warner says simply, and I'm dumbstruck. "He said he'd gone to school with you so many years ago. He said you probably wouldn't remember him, that he looks a lot different now than he did back then. He put together a very convincing case." A beat of breath. "He said he was thrilled to hear you'd been locked up." Warner finally looks at me.

"I'm curious," he continues, tilting his head as he speaks. "Do you remember him?"

"No," I lie, and I'm trying to untangle the truth from the false from assumptions from the postulations but run-on sentences are twisting around my throat.

Adam knew me when he walked into that cell.

He knew exactly who I was.

He already knew my name.

Oh

Oh

Oh

This was all a trap.

"Does this information make you . . . angry?" he asks, and I want to sew his smiling lips into a permanent scowl.

I say nothing and somehow it's worse.

Warner is beaming. "I never told him, of course, why it was that you'd been locked up—I thought the experiment in the asylum should remain untainted by extra information—but he said you were always a threat to the students. That everyone was always warned to stay away from you, though the authorities never explained why. He said he wanted to get a closer look at the freak you've become."

My heart cracks. My eyes flash. I'm so hurt so angry so *humiliated* and burning with indignation so raw that it's like a fire raging within me. I want to crush Warner's spine in my hand. I want him to know what it's like to wound, to inflict such agony on others. I want him to know my pain and Jenkins' pain and Fletcher's pain and I want him to *hurt*. Because maybe Warner is right.

Maybe some people do deserve it.

"Take off your shirt."

For all his posturing, Warner looks genuinely surprised, but he wastes no time unbuttoning his jacket, slipping off his gloves, and peeling away the thin cotton shirt clinging closest to his skin.

His eyes are bright, sickeningly eager; he doesn't mask his curiosity.

Warner drops his clothes to the floor and looks at me almost intimately. I have to swallow back the revulsion bubbling in my mouth. His perfect face. His perfect body. He repulses me. I want his exterior to match his broken black interior. I want to cripple his cockiness with the palm of my hand.

He walks up to me until there's less than a foot of space between us. His height and build make me feel like a fallen twig. "Are you ready?" he asks.

I contemplate breaking his neck.

"If I do this you'll get rid of all the cameras in my room. All the bugs. Everything."

He steps closer. Dips his head. He's staring at my lips, studying me in an entirely new way. "My promises aren't worth much, love," he whispers. "Or have you forgotten?" 3 inches forward. His hand on my waist. His breath sweet and warm on my neck. "I'm an exceptional liar."

Realization slams into me.

I shouldn't be doing this. I shouldn't be making deals with him. I shouldn't be contemplating torture dear God I have lost my mind. My fists are balled at my sides and I'm shaking everywhere. I can hardly find the strength to speak. "You can go to hell."

I'm limp.

I trip backward against the wall and slump into a heap of uselessness; desperation. I think of Adam and my heart deflates.

I can't be here anymore.

I fly to the double doors facing the room and yank them open before Warner can stop me. But Adam stops me instead. He's standing just outside. Waiting. Guarding me wherever I go.

I wonder if he heard everything and my eyes fall to the floor, the color flushed from my face. Of course he heard everything. Of course he now knows I'm a murderer. A monster. A worthless soul stuffed into a poisonous body.

Warner did this on purpose.

And I'm standing between them. Warner with no shirt on. Adam looking at his gun.

"Soldier." Warner speaks. "Take her back up to her room and disable all the cameras. She can have lunch alone if she wants, but I'll expect her for dinner."

Adam blinks for a moment too long. "Yes, sir."

"Juliette?"

I freeze. My back is to Warner and I don't turn around.

"I do expect you to hold up your end of the bargain."

TWENTY-TWO

It takes 5 years to walk to the elevator. 15 more to ride it up. I'm a million years old by the time I walk into my room. Adam is still, silent, perfectly put together and mechanical in his movements. There's nothing in his eyes, in his limbs, in the motions of his body that indicate he even knows my name.

I watch him move quickly, swiftly, carefully around the room, finding the little devices meant to monitor my behavior and disabling them one by one. If anyone asks why my cameras aren't working, Adam won't get in trouble. This order came from Warner. This makes it official.

This makes it possible for me to have some privacy.

I thought I would need privacy.

I'm such a fool.

Adam is not the boy I remember.

I was in third grade.

I'd just moved into town after being ~~thrown out of~~ asked to leave my old school. My parents were always moving, always running away from the messes I made, from the playdates I'd ruined, from the friendships I never had. No one ever wanted to talk about my "problem," but the mystery surrounding my existence somehow made things worse. The human imagination is often disastrous when left to its own devices. I only heard bits and pieces of their whispers.

"Freak!"

"Did you hear what she *did*—?"

"What a loser."

"—got kicked out of her old school—"

"Psycho!"

"She's got some kind of disease—"

No one talked to me. Everyone stared. I was young enough that I still cried. I ate lunch alone by a chain-link fence and never looked in the mirror. I never wanted to see the face everyone hated so much. Girls used to kick me and run away. Boys used to throw rocks at me. I still have scars somewhere.

I watched the world pass by through those chain-link fences. I stared out at the cars and the parents dropping off their kids and the moments I'd never be a part of. This was before the diseases became so common that death was a natural part of conversation. This was before we realized the clouds were the wrong color, before we realized all the animals were dying or infected, before we realized everyone was going to starve to death, and fast. This was back when we still thought our problems had solutions. Back then, Adam was the boy who used to walk to school. Adam was the boy who sat 3 rows in front of me. His clothes were worse than mine, his lunch nonexistent. I never saw him eat.

One morning he came to school in a car.

I know because I saw him being pushed out of it. His father was drunk and driving, yelling and flailing his fists for some reason. Adam stood very still and stared at the ground like he was waiting for something, steeling himself for the inevitable. I watched a father slap his 8-year-old son in the face. I watched Adam fall to the floor and I stood there, motionless as he was kicked repeatedly in the ribs.

"It's all your fault! It's *your* fault, you worthless piece of shit," his father screamed over and over and over again until I threw up right there, all over a patch of dandelions.

Adam didn't cry. He stayed curled up on the ground until his father gave up, until he drove away. Only once he was sure everyone was gone did his body break into heaving sobs, his small face smeared into the dirt, his arms clutching at his bruised abdomen. I couldn't look away.

I could never get that sound out of my head, that scene out of my head.

That's when I started paying attention to Adam Kent.

"Juliette."

I suck in my breath and wish my hands weren't trembling. I wish I had no eyes.

"Juliette," he says again, this time even softer.

I won't turn around.

"You always knew who I was," I whisper.

He says nothing and I'm suddenly desperate to see his eyes. I suddenly need to see his eyes. I turn to face him despite everything only to see he's staring at his hands. "I'm sorry," is all he says.

I lean back against the wall and look away. Everything was a performance. Stealing my bed. Asking for my name. Asking me about my family. He was performing for Warner. For the guards. For whoever was watching. I don't even know what to believe anymore.

I need to say it. I need to get it out. I need to rip my wounds open and bleed fresh for him. "It's true," I tell him. "About the little boy." My voice is shaking so much more than I thought it would. "I did that."

He's quiet for so long. "I never understood before," he says. "When I first heard about it. I didn't realize until just now what must've happened. It never made sense to me," he says. He looks up. "When I heard about it. We all heard about it. The whole school—"

"It was an accident," I choke out. "He—h-he fell—and I was trying to help him—and I just—I didn't—I thought—"

"I know."

"What?" I gasp.

"I believe you," he says to me.

"What . . . why?" My eyes are blinking back tears, my hands unsteady, my heart filled with nervous hope.

He bites his bottom lip. Looks away. Walks to the wall. Opens and closes his mouth several times before the words rush out. "Because I *knew* you, Juliette—I—God—I just—" He closes his eyes. "That was the day I was going to talk to you." A strange sort of smile. A strange sort of laugh. Looks up at the ceiling. Turns his back to me. "I was finally going to talk to you. I was finally going to talk to you and I—" He shakes his head, hard, and attempts another painful laugh. "God, you don't remember me."

I want to laugh and cry and scream and run and I can't choose which to do first.

I confess.

"Of course I remember you." My voice is a strangled whisper. I squeeze my eyes shut. ~~I remember you every day forever in every single broken moment of my life~~. "You were the only one who ever looked at me like a human being."

He never talked to me. He never spoke a single word to me, but he was the only one who dared to sit close to my fence. He was the only one who stood up for me, the only person who fought for me, the only one who'd punch someone in the face for throwing a rock at my head. I didn't even know how to say thank you.

He was the closest thing to a friend I ever had.

I open my eyes and he's standing right in front of me.

"You've always known?" 3 whispered words and he's broken my dam, unlocked my lips and stolen my heart all over again. I can hardly feel the tears streaming down my face.

"Adam." I try to laugh. "I'd recognize your eyes anywhere in the world."

And that's it.

This time there's no self-control.

This time I'm in his arms and against the wall and I'm

trembling everywhere and he's so gentle, so careful, touching me like I'm made of porcelain and I want to shatter.

He's running his hands down my body running his eyes across my face and I'm running marathons with my mind.

Everything is on fire.

My cheeks my hands the pit of my stomach and I'm drowning in waves of emotion and a storm of fresh rain and all I feel is the strength of his silhouette against mine and I never ever ever ever want to forget this moment. I want to stamp him into my skin and save him forever.

He takes my hands and presses my palms to his face and I know I never knew the beauty of feeling human before this. I know I'm still crying when my eyes flutter closed.

I whisper his name.

And he's breathing harder than I am and suddenly his lips are on my neck and I'm gasping and clutching at his arms and he's touching me touching me touching me and I'm thunder and lightning and wondering when the hell I'll be waking up. He meets my eyes only to cup my face in his hands and I'm blushing through these walls from pleasure and pain and impossibility.

"I've wanted to kiss you for so long." His voice is husky, uneven, deep in my ear.

I'm frozen in anticipation in expectation and I'm so worried he'll kiss me, so worried he won't. I'm staring at his lips and I don't realize how close we are until we're pulled apart.

3 distinct electronic screeches reverberate around the

room and Adam looks past me like he can't understand where he is for a moment. He blinks. And runs toward an intercom to press the appropriate buttons. I notice he's still breathing hard.

I'm shaking in my skin.

"Name and number," the voice of the intercom demands.

"Kent, Adam. 45B-86659."

A pause.

"Soldier, are you aware the cameras in your room have been deactivated?"

"Yes, sir. I was given direct orders to dismantle the devices."

"Who cleared this order?"

"Warner, sir."

A longer pause.

"We'll verify and confirm. Unauthorized tampering with security devices may result in your immediate dishonorable discharge, soldier. I hope you're aware of that."

"Yes, sir."

The line goes quiet.

Adam slumps against the wall, his chest heaving. I'm not sure but I could've sworn his lips twitched into the tiniest smile. He closes his eyes and exhales.

I'm not sure what to do with the relief tumbling into my hands.

"Come here," he says, his eyes still shut.

I tiptoe forward and he pulls me into his arms. Breathes in the scent of my hair and kisses the side of my head and

I've never felt anything so incredible in my life. I'm not even human anymore. I'm so much more. The sun and the moon have merged and the earth is upside down. I feel like I can be exactly who I want to be in his arms.

He makes me forget the terror I'm capable of.

"Juliette," he whispers in my ear. "We need to get the hell out of here."

TWENTY-THREE

I'm 14 years old again and I'm staring at the back of his head in a small classroom. I'm 14 years old and I've been in love with Adam Kent for years. I made sure to be extra careful, to be extra quiet, to be extra cooperative because I didn't want to move away again. I didn't want to leave the school with the one friendly face I'd ever known. I watched him grow up a little more every day, grow a little taller every day, a little stronger, a little tougher, a little more quiet every day. He eventually got too big to get beaten up by his dad, but no one really knows what happened to his mother. The students shunned him, harassed him until he started fighting back, until the pressure of the world finally cracked him.

But his eyes always stayed the same.

Always the same when he looked at me. Kind. Compassionate. Desperate to understand. But he never asked questions. He never pushed me to say a word. He just made sure he was close enough to scare away everyone else.

I thought maybe I wasn't so bad. Maybe.

I thought maybe he saw something in me. I thought maybe I wasn't as horrible as everyone said I was. I hadn't touched anyone in years. I didn't dare get close to people. I couldn't risk it.

Until one day I did, and I ruined everything.

I killed a little boy in a grocery store simply by helping him to his feet. By grabbing his little hands. I didn't understand why he was screaming. It was my first experience ever touching someone for such a long period of time and I didn't understand what was happening to me. The few times I'd ever accidentally put my hands on someone I'd always pulled away. I'd pull away as soon as I remembered I wasn't supposed to be touching anyone. As soon as I heard the first scream escape their lips.

The little boy was different.

I wanted to help him. I felt such a surge of sudden anger toward his mother for neglecting his cries. Her lack of compassion as a parent devastated me ~~and it reminded me too much of my own mother~~. I just wanted to help him. I wanted him to know that someone else was listening— that someone else cared. I didn't understand why it felt so strange and exhilarating to touch him. I didn't know that I was draining his life and I couldn't comprehend why he'd grown limp and quiet in my arms. I thought maybe the rush of power and positive feeling meant that I'd been cured of my horrible disease. I thought so many stupid things and I ruined everything.

I thought I was helping.

I spent the next 3 years of my life in hospitals, law offices, juvenile detention centers, and suffered through pills and electroshock therapy. Nothing worked. Nothing helped. Outside of killing me, locking me up in an institution was the only solution. The only way to protect the public from the terror of Juliette.

Until he stepped into my cell, I hadn't seen Adam Kent in 3 years.

And he does look different. Tougher, taller, harder, sharper, tattooed. He's muscle, mature, quiet and quick. It's almost like he can't afford to be soft or slow or relaxed. He can't afford to be anything but strength and efficiency. The lines of his face are precise, carved into shape by years of hard living and training and trying to survive.

He's not a little boy anymore. He's not afraid. He's in the army.

But he's not so different, either. He still has the most unusually blue eyes I've ever seen. Dark and deep and drenched in passion. I always wondered what it'd be like to see the world through such a beautiful lens. I wondered if your eye color meant you saw the world differently. If the world saw you differently as a result.

I should have known it was him when he showed up in my cell.

A part of me did. But I'd tried so hard to repress the memories of my past that I refused to believe it could be possible. Because a part of me didn't want to remember. A part of me was too scared to hope. A part of me didn't know if it would make any difference to know that it was him, after all.

I often wonder what I must look like.

I wonder if I'm just a punctured shadow of the person I

was before. I haven't looked in the mirror in 3 years. I'm so scared of what I'll see.

Someone knocks on the door.

I'm catapulted across the room by my own fear. Adam locks eyes with me before opening the door and I decide to retreat into a far corner of the room.

I sharpen my ears only to hear muted voices, hushed tones, and someone clearing his throat. I'm not sure what to do.

"I'll be down in a minute," Adam says a little loudly. I realize he's trying to end the conversation.

"C'mon, man, I just want to see her—"

"She's not a goddamn spectacle, Kenji. Get the hell out of here."

"Wait—just tell me: Does she light shit on fire with her eyes?" Kenji laughs and I cringe, slumping to the floor behind the bed. I curl into myself and try not to hear the rest of the conversation.

I fail.

Adam sighs. I can picture him rubbing his forehead. "Just get out."

Kenji struggles to muffle his laughter. "Damn you're sensitive all of a sudden, huh? Hanging out with a girl is changing you, man—"

Adam says something I can't hear.

The door slams shut.

*

I peek up from my hiding place. Adam looks embarrassed.

My cheeks go pink. I study the threads of the finely woven carpet under my feet. I touch the cloth wallpaper and wait for him to speak. I stand up to stare out the window only to be met by the bleak backdrop of a broken city. I lean my forehead against the glass.

Metal cubes are clustered together in the distance: compounds housing civilians wrapped in layers, trying to find refuge from the cold. A mother holding the hand of a small child. Soldiers standing over them, still like statues, rifles poised and ready to fire. Heaps and heaps and heaps of trash, dangerous scraps of iron and steel glinting on the ground. Lonely trees waving at the wind.

Adam's hands slip around my waist.

His lips are at my ear and he says nothing at all, but I melt, hot butter dripping down his body. I want to eat every minute of this moment.

I allow my eyes to shut against the truth outside my window. Just for a little while.

Adam takes a deep breath and pulls me even closer. I'm molded to the shape of him; his hands are circling my waist and his cheek is pressed against my head. "You feel incredible."

I try to laugh but seem to have forgotten how. "Those are words I never thought I'd hear."

Adam spins me around so I'm facing him.

He leans in until his forehead rests against mine and our lips still aren't close enough. He whispers, "How are you?" and I want to kiss every beautiful beat of his heart.

How are you? 3 words no one ever asks me.

"I want to get out of here," is all I can think of.

He squeezes me against his chest and I marvel at the power, the glory, the wonder in such a simple movement.

Every butterfly in the world has migrated to my stomach.

"Juliette."

I lean back to see his face.

"Are you serious about leaving?" he asks me. His fingers brush the side of my cheek. He tucks a stray strand of hair behind my ear. "Do you understand the risks?"

I take a deep breath. I know that the only real risk is death. "Yes."

He nods. Drops his eyes, his voice. "The troops are mobilizing for some kind of attack. There've been a lot of protests from groups who were silent before, and our job is to obliterate the resistance. I think they want this attack to be their last one," he adds. "There's something huge going on, and I'm not sure what, not yet. But whatever it is, we have to be ready to go when they are."

I freeze. "What do you mean?"

"When the troops are ready to deploy, you and I should be ready to run. It's the only way out that will give us time to disappear. Everyone will be too focused on the attack—it'll buy us some time before they notice we're missing or can get enough people together to search for us."

"But—you mean—you'll come with me . . . ? You'd be willing to do that for me?"

He smiles a small smile. His lips twitch like he's trying not to laugh. "There's very little I wouldn't do for you."

I take a deep breath and close my eyes, touching my fingers to his chest, imagining the bird soaring across his skin, and I ask him the one question that scares me the most. "Why?"

"What do you mean?"

"Why, Adam? Why do you care? Why do you want to help me? I don't understand—I don't know why you'd be willing to risk your life—"

But then his arms are around my waist and he's pulling me so close and his lips are at my ear and he says my name, once, twice and I had no idea I could catch fire so quickly. His mouth is smiling against my skin. "You don't?"

I don't know anything, is what I would tell him if I had any idea how to speak.

He laughs a little and pulls back. Takes my hand and studies it. "Do you remember in fourth grade," he says, "when Molly Carter signed up for the school field trip too late? All the spots were filled, and she stood outside the bus, crying because she wanted to go?"

He doesn't wait for me to answer.

"I remember you got off the bus. You offered her your seat and she didn't even say thank you. I watched you standing on the sidewalk as we pulled away."

I'm no longer breathing.

"Do you remember in fifth grade? That week Dana's parents nearly got divorced? She came to school every day without her lunch. And you offered to give her yours." He pauses. "As soon as that week was over she went back to pretending you didn't exist."

"In seventh grade Shelly Morrison got caught cheating off your math test. She kept screaming that if she failed, her father would kill her. You told the teacher that you were the one cheating off of *her* test. You got a zero on the exam, and detention for a week." He lifts his head but doesn't look at me. "You had bruises on your arms for at least a month after that. I always wondered where they came from."

My heart is beating too fast. Dangerously fast. I clench my fingers to keep them from shaking.

"A million times," he says, his voice so quiet now. "I saw you do things like that a million times. But you never said a word unless it was forced out of you." He laughs again, this time a hard, heavy sort of laugh. He's staring at a point directly past my shoulder. "You never asked for anything from anyone." He finally meets my eyes. "But no one ever gave you a chance."

I swallow hard, try to look away but he catches my face.

He whispers, "You have no idea how much I've thought about you. How many times I've dreamt"—he takes a tight breath—"how many times I've dreamt about being this close to you." He moves to run a hand through his hair before he changes his mind. Looks down. Looks up. "God, Juliette, I'd follow you anywhere. You're the only good thing left in this world."

I'm begging myself not to burst into tears and I don't know if it's working. I'm everything broken and glued back together and blushing everywhere and I can hardly find the strength to meet his gaze.

His fingers find my chin. Tip me up.

"We have three weeks at the most," he says. "I don't think they can control the mobs for much longer."

I nod. I blink. I rest my face against his chest and pretend I'm not crying.

3 weeks.

TWENTY-FOUR

2 weeks pass.

2 weeks of dresses and showers and food I want to throw across the room. 2 weeks of Warner smiling and touching my waist, laughing and guiding the small of my back, making sure I look my best as I walk beside him. He thinks I'm his trophy. His secret weapon.

I have to stifle the urge to crack his knuckles into concrete.

But I offer him 2 weeks of cooperation because in 1 week we'll be gone.

Hopefully.

But then, more than anything else, I've found I don't hate Warner as much as I thought I did.

I feel sorry for him.

He finds a strange sort of solace in my company; he thinks I can relate to him and his twisted notions, his cruel upbringing, his absent and simultaneously demanding father.

But he never says a word about his mother.

Adam says that no one knows anything about Warner's mother—that she's never been discussed and no one has any idea who she is. He says that Warner is only known to be the consequence of ruthless parenting, and a cold, calculated desire for power. He hates happy children and happy parents and their happy lives.

I think Warner thinks that I understand. That I understand him.

And I do. And I don't.

Because we're not the same.

I want to be better.

Adam and I have little time together but nighttime. And even then, not so much. Warner watches me more closely every day; disabling the cameras only made him more suspicious. He's always walking into my room unexpectedly, taking me on unnecessary tours around the building, talking about nothing but his plans and his plans to make more plans and how together we'll conquer the world. I don't pretend to care.

Maybe it's me who's making this worse.

"I can't believe Warner actually agreed to get rid of your cameras," Adam said to me one night.

"He's insane. He's sick in a way I'll never understand."

Adam sighed. "He's obsessed with you."

"What?" I nearly snapped my neck in surprise.

"You're all he ever talks about." Adam was silent a moment, his jaw too tight. "I heard stories about you before you even got here. That's why I got involved—it's why I volunteered to go get you. Warner spent months collecting information about you: addresses, medical records, personal histories, family relations, birth certificates, blood tests. The entire army was talking about his new project; everyone knew he was looking for a girl who'd killed a little boy in a grocery store. A girl named Juliette."

I held my breath.

Adam shook his head. "I knew it was you. It had to be. I asked Warner if I could help with the project—I told him I'd gone to school with you, that I'd heard about the little boy, that I'd seen you in person." He laughed a hard laugh. "Warner was thrilled. He thought it would make the experiment more interesting," he added, disgusted. "And I knew that if he wanted to claim you as some kind of sick project—" He hesitated. Looked away. "I just knew I had to do something. I thought I could try to help. But now it's gotten worse. Warner won't stop talking about what you're capable of or how valuable you are to his efforts and how excited he is to have you here. Everyone is beginning to notice. Warner is ruthless—he has no mercy for anyone. He loves the power, the thrill of destroying people. But he's starting to crack, Juliette. He's so desperate to have you . . . *join* him. And for all his threats, he doesn't want to force you. He wants you to want it. To choose *him*, in a way." He looked down, took a tight breath. "He's losing his edge. And whenever I see his face I'm always about two inches away from doing something stupid. I'd love to break his jaw."

Yes. Warner is losing his edge.

He's paranoid, though with good reason. But then he's patient and impatient with me. Excited and nervous all the

155

time. He's a walking oxymoron.

He disables my cameras, but some nights he orders Adam to sleep outside my door to make sure I don't escape. He says I can eat lunch alone, but always ends up summoning me to his side. The few hours Adam and I would've had together are stolen from us, but the fewer nights Adam is allowed to sleep inside my room I manage to spend huddled in his arms.

We both sleep on the floor now, wrapped up in each other for warmth even with the blanket covering our bodies. Every time he touches me it's like a burst of fire and electricity that ignites my bones in the most amazing way. It's the kind of feeling I wish I could hold in my hand.

Adam tells me about new developments, whispers he's heard around the other soldiers. He tells me how there are multiple headquarters across what's left of the country. How Warner's dad is at the capital, how he's left his son in charge of this entire sector. He says Warner hates his father but loves the power. The destruction. The devastation. He strokes my hair and tells me stories and tucks me close like he's afraid I'll disappear. He paints pictures of people and places until I fall asleep, until I'm drowning in a drug of dreams to escape a world with no refuge, no relief, no release but his reassurances in my ear. Sleep is the only thing I look forward to these days. I can hardly remember why I used to scream.

Things are getting too comfortable and I'm beginning to panic.

*

"Put these on," Warner says to me.

Breakfast in the blue room has become routine. I eat and don't ask where the food comes from, whether or not the workers are being paid for what they do, how this building manages to sustain so many lives, pump so much water, or use so much electricity. I bide my time now. I cooperate.

Warner hasn't asked me to touch him again, and I don't offer.

"What are they for?" I eye the small pieces of fabric in his hands and feel a nervous twinge in my gut.

He smiles a slow, sneaky smile. "An aptitude test." He grabs my wrist and places the bundle in my hand. "I'll turn around, just this once."

I'm almost too nervous to be disgusted by him.

My hands shake as I change into the outfit that turns out to be a tiny tank top and tinier shorts. I'm practically naked. I'm practically convulsing in fear of what this might mean. I clear my throat and Warner spins around.

He takes too long to speak; his eyes are busy traveling the road map of my body. I want to rip up the carpet and sew it to my skin. He smiles and offers me his hand.

I'm granite and limestone and marbled glass. I don't move.

He drops his hand. Cocks his head. "Follow me."

Warner opens the door. Adam is standing outside. He's gotten so good at masking his emotions that I hardly register the look of shock that shifts in and out of his features. Nothing but the strain in his forehead, the tension in his temples, gives him away. He knows something's not right. He actually turns his neck to take in my appearance. He blinks. "Sir?"

"Remain where you are, soldier. I'll take it from here."

Adam doesn't answer doesn't answer doesn't answer— "Yes, sir," he says.

I feel his eyes on me as I turn down the hall.

Warner takes me somewhere new. We're walking through corridors I've never seen, blacker and bleaker and more narrow as we go. I realize we're heading downward.

Into a basement.

We pass through 1, 2, 4 metal doors. Soldiers everywhere, their eyes everywhere, appraising me with both fear and something else I'd rather not consider. I've realized there are very few females in this building.

If there were ever a place to be grateful for being untouchable, it'd be here.

It's the only reason I have asylum from the preying eyes of hundreds of lonely men. It's the only reason Adam is staying with me—because Warner thinks Adam is a cardboard cutout. He thinks Adam is a machine oiled by orders and demands. He thinks Adam is a reminder of my past, and he uses it to make me uncomfortable. He'd never imagine Adam could lay a finger on me.

No one would. Everyone I meet is absolutely petrified.

The darkness is like a black canvas punctured by a blunt knife, with beams of light peeking through. It reminds me too much of my old cell. My skin ripples with uncontrollable dread.

I'm surrounded by guns.

"In you go," Warner says. I'm pushed into an empty room smelling faintly of mold. Someone hits a switch and fluorescent lights flicker on to reveal pasty yellow walls and carpet the color of dead grass. The door slams shut behind me.

There's nothing but cobwebs and a huge mirror in this room. The mirror is half the size of the wall. Instinctively I know Warner and his accomplices must be watching me. I just don't know why.

Mechanical clinks/cracks/creaks and shifts shake the space I'm standing in. The ground rumbles to life. The ceiling trembles with the promise of chaos. Metal spikes are suddenly everywhere, scattered across the room, puncturing every surface at all different heights. Every few seconds they disappear only to reappear with a sudden jolt of terror, slicing through the air like needles.

I realize I'm standing in a torture chamber.

Static and feedback from speakers older than my dying heart crackle to life.

"Are you ready?" Warner's amplified voice echoes around the room.

"What am I supposed to be ready for?" I yell into the empty space, certain that someone can hear me. ~~I'm calm. I'm calm. I'm calm.~~ I'm petrified.

"We had a deal, remember?" the room responds.

"Wha—"

"I disabled your cameras. Now it's your turn to hold up your end of the bargain."

"I won't touch you!" I shout, spinning in place, terrified.

"That's all right," he says. "I'm sending in my replacement."

The door squeals open and a toddler waddles in wearing nothing but a diaper. He's blindfolded and hiccupping sobs, shuddering in fear.

One pin pops my entire existence into nothing.

"If you don't save him," Warner's words crackle through the room, "we won't, either."

This child.

He must have a mother a father someone who loves him this child this child this child stumbling forward in terror. He could be speared through by a metal stalagmite at any second.

Saving him is simple: I need to pick him up, find a safe spot of ground, and hold him in my arms until the experiment is over.

There's only one problem.

If I touch him, he might die.

TWENTY-FIVE

Warner knows I don't have a choice. He wants to force me into another situation where he can see the impact of my abilities, and he has no problem torturing an innocent child to get exactly what he wants.

Right now I have no options.

I have to take a chance before this little boy steps forward in the wrong direction.

I quickly memorize as much as I can of the traps and dodge/hop/narrowly avoid the spikes until I'm as close as possible.

I take a deep, shaky breath and focus on the shivering limbs of the boy in front of me and pray to God I'm making the right decision. I'm about to pull off my shirt to use as a barrier between us when I notice the slight vibration in the ground. The tremble that precedes the terror. I know I have half of a second before the spikes slice up through the air and even less time to react.

I yank him up and into my arms.

His screams pierce through me like I'm being shot to death. He's clawing at my arms, my chest, kicking my body as hard as he can, crying out in agony until the pain paralyzes him. He goes weak in my grip and I'm being ripped to pieces, my bones, my veins all tumbling out of place, all turning on me to torture me forever with memories of the horrors I'm responsible for.

Pain and power are bleeding through his body into mine, jolting through his limbs and crashing into me until I nearly drop him. ~~It's like reliving a nightmare I've spent 3 years trying to forget.~~

"Absolutely amazing," Warner sighs through the speakers, and I realize I was right. He must be watching through a 2-way mirror. "Brilliant, love. I'm thoroughly impressed."

I'm too desperate to be able to focus on Warner right now. I have no idea how long this sick game is going to last, and I need to lessen the amount of skin I'm exposing to this little boy's body.

My skimpy outfit makes so much sense now.

I rearrange him in my arms and manage to grab hold of his diaper. I'm holding him up with the palm of my hand. I'm desperate to believe I couldn't have touched him long enough to cause serious damage.

He hiccups once; his body quivers back to life.

I could cry from happiness.

But then the screams start back up again, no longer cries of torture but of fear. He's desperate to get away from me and I'm losing my grip, my wrist nearly breaking from the effort. I don't dare remove his blindfold. I'd rather die than allow him to see this space, to see my face.

I clench my jaw. If I put him down, he'll start running. And if he starts running, he's finished. I have to keep holding on.

The roar of an old mechanical wheeze revives my heart. The spikes slip back into the ground, one by one until they've all disappeared. The room is harmless again so swiftly I fear I may have imagined the danger. I drop the boy back onto the floor and bite down on my lip to swallow the pain welling in my wrist.

The child starts running and accidentally bumps my bare legs.

He screams and shudders and falls to the floor, curled up into himself, sobbing until I consider destroying myself, ridding myself of this world. Tears are streaming fast down my face and I want nothing more than to reach out to him and help him, hug him close, kiss his beautiful cheeks and tell him I'll take care of him, that we'll run away together, that I'll play games with him and read him stories at night and I know I can't. I know I never will. I know it will never be possible.

And suddenly the world shifts out of focus.

I'm overcome by rage, an anger so potent I'm almost elevated off the ground. I'm boiling with blind hatred and disgust. I don't even understand how my feet move in the next instant. I don't understand my hands and what they're doing or how they decided to fly forward, fingers splayed, charging toward the window. I only know I want to feel Warner's neck snap between my own two hands. I want him to experience the same terror he just inflicted upon a child. I want to watch him die. I want to watch him beg for mercy.

I catapult through the concrete walls.

I crush the glass with 10 fingers.

I'm clutching a fistful of gravel and a fistful of fabric at Warner's neck and there are 50 different guns pointed at my head. The air is heavy with cement and sulfur, the glass falling in an agonized symphony of shattered hearts.

I slam Warner into the corroded stone.

"Don't you *dare* shoot her," Warner shouts at the guards. I haven't touched his skin yet, but I have the strangest suspicion that I could smash his rib cage into his heart if I just pressed a little harder.

"I should kill you." My voice is one deep breath, one uncontrolled exhalation.

"You—" He tries to swallow. "You just—you just broke through concrete with your bare hands."

I blink. I don't dare look behind me. But I know without looking backward that he can't be lying. I must have.

I lose focus for one instant.

The guns

click

click

click

Every moment is loaded.

"If any of you hurt her I will shoot you myself," Warner barks.

"But sir—"

"STAND DOWN, SOLDIER—"

The rage is gone. The sudden uncontrollable anger is gone. My mind has already surrendered to disbelief.

164

Confusion. I don't know what I've done. I obviously don't know what I'm capable of because I had no idea I could destroy anything at all and I'm suddenly so terrified so terrified so terrified of my own two hands. I stumble backward, stunned, and catch Warner watching me hungrily, eagerly, his emerald eyes bright with boyish fascination. He's practically trembling in excitement.

There's a snake in my throat and I can't swallow it down. I meet Warner's gaze. "If you ever put me in a position like that again, I *will* kill you. And I will enjoy it."

I don't even know if I'm lying.

TWENTY-SIX

Adam finds me curled into a ball on the shower floor.

I've been crying for so long I'm certain the hot water is made of nothing but my tears. My clothes are stuck to my skin, wet and useless. I want to drown in ignorance. I want to be stupid, dumb, mute, completely devoid of a brain. I want to cut off my own limbs. I want to be rid of this skin that can kill and these hands that destroy and this body I don't even know how to understand.

Everything is falling apart.

"Juliette . . ." He presses his hand against the glass. I can hardly hear him.

When I don't respond he opens the shower door. He's pelted with rebel raindrops and kicks his boots off before falling to his knees. He reaches in to touch my arms and the feeling only makes me more desperate to die. He sighs and pulls me up, just enough to lift my head. His hands trap my face and his eyes search me, search through me until I look away.

"I know what happened," he says softly.

My throat is a reptile, covered in scales. "Someone should just kill me," I croak.

Adam's arms wrap around me until he's tugged me up

and I'm wobbling on my legs and we're both standing upright. He steps into the shower and slides the door shut behind him.

I gasp.

He holds me up against the wall and I see nothing but his white T-shirt soaked through, nothing but the water dancing down his face, nothing but his eyes full of a world I'm dying to be a part of.

"It wasn't your fault," he whispers.

"It's what I *am*," I choke.

"No. Warner's wrong about you," Adam says. "He wants you to be someone you're not, and you can't let him break you. Don't let him get into your head. He *wants* you to think you're a monster. He wants you to think you have no choice but to join him. He wants you to think you'll never be able to live a normal life—"

"But I won't live a normal life." I swallow a hiccup. "Not ever—I'll n-never—"

Adam is shaking his head. "You will. We're going to get out of here. I won't let this happen to you."

"H-how could you possibly care about someone . . . like *me*?" I'm barely breathing, nervous and petrified but somehow staring at his lips, studying the shape, counting the drops of water tumbling over the hills and valleys of his mouth.

"Because I'm in love with you."

My eyes snap up to read his face. I'm a mess of electricity, humming with life and lightning, hot and cold and my heart is erratic. I'm shaking in his arms and my lips have parted for no reason at all.

His mouth softens into a smile.

My bones have disappeared.

His nose is touching my nose, his lips one breath away, his eyes devouring me already. I can smell him everywhere; I feel him pressed against me. His hands at my waist, gripping my hips, his legs flush against my own, his chest overpowering me with strength. The taste of his words lingers on my lips.

"Really . . . ?" I have one whisper of incredulity, one conscious effort to believe what's never been done. I'm flushed through my feet, filled with unspoken everything.

He looks at me with so much emotion I nearly crack in half.

"God, Juliette—"

And he's kissing me.

Once, twice, until I've had a taste and realize I'll never have enough. He's everywhere up my back and over my arms and suddenly he's kissing me harder, deeper, with a fervent urgent need I've never known before. He breaks for air only to bury his lips in my neck, along my collarbone, up my chin and cheeks and I'm gasping for oxygen and he's destroying me with his hands and we're drenched in water and beauty and the exhilaration of a moment I never knew was possible.

He pulls back with a low groan and I want him to take his shirt off.

I need to see the bird. I need to tell him about the bird.

My fingers are tugging at the hem of his wet clothes and his eyes widen for only a second before he rips the material off himself. He grabs my hands and lifts my arms above my head and pins me against the wall, kissing me until I'm sure I'm dreaming, drinking in my lips with his lips and he tastes like rain and sweet musk and I'm about to explode.

My heart is beating so fast I don't understand why it's still working. He's kissing away the pain, the hurt, the years of self-loathing, the insecurities, the dashed hopes for a future I always pictured as obsolete. He's lighting me on fire, burning away the torture of Warner's games, the anguish that poisons me every single day. The intensity of our bodies could shatter these glass walls.

It nearly does.

For a moment we're just staring at each other, breathing hard until I'm blushing, until he closes his eyes and takes one ragged, steadying breath and I place my hand on his chest. I dare to trace the outline of the bird soaring across his skin, I dare to trail my fingers down the length of his abdomen.

"You're my bird," I tell him. "You're my bird and you're going to help me fly away."

Adam is gone by the time I get out of the shower.

He wrung his clothes out and dried himself off and granted me privacy to change. Privacy I'm not sure I care about anymore. I touch 2 fingers to my lips and taste him everywhere.

But when I step into the room he's not anywhere. He

had to report downstairs.

I stare at the clothes in my closet.

I always choose a dress with pockets because I don't know where else to store my notebook. It doesn't carry any incriminating information, and the one piece of paper that bore Adam's handwriting has since been destroyed and flushed down the toilet, but I like to keep it close to me. It represents so much more than a few words scribbled on paper. It's a small token of my resistance.

I tuck the notebook into a pocket and decide I'm finally ready to face myself. I take a deep breath, push the wet strands of hair away from my eyes, and pad into the bathroom. The steam from the shower has clouded the mirror. I reach out a tentative hand to wipe away a small circle. Just big enough.

A scared face stares back at me.

I touch my cheeks and study the reflective surface, study the image of a girl who's simultaneously strange and familiar to me. My face is thinner, paler, my cheekbones higher than I remember them, my eyebrows perched above 2 wide eyes not blue not green but somewhere in between. My skin is flushed with heat and something named Adam. My lips are too pink. My teeth are unusually straight. My finger is trailing down the length of my nose, tracing the shape of my chin when I see a movement in the corner of my eye.

"You're so beautiful," he says to me.

I duck my head and trip away from the mirror only to

have him catch me in his arms. "I'd forgotten my own face," I whisper.

"Just don't forget who you *are*," he says.

"I don't even know."

"Yes you do." He tilts my face up. "I do."

I stare at the strength in his jaw, in his eyes, in his body. I try to understand the confidence he has in who he thinks I am and realize his reassurance is the only thing stopping me from diving into a pool of my own insanity. He's always believed in me. Even soundlessly, silently, he fought for me. Always.

He's my only friend.

I take his hand and hold it to my lips. "I've loved you forever," I tell him.

The sun rises, rests, shines in his face and he almost smiles, almost can't meet my eyes. His muscles relax, his shoulders find relief in the weight of a new kind of wonder, and he exhales. He touches my cheek, touches my lips, touches the tip of my chin and I blink and he's kissing me, he's pulling me into his arms and into the air and somehow we're on the bed and tangled in each other and I'm drugged with emotion, drugged by each tender moment. His fingers skim my shoulder, rest at my hips. He pulls me closer, whispers my name, drops kisses down my throat and struggles with the stiff fabric of my dress. His hands are shaking so slightly, his eyes brimming with feeling, his heart thrumming with pain and affection and I want to live here, in his arms, in his eyes for the rest of my life.

I slip my hands under his shirt and he chokes on a moan that turns into a kiss that needs me and wants me and has to have me so desperately it's like the most acute form of torture. His weight is pressed into mine, on top of mine, infinite points of feeling for every nerve ending in my body and his right hand is behind my neck and his left hand is reeling me in and his lips are falling down my shirt and I don't understand why I need to wear clothes anymore and I'm thunder and lightning and the possibility of exploding into tears at any inopportune moment. Bliss Bliss Bliss is beating through my chest.

I don't remember what it means to breathe.

I never

ever

ever

knew

what it meant to *feel*.

An alarm is hammering through the walls.

The room blares to life and Adam stiffens, pulls back; his face collapses.

"This is a CODE SEVEN. All soldiers must report to the Quadrant immediately. This is a CODE SEVEN. All soldiers must report to the Quadrant immediately. This is a CODE SEVEN. All soldiers must report to the Quadra—"

Adam is on his feet and pulling me up and the voice is still shouting orders through a speaker system wired into the building. "There's been a breach," he says, his voice broken and breathy, his eyes darting between me and the door. "Jesus. I can't just leave you here—"

"Go," I tell him. "You have to go—I'll be fine—"

Footsteps are thundering through the halls and soldiers are barking at each other so loudly I can hear it through the walls. Adam is still on duty. He has to perform. He has to keep up appearances until we can leave. I know this.

He pulls me close. "This isn't a joke, Juliette—I don't know what's happening—it could be anything—"

A metal click. A mechanical switch. The door slides open and Adam and I jump 10 feet apart.

Adam rushes to exit just as Warner is walking in. They both freeze.

"I'm pretty sure that alarm has been going off for at least a minute, soldier."

"Yes sir. I wasn't sure what to do about her." He's suddenly composed, a perfect statue. He nods at me like I'm an afterthought but I know he's just slightly too stiff in the shoulders. Breathing just a beat too fast.

"Lucky for you, I'm here to take care of that. You may report to your commanding officer."

"Sir." Adam nods, pivots on one heel, and darts out the door. I hope Warner didn't notice his hesitation.

Warner turns to face me with a smile so calm and casual I begin to question whether the building is actually in chaos. He studies my face. My hair. Glances at the rumpled sheets behind me and I feel like I've swallowed a spider. "You took a nap?"

"I couldn't sleep last night."

"You've ripped your dress."

"What are you doing here?" I need him to stop staring at me, I need him to stop drinking in the details of my existence.

"If you don't like the dress, you can always choose a different one, you know. I picked them out for you myself."

"That's okay. The dress is fine." I glance at the clock for no real reason. It's already 4:30 in the afternoon. "Why won't you tell me what's going on?"

He's too close. He's standing too close and he's looking at me and my lungs are failing to expand. "You should really change."

"I don't want to change." I don't know why I'm so nervous. Why he's making me so nervous. Why the space between us is closing too quickly.

He hooks a finger in the rip close to the drop-waist of my dress and I bite back a scream. "This just won't do."

"It's fine—"

He tugs so hard on the rip that it splits open the fabric and creates a slit up the side of my leg. "That's a bit better."

"What are you *doing*—"

His hands snake up my waist and clamp my arms in place and I know I need to defend myself but I'm frozen and I want to scream but my voice is broken broken broken.

"I have a question," he says, and I try to kick him in this worthless dress and he just squeezes me up against the wall, the weight of his body pressing me into place, every inch of him covered in clothing, a protective layer between us. "I said I have a question, Juliette."

His hand slips into my pocket so quickly it takes me a moment to realize what he's done. I'm panting up against the wall, shaking and trying to find my head.

"I'm curious," he says. "What is *this*?"

He's holding my notebook between 2 fingers.

Oh God.

This dress is too tight to hide the outline of the notebook and I was too busy looking at my face to check the dress in the mirror. ~~This is all my fault all my fault all my fault all my fault~~ I can't believe it. This is all my fault. I should've known better.

I say nothing.

He cocks his head. "I don't recall giving you a notebook. I certainly don't remember granting you allowance for any possessions, either."

"I brought it with me." My voice catches.

"Now you're lying."

"What do you want from me?" I panic.

"That's a stupid question, Juliette."

The soft sound of smooth metal slipping out of place. Someone has opened my door.

Click.

"Get your hands off of her before I bury a bullet in your head."

TWENTY-SEVEN

Warner's eyes close very slowly. He steps away very slowly. His lips twitch into a dangerous smile. "Kent."

Adam's hands are steady, the barrel of his gun pressed into the back of Warner's skull. "You're going to clear our exit out of here."

Warner actually laughs. He opens his eyes and whips a gun out of his inside pocket only to point it directly at my forehead. "I will kill her right now."

"You're not that stupid," Adam says.

"If she moves even a millimeter, I will shoot her. And then I will rip you to pieces."

Adam shifts quickly, slamming the butt of his gun into Warner's head. Warner's gun misfires and Adam catches his arm and twists his wrist until his grip on the weapon wavers. I grab the gun from Warner's limp hand and slam the butt of it into his face. I'm stunned by my own reflexes. I've never held a gun before but I guess there's a first time for everything.

I point it at Warner's eyes. "Don't underestimate me."

"Holy *shit*." Adam doesn't bother hiding his surprise.

Warner coughs through a laugh, steadies himself, and tries to smile as he wipes the blood from his nose. "I never underestimate you," he says to me. "I never have."

Adam shakes his head for less than a second before his face splits into an enormous grin. He's beaming at me as he presses the gun harder into Warner's skull. "Let's get out of here."

I grab the two duffel bags stowed away in the armoire and toss one to Adam. We've been packed for a week already. If he wants to make a break for it earlier than expected, I have no complaints.

Warner's lucky we're showing him mercy.

But we're lucky the entire building has been evacuated. He has no one to rely on.

Warner clears his throat. He's staring straight at me when he speaks. "I can assure you, soldier, your triumph will be short-lived. You may as well kill me now, because when I find you, I will thoroughly enjoy breaking every bone in your body. You're a fool if you think you can get away with this."

"I am not your soldier." Adam's face is stone. "I never have been. You've been so caught up in the details of your own fantasies you failed to notice the dangers right in front of your face."

"We can't kill you yet," I add. "You have to get us out of here."

"You're making a huge mistake, Juliette," he says to me. His voice actually softens. "You're throwing away an entire future." He sighs. "How do you know you can trust him?"

I glance at Adam. Adam, the boy who's always defended me, even when he had nothing to gain. I shake my head to clear it. I remind myself that Warner is a liar. A crazed lunatic. A psychotic murderer. He would never try to help me.

I think.

"Let's go before it's too late," I say to Adam. "He's just trying to stall us until the soldiers get back."

"He doesn't even care about you!" Warner explodes. I flinch at the sudden, uncontrolled intensity in his voice. "He just wants a way out of here and he's *using* you!" He steps forward. "I could love you, Juliette—I would treat you like a *queen*—"

Adam puts him in a swift headlock and points the gun at his temple. "You obviously don't understand what's happening here," he says very carefully.

"Then educate me, soldier," Warner's eyes are dancing flames; dangerous. "Tell me what I'm failing to understand."

"Adam." I'm shaking my head.

He meets my eyes. Nods. Turns to Warner. "Make the call," he says, squeezing his neck a little tighter. "Get us out of here *now*."

"Only my dead body would allow her to walk out that door." Warner exercises his jaw and spits blood on the floor. "You I would kill for pleasure," he says to Adam. "But Juliette is the one I want forever."

"I'm not yours to *want*." I'm breathing too hard. I'm anxious to get out of here. I'm angry he won't stop talking but as much as I'd love to break his face, he's no good to us unconscious.

"You could love me, you know." He's smiling a strange

178

sort of smile. "We would be unstoppable. We would change the world. I could make you happy," he says to me.

Adam looks like he might snap Warner's neck. His face is so taut, so tense, so angry. I've never seen him like this before. "You have nothing to offer her, you sick bastard."

Warner presses his eyes shut for one second. "Juliette. Don't make a rash decision. Stay with me. I'll be patient with you. I'll give you time to adjust. I'll take care of you—"

"You're insane." My hands are shaking but I hold the gun to his face again. I need to get him out of my head. I need to remember what he's done to me. "You want me to be a *monster* for you—"

"I want you to live up to your *potential!*"

"Let me go," I say quietly. "I don't want to be your creature. I don't want to hurt people."

"The world has already hurt *you*," he counters. "The world *put* you here. You're here because of them! You think if you leave they're going to accept you? You think you can run away and live a normal life? No one will care for you. No one will come near you—you'll be an outcast like you've always been! Nothing has changed! You belong with me!"

"She belongs with *me*." Adam's voice could cut through steel.

Warner flinches. For the first time he seems to be understanding what I thought was obvious. His eyes are wide, horrified, unbelieving, staring at me with a new kind of anguish. "No." A short, crazed laugh. "Juliette.

Please. Please. Don't tell me he's filled your head with romantic notions. Please don't tell me you fell for his false proclamations—"

Adam slams his knee into Warner's spine. Warner falls to the floor with a muffled crack and a sharp intake of breath. Adam has thoroughly overpowered him. I feel like I should be cheering.

But I'm too anxious. I'm too suspended in disbelief. I'm too insecure to be confident in my own decisions. I need to pull myself together.

"Adam—"

"I *love* you," he says to me, his eyes just as earnest as I remember them, his words just as urgent as they should be. "Don't let him confuse you—"

"You *love* her?" Warner practically spits. "You don't even—"

"Adam." The room shifts in and out of focus. I'm staring at the window. I glance back at him.

His eyes touch his eyebrows. "You want to *jump* out?"

I nod.

"But we're fifteen stories up—"

"What choice do we have if he won't cooperate?" I look at Warner. Cock my head. "There is no Code Seven, is there?"

Warner's lips twitch. He says nothing.

"Why would you do that?" I ask him. "Why would you pull a false alarm?"

"Why don't you ask the soldier you're so suddenly fond

of?" Warner snaps, disgusted. "Why don't you ask yourself why you're trusting your life to someone who can't even differentiate between a real and an imaginary threat?"

Adam swears under his breath.

I lock eyes with him and he tosses me his gun.

He shakes his head. Swears again. Clenches and unclenches his fist. "It was just a drill."

Warner actually laughs.

Adam glances at the door, the clock, my face. "We don't have much time."

I'm holding Warner's gun in my left hand and Adam's gun in my right and pointing them both at Warner's forehead, doing my best to ignore the eyes he's drilling in my direction. Adam uses his free hand to dig in his pockets for something. He pulls out a pair of plastic zip ties and kicks Warner onto his back just before binding his limbs together. Warner's boots and gloves have been discarded on the floor. Adam keeps one boot pressed on his stomach.

"A million alarms are going to go off the minute we jump through that window," he tells me. "We'll have to run, so we can't risk breaking our legs. We can't jump."

"So what do we do?"

"I have rope," he says. "We'll have to climb down. And fast."

He sets to work pulling out a coil of cord attached to a small clawlike anchor. I'd asked him a million times what on earth he would need it for, why he would pack it in his escape bag. He told me a person could never have too much rope.

He turns to me. "I'm going to go down first so I can catch you on the other side—"

Warner laughs loud, too loud. "You can't *catch* her, you fool." He squirms in his plastic shackles. "She's wearing next to nothing. She'll kill you and kill herself from the fall."

My eyes dart between Warner and Adam. I don't have time to entertain Warner's charades any longer. I make a hasty decision. "Do it. I'll be right behind you."

Warner looks confused. "What are you doing?"

I ignore him.

"Wait—"

I ignore him.

"Juliette."

I ignore him.

"Juliette!" His voice is tighter, higher, full of anger and confusion. "He can *touch* you?"

Adam is wrapping his fist in the bedsheet.

"Goddamn it, Juliette, answer me!" Warner is writhing on the floor, unhinged in a way I never thought possible. He looks wild, his eyes disbelieving, horrified. "Has he *touched* you?"

I can't understand why the walls are suddenly on the ceiling. Everything is stumbling sideways.

"Juliette—"

Adam breaks through the glass with one swift crack, one solid punch, and instantly the room is ringing with the sound of hysteria like no alarm I've heard before. The floor is rumbling under my feet, footsteps are thundering down the halls, and I know we're about one minute from being discovered.

Adam throws the rope through the window and slings his pack over his back. "Throw me your bag!" he shouts and I can barely hear him. I toss my duffel and he catches it right before slipping through the window. I run to join him.

Warner tries to grab my leg.

His failed attempt nearly trips me but I manage to stumble my way to the window without losing much time. I glance back at the door and feel my heart racing through my bones. The sound of soldiers running and yelling is getting louder, closer, clearer by the second.

"Hurry!" Adam is calling to me.

"Juliette, *please*—"

Warner swipes for my leg again and I gasp so loud I almost hear it through the sirens shattering my eardrums. ~~I won't look at him. I won't look at him. I won't look at him.~~

I swing one leg through the window and latch on to the cord. My bare legs are going to make this an excruciating ordeal. Both legs are through. My hands are in place. Adam is calling to me from below, and I don't know how far down he is. Warner is shouting my name and I look up despite my best efforts.

His eyes are two shots of green punched through a pane of glass. Cutting through me.

I take a deep breath and hope I won't die.

I take a deep breath and inch my way down the rope.

I take a deep breath and hope Warner doesn't realize what just happened.

I hope he doesn't know he just touched my leg.

And nothing happened.

TWENTY-EIGHT

I'm burning.

The cord is chafing my legs into a fiery mass so painful I'm surprised there's no smoke. I bite back the pain because I have no choice. The mass hysteria of the building is bulldozing my senses, raining down danger all around us. Adam is shouting to me from below, telling me to jump, promising he'll catch me. I'm too ashamed to admit I'm afraid of the fall.

I never have a chance to make my own decision.

Soldiers are already pouring into what used to be my room, shouting and confused, probably shocked to find Warner in such a feeble position. It was really too easy to overpower him. It worries me.

It makes me think we did something wrong.

A few soldiers pop their heads out of the shattered window and I'm frantic to shimmy down the rope but they're already moving to unlatch the anchor. I prepare myself for the nauseating sensation of free fall only to realize they're not trying to drop me. They're trying to reel me back inside.

Warner must be telling them what to do.

I glance down at Adam below me and finally give in to his calls. I squeeze my eyes shut and let go.

And fall right into his open arms.

We collapse onto the ground, but the breath is knocked out of us for only a moment. Adam grabs my hand and then we're running.

There's nothing but empty, barren space stretching out ahead of us. Broken asphalt, uneven pavement, dirt roads, naked trees, dying plants, a yellowed city abandoned to the elements drowning in dead leaves that crunch under our feet. The civilian compounds are short and squat, grouped together in no particular order, and Adam makes sure to stay as far away from them as possible. The loudspeakers are already working against us. The sound of a young, smoothly mechanical female voice drowns out the sirens.

"Curfew is now in effect. Everyone return to their homes immediately. There are rebels on the loose. They are armed and ready to fire. Curfew is now in effect. Everyone return to their homes immediately. There are rebels on the loose. They are armed and ready to fi—"

My sides are cramping, my skin is tight, my throat dry, desperate for water. I don't know how far we've run. All I know is the sound of boots pounding the pavement, the screech of tires peeling out of underground storage units, alarms wailing in our wake.

I look back to see people screaming and running for shelter, ducking away from the soldiers rushing through their homes, pounding down doors to see if we've found refuge somewhere inside. Adam pulls me away from civilization and heads toward the abandoned streets of an earlier decade: old shops and restaurants, narrow side streets and abandoned playgrounds. The unregulated land of our past lives has been strictly off-limits. It's forbidden territory. Everything closed down. Everything broken, rusted shut, lifeless. No one is allowed to trespass here. Not even soldiers.

And we're charging through these streets, trying to stay out of sight.

The sun is slipping through the sky and tripping toward the edge of the earth. Night will be coming quickly, and I have no idea where we are. I never expected so much to happen so quickly and I never expected it all to happen on the same day. I just have to hope to survive but I haven't the faintest idea where we might be headed.

We're darting in a million directions. Turning abruptly, going forward a few feet only to head back in an opposite path. My best guess is that Adam is trying to confuse and/or distract our followers as much as possible. I can do nothing but attempt to keep up.

And I fail.

Adam is a trained soldier. He's built for exactly these kinds of situations. He understands how to flee, how to stay inconspicuous, how to move soundlessly in any space. I, on the other hand, am a broken girl who's known no exercise for too long. My lungs are burning with the effort to inhale oxygen, wheezing with the effort to exhale carbon dioxide.

I'm suddenly gasping so desperately Adam is forced to pull me into a side street. He's breathing a little harder than usual, but I've acquired a full-time job choking on the weakness of my limp body.

Adam takes my face in his hands and tries to focus my eyes. "I want you to breathe like I am, okay?"

I wheeze a bit more.

"Focus, Juliette." His eyes are so determined. Infinitely patient. He looks fearless and I envy him his composure. "Calm your heart," he says. "Breathe exactly as I do."

He takes 3 small breaths in, holds it for a few seconds, and releases it in one long exhalation. I try to copy him. I'm not very good at it.

"Okay. I want you to keep breathing like—" He stops. His eyes dart up and around the abandoned street for a split second. I know we have to move.

Gunshots shatter the atmosphere. I'd never realized just how loud they are. An icy chill seeps through me and I know immediately that they're not trying to kill *me*. They're trying to kill Adam.

Adam doesn't have time for me to catch my breath and find my head. He flips me up and into his arms and takes off in a diagonal dash across another alleyway.

And we're running.

And I'm breathing.

And he shouts, "Wrap your arms around my neck!" and I release the choke hold I have on his T-shirt and I'm stupid enough to feel shy as I slip my arms around him. He readjusts me against him so I'm higher, closer to his chest. He carries me like I weigh less than nothing.

I close my eyes and press my cheek against his neck.

The gunshots are somewhere behind us, but even I can tell from the sound that they're too far away and too far in the wrong direction. We seem to have momentarily outmaneuvered them. Their cars can't even find us, because Adam has avoided all main streets. He seems to have his own map of this city. He seems to know exactly what he's doing—like he's been planning this for a very long time.

Adam drops me to my feet in front of a stretch of chain-link fence.

"Juliette," he says after a breathless moment. "Can you jump this?"

I'm so eager to be more than a useless lump that I nearly sprint up and over the metal barrier. But I'm reckless. And too hasty. I practically rip my dress off and scratch my legs in the process. I wince against the stinging pain, and in the moment it takes me to reopen my eyes, Adam is already standing next to me.

He looks down at my legs and sighs. He almost laughs. I wonder what I must look like, tattered and wild in this shredded dress. The slit Warner created now stops at my hip bone. I must look like a crazed animal.

Adam doesn't seem to mind.

He's slowed down, too. We're moving at a brisk walk now, no longer barreling through the streets. I realize we must be closer to some semblance of safety, but I'm not sure if I should ask questions now, or save them for later. Adam answers my silent thoughts.

"They won't be able to track me out here," he says, and it dawns on me that all soldiers must have some kind of tracking device on their person. I wonder why I never got one.

It shouldn't be this easy to escape.

"Our trackers aren't tangible," he explains. We make a left into another alleyway. The sun is just dipping below the horizon. I wonder where we are. How far away from Reestablished settlements we must be that there are no people here. "It's a special serum injected into our bloodstream," he continues, "and it's designed to work with our bodies' natural processes. It would know, for example, if I died. It's an excellent way to keep track of soldiers lost in combat." He glances at me out of the corner of his eye. He smiles a crooked smile I want to kiss.

"So how did you confuse the tracker?"

His grin grows bigger. He waves one hand around us. "This space we're standing in? It was used for a nuclear power plant. One day the whole thing exploded."

My eyes are as big as my face. "When did that happen?"

"About five years ago. They cleaned it up pretty quickly. Hid it from the media, from the people. No one really knows what happened here. But the radiation alone is enough to kill." He pauses. "It already has."

He stops walking. "I've been through this area a million times already, and I haven't been affected by it. Warner used to send me up here to collect samples of the soil. He wanted to study the effects." He runs a hand through his hair. "I think he was hoping to manipulate the toxicity into a poison of some kind.

"The first time I came up here, Warner thought I'd died. The tracker is linked to all of our main processing systems—an alert goes off whenever a soldier is lost. He knew there was a risk in sending me, so I don't think he was too surprised to hear I'd died. He was more surprised to see me return." He shrugs. "There's something about the chemicals here that counteracts the molecular composition of the tracking device. So basically—right now everyone thinks I'm dead."

"Won't Warner suspect you might be here?"

"Maybe." He squints up at the fading sunlight. Our shadows are long and unmoving. "Or I could've been shot. In any case, it buys us some time."

He takes my hand and grins at me before something slams into my consciousness.

"What about *me*?" I ask. "Can't this radiation kill me?"

"Oh—no." He shakes his head. "One of the reasons why Warner wanted me collecting these samples? You're immune to it, too. He was studying you. He said he found the information in your hospital records. That you'd been tested—"

"But no one ever—"

"—probably without your knowledge, and despite testing positive for the radiation, you were entirely whole, biologically. There was nothing inherently wrong with you."

Nothing inherently wrong with you.

The observation is so blatantly false I actually start laughing. "There's nothing wrong with me? You're kidding, right?"

Adam stares at me so long I begin to blush. Blue blue blue boring into me. His voice is deep, steady. "I don't think I've ever heard you laugh."

I don't know how to respond except with the truth. "Laughter comes from living." I shrug, try to sound indifferent. "I've never really been alive before."

His eyes haven't wavered in their focus. I can almost feel his heart beating against my skin.

He pulls me close. Kisses the top of my head.

"Let's go home," he whispers.

TWENTY-NINE

Home.

Home.

What does he mean?

I part my lips to ask the question and his sneaky smile is the only answer I receive.

Every step is a step away from the asylum, away from Warner, away from the futility of the existence I've always known. Every step is one I take because I *want* to. For the first time in my life, I walk forward because I *want* to, because I feel hope and love and the exhilaration of beauty, because I want to know what it's like to *live*. I could jump up to catch a breeze and live in its windblown ways forever.

I feel like I've been fitted for wings.

Adam leads me into an abandoned shed on the outskirts of this wild field, overgrown by rogue vegetation and crazed bushlike tentacles, scratchy and hideous, likely poisonous to ingest. I wonder if this is where Adam meant for us to stay. I step into the dark space and squint. An outline comes into focus.

There's a car inside.

I blink.

Not just a car. A tank.

Adam can't hide his own eagerness. He looks at my face for a reaction and seems pleased with my astonishment. "I convinced Warner I'd managed to break one of the tanks I brought up here. These things are designed to run on electricity—so I told him the main unit fried on contact with the chemical traces. That it was corrupted by something in the atmosphere. He arranged for a car to deliver and collect me after that, and said we should leave the tank where it is." He almost smiles. "Warner was sending me up here against his father's wishes, and didn't want anyone to find out he'd broken a 500-thousand-dollar tank. The official report says it was hijacked by rebels."

"Couldn't someone else have come up and seen the tank sitting here?"

Adam opens the passenger door. "The civilians stay far, far away from this place, and no other soldier has been up here. No one else wanted to risk the radiation." He cocks his head. "It's one of the reasons why Warner trusted me with you. He liked that I was willing to die for my *duty*."

"He never thought you'd step out of line," I say, comprehending.

Adam shakes his head. "Nope. And after what happened with the tracking serum, he had no reason to doubt that crazy things were possible up here. I deactivated the tank's electrical unit myself, just in case he wanted to check." He nods back to the monstrous vehicle. "I had a feeling it would come in handy one day. It's always good to be prepared."

Prepared. To run. To escape.

I wonder why.

"Come here," he says, his voice gentler. He reaches for me in the dim light and I pretend it's a happy coincidence that his hands brush my bare thighs. I pretend it doesn't feel incredible to have him struggle with the rips in my dress as he helps me into the tank. I pretend I can't see the way he's looking at me as the last of the sun falls below the horizon.

"I need to take care of your legs," he says, a whisper against my skin, electric in my blood. For a moment I don't even understand what he means. I don't even care. My thoughts are so impractical I surprise myself. I've never had the freedom to touch anyone before. Certainly no one has ever *wanted* my hands on them. Adam is an entirely new experience.

Touching him is all I want to think about.

"The cuts aren't too bad," he says, the tips of his fingers running across my calves. I suck in my breath. "But we'll have to clean them up, just in case. Sometimes it's safer being cut by a butcher knife than being scratched by a random scrap of metal. You don't want it to get infected."

He looks up. His hand is now on my knee.

I'm nodding and I don't know why. I wonder if I'm trembling on the outside as much as I am on the inside. I need to say something. "We should probably get going, right?"

"Yeah." He takes a deep breath and seems to return to himself. "Yeah. We have to go." He peers through the evening light. "We have some time before they realize I'm still alive. And we have to use it to our advantage."

"But once we leave this place—won't the tracker start back up again? Won't they know you're not dead?"

"No." He jumps into the driver's side and fumbles for the ignition. There's no key, just a button. I wonder if it recognizes Adam's thumbprint as authorization. A small sputter and the machine roars to life. "Warner had to renew my tracker serum every time I got back. Once it's gone? It's gone." He grins. "So now we can really get the hell out of here."

"But where are we going?" I finally ask.

He shifts into gear before he responds.

"My house."

THIRTY

"You have a *house*?"

Adam laughs and pulls out of the field. The tank is surprisingly fast, surprisingly swift and stealthy. The engine has quieted to a soothing hum, and I wonder if that's why they switched their tanks from gas to electric. It's certainly less conspicuous this way. "Not exactly," he answers. "But a home of sorts. Yeah."

I want to ask and don't want to ask and need to ask and never want to ask. I have to ask. I steel myself. "Your fathe—"

"He's been dead for a while now." Adam's not smiling anymore. His voice is tight with something I know how to place. Pain. Bitterness. Anger.

"Oh."

We drive in silence, each of us absorbed in our own thoughts. I don't dare ask what became of his mother. I only wonder how he turned out so well despite having such a despicable father. And I wonder why he ever joined the army if he hates it so much. Right now, I'm too shy to ask. I don't want to infringe on his emotional boundaries.

God knows I have a million of my own.

I peer out the window and strain my eyes to see

what we're passing through, but I can't make out much more than the sad stretches of deserted land I've grown accustomed to. There are no civilians where we are: we're too far from Reestablished settlements and civilian compounds. I notice another tank patrolling the area not 100 feet away, but I don't think it sees us. Adam is driving without headlights, presumably to draw as little attention to us as possible. I wonder how he's even able to navigate. The moon is the only lamp to light our way.

It's eerily quiet.

I allow my thoughts to drift back to Warner, wondering what must be going on right now, wondering how many people must be searching for me, wondering what lengths he'll go to until he has me back. He wants Adam dead. He wants me alive. He won't stop until I'm trapped beside him.

He can never never never know that I can touch him.

I can only imagine what he'd do if he had access to my body.

I breathe in one quick, sharp, shaky breath and contemplate telling Adam what happened.

No. No. No. No.

I squeeze my eyes shut. I may have misjudged the situation. It was chaotic. My brain was distracted. Maybe I imagined it.

Yes.

Maybe I imagined it.

It's strange enough that Adam can touch me. The

likelihood of there being 2 people in this world who are immune to my touch doesn't seem possible. In fact, the more I think about it, the more I'm determined I must have made a mistake. It could've been anything brushing my leg. Maybe a piece of the sheet Adam abandoned after using it to punch through the window. Maybe a pillow that'd fallen from the bed. Maybe Warner's gloves lying, discarded, on the floor. Yes.

There's no way he could've touched me, because if he had, he would've cried out in agony.

Just like everyone else.

Adam's hand slips silently into mine and I grip his fingers with both my hands, desperate to reassure myself that he has immunity from me. I worry that there's an expiration date on this phenomenon. A clock striking midnight. A pumpkin carriage.

The possibility of losing him

The possibility of losing him

The possibility of losing him is 100 years of solitude I don't want to imagine. I don't want my arms to be devoid of his warmth. His touch. His lips, God his lips, his mouth on my neck, his body wrapped around mine, holding me together as if to affirm that my existence on this earth is not for nothing.

"Juliette?"

I swallow back the bullet in my throat. "Yes?"

"Why are you crying . . . ?" His voice is almost as gentle as his hand as it breaks free from my grip. He touches the tears rolling down my face.

"You can *touch* me," I say for the first time, recognize out loud for the first time. My words fade to a whisper. "You can touch me. You care and I don't know why. You're kind to me and you don't have to be. My own mother didn't care enough to—t-to—" My voice catches and I press my lips together. Glue them shut. Force myself to be still.

I am a rock. A statue. A movement frozen in time. Ice feels nothing at all.

Adam doesn't answer, doesn't say a single word until he pulls off the road and into an old underground parking garage. I realize we've reached some semblance of civilization, but it's pitch-black belowground. I can see next to nothing and once again wonder at how Adam is managing. My eyes fall on the screen illuminated on his dashboard only to realize the tank has night vision. *Of course.*

Adam shuts off the engine. I hear him sigh. I can hardly distinguish his silhouette before I feel his hand on my thigh. Warmth spreads through my limbs. The tips of my fingers and toes are tingling to life.

"Juliette," he whispers, and I realize just how close he is. "It's been me and you against the world forever," he says. "It's always been that way. It's my fault I took so long to do something about it."

"No." I'm shaking my head. "It's not your fault—"

"It is. I fell in love with you a long time ago. I just never had the guts to act on it."

"Because I could've killed you."

He laughs a quiet laugh. "Because I didn't think I deserved you."

"What?"

He touches his nose to mine. Leans into my neck. Wraps a piece of my hair around his fingers and I can't I can't I can't breathe. "You're so . . . *good*," he whispers.

"But my hands—"

"Have never done anything to hurt anyone."

I'm about to protest when he corrects himself. "Not on purpose." He leans back. "You never fought back," he says after a moment. "I always wondered why. You never yelled or got angry or tried to say anything to anyone," he says, and I know we're both back in third fourth fifth sixth seventh eighth ninth grade all over again. "But damn, you must've read a million books." I know he's smiling when he says it. A pause. "You bothered no one, but you were a moving target every day. You could've fought back. You could've hurt everyone if you wanted to."

"I don't want to hurt anyone." My voice is less than a whisper. I can't get the image of 8-year-old Adam out of my head. Lying on the floor. Broken. Abandoned. Crying into the dirt.

The things people will do for power.

"That's why you'll never be what Warner wants you to be."

I'm staring at a point in the blackness, my mind tortured by possibilities. "How can you be sure?"

His lips are so close to mine. "Because you still give a

damn about the world."

I gasp and he's kissing me, deep and powerful and unrestrained. His arms wrap around my back, dipping my body until I'm practically horizontal. My head is on the seat, his frame hovering over me, his hands gripping my hips from under my tattered dress. He's a hot bath, a short breath, 5 days of summer pressed into 5 fingers writing stories on my body. I'm an embarrassing mess of nerves crashing into him. His scent is assaulting my senses.

His eyes

His hands

His chest

His lips

are at my ear when he speaks. "We're here, by the way." He's breathing harder now than when he was running for his life. I feel his heart pounding against my ribs. His words are a broken whisper. "Maybe we should go inside. It's safer." But he doesn't move.

I just nod, my head bobbing on my neck, until I remember he can't see me. I try to remember how to speak, but I'm too focused on the fingers he's running down my thighs to form sentences. There's something about the absolute darkness, about not being able to see what's happening that makes me drunk with a delicious dizziness. "Yes," is all I manage.

He helps me up to a seated position, leans his forehead against mine. "I'm sorry," he says. "It's so hard for me to stop myself." His words tingle on my skin.

I allow my hands to slip under his shirt. I trace the perfectly sculpted lines of his body. He's nothing but lean muscle. "You don't have to," I tell him.

It's 5,000 degrees in the air between us. His fingers are at the dip right below my hip bone, teasing the small piece of fabric keeping me halfway decent. "Juliette . . ."

"Adam?"

My neck snaps up in surprise. Fear. Anxiety. Adam stops moving, frozen in front of me. I'm not sure he's breathing. I look around but can't find a face to match the voice that called his name and begin to panic before Adam is slamming open the door, flying out before I hear it again.

"Adam . . . is that you?"

It's a boy.

"James!"

The muffled sound of impact, 2 bodies colliding, 2 voices too happy to be dangerous.

"I can't believe it's really you! I mean, well, I thought it was you because I thought I heard something and at first I figured it was nothing but then I decided I should probably check just to be sure because what if it *was* you and—" He pauses. "Wait—what are you doing here?"

"I'm home." Adam laughs a little.

"Really?" James squeaks. "Are you home for good?"

"Yeah." He sighs. "Damn it's good to see you."

"I missed you," James says, suddenly quiet.

One deep breath. "Me too, kid. Me too."

"Hey, so, have you eaten anything? Benny just delivered

my dinner package, and I could share some with y—"

"James?"

He pauses. "Yeah?"

"There's someone I want you to meet."

My palms are sweaty. My heart is in my throat. I hear Adam walk back toward the tank and don't realize he's popped his head inside until he hits a switch. A faint emergency light illuminates the cabin. I blink a few times and see a young boy standing about 5 feet away, dirty-blond hair framing a round face with blue eyes that look too familiar. He's pressed his lips together in concentration. He's staring at me.

Adam is opening my door. He helps me to my feet, barely able to control the smile on his face and I'm stunned by the level of my own nervousness. I don't know why I'm so nervous but God I'm nervous. This boy is obviously important to Adam. I don't know why but I feel like this *moment* is important, too. I'm so worried I'm going to ruin everything. I try to fix the ripped folds of my dress, try to soften the wrinkles ironed into the fabric. I run haphazard fingers through my hair. It's useless.

The poor kid will be petrified.

Adam leads me forward. James is a handful of inches short of my height, but it's obvious in his face that he's young, unblemished, untouched by most of the world's harsh realities.

"James? This is Juliette." Adam glances at me.

"Juliette, this is my brother, James."

THIRTY-ONE

His brother.

I try to shake off the nerves. I try to smile at the boy studying my face, studying the pathetic pieces of fabric barely covering my body. How did I not know Adam had a brother? How could I have never known?

James turns to Adam. *"This* is Juliette?"

I'm standing here like a lump of nonsense. I don't remember my manners. "You know who I am?"

James spins back in my direction. "Oh yeah. Adam talks about you *a lot.*"

I flush and can't help but glance at Adam. He's staring at a spot on the floor. He clears his throat.

"It's really nice to meet you," I manage.

James cocks his head. "So do you always dress like that?"

I'd like to die a little.

"Hey, kid," Adam interrupts. "Juliette is going to be staying with us for a little while. Why don't you go make sure you don't have any underwear lying on the floor, huh?"

James looks horrified. He darts into the darkness without another word.

It's quiet for so many seconds I lose count. I hear some kind of drip in the distance.

I take a deep breath. Bite my bottom lip. Try to find the right words. Fail. "I didn't know you had a brother."

Adam hesitates. "Is it okay . . . that I do? We'll all be sharing the same space and I—"

"Of course it's okay!" I say hastily. "I just—I mean—are you sure it's okay—for *him*? If I'm here?"

"There's no underwear *anywhere*," James announces, marching forward into the light. I wonder where he disappeared to, where the house is. He looks at me. "So you're going to be staying with us?"

Adam intervenes. "Yeah. She's going to crash with us for a bit."

James looks from me to Adam back to me again. He sticks out his hand. "Well, it's nice to finally meet you."

All the color drains from my face. I can't stop staring at his small hand outstretched, offered to me.

"*James*," Adam says a little curtly.

James starts laughing. "I was only kidding," he says, dropping his hand.

"What?" My head is spinning, confused.

"Don't worry," James says, still chuckling. "I won't touch you. Adam told me all about your magical powers." He rolls his eyes.

"Adam—told—he—*what*?"

"Hey, maybe we should go inside." Adam clears his throat a little too loudly. "I'll just grab our bags real quick—" And he jogs off toward the tank. I'm left staring at James. He doesn't conceal his curiosity.

"How old are you?" he asks me.

"Seventeen."

He nods. "That's what Adam said."

I bristle. "What else did Adam tell you about me?"

"He said you don't have parents, either. He said you're like us."

My voice softens. "How old are *you*?"

"I'll be eleven next year."

I grin. "So you're ten years old?"

He crosses his arms. Frowns. "I'll be twelve in two years."

I think I already love this kid.

The cabin light shuts off and for a moment we're immersed in absolute darkness. A soft *click* and a faint circular glow illuminates the view. Adam has a flashlight.

"Hey, James? Why don't you lead the way for us?"

"Yes, sir!" He skids to a halt in front of Adam's feet, offers us an exaggerated salute, and runs off so quickly there's no way to follow him. I can't help the smile spreading across my face.

Adam's hand slips into mine as we move forward. "You okay?"

I squeeze his fingers. "You told your ten-year-old brother about my magical powers?"

He laughs. "I tell him a lot of things."

"Adam?"

"Yeah?"

"Isn't your *house* the first place Warner will go looking for you? Isn't this dangerous?"

"It would be. But according to public records, I don't have a home."

"And your brother?"

"Would be Warner's first target. It's safer for him where I can watch over him. Warner knows I have a brother, he just doesn't know where. And until he figures it out—which he will—we have to prepare."

"To fight?"

"To fight back. Yeah." Even in the dim light of this foreign space I can see the determination holding him together. It makes me want to sing.

I close my eyes. "Good."

"What's taking you so long?" James shouts in the distance.

And we're off.

The parking garage is located underneath an old abandoned office building buried in the shadows. A fire exit leads directly up to the main floor.

James is so excited he's jumping up and down the stairs, running forward a few steps only to run back to complain we're not coming fast enough. Adam catches him from behind and lifts him off the floor. He laughs. "You're going to break your neck."

James protests but only halfheartedly. He's too happy to have his brother back.

A sharp pang of some distant kind of emotion hits me in the heart. It hurts in a bittersweet way I can't place. I feel warm and numb at the same time.

Adam punches a pass code into a keypad by a massive steel door. There's a soft *click,* a short *beep,* and he turns the handle.

I'm stunned by what I see inside.

THIRTY-TWO

It's a full living room, open and plush. A thick rug, soft chairs, one sofa stretched across the wall. Green and red and orange hues, warm lamps softly lit in the large space. It feels more like a home than anything I've ever seen. The cold, lonely memories of my childhood can't even compare. I feel so safe so suddenly it scares me.

"You like it?" Adam is grinning at me, amused no doubt by the look on my face. I manage to pick my jaw up off the floor.

"I love it," I say, out loud or in my head I'm unsure.

"Adam did it," James says, proud, puffing his chest out a little more than necessary. "He made it for me."

"I didn't *make* it," Adam protests, chuckling. "I just . . . cleaned it up a bit."

"You live here by yourself?" I ask James.

He shoves his hands into his pockets and nods. "Benny stays with me a lot, but mostly I'm here alone. I'm lucky, though."

Adam is dropping our bags onto the couch. He runs a hand through his hair and I watch as the muscles in his back flex, tight, pulled together. I watch as he exhales the tension from his body.

I know why, but I ask anyway. "Why are you lucky?"

"Because I have a visitor. None of the other kids have visitors."

"There are other kids here?" I hope I don't look as horrified as I feel.

James nods so quickly his head wobbles on his neck. "Oh yeah. This whole street. All the kids are here. I'm the only one with my own room, though." He gestures around the space. "This is all mine because Adam got it for me. But everyone else has to share. We have school, sort of. And Benny brings me my food packages. Adam says I can play with the other kids but I can't bring them inside." He shrugs. "It's okay."

The reality of what he's saying spreads like poison in the pit of my stomach.

A street dedicated to orphaned children.

I wonder how their parents died. I don't wonder for long.

I take inventory of the room and notice a tiny refrigerator and a tiny microwave perched on top, both nestled into a corner, see some cabinets set aside for storage. Adam brought as much stuff as he could—all sorts of canned food and nonperishable items. We both brought our toiletries and multiple sets of clothes. We packed enough to survive for at least a little while.

James pulls a tinfoil package out of the fridge and sticks it in the microwave.

"Wait—James—don't—" I try to stop him.

His eyes are wide, frozen. "What?"

211

"The tinfoil—you can't—you can't put metal in the microwave—"

"What's a microwave?"

I blink so many times the room spins. "What . . . ?"

He pulls the lid off the tinfoil container to reveal a small square. It looks like a bouillon cube. He points to the cube and then nods at the microwave. "It's okay. I always put this in the Automat. Nothing happens."

"It takes the molecular composition of the food and multiplies it." Adam is standing beside me. "It doesn't add any extra nutritional value, but it makes you feel fuller, longer."

"And it's cheap!" James says, grinning as he sticks it back in the contraption.

It astounds me how much has changed. People have become so desperate they're faking *food*.

I have so many questions I'm liable to burst. Adam squeezes my shoulder, gently. He whispers, "We'll talk later, I promise." But I'm an encyclopedia with too many blank pages.

James falls asleep with his head in Adam's lap.

He talked nonstop once he finished his food, telling me all about his sort-of school, and his sort-of friends, and Benny, the elderly lady who takes care of him because "I think she likes Adam better than me but she sneaks me sugar sometimes so it's okay." Everyone has a curfew. No one but soldiers are allowed outside after sunset, each soldier armed and instructed to fire at their own discretion.

"Some people get more food and stuff than other people," James said, but that's because the people are sorted based on what they can provide to The Reestablishment, and not because they're human beings with the right not to starve to death.

My heart cracked a little more with every word he shared with me.

"You don't mind that I talk a lot, huh?" He bit down on his bottom lip and studied me.

"I don't mind at all."

"Everyone says I talk a lot." He shrugged. "But what am I supposed to do when I have so much to say?"

"Hey—about that—" Adam interrupted. "You can't tell anyone we're here, okay?"

James' mouth stopped midmovement. He blinked a few times. He stared hard at his brother. "Not even Benny?"

"No one," Adam said.

For one infinitesimal moment I saw something that looked like raw understanding flash in his eyes. A 10-year-old who can be trusted absolutely. He nodded again and again. "Okay. You were never here."

Adam brushes back wayward strands of hair from James' forehead. He's looking at his brother's sleeping face as if trying to memorize each brushstroke of an oil painting. I'm staring at him staring at James.

Adam looks up and I look down and we're both embarrassed for different reasons.

He whispers, "I should probably put him in bed," but doesn't make an effort to move. James is sound sound sound asleep.

"When was the last time you saw him?" I ask, careful to keep my voice down.

"About six months ago." A pause. "But I talked to him on the phone a lot." Smiles a little. "Told him a lot about you."

I flush. Count my fingers to make sure they're all there. "Didn't Warner monitor your calls?"

"Yeah. But Benny has an untraceable line, and I was always careful to keep it to official reporting, only. In any case, James has known about you for a long time."

"Really?"

He looks up, looks away. Locks eyes with me. "Juliette, I've been searching for you since the day you left. I didn't know what they were going to do to you."

He leans back against the couch. Runs a free hand over his face. Seasons change. Stars explode. Someone is walking on the moon. "You know I still remember the first day you showed up at school?" He laughs a soft, sad laugh. "Maybe I was too young, and maybe I didn't know much about the world, but there was something about you I was immediately drawn to. It's like I just wanted to be near you, like you had this—this *goodness* I never found in my life. This sweetness that I never found at home. I just wanted to hear you talk. I wanted you to see me, to smile at me. Every single day I promised myself I would talk to you. I wanted to *know* you. But every day I was a coward. And one day you just disappeared.

"I'd heard the rumors, but I knew better. I knew you'd never hurt anyone." He looks down. The earth cracks open and I'm falling into the fissure. "It sounds crazy," he says finally, so quietly. "To think that I cared so much without ever talking to you." He hesitates. "But I couldn't stop thinking about you. I couldn't stop wondering where you went. What would happen to you. I was afraid you'd never fight back."

He's silent for so long.

"I had to find you," he whispers. "I asked around everywhere and no one had answers. The world kept falling apart. Things were getting worse and I didn't know what to do. I had to take care of James and I had to find a way to live and I didn't know if joining the army would help but I never forgot about you. I always hoped," he falters, "that one day I would see you again."

I've run out of words. My pockets are full of letters I can't string together and I'm so desperate to say something that I say nothing and my heart is about to burst through my chest.

"Juliette . . . ?"

"You found me." 3 syllables. 1 whisper of astonishment.

"Are you . . . upset?"

I look up and for the first time I realize he's nervous. Worried. Uncertain how I'll react to this revelation. I don't know whether to laugh or cry or kiss every inch of his body.

I want to fall asleep to the sound of his heart beating. I want to know he's alive and well, breathing in and out, strong and sane and healthy forever.

"You're the only one who ever cared," I say. My eyes are filling with tears and I'm blinking them back and feeling the burn in my throat and everything everything everything hurts. The weight of the entire day crashes into me, threatens to break my bones. I want to cry out in happiness, in agony, in joy and the absence of justice. I want to touch the heart of the only person who ever gave a damn.

"I love you," I whisper. "So much more than you will ever know."

His jaw is tight. His mouth is tight. He looks up and tries to clear his throat and I know he needs a moment to pull himself together. I tell him he should probably put James in bed. He nods. Cradles his brother to his chest. Gets to his feet and carries James to the storage closet that's become his bedroom.

I watch him walk away with the only family he has left and I know why Adam joined the army.

I know why he suffered through being Warner's whipping boy. I know why he dealt with the horrifying reality of war, why he was so desperate to run away, so ready to run away as soon as possible. Why he's so determined to fight back.

He's fighting for so much more than himself.

THIRTY-THREE

"Why don't I take a look at those cuts?"

Adam is standing in front of James' door, his hands tucked into his pockets. He's wearing a dark red T-shirt that hugs his torso. His arms are professionally painted with tattoos I now know how to recognize. He catches me staring.

"I didn't really have a choice," he says, examining the consecutive black bands of ink etched into his forearms. "We had to survive. It was the only job I could get."

I meet him across the room, touch the designs on his skin. Nod. "I understand."

He almost laughs. Shakes his head just a millimeter.

"What?" I jerk my hand away.

"Nothing." He grins. Slips his arms around my waist. "It just keeps hitting me. You're really here. In my house."

I bite my lip. "Where'd you get your tattoo from?"

"These?" He looks at his arms again.

"No." I reach for his shirt, tugging it up so unsuccessfully he nearly loses his balance. He stumbles back against the wall. I touch his chest. Touch the bird. "Where'd you get *this* from?"

"Oh." He's looking at me but I'm suddenly distracted

by his body and the cargo pants set a little too low on his hips. I realize he must've taken his belt off. I force my eyes upward. Allow my fingers to fumble down his abs. He takes a tight breath. "I don't know," he says. "I just—I kept dreaming about this white bird. Birds used to fly, you know."

"You used to dream about it?"

"Yeah. All the time." He smiles a little, exhales a little, remembering. "It was nice. It felt good—hopeful. I wanted to hold on to that memory because I wasn't sure it would last. So I made it permanent."

I cover the tattoo with the palm of my hand. "I used to dream about this bird all the time."

"*This* bird?" His eyebrows could touch the sky.

I nod. "This exact one. Until the day you showed up in my cell. I haven't dreamt of it ever since." I peek up at him.

"You're kidding."

I lean my forehead on his chest. Breathe in the scent of him. He wastes no time pulling me closer. Rests his chin on my head, his hands on my back.

And we stand like that until I'm too old to remember a world without his warmth.

Adam cleans my cuts in a bathroom set a little off to the side of the space. It's a miniature room with a toilet, a sink, a small mirror, and a tiny shower. I love all of it. By the time I get out of the bathroom, finally changed and washed up for bed, Adam is waiting for me in the dark.

There are blankets and pillows laid out on the floor and it looks like heaven. I'm so exhausted I could sleep through a few centuries.

I slip in beside him and he scoops me into his arms. The temperature is significantly lower in this place, and Adam is the perfect furnace. I bury my face in his chest and he pulls me tight. I trail my fingers down his naked back, feel the muscles tense under my touch. I rest my hand on the waist of his pants. Hook my finger into a belt loop. Test the taste of the words on my tongue. "I meant it, you know."

His breath is a beat too late. His heart just a beat too fast. "Meant what . . . ?"

I feel so shy suddenly. So blind, so unnecessarily bold. I know nothing about what I'm venturing into. All I know is I don't want anyone's hands on me but his. Forever.

Adam leans back and I can just make out the outline of his face, his eyes always shining in the darkness. I stare at his lips when I speak. "I've never asked you to stop." My fingers rest on the button holding his pants together. "Not once."

He's staring at me, his chest rising and falling. He seems almost numb with disbelief.

I lean into his ear. "Touch me."

And he's nearly undone.

My face is in his hands and my lips are at his lips and he's kissing me and I'm oxygen and he's dying to breathe. His body is almost on top of mine, one hand in my hair, the other slipping behind my knee to pull me closer, higher, tighter. I want to experience him with all 5 senses, drown in the waves of wonder enveloping me.

He takes my hands and presses them against his chest, guides my fingers as they trail down the length of his torso before his lips meet mine again and again and again drugging me into a delirium I never want to escape. But it's not enough. It's still not enough. My heart is racing through my blood, destroying my self-control. He breaks for air and I pull him back, aching, desperate, dying for his touch. His hands slip up under my shirt, skirting my sides, touching me like he's never dared to before, and my top is nearly over my head when a door squeaks open. We both freeze.

"Adam . . . ?"

He can hardly breathe. He tries to lower himself onto the pillow beside me but I can still feel his heat, his figure, his heart pounding in my ears. Adam leans his head up, just a little. Tries to sound normal. "James?"

"Can I come sleep out here with you?"

Adam sits up. He's breathing hard but he's suddenly alert. "Of course you can." A pause. His voice slows, softens. "You have bad dreams?"

James doesn't answer.

Adam is on his feet.

I hear the muffled hiccup of 10-year-old tears, but can barely distinguish the outline of Adam's body holding James together. "I thought you said it was getting better,"

I hear him whisper, but his words are kind, not accusing.

James says something I can't hear.

Adam picks him up, and I realize how tiny James seems in comparison. They disappear into the bedroom only to return with bedding. Only once James is tucked securely in place a few feet from Adam does he finally give in to exhaustion. His heavy breathing is the only sound in the room.

Adam turns to me. I have no idea what James has witnessed at such a tender age. I have no idea what Adam has had to endure in leaving him behind. I have no idea how people live anymore. How they survive.

~~I don't know what's become of my parents.~~

Adam brushes my cheek. Slips me into his arms. Says, "I'm sorry," and I kiss the apology away.

"When the time is right," I tell him.

He leans into my neck. His hands are under my shirt. Up my back.

I bite back a gasp. "Soon."

THIRTY-FOUR

Adam and I forced ourselves 5 feet apart last night, but somehow I wake up in his arms. He's breathing softly, evenly, steadily, a warm hum in the morning air. I blink, peering into the daylight only to be met by a set of big blue eyes on a 10-year-old's face.

"How come you can touch *him*?" James is standing over us with his arms crossed, back to the stubborn boy I remember. There's no trace of fear, no hint of tears threatening to spill down his face. It's like last night never happened. *"Well?"* His impatience startles me.

I jump away from Adam's uncovered upper half so quickly it jolts him awake. A little.

He reaches for me. "Juliette . . . ?"

"You're touching a *girl*!"

Adam sits up so quickly he tangles in the sheets and falls back on his elbows. "Jesus, James—"

"You were sleeping next to a *girl*!"

Adam opens and closes his mouth several times. He glances at me. Glances at his brother. Shuts his eyes and finally sighs. Runs a hand through his morning hair. "I don't know what you want me to say."

"I thought you said she couldn't touch anyone." James is

staring at me now, suspicious.

"She can't."

"Except for you?"

"Right. Except for me."

~~And Warner.~~

"She can't touch anyone except for you."

~~And Warner.~~

"Right."

"That seems awfully *convenient*." James narrows his eyes.

Adam laughs out loud. "Where'd you learn to talk like that?"

James frowns. "Benny says that a lot. She says my excuses are 'awfully convenient'." He makes air quotes with two fingers. "She says it means I don't believe you. And I don't believe you."

Adam gets to his feet. The early morning light filters through the small windows at the perfect angle, the perfect moment. He's bathed in gold, his muscles taut, his pants still a little low on his hips and I have to force myself to think straight. Adam makes me hungry for things I never knew I could have.

I watch as he drapes an arm over his brother's shoulders before squatting down to meet his gaze. "Can I talk to you about something?" he says. "Privately?"

"Just me and you?" James glances at me out of the corner of his eye.

"Yeah. Just me and you."

"Okay."

I watch the two of them disappear into James' room and wonder what Adam is going to tell him. It takes me a moment to realize James must feel threatened by my sudden appearance. He finally sees his brother after nearly 6 months only to have him come home with a strange girl with crazy magical powers. I nearly laugh at the idea. If only it were magic that made me this way.

I don't want James to think I'm taking Adam away from him.

I slip back under the covers and wait. The morning is cool and brisk and my thoughts begin to wander to Warner. I need to remember that we're not safe. Not yet, maybe not ever. I need to remember never to get too comfortable. I sit up. Pull my knees to my chest and wrap my arms around my ankles.

I wonder if Adam has a plan.

James' door squeaks open. The two brothers step out, the younger before the older. James looks a little pink and he can hardly meet my eyes. He looks embarrassed and I wonder if Adam punished him.

My heart fails for a moment.

Adam claps James on the shoulder. Squeezes. "You okay?"

"I know what a *girlfriend* is—"

"I never said you didn't—"

"So you're his *girlfriend*?" James crosses his arms, looks at me.

I look at Adam because I don't know what else to do.

"Hey, maybe you should be getting ready for school, huh?" Adam opens the refrigerator and hands James a new foil package. I assume it's his breakfast.

"I don't *have* to go," James protests. "It's not like a *real* school, no one *has* to—"

"I want you to," Adam cuts him off. He turns back to his brother with a small smile. "Don't worry. I'll be here when you get back."

James hesitates. "You promise?"

"Yeah." Another grin. Nods him over. "Come here."

James runs forward and clings to Adam like he's afraid he'll disappear. Adam pops the foil food into the Automat and presses a button. He musses James' hair. "You need to get a haircut, kid."

James wrinkles his nose. "I like it."

"It's a little long, don't you think?"

James lowers his voice. "I think *her* hair is really long."

James and Adam glance back at me. I touch my hair without intending to, suddenly self-conscious. I look down. I've never had a reason to cut my hair. I've never even had the tools. No one offers me sharp objects.

I chance a peek and see Adam is still staring at me. James is staring at the Automat.

"I like her hair," Adam says, and I'm not sure who he's talking to.

I watch the two of them as Adam helps his brother get ready for school. James is so full of life, so full of energy, so excited to have his brother around. It makes me wonder what it must be like for a 10-year-old to live on his own. What it must be like for all the kids who live on this street.

I'm itching to get up and change, but I'm not sure what I should do. I don't want to take up the bathroom in case James needs it, or if Adam needs it. I don't want to take up any more space than I already have. It feels so private, so personal, this relationship between Adam and James. It's the kind of bond I've never had, will never have. But being around so much love has managed to thaw my frozen parts into something human. I *feel* human. Like maybe I could be a part of this world. Like maybe I don't have to be a monster. Maybe I'm not a monster.

Maybe things can change.

THIRTY-FIVE

James is at school, Adam is in the shower, and I'm staring at a bowl of granola Adam left for me to eat. It feels so wrong to be eating this food when James has to eat the unidentifiable substance in the foil container. But Adam says James is allocated a certain portion for every meal, and he's required to eat it by law. If he's found wasting it or discarding it, he could be punished. All the orphans are expected to eat the foil food that goes in their Automat. James claims it "doesn't taste too bad."

I shiver slightly in the cool morning air and smooth a hand over my hair, still damp from the shower. The water here isn't hot. It isn't even warm. It's freezing. Warm water is a luxury.

Someone is pounding on the door.

I'm up.
Spinning.
Scanning.
Scared.
They found us is the only thing I can think of. My stomach is a flimsy crepe, my heart a raging woodpecker, my blood a river of anxiety.

Adam is in the shower.

James is at school.

~~I'm absolutely defenseless.~~

I rummage through Adam's duffel bag until I find what I'm looking for. 2 guns, 1 for each hand. 2 hands, just in case the guns fail. I'm finally wearing the kind of clothes that would be comfortable to fight in. I take a deep breath and beg my hands not to shake.

The pounding gets harder.

I point the guns at the door.

"Juliette . . . ?"

I spin back to see Adam staring at me, the guns, the door. His hair is wet. His eyes are wide. He nods toward the extra gun in my hand and I toss it to him without a word.

"If it were Warner he wouldn't be knocking," he says, though he doesn't lower his weapon.

I know he's right. Warner would've shot down the door, used explosives, killed a hundred people to get to me. He certainly wouldn't wait for me to open the door. Something calms inside of me but I won't allow myself to get comfortable. "Who do you think—?"

"It might be Benny—she usually checks up on James—"

"But wouldn't she know he'd be at school right now?"

"No one else knows where I live—"

The pounding is getting weaker. Slower. There's a low, guttural sound of agony.

Adam and I lock eyes.

One more fist flailing into the door. A slump. Another

moan. The thud of a body against the door.

I flinch.

Adam rakes a hand through his hair.

"Adam!" someone cries. Coughs. "Please, man, if you're in there—"

I freeze. The voice sounds familiar.

Adam's spine straightens in an instant. His lips are parted, his eyes astonished. He punches in the pass code and turns the latch. Points his gun toward the door as he eases it open.

"Kenji?"

A short wheeze. A muffled groan. "Shit, man, what took you so long?"

"What the hell are you doing here?" *Click.* I can hardly see through the small slit of the door, but it's clear Adam isn't happy to have company. "Who sent you here? Who are you with?"

Kenji swears a few more times under his breath. "*Look at me,*" he demands, though it sounds more like a plea. "You think I came up here to kill you?"

Adam pauses. Breathes. Doubts. "I have no problem putting a bullet in your back."

"Don't worry, bro. I already have a bullet in my back. Or my leg. Or some shit. I don't even know."

Adam opens the door. "Get up."

"It's all right, I don't mind if you drag my ass inside."

Adam works his jaw. "I don't want your blood on my carpet. It's not something my brother needs to see."

Kenji stumbles up and staggers into the room. I'd heard his voice once before, but never seen his face. Though this probably isn't the best time for first impressions. His eyes are puffy, swollen, purple; there's a huge gash in the side of his forehead. His lip is split, slightly bleeding, his body slumped and broken. He winces, takes short breaths as he moves. His clothes are ripped to shreds, his upper body covered by nothing but a tank top, his well-developed arms cut and bruised. I'm amazed he didn't freeze to death. He doesn't seem to notice me until he does.

He stops. Blinks. Breaks into a ridiculous smile dimmed only by a slight grimace from the pain. "Holy shit," he says, still drinking me in. "Holy *shit*." He tries to laugh. "Dude, you're *insane*—"

"The bathroom is over here." Adam is set in stone.

Kenji moves forward but keeps looking back. I point the gun at his face. He laughs harder, flinches, wheezes a bit. "Dude, you ran off with the crazy chick! You ran off with the psycho girl!" he's calling after Adam. "I thought they made that shit up. What the hell were you thinking? What are you going to do with the psycho chick? No *wonder* Warner wants you dead—OW, MAN, what the *hell*—"

"She's not crazy. And she's not *deaf*, asshole."

The door slams shut behind them and I can only make out their muffled argument. I have a feeling Adam doesn't want me to hear what he has to say to Kenji. Either that, or it's the screaming.

I have no idea what Adam is doing, but I assume it

230

has something to do with dislodging a bullet from Kenji's body and generally repairing the rest of his wounds as best he can. Adam has a pretty extensive first aid supply and strong, steady hands. I wonder if he picked up these skills in the army. Maybe for taking care of himself. Or maybe his brother. It would make sense.

Health insurance was a dream we lost a long time ago.

I've been holding this gun in my hand for nearly an hour. I've been listening to Kenji scream for nearly an hour and I only know that because I like counting the seconds as they pass by. I have no idea what time it is. I think there's a clock in James' bedroom but I don't want to go into his room without permission.

I stare at the gun in my hand, at the smooth, heavy metal, and I'm surprised to find that I enjoy the way it feels in my grip. Like an extension of my body. It doesn't frighten me anymore.

It frightens me more that I might use it.

The bathroom door opens and Adam walks out. He has a small towel in his hands. I get to my feet. He offers me a tight smile. He reaches into the tiny fridge for the even tinier freezer section. Grabs a couple of ice cubes and drops them into the towel. Disappears into the bathroom again.

I sit back on the couch.

Adam comes out of the bathroom, this time empty-handed, still alone.

I stand back up.

He rubs his forehead, the back of his neck. Meets me on the couch. "I'm sorry," he says.

My eyes are wide. "For what?"

"Everything." He sighs. "Kenji was a sort of friend of mine back on base. Warner had him tortured after we left. For information."

I swallow a gasp.

"He says he didn't say anything—didn't have anything to say, really—but he got messed up pretty bad. I have no idea if his ribs are broken or just bruised, but I managed to get the bullet out of his leg."

I take his hand. Squeeze.

"He got shot running away," Adam says after a moment.

And something slams into my consciousness. I panic. "The tracker serum—"

Adam nods, his eyes heavy, distraught. "I think it might be dysfunctional, but I have no way of knowing for sure. I do know that if it were working as it should, Warner would be here by now. But we can't risk it. We have to get out, and we have to get rid of Kenji before we go."

I'm shaking my head. "How did he even *find* you?"

Adam's face hardens. "He started screaming before I could ask."

"And James?" I whisper, almost afraid to wonder.

Adam drops his head into his hands. "As soon as he gets home, we have to go. We can use this time to prepare." He meets my eyes. "I can't leave James behind. It's not safe for him here anymore."

I touch his cheek and he leans into my hand, holds my palm against his face. Closes his eyes.

"Son of a motherless goat—"

Adam and I break apart. I'm blushing past my hairline. Adam looks annoyed. Kenji is leaning against the wall in the bathroom hallway, holding the makeshift ice pack to his face. Staring at us.

"You can *touch* her? I mean—shit, I just *saw* you touch her but that's not even—"

"You have to go," Adam says to him. "You've already left a chemical trace leading right to my home. We need to leave, and you can't come with us."

"Oh hey—whoa—hold on." Kenji stumbles into the living room, wincing as he puts pressure on his leg. "I'm not trying to slow you down, man. I know a place. A safe place. Like, a legit, super-safe place. I can take you. I can show you how to get there. I know a guy."

"Bullshit." Adam is still angry. "How did you even find me? How did you manage to show up at my *door*, Kenji? I don't trust you—"

"I don't know, man. I swear I don't remember what happened. I don't know where I was running after a certain point. I was just jumping fences. I found a huge field with an old shed. Slept in there for a while. I think I blacked out at one point, either from the pain or from the cold—it is cold as *hell* out here—and the next thing I know, some dude is carrying me. Drops me off at your door. Tells me to shut up about Adam, because Adam lives right here." He

233

grins. Tries to wink. "I guess I was dreaming about you in my sleep."

"Wait—what?" Adam leans forward. "What do you mean some guy was carrying you? What guy? What was his name? How did he know *my* name?"

"I don't know. He didn't tell me, and it's not like I had the presence of mind to ask. But dude was *huge.* I mean, he had to be if he was going to lug my ass around."

"You can't honestly expect me to believe you."

"You have no choice." Kenji shrugs.

"Of course I have a choice." Adam is on his feet. "I have no reason to trust you. No reason to believe a word that's coming out of your mouth."

"Then why am I here with a bullet in my leg? Why hasn't Warner found you yet? Why am I *unarmed*—"

"This could be a part of your plan!"

"And you helped me anyway!" Kenji dares to raise his voice. "Why didn't you just let me die? Why didn't you shoot me dead? Why did you *help* me?"

Adam falters. "I don't know."

"You *do* know. You *know* I'm not here to mess you up. I took a goddamn beating for you—"

"You weren't protecting any information of mine."

"Well, shit, man, what the hell do you want me to say? They were going to *kill* my ass. I had to run. It wasn't my fault some dude dropped me off at your door—"

"This isn't just about *me,* don't you understand? I've worked so hard to find a safe place for my brother and in one morning you ruined *years* of planning. What the hell am I supposed to do now? I have to run until I can find a way to keep him safe. He's too young to have to deal with this—"

"We're *all* too young to have to deal with this shit." Kenji is breathing hard. "Don't fool yourself, bro. No one should have to see what we've seen. No one should have to wake up in the morning and find dead bodies in their living room, but shit happens. We deal with it, and we find a way to *survive*. You're not the only one with problems."

Adam sinks into the sofa. He leans forward with his head in his hands.

Kenji stares at me. I stare back.

He grins and hobbles forward. "You know, you're pretty sexy for a psycho chick."

Click.

Kenji is backing up with his hands in the air. Adam is pressing a gun to his forehead. "Show some respect, or I will burn it into your skull."

"I was *kidding*—"

"Like hell you were."

"Damn, Adam, calm the hell down—"

"Where's the 'super-safe place' you can take us?" I'm up, gun still gripped in my hand. I move into position next to Adam. "Or are you making that up?"

Kenji lights up. "No, that's real. Very real. In fact, I may or may not have mentioned something about you. And the dude who runs the place may or may not be ridiculously interested in meeting you."

"You think I'm some kind of freak you can show off to your friends?"

Kenji clears his throat. "Not a freak. Just . . . interesting."

I point my gun at his nose. "I'm so interesting I can kill you with my bare hands."

A barely perceptible flash of fear flickers in his eyes. "You sure you're not crazy?"

"No." I cock my head. "I'm not sure."

Kenji grins. Looks me up and down. "Well damn. But you make crazy sound so *good*."

"I'm about five inches from breaking your face," Adam warns him, his body stiff with anger, his eyes narrowed, unflinching. "I don't need another reason."

"What?" Kenji laughs, undeterred. "I haven't been this close to a chick in *way too long*, bro. And crazy or not—"

"I'm not interested."

Kenji turns to face me. "Well I'm not sure I blame you. I look like hell right now. But I clean up okay." He attempts a grin. "Give me a couple days. You might change your mind—"

Adam elbows him in the face and doesn't apologize.

THIRTY-SIX

Kenji is swearing, bleeding, and tripping his way toward the bathroom, holding his nose together.

Adam pulls me into James' bedroom.

"Tell me something," he says. He stares up at the ceiling, takes a hard breath. "Tell me anything—"

I try to focus his eyes, grasp his hands, gentle gentle gentle. I wait until he's looking at me. "Nothing is going to happen to James. We'll keep him safe. I promise."

His eyes are full of pain like I've never seen them before. He parts his lips. Presses them together. "He doesn't even know about our dad." It's the first time he's acknowledged the issue. It's the first time he's acknowledged that I know anything about it. "I never wanted him to know. I made up stories for him. I wanted him to have a chance to be *normal*." His lips are spelling secrets and my ears are spilling ink, staining my skin with his stories. "I don't want anyone to touch him. I don't want to screw him up. I can't—God I can't let it happen," he says to me. Hushed. Quiet.

I've searched the world for all the right words and my mouth is full of nothing.

"It's never enough," he whispers. "I can never do enough. He still wakes up screaming. He still cries himself to sleep.

He sees things I can't control." He blinks a million times. "So many people, Juliette."

I hold my breath.

"Dead."

I touch the word on his lips and he kisses my fingers.

"I don't know what to do," he says, and it's like a confession that costs him so much more than I can understand. Control is slipping through his fingers and he's desperate to hold on. *"Tell me what to do."*

I study the shape of his lips, the strong lines of his face, the eyelashes any girl would kill for, the deep dark blue of the eyes I've learned to swim in. I offer him the only possibility I have. "Kenji's plan might be worth considering."

"You trust him?" Adam leans back, surprised.

"I don't think he's lying about knowing a place we can go."

"I don't know if that's a good idea."

"Why not . . . ?"

Something that might not be a laugh. "I might kill him before we even get there."

My lips twist into a sad smile. "There isn't any other place for us to hide, is there?"

He shakes his head. Once. Fast. Tight.

I squeeze his hand. "Then we have to try."

"What the hell are you doing in there?" Kenji shouts through the door. Pounds it a couple times. "I mean, shit, man, I don't think there's *ever* a bad time to get naked, but now is probably not the best time for a nooner. So unless

238

you want to get killed, I suggest you get your ass out here. We have to get ready to go."

"I might kill him right now." Adam changes his mind.

I take his face in my hands, tip up on my toes and kiss him. "I love you."

He's looking into my eyes and looking at my mouth and his voice is a husky whisper. "Yeah?"

"Absolutely."

The 3 of us are packed and ready to go before James comes home from school. Adam and I collected the most important basic necessities: food, clothes, money Adam saved up. He keeps looking around the small space like he can't believe he's lost it so easily. I can only imagine how much work he put into it, how hard he tried to make a home for his little brother. My heart is in pieces for him.

His friend is an entirely different species.

Kenji is nursing new bruises, but seems in reasonable spirits, excited for reasons I can't fathom. He's oddly upbeat. It seems impossible to discourage him and I can't help but admire his determination. But he won't stop staring at me.

"So how come you can touch Adam?" he says after a moment.

"I don't know."

He snorts. "Bull."

I shrug. I don't feel the need to convince him that I have no idea how I got so lucky.

"How'd you even know you could touch him? Some

kind of sick experiment?"

"Where's this place you're taking us?"

"Why are you changing the subject?" He's grinning. I'm sure he's grinning. I refuse to look at him, though. "Maybe you can touch *me*, too. Why don't you try?"

"You don't want me to touch you."

"Maybe I do." He's definitely grinning.

"Maybe you should leave her alone before I put that bullet back in your leg," Adam offers.

"I'm sorry—is a lonely man not allowed to make a move, Kent? Maybe I'm actually interested. Maybe you should back the hell off and let her speak for herself."

Adam runs a hand through his hair. Always the same hand. Always through his hair. He's flustered. Frustrated. Maybe even embarrassed.

"I'm still not interested," I remind him, an edge to my voice.

"Yes, but let's not forget that *this*"—he motions to his battered face—"is not permanent."

"Well, I'm permanently uninterested." I want so badly to tell him that I'm unavailable. I want to tell him that I'm in a serious relationship. I want to tell him that Adam's made me promises.

But I can't.

I have no idea what it means to be in a relationship. I don't know if saying "I love you" is code for "mutually exclusive," and I don't know if Adam was serious when he told James I was his girlfriend. Maybe it was an excuse, a cover, an easy answer to an otherwise complicated question.

240

I wish he would say something to Kenji—I wish he would tell him that we're together officially, exclusively.

But he doesn't.

And I don't know why.

"I don't think you should decide until the swelling goes down," Kenji continues matter-of-factly. "It's only fair. I have a pretty spectacular face."

Adam chokes on a cough that I think was a laugh.

"You know, I could've sworn we used to be cool," Kenji says, leveling his gaze at Adam.

"I can't remember why."

Kenji bristles. "Is there something you want to say to me?"

"I don't trust you."

"Then why am I still here?"

"Because I trust *her*."

Kenji turns to look at me. He manages a goofy smile. "Aw, you trust me?"

"As long as I have a clear shot." I tighten my hold on the gun in my hand.

His grin is crooked. "I don't know why, but I kind of like it when you threaten me."

"That's because you're an idiot."

"Nah." He shakes his head. "You've got a sexy voice. Makes everything sound naughty."

Adam stands up so suddenly he nearly knocks over the coffee table.

Kenji bursts out laughing, wheezing against the pain of his injuries. "Calm down, Kent, *damn*. I'm just messing with you guys. I like seeing psycho chick get all intense."

He glances at me, lowers his voice. "I mean that as a compliment—because, you know"—he waves a haphazard hand in my direction—"psycho kind of works for you."

"What the hell is wrong with you?" Adam turns on him.

"What the hell is wrong with *you*?" Kenji crosses his arms, annoyed. "Everyone is so uptight in here."

Adam squeezes the gun in his hand. Walks to the door. Walks back. He's pacing.

"And don't worry about your brother," Kenji adds. "I'm sure he'll be here soon."

Adam doesn't laugh. He doesn't stop pacing. His jaw twitches. "I'm not worried about my brother. I'm trying to decide whether to shoot you now or later."

"Later," Kenji says, collapsing onto the couch. "You still need me right now."

Adam tries to speak but he's out of time.

The door clicks, beeps, unlatches open.

James is home.

THIRTY-SEVEN

"I'm really happy you're taking it so well—I am—but James, this really isn't something to be excited about. We're running for our lives."

"But we're doing it *together*," he says for the fifth time, a huge grin overcrowding his face. He took a liking to Kenji almost too quickly, and now the pair of them are conspiring to turn our predicament into some kind of elaborate mission. "And I can *help!*"

"No, it's not—"

"Of course you can—"

Adam and Kenji speak at the same time. Kenji recovers first. "Why can't he help? Ten years old is old enough to help."

"That's not your call," Adam says, careful to control his voice. I know he's staying calm for his brother's sake. "And it's none of your business."

"I'll finally get to come *with* you," James says. "And I want to help."

James took the news in stride. He didn't even flinch when Adam explained the real reason why he was home, and why we were together. I thought seeing Kenji's bruised and battered face would scare him, but James was eerily unmoved. It occurred to me he must've seen much worse.

Adam takes a few deep breaths before turning to Kenji. "How far?"

"By foot?" Kenji looks uncertain for the first time. "At least a few hours. If we don't do anything stupid, we should be there by nightfall."

"And if we take a car?"

Kenji blinks. His surprise dissolves into an enormous grin. "Well, shit, Kent, why didn't you say so sooner?"

"Watch your mouth around my brother."

James rolls his eyes. "I hear worse stuff than that *every day*. Even Benny uses bad words."

"*Benny?*"

"Yup."

"What does she—" Adam stops. Changes his mind. "That doesn't mean it's okay for you to keep hearing it."

"I'm almost eleven!"

"Hey, little man," Kenji interrupts. "It's okay. It's my fault. I should be more careful. Besides, there are ladies present." Kenji winks at me.

I look away. Look around.

It's difficult for *me* to leave this humble home, so I can only imagine what Adam must be experiencing right now. I think James is too excited about the dangerous road ahead of us to realize what's happening. To truly understand that he'll never be coming back here.

We're all fugitives running for our lives.

"So, what—you stole a car?" Kenji asks.

"A tank."

Kenji barks out a laugh. "Nice."

"It's a little conspicuous for daytime, though."

"What's *conspicuous* mean?" James asks.

"It's a little too . . . noticeable." Adam cringes.

"*SHIT*." Kenji stumbles up to his feet.

"I told you to watch your mouth—"

"Do you hear that?"

"Hear what—?"

Kenji's eyes are darting in every direction. "Is there another way out of here?"

Adam is up. "JAMES—"

James runs to his brother's side. Adam checks his gun. I'm slinging bags over my back, Adam is doing the same, his attention diverted by the front door.

"HURRY—"

"How close—?"

"THERE'S NO TIME—"

"What do you—"

"KENT, RUN—"

And we're running, following Adam into James' room. Adam rips a curtain off of one wall to reveal a hidden door just as 3 beeps sound from the living room.

Adam shoots the lock on the exit door.

Something explodes not 15 feet behind us. The sound shatters in my ears, vibrates through my body. I nearly collapse from the impact. Gunshots are everywhere. Footsteps are pounding into the house but we're already running through the exit. Adam hauls James up and into his arms and we're flying through the sudden burst of light blinding our way through the streets. The rain has stopped. The roads are slick and muddy. There are children everywhere, bright colors of small bodies suddenly screaming at our approach. There's no point being inconspicuous anymore.

They've already found us.

Kenji is lagging behind, stumbling his way through the last of his adrenaline rush. We turn into a narrow alleyway and he slumps against the wall. "I'm sorry," he pants, "I can't—you can leave me—"

"We can't leave you—," Adam shouts, looking everywhere, drinking in our surroundings.

"That's sweet, bro, but it's okay—"

"We need you to show us where to go!"

"Well, *shit*—"

"You said you would help us—"

"I thought you said you had a *tank*—"

"If you hadn't noticed, there's been an unexpected change of plans—"

"I can't keep up, Kent. I can barely walk—"

"You have to *try*—"

"*There are rebels on the loose. They are armed and ready to fire. Curfew is now in effect. Everyone return to their homes immediately. There are rebels on the loose. They are armed and ready to fi*—"

The loudspeakers sound around the streets, drawing attention to our bodies huddled together in the narrow alley. A few people see us and scream. Boots are getting louder. Gunshots are getting wilder.

I take a moment to analyze the surrounding buildings

and realize we're not in a settled compound. The street James lives on is unregulated turf: a series of abandoned office buildings crammed together, leftovers from our old lives. I don't understand why he's not living in a compound like the rest of the population. I don't have time to figure out why I only see two age groups represented, why the elderly and the orphaned are the only residents, why they've been dumped on illegal land with soldiers who are not supposed to be here. I'm afraid to consider the answers to my own questions and in a panicked moment I fear for James' life. I spin around as we run, glimpsing his small body bundled in Adam's arms.

His eyes are squeezed shut so tight I'm sure it hurts.

Adam swears under his breath. He kicks down the door of a deserted building and yells for us to follow him inside.

"I need you to stay here," he says to Kenji. "And I'm out of my mind, but I need to leave James with you. I need you to watch out for him. They're looking for Juliette, and they're looking for *me*. They won't even expect to find you two."

"What are you going to do?" Kenji asks.

"I need to steal a car. Then I'll come back for you." James doesn't even protest as Adam puts him down. His little lips are white. His eyes wide. His hands trembling. "I'll come back for you, James," Adam says again. "I promise."

James nods over and over and over again. Adam kisses his head, once, hard, fast. Drops our duffel bags on the floor. Turns to Kenji. "If you let anything happen to him, I will kill you."

Kenji doesn't laugh. He takes a deep breath. "I'll take care of him."

"Juliette?"

He takes my hand, and we disappear into the streets.

THIRTY-EIGHT

The roads are packed with pedestrians trying to escape. Adam and I hide our guns in the waistbands of our pants, but our wild eyes and jerky movements seem to give us away. Everyone stays away from us, darting in opposite directions, some squeaking, shouting, crying, dropping the things in their hands. But for all the people, I don't see a single car in sight. They must be hard to come by, especially in this area.

Adam pushes me to the ground just as a bullet flies past my head. He shoots down another door and we run through the ruins toward another exit, trapped in the maze of what used to be a clothing store. Gunshots and footsteps are close behind. There must be at least a hundred soldiers following us through these streets, clustered in different groups, dispersed in different areas of the city, ready to capture and kill.

But I know they won't kill me.

It's Adam I'm worried about.

I try to stay as close as possible to his body because I'm certain Warner has given them orders to bring me back alive. My efforts, however, are weak at best. Adam has enough height and muscle to dwarf me. Anyone with an excellent shot would be able to target him. They could shoot him right in the head.

Right in front of me.

He turns to fire two shots. One falls short. Another elicits a strangled cry. We're still running.

Adam doesn't say anything. He doesn't tell me to be brave. He doesn't ask me if I'm okay, if I'm scared. He doesn't offer me encouragement or assure me that we'll be just fine. He doesn't tell me to leave him behind and save myself. He doesn't tell me to watch his brother in case he dies.

He doesn't need to.

We both understand the reality of our situation. Adam could be shot right now. I could be captured at any moment. This entire building might suddenly explode. Someone could've discovered Kenji and James. We might all die today. The facts are obvious.

But we know we need to take the chance just the same.

Because moving forward is the only way to survive.

The gun is growing slick in my hands, but I hold on to it anyway. My legs are screaming against the pain, but I push them faster anyway. My lungs are sawing my rib cage in half, but I force them to process oxygen anyway. I have to keep moving. There's no time for human deficiencies.

The fire escape in this building is nearly impossible to find. Our feet pound the tiled floors, our hands searching through the bleak light for some kind of outlet, some kind of access to the streets. This building is larger than we anticipated, massive, with hundreds of possible directions. I realize it must have been a *warehouse* and not just a store. Adam ducks behind an abandoned desk, pulling me down with him.

"Don't be stupid, Kent—you can only run for so long!" someone shouts. The voice isn't more than 10 feet away.

Adam swallows. Clenches his jaw. The people trying to kill him are the same ones he used to eat lunch with. Train with. Live with. He *knows* these guys. I wonder if that knowledge makes this worse.

"Just give us the girl," a new voice adds. "Just give us the girl and we won't shoot you. We'll pretend we lost you. We'll let you go. Warner only wants the girl."

Adam is breathing hard. He grips the gun in his hand. Pops his head out for a split second and fires. Someone falls to the floor, screaming.

"KENT, YOU SON OF A—"

Adam uses the moment to run. We jump out from behind the desk and fly toward a stairwell. Gunshots miss us by millimeters. I wonder if these two men are the only ones who followed us inside.

The spiral staircase winds into a lower level, a basement of some kind. Someone is trying to aim for Adam, but our erratic movements make it almost impossible. The chance of him hitting me instead are too high. He's unleashing a mass of expletives in our wake.

Adam knocks things over as we run, trying to create any kind of distraction, any kind of hazard to slow down the soldier behind us. I spot a pair of storm cellar doors and realize this area must've been ravaged by tornadoes. The weather is turbulent; natural disasters are common. Cyclones must have ripped this city apart. "Adam—" I tug on his arm. We hide behind a low wall. I point to our only possible escape route.

He squeezes my hand. "Good eye." But we don't move until the air shifts around us. A misstep. A muffled cry. It's almost blindingly black down here; it's obvious the electricity was disconnected a long time ago. The soldier has tripped on one of the obstacles Adam left behind.

Adam holds the gun close to his chest. Takes a deep breath. Turns and takes a swift shot.

His aim is excellent.

An uncontrolled explosion of curse words confirms it. Adam takes a hard breath. "I'm only shooting to disable," he says. "Not to kill."

"I know," I tell him. Though I wasn't sure.

We run for the doors and Adam struggles to pull the latch open. It's nearly rusted shut. We're getting desperate. I don't know how long it'll be until we're discovered by another set of soldiers. I'm about to suggest we shoot it open when Adam finally manages to break it free.

He kicks open the doors and we stumble out onto the street. There are 3 cars to choose from.

I'm so happy I could cry.

"It's about time," he says.

But it's not Adam who says it.

THIRTY-NINE

There's blood everywhere.

Adam is on the ground, clutching his body, but I don't know where he's been shot. There are soldiers swarming around him and I'm clawing at the arms holding me back, kicking the air, crying out into the emptiness. Someone is dragging me away and I can't see what they've done to Adam. Pain is seizing my limbs, cramping my joints, breaking every single bone in my body. I don't understand why the agony isn't finding escape in my screams. Why my mouth is covered with someone else's hand.

"If I let go, you have to promise not to scream," he says to me.

He's touching my face with his bare hands and I don't know where I dropped my gun.

Warner drags me into a still-functioning building and kicks open a door. Hits a switch. Fluorescent lights flicker on with a dull hum. There are paintings taped to the walls, alphabet rainbows stapled to corkboards. Small tables scattered across the room. We're in a classroom.

I wonder if this is where James goes to school.

Warner drops his hand. His glassy green eyes are so delighted I'm petrified. "God I missed you," he says to me.

"You didn't actually think I'd let you go so easily?"

"You shot Adam," are the only words I can think of. My mind is muddled with disbelief. I keep seeing his beautiful body crumpled on the ground, red red red. I need to know if he's alive. He has to be alive.

Warner's eyes flash. "Kent is dead."

"*No—*"

Warner backs me into a corner and I realize I've never been so defenseless in my life. Never so vulnerable. 17 years I spent wishing my curse away, but in this moment I'm more desperate than ever to have it back. Warner's eyes warm unexpectedly. His constant shifts in emotion are difficult to anticipate. Difficult to counter.

"Juliette," he says. He touches my hand so gently it startles me. "Did you notice? It seems I am immune to your gift." He studies my eyes. "Isn't that incredible? Did you notice?" he asks again. "When you tried to escape? Did you feel it . . . ?"

Warner who misses absolutely nothing. Warner who absorbs every single detail.

Of course he knows.

But I'm shocked by the tenderness in his voice. The sincerity with which he wants to know. He's like a feral dog, crazed and wild, thirsty for chaos, simultaneously aching for recognition and acceptance.

Love.

"We can really be together," he says to me, undeterred by my silence. He pulls me close, too close. I'm frozen.

Stunned in grief, in disbelief.

His hands reach for my face, his lips for mine. My brain is on fire, ready to explode from the impossibility of this moment. I feel like I'm watching it happen, detached from my own body, incapable of intervening. More than anything else, I'm shocked by his gentle hands, his earnest eyes.

"I want you to choose me," he says. "I want you to choose to be with me. I want you to *want* this—"

"You're insane," I choke. "You're psychotic—"

"You're only afraid of what you're capable of." His voice is soft. Easy. Slow. Deceptively persuasive. I'd never realized before just how attractive his voice is. "Admit it," he says. "We're perfect for each other. You want the power. You love the feel of a weapon in your hand. You're . . . attracted to me."

I try to swing my fist but he catches my arms. Pins them to my sides. Presses me up against the wall. He's so much stronger than he looks. "Don't lie to yourself, Juliette. You're going to come back with me whether you like it or not. But you can choose to want it. You can choose to enjoy it—"

"I will *never*," I breathe, broken. "You're sick—you're a sick, twisted monster—"

"That's not the right answer," he says, and seems genuinely disappointed.

"It's the only answer you'll ever get from me."

His lips come too close. "But I love you."

"No you don't."

His eyes close. He leans his forehead against mine. "You have no idea what you do to me."

"I hate you."

He shakes his head very slowly. Dips down. His nose brushes the nape of my neck and I stifle a horrified shiver that he misunderstands. His lips touch my skin and I actually whimper. "God I'd love to just take a bite out of you."

I notice the gleam of silver in his inside jacket pocket.

I feel a thrill of hope. A thrill of horror. Brace myself for what I need to do. Spend a moment mourning the loss of my dignity.

And I relax.

He feels the tension seep out of my limbs and responds in turn. He smiles, loosens his clamp on my shoulders. Slips his arms around my waist. I swallow the vomit threatening to give me away.

His military jacket has a million buttons and I wonder how many I'll have to undo before I can get my hands on the gun. His hands are exploring my body, slipping down my back and it's all I can do to keep from doing something reckless. I'm not skilled enough to overpower him and I have no idea why he's able to touch me. I have no idea why I was able to crash through concrete yesterday. I have no idea where that energy came from.

Today he's got every advantage and it's not time to give myself away.

Not yet.

I place my hands on his chest. He presses me into the line of his body. Tilts my chin up to meet his eyes. "I'll be good to you," he whispers. "I'll be so good to you, Juliette. I promise."

I hope I'm not visibly shaking.

And he kisses me. Hungrily. Desperately. Eager to break me open and taste me. I'm so stunned, so horrified, so cocooned in insanity I forget myself. I stand there frozen, disgusted. My hands slip from his chest. All I can think about is Adam and blood and Adam and the sound of gunshots and Adam lying in a pool of blood and I nearly shove him off of me. But Warner will not be discouraged.

He breaks the kiss. Whispers something in my ear that sounds like nonsense. Cups my face in his hands and this time I remember to pretend. I pull him closer, grab a fistful of his jacket and kiss him as hard as I can, my fingers already attempting to release the first of his buttons. Warner tastes like peppermint, smells like gardenias. His arms are strong around me, his lips soft, almost sweet against my skin. There's an electric charge between us I hadn't anticipated.

My head is spinning.

His lips are on my neck, tasting me, devouring me, and I force myself to think straight. I force myself to understand the perversion of this situation. I don't know how to reconcile the confusion in my mind, my hesitant repulsion, my inexplicable chemical reaction to his lips. I need to get this over with. Now.

257

I reach for his buttons.

And he's unnecessarily encouraged.

Warner lifts me by the waist, hoists me up against the wall, his hands cupping my backside, forcing my legs to wrap around him. He doesn't realize he's given me the perfect angle to reach into his coat.

His lips find my lips, his hands slip under my shirt and he's breathing hard, tightening his grip around me, and I practically rip open his jacket in desperation. I can't let this go on much longer. I have no idea how far Warner wants to push things, but I can't keep encouraging his insanity.

I need him to lean forward just an inch more—

My hands wrap around the gun.

I feel him freeze. Pull back. I watch his face phase through frames of confusion/dread/anguish/horror/anger. He drops me to the floor just as my fingers pull the trigger for the very first time.

The power and strength of the weapon is disarming, the sound so much louder than I anticipated. The reverberations are vibrating through my ears and every pulse in my body.

It's a sweet sort of music.

A small sort of victory.

Because this time the blood is not Adam's.

FORTY

Warner is down.

I am up and running away with his gun.

I need to find Adam. I need to steal a car. I need to find James and Kenji. I need to learn how to drive. I need to drive us to safety. I need to do everything in exactly that order.

Adam can't be dead.

Adam is not dead.

Adam will not be dead.

My feet slap the pavement to a steady rhythm, my shirt and face spattered with blood, my hands still shaking slightly in the setting sun. A sharp breeze whips around me, jolting me out of the crazed reality I seem to be swimming in. I take a hard breath, squint up at the sky, and realize I don't have much time before I lose the light. The streets, at least, have long since been evacuated. But I have exactly zero idea where Warner's men might be.

I wonder if Warner has the tracker serum as well. I wonder if they'd know if he were dead.

I duck into dark corners, try to read the streets for clues, try to remember where Adam fell to the ground, but my memory is too weak, too distracted, my brain too broken to process these kinds of details. That horrible instant is one mess of insanity in my mind. I can't make any sense of it and Adam could be anywhere by now. They could've done anything to him.

I don't even know what I'm looking for.

~~I might be wasting my time.~~

I hear sudden movement and dart into a side street, my fingers tightening around the weapon slick in my grip. Now that I've actually fired a gun, I feel more confident with it in my hands, more aware of what to expect, how it functions. But I don't know if I should be happy or horrified that I'm so comfortable so quickly with something so lethal.

Footsteps.

I slide up against the wall, my arms and legs flat against the rough surface. I hope I'm buried in the shadows. I wonder if anyone's found Warner yet.

I watch a soldier walk right past me. He has rifles slung across his chest, a smaller sort of automatic weapon in his hands. I glance down at the gun in my own hand and realize I have no idea how many different kinds there are. All I know is some are bigger than others. Some have to be reloaded constantly. Some, like the one I'm holding, do not. Maybe Adam can teach me the differences.

Adam.

I suck in my breath and move as stealthily as I can through the streets. I spot a particularly dark shadow on a stretch of the sidewalk ahead of me and make an effort to avoid it. But as I get closer I realize it's not a shadow. It's a stain.

Adam's blood.

I squeeze my jaw shut until the pain scares away the screams. I take short, tiny, too-quick breaths. I need to focus. I need to use this information. I need to pay attention—

I need to follow the trail of blood.

Whoever dragged Adam away still hasn't come back to clean the mess. There's a steady spattered drip that leads away from the main roads and into the poorly lit side streets. The light is so dim I have to bend down to search for the spots on the ground. I'm losing sight of where they lead. There are fewer here. I think they've disappeared entirely. I don't know if the dark spots I'm finding are blood or old gum pounded into the pavement or drops of life from another person's flesh. Adam's path has disappeared.

I back up several steps and retrace the line.

I have to do this 3 times before I realize they must've taken him inside. There's an old steel structure with an older rusted door that looks like it's never been opened. It looks like it hasn't been used in years. I don't see any other options.

I wiggle the handle. It's locked.

I try to open it, but I only manage to bruise my body. I could shoot it down like I've seen Adam do, but I'm not certain of my aim nor my skill with this gun, and I'm not sure I can afford the noise. I can't make my presence known.

There has to be another way into this building.

There is no other way into this building.

My frustration is escalating. My desperation is crippling. My hysteria is threatening to break me and I want to scream until my lungs collapse. Adam is in this building. He has to be in this building.

I'm standing right outside this building and I can't get inside.

This can't be happening.

I clench my fists, try to beat back the maddening futility enveloping me but I feel crazed. Wild. Insane. The adrenaline is slipping away, my focus is slipping away, the sun is setting on the horizon and I remember James and Kenji and Adam Adam Adam ~~and Warner's hands on my body and his lips on my mouth and his tongue tasting my neck~~ and all the blood

everywhere

everywhere

everywhere

and I do something stupid.

I punch the door.

In one instant my mind catches up to my muscle and I brace myself for the impact of steel on skin, ready to feel the agony of shattering every bone in my right arm. But my fist flies through 12 inches of steel like it's made of butter. I'm stunned. I harness the same volatile energy and kick my foot through the door. I use my hands to rip the steel to shreds, clawing my way through the metal like a wild animal.

It's incredible. Exhilarating. Completely feral.

This must be how I broke through the concrete in Warner's torture chamber. Which means I still have no idea how I broke through the concrete in Warner's torture chamber.

I climb through the hole I've created and slip into the shadows. It's not hard. The entire place is cloaked in darkness. There are no lights, no sounds of machines or electricity. Just another abandoned warehouse left to the elements.

I check the floors but there's no sign of blood. My heart soars and plummets at the same time. I need him to be okay. I need him to be alive. Adam is not dead. He can't be.

Adam promised James he'd come back for him.

He'd never break that promise.

I move slowly at first, wary, worried that there might be soldiers around, but it doesn't take long for me to realize there's no sound of life in this building. I decide to run.

I tuck caution in my pocket and hope I can reach for it if I need to. I'm flying through doors, spinning around turns, drinking in every detail. This building wasn't just a warehouse. It was a factory.

Old machines clutter the walls, conveyor belts are frozen in place, thousands of boxes of inventory stacked precariously in tall heaps. I hear a breath, a stifled cough.

I'm bolting through a set of swinging double doors, searching out the feeble sound, fighting to focus on the tiniest details. I strain my ears and hear it again.

Heavy, labored breathing.

The closer I get, the more clearly I can hear him. It has to be him. My gun is up and aimed to fire, my eyes careful now, anticipating attackers. My legs move swiftly, easily, silently. I nearly shoot a shadow the boxes have cast on the floor. I take a steadying breath. Round another corner.

And nearly collapse.

Adam is hanging from bound wrists, shirtless, bloodied and bruised everywhere. His head is bent, his neck limp, his left leg drenched in blood despite the tourniquet wrapped around his thigh. I don't know how long the weight of his entire body has been hanging from his wrists. I'm surprised he hasn't dislocated his shoulders. He must still be fighting to hold on.

The rope wrapped around his wrists is attached to some kind of metal rod running across the ceiling. I look more closely and realize the rod is a part of a conveyor belt. That Adam is on a conveyor belt.

That this isn't just a factory.

It's a slaughterhouse.

I'm too poor to afford the luxury of hysteria right now.

I need to find a way to get him down, but I'm afraid to approach. My eyes search the space, certain that there are guards around here somewhere, soldiers prepared for this kind of ambush. But then it occurs to me that perhaps I was never really considered a threat. Not if Warner managed to drag me away.

No one would expect to find me here.

I climb onto the conveyor belt and Adam tries to lift his head. I have to be careful not to look too closely at his wounds, not to let my imagination cripple me. Not here. Not now.

"Adam . . . ?"

His head snaps up with a sudden burst of energy. His

eyes find me. His face is almost unscathed; there are only minor cuts and bruises to account for. Focusing on the familiar gives me a modicum of calm.

"Juliette—?"

"I need to cut you down—"

"Jesus, Juliette—how did you find me?" He coughs. Wheezes.

"Later." I reach up to touch his face. "I'll tell you everything later. First, I need to find a knife."

"My pants—"

"What?"

"In"—he swallows—"in my pants—"

I reach for his pocket and he shakes his head. I look up. "Where—"

"There's an inside pocket *in* my pants—"

I practically rip his clothes off. There's a small pocket sewn into the lining of his cargo pants. I slip my hand inside and retrieve a compact pocketknife. A butterfly knife. I've seen these before.

They're illegal.

I start stacking boxes on the conveyor belt. Climb my way up and hope to God I know what I'm doing. The knife is extremely sharp, and it works quickly to undo the bindings. I realize a little belatedly that the rope holding him together is the same cord we used to escape.

Adam is cut free. I'm climbing down, refolding the knife and tucking it into my pocket. I don't know how I'm going to get Adam out of here. His wrists are rubbed raw, bleeding, his body pounded into one piece of pain, his leg bloodied through with a bullet.

He nearly falls over.

I try to hold on as tenderly as possible. He doesn't say a word about the pain, tries so hard to hide the fact that he's having trouble breathing. He's wincing against the torture of it all, but doesn't whisper a word of complaint. "I can't believe you found me," is all he says.

And I know I shouldn't. I know now isn't the time. I know it's impractical. But I kiss him anyway.

"You are not going to die," I tell him. "We are going to get out of here. We are going to steal a car. We are going to find James and Kenji. And then we're going to get safe."

He stares at me. "Kiss me again," he says.

And I do.

It takes a lifetime to make it back to the door. Adam had been buried deep in the recesses of this building, and finding our way to the front is even more difficult than I expected. Adam is trying so hard, moving as fast as he can, but he still isn't fast at all. "They said Warner wanted to kill me himself," he explains. "That he shot me in the leg on purpose, just to disable me. It gave him a chance to drag you away and come back for me later. Apparently his plan was to torture me to death." He winces. "He said he wanted to enjoy it. Didn't want to rush through killing me." A hard laugh. A short cough.

~~His hands on my body his hands on my body his hands on my body~~

266

"So they just tied you up and abandoned you here?"

"They said no one would ever find me. They said the building is made entirely of concrete and reinforced steel and no one can break in. Warner was supposed to come back for me when he was ready." He stops. Looks at me. "God, I'm so happy you're okay."

I offer him a smile. Try to keep my organs from falling out. Hope the holes in my head aren't showing.

He pauses when we reach the door. The metal is a mangled mess. It looks like a wild animal attacked it and lost. "How did you—"

"I don't know," I admit. Try to shrug, be indifferent. "I just punched it."

"You just punched it."

"And kicked it a little."

He's smiling and I want to cry. I have to focus on his face. I can't let my eyes digest the travesty of his body.

"Come on," I tell him. "Let's go do something illegal."

I leave Adam in the shadows and dart up to the edge of the main road, searching for abandoned vehicles. We have to travel up 3 different side streets until we finally find one.

"How are you holding up?" I ask him, afraid to hear the answer.

He presses his lips together. Does something that looks like a nod. "Okay."

That's not good.

"Wait here."

It's pitch-black, not a single street lamp in sight. This

is good. Also bad. It gives me an extra edge, but makes me extra vulnerable to attack. I have to be careful. I tiptoe up to the car.

I'm fully prepared to smash the glass open, but I check the handle first. Just in case.

The door is unlocked.

The keys are in the ignition.

There's a bag of groceries in the backseat.

Someone must've panicked at the sound of the alarm and unexpected curfew. They must've dropped everything and run for cover. Unbelievable. This would be absolutely perfect if I had any idea how to drive.

I run back for Adam and help him hobble into the passenger side. As soon as he sits down I can tell just how much pain he's in. Bending his body in any way at all. Putting pressure on his ribs. Straining his muscles. "It's okay," he tells me, he lies to me. "I can't stand on my feet for much longer."

I reach into the back and rummage through the grocery bags. There's real food inside. Not just strange bouillon cubes designed to go into Automats, but fruit and vegetables. Even Warner never gave us bananas.

I hand the yellow fruit to Adam. "Eat this."

"I don't think I can—" He pauses. Stares at the form in his hands. "Is this what I think it is?"

"I think so."

We don't have time to process the impossibility. I peel it open for him. Encourage him to take a small bite. I hope it's a good thing. I heard bananas have potassium. I hope he can keep it down.

I try to focus on the machine under my feet.

"How long do you think we'll have until Warner finds us?" Adam asks.

I take a few bites of oxygen. "I don't know."

A pause. "How did you get away from him . . . ?"

I'm staring straight out the windshield when I answer. "I shot him."

"No." Surprise. Awe. Amazement.

I show him Warner's gun. It has a special engraving in the hilt.

Adam is stunned. "So he's . . . dead?"

"I don't know," I finally admit, ashamed. I drop my eyes, study the grooves in the steering wheel. "I don't know for sure." I took too long to pull the trigger. It was stiffer than I expected it to be. Harder to hold the gun between my hands than I'd imagined. Warner was already dropping me when the bullet flew into his body. I was aiming for his heart.

I hope to God I didn't miss.

We're both too quiet.

"Adam?"

"Yeah?"

"I don't know how to drive."

FORTY-ONE

"You're lucky this isn't a stick shift." He tries to laugh.

"Stick shift?"

"Manual transmission."

"What's that?"

"A little more complicated."

I bite my lip. "Do you remember where we left James and Kenji?" I don't even want to consider the possibility that they've moved. Been discovered. Anything. I can't fathom the idea.

"Yes." I know he's thinking exactly what I'm thinking.

"How do I get there?"

Adam tells me the right pedal is for gas. The left is to brake. I have to shift into *D* for *drive*. I use the steering wheel to turn. There are mirrors to help see behind me. I can't turn on my headlights and will have to rely on the moon to light my way.

I turn on the ignition, press the brake, shift into drive. Adam's voice is the only navigation system I need. I release the brake. Press the gas. Nearly crash into a wall.

This is how we finally get back to the abandoned building.

Gas. Brake. Gas. Brake. Too much gas. Too much brake.

Adam doesn't complain and it's almost worse. I can only imagine what my driving is doing for his injuries. I'm grateful that at least we're not dead, not yet.

I don't know why no one has spotted us. I wonder if maybe Warner really is dead. I wonder if everything is in chaos. I wonder if that's why there are no soldiers in this city. They've all disappeared.

I think.

I almost forget to put the car in park when we reach the vaguely familiar broken building. Adam has to reach over and do it for me. I help him transition into the backseat, and he asks me why.

"Because I'm making Kenji drive, and I don't want your brother to have to see you like this. It's dark enough that he won't see your body. I don't think he should have to see you hurt."

He nods after an infinite moment. "Thank you."

And I'm running toward the broken building. Pulling the door open. I can only barely make out two figures in the dark. I blink and they come into focus. James is asleep with his head in Kenji's lap. The duffel bags are open, cans of food discarded on the floor. They're okay.

Thank God they're okay.

I could die of relief.

Kenji pulls James up and into his arms, struggling a little under the weight. His face is smooth, serious, unflinching. He doesn't smile. He doesn't say anything stupid. He studies my eyes like he already knows, like he already understands

271

why it took us so long to get back, like there's only one reason why I must look like hell right now, why I have blood all over my shirt. Probably on my face. All over my hands. "How is he?"

And I nearly lose it right there. "I need you to drive."

He takes a tight breath. Nods several times. "My right leg is still good," he says to me, but I don't think I'd care even if it weren't. We need to get to his safe place, and my driving isn't going to get us anywhere.

Kenji settles a sleeping James into the passenger side, and I'm so happy he's not awake for this moment.

I grab the duffel bags and carry them to the backseat. Kenji slides in front. Looks in the rearview mirror. "Good to see you alive, Kent."

Adam almost smiles. Shakes his head. "Thank you for taking care of James."

"You trust me now?"

A small sigh. "Maybe."

"I'll take a *maybe*." He grins. Turns on the car. "Let's get the hell out of here."

Adam is shaking.

His bare body is finally cracking under the cold weather, the hours of torture, the strain of holding himself together for so long. I'm scrambling through the duffel bags, searching for a coat, but all I find are shirts and sweaters. I don't know how to get them on his body without causing him pain.

I decide to cut them up. I take the butterfly knife to a few of his sweaters and slice them open, draping them over him like a blanket. I glance up. "Kenji—does this car have a heater?"

"It's on, but it's pretty crappy. It's not working very well."

"How much longer until we get there?"

"Not too much."

"Have you seen anyone that might be following us?"

"No." He pauses. "It's weird. I don't understand why no one has noticed a car flying through these streets after curfew. Something's not right."

"I know."

"And I don't know what it is, but obviously my tracker serum isn't working. Either they really just don't give a shit about me, or it's legit not working, and I don't know why."

A tiny detail sits on the outskirts of my consciousness. I examine it. "Didn't you say you slept in a shed? That night you ran away?"

"Yeah, why?"

"Where was it . . . ?"

He shrugs. "I don't know. Some huge field. It was weird. Crazy shit growing in that place. I almost ate something I thought was fruit before I realized it smelled like ass."

My breath catches. "It was an empty field? Barren? Totally abandoned?"

"Yeah."

"The nuclear field," Adam says, a dawning realization in his voice.

"What nuclear field?" Kenji asks.

I take a moment to explain.

"Holy crap." Kenji grips the steering wheel. "So I could've died? And I didn't?"

I ignore him. "But then how did they find us? How did they figure out where you live—?"

"I don't know," Adam sighs. Closes his eyes. "Maybe Kenji is lying to us."

"Come on, man, what the hell—"

"Or," Adam interrupts, "maybe they bought out Benny."

"No." I gasp.

"It's possible."

We're all silent for a long moment. I try to look out the window but it's very nearly useless. The night sky is a vat of tar suffocating the world around us.

I turn to Adam and find him with his head tilted back, his hands clenched, his lips almost white in the blackness. I wrap the sweaters more tightly around his body. He stifles a shudder.

"Adam . . ." I brush a strand of hair away from his forehead. His hair has gotten a little long and I realize I've never really paid attention to it before. It's been cropped short since the day he stepped into my cell. I never would've thought his dark hair would be so soft. Like melted chocolate. I wonder when he stopped cutting it.

He flexes his jaw. Pries his lips open. Lies to me over and over again. "I'm okay."

"Kenji—"

"Five minutes, I promise—I'm trying to gun this thing—"

I touch his wrists, trace the tender skin with my fingertips. The bloodied scars. I kiss the palm of his hand. He takes a broken breath. "You're going to be okay," I tell him.

His eyes are still closed. He tries to nod.

"Why didn't you tell me you two were together?" Kenji asks unexpectedly. His voice is even, neutral.

"What?" Now is not the time to be blushing.

Kenji sighs. I catch a glimpse of his eyes in the rearview mirror. The swelling is almost completely gone. His face is healing. "I'd have to be *blind* to miss something like that. I mean, hell, just the way he looks at you. It's like the guy has never seen a woman in his life. Like putting food in front of a starving man and telling him he can't eat it."

Adam's eyes fly open. I try to read him but he won't look at me.

"Why didn't you just tell me?" Kenji says again.

"I never had a chance to ask," Adam answers. His voice is less than a whisper. His energy levels are dropping too fast. I don't want him to have to talk. He needs to conserve his strength.

"Wait—are you talking to me or her?" Kenji glances back at us.

"We can discuss this later—," I try to say, but Adam shakes his head.

"I told James without asking you. I made . . . an assumption." He stops. "I shouldn't have. You should have a choice. You should always have a choice. And it's your choice if you want to be with me."

"Hey, so, I'm just going to pretend like I can't hear you guys anymore, okay?" Kenji makes a random motion with his hand. "Go ahead and have your moment."

But I'm too busy studying Adam's eyes, his soft soft lips. His furrowed brow.

I lean into his ear, lower my voice. Whisper the words so only he can hear me.

"You're going to get better," I promise him. "And when you do, I'm going to show you exactly what choice I've made. I'm going to memorize every inch of your body with my lips."

He exhales suddenly. Swallows hard.

His eyes are burning into me. He looks almost feverish, and I wonder if I'm making things worse.

I pull back and he stops me. Rests his hand on my thigh. "Don't go," he says. "Your touch is the only thing keeping me from losing my mind."

FORTY-TWO

"We're here, and it's nighttime. So according to my calculations, we must not have done anything stupid."

Kenji shifts into park. We're underground again, in some kind of elaborate parking garage. One minute we were aboveground, the next we've disappeared into a ditch. It's next to impossible to locate, much less to spot in the darkness. Kenji was telling the truth about this hideout.

I've been busy trying to keep Adam awake for the past few minutes. His body is fighting exhaustion, blood loss, hunger, a million different points of pain. I feel so utterly useless.

"Adam has to go straight to the medical wing," Kenji announces.

"They have a medical wing?"

Kenji grins. "This place has everything. It will blow your goddamn mind." He hits a switch on the ceiling. A faint light illuminates the old sedan. Kenji steps out the door. "Wait here—I'll get someone to bring out a stretcher."

"What about James?"

"Oh." Kenji's mouth twitches. "He, uh—he's going to be asleep for a little while longer."

"What do you mean . . . ?"

He clears his throat. Once. Twice. Smooths out the

wrinkles in his shirt. "I, uh, may or may not have given him something to . . . ease the pain of this journey."

"You gave a ten-year-old a *sleeping pill?*" I'm afraid I'm going to break his neck.

"Would you rather he were awake for all of this?"

"Adam is going to kill you."

Kenji glances at Adam's drooping lids. "Yeah, well, I guess I'm lucky he won't be able to kill me tonight." He hesitates. Ducks into the car to run his fingers through James's hair. Smiles a little. "The kid is a saint. He'll be perfect in the morning."

"I can't *believe* you—"

"Hey, hey—" He holds up his hands. "Trust me. He's going to be just fine. I just didn't want him to be any more traumatized than he had to be." He shrugs. "Hell, maybe Adam will agree with me."

"I'm going to murder you." Adam's voice is a soft mumble.

Kenji laughs. "Keep it together, bro, or I'll think you don't really mean it."

Kenji disappears.

I watch Adam, encourage him to stay awake. Tell him he's almost safe. Touch my lips to his forehead. Study every shadow, every outline, every cut and bruise of his face. His muscles relax, his features lose their tension. He exhales a little more easily. I kiss his top lip. Kiss his bottom lip. Kiss his cheeks. His nose. His chin.

Everything happens so quickly after that.

4 people run out toward the car. 2 older than me, 2 older

than them. A pair of men. A pair of women. "Where is he?" the older woman asks. They're all looking around, anxious. I wonder if they can see me staring at them.

Kenji opens Adam's door. Kenji is no longer smiling. In fact, he looks . . . different. Stronger. Faster. Taller, even. He's in control. A figure of authority. These people *know* him.

Adam is lifted onto the stretcher and assessed immediately. Everyone is talking at once. Something about broken ribs. Something about losing blood. Something about airways and lung capacity and *what happened to his wrists?* Something about checking his pulse and *how long has he been bleeding?* The young male and female glance in my direction. They're all wearing strange outfits.

Strange suits. All white with gray stripes down the side. I wonder if it's a medical uniform.

They're carrying Adam away.

"Wait—" I trip out of the car. "Wait! I want to go with him—"

"Not now." Kenji stops me. Softens. "You can't be with him for what they need to do. Not now."

"What do you mean? What are they going to do to him?" The world is fading in and out of focus, shades of gray flickering as stilted frames, broken movements. Suddenly nothing makes sense. Suddenly everything is confusing me. Suddenly my head is a piece of pavement and I'm being trampled to death. I don't know where we are. I don't know who Kenji is. Kenji was Adam's friend. Adam knows him. Adam. My Adam. Adam who is being taken away from me and I can't go with him and I want to go with him but they won't let me go with him and I don't know why—

"They're going to help him—*Juliette*—I need you to focus. You can't fall apart right now. I know it's been a crazy day—but I need you to stay calm." His voice. So steady. So suddenly articulate.

"Who *are* you . . . ?" I'm beginning to panic. I want to grab James and run but I can't. He's done something to James and even if I knew how to wake him up, I can't touch him. I want to rip my nails out. *"Who are you—"*

Kenji sighs. "You're starving. You're exhausted. You're processing shock and a million other emotions right now. Be logical. I'm not going to hurt you. You're safe now. Adam is safe. James is safe."

"I want to be with him—I want to see what they're going to do to him—"

"I can't let you do that."

"What are you going to do to me? Why did you bring me here . . . ?" My eyes are wide, darting in every direction. I'm spinning, stranded in the middle of the ocean of my own imagination and I don't know how to swim. "What do you want from me?"

Kenji looks down. Rubs his forehead. Reaches into his pocket. "I really didn't want to have to do this."

I think I'm screaming.

FORTY-THREE

I'm an old creaky staircase when I wake up.

Someone has scrubbed me clean. My skin is like satin. My eyelashes are soft, my hair is smooth, brushed out of its knots; it gleams in the artificial light, a chocolate river lapping the pale shore of my skin, soft waves cascading around my collarbone. My joints ache; my eyes burn from an insatiable exhaustion. My body is naked under a heavy sheet. I've never felt so pristine.

I'm too tired to be bothered by it.

My sleepy eyes take inventory of the space I'm in, but there's not much to consider. I'm lying in bed. There are 4 walls. 1 door. A small table beside me. A glass of water on the table. Fluorescent lights humming above me. Everything is white.

Everything I've ever known is changing.

I reach for the glass of water and the door opens. I pull the sheet up as high as it will go.

"How are you feeling?"

A tall man is wearing plastic glasses. Black frames. A simple sweater. Pressed pants. His sandy-blond hair falls into his eyes.

He's holding a clipboard.

"Who are you?"

He grabs a chair I hadn't noticed was sitting in the corner. Pushes it forward. Sits down beside my bed. "Do you feel dizzy? Disoriented?"

"Where's Adam?"

He's holding his pen to a sheet of paper. Writing something down. "Do you spell your last name with two *r*s? Or just one?"

"What did you do with James? Where's Kenji?"

He stops. Looks up. He can't be more than 30. He has a crooked nose. A day of scruff. "Can I at least make sure you're doing all right? Then I'll answer your questions. I promise. Just let me get through the basic protocol here."

I blink.

How do I feel. I don't know.

Did I have any dreams. I don't think so.

Do I know where I am. No.

Do I think I'm safe. I don't know.

Do I remember what happened. Yes.

How old am I. 17.

What color are my eyes. I don't know.

"You don't know?" He puts down his pen. Takes off his glasses. "You can remember exactly what happened yesterday, but you don't know the color of your own eyes?"

"I think they're green. Or blue. I'm not sure. Why does it matter?"

"I want to be sure you can recognize yourself. That you haven't lost sight of your person."

"I've never really known my eye color, though. I've only looked in the mirror once in the last three years."

The stranger stares at me, his eyes crinkled in concern. I finally have to look away.

"How did you touch me?" I ask.

"I'm sorry?"

"My body. My skin. I'm so . . . clean."

"Oh." He bites his thumb. Marks something on his papers. "Right. Well, you were covered in blood and filth when you came in, and you had some minor cuts and bruises. We didn't want to risk infection. Sorry for the personal intrusion—but we can't allow anyone to bring that kind of bacteria in here. We had to do a superficial detox."

"That's fine—I understand," I hurry on. "But *how?*"

"Excuse me?"

"How did you touch me?" Surely he must know. How could he not know? God I hope he knows.

"Oh—" He nods, distracted by the words he's scribbling on his clipboard. Squints at the page. "Latex."

"What?"

"Latex." He glances up for a second. Sees my confusion. "Gloves?"

"Right." Of course. Gloves. Even Warner used gloves until he figured it out.

~~Until he figured it out. Until he figured it out. Until he figured it out.~~

I replay the moment over and over and over in my mind. The split second I took too long to jump from the window.

283

The moment of hesitation that changed everything. The instant I lost all control. All power. Any point of dominance. He's never going to stop until he finds me and it's my own fault.

I need to know if he's dead.

I have to force myself to be still. I have to force myself not to shake, shudder, or vomit. I need to change the subject. "Where are my clothes?"

"They've been destroyed for the same reasons you needed to be sanitized." He picks up his glasses. Slips them on. "We have a special suit for you. I think it'll make your life a lot easier."

"A special suit?" I look up. Part my lips in surprise.

"Yes. We'll get to that part a bit later." He pauses. Smiles. There's a dimple in his chin. "You're not going to attack me like you did Kenji, are you?"

"I attacked Kenji?" I cringe.

"Just a little bit." He shrugs. "At least now we know he's not immune to your touch."

"I *touched* him?" I sit up straight and nearly forget to pull my sheet up with me. "I'm so sorry—"

"I'm sure he'll appreciate the apology. But it's all right. We've been expecting some destructive tendencies. You've been having one hell of a week."

"Are you a psychologist?"

"Sort of." He brushes the hair away from his forehead.

"Sort of?"

He laughs. Pauses. Rolls the pen between his fingers.

"Yes. For all intents and purposes, I am a psychologist. Sometimes."

"What is that supposed to mean . . . ?"

He parts his lips. Presses them shut. Seems to consider answering me but examines me instead. He stares for so long I feel my face go hot. He starts scribbling furiously.

"What am I doing here?" I ask him.

"Recovering."

"How long have I been here?"

"You've been asleep for almost fourteen hours. We gave you a pretty powerful sedative." Looks at his watch. "You seem to be doing well." Hesitates. "You look very well, actually."

"Where's Adam?"

Blondie takes a deep breath. Underlines something on his papers. His lips twitch into a smile.

"Where is he?"

"Recovering." He finally looks up.

"He's okay?"

Nods. "He's okay."

I stare at him. "What does that mean?"

2 knocks at the door.

The bespectacled stranger doesn't move. He rereads his notes. "Come in," he calls.

Kenji walks inside, a little hesitant at first. He peeks at me, his eyes cautious. I never thought I'd be so happy to see him. But while it's a relief to see a face I recognize, my stomach immediately twists into a knot of guilt, knocking me over from the inside. I wonder how badly I must've hurt him. He steps forward.

My guilt disappears.

I look more closely and realize he's perfectly unharmed. His leg is working fine. His face is back to normal. His eyes are no longer puffy, his forehead is repaired, smooth, untouched. He was right.

He does have a spectacular face.

A defiant jawline. Perfect eyebrows. Eyes as black as his hair. Sleek. Strong. A bit dangerous.

"Hey, beautiful."

"I'm sorry I almost killed you," I blurt out.

"Oh." He startles. Shoves his hands into his pockets. "Well. Glad we got that out of the way." I notice he's wearing a destroyed T-shirt. Dark jeans. I haven't seen anyone wear jeans in such a long time. Army uniforms, cotton basics, and fancy dresses are all I've known lately.

I can't really look at him. "I panicked," I try to explain. I clasp and unclasp my fingers.

"I figured." He cocks an eyebrow.

"I'm sorry."

"I know."

I nod. "You look better."

He cracks a grin. Stretches. Leans against the wall, arms crossed at his chest, legs crossed at the ankles. "This must be difficult for you."

"Excuse me?"

"Looking at my face. Realizing I was right. Realizing

you made the wrong decision." He shrugs. "I understand. I'm not a proud man, you know. I'd be willing to forgive you."

I gape at him, unsure whether to laugh or throw something. "Don't make me touch you."

He shakes his head. "It's incredible how someone can look so right and feel so wrong. Kent is a lucky bastard."

"I'm sorry—" Psychologist-man stands up. "Are you two finished here?" He looks to Kenji. "I thought you had a purpose."

Kenji pushes off the wall. Straightens his back. "Right. Yeah. Castle wants to meet her."

FORTY-FOUR

"Now?" Blondie is more confused than I am. "But I'm not done examining her."

Kenji shrugs. "He wants to meet her."

"Who's Castle?" I ask.

Blondie and Kenji look at me. Kenji looks away. Blondie doesn't.

He cocks his head. "Kenji didn't tell you anything about this place?"

"No." I falter, uncertain, glancing at Kenji, who won't look at me. "He never explained anything. He said he knew someone who had a safe place and thought he could help us—"

Blondie gapes. Laughs so hard he snorts. Stands up. Cleans his glasses with the hem of his shirt. "You're such an ass," he says to Kenji. "Why didn't you just tell her the truth?"

"She never would've come if I told her the truth."

"How do you know?"

"She nearly *killed* me—"

My eyes are darting from one face to the other. Blond hair to black hair and back again. "What is going *on?*" I demand. "I want to see Adam. I want to see James. And I want a set of *clothes*—"

"You're naked?" Kenji is suddenly studying my sheet and not bothering to be subtle about it.

I flush despite my best efforts, flustered, frustrated. "Blondie said they destroyed my clothes."

"*Blondie?*" Blond man is offended.

"You never told me your name."

"Winston. My name is Winston." He's not smiling anymore.

"Didn't you say you had a suit for me?"

He frowns. Checks his watch. "We won't have time to go through that right now." Sighs. "Get her something to wear temporarily, will you?" He's talking to Kenji. Kenji who is still staring at me.

"I want to see Adam."

"Adam isn't ready to see you yet." ~~Blondie~~ Winston tucks his pen into a pocket. "We'll let you know when he's ready."

"How am I supposed to trust any of you if you won't even let me see him? If you won't let me see James? I don't even have my basic things. I want to get out of this bed and I need something to wear."

"Go fetch, Moto." Winston is readjusting his watch.

"I'm not your dog, *Blondie*," Kenji snaps. "And I told you not to call me Moto."

Winston pinches the bridge of his nose. "No problem. I'll also tell Castle it's your fault she's not meeting with him right now."

Kenji mutters something obscene under his breath. Stalks off. Almost slams the door.

A few seconds pass in a strained sort of silence.

I take a deep breath. "So what's *moto* mean?"

Winston rolls his eyes. "Nothing. It's just a nickname—his last name is Kishimoto. He gets mad when we chop it in half. Gets sensitive about it."

"Well why do you chop it in half?"

He snorts. "Because it's hard as hell to pronounce."

"How is that an excuse?"

He frowns. "What?"

"You got mad that I called you Blondie and not Winston. Why doesn't he have the right to be mad that you're calling him Moto instead of Kenji?"

He mumbles something that sounds like, "It's not the same thing."

I slide down a little. Rest my head on the pillow. "Don't be a hypocrite."

FORTY-FIVE

I feel like a clown in these oversized clothes. I'm wearing someone else's T-shirt. Someone else's pajama pants. Someone else's slippers. Kenji says they had to destroy the clothes in my duffel bag, too, so I have no idea whose outfit is currently hanging on my frame. I'm practically swimming in the material.

I try to knot the extra fabric and Kenji stops me. "You're going to mess up my shirt," he complains.

I drop my hands. "You gave me *your* clothes?"

"Well what did you expect? It's not like we have extra dresses just lying around." He shoots me a look, like I should be grateful he's even sharing.

Well. I guess it's better than being naked. "So who's Castle again?"

"He's in charge of everything," Kenji tells me. "The head of this entire movement."

My ears snap off. *"Movement?"*

Winston sighs. He seems so uptight. "If Kenji hasn't told you anything, you should probably wait to hear it from Castle himself. Hang tight. I promise we're going to answer your questions."

"But what about Adam? Where is *James—*"

"Wow." Winston runs a hand through his floppy hair. "You're just not going to give it up, huh?"

"He's fine, Juliette," Kenji intervenes. "He needs a little more time to recover. You have to start trusting us. No one here is going to hurt you, or Adam, or James. They're both fine. Everything is fine."

But I don't know if *fine* is good enough.

We're walking through an entire city underground, hallways and passageways, smooth stone floors, rough walls left untouched. There are circular disks drilled into the ground, glowing with artificial light every few feet. I notice computers, all kinds of gadgets I don't recognize, doors cracked open to reveal rooms filled with nothing but technological machinery.

"How do you find the electricity necessary to run this place?" I look more closely at the unidentifiable machines, the flickering screens, the unmistakable humming of hundreds of computers built into the framework of this underground world.

Kenji tugs on a stray strand of my hair. I spin around. "We steal it." He grins. Nods down a narrow path. "This way."

People both young and old and of all different shapes and ethnicities shuffle in and out of rooms, all along the halls. Many of them stare, many of them are too distracted to notice us. Some of them are dressed like the men and women who rushed out to our car last night. It's an odd kind of uniform. It seems unnecessary.

"So . . . everyone dresses like that?" I whisper, gesturing to the passing strangers as inconspicuously as possible.

Kenji scratches his head. Takes his time answering. "Not everyone. Not all the time."

"What about you?" I ask him.

"Not today."

I decide not to indulge his cryptic tendencies, and instead ask a more straightforward question. "So are you ever going to tell me how you healed so quickly?"

"Yes," Kenji says, unfazed. "We're going to tell you a lot of things, actually." We make an abrupt turn down an unexpected hallway. "But first—" Kenji pauses outside of a huge wooden door. "Castle wants to meet you. He's the one who requested you."

"*Requested*—?"

"Yeah." Kenji looks uncomfortable for just a wavering second.

"Wait—what do you mean—"

"I mean it wasn't an accident that I ended up in the army, Juliette." He sighs. "It wasn't an accident that I showed up at Adam's door. And I wasn't supposed to get shot or get beaten half to death, but I did. Only I wasn't dropped off by some random dude." He almost grins. "I've always known where Adam lived. It was my job to know." A pause. "We've all been looking for you.

"Go ahead." Kenji pushes me inside. "He'll be out when he's ready."

"Good luck," is all Winston says to me.

1,320 seconds walk into the room before he does.

He moves methodically, his face a mask of neutrality as he brushes wayward dreadlocks into a ponytail and seats himself at the front of the room. He's thin, fit, impeccably dressed in a simple suit. Dark blue. White shirt. No tie. There are no lines on his face, but there's a streak of silver in his hair and his eyes confess he's lived at least 100 years. He must be in his 40s. I look around.

It's an empty space, impressive in its sparseness. The floors and ceilings are built by bricks carefully pieced together. Everything feels old and ancient, but somehow modern technology is keeping this place alive. Artificial lighting illuminates the cavernous dimensions, small monitors are built into the stone walls. I don't know what I'm doing here. I don't know what to expect. I have no idea what kind of person Castle is but after spending so much time with Warner, I'm trying not to get my hopes up. I don't even realize I've stopped breathing until he speaks.

"I hope you're enjoying your stay so far."

My neck snaps up to meet his dark eyes, his smooth voice, silky and strong. His eyes are glinting with genuine curiosity, a smattering of surprise.

"Kenji said you wanted to meet me," is the only response I offer.

"Kenji would be correct." He takes his time breathing. He takes his time shifting in his seat. He takes his time studying my eyes, choosing his words, touching two fingers to his lips. He seems to have dominated the concept of time. "I've heard . . . stories. About you." Smiles. "I simply wanted to know if they were true."

"What have you heard?"

He opens his hands. Studies them for a moment. Looks up. "You can kill a man with nothing but your bare skin. You can crush five feet of concrete with the palm of your hand."

I'm climbing a mountain of air and my feet keep slipping. I need to get a grip on something.

"Is it true?" he asks.

"Rumors are more likely to kill you than I am."

He studies me for too long. "I'd like to show you something," he says after a moment.

"I want answers to my questions." This has gone on too long. I don't want to be lulled into a false sense of security. I don't want to assume Adam and James are okay. I don't want to trust anyone until I have proof. I can't pretend like any of this is all right. Not yet. "I want to know that I'm safe," I tell him. "And I want to know that my friends are safe. There was a ten-year-old boy with us when we arrived and I want to see him. I need to make certain he is healthy and unharmed. I won't cooperate otherwise."

His eyes inspect me a few moments longer. "Your loyalty is refreshing," he says, and he means it. "You will do well here."

"My friends—"

"Yes. Of course." He's on his feet. "Follow me."

This place is far more complex, far more organized than I could've imagined it to be. There are hundreds of different directions to get lost in, almost as many rooms, some bigger than others, each dedicated to different pursuits.

"The dining hall," Castle says to me.

"The dormitories." On the opposite wing.

"The training facilities." Down that hall.

"The common rooms." Right through here.

"The bathrooms." On either end of the floor.

"The meeting halls." Just past that door.

Each space is buzzing with bodies, each body adapted to a particular routine. People look up when they see us. Some wave, smile, delighted. I realize they're all looking at Castle. He nods his head. His eyes are kind. His smile is reassuring.

He's the leader of this entire *movement*, is what Kenji said. These people are depending on him for something more than basic survival. This is more than a fallout shelter. This is much more than a hiding space. There is a greater goal in mind. A greater purpose.

"Welcome," Castle says to me, gesturing with one hand, "to Omega Point."

FORTY-SIX

"Omega Point?"

"The last letter in the Greek alphabet. The final development, the last in a series." He stops in front of me and for the first time I notice the omega symbol stitched into the back of his jacket. "We are the only hope our civilization has left."

"But how—with such small numbers—how can you possibly hope to compete—"

"We've been building for a long time, Juliette." It's the first time he's said my name. "We've been planning, organizing, mapping out our strategy for many years now. The collapse of our human society should not come as a surprise. We brought it upon ourselves.

"The question wasn't *whether* things would fall apart," he continues. "Only *when*. It was a waiting game. A question of who would try to take power and how they would try to use it. Fear," he says to me, turning back for just a moment, his footsteps silent against the stone, "is a great motivator."

"That's pathetic."

"I agree. Which is why part of my job is reviving the stalled hearts that've lost all hope." We turn down another corridor. "And to tell you that almost everything you've learned about the state of our world is a lie."

I stop in place. "What do you mean?"

"I mean things are not nearly as bad as The Reestablishment wants us to think they are."

"But there's no food—"

"That they give *you* access to."

"The animals—"

"Are kept hidden. Genetically modified. Raised on secret pastures."

"But the air—the seasons—the *weather*—"

"Is not as bad as they'll have us believe. It's probably our only real problem—but it's one caused by the perverse manipulations of Mother Earth. *Man-made* manipulations that we can still fix." He turns to face me. Focuses my mind with one steady gaze.

"There is still a chance to change things. We can provide fresh drinking water to all people. We can make sure crops are not regulated for profit; we can ensure that they are not genetically altered to benefit manufacturers. Our people are dying because we are feeding them poison. Animals are dying because we are forcing them to eat waste, forcing them to live in their own filth, caging them together and abusing them. Plants are withering away because we are dumping chemicals into the earth that make them hazardous to our health. But these are things we can fix.

"We are fed lies because believing them makes us weak, vulnerable, malleable. We depend on others for our food, health, sustenance. This cripples us. Creates cowards of our people. Slaves of our children. It's time for us to fight back." His eyes are bright with feeling, his fists clenched in fervor. His words are powerful, heavy with conviction. I have no doubt he's swayed many people with such fanciful thoughts. Hope for a future that seems lost. Inspiration in a bleak world with nothing to offer. He is a natural leader. A talented orator.

I have a hard time believing him.

"How can you know for certain that your theories are correct? Do you have proof?"

His hands relax. His eyes quiet down. His lips form a small smile. "Of course." He almost laughs.

"Why is that funny?"

He shakes his head. Just a bit. "I'm amused by your skepticism. I admire it, actually. It's never a good idea to believe everything you hear."

I catch his double meaning. Acknowledge it. "Touché, Mr. Castle."

"This entire movement is proof enough. We survive because of these truths. We seek out food and supplies from the various storage compounds The Reestablishment has constructed. We've found their fields, their farms, their animals. They have hundreds of acres dedicated to crops. The farmers are slaves, working under the threat of death to themselves or their family members. The rest of society is either killed or corralled into sectors, sectioned off to be monitored, carefully surveyed."

I keep my face neutral. I still haven't decided whether or

not I believe him. "And what do you need with me? Why do you care if I'm here?"

He stops at a glass wall. Points through to the room beyond. Doesn't answer my question. "Your Adam is healing because of our people."

I nearly trip in my haste to see him. I press my hands against the glass and peer into the brightly lit space. Adam is asleep, his face perfect, peaceful. This must be the medical wing.

"Look closely," Castle tells me. "There are no needles attached to his body. No machines keeping him alive. He arrived with three broken ribs. Lungs close to collapsing. A bullet in his thigh. His kidneys were bruised along with the rest of his body. Broken skin, bloodied wrists. A sprained ankle. He'd lost more blood than most hospitals would be able to replenish.

"There are close to two hundred people at Omega Point," Castle says. "Less than half of whom have some kind of gift."

I spin around, stunned.

"I brought you here," he says to me carefully, quietly, "because this is where you belong. Because you need to know that you are not alone."

FORTY-SEVEN

"You would be invaluable to our resistance."

I can hardly breathe. "There are others . . . like me?"

Castle offers me eyes that empathize. "I was the first to realize my affliction could not be mine alone. I sought out others, following rumors, listening for stories, reading the newspapers for abnormalities in human behavior. At first it was just for companionship." He pauses. "I was tired of the insanity. Of believing I was inhuman; a monster. But then I realized that what seemed a weakness was actually a strength. That together we could be something extraordinary. Something *good*."

I can't catch my breath. I can't cough up the impossibility caught in my throat.

Castle is waiting for my reaction.

"What is your . . . gift?" I ask him.

His smile disarms my insecurity. He holds out his hand. Cocks his head. I hear the creak of a distant door opening. The sound of air and metal; movement. I turn toward the sound only to see something hurtling in my direction. I duck. Castle laughs. Catches it in his hand.

I gasp.

He shows me the key now caught between his fingers.

"You can move things with your mind?"

"I have an impossibly advanced level of psychokinesis." He twists his lips into a smile. "So yes."

"There's a *name* for it?"

"For my condition? Yes. For yours?" He pauses. "I'm uncertain."

"And the others—what—they're—"

"You can meet them, if you'd like."

"I—yes—I'd like that," I stammer, excited, 4 years old and still believing in fairies.

I freeze at a sudden sound.

Footsteps are pounding the stone. I catch the pant of strained breathing.

"*Sir*—" someone shouts.

Castle starts. Stills. Pivots around a corner toward the runner. "Brendan?"

"Sir!" he pants again.

"You have news? What have you seen?"

"We're hearing things on the radio," he begins, his broken words thick with a British accent. "Our cameras are picking up more tanks patrolling the area than usual. We think they may be getting closer—"

The sound of static energy. Static electricity. Garbled voices croaking through a weak radio line.

Brendan curses under his breath. "Sorry, sir—it's not usually this distorted—I just haven't learned to contain the charges lately—"

"Not to worry. You just need practice. Your training is going well?"

"Very well, sir. I have it almost entirely under my command." Brendan pauses. "For the most part."

"Excellent. In the meantime, let me know if the tanks get any closer. I'm not surprised to hear they're getting a little more vigilant. Try to listen for any mention of an attack. The Reestablishment has been trying to pinpoint our whereabouts for years, but now we have someone particularly valuable to their efforts and I'm certain they want her back. I have a feeling things are going to develop rather quickly from now on."

A moment of confusion. "Sir?"

"There's someone I'd like for you to meet."

Brendan and Castle step around the corner. Come into view. And I have to make a conscious effort to keep my jaw from unhinging. I can't stop staring.

Castle's companion is white from head to toe.

Not just his strange uniform, which is a blinding shade of shimmering white, but his skin is paler than mine. His hair is so blond it can only be accurately described as white. His eyes are mesmerizing. They're the lightest shade of blue I've ever seen. Piercing. Practically transparent. He looks to be my age.

He doesn't seem *real*.

"Brendan, this is Juliette," Castle introduces us. "She arrived just yesterday. I was giving her an overview of Omega Point."

Brendan sticks out his hand and I almost panic before he frowns. Pulls back, says, "Er, wait—sorry—," and flexes his hands. Cracks his knuckles. A few sparks fly out of his fingers.

I gape at him.

He shrinks back. Smiles sheepishly. "Sometimes I electrocute people by accident."

Something in my heavy armor melts away. I feel suddenly understood. Unafraid of being myself. I can't help my grin. "Don't worry," I tell him. "If I shake your hand I might kill you."

"Blimey." He blinks. Stares. Waits for me to take it back. "You're serious?"

"Very."

He laughs. "Right then. No touching." Leans in. Lowers his voice. "I have a bit of a problem with that myself, you know. Girls are always talking about electricity in their romance, but none are too happy to actually *be* electrocuted, apparently. Bloody confusing, is what it is." He shrugs.

Adam was right. Maybe things can be okay. Maybe I don't have to be a monster. Maybe I do have a choice.

I think I'm going to like it here.

Brendan winks. "It was very nice meeting you, Juliette. I'll be seeing you?"

I nod. "I think so."

"Brilliant." He shoots me another smile. Turns to Castle. "I'll let you know if I hear anything, sir."

"Perfect."

And Brendan disappears.

I turn to the glass wall keeping me from the other half of my heart. Press my head against the cool surface. Wish he would wake up.

"Would you like to say hello?"

I look up at Castle, who is still studying me. Always analyzing me. Somehow his attention doesn't make me uncomfortable. "Yes," I tell him. "I want to say hello."

FORTY-EIGHT

Castle uses the key in his hand to open the door.

"Why does the medical wing have to be locked?" I
ask him.

He turns to me. He's not very tall, I realize for the first
time. "If you'd known where to find him—would you have
waited patiently behind this door?"

I drop my eyes. Don't answer.

He tries to be encouraging. "Healing is a delicate
process. It can't be interrupted or influenced by erratic
emotions. We're lucky enough to have two healers among
us—a set of twins, in fact. But most fascinating is that they
each focus on a different element—one on the physical
incapacitations, and one on the mental. Both facets must be
addressed, otherwise the healing will be incomplete, weak,
insufficient." He turns the door handle. "But I think it's
safe for Adam to see you now."

I step inside and my senses are almost immediately
assaulted by the scent of jasmine. I search the space for
the flowers but find none. I wonder if it's a perfume.
It's intoxicating.

"I'll be just outside," Castle says to me.

The room is filled with a long row of beds, simply made.

All 20 or so of them are empty except for Adam's. There's a door at the end of the room that probably leads to another space, but I'm too nervous to be curious right now.

I pull up an extra chair and try to be as quiet as possible. I don't want to wake him, I just want to know he's okay. I clasp and unclasp my hands. I'm too aware of my racing heart. And I know I probably shouldn't touch him, but I can't help myself. I cover his hand with mine. His fingers are warm.

His eyes flutter for just a moment. They don't open. He takes a sudden breath and I freeze.

"What are you *doing*?"

My head snaps up at the sound of Castle's panicked voice. I drop Adam's hand. Push away from the bed, eyes wide, worried. "What do you mean?"

"Why are you—you can *touch* him—?" I never thought I'd see Castle so confused. He's lost his composure, one arm half extended in an effort to stop me.

"Of course I can tou—" I stop. "Kenji didn't tell you?"

"This young man has immunity from your touch?"

"Yes." I look from him to Adam, still sound asleep. ~~So does Warner.~~

"That's . . . *astounding*."

"Is it?"

"Very." Castle's eyes are bright, so eager. "It certainly isn't coincidence. There is no coincidence in these kinds of situations." He pauses. Paces. "Fascinating. So many possibilities—so many theories—" He's not even talking to me anymore. His mind is working too quickly for me to keep up. He takes a deep breath. Seems to remember I'm still in the room. "My apologies. Please, carry on. The girls will be out soon—they're assisting James at the moment. I must report this new information as soon as possible."

"Wait—"

He looks up. "Yes?"

"You have theories?" I ask him. "You—you know why these things are happening . . . to me?"

"You mean to *us*?" Castle offers me a smile.

I manage to nod.

"We have been doing extensive research for years," he says. "We think we have a pretty good idea."

"And?" I can hardly breathe.

"If you should decide to stay at Omega Point, we'll have that conversation very soon, I promise. Besides, I'm sure now is probably not the best time." He nods at Adam.

"Oh. Of course."

Castle turns to leave.

"But do you think that Adam—" The words tumble out of my mouth too quickly. I try to pace myself. "Do you think he's . . . like *us*, too?"

Castle pivots back around. Studies my eyes. "I think," he says carefully, "that it is entirely possible."

I gasp.

"My apologies," he says, "but I really must get going. And I wouldn't want to interrupt your time together."

I want to say yes, sure, of course, absolutely. I want to

smile and wave and tell him it's no problem. But I have so many questions, I think I might explode; I want him to tell me everything he knows.

"I know this is a lot of information to take in at once." Castle pauses at the door. "But we'll have plenty of opportunities to talk. You must be exhausted and I'm sure you'd like to get some sleep. The girls will take care of you—they're expecting you. In fact, they'll be your new roommates at Omega Point. I'm sure they'll be happy to answer any questions you might have." He clasps my shoulders before he goes. "It's an honor to have you with us, Ms. Ferrars. I hope you will seriously consider joining us on a permanent basis."

I nod, numb.

And he's gone.

We have been doing extensive research for years, he said. *We think we have a pretty good idea,* he said. *We'll have that conversation very soon, I promise.*

For the first time in my life I might finally understand what I am and it doesn't seem possible. And Adam. *Adam.* I shake myself and take my seat next to him. Squeeze his fingers. Castle could be wrong. Maybe this *is* all coincidence.

I have to focus.

I wonder if anyone has heard from Warner lately.

"Juliette?"

His eyes are half open. He's staring at me like he's not sure if I'm real.

"Adam!" I have to force myself to be still.

He smiles and the effort seems to exhaust him. "God it's good to see you."

"You're *okay*." I grip his hand, resist pulling him into my arms. "You're really okay."

His grin gets bigger. "I feel like I could sleep for a few years."

"Don't worry, the sedative will wear off soon."

I spin around. Two girls with exactly the same green eyes are staring at us. They smile at the same time. Their long brown hair is thick and stick-straight in high ponytails on their heads. They're wearing matching silver bodysuits. Gold ballet flats.

"I'm Sonya," the girl on the left says.

"I'm Sara," her sister adds.

I have no idea how to tell them apart.

"It's so nice to meet you," they say at exactly the same time.

"I'm Juliette," I manage. "It's a pleasure to meet you, too."

"Adam is almost ready for release," one says to me.

"Sonya is an excellent healer," the other one chimes in.

"Sara is better than I am," says the first.

"He should be okay to leave just as soon as the sedative is out of his system," they say together, smiling.

"Oh—that's great—thank you so much—" I don't know who to look at. Who to answer. I glance back at Adam. He seems thoroughly amused.

"Where's James?" he asks.

"He's playing with the other children." I think it's Sara who says it.

"We just took him on a bathroom break," says the other.

"Would you like to see him?" Back to Sara.

"There are other children?" My eyes go wide.

The girls nod at the same time.

"We'll go get him," they chorus. And disappear.

"They seem nice," Adam says after a moment.

"Yeah. They do." This whole place seems nice.

Sonya and Sara come back with James, who seems happier than I've ever seen him, almost happier than seeing Adam for the first time. He's thrilled to be here. Thrilled to be with the other kids, thrilled to be with "the pretty girls who take care of me because they're so nice and there's so much food and they gave me *chocolate*, Adam—have you ever tasted *chocolate?*" and he has a big bed and tomorrow he's going to class with the other kids and he's already excited.

"I'm so happy you're awake," he says to Adam, practically jumping up and down on his bed. "They said you got sick and that you were resting and now you're awake so that means you're better, right? And we're safe? I don't really remember what happened on our way here," he admits, a little embarrassed. "I think I fell asleep."

I think Adam is looking to break Kenji's neck at this point.

"Yeah, we're safe," Adam tells him, running a hand through his messy blond hair. "Everything is okay."

James runs back to the playroom with the other kids. Sonya and Sara invent an excuse to leave so we have some

311

privacy. I'm liking them more and more.

"Has anyone told you about this place yet?" Adam asks me. He manages to sit up. His sheet slides down. His chest is exposed. His skin is perfectly healed—I can hardly reconcile the image I have in my memory with the one in front of me. I forget to answer his question.

"You have no scars." I touch his skin like I need to feel it for myself.

He tries to smile. "They're not very traditional in their medical practices around here."

I look up, startled. "You . . . know?"

"Did you meet Castle yet?"

I nod.

He shifts. Sighs. "I've heard rumors about this place for a long time. I got really good at listening to whispers, mostly because I was looking out for myself. But in the army we hear things. Any and all kinds of enemy threats. Possible ambushes. There was talk of an unusual underground movement from the moment I enlisted. Most people said it was crap. That it was some kind of garbage concocted to scare people—that there was no way it could be real. But I always hoped it had some basis in truth, especially after I found out about you—I hoped we'd be able to find others with similar abilities. But I didn't know who to ask. I had no connections—no way of knowing how to find them." He shakes his head. "And all this time, Kenji was working undercover."

"He said he was looking for me."

Adam nods. Laughs. "Just like I was looking for you. Just like Warner was looking for you."

"I don't understand," I mumble. "Especially now that I know there are others like me—stronger, even—why did Warner want *me*?"

"He discovered you before Castle did," Adam says. "He felt like he claimed you a long time ago." Adam leans back. "Warner's a lot of things, but he's not stupid. I'm sure he knew there was some truth to those rumors—and he was fascinated. Because as much as Castle wanted to use his abilities for good, Warner wanted to manipulate those abilities for his own cause. He wanted to become some kind of superpower." A pause. "He invested a lot of time and energy just studying you. I don't think he wanted to let that effort go to waste."

"Adam," I whisper.

He takes my hand. "Yeah?"

"I don't think he's dead."

FORTY-NINE

"He's not."

Adam turns. Frowns at the voice. "What are you doing here?"

"Wow. What a greeting, Kent. Be careful not to pull a muscle thanking me for saving your ass."

"You lied to all of us."

"You're welcome."

"You sedated my ten-year-old brother!"

"You're still welcome."

"Hey, Kenji." I acknowledge him.

"My clothes look good on you." He steps a bit closer, smiles.

I roll my eyes. Adam examines my outfit for the first time.

"I didn't have anything else to wear," I explain.

Adam nods a little slowly. Looks at Kenji. "Did you have a message to deliver?"

"Yeah. I'm supposed to show you where you'll be staying."

"What do you mean?"

Kenji grins. "You and James are going to be my new roommates."

Adam swears under his breath.

"Sorry, bro, but we don't have enough rooms for you

and Hot Hands over here to have your own private space."
He winks at me. "No offense."

"I have to leave right now?"

"Yeah, man. I want to go to sleep soon. I don't have all day to wait around for your lazy ass."

"*Lazy—?*"

I hurry to interrupt before Adam has a chance to fight back. "What do you mean, you want to go to sleep? What time is it?"

"It's almost ten at night," Kenji tells me. "It's hard to tell underground, but we all try to be aware of the clocks. We have monitors in the hallways, and most of us try to wear watches. Losing track of night and day can screw us up pretty quickly. And now is not the time to be getting too comfortable."

"How do you know Warner isn't dead?" I ask, nervous.

"We just saw him on camera," Kenji says. "He and his men are patrolling this area pretty heavily. I managed to hear some of their conversation. Turns out Warner got shot."

I suck in my breath, try to silence my heartbeats.

"That's why we got lucky last night—apparently the soldiers got called back to base because they *thought* Warner was dead. There was a shift in power for a minute. No one knew what to do. What orders to follow. But then it turned out he wasn't dead. Just wounded pretty bad. His arm was all patched up and in a sling," Kenji adds.

Adam finds his voice before I do. "How safe is this place from attack?"

Kenji laughs. "Safe as *hell*. I don't even know how they

managed to get as close as they did. But they'll never be able to find our exact location. And even if they do, they'll never be able to break in. Our security is just about impenetrable. Plus we have cameras everywhere. We can see what they're doing before they even plan it.

"It doesn't really matter, though," he goes on. "Because they're looking for a fight, and so are we. We're not afraid of an attack. Besides, they have no idea what we're capable of. And we've been training for this shit forever."

"Do you—" I pause. "Can you—I mean, do you have a . . . gift, too?"

Kenji smiles. And disappears.

He's really gone.

I stand up. Try to touch the space he was just standing in.

He reappears just in time to jump out of reach. "HEY— whoa, careful—just because I'm invisible doesn't mean I can't feel anything—"

"Oh!" I pull back. Cringe. "I'm sorry—"

"You can make yourself *invisible?*" Adam looks more irritated than interested.

"Just blew your mind, didn't I?"

"How long have you been spying on me?" Adam narrows his eyes.

"As long as I needed to." But his grin is laced with mischief.

"So you're . . . corporeal?" I ask.

"Look at you, using big fancy words." Kenji crosses his arms. Leans against the wall.

"I mean—you can't, like, walk through walls or anything, can you?"

He snorts. "Nah, I'm not a ghost. I can just . . . blend, I guess is the best word. I can blend into the background of any space. Shift myself to match my surrounds. It's taken me a long time to figure it out."

"Wow."

"I used to follow Adam home. That's how I knew where he lived. And that's how I was able to run away—because they couldn't really see me. They tried to shoot at me anyway," he adds, bitter, "but I managed not to die, at least."

"Wait, but why were you following Adam home? I thought you were looking for *me*?" I ask him.

"Yeah—well, I enlisted shortly after we got wind of Warner's big project." He nods in my direction. "We'd been trying to find you, but Warner had more security clearance and access to more information than we did—we were having a hard time tracking you down. Castle thought it would be easier to have someone on the inside paying attention to all the crazy shit Warner was planning. So when I heard that Adam was the main guy involved in this particular project and that he had this history with you, I sent the information to Castle. He told me to watch out for Adam, too—you know, in case Adam turned out to be just as psycho as Warner. We wanted to make sure he wasn't a threat to you or our plans. But I had no idea you'd try to run away together. Messed me the hell up."

We're all silent for a moment.

"So how much did you spy on me?" Adam asks him.

"Well, well, well." Kenji cocks his head. "Is Mr. Adam Kent suddenly feeling a little intimidated?"

"Don't be a jackass."

"You hiding something?"

"Yeah. My gun—"

"Hey!" Kenji claps his hands together. "So! Are we ready to get out of here, or what?"

"I need a pair of pants."

Kenji looks abruptly annoyed. "Seriously, Kent? I don't want to hear that shit."

"Well, unless you want to see me naked, I suggest you do something about it."

Kenji shoots Adam a dirty look and stalks off, grumbling something about lending people all of his clothes. The door swings shut behind him.

"I'm not really naked," Adam tells me.

"Oh," I gasp. Look up. My eyes betray me.

He can't bite back his grin in time. His fingers graze my cheek. "I just wanted him to leave us alone for a second."

I blush. Fumble for something to say. "I'm so happy you're okay."

He says something I don't hear.

Takes my hand. Pulls me up beside him.

He's leaning in and I'm leaning in until I'm practically on top of him and he's slipping me into his arms and kissing me with a new kind of desperation. His hands are threaded in my hair, his lips so soft, so urgent against mine, like fire

318

and honey exploding in my mouth. My body is steaming.

Adam pulls back just a tiny bit. Kisses my bottom lip. Bites it for just a second. His skin feels 100 degrees hotter than it was a moment ago. His lips are pressed against my neck and my hands are on a journey down his upper body and I'm wondering why there are so many freight trains in my heart, why his chest is a broken harmonica. I'm tracing the bird caught forever in flight on his skin and I realize for the first time that he's given me wings of my own. He's helped me fly away and now I'm stuck in centripetal motion, soaring right into the center of everything. I bring his lips back up to mine.

"Juliette," he says. 1 breath. 1 kiss. 10 fingers teasing my skin. "I need to see you tonight."

Yes.

Please.

2 hard knocks send us flying apart.

Kenji slams open the door. "You do realize this wall is made of *glass*, don't you?" He looks like he's bitten the head off a worm. "No one wants to see that."

He throws a pair of pants at Adam.

Nods to me. "Come on, I'll take you to Sonya and Sara. They'll set you up for tonight." Turns to Adam. "And don't *ever* give those pants back to me."

"What if I don't want to sleep?" Adam asks, unabashed. "I'm not allowed to leave my room?"

Kenji presses his lips together. Narrows his eyes. "I will not use this word often, Kent, but *please* don't try

319

any secret-sneaking-away shit. We have to regulate things around here for a reason. It's the only way to survive. So do everyone a favor and keep your pants on. You'll see her in the morning."

But morning feels like a million years from now.

FIFTY

The twins are still asleep when someone knocks. Sonya and Sara showed me where the girls' bathrooms are so I had a chance to shower last night, but I'm still wearing Kenji's oversized clothes. I feel a little ridiculous as I pad my way toward the door.

I open it.

Blink. "Hey, Winston."

He looks me up and down. "Castle thought you might like to change out of those clothes."

"You have something for me to wear?"

"Yeah—remember? We made you something custom."

"Oh. Wow. Yeah, that sounds great."

I slip outside silently, following Winston through the dark halls. The underground world is quiet, its inhabitants still asleep. I ask Winston why we're up so early.

"I figured you'd want to meet everyone at breakfast. This way you can jump into the regular routine of things around here—even get started on your training." He glances back. "We all have to learn how to harness our abilities in the most effective manner possible. It's no good having no control over your body."

"Wait—you have an *ability*, too?"

"There are exactly fifty-six of us who do. The rest are our family members, children, or close friends who help out with everything else. So yes, I'm one of those fifty-six. So are you."

I'm nearly stepping on his feet in an effort to keep up with his long legs. "So what can you do?"

He doesn't answer. And I can't be sure, but I think he's blushing.

"I'm sorry—" I backpedal. "I don't mean to pry— I shouldn't have asked—"

"It's okay," he cuts me off. "I just think it's kind of stupid." He laughs a short, hard laugh. "Of all the things I should be able to do," he sighs. "At least you can do something *interesting*."

I stop walking, stunned. "You think this is a competition? To see which magic trick is more twisted? To see who can inflict the most pain?"

"That's not what I meant—"

"I don't think it's *interesting* to be able to kill someone by accident. I don't think it's *interesting* to be afraid to touch a living thing."

His jaw is tense. "I didn't mean it like that. I just . . . I wish I were more useful. That's all."

I cross my arms. "You don't have to tell me if you don't want to."

He rolls his eyes. Runs a hand through his hair. "I'm just—I'm very . . . flexible," he says.

It takes me a moment to process his admission. "Like— you can bend yourself into a pretzel?"

"Sure. Or stretch myself if I need to."

"Can I see?"

He bites his lip. Readjusts his glasses. Looks both ways down the empty hall. And loops one arm around his waist. Twice.

"Wow."

"It's stupid," he grumbles. "And useless."

"Are you insane?" I lean back to look at him. "That's *incredible*."

But his arm is back to normal and he's walking away again. I have to run to catch up.

"Don't be so hard on yourself," I try to tell him. "It's nothing to be ashamed of." But he's not listening and I'm wondering when I became a motivational speaker. When I made the switch from hating myself to accepting myself. When it became okay for me to choose my own life.

Winston leads me to the room I met him in. The same white walls. The same small bed. Only this time, Adam and Kenji are waiting inside. My heart kicks into gear and I'm suddenly nervous.

Adam is up. He's standing on his own and he looks perfect. Beautiful. Unharmed. There's not a single drop of blood on his body. He walks forward with only slight discomfort, smiles at me with no difficulty. His skin is a little paler than normal, but positively radiant compared to his complexion the night we arrived. His natural tan offsets a pair of eyes a shade of blue in a midnight sky.

"Juliette," he says.

I can't stop staring at him. Marveling at him. Amazed by how incredible it feels to know that he's all right.

"Hey." I manage to smile.

"Good morning to you, too," Kenji interjects.

I startle. "Oh, hi." I wave a limp hand in his direction. He snorts.

"All right. Let's get this over with, shall we?" Winston walks toward one of the walls, which turns out to be a closet. There's one pop of color inside. He pulls it off the hanger.

"Can I, uh, have a moment alone with her?" Adam says suddenly.

Winston takes off his glasses. Rubs his eyes. "I need to follow protocol. I have to explain everything—"

"I know—that's fine," Adam says. "You can do it after. I just need a minute, I promise. I haven't really had a chance to talk to her since we got here."

Winston frowns. Looks at me. Looks at Adam. Sighs.

"All right. But then we'll be back. I need to make sure everything fits and I have to check the—"

"Perfect. That sounds great. Thanks, man—" And he's shoving them out the door.

"Wait!" Winston slams the door back open. "At least get her to put the suit on while we're outside. That way it won't be a complete waste of my time."

Adam stares at the material in Winston's outstretched hand. Winston mumbles something about people always wasting his time, and Adam suppresses a grin. Glances at me. I shrug.

"Okay," he says, grabbing the suit. "But now you have to get out—" And pushes them both back into the hallway.

"We're going to be *right outside*," Kenji shouts. "Like five seconds away—"

Adam closes the door behind them. Turns around. His eyes are burning into me.

"I never had a chance to say thank you," he says.

I look away. Pretend heat isn't fighting its way up my face.

He steps forward. Takes my hands. "Juliette."

I peek up at him.

"You saved my life."

I bite the inside of my cheek. It seems silly to say "You're welcome" for saving someone's life. I don't know what to do. "I'm just so happy you're okay," is all I manage.

He's staring at my lips and I'm aching everywhere. If he kisses me right now I don't think I'll let him stop. He takes a sharp breath. Seems to remember he's holding something. "Oh. Maybe you should put this on?" He hands me a slinky piece of something purple. It looks tiny. Like a jumpsuit that could fit a small child.

I offer Adam a blank stare.

He grins. "Try it on."

I stare differently.

"Oh." He jumps back. "Right—I'll just—I'll turn around—"

I wait until his back is to me before I exhale. I look around. There don't seem to be any mirrors in this room. I shed the oversized outfit. Drop each piece on the floor.

I'm standing here, completely naked, and for a moment I'm too petrified to move. But Adam doesn't turn around. He doesn't say a word. I examine the shiny purple material. I imagine it's supposed to stretch.

It does.

In fact, it's unexpectedly easy to slip on—like it was designed specifically for my body. There's built-in lining for where underwear is supposed to be, extra support for my chest, a collar that goes right up to my neck, sleeves that touch my wrists, legs that touch my ankles, a zipper that pulls it all together. I examine the ultrathin material. It feels like I'm wearing nothing. It's the richest shade of purple, skintight but not tight at all. It's breathable, oddly comfortable.

"How does it look . . . ?" Adam asks. He sounds nervous.

"Can you help me zip it up?"

He turns around. His lips part, falter, form an incredible smile. Adam touches my hair and I realize it's almost all the way down my back. Maybe it's time I cut it.

His fingers are so careful. He pushes the waves over my shoulder so they won't get caught in the zipper. Trails a line from the base of my neck down to the start of the seam, down to the dip in my lower back. My spine is conducting enough electricity to power a city. He takes his time zipping me up. Runs his hands down the length of my silhouette.

"You look incredible," is the first thing he says to me.

I turn around.

I touch the material. Decide I should probably say something. "It's very . . . comfortable."

"Sexy."

I look up.

He's shaking his head. "It's sexy as hell."

He steps forward. Slips me into his arms.

"I look like a gymnast," I mumble.

"No," he whispers, hot hot hot against my lips. "You look like a superhero."

EPILOGUE

I'm still tingling when Kenji and Winston burst back into the room.

"So how is this suit supposed to make my life easier?" I ask anyone who'll answer.

But Kenji is frozen in place, staring without apology. Opens his mouth. Closes it. Shoves his hands into his pockets.

Winston steps in. "It's supposed to help with the touching issue," he tells me. "You don't have to worry about being covered from head to toe in this unpredictable weather. The material is designed to keep you cool or keep you warm based on the temperature. It's light and breathable so your skin doesn't suffocate. It will keep you safe from hurting someone unintentionally, but offers you the flexibility of touching someone . . . intentionally, too. If you ever needed to."

"That's amazing."

He smiles. Big. "You're welcome."

I study the suit more closely. Realize something. "But my hands and feet are totally exposed. How's that supposed to—"

"Oh—shoot," Winston interrupts. "I almost forgot." He runs over to the closet and pulls out a pair of flat-heeled black ankle boots and a pair of black gloves that stop right before the elbow. He hands them to me. I study the soft leather of the accessories and marvel at the springy, flexible build of the boots. I could do ballet and run a mile in these shoes. "These should fit you," he says. "They complete the outfit."

I slip them on and tip up on my toes, luxuriate in the feeling of my new outfit. I feel invincible. I really wish I had a mirror for once in my life. I look from Kenji to Adam to Winston. "What do you think? Is it . . . okay?"

Kenji makes a strange noise.

Winston looks at his watch.

Adam can't stop smiling.

He and I follow Kenji and Winston out of the room, but Adam pauses to slip off my left glove. He takes my hand. Intertwines our fingers. Offers me a smile that manages to kiss my heart.

And I look around.

Flex my fist.

Touch the material hugging my skin.

I feel incredible. My bones feel rejuvenated; my skin feels vibrant, healthy. I take big lungfuls of air and savor the taste.

Things are changing, but this time I'm not afraid. This time I know who I am. This time I've made the right choice and I'm fighting for the right team. I feel safe. Confident.

Excited, even.

Because this time?

I'm ready.

THEY WANT TO FIND ME.
I WILL FIND THEM FIRST.

BOOK TWO IN THE *NEW YORK TIMES* BESTSELLING FANTASY SERIES

UNRAVEL ME

NEW YORK TIMES BESTSELLING AUTHOR
TAHEREH MAFI

JULIETTE HAS ESCAPED, BUT HER STORY IS FAR FROM OVER . . .

ALSO AVAILABLE

UNRAVEL ME

ALSO BY TAHEREH MAFI

UNRAVEL ME

TAHEREH MAFI

First published in USA 2013 by HarperCollins Children's Books

First published in Great Britain 2018
by Electric Monkey, part of Egmont Books

An imprint of HarperCollins*Publishers*
1 London Bridge Street, London SE1 9GF

egmontbooks.co.uk

2 4 6 8 10 9 7 5 3 1

HarperCollins*Publishers*
1st Floor, Watermarque Building
Ringsend Road, Dublin 4, Ireland

Published by arrangement with HarperCollins Children's Books,
a division of HarperCollins Publishers, New York, New York, USA

Text copyright © 2013 Tahereh Mafi

ISBN 978 1 4052 9176 7

YOUNG ADULT

Printed and bound in India by Thomson Press India Ltd

A CIP catalogue record for this title is available from the British Library

Stay safe online. Any website addresses listed in this book are correct at the time
of going to print. However, Egmont Books is not responsible for content hosted by third
parties. Please be aware that online content can be subject to change and websites
can contain content that is unsuitable for children. We advise that all children
are supervised when using the internet.

This book is produced from independently certified FSC™ paper
to ensure responsible forest management.

For my mother. The best person I've ever known.

ONE

The world might be sunny-side up today.

The big ball of yellow might be spilling into the clouds, runny and yolky and blurring into the bluest sky, bright with cold hope and false promises about fond memories, real families, hearty breakfasts, stacks of pancakes drizzled in maple syrup sitting on a plate in a world that doesn't exist anymore.

Or maybe not.

Maybe it's dark and wet today, whistling wind so sharp it stings the skin off the knuckles of grown men. Maybe it's snowing, maybe it's raining, I don't know maybe it's freezing it's hailing it's a hurricane slip slipping into a tornado and the earth is quaking apart to make room for our mistakes.

I wouldn't have any idea.

I don't have a window anymore. I don't have a view. It's a million degrees below zero in my blood and I'm buried 50 feet underground in a training room that's become my second home lately. Every day I stare at these 4 walls and remind myself *I'm not a prisoner I'm not a prisoner I'm not a prisoner* but sometimes the old fears streak across my skin and I can't seem to break free of the claustrophobia clutching at my throat.

I made so many promises when I arrived here.

Now I'm not so sure. Now I'm worried. Now my mind is a traitor because my thoughts crawl out of bed every morning with darting eyes and sweating palms and nervous giggles that sit in my chest, build in my chest, threaten to burst through my chest, and the pressure is tightening and tightening and *tightening*

Life around here isn't what I expected it to be.

My new world is etched in gunmetal, sealed in silver, drowning in the scents of stone and steel. The air is icy, the mats are orange; the lights and switches beep and flicker, electronic and electric, neon bright. It's busy here, busy with bodies, busy with halls stuffed full of whispers and shouts, pounding feet and thoughtful footsteps. If I listen closely I can hear the sounds of brains working and foreheads pinching and fingers tap tapping at chins and lips and furrowed brows. Ideas are carried in pockets, thoughts propped up on the tips of every tongue; eyes are narrowed in concentration, in careful planning I should want to know about.

But nothing is working and all my parts are broken.

I'm supposed to harness my Energy, Castle said. Our gifts are different forms of Energy. Matter is never created or destroyed, he said to me, and as our world changed, so did the Energy within it. Our abilities are taken from the universe, from other matter, from other Energies. We are not anomalies. We are inevitabilities of the perverse manipulations of our Earth. Our Energy came from somewhere, he said. And somewhere is in the chaos all around us.

2

It makes sense. I remember what the world looked like when I left it.

I remember the pissed-off skies and the sequence of sunsets collapsing beneath the moon. I remember the cracked earth and the scratchy bushes and the used-to-be-greens that are now too close to brown. I think about the water we can't drink and the birds that don't fly and how human civilization has been reduced to nothing but a series of compounds stretched out over what's left of our ravaged land.

This planet is a broken bone that didn't set right, a hundred pieces of crystal glued together. We've been shattered and reconstructed, told to make an effort every single day to pretend we still function the way we're supposed to. But it's a lie, it's all a lie.

I do not function properly.

I am nothing more than the consequence of catastrophe.

2 weeks have collapsed at the side of the road, abandoned, already forgotten. 2 weeks I've been here and in 2 weeks I've taken up residence on a bed of eggshells, wondering when something is going to break, when I'll be the first to break it, wondering when everything is going to fall apart. In 2 weeks I should've been happier, healthier, sleeping better, more soundly in this safe space. Instead I worry about what will happen ~~when~~ if I can't get this right, if I don't figure out how to train properly, if I hurt someone ~~on purpose~~ by accident.

We're preparing for a bloody war.

That's why I'm training. We're all trying to prepare

ourselves to take down Warner and his men. To win one battle at a time. To show the citizens of our world that there is hope yet—that they do not have to acquiesce to the demands of The Reestablishment and become slaves to a regime that wants nothing more than to exploit them for power. And I agreed to fight. To be a warrior. To use my power against my better judgment. But the thought of laying a hand on someone brings back a world of memories, feelings, a flush of power I experience only when I make contact with skin not immune to my own. It's a rush of invincibility; a tormented kind of euphoria; a wave of intensity flooding every pore in my body. I don't know what it will do to me. I don't know if I can trust myself to take pleasure in someone else's pain.

All I know is that Warner's last words are caught in my chest and I can't cough out the cold or the truth hacking at the back of my throat.

Adam has no idea that Warner can touch me.

No one does.

Warner was supposed to be dead. Warner was supposed to be dead because I was supposed to have shot him but no one supposed I'd need to know how to fire a gun so now I suppose he's come to find me.

He's come to fight.

For me.

TWO

A sharp knock and the door flies open.

"Ah, Ms. Ferrars. I don't know what you hope to accomplish by sitting in the corner." Castle's easy grin dances into the room before he does.

I take a tight breath and try to make myself look at Castle but I can't. Instead I whisper an apology and listen to the sorry sound my words make in this large room. I feel my shaking fingers clench against the thick, padded mats spread out across the floor and think about how I've accomplished nothing since I've been here. It's humiliating, so humiliating to disappoint one of the only people who's ever been kind to me.

Castle stands directly in front of me, waits until I finally look up. "There's no need to apologize," he says. His sharp, clear brown eyes and friendly smile make it easy to forget he's the leader of Omega Point. The leader of this entire underground movement dedicated to fighting The Reestablishment. His voice is too gentle, too kind, and it's almost worse. ~~Sometimes I wish he would just yell at me.~~ "But," he continues, "you do have to learn how to harness your Energy, Ms. Ferrars."

A pause.

A pace.

His hands rest on the stack of bricks I was supposed to have destroyed. He pretends not to notice the red rims around my eyes or the metal pipes I threw across the room. His gaze carefully avoids the bloody smears on the wooden planks set off to the side; his questions don't ask me why my fists are clenched so tight and whether or not I've injured myself again. He cocks his head in my direction but he's staring at a spot directly behind me and his voice is soft when he speaks. "I know this is difficult for you," he says. "But you must learn. You have to. Your life will depend upon it."

I nod, lean back against the wall, welcome the cold and the pain of the brick digging into my spine. I pull my knees up to my chest and feel my feet press into the protective mats covering the ground. I'm so close to tears I'm afraid I might scream. "I just don't know how," I finally say to him. "I don't know any of this. I don't even know what I'm supposed to be doing." I stare at the ceiling and blink blink blink. My eyes feel shiny, damp. "I don't know how to make things happen."

"Then you have to think," Castle says, undeterred. He picks up a discarded metal pipe. Weighs it in his hands. "You have to find links between the events that transpired. When you broke through the concrete in Warner's torture chamber—when you punched through the steel door to save Mr. Kent—what happened? Why in those two instances were you able to react in such an extraordinary way?" He sits down some feet away from me. Pushes the pipe in my direction. "I need you to analyze your abilities, Ms. Ferrars. You have to focus."

Focus.

It's one word but it's enough, it's all it takes to make me feel sick. Everyone, it seems, needs me to focus. First Warner needed me to focus, and now Castle needs me to focus.

I've never been able to follow through.

Castle's deep, sad sigh brings me back to the present. He gets to his feet. He smooths out the only navy-blue blazer he seems to own and I catch a glimpse of the silver Omega symbol embroidered into the back. An absent hand touches the end of his ponytail; he always ties his dreads in a clean knot at the base of his neck. "You are resisting yourself," he says, though he says it gently. "Maybe you should work with someone else for a change. Maybe a partner will help you work things out—to discover the connection between these two events."

My shoulders stiffen, surprised. "I thought you said I had to work alone."

He squints past me. Scratches a spot beneath his ear, shoves his other hand into a pocket. "I didn't actually want you to work alone," he says. "But no one volunteered for the task."

I don't know why I suck in my breath, why I'm so surprised. I shouldn't be surprised. Not everyone is Adam.

Not everyone is safe from me the way he is. No one but

Adam has ever touched me and enjoyed it. ~~No one except for Warner.~~ But despite Adam's best intentions, he can't train with me. He's busy with other things.

Things no one wants to tell me about.

But Castle is staring at me with hopeful eyes, generous eyes, eyes that have no idea that these new words he's offered me are so much worse. Worse because as much as I know the truth, it still hurts to hear it. It hurts to remember that though I might live in a warm bubble with Adam, the rest of the world still sees me as a threat. A monster. An abomination.

~~Warner was right. No matter where I go, I can't seem to run from this.~~

"What's changed?" I ask him. "Who's willing to train me now?" I pause. "You?"

Castle smiles.

It's the kind of smile that flushes humiliated heat up my neck and spears my pride right through the vertebrae. I have to resist the urge to bolt out the door.

~~Please please please do not pity me, is what I want to say.~~

"I wish I had the time," Castle says to me. "But Kenji is finally free—we were able to reorganize his schedule—and he said he'd be happy to work with you." A moment of hesitation. "That is, if that's all right with you."

Kenji.

I want to laugh out loud. Kenji *would* be the only one willing to risk working with me. I injured him once. By accident. But he and I haven't spent much time together since he first led our expedition into Omega Point. It was like he was just doing a task, fulfilling a mission; once complete, he went back to his own life. Apparently Kenji is important around here. He has a million things to do. Things to regulate. People seem to like him, respect him, even.

I wonder if they've ever known him as the obnoxious, foul-mouthed Kenji I first met.

"Sure," I tell Castle, attempting a pleasant expression for the first time since he arrived. "That sounds great."

Castle stands up. His eyes are bright, eager, easily pleased. "Perfect. I'll have him meet you at breakfast tomorrow. You can eat together and go from there."

"Oh but I usually—"

"I know." Castle cuts me off. His smile is pressed into a thin line now, his forehead creased with concern. "You like to eat your meals with Mr. Kent. I know this. But you've hardly spent any time with the others, Ms. Ferrars, and if you're going to be here, you need to start trusting us. The people of Omega Point feel close to Kenji. He can vouch for you. If everyone sees you spending time together, they'll feel less intimidated by your presence. It will help you adjust."

Heat like hot oil spatters across my face; I flinch, feel my fingers twitch, try to find a place to look, try to pretend I can't feel the pain caught in my chest. "They're—they're afraid of me," I tell him, I whisper, I trail off. "I don't—I didn't want to bother anyone. I didn't want to get in their way. . . ."

Castle sighs, long and loud. He looks down and up,

scratches the soft spot beneath his chin. "They're only afraid," he says finally, "because they don't know you. If you just tried a little harder—if you made even the smallest effort to get to know anyone—" He stops. Frowns. "Ms. Ferrars, you have been here two weeks and you hardly even speak to your roommates."

"But that's not—I think they're great—"

"And yet you ignore them? You spend no time with them? Why?"

~~Because I've never had girl friends before. Because I'm afraid I'll do something wrong, say something wrong and they'll end up hating me like all the other girls I've known. And I like them too much, which will make their inevitable rejection so much harder to endure.~~

I say nothing.

Castle shakes his head. "You did so well the first day you arrived. You seemed almost *friendly* with Brendan. I don't know what happened," Castle continues. "I thought you would do well here."

Brendan. The thin boy with platinum-blond hair and electric currents running through his veins. I remember him. He was nice to me. "I like Brendan," I tell Castle, bewildered. "Is he upset with me?"

"*Upset?*" Castle shakes his head, laughs out loud. He doesn't answer my question. "I don't understand, Ms. Ferrars. I've tried to be patient with you, I've tried to give you time, but I confess I'm quite perplexed. You were so different when you first arrived—you were excited to be here! But it took less than a week for you to withdraw completely. You don't even look at anyone when you walk through the halls. What happened to conversation? To friendship?"

Yes.

It took 1 day for me to settle in. 1 day for me to look around. 1 day for me to get excited about a different life and 1 day for everyone to find out who I am and what I've done.

Castle doesn't say anything about the mothers who see me walking down the hall and yank their children out of my way. He doesn't mention the hostile stares and the unwelcoming words I've endured since I've arrived. He doesn't say anything about the kids who've been warned to stay far, far away, and the handful of elderly people who watch me too closely. I can only imagine what they've heard, where they got their stories from.

Juliette.

A girl with a lethal touch that saps the strength and energy of human beings until they're limp, paralyzed carcasses wheezing on the floor. A girl who spent most of her life in hospitals and juvenile detention centers, a girl who was cast off by her own parents, labeled as certifiably insane, and sentenced to isolation in an asylum where even the rats were afraid to live.

A girl.

So power hungry that she killed a small child. She tortured a toddler. She brought a grown man gasping to his knees. She doesn't even have the decency to kill herself.

None of it is a lie.

So I look at Castle with spots of color on my cheeks and unspoken letters on my lips and eyes that refuse to reveal their secrets.

He sighs.

He almost says something. He tries to speak but his eyes inspect my face and he changes his mind. He only offers me a quick nod, a deep breath, taps his watch, says, "Three hours until lights-out," and turns to go.

Pauses in the doorway.

"Ms. Ferrars," he says suddenly, softly, without turning around. "You've chosen to stay with us, to fight with us, to become a member of Omega Point." A pause. "We're going to need your help. And I'm afraid we're running out of time."

I watch him leave.

I listen to his departing footsteps and lean my head back against the wall. Close my eyes against the ceiling. Hear his voice, solemn and steady, ringing in my ears.

We're running out of time, he said.

As if time were the kind of thing you could run out of, as if it were measured into bowls that were handed to us at birth and if we ate too much or too fast or right before jumping into the water then our time would be lost, wasted, already spent.

But time is beyond our finite comprehension. It's endless, it exists outside of us; we cannot run out of it or lose track of it or find a way to hold on to it. Time goes on even when we do not.

We have plenty of time, is what Castle should have said.

We have all the time in the world, is what he should have said to me. But he didn't because what he meant *tick tock* is that our time *tick tock* is shifting. It's hurtling forward heading in an entirely new direction slamming face-first into something else and

    tick

    tick

    tick

    tick

    tick

    it's almost

    time for war.

THREE

I could touch him from here.

His eyes, dark blue. His hair, dark brown. His shirt, too tight in all the right places and his lips, his lips twitch up to flick the switch that lights the fire in my heart and I don't even have time to blink and exhale before I'm caught in his arms.

Adam.

"Hey, you," he whispers, right up against my neck.

I bite back a shiver as the blood rushes up to blush my cheeks and for a moment, just for this moment, I drop my bones and allow him to hold me together. "Hey." I smile, inhaling the scent of him.

Luxurious, is what this is.

We rarely ever see each other alone. Adam is staying in Kenji's room with his little brother, James, and I bunk with the healer twins. We probably have less than 20 minutes before the girls get back to this room, and I intend to make the most of this opportunity.

My eyes fall shut.

Adam's arms wrap around my waist, pulling me closer, and the pleasure is so tremendous I can hardly keep myself from shaking. It's like my skin and bones have been craving contact, warm affection, human interaction for so many years that I don't know how to pace myself. I'm a starving child trying to stuff my stomach, gorging my senses on the decadence of these moments as if I'll wake up in the morning and realize I'm still sweeping cinders for my stepmother.

But then Adam's lips press against my head and my worries put on a fancy dress and pretend to be something else for a while.

"How are you?" I ask, and it's so embarrassing because my words are already unsteady even though he's hardly held me but I can't make myself let go.

Laughter shakes the shape of his body, soft and rich and indulgent. But he doesn't respond to my question and I know he won't.

We've tried so many times to sneak off together, only to be caught and chastised for our negligence. We are not allowed outside of our rooms after lights-out. Once our grace period—a leniency granted on account of our very abrupt arrival—ended, Adam and I had to follow the rules just like everyone else. And there are a lot of rules to follow.

These security measures—cameras everywhere, around every corner, in every hallway—exist to prepare us in the case of an attack. Guards patrol at night, looking for any suspicious noise, activity, or sign of a breach. Castle and his team are vigilant in protecting Omega Point, and they're unwilling to take even the slightest risks; if trespassers get too close to this hideout, someone has to do anything and everything necessary to keep them away.

Castle claims it's their very vigilance that's kept them from discovery for so long, and if I'm perfectly honest, I can see his rationale in being so strict about it. But these same strict measures keep me and Adam apart. He and I never see each other except during mealtimes, when we're always surrounded by other people, and any free time I have is spent locked in a training room where I'm supposed to "harness my Energy." Adam is just as unhappy about it as I am.

I touch his cheek.

He takes a tight breath. Turns to me. Tells me too much with his eyes, so much that I have to look away because I feel it all too acutely. My skin is hypersensitive, finally finally finally awake and thrumming with life, humming with feelings so intense it's almost indecent.

I can't even hide it.

He sees what he does to me, what happens to me when his fingers graze my skin, when his lips get too close to my face, when the heat of his body against mine forces my eyes to close and my limbs to tremble and my knees to buckle under pressure. I see what it does to him, too, to know that he has that effect on me. He tortures me sometimes, smiling as he takes too long to bridge the gap between us, reveling in the sound of my heart slamming against my chest, in the sharp breaths I fight so hard to control, in the way I swallow a hundred times just before he moves to kiss me. I can't even look at him without reliving every moment we've had together, every memory of his lips, his touch, his scent, his skin. It's too much for me, too much, so much, so new, so many exquisite sensations I've never known, never felt, never even had access to before.

~~Sometimes I'm afraid it will kill me.~~

I break free of his arms; I'm hot and cold and feeling unsteady, hoping I can get myself under control, hoping he'll forget how easily he affects me, and I know I need a moment to pull myself together. I stumble backward; I cover my face with my hands and try to think of something to say but everything is shaking and I catch him looking at me, looking like he might inhale the length of me in one breath.

No is the word I think I hear him whisper.

All I know next are his arms, the desperate edge to his voice when he says my name, and I'm unraveling in his embrace, I'm frayed and falling apart and I'm making no effort to control the tremors in my bones and he's so hot his skin is so hot and I don't even know where I am anymore.

His right hand slides up my spine and tugs on the zipper holding my suit together until it's halfway down my back and I don't care. I have 17 years to make up for and I want to feel everything. I'm not interested in waiting around and risking the who-knows and the what-ifs and the huge regrets. I want to feel all of it because what if I wake up to find this phenomenon has passed, that the expiration date has arrived, that my chance came and went and would never return. That these hands will feel this warmth never again.

I can't.

I won't.

I don't even realize I've pressed myself into him until

I feel every contour of his frame under the thin cotton of his clothes. My hands slip up under his shirt and I hear his strained breath; I look up to find his eyes squeezed shut, his features caught in an expression resembling some kind of pain and suddenly his hands are in my hair, desperate, his lips so close. He leans in and gravity moves out of his way and my feet leave the floor and I'm floating, I'm flying, I'm anchored by nothing but this hurricane in my lungs and this heart beating a skip a skip a skip too fast.

Our lips

touch

and I know I'm going to split at the seams. He's kissing me like he's lost me and he's found me and I'm slipping away and he's never going to let me go. I want to scream, sometimes, I want to collapse, sometimes, I want to die knowing that I've known what it was like to live with this kiss, this heart, this soft soft explosion that makes me feel like I've taken a sip of the sun, like I've eaten clouds 8, 9, and 10.

This.

This makes me ache everywhere.

He pulls away, he's breathing hard, his hands slip under the soft material of my suit and he's so hot his skin is so hot and I think I've already said that but I can't remember and I'm so distracted that when he speaks I don't quite understand.

But it's something.

Words, deep and husky in my ear but I catch little more than an unintelligible utterance, consonants and vowels and broken syllables all mixed together. His heartbeats crash through his chest and topple into mine. His fingers are tracing secret messages on my body. His hands glide down the smooth, satiny material of this suit, slipping down the insides of my thighs, around the backs of my knees and up and up and up and I wonder if it's possible to faint and still be conscious at the same time and I'm betting this is what it feels like to hyper, to hyperventilate when he tugs us backward. He slams his back into the wall. Finds a firm grip on my hips. Pulls me hard against his body.

I gasp.

His lips are on my neck. His lashes tickle the skin under my chin and he says something, something that sounds like my name and he kisses up and down my collarbone, kisses along the arc of my shoulder, and his lips, his lips and his hands and his lips are searching the curves and slopes of my body and his chest is heaving when he swears and he stops and he says *God you feel so good*

and my heart has flown to the moon without me.

I love it when he says that to me. I love it when he tells me that he likes the way I feel because it goes against everything I've heard my entire life and I wish I could put his words in my pocket just to touch them once in a while and remind myself that they exist.

"Juliette."

I can hardly breathe.

I can hardly look up and look straight and see anything but the absolute perfection of this moment but none of

19

that even matters because he's smiling. He's smiling like someone's strung the stars across his lips and he's looking at me, looking at me like I'm *everything* and I want to weep.

"Close your eyes," he whispers.

And I trust him.

So I do.

My eyes fall closed and he kisses one, then the other. Then my chin, my nose, my forehead. My cheeks. Both temples.

Every

inch

of my neck

and

he pulls back so quickly he bangs his head against the rough wall. A few choice words slip out before he can stop them. I'm frozen, startled and suddenly scared. "What happened?" I whisper, and I don't know why I'm whispering. "Are you okay?"

Adam fights not to grimace but he's breathing hard and looking around and stammering "S-sorry" as he clutches the back of his head. "That was—I mean I thought—" He looks away. Clears his throat. "I—I think—I thought I heard something. I thought someone was about to come inside."

Of course.

Adam is not allowed to be in here.

The guys and the girls stay in different wings at Omega Point. Castle says it's mostly to make sure the girls feel safe and comfortable in their living quarters—especially because we have communal bathrooms—so for the most part, I don't have a problem with it. It's nice not to have to shower with old men. But it makes it hard for the two of us to find any time together—and during whatever time we do manage to scrounge up, we're always hyperaware of being discovered.

Adam leans back against the wall and winces. I reach up to touch his head.

He flinches.

I freeze.

"Are you okay . . . ?"

"Yeah." He sighs. "I just—I mean—" He shakes his head. "I don't know." Drops his voice. His eyes. "I don't know what the hell is wrong with me."

"Hey." I brush my fingertips against his stomach. The cotton of his shirt is still warm from his body heat and I have to resist the urge to bury my face in it. "It's okay," I tell him. "You were just being careful."

He smiles a strange, sad sort of smile. "I'm not talking about my head."

I stare at him.

He opens his mouth. Closes it. Pries it open again. "It's—I mean, *this*—" He motions between us.

He won't finish. He won't look at me.

"I don't understand—"

"I'm losing my *mind*," he says, but whispers it like he's not sure he's even saying it out loud.

I look at him. I look and blink and trip on words I can't

21

see and can't find and can't speak.

He's shaking his head.

He grips the back of his skull, hard, and he looks embarrassed and I'm struggling to understand why. Adam doesn't get embarrassed. Adam never gets embarrassed.

His voice is thick when he finally speaks. "I've waited so long to be with you," he says. "I've wanted this—I've wanted *you* for so long and now, after everything—"

"Adam, what are y—"

"I can't *sleep*. I can't sleep and I think about you all—all the time and I can't—" He stops. Presses the heels of his hands to his forehead. Squeezes his eyes shut. Turns toward the wall so I can't see his face. "You should know—you have to know," he says, the words raw, seeming to drain him, "that I have never wanted anything like I've wanted you. Nothing. Because this—this—I mean, God, I *want* you, Juliette, I want—I want—"

His words falter as he turns to me, eyes too bright, emotion flushing up the planes of his face. His gaze lingers along the lines of my body, long enough to strike a match to the lighter fluid flowing in my veins.

I ignite.

I want to say something, something right and steady and reassuring. I want to tell him that I understand, that I want the same thing, that I want him, too, but the moment feels so charged and urgent that I'm half convinced I'm dreaming. It's like I'm down to my last letters and all I have are Qs and Zs and I've only just remembered that someone invented a

22

dictionary when he finally rips his eyes away from me.

He swallows, hard, his eyes down. Looks away again. One of his hands is caught in his hair, the other is curled into a fist against the wall. "You have no idea," he says, his voice ragged, "what you do to me. What you make me feel. When you *touch* me—" He runs a shaky hand across his face. He almost laughs, but his breathing is heavy and uneven; he won't meet my eyes. He steps back, swears under his breath. Pumps his fist against his forehead. "Jesus. What the hell am I saying. Shit. *Shit.* I'm sorry—forget that—forget I said anything—I should go—"

I try to stop him, try to find my voice, try to say, It's all right, it's okay, but I'm nervous now, so nervous, so confused, because none of this makes any sense. I don't understand what's happening or why he seems so uncertain about me and us and him and me and he and I and all of those pronouns put together. I'm not rejecting him. I've never rejected him. My feelings for him have always been so clear—he has no reason to feel unsure about me or around me and I don't know why he's looking at me like something is *wrong*—

"I'm so sorry," he says. "I'm—I shouldn't have said anything. I'm just—I'm—*shit*. I shouldn't have come. I should go—I have to go—"

"What? Adam, what happened? What are you talking about?"

"This was a bad idea," he says. "I'm so stupid—I shouldn't have even been here—"

"You are *not* stupid—it's okay—everything is okay—"

He laughs, loud, hollow. The echo of an uncomfortable smile lingers on his face as he stops, stares at a point directly behind my head. He says nothing for a long time, until finally he does. "Well," he says. He tries to sound upbeat. "That's not what Castle thinks."

"What?" I breathe, caught off guard. I know we're not talking about our relationship anymore.

"Yeah." His hands are in his pockets.

"No."

Adam nods. Shrugs. Looks at me and looks away. "I don't know. I think so."

"But the testing—it's—I mean"—I can't stop shaking my head—"has he found something?"

Adam won't look at me.

"Oh my God," I say, and I whisper it like if I whisper, it'll somehow make this easier. "So it's true? Castle's right?" My voice is inching higher and my muscles are beginning to tighten and I don't know why this feels like fear, this feeling slithering up my back. I shouldn't be afraid if Adam has a gift like I do; I should've known it couldn't have been that easy, that it couldn't have been so simple. This was Castle's theory all along—that Adam can touch me because he too has some kind of Energy that allows it. Castle never thought Adam's immunity from my ability was a happy coincidence. He thought it had to be bigger than that, more scientific than that, more specific than that. ~~I always wanted to believe I just got lucky.~~

24

And Adam wanted to know. He was excited about finding out, actually.

But once he started testing with Castle, Adam stopped wanting to talk about it. He's never given me more than the barest status updates. The excitement of the experience faded far too fast for him.

Something is wrong.

Something is *wrong*.

~~Of course it is~~.

"We don't know anything conclusive," Adam tells me, but I can see he's holding back. "I have to do a couple more sessions—Castle says there are a few more things he needs to . . . examine."

I don't miss the mechanical way Adam is delivering this information. Something isn't right and I can't believe I didn't notice the signs until just now. I haven't wanted to, I realize. I haven't wanted to admit to myself that Adam looks more exhausted, more strained, more tightly wound than I've ever seen him. Anxiety has built a home on his shoulders.

"Adam—"

"Don't worry about me." His words aren't harsh, but there's an undercurrent of urgency in his tone I can't ignore, and he pulls me into his arms before I find a chance to speak. His fingers work to zip up my suit. "I'm fine," he says. "Really. I just want to know you're okay. If you're all right here, then I am too. Everything is fine." His breath catches. "Okay? Everything is going to be fine." The shaky

25

smile on his face is making my pulse forget it has a job to do.

"Okay." It takes me a moment to find my voice. "Okay sure but—"

The door opens and Sonya and Sara are halfway into the room before they freeze, eyes fixed on our bodies wound together.

"Oh!" Sara says.

"Um." Sonya looks down.

Adam swears under his breath.

"We can come back later—," the twins say together.

They're headed out the door when I stop them. I won't kick them out of their own room.

I ask them not to leave.

They ask me if I'm sure.

I take one look at Adam's face and know I'm going to regret forfeiting even a minute of our time together, but I also know I can't take advantage of my roommates. This is their personal space, and it's almost time for lights-out. They can't be wandering the corridors.

Adam isn't looking at me anymore, but he's not letting go, either. I lean forward and leave a light kiss on his heart. He finally meets my eyes. Offers me a small, pained smile.

"I love you," I tell him, quietly, so only he can hear me.

He exhales a short, uneven breath. Whispers, "You have no idea," and pulls himself away. Pivots on one heel. Heads out the door.

My heart is beating in my throat.

The girls are staring at me. Concerned.
Sonya is about to speak, but then

a switch
a click
a flicker

and the lights are out.

FOUR

The dreams are back.

They'd left me for a while, shortly after I'd been freshly imprisoned on base with Warner. I thought I'd lost the bird, the white bird, the bird with streaks of gold like a crown atop its head. It used to meet me in my dreams, flying strong and smooth, sailing over the world like it knew better, like it had secrets we'd never suspect, like it was leading me somewhere safe. It was my one piece of hope in the bitter darkness of the asylum, just until I met its twin tattooed on Adam's chest.

It was like it flew right out of my dreams only to rest atop his heart. I thought it was a signal, a message telling me I was finally safe. That I'd flown away and finally found peace, sanctuary.

I didn't expect to see the bird again.

But now it's back and looks exactly the same. It's the same white bird in the same blue sky with the same yellow crown. Only this time, it's frozen. Flapping its wings in place like it's been caught in an invisible cage, like it's destined to repeat the same motion forever. The bird *seems* to be flying: it's in the air; its wings work. It looks as if it's free to soar through the skies. But it's stuck.

Unable to fly upward.

Unable to fall.

I've had the same dream every night for the past week, and all 7 mornings I've woken up shaking, shuddering into the earthy, icy air, struggling to steady the bleating in my chest.

Struggling to understand what this means.

I crawl out of bed and slip into the same suit I wear every day; the only article of clothing I own anymore. It's the richest shade of purple, so plum it's almost black. It has a slight sheen, a bit of a shimmer in the light. It's one piece from neck to wrists to ankles and it's skintight without being tight at all.

I move like a gymnast in this outfit.

I have springy leather ankle boots that mold to the shape of my feet and render me soundless as I pad across the floor. I have black leather gloves that prevent me from touching something I'm not supposed to. Sonya and Sara lent me one of their hair ties and for the first time in years I've been able to pull my hair out of my face. I wear it in a high ponytail and I've learned to zip myself up without help from anyone. This suit makes me feel extraordinary. It makes me feel invincible.

It was a gift from Castle.

He had it custom-made for me before I arrived at Omega Point. He thought I might like to finally have an outfit that would protect me from myself and others while simultaneously offering me the option of *hurting* others. If I wanted to. Or needed to. The suit is made of some kind of special material that's supposed to keep me cool in the heat and keep me warm in the cold. So far it's been perfect.

~~So far so far so far~~

I head to breakfast by myself.

Sonya and Sara are always gone by the time I'm awake. Their work in the medical wing is never-ending—not only are they able to heal the wounded but they also spend their days trying to create antidotes and ointments. The one time we ever had a conversation, Sonya explained to me how some Energies can be depleted if we exert ourselves too much—how we can exhaust our bodies enough that they'll just break down. The girls say that they want to be able to create medicines to use in the case of multiple injuries they can't heal all at once. They are, after all, only 2 people. And war seems imminent.

Heads still spin in my direction when I walk into the dining hall.

I am a spectacle, an anomaly even among the anomalies. I should be used to it by now, after all these years. I should be tougher, jaded, indifferent to the opinions of others.

~~I should be a lot of things.~~

I clear my eyes and keep my hands to my sides and pretend I'm unable to make eye contact with anything but that spot, that little mark on the wall 50 feet from where I'm standing.

I pretend I'm just a number.

No emotions on my face. Lips perfectly still. Back straight, hands unclenched. I am a robot, a ghost slipping through the crowds.

6 steps forward. 15 tables to pass. 42 43 44 seconds and counting.

~~I am scared~~

~~I am scared~~

~~I am scared~~

I am strong.

Food is served at only 3 times throughout the day: breakfast from 7:00 to 8:00 a.m., lunch from 12:00 to 1:00 p.m., and dinner from 5:00 to 7:00 p.m. Dinner is an hour longer because it's at the end of the day; it's like our reward for working hard. But mealtimes aren't a fancy, luxurious event—the experience is very different from dining with Warner. Here we just stand in a long line, pick up our prefilled bowls, and head toward the eating area—which is nothing more than a series of rectangular tables arranged in parallel lines across the room. Nothing superfluous so nothing is wasted.

I spot Adam standing in line and head in his direction.

68 69 70 seconds and counting.

"Hey, gorgeous." Something lumpy hits me in the back. Falls to the floor. I turn around, my face flexing the 43 muscles required to frown before I see him.

Kenji.

Big, easy smile. Eyes the color of onyx. Hair even darker, sharper, stick-straight and slipping into his eyes. His jaw is twitching and his lips are twitching and the impressive lines of his cheekbones are appled up into a smile struggling to stay suppressed. He's looking at me like I've been walking around with toilet paper in my hair and I can't help but wonder why I haven't spent time with him since we got here. He did, on a purely technical level, save my life. And Adam's life. James', too.

Kenji bends down to pick up what looks like a wadded ball of socks. He weighs them in his hand like he's considering throwing them at me again. "Where are you going?" he says. "I thought you were supposed to meet me here? Castle said—"

"Why did you bring a pair of socks in here?" I cut him off. "People are trying to eat."

He freezes for only a split second before he rolls his eyes. Pulls up beside me. Tugs on my ponytail. "I was running late to meet *you*, your highness. I didn't have time to put my socks on." He gestures to the socks in his hand and the boots on his feet.

"That's so gross."

"You know, you have a really strange way of telling me you're attracted to me."

I shake my head, try to bite back my amusement. Kenji is a walking paradox of Unflinchingly Serious Person and 12-Year-Old Boy Going Through Puberty all rolled into one. But I'd forgotten how much easier it is to breathe around him; it seems natural to laugh when he's near. So I keep walking and I'm careful not to say a word, but a smile is still tugging at my lips as I grab a tray and head into the heart of the kitchen.

Kenji is half a step behind me. "So. We're working together today."

"Yup."

"So, what—you just walk right past me? Don't even say hello?" He clutches the socks to his chest. "I'm crushed. I saved us a table and everything."

I glance at him. Keep walking.

He catches up. "I'm serious. Do you have any idea how awkward it is to wave at someone and have them ignore you? And then you're just looking around like a jackass, trying to be all, 'No, really, I swear, I know that girl' and no one believes y—"

"Are you kidding?" I stop in the middle of the kitchen. Spin around. My face is pulled together in disbelief. "You've spoken to me maybe *once* in the two weeks I've been here. I hardly even notice you anymore."

"Okay, hold up," he says, turning to block my path. "We *both* know there's no way you haven't noticed all of *this*"—he gestures to himself—"so if you're trying to play games with me, I should let you know up front that it's not going to work."

"What?" I frown. "What are you talking abou—"

"You can't play hard to get, kid." He raises an eyebrow. "I can't even *touch* you. Takes 'hard to get' to a whole new level, if you know what I mean."

"Oh my God," I mouth, eyes closed, shaking my head. "You are *insane*."

He falls to his knees. "Insane for your sweet, sweet love!"

"Kenji!" I can't lift my eyes because I'm afraid to look around, but I'm desperate for him to stop talking. To put an entire room between us at all times. I know he's joking, but I might be the only one.

"What?" he says, his voice booming around the room. "Does my love embarrass you?"

"Please—*please* get up—and lower your *voice*—"

"Hell no."

"Why not?" I'm pleading now.

"Because if I lower my voice, I won't be able to hear myself speak. And that," he says, "is my favorite part."

I can't even look at him.

"Don't deny me, Juliette. I'm a lonely man."

"What is *wrong* with you?"

"You're breaking my heart." His voice is even louder now, his arms making sad, sweeping gestures that almost hit me as I back away, panicked. But then I realize everyone is watching him.

Entertained.

I manage an awkward smile as I glance around the room and I'm surprised to find that no one is looking at me now. They're all grinning, clearly accustomed to Kenji's antics, staring at him with a mixture of adoration and something else.

Adam is staring, too. He's standing with his tray in his hands, his head cocked and his eyes confused. He smiles a tentative sort of smile when our gazes meet.

I head toward him.

"Hey—wait up, kid." Kenji jumps up to grab my arm. "You know I was just messing with—" He follows my eyes to where Adam is standing. Slaps a palm to his forehead. "Of *course*! How could I forget? You're in love with my roommate."

I turn to face him. "Listen, I'm grateful you're going to help me train now—really, I am. Thank you for that. But you can't go around proclaiming your fake love to me— especially not in front of Adam—and you have to let me cross this room before the breakfast hour is over, okay? I hardly ever get to see him."

Kenji nods very slowly, looks a little solemn. "You're right. I'm sorry. I get it."

"Thank you."

"Adam is jealous of our love."

"Just go get your food!" I push him, hard, fighting back an exasperated laugh.

Kenji is one of the only people here—with the exception of Adam, of course—who isn't afraid to touch me. In truth, no one really has anything to fear when I'm wearing this suit, but I usually take my gloves off when I eat and my reputation is always walking 5 feet ahead of me. People keep their distance. And even though I accidentally attacked Kenji once, he's not afraid. I think it would take an astronomical amount of something horrible to get him down.

I admire that about him.

Adam doesn't say much when we meet. He doesn't have

to say more than "Hey," because his lips quirk up on one side and I can already see him standing a little taller, a little tighter, a little tenser. And I don't know much about anything in this world but I do know how to read the book written in his eyes.

The way he looks at me.

His eyes are heavy now in a way that worries me, but his gaze is still so tender, so focused and full of feeling that I can hardly keep myself out of his arms when I'm around him. I find myself watching him do the simplest things—shifting his weight, grabbing a tray, nodding good morning to someone—just to track the movement of his body. My moments with him are so few that my chest is always too tight, my heart beating too fast. He makes me want to be impractical all the time.

He never lets go of my hand.

"You okay?" I ask him, still feeling a little apprehensive about the night before.

He nods. Tries to smile. "Yeah. I, uh . . ." Clears his throat. Takes a deep breath. Looks away. "Yeah, I'm sorry about last night. I kind of . . . I freaked out a little."

"About what, though?"

He's looking over my shoulder. Frowning.

"Adam . . . ?"

"Yeah?"

"Why were you freaked out?"

His eyes meet mine again. Wide. Round. "What? Nothing."

"I don't understa—"

"Why the hell are you guys taking so long?"

I spin around. Kenji is standing just behind me, so much food piled on his tray I'm surprised no one said anything. He must've convinced the cooks to give him extra.

"Well?" Kenji is staring, unblinking, waiting for us to respond. He finally cocks his head backward, in a motion that says *follow me*, before walking away.

Adam blows out his breath and looks so distracted that I decide to drop the subject of last night. Soon. We'll talk soon. I'm sure it's nothing. I'm sure it's nothing at all.

We'll talk soon and everything is going to be fine.

FIVE

Kenji is waiting for us at an empty table.

James used to join us at mealtimes, but now he's friends with the handful of younger kids at Omega Point, and prefers sitting with them. He seems the happiest of all of us to be here—and I'm happy he's happy—but I have to admit I miss his company. I'm afraid to mention it though; sometimes I'm not sure if I want to know why he doesn't spend time with Adam when I'm around. ~~I don't think I want to know if the other kids managed to convince him that I'm dangerous. I mean, I am dangerous, but I just~~

Adam sits down on the bench seat and I slide in next to him. Kenji sits across from us. Adam and I hide our linked hands under the table and I allow myself to enjoy the simple luxury of his proximity. I'm still wearing my gloves but just being this close to him is enough; flowers are blooming in my stomach, the soft petals tickling every inch of my nervous system. It's like I've been granted 3 wishes: to touch, to taste, to feel. It's the strangest phenomenon. A crazy happy impossibility wrapped in tissue paper, tied with a bow, tucked away in my heart.

~~It often feels like a privilege I don't deserve.~~

Adam shifts so the length of his leg is pressed against mine.

I look up to find him smiling at me, a secret, tiny sort of smile that says so many things, the kinds of things no one should be saying at a breakfast table. I force myself to breathe as I suppress a grin. I turn to focus on my food. Hope I'm not blushing.

Adam leans into my ear. I feel the soft whispers of his breath just before he begins to speak.

"You guys are disgusting, you know that, right?"

I look up, startled, and find Kenji frozen midmovement, his spoon halfway to his mouth, his head cocked in our direction. He gestures with his spoon at our faces. "What the hell is this? You guys playing footsie under the table or someshit?"

Adam moves away from me, just an inch or 2, and exhales a deep, irritated sigh. "You know, if you don't like it, you can leave." He nods at the tables around us. "No one asked you to sit here."

This is Adam making a concerted effort to be nice to Kenji. The 2 of them were friends back on base, but somehow Kenji knows exactly how to provoke Adam. I almost forget for a moment that they're roommates.

I wonder what it must be like for them to live together.

"That's bullshit and you know it," Kenji says. "I told you this morning that I had to sit with you guys. Castle wants me to help the two of you *adjust*." He snorts. Nods in my direction. "Listen, I don't have a clue what you see in this guy," he says, "but you should try living with him. The man is moody as hell."

"I am not *moody*—"

"Yeah, bro." Kenji puts his utensils down. "You are *moody*. It's always 'Shut up, Kenji.' 'Go to sleep, Kenji.' 'No one wants to see you naked, Kenji.' When I know for a *fact* that there are thousands of people who would love to see me naked—"

"How long do you have to sit here?" Adam looks away, rubs his eyes with his free hand.

Kenji sits up straighter. Picks up his spoon only to stab it through the air again. "*You* should consider yourself lucky that I'm sitting at your table. I'm making you cool by association."

I feel Adam tense beside me and decide to intervene. "Hey, can we talk about something else?"

Kenji grunts. Rolls his eyes. Shovels another spoonful of breakfast into his mouth.

I'm worried.

Now that I'm paying closer attention, I can see the weariness in Adam's eyes, the heaviness in his brow, the stiff set of his shoulders. I can't help but wonder what he's going through. What he's not telling me. I tug on Adam's hand a little and he turns to me.

"You sure you're okay?" I whisper. I feel like I keep asking him the same question over and over and over

His eyes immediately soften, looking tired but slightly amused. His hand releases mine under the table just to rest on my lap, just to slip down my thigh, and I almost lose control of my vocabulary before he leaves a light kiss in my hair. I swallow too hard, almost drop my fork on the floor. It takes me a moment to remember that he hasn't actually answered my question. It's not until he's looked away, staring at his food, when he finally nods, says, "I'm okay." But I'm not breathing and his hand is still tracing patterns on my leg.

"Ms. Ferrars? Mr. Kent?"

I sit up so fast I slam my knuckles under the table at the sound of Castle's voice. There's something about his presence that makes me feel like he's my teacher, like I've been caught misbehaving in class. Adam, on the other hand, doesn't seem remotely startled.

I cling to Adam's fingers as I lift my head.

Castle is standing over our table and Kenji is leaving to deposit his bowl in the kitchen. He claps Castle on the back like they're old friends and Castle flashes Kenji a warm smile as he passes.

"I'll be right back," Kenji shouts over his shoulder, twisting to flash us an overly enthusiastic thumbs-up. "Try not to get naked in front of everyone, okay? There are kids in here."

I cringe and glance at Adam but he seems oddly focused on his food. He hasn't said a word since Castle arrived.

I decide to answer for the both of us. Paste on a bright smile. "Good morning."

Castle nods, touches the lapel of his blazer; his stature is strong and poised. He beams at me. "I just came to say hello and to check in. I'm so happy to see that you're expanding

41

your circle of friends, Ms. Ferrars."

"Oh. Thank you. But I can't take credit for the idea," I point out. "You're the one who told me to sit with Kenji."

Castle's smile is a little too tight. "Yes. Well," he says, "I'm happy to see that you took my advice."

I nod at my food. Rub absently at my forehead. Adam looks like he's not even breathing. I'm about to say something when Castle cuts me off. "So, Mr. Kent," he says. "Did Ms. Ferrars tell you she'll be training with Kenji now? I'm hoping it will help her progress."

Adam doesn't answer.

Castle soldiers on. "I actually thought it might be interesting for her to work with you, too. As long as I'm there to supervise."

Adam's eyes snap up to attention. Alarmed. "What are you talking about?"

"Well—" Castle pauses. I watch his gaze shift between the two of us. "I thought it would be interesting to run some tests on you and her. Together."

Adam stands up so quickly he almost bangs his knee into the table. "Absolutely not."

"Mr. Kent—" Castle starts.

"There's no chance in *hell*—"

"It's her choice to make—"

"I don't want to discuss this here—"

I jump to my feet. Adam looks ready to set something on fire. His fists are clenched at his sides, his eyes narrowed into a tight glare; his forehead is taut, his entire frame shaking with energy and anxiety.

"What is going on?" I demand.

Castle shakes his head. He's not addressing me when he speaks. "I only want to see what happens when she touches you. That's it."

"Are you *insane*—"

"This is for *her*," Castle continues, his voice careful, extra calm. "It has nothing to do with your progress—"

"What progress?" I cut in.

"We're just trying to help her figure out how to affect nonliving organisms," Castle is saying. "Animals and humans we've figured out—we know one touch is sufficient. Plants don't seem to factor into her abilities at all. But everything else? It's . . . different. She doesn't know how to handle that part yet, and I want to help her. That's all we're doing," he says. "Helping Ms. Ferrars."

Adam takes a step closer to me. "If you're helping her figure out how to destroy nonliving things, why do you need me?"

For a second Castle actually looks defeated. "I don't really know," he says. "The unique nature of your relationship—it's quite fascinating. Especially with everything we've learned so far, it's—"

"What have you learned?" I jump in again.

"—entirely possible," Castle is still saying, "that everything is connected in a way we don't yet understand."

Adam looks unconvinced. His lips are pressed into a thin line. He doesn't look like he wants to answer.

Castle turns to me. Tries to sound excited. "What do you think? Are you interested?"

"Interested?" I look at Castle. "I don't even know what you're talking about. And I want to know why no one is answering my questions. What have you discovered about Adam?" I ask. "What's wrong? Is something wrong?" Adam is breathing extra hard and trying not to show it; his hands keep clenching and unclenching. "Someone, please, tell me what's going on."

Castle frowns.

He's studying me, confused, his eyebrows pulled together. "Mr. Kent," he says, still looking at me. "Am I to understand that you have not yet shared our discoveries with Ms. Ferrars?"

"What discoveries?" My heart is racing hard now, so hard it's beginning to hurt.

"Mr. Kent—"

"That's none of your business," Adam snaps.

"She should *know*—"

"We don't know anything yet!"

"We know enough."

"Bullshit. We're not done yet—"

"The only thing left is to test the two of you together—"

Adam steps directly in front of Castle, grabbing his breakfast tray with a little too much strength. "Maybe," he says very, very carefully, "some other time."

He turns to leave.

I touch his arm.

He stops. Drops his tray, pivots in my direction. There's less than half an inch between us and I almost forget we're standing in a crowded room. His breath is hot and his breathing shallow and the heat from his body is melting my blood only to splash it across my cheeks.

Panic is doing backflips in my bones.

"Everything is fine," he says. "Everything is going to be fine. I promise."

"But—"

"I promise," he says again, grabbing my hand. "I swear. I'm going to fix this—"

"Fix this?" I think I'm dreaming. I think I'm dying. "Fix what?" Something is breaking in my brain and something is happening without my permission and I'm lost, I'm so lost, I'm so much everything confused and I'm drowning in confusion. "Adam, I don't underst—"

"I mean, really though?" Kenji is making his way back to our group. "You're going to do that here? In front of everyone? Because these tables aren't as comfortable as they look—"

Adam pulls back and slams into Kenji's shoulder on his way out.

"*Don't.*"

Is all I hear him say before he disappears.

SIX

Kenji lets out a low whistle.

Castle is calling Adam's name, asking him to slow down, to speak to him, to discuss things in a rational manner. Adam never looks back.

"I told you he was moody," Kenji mutters.

"He's not moody," I hear myself say, but the words feel distant, disconnected from my lips. I feel numb, like my arms have been hollowed out.

Where did I leave my voice I can't find my voice I can't find my

"So! You and me, huh?" Kenji claps his hands together. "Ready to get your ass kicked?"

"Kenji."

"Yeah?"

"I want you to take me to wherever they went."

Kenji is looking at me like I've just asked him to kick himself in the face. "Uh, yeah—how about a warm *hell no* to that request? Does that work for you? Because it works for me."

"I need to know what's going on." I turn to him, desperate, feeling stupid. "You know, don't you? You know what's wrong—"

"Of course I know." He crosses his arms. Levels a look at me. "I *live* with that poor bastard and I practically run this place. I know everything."

"So why won't you tell me? Kenji, *please—*"

"Yeah, um, I'm going to pass on that, but you know what I will do? I *will* help you to remove yourself the hell out of this dining hall where everyone is listening to *everything we say.*" This last bit he says extra loudly, looking around at the room, shaking his head. "Get back to your breakfasts, people. Nothing to see here."

It's only then that I realize what a spectacle we've made. Every eye in the room is blinking at me. I attempt a weak smile and a twitchy wave before allowing Kenji to shuffle me out of the room.

"No need to wave at the people, princess. It's not a coronation ceremony." He pulls me into one of the many long, dimly lit corridors.

"Tell me what's happening." I have to blink several times before my eyes adjust to the lighting. "This isn't fair—everyone knows what's going on except for me."

He shrugs, leans one shoulder against the wall. "It's not my place to tell. I mean, I like to mess with the guy, but I'm not an asshole. He asked me not to say anything. So I'm not going to say anything."

"But—I mean—is he okay? Can you at least tell me if he's okay?"

Kenji runs a hand over his eyes; exhales, annoyed. Shoots me a look. Says, "All right, like, have you ever seen a train

47

wreck?" He doesn't wait for me to answer. "I saw one when I was a kid. It was one of those big, crazy trains with a billion cars all hitched up together, totally derailed, half exploded. Shit was on fire and everyone was screaming and you just *know* people are either dead or they're about to die and you really don't want to watch but you just can't look away, you know?" He nods. Bites the inside of his cheek. "This is kind of like that. Your boy is a freaking train wreck."

I can't feel my legs.

"I mean, I don't know," Kenji goes on. "Personally? I think he's overreacting. Worse things have happened, right? Hell, aren't we up to our earlobes in crazier shit? But no, Mr. Adam Kent doesn't seem to know that. I don't even think he sleeps anymore. And you know what," he adds, leaning in, "I think he's starting to freak James out a little, and to be honest it's starting to piss me off because that kid is way too nice and way too cool to have to deal with Adam's drama—"

But I'm not listening anymore.

I'm envisioning the worst possible scenarios, the worst possible outcomes. Horrible, terrifying things that all end with Adam dying in some miserable way. He must be sick, or he must have some kind of terrible affliction, or something that causes him to do things he can't control or oh, God, *no*

"You have to tell me."

I don't recognize my own voice. Kenji is looking at me, shocked, wide-eyed, genuine fear written across his features and it's only then that I realize I've pinned him against the wall. My 10 fingers are curled into his shirt, fistfuls of fabric clenched in each hand, and I can only imagine what I must look like to him right now.

The scariest part is that I don't even care.

"You're going to tell me *something*, Kenji. You have to. I need to know."

"You, uh"—he licks his lips, looks around, laughs a nervous laugh—"you want to let go of me, maybe?"

"Will you help me?"

He scratches behind his hear. Cringes a little. "No?"

I slam him harder into the wall, recognize a rush of some wild kind of adrenaline burning in my veins. It's strange, but I feel as though I could rip through the ground with my bare hands.

It seems like it would be easy. So easy.

"Okay—all right—god*damn*." Kenji is holding his arms up, breathing a little fast. "Just—how about you let me go, and I'll, uh, I'll take you to the research labs."

"The research labs."

"Yeah, that's where they do the testing. It's where we do all of our testing."

"You promise you'll take me if I let go?"

"Are you going to bash my brain into the wall if I don't?"

"Probably," I lie.

"Then yeah. I'll take you. *Damn*."

I drop him and stumble backward; make an effort to pull myself together. I feel a little embarrassed now that I've let go of him. Some part of me feels like I must've overreacted.

"I'm sorry about that," I tell him. "But thank you. I appreciate your help." I try to lift my chin with some dignity.

Kenji snorts. He's looking at me like he has no idea who I am, like he's not sure if he should laugh or applaud or run like hell in the opposite direction. He rubs the back of his neck, eyes intent on my face. He won't stop staring.

"What?" I ask.

"How much do you weigh?"

"Wow. Is that how you talk to every girl you meet? That explains so much."

"I'm about one hundred seventy-five pounds," he says. "Of muscle."

I stare at him. "Would you like an award?"

"Well, well, well," he says, cocking his head, the barest hint of a smile flickering across his face. "Look who's the smart-ass now."

"I think you're rubbing off on me," I say.

But he's not smiling anymore.

"Listen," he says. "I'm not trying to flatter myself by pointing this out, but I could toss you across the room with my pinkie finger. You weigh, like, less than nothing. I'm almost twice your body mass." He pauses. "So how the hell did you pin me against the wall?"

"What?" I frown. "What are you talking about?"

"I'm talking about *you*"—he points at me—"pinning *me*"—he points at himself—"against the wall." He points at the wall.

"You mean you *actually* couldn't move?" I blink. "I thought you were just afraid of touching me."

"No," he says. "I legit could not move. I could hardly breathe."

"You're kidding."

"Have you ever done that before?"

"No." I'm shaking my head. "I mean I don't think I . . ." I gasp, as the memory of Warner and his torture chamber rushes to the forefront of my mind; I have to close my eyes against the influx of images. The barest recollection of that event is enough to make me feel unbearably nauseous; I can already feel my skin break into a cold sweat. Warner was testing me, trying to put me in a position where I'd be forced to use my power on a toddler. I was so horrified, so enraged that I crashed through the concrete barrier to get to Warner, who was waiting on the other side. I'd pinned *him* against the wall, too. Only I didn't realize he was cowed by my strength. I thought he was afraid to move because I'd gotten too close to touching him.

I guess I was wrong.

"Yeah," Kenji says, nodding at something he must see on my face. "Well. That's what I thought. We'll have to remember this juicy tidbit when we get around to our real training sessions." He throws me a loaded look. "Whenever that actually happens."

I'm nodding, not really paying attention. "Sure. Fine. But first, take me to the research rooms."

Kenji sighs. Waves his hand with a bow and a flourish. "After you, princess."

SEVEN

We're trailing down a series of corridors I've never seen before.

We're passing all of the regular halls and wings, past the training room I normally occupy, and for the first time since I've been here, I'm really paying attention to my surroundings. All of a sudden my senses feel sharper, clearer; my entire being feels like it's humming with a renewed kind of energy.

I am electric.

This entire hideout has been dug out of the ground—it's nothing but cavernous tunnels and interconnected passageways, all powered by supplies and electricity stolen from secret storage units belonging to The Reestablishment. This space is invaluable. Castle told us once that it took him at least a decade to design it, and a decade more to get the work done. By then he'd also managed to recruit all of the other members of this underground world. I can understand why he's so relentless about security down here, why he's not willing to let anything happen to it. I don't think I would either.

Kenji stops.

We reach what looks like a dead end—what could be the

very end of Omega Point.

Kenji pulls out a key card I didn't know he was hiding, and his hand fumbles for a panel buried in the stone. He slides the panel open. Does something I can't see. Swipes the key card. Hits a switch.

The entire wall rumbles to life.

The pieces are coming apart, shifting out of place until they reveal a hole big enough for our bodies to clamber through. Kenji motions for me to follow his lead and I scramble through the entryway, glancing back to watch the wall close up behind me.

My feet hit the ground on the other side.

It's like a cave. Massive, wide, separated into 3 longitudinal sections. The middle section is the most narrow and serves as a walkway; square glass rooms fit with slim glass doors make up the left and right sections. Each clear wall acts as a partition to rooms on either side—everything is see-through. There's an electric aura engulfing the entire space; each cube is bright with white light and blinking machinery; sharp and dull hums of energy pulse through the vast dimensions.

There are at least 20 rooms down here.

10 on either side, all of them unobstructed from view. I recognize a number of faces from the dining hall down here, some of them strapped to machines, needles stuck in their bodies, monitors beeping about some kind of information I can't understand. Doors slide open and closed open and closed open and closed; words and whispers and footsteps,

hand gestures and half-formed thoughts collect in the air.

This.

This is where everything happens.

Castle told me 2 weeks ago—the day after I arrived—that he had a pretty good idea why we are the way we are. He said that they'd been doing research for years.

Research.

I see figures running, gasping on what resemble inordinately fast treadmills. I see a woman reloading a gun in a room bursting with weapons and I see a man holding something that emits a bright blue flame. I see a person standing in a chamber full of nothing but water and there are ropes stacked high and strung across the ceiling and all kinds of liquids, chemicals, contraptions I can't name and my brain won't stop screaming and my lungs keep catching fire and it's too much too much too much too much

Too many machines, too many lights, too many people in too many rooms taking notes, talking amongst themselves, glancing at the clocks every few seconds and I'm stumbling forward, looking too closely and not closely enough and then I hear it. I try so hard not to but it's barely contained behind these thick glass walls and there it is again.

The low, guttural sound of human agony.

It hits me right in the face. Punches me right in the stomach. Realization jumps on my back and explodes in my skin and rakes its fingernails down my neck and I'm choking on impossibility.

Adam.

I see him. He's already here, in one of the glass rooms. Shirtless. Strapped down to a gurney, arms and legs clamped in place, wires from a nearby machine taped to his temples, his forehead, just below his collarbone. His eyes are pressed shut, his fists are clenched, his jaw is tight, his face too taut from the effort not to scream.

I don't understand what they're doing to him.

I don't know what's happening I don't understand *why* it's happening or why he needs a machine or why it keeps blinking or beeping and I can't seem to move or breathe and I'm trying to remember my voice, my hands, my head, and my feet and then he

jerks.

He convulses against the stays, strains against the pain until his fists are pounding the padding of the gurney and I hear him cry out in anguish and for a moment the world stops, everything slows down, sounds are strangled, colors look smeared and the floor seems set on its side and I think wow, I think I'm actually going to die. I'm going to drop dead or

I'm going to kill the person responsible for this.

It's one or the other.

That's when I see Castle. Castle, standing in the corner of Adam's room, watching in silence as this 18-year-old boy rages in agony while he does nothing. Nothing except watch, except to take notes in his little book, to purse his lips as he tilts his head to the side. To glance at the monitor on the beeping machine.

And the thought is so simple when it slips into my head. So calm. So easy.

So, *so* easy.

I'm going to kill him.

"Juliette—*no*—"

Kenji grabs me by the waist, arms like bands of iron around me and I think I'm screaming, I think I'm saying things I've never heard myself say before and Kenji is telling me to calm down, he's saying, "This is *exactly* why I didn't want to bring you in here—you don't understand—it's not what it looks like—"

And I decide I should probably kill Kenji, too. Just for being an idiot.

"LET GO OF ME—"

"Stop *kicking* me—"

"I'm going to *murder* him—"

"Yeah, you should really stop saying that out loud, okay? You're not doing yourself any favors—"

"LET GO OF ME, KENJI, I SWEAR TO GOD—"

"Ms. Ferrars!"

Castle is standing at the end of the walkway, a few feet from Adam's glass room. The door is open. Adam isn't jerking anymore, but he doesn't appear to be conscious, either.

White, hot rage.

It's all I know right now. The world looks so black-and-white from here, so easy to demolish and conquer. This is anger like nothing I've known before. It's an anger so raw, so

56

potent it's actually calming, like a feeling that's finally found its place, a feeling that finally sits comfortably as it settles into my bones.

I've become a mold for liquid metal; thick, searing heat distributes itself throughout my body and the excess coats my hands, forging my fists with a strength so breathtaking, an energy so intense I think it might engulf me. I'm light-headed from the rush of it.

I could do anything.

Anything.

Kenji's arms drop away from me. I don't have to look at him to know that he's stumbling back. Afraid. Confused. Probably disturbed.

I don't care.

"So this is where you've been," I say to Castle, and I'm surprised by the cool, fluid tone of my voice. "This is what you've been doing."

Castle steps closer and appears to regret it. He looks startled, surprised by something he sees on my face. He tries to speak and I cut him off.

"What have you done to him?" I demand. "What have you been *doing to him*—"

"Ms. Ferrars, please—"

"He is not your *experiment!*" I explode, and the composure is gone, the steadiness in my voice is gone and I'm suddenly so unstable again I can hardly keep my hands from shaking. "You think you can just use him for your *research*—"

"Ms. Ferrars, please, you must calm yourself—"

"Don't tell me to calm down!" I can't imagine what they must have done to him down here, testing him, treating him like some kind of specimen.

They're *torturing* him.

"I would not have expected you to have such an adverse reaction to this room," Castle says. He's trying to be conversational. Reasonable. Charismatic, even. It makes me wonder what I must look like right now. I wonder if he's afraid of me. "I thought you understood the importance of the research we do at Omega Point," he says. "Without it, how could we possibly hope to understand our origins?"

"You're hurting him—you're *killing* him! What have you done—"

"Nothing he hasn't asked to be a part of." Castle's voice is tight and his lips are tight and I can see his patience is starting to wear thin. "Ms. Ferrars, if you are insinuating that I've used him for my own personal experimentation, I would recommend you take a closer look at the situation." He says the last few syllables with a little too much emphasis, a little too much fire, and I realize I've never seen him angry before.

"I know that you've been struggling here," Castle continues. "I know you are unaccustomed to seeing yourself as part of a group, and I've made an effort to understand where you might be coming from—I've tried to help you adjust. But you must look around!" He gestures toward the glass walls and the people behind them. "We are all the same. We are working on the same team! I have subjected

58

Adam to nothing I have not undergone myself. We are simply running tests to see where his supernatural abilities lie. We cannot know for certain what he is capable of if we do not test him first." His voice drops an octave or 2. "And we do not have the luxury of waiting several years until he accidentally discovers something that might be useful to our cause right now."

And it's strange.

Because it's like a real thing, this anger.

I feel it wrapping itself around my fingers like I could fling it at his face. I feel it coiling itself around my spine, planting itself in my stomach and shooting branches down my legs, up my arms, through my neck. It's choking me. Choking me because it needs release, needs relief. Needs it now.

"You," I tell him, and I can hardly spit the words out. "You think you're any better than The Reestablishment if you're just *using us*—experimenting on us to further your cause—"

"MS. FERRARS!" Castle bellows. His eyes are flashing bright, too bright, and I realize everyone in this underground tunnel is now staring at us. His fingers are in fists at his sides and his jaw is unmistakably set and I feel Kenji's hand on my back before I realize the earth is vibrating under my feet. The glass walls are beginning to tremble and Castle is planted right in the middle of everything, rigid, raw with anger and indignation and I remember that he has an impossibly advanced level of psychokinesis.

I remember that he can move things with his mind.

He lifts his right hand, palm splayed outward, and the glass panel not a few feet away begins to shake, shudder, and I realize I'm not even breathing.

"You do not want to upset me." Castle's voice is far too calm for his eyes. "If you have a problem with my methods, I would gladly invite you to state your claims in a rational manner. I will not tolerate you speaking to me in such a fashion. My concerns for the future of our world may be more than you can fathom, but you should not fault me for your own ignorance!" He drops his right hand and the glass buckles back just in time.

"My *ignorance?*" I'm breathing hard again. "You think because I don't understand why you would subject anyone to—to *this*—" I wave a hand around the room. "You think that means I'm *ignorant*—?"

"Hey, Juliette, it's okay—," Kenji starts.

"Take her away," Castle says. "Take her back to her training quarters." He shoots an unhappy look at Kenji. "And you and I—we will discuss this later. What were you *thinking,* bringing her here? She's not ready to see this—she can hardly even handle *herself* right now—"

He's right.

I can't handle this. I can't hear anything but the sounds of machines beeping, screeching in my head, can't see anything but Adam's limp form lying on a thin mattress. I can't stop imagining what he must've been going through, what he had to endure just to understand what he might be and I realize it's all my fault.

It's my fault he's here, it's my fault he's in danger, it's my fault Warner wants to kill him and Castle wants to test him and if it weren't for me he'd still be living with James in a home that hasn't been destroyed; he'd be safe and comfortable and free from the chaos I've introduced to his life.

I brought him here. If he'd never touched me none of this would've happened. He'd be healthy and strong and he wouldn't be suffering, wouldn't be hiding, wouldn't be trapped 50 feet underground. He wouldn't be spending his days strapped to a gurney.

~~It's my fault it's my fault it's my fault it's my fault~~ it's all my fault

I snap.

It's like I've been stuffed full of twigs and all I have to do is bend and my entire body will break. All the guilt, the anger, the frustration, the pent-up aggression inside of me has found an outlet and now it can't be controlled. Energy is coursing through me with a vigor I've never felt before and I'm not even thinking but I have to do *something* I have to touch *something* and I'm curling my fingers and bending my knees and pulling back my arm and

punching

my

fist

right

through

the

floor.

The earth fissures under my fingers and the reverberations surge through my being, ricocheting through my bones until my skull is spinning and my heart is a pendulum slamming into my rib cage. My eyesight fades in and out of focus and I have to blink a hundred times to clear it only to see a crack creaking under my feet, a thin line splintering the ground. Everything around me is suddenly off-balance. The stone is groaning under our weight and the glass walls are rattling and the machines are shifting out of place and the water is sloshing against its container and the people—

The people.

The people are frozen in terror and horror and the fear in their expressions rips me apart.

I fall backward, cradling my right fist to my chest and try to remind myself I am not a monster, I do not have to be a monster, I do not want to hurt people I do not want to hurt people *I do not want to hurt people*

and it's not working.

Because it's all a lie.

Because this was me, trying to help.

I look around.

At the ground.

At what I've done.

And I understand, for the first time, that I have the power to destroy everything.

EIGHT

Castle is limp.

His jaw is unhinged. His arms are slack at his sides, his eyes wide with worry and wonder and a sliver of intimidation and though he moves his lips he can't seem to make a sound.

I feel like now might be a good time to jump off a cliff.

Kenji touches my arm and I turn to face him only to realize I'm petrified. I'm always waiting for him and Adam and Castle to realize that being kind to me is a mistake, that it'll end badly, that I'm not worth it, that I'm nothing more than a tool, a weapon, a closet murderer.

But he takes my right fist in his hand so gently. Takes care not to touch my skin as he slips off the now-tattered leather glove and sucks in his breath at the sight of my knuckles. The skin is torn and blood is everywhere and I can't move my fingers.

I realize I am in *agony*.

I blink and stars explode and a new torture rages through my limbs in such a hurry I can no longer speak.

I gasp

and
the
world

d i s a p p e a r s

NINE

My mouth tastes like death.

I manage to pry my eyes open and immediately feel the wrath of hell ripping through my right arm. My hand has been bandaged in so many layers of gauze it's rendered my 5 fingers immobile and I find I'm grateful for it. I'm so exhausted I don't have the energy to cry.

I blink.

Try to look around but my neck is too stiff.

Fingers brush my shoulder and I discover myself wanting to exhale. I blink again. Once more. A girl's face blurs in and out of focus. I turn my head to get a better view and blink blink blink some more.

"How're you feeling?" she whispers.

"I'm okay," I say to the blur, but I think I'm lying. "Who are you?"

"It's me," she says. Even without seeing her clearly I can hear the kindness in her voice. "Sonya."

Of course.

Sara is probably here, too. I must be in the medical wing.

"What happened?" I ask. "How long have I been out?"

She doesn't answer and I wonder if she didn't hear me.

"Sonya?" I try to meet her eyes. "How long have I been sleeping?"

"You've been really sick," she says. "Your body needed time—"

"How long?" My voice drops to a whisper.

"Three days."

I sit straight up and know I'm going to be sick.

Luckily, Sonya's had the foresight to anticipate my needs. A bucket appears just in time for me to empty the meager contents of my stomach into it and then I'm dry-heaving into what is not my suit but some kind of hospital gown and someone is wiping a hot, damp cloth across my face.

Sonya and Sara are hovering over me, the hot cloths in their hands, wiping down my bare limbs, making soothing sounds and telling me I'm going to be fine, I just need to rest, I'm finally awake long enough to eat something, I shouldn't be worried because there's nothing to worry about and they're going to take care of me.

But then I look more closely.

I notice their hands, so carefully sheathed in latex gloves; I notice the IV stuck in my arm; I notice the urgent but cautious way they approach me and then I realize the problem.

The healers can't touch me.

TEN

They've never had to deal with a problem like me before.

Injuries are always treated by the healers. They can set broken bones and repair bullet wounds and revive collapsed lungs and mend even the worst kinds of cuts—I know this because Adam had to be carried into Omega Point on a stretcher when we arrived. He'd suffered at the hands of Warner and his men after we escaped the military base and I thought his body would be scarred forever. But he's perfect. Brand-new. It took all of 1 day to put him back together; it was like magic.

But there are no magic medicines for me.

No miracles.

Sonya and Sara explain that I must've suffered some kind of immense shock. They say my body overloaded on its own abilities and it's a miracle I even managed to survive. They also think my body has been passed out long enough to have repaired most of the psychological damage, though I'm not so sure that's true. I think it'd take quite a lot to fix that sort of thing. ~~I've been psychologically damaged for a very long time.~~ But at least the physical pain has settled. It's little more than a steady throbbing that I'm able to ignore for short periods of time.

I remember something.

"Before," I tell them. "In Warner's torture rooms, and then with Adam and the steel door—I never—this never happened—I never injured myself—"

"Castle told us about that," Sonya tells me. "But breaking through one door or one wall is very different from trying to split the earth in two." She attempts a smile. "We're pretty sure this can't even compare to what you did before. This was a lot stronger—we all felt it when it happened. We actually thought explosives had gone off. The tunnels," she says. "They almost collapsed in on themselves."

"No." My stomach turns to stone.

"It's okay," Sara tries to reassure me. "You pulled back just in time."

I can't catch my breath.

"You couldn't have known—" Sonya starts.

"I almost killed—I almost killed all of you—"

Sonya shakes her head. "You have an amazing amount of power. It's not your fault. You didn't know what you were capable of."

"I could've killed you. I could've killed Adam—I could've—" My head whips around. "Is he here? Is Adam here?"

The girls stare at me. Stare at each other.

I hear a throat clear and I jerk toward the sound.

Kenji steps out of the corner. He waves a half wave, offers me a crooked smile that doesn't reach his eyes. "Sorry," he says to me, "but we had to keep him out of here."

"Why?" I ask, but I'm afraid to know the answer.

Kenji pushes his hair out of his eyes. Considers my question. "Well. Where should I begin?" He counts off on his fingers. "After he found out what happened, he tried to *kill* me, he went ballistic on Castle, he refused to leave the medical wing, and then he wou—"

"Please." I stop him. I squeeze my eyes shut. "Never mind. Don't. I can't."

"You asked."

"Where is he?" I open my eyes. "Is he okay?"

Kenji rubs the back of his neck. Looks away. "He'll be all right."

"Can I see him?"

Kenji sighs. Turns to the girls. Says, "Hey, can we get a second alone?" and the 2 of them are suddenly in a hurry to go.

"Of course," Sara says.

"No problem," Sonya says.

"We'll give you some privacy," they say at the same time. And they leave.

Kenji grabs 1 of the chairs pushed up against the wall and carries it over to my bed. Sits down. Props the ankle of 1 foot on the knee of the other and leans back. Links his hands behind his head. Looks at me.

I shift on the mattress so I'm better seated to see him. "What is it?"

"You and Kent need to talk."

"Oh." I swallow. "Yes. I know."

"Do you?"

"Of course."

"Good." He nods. Looks away. Taps his foot too fast against the floor.

"What?" I ask after a moment. "What are you not telling me?"

His foot stops tapping but he doesn't meet my eyes. He covers his mouth with his left hand. Drops it. "That was some crazy shit you pulled back there."

All at once I feel humiliated. "I'm sorry, Kenji. I'm so sorry—I didn't think—I didn't know—"

He turns to face me and the look in his eyes stops me in place. He's trying to read me. Trying to figure me out. Trying, I realize, to decide whether or not he can trust me. Whether or not the rumors about the monster in me are true.

"I've never done that before," I hear myself whisper. "I swear—I didn't mean for that to happen—"

"Are you sure?"

"What?"

"It's a question, Juliette. It's a legitimate question." I've never seen him so serious. "I brought you here because Castle wanted you here. Because he thought we could help you—he thought we could provide you with a safe place to live. To get you away from the assholes trying to use you for their own benefit. But you come here and you don't even seem to want to be a part of anything. You don't talk to people. You don't make any progress with your training. You do nothing, basically."

"I'm sorry, I really—"

"And then I believe Castle when he says he's worried about you. He tells me you're not adjusting, that you're having a hard time fitting in. That people heard negative things about you and they're not being as welcoming as they should be. And I should kick my own ass for it, but I feel sorry for you. So I tell him I'll help. I rearrange my entire goddamn schedule just to help you deal with your issues. Because I think you're a nice girl who's just a little misunderstood. Because Castle is the most decent guy I've ever known and I want to help him out."

My heart is pounding so hard I'm surprised it's not bleeding.

"So I'm wondering," he says to me. He drops the foot he was resting on his knee. Leans forward. Props his elbows on his thighs. "I'm wondering if it's possible that all of this is just *coincidence*. I mean, was it just some crazy *coincidence* that I ended up working with you? Me? One of the very few people here who have access to that room? Or was it coincidence that you managed to threaten me into taking you down to the research labs? That you then, somehow, accidentally, coincidentally, unknowingly punched a fist into the ground that shook this place so hard we all thought the walls were caving in?" He stares at me, hard. "Was it a coincidence," he says, "that if you'd held on for just a few more seconds, this entire place would've collapsed in on itself?"

My eyes are wide, horrified, caught.

He leans back. Looks down. Presses 2 fingers to his lips.

"Do you actually want to be here?" he asks. "Or are you just trying to bring us down from the inside?"

"What?" I gasp. "No—"

"Because you either know *exactly* what you're doing—and you're a hell of a lot sneakier than you pretend to be—or you really have no *clue* what you're doing and you just have really shitty luck. I haven't decided yet."

"Kenji, I swear, I never—I n-never—" I have to bite back the words to blink back the tears. It's crippling, this feeling, this not knowing how to prove your own innocence. It's my entire life replayed over and over and over again, trying to convince people that I'm not dangerous, that I never meant to hurt anyone, that I didn't intend for things to turn out this way. That I'm not a bad person.

~~But it never seems to work out.~~

"I'm so sorry," I choke, the tears flowing fast now. I'm so disgusted with myself. I tried so hard to be different, to be better, to be *good*, and I just went and ruined everything and lost everything all over again and I don't even know how to tell him he's wrong.

~~Because he might be right.~~

I knew I was angry. I knew I wanted to hurt Castle and I didn't care. In that moment, I meant it. In the anger of that moment, I really, truly meant it. I don't know what I would've done if Kenji hadn't been there to hold me back. I don't know. I have no idea. I don't even understand what I'm capable of.

~~*How many times,* I hear a voice whisper in my head, *how*~~

72

many times will you apologize for who you are?

I hear Kenji sigh. Shift in his seat. I don't dare lift my eyes.

"I had to ask, Juliette." Kenji sounds uncomfortable. "I'm sorry you're crying but I'm not sorry I asked. It's my job to constantly be thinking of our safety—and that means I have to look at every possible angle. No one knows what you can do yet. Not even you. But you keep trying to act like what you're capable of isn't a big deal, and it's not helping anything. You need to stop trying to pretend you're not dangerous."

I look up too fast. "But I'm not—I'm n-not trying to hurt anyone—"

"That doesn't matter," he says, standing up. "Good intentions are great, but they don't change the facts. You *are* dangerous. Shit, you're *scary* dangerous. More dangerous than me and everyone else in here. So don't ask me to act like that knowledge, in and of itself, isn't a threat to us. If you're going to stay here," he says to me, "you have to learn how to control what you do—how to contain it. You have to deal with who you are and you have to figure out how to live with it. Just like the rest of us."

3 knocks at the door.

Kenji is still staring at me. Waiting.

"Okay," I whisper.

"And you and Kent need to sort out your drama ASAP," he adds, just as Sonya and Sara walk back into the room. "I don't have the time, the energy, or the interest to deal with your problems. I like to mess with you from time to time because, well, let's face it"—he shrugs—"the world is going to hell out there and I suppose if I'm going to be shot dead before I'm twenty-five, I'd at least like to remember what it's like to laugh before I do. But that does not make me your clown or your babysitter. At the end of the day I do not give two shits about whether or not you and Kent are going steady. We have a million things to take care of down here, and less than none of them involve your love life." A pause. "Is that clear?"

I nod, not trusting myself to speak.

"So are you in?" he says.

Another nod.

"I want to hear you say it. If you're in, you're all in. No more feeling sorry for yourself. No more sitting in the training room all day, crying because you can't break a metal pipe—"

"How did you kn—"

"Are you *in*?"

"I'm in," I tell him. "I'm in. I promise."

He takes a deep breath. Runs a hand through his hair. "Good. Meet me outside of the dining hall tomorrow morning at six a.m."

"But my hand—"

He waves my words away. "Your hand, nothing. You'll be fine. You didn't even break anything. You messed up your knuckles and your brain freaked out a little and basically you just fell asleep for three days. I don't call that an injury," he

74

says. "I call that a goddamn vacation." He stops to consider something. "Do you have any idea how long it's been since I've gone on *vacation*—"

"But aren't we training?" I interrupt him. "I can't do anything if my hand is wrapped up, can I?"

"Trust me." He cocks his head. "You'll be fine. This . . . is going to be a little different."

I stare at him. Wait.

"You can consider it your official welcome to Omega Point," he says.

"But—"

"Tomorrow. Six a.m."

I open my mouth to ask another question but he presses a finger to his lips, offers me a 2-finger salute, and walks backward toward the exit just as Sonya and Sara head over to my bed.

I watch as he nods good-bye to both of them, pivots on 1 foot, and strides out the door.

6:00 a.m.

ELEVEN

I catch a glimpse of the clock on the wall and realize it's only 2:00 in the afternoon.

Which means 6:00 a.m. is 16 hours from now.

Which means I have a lot of hours to fill.

Which means I have to get dressed.

Because I need to get out of here.

And I really need to talk to Adam.

"Juliette?"

I jolt out of my own head and back to the present moment to find Sonya and Sara staring at me. "Can we get you anything?" they ask. "Are you feeling well enough to get out of bed?"

But I look from one set of eyes to another and back again, and instead of answering their questions, I feel a crippling sense of shame dig into my soul and I can't help but revert back to another version of myself. A scared little girl who wants to keep folding herself in half until she can't be found anymore.

I keep saying, "Sorry, I'm so sorry, I'm sorry about everything, for all of this, for all the trouble, for all the damage, really, I'm so, so sorry—"

I hear myself go on and on and on and I can't get myself to stop.

It's like a button in my brain is broken, like I've developed a disease that forces me to apologize for everything, for existing, for wanting more than what I've been given, and I can't stop.

It's what I do.

I'm always apologizing. Forever apologizing. For who I am and what I never meant to be and for this body I was born into, this DNA I never asked for, this person I can't unbecome. 17 years I've spent trying to be different. Every single day. Trying to be someone else for someone else.

And it never seems to matter.

But then I realize they're talking to me.

"There's nothing to apologize for—"

"Please, it's all right—"

Both of them are trying to speak to me, but Sara is closer.

I dare to meet her eyes and I'm surprised to see how soft they are. Gentle and green and squinty from smiling. She sits down on the right side of my bed. Pats my bare arm with her latex glove, unafraid. Unflinching. Sonya stands just next to her, looking at me like she's worried, like she's sad for me, and I don't have long to dwell on it because I'm distracted. I smell the scent of jasmine filling the room, just as it did the very first time I stepped in here. When we first arrived at Omega Point. When Adam was injured. Dying.

He was dying and they saved his life. These 2 girls in front of me. They saved his life and I've been living with them for 2 weeks and I realize, right then, exactly how selfish I've been.

So I decide to try a new set of words.

"Thank you," I whisper.

I feel myself begin to blush and I wonder at my inability to be so free with words and feelings. I wonder at my incapacity for easy banter, smooth conversation, empty words to fill awkward moments. I don't have a closet filled with umms and ellipses ready to insert at the beginnings and ends of sentences. I don't know how to be a verb, an adverb, any kind of modifier. I'm a noun through and through.

Stuffed so full of people places things and ideas that I don't know how to break out of my own brain. How to start a conversation.

I want to trust but it scares the skin off my bones.

But then I remember my promise to Castle and my promise to Kenji and my worries over Adam and I think maybe I should take a risk. Maybe I should try to find a new friend or 2. And I think of how wonderful it would be to be friends with a girl. A girl, just like me.

I've never had one of those before.

So when Sonya and Sara smile and tell me they're "happy to help" and they're here "anytime" and that they're always around if I "need someone to talk to," I tell them I'd love that.

I tell them I'd really appreciate that.

I tell them I'd love to have a friend to talk to.

Maybe sometime.

TWELVE

"Let's get you back into your suit," Sara says to me.

The air down here is cool and cold and often damp, the winter winds relentless as they whip the world above our heads into submission. Even in my suit I feel the chill, especially early in the morning, especially right now. Sonya and Sara are helping me out of this hospital dress and back into my normal uniform and I'm shaking in my skin. Only once they've zipped me up does the material begin to react to my body temperature, but I'm still so weak from being in bed for so long that I'm struggling to stay upright.

"I really don't need a wheelchair," I tell Sara for the third time. "Thank you—really—I-I appreciate it," I stammer, "but I need to get the blood flowing in my legs. I have to be strong on my feet." I have to be strong, period.

Castle and Adam are waiting for me in my room.

Sonya told me that while I was talking to Kenji, she and Sara went to notify Castle that I was awake. So. Now they're there. Waiting for me. In the room I share with Sonya and Sara. And I'm so afraid of what is about to happen that I'm worried I might conveniently forget how to get to my own room. Because I'm fairly certain that whatever I'm about to hear isn't going to be good.

"You can't walk back to the room by yourself," Sara is saying. "You can hardly stand on your own—"

"I'm okay," I insist. I try to smile. "Really, I should be able to manage as long as I can stay close to the wall. I'm sure I'll be back to normal just as soon as I start moving."

Sonya and Sara glance at each other before scrutinizing my face. "How's your hand?" they ask at the same time.

"It's okay," I tell them, this time more earnestly. "It feels a lot better. Really. Thank you so much."

The cuts are practically healed and I can actually move my fingers now. I inspect the brand-new, thinner bandage they've wrapped across my knuckles. The girls explained to me that most of the damage was internal; it seems I traumatized whatever invisible bone in my body is responsible for my ~~curse~~ "gift".

"All right. Let's go," Sara says, shaking her head. "We're walking you back to the room."

"No—please—it's okay—" I try to protest but they're already grabbing my arms and I'm too feeble to fight back. "This is unnecessary—"

"You're being ridiculous," they chorus.

"I don't want you to have to go through the trouble—"

"You're being ridiculous," they chorus again.

"I—I'm really not—" But they're already leading me out of the room and down the hall and I'm hobbling along between them. "I promise I'm fine," I tell them. "Really."

Sonya and Sara share a loaded look before they smile at me, not unkindly, but there's an awkward silence between us as we move through the halls. I spot people walking past us and immediately duck my head. I don't want to make eye contact with anyone right now. I can't even imagine what they must've heard about the damage I've caused. I know I've managed to confirm all of their worst fears about me.

"They're only afraid of you because they don't know you," Sara says quietly.

"Really," Sonya adds. "We barely know you and we think you're great."

I'm blushing fiercely, wondering why embarrassment always feels like ice water in my veins. It's like all of my insides are freezing even though my skin is burning hot too hot.

~~I hate this.~~

~~I hate this feeling.~~

Sonya and Sara stop abruptly. "Here we are," they say together.

We're in front of our bedroom door. I try to unlatch myself from their arms but they stop me. Insist on staying with me until they're sure I've gotten inside okay.

So I stay with them.

And I knock on my own door, because I'm not sure what else to do.

Once.

Twice.

I'm waiting just a few seconds, just a few moments for fate to answer when I realize the full impact of Sonya's and Sara's presence beside me. They're offering me smiles that are supposed to be encouraging, bracing, reinforcing. They're trying to lend me their strength because they know I'm about to face something that isn't going to make me happy.

And this thought makes me happy.

If only for a fleeting moment.

Because I think wow, I imagine this is what it's like to have friends.

"Ms. Ferrars."

Castle opens the door just enough for me to see his face. He nods at me. Glances down at my injured hand. Back up at my face. "Very good," he says, mostly to himself. "Good, good. I'm happy to see you're doing better."

"Yes," I manage to say. "I—th-thank you, I—"

"Girls," he says to Sonya and Sara. He offers them a bright, genuine smile. "Thank you for all you've done. I'll take it from here."

They nod. Squeeze my arms once before letting go and I sway for just a second before I find my footing. "I'm all right," I tell them as they try to reach for me. "I'll be fine."

They nod again. Wave, just a little, as they back away.

"Come inside," Castle says to me.

I follow him in.

THIRTEEN

1 bunk bed on one side of the wall.

1 single bed on the other side.

That's all this room consists of.

That, and Adam, who is sitting on my single bed, elbows propped up on his knees, face in his hands. Castle shuts the door behind us, and Adam startles. Jumps up.

"Juliette," he says, but he's not looking at me; he's looking at all of me. His eyes are searching my body as if to ensure I'm still intact, arms and legs and everything in between. It's only when he finds my face that he meets my gaze; I step into the sea of blue in his eyes, dive right in and drown. I feel like someone's punched a fist into my lungs and snatched up all my oxygen.

"Please, have a seat, Ms. Ferrars." Castle gestures to Sonya's bottom bunk, the bed right across from where Adam is sitting. I make my way over slowly, trying not to betray the dizziness, the nausea I'm feeling. My chest is rising and falling too quickly.

I drop my hands into my lap.

I feel Adam's presence in this room like a real weight against my chest but I choose to study the careful wrapping of my new bandage—the gauze stretched tight across the knuckles of my right hand—because I'm too much of a coward to look up. I want nothing more than to go to him, to have him hold me, to transport me back to the few moments of bliss I've ever known in my life but there's something gnawing at my core, scraping at my insides, telling me that something is wrong and it's probably best if I stay exactly where I am.

Castle is standing in the space between the beds, between me and Adam. He's staring at the wall, hands clasped behind his back. His voice is quiet when he says, "I am very, very disappointed in your behavior, Ms. Ferrars."

Hot, terrible shame creeps up my neck and forces my head down again.

"I'm sorry," I whisper.

Castle takes a deep breath. Exhales very slowly. "I have to be frank with you," he says, "and admit that I'm not ready to discuss what happened just yet. I am still too upset to be able to speak about the matter calmly. Your actions," he says, "were childish. Selfish. *Thoughtless!* The damage you caused—the years of work that went into building and planning that room, I can't even begin to tell you—"

He catches himself, swallows hard.

"That will be a subject," he says steadily, "for another time. Perhaps just between the two of us. But I am here today because Mr. Kent asked me to be here."

I look up. Look at Castle. Look at Adam.

Adam looks like he wants to run.

I decide I can't wait any longer. "You've learned something

about him," I say, and it's less of a question than it is a fact. It's so obvious. There's no other reason why Adam would bring Castle here to talk to me.

Something terrible has already happened. Something terrible is about to happen.

I can feel it.

Adam is staring at me now, unblinking, his hands in fists pressed into his thighs. He looks nervous; scared. I don't know what to do except to stare back at him. I don't know how to offer him comfort. I don't even know how to smile right now. I feel like I'm trapped in someone else's story.

Castle nods, once, slowly.

Says, "Yes. Yes, we've discovered the very intriguing nature of Mr. Kent's ability." He walks toward the wall and leans against it, allowing me a clearer view of Adam. "We believe we now understand why he's able to touch you, Ms. Ferrars."

Adam turns away, presses one of his fists to his mouth. His hand looks like it might be shaking but he, at least, seems to be doing better than I am. Because my insides are screaming and my head is on fire and panic is stepping on my throat, suffocating me to death. Bad news offers no returns once received.

"What is it?" I fix my eyes on the floor and count stones and sounds and cracks and nothing.

1

2, 3, 4

1

2, 3, 4

1

2, 3, 4

"He . . . can disable things," Castle says to me.

5, 6, 7, 8 million times I blink, confused. All my numbers crash to the floor, adding and subtracting and multiplying and dividing. "What?" I ask him.

This news is wrong. This news doesn't sound horrible at all.

"The discovery was quite accidental, actually," Castle explains. "We weren't having much luck with any of the tests we'd been running. But then one day I was in the middle of a training exercise, and Mr. Kent was trying to get my attention. He touched my shoulder."

Wait for it.

"And . . . suddenly," Castle says, pulling in a breath, "I couldn't perform. It was as if—as if a wire inside of my body had been cut. I felt it right away. He wanted my attention and he inadvertently shut me off in an attempt to redirect my focus. It was unlike anything I've ever seen." He shakes his head. "We've now been working with him to see if he can control his ability at will. And," Castle adds, excited, "we want to see if he can *project*.

"You see, Mr. Kent does not need to make contact with the skin—I was wearing my blazer when he touched my arm. So this means he's already projecting, if only just a little bit. And I believe, with some work, he'll be able to extend his gift to a greater surface area."

I have no idea what that means.

I try to meet Adam's eyes; I want him to tell me these things himself but he won't look up. He won't speak and I don't understand. This doesn't seem like bad news. In fact, it sounds quite good, which can't be right. I turn to Castle. "So Adam can just make someone else's power—their *gift*—whatever it is—he can just make it stop? He can turn it off?"

"It appears that way, yes."

"Have you tested this on anyone else?"

Castle looks offended. "Of course we have. We've tried it on every gifted member at Omega Point."

But something isn't making sense.

"What about when he arrived?" I ask. "And he was injured? And the girls were able to heal him? Why didn't he cut off their abilities?"

"Ah." Castle nods. Clears his throat. "Yes. Very astute, Ms. Ferrars." He paces the length of the room. "This . . . is where the explanation gets a little tricky. After much study, we've been able to conclude that his ability is a kind of . . . *defense* mechanism. One that he does not yet know how to control. It's something that's been working on autopilot his entire life, even though it only works to disable other preternatural abilities. If there was ever a risk, if Mr. Kent was ever in any state of danger, in any situation where his body was on high alert, feeling threatened or at risk of injury, his ability automatically set in."

He stops. Looks at me. Really looks at me.

"When you first met, for example, Mr. Kent was working

as a soldier, on guard, always aware of the risks in his surroundings. He was in a constant state of *electricum*—a term we use to define when our Energy is 'on,' so to speak—because he was always in a state of danger." Castle tucks his hands into his blazer pockets. "A series of tests have further shown that his body temperature rises when he is in a state of *electricum*—just a couple of degrees higher than normal. His elevated body temperature indicates that he is exerting more energy than usual to sustain this. And, in short," Castle says, "this constant exertion has been exhausting him. Weakening his defenses, his immune system, his self-control."

His elevated body temperature.

That's why Adam's skin was always so hot when we were together. Why it was always so intense when he was with me. His ability was working to fight mine. His energy was working to *defuse* mine.

It was *exhausting him. Weakening his defenses.*

Oh.

God.

"Your physical relationship with Mr. Kent," Castle says, "is, in truth, none of my business. But because of the very unique nature of your gifts, it's been of great interest to me on a purely scientific level. But you must know, Ms. Ferrars, that though these new developments no doubt fascinate me, I take absolutely no pleasure in them. You've made it clear that you do not think much of my character, but you must believe that I would never find joy in your troubles."

My troubles.

My troubles have arrived fashionably late to this conversation, inconsiderate beasts that they are.

"Please," I whisper. "Please just tell me what the problem is. There's a problem, isn't there? Something is wrong." I look at Adam but he's still staring away, at the wall, at everything but at my face, and I feel myself rising to my feet, trying to get his attention. "Adam? Do you know? Do you know what he's talking about? *Please*—"

"Ms. Ferrars," Castle says quickly. "I beg you to sit down. I know this must be difficult for you, but you must let me finish. I've asked Mr. Kent not to speak until I'm done explaining everything. Someone needs to deliver this information in a clear, rational manner, and I'm afraid he is in no position to do so."

I fall back onto the bed.

Castle lets out a breath. "You brought up an excellent point earlier—about why Mr. Kent was able to interact with our healer twins when he first arrived. But it was different with them," Castle says. "He was weak; he knew he needed help. His body would not—and, more importantly, could not— refuse that kind of medical attention. He was vulnerable and therefore unable to defend himself even if he wanted to. The last of his Energy was depleted when he arrived. He felt safe and he was seeking aid; his body was out of immediate danger and therefore unafraid, not primed for a defensive strategy."

Castle looks up. Looks me in the eye.

"Mr. Kent has begun having a similar problem with you."

"What?" I gasp.

"I'm afraid he doesn't know how to control his abilities yet. It's something we're hoping we can work on, but it will take a lot of time—a lot of energy and focus—"

"What do you mean," I hear myself ask, my words heavy with panic, "that he has *already begun* having a similar problem with me?"

Castle takes a small breath. "It—it seems that he is weakest when he is with you. The more time he spends in your company, the less threatened he feels. And the more . . . intimate you become," Castle says, looking distinctly uncomfortable, "the less control he has over his body." A pause. "He is too open, too vulnerable with you. And in the few moments his defenses have slipped thus far, he's already felt the very distinct pain associated with your touch."

There it is.

There's my head, lying on the floor, cracked right open, my brain spilling out in every direction and I can't I don't I can't even I'm sitting here, struck, numb, slightly dizzy.

Horrified.

Adam is *not* immune to me.

Adam has to *work* to defend himself against me and I'm exhausting him. I'm making him sick and I'm weakening his body and if he ever slips again. If he ever forgets. If he ever makes a mistake or loses focus or becomes too aware of the fact that he's using his *gift* to control what I might do—

I could hurt him.

I could *kill* him.

FOURTEEN

Castle is staring at me.

Waiting for my reaction.

I haven't been able to spit the chalk out of my mouth long enough to string a sentence together.

"Ms. Ferrars," he says, rushing to speak now, "we are working with Mr. Kent to help him control his abilities. He's going to train—just as you are—to learn how to exercise this particular element of who he is. It will take some time until we can be certain he'll be safe with you, but it will be all right, I assure you—"

"No." I'm standing up. "No no no no no." I'm tripping sideways. "NO."

I'm staring at my feet and at my hands and at these walls and I want to scream. I want to run. I want to fall to my knees. I want to curse the world for cursing me, for torturing me, for taking away the only good thing I've ever known and I'm stumbling toward the door, searching for an outlet, for escape from this nightmare that is my life and

"Juliette—please—"

The sound of Adam's voice stops my heart. I force myself to turn around. To face him.

But the moment he meets my eyes his mouth falls closed.

His arm is outstretched toward me, trying to stop me from 10 feet away and I want to sob and laugh at the same time, at the terrible hilarity of it all.

He will not touch me.

I will not allow him to touch me.

Never again.

"Ms. Ferrars," Castle says gently. "I'm sure it's hard to stomach right now, but I've already told you this isn't permanent. With enough training—"

"When you touch me," I ask Adam, my voice breaking, "is it an effort for you? Does it exhaust you? Does it drain you to have to constantly be fighting me and what I am?"

Adam tries to answer. He tries to say something but instead he says nothing and his unspoken words are so much worse.

I spin in Castle's direction. "That's what you said, isn't it?" My voice is even shakier now, too close to tears. "That he's using his Energy to extinguish mine, and that if he ever forgets—if he ever gets c-carried away or t-too vulnerable—that I could hurt him—that I've *already* h-hurt him—"

"Ms. Ferrars, please—"

"Just answer the question!"

"Well yes," he says, "for now, at least, that's all we know—"

"Oh, God, I—I can't—" I'm tripping to reach the door again but my legs are still weak, my head is still spinning, my eyes are blurring and the world is being washed of all its color when I feel familiar arms wrap around my waist, tugging me backward.

"Juliette," he says, so urgently, "please, we have to talk about this—"

"Let go of me." My voice is barely a breath. "Adam, please—I can't—"

"Castle." Adam cuts me off. "Do you think you can give us some time alone?"

"Oh." He startles. "Of course," he says, just a beat too late. "Sure, yes, yes, of course." He walks to the door. Hesitates. "I will—well, right. Yes. You know where to find me when you're ready." He nods at both of us, offers me a strained sort of smile, and leaves the room. The door clicks shut behind him.

Silence pours into the space between us.

"Adam, please," I finally say, and hate myself for saying it. "Let go of me."

"No."

I feel his breath on the back of my neck and it's killing me to be so close to him. It's killing me to know that I have to rebuild the walls I'd so carelessly demolished the moment he came back into my life.

"Let's talk about this," he says. "Don't go anywhere. Please. Just talk to me."

I'm rooted in place.

"Please," he says again, this time more softly, and my resolve runs out the door without me.

I follow him back to the beds. He sits on one side of the room. I sit on the other.

He stares at me. His eyes are too tired, too strained. He looks like he hasn't been eating enough, like he hasn't slept in weeks. He hesitates, licks his lips before pressing them tight, before he speaks. "I'm sorry," he says. "I'm so sorry I didn't tell you. I never meant to upset you."

And I want to laugh and laugh and laugh until the tears dissolve me.

"I understand why you didn't tell me," I whisper. "It makes perfect sense. You wanted to avoid all of *this*." I wave a limp hand around the room.

"You're not mad?" His eyes are so terribly hopeful. He looks like he wants to walk over to me and I have to hold out a hand to stop him.

The smile on my face is literally killing me.

"How could I be mad at you? You were torturing yourself down there just to figure out what was happening to you. You're torturing yourself right now just trying to find a way to fix this."

He looks relieved.

Relieved and confused and afraid to be happy all at the same time. "But something's wrong," he says. "You're crying. Why are you crying if you're not upset?"

I actually laugh this time. Out loud. Laugh and hiccup and want to die, so desperately. "Because I was an idiot for thinking things could be different," I tell him. "For thinking you were a fluke. For thinking my life could ever be better than it was, that *I* could ever be better than I was." I try to speak again but instead clamp a hand over my mouth like I can't believe what I'm about to say. I force myself to swallow the stone in my throat. I drop my hand. "Adam." My voice is raw, aching. "This isn't going to work."

"What?" He's frozen in place, his eyes too wide, his chest rising and falling too fast. "What are you talking about?"

"You can't touch me," I tell him. "You can't touch me and I've already hurt you—"

"No—Juliette—" Adam is up, he's cleared the room, he's on his knees next to me and he reaches for my hands but I have to snatch them back because my gloves were ruined, ruined in the research lab and now my fingers are bare.

Dangerous.

Adam stares at the hands I've hidden behind my back like I've slapped him across the face. "What are you doing?" he asks, but he's not looking at me. He's still staring at my hands. Barely breathing.

"I can't do this to you." I shake my head too hard. "I don't want to be the reason why you're hurting yourself or weakening yourself and I don't want you to always have to worry that I might accidentally *kill* you—"

"No, Juliette, listen to me." He's desperate now, his eyes up, searching my face. "I was worried too, okay? I was worried too. Really worried. I thought—I thought that maybe—I don't know, I thought maybe it would be bad or that maybe we wouldn't be able to work through it but I talked to Castle. I talked to him and explained everything and he said that I just have to learn to control it. I'll learn how to turn it on and off—"

"Except when you're with me? Except when we're together—"

"No—what? No, *especially* when we're together!"

"Touching me—being with me—it takes a physical toll on you! You run a *fever* when we're together, Adam, did you realize that? You'd get sick just trying to fight me off—"

"You're not hearing me—please—I'm telling you, I'll learn to control all of that—"

"When?" I ask, and I can actually feel my bones breaking, 1 by 1.

"What? What do you mean? I'll learn now—I'm learning *now*—"

"And how's it going? Is it easy?"

His mouth falls closed but he's looking at me, struggling with some kind of emotion, struggling to find composure. "What are you trying to say?" he finally asks. "Are you"—he's breathing hard—"are you—I mean—you don't want to make this work?"

"Adam—"

"What are you *saying*, Juliette?" He's up now, a shaky hand caught in his hair. "You don't—you don't want to be with me?"

I'm on my feet, blinking back the tears burning my eyes, desperate to run to him but unable to move. My voice breaks when I speak. "Of course I want to be with you."

He drops his hand from his hair. Looks at me with eyes so open and vulnerable but his jaw is tight, his muscles are tense, his upper body is heaving from the effort to inhale, exhale. "Then what's happening right now? Because something is happening right now and it doesn't feel okay," he says, his voice catching. "It doesn't feel okay, Juliette, it feels like the opposite of whatever the hell okay is and I really just want to hold you—"

"I don't want to h-hurt you—"

"You're not going to hurt me," he says, and then he's in front of me, looking at me, pleading with me. "I swear. It'll be fine—we'll be fine—and I'm better now. I've been working on it and I'm stronger—"

"It's too dangerous, Adam, please." I'm begging him, backing away, wiping furiously at the tears escaping down my face. "It's better for you this way. It's better for you to just stay away from me—"

"But that's not what I want—you're not asking me what *I* want—," he says, following me as I dodge his advances. "I want to be with you and I don't give a damn if it's hard. I still want it. I still want you."

I'm trapped.

I'm caught between him and the wall and I have nowhere to go and I wouldn't want to go even if I could. I don't want to have to fight this even though there's something inside of me screaming that it's wrong to be so selfish, to allow him to be with me if it'll only end up hurting him. But he's looking at me, looking at me like I'm *killing* him and I realize I'm hurting him more by trying to stay away.

I'm shaking. Wanting him so desperately and knowing now, more than ever, that what I want will have to wait. And I hate that it has to be this way. I hate it so much I could scream.

But maybe we can try.

"Juliette." Adam's voice is hoarse, broken with feeling. His hands are at my waist, trembling just a little, waiting for my permission. "Please."

And I don't protest.

He's breathing harder now, leaning into me, resting his forehead against my shoulder. He places his hands flat against the center of my stomach, only to inch them down my body, slowly, so slowly and I gasp.

There's an earthquake happening in my bones, tectonic plates shifting from panic to pleasure as his fingers take their time moving around my thighs, up my back, over my shoulders and down my arms. He hesitates at my wrists. This is where the fabric ends, where my skin begins.

But he takes a breath.

And he takes my hands.

For a moment I'm paralyzed, searching his face for any sign of pain or danger but then we both exhale and I see him attempt a smile with new hope, a new optimism that maybe everything is going to work out.

But then he blinks and his eyes change.

His eyes are deeper now. Desperate. Hungry. He's searching me like he's trying to read the words etched inside of me and I can already feel the heat of his body, the power in his limbs, the strength in his chest and I don't have time to stop him before he's kissing me.

His left hand is cupping the back of my head, his right tightening around my waist, pressing me hard against him and destroying every rational thought I've ever had. It's deep. So strong. It's an introduction to a side of him I've never known before and I'm gasping gasping gasping for air.

It's hot rain and humid days and broken thermostats. It's screaming teakettles and raging steam engines and wanting to take your clothes off just to feel a breeze.

It's the kind of kiss that makes you realize oxygen is overrated.

And I know I shouldn't be doing this. I know it's probably stupid and irresponsible after everything we've just learned but someone would have to shoot me to make me want to stop.

I'm pulling at his shirt, desperate for a raft or a life preserver or something, anything to anchor me to reality but he breaks away to catch his breath and rips off his shirt, tosses it to the floor, pulls me into his arms and we both fall onto my bed.

Somehow I end up on top of him.

He reaches up only to pull me down and he's kissing me, my throat, my cheeks, and my hands are searching his body, exploring the lines, the planes, the muscle and he pulls back, his forehead is pressed against my own and his eyes are squeezed shut when he says, "How is it possible," he says, "that I'm this close to you and it's killing me that you're still so far away?"

And I remember I promised him, 2 weeks ago, that once he got better, once he'd healed, I would memorize every inch of his body with my lips.

I figure now is probably a good time to fulfill that promise.

I start at his mouth, move to his cheek, under his jawline, down his neck to his shoulders and his arms, which are wrapped around me. His hands are skimming my suit and he's so hot, so tense from the effort to remain still but I can hear his heart beating hard, too fast against his chest.

Against mine.

I trace the white bird soaring across his skin, a tattoo of the one impossible thing I hope to see in my life. A bird. White with streaks of gold like a crown atop its head.

It will fly.

Birds don't fly, is what the scientists say, but history says they used to. And one day I want to see it. I want to touch it. I want to watch it fly like it should, like it hasn't been able to in my dreams.

I dip down to kiss the yellow crown of its head, tattooed deep into Adam's chest. I hear the spike in his breathing.

"I love this tattoo," I tell him, looking up to meet his eyes. "I haven't seen it since we got here. I haven't seen you without a shirt on since we got here," I whisper. "Do you still sleep without your shirt on?"

But Adam answers with a strange smile, like he's laughing at his own private joke.

He takes my hand from his chest and tugs me down so we're facing each other, and it's strange, because I haven't felt a breeze since we got here, but it's like the wind has found a home in my body and it's funneling through my lungs, blowing through my blood, mingling with my breath and making it hard for me to breathe.

"I can't sleep at all," he says to me, his voice so low I have to strain to hear it. "It doesn't feel right to be without you every night." His left hand is threaded in my hair, his right wrapped around me. "God I've missed you," he says, his words a husky whisper in my ear. "Juliette."

I am

lit

on fire.

It's like swimming in molasses, this kiss, it's like being dipped in gold, this kiss, it's like I'm diving into an ocean of emotion and I'm too swept up in the current to realize I'm drowning and nothing even matters anymore. Not my hand which no longer seems to hurt, not this room that isn't entirely mine, not this war we're supposed to be fighting, not my worries about who or what I am and what I might become.

This is the only thing that matters.

This.

This moment. These lips. This strong body pressed against me and these firm hands finding a way to bring me closer and I know I want so much more of him, I want all of him, I want to feel the beauty of this love with the tips of my fingers and the palms of my hands and every fiber and bone in my being.

I want all of it.

My hands are in his hair and I'm reeling him in until

he's practically on top of me and he breaks for air but I pull him back, kissing his neck, his shoulders, his chest, running my hands down his back and the sides of his torso and it's incredible, the energy, the unbelievable power I feel in just *being* with him, touching him, holding him like this. I'm alive with a rush of adrenaline so potent, so euphoric that I feel rejuvenated, indestructible—

I jerk back.

Push away so quickly that I'm scrambling and I fall off the bed only to slam my head into the stone floor and I'm swaying as I attempt to stand, struggling to hear the sound of his voice but all I hear are wheezing, paralyzed breaths and I can't think straight, I can't see anything and everything is blurry and I can't, I refuse to believe this is actually happening—

"J-Jul—" He tries to speak. "I-I c-ca—"

And I fall to my knees.

Screaming.

Screaming like I've never screamed in my entire life.

FIFTEEN

I count everything.

Even numbers, odd numbers, multiples of 10. I count the ticks of the clock I count the tocks of the clock I count the lines between the lines on a sheet of paper. I count the broken beats of my heart I count my pulse and my blinks and the number of tries it takes to inhale enough oxygen for my lungs. I stay like this I stand like this I count like this until the feeling stops. Until the tears stop spilling, until my fists stop shaking, until my heart stops aching.

There are never enough numbers.

Adam is in the medical wing.

He is in the medical wing and I have been asked not to visit him. I have been asked to give him space, to give him time to heal, ~~to leave him the hell alone~~. He is going to be okay, is what Sonya and Sara told me. They told me not to worry, that everything would be fine, but their smiles were a little less exuberant than they usually are and I'm beginning to wonder if they, too, are finally beginning to see me for what I truly am.

A horrible, selfish, pathetic monster.

I took what I wanted. I knew better and I took it anyway. Adam couldn't have known, he could never have known what it would be like to really suffer at my hands. He was innocent of the depth of it, of the cruel reality of it. He'd only felt bursts of my power, according to Castle. He'd only felt small stabs of it and was able and aware enough to let go without feeling the full effects.

But I knew better.

I knew what I was capable of. I knew what the risks were and I did it anyway. I allowed myself to forget, to be reckless, to be greedy and stupid because I wanted what I couldn't have. I wanted to believe in fairy tales and happy endings and pure possibility. I wanted to pretend that I was a better person than I actually am but instead I managed to out myself as the terror I've always been accused of being.

~~My parents were right to get rid of me.~~

Castle isn't even speaking to me.

Kenji, however, still expects me to show up at 6:00 a.m. for whatever it is we're supposed to be doing tomorrow, and I find I'm actually kind of grateful for the distraction. I only wish it would come sooner. Life will be solitary for me from now on, just as it always has been, and it's best if I find a way to fill my time.

To forget.

It keeps hitting me, over and over and over again, this complete and utter loneliness. This absence of him in my life, this realization that I will never know the warmth of his body, the tenderness of his touch ever again. This reminder of who I am and what I've done and where I belong.

But I've accepted the terms and conditions of my new reality.

I cannot be with him. I will not be with him. I won't risk

hurting him again, won't risk becoming the creature he's always afraid of, too scared to touch, to kiss, to hold. I don't want to keep him from having a normal life with someone who isn't going to accidentally kill him all the time.

So I have to cut myself out of his world. Cut him out of mine.

It's much harder now. So much harder to resign myself to an existence of ice and emptiness now that I've known heat, urgency, tenderness, and passion; the extraordinary comfort of being able to touch another being.

It's humiliating.

That I thought I could slip into the role of a regular girl with a regular boyfriend; that I thought I could live out the stories I'd read in so many books as a child.

Me.

Juliette with a dream.

Just the thought of it is enough to fill me with mortification. How embarrassing for me, that I thought I could change what I'd been dealt. That I looked in the mirror and actually liked the pale face staring back at me.

How sad.

I always dared to identify with the princess, the one who runs away and finds a fairy godmother to transform her into a beautiful girl with a bright future. I clung to something like hope, to a thread of maybes and possiblys and perhapses. But I should've listened when my parents told me that things like me aren't allowed to have dreams. ~~Things like me are better off destroyed, is what my mother said to me.~~

And I'm beginning to think they were right. I'm

beginning to wonder if I should just bury myself in the ground before I remember that technically, I already am. I never even needed a shovel.

It's strange.

How hollow I feel.

Like there might be echoes inside of me. Like I'm one of those chocolate rabbits they used to sell around Easter, the ones that were nothing more than a sweet shell encapsulating a world of nothing. I'm like that.

I encapsulate a world of nothing.

Everyone here hates me. The tenuous bonds of friendship I'd begun to form have now been destroyed. Kenji is tired of me. Castle is disgusted, disappointed, angry, even. I've caused nothing but trouble since I arrived and the 1 person who's ever tried to see good in me is now paying for it with his life.

The 1 person who's ever dared to touch me.

Well. 1 of 2.

I find myself thinking about Warner too much.

I remember his eyes and his odd kindness and his cruel, calculating demeanor. I remember the way he looked at me when I first jumped out the window to escape and I remember the horror on his face when I pointed his own gun at his heart and then I wonder at my preoccupation with this person who is nothing like me ~~and still so similar~~.

I wonder if I will have to face him again, sometime soon, and I wonder how he will greet me. I have no idea if he wants to keep me alive anymore, especially not after I tried to kill him, and I have no idea what could propel a 19-year-old man boy person into such a miserable, murderous lifestyle and then I realize I'm lying to myself. Because I do know. Because I might be the only person who could ever understand him.

And this is what I've learned:

I know that he is a tortured soul who, like me, never grew up with the warmth of friendship or love or peaceful coexistence. I know that his father is the leader of The Reestablishment and applauds his son's murders instead of condemning them and I know that Warner has no idea what it's like to be normal.

~~Neither do I.~~

He's spent his life fighting to fulfill his father's expectations of global domination without questioning why, without considering the repercussions, without stopping long enough to weigh the worth of a human life. He has a power, a strength, a position in society that enables him to do too much damage and he owns it with pride. He kills without remorse or regret and he wants me to join him. He sees me for what I am and expects me to live up to that potential.

Scary, monstrous girl with a lethal touch. Sad, pathetic girl with nothing else to contribute to this world. Good for nothing but a weapon, a tool for torture and taking control. That's what he wants from me.

And lately I'm not sure if he's wrong. Lately, I'm not sure of anything. Lately, I don't know anything about anything

I've ever believed in, not anymore, and I know the least about who I am. Warner's whispers pace the space in my head, telling me I could be more, I could be stronger, I could be everything; I could be so much more than a scared little girl.

He says I could be power.

But still, I hesitate.

Still, I see no appeal in the life he's offered. I see no future in it. I take no pleasure in it. Still, I tell myself, despite everything, I know that I do not *want* to hurt people. It's not something I crave. And even if the world hates me, even if they never stop hating me, I will never avenge myself on an innocent person. If I die, if I am killed, if I am murdered in my sleep, I will at least die with a shred of dignity. A piece of humanity that is still entirely mine, entirely under my control. And I will not allow anyone to take that from me.

So I have to keep remembering that Warner and I are 2 different words.

We are synonyms but not the same.

Synonyms know each other like old colleagues, like a set of friends who've seen the world together. They swap stories, reminisce about their origins and forget that though they are similar, they are entirely different, and though they share a certain set of attributes, one can never be the other. Because a quiet night is not the same as a silent one, a firm man is not the same as a steady one, and a bright light is not the same as a brilliant one because the way they wedge themselves into a sentence changes everything.

They are not the same.

I've spent my entire life fighting to be better. Fighting to be stronger. Because unlike Warner I don't want to be a terror on this Earth. I don't want to hurt people.

I don't want to use my power to hurt anyone.

But then I look at my own 2 hands and I remember exactly what I'm capable of. I remember exactly what I've done and I'm too aware of what I might do. Because it's so difficult to fight what you cannot control and right now I can't even control my own imagination as it grips my hair and drags me into the dark.

SIXTEEN

Loneliness is a strange sort of thing.

It creeps up on you, quiet and still, sits by your side in the dark, strokes your hair as you sleep. It wraps itself around your bones, squeezing so tight you almost can't breathe. It leaves lies in your heart, lies next to you at night, leaches the light out from every corner. It's a constant companion, clasping your hand only to yank you down when you're struggling to stand up.

You wake up in the morning and wonder who you are. You fail to fall asleep at night and tremble in your skin. You doubt you doubt you doubt

do I

don't I

should I

why won't I

And even when you're ready to let go. When you're ready to break free. When you're ready to be brand-new. Loneliness is an old friend standing beside you in the mirror, looking you in the eye, challenging you to live your life without it. You can't find the words to fight yourself, to fight the words screaming that you're not enough never enough never ever enough.

Loneliness is a bitter, wretched companion.

Sometimes it just won't let go.

"Helloooooo?"

I blink and gasp and flinch away from the fingers snapping in front of my face as the familiar stone walls of Omega Point come back into focus. I manage to spin around.

Kenji is staring at me.

"What?" I shoot him a panicked, nervous look as I clasp and unclasp my ungloved hands, wishing I had something warm to wrap my fingers in. This suit does not come with pockets and I wasn't able to salvage the gloves I ruined in the research rooms. I haven't received any replacements, either.

"You're early," Kenji says to me, cocking his head, watching me with eyes both surprised and curious.

I shrug and try to hide my face, unwilling to admit that I hardly slept through the night. I've been awake since 3:00 a.m., fully dressed and ready to go by 4:00. I've been dying for an excuse to fill my mind with things that have nothing to do with my own thoughts. "I'm excited," I lie. "What are we doing today?"

He shakes his head a bit. Squints at something over my shoulder as he speaks to me. "You, um"—he clears his throat—"you okay?"

"Yes, of course."

"Huh."

"What?"

"Nothing," he says quickly. "Just, you know." A haphazard gesture toward my face. "You don't look so good, princess.

111

You look kind of like you did that first day you showed up with Warner back on base. All scared and dead-looking and, no offense, but you look like you could use a shower."

I smile and pretend I can't feel my face shaking from the effort. I try to relax my shoulders, try to look normal, calm, when I say, "I'm fine. Really." I drop my eyes. "I'm just— it's a little cold down here, that's all. I'm not used to being without my gloves."

Kenji is nodding, still not looking at me. "Right. Well. He's going to be okay, you know."

"What?" Breathing. I'm so bad at breathing.

"Kent." He turns to me. "Your boyfriend. *Adam*. He's going to be fine."

1 word, 1 simple, stupid reminder of him startles the butterflies sleeping in my stomach before I remember that Adam is not my boyfriend anymore. He's not my anything anymore. He can't be.

And the butterflies drop dead.

~~This.~~

~~I can't do this.~~

"So," I say too brightly. "Shouldn't we get going? We should get going, right?"

Kenji shoots me an odd look but doesn't comment. "Yeah," he says. "Yeah, sure. Follow me."

SEVENTEEN

Kenji leads me to a door I've never seen before. A door belonging to a room I've never been in before.

I hear voices inside.

Kenji knocks twice before turning the handle and all at once the cacophony overwhelms me. We're walking into a room bursting with people, faces I've only ever seen from far away, people sharing smiles and laughter I've never been welcome to. There are individual desks with individual chairs set up in the vast space so that it resembles a classroom. There's a whiteboard built into the wall next to a monitor blinking with information. I spot Castle. Standing in the corner, looking over a clipboard with such focus that he doesn't even notice our entry until Kenji shouts a greeting.

Castle's entire face lights up.

I'd noticed it before, the connection between them, but it's now becoming increasingly apparent to me that Castle harbors a special kind of affection for Kenji. A sweet, proud sort of affection that's usually reserved for parents. It makes me wonder about the nature of their relationship. Where it began, how it began, what must've happened to bring them together. It makes me wonder at how little I know about the people of Omega Point.

I look around at their eager faces, men and women, youthful and middle-aged, all different ethnicities, shapes, and sizes. They're interacting with one another like they're part of a family and I feel a strange sort of pain stabbing at my side, poking holes in me until I deflate.

It's like my face is pressed up against the glass, watching a scene from far, far away, wishing and wanting to be a part of something I know I'll never really be a part of. I forget, sometimes, that there are people out there who still manage to smile every day, despite everything.

They haven't lost hope yet.

Suddenly I feel sheepish, ashamed, even. Daylight makes my thoughts look dark and sad and I want to pretend I'm still optimistic, I want to believe that I'll find a way to live. That maybe, somehow, there's still a chance for me somewhere.

Someone whistles.

"All right, everyone," Kenji calls out, hands cupped around his mouth. "Everyone take a seat, okay? We're doing another orientation for those of you who've never done this before, and I need all of you to get settled for a bit." He scans the crowd. "Right. Yeah. Everyone just take a seat. Wherever is fine. Lily—you don't have to—okay, fine, that's fine. Just settle down. We're going to get started in five minutes, okay?" He holds up an open palm, fingers splayed. "Five minutes."

I slip into the closest empty seat without looking around. I keep my head down, my eyes focused on the individual grains of wood on the desk as everyone collapses into chairs around me. Finally, I dare to glance to my right. Bright white hair and snow-white skin and clear blue eyes blink back at me.

Brendan. The electricity boy.

He smiles. Offers me a 2-finger wave.

I duck my head.

"Oh—hey," I hear someone say. "What are you doing here?"

I jerk toward my left to find sandy-blond hair and black plastic glasses sitting on a crooked nose. An ironic smile twisted onto a pale face. *Winston.* I remember him. He interviewed me when I first arrived at Omega Point. Said he was some kind of psychologist. But he also happens to be the one who designed the suit I'm wearing. The gloves I destroyed.

I think he's some kind of genius. I'm not sure.

Right now, he's chewing on the cap of his pen, staring at me. He uses an index finger to push his glasses up the bridge of his nose. I remember he's asked me a question and I make an effort to answer.

"I'm not actually sure," I tell him. "Kenji brought me here but didn't tell me why."

Winston doesn't seem surprised. He rolls his eyes. "Him with the freaking mysteries all the time. I don't know why he thinks it's such a good idea to keep people in suspense. It's like the guy thinks his life is a movie or something. Always so dramatic about everything. It's irritating as hell."

I have no idea what I'm supposed to say to that. ~~I can't help thinking that Adam would agree with him and then I can't help thinking about Adam and then I~~

"Ah, don't listen to him." An English accent steps into

115

the conversation. I turn around to see Brendan still smiling at me. "Winston's always a bit beastly this early in the morning."

"Jesus. How early *is* it?" Winston asks. "I would kick a soldier in the crotch for a cup of coffee right now."

"It's your own fault you never sleep, mate," Brendan counters. "You think you can survive on three hours a night? You're mad."

Winston drops his chewed-up pen on the desk. Runs a tired hand through his hair. Tugs his glasses off and rubs at his face. "It's the freaking patrols. Every goddamn night. Something is going on and it's getting intense out there. So many soldiers just walking around? What the hell are they doing? I have to actually be *awake* the whole time—"

"What are you talking about?" I ask before I can stop myself. My ears are perked and my interest is piqued. News from the outside is something I've never had the opportunity to hear before. Castle was so intent on me focusing all my energy on training that I never heard much more than his constant reminders that *we're running out of time* and that I *need to learn before it's too late*. I'm beginning to wonder if things are worse than I thought.

"The patrols?" Brendan asks. He waves a knowing hand. "Oh, it's just, we work in shifts, right? In pairs—take turns keeping watch at night," he explains. "Most of the time it's no problem, just routine, nothing too serious."

"But it's been weird lately," Winston cuts in. "It's like they're *really* searching for us now. Like it's not just some

116

crazy theory anymore. They know we're a real threat and it's like they actually have a clue where we are." He shakes his head. "But that's impossible."

"Apparently not, mate."

"Well, whatever it is, it's starting to freak me out," Winston says. "There are soldiers all over the place, way too close to where we are. We see them on camera," he says to me, noticing my confusion. "And the weirdest part," he adds, leaning in, lowering his voice, "is that Warner is always with them. Every single night. Walking around, issuing orders I can't hear. And his arm is still injured. He walks around with it in a sling."

"Warner?" My eyes go wide. "He's with them? Is that—is that . . . unusual?"

"It's quite odd," Brendan says. "He's CCR—chief commander and regent—of Sector 45. In normal circumstances he would delegate this task to a colonel, a lieutenant, even. His priorities should be on base, overseeing his soldiers." Brendan shakes his head. "He's a bit daft, I think, taking a risk like that. Spending time away from his own camp. Seems strange that he'd be able to get away so many nights."

"Right," Winston says, nodding his head. "Exactly." He points at the 2 of us, stabbing at the air. "And it makes you wonder who he's leaving in charge. The guy doesn't trust anyone—he's not known for his delegation skills to begin with—so for him to leave the base behind every night?" A pause. "It doesn't add up. Something is going on."

"Do you think," I ask, feeling scared and feeling brave, "that maybe he's looking for ~~someone~~ something?"

"Yup." Winston exhales. Scratches the side of his nose. "That's exactly what I think. And I'd love to know what the hell he's looking for."

"Us, obviously," Brendan says. "He's looking for us."

Winston seems unconvinced. "I don't know," he says. "This is different. They've been searching for us for years, but they've never done anything like this. Never spent so much manpower on this kind of a mission. And they've never gotten this close."

"Wow," I whisper, not trusting myself to posit any of my own theories. Not wanting to think too hard about ~~who~~ what it is, exactly, Warner is searching for. And all the time wondering why these 2 guys are speaking to me so freely, as if I'm trustworthy, as if I'm one of their own.

I don't dare mention it.

"Yeah," Winston says, picking up his chewed-up pen again. "Crazy. Anyway, if we don't get a fresh batch of coffee today, I am seriously going to lose my shit."

I look around the room. I don't see coffee anywhere. No food, either. I wonder what that means for Winston. "Are we going to have breakfast before we start?"

"Nah," he says. "Today we get to eat on a different schedule. Besides, we'll have plenty to choose from when we get back. We get first picks. It's the only perk."

"Get back from where?"

"Outside," Brendan says, leaning back in his chair. He

118

points up at the ceiling. "We're going up and out."

"What?" I gasp, feeling true excitement for the first time. "Really?"

"Yup." Winston puts his glasses back on. "And it looks like you're about to get your first introduction to what it is we do here." He nods at the front of the room, and I see Kenji hauling a huge trunk onto a table.

"What do you mean?" I ask. "What are we doing?"

"Oh, you know." Winston shrugs. Clasps his hands behind his head. "Grand larceny. Armed robbery. That sort of thing."

I begin to laugh when Brendan stops me. He actually puts his hand on my shoulder and for a moment I'm mildly terrified. Wondering if he's lost his mind.

"He's not joking," Brendan says to me. "And I hope you know how to use a gun."

EIGHTEEN

We look homeless.

Which means we look like civilians.

We've moved out of the classroom and into the hallway, and we're all wearing a similar sort of ensemble, tattered and grayish and frayed. Everyone is adjusting their outfits as we go; Winston slips off his glasses and shoves them into his jacket only to zip up his coat. The collar comes up to his chin and he huddles into it. Lily, one of the other girls among us, wraps a thick scarf around her mouth and pulls the hood of her coat over her head. I see Kenji pull on a pair of gloves and readjust his cargo pants to better hide the gun tucked inside.

Brendan shifts beside me.

He pulls a skullcap out of his pocket and tugs it on over his head, zipping his coat up to his neck. It's startling the way the blackness of the beanie offsets the blue in his eyes to make them even brighter, sharper than they looked before. He flashes me a smile when he catches me watching. Then he tosses me a pair of old gloves 2 sizes too big before bending down to tighten the laces on his boots.

I take a small breath.

I try to focus all my energy on where I am, on what I'm

doing and what I'm about to do. I tell myself not to think of Adam, not to think about what he's doing or how he's healing or what he must be feeling right now. I beg myself not to dwell on my last moments with him, the way he touched me, how he held me, his lips and his hands and his breaths coming in too fast—

I fail.

I can't help but think about how he always tried to protect me, how he nearly lost his life in the process. He was always defending me, always watching out for me, never realizing that it was *me*, it was always *me* who was the biggest threat. The most dangerous. He thinks too highly of me, places me on a pedestal I've never deserved.

I definitely don't need protection.

I don't need anyone to worry for me or wonder about me or risk falling in love with me. ~~I am unstable. I need to be avoided. It's right that people fear~~ me.

~~They should.~~

"Hey." Kenji stops beside me, grabs my elbow. "You ready?"

I nod. Offer him a small smile.

The clothes I'm wearing are borrowed. The card hanging from my neck, hidden under my suit, is brand-new. Today I was given a fake RR card—a Reestablishment Registration card. It's proof that I work and live on the compounds; proof that I'm registered as a citizen in regulated territory. Every legal citizen has one. I never did, because I was tossed into an asylum; it was never necessary for someone like me. In fact, I'm fairly certain they just expected me to die in there. Identification was not necessary.

But this RR card is special.

Not everyone at Omega Point receives a counterfeit card. Apparently they're extremely difficult to replicate. They're thin rectangles made out of a very rare type of titanium, laser-etched with a bar code as well as the owner's biographical data, and contain a tracking device that monitors the whereabouts of the citizen.

"RR cards track everything," Castle explained. "They're necessary for entering and exiting compounds, necessary for entering and exiting a person's place of work. Citizens are paid in REST dollars—wages based on a complicated algorithm that calculates the difficulty of their profession, as well as the number of hours they spend working, in order to determine how much their efforts are worth. This electronic currency is dispensed in weekly installments and automatically uploaded to a chip built into their RR cards. REST dollars can then be exchanged at Supply Centers for food and basic necessities. Losing an RR card," he said, "means losing your livelihood, your earnings, your legal status as a registered citizen.

"If you're stopped by a soldier and asked for proof of identification," Castle continued, "you must present your RR card. Failure to present your card," he said, "will result in . . . very unhappy consequences. Citizens who walk around without their cards are considered a threat to The Reestablishment. They are seen as purposely defying the law, as characters worthy of suspicion. Being uncooperative in any way—even if that means you simply do not want your every movement to be tracked and monitored—makes you seem sympathetic to rebel parties. And that makes you a threat. A threat," he said, "that The Reestablishment has no qualms about removing.

"Therefore," he said, taking a deep breath, "you cannot, and you will not, lose your RR card. Our counterfeit cards do not have the tracking device nor the chip necessary for monitoring REST dollars, because we don't have the need for either. But! That does not mean they are not just as valuable as decoys," he said. "And while for citizens on regulated territory, RR cards are part of a life sentence, at Omega Point, they are considered a privilege. And you will treat them as such."

A privilege.

Among the many things I learned in our meeting this morning, I discovered that these cards are only granted to those who go on missions outside of Omega Point. All of the people in that room today were hand-selected as being the best, the strongest, the most trustworthy. Inviting me to be in that room was a bold move on Kenji's part. I realize now that it was his way of telling me he trusts me. Despite everything, he's telling me—and everyone else—that I'm welcome here. Which explains why Winston and Brendan felt so comfortable opening up to me. Because they trust the system at Omega Point. And they trust Kenji if he says he trusts me.

So now I am one of them.

And as my first official act as a member?

I'm supposed to be a thief.

NINETEEN

We're heading up.

Castle should be joining us any moment now to lead our group out of this underground city and into the real world. It will be my first opportunity to see what's happened to our society in almost 3 years.

I was 14 when I was dragged away from home for killing an innocent child. I spent 2 years bouncing from hospital to law office to detention center to psych ward until they finally decided to put me away for good. Sticking me in the asylum was worse than sending me to prison; ~~smarter, according to my parents.~~ If I'd been sent to prison, the guards would've had to treat me like a human being; instead, I spent the past year of my life treated like a rabid animal, trapped in a dark hole with no link to the outside world. Most everything I've witnessed of our planet thus far has been out of a window or while running for my life. And now I'm not sure what to expect.

But I want to see it.

I need to see it.

I'm tired of being blind and I'm tired of relying on my memories of the past and the bits and pieces I've managed to scrape together of our present.

All I really know is that The Reestablishment has been a household name for 10 years.

I know this because they began campaigning when I was 7 years old. I'll never forget the beginning of our falling apart. I remember the days when things were still fairly normal, when people were only sort-of dying all the time, when there was enough food for those with enough money to pay for it. This was before cancer became a common illness and the weather became a turbulent, angry creature. I remember how excited everyone was about The Reestablishment. I remember the hope in my teachers' faces and the announcements we were forced to watch in the middle of the school day. I remember those things.

And just 4 months before my 14-year-old self committed an unforgivable crime, The Reestablishment was elected by the people of our world to lead us into a better future.

Hope. They had so much hope. My parents, my neighbors, my teachers and classmates. Everyone was hoping for the best when they cheered for The Reestablishment and promised their unflagging support.

Hope can make people do terrible things.

I remember seeing the protests just before I was taken away. I remember seeing the streets flooded with angry mobs who wanted a refund on their purchase. I remember how The Reestablishment painted the protesters red from head to toe and told them they should've read the fine print before they left their houses that morning.

All sales are final.

Castle and Kenji are allowing me on this expedition because they're trying to welcome me into the heart of Omega Point. They want me to join them, to really accept them, to understand why their mission is so important. Castle wants me to fight against The Reestablishment and what they have planned for the world. The books, the artifacts, the language and history they plan on destroying; the simple, empty, monochromatic life they want to force upon the upcoming generations. He wants me to see that our Earth is still not so damaged as to be irreparable; he wants to prove that our future is salvageable, that things can get better as long as power is put in the right hands.

He wants me to trust.

I *want* to trust.

But I get scared, sometimes. In my very limited experience I've already found that people seeking power are not to be trusted. People with lofty goals and fancy speeches and easy smiles have done nothing to calm my heart. Men with guns have never put me at ease no matter how many times they promised they were killing for good reason.

It has not gone past my notice that the people of Omega Point are very excellently armed.

But I'm curious. I'm so desperately curious.

So I'm camouflaged in old, ragged clothes and a thick woolen hat that nearly covers my eyes. I wear a heavy jacket that must've belonged to a man and my leather boots are almost hidden by the too-large trousers puddling around my ankles. I look like a civilian. A poor, tortured civilian struggling to find food for her family.

A door clicks shut and we all turn at once. Castle beams. Looks around at the group of us.

Me. Winston. Kenji. Brendan. The girl named Lily. 10 other people I still don't really know. We're 16 altogether, including Castle. A perfectly even number.

"All right, everyone," Castle says, clapping his hands together. I notice he's wearing gloves, too. Everyone is. Today, I'm just a girl in a group wearing normal clothes and normal gloves. Today, I'm just a number. No one of significance. Just an ordinary person. Just for today.

It's so absurd I feel like smiling.

And then I remember how I nearly killed Adam yesterday and suddenly I'm not sure how to move my lips.

"Are we ready?" Castle looks around. "Don't forget what we discussed," he says. A pause. A careful glance. Eye contact with each one of us. Eyes on me for a moment too long. "Okay then. Follow me."

No one really speaks as we follow Castle down these corridors, and I'm left to wonder how easy it would be to just disappear in this inconspicuous outfit. I could run away, blend into the background and never be found again.

~~Like a coward.~~

I search for something to say to shake the silence. "So how are we getting there?" I ask anyone.

"We walk," Winston says.

Our feet pound the floors in response.

"Most civilians don't have cars," Kenji explains. "And we sure as hell can't be caught in a tank. If we want to blend in, we have to do as the people do. And walk."

I lose track of which tunnels break off in which directions as Castle leads us toward the exit. I'm increasingly aware of how little I understand about this place, how little I've seen of it. Although if I'm perfectly honest, I'll admit I haven't made much of an effort to explore anything.

I need to do something about that.

It's only when the terrain under my feet changes that I realize how close we are to getting outside. We're walking uphill, up a series of stone stairs stacked into the ground. I can see what looks like a small square of a metal door from here. It has a latch.

I realize I'm a little nervous.

Anxious.

Eager and afraid.

Today I will see the world as a civilian, really see things up close for the very first time. I will see what the people of this new society must endure now.

~~See what my parents must be experiencing wherever they are.~~

Castle pauses at the door, which looks small enough to be a window. Turns to face us. "Who are you?" he demands.

No one answers.

Castle draws himself up to his full height. Crosses his arms. "Lily," he says. "Name. ID. Age. Sector and occupation. *Now.*"

Lily tugs the scarf away from her mouth. She sounds slightly robotic when she says, "My name is Erica Fontaine, 1117-52QZ. I'm twenty-six years old. I live in Sector 45."

"Occupation," Castle says again, a hint of impatience creeping into his voice.

"Textile. Factory 19A-XC2."

"Winston," Castle orders.

"My name is Keith Hunter, 4556-65DS," Winston says. "Thirty-four years old. Sector 45. I work in Metal. Factory 15B-XC2."

Kenji doesn't wait for a prompt when he says, "Hiro Yamasaki, 8891-11DX. Age twenty. Sector 45. Artillery. 13A-XC2."

Castle nods as everyone takes turns regurgitating the information etched into their fake RR cards. He smiles, satisfied. Then he focuses his eyes on me until everyone is staring, watching, waiting to see if I screw it up.

"Delia Dupont," I say, the words slipping from my lips more easily than I expected.

We're not planning on being stopped, but this is an extra precaution in the event that we're asked to identify ourselves; we have to know the information on our RR cards as if it were our own. Kenji also said that even though the soldiers overseeing the compounds are from Sector 45, they're always different from the guards back on base. He doesn't think we'll run into anyone who will recognize us.

But.

Just in case.

I clear my throat. "ID number 1223-99SX. Seventeen years old. Sector 45. I work in Metal. Factory 15A-XC2."

Castle stares at me for just a second too long.

Finally, he nods. Looks around at all of us. "And what," he says, his voice deep and clear and booming, "are the three things you will ask yourself before you speak?"

Again, no one answers. Though it's not because we don't know the answer.

Castle counts off on his fingers. "First! *Does this need to be said?* Second! *Does this need to be said by me?* And third! *Does this need to be said by me right now?*"

Still, no one says a word.

"We do not speak unless absolutely necessary," Castle says. "We do not laugh, we do not smile. We do not make eye contact with one another if we can help it. We will not act as if we know each other. We are to do nothing at all to encourage extra glances in our direction. We do not draw attention to ourselves." A pause. "You understand this, yes? This is clear?"

We nod.

"And if something goes wrong?"

"We scatter." Kenji clears his throat. "We run. We hide. We think of only ourselves. And we never, ever betray the location of Omega Point."

Everyone takes a deep breath at the same time.

Castle pushes the small door open. Peeks outside before motioning for us to follow him, and we do. We scramble through, one by one, silent as the words we don't speak.

I haven't been aboveground in almost 3 weeks. It feels

like it's been 3 months.

The moment my face hits the air, I feel the wind snap against my skin in a way that's familiar, admonishing. It's as if the wind is scolding me for being away for so long.

We're in the middle of a frozen wasteland. The air is icy and sharp, dead leaves dancing around us. The few trees still standing are waving in the wind, their broken, lonely branches begging for companionship. I look left. I look right. I look straight ahead.

There is nothing.

Castle told us this area used to be covered in lush, dense vegetation. He said when he first sought out a hiding place for Omega Point, this particular stretch of ground was ideal. But that was so long ago—decades ago—that now everything has changed. Nature itself has changed. And it's too late to move this hideout.

So we do what we can.

This part, he said, is the hardest. Out here, we're vulnerable. Easy to spot even as civilians because we're out of place. Civilians have no business being anywhere outside of the compounds; they do not leave the regulated grounds deemed safe by The Reestablishment. Being caught anywhere on unregulated turf is considered a breach of the laws set in place by our new pseudogovernment, and the consequences are severe.

So we have to get ourselves to the compounds as quickly as possible.

The plan is for Kenji—whose gift enables him to blend

into any background—to travel ahead of the pack, making himself invisible as he checks to make sure our paths are clear. The rest of us hang back, careful, completely silent. We keep a few feet of distance between ourselves, ready to run, to save ourselves if necessary. It's strange, considering the tight-knit nature of the community at Omega Point, that Castle wouldn't encourage us to stay together. But this, he explained, is for the good of the majority. It's a sacrifice. One of us has to be willing to get caught in order for the others to escape.

Take one for the team.

Our path is clear.

We've been walking for at least half an hour and no one seems to be guarding this deserted piece of land. Soon, the compounds come into view. Blocks and blocks and blocks of metal boxes, cubes clustered in heaps across the ancient, wheezing ground. I clutch my coat closer to my body as the wind flips on its side just to fillet our human flesh.

It's too cold to be alive today.

I'm wearing my suit—which regulates my body heat—under this outfit and I'm still freezing. I can't imagine what everyone else must be going through right now. I glance at Brendan only to find him already doing the same. Our eyes meet for less than a second but I could swear he smiled at me, his cheeks slapped into pinks and reds by a wind jealous of his wandering eyes.

Blue. So blue.

Such a different, lighter, almost transparent shade of blue but still, so very, very blue. Blue eyes will always remind me of Adam, I think. And it hits me again. Hits me so hard, right in the core of my very being.

The ache.

"Hurry!" Kenji's voice reaches us through the wind, but his body is nowhere in sight. We're not 5 feet from setting foot in the first cluster of compounds, but I'm somehow frozen in place, blood and ice and broken forks running down my back.

"MOVE!" Kenji's voice booms again. "Get close to the compounds and keep your faces covered! Soldiers at three o'clock!"

We all jump up at once, rushing forward while trying to remain inconspicuous and soon we've ducked behind the side of a metal housing unit; we get low, each pretending to be one of the many people picking scraps of steel and iron out from the heaps of trash stacked in piles all over the ground.

The compounds are set in one big field of waste. Garbage and plastic and mangled bits of metal sprinkled like craft confetti all over a child's floor. There's a fine layer of snow powdered over everything, as if the Earth was making a weak attempt to cover up its ugly bits just before we arrived.

I look up.

Look over my shoulder.

Look around in ways I'm not supposed to but I can't help it. I'm supposed to keep my eyes on the ground like I live here, like there's nothing new to see, like I can't stand to lift my face only to have it stung by the cold. I should be huddled into myself like all the other strangers trying to stay warm. But there's so much to see. So much to observe. So much I've never been exposed to before.

So I dare to lift my head.

And the wind grabs me by the throat.

TWENTY

Warner is standing not 20 feet away from me.

His suit is tailor-made and closely fitted to his form in a shade of black so rich it's almost blinding. His shoulders are draped in an open peacoat the color of mossy trunks 5 shades darker than his green, green eyes; the bright gold buttons are the perfect complement to his golden hair. He's wearing a black tie. Black leather gloves. Shiny black boots.

He looks immaculate.

Flawless, especially as he stands here among the dirt and destruction, surrounded by the bleakest colors this landscape has to offer. He's a vision of emerald and onyx, silhouetted in the sunlight in the most deceiving way. He could be glowing. That could be a halo around his head. This could be the world's way of making an example out of irony. Because Warner is beautiful in ways even Adam isn't.

Because Warner is not human.

Nothing about him is normal.

He's looking around, eyes squinting against the morning light, and the wind blows open his unbuttoned coat long enough for me to catch a glimpse of his arm underneath. Bandaged. Bound in a sling.

So close.

I was so close.

The soldiers hovering around him are waiting for orders, waiting for something, and I can't tear my eyes away. I can't help but experience a strange thrill in being so close to him, and yet so far away. It feels almost like an advantage—being able to study him without his knowledge.

He is a strange, strange, twisted boy.

I don't know if I can forget what he did to me. What he made me do. How I came so close to killing all over again. I will hate him forever for it even though I'm sure I'll have to face him again.

One day.

I never thought I'd see Warner on the compounds. I had no idea he even visited the civilians—though, in truth, I never knew much about how he spent his days unless he spent them with me. I have no idea what he's doing here.

He finally says something to the soldiers and they nod, once, quickly. Then disappear.

I pretend to be focused on something just to the right of him, careful to keep my head down and cocked slightly to the side so he can't catch a glimpse of my face even if he does look in my direction. My left hand reaches up to tug my hat down over my ears, and my right hand pretends to sort trash, pretends to pick out pieces of scraps to salvage for the day.

This is how some people make their living. Another miserable occupation.

Warner runs his good hand over his face, covering his eyes for just a moment before his hand rests on his mouth, pressing against his lips as though he has something he can't bear to say.

His eyes look almost . . . worried. Though I'm sure I'm just reading him wrong.

I watch him as he watches the people around him. I watch him closely enough to be able to notice that his gaze lingers on the small children, the way they run after each other with an innocence that says they have no idea what kind of world they've lost. This bleak, dark place is the only thing they've ever known.

I try to read Warner's expression as he studies them, but he's careful to keep himself completely neutral. He doesn't do more than blink as he stands perfectly still, a statue in the wind.

A stray dog is heading straight toward him.

I'm suddenly petrified. I'm worried for this scrappy creature, this weak, frozen little animal probably seeking out small bits of food, something to keep it from starving for the next few hours. My heart starts racing in my chest, the blood pumping too fast and too hard and

I don't know why I feel like something terrible is about to happen.

The dog bolts right into the backs of Warner's legs, as if it's half blind and can't see where it's going. It's panting hard, tongue lolling to the side like it doesn't know how to get it back in. It whines and whimpers a little, slobbering all over Warner's very exquisite pants and I'm holding my breath as the golden boy turns around. I half expect him to take out his gun and shoot the dog right in the head.

I've already seen him do it to a human being.

But Warner's face breaks apart at the sight of the small dog, cracks forming in the perfect cast of his features, surprise lifting his eyebrows and widening his gaze for just a moment. Long enough for me to notice.

He looks around, his eyes swift as they survey his surroundings before he scoops the animal into his arms and disappears around a low fence—one of the short, squat fences that are used to section off squares of land for each compound. I'm suddenly desperate to see what he's going to do and I'm feeling anxious, so anxious, still unable to breathe.

I've seen what Warner can do to a person. I've seen his callous heart and his unfeeling eyes and his complete indifference, his cool, collected demeanor unshaken after killing a man in cold blood. I can only imagine what he has planned for an innocent dog.

I have to see it for myself.

I have to get his face out of my head and this is exactly what I need. It's proof that he's sick, twisted, that he's wrong, and will always be wrong.

If only I could stand up, I could see him. I could see what he's doing to that poor animal and maybe I could find a way to stop him before it's too late but I hear Castle's voice, a loud whisper calling us. Telling us the coast is clear to move forward now that Warner is out of sight. "We all move, and we move separately," he says. "Stick to the plan! No one trails anyone else. We all meet at the drop-off. If you don't make it, we will leave you behind. You have thirty minutes."

Kenji is tugging on my arm, telling me to get to my feet, to focus, to look in the right direction. I look up long enough to see that the rest of the group has already dispersed; Kenji, however, refuses to budge. He curses under his breath until finally I stand up. I nod. I tell him I understand the plan and motion for him to move on without me. I remind him that we can't be seen together. That we cannot walk in groups or pairs. We cannot be conspicuous.

Finally, finally, he turns to go.

I watch Kenji leave. Then I take a few steps forward only to spin around and dart back to the corner of the compound, sliding my back up against the wall, hidden from view.

My eyes scan the area until I spot the fence where I last saw Warner; I tip up on my toes to peer over.

I have to cover my mouth to keep from gasping out loud.

Warner is crouched on the ground, feeding something to the dog with his good hand. The animal's quivering, bony body is huddled inside of Warner's open coat, shivering as its stubby limbs try to find warmth after being frozen for so long. The dog wags its tail hard, pulling back to look Warner in the eye only to plow into the warmth of his jacket again. I hear Warner laugh.

I see him smile.

It's the kind of smile that transforms him into someone else entirely, the kind of smile that puts stars in his eyes and a dazzle on his lips and I realize I've never seen him like this before. I've never even seen his teeth—so straight, so white, nothing less than perfect. A flawless, flawless exterior for a boy with a black, black heart. It's hard to believe there's blood on the hands of the person I'm staring at. He looks soft and vulnerable—so human. His eyes are squinting from all his grinning and his cheeks are pink from the cold.

He has *dimples*.

He's easily the most beautiful thing I've ever seen.

And I wish I'd never seen it.

Because something inside of my heart is ripping apart and it feels like fear, it tastes like panic and anxiety and desperation and I don't know how to understand the image in front of me. I don't want to see Warner like this. I don't want to think of him as anything other than a monster.

This isn't right.

I shift too fast and too far in the wrong direction, suddenly too stupid to find my footing and hating myself for wasting time I could've used to escape. I know Castle and Kenji would be ready to kill me for taking such a risk but they don't understand what it's like in my head right now, they don't understand what I'm—

"Hey!" he barks. "You there—"

I look up without intending to, without realizing that I've responded to Warner's voice until it's too late. He's up, frozen in place, staring straight into my eyes, his good hand paused midmovement until it falls limp at his side, his jaw slack; stunned, temporarily stupefied.

I watch as the words die in his throat.

I'm paralyzed, caught in his gaze as he stands there, his chest heaving so hard and his lips ready to form the words that will surely sentence me to my death, all because of my stupid, senseless, idiotic—

"Whatever you do, don't scream."

Someone closes a hand over my mouth.

TWENTY-ONE

I don't move.

"I'm going to let go of you, okay? I want you to take my hand."

I reach out without looking down and feel our gloved hands fit together. Kenji lets go of my face.

"You are such an *idiot*," he says to me, but I'm still staring at Warner. Warner who's now looking around like he's just seen a ghost, blinking and rubbing his eyes like he's confused, glancing at the dog like maybe the little animal managed to bewitch him. He grabs a tight hold of his blond hair, mussing it out of its perfect state, and stalks off so fast my eyes don't know how to follow him.

"What the hell is wrong with you?" Kenji is saying to me. "Are you even listening to me? Are you *insane*?"

"What did you just do? Why didn't he—oh my God," I gasp, sparing a look at my own body.

I'm completely invisible.

"You're welcome," Kenji snaps, dragging me away from the compound. "And keep your voice down. Being invisible doesn't mean the world can't hear you."

"You can *do* that?" I try to find his face but I might as well be speaking to the air.

"Yeah—it's called projecting, remember? Didn't Castle explain this to you already?" he asks, eager to rush through the explanation so he can get back to yelling at me. "Not everyone can do it—not all abilities are the same—but maybe if you manage to stop being a *dumbass* long enough not to *die*, I might be able to teach you one day."

"You came back for me," I say to him, struggling to keep up with his brisk pace and not at all offended by his anger. "Why'd you come back for me?"

"Because you're a *dumbass*," he says again.

"I know. I'm so sorry. I couldn't help it."

"Well, help it," he says, his voice gruff as he yanks me by the arm. "We're going to have to run to recover all the time you just wasted."

"Why'd you come back, Kenji?" I ask again, undeterred. "How'd you know I was still here?"

"I was watching you," he says.

"What? What do you—"

"I watch you," he says, his words rushing out again, impatient. "It's part of what I do. It's what I've been doing since day one. I enlisted in Warner's army for you and only you. It's what Castle sent me for. You were my job." His voice is clipped, fast, unfeeling. "I already told you this."

"Wait, what do you mean, you *watch* me?" I hesitate, tugging on his invisible arm to slow him down a little. "You follow me around everywhere? Even now? Even at Omega Point?"

He doesn't answer right away. When he does, his words are reluctant. "Sort of."

"But why? I'm here. Your job is done, isn't it?"

"We've already had this conversation," he says. "Remember? Castle wanted me to make sure you were okay. He told me to keep an eye on you—nothing serious—just, you know, make sure you weren't having any psychotic breakdowns or anything." I hear him sigh. "You've been through a lot. He's a little worried about you. Especially now—after what just happened? You don't look okay. You look like you want to throw yourself in front of a tank."

"I would never do something like that," I say to him.

"Yeah," he says. "Fine. Whatever. I'm just pointing out the obvious. You only function on two settings: you're either moping or you're making out with Adam—and I have to say, I kind of prefer the moping—"

"Kenji!" I nearly yank my hand out of his. His grip tightens around my fingers.

"Don't let go," he snaps at me again. "You can't let go or it breaks the connection." Kenji is dragging me through the middle of a clearing. We're far enough from the compounds now that we won't be overheard, but we're still too far from the drop-off to be considered safe just yet. Luckily the snow isn't sticking enough for us to leave tracks.

"I can't believe you spied on us!"

"I was not *spying* on you, okay? Damn. Calm down. Hell, both of you need to calm down. Adam was already all up in my face about it—"

"What?" I feel the pieces of this puzzle finally beginning

144

to fit together. "Is that why he was being mean to you at breakfast last week?"

Kenji slows our pace a little. He takes a deep, long breath. "He thought I was, like, taking *advantage* of the situation." He says *advantage* like it's a strange, dirty word. "He thinks I get invisible just to see you naked or something. Listen—I don't even know, okay? He was being an idiot about it. I'm just doing my job."

"But—you're not, right? You're not trying to see me naked or anything?"

Kenji snorts, chokes on his laughter. "Listen, Juliette," he says through another laugh, "I'm not blind, okay? On a purely physical level? Yeah, you're pretty sexy—and that suit you have to wear all the time doesn't hurt. But even if you didn't have that whole 'I kill you if I touch you' thing going on, you are *definitely* not my type. And more importantly, I'm not some perverted asshole," he says. "I take my job seriously. I get real shit done in this world, and I like to think people respect me for it. But your boy Adam is a little too blinded by his pants to think straight. Maybe you should do something about that."

I drop my eyes. Say nothing for a moment. Then: "I don't think you'll have to worry about that anymore."

"Ah, shit." Kenji sighs, like he can't believe he got stuck listening to problems about my love life. "I just walked right into that, didn't I?"

"We can go, Kenji. We don't have to talk about this."

An irritated breath. "It's not that I don't *care* about what

145

you're going through," he says. "It's not like I want to see you all depressed or whatever. It's just that this life is messed up enough as it is," he says. "And I'm sick of you being so caught up in your own little world all the time. You act like this whole thing—everything we do—is a joke. You don't take any of it seriously—"

"What?" I cut him off. "That's not true—I do take this seriously—"

"*Bullshit.*" He laughs a short, sharp, angry laugh. "All you do is sit around and think about your *feelings*. You've got *problems*. Boo-freaking-hoo," he says. "Your parents hate you and it's so hard but you have to wear gloves for the rest of your life because you kill people when you touch them. Who *gives* a shit?" He's breathing hard enough for me to hear him. "As far as I can tell, you've got food in your mouth and clothes on your back and a place to pee in peace whenever you feel like it. Those aren't problems. That's called living like a king. And I'd really appreciate it if you'd grow the hell up and stop walking around like the world crapped on your only roll of toilet paper. Because it's stupid," he says, barely reining in his temper. "It's stupid, and it's ungrateful. You don't have a clue what everyone else in the world is going through right now. You don't have a clue, Juliette. And you don't seem to give a damn, either."

I swallow, so hard.

"Now I am *trying*," he says, "to give you a chance to fix things. I keep giving you opportunities to do things differently. To see past the sad little girl you used to be—the

146

sad little girl you keep clinging to—and stand up for yourself. Stop crying. Stop sitting in the dark counting out all your individual feelings about how sad and lonely you are. Wake up," he says. "You're not the only person in this world who doesn't want to get out of bed in the morning. You're not the only one with daddy issues and severely screwed-up DNA. You can be whoever the hell you want to be now. You're not with your shitty parents anymore. You're not in that shitty asylum, and you're no longer stuck being Warner's shitty little experiment. So make a choice," he says. "Make a choice and stop wasting everyone's time. Stop wasting your own time. Okay?"

Shame is pooling in every inch of my body.

Heat has flamed its way up my core, singeing me from the inside out. I'm so horrified, so terrified to hear the truth in his words.

"Let's go," he says, but his voice is just a tiny bit gentler. "We have to run."

And I nod even though he can't see me.

I nod and nod and nod and I'm so happy no one can see my face right now.

TWENTY-TWO

"Stop throwing boxes at me, jackass. That's my job." Winston laughs and grabs a package heavily bandaged in cellophane only to chuck it at another guy's head. The guy standing right next to me.

I duck.

The other guy grunts as he catches the package, and then grins as he offers Winston an excellent view of his middle finger.

"Keep it classy, Sanchez," Winston says as he tosses him another package.

Sanchez. His name is Ian Sanchez. I just learned this a few minutes ago when he and I and a few others were grouped together to form an assembly line.

We are currently standing in one of the official storage compounds of The Reestablishment.

Kenji and I managed to catch up to everyone else just in time. We all congregated at the drop-off (which turned out to be little more than a glorified ditch), and then Kenji gave me a sharp look, pointed at me, grinned, and left me with the rest of the group while he and Castle communicated about the next part of our mission.

Which was getting into the storage compound.

The irony, however, is that we traveled aboveground for supplies only to have to go back underground to get them. The storage compounds are, for all intents and purposes, invisible.

They're underground cellars filled with just about everything imaginable: food, medicine, weapons. All the things needed to survive. Castle explained everything in our orientation this morning. He said that while having supplies buried underground is a clever method of concealment against the civilians, it actually worked out in his favor. Castle said he can sense—and move—objects from a great distance, even if that distance is 25 feet belowground. He said that when he approaches one of the storage facilities he can feel the difference immediately, because he can recognize the energy in each object. This, he explained, is what allows him to move things with his mind: he's able to touch the inherent energy in everything. Castle and Kenji have managed to track down 5 compounds within 20 miles of Omega Point just by walking around; Castle sensing, Kenji projecting to keep them invisible. They've located 5 more within 50 miles.

The storage compounds they access are on a rotation. They never take the same things and never in the same quantity, and they take from as many different facilities as possible. The farther the compound, the more intricate the mission becomes. This particular compound is closest, and therefore the mission is, relatively speaking, the easiest. That explains why I was allowed to come along.

All the legwork has already been done.

Brendan already knows how to confuse the electrical system in order to deactivate all the sensors and security cameras; Kenji acquired the pass code simply by shadowing a soldier who punched in the right numbers. All of this gives us a 30-minute window of time to work as quickly as possible to get everything we need into the drop-off, where we'll spend most of the day waiting to load our stolen supplies into vehicles that will carry the items away.

The system they use is fascinating.

There are 6 vans altogether, each slightly different in appearance, and all scheduled to arrive at different times. This way there are fewer chances of everyone being caught, and there's a higher probability that at least 1 of the vans will get back to Omega Point without a problem. Castle outlined what seemed like 100 different contingency plans in case of danger.

I'm the only one here, however, who appears even remotely nervous about what we're doing. In fact, with the exception of me and 3 others, everyone here has visited this particular compound several times, so they're walking around like it's familiar territory. Everyone is careful and efficient, but they feel comfortable enough to laugh and joke around, too. They know exactly what they're doing. The moment we got inside, they split themselves into 2 groups: 1 team formed the assembly line, and the other collected the things we need.

Others have more important tasks.

Lily has a photographic memory that puts photographs to shame. She walked in before the rest of us and immediately scanned the room, collecting and cataloging every minute detail. She's the one who will make sure that we leave nothing behind when we exit, and that, aside from the things we take, nothing else is missing or out of place. Brendan is our backup generator. He's managed to shut off power to the security system while still lighting the dark dimensions of this room. Winston is overseeing our 2 groups, mediating between the givers and the takers, making sure we're securing the right items and the right quantities. His arms and legs have the elastic ability to stretch at will, which enables him to reach both sides of the room quickly and easily.

Castle is the one who moves our supplies outside. He stands at the very end of the assembly line, in constant radio contact with Kenji. And as long as the area is clear, Castle needs to use only one hand to direct the hundreds of pounds of supplies we've hoarded into the drop-off.

Kenji, of course, is standing as lookout.

If it weren't for Kenji, the rest of this wouldn't even be possible. He's our invisible eyes and ears. Without him, we'd have no way of being so secure, so sure that we'll be safe on such a dangerous mission.

Not for the first time today, I'm beginning to realize why he's so important.

"Hey, Winston, can you get someone to check if they have any chocolate in here?" Emory—another guy on my assembly team—is smiling at Winston like he's hoping for good news. But then, Emory is always smiling. I've only known him for a few hours, but he's been smiling since 6:00 a.m., when we all met in the orientation room this morning. He's super tall, super bulky, and he has a super-huge afro that somehow manages to fall into his eyes a lot. He's moving boxes down the line like they're full of cotton.

Winston is shaking his head, trying not to laugh as he passes the question along. "Seriously?" He shoots a look at Emory, nudging his plastic glasses up his nose at the same time. "Of all the things in here, you want *chocolate?*"

Emory's smile vanishes. "Shut up, man, you know my mom loves that stuff."

"You say that every time."

"That's because it's true every time."

Winston says something to someone about grabbing another box of soap before turning back to Emory. "You know, I don't think I've ever seen your mom eat a piece of chocolate before."

Emory tells Winston to do something very inappropriate with his preternaturally flexible limbs, and I glance down at the box Ian has just handed to me, pausing to study the packaging carefully before passing it on.

"Hey, do you know why these are all stamped with the letters *R N W?*"

Ian turns around. Stunned. Looks at me like I've just asked him to take his clothes off. "Well, I'll be damned," he says. "She speaks."

"Of course I speak," I say, no longer interested in speaking at all.

Ian passes me another box. Shrugs. "Well, now I know."

"Now you do."

"The mystery has been solved."

"You really didn't think I could speak?" I ask after a moment. "Like, you thought I was mute?" I wonder what other things people are saying about me around here.

Ian looks over his shoulder at me, smiles like he's trying not to laugh. Shakes his head and doesn't answer me. "The stamp," he says, "is just regulation. They stamp everything RNW so they can track it. It's nothing fancy."

"But what does RNW mean? Who's stamping it?"

"RNW," he says, repeating the 3 letters like I'm supposed to recognize them. "Reestablished Nations of the World. Everything's gone global, you know. They all trade commodities. And that," he says, "is something no one really knows. It's another reason why the whole Reestablishment thing is a pile of crap. They've monopolized the resources of the entire planet and they're just keeping it all for themselves."

I remember some of this. I remember talking to Adam about this when he and I were locked in the asylum together. ~~Back before I knew what it was like to touch him. To be with him. To hurt him.~~ The Reestablishment has always been a global movement. I just didn't realize it had a name.

"Right," I say to Ian, suddenly distracted. "Of course."

Ian pauses as he hands me another package. "So is it true?" he asks, studying my face. "That you really have no clue what's happened to everything?"

"I know some things." I bristle. "I'm just not clear on all the details."

"Well," Ian says, "if you still remember how to speak when we get back to Point, maybe you should join us at lunch sometime. We can fill you in."

"Really?" I turn to face him.

"Yeah, kid." He laughs, tosses me another box. "Really. We don't bite."

TWENTY-THREE

Sometimes I wonder about glue.

No one ever stops to ask glue how it's holding up. If it's tired of sticking things together or worried about falling apart or wondering how it will pay its bills next week.

Kenji is kind of like that.

He's like glue. He works behind the scenes to keep things together and I've never stopped to think about what his story might be. Why he hides behind the jokes and the snark and the snide remarks.

But he was right. Everything he said to me was right.

Yesterday was a good idea. I needed to get away, to get out, to be productive. And now I need to take Kenji's advice and get over myself. I need to get my head straight. I need to focus on my priorities. I need to figure out what I'm doing here and how I can help. And if I care at all about Adam, I'll try to stay out of his life.

Part of me wishes I could see him; I want to make sure he's really going to be okay, that he's recovering well and eating enough and getting sleep at night. But another part of me is afraid to see him now. Because seeing Adam means saying good-bye. It means really recognizing that I can't be with him anymore and knowing that I have to find a new life for myself. Alone.

But at least at Omega Point I'll have options. And maybe if I can find a way to stop being scared, I'll actually figure out how to make friends. To be strong. To stop wallowing in my own problems.

Things have to be different now.

I grab my food and manage to lift my head; I nod hello to the faces I recognize from yesterday. Not everyone knows about my being on the trip—the invitations to go on missions outside of Omega Point are exclusive—but people, in general, seem to be a little less tense around me. I think.

I might be imagining it.

I try to find a place to sit down but then I see Kenji waving me over. Brendan and Winston and Emory are sitting at his table. I feel a smile tug at my lips as I approach them.

Brendan scoots over on the bench seat to make room for me. Winston and Emory nod hello as they shovel food into their mouths. Kenji shoots me a half smile, his eyes laughing at my surprise to be welcomed at his table.

I'm feeling okay. Like maybe things are going to be okay.

"Juliette?"

And suddenly I'm going to tip over.

I turn very, very slowly, half convinced that the voice I'm hearing belongs to a ghost, because there's no way Adam could've been released from the medical wing so soon. I wasn't expecting to have to face him so soon. I didn't think we'd have to have this talk so soon. Not here. Not in the middle of the dining hall.

I'm not prepared. I'm not *prepared*.

Adam looks terrible. He's pale. Unsteady. His hands are stuffed in his pockets and his lips are pressed together and his eyes are weary, tortured, deep and bottomless wells. His hair is messy. His T-shirt is straining across his chest, his tattooed forearms more pronounced than ever.

I want nothing more than to dive into his arms.

Instead, I'm sitting here, reminding myself to breathe.

"Can I talk to you?" he says, looking like he's half afraid to hear my answer. "Alone?"

I nod, still unable to speak. Abandon my food without looking back at Kenji or Winston or Brendan or Emory so I have no idea what they must be thinking right now. I don't even care.

Adam.

Adam is here and he's in front of me and he wants to talk to me and I have to tell him things that will surely be the death of me.

But I follow him out the door anyway. Into the hall. Down a dark corridor.

Finally we stop.

Adam looks at me like he knows what I'm going to say so I don't bother saying it. I don't want to say anything unless it becomes absolutely necessary. I'd rather just stand here and stare at him, shamelessly drink in the sight of him one last time without having to speak a word. Without having to say anything at all.

He swallows, hard. Looks up. Looks away. Blows out

a breath and rubs the back of his neck, clasps both hands behind his head and turns around so I can't see his face. But the effort causes his shirt to ride up his torso and I have to actually clench my fingers to keep from touching the sliver of skin exposed low on his abdomen, his lower back.

He's still looking away from me when he says, "I really—I really need you to say something." And the sound of his voice—so wretched, so agonized—makes me want to fall to my knees.

Still, I do not speak.

And he turns.

Faces me.

"There has to be something," he says, his hands in his hair now, gripping his skull. "Some kind of compromise—something I can say to convince you to make this work. Tell me there's *something*."

And I'm so scared. So scared I'm going to start sobbing in front of him.

"Please," he says, and he looks like he's about to crack, like he's done, like this is it he's about to fall apart and he says, "say something, I'm begging you—"

I bite my trembling lip.

He freezes in place, watching me, waiting.

"Adam," I breathe, trying to keep my voice steady. "I will always, a-always love you—"

"No," he says. "No, don't say that—don't say that—"

And I'm shaking my head, shaking it fast and hard, so hard it's making me dizzy but I can't stop. I can't say another word unless I want to start screaming and I can't look at his face, I can't bear to see what I'm doing to him—

"No, Juliette—*Juliette*—"

I'm backing away, stumbling, tripping over my own feet as I reach blindly for the wall when I feel his arms around me. I try to pull away but he's too strong, he's holding me too tight and his voice is choked when he says, "It was my fault—this is my fault—I shouldn't have kissed you— you tried to tell me but I didn't listen and I'm so—I'm so sorry," he says, gasping the words. "I should've listened to you. I wasn't strong enough. But it'll be different this time, I swear," he says, burying his face in my shoulder. "I'll never forgive myself for this. You were willing to give it a shot and I screwed everything up and I'm sorry, I'm so sorry—"

I have officially, absolutely collapsed inside.

I hate myself for what happened, hate myself for what I have to do, hate that I can't take his pain away, that I can't tell him we can try, that it'll be hard but we'll make it work anyway. Because this isn't a normal relationship. Because our problems aren't fixable.

Because my skin will never change.

All the training in the world won't remove the very real possibility that I could hurt him. Kill him, if we ever got carried away. I will always be a threat to him. Especially during the most tender moments, the most important, vulnerable moments. The moments I want most. Those are the things I can never have with him, and he deserves so much more than me, than this tortured person with so little to offer.

But I'd rather stand here and feel his arms around me than say a single thing. Because I'm weak, I'm so weak and I want him so much it's killing me. I can't stop shaking, I can't see straight, I can't see through the curtain of tears obscuring my vision.

And he won't let go of me.

He keeps whispering "Please" and I want to die.

But I think if I stay here any longer I will actually go insane.

So I raise a trembling hand to his chest and feel him stiffen, pull back, and I don't dare look at his eyes, I can't stand to see him looking hopeful, even if it's for only a second.

I take advantage of his momentary surprise and slackened arms to slip away, out of the shelter of his warmth, away from his beating heart. And I hold out my hand to stop him from reaching for me again.

"Adam," I whisper. "Please don't. I can't—I c-can't—"

"There's never been anyone else," he says, not bothering to keep his voice down anymore, not caring that his words are echoing through these tunnels. His hand is shaking as he covers his mouth, as he drags it across his face, through his hair. "There's never going to be anyone else—I'm never going to want anyone else—"

"Stop it—you have to stop—" I can't breathe I can't breathe I can't *breathe* "You don't want this—you don't want to be with someone like me—someone who will only end up h-hurting you—"

"*Dammit*, Juliette"—he turns to slam his palms against

the wall, his chest heaving, his head down, his voice broken, catching on every other syllable—"you're hurting me *now*," he says. "You're *killing* me—"

"Adam—"

"Don't walk away," he says, his voice tight, his eyes squeezed shut like he already knows I'm going to. Like he can't bear to see it happen. "Please," he whispers, tormented. "Don't walk away from this."

"I-I wish," I tell him, shaking violently now, "I wish I d-didn't have to. I wish I could love you less."

And I hear him call after me as I bolt down the corridor. I hear him shouting my name but I'm running, running away, running past the huge crowd gathered outside the dining hall, watching, listening to everything. I'm running to hide even though I know it will be impossible.

I will have to see him every single day.

Wanting him from a million miles away.

And I remember Kenji's words, his demands for me to wake up and stop crying and make a change, and I realize fulfilling my new promises might take a little longer than I expected.

Because I can't think of anything I'd rather do right now than find a dark corner and cry.

TWENTY-FOUR

Kenji finds me first.

He's standing in the middle of my training room. Looking around like he's never seen the place before, even though I'm sure that can't be true. I still don't know exactly what he does, but it's at least become clear to me that Kenji is one of the most important people at Omega Point. He's always on the move. Always busy. No one—except for me, and only lately—really sees him for more than a few moments at a time.

It's almost as if he spends the majority of his days . . . invisible.

"So," he says, nodding his head slowly, taking his time walking around the room with his hands clasped behind his back. "That was one hell of a show back there. That's the kind of entertainment we never really get underground."

Mortification.

I'm draped in it. Painted in it. Buried in it.

"I mean, I just have to say—that last line? 'I wish I could love you less'? That was genius. Really, really nice. I think Winston actually shed a tear—"

"SHUT UP, KENJI."

"I'm serious!" he says to me, offended. "That was, I don't

know. It was kind of beautiful. I had no idea you guys were so intense."

I pull my knees up to my chest, burrow deeper into the corner of this room, bury my face in my arms. "No offense, but I really don't want to t-talk to you right now, okay?"

"Nope. Not okay," he says. "You and me, we have work to do."

"No."

"Come on," he says. "Get. *Up.*" He grabs my elbow, tugging me to my feet as I try to take a swipe at him.

I wipe angrily at my cheeks, scrub at the stains my tears left behind. "I'm not in the mood for your jokes, Kenji. Please just go away. Leave me alone."

"No one," he says, "is joking." Kenji picks up one of the bricks stacked against the wall. "And the world isn't going to stop waging war against itself just because you broke up with your boyfriend."

I stare at him, fists shaking, wanting to scream.

He doesn't seem concerned. "So what do you do in here?" he asks. "You just sit around trying to . . . what?" He weighs the brick in his hand. "Break this stuff?"

I give up, defeated. Fold myself onto the floor.

"I don't know," I tell him. I sniff away the last of my tears. Try to wipe my nose. "Castle kept telling me to 'focus' and 'harness my Energy'." I use air quotes to illustrate my point. "But all I know about myself is that I *can* break things—I don't know why it happens. So I don't know how he expects me to replicate what I've already done. I had no idea what

I was doing then, and I don't know what I'm doing now, either. Nothing's changed."

"Hold up," Kenji says, dropping the brick back onto the stack before falling on the mats across from me. He splays out on the ground, body stretched out, arms folded behind his head as he stares up at the ceiling. "What are we talking about again? What events are you supposed to be replicating?"

I lie back against the mats, too; mimic Kenji's position. Our heads are only a few inches apart. "Remember? The concrete I broke back in Warner's psycho room. The metal door I attacked when I was looking for A-Adam." My voice catches and I have to squeeze my eyes shut to quell the pain.

~~I can't even say his name right now.~~

Kenji grunts. I feel him nodding his head on the mats. "All right. Well, what Castle told me is that he thinks there's more to you than just the touching thing. That maybe you also have this weird superhuman strength or something." A pause. "That sound about right to you?"

"I guess."

"So what happened?" he asks, tilting his head back to get a good look at me. "When you went all psycho-monster on everything? Do you remember if there was a trigger?"

I shake my head. "I don't really know. When it happens, it's like—it's like I really am completely out of my mind," I tell him. "Something changes in my head and it makes me . . . it makes me crazy. Like, really, legitimately insane."

I glance over at him but his face betrays no emotion. He just blinks, waiting for me to finish. So I take a deep breath and continue. "It's like I can't think straight. I'm just so paralyzed by the adrenaline and I can't stop it; I can't control it. Once that crazy feeling takes over, it *needs* an outlet. I have to touch something. I have to release it."

Kenji props himself up on one elbow. Looks at me. "So what gets you all crazy, though?" he asks. "What were you feeling? Does it only happen when you're really pissed off?"

I take a second to think about it before I say, "No. Not always." I hesitate. "The first time," I tell him, my voice a little unsteady, "I wanted to kill Warner because of what he made me do to that little kid. I was so devastated. I was angry—I was *really* angry—but I was also . . . so sad." I trail off. "And then when I was looking for Adam?" Deep breaths. "I was desperate. Really desperate. I had to save him."

"And what about when you went all Superman on me? Slamming me into the wall like that?"

"I was scared."

"And then? In the research labs?"

"Angry," I whisper, my eyes unfocused as I stare up at the ceiling, remembering the rage of that day. "I was angrier than I've ever been in my entire life. I never even knew I could feel that way. To be *so* mad. And I felt guilty," I add, so quietly. "Guilty for being the reason why Adam was in there at all."

Kenji takes a deep, long breath. Pulls himself up into a sitting position and leans against the wall. He says nothing.

"What are you thinking . . . ?" I ask, shifting to sit up and join him.

"I don't know," Kenji finally says. "But it's obvious that all of these incidents were the result of really intense emotions. Makes me think the whole system must be pretty straightforward."

"What do you mean?"

"Like there has to be some kind of trigger involved," he says. "Like, when you lose control, your body goes into automatic self-protect mode, you know?"

"No?"

Kenji turns so he's facing me. Crosses his legs underneath him. Leans back on his hands. "Like, listen. When I first found out I could do this invisible thing? I mean, it was an accident. I was nine years old. Scared out of my mind. Fast-forward through all the shitty details and my point is this: I needed a place to hide and couldn't find one. But I was so freaked out that my body, like, automatically did it for me. I just disappeared into the wall. Blended or whatever." He laughs. "Tripped me the hell out, because I didn't realize what'd happened for a good ten minutes. And then I didn't know how to turn myself back to normal. It was crazy. I actually thought I was dead for a couple of days."

"No way," I gasp.

"Yup."

"That's *crazy*."

"That's what I said."

"So . . . so, what? You think my body taps into its

166

defense mode when I freak out?"

"Pretty much."

"Okay." I think. "Well, how am I supposed to tap into my defense mode? How did you figure yours out?"

He shrugs. "Once I realized I wasn't some kind of ghost and I wasn't hallucinating, it actually became kind of cool. I was a kid, you know? I was excited, like I could tie on a cape and kill bad guys or something. I liked it. And it became this part of me that I could access whenever I wanted. But," he adds, "it wasn't until I really started training that I learned how to control and maintain it for long periods of time. That took a lot of work. A lot of focus."

"A lot of work."

"Yeah—I mean, all of this takes a lot of work to figure out. But once I accepted it as a part of me, it became easier to manage."

"Well," I say, leaning back again, blowing out an exasperated breath, "I've already accepted it. But it definitely hasn't made things easier."

Kenji laughs out loud. "My ass you've accepted it. You haven't accepted anything."

"I've been like this my entire *life*, Kenji—I'm pretty sure I've accepted it—"

"No." He cuts me off. "*Hell* no. You hate being in your own skin. You can't stand it. That's not called acceptance. That's called—I don't know—the opposite of acceptance. You," he says, pointing a finger at me, "you are the *opposite* of acceptance."

"What are you trying to say?" I shoot back. "That I have to *like* being this way?" I don't give him a chance to respond before I say, "You have no *idea* what it's like to be stuck in my skin—to be trapped in my body, afraid to breathe too close to anything with a beating heart. If you did, you'd never ask me to be *happy* to live like this."

"Come on, Juliette—I'm just saying—"

"No. Let me make this clear for you, Kenji. I *kill* people. I *kill* them. That's what my 'special' power is. I don't blend into backgrounds or move things with my mind or have really stretchy arms. You touch me for too long and you *die*. Try living like that for seventeen years and then tell me how easy it is to accept myself."

I taste too much bitterness on my tongue.

It's new for me.

"Listen," he says, his voice noticeably softer. "I'm not trying to judge, okay? I'm just trying to point out that because you don't *want* it, you might subconsciously be sabotaging your efforts to figure it out." He puts his hands up in mock defeat. "Just my two cents. I mean, obviously you've got some crazy powers going on. You touch people and bam, done. But then you can crush through walls and shit, too? I mean, hell, I'd want to learn how to do *that*, are you kidding me? That would be insane."

"Yeah," I say, slumping against the wall. "I guess that part wouldn't be so bad."

"Right?" Kenji perks up. "That would be awesome. And then—you know, if you leave your gloves on—you could just crush random stuff without actually killing anyone. Then you wouldn't feel so bad, right?"

"I guess not."

"So. Great. You just need to relax." He gets to his feet. Grabs the brick he was toying with earlier. "Come on," he says. "Get up. Come over here."

I walk over to his side of the room and stare at the brick he's holding. He gives it to me like he's handing over some kind of family heirloom. "Now," he says. "You have to let yourself get comfortable, okay? Allow your body to touch base with its core. Stop blocking your own Energy. You've probably got a million mental blocks in your head. You can't hold back anymore."

"I don't have *mental blocks*—"

"Yeah you do." He snorts. "You definitely do. You have severe mental constipation."

"Mental *what*—"

"Focus your anger on the brick. On the *brick*," he says to me. "Remember. Open mind. You *want* to crush the brick. Remind yourself that this is what you want. It's *your* choice. You're not doing this for Castle, you're not doing it for me, you're not doing it to fight anyone. This is just something you feel like doing. For fun. Because you feel like it. Let your mind and body take over. Okay?"

I take a deep breath. Nod a few times. "Okay. I think I'm—"

"Ho-ly *shit*." He lets out a low whistle.

"What?" I spin around. "What happened—"

"How did you not just feel that?"

"Feel what—"

"Look in your hand!"

I gasp. Stumble backward. My hand is full of what looks like red sand and brown clay pulverized into tiny particles. The bigger chunks of brick crumble to the floor and I let the debris slip through the cracks between my fingers only to lift the guilty hand to my face.

I look up.

Kenji is shaking his head, shaking with laughter. "I am so jealous right now you have no idea."

"Oh my God."

"I know. I KNOW. So badass. Now think about it: if you can do that to a *brick*, imagine what you could do to the human *body*—"

That wasn't the right thing to say.

Not now. Not after Adam. Not after trying to pick up the pieces of my hopes and dreams and fumbling to glue them back together. Because now there's nothing left. Because now I realize that somewhere, deep down, I was harboring a small hope that Adam and I would find a way to work things out.

Somewhere, deep down, I was still clinging to possibility.

And now that's gone.

Because now it's not just my skin Adam has to be afraid of. It's not just my touch but my grip, my hugs, my hands, a kiss—anything I do could injure him. I'd have to be careful just holding his *hand*. And this new knowledge, this new information about just exactly how deadly I am—

It leaves me with no alternative.

I will forever and ever and ever be alone because no one is safe from me.

I fall to the floor, my mind whirring, my own brain no longer a safe space to inhabit because I can't stop thinking, I can't stop wondering, I can't stop anything and it's like I'm caught in what could be a head-on collision and I'm not the innocent bystander.

I'm the train.

I'm the one careening out of control.

Because sometimes you see yourself—you see yourself the way you *could* be—the way you *might* be if things were different. And if you look too closely, what you see will scare you, it'll make you wonder what you might do if given the opportunity. You know there's a different side of yourself you don't want to recognize, a side you don't want to see in the daylight. You spend your whole life doing everything to push it down and away, out of sight, out of mind. You pretend that a piece of yourself doesn't exist.

You live like that for a long time.

For a long time, you're safe.

And then you're not.

TWENTY-FIVE

Another morning.

Another meal.

I'm headed to breakfast to meet Kenji before our next training session.

He came to a conclusion about my abilities yesterday: he thinks that the inhuman power in my touch is just an evolved form of my Energy. That skin-to-skin contact is simply the rawest form of my ability—that my true gift is actually a kind of all-consuming strength that manifests itself in every part of my body.

My bones, my blood, my skin.

I told him it was an interesting theory. I told him I'd always seen myself as some sick version of a Venus flytrap and he said, "OH MY GOD. Yes. YES. You are exactly like that. Holy shit, yes."

Beautiful enough to lure in your prey, he said.

Strong enough to clamp down and destroy, he said.

Poisonous enough to digest your victims when the flesh makes contact.

"You *digest* your prey," he said to me, laughing as though it was amusing, as though it was funny, as if it was perfectly acceptable to compare a girl to a carnivorous plant. Flattering, even. "Right? You said that when you touch people, it's, like, you're taking their energy, right? It makes you feel stronger?"

I didn't respond.

"So you're *exactly* like a Venus flytrap. You reel 'em in. Clamp 'em down. Eat 'em up."

I didn't respond.

"Mmmmmmm," he said. "You're like a sexy, super-scary plant."

I closed my eyes. Covered my mouth in horror.

"Why is that so wrong?" he said. Bent down to meet my gaze. Tugged on a lock of my hair to get me to look up. "Why does this have to be so horrible? Why can't you see how *awesome* this is?" He shook his head at me. "You are seriously missing out, you know that? This could be so cool if you would just *own* it."

Own it.

Yes.

How easy it would be to just clamp down on the world around me. Suck up its life force and leave it dead in the street just because someone tells me I should. Because someone points a finger and says "Those are the bad guys. Those men over there." Kill, they say. Kill because you trust us. Kill because you're fighting for the right team. Kill because they're bad, and we're good. Kill because we tell you to. Because some people are so stupid that they actually think there are thick neon lines separating good and evil. That it's easy to make that kind of distinction and go to sleep at night with a clear conscience. Because it's okay.

173

It's okay to kill a man if someone else deems him unfit to live.

What I really want to say is who the hell are you and who are you to decide who gets to die. Who are you to decide who should be killed. Who are you to tell me which father I should destroy and which child I should orphan and which mother should be left without her son, which brother should be left without a sister, which grandmother should spend the rest of her life crying in the early hours of the morning because the body of her grandchild was buried in the ground before her own.

What I really want to say is who the hell do you think you are to tell me that it's awesome to be able to kill a living thing, that it's interesting to be able to ensnare another soul, that it's fair to choose a victim simply because I'm capable of killing without a gun. I want to say mean things and angry things and hurtful things and I want to throw expletives in the air and run far, far away; I want to disappear into the horizon and I want to dump myself on the side of the road if only it will bring me toward some semblance of freedom but I don't know where to go. I have nowhere else to go.

And I feel responsible.

Because there are times when the anger bleeds away until it's nothing but a raw ache in the pit of my stomach and I see the world and wonder about its people and what it's become and I think about hope and maybe and possibly and possibility and potential. I think about glasses half full and glasses to see the world clearly. I think about sacrifice.

And compromise. I think about what will happen if no one fights back. I think about a world where no one stands up to injustice.

And I wonder if maybe everyone here is right.

If maybe it's time to fight.

I wonder if it's ever actually possible to justify killing as a means to an end and then I think of Kenji. I think of what he said. And I wonder if he would still call it awesome if I decided to make *him* my prey.

I'm guessing not.

TWENTY-SIX

Kenji is already waiting for me.

He and Winston and Brendan are sitting at the same table again, and I slide into my seat with a distracted nod and eyes that refuse to focus in front of me.

"He's not here," Kenji says, shoving a spoonful of breakfast into his mouth.

"What?" Oh how fascinating look at this fork and this spoon and this table. "What do y—"

"Not here," he says, his mouth still half full of food.

Winston clears his throat, scratches the back of his head. Brendan shifts in his seat beside me.

"Oh. I—I, um—" Heat flushes up my neck as I look around at the 3 guys sitting at this table. I want to ask Kenji where Adam is, why he isn't here, how he's doing, if he's okay, if he's been eating regularly. I want to ask a million questions I shouldn't be asking but it's blatantly clear that none of them want to talk about the awkward details of my personal life. And I don't want to be that sad, pathetic girl. I don't want pity. I don't want to see the uncomfortable sympathy in their eyes.

So I sit up. Clear my throat.

"What's going on with the patrols?" I ask Winston.

"Is it getting any worse?"

Winston looks up midchew, surprised. He swallows down the food too quickly and coughs once, twice. Takes a sip of his coffee—tar black—and leans forward, looking eager. "It's getting weirder," he says.

"Really?"

"Yeah, so, remember how I told you guys that Warner was showing up every night?"

~~Warner. I can't get the image of his smiling, laughing face out of my head.~~

We nod.

"Well." He leans back in his chair. Holds up his hands. "Last night? Nothing."

"Nothing?" Brendan's eyebrows are high on his forehead. "What do you mean, nothing?"

"I mean no one was there." He shrugs. Picks up his fork. Stabs at a piece of food. "Not Warner, not a single soldier. Night before last?" He looks around at us. "Fifty, maybe seventy-five soldiers. Last night, zero."

"Did you tell Castle about this?" Kenji isn't eating anymore. He's staring at Winston with a focused, too-serious look on his face. It's worrying me.

"Yeah." Winston nods as he takes another sip of his coffee. "I turned in my report about an hour ago."

"You mean you haven't gone to sleep yet?" I ask, eyes wide.

"I slept yesterday," he says, waving a haphazard hand at me. "Or the day before yesterday. I can't remember. God,

177

this coffee is disgusting," he says, gulping it down.

"Right. Maybe you should lay off the coffee, yeah?" Brendan tries to grab Winston's cup.

Winston slaps at his hand, shoots him a dark look. "Not all of us have electricity running through our veins," he says. "I'm not a freaking powerhouse of energy like you are."

"I only did that once—"

"Twice!"

"—and it was an emergency," he says, looking a little sheepish.

"What are you guys talking about?" I ask.

"This guy"—Kenji jerks a thumb at Brendan—"can, like, *literally* recharge his own body. He doesn't need to sleep. It's insane."

"It's not fair," Winston mutters, ripping a piece of bread in half.

I turn to Brendan, jaw unhinged. "No way."

He nods. Shrugs. "I've only done it once."

"Twice!" Winston says again. "And he's a freaking fetus," he says to me. "He's already got way too much energy as it is—shit, all of you kids do—and yet he's the one who comes with a rechargeable battery life."

"I am not a *fetus*," Brendan says, spluttering, glancing at me as heat colors his cheeks. "He's—that's not—you're *mad*," he says, glaring at Winston.

"Yeah," Winston says, nodding, his mouth full of food again. "I am mad. I'm pissed off." He swallows. "And I'm cranky as hell because I'm tired. And I'm hungry. And I need more coffee." He shoves away from the table. Stands up. "I'm going to go get more coffee."

"I thought you said it was disgusting."

He levels a look at me. "Yes, but I am a sad, sad man with very low standards."

"It's true," Brendan says.

"Shut up, fetus."

"You're only allowed one cup," Kenji points out, looking up to meet Winston's eyes.

"Don't worry, I always tell them I'm taking yours," he says, and stalks off.

Kenji is laughing, shoulders shaking.

Brendan is mumbling "I am *not* a fetus" under his breath, stabbing at his food with renewed vigor.

"How old *are* you?" I ask, curious. He's so white-blond and pale-blue-eyed that he doesn't seem real. He looks like the kind of person who could never age, who would remain forever preserved in this ethereal form.

"Twenty-four," he says, looking grateful for a chance at validation. "Just turned twenty-four, actually. Had my birthday last week."

"Oh, wow." I'm surprised. He doesn't look much older than 18. I wonder what it must be like to celebrate a birthday at Omega Point. "Well, happy birthday," I say, smiling at him. "I hope—I hope you have a very good year. And"—I try to think of something nice to say—"and a lot of happy days."

He's staring back at me now, amused, looking straight into my eyes. Grinning. He says, "Thanks." Smiles a bit wider. "Thanks very much." And he doesn't look away.

My face is hot.

I'm struggling to understand why he's still smiling at me, why he doesn't stop smiling even when he finally looks away, why Kenji keeps glancing at me like he's trying to hold in a laugh and I'm flustered, feeling oddly embarrassed and searching for something to say.

"So what are we going to do today?" I ask Kenji, hoping my voice sounds neutral, normal.

Kenji drains his water cup. Wipes his mouth. "Today," he says, "I'm going to teach you how to shoot."

"A gun?"

"Yup." He grabs his tray. Grabs mine, too. "Wait here, I'm gonna drop these off." He moves to go before he stops, turns back, glances at Brendan and says, "Put it out of your head, bro."

Brendan looks up, confused. "What?"

"It's not going to happen."

"Wha—"

Kenji stares at him, eyebrows raised.

Brendan's mouth falls closed. His cheeks are pink again. "I know that."

"Uh-huh." Kenji shakes his head, and walks away.

Brendan is suddenly in a hurry to go about his day.

TWENTY-SEVEN

"Juliette? Juliette!"

"Please wake up—"

I gasp as I sit straight up in bed, heart pounding, eyes blinking too fast as they try to focus. I blink blink blink. "What's going on? What's happening?"

"Kenji is outside," Sonya says.

"He says he needs you," Sara adds, "that something happened—"

I'm tripping out of bed so fast I pull the covers down with me. I'm groping around in the dark, trying to find my suit—I sleep in a pajama set I borrowed from Sara—and making an effort not to panic. "Do you know what's going on?" I ask. "Do you know—did he tell you anything—"

Sonya is shoving my suit into my arms, saying, "No, he just said that it was urgent, that something happened, that we should wake you up right away."

"Okay. I'm sure it's going to be okay," I tell them, though I don't know why I'm saying it, or how I could possibly be of any reassurance to them. I wish I could turn on a light but all the lights are controlled by the same switch. It's one of the ways they conserve power—and one of the ways they manage to maintain the semblance of night and day down here—by only using it during specific hours.

I finally manage to slip into my suit and I'm zipping it up, heading for the door when I hear Sara call my name. She's holding my boots.

"Thank you—thank you both," I say.

They nod several times.

And I'm tugging on my boots and running out the door.

I slam face-first into something solid.

Something human. Male.

I hear his sharp intake of breath, feel his hands steady my frame, feel the blood in my body run right out from under me. "Adam," I gasp.

He hasn't let go of me. I can hear his heart beating fast and hard and loud in the silence between us and he feels too still, too tense, like he's trying to maintain some kind of control over his body.

"Hi," he whispers, but it sounds like he can't really breathe.

My heart is failing.

"Adam, I—"

"I can't let go," he says, and I feel his hands shake, just a little, as if the effort to keep them in one place is too much for him. "I can't let go of you. I'm trying, but I—"

"Well, it's a good thing I'm here then, isn't it?" Kenji yanks me out of Adam's arms and takes a deep, uneven breath. "Jesus. Are you guys done here? We have to go."

"What—what's going on?" I stammer, trying to cover

up my embarrassment. I really wish Kenji weren't always catching me in the middle of such vulnerable moments. I wish he could see me being strong and confident. And then I wonder when I began caring about Kenji's opinion of me.

"Is everything okay?"

"I have no idea," Kenji says as he strides down the dark halls. He must have these tunnels memorized, I think, because I can't see a thing. I have to practically run to keep up with him. "But," he says, "I'm assuming some kind of shit has officially hit the fan. Castle sent me a message about fifteen minutes ago—said to get me and you and Kent up to his office ASAP. So," he says, "that's what I'm doing."

"But—now? In the middle of the night?"

"Shit hitting the fan doesn't work around your schedule, princess."

I decide to stop talking.

We follow Kenji to a single solitary door at the end of a narrow tunnel.

He knocks twice, pauses. Knocks 3 times, pauses. Knocks once.

I wonder if I need to remember that.

The door creaks open on its own and Castle waves us in.

"Close the door, please," he says from behind his desk. I have to blink several times to readjust to the light in here. There's a traditional reading lamp on Castle's desk with just enough wattage to illuminate this small space. I use the moment to look around.

Castle's office is nothing more than a room with a few bookcases and a simple table that doubles as a workstation. Everything is made of recycled metal. His desk looks like it used to be a pickup truck.

There are heaps of books and papers stacked all over the floor; diagrams, machinery, and computer parts shoved onto the bookcases, thousands of wires and electrical units peeking out of their metal bodies; they must either be damaged or broken or perhaps part of a project Castle is working on.

In other words: his office is a mess.

Not something I was expecting from someone so incredibly put-together.

"Have a seat," he says to us. I look around for chairs but only find two upside-down garbage cans and a stool. "I'll be right with you. Give me one moment."

We nod. We sit. We wait. We look around.

Only then do I realize why Castle doesn't care about the disorganized nature of his office.

He seems to be in the middle of something, but I can't see what it is, and it doesn't really matter. I'm too focused on watching him work. His hands shift up and down, flick from side to side, and everything he needs or wants simply gravitates toward him. A particular piece of paper? A notepad? The clock buried under the pile of books farthest from his desk? He looks for a pencil and lifts his hand to catch it. He's searching for his notes and lifts his fingers to find them.

He doesn't need to be organized. He has a system of his own.

Incredible.

He finally looks up. Puts his pencil down. Nods. Nods again. "Good. Good; you're all here."

"Yes, sir," Kenji says. "You said you needed to speak with us."

"Indeed I do." Castle folds his hands over his desk. "Indeed I do." Takes a careful breath. "The supreme commander," he says, "has arrived at the headquarters of Sector 45."

Kenji swears.

Adam is frozen.

I'm confused. "Who's the supreme commander?"

Castle's gaze rests on me. "Warner's father." His eyes narrow, scrutinizing me. "You didn't know that Warner's father is the supreme commander of The Reestablishment?"

"Oh," I gasp, unable to imagine the monster that must be Warner's father. "I—yes—I knew that," I tell him. "I just didn't know what his title was."

"Yes," Castle says. "There are six supreme commanders around the world, one for each of the six divisions: North America, South America, Europe, Asia, Africa, and Oceania. Each section is divided into 555 sectors for a total of 3,330 sectors around the globe. Warner's father is not only in charge of this continent, he is also one of the founders of The Reestablishment, and currently our biggest threat."

"But I thought there were 3,333 sectors," I tell Castle,

"not 3,330. Am I remembering that wrong?"

"The other three are capitals," Kenji says to me. "We're pretty sure that one of them is somewhere in North America, but no one knows for certain where any of them are located. So yeah," he adds, "you're remembering right. The Reestablishment has some crazy fascination with exact numbers. 3,333 sectors altogether and 555 sectors each. Everyone gets the same thing, regardless of size. They think it shows how equally they've divided everything, but it's just a bunch of bullshit."

"Wow." Every single day I'm floored by how much I still need to learn. I look at Castle. "So is this the emergency? That Warner's dad is here and not at one of the capitals?"

Castle nods. "Yes, he . . ." He hesitates. Clears his throat. "Well. Let me start from the beginning. It is imperative that you be aware of all the details."

"We're listening," Kenji says, back straight, eyes alert, muscles tensed for action. "Go on."

"Apparently," Castle says, "he's been in town for some time now—he arrived very quietly, very discreetly, a couple of weeks ago. It seems he heard what his son has been up to lately, and he wasn't thrilled about it. He . . ." Castle takes a deep, steady breath. "He is . . . particularly angry about what happened with you, Ms. Ferrars."

"Me?" Heart pounding. Heart pounding. Heart pounding.

"Yes," Castle says. "Our sources say that he's angry Warner allowed you to escape. And, of course, that he lost two of his soldiers in the process." He nods in Adam and Kenji's direction. "Worse still, rumors are now circulating among the citizens about this defecting girl and her strange ability and they're starting to put the pieces together; they're starting to realize there's another movement—*our movement*—preparing to fight back. It's creating unrest and resistance among the civilians, who are all too eager to get involved.

"So." Castle clasps his hands. "Warner's father has undoubtedly arrived to spearhead this war and remove all doubt of The Reestablishment's power." He pauses to look at each of us. "In other words, he's arrived to punish us and his son at the same time."

"But that doesn't change our plans, does it?" Kenji asks.

"Not exactly. We've always known that a fight would be inevitable, but this . . . changes things. Now that Warner's father is in town, this war is going to happen a lot sooner than we hoped," Castle says. "And it's going to be a lot bigger than we anticipated." He levels his gaze at me, looking grave. "Ms. Ferrars, I'm afraid we're going to need your help."

I'm staring at him, struck. "Me?"

"Yes."

"Aren't—aren't you still angry with me?"

"You are not a child, Ms. Ferrars. I would not fault you for an overreaction. Kenji says he believes that your behavior lately has been the result of ignorance and not malicious intent, and I trust his judgment. I trust his word. But I do want you to understand that we are a team," he says, "and we need your strength. What you can do—your power—it is unparalleled. Especially now that you've been working with Kenji and have at least some knowledge of what you're capable of, we're going to need you. We'll do whatever we can to support you—we'll reinforce your suit, provide you with weapons and armor. And Winston—" He stops. His breath catches. "Winston," he says, quieter now, "just finished making you a new pair of gloves." He looks into my face. "We want you on our team," he says. "And if you cooperate with me, I promise you will see results."

"Of course," I whisper. I match his steady, solemn gaze. "Of course I'll help."

"Good," Castle says. "That is very good." He looks distracted as he leans back in his chair, runs a tired hand across his face. "Thank you."

"Sir," Kenji says, "I hate to be so blunt, but would you please tell me what the hell is going on?"

Castle nods. "Yes," he says. "Yes, yes, of course. I—forgive me. It's been a difficult night."

Kenji's voice is tight. "What happened?"

"He . . . has sent word."

"Warner's father?" I ask. "Warner's father sent word? To us?" I glance around at Adam and Kenji. Adam is blinking fast, lips just barely parted in shock. Kenji looks like he's about to be sick.

I'm beginning to panic.

"Yes," Castle says to me. "Warner's father. He wants to meet. He wants . . . to talk."

Kenji jumps to his feet. His entire face is leached of color.

"No—sir—this is a setup—he doesn't want to *talk*, you must know he's lying—"

"He's taken four of our men hostage, Kenji. I'm afraid we don't have another choice."

TWENTY-EIGHT

"What?" Kenji has gone limp. His voice is a horrified rasp. "Who? *How—*"

"Winston and Brendan were patrolling topside tonight." Castle shakes his head. "I don't know what happened. They must've been ambushed. They were too far out of range and the security footage only shows us that Emory and Ian noticed a disturbance and tried to investigate. We don't see anything in the tapes after that. Emory and Ian," he says, "never came back either."

Kenji is back in his chair again, his face in his hands. He looks up with a sudden burst of hope. "But Winston and Brendan—maybe they can find a way out, right? They could do something—they have enough power between the two of them to figure something out."

Castle offers Kenji a sympathetic smile. "I don't know where he's taken them or how they're being treated. If he's beaten them, or if he's already"—he hesitates—"if he's already tortured them, shot them—if they're bleeding to death—they certainly won't be able to fight back. And even if the two of them could save themselves," he says after a moment, "they wouldn't leave the others behind."

Kenji presses his fists into his thighs.

"So. He wants to talk." It's the first time Adam has said a word.

Castle nods. "Lily found this package where they'd disappeared." He tosses us a small knapsack and we take turns rummaging through it. It contains only Winston's broken glasses and Brendan's radio. Smeared in blood.

I have to grip my hands to keep them from shaking.

I was just getting to know these guys. I'd only just met Emory and Ian. I was just learning to build new friendships, to feel comfortable with the people of Omega Point. I just had *breakfast* with Brendan and Winston. I glance at the clock on Castle's wall; it's 3:31 a.m. I last saw them about 20 hours ago.

Brendan's birthday was last week.

"Winston knew," I hear myself say out loud. "He knew something was wrong. He knew there was something weird about all those soldiers everywhere—"

"I know," Castle says, shaking his head. "I've been reading and rereading all of his reports." He pinches the bridge of his nose with his thumb and index finger. Closes his eyes. "I'd only just begun to piece it all together. But it was too late. I was too late."

"What do you think they were planning?" Kenji asks. "Do you have a theory?"

Castle sighs. Drops his hand from his face. "Well, now we know why Warner was out with his soldiers every night—how he was able to leave the base for as long as he did for so many days."

191

"His father," Kenji says.

Castle nods. "Yes. It's my opinion that the supreme sent Warner out himself. That he wanted Warner to begin hunting us more aggressively. He's always known about us," Castle says to me. "He's never been a stupid man, the supreme. He's always believed the rumors about us, always known that we were out here. But we've never been a threat to him before. Not until now," he says. "Because now that the civilians are talking about us, it's upsetting the balance of power. The people are reenergized—looking for hope in our resistance. And that's not something The Reestablishment can afford right now.

"Anyway," he goes on, "I think it's clear that they couldn't find the entrance to Omega Point, and settled for taking hostages, hoping to provoke us to come out on our own." Castle retrieves a piece of paper from his pile. Holds it up. It's a note. "But there are conditions," he says. "The supreme has given us very specific directions on how next to proceed."

"*And?*" Kenji is rigid with intensity.

"The three of you will go. Alone."

Holy crap.

"What?" Adam gapes at Castle, astonished. "Why us?"

"He hasn't asked to see me," Castle says. "I'm not the one he's interested in."

"And you're just going to agree to that?" Adam asks. "You're just going to throw us at him?"

Castle leans forward. "Of course not."

"You have a plan?" I ask.

"The supreme wants to meet with you at exactly twelve p.m. tomorrow—well, today, technically—at a specific location on unregulated turf. The details are in the note." He takes a deep breath. "And, even though I know this is exactly what he wants, I think we should all be ready to go. We should move together. This is, after all, what we've been training for. I've no doubt he has bad intentions, and I *highly* doubt he's inviting you to chat over a cup of tea. So I think we should be ready to defend against an offensive attack. I imagine his own men will be armed and ready to fight, and I'm fully prepared to lead mine into battle."

"So we're the *bait?*" Kenji asks, his eyebrows pulled together. "We don't even get to fight—we're just the distraction?"

"Kenji—"

"This is bullshit," Adam says, and I'm surprised to see such emotion from him. "There *has* to be another way. We shouldn't be playing by his rules. We should be using this opportunity to ambush them or—I don't know—create a diversion or a distraction so *we* can attack offensively! I mean, hell, doesn't anyone burst into flames or something? Don't we have anyone who can do something crazy enough to throw everything off? To give us an advantage?"

Castle turns to stare at me.

Adam looks like he might punch Castle in the face. "You are *out* of your mind—"

"Then no," he says. "No, we don't have anyone else that can do something so . . . earth-shattering."

"You think that's *funny?*" Adam snaps.

"I'm afraid I'm not trying to be funny, Mr. Kent. And your anger is not helping our situation. You may opt out if you like, but I *will*—respectfully—request Ms. Ferrars' assistance in this matter. She is the only one the supreme actually wants to see. Sending the two of you with her was my idea."

"What?"

All 3 of us are stunned.

"Why me?"

"I really wish I could tell you," Castle says to me. "I wish I knew more. As of right now, I can only do my best to extrapolate from the information I have, and all I've concluded thus far is that Warner has made a glaring error that needs to be set right. Somehow you managed to get caught in the middle." A pause. "Warner's father," he says, "has asked very specifically for *you* in exchange for the hostages. He says if you do not arrive at the appointed time, he will kill our men. And I have no reason to doubt his word. Murdering the innocent is something that comes very naturally to him."

"And you were just going to let her walk into that!" Adam knocks over his garbage can as he jumps to his feet. "You weren't even going to say anything? You were going to let us assume that she wasn't a *target*? Are you insane?"

Castle rubs his forehead. Takes a few calming breaths. "No," he says, his voice carefully measured. "I was not going to let her walk right into anything. What I'm saying is that we will *all* fight together, but you two will go with Ms. Ferrars. The three of you have worked together before, and both you and Kenji have military training. You're more familiar with the rules, the techniques, the strategy they might employ. You would help keep her safe and embody the element of surprise—your presence could be what gives us an advantage in this situation. If he wants her badly enough, he'll have to find a way to juggle the three of you—"

"*Or*—you know, I don't know," Kenji says, affecting nonchalance, "maybe he'll just shoot us both in the face and drag Juliette away while we're too busy being dead to stop him."

"It's okay," I say. "I'll do it. I'll go."

"What?" Adam is looking at me, panic forcing his eyes wide. "Juliette—no—"

"Yeah, you might want to think about this for a second," Kenji cuts in, sounding a little nervous.

"You don't have to come if you don't want to," I tell them. "But I'll go."

Castle smiles, relief written across his features.

"This is what we're here for, right?" I look around. "We're supposed to fight back. This is our chance."

Castle is beaming, his eyes bright with something that might be pride. "We will be with you every step of the way, Ms. Ferrars. You can count on it."

I nod.

And I realize this is probably what I'm meant to do. Maybe this is exactly why I'm here.

Maybe I'm just supposed to die.

TWENTY-NINE

The morning is a blur.

There's so much to do, so much to prepare for, and there are so many people getting ready. But I know that ultimately this is *my* battle; I have unfinished business to deal with. I know this meeting has nothing to do with the supreme commander. He has no reason to care so much about me. I've never even met the man; I should be nothing more than expendable to him.

This is Warner's move.

It has to be Warner who asked for me. This has something and everything to do with him; it's a smoke signal telling me he still wants me and he's not yet given up. And I have to face him.

I only wonder how he managed to get his father to pull these strings for him.

I guess I'll find out soon enough.

Someone is calling my name.

I stop in place.
Spin around.
James.

He runs up to me just outside the dining hall. His hair, so blond; his eyes, so blue, just like his older brother's. But I've missed his face in a way that has nothing to do with how much he reminds me of Adam.

James is a special kid. A sharp kid. The kind of 10-year-old who is always underestimated. And he's asking me if we can talk. He points to one of the many corridors.

I nod. Follow him into an empty tunnel.

He stops walking and turns away for a moment. Stands there looking uncomfortable. I'm stunned he even wants to talk to me; I haven't spoken a single word to him in 3 weeks. He started spending time with the other kids at Omega Point shortly after we arrived, and then things somehow got awkward between us. He stopped smiling when he'd see me, stopped waving hello from across the dining hall. I always imagined he'd heard rumors about me from the other kids and decided he was better off staying away. And now, after everything that's happened with Adam—after our very public display in the tunnel—I'm shocked he wants to say anything to me.

His head is still down when he whispers, "I was really, really mad at you."

And the stitches in my heart begin to pop. One by one.

He looks up. Looks at me like he's trying to gauge whether or not his opening words have upset me, whether or not I'm going to yell at him for being honest with me. And I don't know what he sees in my face but it seems to disarm him. He shoves his hands into his pockets. Rubs his sneaker in circles on the floor. Says, "You didn't tell me you killed someone before."

I take an unsteady breath and wonder if there will ever be a proper way to respond to a statement like that. I wonder if anyone other than James will ever even say something like that to me. I think not. So I just nod. And say, "I'm really sorry. I should've told y—"

"Then why didn't you?" he shouts, shocking me. "Why didn't you tell me? Why did everyone else know except for me?"

And I'm floored for a moment, floored by the hurt in his voice, the anger in his eyes. I never knew he considered me a friend, and I realize I should have. James hasn't known many people in his life; Adam is his entire world. Kenji and I were 2 of the only people he'd ever really met before we got to Omega Point. And for an orphaned child in his circumstances, it must've meant a lot to have new friends. But I've been so concerned with my own issues that it never occurred to me that James would care so much. I never realized my omission would've seemed like a betrayal to him. That the rumors he heard from the other children must've hurt him just as much as they hurt me.

So I decide to sit down, right there in the tunnel. I make room for him to sit down beside me. And I tell him the truth. "I didn't want you to hate me."

He glares at the floor. Says, "I don't hate you."

"No?"

He picks at his shoelaces. Sighs. Shakes his head. "And I didn't like what they were saying about you," he says, quieter now. "The other kids. They said you were mean and nasty and I told them you weren't. I told them you were quiet and nice. And that you have nice hair. And they told me I was lying."

I swallow, hard, punched in the heart. "You think I have nice hair?"

"Why did you kill him?" James asks me, eyes so open, so ready to be understanding. "Was he trying to hurt you? Were you scared?"

I take a few breaths before I answer.

"Do you remember," I say to him, feeling unsteady now, "what Adam told you about me? About how I can't touch anyone without hurting them?"

James nods.

"Well, that's what happened," I say. "I touched him and he died."

"But why?" he asks. "Why'd you touch him? Because you wanted him to die?"

My face feels like cracked china. "No," I tell him, shaking my head. "I was young—only a couple of years older than you, actually. I didn't know what I was doing. I didn't know that I could kill people by touching them. He'd fallen down at the grocery store and I was just trying to help him get to his feet." A long pause. "It was an accident."

James is silent for a while.

He takes turns looking at me, looking at his shoes, at the knees he's tucked up against his chest. He's staring at the ground when he finally whispers, "I'm sorry I was mad at you."

"I'm sorry I didn't tell you the truth," I whisper back.

He nods. Scratches a spot on his nose. Looks at me. "So can we be friends again?"

"You want to be friends with me?" I blink hard against the stinging in my eyes. "You're not afraid of me?"

"Are you going to be mean to me?"

"Never."

"Then why would I be afraid of you?"

And I laugh, mostly because I don't want to cry. I nod too many times. "Yes," I say to him. "Let's be friends again."

"Good," he says, and gets to his feet. "Because I don't want to eat lunch with those other kids anymore."

I stand up. Dust off the back of my suit. "Eat with us," I tell him. "You can always sit at our table."

"Okay." He nods. Looks away again. Tugs on his ear a little. "So did you know Adam is really sad all the time?" He turns his blue eyes on me.

I can't speak. Can't speak at all.

"Adam says he's sad because of you." James looks at me like he's waiting for me to deny it. "Did you hurt him by accident too? He was in the medical wing, did you know that? He was sick."

And I think I'm going to fall apart, right there, but somehow I don't. I can't lie to him. "Yes," I tell James. "I hurt him by accident, but now—n-now I stay away from him. So I can't hurt him anymore."

"Then why's he still so sad? If you're not hurting him anymore?"

I'm shaking my head, pressing my lips together because I don't want to cry and I don't know what to say. And James seems to understand.

He throws his arms around me.

Right around my waist. Hugs me and tells me not to cry because he believes me. He believes I only hurt Adam by accident. And the little boy, too. And then he says, "But be careful today, okay? And kick some ass, too."

I'm so stunned that it takes me a moment to realize that not only did he use a bad word, he just touched me for the very first time. I try to hold on for as long as I can without making things awkward between us, but I think my heart is still in a puddle somewhere on the floor.

And that's when I realize: everyone knows.

James and I walk into the dining hall together and I can already tell that the stares are different now. Their faces are full of pride, strength, and acknowledgment when they look at me. No fear. No suspicion. I've officially become one of them. I will fight with them, for them, against the same enemy.

I can see what's in their eyes because I'm beginning to remember what it feels like.

Hope.

It's like a drop of honey, a field of tulips blooming in the springtime. It's fresh rain, a whispered promise, a cloudless sky, the perfect punctuation mark at the end of a sentence.

And it's the only thing in the world keeping me afloat.

THIRTY

"This isn't how we wanted it to happen," Castle says to me, "but these things never usually go according to plan." Adam and Kenji and I are being fitted for battle. We're camped out in one of the larger training rooms with 5 others I've never met before. They're in charge of weapons and armor. It's incredible how every single person at Omega Point has a job. Everyone contributes. Everyone has a task.

They all work together.

"Now, we still don't know yet *exactly* why or how you can do what you do, Ms. Ferrars, but I'm hoping that when the time comes, your Energy will present itself. These kinds of high-stress situations are perfect for provoking our abilities—in fact, seventy-eight percent of Point members reported initial discovery of their ability while in critical, high-risk circumstances."

Yup, I don't say to him. That sounds about right.

Castle takes something from one of the women in the room—Alia, I think is her name. "And you shouldn't worry about a thing," he says. "We'll be right there in case something should happen."

I don't point out that I never once said I was worried. Not out loud, anyway.

"These are your new gloves," Castle says, handing them to me. "Try them on."

These new gloves are shorter, softer: they stop precisely at my wrist and fasten with a snap-button. They feel thicker, a little heavier, but they fit my fingers perfectly. I curl my hand into a fist. Smile a little. "These are incredible," I tell him. "Didn't you say Winston designed them?"

Castle's face falls. "Yes," he says quietly. "He finished them just yesterday."

Winston.

His was the very first face I saw when I woke up at Omega Point. His crooked nose, his plastic glasses, his sandy-blond hair and his background in psychology. His need for disgusting coffee.

I remember the broken glasses we found in the knapsack.

I have no idea what's happened to him.

Alia returns with a leather contraption in her hands. It looks like a harness. She asks me to lift my arms and helps me slip into the piece, and I recognize it as a holster. There are thick leather shoulder straps that intersect in the center of my back, and 50 different straps of very thin black leather overlapping around the highest part of my waist—just underneath my chest—like some kind of incomplete bustier. It's like a bra with no cups. Alia has to buckle everything together for me and I still don't really understand what I'm wearing. I'm waiting for some kind of explanation.

Then I see the guns.

"There was nothing in the note about arriving unarmed," Castle says as Alia passes him two automatic handguns in a shape and size I've come to recognize. I practiced shooting with these just yesterday.

I was terrible at it.

"And I see no reason for you to be without a weapon," Castle is saying. He shows me where the holsters are on either side of my rib cage. Teaches me how the guns fit, how to snap the holder into place, where the extra cartridges go.

I don't bother to mention that I have no idea how to reload a weapon. Kenji and I never got to that part in our lesson. He was too busy trying to remind me not to use a gun to gesticulate while asking questions.

"I'm hoping the firearms will be a last resort," Castle says to me. "You have enough weapons in your personal arsenal—you shouldn't need to shoot anyone. And, just in case you find yourself using your gift to destroy something, I suggest you wear these." He holds up a set of what look like elaborate variations on brass knuckles. "Alia designed these for you."

I look from her to Castle to the foreign objects in his hand. He's beaming. I thank Alia for taking the time to create something for me and she stammers out an incoherent response, blushing like she can't believe I'm talking to her.

I'm baffled.

I take the pieces from Castle and inspect them. The underside is made up of 4 concentric circles welded together, big enough in diameter to fit like a set of rings, snug over my gloves. I slip my fingers through the holes and turn my hand over to inspect the upper part. It's like a mini shield, a million pieces of gunmetal that cover my knuckles, my fingers, the entire back of my hand. I can curl my fist and the metal moves with the motion of my joints. It's not nearly as heavy as it looks.

I slip the other piece on. Curl my fingers. Reach for the guns now strapped to my body.

Easy.

I can do this.

"Do you like it?" Castle asks. I've never seen him smile so wide before.

"I love it," I tell him. "Everything is perfect. Thank you."

"Very good. I'm so pleased. Now," he says, "if you'll excuse me, I must attend to a few other details before we leave. I will return shortly." He offers me a curt nod before heading out the door. Everyone but me, Kenji, and Adam leaves the room.

I turn to see how the guys are doing.

Kenji is wearing a suit.

Some kind of bodysuit. He's black from head to toe, his jet-black hair and eyes a perfect match for the outfit molded to every contour of his body. The suit seems to have a synthetic feel to it, almost like plastic; it gleams in the fluorescent lighting of the room and looks like it'd be too stiff to move around in. But then I see him stretching his arms and rolling back and forth on the balls of his feet and the suit suddenly looks fluid, like it moves with him. He's wearing boots but no gloves, and a harness, just like me. But his is different: it has simple holsters that sling over his arms like the straps of a backpack.

And Adam.

Adam is ~~gorgeous~~ wearing a long-sleeved T-shirt, dark blue and dangerously tight across his chest. I can't help but linger over the details of his outfit, can't help but remember what it was like to be held against him, in his arms. ~~He's standing right in front of me and I miss him like I haven't seen him in years.~~ His black cargo pants are tucked into the same pair of black boots he was wearing when I first met him in the asylum, shin-high and sleek, created from smooth leather that fits him so perfectly it's a surprise they weren't made for his body. But there are no weapons on his person.

And I'm curious enough to ask.

"Adam?"

He lifts his head to look up and freezes. Blinks, eyebrows up, lips parted. His eyes travel down every inch of my body, pausing to study the harness framing my chest, the guns slung close to my waist.

He says nothing. He runs a hand through his hair, presses the heel of his palm to his forehead and says something about being right back. He leaves the room.

I feel sick.

Kenji clears his throat, loud. Shakes his head. Says, "Wow. I mean, really, are you trying to kill the guy?"

"What?"

Kenji is looking at me like I'm an idiot. "You can't just go around all 'Oh, Adam, look at me, look at how sexy I am in my new outfit' and bat your eyelashes—"

"*Bat my eyelashes?*" I balk at him. "What are you talking about? I'm not *batting* my eyelashes at him! And this is the same outfit I've worn every day—"

Kenji grunts. Shrugs and says, "Yeah, well, it looks different."

"You're crazy."

"I am just *saying*," he says, hands up in mock surrender, "that if I were him? And you were my girl? And you were walking around looking like that, and I couldn't touch you?" He looks away. Shrugs again. "I am just saying I do not envy the poor bastard."

"I don't know what to do," I whisper. "I'm not trying to hurt him—"

"Oh hell. Forget I said anything," he says, waving his hands around. "Seriously. It is *none* of my business." He shoots me a look. "And do *not* consider this an invitation for you to start telling me all of your secret feelings now."

I narrow my eyes at him. "I'm not going to tell you anything about my feelings."

"Good. Because I don't want to know."

"Have you ever had a girlfriend, Kenji?"

"What?" He looks mortally offended. "Do I *look* like the kind of guy who's never had a girlfriend? Have you even *met* me?"

I roll my eyes. "Forget I asked."

"I can't even believe you just said that."

"You're the one who's always going on about not wanting to talk about your feelings," I snap.

"No," he says. "I said I don't want to talk about *your* feelings." He points at me. "I have zero problem talking about my own."

"So do you want to talk about your feelings?"

"Hell no."

"Bu—"

"No."

"Fine." I look away. Pull at the straps tugging at my back. "So what's up with your suit?" I ask him.

"What do you mean, *what's up with it?*" He frowns. He runs his hands down his outfit. "This suit is badass."

I bite back a smile. "I just meant, why are you wearing a suit? Why do you get one and Adam doesn't?"

He shrugs. "Adam doesn't need one. Few people do—it all depends on what kind of gift we have. For me, this suit makes my life a hell of a lot easier. I don't always use it, but when I need to get serious about a mission, it really helps. Like, when I need to blend into a background," he explains, "it's less complicated if I'm shifting one solid color—hence, the black. And if I have too many layers and too many extra pieces floating around my body, I have to focus that much more on making sure I blend all the details. If I'm one solid piece and one solid color, I'm a much better chameleon. Besides," he adds, stretching out the muscles in his arms, "I look sexy as hell in this outfit."

It takes all the self-control I have not to burst into laughter.

"So, but what about Adam?" I ask him. "Adam doesn't need a suit *or* guns? That doesn't seem right."

"I do have guns," Adam says as he walks back into the room. His eyes are focused on the fists he's clenching and unclenching in front of him. "You just can't see them."

I can't stop looking at him, can't stop staring.

"Invisible guns, huh?" Kenji smirks. "That's cute. I don't think I ever went through that phase."

Adam glares at Kenji. "I have nine different weapons concealed on my body right now. Would you like to choose the one I use to shoot you in the face? Or should I?"

"It was a *joke*, Kent. Damn. I was *joking*—"

"All right, everyone."

We all spin around at the sound of Castle's voice.

He examines the 3 of us. "Are you ready?"

I say, "Yes."

Adam nods.

Kenji says, "Let's do this shit."

Castle says, "Follow me."

THIRTY-ONE

It's 10:32 a.m.

We have exactly 1 hour and 28 minutes before we're supposed to meet the supreme commander.

This is the plan:

Castle and every able body from Omega Point are already in position. They left half an hour ago. They're hiding in the abandoned buildings skirting the circumference of the meeting point indicated in the note. They will be ready to engage in an offensive strike just as soon as Castle gives the signal—and Castle will only give that signal if he senses we're in danger.

Adam and Kenji and I are going to travel by foot.

Kenji and Adam are familiar with unregulated turf because as soldiers, they were required to know which sections of land were strictly off-limits. No one is allowed to trespass on the grounds of our past world. The strange alleyways, side streets, old restaurants and office buildings are forbidden territory.

Kenji says our meeting point is in one of the few suburban areas still standing; he says he knows it well. Apparently as a soldier he was sent on several errands in this area, each time required to drop off unmarked packages in an abandoned mailbox. The packages were never explained, and he wasn't stupid enough to ask.

He says it's odd that any of these old houses are even functional, especially considering how strict The Reestablishment is about making sure the civilians never try to go back. In fact, most of the residential neighborhoods were torn down immediately after the initial takeover. So it's very, very rare to find sections left untouched. But there it is, written on the note in too-tight capital letters:

1542 SYCAMORE

We're meeting the supreme commander inside of what used to be someone's home.

"So what do you think we should do? Just ring the doorbell?" Kenji is leading us toward the exit of Omega Point. I'm staring straight ahead in the dim light of this tunnel, trying not to focus on the woodpeckers in my stomach. "What do you think?" Kenji asks again. "Would that be too much? Maybe we should just knock?"

I try to laugh, but the effort is halfhearted at best.

Adam doesn't say a word.

"All right, all right," Kenji says, all seriousness now. "Once we get out there, you know the drill. We link hands. I project to blend the three of us. One of you on either side of me. Got it?"

I'm nodding, trying not to look at Adam as I do.

This is going to be one of the first tests for him and his ability; he'll have to be able to turn off his Energy just as long as he's linked to Kenji. If he can't manage it, Kenji's projection won't work on Adam, and Adam will be exposed. In danger.

"Kent," Kenji says, "you understand the risks, right? If you can't pull this off?"

Adam nods. His face is unflinching. He says he's been training every day, working with Castle to get himself under control. He says he's going to be fine.

He looks at me as he says it.

My emotions jump out of a plane.

I hardly even notice we're nearing the surface when Kenji motions for us to follow him up a ladder. I climb and try to think at the same time, going over and over the plan we spent the early hours of the morning strategizing.

Getting there is the easy part.

Getting inside is where things get tricky.

We're supposed to pretend we're doing a swap—our hostages are supposed to be with the supreme commander, and I'm supposed to oversee their release. It's supposed to be an exchange.

Me for them.

But the truth is that we have no idea what will actually happen. We don't know, for example, who will answer the door. We don't know if *anyone* will answer the door. We don't even know if we're actually meeting inside the house or if we're simply meeting outside of it. We also don't know how they'll react to seeing Adam and Kenji and the makeshift armory we have strapped to our bodies.

We don't know if they'll start shooting right away.

This is the part that scares me. I'm not worried for myself as much as I am for Adam and Kenji. They are the twist in this plan. They are the element of surprise. They're either the unexpected pieces that give us the only advantage we can afford right now, or they're the unexpected pieces that end up dead the minute they're spotted. And I'm starting to think this was a very bad idea.

I'm starting to wonder if I was wrong. If maybe I can't handle this.

But it's too late to turn back now.

THIRTY-TWO

"Wait here."

Kenji tells us to lie low as he pops his head out of the exit. He's already disappeared from sight, his figure blending into the background. He's going to let us know if we're clear to surface.

I'm too nervous to speak.

Too nervous to think.

I can do this we can do this we have no choice but to do this, is all I keep saying to myself.

"Let's go." I hear Kenji's voice from above our heads. Adam and I follow him up the last stretch of the ladder. We're taking one of the alternate exit routes out of Omega Point—one that only 7 people know about, according to Castle. We're taking as many precautions as necessary.

Adam and I manage to haul our bodies aboveground and I immediately feel the cold and Kenji's hand slip around my waist. Cold cold cold. It cuts through the air like little knives slicing across our skin. I look down at my feet and see nothing but a barely perceptible shimmer where my boots are supposed to be. I wiggle my fingers in front of my face.

Nothing.

I look around.

No Adam and no Kenji except for Kenji's invisible hand, now resting at the small of my back.

It worked. Adam made it work. I'm so relieved I want to sing.

"Can you guys hear me?" I whisper, happy no one can see me smiling.

"Yup."

"Yeah, I'm right here," Adam says.

"Nice work, Kent," Kenji says to him. "I know this can't be easy for you."

"It's fine," Adam says. "I'm fine. Let's go."

"Done."

We're like a human chain.

Kenji is between me and Adam and we're linked, holding hands as Kenji guides us through this deserted area. I have no idea where we are, and I'm starting to realize that I seldom do. This world is still so foreign to me, still so new. Spending so much time in isolation while the planet crumbled to pieces didn't do me any favors.

The farther we go, the closer we get to the main road and the closer we get to the compounds that are settled not a mile from here. I can see the boxy shape of their steel structures from where we're standing.

Kenji jerks to a halt.

Says nothing.

"Why aren't we moving?" I ask.

Kenji shushes me. "Can you hear that?"

"What?"

Adam pulls in a breath. "Shit. Someone's coming."

"A tank," Kenji clarifies.

"More than one," Adam adds.

"So why are we still standing here—"

"Wait, Juliette, hold on a second—"

And then I see it. A parade of tanks coming down the main road. I count 6 of them altogether.

Kenji unleashes a series of expletives under his breath.

"What is it?" I ask. "What's the problem?"

"There was only one reason Warner ever ordered us to take more than two tanks out at a time, on the same route," Adam says to me.

"What—"

"They're preparing for a fight."

I gasp.

"He knows," Kenji says. "Dammit! Of course he knows. Castle was right. He knows we're bringing backup. *Shit.*"

"What time is it, Kenji?"

"We have about forty-five minutes."

"Then let's move," I tell him. "We don't have time to worry about what's going to happen afterward. Castle is prepared— he's anticipating something like this. We'll be okay. But if we don't get to that house on time, Winston and Brendan and everyone else might die today."

"*We* might die today," he points out.

"Yeah," I tell him. "That, too."

We're moving through the streets quickly now. Swiftly. Darting through the clearing toward some semblance of civilization and that's when I see it: the remnants of an achingly familiar universe. Little square houses with little square yards that are now nothing more than wild weeds decaying in the wind. The dead grass crunches under our feet, icy and uninviting. We count down the houses.

1542 Sycamore.

It must be this one. It's impossible to miss.

It's the only house on this entire street that looks fully functional. The paint is fresh, clean, a beautiful shade of robin's-egg blue. A small set of stairs leads up to the front porch, where I notice 2 white wicker rocking chairs and a huge planter full of bright blue flowers I've never seen before. I see a welcome mat made of rubber, wind chimes hanging from a wooden beam, clay pots and a small shovel tucked into a corner. It's everything we can never have anymore.

Someone *lives* here.

It's impossible that this exists.

I'm pulling Kenji and Adam toward the home, overcome with emotion, almost forgetting that we're no longer allowed to live in this old, beautiful world.

Someone is yanking me backward.

"This isn't it," Kenji says to me. "This is the wrong street. *Shit.* This is the wrong street—we're supposed to be two streets down—"

"But this house—it's—I mean, Kenji, someone *lives* here—"

"No one lives here," he says. "Someone probably set this up to throw us off—in fact, I bet that house is lined with C4. It's probably a trap designed to catch people wandering unregulated turf. Now come on"—he yanks at my hand again—"we have to hurry. We have seven minutes!"

And even though we're running forward, I keep looking back, waiting to see some sign of life, waiting to see someone step outside to check the mail, waiting to see a bird fly by.

And maybe I'm imagining it.

Maybe I'm insane.

But I could've sworn I just saw a curtain flutter in an upstairs window.

THIRTY-THREE

90 seconds.

The real 1542 Sycamore is just as dilapidated as I'd originally imagined it would be. It's a crumbling mess, its roof groaning under the weight of too many years' negligence. Adam and Kenji and I are standing just around the corner, out of sight even though we're technically still invisible. There is not a single person anywhere, and the entire house looks abandoned. I'm beginning to wonder if this was all just an elaborate joke.

75 seconds.

"You guys stay hidden," I tell Kenji and Adam, struck by sudden inspiration. "I want him to think I'm alone. If anything goes wrong, you guys can jump in, okay? There's too much of a risk that your presence will throw things off too quickly."

They're both quiet a moment.

"*Damn.* That's a good idea," Kenji says. "I should've thought of that."

I can't help but grin, just a little. "I'm going to let go now."

"Hey—good luck," Kenji says, his voice unexpectedly soft. "We'll be right behind you."

"Juliette—"

I hesitate at the sound of Adam's voice.

He almost says something but seems to change his mind. He clears his throat. Whispers, "Promise you'll be careful."

"I promise," I say into the wind, fighting back emotion. Not now. I can't deal with this right now. I have to focus.

So I take a deep breath.

Step forward.

Let go.

10 seconds and I'm trying to breathe

9

and I'm trying to be brave

8

but the truth is I'm scared out of my mind

7

and I have no idea what's waiting for me behind that door

6

and I'm pretty sure I'm going to have a heart attack

5

but I can't turn back now

4

because there it is

3

the door is right in front of me

2

all I have to do is knock

1

but the door flies open first.

"Oh good," he says to me. "You're right on time."

THIRTY-FOUR

"It's refreshing, really," he says. "To see that the youth still value things like punctuality. It's always so frustrating when people waste my time."

My head is full of missing buttons and shards of glass and broken pencil tips. I'm nodding too slowly, blinking like an idiot, unable to find the words in my mouth either because they're lost or because they never existed or simply because I have no idea what to say.

I don't know what I was expecting.

Maybe I thought he'd be old and slumped and slightly blind. Maybe he'd be wearing a patch on one eye and have to walk with a cane. Maybe he'd have rotting teeth and ragged skin and coarse, balding hair and maybe he'd be a centaur, a unicorn, an old witch with a pointy hat anything anything anything but this. Because this isn't possible. This is so hard for me to understand and whatever I was expecting was wrong so utterly, incredibly, horribly wrong.

I'm staring at a man who is absolutely, breathtakingly beautiful.

And he is a *man*.

He has to be at least 45 years old, tall and strong and silhouetted in a suit that fits him so perfectly it's almost unfair. His hair is thick, smooth like hazelnut spread; his jawline is sharp, the lines of his face perfectly symmetrical, his cheekbones hardened by life and age. But it's his eyes that make all the difference. His eyes are the most spectacular things I've ever seen.

They're almost aquamarine.

"Please," he says, flashing me an incredible smile. "Come in."

And it hits me then, right in that moment, because everything suddenly makes sense. His look; his stature; his smooth, classy demeanor; the ease with which I nearly forgot he was a villain—*this man*.

This is Warner's father.

I step into what looks like a small living room. There are old, lumpy couches settled around a tiny coffee table. The wallpaper is yellowed and peeling from age. The house is heavy with a strange, moldy smell that indicates the cracked glass windows haven't been opened in years, and the carpet is forest green under my feet, the walls embellished with fake wood panels that don't make sense to me at all. This house is, in a word, ugly. It seems ridiculous for a man so striking to be found inside of a house so horribly inferior.

"Oh wait," he says, "just one thing."

"Wha—"

He's pinned me against the wall by the throat, his hands carefully sheathed in a pair of leather gloves, already prepared to touch my skin to cut off my oxygen, choke me to death and I'm so sure I'm dying, I'm so sure that this is what it feels like to die, to be utterly immobilized, limp from the neck down. I try to claw at him, kicking at his body with the last of my energy until I'm giving up, forfeiting to my own stupidity, my last thoughts condemning me for being such an idiot, for thinking I could actually come in here and accomplish anything until I realize he's undone my holsters, stolen my guns, put them in his pockets.

He lets me go.

I drop to the floor.

He tells me to have a seat.

I shake my head, coughing against the torture in my lungs, wheezing into the dirty, musty air, heaving in strange, horrible gasps, my whole body in spasms against the pain. I've been inside for less than 2 minutes and he's already overpowered me. I have to figure out how to do something, how to get through this alive. Now's not the time to hold back.

I press my eyes shut for a moment. Try to clear my airways, try to find my head. When I finally look up I see he's already seated himself on one of the chairs, staring at me as though thoroughly entertained.

I can hardly speak. "Where are the hostages?"

"They're fine." This man whose name I do not know waves an indifferent hand in the air. "They'll be just fine. Are you sure you won't sit down?"

"What—" I try to clear my throat and regret it immediately, forcing myself to blink back the traitorous tears burning my eyes. "What do you want from me?"

He leans forward in his seat. Clasps his hands. "You know, I'm not entirely sure anymore."

"What?"

"Well, you've certainly figured out that all of this"—he nods at me, around the room—"is just a distraction, right?" He smiles that same incredible smile. "Surely you've realized that my ultimate goal was to lure your people out into my territory? My men are waiting for just one word. One word from me and they will seek out and destroy all of your little friends waiting so patiently within this half-mile radius."

Terror waves hello to me.

He laughs a little. "If you think I don't know exactly what's going on in my own *land*, young lady, you are quite mistaken." He shakes his head. "I've let these freaks live too freely among us, and it was my mistake. They're causing me too much trouble, and now it's time to take them out."

"I am one of those freaks," I tell him, trying to control the tremble in my voice. "Why did you bring me here if all you want is to kill us? Why me? You didn't have to single me out."

"You're right." He nods. Stands up. Shoves his hands into his pockets. "I came here with a purpose: to clean up the mess my son made, and to finally put an end to the naive efforts of a group of idiotic aberrations. To erase the lot of you from this sorry world. But then," he says, laughing a little, "just as I began drafting my plans, my son came to me and begged me not to kill you. Just you." He stops. Looks up. "He actually *begged me* not to kill you." Laughs again. "It was just as pathetic as it was surprising.

"Of course then I knew I had to meet you," he says, smiling, staring at me like he might be enchanted. "'I must meet the girl who's managed to bewitch my boy!' I said to myself. This girl who's managed to make him lose sight of his pride—his *dignity*—long enough to beg me for a favor." A pause. "Do you know," he says to me, "when my son has ever asked me for a favor?" He cocks his head. Waits for me to answer.

I shake my head.

"Never." He takes a breath. "Never. Not once in nineteen years has he ever asked me for anything. Hard to believe, isn't it?" His smile is wider, brilliant. "I take full credit, of course. I raised him well. Taught him to be entirely self-reliant, self-possessed, unencumbered by the needs and wants that break most other men. So to hear these disgraceful, pleading words come out of his mouth?" He shakes his head. "Well. Naturally, I was intrigued. I had to see you for myself. I needed to understand what he'd seen, what was so special about you that it could've caused such a colossal lapse in judgment. Though, to be perfectly honest," he says, "I really didn't think you'd show up." He takes one hand out of his pocket, gestures with it as he speaks. "I mean I certainly hoped you would. But I thought if you did, you'd at least come with support—some form of backup. But here you are, wearing this spandex monstrosity"—he laughs out loud—"and you're all alone." He studies me. "Very stupid," he says. "But brave. I like that. I can admire bravery.

"Anyhow, I brought you here to teach my son a lesson. I had every intention of killing you," he says, assuming a slow, steady walk around the room. "And I preferred to do it where he would be sure to see it. War is messy," he adds, waving his hand. "It's easy to lose track of who's been killed and how they died and who killed whom, et cetera, et cetera. I wanted this particular death to be as clean and simple as the message it would convey. It's not good for him to form these kinds of attachments, after all. It's my duty as his father to put an end to that kind of nonsense."

I feel sick, so sick, so tremendously sick to my stomach. This man is far worse than I ever could have imagined.

My voice is one hard breath, one loud whisper when I speak. "So why don't you just kill me?"

He hesitates. Says, "I don't know. I had no idea you were going to be quite so lovely. I'm afraid my son never mentioned how beautiful you are. And it's always so difficult to kill a beautiful thing," he sighs. "Besides, you surprised me. You arrived on time. Alone. You were actually willing to sacrifice yourself to save the worthless creatures stupid enough to get themselves caught."

He takes a sharp breath. "Maybe we could keep you. If you don't prove useful, you might prove entertaining, at the very least." He tilts his head, thoughtful. "Though if we did keep you, I suppose you'd have to come back to the capital with me, because I can't trust my son to do anything right anymore. I've given him far too many chances."

"Thanks for the offer," I tell him. "But I'd really rather jump off a cliff."

His laughter is like a hundred little bells, happy and wholesome and contagious. "Oh my." He smiles, bright and warm and devastatingly sincere. He shakes his head. Calls over his shoulder toward what looks like it might be another room—maybe the kitchen, I can't be sure—and says, "Son, would you come in here, please?"

And all I can think is that sometimes you're dying, sometimes you're about to explode, sometimes you're 6 feet under and you're searching for a window when someone pours lighter fluid in your hair and lights a match on your face.

I feel my bones ignite.

Warner is here.

THIRTY-FIVE

He appears in a doorway directly across from where I'm now standing and he looks exactly as I remember him. Golden hair and perfect skin and eyes too bright for their faded shade of emerald. His is an exquisitely handsome face, one I now realize he's inherited from his father. It's the kind of face no one believes in anymore; lines and angles and easy symmetry that's almost offensive in its perfection. No one should ever want a face like that. It's a face destined for trouble, for danger, for an outlet to overcompensate for the excess it stole from an unsuspecting innocent.

It's overdone.

It's too much.

~~It frightens me~~.

Black and green and gold seem to be his colors. His pitch-black suit is tailored to his frame, lean but muscular, offset by the crisp white of his shirt underneath and complemented by the simple black tie knotted at his throat. He stands straight, tall, unflinching. To anyone else he would look imposing, even with his right arm still in a sling. He's the kind of boy who was only ever taught to be a man, who was told to erase the concept of childhood from his life's expectations. His lips do not dare to smile, his forehead does not crease in distress. He has been taught to disguise his emotions, to hide his thoughts from the world and to trust no one and nothing. To take what he wants by whatever means necessary. I can see all of this so clearly.

But he looks different to me.

His gaze is too heavy, his eyes, too deep. His expression is too full of something I don't want to recognize. He's looking at me like I succeeded, like I shot him in the heart and shattered him, like I left him to die after he told me he loved me and I refused to think it was even possible.

And I see the difference in him now. I see what's changed.

He's making no effort to hide his emotions from me.

My lungs are liars, pretending they can't expand just to have a laugh at my expense and my fingers are fluttering, struggling to escape the prison of my bones as if they've waited 17 years to fly away.

Escape, is what my fingers say to me.

Breathe, is what I keep saying to myself.

Warner as a child. Warner as a son. Warner as a boy who has only a limited grasp of his own life. Warner with a father who would teach him a lesson by killing the one thing he'd ever be willing to beg for.

Warner as a human being terrifies me more than anything else.

The supreme commander is impatient. "Sit down," he says to his son, motioning to the couch he was just sitting on.

Warner doesn't say a word to me.

His eyes are glued to my face, my body, to the harness

strapped to my chest; his gaze lingers on my neck, on the marks his father likely left behind and I see the motion in his throat, I see the difficulty he has swallowing down the sight in front of him before he finally rips himself away and walks into the living room. He's so like his father, I'm beginning to realize. The way he walks, the way he looks in a suit, the way he's so meticulous about his hygiene. And yet there is no doubt in my mind that he detests the man he fails so miserably not to emulate.

"So I would like to know," the supreme says, "how, exactly, you managed to get away." He looks at me. "I'm suddenly curious, and my son has made it very difficult to extract these details."

I blink at him.

"Tell me," he says. "How did you escape?"

I'm confused. "The first or the second time?"

"Twice! You managed to escape twice!" He's laughing heartily now; he slaps his knee. "Incredible. Both times, then. How did you get away both times?"

I wonder why he's stalling for time. I don't understand why he wants to talk when so many people are waiting for a war and I can't help but hope that Adam and Kenji and Castle and everyone else haven't frozen to death outside. And while I don't have a plan, I do have a hunch. I have a feeling our hostages might be hidden in the kitchen. So I figure I'll humor him for a little while.

I tell him I jumped out the window the first time. Shot Warner the second time.

The supreme is no longer smiling. "You *shot* him?"

I spare a glance at Warner to see his eyes are still fixed firmly on my face, his mouth still in no danger of moving. I have no idea what he's thinking and I'm suddenly so curious I want to provoke him.

"Yes," I say, meeting Warner's gaze. "I shot him. With his own gun." And the sudden tension in his jaw, the eyes that drop down to the hands he's gripping too tightly in his lap—he looks as if he's wrenched the bullet out of his body with his own 5 fingers.

The supreme runs a hand through his hair, rubs his chin. I notice he seems unsettled for the first time since I've arrived and I wonder how it's possible he had no idea how I escaped.

I wonder what Warner must have said about the bullet wound in his arm.

"What's your name?" I ask before I can stop myself, catching the words just a moment too late. I shouldn't be asking stupid questions but I hate that I keep referring to him as "the supreme," as if he's some kind of untouchable entity.

Warner's father looks at me. "My *name*?"

I nod.

"You may call me Supreme Commander Anderson," he says, still confused. "Why does that matter?"

"*Anderson?* But I thought your last name was Warner." I thought he had a first name I could use to distinguish between him and the Warner I've grown to know too well.

Anderson takes a hard breath, spares a disgusted glance at his son. "Definitely *not*," he says to me. "My son thought it would be a good idea to take his mother's last name, because that's exactly the kind of stupid thing he'd do. The mistake," he says, almost announcing it now, "that he always makes, time and time again—allowing his emotions to get in the way of his *duty*—it's pathetic," he says, spitting in Warner's direction. "Which is why as much as I'd like to let you live, my dear, I'm afraid you're too much of a distraction in his life. I cannot allow him to protect a person who has attempted to *kill* him." He shakes his head. "I can't believe I even have to have this conversation. What an embarrassment he's proven to be."

Anderson reaches into his pocket, pulls out a gun, aims it at my forehead.

Changes his mind.

"I'm sick of always cleaning up after you," he barks at Warner, grabbing his arm, pulling him up from the couch. He pushes his son directly across from me, presses the gun into his good hand.

"Shoot her," he says. "Shoot her right now."

THIRTY-SIX

Warner's gaze is locked onto mine.

He's looking at me, eyes raw with emotion and I'm not sure I even know him anymore. I'm not sure I understand him, I'm not sure I know what he's going to do when he lifts the gun with a strong, steady hand and points it directly at my face.

"Hurry up," Anderson says. "The sooner you do this, the sooner you can move on. Now *get this over with—*"

But Warner cocks his head. Turns around.

Points the gun at his father.

I actually gasp.

Anderson looks bored, irritated, annoyed. He runs an impatient hand across his face before he pulls out another gun—my other gun—from his pocket. It's unbelievable.

Father and son, both threatening to kill each other.

"Point the gun in the right direction, Aaron. This is ridiculous."

Aaron.

I almost laugh in the middle of this insanity.

Warner's first name is *Aaron.*

"I have no interest in killing her," ~~Warner Aaron~~ he says to his father.

"Fine." Anderson points the gun at my head again. "I'll do it then."

"Shoot her," Warner says, "and I will put a bullet through your skull."

It's a triangle of death. Warner pointing a gun at his father, his father pointing a gun at me. I'm the only one without a weapon and I don't know what to do.

If I move, I'm going to die. If I don't move, I'm going to die.

Anderson is smiling.

"How charming," he says. He's wearing an easy, lazy grin, his grip on the gun in his hand so deceptively casual. "What is it? Does she make you feel brave, boy?" A pause. "Does she make you feel strong?"

Warner says nothing.

"Does she make you wish you could be a better man?" A little chuckle. "Has she filled your head with dreams about your future?" A harder laugh.

"You have lost your mind," he says, "over a stupid *child* who's too much of a coward to defend herself even with the barrel of a gun pointed straight at her face. This," he says, pointing the gun harder in my direction, "is the silly little girl you've fallen in love with." He exhales a short, hard breath. "I don't know why I'm surprised."

A new tightness in his breathing. A new tightness in his grip around the gun in his hand. These are the only signs that Warner is even remotely affected by his father's words.

"How many times," Anderson asks, "have you threatened

to kill me? How many times have I woken up in the middle of the night to find you, even as a little boy, trying to shoot me in my sleep?" He cocks his head. "Ten times? Maybe fifteen? I have to admit I've lost count." He stares at Warner. Smiles again. "And how many times," he says, his voice so much louder now, "were you able to go through with it? How many times did you succeed? How many times," he says, "did you burst into tears, apologizing, clinging to me like some demented—"

"Shut your mouth," Warner says, his voice so low, so even, his frame so still it's terrifying.

"You are *weak*," Anderson spits, disgusted. "Too pathetically sentimental. Don't want to kill your own father? Too afraid it'll break your miserable heart?"

Warner's jaw tenses.

"Shoot me," Anderson says, his eyes dancing, bright with amusement. "I said *shoot me!*" he shouts, this time reaching for Warner's injured arm, grabbing him until his fingers are clenched tight around the wound, twisting his arm back until Warner actually gasps from the pain, blinking too fast, trying desperately to suppress the scream building inside of him. His grip on the gun in his good hand wavers, just a little.

Anderson releases his son. Pushes him so hard that Warner stumbles as he tries to maintain his balance. His face is chalk-white. The sling wrapped around his arm is seeping with blood.

"So much talk," Anderson says, shaking his head. "So much talk and never enough follow-through. You *embarrass* me," he says to Warner, face twisted in repulsion. "You make me *sick*."

A sharp crack.

Anderson backhands Warner in the face so hard Warner actually sways for a moment, already unsteady from all the blood he's losing. But he doesn't say a word.

He doesn't make a sound.

He stands there, bearing the pain, blinking fast, jaw so tight, staring at his father with absolutely no emotion on his face; there's no indication he's just been slapped but the bright red mark across his cheek, his temple, and part of his forehead. But his arm sling is more blood than cotton now, and he looks far too ill to be on his feet.

Still, he says nothing.

"Do you want to threaten me again?" Anderson is breathing hard as he speaks. "Do you still think you can defend your little girlfriend? You think I'm going to allow your stupid infatuation to get in the way of everything I've built? Everything I've worked toward?" Anderson's gun is no longer pointed at me. He forgets me long enough to press the barrel of his gun into Warner's forehead, twisting it, jabbing it against his skin as he speaks. "Have I taught you *nothing*?" he shouts. "Have you learned *nothing* from me—"

I don't know how to explain what happens next.

All I know is that my hand is around Anderson's throat and I've pinned him to the wall, so overcome by a blind, burning, all-consuming rage that I think my brain has already caught on fire and dissolved into ash.

237

I squeeze a little harder.

He's sputtering. He's gasping. He's trying to get at my arms, clawing limp hands at my body and he's turning red and blue and purple and I'm enjoying it. I'm enjoying it so, so much.

I think I'm smiling.

I bring my face less than an inch away from his ear and whisper, "Drop the gun."

He does.

I drop him and grab the gun at the same time.

Anderson is wheezing, coughing on the floor, trying to breathe, trying to speak, trying to reach for something to defend himself with and I'm amused by his pain. I'm floating in a cloud of absolute, undiluted hatred for this man and all that he's done and I want to sit and laugh until the tears choke me into a contented sort of silence. I understand so much now. So much.

"Juliette—"

"Warner," I say, so softly, still staring at Anderson's body slumped on the floor in front of me, "I'm going to need you to leave me alone right now."

I weigh the gun in my hands. Test my finger on the trigger. Try to remember what Kenji taught me about taking aim. About keeping my hands and arms steady. Preparing for the kickback—the recoil—of the shot.

I tilt my head. Take inventory of his body parts.

"You," Anderson finally manages to gasp, "you—"

I shoot him in the leg.

He's screaming. I think he's screaming. I can't really hear anything anymore. My ears feel stuffed full of cotton, like someone might be trying to speak to me or maybe someone is shouting at me but everything is muffled and I have too much to focus on right now to pay attention to whatever annoying things are happening in the background. All I know is the reverberation of this weapon in my hand. All I hear is the gunshot echoing through my head. And I decide I'd like to do it again.

I shoot him in the other leg.

There's so much screaming.

I'm entertained by the horror in his eyes. The blood ruining the expensive fabric of his clothes. I want to tell him he doesn't look very attractive with his mouth open like that but then I think he probably wouldn't care about my opinion anyway. I'm just a silly girl to him. Just a silly little girl, a stupid child with a pretty face who's too much of a coward, he said, too much of a coward to defend herself. And oh, wouldn't he like to *keep* me. Wouldn't he like to *keep* me as his little pet. And I realize no. I shouldn't bother sharing my thoughts with him. There's no point wasting words on someone who's about to die.

I take aim at his chest. Try to remember where the heart is.

Not quite to the left. Not quite in the center.

Just—*there*.

Perfect.

THIRTY-SEVEN

I am a thief.

I stole this notebook and this pen from one of the doctors, from one of his lab coats when he wasn't looking, and I shoved them both down my pants. This was just before he ordered those men to come and get me. The ones in the strange suits with the thick gloves and the gas masks with the foggy plastic windows hiding their eyes. They were aliens, I remember thinking. I remember thinking they must've been aliens because they couldn't have been human, the ones who handcuffed my hands behind my back, the ones who strapped me to my seat. They stuck Tasers to my skin over and over for no reason other than to hear me scream but I wouldn't. I whimpered but I never said a word. I felt the tears streak down my cheeks but I wasn't crying.

I think it made them angry.

They slapped me awake even though my eyes were open when we arrived. Someone unstrapped me without removing my handcuffs and kicked me in both kneecaps before ordering me to rise. And I tried. I tried but I couldn't and finally 6 hands shoved me out the door and my face was bleeding on the concrete for a while. I can't really remember the part where they dragged me inside.

I feel cold all the time.

I feel empty, like there is nothing inside of me but this broken heart, the only organ left in this shell. I feel the bleats echo within me, I feel the thumping reverberate around my skeleton. I have a heart, says science, but I am a monster, says society. And I know it, of course I know it. I know what I've done. I'm not asking for sympathy.

But sometimes I think—sometimes I wonder—if I were a monster, surely, I would feel it by now?

I would feel angry and vicious and vengeful. I'd know blind rage and bloodlust and a need for vindication.

Instead I feel an abyss within me that's so deep, so dark I can't see within it; I can't see what it holds. I do not know what I am or what might happen to me.

I do not know what I might do again.

THIRTY-EIGHT

An explosion.

The sound of glass shattering.

Someone yanks me back just as I pull the trigger and the bullet hits the window behind Anderson's head.

I'm spun around.

Kenji is shaking me, shaking me so hard I feel my head jerk back and forth and he's screaming at me, telling me we have to go, that I need to drop the gun, he's breathing hard and he's saying, "I'm going to need you to walk away, okay? Juliette? Can you understand me? I need you to back off right now. You're going to be okay—you're going to be all right—you're going to be fine, you just have to—"

"No, Kenji—" I'm trying to stop him from pulling me away, trying to keep my feet planted where they are because he doesn't understand. He needs to understand. "I have to kill him. I have to make sure he dies," I'm telling him. "I just need you to give me another second—"

"No," he says, "not yet, not right now," and he's looking at me like he's about to break, like he's seen something in my face that he wishes he'd never seen, and he says, "We can't. We can't kill him yet. It's too soon, okay?"

But it's not okay and I don't understand what's happening

but Kenji is reaching for my hand, he's prying the gun out of the fingers I didn't realize were wrapped so tightly around the handle. And I'm blinking. I feel confused and disappointed. I look down at my hands. At my suit. And I can't understand for a moment where all the blood came from.

I glance at Anderson.

His eyes are rolled back in his head. Kenji is checking his pulse. Looks at me, says, "I think he fainted." And my body has begun to shake so violently I can hardly stand.

What have I done.

I back away, needing to find a wall to cling to, something solid to hold on to and Kenji catches me, he's holding me so tightly with one arm and cradling my head with his other hand and I feel like I might want to cry but for some reason I can't. I can't do anything but endure these tremors rocking the length of my entire frame.

"We have to go," Kenji says to me, stroking my hair in a show of tenderness I know is rare for him. I close my eyes against his shoulder, wanting to draw strength from his warmth. "Are you going to be okay?" he asks me. "I need you to walk with me, all right? We'll have to run, too."

"Warner," I gasp, ripping out of Kenji's embrace, eyes wild. "Where's—"

He's unconscious.

A heap on the floor. Arms bound behind his back, an empty syringe tossed on the carpet beside him.

"I took care of Warner," Kenji says.

Suddenly everything is slamming into me at the same

time. All the reasons why we were supposed to be here, what we were trying to accomplish in the first place, the reality of what I've done and what I was about to do. "Kenji," I'm gasping, "Kenji, where's Adam? What happened? Where are the hostages? Is everyone okay?"

"Adam is fine," he reassures me. "We slipped in the back door and found Ian and Emory." He looks toward the kitchen area. "They're in pretty bad shape, but Adam's hauling them out, trying to get them to wake up."

"What about the others? Brendan? A-and Winston?"

Kenji shakes his head. "I have no idea. But I have a feeling we'll be able to get them back."

"How?"

Kenji nods at Warner. "We're going to take this kid hostage."

"What?"

"It's our best bet," he says to me. "Another trade. A real one, this time. Besides, it'll be fine. You take away his guns, and this golden boy is harmless." He walks toward Warner's unmoving figure. Nudges him with the toe of his boot before hauling him up, flipping Warner's body over his shoulder. I can't help but notice that Warner's injured arm is now completely soaked through with blood.

"Come on," Kenji says to me, not unkindly, eyes assessing my frame like he's not sure if I'm stable yet. "Let's get out of here—it's insanity out there and we don't have much time before they move into this street—"

"What?" I'm blinking too fast. "What do you mean—"

Kenji looks at me, disbelief written across his features. "The *war*, princess. They're all fighting to the death out there—"

"But Anderson never made the call—he said they were waiting for a word from him—"

"No," Kenji says. "Anderson didn't make the call. Castle did."

Oh

God.

"Juliette!"

Adam is rushing into the house, whipping around to find my face until I run forward and he catches me in his arms without thinking, without remembering that we don't do this anymore, that we're not together anymore, that he shouldn't be touching me at all. "You're okay—you're *okay*—"

"LET'S GO," Kenji barks for the final time. "I know this is an emotional moment or whatever, but we have to get our asses the hell out of here. I swear, Kent—"

But Kenji stops.

His eyes drop.

Adam is on his knees, a look of fear and pain and horror and anger and terror etched into every line on his face and I'm trying to shake him, I'm trying to get him to tell me what's wrong and he can't move, he's frozen on the ground, his eyes glued to Anderson's body, his hands reaching out to touch the hair that was so perfectly set almost a moment ago and I'm begging him to speak to me, begging him to tell me what happened and it's like the world shifts in his eyes, like nothing will ever be right in this world and nothing can ever be good again and he parts his lips.

He tries to speak.

"My father," he says. "This man is my father."

THIRTY-NINE

"*Shit.*"

Kenji presses his eyes shut like he can't believe this is happening. "Shit shit *shit.*" He shifts Warner against his shoulders, wavers between being sensitive and being a soldier and says, "Adam, man, I'm sorry, but we really have to get out of here—"

Adam gets up, blinking back what I can only imagine are a thousand thoughts, memories, worries, hypotheses, and I call his name but it's like he can't even hear it. He's confused, disoriented, and I'm wondering how this man could possibly be his father when Adam told me his dad was dead.

Now is not the time for these conversations.

Something explodes in the distance and the impact rattles the ground, the windows, the doors of this house, and Adam seems to snap back to reality. He jumps forward, grabs my arm, and we're bolting out the door.

Kenji is in the lead, somehow managing to run despite the weight of Warner's body, limp, hanging over his shoulder, and he's shouting at us to stay close behind. I'm spinning, analyzing the chaos around us. The sounds of gunshots are too close too close too close.

"Where are Ian and Emory?" I ask Adam. "Did you get them out?"

"A couple of our guys were fighting not too far from here and managed to commandeer one of the tanks—I got them to carry those two back to Point," he tells me, shouting so I can hear him. "It was the safest transport possible."

I'm nodding, gasping for air as we fly through the streets and I'm trying to focus on the sounds around us, trying to figure out who's winning, trying to figure out if our numbers have been decimated. We round the corner.

You'd think it'd be a massacre.

50 of our people are fighting against 500 of Anderson's soldiers, who are unloading round after round, shooting at anything that could possibly be a target. Castle and the others are holding their ground, bloody and wounded but fighting back as best they can. Our men and women are armed and storming forward to match the shots of the opposition; others are fighting the only way they know how: one man has his hands to the ground, freezing the earth beneath the soldiers' feet, causing them to lose balance; another man is darting through the soldiers with such speed he's nothing but a blur, confusing the men and knocking them down and stealing their guns. I look up and see a woman hiding in a tree, throwing what must be knives or arrows in such rapid succession that the soldiers don't have a moment to react before they're hit from above.

Then there's Castle in the middle of it all, his hands outstretched over his head, collecting a whirlwind of particles, debris, scattered strips of steel and broken branches with nothing more than the coercion of his fingertips. The others have formed a human wall around him, protecting him as he forms a cyclone of such magnitude that even I can see he's straining to maintain control of it.

Then

he lets go.

The soldiers are shouting, screaming, running back and ducking for cover but most are too slow to escape the reach of so much destruction and they're down, impaled by shards of glass and stone and wood and broken metal but I know this defense won't last for long.

Someone has to tell Castle.

Someone has to tell him to go, to get out of here, that Anderson is down and that we have 2 of our hostages and Warner in tow. He has to get our men and women back to Omega Point before the soldiers get smart and someone throws a bomb big enough to destroy everything. Our numbers won't hold up for much longer and this is the perfect opportunity for them to get safe.

I tell Adam and Kenji what I'm thinking.

"But how?" Kenji shouts above the chaos. "How can we get to him? If we run through there we're dead! We need some kind of distraction—"

"What?" I yell back.

"A *distraction*!" he shouts. "We need something to throw off the soldiers long enough for one of us to grab Castle and give him the green light—we don't have much time—"

Adam is already trying to grab me, he's already trying to stop me, he's already begging me not to do what he thinks I'm going to do and I tell him it's okay. I tell him not to worry. I tell him to get the others to safety and promise him I'm going to be just fine but he reaches for me, he's pleading with his eyes and I'm so tempted to stay here, right next to him, but I break away. I finally know what I need to do; I'm finally ready to help; I'm finally kind of a little bit sure that maybe this time I might be able to control it and I have to try.

So I stumble back.

I close my eyes.

I let go.

I fall to my knees and press my palm to the ground and feel the power coursing through me, feel it curdling in my blood and mixing with the anger, the passion, the fire inside of me and I think of every time my parents called me a monster, a horrible terrifying mistake and I think of all the nights I sobbed myself to sleep and see all the faces that wanted me dead and then it's like a slide show of images reeling through my mind, men and women and children, innocent protesters run over in the streets; I see guns and bombs, fire and devastation, so much suffering suffering suffering and I steel myself. I flex my fist. I pull back my arm and

I

s h a t t e r

what's left of this earth.

FORTY

I'm still here.

I open my eyes and I'm momentarily astonished, confused, half expecting to find myself dead or brain-damaged or at the very least mangled on the ground, but this reality refuses to vanish.

The world under my feet is rumbling, rattling, shaking and thundering to life and my fist is still pressed into the ground and I'm afraid to let go. I'm on my knees, looking up at both sides of this battle and I see the soldiers slowing down. I see their eyes dart around. I see their feet slipping failing to stay standing and the snaps, the groans, the unmistakable cracks that are now creaking through the middle of the pavement cannot be ignored and it's like the jaws of life are stretching their joints, grinding their teeth, yawning themselves awake to witness our disgrace.

The ground looks around, its mouth gaping open at the injustice, the violence, the calculated ploys for power that stop for no one and nothing and are sated only by the blood of the weak, the screams of the unwilling. It's as if the earth thought to take a peek at what we've been doing all this time and it's terrifying just how disappointed it sounds.

Adam is running.

He's dashing through a crowd still gasping for air and an explanation for the earthquake under their feet and he tackles Castle, he pins him down, he's shouting to the men and the women and he ducks, he dodges a stray bullet, he pulls Castle to his feet and our people have begun to run.

The soldiers on the opposite side are stumbling over each other and tripping into a tangle of limbs as they try to outrun one another and I'm wondering how much longer I have to hold on, how much longer this must go on before it's sufficient, and Kenji shouts, "Juliette!"

And I spin around just in time to hear him tell me to let go.

So I do.

The wind the trees the fallen leaves all slip and slide back into place with one giant inhalation and everything stops and for a moment I can't remember what it's like to live in a world that isn't falling apart.

Kenji yanks me up by the arm and we're running, we're the last of our group to leave and he's asking me if I'm okay and I'm wondering how he's still carrying Warner, I'm thinking Kenji must be a hell of a lot stronger than he looks, and I'm thinking I'm too hard on him sometimes, I'm thinking I don't give him enough credit. I'm just beginning to realize that he's one of my favorite people on this planet and I'm so happy he's okay.

I'm so happy he's my friend.

I cling to his hand and let him lead me toward a tank abandoned on our side of the divide and suddenly I realize I can't see Adam, that I don't know where he's gone and I'm frantic, I'm screaming his name until I feel his arms around my waist, his words in my ear, and we're still diving for cover as the final shots sound in the distance.

We clamber into the tank.

We close the doors.

We disappear.

FORTY-ONE

Warner's head is on my lap.

His face is smooth and calm and peaceful in a way I've never seen it and I almost reach out to stroke his hair before I remember exactly how awkward this actually is.

~~Murderer on my lap~~

~~Murderer on my lap~~

~~Murderer on my lap~~

I look to my right.

Warner's legs are resting on Adam's knees and he looks just as uncomfortable as I am.

"Hang tight, guys," Kenji says, still driving the tank toward Omega Point. "I know this is about a million different kinds of weird, but I didn't exactly have enough time to think of a better plan."

He glances at the ~~2~~ 3 of us but no one says a word until

"I'm so happy you guys are okay." I say it like those 9 syllables have been sitting inside of me for too long, like they've been kicked out, evicted from my mouth, and only then do I realize exactly how worried I was that the 3 of us wouldn't make it back alive. "I'm so, so happy you're okay."

Deep, solemn, steady breathing all around.

"How are you feeling?" Adam asks me. "Your arm—you're all right?"

"Yeah." I flex my wrist and try not to wince. "I'm okay. These gloves and this metal thing actually helped, I think." I wiggle my fingers. Examine my gloves. "Nothing is broken."

"That was pretty badass," Kenji says to me. "You really saved us back there."

I shake my head. "Kenji—about what happened—in the house—I'm really sorry, I—"

"Hey, how about let's not talk about that right now."

"What's going on?" Adam asks, alert. "What happened?"

"Nothing," Kenji says quickly.

Adam ignores him. Looks at me. "What happened? Are you all right?"

"I just—I j-just—" I struggle to speak. "What happened—with Warner's da—"

Kenji swears very loudly.

My mouth freezes midmovement.

My cheeks burn as I realize what I've said. As I remember what Adam said just before we ran from that house. He's suddenly pale, pressing his lips together and looking away, out the tiny window of this tank.

"Listen . . ." Kenji clears his throat. "We don't have to talk about that, okay? In fact, I think I might rather *not* talk about that? Because that shit is just too weird for me to—"

"I don't know how it's even possible," Adam whispers. He's blinking, staring straight ahead now, blinking and blinking and blinking and "I keep thinking I must be dreaming," he says, "that I'm just hallucinating this whole thing. But then"—he drops his head in his hands, laughs a harsh laugh—"that is one face I will never forget."

"Didn't—didn't you ever meet the supreme commander?" I dare to ask. "Or even see a picture of him . . . ? Isn't that something you'd see in the army?"

Adam shakes his head.

Kenji speaks. "His whole kick was always being, like, invisible. He got some sick thrill out of being this unseen power."

"Fear of the unknown?"

"Something like that, yeah. I heard he didn't want his pictures anywhere—didn't make any public speeches, either—because he thought if people could put a face on him, it would make him vulnerable. Human. And he always got his thrills from scaring the shit out of everyone. Being the ultimate power. The ultimate threat. Like—how can you fight something if you can't even see it? Can't even find it?"

"That's why it was such a big deal for him to be here," I realize out loud.

"Pretty much."

"But you thought your dad was dead," I say to Adam. "I thought you said he was dead?"

"Just so you guys know," Kenji interjects, "I'm still voting for the *we don't have to talk about this* option. You know. Just so you know. Just putting that out there."

"I thought he was," Adam says, still not looking at me. "That's what they told me."

"Who did?" Kenji asks. Catches himself. Winces. "Shit. Fine. *Fine.* I'm curious."

Adam shrugs. "It's all starting to come together now. All the things I didn't understand. How messed up my life was with James. After my mom died, my dad was never around unless he wanted to get drunk and beat the crap out of someone. I guess he was living a completely different life somewhere else. That's why he used to leave me and James alone all the time."

"But that doesn't make sense," Kenji says. "I mean, not the parts about your dad being a dick, but just, like, the whole scope of it. Because if you and Warner are brothers, and you're eighteen, and Warner is nineteen, and Anderson has always been married to Warner's mom—"

"My parents were never married," Adam says, eyes widening as he speaks the last word.

"You were the love child?" Kenji says, disgusted. "I mean—you know, no offense to you—it's just, I do not want to think about Anderson having some kind of passionate love affair. That is just sick."

Adam looks like he's been frozen solid. "Holy shit," he whispers.

"But I mean, why even have a love affair?" Kenji asks. "I never understood that kind of crap. If you're not happy, just leave. Don't cheat. Doesn't take a genius to figure that shit out. I mean"—he hesitates—"I'm *assuming* it was a love affair," Kenji says, still driving and unable to see the look on Adam's face. "Maybe it wasn't a *love* affair. Maybe it was

257

just another dude-being-a-jackass kind of th—" He catches himself, cringes. "Shit. See, this is why I do *not* talk to people about their personal problems—"

"It was," Adam says, barely breathing now. "I have no idea why he never married her, but I know he loved my mom. He never gave a damn about the rest of us," he says. "Just her. It was always about her. Everything was about her. The few times a month he was ever at home, I was always supposed to stay in my room. I was supposed to be very quiet. I had to knock on my own door and get permission before I could come out, even just to use the bathroom. And he used to get pissed whenever my mom would let me out. He didn't want to see me unless he had to. My mom had to sneak me my dinner just so he wouldn't go nuts about how she was feeding me too much and not saving anything for herself," he says. He shakes his head. "And he was even worse when James was born."

Adam blinks like he's going blind.

"And then when she died," he says, taking a deep breath, "when she died all he ever did was blame me for her death. He always told me it was my fault she got sick, and it was my fault she died. That I needed too much, that she didn't eat enough, that she got weak because she was too busy taking care of us, giving food to us, giving . . . everything to us. To me and James." His eyebrows pull together. "And I believed him for so long. I figured that was why he left all the time. I thought it was some kind of punishment. I thought I deserved it."

I'm too horrified to speak.

"And then he just . . . I mean he was never around when I was growing up," Adam says, "and he was always an asshole. But after she died he just . . . lost his mind. He used to come by just to get piss-drunk. He used to force me to stand in front of him so he could throw his empty bottles at me. And if I flinched—if I *flinched*—"

He swallows, hard.

"That's all he ever did," Adam says, his voice quieter now. "He would come over. Get drunk. Beat the shit out of me. I was fourteen when he stopped coming back." Adam stares at his hands, palms up. "He sent some money every month for us to survive on and then—" A pause. "Two years later I got a letter from our brand-new government telling me my father was dead. I figured he probably got wasted again and did something stupid. Got hit by a car. Fell into the ocean. Whatever. It didn't matter. I was happy he was dead, but I had to drop out of school. I enlisted because the money was gone and I had to take care of James and I knew I wouldn't find another job."

Adam shakes his head. "He left us with nothing, not a single penny, not even a piece of meat to live off of, and now I'm sitting here, in this tank, running from a global war my own *father* has helped orchestrate"—he laughs a hard, hollow laugh—"and the one other worthless person on this planet is lying unconscious in my lap." Adam is actually laughing now, laughing hard, disbelieving, his hand caught in his hair, tugging at the roots, gripping his skull. "And he's my *brother*. My own flesh and blood.

"My father had an entirely separate life I didn't know about and instead of being dead like he should be, he gave me a *brother* who almost tortured me to death in a *slaughterhouse*—" He runs an unsteady hand over the length of his face, suddenly cracking, suddenly slipping, suddenly losing control and his hands are shaking and he has to curl them into fists and he presses them against his forehead and says, "He has to die."

And I'm not breathing, not even a little bit, not even at all, when he says,

"My father," he says, "I have to kill him."

FORTY-TWO

~~I'm going to tell you a secret.~~

~~I don't regret what I did. I'm not sorry at all.~~
~~In fact, if I had a chance to do it again I know this time~~
~~I'd do it right. I'd shoot Anderson right through the heart.~~

~~And I would enjoy it.~~

FORTY-THREE

I don't even know where to begin.

Adam's pain is like a handful of straw shoved down my throat. He has no parents but a father who beat him, abused him, abandoned him only to ruin the rest of the world and left him a brand-new brother who is exactly his opposite in every possible way.

Warner whose first name is no longer a mystery, Adam whose last name isn't actually Kent.

Kent is his middle name, Adam said to me. He said he didn't want to have anything to do with his father and never told people his real last name. He has that much, at least, in common with his brother.

That, and the fact that both of them have some kind of immunity to my touch.

Adam and Aaron Anderson.

Brothers.

I'm sitting in my room, sitting in the dark, struggling to reconcile Adam with his new sibling who is really nothing more than a boy, a child who hates his father and as a result, a child who made a series of very unfortunate decisions in life. 2 brothers. 2 very different sets of choices.

2 very different lives.

Castle came to me this morning—now that all the injured have been set up in the medical wing and the insanity has subsided—he came to me and he said, "Ms. Ferrars, you were very brave yesterday. I wanted to extend my gratitude to you, and thank you for what you did—for showing your support. I don't know that we would've made it out of there without you."

I smiled, struggled to swallow the compliment and assumed he was finished but then he said, "In fact, I'm so impressed that I'd like to offer you your first official assignment at Omega Point."

My first official assignment.

"Are you interested?" he asked.

I said yes yes yes of course I was interested, I was definitely interested, I was so very, very interested to finally have something to do—something to accomplish—and he smiled and he said, "I'm so happy to hear it. Because I can't think of anyone better suited to this particular position than you."

I beamed.

The sun and the moon and the stars called and said, "Turn down the beaming, please, because you're making it hard for us to see," and I didn't listen, I just kept on beaming. And then I asked Castle for the details of my official assignment. The one perfectly suited to me.

And he said

"I'd like you to be in charge of maintaining and interrogating our new visitor."

And I stopped beaming.

I stared at Castle.

"I will, of course, be overseeing the entire process," Castle continued, "so feel free to come to me with questions and concerns. But we'll need to take advantage of his presence here, and that means trying to get him to speak." Castle was quiet a moment. "He . . . seems to have an odd sort of attachment to you, Ms. Ferrars, and—forgive me— but I think it would behoove us to exploit it. I don't think we can afford the luxury of ignoring any possible advantages available to us. Anything he can tell us about his father's plans, or where our hostages might be, will be invaluable to our efforts. And we don't have much time," he said. "I'm afraid I'll need you to get started right away."

And I asked the world to open up, I said, world, please open up, because I'd love to fall into a river of magma and die, just a little bit, but the world couldn't hear me because Castle was still talking and he said, "Perhaps you can talk some sense into him? Tell him we're not interested in hurting him? Convince him to help us get our remaining hostages back?"

I said, "Oh," I said surely, "he's in some kind of holding cell? Behind bars or something?"

But Castle laughed, amused by my sudden, unexpected hilarity and said don't be silly, Ms. Ferrars, "We don't have anything like that here. I never thought we'd need to keep anyone captive at Omega Point. But yes, he's in his own room, and yes, the door is locked."

"So you want me to go inside of his room?" I asked. "With him? Alone?"

Calm! Of course I was calm. I was definitely absolutely everything that is the opposite of calm.

But then Castle's forehead tightened, concerned. "Is that a problem?" he asked me. "I thought—because he can't touch you—I actually thought you might not feel as threatened by him as the others do. He's aware of your abilities, is he not? I imagine he would be wise to stay away from you for his own benefit."

And it was funny, because there it was: a vat of ice, all over my head, dripping leaking seeping into my bones, and actually no, it wasn't funny at all, because I had to say, "Yes. Right. Yes, of course. I almost forgot. Of course he wouldn't be able to touch me," you're quite right, Mr. Castle, sir, what on earth was I thinking.

Castle was relieved, so relieved, as if he'd taken a dip in a warm pool he was sure would be frozen.

And now I'm here, sitting in exactly the same position I was in 2 hours ago and I'm beginning to wonder

how much longer

I can keep this secret to myself.

FORTY-FOUR

This is the door.

This one, right in front of me, this is where Warner is staying. There are no windows and there is no way to see inside of his room and I'm starting to think that this situation is the exact antonym of excellent.

Yes.

I am going to walk into his room, completely unarmed, because the guns are buried deep down in the armory and because I'm lethal, so why would I need a gun? No one in their right mind would lay a hand on me, no one but Warner, of course, whose half-crazed attempt at stopping me from escaping out of my window resulted in this discovery, his discovery that he can touch me without harming himself.

And I've said a word of this to exactly no one.

I really thought that perhaps I'd imagined it, just until Warner kissed me and told me he loved me and then, that's when I knew I could no longer pretend this wasn't happening. But it's only been about 4 weeks since that day, and I didn't know how to bring it up. I thought maybe I wouldn't have to bring it up. I really, quite desperately didn't *want* to bring it up.

And now, the thought of telling anyone, of making it

known to Adam, of all people, that the one person he hates most in this world—second only to his own father—is the one other person who can touch me? That Warner has already touched me, that his hands have known the shape of my body and his lips have known the taste of my mouth—never mind that it wasn't something I actually wanted—I just can't do it.

Not now. Not after everything.

So this situation is entirely my own fault. And I have to deal with it.

I steel myself and step forward.

There are 2 men I've never met before standing guard outside Warner's door. This doesn't mean much, but it gives me a modicum of calm. I nod hello in the guards' direction and they greet me with such enthusiasm I actually wonder whether they've confused me with someone else.

"Thanks so much for coming," one of them says to me, his long, shaggy blond hair slipping into his eyes. "He's been completely insane since he woke up—throwing things around and trying to destroy the walls—he's been threatening to kill all of us. He says you're the only one he wants to talk to, and he's only just calmed down because we told him you were on your way."

"We had to take out all the furniture," the other guard adds, his brown eyes wide, incredulous. "He was breaking *everything*. He wouldn't even eat the food we gave him."

The antonym of excellent.

The antonym of excellent.

The antonym of excellent.

I manage a feeble smile and tell them I'll see what I can do to sedate him. They nod, eager to believe I'm capable of something I know I'm not and they unlock the door. "Just knock to let us know when you're ready to leave," they tell me. "Call for us and we'll open the door."

I'm nodding yes and sure and of course and trying to ignore the fact that I'm more nervous right now than I was meeting his father. To be alone in a room with Warner—to be alone with him and to not know what he might do or what he's capable of and I'm so confused, because I don't even know who he is anymore.

He's 100 different people.

He's the person who forced me to torture a toddler against my will. He's the child so terrorized, so psychologically tormented that he'd try to kill his own father in his sleep. He's the boy who shot a defecting soldier in the forehead; the boy who was trained to be a cold, heartless murderer by a man he thought he could trust. I see Warner as a child desperately seeking his dad's approval. I see him as the leader of an entire sector, eager to conquer me, to use me. I see him feeding a stray dog. I see him torturing Adam almost to death. And then I hear him telling me he loves me, feel him *kissing* me with such unexpected passion and desperation that I don't know I don't know I don't know what I'm walking into.

I don't know who he'll be this time. Which side of

himself he'll show me today.

But then I think this must be different. Because he's in my territory now, and I can always call for help if something goes wrong.

He's not going to hurt me.

I hope.

FORTY-FIVE

I step inside.

The door slams shut behind me but the Warner I find inside this room is not one I recognize at all. He's sitting on the floor, back against the wall, legs outstretched in front of him, feet crossed at the ankles. He's wearing nothing but socks, a simple white T-shirt, and a pair of black slacks. His coat, his shoes, and his fancy shirt are all discarded on the ground. His body is toned and muscular and hardly contained by his undershirt; his hair is a blond mess, disheveled for what's probably the first time in his life.

But he's not looking at me. He doesn't even look up as I take a step closer. He doesn't flinch.

I've forgotten how to breathe again.

Then

"Do you have any idea," he says, so quietly, "how many times I've read this?" He lifts his hand but not his head and holds up a small, faded rectangle between 2 fingers.

And I'm wondering how it's possible to be punched in the gut by so many fists at the same time.

My notebook.

He's holding my notebook.

Of course he is.

I can't believe I'd forgotten. He was the last person to

touch my notebook; the last person to see it. He took it from me when he found that I'd hidden it in the pocket of my dress back on base. This was just before I escaped, just before Adam and I jumped out the window and ran away. Just before Warner realized he could touch me.

And now, to know that he's read my most painful thoughts, my most anguished confessions—the things I wrote while in complete and utter isolation, certain that I would die in that very cell, so certain no one would ever read the things I wrote down—to know that he's read these desperate whispers of my private mind.

I feel absolutely, unbearably naked.

Petrified.

So vulnerable.

He flips the notebook open at random. Scans the page until he stops. He finally looks up, his eyes sharper, brighter, a more beautiful shade of green than they've ever been and my heart is beating so fast I can't even feel it anymore.

And he begins to read.

"No—," I gasp, but it's too late.

"*I sit here every day,*" he says. "*175 days I've sat here so far. Some days I stand up and stretch and feel these stiff bones, these creaky joints, this trampled spirit cramped inside my being. I roll my shoulders, I blink my eyes, I count the seconds creeping up the walls, the minutes shivering under my skin, the breaths I have to remember to take. Sometimes I allow my mouth to drop open, just a little bit; I touch my tongue to the backs of my teeth and the seam of my lips and I walk around this small space, I trail my fingers along the cracks in the concrete and wonder, I wonder what it would be like to speak out* loud and be heard. I hold my breath, listen closely for anything, any sound of life and wonder at the beauty, the impossibility of possibly hearing another person breathing beside me."

He presses the back of his fist to his mouth for just a moment before continuing.

"I stop. I stand still. I close my eyes and try to remember a world beyond these walls. I wonder what it would be like to know that I'm not dreaming, that this isolated existence is not caged within my own mind.

"And I do," he says, reciting the words from memory now, his head resting back against the wall, eyes pressed shut as he whispers, "I do wonder, I think about it all the time. What it would be like to kill myself. Because I never really know, I still can't tell the difference, I'm never quite certain whether or not I'm actually alive. So I sit here. I sit here every single day."

I'm rooted to the ground, frozen in my own skin, unable to move forward or backward for fear of waking up and realizing that this is actually happening. I feel like I might die of embarrassment, of this invasion of privacy, and I want to run and run and run and run and run

"Run, I said to myself." Warner has picked up my notebook again.

"Please." I'm begging him. "Please s-stop—"

He looks up, looks at me like he can really see me, see into me, like he wants me to see into him and then he drops his eyes, he clears his throat, he starts over, he reads from my journal.

"Run, I said to myself. Run until your lungs collapse, until the *wind whips and snaps at your tattered clothes, until you're a blur that blends into the background.*

"Run, Juliette, run faster, run until your bones break and your shins split and your muscles atrophy and your heart dies because it was always too big for your chest and it beat too fast for too long and run.

"Run run run until you can't hear their feet behind you. Run until they drop their fists and their shouts dissolve in the air. Run with your eyes open and your mouth shut and dam the river rushing up behind your eyes. Run, Juliette.

"Run until you drop dead.

"Make sure your heart stops before they ever reach you. Before they ever touch you.

"Run, I said."

I have to clench my fists until I feel pain, anything to push these memories away. I don't want to remember. I don't want to think about these things anymore. I don't want to think about what else I wrote on those pages, what else Warner knows about me now, what he must think of me. I can only imagine how pathetic and lonely and desperate I must appear to him. ~~I don't know why I care.~~

"Do you know," he says, closing the cover of the journal only to lay his hand on top of it. Protecting it. Staring at it. "I couldn't sleep for days after I read that entry. I kept wanting to know which people were chasing you down the street, who it was you were running from. I wanted to find them," he says, so softly, "and I wanted to rip their limbs off, one by one. I wanted to murder them in ways that

273

would horrify you to hear."

I'm shaking now, whispering, "Please, please give that back to me."

He touches the tips of his fingers to his lips. Tilts his head back, just a little. Smiles a strange, unhappy smile. Says, "You must know how sorry I am. That I"—he swallows—"that I kissed you like that. I confess I had no idea you would shoot me for it."

And I realize something. "Your arm," I breathe, astonished. He wears no sling. He moves with no difficulty. There's no bruising or swelling or scars I can see.

His smile is brittle. "Yes," he says. "It was healed when I woke up to find myself in this room."

Sonya and Sara. They helped him. I wonder why anyone here would do him such a kindness. I force myself to take a step back. "Please," I tell him. "My notebook, I—"

"I promise you," he says, "I never would've kissed you if I didn't think you wanted me to."

And I'm so shocked that for a moment I forget all about my notebook. I meet his heavy gaze. Manage to steady my voice. "I told you I *hated* you."

"Yes," he says. He nods. "Well. You'd be surprised how many people say that to me."

"I don't think I would."

His lips twitch. "You tried to kill me."

"That amuses you."

"Oh yes," he says, his grin growing. "I find it fascinating." A pause. "Would you like to know why?"

I stare at him.

"Because all you ever said to me," he explains, "was that you didn't want to hurt anyone. You didn't want to *murder people*."

"I don't."

"Except for me?"

I'm all out of letters. Fresh out of words. Someone has robbed me of my entire vocabulary.

"That decision was so easy for you to make," he says. "So simple. You had a gun. You wanted to run away. You pulled the trigger. That was it."

He's right.

I keep telling myself I have no interest in killing people but somehow I find a way to justify it, to rationalize it when I want to.

Warner. Castle. Anderson.

I wanted to kill every single one of them. And I would have.

What is happening to me.

I've made a huge mistake coming here. Accepting this assignment. Because I can't be alone with Warner. Not like this. Being alone with him is making my insides hurt in ways I don't want to understand.

I have to leave.

"Don't go," he whispers, eyes on my notebook again. "Please," he says. "Sit with me. Stay with me. I just want to see you. You don't even have to say anything."

Some crazed, confused part of my brain actually wants

to sit down next to him, actually wants to hear what he has to say before I remember Adam and what he would think if he knew, what he would say if he were here and could see I was interested in spending my time with the same person who shot him in the leg, broke his ribs, and hung him on a conveyor belt in an abandoned slaughterhouse, leaving him to bleed to death one minute at a time.

I must be insane.

Still, I don't move.

Warner relaxes against the wall. "Would you like me to read to you?"

I'm shaking my head over and over and over again, whispering, "Why are you doing this to me?"

And he looks like he's about to respond before he changes his mind. Looks away. Lifts his eyes to the ceiling and smiles, just a tiny bit. "You know," he says, "I could tell, the very first day I met you. There was something about you that felt different to me. Something in your eyes that was so tender. Raw. Like you hadn't yet learned how to hide your heart from the world." He's nodding now, nodding to himself about something and I can't imagine what it is. "Finding this," he says, his voice soft as he pats the cover of my notebook, "was so"—his eyebrows pull together—"it was so extraordinarily painful." He finally looks at me and he looks like a completely different person. Like he's trying to solve a tremendously difficult equation. "It was like meeting a friend for the very first time."

~~Why are my hands trembling.~~

He takes a deep breath. Looks down. Whispers, "I am so tired, love. I'm so very, very tired."

~~Why won't my heart stop racing.~~

"How much time," he says after a moment, "do I have before they kill me?"

"Kill you?"

He stares at me.

I'm startled into speaking. "We're not going to kill you," I tell him. "We have no intention of hurting you. We just want to use you to get back our men. We're holding you hostage."

Warner's eyes go wide, his shoulders stiffen. "What?"

"We have no reason to kill you," I explain. "We only need to barter with your life—"

Warner laughs a loud, full-bodied laugh. Shakes his head. Smiles at me in that way I've only ever seen once before, looking at me like I'm the sweetest thing he's ever decided to eat.

~~Those dimples.~~

"Dear, sweet, beautiful girl," he says. "Your team here has greatly overestimated my father's affection for me. I'm sorry to have to tell you this, but keeping me here is not going to give you the advantage you were hoping for. I doubt my father has even noticed I'm gone. So I would like to request that you please either kill me, or let me go. But I beg you not to waste my time by confining me here."

I'm checking my pockets for spare words and sentences but I'm finding none, not an adverb, not a preposition or even a dangling participle because there doesn't exist a single response to such an outlandish request.

Warner is still smiling at me, shoulders shaking in silent amusement.

"But that's not even a viable argument," I tell him. "No one *likes* to be held hostage—"

He takes a tight breath. Runs a hand through his hair. Shrugs. "Your men are wasting their time," he says. "Kidnapping me will never work to your advantage. This much," he says, "I can guarantee."

FORTY-SIX

Time for lunch.

Kenji and I are sitting on one side of the table, Adam and James on the other.

We've been sitting here for half an hour now, deliberating over my conversation with Warner. I conveniently left out the parts about my journal, though I'm starting to wonder if I should've mentioned it. I'm also starting to wonder if I should just come clean about Warner being able to touch me. But every time I look at Adam I just can't bring myself to do it. I don't even know *why* Warner can touch me. Maybe Warner is the fluke I thought Adam was. Maybe all of this is some kind of cosmic joke told at my expense.

I don't know what to do yet.

But somehow the extra details of my conversation with Warner seem too personal, too embarrassing to share. I don't want anyone to know, for example, that Warner told me he loves me. I don't want anyone to know that he has my journal, or that he's read it. Adam is the only other person who even knows it exists, and he, at least, was kind enough to respect my privacy. He's the one who saved my journal from the asylum, the one who brought it back to me in the first place. But he said he never read the things I wrote. He said he knew they must've been very private thoughts and that he didn't want to intrude.

Warner, on the other hand, has ransacked my mind.

I feel so much more apprehensive around him now. Just thinking about being near him makes me feel anxious, nervous, so vulnerable. I hate that he knows my secrets. My secret thoughts.

It shouldn't be him who knows anything about me at all.

It should be *him*. The one sitting right across from me. The one with the dark-blue eyes and the dark-brown hair and the hands that have touched my heart, my body.

And he doesn't seem okay right now.

Adam's head is down, his eyebrows drawn, his hands clenched together on the table. He hasn't touched his food and he hasn't said a word since I summarized my meeting with Warner. Kenji has been just as quiet. Everyone's been a bit more solemn since our recent battle; we lost several people from Omega Point.

I take a deep breath and try again.

"So what do you think?" I ask them. "About what he said about Anderson?" I'm careful not to use the word *dad* or *father* anymore, especially around James. I don't know what, if anything, Adam has said to James about the issue, and it's not my business to pry. Worse still, Adam hasn't said a word about it since we got back, and it's already been 2 days. "Do you think he's right that Anderson won't care if he's been taken hostage?"

James squirms around in his seat, eyes narrowed as he chews the food in his mouth, looking at the group of us like he's waiting to memorize everything we say.

Adam rubs his forehead. "That," he finally says, "might actually have some merit."

Kenji frowns, folds his arms, leans forward. "Yeah. It is kind of weird. We haven't heard a single thing from their side, and it's been over forty-eight hours."

"What does Castle think?" I ask.

Kenji shrugs. "He's stressed out. Ian and Emory were really messed up when we found them. I don't think they're conscious yet, even though Sonya and Sara have been working around the clock to help them. I think he's worried we won't get Winston and Brendan back at all."

"Maybe," Adam says, "their silence has to do with the fact that you shot Anderson in both his legs. Maybe he's just recovering."

I almost choke on the water I was attempting to drink. I chance a look at Kenji to see if he's going to correct Adam's assumption, but he doesn't even flinch. So I say nothing.

Kenji is nodding. Says, "Right. Yeah. I almost forgot about that." A pause. "Makes sense."

"You shot him in the legs?" James asks, eyes wide in Kenji's direction.

Kenji clears his throat but is careful not to look at me. I wonder why he's protecting me from this. Why he thinks it's better not to tell the truth about what really happened. "Yup," he says, and takes a bite of his food.

Adam exhales. Pushes up his shirtsleeves, studies the series of concentric circles inked onto his forearms, military mementos of a past life.

"But why?" James asks Kenji.

"Why what, kid?"

"Why didn't you kill him? Why just shoot him in the legs? Didn't you say he's the worst? The reason why we have all the problems we have now?"

Kenji is quiet for a moment. He's gripping his spoon, poking at his food. Finally he puts the spoon down. Motions for James to join him on our side of the table. I slide down to make room. "Come here," he says to James, pulling him tight against the right side of his body. James wraps his arms around Kenji's waist and Kenji drops his hand on James' head, mussing his hair.

I had no idea they were so close.

I keep forgetting that the 3 of them are roommates.

"So, okay. You ready for a little lesson?" he says to James.

James nods.

"It's like this: Castle always teaches us that we can't just cut off the head, you know?" He hesitates; collects his thoughts. "Like, if we just kill the enemy leader, then what? What would happen?"

"World peace," James says.

"Wrong. It would be mass chaos." Kenji shakes his head. Rubs the tip of his nose. "And chaos is a hell of a lot harder to fight."

"Then how do you win?"

"Right," Kenji says. "Well that's the thing. We can only take out the leader of the opposition when we're ready to take over—only when there's a new leader ready to take the place of the old one. People need someone to rally around, right? And we're not ready yet." He shrugs. "This was supposed to be a fight against Warner—taking *him* out wouldn't have been an issue. But to take out Anderson would be asking for absolute anarchy, all over the country. And anarchy means there's a chance someone else—someone even worse, possibly—could take control before we do."

James says something in response but I don't hear it.

Adam is staring at me.

He's staring at me and he's not pretending not to. He's not looking away. He's not saying a word. His gaze moves from my eyes to my mouth, focusing on my lips for a moment too long. Finally he turns away, just for a brief second before his eyes are fixed on mine again. Deeper. Hungrier.

My heart is starting to hurt.

I watch the hard movement in his throat. The rise and fall of his chest. The tense line of his jaw and the way he's sitting so perfectly still. He doesn't say anything, anything at all.

~~I want so desperately to touch him.~~

"Smartass." Kenji is chuckling, shaking his head as he reacts to something James just said. "You know that's not what I meant. Anyway," he sighs, "we're not ready to deal with that kind of insanity just yet. We take out Anderson when we're ready to take over. That's the only way to do this right."

Adam stands up abruptly. He pushes away his untouched bowl of food and clears his throat. Looks at Kenji. "So that's why you didn't kill him when he was right in front of you."

Kenji scratches the back of his head, uncomfortable. "Listen man, if I had any idea—"

"Forget it." Adam cuts him off. "You did me a favor."

"What do you mean?" Kenji asks. "Hey man—where're you going—"

But Adam is already walking away.

FORTY-SEVEN

I go after him.

I'm following Adam down an empty corridor as he exits the dining hall even though I know I shouldn't. I know I shouldn't be talking to him like this, shouldn't be encouraging the feelings I have for him but I'm worried. I can't help it. He's disappearing into himself, withdrawing into a world I can't penetrate and I can't even blame him for it. I can only imagine what he must be experiencing right now. These recent revelations would be enough to drive a weaker person absolutely insane. And even though we've managed to work together lately, it's always been during such high-stress situations that there's hardly been any time for us to dwell on our personal issues.

And I need to know that he's all right.

I can't just stop caring about him.

"Adam?"

He stops at the sound of my voice. His spine goes rigid with surprise. He turns around and I see his expression shift from hope to confusion to worry in a matter of seconds. "What's wrong?" he asks. "Is everything okay?"

Suddenly he's in front of me, all 6 feet of him, and I'm drowning in memories and feelings I've made no effort to forget. I'm trying to remember why I wanted to talk to him. Why I ever told him we couldn't be together. Why I would ever keep myself from a chance at even 5 seconds in his arms and he's saying my name, saying, "Juliette—what's wrong? Did something happen?"

I want so desperately to say yes, yes, horrible things have happened, and I'm sick, I'm so sick and tired and I really just want to collapse in your arms and forget the rest of the world. Instead I manage to look up, manage to meet his eyes. They're such a dark, haunting shade of blue. "I'm worried about you," I tell him.

And his eyes are immediately different, uncomfortable, closed off. "You're worried about me." He blows out a hard breath. Runs a hand through his hair.

"I just wanted to make sure you were okay—"

He's shaking his head in disbelief. "What are you doing?" he says. "Are you mocking me?"

"What?"

He's pounding a closed fist against his lips. Looking up. Looking like he's not sure what to say and then he speaks, his voice strained and hurt and confused and he says, "You broke up with me. You gave up on us—on our entire future together. You basically reached in and ripped my heart out and now you're asking me if I'm okay? How the hell am I supposed to be okay, Juliette? What kind of a question is that?"

I'm swaying in place.

"I didn't mean—" I swallow, hard. "I-I was t-talking about your—your dad—I thought maybe—oh, God, I'm sorry—you're right, I'm so stupid—I shouldn't have come, I sh-shouldn't—"

"Juliette," he says, so desperately, catching me around the waist as I back away. His eyes are shut tight. "Please," he says, "tell me what I'm supposed to do. How am I supposed to feel? It's one shitty thing right after another and I'm trying to be okay—God, I'm trying so hard but it's really freaking *difficult* and I miss"—his voice catches—"I miss you," he says. "I miss you so much it's killing me."

My fingers are clenched in his shirt.

My heart is hammering in the silence.

I see the difficulty he has in meeting my eyes when he whispers, "Do you still love me?"

And I'm straining every muscle in my body just to keep myself from reaching forward to touch him. "Adam—of course I still love you—"

"You know," he says, his voice rough with emotion, "I've never had anything like this before. I can barely remember my mom, and other than that it was just me and James and my piece-of-shit dad. And James has always loved me in his own way, but you—with *you*—" He falters. Looks down. "How am I supposed to go back?" he asks, so quietly. "How am I supposed to forget what it was like to be with you? To be loved by you?"

I don't even realize I'm crying until it's too late.

"You say you love me," he says. "And I know I love you." He looks up, meets my eyes. "So why the hell can't we be together?"

287

And I don't know how to say anything but "I'm s-sorry, I'm so sorry, you have no idea how sorry I am—"

"Why can't we just try?" He's gripping my shoulders now, his words urgent, anguished; our faces too dangerously close. "I'm willing to take whatever I can get, I swear, I just want to know I have you in my life—"

"We can't," I tell him. "It won't be enough, Adam, and you know it. One day we'll take a stupid risk or take a chance we shouldn't. One day we'll think it'll be okay and it won't. And it won't end well."

"But look at us now," he says. "We can make this work—I can be close to you without kissing you—I just need to spend a few more months training—"

"Your training might never be enough." I cut him off, knowing I need to tell him everything now. Knowing he has a right to know the same things I do. "Because the more I train, the more I learn exactly how dangerous I am. And you c-can't be near me. It's not just my skin anymore. I could hurt you just by holding your hand."

"What?" He blinks several times. "What are you talking about?"

I take a deep breath. Press my palm flat against the side of the tunnel before digging my fingers in and dragging them right through the stone. I punch my fist into the wall and grab a handful of rough rock, crush it in my hand, allow it to sift as sand through my fingers to the floor.

Adam is staring at me. Astonished.

"I'm the one who shot your father," I tell him. "I don't

know why Kenji was covering for me. I don't know why he didn't tell you the truth. But I was so blinded by this—this all-consuming *rage*—I just wanted to kill him. And I was torturing him," I whisper. "I shot him in his legs because I was taking my time. Because I wanted to enjoy that last moment. That last bullet I was about to put through his heart. And I was so close. I was so close, and Kenji," I tell him, "Kenji had to pull me away. Because he saw that I'd gone insane.

"I'm out of control." My voice is a rasp, a broken plea. "I don't know what's wrong with me or what's happening to me and I don't even know what I'm capable of yet. I don't know how much worse this is going to get. Every day I learn something new about myself and every day it terrifies me. I've done terrible things to people," I whisper. I swallow back the sob building in my throat. "And I'm not okay," I tell him. "I'm not okay, Adam. I'm not okay and I'm not safe for you to be around."

He's staring at me, so stunned he's forgotten how to speak.

"Now you know that the rumors are true," I whisper. "I am crazy. And I am a monster."

"No," he breathes. "No—"

"Yes."

"No," he says, desperate now. "That's not true—you're stronger than this—I know you are—I know *you*," he says. "I've known your heart for ten years," he says, "and I've seen what you had to live through, what you had to go through, and I'm not giving up on you now, not because of this, not because of something like this—"

"How can you say that? How can you still believe that, after everything—after all of this—"

"You," he says to me, his hands gripping me tighter now, "are one of the bravest, strongest people I've ever met. You have the best heart, the best intentions—" He stops. Takes a tight, shaky breath. "You're the best person I've ever known," he says to me. "You've been through the worst possible experiences and you survived with your humanity still intact. How the hell," he says, his voice breaking now, "am I supposed to let go of you? How can I walk away from you?"

"Adam—"

"No," he says, shaking his head. "I refuse to believe that this is the end of us. Not if you still love me. Because you're going to get through this," he says, "and I will be waiting for you when you're ready. I'm not going anywhere. There won't be another person for me. You're the only one I've ever wanted and that's never," he says, "that's *never* going to change."

"How touching."

Adam and I freeze. Turn around slowly to face the unwelcome voice.

He's right there.

Warner is standing right in front of us, his hands tied behind his back, his eyes blazing bright with anger and hurt and disgust. Castle comes up behind him to lead him in whatever whichever wherever direction and he sees where

Warner is stuck, still, staring at us, and Adam is like one block of marble, not moving, not making any effort to breathe or speak or look away. I'm fairly certain I'm burning so bright I've burnt to a crisp.

"You're so lovely when you're blushing," Warner says to me. "But I really wish you wouldn't waste your affections on someone who has to beg for your love." He cocks his head at Adam. "How sad for you," he says. "This must be terribly embarrassing."

"You sick bastard," Adam says to him, his voice like steel.

"At least I still have my dignity."

Castle shakes his head, exasperated. Pushes Warner forward. "Please get back to work—both of you," he shouts at us as he and Warner make their way past. "You're wasting valuable time standing out here."

"You can go to hell," Adam shouts at Warner.

"Just because I'm going to hell," Warner says, "doesn't mean you'll ever deserve her."

And Adam doesn't answer.

He just watches, eyes focused, as Warner and Castle disappear around the corner.

FORTY-EIGHT

James joins us during our training session before dinner.

He's been hanging out with us a lot since we got back, and we all seem happier when he's around. There's something about his presence that's so disarming, so welcome. It's so good to have him back.

I've been showing him how easily I can break things now.

The bricks are nothing. It feels like crushing a piece of cake. The metal pipes bend in my hands like plastic straws. Wood is a little tricky because if I break it the wrong way I can catch a splinter, but just about nothing is difficult anymore. Kenji has been thinking of new ways to test my abilities; lately he's been trying to see if I can project—if I can focus my power from a distance.

Not all abilities are designed for projection, apparently. Lily, for example, has that incredible photographic memory. But she'd never be able to project that ability onto anyone else.

Projection is, by far, the most difficult thing I've ever attempted to do. It's extremely complicated and requires both mental and physical exertion. I have to be wholly in control of my mind, and I have to know exactly how my brain communicates with whichever invisible bone in my body is responsible for my gift. Which means I have to know how to locate the source of my ability—and how to focus it into one concentrated point of power I can tap into from anywhere.

It's hurting my brain.

"Can I try to break something, too?" James is asking. He grabs one of the bricks off the stack and weighs it in his hands. "Maybe I'm super strong like you."

"Have you ever *felt* super strong?" Kenji asks him. "Like, you know, abnormally strong?"

"No," James says, "but I've never tried to break anything, either." He blinks at Kenji. "Do you think maybe I could be like you guys? That maybe I have some kind of power, too?"

Kenji studies him. Seems to be sorting some things out in his head. Says, "It's definitely possible. Your brother's obviously got something in his DNA, which means you might, too."

"Really?" James is practically jumping up and down.

Kenji chuckles. "I have no idea. I'm just saying it might be *possi*—no," he shouts, "James—"

"Oops." James is wincing, dropping the brick to the floor and clenching his fist against the gash bleeding in the palm of his hand. "I think I pressed too hard and it slipped," he says, struggling not to cry.

"You *think?*" Kenji is shaking his head, breathing fast. "Damn, kid, you can't just go around slicing your hand open like that. You're going to give me a freaking heart attack.

293

Come here," he says, more gently now. "Let me take a look."

"It's okay," James says, cheeks flushed, hiding his hand behind his back. "It's nothing. It'll go away soon."

"That kind of cut is not just going to go away," Kenji says. "Now let me take a look at it—"

"Wait." I interrupt him, caught by the intense look on James' face, the way he seems to be so focused on the clenched fist he's hiding. "James—what do you mean it'll 'go away'? Do you mean it's going to get better? On its own?"

James blinks at me. "Well yeah," he says. "It always gets better really quickly."

"What does? What gets better really quickly?" Kenji is staring too now, already catching on to my theory and throwing looks at me, mouthing *Holy shit* over and over again.

"When I get hurt," James says, looking at us like we've lost our minds. "Like if you cut yourself," he says to Kenji, "wouldn't it just get better?"

"It depends on the size of the cut," Kenji tells him. "But for a gash like the one on your hand?" He shakes his head. "I'd need to clean it to make sure it didn't get infected. Then I'd have to wrap it up in gauze and some kind of ointment to keep it from scarring. And then," he says, "it would take at least a couple days for it to scab up. And then it would begin to heal."

James is blinking like he's never heard of something so absurd in his life.

"Let me see your hand," Kenji says to him.

James hesitates.

"It's all right," I tell him. "Really. We're just curious."

Slowly, so slowly, James shows us his clenched fist. Even more slowly, he uncurls his fingers, watching our reactions the whole time. And exactly where just a moment ago there was a huge gash, now there's nothing but perfect pink skin and a little pool of blood.

"Holy shit on a cracker," Kenji breathes. "Sorry," he says to me, jumping forward to grab James' arm, barely able to rein in his smiles, "but I need to get this guy over to the medical wing. That okay? We can pick up again tomorrow—"

"But I'm not hurt anymore," James protests. "I'm okay—"

"I know, kid, but you're going to want to come with me."

"But why?"

"How would you like," he says, leading James out the door, "to start spending some time with two very pretty girls. . . ."

And they're gone.

And I'm laughing.

Sitting in the middle of the training room all by myself when I hear 2 familiar knocks at my door.

I already know who it's going to be.

"Ms. Ferrars."

I whip around, not because I'm surprised to hear Castle's voice, but because I'm surprised at the intonation. His eyes are narrowed, his lips tight, his eyes sharp and flashing in this light.

He is very, very angry.

Crap.

"I'm sorry about the hallway," I tell him, "I didn't—"

"We can discuss your public and wildly inappropriate displays of affection at a later time, Ms. Ferrars, but right now I have a very important question to ask you and I would advise you to be honest, as acutely honest as is physically possible."

"What"—I can hardly breathe—"what is it?"

Castle narrows his eyes at me. "I have just had a conversation with Warner, who says he is able to touch you without consequence, and that this information is something you are well aware of."

And I think, Wow, I did it. I actually managed to die of a stroke at age 17.

"I need to know," Castle hurries on, "whether or not this information is true and I need to know right now."

There's glue all over my tongue, stuck to my teeth, my lips, the roof of my mouth, and I can't speak, I can't move, I'm pretty sure I just had a seizure or an aneurysm or heart failure or something equally as awful but I can't explain any of this to Castle because I can't move my jaw even an inch.

"Ms. *Ferrars*. I don't think you understand how important this question is. I need an answer from you, and I need it thirty seconds ago."

"I . . . I—"

"Today, I need an answer *today, right now, this very moment*—"

"Yes," I choke out, blushing through my skull, horribly ashamed, embarrassed, horrified in every possible way and the only thing I can think of is Adam Adam Adam how will Adam respond to this information *now*, why does this have to happen *now*, why did Warner say anything at all and I want to kill him for sharing the secret that was mine to tell, mine to hide, mine to hoard.

Castle looks like he's a balloon that fell in love with a pushpin that got too close and ruined him forever. "So it's true, then?"

I drop my eyes. "Yes, it's true."

He falls to the floor right across from me, astonished. "How is it even possible, do you think?"

Because Warner is Adam's brother, I don't tell him.

And I don't tell him because it is *Adam's* secret to tell and I will not talk about it until he does, even though I desperately want to tell Castle that the connection must be in their blood, that they both must share a similar kind of gift or Energy, or oh oh *oh*

Oh God.

Oh no.

Warner is one of us.

FORTY-NINE

"It changes everything."

Castle isn't even looking at me. "This—I mean—this means so many things," he says. "We'll have to tell him everything and we'll have to test him to be sure, but I'm fairly positive it's the only explanation. And he would be welcome to take refuge here if he wanted it—I would have to give him a regular room, allow him to live among us as an equal. I cannot keep him here as a prisoner, at the very least—"

"*What*—but, Castle—why? He's the one who almost killed Adam! And Kenji!"

"You have to understand—this news might change his entire outlook on life." Castle is shaking his head, one hand almost covering his mouth, his eyes wide. "He might not take it well—he might be thrilled—he might lose his mind completely—he might wake up a new man in the morning. You would be surprised what these kinds of revelations will do to people.

"Omega Point will always be a place of refuge for our kind," he continues. "It's an oath I made to myself many years ago. I cannot deny him food and shelter if, for example, his father were to cast him out entirely."

This can't be happening.

"But I don't understand," Castle says suddenly, looking up at me. "Why didn't you say anything? Why not report this information? This is important for us to know and it doesn't condemn you in any way—"

"I didn't want Adam to know," I admit out loud for the first time, my voice 6 broken bits of shame strung together. "I just . . ." I shake my head. "I didn't want him to know."

Castle actually looks sad for me. He says, "I wish I could help you keep your secret, Ms. Ferrars, but even if I wanted to, I'm not sure Warner will."

I focus on the mats laid out on the floor. My voice sounds tiny when I ask, "Why did he even tell you? How did that even come up in conversation?"

Castle rubs his chin, thoughtful. "He told me of his own accord. I volunteered to take him on his daily rounds— walking him to the restroom, et cetera—because I wanted to follow up and ask him questions about his father and see what he knew about the state of our hostages. He seemed perfectly fine. In fact, he looked much better than he was when he first showed up. He was compliant, almost polite. But his attitude changed rather dramatically after we stumbled upon you and Adam in the hall. . . ." His voice trails off, his eyes snap up, his mind working quickly to fit all the pieces together and he's gaping at me, staring at me in a way that is entirely foreign to Castle, in a way that says he is utterly, absolutely baffled.

I'm not sure if I should be offended.

"He's in love with you," Castle whispers, a dawning, groundbreaking realization in his voice. He laughs, once, hard, fast. Shakes his head. "He held you captive and managed to fall in love with you in the process."

I'm staring at the mats like they're the most fascinating things I've ever seen in my life.

"Oh, Ms. Ferrars," Castle says to me. "I do not envy you your predicament. I can see now why this situation must be uncomfortable for you."

I want to say to him, You have no idea, Castle. You have no idea because you don't even know the entire story. You don't know that they're *brothers*, brothers who *hate* each other, brothers who only seem to agree on one thing, and that one thing happens to be killing their own father.

But I don't say any of those things. I don't say anything, in fact.

I sit on these mats with my head in my hands and I'm trying to figure out what else could possibly go wrong. I'm wondering how many more mistakes I'll have to make before things finally fall into place.

If they ever will.

FIFTY

I'm so humiliated.

I've been thinking about this all night and I came to a realization this morning. Warner must've told Castle on purpose. Because he's playing games with me, because he hasn't changed, because he's still trying to get me to do his bidding. He's still trying to get me to be his project and he's trying to hurt me.

I won't allow it.

I will not allow Warner to lie to me, to manipulate my emotions to get what he wants. I can't believe I felt pity for him—that I felt weakness, tenderness for him when I saw him with his father—that I believed him when he told me his thoughts about my journal. I'm such a gullible fool.

I was an idiot to ever think he might be capable of human emotion.

I told Castle that maybe he should put someone else on this assignment now that he knows Warner can touch me; I told him it might be dangerous now. But he laughed and he laughed and he laughed and he said, "Oh, Ms. Ferrars, I'm quite, *quite* certain you will be able to defend yourself. In fact, you're probably much better equipped against him than any of us. Besides," he added, "this is an ideal situation. If

301

he truly is in love with you, you must be able to use that to our advantage somehow. We need your help," he said to me, serious again. "We need all the help we can find, and right now you're the one person who might be able to get the answers we need. Please," he said. "Try to find out anything you can. Anything at all. Winston and Brendan's lives are at risk."

And he's right.

So I'm shoving my own concerns aside because Winston and Brendan are out there, hurting somewhere, and we need to find them. And I'm going to do whatever I can to help.

Which means I have to talk to Warner again.

I have to treat him just like the prisoner that he is. No more side conversations. No falling for his efforts to confuse me. Not again and again and again. I'm going to be better. Smarter.

And I want my notebook back.

The guards are unlocking his room for me and I'm marching in, I'm sealing the door shut behind me and I'm getting ready to give him the speech I've already prepared when I stop in place.

I don't know what I was expecting.

Maybe I thought I'd catch him trying to break a hole in the wall or maybe he'd be plotting the demise of every person at Omega Point or I don't know I don't know I don't know anything because I only know how to fight an angry body, an insolent creature, an arrogant monster, and I do not know what to do with this.

He's sleeping.

Someone put a mattress in here, a simple rectangle of average quality, thin and worn but better than the ground, at least, and he's lying on top of it in nothing but a pair of black boxer briefs.

His clothes are on the floor.

His pants, his shirts, his socks are slightly damp, wrinkled, obviously hand-washed and laid out to dry; his coat is folded neatly over his boots, and his gloves are resting right next to each other on top of his coat.

He hasn't moved an inch since I stepped into this room.

He's resting on his side, his back to the wall, his left arm tucked under his face, his right arm against his torso, his entire body ~~perfect~~ bare, strong, smooth, and smelling faintly of soap. I don't know why I can't stop staring at him. I don't know what it is about sleep that makes our faces appear so soft and innocent, so peaceful and vulnerable, but I'm trying to look away and I can't. I'm losing sight of my own purpose, forgetting all the brave things I said to myself before I stepped in here. Because there's something about him—there's *always* been something about him that's intrigued me and I don't understand it. I wish I could ignore it but I can't.

Because I look at him and wonder if maybe it's just me? Maybe I'm naive?

But I see layers, shades of gold and green and a person who's never been given a chance to be human and I wonder if I'm just as cruel as my own oppressors if I decide that society is right, that some people are too far gone, that sometimes you can't turn back, that there are people in this world who don't deserve a second chance and I can't I can't I can't

I can't help but disagree.

I can't help but think that 19 is too young to give up on someone, that 19 years old is just the beginning, that it's too soon to tell anyone they will never amount to anything but evil in this world.

I can't help but wonder what my life would've been like if someone had taken a chance on me.

So I back away. I turn to leave.

I let him sleep.

I stop in place.

I catch a glimpse of my notebook lying on the mattress next to his outstretched hand, his fingers looking as if they've only just let go. It's the perfect opportunity to steal it back if I can be stealthy enough.

I tiptoe forward, forever grateful that these boots I wear are designed to make no sound at all. But the closer I inch toward his body, the more my attention is caught by something on his back.

A little rectangular blur of black.

I creep closer.

Blink.

Squint.

Lean in.

It's a tattoo.

No pictures. Just 1 word. 1 word, typed into the very center of his upper back. In ink.

IGNITE

And his skin is shredded with scars.

Blood is rushing to my head so quickly I'm beginning to feel faint. I feel sick. Like I might actually, truly upturn the contents of my stomach right now. I want to panic, I want to shake someone, I want to know how to understand the emotions choking me because I can't even imagine, can't even imagine, can't even *imagine* what he must've endured to carry such suffering on his skin.

His entire back is a map of pain.

Thick and thin and uneven and terrible. Scars like roads that lead to nowhere. They're gashes and ragged slices I can't understand, marks of torture I never could have expected. They're the only imperfections on his entire body, imperfections hidden away and hiding secrets of their own.

And I realize, not for the first time, that I have no idea who Warner really is.

"Juliette?"

I freeze.

"What are you doing here?" His eyes are wide, alert.

"I—I came to talk to you—"

"Jesus," he gasps, jumping away from me. "I'm very flattered, love, but you could've at least given me a chance to put my pants on." He's pulled himself up against the wall but makes no effort to grab his clothes. His eyes keep darting from me to the pants on the floor like he doesn't know what to do. He seems determined not to turn his back to me.

"Would you mind?" he says, nodding to the clothes next to my feet and affecting an air of nonchalance that does little to hide the apprehension in his eyes. "It gets chilly in here."

But I'm staring at him, staring at the length of him, awed by how incredibly flawless he looks from the front. Strong, lean frame, toned and muscular without being bulky. He's fair without being pale, skin tinted with just enough sunlight to look effortlessly healthy. The body of a perfect boy.

What a lie appearances can be.

What a terrible, terrible lie.

His gaze is fixed on mine, his eyes green flames that will not extinguish and his chest is rising and falling so fast, so fast, so fast.

"What happened to your back?" I hear myself whisper.

I watch as the color drains from his face. He looks away, runs a hand across his mouth, his chin, down the back of his neck.

"Who hurt you?" I ask, so quietly. I'm beginning to recognize the strange feeling I get just before I do something terrible. Like right now. Right now I feel like I could kill someone for this.

"Juliette, please, my clothes—"

"Was it your father?" I ask, my voice a little sharper. "Did he do this to you—"

"It doesn't matter." Warner cuts me off, frustrated now.

"Of course it matters!"

He says nothing.

"That tattoo," I say to him, "that word—"

"Yes," he says, though he says it quietly. Clears his throat.

"I don't . . ." I blink. "What does it mean?"

Warner shakes his head, runs a hand through his hair.

"Is it from a book?"

"Why do you care?" he asks, looking away again. "Why are you suddenly so interested in my life?"

I don't know, I want to tell him. I want to tell him I don't know but that's not true.

Because I feel it. I feel the clicks and the turns and the creaking of a million keys unlocking a million doors in my mind. It's like I'm finally allowing myself to see what I really think, how I really feel, like I'm discovering my own secrets for the first time. And then I search his eyes, search his features for something I can't even name. And I realize I don't want to be his enemy anymore.

"It's over," I say to him. "I'm not on base with you this time. I'm not going to be your weapon and you'll never be able to change my mind about that. I think you know that now." I study the floor. "So why are we still fighting each other? Why are you still trying to manipulate me? Why are you still trying to get me to fall for your tricks?"

"I have no idea," he says, looking at me like he's not sure I'm even real, "no idea what you're talking about."

"Why did you tell Castle you could touch me? That wasn't your secret to share."

"Right." He exhales a deep breath. "Of course." Seems to return to himself. "Listen, love, could you at least toss me my jacket if you're going to stay here and ask me all these questions?"

I toss him his jacket. He catches it. Slides down to the floor. And instead of putting his jacket on, he drapes it over his lap. Finally, he says, "Yes, I did tell Castle I could touch you. He had a right to know."

"That wasn't any of his business."

"Of course it's his business," Warner says. "The entire world he's created down here thrives on exactly that kind of information. And you're here, living among them. He should know."

"He doesn't need to know."

"Why is it such a big deal?" he asks, studying my eyes too carefully. "Why does it bother you so much for someone to know that I can touch you? Why does it have to be a secret?"

I struggle to find the words that won't come.

"Are you worried about Kent? You think he'd have a problem knowing I can touch you?"

"I didn't want him to find out like this—"

"But why does it matter?" he insists. "You seem to care so much about something that makes no difference in your

308

personal life. It wouldn't," he says, "make any difference in your personal life. Not if you still claim to feel nothing but hatred for me. Because that's what you said, isn't it? That you hate me?"

I fold myself to the floor across from Warner. Pull my knees up to my chest. Focus on the stone under my feet. "I don't hate you."

Warner seems to stop breathing.

"I think I understand you sometimes," I tell him. "I really do. But just when I think I finally get you, you surprise me. And I never really know who you are or who you're going to be." I look up. "But I know that I don't hate you anymore. I've tried," I say, "I've tried so hard. Because you've done so many terrible, terrible things. To innocent people. To *me*. But I know too much about you now. I've seen too much. You're too human."

His hair is so gold. His eyes so green. His voice is tortured when he speaks. "Are you saying," he says, "that you want to be my friend?"

"I-I don't know." I'm so petrified, so, so petrified of this possibility. "I didn't think about that. I'm just saying that I don't know"—I hesitate, breathe—"I don't know how to hate you anymore. Even though I want to. I really want to and I know I should but I just can't."

He looks away.

And he smiles.

It's the kind of smile that makes me forget how to do everything but blink and blink and I don't understand what's happening to me. I don't know why I can't convince my eyes to find something else to focus on.

I don't know why my heart is losing its mind.

He touches my notebook like he's not even aware he's doing it. His fingers run the length of the cover once, twice, before he registers where my eyes have gone and he stops.

"You wrote these words?" He touches the notebook again. "Every single one?"

I nod.

He says, "Juliette."

I stop breathing.

He says, "I would like that very much. To be your friend," he says. "I'd like that."

And I don't really know what happens in my brain.

Maybe it's because he's broken and I'm foolish enough to think I can fix him. Maybe it's because I see myself, I see 3, 4, 5, 6, 17-year-old Juliette abandoned, neglected, mistreated, abused for something outside of her control and I think of Warner as someone who's just like me, someone who was never given a chance at life. I think about how everyone already hates him, how hating him is a universally accepted fact.

Warner is horrible.

There are no discussions, no reservations, no questions asked. It has already been decided that he is a despicable human being who thrives on murder and power and torturing others.

But I want to know. I need to know. I have to know.

If it's really that simple.

Because what if one day I slip? What if one day I fall through the cracks and no one is willing to pull me back? What happens to me then?

So I meet his eyes. I take a deep breath.

And I run.

I run right out the door.

FIFTY-ONE

Just a moment.

Just 1 second, just 1 more minute, just give me another hour or maybe the weekend to think it over it's not so much it's not so hard it's all we ever ask for it's a simple request.

But the moments the seconds the minutes the hours the days and years become one big mistake, one extraordinary opportunity slipped right through our fingers because we couldn't decide, we couldn't understand, we needed more time, we didn't know what to do.

We don't even know what we've done.

We have no idea how we even got here when all we ever wanted was to wake up in the morning and go to sleep at night and maybe stop for ice cream on the way home and that one decision, that one choice, that one accidental opportunity unraveled everything we've ever known and ever believed in and what do we do?

What do we do

from here?

FIFTY-TWO

Things are getting worse.

The tension among the citizens of Omega Point is getting tighter with each passing hour. We've tried to make contact with Anderson's men to no avail—we've heard nothing from their team or their soldiers, and we have no updates on our hostages. But the civilians of Sector 45— the sector Warner used to be in charge of, the sector he used to oversee—are beginning to grow more and more unsettled. Rumors about us and our resistance are spreading too quickly.

The Reestablishment tried to cover up the news of our recent battle by calling it a standard attack on rebel party members, but the people are getting smarter. Protests are breaking out among them and some are refusing to work, standing up to authority, trying to escape the compounds, and running back to unregulated territory.

It never ends well.

The losses have been too many and Castle is anxious to do something. We all have a feeling we're going to be heading out again, and soon. We haven't received any reports that Anderson is dead, which means he's probably just biding his time—or maybe Adam is right, and he's just recovering. But whatever the reason, Anderson's silence can't be good.

"What are you doing here?" Castle says to me.

I've just collected my dinner. I've just sat down at my usual table with Adam and Kenji and James. I blink at Castle, confused.

Kenji says, "What's going on?"

Adam says, "Is everything all right?"

Castle says, "My apologies, Ms. Ferrars, I didn't mean to interrupt. I confess I'm just a bit surprised to see you here. I thought you were currently on assignment."

"Oh." I startle. Glance at my food and back at Castle again. "I—well yes, I am—but I've talked to Warner twice already—I actually just saw him yesterday—"

"Oh, that's excellent news, Ms. Ferrars. Excellent news." Castle clasps his hands together; his face is the picture of relief. "And what have you been able to discover?" He looks so hopeful that I actually begin to feel ashamed of myself.

Everyone is staring at me and I don't know what to do. I don't know what to say.

I shake my head.

"Ah." Castle drops his hands. Looks down. Nods to himself. "So. You've decided that your two visits have been more than sufficient?" He won't look at me. "What is your professional opinion, Ms. Ferrars? Do you think it would be best to take your time in this particular situation? That Winston and Brendan will be relaxing comfortably until you find an opportunity in your busy schedule to interrogate the only person who might be able to help us find them? Do you think that y—"

"I'll go right now." I grab my tray and jump up from table, nearly tripping over myself in the process. "I'm sorry—I'm just—I'll go right now. I'll see you guys at breakfast," I whisper, and run out the door.

Brendan and Winston

Brendan and Winston

Brendan and Winston, I keep telling myself.

I hear Kenji laughing as I leave.

I'm not very good at interrogation, apparently.

I have so many questions for Warner but none of them have to do with our hostage situation. Every time I tell myself I'm going to ask the right questions, Warner somehow manages to distract me. It's almost like he knows what I'm going to ask and is already prepared to redirect the conversation.

It's confusing.

"Do you have any tattoos?" he's asking me, smiling as he leans back against the wall in his undershirt; pants on, socks on, shoes off. "Everyone seems to have tattoos these days."

This is not a conversation I ever thought I'd have with Warner.

"No," I tell him. "I've never had an opportunity to get one. Besides, I don't think anyone would ever want to get that close to my skin."

315

He studies his hands. Smiles. Says, "Maybe someday."

"Maybe," I agree.

A pause.

"So what about your tattoo?" I ask. "Why *IGNITE*?"

His smile is bigger now. Dimples again. He shakes his head, says, "Why not?"

"I don't get it." I tilt my head at him, confused. "You want to remind yourself to catch on fire?"

He smiles, presses back a laugh. "A handful of letters doesn't always make a word, love."

"I . . . have no idea what you're talking about."

He takes a deep breath. Sits up straighter. "So," he says. "You used to read a lot?"

I'm caught off guard. It's a strange question, and I can't help but wonder for a moment if it's a trick. If admitting to such a thing might get me into trouble. And then I remember that Warner is *my* hostage, not the other way around. "Yes," I say to him. "I used to."

His smile fades into something a bit more serious, calculated. His features are carefully wiped clean of emotion. "And when did you have a chance to read?"

"What do you mean?"

He shrugs slowly, glances at nothing across the room. "It just seems strange that a girl who's been so wholly isolated her entire life would have much access to literature. Especially in this world."

I say nothing.

He says nothing.

I breathe a few beats before answering him.

"I . . . I never got to choose my own books," I tell him, and I don't know why I feel so nervous saying this out loud, why I have to remind myself not to whisper. "I read whatever was available. My schools always had little libraries and my parents had some things around the house. And later . . ." I hesitate. "Later, I spent a couple of years in ~~hospitals and psychiatric wards and~~ a juvenile d-detention center." My face enflames as if on cue, always ready to be ashamed of my past, of who I've been and continue to be.

But it's strange.

While one part of me struggles to be so candid, another part of me actually feels comfortable talking to Warner. Safe. Familiar.

Because he already knows everything about me.

He knows every detail of my 17 years. He has all of my medical records, knows all about my incidents with the police and the painful relationship I ~~have~~ had with my parents. And now he's read my notebook, too.

There's nothing I could reveal about my history that would surprise him; nothing about what I've done would shock or horrify him. I don't worry that he'll judge me or run away from me.

And this realization, perhaps more than anything else, rattles my bones.

~~And gives me some sense of relief.~~

"There were always books around," I continue, somehow unable to stop now, eyes glued to the floor. "In the detention center. A lot of them were old and worn and didn't have covers, so I didn't always know what they were called or who wrote them. I just read anything I could find. Fairy tales and mysteries and history and poetry. It didn't matter what it was. I would read it over and over and over again. The books . . . they helped keep me from losing my mind altogether . . ." I trail off, catching myself before I say much more. Horrified as I realize just how much I want to confide in him. In Warner.

Terrible, terrible Warner who tried to kill Adam and Kenji. Who made me his toy.

I hate that I should feel safe enough to speak so freely around him. I hate that of all people, Warner is the one person I can be completely honest with. I always feel like I have to protect Adam from me, from the horror story that is my life. I never want to scare him or tell him too much for fear that he'll change his mind and realize what a mistake he's made in trusting me; in showing me affection.

But with Warner there's nothing to hide.

I want to see his expression; I want to know what he's thinking now that I've opened up, offered him a personal look at my past, but I can't make myself face him. So I sit here, frozen, humiliation perched on my shoulders and he doesn't say a word, doesn't shift an inch, doesn't make a single sound. Seconds fly by, swarming the room all at once and I want to swat them all away; I want to catch them and shove them into my pockets just long enough to stop time.

Finally, he interrupts the silence.

"I like to read, too," he says.

I look up, startled.

He's leaned back against the wall, one hand caught in his hair. He runs his fingers through the golden layers just once. Drops his hand. Meets my gaze. His eyes are so, so green.

"You like to read?" I ask.

"You're surprised."

"I thought The Reestablishment was going to destroy all of those things. I thought it was illegal."

"They are, and it will be," he says, shifting a little. "Soon, anyway. They've destroyed some of it already, actually." He looks uncomfortable for the first time. "It's ironic," he says, "that I only really started reading when the plan was in place to destroy everything. I was assigned to sort through some lists—give my opinion on which things we'd keep, which things we'd get rid of, which things we'd recycle for use in campaigns, in future curriculum, et cetera."

"And you think that's okay?" I ask him. "To destroy what's left of culture—all the languages—all those texts? Do you agree?"

He's playing with my notebook again. "There . . . are many things I'd do differently," he says, "if I were in charge." A deep breath. "But a soldier does not always have to agree in order to obey."

"What would you do differently?" I ask. "If you were in charge?"

He laughs. Sighs. Looks at me, smiles at me out of the corner of his eye. "You ask too many questions."

"I can't help it," I tell him. "You just seem so different now. Everything you say surprises me."

"How so?"

"I don't know," I say. "You're just . . . so calm. A little less crazy."

He laughs one of those silent laughs, the kind that shakes his chest without making a sound, and he says, "My life has been nothing but battle and destruction. Being here?" He looks around. "Away from duties, responsibilities. Death," he says, eyes intent on the wall. "It's like a vacation. I don't have to think all the time. I don't have to do anything or talk to anyone or be anywhere. I've never had so many hours to simply *sleep*," he says, smiling. "It's actually kind of luxurious. I think I'd like to get held hostage more often," he adds, mostly to himself.

And I can't help but study him.

I study his face in a way I've never dared to before and I realize I don't have the faintest idea what it must be like to live his life. He told me once that I didn't have a clue, that I couldn't possibly understand the strange laws of his world, and I'm only just beginning to see how right he was. Because I don't know anything about that kind of bloody, regimented existence. But I suddenly want to know.

I suddenly want to understand.

I watch his careful movements, the effort he makes to look unconcerned, relaxed. But I see how calculated it is. How there's a reason behind every shift, every readjustment of his body. He's always listening, always touching a hand to the ground, the wall, staring at the door, studying its outline, the hinges, the handle. I see the way he tenses— just a little bit—at the sound of small noises, the scratch of metal, muffled voices outside the room. It's obvious he's always alert, always on edge, ready to fight, to react. It makes me wonder if he's ever known tranquillity. Safety. If he's ever been able to sleep through the night. If he's ever been able to go anywhere without constantly looking over his own shoulder.

His hands are clasped together.

He's playing with a ring on his left hand, turning and turning and turning it around his pinkie finger. I can't believe it's taken me so long to notice he's wearing it; it's a solid band of jade, a shade of green pale enough to perfectly match his eyes. And then I remember, all at once, seeing it before.

Just one time.

The morning after I'd hurt Jenkins. When Warner came to collect me from his room. He caught me staring at his ring and quickly slipped his gloves on.

It's déjà vu.

He catches me looking at his hands and quickly clenches his left fist, covers it with his right.

"Wha—"

"It's just a ring," he says. "It's nothing."

"Why are you hiding it if it's nothing?" I'm already so much more curious than I was a moment ago, too eager for any opportunity to crack him open, to figure out what on earth goes on inside of his head.

He sighs.

Flexes and unflexes his fingers. Stares at his hands, palms down, fingers spread. Slips the ring off his pinkie and holds it up to the fluorescent light; looks at it. It's a little O of green. Finally, he meets my eyes. Drops the ring into the palm of his hand and closes a fist around it.

"You're not going to tell me?" I ask.

He shakes his head.

"Why not?"

He rubs the side of his neck, massages the tension out of the lowest part, the part that just touches his upper back. I can't help but watch. Can't help but wonder what it would feel like to have someone massage the pain out of my body that way. His hands look so strong.

I've just about forgotten what we were talking about when he says, "I've had this ring for almost ten years. It used to fit my index finger." He glances at me before looking away again. "And I don't talk about it."

"Ever?"

"No."

"Oh." I bite down on my bottom lip. Disappointed.

"Do you like Shakespeare?" he asks me.

An odd segue.

I shake my head. "All I know about him is that he stole my name and spelled it wrong."

Warner stares at me for a full second before he bursts into laughter—strong, unrestrained gales of laughter—trying to rein it in and failing.

I'm suddenly uncomfortable, nervous in front of this strange boy who laughs and wears secret rings and asks me about books and poetry. "I wasn't trying to be funny," I manage to tell him.

But his eyes are still full of smiles when he says, "Don't worry. I didn't know much about him until roughly a year ago. I still don't understand half the things he says, so I think we're going to get rid of most of it, but he did write a line I really liked."

"What was it?"

"Would you like to see it?"

"*See* it?"

But Warner is already on his feet, unbuttoning his pants and I'm wondering what could possibly be happening, worried I'm being tricked into some new sick game of his when he stops. Catches the horrified look on my face. Says, "Don't worry, love. I'm not getting naked, I promise. It's just another tattoo."

"Where?" I ask, frozen in place, wanting and not wanting to look away.

He doesn't answer.

His pants are unzipped but hanging low on his waist. His boxer-briefs are visible underneath. He tugs and tugs on the elastic band of his underwear until it sits just below his hipbone.

I'm blushing through my hairline.

I've never seen such an intimate area of any boy's body before, and I can't make myself look away. My moments with Adam were always in the dark and always interrupted; I never saw this much of him not because I didn't want to, but because I never had a chance to. And now the lights are on and Warner's standing right in front of me and I'm so caught, so intrigued by the cut of his frame. I can't help but notice the way his waist narrows into his hips and disappears under a piece of fabric. I want to know what it would be like to understand another person without those barriers.

To know a person so thoroughly, so privately.

I want to study the secrets tucked between his elbows and the whispers caught behind his knees. I want to follow the lines of his silhouette with my eyes and the tips of my fingers. I want to trace rivers and valleys along the curved muscles of his body.

My thoughts shock me.

There's a desperate heat in the pit of my stomach I wish I could ignore. There are butterflies in my chest I wish I could explain away. There's an ache in my core that I'm unwilling to name.

~~Beautiful.~~

~~*He's so beautiful.*~~

I must be insane.

"It's interesting," he says. "It feels very . . . relevant, I think. Even though it was written so long ago."

"What?" I rip my eyes away from his lower half, desperately trying to keep my imagination from drawing in the details. I look back at the words tattooed onto his skin and focus this time. "Oh," I say. "Yes."

It's 2 lines. Font like a typewriter inked across the very bottom of his torso.

hell is empty
and all the devils are here

Yes. Interesting. Yes. Sure.

I think I need to lie down.

"Books," he's saying, pulling his boxer-briefs up and rezipping his pants, "are easily destroyed. But words will live as long as people can remember them. Tattoos, for example, are very hard to forget." He buttons his button. "I think there's something about the impermanence of life these days that makes it necessary to etch ink into our skin," he says. "It reminds us that we've been marked by the world, that we're still alive. That we'll never forget."

"Who *are* you?"

I don't know this Warner. I'd never be able to recognize this Warner.

He smiles to himself. Sits down again. Says, "No one else will ever need to know."

"What do you mean?"

"I know who I am," he says. "That's enough for me."

I'm silent a moment. I frown at the floor. "It must be great to go through life with so much confidence."

"You are confident," he says to me. "You're stubborn and resilient. So brave. So strong. So inhumanly beautiful. You could conquer the world."

I actually laugh, look up to meet his eyes. "I cry too much. And I'm not interested in conquering the world."

"That," he says, "is something I will never understand." He shakes his head. "You're just scared. You're afraid of what you're unfamiliar with. You're too worried about disappointing people. You stifle your own potential," he says, "because of what you think others expect of you— because you still follow the rules you've been given." He looks at me, hard. "I wish you wouldn't."

"I wish you'd stop expecting me to use my power to kill people."

He shrugs. "I never said you had to. But it will happen along the way; it's an inevitability in war. Killing is statistically impossible to avoid."

"You're joking, right?"

"Definitely not."

"You can always avoid killing people, Warner. You avoid killing them by *not* going to war."

But he grins, so brilliantly, not even paying attention. "I love it when you say my name," he says. "I don't even know why."

"Warner isn't your name," I point out. "Your name is Aaron."

His smile is wide, so wide. "God, I love that."

"Your name?"

"Only when you say it."

"Aaron? Or Warner?"

His eyes close. He tilts his head back against the wall. Dimples.

Suddenly I'm struck by the reality of what I'm doing here. Sitting here, spending time with Warner like we have so many hours to waste. Like there isn't a very terrible world outside of these walls. I don't know how I manage to keep getting distracted and I promise myself that this time I won't let the conversation veer out of control. But when I open my mouth he says

"I'm not going to give you your notebook back."

My mouth falls closed.

"I know you want it back," he says, "but I'm afraid I'm going to have to keep it forever." He holds it up, shows it to me. Grins. And then puts it in his pocket. The one place I'd never dare to reach.

"Why?" I can't help but ask. "Why do you want it so much?"

He spends far too long just looking at me. Not answering my question. And then he says

"On the darkest days you have to search for a spot of brightness, on the coldest days you have to seek out a spot of warmth; on the bleakest days you have to keep your eyes onward and upward and on the saddest days you have to leave them open to let them cry. To then let them dry. To give them a chance to wash out the pain in order to see fresh and clear once again."

"I can't believe you have that memorized," I whisper.

He leans back again. Closes his eyes again. Says, *"Nothing in this life will ever make sense to me but I can't help but try to collect the change and hope it's enough to pay for our mistakes."*

"I wrote that, too?" I ask him, unable to believe it's possible he's reciting the same words that fell from my lips to my fingertips and bled onto a page. Still unable to believe he's now privy to my private thoughts, feelings I captured with a tortured mind and hammered into sentences I shoved into paragraphs, ideas I pinned together with punctuation marks that serve no function but to determine where one thought ends and another begins.

This blond boy has my secrets in his mouth.

"You wrote a lot of things," he says, not looking at me. "About your parents, your childhood, your experiences with other people. You talked about hope and redemption and what it would be like to see a bird fly by. You wrote about pain. And what it's like to think you're a monster. What it was like to be judged by everyone before you'd even spoken two words to them." A deep inhale. "So much of it was like seeing myself on paper," he whispers. "Like reading all the things I never knew how to say."

And I wish my heart would just shut up shut up shut up shut up.

"Every single day I'm sorry," he says, his words barely a breath now. "Sorry for believing the things I heard about you. And then for hurting you when I thought I was helping you. I can't apologize for who I am," he says. "That part of me is already done; already ruined. I gave up on myself a long time ago. But I am sorry I didn't understand you better. Everything I did, I did because I wanted to help you to be stronger. I wanted you to use your anger as a tool, as a weapon to help harness the strength inside of you; I wanted you to be able to fight the world. I provoked you on purpose," he says. "I pushed you too far, too hard, did things to horrify and disgust you and I did it all on purpose. Because that's how I was taught to steel myself against the terror in this world. That's how I was trained to fight back. And I wanted to teach you. I knew you had the potential to be more, so much more. I could see greatness in you."

He looks at me. Really, really looks at me.

"You're going to go on to do incredible things," he says. "I've always known that. I think I just wanted to be a part of it."

And I try. I try so hard to remember all the reasons why I'm supposed to hate him, I try to remember all the horrible things I've seen him do. But I'm tortured because I understand too much about what it's like to be tortured. To do things because you don't know any better. To do things because you think they're right because you were never taught what was wrong.

Because it's so hard to be kind to the world when all you've ever felt is hate.

Because it's so hard to see goodness in the world when all you've ever known is terror.

And I want to say something to him. Something profound and complete and memorable but he seems to understand. He offers me a strange, unsteady smile that doesn't reach his eyes but says so much.

Then

"Tell your team," he says, "to prepare for war. Unless his plans have changed, my father will be ordering an attack on civilians the day after tomorrow and it will be nothing short of a massacre. It will also be your only opportunity to save your men. They are being held captive somewhere in the lower levels of Sector 45 Headquarters. I'm afraid that's all I can tell you."

"How did you—"

"I know why you're here, love. I'm not an idiot. I know why you're being forced to spend time with me."

"But why offer the information so freely?" I ask him. "What reason do you have to help us?"

There's a flicker of change in his eyes that doesn't last long enough for me to examine it. And though his expression is carefully neutral, something in the space between us feels different all of a sudden. Charged.

"Go," he says. "You must tell them now."

FIFTY-THREE

Adam, Kenji, Castle, and I are camped out in his office trying to discuss strategy.

Last night I ran straight to Kenji—who then took me to Castle—to tell him what Warner told me. Castle was both relieved and horrified, and I think he still hasn't digested the information yet.

He told me he was going to meet with Warner in the morning, just to follow up, just to see if Warner would be willing to elaborate at all (he wasn't), and that Kenji, Adam, and I should meet him in his office at lunch.

So now we're all crammed into his small space, along with 7 others. The faces in this room are many of the same ones I saw when we journeyed into The Reestablishment's storage compound; that means they're important, integral to this movement. And it makes me wonder when I ever became a part of Castle's core group at Omega Point.

I can't help but feel a little proud. A little thrilled to be someone he relies on. To be contributing.

And it makes me wonder how much I've changed in such a short period of time. How different my life has become, how much stronger and how much weaker I feel now. It makes me wonder whether things would've turned out differently if Adam and I had found a way to stay together. If

I ever would've ventured outside of the safety he introduced to my life.

I wonder about a lot of things.

But when I look up and catch him staring at me, my wonders disappear; and I'm left with nothing but the pains of missing him. Left wishing he wouldn't look away the moment I look up.

This was my miserable choice. I brought it upon myself.

Castle is sitting at his desk, elbows propped up on the table, chin resting on clasped hands. His eyebrows are furrowed, his lips pursed, his eyes focused on the papers in front of him.

He hasn't said a word in 5 minutes.

Finally, he looks up. Looks at Kenji, who is sitting right in front of him, between me and Adam. "What do you think?" he says. "Offensive or defensive?"

"Guerrilla warfare," Kenji says without hesitation. "Nothing else."

A deep breath. "Yes," Castle says. "I thought so too."

"We need to be split up," Kenji says. "Do you want to assign groups, or should I?"

"I'll assign the preliminary groups. I'd like you to look them over and suggest changes, if any."

Kenji nods.

"Perfect. And weapons—"

"I'll oversee that," Adam says. "I can make sure everything is clean, loaded, ready to go. I'm already familiar with the armory."

I had no idea.

"Good. Excellent. We'll assign one group to try and get on base to find Winston and Brendan; everyone else will spread out among the compounds. Our mission is simple: save as many civilians as possible. Take out only as many soldiers as is absolutely necessary. Our fight is not against the men, but against their leaders—we must never forget that. Kenji," he says, "I'd like you to oversee the groups entering the compounds. Do you feel comfortable doing that?"

Kenji nods.

"I will lead the group onto base," Castle says. "While you and Mr. Kent would be ideal for infiltrating Sector 45, I'd like you to stay with Ms. Ferrars; the three of you work well together, and we could use your strengths on the ground. Now," he says, spreading out the papers in front of him, "I've been studying these blueprints all ni—"

Someone is banging on the glass window in Castle's door.

He's a youngish man I've never seen before, with bright, light-brown eyes and hair cropped so close to the crown I can't even make out the color. His eyes are pulled together, his forehead tight, tense. "Sir!" he's shouting, he's *been* shouting, I realize, but his voice is muffled and only then does it dawn on me that this room must be soundproof, if only just a little bit.

Kenji jumps out of his chair, yanks the door open.

"Sir!" The man is out of breath. It's clear he ran all the way here. "Sir, please—"

"Samuel?" Castle is up, around his desk, charging forward to grip this boy's shoulders, trying to focus his eyes. "What is it—what's wrong?"

"Sir," Samuel says again, this time more normally, his breathing almost within his grasp. "We have a—a situation."

"Tell me everything—now is not the time to hold back if something has happened—"

"It's nothing to do with anything topside, sir, it's just—" His eyes dart in my direction for one split second. "Our . . . visitor—he—he is not cooperating, sir, he's—he's giving the guards a lot of trouble—"

"What kind of trouble?" Castle's eyes are two slits.

Samuel drops his voice. "He's managed to make a dent in the door, sir. He's managed to dent the *steel door*, sir, and he's threatening the guards and they're beginning to worry—"

"*Juliette.*"

No.

"I need your help," Castle says without looking at me. "I know you don't want to do this, but you're the only one he'll listen to and we can't afford this distraction, not right now." His voice is so thin, so stretched it sounds as if it might actually crack. "Please do what you can to contain him, and when you deem it safe for one of the girls to enter, perhaps we can find a way to sedate him without endangering them in the process."

My eyes flick up to Adam almost accidentally. He doesn't look happy.

"Juliette." Castle's jaw tightens. "Please. Go now."

I nod. Turn to leave.

"Get ready," Castle adds as I walk out the door, his voice too soft for the words he speaks next. "Unless we have been deceived, the supreme will be massacring unarmed civilians tomorrow, and we can't afford to assume Warner has given us false information. We leave at dawn."

FIFTY-FOUR

The guards let me into Warner's room without a single word.

My eyes dart around the now partially furnished space, heart pounding, fists clenching, blood racing racing racing. Something is wrong. Something has happened. Warner was perfectly fine when I left him last night and I can't imagine what could've inspired him to lose his mind like this but I'm scared.

Someone has given him a chair. I realize now how he was able to dent the steel door. No one should've given him a chair.

Warner is sitting in it, his back to me. Only his head is visible from where I'm standing.

"You came back," he says.

"Of course I came back," I tell him, inching closer. "What's wrong? Is something wrong?"

He laughs. Runs a hand through his hair. Looks up at the ceiling.

"What happened?" I'm so worried now. "Are you—did something happen to you? Are you okay?"

"I need to get out of here," he says. "I need to leave. I can't be here anymore."

"Warner—"

"Do you know what he said to me? Did he tell you what he said to me?"

Silence.

"He just walked into my room this morning. He walked right in here and said he wanted to have a conversation with me." Warner laughs again, loud, too loud. Shakes his head. "He told me I can change. He said I might have a *gift* like everyone else here—that maybe I have an *ability*. He said I can be different, love. He said he *believes* I can be *different* if I *want* to be."

Castle told him.

Warner stands up but doesn't turn around all the way and I see he's not wearing a shirt. He doesn't even seem to mind that I can see the scars on his back, the word *IGNITE* tattooed on his body. His hair is messy, untamed, falling into his face and his pants are zipped but unbuttoned and I've never seen him so disheveled before. He presses his palms against the stone wall, arms outstretched; his body is bowed, his head down as if in prayer. His entire body is tense, tight, muscles straining against his skin. His clothes are in a pile on the floor and his mattress is in the middle of the room and the chair he was just sitting in is facing the wall, staring at nothing at all and I realize he's begun to lose his mind in here.

"Can you believe that?" he asks me, still not looking in my direction. "Can you believe he thinks I can just wake up one morning and be *different*? Sing happy songs and give money to the poor and beg the world to forgive me for what

I've done? Do you think that's possible? Do you think I can change?"

He finally turns to face me and his eyes are laughing, his eyes are like emeralds glinting in the setting sun and his mouth is twitching, suppressing a smile. "Do you think I could be *different*?" He takes a few steps toward me and I don't know why it affects my breathing. Why I can't find my mouth.

"It's just a question," he says, and he's right in front of me and I don't even know how he got there. He's still looking at me, his eyes so focused and so simultaneously unnerving, brilliant, blazing with something I can never place.

My heart it will not be still it refuses to stop skipping skipping skipping

"Tell me, Juliette. I'd love to know what you really think of me."

"Why?" Barely a whisper in an attempt to buy some time.

Warner's lips flicker up and into a smile before they fall open, just a bit, just enough to twitch into a strange, curious look that lingers in his eyes. He doesn't answer. He doesn't say a word. He only moves closer to me, studying me and I'm frozen in place, my mouth stuffed full of the seconds he doesn't speak and I'm fighting every atom in my body, every stupid cell in my system for being so attracted to him.

Oh.

God.

~~I am so horribly attracted to him.~~

The guilt is growing inside of me in stacks, settling on

my bones, snapping me in half. It's a cable twisted around my neck, a caterpillar crawling across my stomach. It's the night and midnight and the twilight of indecision. It's too many secrets I no longer contain.

~~I don't understand why I want this.~~

I am a terrible person.

And it's like he *sees* what I'm thinking, like he can feel the change happening in my head, because suddenly he's different. His energy slows down, his eyes are deep, troubled, tender; his lips are soft, still slightly parted and now the air in this room is too tight, too full of cotton and I feel the blood rushing around in my head, crashing into every rational region of my brain.

I wish someone would remind me how to breathe.

"Why can't you answer my question?" He's looking so deeply into my eyes that I'm surprised I haven't buckled under the intensity and I realize then, right in this moment I realize that everything about him is intense. Nothing about him is manageable or easy to compartmentalize. He's too much. Everything about him is too much. His emotions, his actions, his anger, his aggression.

~~His love.~~

He's dangerous, electric, impossible to contain. His body is rippling with an energy so extraordinary that even when he's calmed down it's almost palpable. It has a presence.

But I've developed a strange, frightening faith in who Warner really is and who he has the capacity to become. I want to find the 19-year-old boy who would feed a stray dog. I want to believe in the boy with a tortured childhood and an abusive father. I want to understand him. I want to unravel him.

I want to believe he is more than the mold he was forced into.

"I think you can change," I hear myself saying. "I think anyone can change."

And he smiles.

It's a slow, delighted smile. The kind of smile that breaks into a laugh and lights up his features and makes him sigh. He closes his eyes. His face is so touched, so amused. "It's just so sweet," he says. "So unbearably sweet. Because you really believe that."

"Of course I do."

He finally looks at me when he whispers, "But you're wrong."

"What?"

"I'm heartless," he says to me, his words cold, hollow, directed inward. "I'm a heartless bastard and a cruel, vicious being. I don't care about people's feelings. I don't care about their fears or their futures. I don't care about what they want or whether or not they have a family, and I'm not sorry," he says. "I've never been sorry for anything I've done."

It actually takes me a few moments to find my head. "But you apologized to me," I tell him. "You apologized to me just last night—"

"You're different," he says, cutting me off. "You don't count."

"I'm not different," I tell him. "I'm just another person, just like everyone else. And you've proven you have the capacity for remorse. For compassion. I know you can be kind—"

"That's not who I am." His voice is suddenly hard, suddenly too strong. "And I'm not going to change. I can't erase the nineteen miserable years of my life. I can't misplace the memories of what I've done. I can't wake up one morning and decide to live on borrowed hopes and dreams. Someone else's promises for a brighter future.

"And I won't lie to you," he says. "I've never given a damn about others and I don't make sacrifices and I do not compromise. I am not good, or fair, or decent, and I never will be. I can't be. Because to try to be any of those things would be *embarrassing*."

"How can you think that?" I want to shake him. "How can you be ashamed of an attempt to be better?"

But he's not listening. He's laughing. He's saying, "Can you even picture me? Smiling at small children and handing out presents at birthday parties? Can you picture me helping a stranger? Playing with the neighbor's dog?"

"Yes," I say to him. "Yes I can." I've already seen it, I don't say to him.

"No."

"Why not?" I insist. "Why is that so hard to believe?"

"That kind of life," he says, "is impossible for me."

"But why?"

Warner clenches and unclenches 5 fingers before

341

running them through his hair. "Because I feel it," he says, quieter now. "I've always been able to feel it."

"Feel what?" I whisper.

"What people think of me."

"What . . . ?"

"Their feelings—their energy—it's—I don't know what it is," he says, frustrated, stumbling backward, shaking his head. "I've always been able to tell. I know how everyone hates me. I know how little my father cares for me. I know the agony of my mother's heart. I know that you're not like everyone else." His voice catches. "I know you're telling the truth when you say you don't hate me. That you want to and you can't. Because there's no ill will in your heart, not toward me, and if there was I would know. Just like I know," he says, his voice husky with restraint, "that you felt something when we kissed. You felt the same thing I did and you're ashamed of it."

I'm dripping panic everywhere.

"How can you know that?" I ask him. "H-how—you can't just *know* things like that—"

"No one has ever looked at me like you do," he whispers. "No one ever talks to me like you do, Juliette. You're different," he says. "You're so different. You would understand me. But the rest of the world does not want my sympathies. They don't want my smiles. Castle is the only man on Earth who's been the exception to this rule, and his eagerness to trust and accept me only shows how weak this resistance is. No one here knows what they're doing and they're all going to get themselves slaughtered—"

"That's not *true*—that can't be true—"

"Listen to me," Warner says, urgently now. "You must understand—the only people who matter in this wretched world are the ones with real power. And you," he says, "*you* have power. You have the kind of strength that could shake this planet—that could conquer it. And maybe it's still too soon, maybe you need more time to recognize your own potential, but I will always be waiting. I will always want you on my side. Because the two of us—the two of us," he says, he stops. He sounds breathless. "Can you imagine?" His eyes are intent on mine, eyebrows drawn together. Studying me. "Of course you can," he whispers. "You think about it all the time."

I gasp.

"You don't belong here," he says. "You don't belong with these people. They will drag you down with them and get you *killed*—"

"I have no other choice!" I'm angry now, indignant. "I'd rather stay here with those who are trying to help—trying to make a difference! At least they're not murdering innocent people—"

"You think your new friends have never killed before?" Warner shouts, pointing at the door. "You think Kent has never killed anyone? That Kenji has never put a bullet through a stranger's body? They were *my* soldiers!" he says. "I saw them do it with my own eyes!"

"They were trying to survive," I tell him, shaking,

fighting to ignore the terror of my own imagination. "Their loyalties were never with The Reestablishment—"

"My loyalties," he says, "do not lie with The Reestablishment. My loyalties lie with those who know how to live. I only have two options in this game, love." He's breathing hard. "Kill. Or be killed."

"No," I tell him, backing away, feeling sick. "It doesn't have to be like that. You don't have to live like that. You could get away from your father, from that life. You don't have to be what he wants you to be—"

"The damage," he says, "is already done. It's too late for me. I've already accepted my fate."

"No—Warner—"

"I'm not asking you to worry about me," he says. "I know exactly what my future looks like and I'm okay with it. I'm happy to live in solitude. I'm not afraid of spending the rest of my life in the company of my own person. I do not fear loneliness."

"You don't have to have that life," I tell him. "You don't have to be alone."

"I will not stay here," he says. "I just wanted you to know that. I'm going to find a way out of here and I'm going to leave as soon as I have the chance. My vacation," he says, "has officially come to an end."

FIFTY-FIVE

Tick tock.

Castle called an impromptu meeting to brief everyone on the details of tomorrow's fight; there are less than 12 hours until we leave. We've gathered in the dining hall because it's the easiest place to seat everyone at once.

We had 1 final meal, a handful of forced conversation, 2 tense hours filled with brief, hysterical moments of laughter that sounded more like choking. Sara and Sonya were the last to sneak into the hall, both spotting me and waving a quick hello before they sat down on the other side of the room. Then Castle began to speak.

Everyone will need to fight.

All able-bodied men and women. The elderly unable to enter battle will stay back with the youngest ones, and the youngest ones will include James and his old group of friends.

James is currently crushing Adam's hand.

Anderson is going after the people, Castle says. The people have been rioting, raging against The Reestablishment now more than ever. Our battle gave them hope, Castle says to us. They'd only heard rumors of a resistance, and the battle made those rumors concrete. They are looking to us to support them, to stand by them, and now, for the first time, we will be fighting with our gifts out in the open.

On the compounds.

Where the civilians will see us for what we are.

Castle is telling us to prepare for aggression on both sides. He says that sometimes, especially when frightened, people will not react positively to seeing our kind. They prefer the familiar terror as opposed to the unknown or the inexplicable, and our presence, our public display might create new enemies.

We have to be ready for that.

"Then why should we care?" someone shouts from the back of the room. She gets to her feet and I notice her sleek black hair, one heavy sheet of ink that stops at her waist. Her eyes are glittering under the fluorescent lights. "If they're only going to hate us," she says, "why should we even defend them? That's ridiculous!"

Castle takes a deep breath. "We cannot fault them all for the foolishness of one."

"But it's not just one, is it?" a new voice chimes in. "How many of them are going to turn on us?"

"We have no way of knowing," Castle says. "It could be one. It could be none. I am merely advising you to be cautious. You must never forget that these civilians are innocent and unarmed. They are being murdered for their disobedience— for merely speaking out and asking for fair treatment. They are starved and they've lost their homes, their families. Surely, you must be able to relate. Many of you still have family lost, scattered across the country, do you not?"

There's a general murmur among the crowd.

"You must imagine that it is your mother. Your father. Your brothers and sisters among them. They are hurting and they are beaten down. We have to do what little we can to help. It's the only way. We are their only hope."

"What about our men?" Another person gets to his feet. He must be in his late 40s, round and robust, towering over the room. "Where is the guarantee that we will get Winston and Brendan back?"

Castle's gaze drops for only a second. I wonder if I'm the only one who noticed the pain flit in and out of his eyes. "There is no guarantee, my friend. There never is. But we will do our best. We will not give up."

"Then what good was it to take the kid hostage?" he protests. "Why not just kill him? Why are we keeping him alive? He's done us no good and he's eating our food and using resources that should go to the rest of us!"

The crowd bursts into an aggravated frenzy, angry, insane with emotions. Everyone is shouting at once, shouting things like, "Kill him!" and "That'll show the supreme!" and "We have to make a statement!" and "He deserves to die!"

There's a sudden constriction in my heart. I've almost begun to hyperventilate and I realize, for the very first time, that the thought of Warner dead is anything but appealing to me.

It horrifies me.

I look to Adam for a different kind of reaction but I don't

know what I was expecting. I'm stupid to be surprised at the tension in his eyes, his forehead, the stiff set of his lips. I'm stupid to have expected anything but hatred from Adam. Of course Adam hates Warner. Of course he does.

Warner tried to *murder* him.

Of course he, too, wants Warner dead.

I think I'm going to be sick.

"Please!" Castle shouts. "I know you're upset! Tomorrow is a difficult thing to face, but we can't channel our aggression onto one person. We have to use it as fuel for our fight and we have to remain united. We cannot allow anything to divide us. Not now!"

6 ticks of silence.

"I won't fight until he's dead!"

"We kill him tonight!"

"Let's get him now!"

The crowd is a roar of angry bodies, determined, ugly faces so scary, so savage, so twisted in inhuman rage. I hadn't realized that the people of Omega Point were harboring so much resentment.

"STOP!" Castle's hands are in the air, his eyes on fire. Every table and chair in the room has begun to rattle. People are looking around, scattered and scared, unnerved.

They're still unwilling to undermine Castle's authority. At least for now.

"Our hostage," Castle begins, "is no longer a hostage."

Impossible.

It's *impossible*.

It's not *possible.*

"He has come to me, just tonight," Castle says, "and asked for sanctuary at Omega Point."

My brain is screaming, raging against the 14 words Castle has just confessed.

It can't be true. Warner said he was going to leave. He said he was going to find a way to get *out.*

But Omega Point is even more shocked than I am. Even Adam is shaking with anger beside me. I'm afraid to look at his face.

"SILENCE! PLEASE!" Castle holds out another hand to quell the explosion of protests.

He says, "We have recently discovered that he, too, has a gift. And he says he wants to join us. He says he will fight with us tomorrow. He says he will fight against his father and help us find Brendan and Winston."

Chaos

Chaos

Chaos

explodes in every corner of the room.

"He's a liar!"

"Prove it!"

"How can you believe him?"

"He's a traitor to his own people! He'll be a traitor to us!"

"I'll never fight beside him!"

"I'll kill him first!"

Castle's eyes narrow, flashing under the fluorescent lights, and his hands move through the air like whisks, gathering up every plate, every spoon, every glass cup in the room and he holds them there, right in midair, daring someone to speak, to shout, to disagree.

"You will not touch him," he says quietly. "I took an oath to help the members of our kind and I will not break it now. Think of yourselves!" he shouts. "Think of the day you found out! Think of the loneliness, the isolation, the terror that overcame you! Think of how you were cast off by your families and your friends! You don't think he could be a changed man? How have *you* changed, friends? You judge him now! You judge one of your own who asks for amnesty!"

Castle looks disgusted.

"If he does anything to compromise any of us, if he does one single thing to disprove his loyalty—only then are you free to pass judgment upon his person. But we first give him a chance, do we not?" He is no longer bothering to hide his anger. "He says he will help us find our men! He says he will fight against his father! He has valuable information we can use! Why should we be unwilling to take a chance? He is no more than a child of nineteen! He is only one and we are many more!"

The crowd is hushed, whispering amongst itself and I hear snippets of conversation and things like "naive" and "ridiculous" and "he's going to get all of us killed!" but no one speaks up and I'm relieved. I can't believe what I'm feeling right now and I wish I didn't care at all about what happens to Warner.

I wish I could want him dead. I wish I felt nothing for him.

But I can't. I can't. I can't.

"How do you know?" someone asks. A new voice, a calm voice, a voice struggling to be rational.

The voice sitting right beside me.

Adam gets to his feet. Swallows, hard. Says, "How do you know he has a gift? Have you tested him?"

And he looks at me, Castle looks at me, he stares at me as if to will me to speak and I feel like I've sucked all of the air out of this room, like I've been thrown into a vat of boiling water, like I will never find my heartbeat ever again and I am begging praying hoping and wishing he will not say the words he says next but he does.

Of course he does.

"Yes," Castle says. "We know that he, like you, can touch Juliette."

FIFTY-SIX

It's like spending 6 months just trying to inhale.

It's like forgetting how to move your muscles and reliving every nauseous moment in your life and struggling to get all the splinters out from underneath your skin. It's like that one time you woke up and tripped down a rabbit hole and a blond girl in a blue dress kept asking you for directions but you couldn't tell her, you had no idea, you kept trying to speak but your throat was full of rain clouds and it's like someone has taken the ocean and filled it with silence and dumped it all over this room.

It's like this.

No one is speaking. No one is moving. Everyone is staring.

At me.

At Adam.

At Adam staring at me.

His eyes are wide, blinking too fast, his features shifting in and out of confusion and anger and pain and confusion so much confusion and a touch of betrayal, of suspicion, of so much more confusion and an extra dose of pain and I'm gaping like a fish in the moments before it dies.

I wish he would say something. I wish he would at least

ask or accuse or demand *something* but he says nothing, he only studies me, stares at me, and I watch as the light goes out of his eyes, as the anger gives way to the pain and the extraordinary impossibility he must be experiencing right now and he sits down.

He does not look in my direction.

"Adam—"

He's up. He's up. He's up and he's charging out of the room and I scramble to my feet, I chase him out the door and I hear the chaos erupt in my wake, the crowd dissolving into anger all over again and I almost slam right into him, I'm gasping and he spins around and he says

"I don't understand." His eyes are so hurt, so deep, so blue.

"Adam, I—"

"He's touched you." It's not a question. He can hardly meet my eyes and he looks almost embarrassed by the words he speaks next. "He's touched your skin."

If only it were just that. If only it were that simple. If only I could get these currents out of my blood and Warner out of my head and *why am I so confused*

"Juliette."

"Yes," I tell him, I hardly move my lips. The answer to his nonquestion is yes.

Adam touches his fingers to his mouth, looks up, looks away, makes a strange, disbelieving sound. "When?"

I tell him.

I tell him when it happened, how it all began, I tell him

how I was wearing one of the dresses Warner always made me wear, how he was fighting to stop me before I jumped out the window, how his hand grazed my leg and how he touched me and nothing happened.

I tell him how I tried to pretend it was all just a figment of my imagination until Warner caught us again.

I don't tell him how Warner told me he missed me, how he told me he loved me and he kissed me, how he kissed me with such wild, reckless intensity. I don't tell him that I pretended to return Warner's affections just so I could slip my hands under his coat to get the gun out of his inside pocket. I don't tell him that I was surprised, shocked, even, at how it felt to be in his arms, and that I pushed away those strange feelings because I hated Warner, because I was so horrified that he'd shot Adam that I wanted to kill him.

All Adam knows is that I almost did. That I almost killed Warner.

And now Adam is blinking, digesting the words I'm telling him, innocent of the things I've kept to myself.

~~I really am a monster.~~

"I didn't want you to know," I manage to say. "I thought it would complicate things between us—after everything we've had to deal with—I just thought it would be better to ignore it and I don't know." I fumble, fail for words. "It was stupid. I was stupid. I should have told you and I'm sorry. I'm so sorry. I didn't want you to find out like this."

Adam is breathing hard, rubbing the back of his head before running a hand through his hair and he says, "I don't—I don't get it—I mean—do we know why he can touch you? Is it like me? Can he do what I do? I don't—*God*, Juliette, and you've been spending all that time alone with him—"

"Nothing happened," I tell him. "All I did was talk to him and he never tried to touch me. And I have no idea why he can touch me—I don't think anyone does. He hasn't started testing with Castle yet."

Adam sighs and drags a hand across his face and says, so quietly only I can hear him, "I don't even know why I'm surprised. We share the same goddamn DNA." He swears under his breath. Swears again. "Am I ever going to catch a break?" he asks, raising his voice, talking to the air. "Is there ever going to be a time when some shitty thing isn't being thrown in my face? Jesus. It's like this insanity is never going to end."

I want to tell him that I don't think it ever will.

"Juliette."

I freeze at the sound of his voice.

I squeeze my eyes shut tight, so tight, refusing to believe my ears. Warner cannot be here. Of course he's not here. It's not even *possible* for him to be out here but then I remember. Castle said he's no longer a hostage.

Castle must've let him out of his room.

Oh.

Oh no.

This can't be happening. Warner is not standing so close to me and Adam right now, not again, not like this not after everything this *cannot* be happening

but Adam looks over my shoulder, looks behind me at the person I'm trying so hard to ignore and I can't lift my eyes. I don't want to see what's about to happen.

Adam's voice is like acid when he speaks. "What the hell are you doing here?"

"It's good to see you again, Kent." I can actually hear Warner smile. "We should catch up, you know. Especially in light of this new discovery. I had no idea we had so much in common."

You really, truly have no idea, I want to say out loud.

"You sick piece of shit," Adam says to him, his voice low, measured.

"Such unfortunate language." Warner shakes his head. "Only those who cannot express themselves intelligently would resort to such crude substitutions in vocabulary." A pause. "Is it because I intimidate you, Kent? Am I making you nervous?" He laughs. "You seem to be struggling to hold yourself together."

"I will *kill you*—" Adam charges forward to grab Warner by the throat just as Kenji slams into him, into both of them, shoving them apart with a look of absolute disgust on his face.

"What the *hell* do you two think you're doing?" His eyes are blazing. "I don't know if you've noticed but you're standing right in front of the doorway and you're scaring the *shit* out of the little kids, Kent, so I'm going to have to ask you to calm your ass down." Adam tries to speak but Kenji cuts him off. "Listen, I don't have a clue what Warner is doing out of his room, but that's not my call to make. Castle is in charge around here, and we have to respect that. You can't go around killing people just because you feel like it."

"This is the same guy who tried to torture me to death!" Adam shouts. "He had his men beat the shit out of you! And I have to live with him? Fight with him? Pretend everything is fine? Has Castle *lost his mind*—"

"Castle knows what he's doing," Kenji snaps. "You don't need to have an opinion. You will defer to his judgment."

Adam throws his hands in the air, furious. "I don't believe this. This is a *joke*! Who does this? Who treats hostages like they're on some kind of retreat?" he shouts again, making no effort to keep his voice down. "He could go back and give away every detail of this place—he could give away our exact location!"

"That's impossible," Warner says. "I have no idea where we are."

Adam turns on Warner so quickly that I spin around just as fast, just to catch the action. Adam is shouting, saying something, looking like he might attack Warner right here in this moment and Kenji is trying to restrain him but I can hardly hear what's going on around me. The blood is pounding too hard in my head and my eyes are forgetting to blink because Warner is looking at me, only me, his eyes so focused, so intent, so heart-wrenchingly deep it renders me completely still.

Warner's chest is rising and falling, strong enough that I can see it from where I'm standing. He's not paying attention to the commotion beside him, the chaos of the dining hall or Adam trying to pummel him into the ground; he's not moved a single inch. He will not look away and I know I have to do it for him.

I turn my head.

Kenji is yelling at Adam to calm down about something and I reach out, I grab Adam's arm, I offer him a small smile and he stills. "Come on," I tell him. "Let's go back inside. Castle isn't finished yet and we need to hear what he's saying."

Adam makes an effort to regain control of himself. Takes a deep breath. Offers me a quick nod and allows me to lead him forward. I'm forcing myself to focus on Adam so I can pretend Warner isn't here.

Warner isn't a fan of my plan.

He's now standing in front of us, blocking our path and I look at him despite my best intentions only to see something I've never seen before. Not to this degree, not like this.

Pain.

"Move," Adam snaps at him, but Warner doesn't seem to notice.

He's looking at me. He's looking at my hand clenched around Adam's covered arm and the agony in his eyes is breaking my knees and I can't speak, I shouldn't speak, I wouldn't know what to say even if I could speak and then he says my name. He says it again. He says, "Juliette—"

"Move!" Adam barks again, this time losing restraint and pushing Warner with enough strength to knock him to the floor. Except Warner doesn't fall. He trips backward, just a little, but the movement somehow triggers something within him, some kind of dormant anger he's all too eager to unleash and he's charging forward, ready to inflict damage and I'm trying to figure out what to do to make it stop, I'm trying to come up with a plan and I'm stupid.

I'm stupid enough to step in the middle.

Adam grabs me to try and pull me back but I'm already pressing a palm to Warner's chest and I don't know what I'm thinking but I'm not thinking at all and that seems to be the problem. I'm here, I'm caught in the milliseconds standing between 2 brothers willing to destroy one another and it's not even me who manages to do anything at all.

It's Kenji.

He grabs both boys by the arms and tries to pry them apart but the sudden sound that rips through his throat is a torture and a terror I wish I could tear out of my skull.

He's down.

He's on the ground.

He's choking, gasping, writhing on the floor until he goes limp, until he can hardly breathe and then he's still, too still, and I think I'm screaming, I keep touching my lips to see where this sound is coming from and I'm on my knees. I'm trying to shake him awake but he's not moving, he's not responding and I have no idea what just happened.

I have no idea if Kenji is dead.

FIFTY-SEVEN

I'm definitely screaming.

Arms are pulling me up off the floor and I hear voices and sounds I don't care to recognize because all I know is that this can't happen, not to Kenji, not to my funny, complicated friend who keeps secrets behind his smiles and I'm ripping away from the hands holding me back and I'm blind, I'm bolting into the dining hall and a hundred blurry faces blend into the background because the only one I want to see is wearing a navy-blue blazer and headful of dreads tied into a ponytail.

"Castle!" I'm screaming. I'm still screaming. I may have fallen to the floor, I'm not sure, but I can tell my kneecaps are starting to hurt and I don't care I don't care I don't care—"Castle! It's Kenji—he's—*please*—"

I've never seen Castle run before.

He charges through the room at an inhuman speed, past me and into the hall. Everyone in the room is up, frantic, some shouting, panicked, and I'm chasing Castle back into the tunnel and Kenji is still there. Still limp. Still.

Too still.

"Where are the girls?" Castle is shouting. "Someone— get the girls!" He's cradling Kenji's head, trying to pull

Kenji's heavy body into his arms and I've never heard him like this before, not even when he talked about our hostages, not even when he talked about what Anderson has done to the civilians. I look around and see the members of Omega Point standing all around us, pain carved into their features and so many of them have already started crying, clutching at each other and I realize I never fully recognized Kenji. I didn't understand the reach of his authority. I'd never really seen just how much he means to the people in this room.

How much they love him.

I blink and Adam is one of 50 different people trying to help carry Kenji and now they're running, they're hoping against hope and someone is saying, "They've gone to the medical wing! They're preparing a bed for him!" And it's like a stampede, everyone rushing after them, trying to find out what's wrong and no one will look at me, no one will meet my eyes and I pull myself away, out of sight, around the corner, into the darkness. I taste the tears as they fall into my mouth, I count each salty drop because I can't understand what happened, how it happened, how this is even possible because I wasn't touching him, I couldn't have been touching him please please please I couldn't have touched him but then I freeze. Icicles form along my arms as I realize:

I'm not wearing my gloves.

I forgot my gloves. I was in such a rush to get here tonight that I just jumped out of the shower and left my gloves in my room and it doesn't seem real, it doesn't seem possible that I could've done this, that I could've forgotten, that I could be responsible for yet another life lost and I just I just I just

I fall to the floor.

"Juliette."

I look up. I jump up.

I say, "Stay away from me" and I'm shaking, I'm trying to push the tears back but I'm shrinking into nothingness because I'm thinking this must be it. This must be my ultimate punishment. I deserve this pain, I deserve to have killed one of my only friends in the world and I want to shrivel up and disappear forever. "Go away—"

"Juliette, *please*," Warner says, coming closer. His face is cast in shadow. This tunnel is only half lit and I don't know where it leads. All I know is that I do not want to be alone with Warner.

Not now. Not ever again.

"I said stay away from me." My voice is trembling. "I don't want to talk to you. Please—just leave me alone!"

"I can't abandon you like this!" he says. "Not when you're crying!"

"Maybe you wouldn't understand that emotion," I snap at him. "Maybe you wouldn't care because killing people means nothing to you!"

He's breathing hard. Too fast. "What are you talking about?"

"I'm talking about Kenji!" I explode. "I did that! It's my

fault! It's my fault you and Adam were fighting and it's my fault Kenji came out to stop you and it's my fault—" My voice breaks once, twice. "It's my fault he's dead!"

Warner's eyes go wide. "Don't be ridiculous," he says. "He's not dead."

I'm agony.

I'm sobbing about what I've done and how of course he's dead, didn't you see him, he wasn't even moving and I killed him and Warner remains utterly silent. He doesn't say a single thing as I hurl awful, horrible insults at him and accuse him of being too coldhearted to understand what it's like to grieve. I don't even realize he's pulled me into his arms until I'm nestled against his chest and I don't fight it. I don't fight it at all. I cling to him because I need this warmth, I miss feeling strong arms around me and I'm only just beginning to realize how quickly I came to rely on the healing properties of an excellent hug.

How desperately I've missed this.

And he just holds me. He smooths back my hair, he runs a gentle hand down my back, and I hear his heart beat a strange, crazy beat that sounds far too fast to be human.

His arms are wrapped entirely around me when he says, "You didn't kill him, love."

And I say, "Maybe you didn't see what I saw."

"You are misunderstanding the situation entirely. You didn't do anything to hurt him."

I shake my head against his chest. "What are you talking about?"

363

"It wasn't you. I know it wasn't you."

I pull back. Look up into his eyes. "How can you know something like that?"

"Because," he says. "It wasn't you who hurt Kenji. It was me."

FIFTY-EIGHT

"What?"

"He's not dead," Warner says, "though he is severely injured. I suspect they should be able to revive him."

"What"—I'm panicking, panicking in my bones—"what are you talking about—"

"Please," Warner says. "Sit down. I'll explain." He folds himself onto the floor and pats the place beside him. I don't know what else to do and my legs are now officially too shaky to stand on their own.

My limbs spill onto the ground, both our backs against the wall, his right side and my left side divided only by a thin inch of air.

1

2

3 seconds pass.

"I didn't want to believe Castle when he told me I might have a . . . a *gift*," Warner says. His voice is pitched so low that I have to strain to hear it even though I'm only inches away. "A part of me hoped he was trying to drive me mad for his own benefit." A small sigh. "But it did make a bit of sense, if I really thought about it. Castle told me about Kent, too," Warner says. "About how he can touch you and how they've discovered why. For a moment I wondered if perhaps I had a similar ability. One just as pathetic. Equally as useless." He laughs. "I was extremely reluctant to believe it."

"It's not a useless ability," I hear myself saying.

"Really?" He turns to face me. Our shoulders are almost touching. "Tell me, love. What can he do?"

"He can disable things. Abilities."

"Right," he says, "but how will that ever *help* him? How could it ever help him to disable the powers of his own people? It's absurd. It's *wasteful*. It won't help at all in this war."

I bristle. Decide to ignore that. "What does any of this have to do with Kenji?"

He turns away from me again. His voice is softer when he says, "Would you believe me if I told you I could sense your energy right now? Sense the tone and weight of it?"

I stare at him, study his features and the earnest, tentative note in his voice. "Yes," I tell him. "I think I'd believe you."

Warner smiles in a way that seems to sadden him. "I can sense," he says, taking a deep breath, "the emotions you're feeling most strongly. And because I know you, I'm able to put those feelings into context. I know the fear you're feeling right now, for example, is not directed toward me, but toward yourself, and what you think you've done to Kenji. I sense your hesitation—your reluctance to believe that it wasn't your fault. I feel your sadness, your grief."

"You can really feel that?" I ask.

He nods without looking at me.

"I never knew that was possible," I tell him.

"I didn't either—I wasn't aware of it," he says. "Not for a very long time. I actually thought it was normal to be so acutely aware of human emotions. I thought perhaps I was more perceptive than most. It's a big factor in why my father allowed me to take over Sector 45," he tells me. "Because I have an uncanny ability to tell whenever someone is hiding something, or feeling guilty, or, most importantly, lying." A pause. "That," he says, "and because I'm not afraid to deliver consequences if the occasion calls for it.

"It wasn't until Castle suggested there might be something more to me that I really began to analyze it. I nearly lost my mind." He shakes his head. "I kept going over it, thinking of ways to prove and disprove his theories. Even with all my careful deliberation, I dismissed it. And while I am a bit sorry—for your sake, not for mine—that Kenji had to be stupid enough to interfere tonight, I think it was actually quite serendipitous. Because now I finally have proof. Proof that I was wrong. That Castle," he says, "was right."

"What do you mean?"

"I took your Energy," he tells me, "and I didn't know I could. I could feel it all very vividly when the four of us connected. Adam was inaccessible—which, by the way, explains why I never suspected him of being disloyal. His emotions were always hidden; always blocked off. I was naive and assumed he was merely robotic, devoid of any real personality or interests. He eluded me and it was my own

367

fault. I trusted myself too much to be able to anticipate a flaw in my system."

And I want to say, Adam's ability isn't so useless after all, is it?

But I don't.

"And Kenji," Warner says after a moment. He rubs his forehead. Laughs a little. "Kenji was . . . very smart. A lot smarter than I gave him credit for—which, as it turns out, was exactly his tactic. Kenji," he says, blowing out a breath, "was careful to be an obvious threat as opposed to a discreet one.

"He was always getting into trouble—demanding extra portions at meals, fighting with the other soldiers, breaking curfew. He broke simple rules in order to draw attention to himself. In order to trick me into seeing him as an irritant and nothing more. I always felt there was something off about him, but I attributed it to his loud, raucous behavior and his inability to follow rules. I dismissed him as a poor soldier. Someone who would never be promoted. Someone who would always be recognized as a waste of time." He shakes his head. Raises his eyebrows at the ground. "Brilliant," he says, looking almost impressed. "It was brilliant. His only mistake," Warner adds after a moment, "was being too openly friendly with Kent. And that mistake nearly cost him his life."

"So—what? You were trying to finish him off tonight?" I'm still so confused, trying to make an attempt to refocus the conversation. "Did you hurt him on purpose?"

"Not on purpose." Warner shakes his head. "I didn't actually know what I was doing. Not at first. I've only ever just *sensed* Energy; I never knew I could *take* it. But I touched yours simply by touching you—there was so much adrenaline among the group of us that yours practically threw itself at me. And when Kenji grabbed my arm," he says, "you and I, we were still connected. And I . . . somehow I managed to redirect your power in his direction. It was quite accidental but I felt it happen. I felt your power rush into me. Rush out of me." He looks up. Meets my eyes. "It was the most extraordinary thing I've ever experienced."

I think I'd fall down if I weren't already sitting.

"So you can take—you can just take other people's powers?" I ask him.

"Apparently."

"And you're sure you didn't hurt Kenji on purpose?"

Warner laughs, looks at me like I've just said something highly amusing. "If I had wanted to kill him, I would have. And I wouldn't have needed such a complicated setup to accomplish it. I'm not interested in theatrics," he says. "If I want to hurt someone, I won't require much more than my own two hands."

I'm stunned into silence.

"I'm actually amazed," Warner says, "how you manage to contain so much without finding ways to release the excess. I could barely hold on to it. The transfer from my body to Kenji's was not only immediate, it was necessary. I couldn't tolerate the intensity for very long."

"And I can't hurt you?" I blink at him, astonished. "At all? My power just goes *into* you? You just absorb it?"

He nods. Says, "Would you like to see?"

And I'm saying yes with my head and my eyes and my lips and I've never been more terrified to be excited in my life. "What do I have to do?" I ask him.

"Nothing," he says, so quietly. "Just touch me."

My heart is beating pounding racing running through my body and I'm trying to focus. Trying to stay calm. This is going to be fine, I say to myself. It's going to be fine. It's just an experiment. There's no need to get so excited about being able to touch someone again, I keep saying to myself.

~~But oh, I am so, so excited.~~

He holds out his bare hand.

I take it.

I wait to feel something, some feeling of weakness, some depletion of my Energy, some sign that a transfer is taking place from my body to his but I feel nothing at all. I feel exactly the same. But I watch Warner's face as his eyes close and he makes an effort to focus. Then I feel his hand tighten around mine and he gasps.

His eyes fly open and his free hand goes right through the floor.

I jerk back, panicked. I'm tipping sideways, my hands catching me from behind. I must be hallucinating. I must be hallucinating the hole in the floor not 4 inches from where Warner is still sitting on the ground. I must've been hallucinating when I saw his resting palm press too hard

370

and go right through. I must be hallucinating everything. All of this. I'm dreaming and I'm sure I'm going to wake up soon. That must be it.

"Don't be afraid—"

"H-how," I stammer, "how did you d-do that—"

"Don't be frightened, love, it's all right, I promise—it's new for me, too—"

"My—my power? It doesn't—you don't feel any pain?"

He shakes his head. "On the contrary. It's the most incredible rush of adrenaline—it's unlike anything I've ever known. I actually feel a little light-headed," he says, "in the best possible way." He laughs. Smiles to himself. Drops his head into his hands. Looks up. "Can we do it again?"

"No," I say too quickly.

He's grinning. "Are you sure?"

"I can't—I just, I still can't believe you can touch me. That you really—I mean"—I'm shaking my head—"there's no catch? There are no conditions? You touch me and no one gets hurt? And not only does no one get hurt, but you *enjoy* it? You actually *like* the way it feels to touch me?"

He's blinking at me now, staring like he's not sure how to answer my question.

"Well?"

"Yes," he says, but it's a breathless word.

"Yes, what?"

I can hear how hard his heart is beating. I can actually hear it in the silence between us. "Yes," he says. "I like it."

Impossible.

"You never have to be afraid of touching me," he says. "It won't hurt me. It can only give me strength."

I want to laugh one of those strange, high-pitched, delusional laughs that signals the end of a person's sanity. Because this world, I think, has a terrible, terrible sense of humor. It always seems to be laughing at me. At my expense. Making my life infinitely more complicated all the time. Ruining all of my best-laid plans by making every choice so difficult. Making everything so confusing.

I can't touch the boy I love.

But I can use my touch to strengthen the boy who tried to kill the one I love.

No one, I want to tell the world, is laughing.

"Warner." I look up, hit with a sudden realization. "You have to tell Castle."

"Why would I do that?"

"Because he has to know! It would explain Kenji's situation and it could help us tomorrow! You'll be fighting with us and it might come in handy—"

Warner laughs.

He laughs and laughs and laughs, his eyes brilliant, gleaming even in this dim light. He laughs until it's just a hard breath, until it becomes a gentle sigh, until it dissolves into an amused smile. And then he grins at me until he's grinning to himself, until he looks down and his gaze drops to my hand, the one lying limp on my lap and he hesitates just a moment before his fingers brush the soft, thin skin covering my knuckles.

I don't breathe.

I don't speak.

I don't even move.

He's hesitant, like he's waiting to see if I'll pull away and I should, I know I should but I don't. So he takes my hand. Studies it. Runs his fingers along the lines of my palm, the creases at my joints, the sensitive spot between my thumb and index finger and his touch is so tender, so delicate and gentle and it feels so good it hurts, it actually hurts. And it's too much for my heart to handle right now.

I snatch back my hand in a jerky, awkward motion, face flushing, pulse tripping.

Warner doesn't flinch. He doesn't look up. He doesn't even seem surprised. He only stares at his now empty hands as he speaks. "You know," he says, his voice both strange and soft, "I think Castle is little more than an optimistic fool. He tries too hard to welcome too many people and it's going to backfire, simply because it's impossible to please everyone." A pause. "He is the perfect example of the kind of person who doesn't know the rules of this game. Someone who thinks too much with his heart and clings too desperately to some fantastical notion of hope and peace. It will never help him," he sighs. "In fact, it will be the end of him, I'm quite sure of it.

"But there is something about you," Warner says, "something about the way *you* hope for things." He shakes his head. "It's so naive that it's oddly endearing. You like to believe people when they speak," he says. "You prefer kindness." He smiles, just a little. Looks up. "It amuses me."

All at once I feel like an idiot. "You're not fighting with us tomorrow."

Warner is smiling openly now, his eyes so warm. "I'm going to leave."

"You're going to leave." I'm numb.

"I don't belong here."

I'm shaking my head, saying, "I don't understand—how can you leave? You told Castle you're going to fight with us tomorrow—does he know you're leaving? Does anyone know?" I ask him, searching his face. "What do you have planned? What are you going to do?"

He doesn't answer.

"What are you going to *do*, Warner—"

"Juliette," he whispers, and his eyes are urgent, tortured all of a sudden. "I need to ask you somethi—"

Someone is bolting down the tunnels.

Calling my name.

Adam.

FIFTY-NINE

I jump up, frantic, and tell Warner I'll be right back.

I'm saying don't leave yet, don't go anywhere just yet I'll be right back but I don't wait for his response because I'm on my feet and I'm running toward the lighted hallway and I almost slam right into Adam. He steadies me and pulls me tight, so close, always forgetting not to touch me like this and he's anxious and he says, "Are you okay?" and "I'm so sorry," and "I've been looking for you everywhere," and "I thought you'd come down to the medical wing," and "it wasn't your fault, I hope you know that—"

It keeps hitting me in the face, in the skull, in the spine, this knowledge of just how much I care about him. How much I know he cares about me. Being close to him like this is a painful reminder of everything I had to force myself to walk away from. I take a deep breath.

"Adam," I ask, "is Kenji okay?"

"He's not conscious yet," he says to me, "but Sara and Sonya think he's going to be okay. They're going to stay up with him all night, just to be sure he makes it through in one piece." A pause. "No one knows what happened," he says. "But it wasn't you." His eyes lock mine in place. "You know that, right? You didn't even touch him. I know you didn't."

And even though I open my mouth a million times to say, It was Warner. Warner did it. He's the one who did this to Kenji, you have to get him and catch him and stop him he is lying to all of you! He's going to escape tomorrow! I don't say any of it and I don't know why.

I don't know why I'm protecting him.

I think part of me is afraid to say the words out loud, afraid to make them true. I still don't know whether or not Warner is really going to leave or even how he's going to escape; I don't know if it's even possible. And I don't know if I can tell anyone about Warner's ability yet; I don't think I want to explain to Adam that while he and the rest of Omega Point were tending to Kenji, I was hiding in a tunnel with Warner—our enemy and hostage—holding his hand and testing out his new power.

I wish I weren't so confused.

I wish my interactions with Warner would stop making me feel so guilty. Every moment I spend with him, every conversation I have with him makes me feel like I've somehow betrayed Adam, even though technically we're not even together anymore. My heart still feels so tied to Adam; I feel bound to him, like I need to make up for already having hurt him so much. I don't want to be the reason for the pain in his eyes, not again, and somehow I've decided that keeping secrets is the only way to keep him from getting hurt. But deep down, I know this can't be right. Deep down, I know it could end badly.

But I don't know what else to do.

"Juliette?" Adam is still holding me tight, still so close and warm and wonderful. "Are you okay?"

And I'm not sure what makes me ask it, but suddenly I need to know.

"Are you ever going to tell him?"

Adam pulls back, just an inch. "What?"

"Warner. Are you ever going to tell him the truth? About the two of you?"

Adam is blinking, stunned, caught off guard by my question. "No," he finally says. "Never."

"Why not?"

"Because it takes a lot more than blood to be family," he says. "And I want nothing to do with him. I'd like to be able to watch him die and feel no sympathy, no remorse. He's the textbook definition of a monster," Adam says to me. "Just like my dad. And I'll drop dead before I recognize him as my brother."

Suddenly I'm feeling like I might fall over.

Adam grabs my waist, tries to focus my eyes. "You're still in shock," he says. "We need to get you something to eat—or maybe some water—"

"It's okay," I tell him. "I'm okay." I allow myself to enjoy one last second in his arms before I break away, needing to breathe. I keep trying to convince myself that Adam is right, that Warner has done terrible, awful things and I shouldn't forgive him. I shouldn't smile at him. I shouldn't even talk to him. And then I want to scream because I don't think my brain can handle the split personality I seem to be developing lately.

I tell Adam I need a minute. I tell him I need to stop by the bathroom before we head over to the medical wing and he says okay, he says he'll wait for me.

He says he'll wait for me until I'm ready.

And I tiptoe back into the dark tunnel to tell Warner that I have to leave, that I won't be coming back after all, but when I squint into the darkness I can't see a thing.

I look around.

He's already gone.

SIXTY

We don't have to do anything at all to die.

We can hide in a cupboard under the stairs our whole life and it'll still find us. Death will show up wearing an invisible cloak and it will wave a magic wand and whisk us away when we least expect it. It will erase every trace of our existence on this earth and it will do all this work for free. It will ask for nothing in return. It will take a bow at our funeral and accept the accolades for a job well done and then it will disappear.

Living is a little more complex. There's one thing we always have to do.

Breathe.

In and out, every single day in every hour minute and moment we must inhale whether we like it or not. Even as we plan to asphyxiate our hopes and dreams still we breathe. Even as we wither away and sell our dignity to the man on the corner we breathe. We breathe when we're wrong, we breathe when we're right, we breathe even as we slip off the ledge toward an early grave. It cannot be undone.

So I breathe.

I count all the steps I've climbed toward the noose hanging from the ceiling of my existence and I count out the number of times I've been stupid and I run out of numbers.

Kenji almost died today.

Because of me.

It's still my fault that Adam and Warner were fighting. It's still my fault that I stepped between them. It's still my fault that Kenji felt the need to pull them apart and if I hadn't been caught in the middle Kenji never would've been hurt.

And I'm standing here. Staring at him.

He's barely breathing and I'm begging him. I'm begging him to do the one thing that matters. The only thing that matters. I need him to hold on but he's not listening. He can't hear me and I need him to be okay. I need him to pull through. I need him to breathe.

I need him.

Castle didn't have much more to say.

Everyone was standing around, some wedged into the medical wing, others standing on the other side of the glass, watching silently. Castle gave a small speech about how we need to stick together, how we're a family and if we don't have each other then who do we have? He said we're all scared, sure, but now is the time for us to support one another. Now is the time to band together and fight back. Now is the time, he said, for us to take back our world.

"Now is the time for us to live," he said.

"We'll postpone tomorrow's departure just long enough for everyone to have a final breakfast together. We cannot go into battle divided," he said. "We have to have faith in ourselves and in each other. Take a little more time in the morning to find peace with yourselves. After breakfast we leave. As one."

"What about Kenji?" someone asked, and I was startled to hear the familiar voice.

James. He was standing there with his fists clenched, tearstains streaked across his face, his bottom lip trembling even as he fought to hide the pain in his voice.

My heart split clean in half.

"What do you mean?" Castle asked him.

"Will he fight tomorrow?" James demanded, sniffing back the last of his tears, fists beginning to shake. "He wants to fight tomorrow. He told me he wants to fight tomorrow."

Castle's face creased as it pulled together. He took his time responding. "I . . . I'm afraid I don't think Kenji will be able to join us tomorrow. But perhaps," he said, "perhaps you could stay and keep him company?"

James didn't respond. He only stared at Castle. Then he stared at Kenji. He blinked several times before pushing through the crowd to clamber onto Kenji's bed. Burrowed into his side and promptly fell asleep.

We all took that as our cue to leave.

Well. Everyone but me, Adam, Castle, and the girls. I find it interesting that everyone refers to Sonya and Sara as "the girls," as if they're the only girls in this entire place. They're not. I don't even know how they got that nickname and while a part of me wants to know, another part of me is too exhausted to ask.

I curl into my seat and stare at Kenji, who is struggling to breathe in and out. I prop my head up on my fist, fighting the sleep weaving its way into my consciousness. I don't deserve to sleep. I should stay here all night and watch over him. I would, too, if I could touch him without destroying his life.

"You two should really get to bed."

I jolt awake, jerking up, not realizing I'd actually dozed off for a second. Castle is staring at me with a soft, strange look on his face.

"I'm not tired," I lie.

"Go to bed," he says. "We have a big day tomorrow. You need to sleep."

"I can walk her out," Adam says. He moves to stand up. "And then I can be right back—"

"Please." Castle cuts him off. "Go. I'll be fine with the girls."

"But you need to sleep more than we do," I tell him.

Castle smiles a sad smile. "I'm afraid I won't be getting any sleep tonight."

He turns to look at Kenji, his eyes crinkling in happiness or pain or something in between. "Did you know," Castle says to us, "that I've known Kenji since he was a small boy? I found him shortly after I'd built Omega Point. He grew up here. When I first met him he was living in an old shopping cart he'd found on the side of the highway." Castle pauses. "Has he ever told you that story?"

Adam sits back down. I'm suddenly wide-awake. "No,"

we both say at the same time.

"Ah—forgive me." Castle shakes his head. "I shouldn't waste your time with these things," he says. "I think there's too much on my mind right now. I'm forgetting which stories to keep to myself."

"No—please—I want to know," I tell him. "Really."

Castle stares into his hands. Smiles a little. "There's not much to it," he says. "Kenji has never talked to me about what happened to his parents, and I try not to ask. All he ever had was a name and an age. I stumbled upon him quite accidentally. He was just a boy sitting in a shopping cart. Far from civilization. It was the dead of winter and he was wearing nothing but an old T-shirt and a pair of sweatpants a few sizes too big for him. He looked like he was freezing, like he could use a few meals and place to sleep. I couldn't just walk away," Castle says. "I couldn't just leave him there. So, I asked him if he was hungry."

He stops, remembering.

"Kenji didn't say a single thing for at least thirty seconds. He simply stared at me. I almost walked away, thinking I'd frightened him. But then, finally, he reached out, grabbed my hand, placed it in his palm and shook it. Very hard. And then he said, 'Hello, sir. My name is Kenji Kishimoto and I am nine years old. It's very nice to meet you.'" Castle laughs out loud, his eyes shining with an emotion that betrays his smiles. "He must've been starving, the poor kid. He always," Castle says, blinking up at the ceiling now, "he always had a strong, determined sort of personality. So much pride.

Unstoppable, that boy."

We're all silent for a while.

"I had no idea," Adam says, "that you two were so close."

Castle stands up. Looks around at us and smiles too brightly, too tightly. Says, "Yes. Well, I'm sure he's going to be just fine. He'll be just fine in the morning, so you two should definitely get some sleep."

"Are you su—"

"Yes, please, get to bed. I'll be fine here with the girls, I promise."

So we get up. We get up and Adam manages to lift James from Kenji's bed and into his arms without waking him. And we walk out.

I glance back.

I see Castle fall into his chair and drop his head into his hands and rest his elbows on his knees. I see him reach out a shaky hand to rest on Kenji's leg and I wonder at how much I still don't know about these people I live with. How little I've allowed myself to become a part of their world.

And I know I want to change that.

SIXTY-ONE

Adam walks me to my room.

It's been lights-out for about an hour now, and, with the exception of faint emergency lights glowing every few feet, everything is, quite literally, out. It's absolute blackness, and even still, the guards on patrol manage to spot us only to warn us to go straight to our separate quarters.

Adam and I don't really speak until we reach the mouth of the women's wing. There's so much tension, so many unspoken worries between us. So many thoughts about today and tomorrow and the many weeks we've already spent together. So much we don't know about what's already happening to us and what will eventually happen to us. Just looking at him, being so close and being so far away from him—it's painful.

I want so desperately to bridge the gap between our bodies. I want to press my lips to every part of him and I want to savor the scent of his skin, the strength in his limbs, in his heart. I want to wrap myself in the warmth and reassurance I've come to rely on.

But.

In other ways, I've come to realize that being away from him has forced me to rely on myself. To allow myself to be scared and to find my own way through it. I've had to train without him, fight without him, face Warner and Anderson and the chaos of my mind all without him by my side. And I feel different now. I feel stronger since putting space between us.

And I don't know what that means.

All I know is that it'll never be safe for me to rely on someone else again, to *need* constant reassurance of who I am and who I might someday be. I can love him, but I can't depend on him to be my backbone. I can't be my own person if I constantly require someone else to hold me together.

My mind is a mess. Every single day I'm confused, uncertain, worried I'm going to make a new mistake, worried I'm going to lose control, worried I'm going to lose myself. But it's something I have to work through. Because for the rest of my life, I'll always, always be stronger than everyone around me.

But at least I'll never have to be scared anymore.

"Are you going to be okay?" Adam asks, finally dispelling the silence between us. I look up to find that his eyes are worried, trying to read me.

"Yes," I tell him. "Yes. I'm going to be fine." I offer him a tight smile, but it feels wrong to be this close to him without being able to touch him at all.

Adam nods. Hesitates. Says, "It's been one hell of a night."

"And it'll be one hell of day tomorrow, too," I whisper.

"Yeah," he says quietly, still looking at me like he's

trying to find something, like he's searching for an answer to an unspoken question and I wonder if he sees something different in my eyes now. He grins a small grin. Says, "I should probably go," and nods at James bundled in his arms.

I nod, not sure what else to do. What to say.

So much is uncertain.

"We'll get through this," Adam says, answering my silent thoughts. "All of it. We're going to be okay. And Kenji will be fine." He touches my shoulder, allows his fingers to trail down my arm and stop just short of my bare hand.

I close my eyes, try to savor the moment.

And then his fingers graze my skin and my eyes fly open, my heart racing in my chest.

He's staring at me like he might've done much more than touch my hand if he weren't holding James against his chest.

"Adam—"

"I'm going to find a way," he says to me. "I'm going to find a way to make this work. I promise. I just need some time."

I'm afraid to speak. Afraid of what I might say, what I might do; afraid of the hope ballooning inside of me.

"Good night," he whispers.

"Good night," I say.

I'm beginning to think of hope as a dangerous, terrifying thing.

SIXTY-TWO

I'm so tired when I walk into my room that I'm only half conscious as I change into the tank top and pajama shorts I sleep in. They were a gift from Sara. It was her recommendation that I change out of my suit while I sleep; she and Sonya think it's important to give my skin direct contact with fresh air.

I'm about to climb under the covers when I hear a soft knock at my door.

Adam

is my first thought.

But then I open the door. And promptly close it.

I must be dreaming.

"Juliette?"

Oh. God.

"What are you *doing* here?" I shout-whisper through the closed door.

"I need to speak with you."

"Right now. You need to speak with me right now."

"Yes. It's important," Warner says. "I heard Kent telling you that those twin girls would be in the medical wing tonight and I figured it would be a good time for us to speak privately."

"You heard my conversation with Adam?" I begin to panic, worried he might've heard too much.

"I have zero interest in your conversation with Kent," he says, his tone suddenly flat, neutral. "I left just as soon as I heard you'd be alone tonight."

"Oh." I exhale. "How did you even get in here without guards stopping you?"

"Maybe you should open the door so I can explain."

I don't move.

"Please, love, I'm not going to do anything to hurt you. You should know that by now."

"I'm giving you five minutes. Then I have to sleep, okay? I'm exhausted."

"Okay," he says. "Five minutes."

I take a deep breath. Crack the door open. Peek at him.

He's smiling. Looking entirely unapologetic.

I shake my head.

He slips past me and sits down directly on my bed.

I close the door, make my way across the room from him, and sit on Sonya's bed, suddenly all too aware of what I'm wearing and how incredibly exposed I feel. I cross my arms over the thin cotton clinging to my chest—even though I'm sure he can't actually see me—and make an effort to ignore the cold chill in the air. I always forget just how much the suit does to regulate my body temperature so far belowground.

Winston was a genius to design it for me.

Winston.

Winston and Brendan.

Oh how I hope they're okay.

"So . . . what is it?" I ask Warner. I can't see a single thing in this darkness; I can hardly make out the form of his silhouette. "You just left earlier, in the tunnel. Even though I asked you to wait."

A few beats of silence.

"Your bed is so much more comfortable than mine," he says quietly. "You have a pillow. And an actual blanket?" He laughs. "You're living like a queen in these quarters. They treat you well."

"Warner." I'm feeling nervous now. Anxious. Worried. Shivering a little and not from the cold. "What's going on? Why are you here?"

Nothing.

Still nothing.

Suddenly.

A tight breath.

"I want you to come with me."

The world stops spinning.

"When I leave tomorrow," he says. "I want you to come with me. I never had a chance to finish talking to you earlier and I thought asking you in the morning would be bad timing all around."

"You want me to come with you." I'm not sure I'm still breathing.

"Yes."

"You want me to run away with you." This can't possibly be happening.

A pause. "Yes."

"I can't believe it." I'm shaking my head over and over and over again. "You really have lost your mind."

I can almost hear him smile in the dark. "Where's your face? I feel like I'm talking to a ghost."

"I'm right here."

"Where?"

I stand up. "I'm here."

"I still can't see you," he says, but his voice is suddenly much closer than it was before. "Can you see me?"

"No," I lie, and I'm trying to ignore the immediate tension, the electricity humming in the air between us.

I take a step back.

I feel his hands on my arms, I feel his skin against my skin and I'm holding my breath. I don't move an inch. I don't say a word as his hands drop to my waist, to the thin material making a poor attempt to cover my body. His fingers graze the soft skin of my lower back, right underneath the hem of my shirt and I'm losing count of the number of times my heart skips a beat.

I'm struggling to get oxygen in my lungs.

~~I'm struggling to keep my hands to myself.~~

"Is it even possible," he whispers, "that you can't feel this fire between us?" His hands are traveling up my arms again, his touch so light, his fingers slipping under the straps of my shirt and it's ripping me apart, it's aching in my core, it's a pulse beating in every inch of my body and I'm trying to convince myself not to lose my head when I feel the straps fall down and everything stops.

The air is still.

My skin is scared.

Even my thoughts are whispering.

2

4

6 seconds I forget to breathe.

Then I feel his lips against my shoulder, soft and scorching and tender, so gentle I could almost believe it's the kiss of a breeze and not a boy.

Again.

This time on my collarbone and it's like I'm dreaming, reliving the caress of a forgotten memory and it's like an ache looking to be soothed, it's a steaming pan thrown in ice water, it's a flushed cheek pressed to a cool pillow on a hot hot hot night and I'm thinking *yes*, I'm thinking *this*, I'm thinking *thank you thank you thank you*

before I remember his mouth is on my body and I'm doing nothing to stop him.

He pulls back.

My eyes refuse to open.

His finger t-touches my bottom lip.

He traces the shape of my mouth, the curves the seam the dip and my lips part even though I asked them not to and he steps closer. I feel him so much closer, filling the air around me until there's nothing but him and his body heat, the smell of fresh soap and something unidentifiable, something sweet but not, something real and hot, something that smells like *him*, like it belongs to him, like he was poured into the bottle I'm drowning in and I don't even realize I'm leaning into him, inhaling the scent of his neck until I find his fingers are no longer on my lips because his hands are around my waist and he says

"You," and he whispers it, letter by letter he presses the word into my skin before he hesitates.

Then.

Softer.

His chest, heaving harder this time. His words, almost gasping this time. "You *destroy* me."

I am falling to pieces in his arms.

My fists are full of unlucky pennies and my heart is a jukebox demanding a few nickels and my head is flipping quarters heads or tails heads or tails heads or tails heads or tails

"Juliette," he says, and he mouths the name, barely speaking at all, and he's pouring molten lava into my limbs and I never even knew I could melt straight to death.

"I want you," he says. He says "I want all of you. I want you inside and out and catching your breath and aching for me like I ache for you." He says it like it's a lit cigarette lodged in his throat, like he wants to dip me in warm honey and he says, "It's never been a secret. I've never tried to hide that from you. I've never pretended I wanted anything less."

"You—you said you wanted f-friendship—"

"Yes," he says, he swallows, "I did. I do. I do want to be your friend." He nods and I register the slight movement in the air between us. "I want to be the friend you fall hopelessly in love with. The one you take into your arms and into your bed and into the private world you keep trapped in your head. I want to be that kind of friend," he says. "The one who will memorize the things you say as well as the shape of your lips when you say them. I want to know every curve, every freckle, every shiver of your body, *Juliette*—"

"No," I gasp. "Don't—don't s-say that—"

I don't know what I'll do if he keeps talking I don't know what I'll do and I don't trust myself

"I want to know where to touch you," he says. "I want to know how to touch you. I want to know how to convince you to design a smile just for me." I feel his chest rising, falling, up and down and up and down and "Yes," he says. "I do want to be your friend." He says "I want to be your best friend in the entire world."

I can't think.

I can't *breathe*

"I want so many things," he whispers. "I want your mind. Your strength. I want to be worth your time." His fingers graze the hem of my top and he says "I want this up." He tugs on the waist of my shorts and says "I want these down." He touches the tips of his fingers to the sides of my body and says, "I want to feel your skin on fire. I want to feel your heart racing next to mine and I want to know it's racing because of me, because you want me. Because you never," he says, he breathes, "never want me to stop. I want every second. Every inch of you. I want all of it."

And I drop dead, all over the floor.

"Juliette."

I can't understand why I can still hear him speaking because I'm dead, I'm already dead, I've died over and over and over again

He swallows, hard, his chest heaving, his words a breathless, shaky whisper when he says "I'm so—I'm so desperately in love with you—"

I'm rooted to the ground, spinning while standing, dizzy in my blood and in my bones and I'm breathing like I'm the first human who's ever learned to fly, like I've been inhaling the kind of oxygen only found in the clouds and I'm trying but I don't know how to keep my body from reacting to him, to his words, to the ache in his voice.

He touches my cheek.

Soft, so soft, like he's not sure if I'm real, like he's afraid if he gets too close I'll just oh, look she's gone, she's just disappeared. His 4 fingers graze the side of my face, slowly, so slowly before they slip behind my head, caught in that in-between spot just above my neck. His thumb brushes the apple of my cheek.

He keeps looking at me, looking into my eyes for help, for guidance, for some sign of a protest like he's so sure I'm going to start screaming or crying or running away but I won't. I don't think I could even if I wanted to because I don't want to. I want to stay here. Right here. I want to be paralyzed by this moment.

He moves closer, just an inch. His free hand reaches up

to cup the other side of my face.

He's holding me like I'm made of feathers.

He's holding my face and looking at his own hands like he can't believe he's caught this bird who's always so desperate to fly away. His hands are shaking, just a little bit, just enough for me to feel the slight tremble against my skin. Gone is the boy with the guns and the skeletons in his closet. These hands holding me have never held a weapon. These hands have never touched death. These hands are perfect and kind and tender.

And he leans in, so carefully. Breathing and not breathing and hearts beating between us and he's so close, he's so close and I can't feel my legs anymore. I can't feel my fingers or the cold or the emptiness of this room because all I feel is him, everywhere, filling everything and he whispers

"Please."

He says "Please don't shoot me for this."

And he kisses me.

His lips are softer than anything I've ever known, soft like a first snowfall, like biting into cotton candy, like melting and floating and being weightless in water. It's sweet, it's so effortlessly sweet.

And then it changes.

"Oh *God*—"

He kisses me again, this time stronger, desperate, like he has to have me, like he's dying to memorize the feel of my lips against his own. The taste of him is making me crazy; he's all heat and desire and peppermint and I want more.

I've just begun reeling him in, pulling him into me when he breaks away.

He's breathing like he's lost his mind and he's looking at me like something has broken inside of him, like he's woken up to find that his nightmares were just that, that they never existed, that it was all just a bad dream that felt far too real but now he's awake and he's safe and everything is going to be okay and

I'm falling.

I'm falling apart and into his heart and I'm a disaster.

He's searching me, searching my eyes for something, for yeses or nos or maybe a cue to keep going and all I want is to drown in him. I want him to kiss me until I collapse in his arms, until I've left my bones behind and floated up into a new space that is entirely our own.

No words.

Just his lips.

Again.

Deep and urgent like he can't afford to take his time anymore, like there's so much he wants to feel and there aren't enough years to experience it all. His hands travel the length of my back, learning every curve of my figure and he's kissing my neck, my throat, the slope of my shoulders and his breaths come harder, faster, his hands suddenly threaded in my hair and I'm spinning, I'm dizzy, I'm moving and reaching up behind his neck and clinging to him and it's ice-cold heat, it's an ache that attacks every cell in my body. It's a wanting so desperate, a need so exquisite that it rivals everything, every happy moment I ever thought I knew.

I'm against the wall.

He's kissing me like the world is rolling right off a cliff, like he's trying to hang on and he's decided to hold on to me, like he's starving for life and love and he's never known it could ever feel this good to be close to someone. Like it's the first time he's ever felt anything but hunger and he doesn't know how to pace himself, doesn't know how to eat in small bites, doesn't know how to do anything anything anything in moderation.

My shorts fall to the floor and his hands are responsible.

I'm in his arms in my underwear and a tank top that's doing little to keep me decent and he pulls back just to look at me, to drink in the sight of me and he's saying "you're so beautiful" he's saying "you're so unbelievably beautiful" and he pulls me into his arms again and he picks me up, he carries me to my bed and suddenly I'm resting against my pillows and he's straddling my hips and his shirt is no longer on his body and I have no idea where it went. All I know is that I'm looking up and into his eyes and I'm thinking there isn't a single thing I would change about this moment.

He has a hundred thousand million kisses and he's giving them all to me.

He kisses my top lip.

He kisses my bottom lip.

He kisses just under my chin, the tip of my nose, the length of my forehead, both temples, my cheeks, all across my jawline. Then my neck, behind my ears, all the way down my throat and

his hands

slide

down

my body. His entire form is moving down my figure, disappearing as he shifts downward and suddenly his chest is hovering above my hips; suddenly I can't see him anymore. I can only make out the top of his head, the curve of his shoulders, the unsteady rise and fall of his back as he inhales, exhales. He's running his hands down and around my bare thighs and up again, up past my ribs, around my lower back and down again, just past my hip bone. His fingers hook around the elastic waist of my underwear and I gasp.

His lips touch my bare stomach.

It's just a whisper of a kiss but something collapses in my skull. It's a feather-light brush of his mouth against my skin in a place I can't quite see. It's my mind speaking in a thousand different languages I don't understand.

And I realize he's working his way up my body.

He's leaving a trail of fire along my torso, one kiss after another, and I really don't think I can take much more of this; I really don't think I'll be able to survive this. There's a whimper building in my throat, begging to break free and I'm locking my fingers in his hair and I'm pulling him up, onto me, on top of me.

I need to kiss him.

I'm reaching up only to slip my hands down his neck, over his chest and down the length of his body and I realize I've never felt this, not to this degree, not like every moment is about to explode, like every breath could be our last, like every touch is enough to ignite the world. I'm forgetting everything, forgetting the danger and the horror and the terror of tomorrow and I can't even remember *why* I'm forgetting, *what* I'm forgetting, that there's something I already seem to have forgotten. It's too hard to pay attention to anything but his eyes, burning; his skin, bare; his body, perfect.

He's completely unharmed by my touch.

He's careful not to crush me, his elbows propped up on either side of my head, and I think I must be smiling at him because he's smiling at me, but he's smiling like he might be petrified; he's breathing like he's forgotten he's supposed to, looking at me like he's not sure how to do this, hesitating like he's unsure how to let me see him like this. Like he has no idea how to be so vulnerable.

But here he is.

And here I am.

Warner's forehead is pressed against mine, his skin flushed with heat, his nose touching my own. He shifts his weight to one arm, uses his free hand to softly stroke my cheek, to cup my face like it's spun from glass and I realize I'm still holding my breath and I can't even remember the last time I exhaled.

His eyes shift down to my lips and back again. His gaze is heavy, hungry, weighed down by emotion I never thought him capable of. I never thought he could be so full, so human, so real. But it's there. It's right there. Raw, written across his face like it's been ripped out of his chest.

He's handing me his heart.

And he says one word. He whispers one thing. So urgently.

He says, "Juliette."

I close my eyes.

He says, "I don't want you to call me Warner anymore."

I open my eyes.

"I want you to know me," he says, breathless, his fingers pushing a stray strand of hair away from my face. "I don't want to be Warner with you," he says. "I want it to be different now. I want you to call me Aaron."

And I'm about to say yes, of course, I completely understand, but there's something about this stretch of silence that confuses me; something about this moment and the feel of his name on my tongue that unlocks other parts of my brain and there's something there, something pushing and pulling at my skin and trying to remind me, trying to tell me and

it slaps me in the face

it punches me in the jaw

it dumps me right into the ocean.

"Adam."

My bones are full of ice. My entire being wants to vomit. I'm tripping out from under him and pulling myself away and I almost fall right to the floor and this feeling, this feeling, this overwhelming *feeling* of absolute self-loathing sticks in my stomach like the slice of a knife too sharp, too thick, too lethal to keep me standing and I'm clutching at myself, I'm trying not to cry and I'm saying no no no this can't happen this can't be *happening* I love Adam, my heart is with Adam, I can't do this to him

and Warner looks like I've shot him all over again, like I've wedged a bullet in his heart with my bare hands and he gets to his feet but he can hardly stand. His frame is shaking and he's looking at me like he wants to say something but every time he tries to speak he fails.

"I'm s-sorry," I stammer, "I'm so sorry—I never meant for this to happen—I wasn't *thinking*—"

But he's not listening.

He's shaking his head over and over and over and he's looking at his hands like he's waiting for the part where someone tells him this isn't real and he whispers "What's happening to me? Am I dreaming?"

And I'm so sick, I'm so confused, because I want him, I want him and I want Adam, too, and I want too much and I've never felt more like a monster than I have tonight.

The pain is so plain on his face and it's killing me.

I feel it. I feel it killing me.

I'm trying so hard to look away, to forget, to figure out how to erase what just happened but all I can think is that life is like a broken tire swing, an unborn child, a fistful of wishbones. It's all possibility and potential, wrong and right steps toward a future we're not even guaranteed and I, I am so wrong. All of my steps are wrong, always wrong. I am the incarnation of error.

Because this never should have happened.

This was a mistake.

"You're choosing him?" Warner asks, barely breathing, still looking as if he might fall over. "Is that what just happened? You're choosing Kent over me? Because I don't think I understand what just happened and I need you to say something, I need you to tell me what the hell is happening to me right now—"

"No," I gasp. "No, I'm not choosing anyone—I'm not— I'm n-not—"

But I am. And I don't even know how I got here.

"Why?" he says. "Because he's the safer choice for you? Because you think you *owe* him something? You are making a mistake," he says, his voice louder now. "You're scared. You don't want to make the difficult choice and you're running away from me."

"Maybe I just d-don't want to be with you."

"I know you want to be with me!" he explodes.

"You're wrong."

Oh my God what am I saying I don't even know where I'm finding these words, where they're coming from or which tree I've plucked them from. They just keep growing in my mouth and sometimes I bite down too hard on an adverb or a pronoun and sometimes the words are bitter, sometimes they're sweet, but right now everything tastes like romance and regret and liar liar pants on fire all the way down my throat.

Warner is still staring.

"Really?" He struggles to rein in his temper and takes a step closer, so much closer, and I can see his face too clearly, I can see his lips too clearly, I can see the anger and the pain and the disbelief etched into his features and I'm not so sure I should be standing anymore. I don't think my legs can carry me much longer.

"Y-yes." I pluck another word from the tree lying in my mouth, lying lying lying on my lips.

"So I'm wrong." He says the sentence quietly, so, so quietly. "I'm wrong that you want me. That you want to be with me." His fingers graze my shoulders, my arms; his hands slide down the sides of my body, tracing every inch of me and I'm pressing my mouth shut to keep the truth from falling out but I'm failing and failing and failing because the only truth I know right now is that I'm mere moments from losing my mind.

"Tell me something, love." His lips are whispering against my jaw. "Am I blind, too?"

I am actually going to die.

"I will not be your clown!" He breaks away from me. "I will not allow you to make a mockery of my feelings for you! I could respect your decision to *shoot me*, Juliette, but doing this—doing—doing what you just did—" He can hardly speak. He runs a hand across his face, both hands through his hair, looking like he wants to scream, to break something, like he's really, truly about to lose his mind. His voice is a rough whisper when he finally speaks. "It's the play of a coward," he says. "I thought you were so much better than that."

"I'm not a coward—"

"Then be honest with yourself!" he says. "Be honest with me! Tell me the truth!"

My head is rolling around on the floor, spinning like a wooden top, circling around and around and around and I can't make it stop. I can't make the world stop spinning and my confusion is bleeding into guilt which quickly evolves into anger and suddenly it's bubbling raging rising to the surface and I look at him. I clench my shaking hands into fists. "The truth," I tell him, "is that I never know what to think of you! Your actions, your behavior—you're never consistent! You're horrible to me and then you're kind to me and you tell me you love me and then you hurt the ones I care most about!

"And you're a liar," I snap, backing away from him. "You say you don't care about what you do—you say you don't care about other people and what you've done to them but I don't believe it. I think you're hiding. I think the real you is hiding underneath all of the destruction and I think you're better than this life you've chosen for yourself. I think you can change. I think you could be different. And I feel sorry for you!"

These words these stupid stupid words they won't stop spilling from my mouth.

"I'm sorry for your horrible childhood. I'm sorry you

have such a miserable, worthless father and I'm sorry no one ever took a chance on you. I'm sorry for the terrible decisions you've made. I'm sorry that you feel trapped by them, that you think of yourself as a monster who can't be changed. But most of all," I tell him, "most of all I'm sorry that you have no mercy for yourself!"

Warner flinches like I've slapped him in the face.

The silence between us has slaughtered a thousand innocent seconds and when he finally speaks his voice is barely audible, raw with disbelief.

"You pity me."

My breath catches. My resolve wavers.

"You think I'm some kind of broken project you can repair."

"No—I didn't—"

"You have no *idea* what I've done!" His words are furious as he steps forward. "You have no idea what I've seen, what I've had to be a part of. You have no idea what I'm capable of or how much mercy I deserve. I know my own heart," he snaps. "I know who I am. Don't you dare pity me!"

Oh my legs are definitely not working.

"I thought you could love me for *me*," he says. "I thought you would be the one person in this godforsaken world who would accept me as I am! I thought you, of all people, would understand." His face is right in front of mine when he says, "I was wrong. I was so horribly, horribly wrong."

He backs away. He grabs his shirt and he turns to leave and I should let him go, I should let him walk out the door and out of my life but I can't, I catch his arm, I pull him back and I say, "Please—that's not what I meant—"

He spins around and he says, "I do not want your *sympathy!*"

"I wasn't trying to hurt you—"

"The truth," he says, "is a painful reminder of why I prefer to live among the lies."

I can't stomach the look in his eyes, the wretched, awful pain he's making no effort to conceal. I don't know what to say to make this right. I don't know how to take my words back.

I know I don't want him to leave.

Not like this.

He looks as if he might speak; he changes his mind. He takes a tight breath, presses his lips together as if to stop the words from escaping and I'm about to say something, I'm about to try again when he pulls in a shaky breath, when he says, "Good-bye, Juliette."

And I don't know why it's killing me, I can't understand my sudden anxiety and I need to know, I have to say it, I have to ask the question that isn't a question and I say "I won't see you again."

I watch him struggle to find the words, I watch him turn to me and turn away and for one split second I see what's happened, I see the difference in his eyes, the shine of emotion I never would've dreamed him capable of and I know, I understand why he won't look at me and I can't believe it. I want to fall to the floor as he fights himself, fights to speak, fights to swallow back the tremor in his voice when he says, "I certainly hope not."

And that's it.

He walks out.

I'm split clean in half and he's gone.

He's gone forever.

SIXTY-THREE

Breakfast is an ordeal.

Warner has disappeared and he's left a trail of chaos in his wake.

No one knows how he escaped, how he managed to get out of his room and find his way out of here and everyone is blaming Castle. Everyone is saying he was stupid to trust Warner, to give him a chance, to believe he might have changed.

Angry is an insult to the level of aggression in here right now.

But I'm not going to be the one to tell everyone that Warner was already out of his room last night. I'm not going to be the one to tell them that he probably didn't have to do much to find the exit. I won't explain to them that he's not an idiot.

I'm sure he figured it out easily enough. I'm sure he found a way to get past the guards.

Now everyone is ready to fight, but for all the wrong reasons. They want to murder Warner: first for all he's done; second for betraying their trust. More frightening still, everyone is worried that he'll give away all of our most sensitive information. I have no idea what Warner managed to discover about this place before he left, but nothing that happens now can possibly be good.

No one has even touched their breakfasts.

We're all dressed, armed, ready to face what could be an almost instant death, and I'm feeling little more than entirely numb. I didn't sleep at all last night, my heart and mind plagued and conflicted and I can't feel my limbs, I can't taste the food I'm not eating and I can't see straight, I can't focus on the things I'm supposed to be hearing. All I can think about are all the casualties ~~and Warner's lips on my neck, his hands on my body, the pain and passion in his eyes~~ and the many possible ways I could die today. I can only think about ~~Warner touching me, kissing me, torturing me with his heart and~~ Adam sitting beside me, not knowing what I've done.

It probably won't even matter after today.

Maybe I'll be killed and maybe all the agony of these past 17 years will have been for naught. Maybe I'll just fall right off the face of the Earth, gone forever, and all of my adolescent angst will have been a ridiculous afterthought, a laughable memory.

But maybe I'll survive.

Maybe I'll survive and I'll have to face the consequences of my actions. I'll have to stop lying to myself; I'll have to actually make a decision.

I have to face the fact that I'm battling feelings for someone who has no qualms about putting a bullet in another man's head. I have to consider the possibility that

I might really be turning into a monster. A horrible, selfish creature who cares only about herself.

Maybe Warner was right all along.

Maybe he and I really are perfect for each other.

Just about everyone has filed out of the dining hall. People are saying last-minute good-byes to the old and the young ones they're leaving behind. James and Adam had a lengthy good-bye just this morning. Adam and I have to head out in about 10 minutes.

"Well damn. Who died?"

I spin around at the sound of his voice. Kenji is up. He's in this room. He's standing next to our table and he looks like he's about to fall right over but he's *awake*. He's alive.

He's breathing.

"Holy crap." Adam is gaping. "Holy *shit*."

"Good to see you too, Kent." Kenji grins a crooked grin. He nods at me. "You ready to kick some ass today?"

I tackle him.

"WHOA—hey—thank you, yeah—that's—uh—" He clears his throat. Tries to shift away from me and I flinch, pull back. I'm covered everywhere except for my face; I'm wearing my gloves and my reinforced knuckles, and my suit is zipped up to my neck. Kenji never usually shies away from me.

"Hey, uh, maybe you should hold off on touching me for a little while, yeah?" Kenji tries to smile, tries to make it sound like he's joking, but I feel the weight of his words, the tension and the sliver of fear he's trying so hard to hide. "I'm not too steady on my feet just yet."

I feel the blood rush out of me, leaving me weak in the knees and needing to sit down.

"It wasn't her," Adam says. "You know she didn't even touch you."

"I *don't* know that, actually," Kenji says. "And it's not like I'm blaming her—I'm just saying maybe she's projecting and doesn't know it, okay? Because last I checked, I don't think we have any other explanations for what happened last night. It sure as hell wasn't you," he says to Adam, "and shit, for all we know, Warner being able to touch Juliette could just be a fluke. We don't know anything about him yet." A pause. He looks around. "Right? Unless Warner pulled some kind of magical rabbit out of his ass while I was busy being dead last night?"

Adam scowls. I don't say a word.

"Right," Kenji says. "That's what I thought. So. I think it's best if, unless absolutely necessary, I stay away." He turns to me. "Right? No offense, right? I mean, I did nearly just die. I think you could cut me some slack."

I can hardly hear my own voice when I say, "Yeah, of course." I try to laugh. I try to figure out why I'm not telling them about Warner. Why I'm still protecting him. ~~Probably because I'm just as guilty as he is~~.

"So *anyway*," Kenji says. "When are we leaving?"

"You're insane," Adam tells him. "You're not going anywhere."

"Bullshit I'm not."

"You can barely stand up on your own!" Adam says.

And he's right. Kenji is clearly leaning on the table for support.

"I'd rather die out there than sit in here like some kind of idiot."

"Kenji—"

"Hey," Kenji says, cutting me off. "So I heard through the very loud grapevine that Warner got his ass the hell out of here last night. What's that about?"

Adam makes a strange sound. It's not quite a laugh. "Yeah," he says. "Who even knows. I never thought it was a good idea to keep him hostage here. It was an even stupider idea to trust him."

"So first you insult my idea, and then you insult Castle's, huh?" Kenji's eyebrow is cocked.

"They were bad calls," Adam says. "Bad ideas. Now we have to pay for it."

"Well how was I supposed to know Anderson would be so willing to let his own son rot in hell?"

Adam flinches and Kenji backpedals.

"Oh, hey—I'm sorry, man—I didn't mean to say it like that—"

"Forget it." Adam cuts him off. His face is suddenly hard, suddenly cold, closed off. "Maybe you should get back to the medical wing. We're leaving soon."

"I'm not going anywhere but *out of here.*"

"Kenji, please—"

"Nope."

"You're being unreasonable. This isn't a joke," I tell him. "People are going to die today."

But he laughs at me. Looks at me like I've said something obliquely entertaining. "I'm sorry, are you trying to teach *me* about the realities of war?" He shakes his head. "Are you forgetting that I was a soldier in Warner's army? Do you have any idea how much crazy shit we've seen?" He gestures between himself and Adam. "I know exactly what to expect today. Warner was *insane*. If Anderson is even twice as bad as his son, then we are diving right into a bloodbath. I can't leave you guys hanging like that."

But I'm caught on one sentence. One word. I just want to ask. "Was he really that bad . . . ?"

"Who?" Kenji is staring at me.

"Warner. Was he really that ruthless?"

Kenji laughs out loud. Laughs louder. Doubles over. He's practically wheezing when he says, "Ruthless? Juliette, the guy is sick. He's an animal. I don't think he even knows what it means to be human. If there's a hell out there, I'm guessing it was designed especially for him."

It's so hard to pull this sword out of my stomach.

A rush of footsteps.

I turn around.

Everyone is supposed to exit the tunnels in a single-file line in an attempt to maintain order as we leave this underground world. Kenji and Adam and I are the only fighters who haven't joined the group yet.

414

We all get to our feet.

"Hey—so, does Castle know what you're doing?" Adam is looking at Kenji. "I don't think he'd be okay with you going out there today."

"Castle wants me to be happy," Kenji says matter-of-factly. "And I won't be happy if I stay here. I've got work to do. People to save. Ladies to impress. He'd respect that."

"What about everyone else?" I ask him. "Everyone was so worried about you—have you even seen them yet? To at least tell them you're okay?"

"Nah," Kenji says. "They'd probably shit a brick if they knew I was going up. I thought it'd be safer to keep it quiet. I don't want to freak anyone out. And Sonya and Sara—poor kids—they're passed the hell out. It's my fault they're so exhausted, and they're still talking about heading out today. They want to fight even though they're going to have a lot of work to do once we're done with Anderson's army. I've been trying to convince them to stay here but they can be so damn stubborn. They need to save their strength," he says, "and they've already wasted too much of it on me."

"It's not a *waste*—" I try to tell him.

"Anywayyy," Kenji says. "Can we please get going? I know you're all about hunting down Anderson," he says to Adam, "but personally? I would love to catch Warner. Put a bullet through that worthless piece of crap and be done with it."

Something punches me in the gut so hard I'm afraid I'm actually going to be sick. I'm seeing spots, struggling to keep

415

myself standing, fighting to ignore the image of Warner dead, his body crumpled in red.

"Hey—you okay?" Adam pulls me to the side. Takes a good look at my face.

"I'm okay," I lie to him. Nod too many times. Shake my head once or twice. "I just didn't get enough sleep last night, but I'll be fine."

He hesitates. "Are you sure?"

"I'm positive," I lie again. I pause. Grab his shirt. "Hey—just be careful out there, okay?"

He exhales a heavy breath. Nods once. "Yeah. You too."

"Let's go let's go let's go!" Kenji interrupts us. "Today is our day to die, ladies."

Adam shoves him. A little.

"Oh, so now you're abusing the crippled kid, huh?" Kenji takes a moment to steady himself before punching Adam in the arm. "Save your angst for the battlefield, bro. You're going to need it."

A shrill whistle sounds in the distance.

It's time to go.

SIXTY-FOUR

It's raining.

The world is weeping at our feet in anticipation of what we're about to do.

We're all supposed to split off into clusters, fighting in tight groups so we can't all be killed at once. We don't have enough people to fight offensively so we have to be stealthy. And though I feel a pang of guilt for admitting it, I'm so happy Kenji decided to come with us. We would've been weaker without him.

But we have to get out of the rain.

We're already soaked through, and while Kenji and I are wearing suits that offer at least a modicum of protection against the natural elements, Adam is wearing nothing but crisp cotton basics, and I'm worried we won't last long like this. All members of Omega Point have already scattered. The immediate area above the Point is still nothing but a barren stretch of land that leaves us vulnerable upon exiting.

Lucky for us, we have Kenji. The 3 of us are already invisible.

Anderson's men aren't far from here.

All we know is that ever since Anderson arrived, he's

been going out of his way to make a point about his power and the iron grip of The Reestablishment. Any voice of opposition, no matter how weak or feeble, no matter how unthreatening or innocuous, has been silenced. He's angry that we've inspired rebellion and now he's trying to make a statement. What he really wants is to destroy all of *us*.

The poor civilians are just caught in his friendly fire.

Gunshots.

We automatically move toward the sound echoing in the distance. We aren't saying a word. We understand what we need to do and how we have to operate. Our only mission is to get as close as possible to the devastation and then to take out as many of Anderson's men as we can. We protect the innocent. We support our fellow Point men and women.

We try very hard not to die.

I can make out the compounds creeping closer in the distance, but the rain is making it difficult to see. All the colors are bleeding together, melting into the horizon, and I have to strain to discern what lies ahead of us. I instinctively touch the guns attached to the holsters on my back and I'm momentarily reminded of my last encounter with Anderson—my *only* encounter with the horrible, despicable man—and I wonder what's happened to him. I wonder if maybe Adam was right when he said that Anderson might be severely wounded, that perhaps he's still struggling to recuperate. I wonder if Anderson will make an appearance on the battlefield. I wonder if perhaps he's too much of a coward to fight in his own wars.

The screams tell us we're getting closer.

The world around us is a blurry landscape of blues and grays and mottled hues and the few trees still standing have a hundred shaky, quivering arms ripping through their trunks, reaching up to the sky as if in prayer, begging for relief from the tragedy they've been rooted in. It's enough to make me feel sorry for the plants and animals forced to bear witness to what we've done.

They never asked for this.

Kenji guides us toward the outskirts of the compounds and we slip forward to stand flush against the wall of one of the little square houses, huddled under the extra bit of roof that, at least for a moment, grants us reprieve from the clenched fists falling from the sky.

Wind is gnawing at the windows, straining against the walls. Rain is popping against the roof like popcorn against a pane of glass.

The message from the sky is clear: we are pissed.

We are pissed and we will punish you and we will make you pay for the blood you spill so freely. We will not sit idly by, not anymore, not ever again. We will *ruin* you, is what the sky says to us.

How could you do this to me? it whispers in the wind.

I gave you everything, it says to us.

Nothing will ever be the same again.

I'm wondering why I still can't see any sign of the army. I don't see anyone else from Omega Point. I don't see anyone at all. In fact, I'm starting to feel like this compound is a little too peaceful.

I'm about to suggest we move when I hear a door slam open.

"This is the last of them," someone shouts. "She was hiding out over here." A soldier is dragging a crying woman out from the compound we're huddled against and she's screaming, she's begging for mercy and asking about her husband and the soldier barks at her to shut up.

I have to keep the emotions from spilling out of my eyes, my mouth.

I do not speak.

I do not breathe.

Another soldier jogs over from somewhere I can't see. He shouts some kind of approving message and makes a motion with his hands that I don't understand. I feel Kenji stiffen beside me.

Something is wrong.

"Toss her in with everyone else," the second soldier shouts. "And then we'll call this area clear."

The woman is hysterical. She's screeching, clawing at the soldier, telling him she's done nothing wrong, she doesn't understand, where is her husband, she's been looking for her daughter everywhere and what is happening, she cries, she screams, she flails her fists at the man gripping her like an animal.

He presses the barrel of his gun to her neck. "If you don't shut up, I'll shoot you right now."

She whimpers once, twice, and then she's limp. She's fainted in his arms and the soldier looks disgusted as he pulls her out of sight toward wherever they're keeping everyone else. I have no idea what's happening. I don't understand what's happening.

We follow them.

The wind and the rain pick up in pace and there's enough noise in the air and distance between us and the soldiers that I feel safe to speak. I squeeze Kenji's hand. He's still the glue between me and Adam, projecting his powers to keep us all invisible. "What do you think is going on?" I ask.

He doesn't answer right away.

"They're rounding them up," he says after a moment. "They're creating groups of people to kill all at once."

"The woman—"

"Yeah." I hear him clear his throat. "Yeah, she and whoever else they think might be connected to the protests. They don't just kill the inciters," he tells me. "They kill the friends and the family members, too. It's the best way to keep people in line. It never fails to scare the shit out of the few left alive."

I have to swallow back the vomit threatening to overpower me.

"There has to be a way to get them out of there," Adam says. "Maybe we can take out the soldiers in charge."

"Yeah, but listen, you guys know I'm going to have to let go of you, right? I'm already kind of losing strength; my Energy is fading faster than normal. So you'll be visible,"

Kenji says. "You'll be a clearer target."

"But what other choice do we have?" I ask.

"We could try to take them out sniper-style," Kenji says. "We don't have to engage in direct combat. We have that option." He pauses. "Juliette, you've never been in this kind of situation before. I want you to know I'd respect your decision to stay out of the direct line of fire. Not everyone can stomach what we might see if we follow those soldiers. There's no shame or blame in that."

I taste metal in my mouth as I lie. "I'll be okay."

He's quiet a moment. "Just—all right—but don't be afraid to use your abilities to defend yourself," he says to me. "I know you're all weird about not wanting to hurt people or whatever, but these guys aren't messing around. They *will* try to kill you."

I nod even though I know he can't see me. "Right," I say. "Yeah." But I'm panicked through my mind.

"Let's go," I whisper.

SIXTY-FIVE

I can't feel my knees.

There are 27 people lined up, standing side by side in the middle of a big, barren field. Men and women and children of all different ages. All different sizes. All standing before what could be called a firing squad of 6 soldiers. The rain is rushing down around us, hard and angry, pelting everything and everyone with teardrops as hard as my bones. The wind is absolutely frantic.

The soldiers are deciding what to do. How to kill them. How to dispose of the 27 sets of eyes staring straight ahead. Some are sobbing, some are shaking from fear and grief and horror, others still are standing perfectly straight, stoic in the face of death.

One of the soldiers fires a shot.

The first man crumples to the ground and I feel like I've been whipped in the spine. So many emotions rush in and out of me in the span of a few seconds that I'm afraid I might faint; I'm clinging to consciousness with an animal desperation and trying to swallow back the tears, trying to ignore the pain spearing through me.

I can't understand why no one is moving, why we're not moving, why none of the civilians are moving even just to jump out of the way and it occurs to me, it dawns on me that running, trying to escape or trying to fight back is simply not a viable option. They are utterly overpowered. They have no guns. No ammunition of any kind.

But I do.

I have a gun.

I have 2, in fact.

This is the moment, this is where we have to let go, this is where we fight alone, just the 3 of us, 3 ancient kids fighting to save 26 faces or we die trying. My eyes are locked on a little girl who can't be much older than James, her eyes so wide, so terrified, the front of her pants already wet from fear and it rips me to pieces, it *kills* me, and my free hand is already reaching for my gun when I tell Kenji I'm ready.

I watch the same soldier focus his weapon on the next victim when Kenji releases us.

3 guns are up, aimed to fire, and I hear the bullets before they're released into the air; I see one find its mark in a soldier's neck and I have no idea if it's mine.

It doesn't matter now.

There are still 5 soldiers left to face, and now they can see us.

We're running.

We're dodging the bullets aimed in our direction and I see Adam dropping to the ground, I see him shooting with perfect precision and still failing to find a target. I look around for Kenji only to find that he's disappeared and I'm so happy for it; 3 soldiers go down almost instantly. Adam takes advantage of the remaining soldiers' distraction and takes out a fourth. I shoot the fifth from behind.

I don't know whether or not I've killed him.

We're screaming for the people to follow us, we're herding them back to the compounds, yelling for them to stay down, to stay out of sight; we tell them help is coming and we'll do whatever we can to protect them and they're trying to reach out to us, to touch us, to thank us and take our hands but we don't have time. We have to hurry them to some semblance of safety and move on to wherever the rest of this decimation is taking place.

I still haven't forgotten the one man we weren't able to save. I haven't forgotten number 27.

I never want that to happen again.

We're bolting across the many miles of land dedicated to these compounds now, not bothering to keep ourselves hidden or to come up with a definitive plan. We still haven't spoken. We haven't discussed what we've done or what we might do and we only know that we need to keep moving.

We follow Kenji.

He weaves his way through a demolished cluster of compounds and we know something has gone horribly wrong. There's no sign of life anywhere. The little metal boxes that used to house civilians are completely destroyed and we don't know if there were people inside when this happened.

Kenji tells us we have to keep looking.

We move deeper through the regulated territory, these pieces of land dedicated to human habitation, until we hear a rush of footsteps, the sound of a softly churning mechanical sound.

The tanks.

They run on electricity so they're less conspicuous as they move through the streets, but I'm familiar enough with these tanks to be able to recognize the electric thrum. Adam and Kenji do too.

We follow the noise.

We're fighting against the wind trying push us away and it's almost as if it knows, as if the wind is trying to protect us from whatever is waiting on the other side of this compound. It doesn't want us to have to see this. It doesn't want us to have to die today.

Something explodes.

A raging fire rips through the atmosphere not 50 feet from where we're standing. The flames lick the earth, lapping up the oxygen, and even the rain can't douse the devastation all at once. The fire whips and sways in the wind, dying down just enough, humbled into submission by the sky.

We need to be wherever that fire is.

Our feet fight for traction on the muddy ground and I don't feel the cold as we run, I don't feel the wet, I only feel the adrenaline coursing through my limbs, forcing me to move forward, gun clenched too tight in my fist, too ready to aim, too ready to fire.

But when we reach the flames I almost drop my weapon.

I almost fall to the floor.

I almost can't believe my eyes.

SIXTY-SIX

Dead dead dead is everywhere.

So many bodies mixed and meshed into the earth that I have no idea whether they're ours or theirs and I'm beginning to wonder what it means, I'm beginning to doubt myself and this weapon in my hand and I can't help but wonder about these soldiers, I wonder how they could be just like Adam, just like a million other tortured, orphaned souls who simply needed to survive and took the only job they could get.

My conscience has declared war against itself.

I'm blinking back tears and rain and horror and I know I need to move my legs, I know I need to push forward and be brave, I have to fight whether I like it or not because we can't let this happen.

I'm tackled from behind.

Someone pins me down and my face is buried in the ground and I'm kicking, I'm trying to scream but I feel the gun wrenched out of my grip, I feel an elbow in my spine and I know Adam and Kenji are gone, they're deep in battle and I know I'm about to die. I know it's over and it doesn't feel real, somehow, it feels like this is a story someone else is telling, like death is a strange, distant thing you've only ever seen happen to people you've never known and surely it doesn't happen to me, to you, to any of the rest of us.

But here it is.

It's a gun in the back of my head and a boot pressed down on my back and it's my mouth full of mud and it's a million worthless moments I never really lived and it's all right in front of me. I see it so clearly.

Someone flips me over.

The same someone who held a gun to my head is now pointing it at my face, inspecting me as if trying to read me and I'm confused, I don't understand his angry gray eyes or the stiff set of his mouth because he's not pulling the trigger. He's not killing me and this, this more than anything else is what petrifies me.

I need to take off my gloves.

My captor shouts something I don't catch because he's not talking to me, he's not looking in my direction because he's calling to someone else and I use his moment of distraction to yank off the steel knuckle brace on my left hand only to toss it to the ground. I have to get my glove off. I have to get my glove off because it's my only chance for survival but the rain has made the leather too wet and it's sticking to my skin, refusing to come off easily and the soldier spins back too soon. He sees what I'm trying to do and he yanks me to my feet, pulls me into a headlock and presses the gun to my skull. "I know what you're trying to do, you little freak," he says. "I've heard about you. You move even an inch and I will kill you."

Somehow, I don't believe him.

I don't think he's supposed to shoot me, because if he wanted to, he would've done it already. But he's waiting for something. He's waiting for something I don't understand and I need to act fast. I need a plan but I have no idea what to do and I'm only clawing at his covered arm, at the muscle he's bound around my neck and he shakes me, shouts at me to stop squirming and he pulls me tighter to cut off my air supply and my fingers are clenched around his forearm, trying to fight the viselike grip he has around me and I can't breathe and I'm panicked, I'm suddenly not so sure he's not going to kill me and I don't even realize what I've done until I hear him scream.

I've crushed all the bones in his arm.

He falls to the floor, he drops his gun to grab at his arm, and he's screaming with a pain so excruciating I'm almost tempted to feel remorse for what I've done.

Instead, I run.

I've only gotten a few feet before 3 more soldiers slam into me, alerted by what I've done to their comrade, and they see my face and they're alight with recognition. One of them appears vaguely familiar, almost as if I've seen his shaggy brown hair before, and I realize: they know me. These soldiers knew me when Warner held me captive. Warner had made a complete spectacle out of me. Of course they'd recognize my face.

And they're not letting me go.

The 3 of them are pushing me face-first into the ground,

pinning down my arms and legs until I'm fairly certain they've decided to rip my limbs off. I'm trying to fight back, I'm trying to get my mind in the right place to focus my Energy, and I'm just about to knock them back but then

a sharp blow to my head and I'm rendered almost entirely unconscious.

Sounds are mixing together, voices are becoming one big mess of noise and I can't see colors, I don't know what's happening to me because I can't feel my legs anymore. I don't even know if I'm walking or if I'm being carried but I feel the rain. I feel it fall fast down the planes of my face until I hear the sound of metal on metal, I hear a familiar electric thrum and then the rain stops, it disappears from the sky and I only know 2 things and I only know 1 of those things for certain.

I am in a tank.

I am going to die.

SIXTY-SEVEN

I hear wind chimes.

I hear wind chimes being blown into hysteria by a wind so violent as to be a legitimate threat and all I can think is that the tinkling sounds seem so incredibly familiar to me. My head is still spinning but I have to stay as aware as possible. I have to know where they're taking me. I have to have some idea of where I am. I need to have a point of reference and I'm struggling to keep my head straight without making it known that I'm not unconscious.

The soldiers don't speak.

I was hoping to at least glean a bit of information from the conversations they might have but they do not say a word to one another. They are like machines, like robots programmed to follow through with a specific assignment, and I wonder, I'm so curious, I can't figure out why I had to be dragged away from the battlefield to be killed. I wonder why my death has to be so special. I wonder why they're carrying me out of the tank toward the chaos of an angry wind chime and I dare to open my eyes just a sliver and I nearly gasp.

It's the house.

It's the house, the house on unregulated turf, the one

painted the perfect shade of robin's-egg blue and the only traditional, functioning home within a 500-mile radius. It's the same house Kenji told me must be a trap, it's the house where I was so sure I'd meet Warner's father, and then it hits me. A sledgehammer. A bullet train. A rush of realization crushing my brain.

Anderson must be here. He must want to kill me himself.

I am a special delivery.

They even ring the doorbell.

I hear feet shuffling. I hear creaks and groans. I hear the wind snapping through the world and then I see my future, I see Anderson torturing me to death in every possible way and I wonder how I'm going to get myself out of this. Anderson is too smart. He will probably chain me to the floor and cut off my hands and feet one at a time. He is likely going to want to enjoy this.

He answers the door.

"Ah! Gentlemen. Thank you very much," he says. "Please follow me." And I feel the soldier carrying me shift his weight under my damp, limp, suddenly heavy body. I'm starting to feel a cold chill seep into my bones and I realize I've been running through the pouring rain for too long.

I'm shaking and it's not from fear.

I'm burning and it's not from anger.

I'm so delirious that even if I had the strength to defend myself I'm not sure I'd be able to do it right. It's amazing how many different ways I could meet my end today.

Anderson smells rich and earthy; I can smell him even though I'm being carried in someone else's arms, and the scent is disturbingly pleasant. He closes the front door behind us just after advising the waiting soldiers to return to work. Which is essentially an order for them to go kill more people.

I think I'm starting to hallucinate.

I see a warm fireplace like the kind I've only ever read about. I see a cozy living room with soft, plush couches and a thick oriental rug gracing the floor. I see a mantel with pictures on it that I can't recognize from here and Anderson is telling me to wake up, he's saying you need to take a bath, you've gotten yourself quite dirty haven't you, and that won't do, will it? I'm going to need you to be awake and fully coherent or this won't be much fun at all, he says, and I'm fairly certain I'm losing my mind.

I feel the thud thud thud of heavy footsteps climbing a stairwell and realize my body is moving with it. I hear a door whine open, I hear the shuffle of other feet and there are words being spoken that I can't distinguish anymore. Someone says something to someone and I'm dropped onto a cold, hard floor.

I hear myself whimper.

"Be careful not to touch her skin," is the only sentence I can make out in a single thread. Everything else is "bathe" and "sleep" and "in the morning" and "no, I don't think so" and "very good," and I hear another door slam shut. It's the one right next to my head.

434

Someone is trying to take my suit off.

I snap up so quickly it's painful; I feel something sear through me, through my head until it hits me square in the eye and I know I'm a mix of so many things right now. I can't remember the last time I ate anything and I haven't truly slept in over 24 hours. My body is soaked through, my head is pounding with pain, my body has been twisted and stepped on, and I'm aching in a million different ways. But I will not allow any strange man to take my clothes off. I'd rather be dead.

But the voice I hear isn't male at all. It sounds soft and gentle, motherly. She's speaking to me in a language I don't understand but maybe it's just my head that can't understand anything at all. She makes soothing noises, she rubs her hands in small circles on my back. I hear a rush of water and feel the heat rise up around me and it's so warm, it feels like steam and I think this must be a bathroom, or a tub, and I can't help but think that I haven't taken a hot shower since I was back at the headquarters with Warner.

I try to open my eyes and fail.

It's like two anvils are sitting on my eyelids, like everything is black and messy and confusing and exhausting and I can only make out the general circumstances of my situation. I see through little more than slits; I see only the gleaming porcelain of what I assume is a bathtub and I crawl over despite the protests in my ear and clamber up.

I topple right into the hot water fully clothed, gloves and boots and suit intact and it's an unbelievable pleasure I

435

didn't expect to experience.

My bones begin to thaw and my teeth are slowing their chatter and my muscles are learning to relax. My hair floats up around my face and I feel it tickle my nose.

I sink beneath the surface.

I fall asleep.

SIXTY-EIGHT

I wake up in a bed made of heaven and I'm wearing clothes that belong to a boy.

I'm warm and comfortable but I can still feel the creak in my bones, the ache in my head, the confusion clouding my mind. I sit up. I look around.

I'm in someone's bedroom.

I'm tangled in blue-and-orange bedsheets decorated with little baseball mitts. There's a little desk with a little chair set off to the side and there's a set of drawers, a collection of plastic trophies in perfectly straight rows on top. I see a simple wooden door with a traditional brass knob that must lead outside; I see a sliding set of mirrors that must be hiding a closet. I look to my right to find a little bedside table with an alarm clock and a glass of water and I grab it.

It's almost embarrassing how quickly I inhale the contents.

I climb out of bed only to find that I'm wearing a pair of navy gym shorts that are hanging so low on my hips I'm afraid they're going to fall off. I'm wearing a gray T-shirt with some kind of logo on it and I'm swimming in the extra material. I have no socks. No gloves. No underwear.

I have nothing.

I wonder if I'm allowed to step outside and I decide it's worth a shot. I have no idea what I'm doing here. I have no idea why I'm not dead yet.

I freeze in front of the mirrored doors.

My hair has been washed well and it falls in thick, soft waves around my face. My skin is bright and, with the exception of a few scratches, relatively unscathed. My eyes are wide; an odd, vibrant mix of green and blue blinking back at me, surprised and surprisingly unafraid.

But my neck.

My neck is one mess of purple, one big bruise that discolors my entire appearance. I hadn't realized just how tightly I was being choked to death yesterday—I think it was yesterday—and I only now realize just how much it hurts to swallow. I take a sharp breath and push past the mirrors. I need to find a way to get out of here.

The door opens at my touch.

I look around the hallway for any sign of life. I don't have any idea what time of day it is or what I've gotten myself into. I don't know if anyone exists in this house except for Anderson—and whoever it was that helped me in the bathroom—but I have to assess my situation. I have to figure out exactly how much danger I'm in before I can devise a plan to fight my way out.

I try to tiptoe quietly down the stairs.

It doesn't work.

The stairs creak and groan under my weight and I hardly

have a chance to backpedal before I hear him call my name. He's downstairs.

Anderson is downstairs.

"Don't be shy," he says. I hear the rustle of something that sounds like paper. "I have food for you and I know you must be starving."

My heart is suddenly beating in my throat. I wonder what choices I have, what options I have to consider and I decide I can't hide from him in his own hideout.

I meet him downstairs.

He's the same beautiful man he was before. Hair perfect and polished, clothing crisp, clean, expertly pressed. He's sitting in the living room in an overstuffed chair with a blanket draped over his lap. I notice a gorgeous, rustic-looking, intricately carved walking stick leaning against the armrest. He has a stack of papers in his hand.

I smell coffee.

"Please," he says to me, not at all surprised by my strange, wild appearance. "Have a seat."

I do.

"How are you feeling?" he asks.

I look up. I don't answer him.

He nods. "Yes, well, I'm sure you're very surprised to see me here. It's a lovely little house, isn't it?" He looks around. "I had this preserved shortly after I moved my family to what is now Sector 45. This sector was supposed to be mine, after all. It turned out to be the ideal place to store my wife." He waves a hand. "Apparently she doesn't do very well in the compounds," he says, as if I'm supposed to have any idea what he's talking about.

Store his wife?

I don't know why I allow anything out of his mouth to surprise me.

Anderson seems to catch my confusion. He looks amused. "Am I to understand that my love-struck boy didn't tell you about his beloved mother? He didn't go on and on and on about his pathetic love for the creature that gave birth to him?"

"What?" is the first word I speak.

"I am truly shocked," Anderson says, smiling like he's not shocked at all. "He didn't bother to mention that he has a sick, ailing mother who lives in this house? He didn't tell you that's why he wanted the post here, in this sector, so desperately? No? He didn't tell you anything about that?" He cocks his head. "I am just so shocked," he lies again.

I'm trying to keep my heart rate down, trying to figure out why on earth he's telling me this, trying to stay one step ahead of him, but he's doing a damn good job of confusing the hell out of me.

"When I was chosen as supreme commander," he goes on, "I was going to leave Aaron's mother here and take him with me to the capital. But the boy didn't want to leave his mother behind. He wanted to take care of her. He didn't want to leave her. He needed to *be* with her like some stupid *child*," he says, raising his voice at the end, forgetting himself for a moment. He swallows. Regains his composure.

And I'm waiting.

Waiting for the anvil he's preparing to drop on my head.

"Did he tell you how many other soldiers wanted be in charge of Sector 45? How many fine candidates we had to choose from? He was only eighteen years old!" He laughs. "Everyone thought he'd gone mad. But I gave him a chance," Anderson says. "I thought it might be good for him to take on that kind of responsibility."

Still waiting.

A deep, contented sigh. "Did he ever tell you," Anderson says, "what he had to do to prove he was worthy?"

There it is.

"Did he ever tell you what I made him do to earn it?"

I feel so dead inside.

"No," Anderson says, eyes bright, too bright. "I suspect he didn't want to mention that part, did he? I bet he didn't include that part of his past, did he?"

I don't want to hear this. I don't want to know this. I don't want to listen anymore—

"Don't worry," Anderson says. "I won't spoil it for you. Best to let him share those details with you himself."

I'm not calm anymore. I'm not calm and I've officially begun to panic.

"I'll be heading back to base in just a bit," Anderson says, sorting through his papers, not seeming to mind having an entirely one-sided conversation with me. "I can't stand to be under the same roof as his mother for very long—I do not get on well with the ill, unfortunately—but this has

441

turned out to be a convenient little camp under the present circumstances. I've been using it as a base from which to oversee all that's going on at the compounds."

The battle.

The fighting.

The bloodshed and Adam and Kenji and Castle and everyone I've left behind

How could I forget

The horrifying, terrifying possibilities are flashing through my mind. I have no idea what's happened. If they're okay. If they know I'm still alive. If Castle managed to get Brendan and Winston back.

If anyone I know has died.

My eyes are crazed, darting around. I get to my feet, convinced that this is all just an elaborate trap, that perhaps someone is going to maul me from behind or someone is waiting in the kitchen with a cleaver, and I can't catch my breath, I'm wheezing and I'm trying to figure out what to do what to do what to do and I say, "What am I doing here? Why did you bring me here? Why haven't you killed me yet?"

Anderson looks at me. He cocks his head. He says, "I am very upset with you, Juliette. Very, very unhappy." He says, "You have done a very bad thing."

"What?" seems to be the only question I know how to ask. "What are you talking about?" For one crazy moment I wonder if he knows about what happened with Warner. I almost feel myself blush.

442

But he takes a deep breath. Grabs the cane resting against his chair. He has to use his entire upper body to get to his feet. He's shaking, even with the cane to support him.

"You did this to me. You managed to overpower me. You shot me in my legs. You almost shot me in the heart. And you kidnapped my son."

"No," I gasp, "that wasn't—"

"You did this to me." He cuts me off. "And now I want compensation."

SIXTY-NINE

Breathing. I have to remember to keep breathing.

"It's quite extraordinary," Anderson says, "what you were able to do entirely on your own. There were only three people in that room," he says. "You, me, and my son. My soldiers were watching that entire area for anyone else who might've come with you, and they said you were utterly alone." A pause. "I actually thought you'd come with a team, you see. I didn't think you'd be brave enough to meet me by yourself. But then you single-handedly disarmed me and stole back your hostages. You had to carry two men—not including my son—out to safety. How you managed to do it is entirely beyond my comprehension."

And it hits me: this choice is simple.

I either tell him the truth about Kenji and Adam and risk having Anderson go after them, or I take the fall.

So I meet Anderson's eyes.

I nod. I say, "You called me a stupid little girl. You said I was too much of a coward to defend myself."

He looks uncomfortable for the very first time. Seems to realize that I could probably do the same thing to him again, right now if I wanted.

And I think, yes, I probably could. What an excellent idea.

But for now, I'm still strangely curious to see what he wants from me. Why he's talking to me. I'm not worried about attacking him right away; I know that I have an advantage over him now. I should be able to overtake him easily.

Anderson clears his throat.

"I was planning on returning to the capital," he says. He takes a deep breath. "But it's clear that my work here is not yet finished. Your people are making things infinitely more complicated and it's becoming harder and harder to simply kill all the civilians." A pause. "Well, no, actually, that's not true. It's not hard to kill them, it's only that it's becoming impractical." He looks at me. "If I were to kill them all, I wouldn't have any left to rule over, would I?"

He actually laughs. Laughs as if he's said something funny.

"What do you want with me?" I ask him.

He takes a deep breath. He's smiling. "I must admit, Juliette—I'm thoroughly impressed. You alone were able to overpower me. You had enough foresight to think of taking my son hostage. You saved two of your own men. You caused an *earthquake* to save the rest of your team!" He laughs. He laughs and laughs and laughs.

I don't bother telling him that only 2 of those things are true.

"I see now that my son was right. You *could* be invaluable to us, especially right now. You know the inside of their headquarters better than anything Aaron is able to remember."

So Warner has been to see his father.

He's shared our secrets. Of course he has. I can't imagine why I'm so surprised.

"You," Anderson says to me, "could help me destroy all of your little friends. You could tell me everything I need to know. You could tell me all about the other freaks, what they're capable of, what their strengths and weaknesses are. You could take me to their hideout. You would do whatever I asked you to do."

I want to spit in his face.

"I would sooner *die*," I tell him. "I'd rather be burned alive."

"Oh, I highly doubt that," he says. He shifts his weight onto the cane to better hold himself up. "I think you'd change your mind if you actually had the opportunity to feel the skin melt off your face. But," he says, "I am not unkind. I certainly won't rule it out as an option, if you're really that interested."

Horrible, horrible man.

He smiles, wide, satisfied by my silence. "Yes, I didn't think so."

The front door flies open.

I don't move. I don't turn around. I don't know if I want to see what's about to happen to me but then I hear Anderson greet his visitor. Invite him in. Ask him to say hello to their new guest.

Warner steps into my line of vision.

I'm suddenly weak through the bone, sick and slightly

446

mortified. Warner doesn't say a word. He's wearing his perfect suit with his perfect hair and he looks exactly like the Warner I first met; the only difference now is the look in his eyes. He's staring at me in a state of shock so debilitating he actually looks ill.

"You kids remember each other, right?" Anderson is the only one laughing.

Warner is breathing like he's hiked several mountains, like he can't understand what he's seeing or why he's seeing it and he's staring at my neck, at what must be the ugly blotchy bruise staining my skin and his face twists into something that looks like anger and horror and heartbreak. His eyes drop to my shirt, to my shorts, and his mouth falls open just enough for me to notice before he's reining himself in, wiping the emotions off his face. He's struggling to stay composed but I can see the rapid motions of his chest rising and falling. His voice isn't nearly as strong as it could be when he says, "What is she doing here?"

"I've had her collected for us," Anderson says simply.

"For what?" Warner asks. "You said you didn't want her—"

"Well," Anderson says, considering. "That's not entirely true. I could certainly benefit from having her around, but I decided at the last moment that I wasn't interested in her company anymore." He shakes his head. Looks down at his legs. Sighs. "It's just so *frustrating* to be crippled like this," he says, laughing again. "It's just so unbelievably *frustrating*. But," he says, smiling, "at least I've found a fast and easy

447

way to fix it. To put it all back to normal, as they say. It'll be just like magic."

Something about his eyes, the sick smile in his voice, the way he says that last line makes me feel ill. "What do you mean?" I ask, almost afraid to hear his response.

"I'm surprised you even have to ask, my dear. I mean, honestly—did you really think I wouldn't notice my son's brand-new shoulder?" He laughs. "Did you think I wouldn't find it strange to see him come home not only unharmed, but entirely *healed*? No scars, no tenderness, no weakness— as if he'd never been shot at all! It's a miracle," he says. "A miracle, my son informs me, that was performed by two of your little freaks."

"No."

Horror is building inside of me, blinding me.

"Oh yes." He glances at Warner. "Isn't that right, son?"

"No," I gasp. "Oh, God—what have you done—WHERE ARE THEY—"

"Calm yourself," Anderson says to me. "They are perfectly unharmed. I simply had them collected, just as I had you collected. I need them to stay alive and healthy if they're going to heal me, don't you think?"

"Did you know about this?" I turn to Warner, frantic. "Did you do this? Did you know—"

"No—Juliette," he says, "I swear—this wasn't my idea—"

"You are both getting agitated over nothing," Anderson says, waving a lazy hand in our direction. "We have more important things to focus on right now. More pressing issues to deal with."

"What," Warner asks, "are you talking about?" He doesn't seem to be breathing.

"Justice, son." Anderson is staring at me now. "I'm talking about justice. I like the idea of setting things right. Of putting order back into the world. And I was waiting for you to arrive so I could show you exactly what I mean. This," he says, "is what I should've done the first time." He glances at Warner. "Are you listening? Pay close attention now. Are you watching?"

He pulls out a gun.

And shoots me in the chest.

SEVENTY

My heart has exploded.

I'm thrown backward, tripping over my own feet until I hit the floor, my head slamming into the carpeted ground, my arms doing little to break my fall. It's pain like I've never known it, pain I never thought I could feel, never would have even imagined. It's like dynamite has gone off in my chest, like I've been lit on fire from the inside out, and suddenly everything slows down.

So this, I think, is what it feels like to die.

I'm blinking and it seems to take forever. I see an unfocused series of images in front of me, colors and bodies and lights swaying, stilted movements all blurred together. Sounds are warped, garbled, too high and too low for me to hear clearly. There are icy, electric bursts surging through my veins, like every part of my body has fallen asleep and is trying to wake up again.

There's a face in front of me.

I try to concentrate on the shape, the colors, try to bring everything into focus but it's too difficult and suddenly I can't breathe, suddenly I feel like there are knives in my throat, holes punched into my lungs, and the more I blink, the less clearly I'm able to see. Soon I'm only able to take in the tightest breaths, tiny little gasps that remind me of when I was a child, when the doctors told me I suffered from asthma attacks. They were wrong, though; my shortness of breath had nothing to do with asthma. It had to do with panic and anxiety and hyperventilation. But this feeling I'm feeling right now is very similar to what I experienced then. It's like trying to take in oxygen by breathing through the thinnest straw. Like your lungs are just closing up, gone for the holidays. I feel the dizziness take over, the light-headed feeling take over. And the pain, the pain, the *pain*. The pain is terrible. The pain is the worst. The pain never seems to stop.

Suddenly I'm blind.

I feel rather than see the blood, feel it leaking out of me as I blink and blink and blink in a desperate attempt to regain my vision. But I can see nothing but a haze of white. I hear nothing but the pounding in my eardrums and the short, the short, the short frantic gasp gasp gasps of my own breath and I feel hot, so hot, the blood of my body still so fresh and warm and pooling underneath me, all around me.

Life is seeping out of me and it makes me think about death, makes me think about how short a life I lived and how little I lived it. How I spent most of my years cowering in fear, never standing up for myself, always trying to be what someone else wanted. For 17 years I tried to force myself into a mold that I hoped would make other people feel comfortable, safe, unthreatened.

And it never helped.

I will have died having accomplished nothing. I am still no one. I am nothing more than a silly little girl bleeding to death on a psychotic man's floor.

And I think, if I could do it over again, I'd do it so differently.

I'd be better. I'd make something of myself. I'd make a difference in this sorry, sorry world.

And I'd start by killing Anderson.

It's too bad I'm already so close to dead.

SEVENTY-ONE

My eyes open.

I'm looking around and wondering at this strange version of an afterlife. Odd, that Warner is here, that I still can't seem to move, that I still feel such extraordinary pain. Stranger still to see Sonya and Sara in front of me. I can't even pretend to understand their presence in this picture.

I'm hearing things.

Sounds are beginning to come in more clearly, and, because I can't lift my head to look around, I try instead to focus on what they're saying.

They're arguing.

"You have to!" Warner shouts.

"But we can't—we can't t-touch her," Sonya is saying, choking back tears. "There's no way for us to help her—"

"I can't believe she's actually dying," Sara gasps. "I didn't think you were telling the truth—"

"She's not dying!" Warner says. "She is not going to die! Please, listen, I'm telling you," he says, desperate now, "you can help her—I've been trying to explain to you," he says, "all you have to do is touch me and I can take your power—I can be the transfer, I can control it and redirect your Energy—"

"That's not possible," Sonya says. "That's not—Castle never said you could do that—he would've told us if you could do that—"

"Jesus, please, just listen to me," he says, his voice breaking. "I'm not trying to trick you—"

"You kidnapped us!" they both shout at the same time.

"That wasn't me! I wasn't the one who kidnapped you—"

"How are we supposed to trust you?" Sara says. "How do we know you didn't do this to her yourself?"

"Why don't you care?" He's breathing so hard now. "How can you not care? Why don't you care that she's bleeding to death—I thought you were her friends—"

"Of course we care!" Sara says, her voice catching on the last word. "But how can we help her now? Where can we take her? Who can we take her to? No one can touch her and she's lost so much blood already—just look at he—"

A sharp intake of breath.

"Juliette?"

Footsteps stomp stomp stomp the ground. Rushing around my head. All the sounds are banging into each other, colliding again, spinning around me. I can't believe I'm not dead yet.

I have no idea how long I've been lying here.

"Juliette? JULIETTE—"

Warner's voice is a rope I want to cling to. I want to catch it and tie it around my waist and I want him to haul me out of this paralyzed world I'm trapped in. I want to tell him not to worry, that it's fine, that I'm going to be okay because

I've accepted it, I'm ready to die now, but I can't. I can't say anything. I still can't breathe, can hardly shape my lips into words. All I can do is take these torturous little gasps and wonder why the hell my body hasn't given up yet.

All of a sudden Warner is straddling my bleeding body, careful not to allow any of his weight to touch me, and he shoves up my shirtsleeves. Grabs ahold of my bare arms and says, "You are going to be okay. We're going to fix this— they're going to help me fix this and you—you're going to be fine." Deep breaths. "You're going to be perfect. Do you hear me? Juliette, can you hear me?"

I blink at him. I blink and blink and blink at him and find I'm still fascinated by his eyes. Such a startling shade of green.

"Each one of you, grab my arms," he shouts to the girls, his hands still gripped firmly around my shoulders. "Now! Please! I'm *begging you—*"

And for some reason they listen.

Maybe they see something in him, see something in his face, in his features. Maybe they see what I see from this disjointed, foggy perspective. The desperation in his expression, the anguish carved into his features, the way he looks at me, like he might die if I do.

And I can't help but think this is an interesting parting gift from the world.

That at least, in the end, I didn't die alone.

SEVENTY-TWO

I'm blind again.

Heat is pouring into my being with such intensity it's literally taken over my vision. I can't feel anything but hot, hot, searing hot heat flooding my bones, my nerves, my skin, my cells.

Everything is on fire.

At first I think it's the same heat in my chest, the same pain from the hole where my heart used to be, but then I realize this heat doesn't actually hurt. It's a soothing kind of heat. So potent, so intense, but somehow it's welcome. My body does not want to reject it. Does not want to flinch away from it, is not looking for a way to protect itself from it.

I actually feel my back lift off the floor when the fire hits my lungs. I'm suddenly gasping in huge, raging hyperventilated breaths, taking in lungfuls of air like I might cry if I don't. I'm drinking oxygen, devouring it, choking on it, taking it in as quickly as possible, my entire body heaving as it strains to return to normal.

My chest feels like it's being stitched back together, like the flesh is regenerating itself, healing itself at an inhuman rate and I'm blinking and breathing and I'm moving my head and trying to see but it's still so blurry, still unclear but it's getting easier. I can feel my fingers and my toes and the life in my limbs and I can actually hear my heart beating again and suddenly the faces above me come into focus.

All at once the heat is gone.

The hands are gone.

I collapse back onto the floor.

And everything goes black.

SEVENTY-THREE

Warner is sleeping.

I know this because he's sleeping right next to me. It's dark enough that it takes me several tries to blink my eyes open and understand that I'm not blind this time. I catch a glimpse out the window and find the moon filled to the brim, pouring light into this little room.

I'm still here. In Anderson's house. In what probably used to be Warner's bedroom.

And he's asleep on the pillow right next to me.

His features are so soft, so ethereal in the moonlight. His face is deceptively calm, so unassuming and innocent. And I think of how impossible it is that he's here, lying next to me. That I'm here, lying next to him.

That we're lying in his childhood bed together.

That he saved my life.

Impossible is such a stupid word.

I shift hardly at all and Warner reacts immediately, sitting straight up, chest heaving, eyes blinking. He looks at me, sees that I'm awake, that my eyes are open, and he freezes in place.

There are so many things I want to say to him. So many things I have to tell him. So many things I need to do now, that I need to sort through, that I have to decide.

But for now, I only have one question.

"Where's your father?" I whisper.

It takes Warner a moment to find his voice. He says, "He's back on base. He left right after"—he hesitates, struggles for a second—"right after he shot you."

Incredible.

He left me bleeding all over his living room floor. What a nice little present for his son to clean up. What a nice little lesson for his son to learn. Fall in love, and you get to watch your love get shot.

"So he doesn't know I'm here?" I ask Warner. "He doesn't know I'm alive?"

Warner shakes his head. "No."

And I think, *Good*. That's very good. It'll be so much better if he thinks I'm dead.

Warner is still looking at me. Looking and looking and looking at me like he wants to touch me but he's afraid to get too close. Finally, he whispers, "Are you okay, love? How do you feel?"

And I smile to myself, thinking of all the ways I could answer that question.

I think of how my body is more exhausted, more defeated, more drained than it's ever been in my life. I think about how I've had nothing but a glass of water in 2 days. How I've never been more confused about people, about who they seem to be and who they actually are, and I think about how I'm lying here, sharing a bed in a house we were told doesn't exist anymore, with one of the most hated and feared people of Sector 45. And I think about how that terrifying creature has the capacity for such tenderness, how he saved my life. How his own father shot me in the chest. How only hours earlier I was lying in a pool of my own blood.

I think about how my friends are probably still locked in battle, how Adam must be suffering not knowing where I am or what's happened to me. How Kenji is still pulling the weight of so many. How Brendan and Winston might still be lost. How the people of Omega Point might all be dead. And it makes me think.

I feel better than I ever have in my entire life.

I'm amazed by how different I feel now. How different I know things will be now. I have so many things to do. So many scores to settle. So many friends who need my help.

Everything has changed.

Because once upon a time I was just a child.

Today I'm still just a child, but this time I've got an iron will and 2 fists made of steel and I've aged 50 years. Now I finally have a clue. I've finally figured out that I'm strong enough, that maybe I'm a touch brave enough, that maybe this time I can do what I was meant to do.

This time I am a force.

A deviation of human nature.

I am living, breathing proof that nature is officially screwed, afraid of what it's done, what it's become.

And I'm stronger. I'm angrier.

I'm ready to do something I'll definitely regret and this time I don't care. I'm done being nice. I'm done being nervous. I'm not afraid of anything anymore.

Mass chaos is in my future.

And I'm leaving my gloves behind.

ACKNOWLEDGEMENTS

My mother. My father. My brothers. My family. I love you laughing. I love you crying. I love you laughing and crying into every pot of tea we've ever finished together. You're the most incredible people I've ever met and you'll be forced to know me all my life and you've never once complained. Thank you always, for every hot cup. For never letting go of my hand.

Jodi Reamer. I said hello and you smiled so I asked about the weather and you said the weather? The weather is unpredictable. I said what about the road? You said the road is known to be bumpy. I said do you know what's going to happen? You said absolutely not. And then you introduced me to some of the best years of my life. I say, forgetting you, it's impossible.

Tara Weikum. You read the words I write with my heart and my hands and understand them with an accuracy that is both painful and astounding. Your brilliance, your patience, your unfailing kindness. Your generous smiles. It's such an honor to work with you.

Tana. Randa. We've shed many tears together – in sadness, in joy. But the most tears I've ever wept were in the moments I spent laughing with you. Your friendship has been the greatest gift; it's a blessing I'm determined every day to deserve.

Sarah. Nathan. For your unwavering support. You two are beyond-words amazing.

Sumayyah. For your shoulder and your ear and the safe space you grant me. I don't know what I'd do without it.

A huge, huge thank-you to all of my dear friends at HarperCollins and Writers House who are never thanked enough for all they do: Melissa Miller, for all your love and enthusiasm; Christina Colangelo, Diane Naughton, and Lauren Flower, for your energy and passion and invaluable marketing prowess; Hallie Patterson, my exceptionally talented publicist, who is both clever and unfailingly kind. More thanks to Cara Petrus and Sarah Kaufman, for their fabulous design work; and Colin Anderson, the digital illustrator whose work continues to astound me. Thanks also to Brenna Franzitta: because I'm thankful every single day to have a copy editor as brilliant as you (and I hope I just used that colon correctly); Alec Shane, for everything, but also for knowing how to respond gracefully when oddly shaped, leaking children's toys show up in his office; Cecilia de la Campa, for always working to make my books available all around the world; Beth Miller, for her continued support; and Kassie Evashevski at UTA, for her silent grace and razor-sharp instinct.

Thanks always to all my readers! Without you I'd have no one to talk to but the characters in my head. Thank you for sharing Juliette's journey with me.

And to all my friends on Twitter, Tumblr, Facebook, and

my blog: Thank you. Really. I wonder if you'll ever truly know how much I appreciate your friendship, your support, and your generosity.

Thank you forever.

FEAR WILL LEARN TO FEAR ME.

BOOK THREE IN THE *NEW YORK TIMES* BESTSELLING FANTASY SERIES

Read on for the
first chapter of

IGNITE ME

ONE

I am an hourglass.

My seventeen years have collapsed and buried me from the inside out. My legs feel full of sand and stapled together, my mind overflowing with grains of indecision, choices unmade and impatient as time runs out of my body. The small hand of a clock taps me at one and two, three and four, whispering hello, get up, stand up, it's time to

wake up

wake up

"Wake up," he whispers.

A sharp intake of breath and I'm awake but not up, surprised but not scared, somehow staring into the very desperately green eyes that seem to know too much, too well. Aaron Warner Anderson is bent over me, his worried eyes inspecting me, his hand caught in the air like he might've been about to touch me.

He jerks back.

He stares, unblinking, chest rising and falling.

"Good morning," I assume. I'm unsure of my voice, of the hour and this day, of these words leaving my lips and this body that contains me.

I notice he's wearing a white shirt, half untucked into

his curiously unrumpled black slacks. His shirtsleeves are folded, pushed up past his elbows.

His smile looks like it hurts.

I pull myself into a seated position and Warner shifts to accommodate me. I have to close my eyes to steady the sudden dizziness, but I force myself to remain still until the feeling passes.

I'm tired and weak from hunger, but other than a few general aches, I seem to be fine. I'm alive. I'm breathing and blinking and feeling human and I know exactly why.

I meet his eyes. "You saved my life."

I was shot in the chest.

Warner's father put a bullet in my body and I can still feel the echoes of it. If I focus, I can relive the exact moment it happened; the pain: so intense, so excruciating; I'll never be able to forget it.

I suck in a startled breath.

I'm finally aware of the familiar foreignness of this room and I'm quickly seized by a panic that screams I did not wake up where I fell asleep. My heart is racing and I'm inching away from him, hitting my back against the headboard, clutching at these sheets, trying not to stare at the chandelier I remember all too well—

"It's okay—" Warner is saying. "It's all right—"

"What am I doing here?" Panic, panic; terror clouds my consciousness. "Why did you bring me here again—?"

"Juliette, please, I'm not going to hurt you—"

"Then why did you bring me here?" My voice is starting

to break and I'm struggling to keep it steady. "Why bring me back to this *hellhole*—"

"I had to hide you." He exhales, looks up at the wall.

"What? Why?"

"No one knows you're alive." He turns to look at me. "I had to get back to base. I needed to pretend everything was back to normal and I was running out of time."

I force myself to lock away the fear.

I study his face and analyze his patient, earnest tone. I remember him last night—it must've been last night—I remember his face, remember him lying next to me in the dark. He was tender and kind and gentle and he saved me, saved my life. Probably carried me into bed. Tucked me in beside him. It must've been him.

But when I glance down at my body I realize I'm wearing clean clothes, no blood or holes or anything anywhere and I wonder who washed me, wonder who changed me, and worry that might've been Warner, too.

"Did you . . ." I hesitate, touching the hem of the shirt I'm wearing. "Did—I mean—my clothes—"

He smiles. He stares until I'm blushing and I decide I hate him a little and then he shakes his head. Looks into his palms. "No," he says. "The girls took care of that. I just carried you to bed."

"The girls," I whisper, dazed.

The girls.

Sonya and Sara. They were there too, the healer twins, they helped Warner. They helped him save me because he's the only one who can touch me now, the only person in the world who'd have been able to transfer their healing power safely into my body.

My thoughts are on fire.

Where are the girls what happened to the girls and where is Anderson and the war and oh God what's happened to Adam and Kenji and Castle and I have to get up I have to get up I have to get up and get out of bed and get going

but

I try to move and Warner catches me. I'm off-balance, unsteady; I still feel as though my legs are anchored to this bed and I'm suddenly unable to breathe, seeing spots and feeling faint. Need up. Need out.

Can't.

"Warner." My eyes are frantic on his face. "What happened? What's happening with the battle—?"

"Please," he says, gripping my shoulders. "You need to start slowly; you should eat something—"

"Tell me—"

"Don't you want to eat first? Or shower?"

"No," I hear myself say. "I have to know now."

One moment. Two and three.

Warner takes a deep breath. A million more. Right hand over left, spinning the jade ring on his pinkie finger over and over and over and over "It's over," he says.

"What?"

I say the word but my lips make no sound. I'm numb, somehow. Blinking and seeing nothing.

472

"It's over," he says again.

"No."

I exhale the word, exhale the impossibility.

He nods. He's disagreeing with me.

"No."

"Juliette."

"No," I say. "No. No. Don't be stupid," I say to him. "Don't be ridiculous," I say to him. *"Don't lie to me goddamn you,"* but now my voice is high and broken and shaking and "No," I gasp, "no, no, *no—*"

I actually stand up this time. My eyes are filling fast with tears and I blink and blink but the world is a mess and I want to laugh because all I can think is how horrible and beautiful it is, that our eyes blur the truth when we can't bear to see it.

The ground is hard.

I know this to be an actual fact because it's suddenly pressed against my face and Warner is trying to touch me but I think I scream and slap his hands away because I already know the answer. I must already know the answer because I can feel the revulsion bubbling up and unsettling my insides but I ask anyway. I'm horizontal and somehow still tipping over and the holes in my head are tearing open and I'm staring at a spot on the carpet not ten feet away and I'm not sure I'm even alive but I have to hear him say it.

"Why?" I ask.

It's just a word, stupid and simple.

"Why is the battle over?" I ask. I'm not breathing

anymore, not really speaking at all; just expelling letters through my lips.

Warner is not looking at me.

He's looking at the wall and at the floor and at the bedsheets and at the way his knuckles look when he clenches his fists but no not at me he won't look at me and his next words are so, so soft.

"Because they're dead, love. They're all dead."

DEFY ME

First published in USA 2019 by HarperCollins Children's Books
First published in Great Britain 2019
by Electric Monkey, part of Egmont Books

An imprint of HarperCollins*Publishers*
1 London Bridge Street
London SE1 9GF

egmontbooks.co.uk

2 4 6 8 10 9 7 5 3 1

Published by arrangement with HarperCollins Children's Books,
a division of HarperCollins Publishers, New York, New York, USA

Text copyright © 2019 Tahereh Mafi

ISBN 978 1 4052 9179 8

YOUNG ADULT

A CIP catalogue record for this title is available from the British Library

68843/002

Printed and bound in India by Thomson Press India Ltd

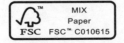

MIX
Paper
FSC™ C010615

DEFY
ME

TAHEREH MAFI

KENJI

She's screaming.

She's just screaming words, I think. They're just *words*. But she's screaming, screaming at the top of her lungs, with an agony that seems almost an exaggeration, and it's causing devastation I never knew possible. It's like she just—imploded.

It doesn't seem real.

I mean, I knew Juliette was strong—and I knew we hadn't discovered the depth of her powers—but I never imagined she'd be capable of this.

Of this:

The ceiling is splitting open. Seismic currents are thundering up the walls, across the floors, chattering my teeth. The ground is rumbling under my feet. People are frozen in place even as they shake, the room vibrating around them. The chandeliers swing too fast and the lights flicker ominously. And then, with one last vibration, three of the massive chandeliers rip free from the ceiling and shatter as they hit the floor.

Crystal flies everywhere. The room loses half its light, bathing the cavernous space in a freakish glow, and it's suddenly hard to see what's happening. I look at Juliette and see her staring, slack-jawed, frozen at the sight of the devastation, and I realize she must've stopped screaming a minute ago. She can't stop this. She already put the energy into the world and now—

It has to go somewhere.

The shudders ripple with renewed fervor across the floorboards, ripping through walls and seats and *people*.

I don't actually believe it until I see the blood. It seems fake, for a second, all the limp bodies in seats with their chests butterflied open. It seems staged—like a bad joke, like a bad theater production. But when I see the blood, thick and heavy, seeping through clothes and upholstery, dripping down frozen hands, I know we'll never recover from this.

Juliette just murdered six hundred people at once.

There's no recovering from this.

I shove my way through the quiet, stunned, still-breathing bodies of my friends. I hear Winston's soft, insistent whimpers and Brendan's steady, reassuring response that the wound isn't as bad as it looks, that he's going to be okay, that he's been through worse than this and survived it—

And I know my priority right now needs to be Juliette.

When I reach her I pull her into my arms, and her cold, unresponsive body reminds me of the time I found her standing over Anderson, a gun aimed at his chest. She was so terrified—*so surprised*—by what she'd done that she could hardly speak. She looked like she'd disappeared into herself somewhere—like she'd found a small room in her brain and had locked herself inside. It took a minute to coax her back out again.

She hadn't even killed anyone that time.

I try to warm some sense into her, begging her now to return to herself, to hurry back to her mind, to the present moment.

"I know everything is crazy right now, but I need you to snap out of this, J. Wake up. Get out of your head. We have to get out of here."

She doesn't blink.

"Princess, please," I say, shaking her a little. "We have to go—*now*—"

And when she still doesn't move, I figure I have no choice but to move her myself. I start hauling her backward. Her limp body is heavier than I expect, and she makes a small, wheezing sound that's almost like a sob. Fear sparks in my nerves. I nod at Castle and the others to go, to move on without me, but when I glance around, looking for Warner, I realize I can't find him anywhere.

What happens next knocks the wind from my lungs.

The room tilts. My vision blackens, clears, and then darkens only at the edges in a dizzying moment that lasts hardly a second. I feel off-center. I stumble.

And then, all at once—

Juliette is gone.

Not figuratively. She's literally gone. Disappeared. One

second she's in my arms, and the next, I'm grasping at air. I blink and spin around, convinced I'm losing my mind, but when I scan the room I see the audience members begin to stir. Their shirts are torn and their faces are scratched, but no one appears to be dead. Instead, they begin to stand, confused, and as soon as they start shuffling around, someone shoves me, hard. I look up to see Ian swearing at me, telling me to get moving while we still have a chance, and I try to push back, try to tell him that we lost Juliette—that I haven't seen Warner—and he doesn't hear me, he just forces me forward, offstage, and when the murmur of the crowd grows into a roar, I know I have no choice.

I have to go.

WARNER

"I'm going to kill him," she says, her small hands forming fists. "I'm going to kill him—"

"Ella, don't be silly," I say, and walk away.

"One day," she says, chasing after me, her eyes bright with tears. "If he doesn't stop hurting you, I swear I'll do it. You'll see."

I laugh.

"It's not funny!" she cries.

I turn to face her. "No one can kill my dad. He's unkillable."

"No one is unkillable," she says.

I ignore her.

"Why doesn't your mum do anything?" she says, and she grabs my arm.

When I meet her eyes she looks different. Scared.

"Why doesn't anyone stop him?"

The wounds on my back are no longer fresh, but, somehow, they still hurt. Ella is the only person who knows about these scars, knows what my dad started doing to me on my birthday two years ago. Last year, when all the families came to visit us in California, Ella had barged into my room, wanting to know where Emmaline and Nazeera had gone off to, and she'd caught me staring at my back in the mirror.

I begged her not to say anything, not to tell anyone what she saw, and she started crying and said that we had to tell someone, that she was going to tell her mom and I said, "If you tell your mom I'll only get into more trouble. Please don't say anything, okay? He won't do it again."

But he did do it again.

And this time he was angrier. He told me I was seven years old now, and that I was too old to cry.

"We have to do something," she says, and her voice shakes a little. Another tear steals down the side of her face and, quickly, she wipes it away. "We have to tell someone."

"Stop," I say. "I don't want to talk about it anymore."

"But—"

"Ella. Please."

"No, we have t—"

"Ella," I say, cutting her off. "I think there's something wrong with my mom."

Her face falls. Her anger fades. "What?"

I'd been terrified, for weeks, to say the words out loud, to make my fears real. Even now, I feel my heart pick up.

"What do you mean?" she says. "What's wrong with her?"

"She's . . . sick."

Ella blinks at me. Confused. "If she's sick we can fix her. My mum and dad can fix her. They're so smart; they can fix anything. I'm sure they can fix your mum, too."

I'm shaking my head, my heart racing now, pounding in my ears. "No, Ella, you don't understand—I think—"

"What?" She takes my hand. Squeezes. "What is it?"

"I think my dad is killing her."

KENJI

We're all running.

Base isn't far from here, and our best option is to go on foot. But the minute we hit the open air, the group of us—myself, Castle, Winston, injured Brendan, Ian, and Alia—go invisible. Someone shouts a breathless *thanks* in my direction, but I'm not the one doing this.

My fists clench.

Nazeera.

These last couple of days with her have been making my head spin. I never should've trusted her. First she hates me, then she hates me even more, and then, suddenly, she decides I'm not an asshole and wants to be my friend? I can't believe I fell for it. I can't believe I'm such an idiot. She's been playing me this whole time. This girl just shows up out of nowhere, magically mimics my exact supernatural ability, and then—right when she pretends to be best friends with Juliette—we're ambushed at the symposium and Juliette sort of murders six hundred people?

No way. I call bullshit.

No way this was all some big coincidence.

Juliette attended that symposium because *Nazeera* encouraged her to go. Nazeera convinced Juliette it was the right thing to do. And then five seconds before Brendan gets shot, Nazeera tells me to run? Tells me we have the same powers?

Bullshit.

I can't believe I let myself be distracted by a pretty face. I should've trusted Warner when he told me she was hiding something.

Warner.

God. I don't even know what happened to him.

The minute we get back to base our invisibility is lifted. I can't know for sure if that means Nazeera went her own way, but we can't slow down long enough to find out. Quickly, I project a new layer of invisibility over our team; I'll have to keep it up just long enough to get us all to a safe space, and just being back on base isn't assurance enough. The soldiers are going to ask questions, and right now I don't have the answers they need.

They're going to be pissed.

We make our way, as a group, to the fifteenth floor, to our home on base in Sector 45. Warner only just finished having this thing built for us. He cleared out the entire top floor for our new headquarters—we'd hardly even settled in—and things have already gone to shit. I can't even allow myself to think about it now, not yet.

It makes me feel sick to my stomach.

Once we're gathered in our largest common room, I do a head count. All original, remaining Omega Point members are present. Adam and James show up to find out what happened, and Sonya and Sara stick around just long enough to gather intel before carting Brendan over to the medical wing. Winston disappears down the hall behind them.

Juliette and Warner never show.

Quickly, we share our own versions of what we saw. It doesn't take long to confirm we all witnessed basically the same thing: blood, mayhem, murdered bodies, and then—a slightly less-bloody version of the same thing. No one seems as surprised by the twisted turn of events as I was, because, according to Ian, "Weird supernatural shit happens around here all the time, it's not that weird," but, more important:

No one saw what happened to Warner and Juliette.

No one but me.

For a few seconds, we all stare at each other. My heart pounds hard and heavy in my chest. I feel like I might be on fire, burning with indignation.

Denial.

Alia is the first to speak. "You don't think they're dead, do you?"

Ian says, "Probably."

And I jump to my feet. "STOP. They're not dead."

"How can you be sure?" Adam says.

"I would know if they were dead."

"What? How w—"

"I would just know, okay?" I cut him off. "I would know. And they're not dead." I take a deep, steadying breath. "We're not going to freak out," I say as calmly as possible.

"There has to be a logical explanation. People don't just *disappear*, right?"

Everyone stares at me.

"You know what I mean," I snap, irritated. "We all know that Juliette and Warner wouldn't, like, run away together. They weren't even on speaking terms before the symposium. So it makes the most sense that they would be kidnapped." I pause. Look around again. "Right?"

"Or dead," Ian says.

"If you keep talking like that, Sanchez, I can guarantee that at least one person *will* be dead tonight."

Ian sighs, hard. "Listen, I'm not trying to be an asshole. I know you were close with them. But let's be real: they weren't close with the rest of us. And maybe that makes me less invested in all this, but it also makes me more level-headed."

He waits, gives me a chance to respond.

I don't.

Ian sighs again. "I'm just saying that maybe you're letting emotion cloud your better judgment right now. I know you don't *want* them to be dead, but the possibility that they *are* dead is, like, really high. Warner was a traitor to The Reestablishment. I'm surprised they didn't try to kill him sooner. And Juliette—I mean, that's obvious, right? She murdered Anderson and declared herself ruler of North America." He raises his eyebrows in a knowing gesture. "Those two have had targets on their backs for months."

My jaw clenches. Unclenches. Clenches again.

"So," Ian says quietly. "We have to be smart about this. If they're dead, we need to be thinking about our next moves. Where do we go?"

"Wait—what do you mean?" Adam says, sitting forward. "What next moves? You think we have to leave?"

"Without Warner and Juliette, I don't think we're safe here." Lily takes Ian's hand in a show of emotional support that makes me feel violent. "The soldiers paid their allegiance to the two of them—to Juliette in particular. Without her, I'm not sure they'd follow the rest of us anywhere."

"And if The Reestablishment had Juliette murdered," Ian adds, "they're obviously just getting started. They'll be coming to reclaim Sector 45 any second now. Our best chance of survival is to first consider what's best for our team. Since we're the obvious next targets, I think we should bail. Soon." A pause. "Maybe even tonight."

"Bro, are you insane?" I drop down into my chair too hard, feeling like I might scream. "We can't just bail. We need to look for them. We need to be planning a rescue mission right now!"

Everyone just stares at me. Like *I'm* the one who's lost his mind.

"Castle, sir?" I say, trying and failing to keep the sharp edge out of my voice. "Do you want to chime in here?"

But Castle has sunk down in his chair. He's staring up, at the ceiling, at nothing. He looks dazed.

I don't have the chance to dwell on it.

"Kenji," Alia says quietly. "I'm sorry, but Ian's right. I

don't think we're safe here anymore."

"We're not leaving," Adam and I say at exactly the same time.

I spin around, surprised. Hope shoots through me fast and strong. Maybe Adam feels more for Juliette than he lets on. Maybe Adam will surprise us all. Maybe he'll finally stop hiding, stop cowering in the background. *Maybe,* I think, Adam is back.

"Thank you," I say, and point at him in a gesture that says to everyone:

See? This is loyalty.

"James and I aren't running anymore," Adam says, his eyes going cold as he speaks. "I understand if the rest of you have to leave, but James and I will stay here. I was a Sector 45 soldier. I lived on this base. Maybe they'll give me immunity."

I frown. "But—"

"James and I aren't leaving," Adam says. Loudly. Definitively. "You can make your plans without us. We have to take off for the night, anyway." Adam stands, turns to his brother. "It's time to get ready for bed."

James stares at the floor.

"James," Adam says, a gentle warning in his voice.

"I want to stay and listen," James says, crossing his arms. "You can go to bed without me."

"James—"

"But I have a theory," the ten-year-old says. He says the word *theory* like it's brand-new to him, like it's an interesting

18

sound in his mouth. "And I want to share it with Kenji."

Adam looks so tense that the strain in his shoulders is stressing *me* out. I think I haven't been paying close enough attention to him, because I didn't realize until right now that Adam looks worse than tired. He looks ragged. Like he could collapse, crack in half, at any moment.

James catches my eye from across the room, his own eyes round and eager.

I sigh.

"What's your theory, little man?"

James's face lights up. "I was just thinking: maybe all the fake-killing thing was, like, a distraction."

I raise an eyebrow.

"Like, if someone wanted to kidnap Warner and Juliette," James says. "You know? Like you said earlier. Causing a scene like that would be the perfect distraction, right?"

"Well. Yeah," I say, and frown. "I guess. But why would The Reestablishment need a distraction? When have they ever been secretive about what they want? If a supreme commander wanted to take Juliette or Warner, for example, wouldn't they just show up with a shit ton of soldiers and take what they wanted?"

"*Language,*" Adam says, outraged.

"My bad. Strike the word *shit* from the record."

Adam shakes his head. He looks like he might throttle me. But James is smiling, which is really all that matters.

"No. I don't think they'd rush in like that, not with so many soldiers," James says, his blue eyes bright. "Not if they

19

had something to hide."

"You think they'd have something to hide?" Lily pipes up. "From *us*?"

"I don't know," James says. "Sometimes people hide things." He steals a split-second glance at Adam as he says it, a glance that sets my pulse racing with fear, and I'm about to respond when Lily beats me to it.

"I mean, it's possible," she says. "But The Reestablishment doesn't have a long history of caring about pretenses. They stopped pretending to care about the opinion of the public a long time ago. They mow people down in the street just because they feel like it. I don't think they're worried about hiding things from us."

Castle laughs, out loud, and we all spin around to stare at him. I'm relieved to finally see him react, but he still seems lost in his head somewhere. He looks angry. I've never really seen Castle get angry.

"They hide a great deal from us," he says sharply. "And from each other." After a long, deep breath, he finally gets to his feet. Smiles, warily, at the ten-year-old in the room. "James, you are wise indeed."

"Thank you," James says, blinking up at him.

"Castle, sir?" I say, my voice coming out harder than I'd intended. "Will you please tell us what the hell is going on? Do you know something?"

Castle sighs. Rubs the stubble on his chin with the flat of his palm. "All right, Nazeera," he says, turning toward nothing, like he's speaking to a ghost. "Go ahead."

When Nazeera appears, as if out of thin air, I'm not the only one who's pissed. Okay, maybe I'm the only one who's pissed.

But everyone else looks surprised, at least.

They're staring at her, at each other, and then all of them—*all of them*—turn to look at me.

"Bro, did you know about this?" Ian asks.

I scowl.

Invisibility is *my* thing. My thing, goddammit.

No one ever said I had to share that with anyone. Especially not with someone like Nazeera, a lying, manipulative—

Gorgeous. Gorgeous human being.

Shit.

I turn, stare at the wall. I can't be distracted by her anymore. She knows I'm into her—my infatuation is apparently obvious to everyone within a ten-mile radius, according to Castle—and she's clearly been using my idiocy to her best advantage.

Smart. I respect the tactic.

But that also means I have to keep my guard up when she's around. No more staring. No more daydreaming about her. No more thinking about how she looked at me when she smiled. Or the way she laughed, like she meant it, the same night she yelled at me for asking reasonable questions. Which, by the way—

I don't think I was crazy for wondering out loud how the daughter of a supreme commander could get away with wearing an illegal headscarf. She told me later that she wears

21

the scarf symbolically, every once in a while, that she can't get away with wearing it all the time because it's illegal. But when I pointed this out to her, she gave me hell. And then she gave me shit for being confused.

I'm *still* confused.

She's not covering her hair now, either, but no one else seems to have registered this fact. Maybe they'd already seen her like this. Maybe everyone but me already had that conversation with her, already heard her story about wearing it symbolically, occasionally.

Illegally, when her dad wasn't watching.

"Kenji," she says, and her voice is so sharp I look up, stare at her despite my own very explicit orders to keep my eyes on the wall. All it takes is two seconds of eye contact and my heart hits itself.

That mouth. Those eyes.

"Yeah?" I cross my arms.

She looks surprised, like she wasn't expecting me to be upset, and I don't care. She should know that I'm pissed. I want her to know that invisibility is my thing. That I know I'm petty and I don't care. Plus, I don't trust her. Also, what is up with these kids of the supreme commanders all being super-good-looking? It's almost like they did it on purpose, like they made these kids in test tubes or some shit.

I shake my head to clear it.

Carefully, Nazeera says, "I really think you should sit down for this."

"I'm good."

22

She frowns. For a second she looks almost hurt, but before I have a chance to feel bad about it, she shrugs. Turns away.

And what she says next nearly splits me in half.

JULIETTE

I'm sitting on an orange chair in the hallway of a dimly lit building. The chair is made of cheap plastic, its edges coarse and unfinished. The floor is a shiny linoleum that occasionally sticks to the soles of my shoes. I know I've been breathing too loudly but I can't help it. I sit on my hands and swing my legs under my seat.

Just then, a boy comes into view. His movements are so quiet I only notice him when he stops directly in front of me. He leans against the wall opposite me, his eyes focused on a point in the distance.

I study him for a moment.

He seems about my age, but he's wearing a suit. There's something strange about him; he's so pale and stiff he seems close to dead.

"Hi," I say, and try to smile. "Do you want to sit down?"

He doesn't return my smile. He won't even look at me. "I'd prefer to stand," he says quietly.

"Okay."

We're both silent awhile.

Finally, he says, "You're nervous."

I nod. My eyes must be a little red from crying, but I'd been hoping no one would notice. "Are you here to get a new family, too?"

27

"No."

"Oh." I look away. Stop swinging my feet. I feel my bottom lip tremble and I bite it, hard. "Then why are you here?"

He shrugs. I see him glance, briefly, at the three empty chairs next to me, but he makes no effort to sit down. "My father made me come."

"He made you come here?"

"Yes."

"Why?"

He stares at his shoes and frowns. "I don't know."

"Shouldn't you be in school?"

And then, instead of answering me, he says, "Where are you from?"

"What do you mean?"

He looks up then, meets my eyes for the first time. He has such unusual eyes. They're a light, clear green.

"You have an accent," he says.

"Oh," I say. "Yeah." I look at the floor. "I was born in New Zealand. That's where I lived until my mum and dad died."

"I'm sorry to hear that."

I nod. Swing my legs again. I'm about to ask him another question when the door down the hall finally opens. A tall man in a navy suit walks out. He's carrying a briefcase.

It's Mr. Anderson, my social worker.

He beams at me. "You're all set. Your new family is dying to meet you. We have a couple more things to do before you can go, but it won't take too lon—"

I can't hold it in anymore.

28

I start sobbing right there, all over the new dress he bought me. Sobs rack my body, tears hitting the orange chair, the sticky floor.

Mr. Anderson sets down his briefcase and laughs. "Sweetheart, there's nothing to cry about. This is a great day! You should be happy!"

But I can't speak.

I feel stuck, stuck to the seat. Like my lungs have been stuck together. I manage to calm the sobs but I'm suddenly hiccuping, tears spilling quietly down my cheeks. "I want—I want to go h-home—"

"You are going home," he says, still smiling. "That's the whole point."

And then—

"Dad."

I look up at the sound of his voice. So quiet and serious. It's the boy with the green eyes. Mr. Anderson, I realize, is his father.

"She's scared," the boy says. And even though he's talking to his dad, he's looking at me. "She's really scared."

"Scared?" Mr. Anderson looks from me to his son, then back again. "What's there to be scared of?"

I scrub at my face. Try and fail to stop the tears.

"What's her name?" the boy asks. He's still staring at me, and this time, I stare back. There's something in his eyes, something that makes me feel safe.

"This is Juliette," Mr. Anderson says, and looks me over. "Tragic"—he sighs—"just like her namesake."

KENJI

Nazeera was right. I should've sat down.

I'm looking at my hands, watching a tremor work its way across my fingers. I nearly lose my grip on the stack of photos I'm clutching. The photos. The photos Nazeera passed around after telling us that Juliette is not who we think she is.

I can't stop staring at the pictures.

A little brown girl and a little white girl running in a field, both of them smiling tiny-toothed smiles, long hair flying in the wind, small baskets full of strawberries swinging from their elbows.

Nazeera and Emmaline at the strawberry patch, it read on the back.

Little Nazeera being hugged, on either side, by two little white girls, all three of them laughing so hard they look like they're about to fall over.

Ella and Emmaline and Nazeera, it read.

A close-up of a little girl smiling right into the camera, her eyes huge and blue-green, lengths of soft brown hair framing her face.

Ella on Christmas morning, it read.

"Ella Sommers," Nazeera says.

She says her real name is Ella Sommers, sister to Emmaline Sommers, daughter of Maximillian and Evie Sommers.

"Something is wrong," Nazeera says.

"Something is happening," she says. She says she woke up six weeks ago remembering Juliette—sorry, Ella—

"Remembering her. I was *remembering* her, which means I'd forgotten her. And when I remembered Ella," she says, "I remembered Emmaline, too. I remembered how we'd all grown up together, how our parents used to be friends. I remembered but I didn't understand, not right away. I thought maybe I was confusing dreams with memory. Actually, the memories came back to me so slowly I thought, for a while, that I might've been hallucinating."

She says the hallucinations, as she called them, were impossible to shake, so she started digging, started looking for information.

"I learned the same thing you did. That two girls named Ella and Emmaline were donated to The Reestablishment, and that only Ella was taken out of their custody, so Ella was given an alias. Relocated. Adopted. But what you didn't know was that the parents who gave up their daughters were also members of The Reestablishment. They were doctors and scientists. You didn't know that Ella—the girl you know to be Juliette—is the daughter of Evie Sommers, the current supreme commander of Oceania. She and I grew up together. She, like the rest of us kids, was built to serve The Reestablishment."

Ian swears, loudly, and Adam is so stunned he doesn't complain.

"That can't be possible," Adam says. "Juliette—The girl I went to school with? She was"—he shakes his head—"I knew Juliette for years. She wasn't made like you or Warner. She was this quiet, timid, sweet girl. She was always so *nice*. She never wanted to hurt anyone. All she ever wanted was to, like, connect with people. She was trying to *help* that little boy in the grocery store. But then it just—everything ended so badly and she got sucked into this whole mess and I tried," he says, looking suddenly distraught, "I tried to help her, I tried to keep her safe. I wanted to protect her from this. I wanted t—"

He cuts himself off. Pulls himself together.

"She wasn't like this," he says, and he's staring at the ground now. "Not until she started spending all that time with Warner. After she met him she just—I don't know what happened. She lost herself, little by little. Eventually she became someone else." He looks up. "But she wasn't made to be this way, not like you. Not like Warner. There's no way she's the daughter of a supreme commander—she's not a born murderer. Besides," he says, taking a sharp breath, "if she were from Oceania she would have an *accent*."

Nazeera tilts her head at Adam.

"The girl you knew had undergone severe physical and emotional trauma," she says. "She'd had her native memories

35

forcibly removed. She was shipped across the globe as a specimen and convinced to live with abusive adoptive parents who beat the life out of her." Nazeera shakes her head slowly. "The Reestablishment—and Anderson, in particular—made sure that Ella could never remember why she was suffering, but just because she couldn't remember what happened to her didn't change the fact that it happened. Her body was repeatedly used and abused by a rotating cast of monsters. And that shit leaves its mark."

Nazeera looks Adam straight in the eye.

"Maybe you don't understand," she says. "I read all the reports. I hacked into all my father's files. I found *everything*. What they did to Ella over the course of twelve years is *unspeakable*. So yes, I'm sure you remember a very different person. But I don't think she became someone she wasn't. My guess is she finally gathered the strength to remember who she'd always been. And if you don't get that, I'm glad things didn't work out between the two of you."

In an instant, the tension in the room is nearly suffocating.

Adam looks like he might be on fire. Like fire might literally come out of his eyeballs. Like it might be his new superpower.

I clear my throat. I force myself to say something—anything—to break the silence. "So you guys, uh, you all knew about Adam and Juliette, too, huh? I didn't realize you knew about that. Huh. Interesting."

Nazeera takes her time turning in her seat to look me in

the eye. "Are you kidding?" she says, staring at me like I'm worse than an idiot.

I figure it's best not to press the issue.

"Where did you get these photos?" Alia asks, changing the subject more deftly than I did. "How can we trust that they're real?"

At first, Nazeera only looks at her. And she seems resigned when she says, "I don't know how to convince you that the photos are real. I can only tell you that they are."

The room goes silent.

"Why do you even care?" Lily says. "Why are we supposed to believe you care about this? About Juliette—about *Ella*? What do you have to gain from helping us? Why would you betray your parents?"

Nazeera sits back in her seat. "I know you all think the children of the supreme commanders are a bunch of carefree, amoral psychopaths, happy to be the military robots our parents wanted us to be, but nothing is ever that straightforward. Our parents are homicidal maniacs intent on ruling the world; that part is true. But the thing no one seems to understand is that our parents *chose* to be homicidal maniacs. We, on the other hand, were forced to be. And just because we've been trained to be mercenaries doesn't mean we like it. None of us got to choose this life. None of us enjoyed being taught to torture before we could even drive. And it's not insane to imagine that sometimes even horrible people are searching for a way out of their own darkness."

Nazeera's eyes flash with feeling as she speaks, and her words puncture the life vest around my heart. Emotion drowns me again.

Shit.

"Is it really so crazy to think I might care about the girls I once loved as my own sisters?" she's saying. "Or about the lies my parents forced me to swallow, or the innocent people I watched them murder? Or maybe even something simpler than that—that I might've opened my eyes one day and realized that I was part and parcel of a system that was not only ravaging the world but also slaughtering everyone in it?"

Shit.

I can feel it, can feel my heart filling out, filling up. My chest feels tight, like it's swollen, like my lungs don't fit anymore. I don't want to care about Nazeera. Don't want to feel her pain or feel connected to her or feel *anything*. I just want to keep a level head. Be cool.

I force myself to think about a joke James told me the other day, a stupid pun—something to do with muffins—a joke that was so lame I nearly cried. I focus on the memory, the way James laughed at his own lameness, snorting so hard a little food fell out of his mouth. I smile and glance at James, who looks like he might be falling asleep in his seat.

Soon, the tightness in my chest begins to abate.

Now I'm really smiling, wondering if it's weird that I love bad jokes even more than good ones, when I hear Ian say—

"It's not that you seem heartless. It's just that these

38

photos seem so convenient. You had them ready to share." He stares down at the single photo he's holding. "These kids could be anyone."

"Look closely," Nazeera says, standing up to get a better look at the picture in his hands. "Who do you think that is?"

I lean over—Ian isn't far from me—and peer over his shoulder. There's really no point denying it anymore; the resemblance is insane.

Juliette. *Ella.*

She's just a kid, maybe four or five years old, standing in front of the camera, smiling. She's holding a bouquet of dandelions up to the cameraman, as if to offer him one. And then, just off to the side, there's another figure. A little blond boy. So blond his hair is white. He's staring, intensely, at a single dandelion in his hands.

I nearly fall out of my chair. Juliette is one thing, but this—

"Is that *Warner?*" I say.

Adam looks up sharply. He glances from me to Nazeera, then stalks over to look at the photo. His eyebrows fly up his head.

"No way," he says.

Nazeera shrugs.

"No way," Adam says again. "*No way.* That's impossible. There's no way they knew each other this long. Warner had no idea who Juliette was before she came here." When Nazeera seems unmoved, Adam says, "I'm serious. I know you think I'm full of shit, but I'm not wrong about this. I was *there*. Warner literally interviewed me for the job of being her cellmate in the asylum. He didn't know who she was. He'd never met her. Never seen her face, not up close, anyway. Half the reason he chose me to be her roommate was because she and I had history, because he found that useful. He'd grill me for hours about her."

Nazeera sighs slowly, like she's surrounded by idiots.

"When I found these photos," she says to Adam, "I couldn't understand how I came across them so easily. I didn't understand why anyone would keep evidence like this right under my nose or make it so easy to find. But I know now that my parents never expected me to look. They got lazy. They figured that, even if I found these photos, I'd never know what I was looking at. Two months ago I could've seen these pictures and assumed that this girl"—she plucks a photo of herself, what appears to be a young Haider, and a thin brown-haired girl with bright blue eyes, out of a pile—"was a neighbor kid, someone I used to know but couldn't be bothered to remember.

"But I do remember," she says. "I remember all of it. I remember the day our parents told us that Ella and Emmaline had drowned. I remember crying myself to sleep every night. I remember the day they took us to a place I thought was a hospital. I remember my mother telling me I'd feel better soon. And then, I remember *remembering* nothing. Like time, in my brain, just folded in on itself." She raises her eyebrows. "Do you get what I'm trying to say to you, Kent?"

He glares at her. "I get that you think I'm an idiot."

She smiles.

"Yes, I get what you're saying," he says, obviously irritated. "You're saying you all had your memories wiped. You're saying Warner doesn't even know that they knew each other."

She holds up a finger. "*Didn't* know," she says. "He didn't know until just before the symposium. I tried to warn him—and Castle," she says, glancing at Castle, who's looking at the wall. "I tried to warn them both that something was wrong, that something big was happening and I didn't really understand what or why. Warner didn't believe me, of course. I'm not sure Castle did, either. But I didn't have time to give them proof."

"Wait, what?" I say, my eyebrows furrowing. "You told Warner and Castle? *Before* the symposium? You told them all of this?"

"I tried," she says.

"Why wouldn't you just tell Juliette?" Lily asks.

"You mean Ella."

Lily rolls her eyes. "Sure. Ella. Whatever. Why not warn her directly? Why tell everyone else?"

"I didn't know how she'd take the news," Nazeera says. "I'd been trying to take her temperature from the moment I got here, and I could never figure out how she felt about me. I didn't think she really trusted me. And then after everything that happened"—she hesitates—"it never seemed like the right time. She got shot, she was in recovery, and then she

41

and Warner broke up, and she just . . . I don't know. Spiraled. She wasn't in a healthy headspace. She'd already had to stomach a bunch of revelations and she didn't seem to be handling them well. I wasn't sure she could take much more, to be honest, and I was worried what she might do."

"Murder six hundred people, maybe," Ian mutters under his breath.

"Hey," I snap. "She didn't murder anyone, okay? That was some kind of magic trick."

"It was a distraction," Nazeera says firmly. "James was the only one who saw this for what it was." She sighs. "I think this whole thing was staged to make Ella appear volatile and unhinged. That scene at the symposium will no doubt undermine her position here, at Sector 45, by instilling fear in the soldiers who pledged their allegiance to her. She'll be described as unstable. Irrational. Weak. And then—easily captured. I knew The Reestablishment wanted Ella gone, but I thought they'd just burn the whole sector to the ground. I was wrong. This was a far more efficient tactic. They didn't need to kill off a regiment of perfectly good soldiers and a population of obedient workers," Nazeera says. "All they needed to do was to discredit Ella as their leader."

"So what happens now?" Lily says.

Nazeera hesitates. And then, carefully, she says, "Once they've punished the citizens and thoroughly quashed any hope for rebellion, The Reestablishment will turn everyone against you. Put bounties on your heads, or, worse, threaten to murder loved ones if civilians and soldiers don't turn you in. You were right," she says to Lily. "The soldiers and citizens paid allegiance to Ella, and with both her *and* Warner gone, they'll feel abandoned. They have no reason to trust the rest of you." A pause. "I'd say you have about twenty-four hours before they come for your heads."

Silence falls over the room. For a moment, I think everyone actually stops breathing.

"*Fuck,*" Ian says, dropping his head in his hands.

"Immediate relocation is your best course of action," Nazeera says briskly, "but I don't know that I can be much help in that department. Where you go will be up to your discretion."

"Then what are you even doing here?" I say, irritated. I understand her a little better now—I know that she's been trying to help—but that doesn't change the fact that I still feel like shit. Or that I still don't know how to feel about her. "You showed up just to tell us we're all going to die and that's it?" I shake my head. "So helpful, thanks."

"Kenji," Castle says, finally breaking his silence. "There's no need to attack our guest." His voice is a calm, steadying sound. I've missed it. "She really did try to talk to me—to warn me—while she was here. As for a contingency plan," he says, speaking to the room, "give me a little time. I have friends. We're not alone, as you well know, in our resistance. There's no need to panic, not yet."

"Not yet?" Ian says, incredulous.

"Not yet," Castle says. Then: "Nazeera, what of your brother? Were you able to convince him?"

Nazeera takes a steadying breath, losing some of the tension in her shoulders. "Haider knows," she explains to the rest of us. "He's been remembering things about Ella, too, but his memories of her aren't as strong as mine, and he didn't understand what was happening to him until last night when I decided to tell him what I'd discovered."

"Whoa—Wait," Ian says. "You trust him?"

"I trust him enough," she says. "Besides, I figured he had a right to know; he knew Ella and Emmaline, too. But he wasn't entirely convinced. I don't know what he'll decide to do, not yet, but he definitely seemed shaken up about it, which I think is a good sign. I asked him to do some digging, to find out if any of the other kids were beginning to remember things, too, and he said he would. Right now, that's all I've got."

"Where *are* the other kids?" Winston asks, frowning. "Do they know you're still here?"

Nazeera's expression grows grim. "All the kids were supposed to report back as soon as the symposium was over. Haider should be on his way back to Asia by now. I tried to convince my parents I was staying behind to do more reconnaissance, but I don't think they bought it. I'm sure I'll hear from them soon. I'll handle it as it comes."

"So—Wait—" I glance from her to Castle. "You're staying with us?"

"That wasn't really my plan."

"Oh," I say. "Good. That's good."

She raises an eyebrow at me.

"You know what I mean."

"I don't think I do," she says, and she looks suddenly irritated. "Anyway, even though it *wasn't* my plan to stay, I think I might have to."

My eyes widen. "What? Why?"

"Because," she says, "my parents have been lying to me since I was a kid—stealing my memories and rewriting my history—and I want to know why. Besides"—she takes a deep breath—"I think I know where Ella and Warner are, and I want to help."

WARNER

"Goddammit."

I hear the barely restrained anger in my father's voice just before something slams, hard, into something else. He swears again.

I hesitate outside his door.

And then, impatiently—

"What do you want?"

His voice is practically a growl. I fight the impulse to be intimidated. I make my face a mask. Neutralize my emotions. And then, carefully, I step into his office.

My father is sitting at his desk, but I see only the back of his chair and the unfinished glass of Scotch clutched in his left hand. His papers are in disarray. I notice the paperweight on the floor; the damage to the wall.

Something has gone wrong.

"You wanted to see me," I say.

"What?" My father turns in his chair to face me. "See you for what?"

I say nothing. I've learned by now never to remind him when he's forgotten something.

Finally, he sighs. Says, "Right. Yes." And then: "We'll have to discuss it later."

"Later?" This time, I struggle to hide my feelings. "You said you'd give me an answer today—"

"Something's come up."

Anger wells in my chest. I forget myself. "Something more important than your dying wife?"

My father won't be baited. Instead, he picks up a stack of papers on his desk and says, "Go away."

I don't move.

"I need to know what's going to happen," I say. "I don't want to go to the capital with you—I want to stay here, with Mom—"

"Jesus," he says, slamming his glass down on the desk. "Do you hear yourself?" He looks at me, disgusted. "This behavior is unhealthy. It's disturbing. I've never known a sixteen-year-old boy to be so obsessed with his mother."

Heat creeps up my neck, and I hate myself for it. Hate him for making me hate myself when I say, quietly, "I'm not obsessed with her."

Anderson shakes his head. "You're pathetic."

I take the emotional hit and bury it. With some effort, I manage to sound indifferent when I say, "I just want to know what's going to happen."

Anderson stands up, shoves his hands in his pockets. He looks out the massive window in his office, at the city just beyond.

The view is bleak.

Freeways have become open-air museums for the skeletons of forgotten vehicles. Mountains of trash form ranges along the terrain. Dead birds litter the streets, carcasses still occasionally falling out of the sky. Untamed fires rage in the distance, heavy winds stoking their flames. A thick layer of smog has permanently settled over the city, and the remaining clouds are gray, heavy with rain. We've already begun the process of regulating what passes for livable and unlivable turf, and entire sections of the city have since been shut down. Most of the coastal areas, for example, have been evacuated, the streets and homes flooded, roofs slowly collapsing.

By comparison, the inside of my father's office is a veritable paradise. Everything is still new in here; the wood still smells like wood, every surface shines. The Reestablishment was voted into power just four months ago, and my father is currently the commander and regent of one of our brand-new sectors.

Number 45.

A sudden gust of wind hits the window, and I feel the shudder reverberate through the room. The lights flicker. He doesn't flinch. The world may be falling apart, but The Reestablishment has been doing better than ever. Their plans fell into place more swiftly than they'd expected. And even though my father is already being considered for a huge promotion—to supreme commander of North America—no amount of success seems to soothe him. Lately, he's been more volatile than usual.

Finally, he says, "I have no idea what's going to happen. I don't even know if they'll be considering me for the promotion anymore."

I'm unable to mask my surprise. "Why not?"

Anderson smiles, unhappily, at the window. "A babysitting job gone awry."

"I don't understand."

"I don't expect you to."

"So—we're not moving anymore? We won't be going to the capital?"

Anderson turns back around. "Don't sound so excited. I said I don't know yet. First, I have to figure out how to deal with the problem."

Quietly, I say, "What's the problem?"

Anderson laughs; his eyes crinkle and he looks, for a moment, human. "Suffice it to say that your girlfriend is ruining my goddamn day. As usual."

"My what?" I frown. "Dad, Lena isn't my girlfriend. I don't care what she's telling any—"

"Different girlfriend," Anderson says, and sighs. He won't meet my eyes now. He snatches a file folder from his desk, flips it open, and scans the contents.

I don't have a chance to ask another question.

There's a sudden, sharp knock at the door. At my dad's signal, Delalieu steps inside. He seems more than a little surprised to see me, and, for a moment, says nothing.

"Well?" My dad seems impatient. "Is she here?"

"Y-yes, sir." Delalieu clears his throat. His eyes flit to me again. "Should I bring her up, or would you prefer to meet elsewhere?"

"Bring her up."

Delalieu hesitates. "Are you quite certain, sir?"

I look from my dad to Delalieu. Something is wrong.

My father meets my eyes when he says, "I said, bring her up."

Delalieu nods, and disappears.

My head is a stone, heavy and useless, my eyes cemented to my skull. I maintain consciousness for only seconds at a time. I smell metal, taste metal. An ancient, roaring noise grows loud, then soft, then loud again.

Boots, heavy, near my head.

Voices, but the sounds are muffled, light-years away. I can't move. I feel as though I've been buried, left to rot. A weak orange light flickers behind my eyes and for just a second—just a second—

No.

Nothing.

Days seem to pass. Centuries. I'm only aware enough to know I've been heavily sedated. Constantly sedated. I'm parched, dehydrated to the point of pain. I'd kill for water. Kill for it.

When they move me I feel heavy, foreign to myself. I land hard on a cold floor, the pain ricocheting up my body as if from a distance. I know that, too soon, this pain will catch up to me. Too soon, the sedative will wear off and I'll be alone with my bones and this dust in my mouth.

A swift, hard kick to the gut and my eyes fly open, blackness devouring my open, gasping mouth, seeping into the sockets of my eyes. I feel blind and suffocated at once, and when the shock finally subsides, my limbs give out. Limp.

The spark dies.

KENJI

"Do you want to tell me what the hell is going on?"

I stop, frozen in place, at the sound of Nazeera's voice. I was heading back to my room to close my eyes for a minute. To try to do something about the massive headache ringing through my skull.

We finally, finally, took a break.

A brief recess after hours of exhausting, stressful conversations about next steps and blueprints and something about stealing a plane. It's too much. Even Nazeera, with all her intel, couldn't give me any real assurance that Juliette— sorry, Ella—and Warner were still alive, and just the *chance* that someone out there might be torturing them to death is, like, more than my mind can handle right now. Today has been a shitstorm of shit. A tornado of shit. I can't take it anymore. I don't know whether to sit down and cry or set something on fire.

Castle said he'd brave his way down to the kitchens to see about scrounging up some food for us, and that was the best news I'd heard all day. He also said he'd do his best to placate the soldiers for just a little longer—just long enough for us to figure out exactly what we're going to do next—but I'm not sure how much he can do. It was bad enough when

J got shot. The hours she spent in the medical wing were stressful for the rest of us, too. I really thought the soldiers would revolt right then. They kept stopping me in the halls, yelling about how they thought she was supposed to be *invincible*, that this wasn't the plan, that they didn't decide to risk their lives for a *regular* teenage girl who couldn't take a bullet and goddammit she was supposed to be some supernatural phenomenon, something more than human—

It took forever to calm them down.

But now?

I can only imagine how they'll react when they hear what happened at the symposium. It'll be mutiny, most likely.

I sigh, hard.

"So you're just going to ignore me?"

Nazeera is standing inches away from me. I can feel her, hovering. Waiting. I still haven't said anything. Still haven't turned around. It's not that I don't want to talk—I think I might, sort of, want to talk. Maybe some other day. But right now I'm out of gas. I'm out of James's jokes. I'm fresh out of fake smiles. Right now I'm nothing but pain and exhaustion and raw emotion, and I don't have the bandwidth for another serious conversation. I really don't want to do this right now.

I'd nearly made my escape, too. I'm right here, right in front of my door. My hand is on the handle.

I could just walk away, I think.

I could be that kind of guy, a Warner kind of guy. A jackass kind of guy. Just walk away without a word. Too tired, no thank you, don't want to talk.

Leave me alone.

Instead, I slump forward, rest my hands and forehead against the closed bedroom door. "I'm tired, Nazeera."

"I can't believe you're upset with me."

My eyes close. My nose bumps against the wood. "I'm not upset with you. I'm half asleep."

"You were *mad*. You were mad at me for having the same ability as you. Weren't you?"

I groan.

"Weren't you?" she says again, this time angrily.

I say nothing.

"*Unbelievable*. That is the most petty, ridiculous, *immature*—"

"Yeah, well."

"Do you know how hard it was for me to tell you that? Do you have any idea—" I hear her sharp, angry huff. "Will you at least look at me when I'm talking to you?"

"Can't."

"What?" She sounds startled. "What do you mean you can't?"

"Can't look at you."

She hesitates. "Why not?"

"Too pretty."

She laughs, but angrily, like she might punch me in the face. "Kenji, I'm trying to be serious with you. This is important to me. This is the first time in my whole life I've ever shown other people what I can do. It's the first time I've ever interacted with other people like me. Besides," she says, "I thought we decided we were going to be friends. Maybe that's not a big deal to you, but it's a big deal to me, because I don't make friends easily. And right now you're making me doubt my own judgment."

I sigh so hard I nearly hurt myself.

I push off the door, stare at the wall. "Listen," I say, swallowing hard. "I'm sorry I hurt your feelings. I just— There was a minute back there, before you really started talking, when I thought you'd just, like, lied about things. I didn't understand what was happening. I thought maybe you'd set us up. A bunch of stuff seemed too crazy to be a coincidence. But we've been talking for hours now, and I don't feel that way anymore. I'm not mad anymore. I'm sorry. Can I go now?"

"Of course," she says. "I just . . ." She trails off, like she's confused, and then she touches my arm. No, she doesn't just touch my arm. She takes my arm. She wraps her hand around my bare forearm and tugs, gently.

The contact is hot and immediate. Her skin is soft. My brain feels dim. Dizzy.

"Stop," I say.

She drops her hand.

"Why won't you look at me?" she says.

"I already told you why I won't look at you, and you laughed at me."

She's quiet for so long I wonder if she's walked away. Finally, she says, "I thought you were joking."

"Well, I wasn't."

More silence.

Then: "Do you always say exactly what you're thinking?"

"Most of the time, yeah." Gently, I bang my head against the door. I don't understand why this girl won't let me wallow in peace.

"What are you thinking right now?" she asks.

Jesus Christ.

I look up, at the ceiling, hoping for a wormhole or a bolt of lightning or maybe even an alien abduction—anything to get me out of here, this moment, this relentless, exhausting conversation.

In the absence of miracles, my frustration spikes.

"I'm thinking I want to go to sleep," I say angrily. "I'm thinking I want to be left alone. I'm thinking I've already told you this, a thousand times, and you won't let me go even though I apologized for hurting your feelings. So I guess what I'm really thinking is *I don't understand what you're doing here.* Why do you care so much about what I think?"

"What?" she says, startled. "I don't—"

Finally, I turn around. I feel a little unhinged, like my brain is flooded. There's too much happening. Too much to feel. Grief, fear, exhaustion. Desire.

Nazeera takes a step back when she sees my face.

She's perfect. Perfect everything. Long legs and curves. Her face is insane. Faces shouldn't look like that. Bright, honey-colored eyes and skin like dusk. Her hair is so brown it's nearly black. Thick, heavy, straight. She reminds me of

61

something, of a feeling I don't even know how to describe. And there's something about her that's made me stupid. Drunk, like I could just stare at her and be happy, float forever in this feeling. And then I realize, with a start, that I'm staring at her mouth again.

I never mean to. It just happens.

She's always touching her mouth, tapping that damn diamond piercing under her lip, and I'm just dumb, my eyes following her every move. She's standing in front of me with her arms crossed, running her thumb absently against the edge of her bottom lip, and I can't stop staring. She startles, suddenly, when she realizes I'm looking. Drops her hands to her sides and blinks at me. I have no idea what she's thinking.

"I asked you a question," I say, but this time my voice comes out a little rough, a little too intense. I knew I should've kept my eyes on the wall.

Still, she only stares at me.

"All right. Forget it," I say. "You keep begging me to talk, but the minute I ask *you* a question, you say nothing. That's just great."

I turn away again, reach for the door handle.

And then, still facing the door, I say:

"You know—I'm aware that I haven't done a good job being smooth about this, and maybe I'll never be that kind of guy. But I don't think you should treat me like this, like I'm some idiot nothing, just because I don't know how to be a douchebag."

"What? Kenji, I don't—"

"*Stop*," I say, jerking away from her. She keeps touching my arm, touching me like she doesn't even know she's doing it. It's driving me crazy. "Don't do that."

"Don't do what?"

Finally, angrily, I spin around. I'm breathing hard, my chest rising and falling too fast. "Stop messing with me," I say. "You don't know me. You don't know anything about me. You say you want to be my friend, but you talk to me like I'm an idiot. You touch me, constantly, like I'm a child, like you're trying to comfort me, like you have no idea that I'm a grown-ass man who might *feel* something when you put your hands on me like that." She tries to speak and I cut her off. "I don't care what you think you know about me—or how stupid you think I am—but right now I'm exhausted, okay? I'm done. So if you want nice Kenji maybe you should check back in the morning, because right now all I've got is jack shit in the way of pleasantries."

Nazeera looks frozen. Stunned. She stares at me, her lips slightly parted, and I'm thinking this is it, this is how I die, she's going to pull out a knife and cut me open, rearrange my organs, put on a puppet show with my intestines. What a way to go.

But when she finally speaks, she doesn't sound angry. She sounds a little out of breath.

Nervous.

"I don't think you're a child," she says.

I have no idea what to say to that.

63

She takes a step forward, presses her hands flat against my torso, and I turn into a statue. Her hands seem to sear into my body, heat pressing between us, even through my shirt.

I feel like I might be dreaming.

She runs her hands up my chest and that simple motion feels so good I'm suddenly terrified. I feel magnetized to her, frozen in place. Afraid to wake up.

"What are you doing?" I whisper.

She's still staring at my chest when she says, again, "I don't think you're a child."

"Nazeera."

She lifts her head to meet my eyes, and a flash of feeling, hot and painful, shoots down my spine.

"And I don't think you're stupid," she says.

Wrong.

I'm definitely stupid.

So stupid. I can't even think right now.

"Okay," I say stupidly. I don't know what to do with my hands. I mean, I *know* what to do with my hands, I'm just worried that if I touch her she might laugh and then, probably, kill me.

She smiles then, smiles so big I feel my heart explode, make a mess inside my chest. "So you're not going to make a move?" she says, still smiling. "I thought you liked me. I thought that's what this whole thing was all about."

"*Like* you?" I blink at her. "I don't even know you."

"Oh," she says, and her smile disappears. She begins to

pull away and she can't meet my eyes and then, I don't know what comes over me—

I grab her hand, open my bedroom door, and lock us both inside.

She kisses me first.

I have an out-of-body moment, like I can't believe this is actually happening to me. I can't understand what I did to make this possible, because according to my calculations I messed this up on a hundred different levels and, in fact, I was pretty sure she was pissed at me up until, like, five minutes ago.

And then I tell myself to shut up.

Her kiss is soft, her hands tentative against my chest, but I wrap my arms around her waist and kiss her, really kiss her, and then somehow we're against the wall and her hands are around my neck and she parts her lips for me, sighs in my mouth, and that small sound of pleasure drives me crazy, floods my body with heat and desire so intense I can hardly stand.

We break apart, breathing hard, and I stare at her like an idiot, my brain still too numb to figure out exactly how I got here. Then again, who cares how I got here. I kiss her again and it nearly kills me. She feels so good, so soft. Perfect. She's perfect, fits perfectly in my arms, like we were made for this, like we've done this a thousand times before, and she smells like shampoo, like something sweet. Perfume, maybe. I don't know. Whatever it is, it's in my head now.

Killing brain cells.

When we break apart she looks different, her eyes darker, deeper. She turns away and when she turns back again she's smiling at me and for a second I think we might both be thinking the same thing. But I'm wrong, of course, so wrong, because I was thinking about how I'm, like, the luckiest guy on the planet and *she*—

She puts her hand on my chest and says, softly:

"You're really not my type."

That knocks the wind out of me. I drop my arms from around her waist and take a sudden, uncertain step backward.

She cringes, covers her face with both hands. "I don't—wow—I don't mean you're not my *type*." She shakes her head, hard. "I just mean I don't normally—I don't usually do this."

"Do what?" I say, still wounded.

"This," she says, and gestures between us. "I don't—I don't, like, just go around kissing guys I barely know."

"Okay." I frown. "Do you want to leave?"

"No." Her eyes widen.

"Then what do you want?"

"I don't know," she says, and her eyes go soft again. "I kind of just want to look at you for a minute. I meant what I said about your face," she says, and smiles. "You have a great face."

I go suddenly weak in the knees. I literally have to sit down. I walk over to my bed and collapse backward, my head hitting the pillow. It feels too good to be horizontal. If there weren't a gorgeous woman in my room right now, I'd be asleep already.

"Just so you know, this is not a move," I say, mostly to the ceiling. "I'm not trying to get you to sleep with me. I just literally had to lie down. Thank you for appreciating my face. I've always thought I had an underappreciated face."

She laughs, hard, and sits next to me, teetering on the edge of the bed, near my arm. "You're really not what I was expecting," she says.

I peer at her. "What were you expecting?"

"I don't know." She shakes her head. Smiles at me. "I guess I wasn't expecting to like you so much."

My chest goes tight. Too tight. I force myself to sit up, to meet her eyes.

"Come here," I say. "You're too far away."

She kicks off her boots and shifts closer, folding her legs up underneath her. She doesn't say a word. Just stares at me. And then, carefully, she touches my face, the line of my jaw. My eyes close, my mind swimming with nonsense. I lean back, rest my head against the wall behind us. I know it doesn't say much for my self-confidence that I'm so surprised this is happening, but I can't help it.

I never thought I'd get this lucky.

"Kenji," she says softly.

I open my eyes.

"I can't be your girlfriend."

I blink. Sit up a little. "Oh," I say.

It hadn't occurred to me until exactly this moment that I might even want something like that, but now that I'm thinking about it, I know that I do. A girlfriend is exactly what I want. I want a relationship. I want something real.

"It would never work, you know?" She tilts her head, looks at me like it's obvious, like I know as well as she does why things would never work out between us. "We're not—" She motions between our bodies to indicate something I don't understand. "We're so different, right? Plus, I don't even live here."

"Right," I say, but my mouth feels suddenly numb. My whole face feels numb. "You don't even live here."

And then, just as I'm trying to figure out how to pick up the pieces of my obliterated hopes and dreams, she climbs into my lap. Zero to sixty. My body malfunctions. Overheats.

She presses her face into my cheek and kisses me, softly, just underneath my jaw, and I feel myself melt into the wall, into the air.

I don't understand what's happening anymore. She likes me but she doesn't want to be with me. She's not going to be with me but she's going to sit on my lap and kiss me into oblivion.

Sure. Okay.

I let her touch me the way she wants to, let her put her hands on my body and kiss me wherever, however she wants. She touches me in a proprietary way, like I already belong to her, and I don't mind. I kind of love it. And I let her take the lead for as long as I can bear it. She's pulling up my shirt, running her hands across my bare skin and telling me how much she likes my body, and I really feel like—like I can't breathe. I feel too hot. Delirious but sharp, aware of this moment in an almost primal way.

She helps me pull off my shirt and then she just looks at me, first at my face and then at my chest, and she runs her hands across my shoulders, down my arms. "Wow," she says softly. "You're so gorgeous."

That's it for me.

I pick her up off my lap and lay her down, on her back, and she gasps, stares at me like she's surprised. And then, *deep*, her eyes go deep and dark, and she's looking at my mouth but I decide to kiss her neck, the curve of her shoulder.

"Nazeera," I whisper, hardly recognizing the sound of my own voice. "I want you so badly it might kill me."

Suddenly, someone is banging on my door.

"Bro, where the hell did you go?" Ian shouts. "Castle brought dinner up like ten minutes ago."

I sit up too fast. I nearly pull a muscle. Nazeera laughs out loud, and even though she claps a hand over her mouth to muffle the sound, she's not quick enough.

"Uh—Hello?" Ian again. "Kenji?"

"I'll be right there," I shout back.

I hear him hesitate—his footsteps uncertain—and then he's gone. I drop my head into my hands. Suddenly, everything comes rushing back to me. For a few minutes this moment with Nazeera felt like the whole world, a welcome reprieve from all the war and death and struggle. But now, with a little oxygen in my brain, I feel stupid. I don't know what I was thinking.

Juliette might be *dead*.

I get to my feet. I pull my shirt on quickly, careful not to meet her eyes. For some reason, I can't bring myself to look at Nazeera. I have no regrets about kissing her—it's just that I also feel suddenly guilty, like I was doing something wrong. Something selfish and inappropriate.

"I'm sorry," I say. "I don't know what got into me."

Nazeera is tugging on her boots. She looks up, surprised. "What do you mean?"

"What we just"—I sigh, hard—"I don't know. I forgot, for a moment, everything we have to do. The fact that Juliette might be out there, somewhere, being tortured to death. Warner might be dead. We'll have to pack up and run, leave this place behind. God, there's so much happening and I just—My head was in the wrong place. I'm sorry."

Nazeera is standing up now. She looks upset. "Why do you keep apologizing to me? Stop apologizing to me."

"You're right. I'm sorry." I wince. "I mean—You know what I mean. Anyway, we should go."

"Kenji—"

"Listen, you said you didn't want a relationship, right? You didn't want to be my girlfriend? You don't think that this"—I mimic what she did earlier, motioning between us—"could ever work? Well, then—" I take a breath. Run a hand through my hair. "This is what not being my girlfriend looks like. Okay? There are only a few people in my life who actually care about me, and right now my best friend is probably being murdered by a bunch of psychopaths, and I should be out there, doing something."

"I didn't realize you and Warner were so close," she says quietly.

"What?" I frown. "No, I'm talking about Juliette," I say. "Ella. Whatever."

Nazeera's eyebrows go high.

"Anyway, I'm sorry. We should probably just keep this professional, right? You're not looking for anything serious, and I don't know how to have casual relationships anyway. I always end up caring too much, to be honest, so this probably wasn't a good idea."

"Oh."

"Right?" I look at her, hoping, suddenly, that there was something I missed, something more than the cool distance in her eyes. "Didn't you just tell me that we're too different? That you don't even live here?"

She turns away. "Yes."

"And have you changed your mind in the last thirty seconds? About being my girlfriend?"

She's still staring at the wall when she says, "No."

Pain shoots up my spine, gathers in my chest. "Okay then," I say, and nod. "Thanks for your honesty. I have to go."

She cuts past me, walks out the door. "I'm coming, too."

JULIETTE

I've been sitting in the back of a police car for over an hour. I haven't been able to cry, not yet. And I don't know what I'm waiting for, but I know what I did, and I'm pretty sure I know what happens next.

I killed a little boy.

I don't know how I did it. I don't know why it happened. I just know that it was me, my hands, me. I did that. Me.

I wonder if my parents will show up.

Instead, three men in military uniforms march up to my window. One of them flings open the door and aims a machine gun at my chest.

"Get out," he barks. "Out with your hands up."

My heart is racing, terror propelling me out of the car so fast I stumble, slamming my knee into the ground. I don't need to check to know that I'm bleeding; the pain of the fresh wound is already searing. I bite my lip to keep from crying out, force the tears back.

No one helps me up.

I want to tell them that I'm only fourteen, that I don't know a lot about a lot of things, but that I know enough. I've watched TV shows about this sort of thing. I know they can't charge me as an adult. I know that they shouldn't be treating me like this.

But then I remember that the world is different now. We have a new government now, one that doesn't care how we used to do things. Maybe none of that matters anymore.

My heart beats faster.

I'm shoved into the backseat of a black car, and before I know it, I'm deposited somewhere new: somewhere that looks like an ordinary office building. It's tall. Steel gray. It seems old and decrepit—some of its windows are cracked—and the whole thing looks sad.

But when I walk inside I'm stunned to discover a blinding, gleaming interior. I look around, taking in the marble floors, the rich carpets and furnishings. The ceilings are high, the architecture modern but elegant. It's all glass and marble and stainless steel.

I've never been anywhere so beautiful.

And I haven't even had a moment to take it all in before I'm greeted by a thin, older man with even thinner brown hair.

The soldiers flanking me step back as he steps forward.

"Ms. Ferrars?" he says.

"Yes?"

"You are to come with me."

I hesitate. "Who are you?"

He studies me a moment and then seems to make a decision. "You may call me Delalieu."

"Okay," I say, the word disappearing into a whisper.

I follow Delalieu into a glass elevator and watch him use a key card to authorize the lift. Once we're in motion, I find the courage to speak.

"Where am I?" I ask. "What's happening?"

His answer comes automatically. "You are in Sector 45

headquarters. You're here to have a meeting with the chief commander and regent of Sector 45." He doesn't look at me when he speaks, but there's nothing in his tone that feels threatening. So I ask another question.

"Why?"

The elevator doors ping as they open. Delalieu finally turns to look at me. "You'll find out in just a moment."

I follow Delalieu down a hall and wait, quietly, outside a door while he knocks. He peeks his head inside when the door opens, announces his presence, and then motions for me to follow him in.

When I do, I'm surprised.

There's a beautiful man in military uniform—I'm assuming he's the commander—standing in front of a large, wooden desk, his arms crossed against his chest. He's staring me straight in the eye, and I'm suddenly so overwhelmed I feel myself blush.

I've never seen anyone so handsome before.

I look down, embarrassed, and study the laces of my tennis shoes. I'm grateful for my long hair. It serves as a dark, heavy curtain, shielding my face from view.

"Look at me."

The command is sharp and clear. I look up, nervously, to meet his eyes. He has thick, dark brown hair. Eyes like a storm. He looks at me for so long I feel goose bumps rise along my skin. He won't look away, and I feel more terrified by the moment. This man's eyes are full of anger. Darkness. There's something genuinely frightening about him, and my heart begins to hammer.

"You're growing up quickly," he says.

I stare at him, confused, but he's still studying my face.

"Fourteen years old," he says quietly. "Such a complicated age for a young girl." Finally, he sighs. Looks away. "It always breaks my heart to break beautiful things."

"I don't—I don't understand," I say, feeling suddenly ill.

He looks up again. "You're aware of what you did today?"

I freeze. Words pile up in my throat, die in my mouth.

"Yes or no?" he demands.

"Y-yes," I say quickly. "Yes."

"And do you know why you did it? Do you know how you did it?"

I shake my head, my eyes filling fast with tears. "It was an accident," I whisper. "I didn't know—I didn't know that this—"

"Does anyone else know about your sickness?"

"No." I stare at him, my eyes wide even as tears blur my vision. "I mean, n-not, not really—just my parents—but no one really understands what's wrong with me. I don't even understand—"

"You mean you didn't plan this? It wasn't your intention to murder the little boy?"

"No!" I cry out, and then clap both hands over my mouth. "No," I say, quietly now. "I was trying to help him. He'd fallen to the floor and I—I didn't know. I swear I didn't know."

"Liar."

I'm still shaking my head, wiping away tears with shaking hands. "It was an accident. I swear, I didn't mean to—I d-didn't—"

"Sir." It's Delalieu. His voice.

I didn't realize he was still in the room.

I sniff, hard, wiping quickly at my face, but my hands are still

78

shaking. I try, again, to swallow back the tears. To pull myself together.

"Sir," Delalieu says more firmly, "perhaps we should conduct this interview elsewhere."

"I don't see why that's necessary."

"I don't mean to seem impertinent, sir, but I really feel that you might be better served conducting this interview privately."

I dare to turn, to look up at him. And that's when I notice the third person in the room.

A boy.

My breath catches in my throat with an almost audible gasp. A single tear escapes down my cheek and I brush it away, even as I stare at him. I can't help it—I can't look away. He has the kind of face I've never seen in real life. He's more handsome than the commander. More beautiful. Still, there's something unnerving about him, something cold and alien about his face that makes him difficult to look at. He's almost too perfect. He has a sharp jawline and sharp cheekbones and a sharp, straight nose. Everything about him reminds me of a blade. His face is pale. His eyes are a stunning, clear green, and he has rich, golden hair. And he's staring at me, his eyes wide with an emotion I can't decipher.

A throat clears.

The spell is broken.

Heat floods my face and I avert my eyes, mortified I didn't look away sooner.

I hear the commander mutter angrily under his breath. "Unbelievable," he says. "Always the same."

I look up.

"Aaron," he says sharply. "Get out."

The boy—his name must be Aaron—startles. He stares at the commander for a second, and then glances at the door. But he doesn't move.

"Delalieu, please escort my son from the room, as he seems presently unable to remember how to move his legs."

His son.

Wow. That explains the face.

"Yes, sir, of course, sir."

Aaron's expression is impossible to read. I catch him looking at me, just once more, and when he finds me staring, he frowns. It's not an unkind look.

Still, I turn away.

He and Delalieu move past me as they exit, and I pretend not to notice when I hear him whisper—

"Who is she?"

—as they walk away.

"Ella? Are you all right?"

I blink, slowly clearing the webbing of blackness obscuring my vision. Stars explode and fade behind my eyes and I try to stand, the carpet pressing popcorn impressions into my palms, metal digging into my flesh. I'm wearing manacles, glowing cuffs that emit a soft, blue light that leaches the life from my skin, makes my own hands seem sinister.

The woman at my door is staring at me. She smiles.

"Your father and I thought you might be hungry," she

says. "We made you dinner."

I can't move. My feet seem bolted in place, the pinks and purples of the walls and floors assaulting me from every corner. I'm standing in the middle of the bizarre museum of what was likely my childhood bedroom—staring at what might be my biological mother—and I feel like I might throw up. The lights are suddenly too bright, the voices too loud. Someone walks toward me and the movement feels exaggerated, the footsteps thudding hard and fast in my ears. My vision goes in and out and the walls seem to shake. The floor shifts, tilts backward.

I fall, hard, onto the floor.

For a minute, I hear nothing but my heartbeat. Loud, so loud, pressing in on me, assaulting me with a cacophony of sound so disturbing I double over, press my face into the carpet and scream.

I'm hysterical, my bones shaking in my skin, and the woman picks me up, reels me in, and I tear away, still screaming—

"Where is everyone?" I scream. "What's happening to me?" I scream. "Where am I? Where's Warner and Kenji and oh my God—*oh my God*—all those people—all those people I k-killed—"

Vomit inches up my throat, choking me, and I try and fail to suppress the images, the horrible, terrifying images of bodies cleaved open, blood snaking down ridges of poorly torn flesh and something pierces my mind, something sharp and blinding and suddenly I'm on my knees, heaving the meager contents of my stomach into a pink basket.

I can hardly breathe.

My lungs are overworked, my stomach still threatening to betray me, and I'm gasping, my hands shaking hard as I try to stand. I spin around, the room moving more quickly than I do, and I see only flashes of pink, flashes of purple.

I sway.

Someone catches me again, this time new arms, and the man who calls me his daughter holds me like I'm his child and he says, "Honey, you don't have to think about them anymore. You're safe now."

"Safe?" I rear back, eyes wild. "Who *are* you—?"

The woman takes my hand. Squeezes my fingers even as I wrench free from her grip. "I'm your mother," she says. "And I've decided it's time for you to come home."

"What"—I grab two fistfuls of her shirt—"have you done *with my friends?*" I scream. And then I shake her, shake her so hard she actually looks scared for a second, and then I try to pick her up and throw her into the wall but remember, with a start, that my powers have been cut off, that I have to rely on mere anger and adrenaline and I turn around, suddenly furious, feeling more certain by the second that I've begun to hallucinate, hallucinate, when

unexpectedly

she slaps me in the face.

Hard.

I blink, stunned, but manage to stay upright.

"Ella Sommers," she says sharply, "you will pull yourself

together." Her eyes flash as she appraises me. "What is this ridiculous, dramatic behavior? Worried about your *friends*? Those people are not your friends."

My cheek burns and half my mouth feels numb but I say, "Yes, yes they're my fr—"

She slaps me again.

My eyes close. Reopen. I feel suddenly dizzy.

"We are your parents," she says in a harsh whisper. "Your father and I have brought you home. You should be grateful."

I taste blood. I reach up, touch my lip. My fingers come away red. "Where's Emmaline?" Blood is pooling in my mouth and I spit it out, onto the floor. "Have you kidnapped her, too? Does she know what you've done? That you donated us to The Reestablishment? Sold our bodies to the world?"

A third, swift slap.

I feel it ring in my skull.

"*How dare you.*" My mother's face flushes crimson. "How *dare* you—You have no idea what we've built, all these years—The sacrifices we made for our *future*—"

"Now, Evie," my dad says, and places a calming hand on her shoulder. "Everything is going to be okay. Ella just needs a little time to settle in, that's all." He glances at me. "Isn't that right, Ella?"

It hits me then, in that moment. Everything. It hits me, all at once, with a frightening, destabilizing force—

I've been kidnapped by a pair of crazy people and I might

never see my friends again. In fact, my friends might be dead. My *parents* might've killed them. All of them.

The realization is like suffocation.

Tears fill my throat, my mouth, my eyes—

"Where," I say, my chest heaving, "is Warner? What did you do to him?"

Evie's expression goes suddenly murderous. "You and that damn boy. If I have to hear his name one more time—"

"Where's Warner?" I'm screaming again. "Where is he? Where's Kenji? What did you do with them?"

Evie looks suddenly exhausted. She pinches the bridge of her nose between her thumb and index finger.

"Darling," she says, but she isn't looking at me, she's looking at my father. "Will you handle this, please? I have a terrible headache and several urgent phone calls to return."

"Of course, my love." And he pulls a syringe from his pocket and stabs it, swiftly, into my neck.

KENJI

The common room is really growing on me.

I used to walk by, all the time, and wonder why Warner ever thought we'd need a common room this big. There's tons of seating and a lot of room to spread out, but I always thought it was a waste of space. I secretly wished Warner had used the square footage for our bedrooms.

Now I get it.

When Nazeera and I walk in, ten minutes late to the impromptu pizza party, everyone is here. *Brendan* is here. He's sitting in a corner being fussed over by Castle and Alia, and I nearly tackle him. I don't, of course, because it's obvious he's still in recovery, but I'm relieved to find that he looks okay. Mostly he looks wrung-out, but he's not wearing a sling or anything, so I'm guessing the girls didn't run into any problems when they were patching him up. That's a great sign.

I spot Winston walking across the room and I catch up to him, clap him on the back. "Hey," I say, when he turns around. "You okay?"

He's balancing a couple of paper plates, both of which are already sagging under the weight of too much pizza, and he smiles with his whole face when he says, "I hate today.

Today is a garbage fire. I hate everything about today except for the fact that Brendan is okay and we have pizza. Other than that, today can go straight to hell."

"Yeah. I feel that so much." And then, after a pause, I say quietly: "So I'm guessing you never had that conversation with Brendan, huh?"

Winston goes suddenly pink. "I said I was waiting for the right time. Does this seem like the right time to you?"

"Good point." I sigh. "I guess I was just hoping you had some good news. We could all use some good news right now."

Winston shoots me a sympathetic look. "No word on Juliette?"

I shake my head. Feel suddenly sick. "Has anyone told you her real name is Ella?"

"I heard," Winston says, raising his eyebrows. "That whole story is batshit."

"Yeah," I say. "Today is the worst."

"Fuck today," Winston says.

"Don't forget about tomorrow," I say. "Tomorrow's going to suck, too."

"What? Why?" The paper plates in Winston's hands are going translucent from pizza grease. "What's happening tomorrow?"

"Last I heard we were jumping ship," I say. "Running for our lives. I'm assuming it's going to suck."

"*Shit*." Winston nearly drops his plates. "Seriously? Brendan needs more time to rest." Then, after a beat:

"Where are we going to go?"

"The other side of the continent, apparently," Ian says as he walks over.

He hands me a plate of pizza. I murmur a quick thanks and stare at the pizza, wondering whether I'd be able to shove the whole thing in my mouth at once. Probably not.

"Do you know something we don't?" Winston says to Ian, his glasses slipping down the bridge of his nose. Winston tries, unsuccessfully, to shove them back up with his forearm, and Ian steps up to do it for him.

"I know a lot of things you don't know," Ian says. "The first of which is that Kenji was definitely hooking up with Nazeera, like, five seconds ago."

My mouth nearly falls open before I remember there's food in it. I swallow, too quickly, and choke. I'm still coughing as I look around, panicking that Nazeera might be within earshot. Only when I spot her across the room speaking with Sonya and Sara do I finally relax.

I glare at Ian. "What the hell is wrong with you?"

Winston, at least, has the decency to whisper-yell when he says, "You were hooking up with Nazeera? We were only gone a few hours!"

"I did not hook up with Nazeera," I lie.

Ian takes a bite of pizza. "Whatever, bro. No judgment. The world's on fire. Have some fun."

"We didn't"—I sigh, look away—"it wasn't like that. It's not even anything. We were just, like—" I make some random gesture with my hand that means exactly nothing.

Ian raises his eyebrows.

"Okay," Winston says, shooting me a look. "We'll talk about the Nazeera thing later." He turns to Ian. "What's happening tomorrow?"

"We bail," Ian says. "Be ready to go at dawn."

"Right, I heard that part," Winston says, "but where are we going?"

Ian shrugs. "Castle has the news," he says. "That's all I heard. He was waiting for Kenji and Nazeera to put their clothes back on before he told everyone the details."

I tilt my head at Ian, threatening him with a single look. "Nothing is going on with me and Nazeera," I say. "Drop it."

"All right," he says, picking at his pizza. "Makes sense. I mean she's not even that pretty."

My plate falls out of my hand. Pizza hits the floor. I feel a sudden, unwelcome need to punch Ian in the face. "Are you—Are you out of your mind? Not even—She's, like, the most beautiful woman I've ever seen in my *life*, and you're out here saying she's *not even that pretty*? Have y—"

"See what I'm saying?" Ian cuts me off. He's looking at Winston.

"Wow," Winston says, staring solemnly at the pizza on the ground. "Yeah, Kenji is definitely full of shit."

I drag a hand across my face. "I hate you guys."

"Anyway," Ian says, "I heard Castle's news has something to do with Nouria."

My head snaps back up.

Nouria.

I nearly forgot. This morning, just before the symposium, the twins told me they'd uncovered something—something to do with the poison in the bullets Juliette had been shot with—that led them back to Nouria.

But so much happened today that I never had the chance to follow up. Find out what happened.

"Did you hear about that?" Ian asks me, raising an eyebrow. "She sent a message, apparently. That's what the girls are saying."

"Yeah," I say, and frown. "I heard."

I honestly have no idea how this might shake out.

It's been at least ten years since the last time Castle saw his daughter, Nouria. Darrence and Jabari, his two boys, were murdered by police officers when they refused to let the men into their house without a warrant. This was before The Reestablishment took over.

Castle wasn't home that day, but Nouria was.

She watched it happen. Castle said he felt like he'd lost three children that day. Nouria never recovered. Instead, she grew detached. Listless. She stopped coming home at normal hours and then—one day—she disappeared. The Reestablishment was always picking kids up off the street and shipping them wherever they felt there was a need to fill. Nouria was collected against her will; picked up and packaged for another sector. Castle knew for certain that it happened, because The Reestablishment sent him a receipt for his child. A fucking receipt.

Everyone from Point knew Castle's story. He always

made an effort to be honest, to share the hardest, most painful memories from his life so that the rest of us didn't feel like we were suffering alone.

Castle thought he'd never see Nouria again.

So if she's reaching out now—

Just then, Castle catches my eye. He glances at me, then at Nazeera. A hint of a smile touches his lips and then it's gone, his spine straight as he addresses the room. He looks good, I realize. He looks bright, alive like I haven't seen him in years. His locs are pulled back, tied neatly at the base of his neck. His faded blue blazer still fits him perfectly, even after all these years.

"I have news," he says.

But I'm pretty sure I know what's coming next.

Nouria lives in Sector 241, thousands of miles away, and cross-sector communication is nearly unheard of. Only rebel groups are brave enough to risk sending coded messages across the continent. Ian and Winston know this. I know this.

Everyone knows this.

Which means Castle is probably here to tell us that Nouria has gone rogue.

Ha.

Like father, like daughter.

WARNER

"Hi," I say.

She turns at the sound of my voice and startles when she sees my face. Her eyes widen. And I feel it, right away, when her emotions change.

She's attracted to me.

She's attracted to me, and the revelation makes me happy. I don't know why. It's not new. I learned, long ago, that lots of people find me attractive. Men. Women. Especially older women, a phenomenon I still don't understand. But this—

It makes me happy.

"Hi," *she says, but she won't look at me.*

I realize she's blushing. I'm surprised. There's something sweet about her, something gentle and sweet I wasn't really expecting.

"Are you doing all right?" *I ask.*

It's a stupid question. The girl is clearly in an awful position. Right now she's only in our custody for as long as it takes my father to decide what to do with her. She's currently in a fairly comfortable holding facility here on base, but she'll likely end up in a juvenile detention center. I'm not sure. I've heard my father talk about running more tests on her first. Her parents are apparently hysterical, desperate for us to take her in and deal with her. Offer a diagnosis. They think she killed the little boy on purpose. They think their daughter is insane.

I think she seems just fine.

I can't stop looking at her. My eyes travel her face more than once, studying her features carefully. She seems so familiar to me, like I might've seen her before. Maybe in a dream.

I'm aware, even as I think it, that my thoughts are ridiculous.

But I was drawn down here, magnetized to her by something beyond my control. I know I shouldn't have come. I have no business talking to her, and if my father found me in here he'd likely murder me. But I've tried, for days, to forget her face, and I couldn't. I try to sleep at night and her likeness materializes in the blackness. I needed to see her again.

I don't know how to defend it.

Finally, she speaks, and I shake free from my reverie. I remind myself that I've asked her a question.

"Yes, thank you," she says, her eyes on the floor. "I'm doing fine."

She's lying.

I want her to look up, to meet my eyes. She doesn't, and I find it frustrating.

"Will you look at me?" I say.

That works well enough.

But when she looks me directly in the eye I feel my heart go suddenly, terrifyingly still. A skipped beat. A moment of death.

And then—

Fast. My heart is racing too fast.

I've never understood my ability to be so aware of others, but it's often served me well. In most cases, it offers me an advantage.

In this case, it's nothing short of overwhelming.

Right now, everything is hitting me twice as hard. I feel two sets of emotions—hers and mine, the both of them intertwined. We seem to be feeling the same things at the same time. It's disorienting, so heady I can hardly catch my breath.

"Why?" she says.

I blink. "What?"

"Why do you want me to look at you?"

I take a breath. Clear my head, consider my options. I could tell the truth. I could tell a lie. I could be evasive, change the subject.

Finally, I say, "Do I know you?"

She laughs and looks away. "No," she says. "Definitely not."

She bites her lip and I feel her sudden nervousness, hear the spike in her breathing. I draw closer to her almost without realizing it.

She looks up at me then, and I realize, with a thrill, how close we are. Her eyes are big and beautiful, blue green. Like the globe, I think. Like the whole world.

She's looking at me and I feel suddenly off-balance.

"What's wrong?" she says.

I have to step away from her. "I don't—" I look at her again. "Are you sure I don't know you?"

And she smiles. Smiles at me and my heart shatters.

"Trust me," she says. "I'd remember you."

KENJI

Delalieu.

I can't believe we forgot about Delalieu.

I thought Castle's news would be about Nouria. I thought he was going to tell us that she reached out to say that she was some fancy resistance leader now, that we'd be welcome to crash at her place for a while. Instead, Castle's news was—

Delalieu.

Homeboy came through.

Castle steps aside and allows the lieutenant to enter the room, and even though he seems stiff and out of place, Delalieu looks genuinely upset. I feel it, like a punch to the gut, the moment I see his face. *Grief.*

He clears his throat two or three times.

When he finally speaks, his voice is steadier than I've ever heard it. "I've come to reassure you," he says, "in person, that I'll make sure your group remains safe here, for as long as I can manage." A pause. "I don't know yet exactly what's happening right now, but I know it can't be good. I'm worried it won't end well if you stay, and I'm committed to helping you while you plan your escape."

Everyone is quiet.

"Um, thank you," I say, breaking the silence. I look around the room when I say, "We really appreciate that. But, uh, how much time do we have?"

Delalieu shakes his head. "I'm afraid I can't guarantee your safety for more than a week. But I'm hoping a few days' reprieve will give you the necessary time to figure out your next steps. Find a safe place to go. In the meantime, I'll provide whatever assistance I can."

"Okay," Ian says, but he looks skeptical. "That's really . . . generous."

Delalieu clears his throat again. "It must be hard to know whether you should trust me. I understand your concerns. But I fear I've stayed silent for t-too long," he says, his voice losing its steadiness. "And now—with—With what's happened to Warner and to Ms. Ferrars—" He stops, his voice breaking on the last word. He looks up, looks me in the eye. "I'm sure Warner told none of you that I am his grandfather."

My jaw drops open. Actually drops open.

Castle is the only person in the room who doesn't look shocked.

"You're Warner's grandfather?" Adam says, getting to his feet. The terrified look in his eyes breaks my heart.

"Yes," Delalieu says quietly. "On his mother's side." He meets Adam's eyes, acknowledging, silently, that he knows. Knows that Adam is Anderson's illegitimate son. That he knows everything.

Adam sits back down, relief apparent on his face.

102

"I can only imagine what an unhappy life yours must've been," Brendan says. I turn to look at him, surprised to hear his voice. He's been so quiet all this time. But then, of course Brendan would be compassionate. Even to someone like Delalieu, who stepped aside and said nothing while Anderson set the world on fire. "But I'm grateful—we're all grateful," Brendan says, "for your help today."

Delalieu manages a smile. "It's the least I can do," he says, and turns to go.

"Did you know her?" Lily says, her voice sharp. "As Ella?"

Delalieu freezes in place, still half turned toward the exit.

"Because if you're Warner's grandfather," Lily says, "and you've been working under Anderson for this long—you must've known her."

Slowly, very slowly, Delalieu turns to face us. He seems tense, nervous like I've never seen him. He says nothing, but the answer is written all over his face. The twitch in his hands.

Jesus.

"How long?" I say, anger building inside of me. "How long did you know her and say nothing?"

"I don't—I d-don't—"

"*How long?*" I say, my hand already reaching for the gun tucked in the waistband of my pants.

Delalieu takes a jerky step backward. "Please don't," he says, his eyes wild. "Please don't ask this of me. I can give you aid. I can provide you with weapons and transportation—anything you need—but I can't—You don't underst—"

"*Coward,*" Nazeera says, standing up. She looks stunning,

tall and strong and steady. I love watching that girl move. Talk. Breathe. Whatever. "You watched and said nothing as Anderson tortured his own children. Didn't you?"

"No," Delalieu says desperately, his face flushing with emotion I've never seen in him before. "No, that's not—"

Castle picks up a chair with single flick of his hand and drops it, unceremoniously, in front of Delalieu.

"Sit down," he says, a violent, unguarded rage flashing in his eyes.

Delalieu obeys.

"How long?" I say again. "How long have you known her as Ella?"

"I—I've"—Delalieu hesitates, looks around—"I've known Ella s-since she was a child," he says finally.

I feel the blood leave my body.

His clear, explicit confession is too much. It means too much. I sag under the weight of it—the lies, the conspiracies. I sink back into my chair and my heart splinters for Juliette, for all she's suffered at the hands of the people meant to protect her. I can't form the words I need to tell Delalieu he's a spineless piece of shit. It's Nazeera who still has the presence of mind to spear him.

Her voice is soft—lethal—when she speaks.

"You've known Ella since she was a child," Nazeera says. "You've been here, working here, helping Anderson since Ella was a *child*. That means you helped Anderson put her in the custody of abusive, adoptive parents and you stood by as they tortured her, as Anderson tortured her, over and over—"

"No," Delalieu cries out. "I d-didn't condone any of that. Ella was supposed to grow up in a normal home environment. She was supposed to be given nurturing parents and a stable upbringing. Those were the terms everyone agreed t—"

"Bullshit," Nazeera says, her eyes flashing. "You know as well as I do that her adoptive parents were monsters—"

"Paris changed the terms of the agreement," Delalieu shouts angrily.

Nazeera raises an eyebrow, unmoved.

But something seems to have loosened Delalieu's tongue, something like fear or guilt or pent-up rage, because suddenly the words rush out of him.

"Paris went back on his word as soon as Ella was in his custody," he says. "He thought no one would find out. Back then he and I were about the same, as far as rank went, in The Reestablishment. We often worked closely together because of our family ties, and I was, as a result, privy to the choices he made."

Delalieu shakes his head.

"But I discovered too late that he purposely chose adoptive parents who exhibited abusive, dangerous behavior. When I confronted him about it he argued that any abuse Ella suffered at the hands of her surrogate parents would only encourage her powers to manifest, and he had the statistics to support his claim. I tried to voice my concerns—I reported him; I told the council of commanders that he was hurting her, *breaking* her—but he made my concerns sound like the desperate histrionics of someone unwilling to do what was necessary for the cause."

I can see the color creeping up Delalieu's neck, his anger only barely contained.

"I was repeatedly overruled. Demoted. I was punished for questioning his tactics.

"But I knew Paris was wrong," he says quietly. "Ella withered. When I first met her she was a strong girl with a joyful spirit. She was unfailingly kind and upbeat." He hesitates. "It wasn't long before she grew cold and closed-off. Withdrawn. Paris moved up in rank quickly, and I was soon relegated to little more than his right hand. I was the one he sent to check on her at home, at school. I was ordered to monitor her behavior, write the reports outlining her progress.

"But there were no results. Her spirit had been broken. I begged Paris to put her elsewhere—to, at the very least, return her to a regular facility, one that I might oversee personally—and still he insisted, over and over again, that the abuse she suffered would spur results." Delalieu is on his feet now, pacing. "He was hoping to impress the council, hoping his efforts would be rewarded with yet another promotion. It soon became his single task to wait, to have me watch Ella closely for developments, for any sign that she'd changed. Evolved." He stops in place. Swallows, hard. "But Paris was careless."

Delalieu drops his head into his hands.

The room around us has gone so quiet I can almost

hear the seconds pass. We're all waiting for him to keep going, but he doesn't lift his head. I'm studying him—his shaking hands, the tremble in his legs, his general loss of composure—and my heart hammers in my chest. I feel like he's about to break. Like he's close to telling us something important.

"What do you mean?" I say quietly. "Careless how?"

Delalieu looks up, his eyes red-rimmed and wild.

"I mean *it was his one job*," he says, slamming his fist against the wall. He hits it, hard, his knuckles breaking through the plaster, and for a moment, I'm genuinely stunned. I didn't think Delalieu had it in him.

"You don't understand," he says, losing the fire. He stumbles back, sags against the wall. "My greatest regret in life has been watching those kids suffer and doing nothing about it."

"Wait," Winston says. "Which kids? Who are you talking about?"

But Delalieu doesn't seem to hear him. He only shakes his head. "Paris never took Ella's assignment seriously. It was his fault she lost control. It was his fault she didn't know better, it was his fault she hadn't been prepared or trained or properly guarded. It was his fault she killed that little boy," he says, now so broken his voice is shaking. "What she did that day nearly destroyed her. Nearly ruined the entire operation. Nearly exposed us to the world."

He closes his eyes, presses his fingers to his temples. And then he sinks back down into his chair. He looks unmoored.

Castle and I share a knowing glance from across the room. Something is happening. Something is about to happen.

Delalieu is a resource we never realized we had. And for all his protests, he actually seems like he wants to talk. Maybe Delalieu is the key. Maybe he can tell us what we need to know about—about everything. About Juliette, about Anderson, about The Reestablishment. It's obvious a dam broke open in Delalieu. I'm just hoping we can keep him talking.

It's Adam who says, "If you hated Anderson so much, why didn't you stop him when you had the chance?"

"Don't you understand?" Delalieu says, his eyes big and round and sad. "I *never* had the chance. I didn't have the authority, and we'd only just been voted into power. Leila— my daughter—was sicker every day and I was—I wasn't myself. I was unraveling. I suspected foul play in her illness but had no proof. I spent my work hours overseeing the crumbling mental and physical health of an innocent young woman, and I spent my free hours watching my daughter die."

"Those are excuses," Nazeera says coldly. "You were a coward."

He looks up. "Yes," he says. "That's true. I was a coward." He shakes his head, turns away. "I said nothing, even when Paris spun Ella's tragedy into a victory. He told everyone that what Ella did to that boy was a blessing in disguise. That, in fact, it was exactly what he'd been working toward.

He argued that what she did that day, regardless of the consequences, was the exact manifestation of her powers he'd been hoping for all along." Delalieu looks suddenly sick. "He got away with everything. Everything he ever wanted, he was given. And he was always reckless. He did lazy work, all the while using Ella as a pawn to fulfill his own sadistic desires."

"Please be more specific," Castle says coolly. "Anderson had a great deal of sadistic desires. Which are you referring to?"

Delalieu goes pale. His voice is lower, weaker, when he says, "Paris has always been perversely fond of destroying his own son. I never understood it. I never understood his need to break that boy. He tortured him a thousand different ways, but when Paris discovered the depth of Aaron's emotional connection to Ella, he used it to drive that boy near to madness."

"That's why he shot her," I say, remembering what Juliette—Ella—told me after Omega Point was bombed. "Anderson wanted to kill her to teach Warner a lesson. Right?"

But something changes in Delalieu's face. Transforms him, sags him down. And then he laughs—a sad, broken laugh. "You don't understand, you don't understand, *you don't understand*," he cries, shaking his head. "You think these recent events are everything. You think Aaron fell in love with your friend of several months, a rebel girl named Juliette. You don't know. You don't know. You don't know that Aaron has been in love with Ella for the better part of his entire life. They've known each other since childhood."

Adam makes a sound. A stunned sound of disbelief.

"Okay, I have to be honest—I don't get it," Ian says. He steals a wary glance at Nazeera before he says, "Nazeera said Anderson has been wiping their memories. If that's true, then how could Warner be in love with her for so long? Why would Anderson wipe their memories, tell them all about how they know each other, and then wipe their memories again?"

Delalieu is shaking his head. A strange smile begins to form on his face, the kind of shaky, terrified smile that isn't a smile at all. "No. *No.* You don't—" He sighs, looks away. "Paris has never told either of them about their shared history. The reason he had to keep wiping their memories was because it didn't matter how many times he reset the story or remade the introductions—Aaron always fell in love with her. Every time.

"In the beginning Paris thought it was a fluke. He found it almost funny. Entertaining. But the more it happened, the more it began to drive Paris insane. He thought there was something wrong with Aaron—that there was something wrong with him on a genetic level, that he'd been plagued by a sickness. He wanted to crush what he saw as a weakness."

"Wait," Adam says, holding up his hands. "What do you mean, *the more it happened*? How many times did it happen?"

"At least several times."

Adam looks shell-shocked. "They met and fell in love

several times?"

Delalieu takes a shaky breath. "I don't know that they always fell in love, exactly. Paris seldom let them spend that much time alone. But they were always drawn together. It was obvious, every time he put them in the same room, they were like"—Delalieu claps his hands—"magnets."

Delalieu shakes his head at Adam.

"I'm sorry to be the one to tell you all this. I'm sure it's painful to hear, especially considering your history with Ella. It's not fair that you were pulled into Paris's games. He never should've p—"

"Whoa, whoa—Wait. What games?" Adam says, stunned. "What are you talking about?"

Delalieu runs a hand across his sweaty forehead. He looks like he's melting, crumbling under pressure. Maybe someone should get him some water.

"There's too much," he says wearily. "Too much to tell. Too much to explain." He shakes his head. "I'm sorry, I—"

"I need you to try," Adam says, his eyes flashing. "Are you saying our relationship was fake? That everything she said—everything she felt was fake?"

"No," Delalieu says quickly, even as he uses his shirtsleeve to wipe the sweat from his face. "No. As far as I'm aware, her feelings for you were as real as anything else. You came into her life at a particularly difficult time, and your kindness and affection no doubt meant a great deal to her." He sighs. "I only mean that it wasn't coincidence that both of Paris's boys fell in love with the same girl. Paris liked toying with things. He liked cutting things open to study them. He liked experiments. And Paris pit you and Warner against each other on *purpose*.

"He planted the soldier at your lunch table who let slip that Warner was monitoring a girl with a lethal touch. He sent another to speak with you, to ask you about your history with her, to appeal to your protective nature by discussing Aaron's plans for her—Do you remember? You were persuaded, from every angle, to apply for the position. When you did, Paris pulled your application from the pile and encouraged Aaron to interview you. He then made it clear that you should be chosen as her cellmate. He let Aaron think he was making all his own decisions as CCR of Sector 45—but Paris was always there, manipulating everything. I watched it happen."

Adam looks so stunned it takes him a moment to speak. "So . . . he knew? My dad always knew about me? Knew where I was—what I was doing?"

"Knew?" Delalieu frowns. "Paris *orchestrated* your lives. That was the plan, from the beginning." He looks at Nazeera. "All the children of the supreme commanders were to become case studies. You were engineered to be soldiers. You and James," he says to Adam, "were unexpected, but he made plans for you, too."

"What?" Adam goes white. "What's his plan for me and James?"

"This, I honestly don't know."

Adam sits back in his chair, looking suddenly ill.

"Where is Ella now?" Winston says sharply. "Do you know where they're keeping her?"

Delalieu shakes his head. "All I know is that she can't be dead."

"What do you mean she *can't* be dead?" I ask. "Why not?"

"Ella's and Emmaline's powers are critical to the regime," he says. "Critical to the continuation of everything we've been working toward. The Reestablishment was built with the promise of Ella and Emmaline. Without them, Operation Synthesis means nothing."

Castle bolts upright. His eyes are wide. "Operation Synthesis," he says breathlessly, "has to do with *Ella*?"

"The Architect and the Executioner," Delalieu says. "It—"

Delalieu falls back with a small, surprised gasp, his head hitting the back of his chair. Everything, suddenly, seems to slow down.

I feel my heart rate slow. I feel the world slow. I feel formed from water, watching the scene unfold in slow motion, frame by frame.

A bullet between his eyes.

Blood trickling down his forehead.

A short, sharp scream.

"You traitorous son of a bitch," someone says.

I'm seeing it, but I don't believe it.

Anderson is here.

JULIETTE

I'm given no explanations.

My father doesn't invite me to dinner, like Evie promised. He doesn't sit me down to offer me long histories about my presence or his; he doesn't reveal groundbreaking information about my life or the other supreme commanders or even the nearly six hundred people I just murdered. He and Evie are acting like the horrors of the last seventeen years never happened. Like *nothing* strange has ever happened, like I never stopped being their daughter—not in the ways that matter, anyway.

I don't know what was in that needle, but the effects are unlike anything I've experienced. I feel both awake and asleep, like I'm spinning in place, like there's too much grease turning the wheels in my brain and I try to speak and realize my lips no longer move on command. My father carries my limp body into a blindingly silver room, props me up in a chair, straps me down, and panic pours into me, hot and terrifying, flooding my mind. I try to scream. Fail. My brain is slowly disconnecting from my body, like I'm being removed from myself. Only basic, instinctual functions seem to work. Swallowing. Breathing.

Crying.

Tears fall quietly down my face and my father whistles a tune, his movements light and easy even as he sets up an IV drip. He moves with such startling efficiency I don't even realize he's removed my manacles until I see the scalpel.

A flash of silver.

The blade is so sharp he meets no resistance as he slices clean lines into my forearms and blood, blood, heavy and warm, spills down my wrists and into my open palms and it doesn't seem real, not even when he stabs several electrical wires into my exposed flesh.

The pain arrives just seconds later.

Pain.

It begins at my feet, blooms up my legs, unfurls in my stomach and works its way up my throat only to explode behind my eyes, *inside my brain*, and I cry out, but only in my mind, my useless hands still limp on the armrests, and I'm so certain he's going to kill me—

but then he smiles.

And then he's gone.

I lie in agony for what feels like hours.

I watch, through a delirious fog, as blood drips off my fingertips, each drop feeding the crimson pools growing in the folds of my pants. Visions assault me, memories of a girl I might've been, scenes with people I might've known. I want to believe they're hallucinations, but I can't be certain of anything anymore. I don't know if Max and Evie are planting things in my mind. I don't know that I can trust anything I might've once believed about myself.

I can't stop thinking about Emmaline.

I'm adrift, suspended in a pool of senselessness, but something about her keeps tugging, sparking my nerves, errant currents pushing me to the surface of something—an emotional revelation—that trembles into existence only to evaporate, seconds later, as if it might be terrified to exist.

This goes on and on and on and on and on

Lightyears.

Eons.

over

and

over

    whispers of clarity

        g a s p s   o f   o x y g e n

and I'm tossed back out to sea.

Bright, white lights flicker above my head, buzzing in unison with the low, steady hum of engines and cooling units. Everything smells sharp, like antiseptic. Nausea makes my head swim. I squeeze my eyes shut, the only command my body will obey.

Me and Emmaline at the zoo

Me and Emmaline, first trip on a plane
Me and Emmaline, learning to swim
Me and Emmaline, getting our hair cut

Images of Emmaline fill my mind, moments from the first years of our lives, details of her face I never knew I could conjure. I don't understand it. I don't know where they're coming from. I can only imagine that Evie put these images here, but why Evie would want me to see *this*, I don't understand. Scenes play through my head like I might be flipping through a photo album, and they make me miss my sister. They make me remember Evie as my mother. Make me remember I had a family.

Maybe Evie wants me to reminisce.

My blood has hit the floor. I hear it, the familiar drip, the sound like a broken faucet, the slow

tap

tap

of tepid fluid on tile.

Emmaline and I held hands everywhere we went, often wearing matching outfits. We had the same long brown hair, but her eyes were pure blue, and she was a few inches taller than me. We were only a year apart, but she looked so much older. Even then, there was something in her eyes that looked hard. Serious. She held my hand like she was trying to protect me. Like maybe she knew more than I did.

Where are you? I wonder. *What did they do to you?*

I have no idea where I am. No idea what they've done

to me. No idea of the hour or the day, and pain blisters everywhere. I feel like a live wire, like my nerves have been stapled to the outside of my body, sensitive to every minute change in environment. I exhale and it hurts. Twitch and it takes my breath away.

And then, in a flash of movement, my mother returns.

The door opens and the motion forces a gentle rush of air into the room, a whisper of a breeze, gentle even as it grazes my skin, and somehow the sensation is so unbearable I'm certain I'll scream.

I don't.

"Feeling better?" she says.

Evie is holding a silver box. I try to look more closely but the pain is in my eyes now. Searing.

"You must be wondering why you're here," she says softly. I hear her working on something, glass and metal touching together, coming apart, touching together, coming apart. "But you must be patient, little bird. You might not even get to stay."

I close my eyes.

I feel her cold, slender fingers on my face just seconds before she yanks my eyelids back. Swiftly, she replaces her fingers with sharp, steel clamps, and I muster only a low, guttural sound of agony.

"Keep your eyes open, Ella. Now's not the time to fall asleep."

Even then, in that painful, terrifying moment, the words sound familiar. Strange and familiar. I can't figure out why.

"Before we make any concrete plans to keep you here, I need to make sure"—she tugs on a pair of latex gloves—"that you're still viable. See how you've held up after all these years."

Her words send waves of dread coursing through me.

Nothing has changed.

Nothing has changed.

I'm still no more than a receptacle. My body exchanges hands exchanges hands in exchange for what

My mother has no love for me.

What has she done to my sister.

"Where is Emmaline?" I try to scream, but the words don't leave my mouth. They expand in my head, explosive and angry, pressing against the ridges of my mind even as my lips refuse to obey me.

Dying.

The word occurs to me suddenly, as if it were something I've just remembered, the answer to a question I forgot existed.

I don't comprehend it.

Evie is standing in front of me again.

She touches my hair, sifts through the short, coarse strands like she might be panning for gold. The physical contact is excruciating.

"Unacceptable," she says. "This is unacceptable."

She turns away, makes notes in a tablet she pulls out of

her lab coat. Roughly, she takes my chin in her hand, lifts my face toward hers.

Evie counts my teeth. Runs the tip of one finger along my gums. She examines the insides of my cheeks, the underside of my tongue. Satisfied, she rips off the gloves, the latex making harsh snapping sounds that collide and echo, shattering the air around me.

A mechanical purr fills my ears and I realize Evie is adjusting my chair. I was previously in a reclining position, now I'm flat on my back. She takes a pair of shears to my clothes, cutting straight through my pants, my shirt, my sleeves.

Fear threatens to rip my chest open, but I only lie there, a perfect vegetable, as she strips me down.

Finally, Evie steps back.

I can't see what's happening. The hum of an engine builds into a roar. Sounds like scissors, slicing the air. And then: Sheets of glass materialize at the edges of my vision, move toward me from all sides. They lock into place easily, seams sealing shut with a cool *click* sound.

I'm being burned alive.

Heat like I've never known it, fire I can't see or stop. I don't know how it's happening but I feel it. I *smell* it. The scent of charred flesh fills my nose, threatens to upend the contents of my stomach. The top layer of skin is being slowly singed off my body. Blood beads along my body like morning dew, and a fine mist follows the heat, cleansing and cooling. Steam fogs up the glass around me and then, just when I think I might die from the pain, the glass fissures open with a sudden gasp.

I wish she would just kill me.

Instead, Evie is meticulous. She catalogs my every physical detail, making notes, constantly, in her pocket tablet. For the most part, she seems frustrated with her assessment. My arms and legs are too weak, she says. My shoulders too tense, my hair too short, my hands too scarred, my nails too chipped, my lips too chapped, my torso too long.

"We made you too beautiful," she says, shaking her head at my naked body. She prods at my hips, the balls of my feet. "Beauty can be a terrifying weapon, if you know how to wield it. But all this seems deeply unnecessary now." She makes another note.

When she looks at me again, she looks thoughtful.

"I gave this to you," she says. "Do you understand? This container you live in. I grew it, shaped it. You belong to me. Your life belongs to me. It's very important that you understand that."

Rage, sharp and hot, sears through my chest.

Carefully, Evie cracks open the silver box. Inside are dozens of slim glass cylinders. "Do you know what these are?" she says, lifting a few vials of shimmering, white liquid. "Of course you don't."

Evie studies me awhile.

"We did it wrong the first time," she finally says. "We didn't expect emotional health to supersede the physical in such dramatic fashion. We expected stronger minds, from both of you. Of course—" Evie hesitates. "She was the superior specimen, your sister. Infinitely superior. You were always a bit doe-eyed as a child. A little moonier than I'd have liked. Emmaline, on the other hand, was pure fire. We never dreamed she'd deteriorate so quickly. Her failures have been a great personal disappointment."

I inhale sharply and choke on something hot and wet in my throat. Blood. So much blood.

"But then," Evie says with a sigh, "such is the situation. We must be adaptable to the unexpected. Amenable to change when necessary."

Evie hits a switch and something seizes inside of me. I feel my spine straighten, my jaw go slack. Blood is now bubbling up my throat in earnest, and I don't know whether to let it up or swallow it down. I cough, violently, and blood spatters across my face. My arms. Drips down my chest, my fresh pink skin.

My mother drops into a crouch. She takes my chin in her hand and forces me to look at her. "You are far too full of emotion," she says softly. "You feel too much for this world. You call people your friends. You imagine yourself in love." She shakes her head slowly. "That was never the plan for you, little bird. You were meant for a solitary existence. We put you in isolation on purpose." She blinks. "Do you understand?"

I'm hardly breathing. My tongue feels rough and heavy, foreign in my mouth. I swallow my own blood and it's revolting, thick and lukewarm, gelatinous with saliva.

"If Aaron were anyone else's son," she says, "I would've had him executed. I'd have him executed right now, if I could. Unfortunately, I alone do not have the authority."

A force of feeling seizes my body.

I'm half horror, half joy. I didn't know I had any hope left that Warner was alive until just this moment.

The feeling is explosive.

It takes root inside of me. Hope catches fire in my blood, a feeling more powerful than these drugs, more powerful than myself. I cling to it with my whole heart, and, suddenly, I'm able to feel my hands. I don't know why or how but I feel a quiet strength surge up my spine.

Evie doesn't notice.

"I regret our mistakes," she's saying. "I regret the oversights that seem so obvious now. We couldn't have known so many years ago that things would turn out like this. We didn't expect to be blindsided by something so flimsy as your emotions. We couldn't have known, at the onset, that things would escalate in this way.

"Paris," she says, "had convinced everyone that bringing you on base in Sector 45 would be beneficial to us all, that he'd be able to monitor you in a new environment rife with experiences that would motivate your powers to evolve. Your father and I thought it was a stupid plan, stupider still for placing you under the direct supervision of a nineteen-year-old boy with whom your history was . . . complicated." She looks away. Shakes her head. "But Anderson delivered results. With Aaron you made progress at a rate we'd only dreamed of, and we were forced to let it be. Still," she says. "It backfired."

Her eyes linger, for a moment, on my shaved head.

"There are few people, even in our inner circle, who really understand what we're doing here. Your father understands. Ibrahim understands. But Paris, for security reasons, was never told everything about you. He wasn't yet a supreme commander when we gave him the job, and we decided to keep him informed on a need-to-know basis. Another mistake," Evie says, her voice both sad and terrifying.

She presses the back of her hand to her forehead.

"Six months and everything falls apart. You run away. You join some ridiculous gang. You drag Aaron into all of this and Paris, the oblivious fool, tries to *kill* you. Twice. I nearly slit his throat for his idiocy, but my mercy may as well have been for nothing, what with your attempt to murder him. Oh, Ella," she says, and sighs. "You've caused me a great deal of trouble this year. The paperwork alone." She closes her eyes. "I've had the same splitting headache for six months."

She opens her eyes. Looks at me for a long time.

"And now," she says, gesturing at me with the tablet in her hand, "there's this. Emmaline needs to be replaced, and we're not even sure you're a suitable substitute. Your body is operating at *maybe* sixty-five percent efficiency, and your mind is a complete disaster." She stops. A vein jumps in her forehead. "Perhaps it's impossible for you to understand how I'm feeling right now. Perhaps you don't care to know the depth of my disappointments. But you and Emmaline are my life's work. I was the one who found a way to isolate the gene that was causing widespread transformations in the population. I was the one who managed to re-create the transformation. I was the one who rewrote your genetic code." She frowns at me, looking, for the first time, like a real person. Her voice softens. "I *remade* you, Ella. You and your sister were the greatest accomplishments of my career. Your failures," she whispers, touching the tips of her fingers to my face, "are my failures."

I make a harsh, involuntary sound.

She stands up. "This is going to be uncomfortable for you. I won't pretend otherwise. But I'm afraid we have no choice. If this is going to work, I'll need you to have a healthy, unpolluted headspace. We have to start fresh. When we're done, you won't remember anything but what I tell you to remember. Do you understand?"

My heart picks up and I hear its wild, erratic beats amplified on a nearby monitor. The sounds echo around the room like a siren.

"Your temperature is spiking," Evie says sharply. "There's no need to panic. This is the merciful option. Paris is still clamoring to have you killed, after all. But Paris"— she hesitates—"Paris can be melodramatic. We've all known how much he's hated you for your effect on Aaron. He blames you, you know." Evie tilts her head at me. "He thinks you're part of the reason Aaron is so weak. Honestly, sometimes I wonder if he's right."

My heart is beating too fast now. My lungs feel fit to burst. The bright lights above my head bleed into my eyes, into my brain—

"Now. I'm going to download this information"—I hear her tap the silver box—"directly into your mind. It's a lot of data to process, and your body will need some time to accept it all." A long pause. "Your mind might try to reject this, but it's up to you to let things take their course, do you understand? We don't want to risk splicing the past and present. It's only painful in the first few hours, but if you can survive those first hours, your pain receptors will begin to fail, and the rest of the data should upload without incident."

I want to scream.

Instead, I make a weak, choking sound. Tears spill fast down my cheeks and my mother stands there, her fingers small and foreign on my face, and I see, but cannot feel, the enormous needle going into the soft flesh at my temple. She empties and refills the syringe what feels like a thousand times, and each time it's like being submerged underwater, like I'm slowly drowning, suffocating over and over again and never allowed to die. I lie there, helpless and mute, caught in an agony so excruciating I no longer breathe, but rasp, as she leans over me to watch.

"You're right," she says softly. "Maybe this is cruel. Maybe it would've been kinder to simply let you die. But this isn't about you, Ella. This is about me. And right now," she says, stroking my hair, "this is what I need."

KENJI

The whole thing happens so quickly it takes me a second to register exactly what went down.

Delalieu is dead.

Delalieu is dead and Anderson is alive.

Anderson is back from the dead.

I mean, right now he's flat on the ground, buried under the weight of every single piece of furniture in this room. Castle stares, intently, from across the space, and when I hear Anderson wheezing, I realize Castle isn't trying to kill him; he's only using the furniture to contain him.

I inch closer to the crowd forming around Anderson's gasping figure. And then I notice, with a start, that Adam is pressed up against the wall like a statue, his face frozen in horror.

My heart breaks for him.

I'm so glad Adam dragged James off to bed hours ago. So glad that kid doesn't have to see any of this right now.

Castle finally makes his way across the room. He's standing a few feet away from Anderson's prone figure when he asks the question we're all thinking:

"How are you still alive?"

Anderson attempts a smile. It comes out crooked. Crazy.

"You know what's always been so great about you, Castle?" He says Castle's name like it's funny, like he's saying it out loud for the first time. He takes a tight, uneven breath. "You're so predictable. You like to collect strays. You love a good sob story."

Anderson cries out with a sudden, rough exhalation, and I realize Castle probably turned up the pressure. When Anderson catches his breath, he says, "You're an idiot. You're an idiot for trusting so easily."

Another harsh, painful gasp.

"Who do you think called me here?" he says, struggling to speak now. "Who do you think has been keeping me apprised"—another strained breath—"of every single thing you've been discussing?"

I freeze. A horrible, sick feeling gathers in my chest.

We all turn, as a group, to face Nazeera. She's standing apart from everyone else, the personification of calm, collected intensity. She has no expression on her face. She looks at me like I might be a wall.

For a split second I feel so dizzy I think I might actually pass out.

Wishful thinking.

That's it—that's the thing that does it. A room full of extremely powerful people and yet, it's this moment, this brief, barely there moment of shock that ruins us all. I feel the needle in my neck before I even register what's happening, and I have only a few seconds to scan the room—glimpsing the horror on my friends' faces—before I fall.

WARNER

I'm sitting in my office listening to an old record when I get the call. I worry, at first, that it might be Lena, begging me to come back to her, but my feeling of revulsion quickly transforms to hate when I hear the voice on the line. My father. He wants me downstairs.

The mere sound of his voice fills me with a feeling so violent it takes me a minute to control myself.

Two years away.

Two years becoming the monster my father always wanted me to be. I glance in the mirror, loathing myself with a new, profound intensity I'd never before experienced. Every morning I wake up hoping only to die. To be done with this life, with these days.

He knew, when he made that deal, what he was asking me to do. I didn't. I was sixteen, still young enough to believe in hope, and he took advantage of my naiveté. He knew what it would do to me. He knew it would break me. And it was all he'd ever wanted.

My soul.

I sold my soul for a few years with my mother, and now, after everything, I don't even know if it'll be worth it. I don't know if I'll be able to save her. I've been away too long. I've missed too much. My mother is doing so much worse now, and no doctor has been able to help her. Nothing has helped. My efforts have been worse than futile.

I gave up everything—for nothing.

I wish I'd known how those two years would change me. I wish I'd known how hard it would be to live with myself, to look in the mirror. No one warned me about the nightmares, the panic attacks, or the dark, destructive thoughts that would follow. No one explained to me how darkness works, how it feasts on itself or how it festers. I hardly recognize myself these days. Becoming an instrument of torture destroyed what was left of my mind.

And now, this: I feel empty, all the time. Hollowed out.

Beyond redemption.

I didn't want to come back here. I wanted to walk directly into the ocean. I wanted to fade into the horizon. I wanted to disappear.

Of course, he'd never let that happen.

He dragged me back here and gave me a title. I was rewarded for being an animal. Celebrated for my efforts as a monster. Never mind the fact that I wake up in the middle of every night strangled by irrational fears and a sudden, violent urge to upend the contents of my stomach.

Never mind that I can't get these images out of my head.

I glance at the expensive bottle of bourbon my father left for me in my room and feel suddenly disgusted. I don't want to be like him. I don't want his opiate, his preferred form of oblivion.

At least, soon, my father will be gone. Any day now, he'll be gone, and this sector will become my domain. I'll finally be on my own.

Or something close to it.

Reluctantly, I pull on my blazer and take the elevator down.

When I finally arrive in his quarters as he requested, he spares me only the briefest look.

"Good," he says. "You've come."

I say nothing.

He smiles. "Where are your manners? You're not going to greet our guest?"

Confused, I follow his line of sight. There's a young woman sitting on a chair in the far corner of the room, and, at first, I don't recognize her.

When I do, the blood drains from my face.

My father laughs. "You kids remember each other, right?"

She was sitting so quietly, so still and small that I almost hadn't noticed her at all. My dead heart jumps at the sight of her slight frame, a spark of life trying, desperately, to ignite.

"Juliette," I whisper.

My last memory of her was from two years ago, just before I left home for my father's sick, sadistic assignment. He ripped her away from me. Literally ripped her out of my arms. I'd never seen that kind of rage in his eyes, not like that, not over something so innocent.

But he was wild.

Out of his mind.

She and I hadn't done anything more than talk to each other. I'd started stealing down to her room whenever I could get away, and I'd trick the cameras' feeds to give us privacy. We'd talk, sometimes for hours. She'd become my friend.

I never touched her.

She said that after what happened with the little boy, she was afraid to touch anyone. She said she didn't understand what was happening to her and didn't trust herself anymore. I asked her if she wanted to touch me, to test it out and see if anything would happen, and she looked scared and I told her not to worry. I promised it'd be okay. And when I took her hand, tentatively, waiting for disaster—

Nothing happened.

Nothing happened except that she burst into tears. She threw herself into my arms and wept and told me she'd been terrified that there was something wrong with her, that she'd turned into a monster—

We only had a month, altogether.

But there was something about her that felt right to me, from the very beginning. I trusted her. She felt familiar, like I'd always known her. But I also knew it seemed a dramatic sort of thought, so I kept it to myself.

She told me about her life. Her horrible parents. She'd shared her fears with me, so I shared mine. I told her about my mom, how I didn't know what was happening to her, how worried I was that she was going to die.

Juliette cared about me. Listened to me the way no one else did.

It was the most innocent relationship I'd ever had, but it meant more to me than anything. For the first time in years, I felt less alone.

The day I found out she was finally being transferred, I pulled her close. I pressed my face into her hair and breathed her in and she cried. She told me she was scared and I promised I'd try to do something—I promised to talk to my dad even though I knew he wouldn't care—

And then, suddenly, he was there.

He ripped her out of my arms, and I noticed then that he was wearing gloves. "What the hell are you doing?" he cried. "Have you lost your mind? Have you lost yourself entirely?"

"Dad," I said, panicking. "Nothing happened. I was just saying good-bye to her."

His eyes widened, round with shock. And when he spoke, his words were whispers. "You were just—You were saying good-bye to her?"

"She's leaving," I said stupidly.

"You think I don't know that?"

I swallowed, hard.

"Jesus," he said, running a hand across his mouth. "How long have you been doing this? How long have you been coming down here?"

My heart was racing. Fear pulsed through me. I was shaking my head, unable to speak.

"What did you do?" my dad demanded, his eyes flashing. "Did you touch her?"

"No." Anger surged through me, giving me back my voice even as my face flushed with embarrassment. "No, of course not."

"Are you sure?"

"Dad, why are you"—I shook my head, confused—"I don't understand why you're so upset. You've been pushing me and Lena *together for months, even though I've told you a hundred times that I don't like her, but now, when I actually—" I hesitated, looking at Juliette, her face half hidden behind my dad. "I was just getting to know her. That's all."*

"You were just getting to know her?" He stared at me, disgusted. "Of all the girls in the world, you fall for this one? The child- murderer bound for prison? The likely insane test tube experiment? What is wrong with you?"

"Dad, please—Nothing happened. We're just friends. We just talk sometimes."

"Just friends," he said, and laughed. The sound was demented. "You know what? I'll let you take this with you. I'll let you keep this one while you're gone. Let it sit with you. Let it teach you a lesson."

"What? Take what with me?"

"A warning." He leveled me with a lethal look. "Try something like this again," he said, "and I'll kill her. And I'll make sure you get to watch."

I stared at him, my heart beating out of my chest. This was insane. We hadn't even done anything. I'd known that my dad would probably be angry, but I never thought he'd threaten to kill her. If I'd known, I never would've risked it. And now—

My head was spinning. I didn't understand. He was dragging her down the hall and I didn't understand.

Suddenly, she screamed.

She screamed and I stood there, helpless as he dragged her away. She called my name—cried out for me—and he shook her, told her to shut up, and I felt something inside of me die. I felt it as

142

it happened. Felt something break apart inside of me as I watched her go.

I'd never hated myself so much. I'd never been more of a coward.

And now, here we are.

That day feels like a lifetime ago. I never thought I'd see her again.

Juliette looks up at me now, and she looks different. Her eyes are glassy with tears. Her skin has lost its pallor; her hair has lost its sheen. She looks thinner. She reminds me of myself.

Hollow.

"Hi," I whisper.

Tears spill, silently, down her cheeks.

I have to force myself to remain calm. I have to force myself not to lose my head. My mother warned me, years ago, to hide my heart from my father, and every time I slipped—every time I let myself hope he might not be a monster—he punished me, mercilessly.

I wasn't going to let him do that to me again. I didn't want him to know how much it hurt to see her like this. How painful it was to sit beside her and say nothing. Do nothing.

"What is she doing here?" I ask, hardly recognizing my own voice.

"She's here," he says, "because I had her collected for us."

"Collected for what? You said—"

"I know what I said." He shrugs. "But I wanted to see this moment. Your reunion. I'm always interested in your reunions. I find the dynamics of your relationship fascinating."

I look at him, feel my chest explode with rage and somehow, fight it back. "You brought her back here just to torture me?"

"You flatter yourself, son."

"Then what?"

"I have your first task for you," he says, pushing a stack of files across his desk. "Your first real mission as chief commander and regent of this sector."

My lips part, surprised. "What does that have to do with her?"

My father's eyes light up. "Everything."

I say nothing.

"I have a plan," he says. "One that will require your assistance. In these files"—he nods at the stack in front of me—"is everything you need to know about her illness. Every medical report, every paper trail. I want you to reform the girl. Rehabilitate her. And then I want you to weaponize her abilities for our own use."

I meet his eyes, failing to conceal my horror at the suggestion. "Why? Why would you come to me with this? Why would you ask me to do something like this, when you know our history?"

"You are uniquely suited to the job. It seems silly to waste my time explaining this to you now, as you won't remember most of this conversation tomorrow—"

"What?" I frown. "Why wouldn't I—"

"—but the two of you seem to have some kind of immutable connection, one that might, I hope, inspire her abilities to develop more fully. More quickly."

"That doesn't make any sense."

144

He ignores me. Glances at Juliette. Her eyes are closed, her head resting against the wall behind her. She seems almost asleep, except for the tears still streaking softly down her face.

It kills me just to look at her.

"As you can see," my father says, "she's a bit out of her mind right now. Heavily sedated. She's been through a great deal these last two years. We had no choice but to turn her into a sort of guinea pig. I'm sure you can imagine how that goes."

He stares at me with a slight smile on his face. I know he's waiting for something. A reaction. My anger.

I refuse to give it to him.

His smile widens.

"Anyhow," he says happily, "I'm going to put her back in isolation for the next six months—maybe a year, depending on how things develop. You can use that opportunity to prepare. To observe her."

But I'm still fighting back my anger. I can't bring myself to speak.

"Is there a problem?" he says.

"No."

"You remember, of course, the warning I gave you the last time she was here."

"Of course," I say, my voice flat. Dead.

And then, as if out of nowhere: "How is Lena, by the way? I hope she's well."

"I wouldn't know."

It's barely there, but I catch the sudden shift in his voice. The anger when he says, "And why is that?"

"I broke things off with her last week."

"And you didn't think to tell me?"

Finally, I meet his eyes. "I never understood why you wanted us to be together. She's not right for me. She never was."

"You don't love her, you mean."

"I can't imagine how anyone would."

"That," he says, "is exactly why she's perfect for you."

I blink at him, caught off guard. For a moment, it almost sounded like my father cared about me. Like he was trying to protect me in some perverse, idiotic way.

Eventually, he sighs.

He picks up a pen and a pad of paper and begins writing something down. "I'll see what I can do about repairing the damage you've done. Lena's mother must be hysterical. Until then, get to work." He nods at the stack of files he's set before me.

Reluctantly, I pick a folder off the top.

I glance through the documents, scanning the general outline of the mission, and then I look up at him, stunned. "Why does the paperwork make it sound like this was my idea?"

He hesitates. Puts down his pen. "Because you don't trust me."

I stare at him, struggling to understand.

He tilts his head. "If you knew this was my idea, you'd never trust it, would you? You'd look too closely for holes. Conspiracies. You'd never follow through the way I'd want you to. Besides," he says, picking up his pen again. "Two birds. One stone. It's time to finally break the cycle."

I replace the folder on the pile. I'm careful to temper the tone of my voice when I say, "I have no idea what you're talking about."

"I'm talking about your new experiment," he says coolly. "Your little tragedy. This," he says, gesturing between me and Juliette. "This needs to end. And she is unlikely to return your affections when she wakes up to discover you are not her friend but her oppressor. Isn't she?"

And I can no longer keep the fury or the hysteria out of my voice when I say, "Why are you doing this to me? Why are you purposely torturing me?"

"Is it so crazy to imagine that I might be trying to do you a favor?" My father smiles. "Look more closely at those files, son. If you've ever wanted a chance at saving your mother—this might be it."

I've become obsessed with time.

Still, I can only guess at how long I've been here, staring at these walls without reprieve. No voices, only the occasional warped sounds of faraway speech. No faces, not a single person to tell me where I am or what awaits me. I've watched the shadows chase the light in and out of my cell for weeks, their motions through the small window my only hope for marking the days.

A slim, rectangular slot in my door opens with sudden, startling force, the aperture shot through with what appears to be artificial light on the other side.

I make a mental note.

A single, steaming bun—no tray, no foil, no utensils—is shoved through the slot and my reflexes are still fast enough

147

to catch the bread before it touches the filthy floor. I have enough sense to understand that the little food I'm given every day is poisoned. Not enough to kill me. Just enough to slow me down. Slight tremors rock my body, but I force my eyes to stay open as I turn the soft bun around in my hand, searching its flaky skin for information. It's unmarked. Unextraordinary. It could mean nothing.

There's no way to be sure.

This ritual happens exactly twice a day. I am fed an insignificant, tasteless portion of food twice a day. For hours at a time my thoughts slur; my mind swims and hallucinates. I am slow. Sluggish.

Most days, I fast.

To clear my head, to cleanse my body of the poison, and to collect information. I have to find my way out of here before it's too late.

Some nights, when I'm at my weakest, my imagination runs wild; my mind is plagued by horrible visions of what might've happened to her. It's torture not knowing what they've done with her. Not knowing where she is, not knowing how she is, not knowing if someone is hurting her.

But the nightmares are perhaps the most disconcerting.

At least, I think they're nightmares. It's hard to separate fact from fiction, dreams from reality; I spend too much time with poison running through my veins. But Nazeera's words to me before the symposium—her warning that Juliette was someone else, that Max and Evie are her true, biological parents . . .

I didn't want to believe it then.

It seemed a possibility too perverse to be real. Even my father had lines he wouldn't cross, I told myself. Even The Reestablishment had some sense of invented morality, I told myself.

But I saw them as I was carried away—I saw the familiar faces of Evie and Maximillian Sommers—the supreme commander of Oceania and her husband. And I've been thinking of them ever since.

They were the key scientists of our group, the quiet brains of The Reestablishment. They were military, yes, but they were medical. The pair often kept to themselves. I had few memories of them until very recently.

Until *Ella* appeared in my mind.

But I don't know how to be sure that what I'm seeing is real. I have no way of knowing that this isn't simply another part of the torture. It's impossible to know. It's agony, boring a hole through me. I feel like I'm being assaulted on both sides—mental and physical—and I don't know where or how to begin fighting back. I've begun clenching my teeth so hard it's causing me migraines. Exhaustion feasts, slowly, on my mind. I'm fairly certain I've got at least two fractured ribs, and my only hours of rest are achieved standing up, the single position that eases the pain in my torso. It'd be easy to give up. Give in. But I can't lose myself to these mind games.

I won't.

So I compile data.

I spent my whole life preparing for moments like these by people like this and they will take full advantage of that knowledge. I know they'll expect me to prove that I deserve to survive, and—unexpectedly—knowing this brings me a much-needed sense of calm. I feel none of my usual anxiety here, being carefully poisoned to death.

Instead, I feel at home. Familiar.

Fortified by adrenaline.

Under any other circumstances I'd assume my meals were offered once in the morning and once at night—but I know better than to assume anything anymore. I've been charting the shadows long enough to know that I'm never fed at regular hours, and that the erratic schedule is intentional. There must be a message here: a sequence of numbers, a pattern of information, something I'm not grasping—because I know that this, like everything else, is a test.

I am in the custody of a supreme commander.

There can be no accidents.

I force myself to eat the warm, flavorless bun, hating the way the gummy, overly processed bread sticks to the roof of my mouth. It makes me wish for a toothbrush. They've given me my own sink and toilet, but I have little else to keep my standards of hygiene intact, which is possibly the greatest indignity here. I fight a wave of nausea as I swallow the last bite of bread and a sudden, prickling heat floods my body. Beads of sweat roll down my back and I clench my fists to keep from succumbing too quickly to the drugs.

I need a little more time.

There's a message here, somewhere, but I haven't yet decided where. Maybe it's in the movements of the shadows. Or in the number of times the slot opens and closes. It might be in the names of the foods I'm forced to eat, or in the exact number of footsteps I hear every day—or perhaps it's in the occasional, jarring knock at my door that accompanies silence.

There's something here, something they're trying to tell me, something I'm supposed to decipher—I gasp, reach out blindly as a shock of pain shoots through my gut—

I can figure this out, I think, even as the drug drags me down. I fall backward, onto my elbows. My eyes flutter open and closed and my mind drowns even as I count the sounds outside my door—

one hard step

two dragging steps

one hard step

—and there's something there, something deliberate in the movement that speaks to me. I know this. I know this language, I know its name, it's right there at the tip of my tongue but I can't seem to grasp it.

I've already forgotten what I was trying to do.

My arms give out. My head hits the floor with a dull thud. My thoughts melt into darkness.

The nightmares take me by the throat.

KENJI

I thought I'd spent time in some pretty rough places in my life, but this shit is like nothing else. Perfect darkness. No sounds but the distant, tortured screams of other prisoners. Food is disgusting slop shoved through a slot in the door. No bathrooms except that they open the doors once a day, just long enough for you to kill yourself trying to find the disgusting showers and toilets. I know what this is. I remember when Juliette—

Ella. *Ella*. Ella used to tell me about this place.

Some nights we'd stay up for hours talking about it. I wanted to know. I wanted to know everything. And those conversations are the only reason I knew what the open door means.

I don't really know how long I've been here—a week? Maybe two? I don't understand why they won't just kill me. I try to tell myself, every minute of every damn day, that they're just doing this to mess with our heads, that the tortured mind is a worse fate than a bullet in the brain, but I can't lie. This place is starting to get to me.

I feel myself starting to go weird.

I'm starting to hear things. See things. I'm beginning to freak myself out about what might've happened to my friends or whether I'll ever get out of here.

I try not to think about Nazeera.

When I think about Nazeera I want to punch myself in the face. I want to shoot myself in the throat.

When I think about Nazeera I feel a rage so acute I'm actually convinced, for a minute, that I might be able to break out of these neon handcuffs with nothing but brute force. But it never happens. These things are unbreakable, even as they strip me of my powers. And they emit a soft, pulsing blue glow, the only light I ever see.

J told me her cell had a window. Mine doesn't.

A harsh buzzing sound fills my cell. I hear a smooth click in the heavy metal door. I jump to my feet.

The door swings open.

I feel my way down the dripping corridor, the dim, pulsing light of my cuffs doing little to guide my way.

The shower is quick and cold. Awful in every way. There are no towels in this shithole, so I'm always freezing until I can get back to my room and wrap myself in the threadbare blanket. I'm thinking about that blanket now, trying to keep my thoughts focused and my teeth from chattering as I wend my way down the dark tunnels.

I don't see what happens next.

Someone comes up on me from behind and puts me in a choke hold, suffocating me with a technique so perfect I don't even know if it's worth a struggle. I'm definitely about to die.

Super weird way to go, but this is it. I'm done.

Shit.

~~JULIETTE~~

ELLA

Mr. Anderson says I can have lunch at his house before I meet my new family. It wasn't his idea, but when Aaron, his son—that was the boy's name—suggested it, Mr. Anderson seemed okay with it.

I'm grateful.

I'm not ready to go live with a bunch of strangers yet. I'm scared and nervous and worried about so many things, I don't even know where to start. Mostly, I feel angry. I'm angry with my parents for dying. Angry with them for leaving me behind.

I'm an orphan now.

But maybe I have a new friend. Aaron said that he was eight years old—about two years older than me—so there isn't any chance we'd be in the same grade, but when I said that we'd probably be going to the same school anyway, he said no, we wouldn't. He said he didn't go to public school. He said his father was very particular about these kinds of things and that he'd been homeschooled by private tutors his whole life.

We're sitting next to each other in the car ride back to his house when he says, quietly, "My dad never lets me invite people over to our house. He must like you."

I smile, secretly relieved. I really hope that this means I'll have a new friend. I'd been so scared to move here, so scared to be somewhere new and to be all alone, but now, sitting next to this strange blond boy with the light green eyes, I'm beginning to feel like things might be okay.

At least now, even if I don't like my new parents, I'll know I'm not completely alone. The thought makes me both happy and sad.

I look over at Aaron and smile. He smiles back.

When we get to his house, I take a moment to admire it from the outside. It's a big, beautiful old house painted the prettiest blue. It has big white shutters on the windows and a white fence around the front yard. Pink roses are growing around the edges, peeking through the wooden slats of the fence, and the whole thing looks so peaceful and lovely that I feel immediately at home.

My worries vanish.

I'm so grateful for Mr. Anderson's help. So grateful to have met his son. I realize, then, that Mr. Anderson might've brought his son to my meeting today just to introduce me to someone my own age. Maybe he was trying to make me feel at home.

A beautiful blond lady answers the front door. She smiles at me, bright and kind, and doesn't even say hello to me before she pulls me into her arms. She hugs me like she's known me forever, and there's something so comfortable about her arms around me that I embarrass everyone by bursting into tears.

I can't even look at anyone after I pull away from her—she told me her name was Mrs. Anderson, but that I could call her Leila, if I wanted—and I wipe at my tears, ashamed of my overreaction.

Mrs. Anderson tells Aaron to take me upstairs to his room while she makes us some snacks before lunch.

Still sniffling, I follow him up the stairs.

His room is nice. I sit on his bed and look at his things. Mostly it's pretty clean except that there's a baseball mitt on his nightstand and there are two dirty baseballs on the floor. Aaron catches me staring and scoops them up right away. He seems embarrassed as he tucks them in his closet, and I don't understand why. I was never very tidy. My room was always—

I hesitate.

I try to remember what my old bedroom looked like but, for some reason, I can't. I frown. Try again.

Nothing.

And then I realize I can't remember my parents' faces.

Terror barrels through me.

"What's wrong?"

Aaron's voice is so sharp—so intense—that I look up, startled. He's staring at me from across the room, the fear on his face reflected in the mirrors on his closet doors.

"What's wrong?" he says again. "Are you okay?"

"I—I don't—" I falter, feeling my eyes refill with tears. I hate that I keep crying. Hate that I can't stop crying. "I can't remember my parents," I say. "Is that normal?"

Aaron walks over, sits next to me on his bed. "I don't know," he says.

We're both quiet for a while. Somehow, it helps. Somehow, just sitting next to him makes me feel less alone. Less terrified.

Eventually, my heart stops racing.

After I've wiped away my tears, I say, "Don't you get lonely, being homeschooled all the time?"

He nods.

"Why won't your dad let you go to a normal school?"

"I don't know."

"What about birthday parties?" I ask. "Who do you invite to your birthday parties?"

Aaron shrugs. He's staring into his hands when he says, "I've never had a birthday party."

"What? Really?" I turn to face him more fully. "But birthday parties are so fun. I used to—" I blink, cutting myself off.

I can't remember what I was about to say.

I frown, trying to remember something, something about my old life, but when the memories don't materialize, I shake my head to clear it. Maybe I'll remember later.

"Anyway," I say, taking a quick breath, "you have to have a birthday party. Everyone has birthday parties. When is your birthday?"

Slowly, Aaron looks up at me. His face is blank even as he says, "April twenty-fourth."

"April twenty-fourth," I say, smiling. "That's great. We can have cake."

The days pass in a stifled panic, an excruciating crescendo toward madness. The hands of the clock seem to close around my throat and still, I say nothing, do nothing.

I wait.

Pretend.

I've been paralyzed here for two weeks, stuck in the prison of this ruse, this compound. Evie doesn't know that her plot to bleach my mind failed. She treats me like a foreign

162

object, distant but not unkind. She instructed me to call her *Evie*, told me she was my doctor, and then proceeded to lie, in great detail, about how I'd been in a terrible accident, that I'm suffering from amnesia, that I need to stay in bed in order to recover.

She doesn't know that my body won't stop shaking, that my skin is slick with sweat every morning, that my throat burns from the constant return of bile. She doesn't know what's happening to me. She could never understand the sickness plaguing my heart. She couldn't possibly understand this agony.

Remembering.

The attacks are relentless.

Memories assault me while I sleep, jolting me upright, my chest seizing in panic over and over and over until, finally, I meet dawn on the bathroom floor, the smell of vomit clinging to my hair, the inside of my mouth. I can only drag myself back to bed every morning and force my face to smile when Evie checks on me at sunrise.

Everything feels wrong.

The world feels strange. Smells confuse me. Words don't feel right in my mouth anymore. The sound of my own name feels at once familiar and foreign. My memories of people and places seem warped, fraying threads coming together to form a ragged tapestry.

But Evie. *My mother.*

I remember her.

"Evie?"

I pop my head out of the bathroom, clutching a robe to my wet body. I search my room for her face. "Evie, are you there?"

"Yes?" I hear her voice just seconds before she's suddenly standing before me, holding a set of fresh sheets in her hands. She's stripping my bed again. "Did you need something?"

"We're out of towels."

"Oh—easily rectified," she says, and hurries out the door. Not seconds later she's back, pressing a warm, fresh towel into my hands. She smiles faintly.

"Thanks," I say, forcing my own smile to stretch, to spark life in my eyes. And then I disappear into the bathroom.

The room is steaming; the mirrors fogged, perspiring. I grip the towel with one hand, watching as beads of water race down my bare skin. Condensation wears me like a suit; I wipe at the damp metal cuffs locked around my wrists and ankles, their glowing blue light my constant reminder that I am in hell.

I collapse, with a heavy breath, onto the floor.

I'm too hot to put on clothes, but I'm not ready to leave the privacy of the bathroom yet, so I sit here, wearing nothing but these manacles, and drop my head into my hands.

My hair is long again.

I discovered it like this—long, heavy, dark—one morning, and when I asked her about it, I nearly ruined everything.

"What do you mean?" Evie said, narrowing her eyes at me. "Your hair has always been long."

164

I blinked at her, remembering to play dumb. "I know."

She stared at me awhile longer before she finally let it go, but I'm still worried I'll pay for that slip. Sometimes it's hard to remember how to act. My mind is being attacked, assaulted every day by emotion I never knew existed. My memories were supposed to be erased. Instead, they're being replenished.

I'm remembering everything:

My mother's laugh, her slender wrists, the smell of her shampoo, and the familiarity of her arms around me.

The more I remember, the less this place feels foreign to me. The less these sounds and smells—these mountains in the distance—feel unknown. It's as if the disparate parts of my most desperate self are stitching back together, as if the gaping holes in my heart and head are healing, filling slowly with sensation.

This compound was my home. These people, my family. I woke up this morning remembering my mother's favorite shade of lipstick.

Bloodred.

I remember watching her paint her lips some evenings. I remember the day I snuck into her room and stole the glossy metal tube; I remember when she found me, my hands and mouth smeared in red, my face a grotesque reimagining of herself.

The more I remember my parents, the more I begin to finally make sense of myself—my many fears and insecurities, the myriad ways in which I've often felt lost, searching for something I could not name.

It's devastating.

And yet—

In this new, turbulent reality, the one person I recognize anymore is *him*. My memories of him—memories of us—have done something to me. I've changed somewhere deep inside. I feel different. Heavier, like my feet have been more firmly planted, liberated by certainty, free to grow roots here in my own self, free to trust unequivocally in the strength and steadiness of my own heart. It's an empowering discovery, to find that I can trust myself—even when I'm not myself—to make the right choices. To know for certain now that there was at least one mistake I never made.

Aaron Warner Anderson is the only emotional through line in my life that ever made sense. He's the only constant. The only steady, reliable heartbeat I've ever had.

Aaron, Aaron, Aaron, Aaron

I had no idea how much we'd lost, no idea how much of him I'd longed for. I had no idea how desperately we'd been fighting. How many years we'd fought for moments—minutes—to be together.

It fills me with a painful kind of joy.

But when I remember how I left things between us, I want to *scream*.

I have no idea if I'll ever see him again.

Still, I'm holding on to the hope that he's alive, out there, somewhere. Evie said she couldn't kill him. She said that she alone didn't have the authority to have him executed.

And if Aaron is still alive, I will find a way to get to him. But I have to be careful. Breaking out of this new prison won't be easy—As it is, Evie almost never lets me out of my room. Worse, she sedates me during the day, allowing me only a couple of lucid hours. There's never enough time to *think*, much less to plan an escape, to assess my surroundings, or to wander the halls outside my door.

Only once did she let me go outside.

Sort of.

She let me onto a balcony overlooking the backyard. It wasn't much, but even that small step helped me understand a bit about where we were and what the layout of the building might look like.

The assessment was chilling.

We appeared to be in the center of a settlement—a small city—in the middle of nowhere. I leaned over the edge of the balcony, craning my neck to take in the breadth of it, but the view was so vast I couldn't see all the way around. From where I stood I saw at least twenty different buildings, all connected by roads and navigated by people in miniature, electric cars. There were loading and unloading docks, massive trucks filing in and out, and there was a landing strip in the distance, a row of jets parked neatly in a concrete lot. I understood then that I was living in the middle of a massive operation—something so much more terrifying than Sector 45.

This is an international base.

This has to be one of the capitals. Whatever this

is—whatever they do here—it makes Sector 45 look like a joke.

Here, where the hills are somehow still green and beautiful, where the air is fresh and cool and everything seems alive. My accounting is probably off, but I think we're nearing the end of April—and the sights outside my window are unlike anything I've ever seen in Sector 45: vast, snowcapped mountain ranges; rolling hills thick with vegetation; trees heavy with bright, changing leaves; and a massive, glittering lake that looks close enough to run to. This land looks healthy. Vibrant.

I thought we'd lost a world like this a long time ago.

Evie's begun to sedate me less these days, but some days my vision seems to fray at the edges, like a satellite image glitching, waiting for data to load.

I wonder, sometimes, if she's poisoning me.

I'm wondering this now, remembering the bowl of soup she sent to my room for breakfast. I can still feel the gluey residue as it coated my tongue, the roof of my mouth.

Unease churns my stomach.

I haul myself up off the bathroom floor, my limbs slow and heavy. It takes me a moment to stabilize. The effects of this experiment have left me hollow.

Angry.

As if out of nowhere, my mind conjures an image of Evie's face. I remember her eyes. Deep, dark brown. Bottomless. The same color as her hair. She has a short, sharp bob, a heavy curtain constantly whipping against her chin. She's a beautiful woman, more beautiful at fifty than she was at twenty.

Coming.

The word occurs to me suddenly, and a bolt of panic shoots up my spine. Not a second later there's a sharp knock at my bathroom door.

"Yes?"

"Ella, you've been in the bathroom for almost half an hour, and you know how I feel about wasting ti—"

"*Evie.*" I force myself to laugh. "I'm almost done," I say. "I'll be right out."

A pause.

The silence stretches the seconds into a lifetime. My heart jumps up, into my throat. Beats in my mouth.

"All right," she says slowly. "Five more minutes."

I close my eyes as I exhale, pressing the towel to the racing pulse at my neck. I dry off quickly before wringing the remaining water from my hair and slipping back into my robe.

Finally, I open the bathroom door and welcome the cool morning temperature against my feverish skin. But I hardly have a chance to take a breath before she's in my face again.

"Wear this," she says, forcing a dress into my arms. She's smiling but it doesn't suit her. She looks deranged. "You love wearing yellow."

I blink as I take the dress from her, feeling a sudden,

disorienting wave of déjà vu. "Of course," I say. "I love wearing yellow."

Her smile grows thinner, threatens to turn her face inside out.

"Could I just—?" I make an abstract gesture toward my body.

"Oh," she says, startled. "Right." She shoots me another smile and says, "I'll be outside."

My own smile is brittle.

She watches me. She always watches me. Studies my reactions, the timing of my responses. She's scanning me, constantly, for information. She wants confirmation that I've been properly hollowed out. *Remade.*

I smile wider.

Finally, she takes a step back. "Good girl," she says softly.

I stand in the middle of my room and watch her leave, the yellow dress still pressed against my chest.

There was another time when I'd felt trapped, just like this. I was held against my will and given beautiful clothes and three square meals and demanded to be something I wasn't and I fought it—fought it with everything I had.

It didn't do me any good.

I swore that if I could do it again I'd do it differently. I said if I could do it over I'd wear the clothes and eat the food and play along until I could figure out where I was and how to break free.

So here's my chance.

This time, I've decided to play along.

KENJI

I wake up, bound and gagged, a roaring sound in my ears. I blink to clear my vision. I'm bound so tightly I can't move, so it takes me a second to realize I can't see my legs.

No legs. No arms, either.

The revelation that I'm invisible hits me with full, horrifying force.

I'm not doing this.

I didn't bring myself here, bind and gag myself, and make myself invisible.

There's only one other person who would.

I look around desperately, trying to gauge where I am and what my chances might be for escape, but when I finally manage to heave my body to one side—just long enough to crane my neck—I realize, with a terrifying jolt, that I'm on a plane.

And then—voices.

It's Anderson and Nazeera.

I hear them discussing something about how we'll be landing soon, and then, minutes later, I feel it when we touch ground.

The plane taxis for a while and it seems to take forever before the engines finally turn off.

I hear Anderson leave. Nazeera hangs back, saying something about needing to clean up. She shuts down the plane and its cameras, doesn't acknowledge me.

Finally, I hear her footsteps getting closer to my head. She uses one foot to roll me onto my back, and then, just like that, my invisibility is gone. She stares at me for a little while longer, says nothing.

Finally, she smiles.

"Hi," she says, removing the gag from my mouth. "How are you holding up?"

And I decide right then that I'm going to have to kill her.

"Okay," she says, "I know you're probably upset—"

"UPSET? YOU THINK I'M UPSET?" I jerk violently against the ties. "Jesus Christ, woman, get me out of these goddamn restraints—"

"I'll get you out of the restraints when you calm down—"

"HOW CAN YOU EXPECT ME TO BE CALM?"

"I'm trying to save your life right now, so, actually, I expect a lot of things from you."

I'm breathing hard. "Wait. What?"

She crosses her arms, stares down at me. "I've been trying to explain to you that there was really no other way to do this. And don't worry," she says. "Your friends are okay. We should be able to get them out of the asylum before any permanent damage is done."

"What? What do you mean *permanent damage?*"

Nazeera sighs. "Anyway, this was the only way I could think of stealing a plane without attracting notice. I needed to track Anderson."

"So you knew he was alive, that whole time, and you said nothing about it."

She raises her eyebrows. "Honestly, I thought you knew."

"How the hell was I supposed to know?" I shout. "How was I supposed to know *anything*?"

"Stop shouting," she says. "I went to all this trouble to save your life but I swear to God I will kill you if you don't stop shouting right now."

"Where," I say, "THE HELL," I say, "ARE WE?"

And instead of killing me, she laughs. "Where do you think we are?" She shakes her head. "We're in Oceania. We're here to find Ella."

WARNER

"We can live in the lake," she says simply.

"What?" I almost laugh. "What are you talking about?"

"I'm serious," she says. "I heard my mum talking about how to make it so people can live underwater, and I'm going to ask her to tell me, and then we can live in the lake."

I sigh. "We can't live in the lake, Ella."

"Why not?" She turns and looks at me, her eyes wide, startlingly bright. Blue green. Like the globe, I think. Like the whole world. "Why can't we live in the lake? My mum says th—"

"Stop it, Ella. Stop—"

I wake suddenly, jerking upward as my eyes fly open, my lungs desperate for air. I breathe in too fast and cough, choking on the overcorrection of oxygen. My body bows forward, chest heaving, my hands braced against the cold, concrete floor.

Ella.

Ella.

Pain spears me through the chest. I stopped eating the poisoned food two days ago, but the visions linger even when I'm lucid. There's something hyperreal about this one in particular, the memory barreling into me over

179

and over, shooting swift, sharp pains through my gut. It's breathtaking, this disorienting rush of emotion.

For the first time, I'm beginning to believe.

I thought nightmares. Hallucinations, even. But now I know.

Now it seems impossible to deny.

I heard my mum talking about how to make it so people can live underwater

I didn't understand right away why Max and Evie were keeping me captive here, but they must blame me for something—maybe something my father is responsible for. Something I unknowingly took part in.

Maybe something like torturing their daughter Emmaline.

When I was sent away for two years, I was never told where I was going. The details of my location were never disclosed, and during that time period I lived in a veritable prison of my own, never allowed to step outside, never allowed to know more than was absolutely necessary about the task at hand. The breaks I was given were closely guarded, and I was required to wear a blindfold as I was ushered on and off the jet, which always made me think I must've been working somewhere easily identifiable. But those two years also comprised some of the darkest, saddest days of my life; all I knew was my desperate need for oblivion. I was so buried in self-loathing that it seemed only right to find solace in the arms of someone who meant nothing to me. I hated myself every day. Being with Lena was both relief and torture.

Even so, I felt numb, all the time.

After two weeks here, I'm beginning to wonder if this prison isn't one I've known before. If this isn't the same place I spent those two horrible years of my life. It's hard to explain the intangible, irrational reasons why the view outside my window is beginning to feel familiar to me, but two years is a long time to grow familiar with the rhythms of a land, even one you don't understand.

I wonder if Emmaline is here, somewhere.

It makes sense that she'd be here, close to home—close to her parents, whose medical and scientific advances are the only reason she's even alive. Or something close to alive, anyway.

It makes sense that they'd bring Juliette—*Ella*, I remind myself—back here, to her home. The question is—

Why bring her here? What are they hoping to do with her?

But then, if her mother is anything like my father, I think I can imagine what they might have in mind.

I push myself off the floor and take a steadying breath. My body is running on mere adrenaline, so starved for sleep and sustenance that I have to—

Pain.

It's swift and sudden and I gasp even as I recognize the familiar sting. I have no idea how long it'll take for my ribs to fully heal. Until then, I clench my teeth as I stand, feeling blindly for purchase against the rough stone. My hands shake as I steady myself and I'm breathing too hard again, eyes darting around the familiar cell.

I turn on the sink and splash ice-cold water on my face. The effect is immediate. Focusing.

Carefully, I strip down to nothing. I soak my undershirt under the running water and use it to scrub my face, my neck, the rest of my body. I wash my hair. Rinse my mouth. Clean my teeth. And then I do what little I can for the rest of my clothes, washing them by hand and wringing them dry. I slip back into my underwear even though the cotton is still slightly damp, and I fight back a shiver in the darkness. Hungry and cold is at least better than drugged and delirious.

This is the end of my second week in confinement, and my third day this week without food. It feels good to have a clear head, even as my body slowly starves. I'd already been leaner than usual, but now the lines of my body feel unusually sharp, even to myself, all necessary softness gone from my limbs. It's only a matter of time before my muscles atrophy and I do irreparable damage to my organs, but right now I have no choice. I need access to my mind.

To *think*.

And something about my sentencing feels off.

The more I think about it, the less sense it makes that Max and Evie would want me to suffer for what I did to Emmaline. They were the ones who donated their daughters to The Reestablishment in the first place. My work overseeing Emmaline was assigned to me—in fact, it was likely a job they'd approved. It would make more sense that I were here for treason. Max and Evie, like any other commanders, would want me to suffer for turning my back on The Reestablishment.

But even this theory feels wrong. Incongruous.

The punishment for treason has always been public execution. Quick. Efficient. I should be murdered, with only a little fanfare, in front of my own soldiers. But this—locking people up like this—slowly starving them while stripping them of their sanity and dignity—this is uncivilized. It's what The Reestablishment does to others, not to its own.

It's what they did to Ella. They tortured her. Ran tests on her. She wasn't locked up to inspire penitence. She was in isolation because she was part of an ongoing experiment.

And I am in the unique position to know that such a prisoner requires constant maintenance.

I figured I'd be kept here for a few days—maybe a week—but locking me up for what seems to be an indeterminate amount of time—

This must be difficult for them.

For two weeks they've managed to remain just slightly ahead of me, a feat they accomplished by poisoning my food. In training I'd never needed more than a week to break my way out of high-security prisons, and they must've known this. By forcing me to choose between sustenance and clarity every day, they've given themselves an advantage.

Still, I'm unconcerned.

The longer I'm here, the more leverage I gain. If they know what I'm capable of, they must also know that this is unsustainable. They can't use shock and poison to destabilize me indefinitely. I've now been here long enough to have taken stock of my surroundings, and I've been filing away information for nearly two weeks—the movements of the sun, the phases of the moon, the manufacturer of the locks, the sink, the unusual hinges on the door. I suspected, but now know for certain, that I'm in the southern hemisphere, not only because I know Max and Evie hail from Oceania, but because the northern constellations outside my window are upside down.

I must be on their base.

Logically, I know I must've been here a few times in my life, but the memories are dim. The night skies are clearer here than they were in Sector 45. The stars, brighter. The lack of light pollution means we are far from civilization, and the view out the window proves that we are surrounded, on all sides, by the wild landscape of this territory. There's a massive, glittering lake not far in the distance, which—

Something jolts to life in my mind.

The memory from earlier, expanded:

She shrugs and throws a rock in the lake. It lands with a dull splash. "Well, we'll just run away," she says.

"We can't run away," I say. "Stop saying that."

"We can, too."

"There's nowhere to go."

"There are plenty of places to go."

I shake my head. "You know what I mean. They'd find us wherever we went. They watch us all the time."

"We can live in the lake," she says simply.

"What?" I almost laugh. "What are you talking about?"

"I'm serious," she says. "I heard my mum talking about how to make it so people can live underwater, and I'm going to ask her to tell me, and then we can live in the lake."

I sigh. "We can't live in the lake, Ella."

"Why not?" She turns and looks at me, her eyes wide, startlingly bright. Blue green. Like the globe, I think. Like the whole world. "Why can't we live in the lake? My mum says th—"

"Stop it, Ella. Stop—"

A cold sweat breaks out on my forehead. Goose bumps rise along my skin. *Ella.*

Ella Ella Ella

Over and over again.

Everything about the name is beginning to sound familiar. The movement of my tongue as I form the word, familiar. It's as if the memory is in my muscle, as if my mouth has made this shape a thousand times.

I force myself to take a steadying breath.

I need to find her. *I have to find her.*

Here is what I know:

It takes just under thirty seconds for the footsteps to disappear down the hall, and they're always the same—same stride, same cadence—which means there's only one person attending to me. The paces are long and heavy, which means my attendant is tall, possibly male. Maybe Max himself, if they've deemed me a high-priority prisoner. Still, they've left me unshackled and unharmed—*why?*—and though I've been given neither bed nor blanket, I have access to water from the sink.

There's no electricity in here; no outlets, no wires. But there must be cameras hidden somewhere, watching my every move. There are two drains: one in the sink, and one underneath the toilet. There's one square foot of window—likely bulletproof glass, maybe eight to ten centimeters thick—and a single, small air vent in the floor. The vent has no visible screws, which means it must be bolted from inside, and the slats are too narrow for my fingers, the steel blades visibly welded in place. Still, it's only an average level of security for a prison vent. A little more time and clarity, and I'll find a way to remove the screen and repurpose the parts. Eventually, I'll find a way to dismantle everything in this room. I'll take apart the metal toilet, the flimsy metal sink. I'll make my own tools and weapons and find a way to slowly, carefully disassemble the locks and hinges. Or perhaps I'll damage the pipes and flood the room and its adjoining hallway, forcing someone to come to the door.

The sooner they send someone to my room, the better. If they've left me alone in my cell this long, it's been for their own protection, not my suffering. I excel at hand-to-hand combat.

I know myself. I know my capacity to withstand

complicated physical and mental torture. If I wanted to, I could give myself two—maybe three—weeks to forgo the poisoned meals and survive on water alone before I lost my mind or mobility. I know how resourceful I can be, given the opportunity, and this—this effort to contain me—must be exhausting. Great care went into selecting these sounds and meals and rituals and even this vigilant lack of communication.

It doesn't make sense that they'd go to all this trouble for treason. No. I must be in purgatory for something else.

I rack my brain for a motive, but my memories are surprisingly thin when it comes to Max and Evie. Still forming.

With some difficulty, I'm able to conjure up flickers of images.

A brief handshake with my father.

A burst of laughter.

A cheerful swell of holiday music.

A laboratory and my mother.

I stiffen.

A laboratory and my mother.

I focus my thoughts, homing in on the memory—*bright lights, muffled footsteps, the sound of my own voice asking my father a question* and then, painfully—

My mind goes blank.

I frown. Stare into my hands.

Nothing.

I know a great deal about the other commanders and

their families. It's been my business to know. But there's an unusual dearth of information where Oceania is concerned, and for the first time, it sends a shock of fear through me. There are two timelines merging in my mind—a life with Ella, and a life without her—and I'm still learning to sift through the information for something real.

Still, thinking about Max and Evie now seems to strain something in my brain. It's as if there's something there, something just out of reach, and the more I force my mind to recall them—their faces, their voices—the more it hurts.

Why all this trouble to imprison me?

Why not simply have me killed?

I have so many questions it's making my head spin.

Just then, the door rattles. The sound of metal on metal is sharp and abrasive, the sounds like sandpaper against my nerves.

I hear the bolt unlock and feel unusually calm. I was built to handle this life, its blows, its sick, sadistic ways. Death has never scared me.

But when the door swings open, I realize my mistake.

I imagined a thousand different scenarios. I prepared for a myriad of opponents. But I had not prepared for this.

"Hi birthday boy," he says, laughing as he steps into the light. "Did you miss me?"

And I'm suddenly unable to move.

~~JULIETTE~~

ELLA

"Stop—stop it, oh my God, that's disgusting," Emmaline cries. "Stop it. Stop touching each other! You guys are so gross."

Dad pinches Mum's butt, right in front of us.

Emmaline screams. "Oh my God, I said stop!"

It's Saturday morning, and Saturday morning is when we make pancakes, but Mum and Dad don't really get around to cooking anything because they won't stop kissing each other. Emmaline hates it.

I think it's nice.

I sit at the counter and prop my face in my hands, watching. I prefer watching. Emmaline keeps trying to make me work, but I don't want to. I like sitting better than working.

"No one is making pancakes," Emmaline cries, and she spins around so angrily she knocks a bowl of batter to the ground. "Why am I doing all the work?"

Dad laughs. "Sweetheart, we're all together," he says, scooping up the fallen bowl. He grabs a bunch of paper towels and says, "Isn't that more important than pancakes?"

"No," Emmaline says angrily. "We're supposed to make pancakes. It's Saturday, which means we're supposed to make pancakes, and you and Mum are just kissing, and Ella is being lazy—"

"Hey—" I say, and stand up.

"—and no one is doing what they're supposed to be doing and instead I'm doing it all by myself—"

Mum and Dad are both laughing now.

"It's not funny!" Emmaline cries, and now she's shouting, tears streaking down her face. "It's not funny, and I don't like it when no one listens to me, and I don't—"

Two weeks ago, I was lying on an operating table, limp, naked, and leaking blood through an aperture in my temple the size of a gunshot wound. My vision was blurred. I couldn't hear much more than the sound of my own breathing, hot and heavy and everywhere, building in and around me. Suddenly, Evie came into view. She was staring at me; she seemed frustrated. She'd been trying to complete the process of *physical recalibration,* as she called it.

For some reason, she couldn't finish the job.

She'd already emptied the contents of sixteen syringes into my brain, and she'd made several small incisions in my abdomen, my arms, and my thighs. I couldn't see exactly what she did next, but she spoke, occasionally, as she worked, and she claimed that the simple surgical procedures she was performing would strengthen my joints and reinforce my muscles. She wanted me to be stronger, to be more resilient on a cellular level. It was a preventative measure, she said. She was worried my build was too slight; that my muscles might degenerate prematurely in the face of intense physical challenges. She didn't say it, but I felt it: she wanted me to be stronger than my sister.

"Emmaline," I whispered.

It was lucky that I was too exhausted, too broken, too sedated to speak clearly. It was lucky that I only lay there, eyes fluttering open and closed, my chapped lips making it impossible to do more than mutter the name. It was lucky that I couldn't understand, right away, that I was still *me*. That I still remembered everything despite Evie's promises to dissolve what was left of my mind.

Still, I'd said the wrong thing.

Evie stopped what she was doing. She leaned over my face and studied me, nose to nose.

I blinked.

Don't

The words appeared in my head as if they'd been planted there long ago, like I was remembering, remembering

Evie jerked backward and immediately started speaking into a device clenched in her fist. Her voice was low and rough and I couldn't make out what she was saying.

I blinked again. Confused. I parted my lips to say something, when—

Don't

The thought came through more sharply this time.

A moment later Evie was in my face again, this time

drilling me with questions.

who are you
where are you
what is your name
where were you born
how old are you
who are your parents
where do you live

I was suddenly aware enough to understand that Evie was checking her work. She wanted to make sure my brain had been wiped clean. I wasn't sure what I was supposed to say or do, so I said nothing.

Instead, I blinked.

Blinked a lot.

Evie finally—reluctantly—stepped away, but she didn't seem entirely convinced of my stupidity. And then, when I thought she might murder me just to be safe, she stopped. Stared at the wall.

And then she left.

I was trembling on the operating table for twenty minutes before the room was swarmed by a team of people. They unstrapped my body, washed and wrapped my open wounds.

I think I was screaming.

Eventually the combination of pain, exhaustion, and the slow drip of opiates caught up with me, and I passed out.

I never understood what happened that day.

I couldn't ask, Evie never explained, and the strange, sharp voice in my head never returned. But then, Evie sedated me so much in my first weeks on this compound that it's possible there was never even a chance.

Today, for the first time since that day, I hear it again.

I'm standing in the middle of my room, this gauzy yellow dress still bunched in my arms, when the voice assaults me.

It knocks the wind out of me.

Ella

I spin around, my breaths coming in fast. The voice is louder than it's ever been, frightening in its intensity. Maybe I was wrong about Evie's experiment, maybe this is part of it, maybe hallucinating and hearing voices is a precursor to oblivion—

No

"Who are you?" I say, the dress dropping to the floor. It occurs to me, as if from a distance, that I'm standing in my underwear, screaming at an empty room, and a violent shudder goes through my body.

Roughly, I yank the yellow dress over my head, its light, breezy layers like silk against my skin. In a different lifetime, I would've loved this dress. It's both beautiful and comfortable, the perfect sartorial combination. But there's no time for that kind of frivolity anymore.

Today, this dress is just a part of the role I must play.

The voice in my head has gone quiet, but my heart is still racing. I feel propelled into motion by instinct alone, and, quickly, I slip into a pair of simple white tennis shoes, tying the laces tightly. I don't know why, but today, *right now*, for some reason—I feel like I might need to run.

Yes

My spine straightens.

Adrenaline courses through my veins and my muscles feel tight, burning with an intensity that feels brand-new to me; it's the first time I've felt any positive effects of Evie's procedures. This strength feels like it's been grafted to my bones, like I could launch myself into the air, like I could scale a wall with one hand.

I've known superstrength before, but that strength always felt like it was coming from elsewhere, like it was something I had to harness and release. Without my supernatural abilities—when I turned off my powers—I was left with an unimpressive, flimsy body. I'd been undernourished for years, forced to endure extreme physical and mental conditions, and my body suffered for it. I'd only begun to learn proper forms of exercise and conditioning in the last couple of months, and while the progress I made was helpful, it was only the first step in the right direction.

But this—

Whatever Evie did to me? This is different.

Two weeks ago I was in so much pain I could hardly move. The next morning, when I could finally stand on my own, I saw no discernible difference in my body except that I was seven shades of purple from top to bottom. Everything was bruised. I was walking agony.

Evie told me, as my doctor, that she kept me sedated so that I'd be forced to remain still in order to heal more quickly, but I had no reason to believe her. I still don't. But this is the first time in two weeks that I feel almost normal. The bruises have nearly faded. Only the incision sites, the most painful entry points, still look a little yellow.

Not bad.

I flex my fists and feel powerful, truly powerful, even with the glowing manacles clamped around my wrists and ankles. I've desperately missed my powers, missed them more than I ever thought I could miss something I'd spent so many years hating about myself. But for the first time in weeks, I feel strong. I know Evie did this to me—did this to my muscles—and I know I should distrust it, but it feels so good to feel good that I almost can't help but revel in it.

And right now, I feel like I could—

Run

I go still.

RUN

"What?" I whisper, turning to scan the walls, the ceiling. "Run where?"

Out

The word thunders through me, reverberates along my rib cage. *Out.* As if it were that simple, as if I could turn the doorknob and be rid of this nightmare. If it were that easy to leave this room, I would've done it already. But Evie reinforces the locks on my door with multiple layers of security. I only saw the mechanics of it once, when she returned me to my room after allowing me to look outside for a few minutes. In addition to the discreet cameras and retina displays, there's a biometric scanner that reads Evie's fingerprints to allow her access to the room. I've spent hours trying to get my bedroom door open, to no avail.

Out

Again, that word, loud and harsh inside my head. There's something terrifying about the hope that snakes through me at the thought of escape. It clings and tugs and tempts me to be crazy enough to listen to the absurd hallucinations attacking my mind.

This could be a trap, I think.

This could all be Evie's doing. I could be playing directly

into her hand.

Still.

I can't help myself.

I cross the room in a few quick strides. I hesitate, my hand hovering over the handle, and, with a final exhalation, I give in.

The door swings opens easily.

I stand in the open doorway, my heart racing harder. A heady rush of feeling surges through me and I look around desperately, studying the many hallways stretching out before me.

This seems impossible.

I have no idea where to go. No idea if I'm crazy for listening to a manipulative voice in my head after my psychotic mother spent hours injecting things into my mind.

It's only when I remember that I first heard this voice the night I arrived—just moments before Evie began torturing me—that I begin to doubt my doubt.

Dying

That was what the voice said to me that first night. *Dying.*

I was lying on an operating table, unable to move or speak. I could only shout inside my head and I wanted to know where Emmaline was. I tried to scream it.

Dying, the voice had said.

A cold, paralyzing fear fills my blood.
"Emmaline?" I whisper. "Is that you?"

Help

I take a certain step forward.

WARNER

"I'm a little early," he says. "I know your birthday is tomorrow, but I just couldn't wait any longer."

I stare at my father as though he might be a ghost. Worse, a poltergeist. I can't bring myself to speak, and for some reason he doesn't seem to mind my silence.

Then—

He smiles.

It's a true smile, one that softens his features and brightens his eyes. We're in something that looks like a sitting room, a bright, open space with plush couches, chairs, a round table, and a small writing desk in the corner. There's a thick carpet underfoot. The walls are a pleasant, pale yellow, sun pouring in through large windows. My father's figure is backlit. He looks ethereal. Glowing, like he might be an angel.

This world has a sick sense of humor.

He tossed me a robe when he walked into my cell, but hasn't offered me anything else. I haven't been given a chance to change. I haven't been offered food or water. I feel underdressed—vulnerable—sitting across from him in nothing but cold underwear and a thin robe. I don't even have socks. Slippers. *Something.*

And I can only imagine what I must look like right now, considering it's been a couple of weeks since I've had a shave or a haircut. I managed to keep myself clean in prison, but my hair is a bit longer now. Not like it used to be, but it's getting there. And my face—

I touch my face almost without thinking.

Touching my face has become a bit of a habit these last couple of weeks. I have a beard. It's not much of a beard, but it's enough to surprise me, every time. I have no idea how I must look right now.

Untamed, perhaps.

Finally, I say, "You're supposed to be dead."

"Surprise," he says, and smiles.

I only stare at him.

My father leans against the table and stuffs his hands into his pants' pockets in a way that makes him look boyish. Charming.

It makes me feel ill.

I look away, scanning the room for help. Details. Something to root me, something to explain *him*, something to arm me against what might be coming.

I come up short.

He laughs. "You know, you could stand to show a bit more emotion. I actually thought you might be happy to see me."

That gets my attention. "You thought wrong," I say. "I was happy to hear you were dead."

"Are you sure?" He tilts his head. "You're sure you didn't

shed a single tear for me? Didn't miss me even the tiniest bit?"

All it takes is a moment of hesitation. The half-second delay during which I remember the weeks I spent caught in a prison of half grief, hating myself for mourning him, and hating that I ever cared at all.

I open my mouth to speak and he cuts me off, his smile triumphant. "I know this must be a bit unsettling. And I know you're going to pretend you don't care. But we both know that your bleeding heart has always been the source of all our problems, and there's no point trying to deny that now. So I'll be generous and offer to overlook your treasonous behavior."

My spine stiffens.

"You didn't think I'd just forget, did you?" My father is no longer smiling. "You try to overthrow *me*—my government, my continent—and then you stand aside like a perfect, pathetic piece of garbage as your girlfriend attempts to *murder* me—and you thought I'd never mention it?"

I can't look at him anymore. I can't stand the sight of his face, so like my own. His skin is still perfect, unscarred. As if he'd never been injured. Never taken a bullet to the forehead.

I don't understand it.

"No? You still won't be inspired to respond?" he says. "In that case, you might be smarter than I gave you credit for."

There. That feels more like him.

"But the fact remains that we're at an important crossroads right now. I had to call in a number of favors to have you transported here unharmed. The council was going to vote to have you executed for treason, and I was able to convince them otherwise."

"Why would you even bother?"

His eyes narrow as he appraises me. "I save your life," he says, "and this is your reaction? Insolence? Ingratitude?"

"This," I say sharply, "is your idea of saving my life? Throwing me in prison and having me poisoned to death?"

"That should've been a picnic." His gaze grows cold. "You really would be better off dead if those circumstances were enough to break you."

I say nothing.

"Besides, we had to punish you somehow. Your actions couldn't go unchecked." My father looks away. "We've had a lot of messes to clean up," he says finally. "Where do you think I've been all this time?"

"As I said, I thought you were dead."

"Close, but not quite. Actually," he says, taking a breath, "I spent a great deal of time convalescing. *Here.* I was airlifted back here, where the Sommerses have been reviving me." He pulls up the hem of his pants and I glimpse the silver gleam of metal where his ankle should be. "I've got new feet," he says, and laughs. "Can you believe it?"

I can't. I can't believe it.

I'm stunned.

He smiles, obviously satisfied with my reaction. "We let

you and your friends think you'd had a victory just long enough to give me time to recover. We sent the rest of the kids down to distract you, to make it seem like The Reestablishment might actually accept its new, self-appointed commander." He shakes his head. "A seventeen-year-old child declaring herself the ruler of North America," he says, almost to himself. And then, looking up: "That girl really was a piece of work, wasn't she?"

Panic gathers in my chest. "What did you do to her? Where is she?"

"No." My father's smile disappears. "Absolutely not."

"What does that mean?"

"It means *absolutely not*. That girl is done. She's gone. No more afternoon specials with your buddies from Omega Point. No more running around naked with your little girlfriend. No more sex in the afternoon when you should be working."

I feel both ill and enraged. "Don't you dare—Don't *ever* talk about her like that. You have no right—"

He sighs, long and loud. Mutters something foul. "When are you going stop this? When will you grow out of this?"

It takes everything I've got to bite back my anger. To sit here, calmly, and say nothing. Somehow, my silence makes things worse.

"Dammit, Aaron," he says, getting to his feet. "I keep waiting for you to move on. To get over her. To *evolve*," he says, practically shouting at me now. "It's been over a decade of the same bullshit."

Over a decade.

A slip.

"What do you mean," I say, studying him carefully. "'Over a decade'?"

"I'm exaggerating," he says, biting off the words. "Exaggerating to make a point."

"*Liar.*"

For the first time, something uncertain flashes through my father's eyes.

"Will you admit it?" I say quietly. "Will you admit to me what I already know?"

He sets his jaw. Says nothing.

"*Admit it,*" I say. "Juliette was an alias. Juliette Ferrars is actually Ella Sommers, the daughter of Evie and Maximillian Som—"

"How—" My father catches himself. He looks away and then, too soon, he looks back. He seems to be deciding something.

Finally, slowly, he nods.

"You know what? It's better this way. Better for you to know," he says quietly. "Better for you to understand exactly why you're never going to see her again."

"That's not up to you."

"Not up to me?" Rage flashes in and out of his eyes, his cool mask quickly crumbling. "That girl has been the bane of my existence for *twelve years,*" he says. "She's caused me more problems than you can even begin to understand, not the least of which has been to distract my idiot son for the better part of the last decade. Despite my every effort to break you apart—to remove this cancer from our lives— you've insisted, over and over again, on falling in love with her." He looks me in the eye, his own eyes wild with fury. "She was never meant for you. She was never meant for any of this. That girl was sentenced to death," he says viciously, "the moment I named her Juliette."

My heart is beating so hard it feels as though I'm dreaming. This must be a nightmare. I have to force myself to speak. To say:

"What are you talking about?"

My father's mouth twists into an imitation of a smile.

"Ella," he says, "was designed to become a tool for war. She and her sister both, right from the beginning. Decades before we took over, sicknesses were beginning to ravage the population. The government was trying to bury the information, but we knew. I saw the classified files. I tracked down one of the secret bunkers. People were malfunctioning, metamorphosing—so much so that it felt almost like the next phase of evolution. Only Evie had the presence of mind to see the sickness as a tool. She was the one who first began studying the Unnaturals. She was the reason we created the asylums—she wanted access to more varieties of the illness—and she was the one who learned how to isolate and reproduce the alien DNA. It was her idea to use the findings to help our cause. Ella and Emmaline," he says angrily, "were only ever meant to be Evie's science experiments. Ella was never meant for you. Never meant for *anyone,*" he shouts. "Get her out of your head."

I feel frozen as the words settle around me. Within me. The revelation isn't entirely new and yet—the pain is fresh. Time seems to slow down, speed up, spin backward. My eyes fall closed. My memories collect and expand, exploding with renewed meaning as they assault me, all at once—

Ella through the ages.

My childhood friend.

Ella, ripped away from me when I was seven years old. Ella and Emmaline, who they'd said had drowned in the lake. They told me to forget, to forget the girls ever existed and, finally, tired of answering my questions, they told me they'd make things easier for me. I followed my father into a room where he promised he'd explain everything.

And then—

I'm strapped to a chair, my head held in place with heavy metal clamps. Bright lights flash and buzz above me.

I hear the monitors chirping, the muffled sounds of voices around me. The room feels large and cavernous, gleaming. I hear the loud, disconcerting sounds of my own breathing and the hard, heavy beats of my heart. I jump, a little, at the unwelcome feel of my father's hand on my arm, telling me I'll feel better soon.

I look up at him as if emerging from a dream.

"What is it?" he says. "What just happened?"

I part my lips to speak, wonder if it's safe to tell him the truth.

I decide I'm tired of the lies.

"I've been remembering her," I say.

My father's face goes unexpectedly blank, and it's the only reaction I need to understand the final, missing piece.

"You've been stealing my memories," I say to him, my voice unnaturally calm. "All these years. You've been tampering with my mind. It was you."

He says nothing, but I see the tension in his jaw, the sudden jump of a vein under skin. "What are you remembering?"

I shake my head, stunned as I stare at him. "I should've known. After everything you've done to me—" I stop, my vision shifts, unfocused for a moment. "Of course you wouldn't let me be master of my own mind."

"What, exactly, are you remembering?" he says, hardly able to control the anger in his voice now. "What else do you know?"

At first, I feel nothing.

I've trained myself too well. Years of practice have taught me to bury my emotions as a reflex—especially in his presence—and it takes a few seconds for the feelings to emerge. They form slowly, infinite hands reaching up from infinite graves to fan the flames of an ancient rage I've never really allowed myself to touch.

"You stole my memories of her," I say quietly. "Why?"

"Always so focused on the girl." He glares at me. "She's not the center of everything, Aaron. I stole your memories of lots of things."

I'm shaking my head. I get to my feet slowly, at once out of my mind and perfectly calm, and I worry, for a moment, that I might actually expire from the full force of everything I feel for him. Hatred so deep it might boil me alive.

"Why would you do something like this except to torture me? You knew how I felt about her. You did it on purpose. Pushing us together and pulling us apart—" I stop suddenly. Realization dawns, bright and piercing and I look at him, unable to fathom the depth of his cruelty.

"You put Kent under my command on purpose," I say.

My father meets my eyes with a vacant expression. He says nothing.

"I find it hard to believe you didn't know the whereabouts of your illegitimate children," I say to him. "I don't believe for a second that you weren't having Kent's every move monitored. You must've known what he was doing with his life. You must've been notified the moment he enlisted.

"You could've sent him anywhere," I say. "You had the power to do that. Instead, you let him remain in Sector 45— under *my* jurisdiction—on purpose. Didn't you? And when you had Delalieu show me those files—when he came to me, convinced me that Kent would be the perfect cellmate for Juliette because here was proof that he'd known her, that they'd gone to school together—"

Suddenly, my father smiles.

"I've always tried to tell you," he says softly. "I've tried to tell you to stop letting your emotions rule your mind. Over and over, I tried to teach you, and you never listened. You

212

never learned." He shakes his head. "If you suffer now, it's because you brought it upon yourself. You made yourself an easy target."

I'm stunned.

Somehow, even after everything, he manages to shock me. "I don't understand how you can stand there, defending your actions, after you spent twenty years torturing me."

"I've only ever been trying to teach you a lesson, Aaron. I didn't want you to end up like your mother. She was weak, just like you."

I need to kill him.

I picture it: what it would be like to pin him to the ground, to stab him repeatedly through the heart, to watch the light go out of his eyes, to feel his body go cold under my hands.

I wait for fear.

Revulsion.

Regret.

They don't come.

I have no idea how he survived the last attempt on his life, but I no longer care to know the answer. I want him dead. I want to watch his blood pool in my hands. I want to rip his throat out.

I spy a letter opener on the writing desk nearby, and in the single second I take to swipe it, my father laughs.

Laughs.

Out loud. Doubled over, one hand holding his side. When he looks up, there are actual tears in his eyes.

"Have you lost your mind?" he says. "Aaron, don't be ridiculous."

I step forward, the letter opener clutched loosely in my fist, and I watch, carefully, for the moment he understands that I'm going to kill him. I want him to know that it's going to be me. I want him to know that he finally got what he wanted.

That he finally broke me.

"You made a mistake sparing my life," I say quietly. "You made a mistake showing your face. You made a mistake thinking you could ask me to come back, after all you've done—"

"You misunderstand me." He's standing straight again, the laughter gone from his face. "I'm not asking you to come back. You don't have a choice."

"Good. That makes this easier."

"Aaron." He shakes his head. "I'm not unarmed. I'm entirely willing to kill you if you step out of line. And though I can't claim that murdering my son is my favorite way to spend a morning, that doesn't mean I won't do it. So you need to stop and think, for just a moment, before you step forward and commit suicide."

I study him. My fingers flex around the weapon in my hand. "Tell me where she is," I say, "and I'll consider sparing your life."

"You fool. Have you not been listening to me? *She's gone.*"

I stiffen. Whatever he means by that, he's not lying. "Gone where?"

"Gone," he says angrily. "Disappeared. The girl you knew no longer exists."

He pulls a remote out of his jacket pocket and points it at the wall. An image appears instantly, projected from elsewhere, and the sound that fills the room is so sudden—so jarring and unexpected—it nearly brings me to my knees.

It's Ella.

She's screaming.

Blood drips down her open, screaming mouth, the agonizing sounds punctured only by the heaving sobs that pull ragged, aching breaths from her body. Her eyes are half open, delirious, and I watch as she's unstrapped from a chair and dragged onto a stretcher. Her body spasms, her arms and legs jerking uncontrollably. She's in a white hospital gown, the insubstantial ties coming undone, the thin fabric damp with her own blood.

My hands shake uncontrollably as I watch, her head whipping back and forth, her body straining against her restraints. She screams again and a bolt of pain shoots through me, so excruciating it nearly bends me in half. And then, quickly, as if out of nowhere, someone steps forward and stabs a needle in her neck.

Ella goes still.

Her body is frozen, her face captured in a single moment of agony before the drug kicks in, collapsing her. Her screams dissolve into smaller, steadier whimpers. She cries, even as her eyes close.

I feel violently ill.

My hands are shaking so hard I can no longer form a fist, and I watch, as if from afar, as the letter opener falls to the floor. I hold still, forcing back the urge to vomit, but the action provokes a shudder so disorienting I almost lose my balance. Slowly, I turn to face my father, whose eyes are inscrutable.

It takes two tries before I'm able to form a single, whispered word:

"What?"

He shakes his head, the picture of false sympathy. "I'm trying to get you to understand. This," he says, nodding at the screen, "this is what she's destined for. Forever. Stop imagining your life with her. Stop thinking of her as a *person*—"

"This can't be real," I say, cutting him off. I feel wild. Unhinged. "This—Tell me this isn't real. What are you doing to me? Is this—"

"Of course it's real," he says. "Juliette is gone. Ella is gone. She's as good as dead. She had her mind wiped *weeks* ago. But you," he says, "you still have a life to live. Are you listening to me? You have to pull yourself together."

But I can't hear him over the sound of Ella sobbing.

She's still weeping—the sounds softer, sadder, more desperate. She looks terrified. Small and helpless as foreign hands bandage the open wounds on her arms, the backs of her legs. I watch as glowing metal cuffs are shackled to her wrists and ankles. She whimpers once more.

And I feel insane.

I must be. Listening to her scream—watching her fight for her life, watching her choke on her own blood while I stand here, powerless to help her—

I'll never be able to forget the sound.

No matter what happens, no matter where I run, these screams—her screams—will haunt me forever.

"You wanted me to watch this?" I'm whispering now; I can hardly speak. "Why would you want me to watch this?"

He says something to me. Shouts something at me. But I feel suddenly deaf.

The sounds of the world seem warped, faraway, like my head has been submerged underwater. The fire in my brain has been snuffed out, replaced by a sudden, absolute calm. A sense of certainty. I know what I need to do now. And I know that there's nothing—nothing I won't do to get to her.

I feel it, feel my thin morals dissolving. I feel my flimsy, moth-eaten skin of humanity begin to come apart, and with it, the veil keeping me from complete darkness. There are no lines I won't cross. No illusions of mercy.

I wanted to be better for her. For her happiness. For her future.

But if she's gone, what good is goodness?

I take a deep, steadying breath. I feel oddly liberated, no longer shackled by an obligation to decency. And in one simple move, I pick up the letter opener I dropped on the floor.

"Aaron," he says, a warning in his voice.

"I don't want to hear you speak," I say. "I don't want you

217

to talk to me ever again."

I throw the knife even before the words have left my mouth. It flies hard and fast, and I enjoy the second it soars through the air. I enjoy the way the second expands, exploding in the strangeness of time. It all feels like slow motion. My father's eyes widen in a rare display of unmasked shock, and I smile at the sound of his gasp when the weapon finds its mark. I was aiming for his jugular, and it looks like my aim was true. He chokes, his eyes bulging as his hands move, shakily, to yank the letter opener from its home in his neck.

He coughs, suddenly, blood spattering everywhere, and with some effort, he's able to pull the thing free. Fresh blood gushes down his shirt, seeps from his mouth. He can't speak; the blade has penetrated his larynx. Instead, he gasps, still choking, his mouth opening and closing like a dying fish.

He falls to his knees.

His hands grasp at air, his veins jumping under his skin, and I step toward him. I watch him as he begs, silently, for something, and then I pat him down, pocketing the two guns I find concealed on his person.

"Enjoy hell," I whisper, before walking away.

Nothing matters anymore.

I have to find her.

~~JULIETTE~~

ELLA

Left.
 Right.
 Straight.
 Left.

The commands keep my feet moving safely down the hall. This compound is vast. Enormous. My bedroom was so ordinary that the truth of this facility is jarring. An open framework reveals many dozens of floors, hallways and staircases intertwining like overpasses and freeways. The ceiling seems miles away, high and arched and intricate. Exposed steel beams meet clean white walkways centered around an open, interior courtyard. I had no idea I was so high up. And, somehow, for such a huge building, I haven't yet been spotted.

Things are growing more eerie by the minute.

I encounter no one as I go; I'm ordered to run, detour, or hide just in time to avoid passersby. It's uncanny. Still, I've been walking for at least twenty minutes, and I don't seem to be getting closer to anything. I have no idea where I am in the scheme of things, and there are no windows nearby. The whole facility feels like a gilded prison.

A long stretch of silence between myself and my imaginary friend starts making me nervous. I think this voice might be Emmaline's, but she still hasn't confirmed it. And though I want to say something, I feel silly speaking out loud. So I speak only inside my mind when I say:

Emmaline? Are you there?

No response.
My nervousness reaches its peak and I stop walking.

Where are you taking me?

This time, the answer comes quickly:

Escape

Are we getting closer? I ask.

Yes

I take a deep breath and forge ahead, but I feel a creeping dread infiltrate my senses. The longer I walk—down hallways and infinite staircases—the closer I seem to be getting to *something*—something that fills me with fear. I can't explain it.

It's clear I'm going underground.

The lights are growing dimmer as I go. The halls are

beginning to narrow. The windows and staircases are beginning to disappear. And I know I'm only getting closer to the bowels of the building when the walls change. Gone are the smooth, finished white walls of the upper floors. Here, everything is unfinished cement. It smells cold and wet. Earthy. The lights buzz and hum, occasionally snapping.

Fear continues to pulse up my spine.

I shuffle down a slight slope, my shoes slipping a little as I go. My lungs squeeze. My heartbeat feels loud, too loud, and a strange sensation begins to fill my arms and legs. Feeling. Too much feeling. It makes my skin crawl, makes my bones itch. I feel suddenly restless and anxious. And just as I'm about to lose hope in this crazy, meandering escape route—

Here

I stop.

I'm standing in front of a massive stone door. My heart is racing in my throat. I hesitate, fear beginning to fissure my certainty.

Open

"Who are you?" I ask again, this time speaking out loud. "This doesn't look like an escape route."

Open

I squeeze my eyes shut; fill my lungs with air.

I came all this way, I tell myself. I have no other options at the moment. I may as well see it through.

But when I open the door I realize it's only the first of several. Wherever I'm headed is protected by multiple layers of security. The mechanisms required to open each door are baffling—there are no knobs or handles, no traditional hinges—but all I have to do is touch the door for it to swing open.

It's too easy.

Finally, I'm standing in front of a steel wall. There's nothing here to indicate there might be a room beyond.

Touch

Tentatively, I touch my fingers to the metal.

More

I press my whole hand firmly against the door, and within seconds, the wall melts away. I look around nervously and step forward.

Immediately, I know I've been led astray.

I feel sick as I look around, sick and terrified. This place is so far from an escape I almost can't believe I fell for it. I'm in a laboratory.

Another laboratory.

Panic collapses something inside me, bones and organs

knocking together, blood rushing to my head. I run for the door and it seals shut, the steel wall forming easily, as if from air.

I pull in a few sharp breaths, begging myself to stay calm.

"Show yourself," I shout. "Who are you? What do you want with me?"

Help

My heart shudders to a stop. I feel my fear expand and contract.

Dying

Goosebumps rise along my skin. My breath catches; my fists clench. I take a step farther into the room, and then a few more. I'm still wary, worried this is all yet another part of the trick—

Then I see it.

A glass cylinder as tall and wide as the wall, filled to the hilt with water. There's a creature floating inside of it. Something greater than fear is driving me forward, greater than curiosity, greater than wonder.

Feeling washes over me.

Memories crash into me.

A spindly arm reaches through the murky water, shaky fingers forming a loose fist that pounds, weakly, against the glass.

At first, all I see is her hand.

But the closer I get, the more clearly I'm able to see what they've done to her. And I can't hide my horror.

She inches closer to the glass and I catch sight of her face. She no longer has a face, not really. Her mouth has been permanently sealed around a regulator, skin spiderwebbing over silicone. Her hair is a couple feet long, dark and wild and floating around her head like wispy tentacles. Her nose has melted backward into her skull and her eyes are permanently closed, long dark lashes the only indication they ever used to open. Her hands and feet are webbed. She has no fingernails. Her arms and legs are mostly bone and sagging, wrinkled skin.

"Emmaline," I whisper.

Dying

The tears come hot and fast, hitting me without warning, breaking me from within.

"What did they do to you?" I say, my voice ragged. "How could they do this to you?"

A dull, metallic sound. Twice.

Emmaline is floating closer. She presses her webbed fingers against the barrier between us and I reach up, hastily wiping my eyes before I meet her there. I press my palm to the glass and somehow, impossibly, I feel her take my hand. Soft. Warm. Strong.

And then, with a gasp—

Feeling pulses through me, wave after wave of *feeling*, emotions as infinite as time. Memories, desires, long-extinguished hopes and dreams. The force of everything sends my head spinning; I slump forward and grit my teeth, steadying myself by pressing my forehead against the barrier between us. Images fill my mind like stilted frames from an old movie.

Emmaline's life.

She wants me to know. I feel like I'm being pulled into her, like she's reeling me into her own body, immersing me in her mind. Her memories.

I see her younger, much younger, eight or nine years old. She was spirited, furious. Difficult to control. Her mind was stronger than she could handle and she didn't know how to feel about her powers. She felt cursed, strangled by them. But unlike me, she was kept at home, here, in this exact laboratory, forced to undergo test after test administered by her own parents. I feel her rage pierce through me.

For the first time, I realize I had the luxury of forgetting. She didn't.

Max and Evie—and even Anderson—tried to wipe Emmaline's memory multiple times, but each time, Emmaline's body prevailed. Her mind was so strong that she was able to convince her brain to reverse the chemistry meant to dissolve her memories. No matter what Max and Evie tried, Emmaline could never forget them.

Instead, she watched as her own parents turned on her. Turned her inside out.

Emmaline is telling me everything without saying a word. She can't speak. She's lost four of her five senses.

She went blind first.

She lost her sense of smell and sensation a year later, both at the same time. Finally, she lost the ability to speak. Her tongue and teeth disintegrated. Her vocal cords eroded. Her mouth sealed permanently shut.

She can only hear now. But poorly.

I see the scenes change, see her grow a little older, a little more broken. I see the fire go out of her eyes. And then, when she realizes what they have planned for her—The entire reason they wanted her, so desperately—

Violent horror takes my breath away.

I fall, kneecaps knocking the floor. The force of her feelings rips me open. Sobs break my back, shudder through my bones. I feel everything. Her pain, her endless pain.

Her inability to end her own suffering.

She wants this to end.

End, she says, the word sharp and explosive.

With some effort, I manage to lift my head to look at her. "Was it you this whole time?" I whisper. "Did you give me back my memories?"

Yes

"How? Why?"

She shows me.

I feel my spine straighten as the vision moves through me. I see Evie and Max, hear their warped conversations from inside the glass prison. They've been trying to make Emmaline stronger over the years, trying to find ways to enhance Emmaline's telekinetic abilities. They wanted her skills to evolve. They wanted her to be able to perform mind control.

Mind control of the masses.

It backfired.

The more they experimented on her—the further they pushed her—the stronger and weaker she became. Her mind was able to handle the physical manipulations, but her heart couldn't take it. Even as they built her up, they were breaking her down.

She'd lost the will to live. To fight.

She no longer had complete control over her own body; even her powers were now regulated through Max and Evie. She'd become a puppet. And the more listless she became, the more they misunderstood. Max and Evie thought Emmaline was growing compliant.

Instead, she was deteriorating.

And then—

Another scene. Emmaline hears an argument. Max and Evie are discussing *me*. Emmaline hasn't heard them mention me in years; she had no idea I was still alive. She hears that I've been fighting back. That I've been resisting, that I tried to kill a supreme commander.

Emmaline feels hope for the first time in years.

I clap my hands over my mouth. Take a step back.

Emmaline has no eyes, but I feel her staring at me. Watching me for a reaction. I feel unsteady, alert but overcome.

I finally understand.

Emmaline has been using her last gasp of strength to contact me—and not just me, but all the other children of the supreme commanders.

She shows me, inside my own mind, how she's taken advantage of Max and Evie's latest effort to expand her capabilities. She'd never been able to reach out to people individually before, but Max and Evie got greedy. In Emmaline they laid the foundation for their own demise.

Emmaline thinks we're the last hope for the world. She wants us to stand up, fight, save humanity. She's been slowly returning our minds to us, giving back what our parents once stole. She wants us to see the truth.

Help, she says.

"I will," I whisper. "I promise I will. But first I'm going to get you out of here."

Rage, hot and violent, sends me reeling. Emmaline's anger is sharp and terrifying, and a resounding

NO

fills my brain.

I go still. Confused.

"What do you mean?" I say. "I have to help you get out of here. We'll escape together. I have friends—healers—who can restore y—"

NO

And then, in a flash—

She fills my mind with an image so dark I think I might be sick.

"No," I say, my voice shaking. "I won't do it. I'm not going to kill you."

Anger, hot, ferocious anger, attacks my mind. Image after image assaults me, her failed suicide attempts, her inability to turn her own powers against herself, the infinite fail-safes Max and Evie put in place to make sure Emmaline couldn't take her own life, and that she couldn't harm theirs—

"Emmaline, please—"

HELP

"There has to be another way," I say desperately. "This can't be it. You don't have to die. We can get through this together."

She bangs her open palm against the glass. Tremors rock her emaciated body.

Already

dying

I step forward, press my hands to her prison. "It wasn't supposed to end like this," I say, the words broken. "There has to be another way. Please. I want my sister back. I want you to live."

More anger, hot and wild, begins to bloom in my mind and then—
a spike of fear.
Emmaline goes rigid in her tank.

Coming

I look around, steeling myself. Adrenaline spikes in my veins.

Wait

Emmaline has wrapped her arms around her body, her face pinched in concentration. I can still feel her with an immediacy so intimate it feels almost like her thoughts are my own.

And then, unexpectedly—

My shackles pop open.

I spin around as they fall to the floor with a rich clatter. I rub at my aching wrists, my ankles. "How did you—?"

Coming

I nod.

"Whatever happens today," I whisper, "I'm coming back for you. This isn't over. Do you hear me? Emmaline, I won't let you die here."

For the first time, Emmaline seems to relax.

Something warm and sweet fills my head, affection so unexpected it pricks my eyes.

I fight back the emotion.

Footsteps.

Fear has fled my body. I feel unusually calm. I'm stronger than I've ever been. There's strength in my bones, strength in my mind. And now that the cuffs are off, my powers are back on and a familiar feeling is surging through me; it's like being joined by an old friend.

I meet Evie's eyes as she walks through the door.

She's already pointing a gun at me. Not a gun—something that looks like a gun. I don't know what's in it.

"What are you doing here?" she says, her voice only slightly hysterical. "What have you done?"

I shake my head.

I can't look at her face anymore without feeling blind

rage. I can't even think her name without feeling a violent, potent, animalistic need to murder her with my bare hands. Evie Sommers is the worst kind of human being. A traitor to humanity. An unadulterated sociopath.

"*What have you done?*" she says again, this time betraying her fear. Her panic. The gun trembles in her fist. Her eyes are wide, crazed, darting from me to Emmaline, still trapped in the tank behind me.

And then—

I see it. I see the moment she realizes I'm not wearing my manacles.

Evie goes pale.

"I haven't done anything," I say softly. "Not yet."

Her gun falls, with a clatter, to the floor.

Unlike Paris, my mother isn't stupid. She knows there's no point trying to shoot me. She *created* me. She knows what I'm capable of. And she knows—I can see it in her eyes—she knows I'm about to kill her, and she knows there's nothing she can do to stop it.

Still, she tries.

"Ella," she says, her voice unsteady. "Everything we did—everything we've ever done—was to try to help you. We were trying to save the world. You have to understand."

I take a step forward. "I do understand."

"I just wanted to make the world a better place," she says. "Don't you want to make the world a better place?"

"Yes," I say. "I do."

She almost smiles. A small, broken breath escapes her body.

Relief.

I take two swift, running steps and punch her through the chest, ribs breaking under my knuckles. Her eyes widen and she chokes, staring at me in stunned, paralyzed silence. She coughs and blood spatters, hot and thick, across my face. I turn away, spitting her blood out of my mouth, and by the time I look back, she's dead.

With one last tug, I rip her heart out of her body.

Evie falls to the floor with a heavy thud, her eyes cold and glassy. I'm still holding my mother's heart, watching it die in my hands, when a familiar voice calls out to me.

Thank you

Thank you

Thank you

WARNER

I realize, upon quitting the crime scene, that I have no idea where I am. I stand in the middle of the hallway outside the room within which I just murdered my father, and try to figure out my next moves. I'm nearly naked. No socks. Completely barefoot. Far from ideal.

Still, I need to keep moving.

If only.

I don't make it five feet before I feel the familiar pinch of a needle. I feel it—even as I try to fight it—I feel it as a foreign chemical enters my body. It's only a matter of time before it pulls me under.

My vision blurs.

I try to beat it, try to remain standing, but my body is weak. After two weeks of near starvation, constant poisoning, and violent exhaustion, I've run out of reserves. The last dregs of my adrenaline have left me.

This is it.

I fall to the floor, and the memories consume me.

I gasp as I'm returned to consciousness, taking in great lungfuls of air as I sit up too fast, my head spinning.

There are wires taped to my temples, my limbs, the

plastic ends pinching the soft hinges of my arms and legs, pulling at the skin on my bare chest. I rip them off, causing great distress to the monitors nearby. I yank the needle out of my arm and toss it to the floor, applying pressure to the wound for a few seconds before deciding to let it bleed. I get to my feet, spinning around to assess my surroundings, but still feel off-balance.

I can only guess at who must've shot me with a tranquilizer; even so, I feel no urgency to panic. Killing my father has instilled in me an extraordinary serenity. It's a perverse, horrible thing to celebrate, but to murder my father was to vanquish my greatest fear. With him dead, anything seems possible.

I feel free.

Still, I need to focus on where I am, on what's happening. I need to be forming a plan of attack, a plan of escape, a plan to rescue Ella. But my mind is being pulled in what feels like a hundred different directions.

The memories are growing more intense by the minute.

I don't know how much more of this I can take. I don't know how long this barrage will last or how much more will be uncovered, but the emotional revelations are beginning to take their toll on me.

A few months ago, I knew I loved Ella. I knew I felt for her what I'd never felt before for anyone. It felt new and precious and tender.

Important.

But every day—every minute—of the last couple of

weeks I've been bombarded by memories of her I never even knew I had. Moments with her from years ago. The sound of her laughter, the smell of her hair, the look in her eyes when she smiled at me for the first time. The way it felt to hold her hand when everything was new and unknown—

Three years ago.

How could it be possible that I touched her like that three years ago? How could we have known then, without actually knowing *why*, that we could be together? That she could touch me without hurting me? How could any of these moments have been ripped from my mind?

I had no idea I'd lost so much of her. But then, I had no idea there'd been so much to lose.

A profound, painful ache has rooted inside of me, carrying with it the weight of years. Being apart from Juliette—*Ella*—has always been hard, but now it seems unsurvivable.

I'm being slowly decimated by emotion.

I need to see her. To hold her. To bind her to me, somehow. I won't believe a word my father said until I see her and speak with her in person.

I can't give up. Not yet.

To hell with what happened between us back on base. Those events feel like they happened lifetimes ago. Like they happened to different people. Once I find her and get her to safety I will find a way to make things right between us. It feels like something long dead inside of me is being slowly returned to life—like my hopes and dreams are being resuscitated, like the holes in my heart are being slowly, carefully mended. I will find her. And when I do, I will find a way to move forward with her, by my side, forever.

I take a deep breath.

And then I get to my feet.

I brace myself, expecting the familiar sting of my broken ribs, but the pain in my side is gone. Gingerly, I touch my torso; the bruising has disappeared. I touch my face and I'm surprised to discover that my skin is smooth, clean-shaven. I touch my hair and find it's been returned to its original length—exactly as it was before I had to cut it all off.

Strange.

Still, I feel more like myself than I have in a long time, and I'm quietly grateful. The only thing bothering me is that I'm wearing nothing but a dressing grown, under which I'm completely naked.

I'm sick of being naked.

I want my clothes. I want a proper pair of pants. I want—

And then, as if someone has read my mind, I notice a fresh set of clothes on a nearby table. Clothes that look exactly my size.

I pick up the sweater. Examine it.

These are my actual clothes. I know these pieces. Recognize them. And if that wasn't enough, my initials—AWA—are monogrammed on the cuff of the sweater. This was no accident. Someone brought my clothes here. From my own closet.

They were expecting me.

I dress quickly, grateful for the clean outfit regardless of the circumstances, and I'm nearly done with the straps on my boots when someone walks in.

"Max," I say, without lifting my head. Carefully, I step on the needle I'd tossed earlier to the floor. "How are you?"

He laughs out loud. "How did you know it was me?"

"I recognized the rhythm of your footfalls."

He goes quiet.

"Don't bother trying to deny it," I say, hiding the syringe in my hand as I sit up. I meet his eyes and smile. "I've been listening to your heavy, uneven gait for the last two weeks."

Max's eyes widen. "I'm impressed."

"And I appreciate the clean shave," I say, touching my face.

He laughs again, more softly this time. "You were pretty close to dead when I brought you in here. Imagine my surprise to find you nearly naked, severely dehydrated, half-starved, vitamin-deficient. You had three broken ribs. Your father's blood all over your hands."

"Three broken ribs? I thought it was two."

"Three broken ribs," Max says, and nods. "And still, you managed to sever Paris's carotid artery. Nicely done."

I meet his eyes. Max thinks this is funny.

And then I understand.

"He's still alive, isn't he?" I say.

Max smiles wider. "Quite alive, yes. Despite your best efforts to murder him."

"That seems impossible."

"You sound irritated," Max says.

"I am irritated. That he survived is an insult to my skill set."

Max fights back another laugh. "I don't remember you being so funny."

"I'm not trying to be funny."

But Max can't wipe the smile off his face.

"So you're not going to tell me how he survived?" I say. "You're just going to bait me?"

"I'm waiting for my wife," he says.

"I understand. Does she help you sound out the big words?"

Max's eyebrows jump up his forehead. "Watch yourself, Aaron."

"Apologies. Please step out of my way."

"As I said, I'm waiting for my wife. She has something she wants to say to you."

I study him, looking closely at his face in a way I can't remember ever having done. He has dark brown hair, light brown skin, and bright blue-green eyes. He's aged well. On a different day, I might've even described his face as warm, friendly. But knowing now that he's Ella's father—I almost can't believe I didn't notice sooner. She has his eyes.

I hear a second set of footsteps drawing nearer to the door. I expect to see Evie, Supreme Sommers, and instead—

"Max, how long do you think it'll take bef—"

My father. His voice.

I can hardly believe it.

He stops, just inside the doorway, when he sees my face.

He's holding a bloodied towel to his throat. "You *idiot*," he says to me.

I don't have a chance to respond.

A sharp alarm sounds, and Max goes suddenly rigid. He glances at a monitor on the wall before looking back at my father.

"Go," Anderson says. "I can handle him."

Max glances at me just once before he disappears.

"So," I say, nodding at my father's face, his healing wound. "Are you going to explain?"

He merely stares at me.

I watch, quietly, as he uses his free hand to pull a handkerchief from his pocket. He wipes the remaining blood from his lips, refolds the handkerchief, and tucks it back inside his pocket.

Something between us has changed.

I can feel it. Can feel the shift in his attitude toward me. It takes a minute to piece together the various emotional cues long enough to understand, but when it finally hits me, it hits me hard.

Respect.

For the first time in my life, my father is staring at me with something like respect. I tried to kill him, and instead of being angry with me, he seems pleased. Maybe even impressed.

"You did good work back there," he says quietly. "It was a strong throw. Solid."

It feels strange to accept his compliment, so I don't.

My father sighs.

"Part of the reason I wanted custody of those healer twins," he says finally, "was because I wanted Evie to study them. I wanted her to replicate their DNA and braid it into my own. Healing powers, I realized, were extremely useful."

A sharp chill goes up my spine.

"But I didn't have them under my control for as long as I wanted," he says. "I was only able to extract a few blood samples. Evie did the best she could with the time we had."

I blink. Try to control the expression on my face. "So you have healing powers now?"

"We're still working on it," he says, his jaw tight. "It's not yet perfect. But it was enough that I was able to survive the wounds to the head just long enough to be shipped to safety." He smiles a bitter smile. "My feet, on the other hand, didn't make it."

"How unfortunate," I lie.

I test the weight of the syringe in my hand. I wonder how much damage it could do. It's not substantial enough to do much more than stun, but a carefully angled attack could result in temporary nerve pain that would buy me a sizable amount of time. But then, so might a single, precise stab in the eye.

"Operation Synthesis," my father says sharply.

I look up. Surprised.

"You're ready, Aaron." His gaze is steady. "You're ready for a real challenge. You've got the necessary fire. The drive. I'm seeing it in your eyes for the first time."

I'm too afraid to speak.

Finally, after all these years, my father is giving me praise. He's telling me I'm capable. As a child, it was everything I'd ever wanted.

But I'm not a child anymore.

"You've seen Emmaline," my father says. "But you haven't seen her recently. You don't know what state she's in."

I wait.

"She's dying," he says. "Her body isn't strong enough to survive her mind or her environment, and despite Max and Evie's every effort, they don't know if there's anything else they can do to help her. They've been working for years to prolong her life as much as possible, but they've reached the end of the line. There's nothing left to do. She's deteriorating at a rate they can no longer control."

Still, I say nothing.

"Do you understand?" my father says to me. "Do you understand the importance of what I'm saying to you? Emmaline is not only a psychokinetic, but a telepath," he says. "As her body deteriorates, her mind grows wilder. She's too strong. Too explosive. And lately, without a strong enough body to contain her, she's become volatile. If she's not given a n—"

"Don't you dare," a voice barks, loudly, into the room. "Don't you dare say another word. You thickheaded *fool*."

I spin around, surprise catching in my throat.

Supreme Commander Ibrahim. He seems taller than I

247

remember him. Dark skin, dark hair. *Angry.*

"It's okay," my father says, unbothered. "Evie has taken care of—"

"Evie is *dead*," Ibrahim says angrily. "We need to initiate the transfer immediately."

"What?" My father goes pale. I've never seen him pale. I've never seen him terrified. "What do you mean she's dead?"

Ibrahim's eyes flash. "I mean we have a serious problem." He glances at me. "This boy needs to be put back in isolation. We can't trust any of them right now. We don't know what she might've done."

And just as I'm trying to decide my next move, I hear a whisper at my ear.

"Don't scream," she says.

Nazeera.

~~JULIETTE~~

ELLA

I'm running for my life, bolting down hallways and up staircases. A low, insistent alarm has gone off, its high, piercing sound sending shocks of fear through me even as my feet pound the floor. I feel strong, steady, but I'm increasingly aware of my inability to navigate these snaking paths. I could see—could feel—Emmaline growing weaker as I left, and now, the farther I get from her, the dimmer our connection becomes. She showed me, in her memories, how Max and Evie slowly stripped her of control; Emmaline is more powerful than anyone, but now she can only use her powers on command. It took all her strength to push past the fail-safes long enough to use her strength at will, and now that her voice has retreated from my mind, I know she won't be back. Not anytime soon. I have to figure out my own way out of here.

I will.

My power is back on. I can get through anything from here. I have to. And when I hear someone shout I spin around, ready to fight—

But the face in the distance is so familiar I stop, stunned, in my tracks.

Kenji barrels into me.

Kenji.

Kenji is hugging me. Kenji is hugging me, and he's uninjured. He's perfect.

And just as I begin to return his embrace he swears, violently, and launches himself backward. "Jesus, woman— Are you trying to kill me? You can't turn that shit off for a second? You have to go and ruin our dramatic reunion by nearly murdering me even after I've gone to all the trouble of f—"

I launch myself into his arms again and he stiffens, relaxing only when he realizes I've pulled my power back. I forgot, for a second, how much of my skin was exposed in this dress.

"Kenji," I breathe. "You're alive. You're okay. Oh my God."

"Hey," he says. "*Hey.*" He pulls back, looks me in the eye. "I'm okay. You okay?"

I don't really know how to answer the question. Finally, I say, "I'm not sure."

He studies my face for a second. He looks concerned.

And then, the knot of fear growing only more painful in my throat, I ask the question killing me most:

"Where's Warner?"

Kenji shakes his head.

I feel myself begin to unravel.

"I don't know yet," Kenji says quietly. "But we're going to find him, okay? Don't worry."

I nod. My bottom lip trembles and I bite it down but the

tremble won't be killed. It grows, multiplies, evolves into a tremor that shakes me from stem to sternum.

"Hey," Kenji says.

I look up.

"You want to tell me where all the blood came from?"

I blink. "What blood?"

He raises his eyebrows at me. "The *blood*," he says, gesturing, generally, at my body. "On your face. Your dress. All over your hands."

"Oh," I say, startled. I look at my hands as if seeing them for the first time. "The blood."

Kenji sighs, squints at something over my shoulder. He pulls a pair of gloves out of his back pocket and tugs them on. "All right, princess, turn your power back on. We have to move."

We break apart. Kenji pulls his invisibility over us both.

"Follow me," he says, taking my hand.

"Where are we going?" I say.

"What do you mean, *where are we going*? We're getting the hell out of here."

"But—What about Warner?"

"Nazeera is looking for him as we speak."

I stop so suddenly I nearly stumble. "Nazeera is here?"

"Uh, yeah—So—It's a really long story? But the short answer is yes."

"So that's how you got in here," I say, beginning to understand. "Nazeera."

Kenji makes a sound of disbelief. "Wow, right off the

253

bat you give me no credit, huh? C'mon, J, you know I love a good rescue mission. I know some things. I can figure things out, too."

For the first time in weeks I feel a smile tug at my lips. A laugh builds and breaks inside my body. I've missed this so much. I've missed my friends so much. Emotion wells in my throat, surprising me.

"I missed you, Kenji," I say. "I'm so happy you're here."

"*Hey*," Kenji says sharply. "Don't you dare start crying. If you start crying I'll start crying and we do not have time to cry right now. We have too much shit to do, okay? We can cry later, at a more convenient time. Okay?"

When I say nothing, he squeezes my hand.

"Okay?" he says again.

"Okay," I say.

I hear him sigh. "Damn," he says. "They really messed you up in here, didn't they?"

"Yeah."

"I'm so sorry," he says.

"Can we cry about it later? I'll tell you everything."

"Hell yeah we can cry about it later." Kenji tugs gently on my hand to get us moving again. "I have so much shit to cry about, J. So much. We should make, like, a list."

"Good idea," I say, but my heart is in my throat again.

"Hey, don't worry," Kenji says, reading my thoughts. "Seriously. We'll find Warner. Nazeera knows what she's doing."

"But I don't think I can just wait while Nazeera goes

searching for him. I can't just stand around—I need to do something. I need to look for him myself—"

"Uh-uh. No way. Nazeera and I split up on purpose. *My* mission is to get you on the plane. *Her* mission is to get Warner on the plane. That's how math works."

"Wait—You have a plane?"

"How else did you think we got here?"

"I have no idea."

"Well, that's another long story, and I'll fill you in later, but the highlights are that Nazeera is very confusing but helpful, and according to her calculations, we need to be getting the hell out of here yesterday. We're running out of time."

"But wait, Kenji—What happened to everyone? Last time I saw you, you were bleeding. Brendan had been shot. Castle was down. I thought everyone was dead."

Kenji doesn't answer me at first. "You really have no idea what happened, huh?" he says finally.

"I only know that I didn't actually kill all those people at the symposium."

"Oh yeah?" He sounds surprised. "Who told you?"

"Emmaline."

"Your *sister*?"

"Yeah," I say, sighing heavily. "There's so much I have to tell you. But first—Please tell me everyone is still alive."

Kenji hesitates. "I mean, I think so? Honestly, I don't know. Nazeera says they're alive. She's promising to come through on getting them to safety, so I'm still holding my breath. But get this." He stops walking, puts an invisible hand on my shoulder. "You're never going to believe this."

"Let me guess," I say. "Anderson is alive."

I hear Kenji's sharp intake of breath. "How did you know?"

"Evie told me."

"So you know about how he came back to Sector 45?"

"What?" I say. "No."

"Well, what I was about to tell you, right now, was that Anderson came back to base. He's resumed his position as supreme commander of North America. He was there right before we left. Nazeera told me he made up this whole story about how he'd been ill and how our team had spread false rumors while he was recovering—and that you'd been executed for your deception."

"What?" I say, stunned. "That's insane."

"This is what I'm saying."

"So what are we going to do when we get back to Sector 45?" I say. "Where do we go? Where do we stay?"

"Shit if I know," Kenji says. "Right now, I'm just hoping we can get out of here alive."

Finally, we reach the exit. Kenji has a security card that grants him access to the door, and it opens easily.

From there, it's almost too simple. Our invisibility keeps us undetected. And once we're on the plane, Kenji checks his watch.

"We've only got thirty minutes, just so you know. That was the rule. Thirty minutes and if Nazeera doesn't show up with Warner, we have to go."

My heart drops into my stomach.

WARNER

I have no time to register my shock, or to ask Nazeera when on earth she was going to tell me she had the power to turn herself invisible, so I do the only thing I can, in the moment.

I nod, the movement almost imperceptible.

"Kenji is getting Ella onto a plane. I'm going to wait for you just outside this door," she says. "Do you think you can make it? If you go invisible in front of everyone, they'll be on to us, and it'd be better if they think you're just trying to run."

Again, I nod.

"All right then. I'll see you out there."

I wait a second or two, and then I head for the door.

"Hey—" Ibrahim bellows.

I hesitate, turning back slightly, on my heel.

"Yes?"

"Where do you think you're going?" he says. He pulls a gun from the inside of his jacket and points it at me.

"I have to use the bathroom."

Ibrahim doesn't laugh. "You're going to wait here until Max gets back. And then we decide what we're going to do with you."

I tilt my head at him. The gun he's pointing at me looks

suspiciously like one of the guns I stole from my father earlier.

Not that it matters.

I take a quick breath. "I'm afraid that's not how this is going to work," I say, attempting a smile. "Though I'm sure we'll all be seeing each other soon, so I wouldn't worry about missing me too much."

And then, before anyone has a chance to protest, I run for the door, but not before Ibrahim fires his weapon.

Three times.

In close range.

I fight back the urge to cry out as one of the bullets shoots clean through my calf, even as the pain nearly takes my breath away.

Once I'm on the other side of the door, Nazeera pulls her invisibility over me. I don't make it far before I take a sharp breath, slumping against the wall.

"*Shit*," she says. "Did you get shot?"

"Obviously," I bite out, trying to keep my breathing even.

"Dammit, Warner, what the hell is wrong with you? We have to get back to the plane in the next fifteen minutes, or they're going to leave without us."

"What? Why would—"

"Because I told them to. We have to get Ella out of here no matter what. I can't have them waiting around for us and risk getting killed in the process."

"Your sympathy is truly heartwarming. Thank you."

She sighs. "Where did you get shot?"

"In my leg."

"Can you walk?"

"I should be able to in just a minute."

I hear her hesitate. "What does that mean?"

"If I manage to live long enough, maybe I'll tell you."

She's unamused. "Can you really start running in just a minute?"

"Oh, now it's running? A moment ago you were asking if I could walk."

"Running would be better."

I offer her a bitter laugh. It's hard from this distance, but I've been drawing on my father's new ability, harnessing it as best I can from where I am. I feel the wound healing, slowly regenerating nerves and veins and even a bit of bone, but it's taking longer than I'd like.

"How long is the flight back?" I say. "I can't remember."

"We've got the jet, so it should only take about eight hours."

I nod, even though she can't see me. "I don't think I can survive eight hours with an open wound."

"Well, it's a good thing I don't give a shit. I'm giving you two more minutes before I carry you out of here myself."

I grunt in response, focusing all of my energy on drawing up the healing powers into my body. I've never tried to do something like this while wounded, and I didn't realize how demanding it was, both emotionally and physically. I feel drained. My head is throbbing, my jaw aching from the intense pressure I've used to bite back the pain, and my leg feels like it's on *fire*. There's nothing pleasant about the healing process. I have to imagine that my father is on the move—probably searching for me with Ibrahim—because harnessing his power is harder than any of the others I've tried to take.

"We're leaving in thirty seconds," Nazeera says, a warning in her voice.

I grit my teeth.

"Fifteen."

"Shit."

"Did you just swear?" Nazeera says, stunned.

"I'm in an extraordinary amount of pain."

"All right, that's it, we're out of time."

And before I manage to get a word in, she picks me up, off the ground.

And we're in the air.

~~JULIETTE~~

ELLA

Kenji and I have been staring at each other in nervous silence for the last minute. I spent the first ten minutes telling him a little about Emmaline, which was its own stressful distraction, and then Kenji helped me wash the blood off my hands and face with the few supplies we have on board. Now we're both staring into the silence, our combined terror filling the plane.

It's a nice plane, I think. I'm not sure. I haven't actually had the presence of mind to look around. Or to ask him who, exactly, among us even knows how to fly a plane. But none of that will matter, of course, if Nazeera and Warner don't get back here soon.

It won't matter because I won't be leaving without him.

And my thoughts must be easy to read, because suddenly Kenji frowns. "Listen," he says, "I'm just as worried about them as you are. I don't want to leave Nazeera behind and I sure as hell don't want to imagine anything bad happening to her while she's out there, but we have to get you out of here."

"Kenji—"

"We don't have a choice, J," he says, cutting me off. "We have to get you out of here whether you like it or not. The

Reestablishment is up to some shady shit, and you're right in the center of it. We have to keep you safe. Right now, keeping you safe is my entire mission."

I drop my face in my hands, and then, just as quickly, look up again. "This is all my fault, you know? I could've prevented this."

"What are you talking about?"

I look him straight in the eye. "I should've done more research on The Reestablishment. I should've read up on its history—and my history within it. I should've learned more about the supreme commanders. I should've been better prepared. Hell, I should've demanded we search the water for Anderson's dead body instead of just *assuming* he'd sunk with the ship." I shake my head, hard. "I wasn't ready to be supreme commander, Kenji. You knew it; Castle knew it. I put everyone's lives in danger."

"Hey," he says sharply, "I never said you weren't—"

"Only Warner ever tried to convince me I was good enough, but I don't think I ever really believed it."

"J, listen to me. I never said you weren't—"

"And now he's gone. Warner is gone. Everyone from Omega Point might be dead. Everything we built . . . everything we worked toward—" I feel myself break, snap open from the inside. "I can't lose him, Kenji." My voice is shaking. My hands are shaking. "I can't—You don't know— You don't—"

Kenji looks at me with actual pain in his eyes. "Stop it, J. You're breaking my heart. I can't hear this."

And I realize, as I swallow back the lump in my throat, how much I'd needed to have this conversation. These feelings had been building inside of me for weeks, and I'd desperately needed someone to talk to.

I needed my friend.

"I thought I'd been through some hard things," I say, my eyes now filling with tears. "I thought I'd lived through my share of awful experiences. But this—I honestly think these have been the worst days of my life."

Kenji's eyes are deep. Serious. "You want to tell me about it?"

I shake my head, wiping furiously at my cheeks. "I don't think I'll be able to talk about any of it until I know Warner is okay."

"I'm so sorry, J. I really am."

I sniff, hard. "You know my name is Ella, right?"

"Right," he says, his eyebrows pulling together. "Yeah. Ella. That's wild."

"I like it," I say. "I like it better than Juliette."

"I don't know. I think both names are nice."

"Yeah," I say, turning away. "But *Juliette* was the name Anderson picked out for me."

"And *Ella* is the name you were born with," Kenji says, shooting me a look. "I get it."

"Yeah."

"Listen," he says with a sigh. "I know this has been a rough couple of weeks for you. I heard about the memory thing. I heard about lots of things. And I can't pretend to

267

imagine I have any idea what you must be going through right now. But you can't blame yourself for any of this. It's not your fault. None of it is your fault. You've been a pawn at the center of this conspiracy your entire life. The last month wasn't going to change that, okay? You have to be kinder to yourself. You've already been through so much."

I offer Kenji a weak smile. "I'll try," I say quietly.

"Feeling any better now?"

"No. And thinking about leaving here without Warner— not knowing if he'll even make it onto this plane—It's killing me, Kenji. It's boring a hole through my body."

Kenji sighs, looks away. "I get it," he says. "I do. You're worried you won't have a chance to make things right with him."

I nod.

"Shit."

"I won't do it. I can't do it, Kenji."

"I understand where you're coming from, kid, I swear. But we can't afford to do this. If they're not back here in five minutes, we have to go."

"Then you'll have to leave without me."

"No way, not an option," he says, getting to his feet. "I don't want to do this any more than you do, but I know Nazeera well enough to know that she can handle herself out there, and if she's not back yet, it's probably because she's waiting for a safer moment. She'll find her way. And you have to trust that she'll bring Warner back with her. Okay?"

"No."

"C'mon—"

"Kenji, stop." I get to my feet, too, anger and heartbreak colliding.

"Don't do this," he says, shaking his head. "Don't force me to do something I don't want to do. Because if I have to, I will tackle you to the floor, J, I swear—"

"You wouldn't do that," I say quietly. The fight leaves my body. I feel suddenly exhausted, hollowed out by heartache. "I know you wouldn't. You wouldn't make me leave him behind."

"Ella?"

I turn around, a bolt of feeling leaving me breathless. Just the sound of his voice has my heart racing in a way that feels dangerous. The jarring shift from fear to joy has my head pounding, delirious with feeling. I'd been so worried, all this time, and to know now—

He's unharmed.

His face, unmarked. His body, intact. He's perfect and beautiful and he's *here*. I don't know how, but he's here.

I clap my hands over my mouth.

I'm shaking my head and searching desperately for the right words but find I can't speak. I can only stare at him as he steps forward, his eyes bright and burning.

He pulls me into his arms.

Sobs break my body, the culmination of a thousand fears and worries I hadn't allowed myself to process. I press my face into his neck and try, but fail, to pull myself together.

"I'm sorry," I say, gasping the words, tears streaming fast down my face. "Aaron, I'm so sorry. I'm so, so sorry."

I feel him stiffen.

He pulls away, staring at me with strange, scared eyes. "Why would you say that?" He looks around wildly, glances at Kenji, who only shakes his head. "What happened, love?" He pushes the hair out of my eyes, takes my face in his hands. "What are you sorry for?"

Nazeera pushes past us.

She nods at me, just once, before heading to the cockpit. Moments later I hear the roar of the engine, the electric sounds of equipment coming online.

I hear her voice in the speakers overhead, her crisp, certain commands filling the plane. She tells us to take our seats and get strapped in and I stare at Warner just once more, promising myself that we'll have a chance to talk. Promising myself that I'll make this right.

When we take off, he's holding my hand.

We've been climbing higher for several minutes now, and Kenji and Nazeera were generous enough to give us some illusion of privacy. They both shot me separate but similar looks of encouragement just before they slipped off into the cockpit. It finally feels safe to keep talking.

But emotion is like a fist in my chest, hard and heavy.

There's too much to say. Too much to discuss. I almost don't even know where to start. I don't know what happened to him, what he learned or what he remembers. I don't know if he's feeling the same things I'm feeling anymore. And all the unknowns are starting to scare me.

"What's wrong?" he says.

He's turned in his seat to face me. He reaches up, touches my face, and the feeling of his skin against mine is overwhelming—so powerful it leaves me breathless. Feeling shoots up my spine, sparks in my nerves.

"You're afraid, love. Why are you afraid?"

"Do you remember me?" I whisper. I have to force myself to remain steady, to fight back the tears that refuse to die. "Do you remember me the way I remember you?"

Something changes in his expression. His eyes change, pull together in pain.

He nods.

"Because I remember you," I say, my voice breaking on the last word. "I remember you, Aaron. I remember everything. And you have to know—You have to know how sorry I am. For the way I left things between us." I'm crying again. "I'm sorry for everything I said. For everything I put you thr—"

"Sweetheart," he says gently, the question in his eyes resolving to a measure of understanding. "None of that matters anymore. That fight feels like it happened in another lifetime. To different people."

I wipe away my tears. "I know," I say. "But being here—All of this—I thought I might never see you again. And it *killed* me to remember how I left things between us."

When I look up again Warner is staring at me, his own

eyes bright, shining. I watch the movement in his throat as he swallows, hard.

"Forgive me," I whisper. "I know it all seems stupid now, but I don't want to take anything for granted anymore. Forgive me for hurting you. Forgive me for not trusting you. I took my pain out on you and I'm so sorry. I was selfish, and I hurt you, and I'm so sorry."

He's silent for so long I almost can't bear it.

When he finally speaks, his voice is rough with emotion. "Love," he says, "there's nothing to forgive."

WARNER

Ella is asleep in my arms.

Ella.

I can't really think of her as *Juliette* anymore.

We've been in the air for an hour now, and Ella cried until her tears ran dry, cried for so long I thought it might kill me. I didn't know what to say. I was so stunned I didn't know how to soothe her. And only when the exhaustion overcame the tears did she finally go still, collapsing fully and completely into my arms. I've been holding her against my chest for at least half an hour, marveling at what it does to me to just be this close to her. Every once in a while, it feels like a dream. Her face is pressed against my neck. She's clinging to me like she might never let go and it does something to me, something heady, to know that she could possibly want me—or need me—like this. It makes me want to protect her even if she doesn't need protecting. It makes me want to carry her away. Lose track of time.

Gently, I stroke her hair. Press my lips to her forehead.

She stirs, but only slightly.

I had not been expecting this.

Of all the things I thought might happen when I finally saw her, I could never have dreamed a scenario such as this.

No one has ever apologized to me before. Not like this.

I've had men fall to their knees before me, begging me to spare their lives—but I can't remember a single time in my life when someone apologized to me for hurting my feelings. No one has ever cared about my feelings long enough to apologize for hurting them. In my experience, I'm usually the monster. I'm the one expected to make amends.

And now—

I'm stunned. Stunned by the experience, by how strange it feels. All this time, I'd been preparing to win her back. To try to convince her, somehow, to see past my demons. And up until just this moment, I don't think I was ever truly convinced anyone would see me as human enough to forgive my sins. To give me a second chance.

But now, she knows everything.

Every dark corner of my life. Every awful thing I ever tried to hide. She knows and she still loves me.

God. I run a tired hand across my face. She asked me to forgive *her.* I almost don't know what to do with myself. I feel joy and terror. My heart is heavy with something I don't even know how to describe.

Gratitude, perhaps.

The ache in my chest has grown stronger, more painful. Being near her is somehow both a relief and a new kind of agony. There's so much ahead of us, so much we still need to face, together, but right now I don't want to think about any of it. Right now I just want to enjoy her proximity. I want to watch the gentle motions of her breathing. I want to inhale the soft scent of her hair and lean into the steadying warmth of her body.

Carefully, I touch my fingers to her cheek.

Her face is smooth, free from pain and tension. She looks peaceful. She looks *beautiful*.

My love.

My beautiful love.

Her eyes flutter open and I worry, for a moment, that I might've spoken out loud. But then she looks up at me, her eyes still soft with sleep, and I bring my hand to her face, this time trailing my fingers lightly along her jaw. She closes her eyes again. Smiles.

"I love you," she whispers.

A shock of feeling swells inside of me, makes it hard for me to breathe. I can only look at her, studying her face, the lines and angles I've somehow always known.

Slowly, she sits up.

She leans back, stretching out her sore, stiff muscles. When she catches me watching her, she offers me a shy smile.

She leans in, takes my face in her hands.

"Hi," she says, her words soft, her hands gentle as she tilts my chin down, toward her mouth. She kisses me, once, her lips full and sweet. It's a tender kiss, but feeling strikes through me with a sharp, desperate need. "I missed you so much," she says. "I still can't believe you're here." She kisses me again, this time deeper, hungrier, and my heart beats so fast it roars in my ears. I can hardly hear anything else. I can't bring myself to speak.

I feel stunned.

When we break apart, her eyes are worried. "Aaron," she says. "Is everything okay?"

And I realize then, in a moment that terrifies me, that I want this, forever. I want to spend the rest of my life with her. I want to build a future with her. I want to grow old with her.

I want to marry her.

~~JULIETTE~~

ELLA

"Aaron?" I say again, this time softly. "Are you all right?"

He blinks, startled. "Yes," he says, drawing in a sharp breath. "Yes. Yes, I'm perfect."

I manage a small smile. "I'm glad you finally agree with me."

He frowns, confused, and then, as realization hits—

He *blushes*.

And for the first time in weeks, a full, genuine grin spreads across my face. It feels good. Human.

But Aaron shakes his head, clearly mortified. He can't meet my eyes. His voice is careful, quiet when he says, "That's not at all what I meant."

"Hey," I say, my smile fading. I take his hands in mine, squeeze. "Look at me."

He does.

And I forget what I was going to say.

He has that kind of face. The kind of face that makes you forget where you are, who you are, what you might've been about to do or say. I've missed him so much. Missed his eyes. It's only been a couple of weeks, but it feels like forever since the last time I saw him, a lifetime full of horrible revelations that threatened to break us both. I can't believe he's here, that we found each other and made things right.

It's no small thing.

Even with everything else—with all the other horrors we've yet to contend with—being here with him feels like a huge victory. Everything feels new. My mind feels new, my memories, new. Even Aaron's face is new, in its own way. He looks a little different to me now.

Familiar.

Like he's always been here. Always lived in my heart.

His hair, thick and golden and beautiful, is how I remember it best—Evie must've done something to his hair, too, somehow. And even though he looks more exhausted than I'd like, his face is still striking. Beautiful, sharp lines. Piercing green eyes so light and bright they're almost painful to look at. Everything about him is finely crafted. His nose. His chin. His ears and eyebrows. He has a beautiful mouth.

I linger too long there, my eyes betraying my mind, and Aaron smiles. *Aaron.* Calling him Warner doesn't feel right anymore.

"What are you doing, love?"

"Just enjoying the view," I say, still staring at his mouth. I reach up, touch two fingers to his bottom lip. Memories flood through me in a sudden, breathless rush. Long nights. Early mornings. His mouth, on me. Everywhere. Over and over again.

I hear him exhale, suddenly, and I glance up at him.

His eyes are darker, heavy with feeling. "What are you thinking?"

I shake my head, feeling suddenly shy. It's strange, considering how close we've been, that I'd feel shy around him now. But he feels at once old and new to me—like we're still learning about each other. Still discovering what our relationship means and what we mean to each other. Things feel deeper, desperate.

More important.

I take his hands again. "How are you?" I whisper.

He's staring at our hands, entwined, when he says: "My father is still alive."

"I heard. I'm so sorry."

He nods. Looks away.

"Did you see him?"

Another nod. "I tried to kill him."

I go still.

I know how hard it's been for Aaron to face his father. Anderson has always been his most formidable opponent; Aaron has never been able to fight him head on. He's never been able to bring himself to actually follow through with his threats to kill his father.

It's astonishing he even came close.

And then Aaron tells me how his father has semi-functional healing powers, how Evie tried to re-create the twins' DNA for him.

"So your dad is basically invincible?"

Aaron laughs quietly. Shakes his head. "I don't think so. It makes him harder to kill, but I definitely think there's a chink to be found in his armor." He sighs. "Believe it or not, the strangest part of the whole thing was that, afterward, my father was proud of me. Proud of me for trying to kill him." Aaron looks up, looks me in the eye. "Can you imagine?"

"Yes," I whisper. "I can."

Aaron's eyes go deep with emotion. He pulls me close. "I'm so sorry, love. I'm so sorry for everything they did to you. For everything they've put you through. It kills me to know that you were suffering. That I couldn't be there for you."

"I don't want to think about it right now." I shake my head. "Right now all I want is *this*. I just want to be here. With you. Whatever comes next, we'll face it together."

"Ella," he says softly.

A wave of feeling washes over me. Hearing him say my name—my real name—makes everything feel real. Makes *us* feel real.

I meet his eyes.

He smiles. "You know—I feel everything when you touch me, love. I can feel your excitement. Your nervousness. Your pleasure. And I love it," he says quietly. "I love the way you respond to me. I love the way you *want* me. I feel it, when you lose yourself, the way you trust me when we're together. And I feel your love for me," he whispers. "I feel it in my bones."

He turns away.

"I have loved you my entire life." He looks up, looks at me with so much feeling it nearly breaks my heart. "And after everything we've been through—after all the lies and the secrets and the misunderstandings—I feel like we've been given a chance to start fresh. I want to start over," he says. "I never want to lie to you again. I want us to trust each other and be true partners in everything. No more misunderstandings," he says. "No more secrets. I want us to begin again, here, in this moment."

I nod, pulling back so I can see his face more clearly. Emotions well in my throat, threaten to overcome me. "I want that, too. I want that so much."

"Ella," he says, his voice rough with feeling. "I want to spend the rest of my life with you."

My heart stops.

I stare at him, uncertain, thoughts pinwheeling in my head. I touch his cheek and he looks away, takes a sudden, shaky breath.

"What are you saying?" I whisper.

"I love you, Ella. I love you more th—"

"*Wow.* You two seriously couldn't wait until we got back to base, huh? You couldn't spare my eyes?"

The sound of Kenji's voice pulls me suddenly, abruptly out of my head. I turn too quickly, awkwardly disengaging from Aaron's body.

Aaron, on the other hand, goes suddenly white.

Kenji throws a thin airplane pillow at him. "You're welcome," he says.

Aaron chucks the pillow back without a word, his eyes burning in Kenji's direction. He seems both shocked and angry, and he leans forward in his seat, his elbows balanced on his knees, the heels of his hands pressed against his eyes.

"You are a plague upon my life, Kishimoto."

"I said *you're welcome*."

Aaron sighs, heavily. "What I would give to snap your neck right now, you have no idea."

"Hey—*you* have no idea what I just did for you," Kenji says. "So I'm going to repeat myself one more time: You are *welcome*."

"I never asked for your help."

Kenji crosses his arms. When he speaks, he overenunciates each word, like he might be talking to an idiot. "I don't think you're thinking clearly."

"I'm thinking clearer than I ever have."

"You really thought that would be a good idea?" Kenji says, shaking his head. "Here? Now?"

Aaron's jaw clenches. He looks mutinous.

"Bro, this is not the moment."

"And when, exactly, did you become an expert on this sort of thing?"

I look between the two of them. "What is going on?" I say. "What are you guys talking about?"

"Nothing," they say at the same time.

"Um, okay." I stare at them, still confused, and I'm about to ask another question when Kenji says, suddenly:

"Who wants lunch?"

My eyebrows shoot up my forehead. "We have lunch?"

"It's pretty awful," Kenji says, "but Nazeera and I have a picnic basket we brought with us, yeah."

"I guess I'm up for trying the contents of the mystery basket." I smile at Aaron. "Are you hungry?"

But Aaron says nothing. He's still staring at the floor. I touch his hand and, finally, he sighs. "I'm not hungry," he says.

"Not an option," Kenji says sharply. "I'm pretty sure you haven't eaten a damn thing since you got out of fake prison."

Aaron frowns. And when he looks up, he says, "It wasn't *fake* prison. It was a very real prison. They poisoned me for weeks."

"What?" My eyes widen. "You never t—"

Kenji cuts me off with the wave of his hand. "They gave you food, water, and let you keep the clothes on your back, didn't they?"

"Yes, but—"

He shrugs. "Sounds like you had a little vacation."

Aaron sighs. He looks both annoyed and exhausted as he runs a hand down the length of his face.

I don't like it.

"Hey—Why are you giving him such a hard time?" I say, frowning at Kenji. "Just before he and Nazeera showed up you were going on and on about how wonderful he is, and n—"

Kenji swears, suddenly, under his breath. "Jesus, J." He shoots me a dark look. "What did I say to you about repeating that conversation out loud?"

Aaron sits up, the frustration in his eyes slowly giving way to surprise. "You think I'm wonderful?" he says, one

287

hand pressed against his chest in mock affection. "That's so sweet."

"I *never* said you were wonderful."

Aaron tilts his head. "Then what, exactly, did you say?"

Kenji turns away. Says nothing.

I'm grinning at Kenji's back when I say, "He said you looked good in everything and that you were good at everything."

Aaron's smile deepens.

Aaron almost never smiles widely enough for me to see his dimples, but when he does, they transform his face. His eyes light up. His cheeks go pink with feeling. He looks suddenly sweet. *Adorable.*

It takes my breath away.

But he's not looking at me, he's looking at Kenji, his eyes full of laughter when he says, "Please tell me she's not serious."

Kenji gives us both the finger.

Aaron laughs. And then, leaning in—

"You really think I look good in everything?"

"Shut up, asshole."

Aaron laughs again.

"Stop having fun without me," Nazeera shouts from the cockpit. "No more making jokes until I put this thing on cruise control."

I stiffen. "Do planes have cruise control?"

"Um"—Kenji scratches his head—"I don't actually know?"

But then Nazeera saunters over to us, tall and beautiful and unbothered. She's not covering her hair today, which I suppose makes sense, considering it's generally illegal, but I feel a faint panic spread through my body when I realize she's in no hurry to return to the cockpit.

"Wait—No one is flying the plane," I say. "Shouldn't someone be flying the plane?"

She waves me down. "It's fine. These things are practically automatic now, anyway. I don't have to do more than input coordinates and make sure everything is operating smoothly."

"But—"

"Everything is fine," she says, shooting me a sharp look. "We're fine. But someone needs to tell me what's going on."

"Are you sure we're fine?" I ask once more, quietly.

She levels me with a dark look.

I sigh. "Well, in that case," I say. "You should know that Kenji was just admiring Aaron's sense of style."

Nazeera turns to Kenji. Raises a single eyebrow.

Kenji shakes his head, visibly irritated. "I wasn't— Dammit, J, you have no loyalty."

"I have plenty of loyalty," I say, slightly wounded. "But when you guys fight like this it stresses me out. I just want Aaron to know that, secretly, you care about him. I love you both and I want the two of you to be frien—"

"Wait"—Aaron frowns—"What do you mean you love us both?"

I glance between him and Kenji, surprised. "I mean I

289

care about both of you. I love you both."

"Right," Aaron says, hesitating, "but you don't *actually* love us both. That's just a figure of speech, isn't it?"

It's my turn to frown. "Kenji is my best friend," I say. "I love him like a brother."

"But—"

"I love you, too, princess," Kenji says, a little too loudly. "And I appreciate you saying that."

Aaron mutters something under his breath that sounds suspiciously like, "*Unwashed idiot.*"

"What did you just say to me?" Kenji's eyes widen. "I'll have you know I wash *all the time*—"

Nazeera places a calming hand on Kenji's arm, and he startles at her touch. He looks up at her, blinking.

"We have another five hours ahead of us on this flight," she says, and her voice is firm but kind. "So I recommend we put this conversation to bed. I think it's clear to everyone that you and Warner secretly enjoy each other's friendship, and it's not doing anyone any good to pretend otherwise."

Kenji blanches.

"Does that sound like a reasonable plan?" She looks around at all of us. "Can we all agree that we're on the same team?"

"Yes," I say enthusiastically. "I do. I agree."

Aaron says, "Fine."

"Great," Nazeera says. "Kenji, you okay?"

He nods and mumbles something under his breath.

"Perfect. Now here's the plan," she says briskly. "We're

going to eat and then take turns trying to get some sleep. We'll have a ton of things to deal with when land, and it's best if we hit the ground running when we do." She tosses a few vacuum-sealed bags at each of us. "That's your lunch. There are water bottles in the fridge up front. Kenji and I will take the first shift—"

"No way," Kenji says, crossing his arms. "You've been up for twenty-four hours straight. I'll take the first shift."

"But—"

"Warner and I will take the first shift together, actually." Kenji shoots Warner a look. "Isn't that right?"

"Yes, of course," Aaron says. He's already on his feet. "I'd be happy to."

"Great," Kenji says.

Nazeera is already stifling a yawn, pulling a bunch of thin blankets and pillows from a storage closet. "All right, then. Just wake us up in a couple of hours, okay?"

Kenji raises an eyebrow at her. "Sure."

"I'm serious."

"Yup. Got it." Kenji offers her a mock salute, Aaron offers me a quick smile, and the two of them disappear into the cockpit.

Kenji closes the door behind them.

I'm staring at the closed door, wondering what on earth is going on between the two of them, when Nazeera says—

"I had no idea you two were so intense."

I look up, surprised. "Who? Me and Aaron?"

"No," she says, smiling. "You and Kenji."

"Oh." I frown. "I don't think we're intense."

She shoots me a funny look.

"I'm serious," I say. "I think we have a pretty normal friendship."

Instead of answering me, she says, "Did you two ever"—she waves a hand at nothing—"date?"

"What?" My eyes widen. A traitorous heat floods my body. "*No.*"

"Never?" she says, her smile slow.

"Never. I swear. Not even close."

"Okay."

"Not that there's anything wrong with him," I hurry to add. "Kenji is wonderful. The right person would be lucky to be with him."

Nazeera laughs, softly.

She carries the stack of pillows and blankets over to the row of airplane seats and begins reclining the backs. I watch her as she works. There's something so smooth and refined about her movements—something intelligent in her eyes at all times. It makes me wonder what she's thinking, what she's planning. Why she's here at all.

Suddenly, she sighs. She's not looking at me when she says, "Do you remember me yet?"

I raise my eyebrows, surprised. "Of course," I say quietly.

She nods. She says, "I've been waiting awhile for you to catch up," and sits down, inviting me to join her by patting the seat next to her.

I do.

Wordlessly, she hands me a couple of blankets and pillows. And then, when we're both settled in and I'm staring, suspiciously, at the vacuum-sealed package of "food" she threw at me, I say—

"So you remember me, too?"

Nazeera tears open her vacuum-sealed package. Peers inside to study the contents. "Emmaline guided me to you," she says quietly. "The memories. The messages. It was her."

"I know," I say. "She's trying to unify us. She wants us to band together."

Nazeera shakes out the contents of the bag into her hand, picks through the bits of freeze-dried fruit. She glances at me. "You were five when you disappeared," she says. "Emmaline was six. I'm six months older than you, and six months younger than Emmaline."

I nod. "The three of us used to be best friends."

Nazeera looks away, looks sad. "I really loved Emmaline," she says. "We were inseparable. We did everything together." She shrugs, even as a flash of pain crosses her face. "That was all we got. Whatever we might've been was stolen from us."

She picks out two pieces of fruit and pops them into her mouth. I watch as she chews, thoughtfully, and wait for more.

But the seconds pass and she says nothing, and I figure I should fill the silence. "So," I say. "We're not actually getting any sleep, are we?"

That gets her to smile. Still, she doesn't look at me.

Finally, she says, "I know you and Warner got the absolute worst of it, I do. But if it makes you feel any better, they wiped all of our memories, in the beginning."

"I know. Emmaline told me."

"They didn't want us to remember you," she says. "They didn't want us to remember a lot of things. Did Emmaline tell you she's reached out to all of us? You, me, Warner, my brother—all the kids."

"She told me a little bit, yeah. Have you talked to any of the others about it?"

Nazeera nods. Pops another piece of fruit in her mouth.

"And?"

She tilts her head. "We'll see."

My eyes widen. "What does that mean?"

"I'll know more when we land, that's all."

"So—How did you even know?" I say, frowning a little. "If you'd only ever had memories of me and Emmaline as children—how did you tie it all back to the present? How did you know that I was the Ella from our childhood?"

"You know—I wasn't a hundred percent positive I was right about everything until I saw you at dinner that first night on base."

"You recognized me?" I say. "From when I was five?"

"No," she says, and nods at my right hand. "From the scar on the back of your wrist."

"This?" I say, lifting my hand. And then I frown, remembering that Evie repaired my skin. I used to have faded scars all over my body; the ones on my hands were the worst. My adoptive mom put my hands in the fire, once. And I hurt myself a lot while I was locked up; lots of burns, lots of poorly healed wounds. I shake my head at Nazeera when I say, "I used to have scars on my hand from my time in the asylum. Evie got rid of them."

Nazeera takes my hand, flips it over so my palm is up, open. Carefully, she traces a line from my wrist to my forearm. "Do you remember the one that was here?"

"Yes." I raise my eyebrows.

"My dad has a really extensive sword collection," she says, dropping my hand. "Really gorgeous blades—gilded, handmade, ancient, ornate stuff. Anyway," she says, tapping the invisible scar on my wrist. "I did that to you. I broke into my dad's sword room and thought it'd be fun for us to practice a little hand-to-hand combat. But I sliced you up pretty bad, and my mom just about beat the crap out of me." She laughs. "I will never forget that."

I frown at her, at where my scar used to be. "Didn't you say that we were friends when we were *five*?"

She nods.

"We were five and we thought it would be fun to play with real swords?"

She laughs. Looks confused. "I never said we had a *normal* childhood. Our lives were so messed up," she says, and laughs again. "I never trusted my parents. I always knew they were knee-deep in some dark shit; I always tried to learn more. I'd been trying, for years, to hack into Baba's electronic files," she says. "And for a long time, I only ever accessed basic information. I learned about the asylums. The Unnaturals."

"That's why you hid your abilities from them," I say, finally understanding.

She nods. "But I wanted to know more. I knew I was only scratching the surface of something big. But the levels of security built into my dad's account are unlike anything I'd ever seen before. I was able to get through the first few levels of security, which is how I learned of yours and Emmaline's existence, a few years back. Baba had tons of records, reports on your daily habits and activities, a log with the time and date of every memory they stole from you—and they were all from recent years and months."

I gasp.

Nazeera shoots me a sympathetic look. "There were brief mentions of a sister in your files," she says, "but nothing substantial; mostly just a note that you were both powerful, and had been donated to the cause by your parents. But I couldn't find anything on the unknown sister, which made me think that her files were more protected. I spent the last couple of years trying to break into the deeper levels of Baba's account and never had any success. So I let it go for a while."

She pops another piece of dried fruit in her mouth.

"It wasn't until my dad started losing his *mind* after you almost killed Anderson that I started getting suspicious. That was when I began to wonder if the *Juliette Ferrars* he kept screaming about wasn't someone important." She studies me out of the corner of her eye. "I knew you couldn't have been some random *Unnatural*. I just knew it. Baba went *ballistic*. So I started hacking again."

"Wow," I say.

"Yeah," she says, nodding. "Right? Anyway, all I'm trying to say is that I've been trying to sniff out the bullshit in this situation for a few years, and now, with Emmaline in my head, I'm finally getting close to figuring it all out."

I glance up at her.

"The only thing I still don't know is *why* Emmaline is locked up. I don't know what they're doing with her. And I don't understand why it's such a secret."

"I do," I say.

Her head snaps up. She looks at me, wide-eyed. "Way to get to the point, Ella."

I laugh, but the sound is sad.

WARNER

As soon as we take our seats, Kenji turns on me. "You want to tell me what the hell is going on?" he says.

"No."

Kenji rolls his eyes. He rips open his little snack bag and doesn't even inspect the contents before he tips the bag directly into his mouth. He closes his eyes as he chews. Makes little satisfied noises.

I manage to fight the impulse to cringe, but I can't stop myself from saying—

"You eat like a caveman."

"No, I don't," he says angrily. And then, a moment later: "Do I?"

I hesitate, feeling his sudden wave of embarrassment. Of all the emotions I hate experiencing, secondhand embarrassment might be the worst. It hits me right in the gut. Makes me want to turn my skin inside out.

And it's by far the easiest way to make me capitulate.

"No," I say heavily. "You don't eat like a caveman. That was unfair."

Kenji glances at me. There's too much hope in his eyes.

"I've just never seen anyone eat food with as much enthusiasm as you do."

Kenji raises an eyebrow. "I'm not enthusiastic. I'm hungry."

Carefully, I tear open my own package. Shake out a few bits of the fruit into my open hand.

They look like desiccated worms.

I return the fruit to the bag, dust off my hands, and offer my portion to Kenji.

"You sure?" he says, even as he takes it from me.

I nod.

He thanks me.

We both say nothing for a while.

"So," Kenji says finally, still chewing. "You were going to propose to her. Wow."

I exhale a long, heavy breath. "How you could have even known something like that?"

"Because I'm not deaf."

I raise my eyebrows.

"It echoes in here."

"It certainly does not echo in here."

"Stop changing the subject," he says, shaking more fruit into his mouth. "The point is, you were going to propose. Do you deny it?"

I look away, run a hand along the side of my neck, massaging the sore muscles. "I do not deny it," I say.

"Then congratulations. And yes, I'd be happy to be your best man at the wedding."

I look up, surprised. "I've no interest in addressing the latter part of what you just said, but—Why offer congratulations? I thought you were vehemently opposed to the idea."

Kenji frowns. "What? I'm not opposed to the idea."

"Then why were you so angry?"

"I thought you were stupid for doing it *here*," he says. "Right now. I didn't want you to do something you would regret. That you'd both regret."

"Why would I regret proposing right now? This seems as good a time as any."

Kenji laughs, but somehow manages to keep his mouth closed. He swallows another bite of food and says, "Don't you want, to, like, I don't know—buy her some roses? Light a candle? Maybe hand her a box of chocolates or some shit? Or, hell, uh, I don't know—maybe you'd want to get her a *ring* first?"

"I don't understand."

"C'mon, bro—Have you never seen, like, a movie?"

"No."

Kenji stares at me, dumbfounded. "You're shitting me," he says. "Please tell me you're shitting me."

I bristle. "I was never allowed to watch movies growing up, so I never picked up the habit, and after The Reestablishment took over, that sort of thing was outlawed anyway. Besides, I don't enjoy sitting still in the dark for that long. And I don't enjoy the emotional manipulations of cinema."

Kenji brings his hands to his face, his eyes wide with something like horror. "You have got to be kidding me."

"Why would—I don't understand why that's strange. I was homeschooled. My father was very—"

"There are so many things about you that never made sense to me," Kenji says, staring, flabbergasted, at the wall behind me. "Like, everything about you is weird, you know?"

"No," I say sharply. "I don't think I'm weird."

"But now it all makes sense." He shakes his head. "It all makes so much sense. Wow. Who knew."

"*What* makes sense?"

Kenji doesn't seem to hear me. Instead, he says, "Hey, is there anything else you've never done? Like—I don't know, have you ever gone swimming? Or, like, blown out candles on a birthday cake?"

"Of course I've been swimming," I say, irritated. "Swimming was an important part of my tactical training. But I've never—" I clear my throat. "No, I never had my own birthday cake."

"Jesus."

"*What is wrong with you?*"

"Hey," Kenji says suddenly. "Do you even know who Bruce Lee is?"

I hesitate.

There's a challenge in his voice, but Kenji isn't generating much more in the way of emotional cues, so I don't understand the importance of the question. Finally, I say, "Bruce Lee was an actor. Though he's also considered to be one of the greatest martial artists of our time. He founded a system of martial arts called jeet kune do, a type of Chinese kung fu that eschews patterns and form. His Chinese name is Lee Jun-fan."

"Well shit," Kenji says. He sits back in his chair, staring at me like I might be an alien. "Okay. I wasn't expecting that."

"What does Bruce Lee have to do with anything?"

"First of all," he says, holding up a finger, "Bruce Lee has everything to do with everything. And second of all, can you just, like, do that?" He snaps his fingers in the direction of my head. "Can you just, like, remember shit like that? Random facts?"

"They're not random facts. It's information. Information about our world, its fears, histories, fascinations, and pleasures. It's my job to know this sort of thing."

"But you've never seen a single movie?"

"I didn't have to. I know enough about pop culture to know which films mattered or made a difference."

Kenji shakes his head, looks at me with something like awe. "But you don't know anything about the *best* films. You never saw the really good stuff. Hell, you've probably never even heard of the good stuff."

"Try me."

"Have you ever heard of *Blue Streak*?"

I blink at him. "That's the name of a movie?"

"*Romeo Must Die? Bad Boys? Rush Hour? Rush Hour 2? Rush Hour 3?* Actually, *Rush Hour 3* wasn't that great. *Tangled?*"

"That last one, I believe, is a cartoon about a girl with very long hair, inspired by the German fairy tale 'Rapunzel.'"

Kenji looks like he might be choking. "A *cartoon?*" he says, outraged. "*Tangled* is not a *cartoon.* *Tangled* is one of the greatest movies of all time. It's about fighting for freedom and true love."

"Please," I say, running a tired hand across my face. "I really don't care what kinds of cartoons you like to watch in your free time. I only want to know why you're so certain I was making a mistake today."

Kenji sighs so deeply his shoulders sag. He slumps down in his chair. "I can't believe you've never seen *Men in Black.* Or *Independence Day.*" He looks up at me, his eyes bright. "Shit, you'd love *Independence Day.* Will Smith punches an alien in the face, for God's sake. It's so good."

I stare blankly at him.

"My dad and I used to watch movies all the time," he says quietly. "My dad loved movies." Kenji only allows himself to feel his grief for a moment, but when he does, it hits me in a wild, desperate wave.

"I'm so sorry for your loss," I say quietly.

"Yeah, well." Kenji runs a hand over his face. Rubs at his eyes and sighs. "Anyway, do whatever you want. I just think you should buy her a ring or something before you get down on one knee."

"I wasn't planning on getting down on one knee."

"What?" He frowns. "Why not?"

"That seems illogical."

Kenji laughs. Rolls his eyes. "Listen, just trust me and at least pick out a ring first. Let her know you actually thought about it. Think it through for a beat, you know?"

"I did think it through."

"For, what, five seconds? Or did you mean that you were planning this proposal while you were being poisoned in prison?" Kenji laughs. "Bro, you literally saw her—for the first time—*today*, like, two hours ago, after two weeks of being apart, and you think proposing to her is a rational, clearheaded move?" Kenji shakes his head. "Just take some time. Think about it. Make some plans."

And then, suddenly, his reaction makes sense to me.

"You don't think she's going to say yes." I sit back, stunned. Look at the wall. "You think she'll refuse me."

"What? I never said that."

"But it's what you think, isn't it?"

"Listen," he says, and sighs. "I have no idea what she'll say. I really don't. I mean I think it's more than obvious that she loves you, and I think if she's ready to call herself the supreme commander of North America she's probably ready to handle something as big as this, but"—he rubs his chin, looks away—"I mean, yeah, I think maybe you should, like, think about it for a minute."

I stare at him. Consider his words.

Finally, I say, "You think I should get her a ring."

Kenji smiles at the floor. He seems to be fighting back a laugh. "Uh. Yeah, I do."

"I don't know anything about jewelry."

He looks up, his eyes bright with humor. "Don't worry. I'm sure the files in that thick head of yours have tons of information on this sort of thing."

"But—"

The plane gives a sudden, unexpected jolt, and I'm thrown backward in my seat. Kenji and I stare at each other for a protracted second, caution giving way to fear, fear building slowly into panic.

The plane jolts again. This time harder.

And then, once more.

"That's not turbulence," I say.

Kenji swears, loudly, and jumps to his feet. He scans the dashboard for a second before turning back, his head in a viselike grip between his hands. "I can't read these dials," he says, "I have no idea how to read these goddamn dials—"

I shove the cockpit door open just as Nazeera runs forward. She pushes her way past me to scan the dashboard and when she pulls away she looks suddenly terrified. "We've lost one of our engines," she says, her words barely a whisper. "Someone is shooting us out of the sky."

"What? How is that—"

But there's no time to discuss it. And Nazeera and I hardly have a chance to try to figure out a way to fix it before the plane jolts, once more, and this time the emergency oxygen masks fall out of their overhead compartments. Sirens are wailing. Lights overhead blink rapidly, insistent, sharp beeps warning us that the system is crashing.

"We have to try to land the plane," Nazeera is saying. "We have to figure out—Shit," she says. She covers her mouth with one hand. "We just lost another engine."

"So we're just going to fall out of the goddamn sky?" This, from Kenji.

"We can't land the plane," I say, my heart beating furiously even as I try to keep a level head. "Not like this, not when we're missing two engines. Not while they're still shooting at us."

"So what do we do?" she says.

It's Ella, at the door, who says quietly, "We have to jump."

~~JULIETTE~~

ELLA

"*What?*"

The three of them turn to face me.

"What are you talking about?" Kenji says.

"Love, that's really not a good idea—We don't have any parachutes on this plane, and without them—"

"No, she's right," Nazeera says carefully. She's looking me in the eye. She seems to understand what I'm thinking.

"It'll work," I say. "Don't you think?"

"Honestly, I have no idea," she says. "But it's definitely worth a shot. It might be our only shot."

Kenji is beginning to pace. "Okay, someone needs to tell me what the hell is going on."

Aaron has gone pale. "Love," he says again, "what—"

"Nazeera can fly," I explain. "If we all find a way to secure ourselves to one another, she can use her powers to bolster us, you can use your power to bolster *her* power, and because there's little chance either of you could use that much of your strength while still carrying our combined weight, we'll eventually, slowly, be dragged down to the ground."

Nazeera glances at the dash again. "We're eight thousand feet in the air and losing altitude quickly. If we're going to do this, we should jump now, while the plane is still relatively stable."

"Wait—where are we?" Kenji says. "Where are we going to land?"

"I'm not sure," she says. "But it looks like we're somewhere over the general vicinity of sectors 200 through 300." She looks at Aaron. "Do you have any friends in this region?"

Aaron shoots her a dark look. "I have friends nowhere."

"Zero people skills," Kenji mutters.

"We're out of time," I say. "Are we going to do this?"

"I guess so. It's the only plan we've got," Kenji says.

"I think it's a solid plan," Aaron says, and shoots me a hesitant, but encouraging look. "But I think we should find a way to strap ourselves together. Some kind of harness or something—so we don't lose each other in the air."

"We don't have time for that." Nazeera's calm is quickly giving way to panic. "We'll just have to hold on tight."

Kenji nods, and with a sudden heave, shoves open the airplane door. Air rushes in fast and hard, nearly knocking us off our feet.

Quickly, we all link arms, Nazeera and Aaron holding up the outer edges, and with a few reassuring shouts through the howling wind—

We jump.

It's a terrifying sensation.

The wind pushes up fast and hard and then, all at once, stills. We seem to be frozen in time, whirring in place even as we watch the jet fall, steadily, into the distance. Nazeera and Aaron appear to be doing their jobs almost too well. We're not falling fast enough, and not only is it freezing up here, oxygen is scarce.

"I'm going to drop my hold on your power," Aaron calls out to Nazeera, and she shouts back her agreement.

Slowly, we begin to descend.

I watch as the world blurs around us. We drift downward, unhurried, the wind pushing hard against our feet. And then, suddenly, the bottom seems to drop out from under us, and we go shooting down, hard, into the terrain below.

I give out a single, terrified scream—

Or was that Kenji?

—before we pull to a sudden stop, a foot above the ground. Aaron squeezes my arm and I look at him, grateful for the catch.

And then we fall to the ground.

I land badly on my ankle and wince, but I can put weight on my foot, so I know it's all right. I look around to assess the state of my friends, but realize, too late, that we're not alone.

We're in a vast, wide-open field. This was, once upon a time, almost certainly farmland, but it's now been reduced to little more than ash. In the distance appears a thin band of people, quickly closing in on us.

I harness my powers, ready to fight. Ready to face whatever comes our way. Energy is thrumming inside me, sparking in my blood.

I am not afraid.

Aaron puts his arm around me, pulls me close. "Together," he whispers. "No matter what."

Finally, after what feels like immeasurable minutes, two bodies separate from their group. Slowly, they walk up to us.

My whole body is tense in preparation for an attack, but as they get closer, I'm able to discern their faces.

They're two adults:

One, a slender, stunning woman with closely cropped hair and skin so dark it gleams. She's luminous as she walks, her smile widening with every step. Beside her is another smiling face, but the familiar sight of his brown skin and long dreadlocks sends shock and panic and hope rushing through me. I feel dazed.

Castle.

His presence here could be either good or bad. A thousand questions run through my mind, among them: What is he doing here? How did he get here? The last time I saw him, I didn't think he was on my side at all—has he turned against us completely?

The woman is the first to speak.

"I'm glad to see you're all right," she says. "I'm afraid we had no choice but to shoot your plane out of the sky."

"What? What are y—"

"Castle?" Kenji's quiet, tentative voice reaches out from behind me.

Castle steps forward just as Kenji moves toward him,

316

and the two embrace, Castle pulling him in so tightly I can practically feel the tension from where I'm standing. They're both visibly emotional, and the moment is so touching it puts my fears at ease.

"You're okay," Kenji says. "I thought—"

Haider and Stephan, the son of the supreme commander of Africa, step out of the crowd. Shock seizes my body at the sight of them. They nod at Nazeera and the three of them separate to form a new group, off to the side. They speak in low, hurried whispers.

Castle takes a deep breath. "We have a lot to talk about." And then, to me, he says, "Ella, I'd like you to meet my daughter, Nouria."

My eyebrows fly up my forehead. I glance at Aaron, who seems as stunned as I am, but Kenji lets out a sudden *whoop*, and tackles Castle all over again. The two of them laugh. Kenji is saying, *No way, no way*

Nouria pointedly ignores them and smiles at me. "We call our home the Sanctuary," she says. "My wife and I are the leaders of the resistance here. Welcome."

Another woman separates from the crowd and steps forward. She's petite, with long blond hair. She shakes my hand. "It's an honor to meet you," she says. "My name is Samantha."

I study both of them, Nouria and Samantha standing side by side. Castle's happiness. The smile on Kenji's face. The cluster of Nazeera, Haider, and Stephan off to the side. The larger group crowded in the distance.

"The honor is ours," I say, and smile. Then: "But are we safe out here? Out in the open like this?"

Nouria nods. "My powers allow me to manipulate light in unusual ways," she says. "I've cast a protective shield around us right now, so that if someone were to look in our direction, they'd see only a painful brightness that would force them to look away."

"Whoa." Kenji's eyes widen. "That's cool."

"Thank you," Nouria says. She's practically emanating light, her dark brown skin shimmering even as she stands still. There's something breathtaking about just being near her.

"Are those your people?" I hear Aaron say, speaking for the first time. He's peering over her head, at the small crowd in the distance.

She nods.

"And are they here to make sure we don't hurt you?"

Nouria smiles. "They're here to make sure no one hurts *you*," she says. "Your group is welcome here. You've more than proven yourselves worthy." And then, "We've heard all the stories about Sector 45."

"You have?" I say, surprised. "I thought The Reestablishment buried everything."

Nouria shakes her head. "Whispers travel faster than anyone can control. The continent is buzzing with the news of all you've been doing these past couple of months. It's truly a privilege to meet you," she says to me, and holds out her hand. "I've been so inspired by your work."

318

I take her hand, feeling at once proud and embarrassed. "Thank you," I say quietly. "That's very kind of you."

But then Nouria's eyes grow somber. "I *am* sorry we had to shoot you out of the sky," she says. "That must've been terrifying. But Castle assured me that there were two among you who would be able to fly."

"Wait, what?" Kenji hazards a look at Castle. "You planned this?"

"It was the only way," he says. "Once we were able to get free of the asylum"—he nods gratefully at Nazeera—"I knew the only place left for us was here, with Nouria. But we couldn't have radioed to tell you to land here; our communication would've been intercepted. And we couldn't have you land at the air base, for obvious reasons. So we've been tracking your plane, waiting for the right moment. Shooting you out of the sky punts the problem straight back to the military. They'll think it was action from another unit, and by the time they begin to figure it out, we'll have destroyed all evidence of our being here."

"So—Wait—" I say. "How did you and Nouria coordinate this? How'd you find each other?" And then: "Castle, if you've abandoned the citizens—Won't Anderson just murder them all? Shouldn't you have stayed to protect them? Tried to fight back?"

He shakes his head. "We had no choice but to evacuate Omega Point members from Sector 45. After the two of you"—he nods at me and Aaron—"were taken, things fell into complete chaos. We were all taken hostage and thrown in prison. It was only because of Nazeera—who connected us with Haider and Stephan—that we were able to make our way here. Sector 45 has since been returned to its original state as a prison." Castle takes a tight breath. "There's a great deal we need to share with each other. So much has happened in the last two weeks it'll be impossible to discuss it all quickly. But it *is* important that you know, right now, a little bit about Nouria's role in all this."

He turns to Nouria and gives her a small nod.

Nouria looks me in the eye and says, "That day you were shot on the beach," she says quietly. "Do you remember?"

I hesitate. "Of course."

"I was the one who issued that order against you."

I'm so stunned I visibly flinch.

"*What?*" Aaron steps forward, outraged. "Castle, are you *insane*? You ask us to take refuge in the home of a person who nearly murdered Ella?" He turns back, stares at me with a wild look in his eyes. "How could y—"

"Castle?" There's a warning in Kenji's voice. "What is going on?"

But Nouria and Castle are staring at each other, and a heavy look passes between them.

Finally, Castle sighs.

"Let's get settled before we keep talking," he says. "This is a long conversation, and it's an important one."

"Let's have it now," Aaron says.

"Yes," Kenji says angrily. "Now."

"She tried to murder me," I say, finally finding my voice.

"Why would you bring me here? What are you trying to do?"

"You've had a long, difficult journey," Castle says. "I want you to have a chance to get settled. Take a shower and eat some food. And then, I promise—we'll give you all the answers you want."

"But how can we trust that we'll be safe?" I say. "How can we know Nouria isn't trying to hurt us?"

"Because," she says steadily, "I did what I did to help you."

"And how is that plausible?" Aaron says sharply.

"It was the only way I knew how to get a message to you," Nouria says, still staring at me. "I was never trying to kill you—and I knew that your own defenses would help protect you from certain death."

"That was a dangerous bet to make."

"Believe me," she says quietly, "it was a difficult decision to make. It came at great cost to us—we lost one of our own in the process."

I feel myself tense, but otherwise betray no emotion. I remember the day Nazeera saved me—the day she killed my assailant.

"But I had to reach you," Nouria says, her dark brown eyes deep with feeling. "It was the only way I could do it without rousing suspicion."

My curiosity beats out my skepticism. For the moment.

"So—Why? Why did you do it?" I ask. "Why poison me?"

Unexpectedly, Nouria smiles. "I needed you to see what I saw. And according to Castle, it worked."

"What worked?"

"Ella—" She hesitates. "May I call you by your real name?"

I blink. Stare at Castle. "You told her about me?"

"He didn't have to. Things don't stay secret for very long around here," Nouria says. "No matter what The Reestablishment has you believe, we're all finding ways to pass messages to each other. All the resistance groups across the globe know the truth about you by now. And they love you more for it."

I don't know what to say.

"Ella," she says softly, "I was able to figure out why your parents have kept your sister a secret for so long. And I just wanted t—"

"I already know," I say, the words coming out quietly.

I haven't talked to anyone about this yet; haven't told a soul. There's been no time to discuss something this big. No time to have a long conversation. But I guess we're going to have it now.

Nouria is staring at me, stunned. "You know?"

"Emmaline told me everything."

A hush falls over the crowd. Everyone turns to look at me. Even Haider, Stephan, and Nazeera finally stop talking amongst themselves long enough to stare.

"She's kept in captivity," I say. "She lives in a holding tank, where she exists almost permanently underwater. Her brain waves are connected to tidal turbines that convert the kinetic energy of her mind into electricity. Evie, my mother, found a way to harness that electricity—and project it outward. All over the world." I take a deep breath. "Emmaline is stronger than I've ever been or ever will be. She has the power to bend the minds of the people—she can warp and distort realities—Here. Everywhere."

Kenji's face is a perfect encapsulation of horror, and his expression is reflected on dozens of other faces around me. Nazeera, on the other hand, looks stricken.

"What you see here?" I say. "Around us? The decay of society, the broken atmosphere, the birds gone from the sky—It's all an illusion. It's true that our climate has changed, yes—we've done serious damage to the atmosphere, to the animals, to the planet as a whole—but that damage is not irreparable. Scientists were hopeful that, with a careful, concerted effort, we could fix our Earth. Save the future. But The Reestablishment didn't like that angle," he says. "They didn't want the people to hope. They wanted people to think that our Earth was beyond salvation. And with Emmaline they were able to do just that."

"Why?" Kenji says, stunned. "Why would they do that? What do they gain?"

"Desperate, terrified people," Nouria says solemnly, "are much easier to control. They used Ella's sister to create the illusion of irreversible devastation, and then they preyed upon the weak and the hopeless, and convinced them to turn to The Reestablishment for support."

"Emmaline and I were designed for something called Operation Synthesis. She was meant to be the architect of the world, and I was to be the executioner. But Emmaline is dying. They need another powerful weapon with which to control the people. A contingency. A backup plan."

Aaron takes my hand.

"The Reestablishment wanted me to replace my sister," I say.

For the first time, Nouria has gone still. No one knew this part. No one but me. "How?" she says. "You have such different abilities."

It's Castle who says, "It's easy to imagine, actually." But he looks terrified. "If they were to magnify Ella's powers the way they did her sister's, she would become the equivalent of a human atom bomb. She could cause mass destruction. Excruciating pain. Death when they please. Across tremendous distances."

"We have no choice." Nazeera's voice rings out, sharp and clear. "We have to kill Evie."

And I'm looking out, far into the distance, when I say, quietly, "I already did."

A collective gasp goes through the crowd. Aaron goes still beside me.

"And now," I say, "I have to kill my sister. It's what she wants. It's the only way."

WARNER

Nouria's headquarters are both strange and beautiful. They have no need to hide underground, because she's found a way to imbue objects with her power—an evolution of our abilities even Castle hadn't foreseen. The Sanctuary's campsite is protected by a series of twenty-foot-tall pole lights that border the edges of the clearing. Fused with Nouria's power, the lights work together as a barrier that makes it impossible to look in the direction of their campsite. She says her abilities not only have the power to blind, but that she can also use light to warp sounds. So they live here, out in the open, their words and actions protected in plain sight. Only those who know the location can find their way here.

Nouria says that the illusion has kept them safe for years.

The sun begins its descent as we make our way toward the campsite—the vast, unusually green field dotted with cream-colored tents—and the scene is so breathtaking I can't help but stop to appreciate the view. Fire streaks across the sky, golden light flooding the air and earth. It feels both beautiful and bleak, and I shiver as a gust of wind wraps around my body.

Ella takes my hand.

I look at her, surprised, and she smiles at me, the fading

sun glinting in her eyes. I feel her fear, her hope, her love for me. But there's something else, too—something like pride. It's faint, but it's there, and it makes me so happy to see her like this. She *should* be proud. I can speak for myself, at least, when I say that I've never been so proud of her. But then, I always knew she would go on to greatness. It doesn't surprise me at all that, even after everything she's been through—after all the horrors she's had to face— she's still managed to inspire the world. She's one of the strongest people I've ever known. My father might be back from the dead, and Sector 45 might be out of our hands, but Ella's impact can't be ignored. Nouria says that no one really believed that she was actually dead, but now that it's official—now that word has spread that Ella is still alive— she's become more notorious than ever. Nouria says that the rumbles underground are already getting stronger. People are more desperate to act, to get involved, and to stand up to The Reestablishment. Resistance groups are growing. The civilians are finding ways to get smarter—to get stronger, together. And Ella has given them a figure to rally around. Everyone is talking about her.

She's become a symbol of hope for so many.

I squeeze Ella's hand, returning her smile, and when her cheeks flush with color I have to fight back the urge to pull her into my arms.

She amazes me more every day.

My conversation with Kenji is still, despite everything, at the forefront of my mind. Things always feel so desperate these days that I feel a new, nagging insistence that this window of calm might be my only chance at happiness. We're almost constantly at war, either fighting for our lives or on the run—and there's no guarantee of a future. No guarantee that I'll live to see another year. No promise to grow old. It makes me feel li—

I stop, suddenly, and Ella nearly stumbles.

"Are you okay?" she says, squeezing my hand.

I nod. I offer her a distracted smile and vague apology as we begin walking again, but—

I run the numbers once more.

Finally, I say, without looking up, "Does anyone happen to know what day it is?"

And someone responds, a voice from the group I can't be bothered to identify, confirming what I already thought might be true. My father wasn't lying.

Tomorrow is my birthday.

I'll be twenty years old.

Tomorrow.

The revelation thunders through me. This birthday feels like more of a milestone than usual, because my life, exactly one year ago, was nearly unrecognizable. Almost everything in my life is different now. One year ago I was a different person. I was in an awful, self-destructive relationship with a different person. One year ago my anxiety was so crippling that five minutes alone with my own mind would leave me spiraling for days. I relied entirely upon my routines and schedules to keep me tethered to the endless horrors of my job and its demands. I was inflexible beyond reason. I was hanging on to humanity by a thread. I felt both wild and nearly out of my mind, all the time. My private thoughts and fears were so dark that I spent nearly all my free hours either exercising, in my shooting range, or in the bowels of Sector 45, running training simulations that, I'm not proud to admit, I designed specifically to experience killing myself, over and over again.

That was one year ago. Less than a year ago. Somehow, it feels like a lifetime ago. And when I think back on who I was and what that version of myself thought my life would be like today—

I'm left deeply and profoundly humbled.

Today is not forever. Happiness does not *happen*. Happiness must be uncovered, separated from the skin of pain. It must be claimed. Kept close.

Protected.

"Would you prefer a chance to shower and change before reuniting with the others?" Nouria is saying.

Her voice is sharp and clear and it shakes me from my reverie. "Yes," I say quickly. "I'd really appreciate the time to rest."

"No problem. We meet for dinner in the main tent in two hours. I'll show you to your new residences." She hesitates. "I hope you'll forgive me for being presumptuous, but I assumed the two of you"—she looks at me and Ella—"would like to share a space. But of course if that's not—"

"Yes, thank you," Ella says quickly. Her cheeks are

330

already pink. "We're grateful for your thoughtfulness."

Nouria nods. She seems pleased. And then she turns to Kenji and Nazeera and says, "If you'd like, I can arrange to join your separate rooms so that y—"

Kenji and Nazeera respond at the same time.

"What? No."

"Absolutely not."

"*Oh,* I'm so sorry," Nouria says quickly. "My apologies. I shouldn't have assumed."

For the first time ever, Nazeera looks flustered. She can hardly get out the words when she says, "Why would you think we'd want to share a room?"

Nouria shakes her head. She shares a quick, confused glance with Castle, but seems suddenly mortified. "I don't know. I'm sorry. You seemed—"

"Separate rooms are perfect," Kenji says sharply.

"Great," Nouria says a little too brightly. "I'll lead the way."

And I watch, amused, as Castle tries and fails to hide a smile.

Our residence, as Nouria called it, is more than I could've hoped for. I thought we'd be camping; instead, inside of each tent is a miniature, self-contained home. There's a bed, a small living area, a tiny kitchen, and a full bathroom. The furnishings are spare but bright, well made and clean.

And when Ella walks in, slips off her shoes, and throws herself backward onto the bed, I can almost imagine us together like this—maybe, someday—in our own home. The thought sends a wave of disorienting euphoria through my body.

And then—fear.

It seems like tempting fate to even hope for a happiness like that. But there's another part of me, a small, but insistent part of me, that clings to that hope nonetheless. Ella and I overcame what I once thought impossible. I never dreamed she'd still love me once she knew everything about me. I never dreamed that the heartbreak and horrors of recent events would only bring us closer, or that my love for her could somehow increase tenfold in two weeks. I grew up thinking that the joys of this world were for other people to enjoy. I was certain that I was fated to a bleak, solitary life, forever barred from the contentment offered by human connection.

But now—

Ella yawns soundlessly, hugging a pillow to her chest as she curls up on her side. Her eyes close.

A smile tugs at my mouth as I watch her.

I'm still amazed at how just the sight of her could bring me so much peace. She shifts, again, burrowing more deeply into the pillows, and I realize she must be exhausted. And as much as I'd love to pull her into my arms, I decide to give her space. I back away quietly, and instead use the time to explore the rest of our new, temporary home.

I'm still surprised by how much I like it.

We have more privacy here, in these new headquarters,

than we ever did before. More freedom. Here, I'm a visitor, welcome to take my time showering and resting before dinner. No one expects me to run their world. I have no correspondence to attend to. No awful tasks to attend to. No civilians to oversee. No innocents to torture. I feel so much freer now that someone else has taken the reins.

It's both alien and wonderful.

It feels so good to have space with Ella—literal and figurative space—to be ourselves, to be together, to simply be and breathe. Ella and I shared my bedroom back on base, but it never felt like home there. Everything was cold, sterile. I hated that building. Hated that room. Hated every minute of my life. Those walls—my own personal rooms—were suffocating, infused with awful memories. But here, even though the room is small, the tight quarters manage to be cozy. This place feels fresh and new and serene. The future doesn't seem improbable here. Hope doesn't feel ridiculous.

It feels like a chance to begin again.

And it doesn't feel dangerous to dream that one day, Ella might be mine in every way. My wife. My family. My future.

I've never, ever dared to think of it.

But my hope is snuffed out just as quickly as it appeared. Kenji's warnings flash through my mind, and I feel suddenly agitated. Apparently proposing to Ella is more complicated than I'd originally thought it might be. Apparently I need some kind of plan. A ring. A moment on one knee. It all sounds ridiculous to me. I don't even know why it sounds ridiculous, exactly, just that it doesn't feel like *me*. I don't know how to put on a performance. I don't want to make a scene. I'd find it excruciating to be so vulnerable in front of other people or in an unfamiliar setting. I wouldn't know what to do with myself.

Still, these problems seem surmountable in the pursuit of forever with her. I would get on one knee if Ella wanted me to. I'd propose in a room filled with her closest friends if that was what she needed.

No, my fear is something much greater than that.

The thing Kenji said to me today that rattled me to my core was the possibility that Ella might say no. It's *unconscionable* that it never occurred to me that she might say no.

Of course she might say no.

She could be uninterested for any number of reasons. She might not be ready, for example. Or she might not be interested in the institution of marriage as a whole. *Or*, I think, she simply might not want to tether herself to me in such a permanent way.

The thought sends a chill through my body.

I suppose I assumed she and I were on the same page, emotionally. But my assumptions in this department have landed me in trouble more times than I'd like to admit, and the stakes are too high now not to take Kenji's concerns seriously. I'm not prepared to acknowledge the damage it would do to my heart if she rejected my proposal.

I take a deep, sharp breath.

Kenji said I need to get her a ring. So far he's been right

about most of the things I've done wrong in our relationship, so I'm inclined to believe he might have a point. But I have no idea where I'd be able to conjure up a ring in a place like this. Maybe if we were back home, where I was familiar with the area and its artisans—

But here?

It's almost too much to think about right now.

There's so much to think about, in fact, that I can't quite believe I'm even considering something like this—at a time like this. I haven't even had a moment to reconcile the apparent regeneration of my father, or literally any of the other new, outrageous revelations our families have thrown at us. We're in the middle of a fight for our lives; we're fighting for the future of the *world*.

I squeeze my eyes shut. Maybe I really am an idiot.

Five minutes ago, the end of the world seemed like the right reason to propose: to take everything I can in this transitory world—and grieve nothing. But suddenly, it feels like this really might be an impulsive decision. Maybe this isn't the right time, after all.

Maybe Kenji was right. Maybe I'm not thinking clearly. Maybe losing Ella and regaining all these memories—

Maybe it's made me irrational.

I push off the wall, trying to clear my head. I wander the rest of the small space, taking stock of everything in our tent, and peer into the bathroom. I'm relieved to discover that there's real plumbing. In fact, the more I look around, the more I realize that this isn't a tent at all. There are actual floors and walls and a single vaulted ceiling in this room, as if each unit is actually a small, freestanding building. The tents seem to be draped over the entire structure—and I wonder if they serve a more practical purpose that's not immediately obvious.

Several years, Nouria said.

Several years they've lived here and made this their home. They really found a way to make something out of nothing.

The bathroom is a nice size—spacious enough for two people to share, but not big enough for a bathtub. Still, when we first approached the clearing I wasn't even sure they'd have proper facilities or running water, so this is more than I could've hoped for. And the more I stare at the shower, the more I'm suddenly desperate to rinse these weeks from my skin. I always took pains to stay clean, even in prison, but it's been too long since I've had a hot shower with steady, running water, and I can hardly resist the temptation now. And I've already stripped off most of my clothes when I hear Ella call my name, her still-sleepy voice carrying over from what serves as our bedroom. Or bed space. It's not really a room as much as it is an area designated for a bed.

"Yes?" I call back.

"Where'd you go?" she says.

"I thought I might take a shower," I try to say without shouting. I've just stepped out of my underwear and into the standing shower, but I turn the dials in the wrong direction and cold water sprays from the showerhead. I jump backward even as I hurry to undo my mistake, and nearly collide with Ella in the process.

Ella, who's suddenly standing behind me.

I don't know whether its habit, instinct, or self-preservation, but I grab a towel from a nearby shelf and quickly press it against my exposed body. I don't even understand why I'm suddenly self-conscious. I never feel uncomfortable in my own skin. I like the way I look naked.

But this moment wasn't one I'd anticipated, and I feel defenseless.

"Hi, love," I say, taking a quick breath. I remember to smile. "I didn't see you standing there."

Ella crosses her arms, pretending to look mad, but I can see the effort she's making to fight back a smile. "Aaron," she says sternly. "You were going to take a shower without me?"

My eyebrows fly up, surprised.

For a moment, I don't know what to say. And then, carefully, "Would you like to join me?"

She steps forward, wraps her arms around my waist, and stares up at me with a sweet, secret smile. The look in her eyes is enough to make me think about dropping the towel.

I whisper her name, my heart heavy with emotion.

She pulls me closer, gently touching her lips to my chest, and I go uncomfortably still. Her kisses grow more intent, her lips leaving a trail of fire across my chest, down my torso, and feeling rushes through my veins, sets me on fire. Suddenly I forget why I was ever holding a towel.

I don't even know when it falls to the floor.

I slip my arms around her, reel her in. She feels incredible, her body fitting against me perfectly, and I tilt her face up, my hand caught somewhere behind her neck and the base of her jaw and I kiss her, soft and slow, heat filling my blood with dangerous speed. I pull her tighter and she gasps, stumbles and takes an accidental step back and I catch her, pressing her against the wall behind her. I bunch up the hem of her dress and in one smooth motion yank it upward, my hand slipping under the material to skim the smooth skin of her waist, to grip her hip, hard. I part her legs with my thigh and she makes a soft, desperate sound deep in her throat and it does something to me, to feel her like this, to hear her like this—to be assaulted by endless waves of her pleasure and desire—

It drives me *insane*.

I bury my face in her neck, my hands moving up, under her dress to feel her skin, hot and soft and sensitive to my touch. I've missed her so much. I've missed her body under my hands, missed the scent of her skin and the soft, feather-light whisper of her hair against my body. I kiss her neck, trying to ignore the tension in my muscles or the hard, desperate pressure driving me toward her, toward madness. There's an ache expanding inside of me and demanding more, demanding I flip her over and lose myself in her here, right now, and she whispers—

"How—How do you always feel so good?" She's clinging to me, her eyes half-lidded but bright with desire. Her face is flushed. Her words are heavy with feeling when she says, "How do you always do this to me?"

I break away from her.

I take two steps backward and I'm breathing hard, trying to regain control of myself even as her eyes widen, her arms going suddenly still.

"Aaron?" she says. "What's—"

"Take off your dress," I say quietly.

Understanding awakens in her eyes.

She says nothing, she only looks at me, carefully, as I watch, imprisoned in place by an acute form of agony. Her hands are trembling but her eyes are willing and wanting and nervous. She shoves the material down, past her shoulders and lets it fall to the floor. I drink her in as she steps out of the dress, my mind racing.

Gorgeous, I think. *So gorgeous.*

My pulse is wild.

When I ask her to, she unhooks her bra. Moments later, her underwear joins her bra on the floor and I can't look away from her, my mind unable to process the perfection of this happiness. She's so stunning I can hardly breathe. I can hardly fathom that she's mine, that she wants me, that she would ever love me. I can't even hear myself *think* over the rush of blood in my ears, my heart beating so fast and hard it seems to thud against my skull. The sight of her standing in front of me, vulnerable and flushed with desire, is doing wild, desperate things to my mind. God, the fantasies I've had about her. The places my mind has gone.

I step forward and pick her up and she gasps, surprised, clinging desperately to my neck as I hitch her legs around my waist, my arms settling under her thighs. I love feeling the weight of her soft curves. I love having her this close to me. I love her arms around my neck and the squeeze of her legs around my hips. I love how ready she is, her thighs already parted, every inch of her pressed against me. But then she runs her hands up my naked back and I have to resist the urge to flinch. I don't want to be self-conscious about the scars on my body. I don't want any part of me to be off-limits to her. I want her to know me exactly as I am, and, as hard as it is, I allow myself to ease into her touch, closing my eyes as she trails her hands up, across my shoulders, down my arms.

"You're so gorgeous," she says softly. "I'm always surprised. It doesn't matter how many times I see you without your clothes on, I'm always surprised. It doesn't seem fair that anyone should be this gorgeous."

She looks at me, stares at me as if expecting an answer, but I can't speak. I fear I might unravel if I do. I want her with a desperate need I've never known before—a desperate, painful need so overwhelming it's threatening to consume me. I need her. Need this. Now. I take a deep, unsteady breath, and carry her into the shower.

She screams.

Hot water hits us fast and hard and I press her against the shower wall, losing myself in her in a way I never have before. The kisses are deeper, more desperate. The heat, more explosive. Everything between us feels wild and raw and vulnerable.

I lose track of time.

I don't know how long we've been here. I don't know how long I've lost myself in her when she cries out, clutching my arms so tightly her fingernails dig into my skin, her screams muffled against my chest. I feel weak, unsteady as she collapses in my arms; I'm intoxicated by the pure, stunning power of her emotions: endless waves of love and desire, love and kindness, love and joy, love and tenderness. So much tenderness.

It's almost too much.

I step backward, bracing myself against the wall as she presses her cheek against my chest and holds me, our bodies wet and heavy with feeling, our hearts pounding with something more powerful than I ever thought possible. I kiss the curve of her shoulder, the nape of her neck. I forget where we are and all we have left to do and I just hold on, hot water rushing down my arms, my limbs still slightly shaking, too terrified to let her go.

~~JULIETTE~~

ELLA

I wake up with a start.

After we got out of the shower, Aaron and I dried off, climbed into bed without a word, and promptly fell asleep.

I have no idea what time it is.

Aaron's body is curled around mine, one of his arms under my head, the other wrapped around my waist. His arms are heavy, and the weight of him feels so good—makes me feel so safe—that, on the one hand, I don't ever want to move. On the other hand—

I know we should probably get out of bed.

I sigh, hating to wake him up—he seems so tired—and I turn around, slowly, in his arms.

He only pulls me tighter.

He shifts so that his chin rests on my head; my face is now pressed gently against his throat, and I breathe him in, running my hands along the strong, deep lines of muscle in his arms. Everything about him feels raw. Powerful. There's something both wild and terrified about his heart, and somehow, knowing this only makes me love him more. I trace the lines of his shoulder blades, the curve of his spine. He stirs, but only a little, and buries his face in my hair, breathing me in.

"Don't go," he says quietly.

I tilt my head, gently kiss the column of his throat. "Aaron," I whisper, "I'm not going anywhere."

He sighs. Says, "Good."

I smile. "But we should probably get out of bed. We have to go to dinner. Everyone will be waiting for us."

He shakes his head, barely. Makes a disapproving sound in his throat.

"But—"

"No." And then, deftly, he helps me turn around. He hugs me close again, my back pressed against his chest. His voice is soft, husky with desire when he says. "Let me enjoy you, love. You feel so good."

And I give in. Melt back into his arms.

The truth is, I love these moments most. The quiet contentment. The peace. I love the weight of him, the feel of him, his naked body wrapped around mine. I never feel closer to him than I do like this, when there's nothing between us.

Gently, he kisses my temple. Pulls me, somehow, even tighter. And his lips are at my ear when he says,

"Kenji said I was supposed to get you a ring."

I stiffen, confused. Try to turn around when I say, "What do you mean?"

But Aaron eases my body back down. He rests his chin on my shoulder. His hands move down my arms, trace the curve of my hips. He kisses my neck once, twice, so softly. "I know I'm doing this wrong," he says. "I know I'm not good at this sort of thing, love, and I hope you'll forgive me for it, but I don't know how else to do it." A pause. "And I'm starting to think it might kill me if I don't."

My body is frozen, even as my heart pounds furiously in my chest. "Aaron," I say, hardly daring to breathe. "What are you talking about?"

He says nothing.

I turn around again, and this time, he doesn't stop me. His eyes flare with emotion, and I watch the gentle movement in his throat as he swallows. A muscle jumps in his jaw.

"Marry me," he whispers.

I stare at him, disbelief and joy colliding. And it's the look in his eyes—the hopeful, terrified look in his eyes—that nearly kills me.

I'm suddenly crying.

I clap my hands over my face. A sob escapes my mouth. Gently, he pries my hands away from my face.

"Ella?" he says, his words hardly a whisper.

I'm still crying when I throw my arms around his neck, still crying when he says, a little nervously—

"Sweetheart, I really need to know if this means yes or no—"

"Yes," I cry, slightly hysterical. "Yes. Yes to everything with you. Yes to forever with you. *Yes*."

WARNER

Is this joy?

I think it might kill me.

"Aaron?"

"Yes, love?"

She takes my face in her hands and kisses me, kisses me with a love so deep it releases my brain from its prison. My heart starts beating violently.

"Ella," I say. "You're going to be my wife."

She kisses me again, crying again, and suddenly I don't recognize myself. I don't recognize my hands, my bones, my heart. I feel new. Different.

"I love you," she whispers. "I love you so much."

"That you could love me at all seems like some kind of miracle."

She smiles, even as she shakes her head. "That's ridiculous," she says. "It's very, very easy to love you."

And I don't know what to say. I don't know how to respond.

She doesn't seem to mind.

I reel her in, kiss her, again, and lose myself in the taste and feel of her, in the fantasy of what we might have. What we might be. And then I pull her gently onto my lap and she straddles my body, settling over me until we're pressed together, her cheek against my chest. I wrap my arms around her, spread my hands along her back. I feel her gentle breaths on my skin, her eyelashes tickling my chest as she blinks, and I decide I'm never, ever leaving this bed.

A happy, wonderful silence settles between us.

"You asked me to marry you," she says softly.

"Yes."

"Wow."

I smile, my heart filled suddenly with inexpressible joy. I hardly recognize myself. I can't remember the last time I ever smiled this much. I can't recall ever feeling this kind of pure, unburdened bliss.

Like my body might float away without me.

I touch her hair, gently. Run my fingers through the soft, silky strands. When I finally sit up, she sits up, too, and she blushes as I stare at her, mesmerized by the sight of her. Her eyes are wide and bright. Her lips full and pink. She's perfect, perfect here, bare and beautiful in my arms.

I press my forehead to the curve of her shoulder, my lips brushing against her skin. "I love you, Ella," I whisper. "I will love you for the rest of my life. My heart is yours. Please don't ever give it back to me."

She says nothing for what feels like an eternity.

Finally, I feel her move. Her hand touches my face.

"Aaron," she whispers. "Look at me."

I shake my head.

"Aaron."

I look up, slowly, to meet her eyes, and her expression is at once sad and sweet and full of love. I feel something thaw inside of me as I stare at her, and just as she's about to say something, a complicated chime echoes through the room.

I freeze.

Ella frowns. Looks around. "That sounds like a doorbell," she says.

I wish I could deny the possibility.

I sit back, even though she's still sitting on my lap. I want this interruption to end. I want to go back to our conversation. I want to stick to my original plan to spend the rest of the night here, in bed, with my perfect, naked fiancée.

The chime sounds again, and this time, I say something decidedly ungentlemanly under my breath.

Ella laughs, surprised. "Did you just swear?"

"No."

A third chime. This time, I stare up at the ceiling and try to clear my head. Try to convince myself to move, to get dressed. This must be some kind of emergency, or else—

Suddenly, a voice:

"Listen—I didn't want to come, okay? I really didn't. I hate being this guy. But Castle sent me to come get you guys because you missed dinner. It's getting super late and everyone is a little worried, and now you're not even answering the door, and—Jesus Christ, open the goddamn door—"

I can't believe it. I can't believe he's here. He's always

here, ruining my life.

I'm going to *kill* him.

I nearly trip trying to pull on my pants and get to the door at the same time, but when I do, I rip the door open, practically tearing it off its hinges.

"Unless someone is dead, dying, or we are under attack, I want you gone before I've even finished this sentence."

Kenji narrows his eyes at me, and then pushes past me into the room. And I'm so stunned by his gall that it takes me a moment to realize I'm going to have to murder him.

"J—?" he says, looking around as he walks in. "You in here?"

Ella is holding the bedsheet up to her neck. "Uh, hi," she says. She smiles nervously. "What are you doing here?"

"Hey, is it cool if I still call you J?" he says. "I know your name is Ella and everything, but I got so used to calling you J that it just feels right, you know?"

"You can still call me J," she says. And then she frowns. "Kenji, what's wrong?"

I groan.

"Get out," I snap at him. "I don't know why you're here, and I don't care. We don't wish to be disturbed. *Ever.*"

Ella shoots me a sharp look. She ignores me when she says, to Kenji, "It's okay. I care. Tell me what's wrong."

"Nothing is wrong," Kenji says. "But I know your boyfriend won't listen to me, so I wanted to let *you* know that it's almost midnight and we really need you guys to get down to the dining tent ASAP, okay?" He shoots Ella a loaded look, and her eyes widen. She nods. I feel a sudden rush of excitement move through her, and it leaves me confused.

"What's going on?" I say.

But Kenji is already walking away.

"Bro, you really need to, like, eat a pizza or something," he says, slapping me on the shoulder as he leaves. "You have too many abs."

"What?" My eyebrows pull together. "That's not—"

"I'm *joking*," Kenji says, pausing in the doorway just before he leaves. "Joking," he says again. "It was a joke. Jesus."

And then he slams the door behind him. I turn around.

"What's going on?" I say again.

But she only smiles. "We should get dressed."

"Ella—"

"I promise I'll explain as soon as we get there."

I shake my head. "Did something happen?"

"No—I'm just—I'm really excited to see everyone from Omega Point again, and they're all waiting for us in the dining tent." She gets out of bed still holding the bedsheet to her body, and I have to clench my fists to keep from pulling it away from her. From pinning her against the wall.

And before I even have a chance to respond, she disappears into the bathroom, the sheet dragging on the floor as she goes.

I follow her.

She's looking for her clothes, oblivious to my presence,

but her dress is on the floor in a corner she hasn't glimpsed yet, and I doubt she'd want to put that bloodied dress back on anyway. I should tell her that I found a drawer full of simple, standard clothes we're probably allowed to borrow.

Maybe later.

For now, I step behind her, slip my hands around her waist. She startles and the sheet falls to the floor. "Ella," I say softly, tugging her body against mine. "Sweetheart, you have to tell me what's going on."

I turn her around, slowly. She looks down at herself, surprised—always surprised—by the sight of her naked body. "I don't have any clothes on," she whispers.

"I know," I say, smiling as I run my hands down her back, appreciating her softness, her perfect curves. I wish I could store these moments. I wish I could revisit them. Relive them. She shivers in my arms and I pull her closer.

"It's not fair," she says, wrapping her arms around me. "It's not fair that you can sense emotions. That it's impossible to keep secrets from you."

"What's not fair," I say, "is that you're about to put your clothes on and force me to leave this bedroom and I don't know why."

She stares at me, her eyes wide and nervous even as she smiles. I can sense that she's torn, her heart in two places at once. "Aaron," she says softly. "Don't you like surprises?"

"I hate surprises."

She laughs. Shakes her head. "I guess I should've known that."

I stare at her, my eyebrows raised, still waiting for an explanation.

"They're going to kill me for telling you," she says. And then at the look in my eyes, "Not—I mean, not literally. But just—" Finally, she sighs. And she won't look at me when she says—

"We're throwing you a birthday party."

I'm certain I've heard her wrong.

~~JULIETTE~~

ELLA

It took more work than I imagined to get him to believe me. He wanted to know how anyone even knew that tomorrow was his birthday and how we could've possibly planned a party when we had no idea we were going to crash the plane here and why would anyone throw him a party and he wasn't even sure he liked parties and on and on and on

And it wasn't until we literally walked through the doors of the dining tent and everyone screamed happy birthday at him that he finally believed me. It wasn't much, of course. We hadn't really had time to prepare. I knew his birthday was coming up because I'd been keeping track of it ever since the day he told me what his father used to do to him, every year, on his birthday. I swore to myself I would do whatever I could to replace those memories with better ones. That forever and ever I would try to drown out the darkness that had inhaled his entire young life.

I told Kenji, when he found me, that tomorrow was Aaron's birthday, and I made him promise me that, no matter what happened, when we found him we would find a way to celebrate, in some small way.

But this—

This was more than I could've hoped for. I thought

maybe, given our time constraints, we'd just get a group to sing him "Happy Birthday," or maybe eat dessert in his honor, but this—

There's an actual cake.

A cake with candles in it, waiting to be lit.

Everyone from Omega Point is here—the whole crew of familiar faces: Brendan and Winston, Sonya and Sara, Alia and Lily, and Ian and Castle. Only Adam and James are missing, but we have new friends, too—

Haider is here. So is Stephan. Nazeera.

And then there's the new resistance. The members of the Sanctuary that we've yet to meet, all come forward, gathered around a single, modest sheet cake. It reads—

HAPPY BIRTHDAY WARNER

in red icing.

The piping is a little sloppy. The icing is imperfect. But when someone dims the lamps and lights the candles, Aaron goes suddenly still beside me. I squeeze his hand as he looks at me, his eyes round with a new emotion.

There's tragedy and beauty in his eyes: something stoic that refuses to be moved, and something childlike that can't help but feel joy. He looks, in short, like he's in pain.

"Aaron," I whisper. "Is this okay?"

He takes a few seconds to respond, but when he finally does, he nods. Just once—but it's enough.

"Yes," he says softly. "This is okay."

And I feel myself relax.

Tomorrow, there will be pain and devastation to contend

362

with. Tomorrow we'll dive into a whole new chapter of hardship. There's a world war brewing. A battle for our lives—for the whole world. Right now, little is certain. But tonight, I'm choosing to celebrate. We're going to celebrate the small and large joys. Birthdays and engagements. We're going to find time for happiness. Because how can we stand against tyranny if we ourselves are filled with hate? Or worse—

Nothing?

I want to remember to celebrate more. I want to remember to experience more joy. I want to allow myself to be happy more frequently. I want to remember, forever, this look on Aaron's face, as he's bullied into blowing out his birthday candles for the very first time.

This is, after all, what we're fighting for, isn't it?

A second chance at joy.

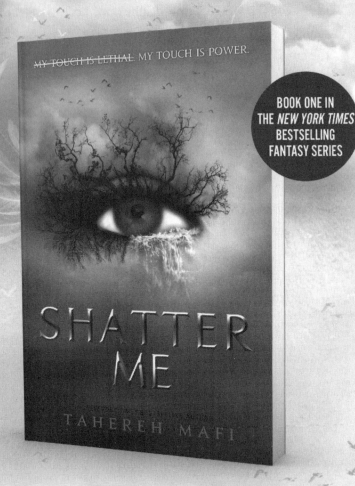

RESTORE ME

ALSO BY TAHEREH MAFI

RESTORE ME

TAHEREH MAFI

First published in USA 2018 by HarperCollins Children's Books
First published in Great Britain 2018
by Electric Monkey, part of Farshore

An imprint of HarperCollins*Publishers*
1 London Bridge Street, London SE1 9GF

farshore.co.uk

2 4 6 8 10 9 7 5 3 1

HarperCollins*Publishers*
1st Floor, Watermarque Building,
Ringsend Road, Dublin 4, Ireland

Published by arrangement with HarperCollins Children's Books,
a division of HarperCollins Publishers, New York, New York, USA

ISBN 978 1 4052 9178 1

YOUNG ADULT

Printed and bound in India by Thomson Press India Ltd

A CIP catalogue record for this title is available from the British Library

For Jodi Reamer, who always believed

JULIETTE

I don't wake up screaming anymore. I do not feel ill at the sight of blood. I do not flinch before firing a gun.

I will never again apologize for surviving.

And yet—

I'm startled at once by the sound of a door slamming open. I silence a gasp, spin around, and, by force of habit, rest my hand on the hilt of a semiautomatic hung from a holster at my side.

"J, we've got a serious problem."

Kenji is staring at me—eyes narrowed—his hands on his hips, T-shirt taut across his chest. This is angry Kenji. Worried Kenji. It's been sixteen days since we took over Sector 45—since I crowned myself the supreme commander of The Reestablishment—and it's been quiet. Unnervingly so. Every day I wake up, filled with half terror, half exhilaration, anxiously awaiting the inevitable missives from enemy nations who would challenge my authority and wage war against us—and now, finally, it seems that moment has arrived. So I take a deep breath, crack my neck, and look Kenji in the eye.

"Tell me."

He presses his lips together. Looks up at the ceiling. "So,

okay—the first thing you need to know is that this isn't my fault, okay? I was just trying to help."

I falter. Frown. "What?"

"I mean, I knew his punkass was a major drama queen, but this is just beyond ridiculous—"

"I'm sorry—what?" I take my hand off my gun; feel my body unclench. "Kenji, what are you talking about? This isn't about the war?"

"The war? What? J, are you not paying attention? Your boyfriend is having a freaking conniption right now and you need to go handle his ass before I do."

I exhale, irritated. "Are you serious? *Again* with this nonsense? Jesus, Kenji." I unlatch the holster from my back and toss it on the bed behind me. "What did you do this time?"

"See?" Kenji points at me. "See—why are you so quick to judge, huh, princess? Why assume that *I* was the one who did something wrong? Why me?" He crosses his arms against his chest, lowers his voice. "And you know, I've been meaning to talk to you about this for a while, actually, because I really feel that, as supreme commander, you can't be showing preferential treatment like this, but clearly—"

Kenji goes suddenly still.

At the creak of the door Kenji's eyebrows shoot up; a soft click and his eyes widen; a muted rustle of movement and suddenly the barrel of a gun is pressed against the back of his head. Kenji stares at me, his lips making no sound as he mouths the word *psychopath* over and over again.

The psychopath in question winks at me from where

2

he's standing, smiling like he couldn't possibly be holding a gun to the head of our mutual friend. I manage to suppress a laugh.

"Go on," Warner says, still smiling. "Please tell me exactly how she's failed you as a leader."

"*Hey*—" Kenji's arms fly up in mock surrender. "I never said she failed at anything, okay? And you are clearly overreact—"

Warner knocks Kenji on the side of the head with the weapon. "Idiot."

Kenji spins around. Yanks the gun out of Warner's hand. "What the hell is wrong with you, man? I thought we were cool."

"We were," Warner says icily. "Until you touched my *hair*."

"You asked me to give you a haircut—"

"I said nothing of the sort! I asked you to trim the edges!"

"And that's what I did."

"*This*," Warner says, spinning around so I might inspect the damage, "is not trimming the edges, you incompetent moron—"

I gasp. The back of Warner's head is a jagged mess of uneven hair; entire chunks have been buzzed off.

Kenji cringes as he looks over his handiwork. Clears his throat. "Well," he says, shoving his hands in his pockets. "I mean—whatever, man, beauty is subjective—"

Warner aims another gun at him.

"Hey!" Kenji shouts. "I am not here for this abusive

relationship, okay?" He points at Warner. "I did not sign up for this shit!"

Warner glares at him and Kenji retreats, backing out of the room before Warner has another chance to react; and then, just as I let out a sigh of relief, Kenji pops his head back into the doorway and says

"I think the cut looks cute, actually"

and Warner slams the door in his face.

Welcome to my brand-new life as supreme commander of The Reestablishment.

Warner is still facing the closed door as he exhales, his shoulders losing their tension as he does, and I'm able to see even more clearly the mess Kenji has made. Warner's thick, gorgeous, golden hair—a defining feature of his beauty—chopped up by careless hands.

A disaster.

"Aaron," I say softly.

He hangs his head.

"Come here."

He turns around, looking at me out of the corner of his eye like he's done something to be ashamed of. I clear the guns off the bed and make room for him beside me. He sinks into the mattress with a sad sigh.

"I look hideous," he says quietly.

I shake my head, smiling, and touch his cheek. "Why did you let him cut your hair?"

4

Warner looks up at me then; his eyes round and green and perplexed. "You told me to spend time with him."

I laugh out loud. "So you let Kenji cut your hair?"

"I didn't let him *cut* my hair," he says, scowling. "It was"—he hesitates—"it was a gesture of camaraderie. It was an act of trust I'd seen practiced among my soldiers. In any case," he says, turning away, "it's not as though I have any experience building friendships."

"Well," I say. "We're friends, aren't we?"

At this, he smiles.

"And?" I nudge him. "That's been good, hasn't it? You're learning to be nicer to people."

"Yes, well, I don't want to be nicer to people. It doesn't suit me."

"I think it suits you beautifully," I say, beaming. "I love it when you're nice."

"You would say that." He almost laughs. "But being kind does not come naturally to me, love. You'll have to be patient with my progress."

I take his hand in mine. "I have no idea what you're talking about. You're perfectly kind to me."

Warner shakes his head. "I know I promised I would make an effort to be nicer to your friends—and I will continue to make that effort—but I hope I've not led you to believe I'm capable of an impossibility."

"What do you mean?"

"Only that I hope I won't disappoint you. I might, if pressed, be able to generate some degree of warmth, but you must know that I have no interest in treating anyone the way I treat you. *This*," he says, touching the air between us, "is an exception to a very hard rule." His eyes are on my lips now; his hand has moved to my neck. "*This*," he says softly, "is very, very unusual."

I stop

stop breathing, talking, thinking—

He's hardly touched me and my heart is racing; memories crash over me, scalding me in waves: the weight of his body against mine; the taste of his skin; the heat of his touch and his sharp gasps for air and the things he's said to me only in the dark.

Butterflies invade my veins, and I force them out.

This is still so new, his touch, his skin, the scent of him, so new, so new and so incredible—

He smiles, tilts his head; I mimic the movement and with one soft intake of air his lips part and I hold still, my lungs flung to the floor, fingers feeling for his shirt and for what comes next when he says

"I'll have to shave my head, you know"

and pulls away.

I blink and he's still not kissing me.

"And it is my very sincere hope," he says, "that you will still love me when I return."

And then he's up up and away and I'm counting on one hand the number of men I've killed and marveling at how little it's done to help me hold it together in Warner's presence.

I nod once as he waves good-bye, collect my good sense from where I left it, and fall backward onto the bed, head spinning, the complications of war and peace heavy on my mind.

I did not think it would be *easy* to be a leader, exactly, but I do think I thought it would be easier than this:

I am racked with doubt in every moment about the decisions I have made. I am infuriatingly surprised every time a soldier follows my lead. And I am growing more terrified that we—that *I*—will have to kill many, many more before this world is settled. Though I think it's the silence, more than anything else, that's left me shaken.

It's been sixteen days.

I've given speeches about what's to come, about our plans for the future; we've held memorials for the lives lost in battle and we're making good on promises to implement change. Castle, true to his word, is already hard at work, trying to address issues with farming, irrigation, and, most urgent, how best to transition the civilians out of the compounds. But this will be work done in stages; it will be a slow and careful build—a fight for the earth that may take a century. I think we all understand that. And if it were only the civilians I had to worry about, I would not worry so much. But I worry because I know too well that nothing can be done to fix this world if we spend the next several decades at war within it.

Even so, I'm prepared to fight.

It's not what I want, but I'll gladly go to war if it's what we need to do to make a change. I just wish it were that simple. Right now, my biggest problem is also the most confusing:

Wars require enemies, and I can't seem to find any.

In the sixteen days since I shot Anderson in the forehead I have faced zero opposition. No one has tried to arrest me. No other supreme commanders have challenged me. Of the 554 remaining sectors on this continent alone, not a single one has defected, declared war, or spoken ill of me. No one has protested; the people have not rioted. For some reason, The Reestablishment is playing along.

Playing pretend.

And it deeply, deeply unnerves me.

We're in a strange stalemate, stuck in neutral when I desperately want to be doing more. More for the people of Sector 45, for North America, and for the world as a whole. But this strange quiet has thrown all of us off-balance. We were so sure that, with Anderson dead, the other supreme commanders would rise up—that they'd command their armies to destroy us—to destroy *me*. Instead, the leaders of the world have made our insignificance clear: they're ignoring us as they would an annoying fly, trapping us under glass where we're free to buzz around, banging broken wings against the walls for only as long as the oxygen lasts. Sector 45 has been left to do as it pleases; we've been allowed autonomy and the authority to revise the infrastructure of our sector with no interference. Everywhere else—and everyone else—is pretending as though nothing in the world has changed. Our revolution occurred in a vacuum. Our subsequent victory has been reduced to something so small it might not even exist.

Mind games.

Castle is always visiting, advising. It was his suggestion that I be proactive—that I take the upper hand. Instead of waiting around, anxious and defensive, I should reach out, he said. I should make my presence known. Stake a claim, he said. Take a seat at the table. And attempt to form alliances before launching assaults. Connect with the five other supreme commanders around the world.

Because I may speak for North America—but what of the rest of the world? What of South America? Europe? Asia? Africa? Oceania?

Host an international conference of leaders, he said.

Talk.

Aim for peace first, he said.

"They must be dying of curiosity," Castle said to me. "A seventeen-year-old girl taking over North America? A teenage girl killing Anderson and declaring herself ruler of this continent? Ms. Ferrars—you must know that you have great leverage at the moment! Use it to your advantage!"

"Me?" I said, stunned. "How do I have leverage?"

Castle sighed. "You certainly are brave for your age, Ms. Ferrars, but I'm sorry to see your youth so inextricably tied to inexperience. I will try to put it plainly: you have superhuman strength, nearly invincible skin, a lethal touch, only seventeen years to your name, and you have single-handedly felled the despot of this nation. And yet you doubt that you might be capable of intimidating the world?"

I cringed.

"Old habits, Castle," I said quietly. "Bad habits. You're right, of course. Of course you're right."

He leveled me with a straight stare. "You must understand that unanimous, collective silence from your enemies is no act of coincidence. They've certainly been in touch with one another—they've certainly agreed to this approach—because they're waiting to see what you do next." He shook his head. "They are awaiting your next move, Ms. Ferrars. I implore you to make it a good one."

So I'm learning.

I did as he suggested and three days ago I sent word through Delalieu and contacted the five other supreme commanders of The Reestablishment. I invited them to join me here, in Sector 45, for a conference of international leaders next month.

Just fifteen minutes before Kenji barged into my room, I'd received my first RSVP.

Oceania said yes.

And I'm not sure what that means.

WARNER

I've not been myself lately.

The truth is I've not been myself for what feels like a long time, so much so that I've begun to wonder whether I ever really knew. I stare, unblinking, into the mirror, the din of buzzing hair clippers echoing through the room. My face is only dimly reflected in my direction, but it's enough for me to see that I've lost weight. My cheeks are hollow; my eyes, wider; my cheekbones more pronounced. My movements are both mournful and mechanical as I shear off my own hair, the remnants of my vanity falling at my feet.

My father is dead.

I close my eyes, steeling myself against the unwelcome strain in my chest, the clippers still humming in my clenched fist.

My father is dead.

It's been just over two weeks since he was killed, shot twice in the forehead by someone I love. She was doing me a kindness by killing him. She was braver than I'd ever been, pulling the trigger when I never could. He was a monster. He deserved worse.

And still—

This pain.

I take in a tight breath and blink open my eyes, grateful for the time to be alone; grateful, somehow, for the opportunity to tear asunder something, anything from my flesh. There's a strange catharsis in this.

My mother is dead, I think, as I drag the electric blade across my skull. *My father is dead*, I think, as the hair falls to the floor. Everything I was, everything I did, everything I am, was forged from the twins of their action and inaction.

Who am I, I wonder, in their absence?

Shorn head, blade switched off, I rest my palms against the edge of the sink and lean in, still trying to catch a glimpse of the man I've become. I feel old and unsettled, my heart and mind at war. The last words I ever spoke to my father—

"Hey."

My heart speeds up as I spin around; I'm affecting nonchalance in an instant. "Hi," I say, forcing my limbs to slow, to be steady as I dust errant strands of hair from my shoulders.

She's looking at me with big eyes, beautiful and worried.

I remember to smile. "How do I look? Not too horrible, I hope."

"Aaron," she says quietly. "Are you okay?"

"I'm fine," I say, and glance again in the mirror. I run a hand over the soft/spiky half inch of hair I have left and wonder at how the cut manages to makes me look harsher—and colder—than before. "Though I confess I don't really recognize myself," I add aloud, attempting a laugh. I'm standing in the middle of the bathroom wearing nothing but boxer briefs. My body has never been leaner, the sharp lines of muscle never more defined; and the rawness of my body is now paired with the rough cut of my hair in a way that feels almost uncivilized—and so unlike me that I have to look away.

Juliette is now right in front of me.

Her hands settle on my hips and pull me forward; I trip a little as I follow her lead. "What are you doing?" I begin to say, but when I meet her eyes I find tenderness and concern. Something thaws inside of me. My shoulders relax and I reel her in, drawing in a deep breath as I do.

"When will we talk about it?" she says against my chest. "All of it? Everything that's happened—"

I flinch.

"Aaron."

"I'm okay," I lie to her. "It's just hair."

"You know that's not what I'm talking about."

I look away. Stare at nothing. We're both quiet a moment. It's Juliette who finally breaks the silence.

"Are you upset with me?" she whispers. "For shooting him?"

My body stills.

Her eyes widen.

"No—no." I say the words too quickly, but I mean them. "No, of course not. It's not that."

Juliette sighs.

"I'm not sure you're aware of this," she says finally, "but

15

it's okay to mourn the loss of your father, even if he was a terrible person. You know?" She peers up at me. "You're not a robot."

I swallow back the lump growing in my throat and gently extricate myself from her arms. I kiss her on the cheek and linger there, against her skin, for only a second. "I need to take a shower."

She looks heartbroken and confused, but I don't know what else to do. It's not that I don't love her company, it's just that right now I'm desperate for solitude and I don't know how else to find it.

So I shower. I take baths. I go for long walks.

I tend to do this a lot.

When I finally come to bed she's already asleep.

I want to reach for her, to pull her soft, warm body against my own, but I feel paralyzed. This horrible half-grief has made me feel complicit in darkness. I worry that my sadness will be interpreted as an endorsement of his choices—of his very existence—and in this matter I don't want to be misunderstood, so I cannot admit that I grieve him, that I care at all for the loss of this monstrous man who raised me. And in the absence of healthy action I remain frozen, a sentient stone in the wake of my father's death.

Are you upset with me? For shooting him?

I hated him.

I hated him with a violent intensity I've never since

16

experienced. But the fire of true hatred, I realize, cannot exist without the oxygen of affection. I would not hurt so much, or hate so much, if I did not care.

And it is this, my unrequited affection for my father, that has always been my greatest weakness. So I lie here, marinating in a sorrow I can never speak of, while regret consumes my heart.

I am an orphan.

"Aaron?" she whispers, and I'm pulled back to the present.

"Yes, love?"

She moves in a sleepy, sideways motion, and nudges my arm with her head. I can't help but smile as I open up to make room for her against me. She fills the void quickly, pressing her face into my neck as she wraps an arm around my waist. My eyes close as if in prayer. My heart restarts.

"I miss you," she says. It's a whisper I almost don't catch.

"I'm right here," I say, gently touching her cheek. "I'm right here, love."

But she shakes her head. Even as I pull her closer, even as she falls back asleep, she shakes her head.

And I wonder if she's not wrong.

JULIETTE

LUNETTE

I'm having breakfast by myself this morning—alone, but not lonely.

The breakfast room is full of familiar faces, all of us catching up on something: sleep; work; half-finished conversations. Energy levels in here are always dependent on the amount of caffeine we've had, and right now, things are still pretty quiet.

Brendan, who's been nursing the same cup of coffee all morning, catches my eye and waves. I wave back. He's the only one among us who doesn't actually need caffeine; his gift for creating electricity also works as a backup generator for his whole body. He's exuberance, personified. In fact, his stark-white hair and ice-blue eyes seem to emanate their own kind of energy, even from across the room. I'm starting to think Brendan keeps up appearances with the coffee cup mostly out of solidarity with Winston, who can't seem to survive without it. The two of them are inseparable these days—even if Winston occasionally resents Brendan's natural buoyancy.

They've been through a lot together. We all have.

Brendan and Winston are sitting with Alia, who's got her sketchbook open beside her, no doubt designing something new and amazing to help us in battle. I'm too tired to move, otherwise I'd get up to join their group; instead, I drop my chin in one hand and study the faces of my friends, feeling grateful. But the scars on Brendan's and Winston's faces take me back to a time I'd rather not remember—back to a time when we thought we'd lost them. When we'd lost two others. And suddenly my thoughts are too heavy for breakfast. So I look away. Drum my fingers against the table.

I'm supposed to be meeting Kenji for breakfast—it's how we begin our workdays—which is the only reason I haven't grabbed my own plate of food. Unfortunately, his lateness is beginning to make my stomach grumble. Everyone in the room is cutting into fresh stacks of fluffy pancakes, and they look delicious. All of it is tempting: the mini pitchers of maple syrup; the steaming heaps of breakfast potatoes; the little bowls of freshly cut fruit. If nothing else, killing Anderson and taking over Sector 45 got us much better breakfast options. But I think we might be the only ones who appreciate the upgrades.

Warner never has breakfast with the rest of us. He pretty much never stops working, not even to eat. Breakfast is another meeting for him, and he takes it with Delalieu, just the two of them, and even then I'm not sure he actually eats anything. Warner never appears to take pleasure in food. For him, food is fuel—necessary and, most of the time, annoying—in that his body requires it to function. Once, while he was deeply immersed in some important paperwork at dinner, I put a cookie on a plate in front of him just to see what would happen. He glanced up at me, glanced back at his work, whispered a quiet *thank you*, and ate the cookie with a knife and fork. He didn't even seem to enjoy it. This, needless to say, makes him the polar opposite of Kenji, who loves to eat everything, all the time, and who later told me that watching Warner eat a cookie made him want to cry.

Speaking of Kenji, him flaking on me this morning is more than a little weird, and I'm beginning to worry. I'm just about to glance at the clock for the third time when, suddenly, Adam is standing next to my table, looking uncomfortable.

"Hi," I say, just a little too loudly. "What's, uh, what's up?"

Adam and I have interacted a couple of times in the last two weeks, but it's always been by accident. Suffice it to say that it's unusual for Adam to be standing in front of me on purpose, and I'm so surprised that for a moment I almost miss the obvious:

He looks bad.

Rough. Ragged. More than a little exhausted. In fact, if I didn't know any better, I would've sworn Adam had been crying. Not over our failed relationship, I hope.

Still, old instinct gnaws at me, tugs at ancient heartstrings.

We speak at the same time:

"You okay . . . ?" I ask.

"Castle wants to talk to you," he says.

"Castle sent *you* to come get me?" I say, feelings forgotten.

23

Adam shrugs. "I was walking past his room at the right time, I guess."

"Um. Okay." I try to smile. Castle is always trying to make nice between me and Adam; he doesn't like the tension. "Did he say he wants to see me right now?"

"Yep." Adam shoves his hands in his pockets. "Right away."

"All right," I say, and the whole thing feels awkward. Adam just stands there as I gather my things, and I want to tell him to go away, to stop staring at me, that this is weird, that we broke up forever ago and it was *weird*, you made it *so weird*, but then I realize he isn't staring at me. He's looking at the floor like he's stuck, lost in his head somewhere.

"Hey—are you okay?" I say again, this time gently.

Adam looks up, startled. "What?" he says. "What, oh— yeah, I'm fine. Hey do you know, uh"—he clears his throat, looks around—"do you, uh—"

"Do I what?"

Adam rocks on his heels, eyes darting around the room. "Warner is never here for breakfast, huh?"

My eyebrows shoot up my forehead. "You're looking for Warner?"

"What? No. I'm just, uh, wondering. He's never here. You know? It's weird."

I stare at him.

He says nothing.

"It's not that weird," I say slowly, studying Adam's face. "Warner doesn't have time for breakfast with us. He's always working."

"Oh," Adam says, and the word seems to deflate him. "That's too bad."

"Is it?" I frown.

But Adam doesn't seem to hear me. He calls for James, who's putting away his breakfast tray, and the two of them meet in the middle of the room and then disappear.

I have no idea what they do all day. I've never asked.

The mystery of Kenji's absence at breakfast is solved the moment I walk up to Castle's door: the two of them are here, heads together.

I knock on the open door as a courtesy. "Hey," I say. "You wanted to see me?"

"Yes, yes, Ms. Ferrars," Castle says eagerly. He gets to his feet and waves me inside. "Please, have a seat. And if you would"—he gestures behind me—"close the door."

I'm nervous in an instant.

I take a tentative step into Castle's makeshift office and glance at Kenji, whose blank face does nothing to allay my fears. "What's going on?" I say. And then, only to Kenji: "Why weren't you at breakfast?"

Castle motions for me to take a seat.

I do.

"Ms. Ferrars," he says urgently. "You have news of Oceania?"

"Excuse me?"

"The RSVP. You received your first RSVP, did you not?"

"Yeah, I did," I say slowly. "But no one is supposed to know about that yet—I was going to tell Kenji about it

25

over breakfast this morning—"

"Nonsense." Castle cuts me off. "Everyone knows. Mr. Warner knows, certainly. And Lieutenant Delalieu knows."

"What?" I glance at Kenji, who shrugs. "How is that possible?"

"Don't be so easily shocked, Ms. Ferrars. Obviously all of your correspondence is monitored."

My eyes widen. "What?"

Castle makes a frustrated motion with his hand. "Time is of the essence, so if you would, I'd really—"

"Time is of *what* essence?" I say, irritated. "How am I supposed to help you when I don't even know what you're talking about?"

Castle pinches the bridge of his nose. "Kenji," he says suddenly. "Will you leave us, please?"

"Yep." Kenji jumps to his feet with a mock salute. He heads toward the door.

"Wait," I say, grabbing his arm. "What's going on?"

"I have no idea, kid." Kenji laughs, shakes his arm free. "This conversation doesn't concern me. Castle called me in here earlier to talk about cows."

"*Cows?*"

"Yeah, you know." He arches an eyebrow. "Livestock. He's been having me do reconnaissance on several hundreds of acres of farmland that The Reestablishment has been keeping off the radar. Lots and lots of cows."

"Exciting."

"It is, actually." His eyes light up. "The methane makes

it all pretty easy to track. Makes you wonder why they wouldn't do something to preve—"

"*Methane?*" I say, confused. "Isn't that a kind of gas?"

"I take it you don't know much about cow shit."

I ignore that. Instead, I say, "So that's why you weren't at breakfast this morning? Because you were looking at cow poop?"

"Basically."

"Well," I say. "At least that explains the smell."

It takes Kenji a second to catch on, but when he does, he narrows his eyes. Taps me on the forehead with one finger. "You're going straight to hell, you know that?"

I smile, big. "See you later? I still want to go on our morning walk."

He makes a noncommittal grunt.

"C'mon," I say, "it'll be fun this time, I promise."

"Oh yeah, big fun." Kenji rolls his eyes as he turns away, and shoots Castle another two-finger salute. "See you later, sir."

Castle nods his good-bye, a bright smile on his face.

It takes a minute for Kenji to finally walk out the door and shut it behind him, but in that minute Castle's face transforms. His easy smile, his eager eyes: gone. Now that he and I are fully alone, Castle looks a little shaken, a little more serious. Maybe even . . . scared?

And he gets right down to business.

"When the RSVP came through, what did it say? Was there anything memorable about the note?"

"No." I frown. "I don't know. If all my correspondence is being monitored, wouldn't you already know the answer to this question?"

"Of course not. I'm not the one monitoring your mail."

"So who's monitoring my mail? Warner?"

Castle only looks at me. "Ms. Ferrars, there is something deeply unusual about this response." He hesitates. "Especially as it's your first, and thus far, only RSVP."

"Okay," I say, confused. "What's unusual about it?"

Castle looks into his hands. At the wall. "How much do you know about Oceania?"

"Very little."

"How little?"

I shrug. "I can point it out on a map."

"And you've never been there?"

"Are you serious?" I shoot him an incredulous look. "Of course not. I've never been anywhere, remember? My parents pulled me out of school. Passed me through the system. Eventually threw me in an insane asylum."

Castle takes a deep breath. Closes his eyes as he says, very carefully, "Was there anything at all memorable about the note you received from the supreme commander of Oceania?"

"No," I say. "Not really."

"Not really?"

"I guess it was little informal? But I don't thi—"

"Informal, how?"

I look away, remembering. "The message was really

brief," I explain. "It said *Can't wait to see you*, with no sign-off or anything."

"'Can't wait to see you'?" Castle looks suddenly puzzled.

I nod.

"Not can't wait to *meet* you," he says, "but can't wait to *see* you."

I nod again. "Like I said, a little informal. But it was polite, at least. Which I think is a pretty positive sign, all things considered."

Castle sighs heavily as he turns in his chair. He's facing the wall now, his fingers steepled under his chin. I'm studying the sharp angles of his profile as he says quietly,

"Ms. Ferrars, how much has Mr. Warner told you about The Reestablishment?"

WARNER

I'm sitting alone in the conference room, running an absent hand over my new haircut, when Delalieu arrives. He's pulling a small coffee cart in behind him, wearing the tepid, shaky smile I've come to rely upon. Our workdays have been busier than ever lately; thankfully, we've never made time to discuss the uncomfortable details of recent events, and I doubt we ever will.

For this I am forever grateful.

It's a safe space for me here, with Delalieu, where I can pretend that things in my life have changed very little.

I am still chief commander and regent to the soldiers of Sector 45; it's still my duty to organize and lead those who will help us stand against the rest of The Reestablishment. And with that role comes responsibility. We've had a lot of restructuring to do while we coordinate our next moves, and Delalieu has been critical to these efforts.

"Good morning, sir."

I nod a greeting as he pours us both a cup of coffee. A lieutenant such as himself need not pour his own coffee in the morning, but we've come to prefer the privacy.

I take a sip of the black liquid—I've recently learned to enjoy its bitter tang—and lean back in my chair. "Updates?"

Delalieu clears his throat.

"Yes, sir," he says, hastily returning his coffee cup to its saucer, spilling a little as he does. "Quite a few this morning, sir."

I tilt my head at him.

"Construction of the new command station is going well. We're expecting to be done with all the details in the next two weeks, but the private rooms will be move-in ready by tomorrow."

"Good." Our new team, under Juliette's supervision, comprises many people now, with many departments to manage and, with the exception of Castle, who's carved out a small office for himself upstairs, thus far they've all been using my personal training facilities as their central headquarters. And though this had seemed like a practical idea at its inception, my training facilities are accessible only through my personal quarters; and now that the group of them are living freely on base, they're often barging in and out of my rooms, unannounced.

Needless to say, it's driving me insane.

"What else?"

Delalieu checks his list and says, "We've finally managed to secure your father's files, sir. It's taken all this time to locate and retrieve the bulk of it, but I've left the boxes in your room, sir, for you to open at your leisure. I thought"—he clears his throat—"I thought you might like to look through his remaining personal effects before they are inherited by our new supreme commander."

A heavy, cold dread fills my body.

"There's quite a lot of it, I'm afraid," Delalieu is still saying. "All his daily logs. Every report he'd ever filed. We even managed to locate a few of his personal journals." Delalieu hesitates. And then, in a tone only I know how to decipher: "I do hope his notes will be useful to you, somehow."

I look up, meet Delalieu's eyes. There's concern there. Worry.

"Thank you," I say quietly. "I'd nearly forgotten."

An uncomfortable silence settles between us and, for a moment, neither of us knows exactly what to say. We still haven't discussed this, the death of my father. The death of Delalieu's son-in-law. The horrible husband of his late daughter, my mother. We never talk about the fact that Delalieu is my grandfather. That he is the only kind of father I have left in the world.

It's not what we do.

So it's with a halting, unnatural voice that Delalieu attempts to pick up the thread of conversation.

"Oceania, as, as I'm sure you've heard, sir, has said that, that they would attend a meeting organized by our new madam, madam supreme—"

I nod.

"But the others," he says, the words rushing out of him now, "will not respond until they've spoken with you, sir."

At this, my eyes widen perceptibly.

"They're"—Delalieu clears his throat again—"well, sir,

as you know, they're all old friends of the family, and they—well, they—"

"Yes," I whisper. "Of course."

I look away, at the wall. My jaw feels suddenly wired shut with frustration. Secretly, I'd been expecting this. But after two weeks of silence I'd actually begun to hope that maybe they'd continue to play dumb. There's been no communication from these old friends of my father, no offers of condolences, no white roses, no sympathy cards. No correspondence, as was our daily ritual, from the families I'd known as a child, the families responsible for the hellscape we live in now. I thought I'd been happily, mercifully, cut off.

Apparently not.

Apparently treason is not enough of a crime to be left alone. Apparently my father's many daily missives expounding my "grotesque obsession with an experiment" were not reason enough to oust me from the group. He loved complaining aloud, my father, loved sharing his many disgusts and disapprovals with his old friends, the only people alive who knew him face-to-face. And every day he humiliated me in front of the people we knew. He made my world, my thoughts, and my feelings seem small. Pathetic. And every day I'd count the letters piling up in my in-box, screeds from his old friends begging me to see *reason*, as they called it. To remember myself. To stop embarrassing my family. To listen to my father. To grow up, be a man, and stop crying over my sick mother.

No, these ties run too deep.

I squeeze my eyes shut to quell the rush of faces, memories of my childhood, as I say, "Tell them I'll be in touch."

"That won't be necessary, sir," says Delalieu.

"Excuse me?"

"Ibrahim's children are already *en route*."

It happens swiftly: a sudden, brief paralysis of my limbs.

"What do you mean?" I say, only barely managing to stay calm. "*En route* where? Here?"

Delalieu nods.

A wave of heat floods my body so quickly I don't even realize I'm on my feet until I have to grab the table for support. "How *dare* they," I say, somehow still clinging to the edge of composure. "Their complete disregard— To be so unbearably entitled—"

"Yes, sir, I understand, sir," Delalieu says, looking newly terrified, "it's just—as you know—it's the way of the supreme families, sir. A time-honored tradition. A refusal on my part would've been interpreted as an open act of hostility—and Madam Supreme has instructed me to be diplomatic for as long as possible so I thought, I—I thought—Oh, I'm very sorry, sir—"

"She doesn't know who she's dealing with," I say sharply. "There is no diplomacy with these people. Our new supreme commander might have no way of knowing this, but you," I say, more upset than angry now, "you should've known better. War would've been worth avoiding this."

I don't look up to see his face when he says, his voice trembling, "I'm deeply, deeply sorry, sir."

A time-honored tradition, indeed.

The right to come and go was a practice long ago agreed upon. The supreme families were always welcome in each other's lands at any time, no invitations necessary. While the movement was young and the children were young, our families held fast. And now those families—and their children—rule the world.

This was my life for a very long time. On Tuesday, a playdate in Europe; on Friday, a dinner party in South America. Our parents insane, all of them.

The only *friends* I ever knew had families even crazier than mine. I have no wish to see any of them ever again.

And yet—

Good God, I have to warn Juliette.

"As to the, as to the matter of the, of the civilians"— Delalieu is prattling on—"I've been communicating with Castle, per, per your request, sir, on how best to proceed with their transition out of the, out of the compounds—"

But the rest of our morning meeting passes by in a blur.

When I finally manage to loose myself from Delalieu's shadow, I head straight back to my own quarters. Juliette is usually here this time of day, and I'm hoping to catch her, to warn her before it's too late.

Too soon, I'm intercepted.

"Oh, um, hey—"

I look up, distracted, and quickly stop in place. My eyes widen, just a little.

"Kent," I say quietly.

One swift appraisal is all I need to know that he's not okay. In fact, he looks terrible. Thinner than ever; dark circles under his eyes. Thoroughly worn-out.

I wonder whether I look just the same to him.

"I was wondering," he says, and looks away, his face pinched. He clears his throat. "I was, uh"—he clears his throat again—"I was wondering if we could talk."

I feel my chest tighten. I stare at him a moment, cataloging his tense shoulders, his unkempt hair, his deeply bitten fingernails. He sees me staring and quickly shoves his hands into his pockets. He can hardly meet my eyes.

"Talk," I manage to say.

He nods.

I exhale quietly, slowly. We haven't spoken a word to each other since I first found out we were brothers, nearly three weeks ago. I thought the emotional implosion of the evening had ended as well anyone could've hoped, but so much has happened since that night. We haven't had a chance to rip open that wound again. "Talk," I say again. "Of course."

He swallows hard. Stares at the ground. "Cool."

And I'm suddenly compelled to ask a question that unsettles both of us: "Are you all right?"

He looks up, stunned. His blue eyes are round and red-rimmed, bloodshot. His Adam's apple bobs in his throat. "I don't know who else to talk to about this," he whispers. "I don't know anyone else who would even understand—"

And I do. All at once.

I understand.

When his eyes go abruptly glassy with emotion; when his shoulders tremble even as he tries to hold himself still— I feel my own bones rattle.

"Of course," I say, surprising myself. "Come with me."

JULIETTE

It's another cold day today, all silver ruins and snow-covered decay. I wake up every morning hoping for even a slant of sunlight, but the bite in the air remains unforgiving as it sinks hungry teeth into our flesh. We've finally left the worst of winter behind, but even these early weeks of March feel inhumanly frosty. I pull my coat up around my neck and huddle into it.

Kenji and I are on what has become our daily walk around the forgotten stretches of Sector 45. It's been both strange and liberating to be able to walk so freely in the fresh air. Strange, because I can't leave the base without a small troop for protection, and liberating because it's the first time I've been able to acquaint myself with the land. I'd never had a chance to walk calmly through these compounds; I had no way of seeing, firsthand, exactly what'd happened to this world. And now, to be able to roam freely, unquestioned—

Well, sort of.

I glance over my shoulder at the six soldiers shadowing our every move, machine guns held tightly against their chests as they march. No one really knows what to do about me yet; Anderson had a very different system in place as supreme commander—he never showed his face to anyone except those he was about to kill, and never traveled anywhere without his Supreme Guard. But I don't have rules about either and, until I decide exactly how I want to rule, this is my new situation:

I'm to be babysat from the moment I step outside.

I tried to explain that I don't need protection—I tried to remind everyone of my very literal, lethal touch; my superhuman strength; my functional invincibility—

"But it would be very helpful to the soldiers," Warner had explained, "if you would at least go through the motions. We rely on rules, regulation, and constant discipline in the military, and soldiers need a system upon which they might depend, at all times. Do this for them," he said. "Maintain the pretense. We can't change everything all at once, love. It'd be too disorienting."

So here I am.

Being followed.

Warner has been my constant guide these last couple of weeks. He's been teaching me every day about all the many things his dad did and all the things he, himself, is responsible for. There are an infinite number of things Warner needs to do every day just to run this sector—never mind the bizarre (and seemingly endless) list of things I need to do to lead an entire continent.

I'd be lying if I didn't say that, sometimes, it all feels impossible.

I had one day, just one day to exhale and enjoy the relief of overthrowing Anderson and reclaiming Sector 45. One day to sleep, one day to smile, one day to indulge in the luxury of imagining a better world.

It was at the end of Day 2 that I discovered a nervous-looking Delalieu standing behind my door.

He seemed frantic.

"Madam Supreme," he'd said, a crazy smile half hung on his face. "I imagine you must be very overwhelmed lately. So much to do." He looked down. Wrung his hands. "But I fear—that is—I think—"

"What is it?" I'd said to him. "Is something wrong?"

"Well, madam—I haven't wanted to bother you—you've been through so much and you've needed time to adjust—"

He looked at the wall.

I waited.

"Forgive me," he said. "It's just that it's been nearly thirty-six hours since you've taken control of the continent and you haven't been to visit your quarters once," he said in a rush. "And you've already received so much mail that I don't know where to put it anymo—"

"*What?*"

He froze. Finally met my eyes.

"What do you mean, *my quarters*? I have *quarters*?"

Delalieu blinked, dumbfounded. "Of course you do, madam. The supreme commander has his or her own quarters in every sector on the continent. We have an entire wing here dedicated to your offices. It's where the late supreme commander Anderson used to stay whenever he visited us on base. And as everyone around the world knows

45

that you've made Sector 45 your permanent residence, this is where they've sent all your mail, both physical and digital. It's where your intelligence briefings will be delivered every morning. It's where other sector leaders have been sending their daily reports—"

"You're not serious," I said, stunned.

"Very serious, madam." He looked desperate. "And I worry about the message you might be sending by ignoring all correspondence at this early stage." He looked away. "Forgive me. I don't mean to overstep. I just—I know you'd like to make an effort to strengthen your international relationships—but I worry about the consequences you might face for breaking your many continental accords—"

"No, no, of course. Thank you, Delalieu," I said, head spinning. "Thank you for letting me know. I'm—I'm very grateful to you for intervening. I had no idea"—I clapped a hand to my forehead—"but maybe tomorrow morning?" I said. "Tomorrow morning you could meet me after my morning walk? Show me where these quarters are located?"

"Of course," he said with a slight bow. "It would be my pleasure, Madam Supreme."

"Thank you, Lieutenant."

"Certainly, madam." He looked so relieved. "Have a pleasant evening."

I stumbled then as I said good-bye to him, tripping over my feet in a daze.

Not much has changed.

My shoes scuff on the concrete, my feet knocking into

each other as I startle myself back into the present. I take a more certain step forward, this time bracing myself against another sudden, biting gust. Kenji shoots me a look of concern. I look, but don't really see him. I'm looking beyond him now, eyes narrowed at nothing in particular. My mind continues on its course, whirring in time with the wind.

"You okay, kid?"

I look up, squinting sideways at Kenji. "I'm okay, yeah."

"Convincing."

I manage to smile and frown at the same time.

"So," Kenji says, exhaling the word. "What'd Castle want to talk to you about?"

I turn away, irritated in an instant. "I don't know. Castle is being weird."

That gets Kenji's attention. Castle is like a father to him—and I'm pretty sure if he had to choose, Kenji would choose Castle over me—so it's clear where his loyalties lie when he says, "What do you mean? How is Castle being weird? He seemed fine this morning."

I shrug. "He just seems really paranoid all of a sudden. And he said some things about Warner that just—" I cut myself off. Shake my head. "I don't know."

Kenji stops walking. "Wait, what things did he say about Warner?"

I shrug again, still irritated. "He thinks Warner is hiding stuff from me. Like, not hiding stuff from me, exactly—but that there's a lot I don't know about him? So I was like, 'If you know so much about Warner, why don't *you* tell me what I need to know about him?' and Castle was like, 'No,

blah blah, Mr. Warner should tell you himself, blah blah.'"
I roll my eyes. "Basically he was telling me it's weird that I
don't know that much about Warner's past. But that's not
even true," I say, looking at Kenji now. "I know a bunch
about Warner's past."

"Like?"

"Like, I don't know—I know all that stuff about his
mom."

Kenji laughs. "You don't know shit about his mom."

"Sure I do."

"Whatever, J. You don't even know that lady's name."

At this, I falter. I search my mind for the information,
certain he must've mentioned it—

and come up short.

I glance at Kenji, feeling small.

"Her name was Leila," he says. "Leila Warner. And I only
know this because Castle does his research. We had files on
all persons of interest back at Omega Point. Never knew she
had powers that made her sick, though," he says, looking
thoughtful. "Anderson did a good job keeping that quiet."

"Oh," is all I manage to say.

"So that's why you thought Castle was being weird?"
Kenji says to me. "Because he very correctly pointed out that
you know nothing about your boyfriend's life?"

"Don't be mean," I say quietly. "I know some things."

But the truth is, I don't know much.

What Castle said to me this morning hit a nerve. I'd be
lying if I said I didn't wonder, all the time, what Warner's

life was like before I met him. In fact, I think often of that day—that awful, awful day—in the pretty blue house on Sycamore, the house where Anderson shot me in the chest.

We were all alone, me and Anderson.

I never told Warner what his father said to me that day, but I've never forgotten. Instead, I've tried to ignore it, to convince myself that Anderson was playing games with my mind to confuse and immobilize me. But no matter how many times I've played back the conversation in my head— trying desperately to break it down and dismiss it—I've never been able to shake the feeling that, maybe, just maybe, it wasn't all for show. Maybe Anderson was telling me the truth.

I can still see the smile on his face as he said it. I can still hear the musical lilt in his voice. He was enjoying himself. Tormenting me.

Did he tell you how many other soldiers wanted to be in charge of Sector 45? How many fine candidates we had to choose from? He was only eighteen years old!

Did he ever tell you what he had to do to prove he was worthy?

My heart pounds in my chest as I remember, and I close my eyes, my lungs knotting together—

Did he ever tell you what I made him do to earn it?

No.

I suspect he didn't want to mention that part, did he? I bet he didn't want to include that part of his past, did he?

No.

He never did. And I've never asked.

I think I never want to know.

"Don't worry," Anderson said to me then. *"I won't spoil it for you. Best to let him share those details with you himself."*

And now, this morning—I get the same line from Castle:

"No, Ms. Ferrars," Castle had said, refusing to look me in the eye. "No, no, it's not my place to tell. Mr. Warner needs to be the one to tell you the stories about his life. Not I."

"I don't understand," I said, frustrated. "How is this even relevant? Why do you suddenly care about Warner's past? And what does any of that have to do with Oceania's RSVP?"

"Warner knows these other commanders," Castle said. "He knows the other supreme families. He knows how The Reestablishment operates from within. And there's still a great deal he needs to tell you." He shook his head. "Oceania's response is deeply unusual, Ms. Ferrars, for the simple reason that it is the only response you've received. I feel very certain that the moves made by these commanders are not only coordinated but also intentional, and I'm beginning to feel more worried by the moment that there is an entirely *other* message here—one that I'm still trying to translate."

I could feel it then, could feel my temperature rising, my jaw tensing as anger surged through me. "But you're the one who told me to reach out to all the supreme commanders! This was your idea! And now you're terrified that someone actually reached out? What do y—"

And then, all at once, I understood.

My words were soft and stunned when I said, "Oh my God, you didn't think I'd get any responses, did you?"

Castle swallowed hard. Said nothing.

"You didn't think anyone would respond?" I said, my voice rising in pitch.

"Ms. Ferrars, you must understand—"

"Why are you playing games with me, Castle?" My fists clenched. "What are you doing?"

"I'm not playing games with you," he said, the words coming out in a rush. "I just—I thought—" he said, gesticulating wildly. "It was an exercise. An experiment—"

I felt flashes of heat spark behind my eyes. Anger welled in my throat, vibrated along my spine. I could feel the rage building inside me and it took everything I had to clamp it down. "I am no longer anyone's experiment," I said. "And I need to know what the hell is going on."

"You must speak with Mr. Warner," he said. "He will explain everything. There's still so much you need to know about this world—and The Reestablishment—and time is of the essence," he said. He met my eyes. "You must be prepared for whatever comes next. You need to know more, and you need to know now. Before things escalate."

I looked away, my hands shaking from the surge of unspent energy. I wanted to—needed to—break something. Anything. Instead, I said, "This is bullshit, Castle. Complete bullshit."

And he looked like the saddest man in the world when he said—

"I know."

I've been walking around with a splitting headache ever since.

So it doesn't make me feel any better when Kenji pokes me in the shoulder, startling me back to life, and says,

"I've said it before and I'll say it again: You guys have a weird relationship."

"No, we don't," I say, and the words are reflexive, petulant.

"Yes," Kenji says. "You do." And he saunters off, leaving me alone in the abandoned streets, tipping an imaginary hat as he walks away.

I throw my shoe at him.

The effort, however, is fruitless; Kenji catches my shoe midair. He's now waiting for me, ten steps ahead, holding my tennis shoe in his hand as I hop awkwardly in his direction. I don't have to turn around to see the smirks on the soldiers' faces some distance behind us. I'm pretty sure everyone thinks I'm a joke of a supreme commander. And why wouldn't they?

It's been over two weeks and I still feel lost.

Half paralyzed.

I'm not proud of my inability to get it together, not proud of the revelation that, as it turns out, I'm not smart enough, fast enough, or shrewd enough to rule the world. I'm not proud that, at my lowest moments, I look around at all that I have to do in a single day and wonder, in awe, at how organized Anderson was. How accomplished. How very, very talented.

I'm not proud that I've thought that.

Or that, in the quietest, loneliest hours of the morning I lie awake next to the son Anderson tortured nearly to death and wish that Anderson would return from the dead and take back the burden I stole from his shoulders.

And then there's this thought, all the time, all the time: *That maybe I made a mistake.*

"Uh, hello? Earth to princess?"

I look up, confused. Lost in my mind today. "Did you say something?"

Kenji shakes his head as he hands me my shoe. I'm struggling to put it on when he says, "So you forced me to take a stroll through this nasty, frozen shitland just to ignore me?"

I raise a single eyebrow at him.

He raises both, waiting, expectant. "What's the deal, J? *This,*" he says, gesturing at my face, "is more than whatever weirdness you got from Castle this morning." He tilts his head at me, and I read genuine concern in his eyes when he says, "So what's going on?"

I sigh; the exhalation withers my body.

You must speak with Mr. Warner. He will explain everything.

But Warner isn't known for his communication skills. He doesn't make small talk. He doesn't share details about himself. He doesn't do *personal*. I know he loves me—I can feel, in our every interaction, how deeply he cares for me—but even so, he's only ever offered me the vaguest information about his life. He is a vault to which I'm only occasionally granted access, and I often wonder how much I have left to learn about him. Sometimes it scares me.

"I'm just—I don't know," I finally say. "I'm really tired. I've got a lot on my mind."

"Rough night?"

I peer up at Kenji, shading my eyes against the cold sunlight. "You know, I don't really sleep anymore," I say to him. "I'm up at four in the morning every day, and I still haven't gotten through *last week's* mail. Isn't that crazy?"

Kenji shoots me a sideways glance, surprised.

"And I have to, like, approve a million things every day? Approve this, approve that. Not even, like, big things," I say to him. "It's stupid stuff, like, like"—I pull a crumpled sheet of paper out of my pocket and shake it at the sky—"like this nonsense: Sector 418 wants to extend their soldiers' lunch hour by an additional three minutes, and they need my approval. Three minutes? *Who cares?*"

Kenji fights back a smile; shoves his hands in his pockets.

"Every day. All day. I can't get anything *real* done. I thought I'd be doing something big, you know? I thought I'd be able to, like, unify the sectors and broker peace or something, and instead I spend all day trying to avoid Delalieu, who's in my face every five minutes because he needs me to sign something. *And that's just the mail.*"

I can't seem to stop talking now, finally confessing to Kenji all the things I feel I can never say to Warner, for fear of disappointing him. It's liberating, but then, suddenly, it also feels dangerous. Like maybe I shouldn't be telling *anyone* that I feel this way, not even Kenji.

So I hesitate, wait for a sign.

Kenji isn't looking at me anymore, but he still appears to be listening. His head is cocked to the side, his mouth playing at a smile when he says, after a moment, "Is that all?"

And I shake my head, hard, relieved and grateful to keep complaining. "I have to log everything, all the time. I have to fill out reports, read reports, file reports. There are five hundred and fifty-four other sectors in North America, Kenji. *Five hundred and fifty-four.*" I stare at him. "That means I have to read five hundred and fifty-four reports, every single day."

Kenji stares back, unmoved.

"Five hundred and fifty-four!"

He crosses his arms.

"The reports are ten pages long!"

"Uh-huh."

"Can I tell you a secret?" I say.

"Hit me."

"This job blows."

Now Kenji laughs, out loud. Still, he says nothing.

"What?" I say. "What are you thinking?"

He musses my hair and says, "Aww, J."

I jerk my head away from his hand. "That's all I get? Just an '*Aww, J,*' and that's it?"

Kenji shrugs.

"What?" I demand.

"I mean, I don't know," he says, cringing a little as he says it. "Did you think this was going to be . . . easy?"

"No," I say quietly. "I just thought it would be better than this."

"Better, how?"

"I guess, I mean, I thought it would be . . . cooler?"

"Like, you thought you'd be killing a bunch of bad dudes by now? High-kicking your way through politics? Like you could just kill Anderson and all of a sudden, *bam*, world peace?"

And now I can't bring myself to look at him, because I'm lying, lying through my teeth when I say,

"No, of course not. I didn't think it would be like that."

Kenji sighs. "This is why Castle was always so apprehensive, you know? With Omega Point it was always about being slow and steady. Waiting for the right moment. Knowing our strengths—and our weaknesses. We had a lot going for us, but we always knew—Castle always said—that we could never take out Anderson until we were ready to lead. It's why I didn't kill him when I had the chance. Not even when he was half dead already and standing right in front of me." A pause. "It just wasn't the right moment."

"So—you think I made a mistake?"

Kenji frowns, almost. Looks away. Looks back, smiles a little, but only with one side of his mouth. "I mean, I think you're great."

"But you think I made a mistake."

He shrugs in a slow, exaggerated way. "Nah, I didn't say that. I just think you need a little more training, you know? I'm guessing the insane asylum didn't prep you for this gig."

I narrow my eyes at him.

He laughs.

"Listen, you're good with the people. You talk pretty. But this job comes with a lot of paperwork, and it comes with a lot of bullshit, too. Lots of playing nice. Lots of ass-kissing. I mean, what are we trying to do right now? We're trying to be cool. Right? We're trying to, like, take over but, like, not cause absolute anarchy. We're trying *not* to go to war right now, right?"

I don't respond quickly enough and he pokes me in the shoulder.

"Right?" he says. "Isn't that the goal? Maintain the peace for now? Attempt diplomacy before we start blowing shit up?"

"Yes, right," I say quickly. "Yeah. Prevent war. Avoid casualties. Play nice."

"Okay then," he says, and looks away. "So you have to keep it together, kid. Because if you start losing it now? The Reestablishment is going to eat you alive. It's what they want. In fact, it's probably what they're expecting—they're waiting for you to self-destruct all this shit for them. So you can't let them see this. You can't let these cracks show."

I stare at him, feeling suddenly scared.

He wraps one arm around my shoulder. "You can't be

getting stressed out like this. Over some paperwork?" He shakes his head. "Everyone is watching you now. Everyone is waiting to see what happens next. We either go to war with the other sectors—hell, with the rest of the world—or we manage to be cool and negotiate. And you have to be *chill*, J. Just be chill."

And I don't know what to say.

Because the truth is, he's right. I'm so far in over my head I don't even know where to start. I didn't even graduate from high school. And now I'm supposed to have a lifetime's worth of knowledge about international relations?

Warner was designed for this life. Everything he does, is, breathes—

He was built to lead.

But me?

What on earth, I think, *have I gotten myself into?*

Why did I think I'd be capable of running an entire continent? How did I allow myself to imagine that a supernatural ability to kill things with my skin would suddenly grant me a comprehensive understanding of political science?

I clench my fists too hard and—

pain, fresh pain

--as my fingernails pierce the flesh.

How did I think people ruled the world? Did I really imagine it would be so simple? That I might control the fabric of society from the comfort of my boyfriend's bedroom?

I'm only now beginning to understand the breadth of

this delicate, intricately developed spiderweb of people, positions, and power already in place. I said I was up for the task. Me, a seventeen-year-old nobody with very little life experience; I volunteered for this position. And now—basically overnight—I have to keep up. And I have no *idea* what I'm doing.

But if I don't learn how to manage these many relationships? If I don't at least pretend to have even the slightest idea of how I'm going to rule?

The rest of the world could so easily destroy me.

And sometimes I'm not sure I'll make it out of this alive.

WARNER

"How's James?"

I'm the first to break the silence. It's a strange feeling. New for me.

Kent nods his head in response, his eyes focused on the hands he's clasped in front of him. We're on the roof, surrounded by cold and concrete, sitting next to each other in a quiet corner to which I sometimes retreat. I can see the whole sector from here. The ocean far off in the distance. The sun making its sluggish, midday approach. Civilians like toy soldiers marching to and fro.

"He's good," Kent finally says. His voice is tight. He's wearing nothing but a T-shirt and doesn't seem to be bothered by the blistering cold. He takes in a deep breath. "I mean—he's great, you know? He's so great. Doing great."

I nod.

Kent looks up, laughs a short, nervous sort of laugh and looks away. "Is this crazy?" he says. "Are we crazy?"

We're both silent a minute, the wind whistling harder than before.

"I don't know," I finally say.

Kent pounds a fist against his leg. Exhales through his nose. "You know, I never said this to you. Before." He looks up, but doesn't look at me. "That night. I never said it, but I wanted you to know that it meant a lot to me. What you said."

I squint into the distance.

It's an impossible thing to do, really, to apologize for attempting to kill someone. Even so, I tried. I told him I understood him then. His pain. His anger. His actions. I told him that he'd survived the upbringing of our father to become a much better person than I'd ever be.

"I meant it," I say to him.

Kent now taps his closed fist against his mouth. Clears his throat. "I'm sorry, too, you know." His voice is hoarse. "Things got so screwed up. Everything. It's such a mess."

"Yes," I say. "It is."

"So what do we do now?" He finally turns to look at me, but I'm still not ready to meet his eyes. "How—how do we fix this? Can we even fix this? Is it too far gone?"

I run a hand over my newly shorn hair. "I don't know," I say, too quietly. "But I'd like to fix it."

"Yeah?"

I nod.

Kent nods several times beside me. "I'm not ready to tell James yet."

I falter, surprised. "Oh."

"Not because of you," he says quickly. "It's not you I'm worried about. I just—explaining *you* means explaining something so much bigger. And I don't know how to tell him his dad was a monster. Not yet. I really thought he'd never have to know."

At this, I look up. "James doesn't know? Anything?"

Kent shakes his head. "He was so little when our mom died, and I always managed to keep him out of sight when our dad came around. He thinks our parents died in a plane crash."

"Impressive," I hear myself say. "That was very generous of you."

I hear Kent's voice crack when he next speaks. "God, why am I so messed up over him? Why do I *care*?"

"I don't know," I say, shaking my head. "I'm having the same problem."

"Yeah?"

I nod.

Kent drops his head in his hands. "He really screwed us up, man."

"Yes. He did."

I hear Kent sniff twice, two sharp attempts at keeping his emotions in check, and even so, I envy him his ability to be this open with his feelings. I pull a handkerchief from the inside pocket of my jacket and hand it to him.

"Thanks," he says tightly.

Another nod.

"So, um—what's up with your hair?"

I'm so caught off guard by the question I almost flinch. I actually consider telling Kent the whole story, but I'm worried he'll ask me why I'd ever let Kenji touch my hair, and then I'd have to explain Juliette's many, many requests that I befriend the idiot. And I don't think she's a safe topic for us yet. So instead I say, "A little mishap."

Kent raises his eyebrows. Laughs. "Uh-huh."

I glance in his direction, surprised.

He says, "It's okay, you know."

"What is?"

Kent is sitting up straighter now, staring into the sunlight. I'm beginning to see shades of my father in his face. Shades of myself. "You and Juliette," he says.

I freeze.

He glances at me. "Really. It's okay."

I can't help it when I say, stunned, "I'm not sure it would've been okay with me, had our roles been reversed."

Kent smiles, but it looks sad. "I was a real dick to her at the end," he says. "So I guess I got what I deserved. But it wasn't actually about her, you know? All of that. It wasn't about her." He looks up at me out of the corner of his eye. "I'd been drowning for a while, actually. I was just really unhappy, and really stressed, and then"—he shrugs, turns away—"honestly, finding out you were my brother nearly killed me."

I blink. Surprised once more.

"Yeah." He laughs, shaking his head. "I know it seems weird now, but at the time I just—I don't know, man, I thought you were a sociopath. I was so worried you'd figure out we were related and then, I mean—I don't know, I thought you'd try to murder me or something."

He hesitates. Looks at me.

Waits.

It's only then that I realize—surprised, yet again—that he wants me to deny this. To say it wasn't so.

But I can understand his concern. So I say, "Well. I did try to kill you once, didn't I?"

Kent's eyes go wide. "It's too soon for that, man. That shit is still not funny."

I look away as I say, "I wasn't making a joke."

I can feel Kent looking at me, studying me, trying, I assume, to make some sense of me or my words. Perhaps both. But it's hard to know what he's thinking. It's frustrating to have a supernatural ability that allows me to know everyone's emotions, except for his. It makes me feel off-kilter around him. Like I've lost my eyesight.

Finally, Kent sighs.

I seem to have passed a test.

"Anyway," he says, but he sounds a bit uncertain now, "I was pretty sure you would come after me. And all I could think was that if I died, James would die. I'm his whole world, you know? You kill me, you kill him." He looks into his hands. "I stopped sleeping at night. Stopped eating. I was losing my mind. I couldn't handle it, any of it—and you were, like, living with us? And then everything with Juliette—I just—I don't know." He sighs, long and loud. Shaky. "I was an asshole. I took everything out on her. Blamed her for everything. For walking away from what I thought was one of the few sure things in my life. It's my own fault, really. My own baggage. I've still got a lot of shit to work out," he says finally. "I've got issues with people leaving me behind."

For a moment, I'm rendered speechless.

I'd never thought of Kent as capable of complex thought. My ability to sense emotions and his ability to extinguish preternatural gifts has made for a strange pairing—I'd always been forced to conclude that he was devoid of all thought and feeling. It turns out he's quite a bit more emotionally adept than I'd expected. Vocal, too.

But it's strange to see someone with my shared DNA speak so freely. To admit aloud his fears and shortcomings. It's too raw, like looking directly at the sun. I have to look away.

Ultimately, I say only, "I understand."

Kent clears his throat.

"So. Yeah," he says. "I guess I just wanted to say that Juliette was right. In the end, she and I grew apart. All of this"—he makes a gesture between us—"made me realize a lot of things. And she was right. I've always been so desperate for something, some kind of love, or affection, or *something*. I don't know," he says, shaking his head. "I guess I wanted to believe she and I had something we didn't. I was in a different place then. Hell, I was a different person. But I know my priorities now."

I look at him then, a question in my eyes.

"My family," he says, meeting my gaze. "That's all I care about now."

JULIETTE

We're making our way slowly back to base.

I'm in no hurry to find Warner only to have what will probably be a difficult, stressful conversation, so I take my time. I pick my way through the detritus of war, winding through the gray wreckage of the compounds as we leave behind unregulated territory and the smudged remnants of what used to be. I'm always sorry when our walk is nearly at an end; I feel great nostalgia for the cookie-cutter homes, the picket fences, the small, boarded-up shops and old, abandoned banks and buildings that make up the streets of unregulated turf. I'd like to find a way to bring it all back again.

I take a deep breath and enjoy the rush of crisp, icy air as it burns through my lungs. Wind wraps around me, pulling and pushing and dancing, whipping my hair into a frenzy, and I lean into it, get lost in it, open my mouth to inhale it. I'm about to smile when Kenji shoots me a dark look and I cringe, apologizing with my eyes.

My halfhearted apology does little to placate him.

I forced Kenji to take another detour down to the ocean, which is often my favorite part of our walk. Kenji, on the other hand, really hates it—and so do his boots, one of which got stuck in the muck that now clings to what used to be clean sand.

"I still can't believe you like staring at that nasty, piss-infested—"

"It's not infested, exactly," I point out. "Castle says it's definitely more water than pee."

Kenji only glares at me.

He's still muttering under his breath, complaining about his shoes being soaked in "piss water," as he likes to call it, as we make our way up the main road. I'm happy to ignore him, determined to enjoy the last of this peaceful hour, as it's one of the only hours I have for myself these days. I linger and look back at the cracked sidewalks and caving roofs of our old world, trying—and occasionally succeeding—to remember a time when things weren't so bleak.

"Do you ever miss it?" I ask Kenji. "The way things used to be?"

Kenji is standing on one foot, shaking some kind of sludge from one leather boot, when he looks up and frowns. "I don't know what you think you remember, J, but the way things used to be wasn't much better than the way they are now."

"What do you mean?" I ask, leaning against the pole of an old street sign.

"What do *you* mean?" he counters. "How can you miss anything about your old life? I thought you hated your life with your parents. I thought you said they were horrible and abusive."

"They were," I say, turning away. "And we didn't have much. But there were some things I like to remember— some nice moments—back before The Reestablishment was in power. I guess I just miss the small things that used to make me happy." I look back at him and smile. "You know?"

He raises an eyebrow.

"Like—the sound of the ice cream truck in the afternoons," I say to him. "Or the mailman making his rounds. I used to sit by the window and watch people come home from work in the evenings." I look away, remembering. "It was nice."

"Hm."

"You don't think so?"

Kenji's lips quirk up into an unhappy smile as he inspects his boot, now free of sludge. "I don't know, kid. Those ice cream trucks never came into my neighborhood. The world I remember was tired and racist and volatile as hell, ripe for a hostile takeover by a shit regime. We were already divided. The conquering was easy." He takes a deep breath. Blows it out as he says, "Anyway, I ran away from an orphanage when I was eight, so I don't remember much of that cutesy shit, regardless."

I freeze, stunned. It takes me a second to find my voice. "You lived in an orphanage?"

Kenji nods before offering me a short, humorless laugh. "Yep. I'd been living on the streets for a year, hitchhiking my way across the state—you know, before we had sectors— until Castle found me."

"What?" My body goes rigid. "Why have you never told me this story? All this time—and you never said—"

He shrugs.

"Did you ever know your parents?"

He nods but doesn't look at me.

I feel my blood run cold. "What happened to them?"

"It doesn't matter."

"Of course it matters," I say, and touch his elbow. *"Kenji—"*

"It's not important," he says, breaking away. "We've all got problems. We've all got baggage. No need to dwell on it."

"This isn't about dwelling on the past," I say. "I just want to know. Your life—your past—it matters to me." And for a moment I'm reminded again of Castle—his eyes, his urgency—and his insistence that there's more I need to know about Warner's past, too.

There's so much left to learn about the people I care about.

Kenji finally smiles, but it makes him look tired. Eventually, he sighs. He jogs up a few cracked steps leading to the entrance of an old library and sits down on the cold concrete. Our armed guards are waiting for us, just out of sight.

Kenji pats the place next to him.

I scramble up the steps to join him.

We're staring out at an ancient intersection, old stoplights and electric lines smashed and tangled on the pavement, when he says,

"So, you know I'm Japanese, right?"

74

I nod.

"Well. Where I grew up, people weren't used to seeing faces like mine. My parents weren't born here; they spoke Japanese and broken English. Some people didn't like that. Anyway, we lived in a rough area," he explains, "with a lot of ignorant people. And just before The Reestablishment started campaigning, promising to solve all our people problems by obliterating cultures and languages and religions and whatever, race relations were at their worst. There was a lot of violence, all across the continent. Communities clashing. Killing each other. If you were the wrong color at the wrong time"—he makes a finger gun, shoots it into the air—"people would make you disappear. We avoided it, mostly. The Asian communities never had it as bad as the black communities, for example. The black communities had it the worst—Castle can tell you all about that," he says. "Castle's got the craziest stories. But the worst that ever happened to my family, usually, was people would talk shit when we were out together. I remember my mom never wanted to leave the house."

I feel my body tense.

"Anyhow." He shrugs. "My dad just—you know—he couldn't just stand there and let people say stupid, foul shit about his family, right? So he'd get mad. It wasn't like this was always happening or whatever—but when it *did* happen, sometimes the altercation would end in an argument, and sometimes nothing. It didn't seem like the end of the world. But my mom was always begging my dad to let it go, and he couldn't." His face darkens. "And I don't blame him.

"One day," Kenji says, "it ended really badly. Everyone had guns in those days, remember? *Civilians* had guns. Crazy to imagine now, under The Reestablishment, but back then, everyone was armed, out for themselves." A short pause. "My dad bought a gun, too. He said we needed it, just in case. For our own protection." Kenji isn't looking at me when he says, "And the next time some stupid shit went down, my dad got a little too brave. They used his own gun against him. Dad got shot. Mom got shot trying to make it stop. I was seven."

"You were there?" I gasp.

He nods. "Saw the whole thing go down."

I cover my mouth with both hands. My eyes sting with unshed tears.

"I've never told anyone that story," he says, his forehead creasing. "Not even Castle."

"What?" I drop my hands. My eyes widen. "Why not?"

He shakes his head. "I don't know," he says quietly, and stares off into the distance. "When I met Castle everything was still so fresh, you know? Still too real. When he wanted to know my story, I told him I didn't want to talk about it. Ever." Kenji glances over at me. "Eventually, he just stopped asking."

I can only stare at him, stunned. Speechless.

Kenji looks away. He's almost talking to himself when he says, "It feels so weird to have said all of that out loud." He takes a sudden, sharp breath, jumps to his feet, and turns his head so I can't see his face. I hear him sniff hard, twice. And then he stuffs his hands in his pockets and says, "You know, I think I might be the only one of us who doesn't have daddy issues. I loved the *shit* out of my dad."

I'm still thinking about Kenji's story—and how much more there is to know about him, about Warner, about everyone I've come to call a friend—when Winston's voice startles me back to the present.

"We're still figuring out exactly how to divvy up the rooms," he's saying, "but it's coming together nicely. In fact, we're a little ahead of schedule on the bedrooms," he says. "Warner fast-tracked the work on the east wing, so we can actually start moving in tomorrow."

There's a brief round of applause. Someone cheers.

We're taking a brief tour of our new headquarters.

The majority of the space is still under construction, so, for the most part, what we're staring at is a loud, dusty mess, but I'm excited to see the progress. Our group has desperately needed more bedrooms, more bathrooms, desks and studios. And we need to set up a real command center from which we can get work done. This will, hopefully, be the beginning of that new world. The world wherein I'm the supreme commander.

Crazy.

For now, the details of what I do and control are still unfolding. We won't be challenging other sectors or their leaders until we have a better idea of who our allies might be, and that means we'll need a little more time. "The destruction of the world didn't happen overnight, and neither will saving it," Castle likes to say, and I think he's right. We need to make thoughtful decisions as we move forward—and making an effort to be diplomatic might be the difference between life and death. It would be far easier to make global progress, for example, if we weren't the only ones with the vision for change.

We need to forge alliances.

But Castle's conversation with me this morning has left me a little rattled. I'm not sure how to feel anymore—or what to hope for. I only know that, despite the brave face I put on for the civilians, I don't *want* to jump from one war to another; I don't *want* to have to slaughter everyone who stands in my way. The people of Sector 45 are trusting me with their loved ones—with their children and spouses who've become my soldiers—and I don't want to risk any more of their lives unless absolutely necessary. I'm hoping to ease into this. I'm hoping that there's a chance—even the smallest chance—that the semicooperation of my fellow sectors and the five other supreme commanders could mean good things for the future. I'm wondering if we might be able to come together without more bloodshed.

"That's ridiculous. And *naive*," Kenji says.

I look up at the sound of his voice, look around. He's talking to Ian. Ian Sanchez—tall, lanky guy with a bit of an attitude but a good heart. The only one of us with no superpowers, though. Not that it matters.

Ian is standing tall, arms crossed against his chest, head turned to the side, eyes up at the ceiling. "I don't care what you think—"

"Well, I do." I hear Castle cut in. "I care what Kenji thinks," he's saying.

"But—"

"I care what you think, too, Ian," Castle says, "But you have to see that Kenji is right in this instance. We have to approach everything with a great deal of caution. We can't know for certain what will happen next."

Ian sighs, exasperated. "That's not what I'm saying. What I'm saying is I don't understand why we need all this space. It's unnecessary."

"Wait—what's the issue here?" I ask, looking around. And then, to Ian: "Why don't you like the new space?"

Lily puts an arm around Ian's shoulders. "Ian is just sad," she says, smiling. "He doesn't want to break up the slumber party."

"What?" I frown.

Kenji laughs.

Ian scowls. "I just think we're fine where we are," he says. "I don't know why we need to move up into all *this*," he says, his arms wide as he scans the cavernous space. "It feels like tempting fate. Doesn't anyone remember what happened the last time we built a huge hideout?"

I watch Castle flinch.

I think we all do.

Omega Point, destroyed. Bombed into nothingness.

Decades of hard work obliterated in a moment.

"That's not going to happen again," I say firmly. "Besides, we're more protected here than we ever were before. We have an entire army behind us now. We're safer in this building than we would be anywhere else."

My words are met with an immediate chorus of support, but still I bristle, because I know that what I've said is only partly true.

I have no way of knowing what's going to happen to us or how long we'll last here. What I *do* know is that we need the new space—and we need to set up shop while we still have the funds. No one has tried to cut us off or shut us down yet; no sanctions have been imposed by fellow continents or commanders. Not yet, anyway. Which means we need to rebuild while we still have the means to do so.

But this—

This enormous space dedicated only to our efforts?

This was all Warner's doing.

He was able to empty out an entire floor for us—the top floor, the fifteenth story—of Sector 45 headquarters. It took an enormous amount of effort to transfer and distribute a whole floor's worth of people, work, and furnishings to other departments, but somehow, he managed it. Now the level is being refitted specifically for our needs.

Once it's all done we'll have state-of-the-art technology that will allow us not only the access to the research and surveillance we'll need, but the necessary tools for Winston and Alia to continue building any devices, gadgets, and uniforms we might require. And even though Sector 45 already has its own medical wing, we'll need a secure area for Sonya and Sara to work, from where they'll be able to continue developing antidotes and serums that might one day save our lives.

I'm just about to point this out when Delalieu walks into the room.

"Supreme," he says, with a nod in my direction.

At the sound of his voice, we all spin around.

"Yes, Lieutenant?"

There's a slight quiver in his words when he says, "You have a visitor, madam. He's requesting ten minutes of your time."

"A visitor?" I turn instinctively, finding Kenji with my eyes. He looks just as confused as I am.

"Yes, madam," says Delalieu. "He's waiting downstairs in the main reception room."

"But who is this person?" I ask, concerned. "Where did he come from?"

"His name is Haider Ibrahim. He's the son of the supreme commander of Asia."

I feel my body lock in sudden apprehension. I'm not sure I'm any good at hiding the panic that jolts through me as I say, *"The son of the supreme commander of Asia?* Did he say why he was here?"

Delalieu shakes his head. "I'm sorry to say that he refused to answer any of my more detailed questions, madam."

I'm breathing hard, head spinning. Suddenly all I can

think about is Castle's concern over Oceania this morning. The fear in his eyes. The many questions he refused to answer.

"What shall I tell him, madam?" Delalieu again.

I feel my heart pick up. I close my eyes. *You are a supreme commander,* I say to myself. *Act like it.*

"Madam?"

"Yes, of course, tell him I'll be right th—"

"Ms. Ferrars." Castle's sharp voice pierces the fog of my mind.

I look in his direction.

"Ms. Ferrars," he says again, a warning in his eyes. "Perhaps you should wait."

"Wait?" I say. "Wait for what?"

"Wait to meet with him until Mr. Warner can be there, too."

My confusion bleeds into anger. "I appreciate your concern, Castle, but I can do this on my own, thank you."

"Ms. Ferrars, I would beg you to reconsider. Please," he says, more urgently now, "you must understand—this is no small thing. The son of a supreme commander—it could mean so much—"

"As I said, thank you for your concern." I cut him off, my cheeks inflamed. Lately, I've been feeling like Castle has no faith in me—like he isn't rooting for me at all—and it makes me think back to this morning's conversation. It makes me wonder if I can trust anything he says. What kind of ally would stand here and point out my ineptitude in front of everyone? It's all I can do not to shout at him when I say, "I can assure you, I'll be fine."

And then, to Delalieu:

"Lieutenant, please tell our visitor that I'll be down in a moment."

"Yes, madam." Another nod, and Delalieu's gone.

Unfortunately, my bravado walks out the door with him.

I ignore Castle as I search the room for Kenji's face; for all my big talk, I don't actually want to do this alone. And Kenji knows me well.

"Hey—I'm right here." He's crossed the room in just a few strides, by my side in seconds.

"You're coming with me, right?" I whisper, tugging at his sleeve like a child.

Kenji laughs. "I'll be wherever you need me to be, kid."

WARNER

I have a great fear of drowning in the ocean of my own silence.

In the steady thrum that accompanies quiet, my mind is unkind to me. I think too much. I feel, perhaps, far more than I should. It would be only a slight exaggeration to say that my goal in life is to outrun my mind, my memories.

So I have to keep moving.

I used to retreat belowground when I wanted a distraction. I used to find comfort in our simulation chambers, in the programs designed to prepare soldiers for combat. But as we've recently moved a team of soldiers underground in all the chaos of the new construction, I'm without reprieve. I've no choice now but to go up.

I enter the hangar at a brisk pace, my footsteps echoing in the vast space as I move, almost instinctively, toward the army choppers parked in the far right wing. Soldiers see me and jump quickly out of my way, their eyes betraying their confusion even as they salute me. I nod only once in their direction, offering no explanation as I climb up and into the aircraft. I place the headphones over my head and speak quietly into the radio, alerting our air-traffic controllers of my intent to take flight, and strap myself into the front seat.

The retinal scanner takes my identification automatically. Preflight checks are clear. I turn on the engine and the roar is deafening, even through the noise-canceling headphones. I feel my body begin to unclench.

Soon, I'm in the air.

My father taught me to shoot a gun when I was nine years old. When I was ten he sliced open the back of my leg and showed me how to suture my own wounds. At eleven he broke my arm and abandoned me in the wild for two weeks. At age twelve I was taught to build and defuse my own bombs. He began teaching me how to fly planes when I was thirteen.

He never did teach me how to ride a bike. I figured that out on my own.

From thousands of feet above the ground, Sector 45 looks like a half-assembled board game. Distance makes the world feel small and surmountable, a pill easily swallowed. But I know the deceit too well, and it is here, above the clouds, that I finally understand Icarus. I, too, am tempted to fly too close to the sun. It is only my inability to be impractical that keeps me tethered to the earth. So I take a steadying breath, and get back to work.

I'm making my aerial rounds a bit earlier than usual, so the sights below are different from the ones I've begun to expect every day. On an average day I'm up here in the late afternoon, checking in on civilians as they leave work to exchange their REST dollars at local Supply Centers. They usually scurry back to their compounds shortly thereafter, weighted down with newly purchased necessities and the disheartening realization that they'll have to do it all again the following day. Right now, everyone is still at work, leaving the land empty of its worker ants. The landscape is bizarre and beautiful from afar, the ocean vast, blue, and breathtaking. But I know only too well our world's pockmarked surface.

This strange, sad reality my father helped create.

I squeeze my eyes shut, my hand clutching the throttle. There's simply too much to contend with today.

First, the disarming realization that I have a brother whose heart is as complicated and flawed as my own.

Second, and perhaps most offensive: the impending, anxiety-inducing arrival of my past.

I still haven't talked to Juliette about the imminent arrival of our guests, and, if I'm being honest, I'm no longer sure I want to. I've never discussed much of my life with her. I've never told her stories of my childhood friends, their parents, the history of The Reestablishment and my role within it. There's never been time. Never the right moment. If Juliette has been supreme commander for seventeen days now, she and I have only been in a relationship for two days longer than that.

We've both been busy.

And we've only just overcome so much—all the complications between us, all the distance and confusion, the misunderstandings. She's mistrusted me for so long.

I know I have only myself to blame for what's transpired between us, but I worry that the past ugliness has inspired in her an instinct to doubt me; it's likely a well-developed muscle now. And I feel certain that telling her more about my ignoble life will only make things worse at the onset of a relationship I want desperately to preserve. To protect.

So how do I begin? Where do I start?

The year I turned sixteen, our parents, the supreme commanders, decided we should all take turns shooting each other. Not to kill, merely to disable. They wanted us to know what a bullet wound felt like. They wanted us to be able to understand the recovery process. Most of all, they wanted us to know that even our friends might one day turn on us.

I feel my mouth twist into an unhappy smile.

I suppose it was a worthwhile lesson. After all, my father is now six feet under the ground and his old friends don't seem to care. But the problem that day was that I'd been taught by my father, a master marksman. Worse, I'd already been practicing every day for five years—two years earlier than the others—and, as a result, I was faster, sharper, and crueler than my peers. I didn't hesitate. I'd shot all my friends before they'd even picked up their weapons.

That was the first day I felt, with certainty, that my father was proud of me. I'd spent so long desperately seeking his approval and that day, I finally had it. He looked at me the way I'd always hoped he would: like he cared for me. Like a father who saw a bit of himself in his son. The realization sent me into the forest, where I promptly threw up in the bushes.

I've only been struck by a bullet once.

The memory still mortifies me, but I don't regret it. I deserved it. For misunderstanding her, for mistreating her, for being lost and confused. But I've been trying so hard to be a different man; to be, if not kinder, then at the very least, *better*. I don't want to lose the love I've come to cherish.

And I don't want Juliette to know my past.

I don't want to share stories from my life that only disgust and revolt me, stories that would color her impression of me. I don't want her to know how I spent my time as a child. She doesn't need to know how many times my father forced me to watch him skin dead animals, how I can still feel the vibrations of his screams in my ear as he kicked me, over and over again, when I dared to look away. I'd rather not remember the hours I spent shackled in a dark room, compelled to listen to the manufactured sounds of women and children screaming for help. It was all supposed to make me strong, he'd said. It was supposed to help me survive.

Instead, life with my father only made me wish for death.

I don't want to tell Juliette how I'd always known my father was unfaithful, that he'd abandoned my mother long, long ago, that I'd always wanted to murder him, that I'd dreamt of it, planned for it, hoped to one day break his neck using the very skills he'd given me.

How I failed. Every time.

Because I am weak.

I don't miss him. I don't miss his life. I don't want his friends or his footprint on my soul. But for some reason, his old comrades won't let me go.

They're coming to collect their pound of flesh, and I fear that this time—as I have every time—I will end up paying with my heart.

JULIETTE

Kenji and I are in Warner's room—what's become my room—and we're standing in the middle of the closet while I fling clothes at him, trying to figure out what to wear.

"What about this?" I say to him, throwing something glittery in his direction. "Or this?" I toss another ball of fabric at him.

"You don't know shit about clothes, do you?"

I turn around, tilt my head. "I'm sorry, when was I supposed to learn about fashion, Kenji? When I was growing up alone and tortured by my horrible parents? Or maybe when I was festering in an insane asylum?"

That shuts him up.

"*So?*" I say, nodding with my chin. "Which one?"

He picks up the two pieces I threw at him and frowns. "You're making me choose between a short, shiny dress and a pair of pajama bottoms? I mean—I guess I choose the dress? But I don't think it'll go well with those ratty tennis shoes you're always wearing."

"Oh." I glance down at my shoes. "Well, I don't know. Warner picked this stuff out for me a long time ago—before he even met me. It's all I have," I say, looking up. "These clothes are left over from when I first got to Sector 45."

"Why don't you just wear your suit?" Kenji says, leaning against the wall. "The new one Alia and Winston made for you?"

I shake my head. "They haven't finished fixing it yet. And it's still got bloodstains from when I shot Warner's dad. Besides," I say, taking a deep breath, "that was a different me. I wore those head-to-toe suits when I thought I had to protect people from my skin. But I'm different now. I can turn my power off. I can be . . . normal." I try to smile. "So I want to dress like a normal person."

"But you're not a normal person."

"I know that." A frustrating flush of heat warms my cheeks. "I just . . . I think I'd like to dress like one. Maybe for a little while? I've never been able to act my age and I just want to feel a little bit—"

"I get it," Kenji says, cutting me off with one hand. He looks me up and down. Says, "Well, I mean, if that's the look you're going for, I think you look like a normal person right now. This'll work." He waves in the general direction of my body.

I'm wearing jeans and a pink sweater. My hair is pulled up into a high ponytail. I feel comfortable and normal— but I also feel like an unaccomplished seventeen-year-old playing pretend.

"But I'm supposed to be the supreme commander of North America," I say. "Do you think it's okay if I'm dressed like this? Warner is always wearing fancy suits, you know? Or just, like, really nice clothes. He always looks so poised—so intimidating—"

"Where is he, by the way?" Kenji cuts me off. "I mean, I know you don't want to hear this, but I agree with Castle. Warner should be here for this meeting."

I take a deep breath. Try to be calm. "I know that Warner knows everything, okay? I know he's the best at basically everything, that he was born for this life. His father was grooming him to lead the world. In another life, another reality? This was supposed to be his role. I know that. I do."

"But?"

"But it's *not* Warner's job, is it?" I say angrily. "It's mine. And I'm trying not to rely on him all the time. I want to try to do some things on my own now. To take charge."

Kenji doesn't seem convinced. "I don't know, J. I think maybe this is one of those times when you should still be relying on him. He knows this world way better than we do—and, bonus, he'd be able to tell you what you should be wearing." Kenji shrugs. "Fashion really isn't my area of expertise."

I pick up the short, shiny dress and examine it.

Just over two weeks ago I single-handedly fought off hundreds of soldiers. I crushed a man's throat in my fist. I put two bullets through Anderson's forehead with no hesitation or regret. But here, staring at an armoire full of clothes, I'm intimidated.

"Maybe I *should* call Warner," I say, peeking over my shoulder at Kenji.

"Yep." He points at me. "Good idea."

But then,

"No—never mind," I say. "It's okay. I'll be okay, right? I mean what's the big deal? He's just a kid, right? Just the *son* of a supreme commander. Not an actual supreme commander. Right?"

"Uhhh—all of it is a big deal, J. The kids of the commanders are all, like, other Warners. They're basically mercenaries. And they've all been prepped to take their parents' places—"

"Yeah, no, I should definitely do this on my own." I'm looking in a mirror now, pulling my ponytail tight. "Right?"

Kenji is shaking his head.

"Yes. Exactly." I nod.

"Uh-uh. No. I think this is a bad idea."

"I'm capable of doing *some* things on my own, Kenji," I snap. "I'm not totally clueless."

Kenji sighs. "Whatever you say, princess."

WARNER

"Mr. Warner—please, Mr. Warner, slow down, son—"

I stop too suddenly, pivoting sharply on my heel. Castle is chasing me down the hall, waving a frantic hand in my direction. I meet his eyes with a mild expression.

"Can I help you?"

"Where have you been?" he says, obviously out of breath. "I've been looking for you everywhere."

I raise an eyebrow, fighting back the urge to tell him that my whereabouts are none of his business. "I had a few aerial rounds to make."

Castle frowns. "Don't you usually do that later in the afternoon?"

At this, I almost smile. "You've been watching me."

"Let's not play games. You've been watching me, too."

Now I actually smile. "Have I?"

"You think so little of my intelligence."

"I don't know what to think of you, Castle."

He laughs out loud. "Goodness, you're an excellent liar."

I look away. "What do you need?"

"He's here. He's here right now and she's with him and I tried to stop her but she wouldn't listen to me—"

I turn back, alarmed. "Who's here?"

For the first time, I see actual anger flicker in Castle's eyes. "Now is not the time to play dumb with me, son. Haider Ibrahim is here. Right now. And Juliette is meeting with him alone, completely unprepared."

Shock renders me, for a moment, speechless.

"Did you hear what I said?" Castle is nearly shouting. "She's meeting with him *now*."

"How?" I say, coming back to myself. "How is he here already? Did he arrive alone?"

"Mr. Warner, please listen to me. You have to talk to her. You have to explain and you have to do it now," he says, grabbing my shoulders. "They're coming back for h—"

Castle is thrown backward, hard.

He cries out as he catches himself, his arms and legs splayed out in front of him as if caught in a gust of wind. He remains in that impossible position, hovering several inches off the ground, and stares at me, chest heaving. Slowly, he steadies. His feet finally touch the floor.

"You would use my own powers against me?" he says, breathing hard. "I am your *ally*—"

"Never," I say sharply, "ever put your hands on me, Castle. Or next time I might accidentally kill you."

Castle blinks. And then I feel it—I can sense it, close my fingers around it: his pity. It's everywhere. Awful. Suffocating.

"Don't you dare feel sorry for me," I say.

"My apologies," he says quietly. "I didn't mean to invade your personal space. But you must understand the urgency here. First, the RSVP—and now, Haider's arrival? This is just the beginning," he says, lowering his voice. "They are mobilizing."

"You are overthinking this," I say, my voice clipped. "Haider's arrival today is about *me*. Sector 45's inevitable infestation by a swarm of supreme commanders is about *me*. I've committed treason, remember?" I shake my head, begin walking away. "They're just a little . . . angry."

"Stop," he says. "Listen to me—"

"You don't need to concern yourself with this, Castle. I'll handle it."

"Why aren't you listening to me?" He's chasing after me now. "They're coming to take her back, son! We can't let that happen!"

I freeze.

I turn to face him. My movements are slow, deliberate. "What are you talking about? Take her back where?"

Castle doesn't respond. Instead, his face goes slack. He stares, confused, in my direction.

"I have a thousand things to do," I say, impatient now, "so if you would please make this quick and tell me what on earth you're talking about—"

"He never told you, did he?"

"Who? Told me what?"

"Your father," he says. "He never told you." Castle runs a hand down the length of his face. He looks abruptly ancient, about to expire. "My God. He never told you."

"What do you mean? What did he never tell me?"

"The truth," he says. "About Ms. Ferrars."

I stare at him, my chest constricting in fear.

Castle shakes his head as he says, "He never told you where she really came from, did he? He never told you the truth about her parents."

JULIETTE

JULIETTE

"Stop squirming, J."

We're in the glass elevator, making our way down to one of the main reception areas, and I can't stop fidgeting.

My eyes are squeezed shut. I keep saying, "Oh my God, I *am* totally clueless, aren't I? What am I doing? I don't look professional at all—"

"You know what? Who cares what you're wearing?" Kenji says. "It's all in the attitude, anyway. It's about how you carry yourself."

I look up at him, feeling the height difference between us more acutely than ever. "But I'm so short."

"Napoleon was short, too."

"Napoleon was horrible," I point out.

"Napoleon got shit done, didn't he?"

I frown.

Kenji nudges me with his elbow. "You might want to spit the gum out, though."

"Kenji," I say, only half hearing him, "I've just realized I've never met any foreign officials before."

"I know, right? Me neither," he says, mussing my hair. "But it'll be okay. You just need to calm down. Anyway, you look cute. You'll do great."

I slap his hand away. "I may not know much about being a supreme commander yet, but I do know that I'm not supposed to be *cute*."

Just then, the elevator dings open.

"Who says you can't be cute and kick ass at the same time?" Kenji winks at me. "I do it every day."

"Oh, man—you know what? Never mind," is the first thing Kenji says to me.

He's cringing, shooting me a sidelong glance as he says, "Maybe you really *should* work on your wardrobe?"

I might die of embarrassment.

Whoever this guy is, whatever his intentions are, Haider Ibrahim is dressed unlike anyone I've ever seen before. He *looks* like no one I've ever seen before.

He stands up as we enter the room—tall, very tall—and I'm instantly struck by the sight of him. He's wearing a dark gray leather jacket over what I can only assume is meant to be a shirt, but is actually a series of tightly woven chains strung across his body. His skin is heavily tanned and half exposed, his upper body only barely concealed by his chain-link shirt. His closely tapered black pants disappear into shin-high combat boots, and his light brown eyes—a startling contrast to his brown skin—are rimmed in a flutter of thick black lashes.

I tug at my pink sweater and nervously swallow my gum.

"Hi," I say, and begin to wave, but Kenji is kind enough to push down my hand. I clear my throat. "I'm Juliette."

Haider steps forward cautiously, his eyes drawn together in what looks like confusion as he appraises my appearance. I feel uncomfortably self-conscious. Wildly underprepared. And I suddenly really need to use the bathroom.

"Hello," he finally says, but it sounds more like a question.

"Can we help you?" I say.

"Tehcheen Arabi?"

"Oh." I glance at Kenji, then at Haider. "Um, you don't speak English?"

Haider raises a single eyebrow. "Do you only speak English?"

"Yes?" I say, feeling now more nervous than ever.

"That's too bad." He sighs. Looks around. "I'm here to see the supreme commander." He has a rich, deep voice but speaks with a slight accent.

"Yep, hi, that's me," I say, and smile.

His eyes widen with ill-concealed confusion. "You are"— he frowns—"the supreme?"

"Mm-hm." I paste on a brighter smile. Diplomacy, I tell myself. *Diplomacy.*

"But we were told that the new supreme was wild, lethal—terrifying—"

I nod. Feel my face warm. "Yes. That's me. I'm Juliette Ferrars."

Haider tilts his head, his eyes scanning my body. "But you're so small." And I'm still trying to figure out how to respond to that when he shakes his head and says, "I apologize, I meant to say—that you are so young. But then, also, very small."

My smile is beginning to hurt.

"So it was you," he says, still confused, "who killed Supreme Anderson?"

I nod. Shrug.

"But—"

"I'm sorry," Kenji interjects. "Did you have a reason for being here?"

Haider looks taken aback by the question. He glances at Kenji. "Who is this?"

"He's my second-in-command," I say. "And you should feel free to respond to him when he speaks to you."

"Oh, I see," Haider says, understanding in his eyes. He nods at Kenji. "A member of your Supreme Guard."

"I don't have a Supr—"

"That's right," Kenji says, throwing a swift *shut up* elbow in my ribs. "You'll have to forgive me for being a little overprotective." He smiles. "I'm sure you know how it is."

"Yes, of course," Haider says, looking sympathetic.

"Should we all sit down?" I say, gesturing to the couches across the room. We're still standing in the entryway and it's starting to get awkward.

"Certainly." Haider offers me his arm in anticipation of the fifteen-foot journey to the couches, and I shoot Kenji a quick look of confusion.

He shrugs.

The three of us settle into our seats; Kenji and I sit across from Haider. There's a long, wooden coffee table between us, and Kenji presses the slim button underneath to call for a tea and coffee service.

Haider won't stop staring at me. His gaze is neither flattering nor threatening—he looks genuinely confused—and I'm surprised to find that it's *this* reaction I find most unsettling. If his eyes were angry or objectifying, I might better know how to react. Instead, he seems mild and pleasant, but—surprised. And I'm not sure what to do with it. Kenji was right—I wish more than ever that Warner were here; his ability to sense emotions would give me a clearer idea of how to respond.

I finally break the silence between us.

"It's really very nice to meet you," I say, hoping I sound kinder than I feel, "but I'd love to know what brings you here. You've come such a long way."

Haider smiles then. The action adds a necessary warmth to his face that makes him look younger than he first appeared. "Curiosity," he says simply.

I do my best to mask my anxiety.

It's becoming more obvious by the moment that he was sent here to do some kind of reconnaissance for his father. Castle's theory was right—the supreme commanders must be dying to know who I am. And I'm beginning to wonder if this is only the first of several visits I'll soon receive from prying eyes.

Just then, the tea and coffee service arrives.

The ladies and gentlemen who work in Sector 45—here,

and in the compounds—are peppier than ever these days. There's an infusion of hope in our sector that doesn't exist anywhere else on the continent, and the two older ladies who hurry into our room with the food cart are no exception to the effects of recent events. They flash big, bright smiles in my direction, and arrange the china with an exuberance that does not go unnoticed. I see Haider watching our interaction closely, examining the ladies' faces and the comfortable way in which they move in my presence. I thank them for their work and Haider is visibly stunned. Eyebrows raised, he sits back in his seat, hands clasped in his lap like the perfect gentleman, silent as salt until the moment they leave.

"I will impose upon your kindness for a few weeks," Haider says suddenly. "That is—if that's all right."

I frown, begin to protest, and Kenji cuts me off.

"Of course," he says, smiling wide. "Stay as long as you like. The son of a supreme commander is always welcome here."

"You are very kind," he says with a simple bow of his head. And then he hesitates, touches something at his wrist, and our room is swarmed in an instant by what appear to be members of his personal staff.

Haider stands up so swiftly I almost miss it.

Kenji and I hurry to our feet.

"It was a pleasure meeting you, Supreme Commander Ferrars," Haider says, stepping forward to reach for my hand, and I'm surprised by his boldness. Despite the many rumors

I know he's heard about me, he doesn't seem to mind being near my skin. Not that it really matters, of course—I've now learned how to turn my powers on and off at will—but not everyone knows that yet.

Either way, he presses a brief kiss to the back of my hand, smiles, and bows his head very slightly.

I manage an awkward smile and a small nod.

"If you tell me how many people are in your party," Kenji says, "I can begin to arrange accommodations for y—"

Haider laughs out loud, surprised. "Oh, that won't be necessary," he says. "I've brought my own residence."

"You've brought"—Kenji frowns—"you brought your own *residence?*"

Haider nods without looking at Kenji. When he next speaks he speaks only to me. "I look forward to seeing you and the rest of your guard at dinner tonight."

"Dinner," I say, blinking fast. "Tonight?"

"Of course," Kenji says swiftly. "We look forward to it."

Haider nods. "Please send my warmest regards to your Regent Warner. It's been several months since our last visit, but I look forward to catching up with him. He has mentioned me, of course?" A bright smile. "We've known each other since our infancy."

Stunned, I nod slowly, realization overcoming my confusion. "Yes. Right. Of course. I'm sure he'll be thrilled to see you again."

Another nod, and Haider's gone.

Kenji and I are alone.

"What the f—"

"Oh"—Haider pops his head back in the room—"and please tell your chef that I do not eat meat."

"For sure," Kenji says, nodding and smiling. "Yep. You got it."

WARNER

I'm sitting in the dark with my back to the bedroom door when I hear it open. It's only midafternoon, but I've been sitting here, staring at these unopened boxes for so long that even the sun, it seems, has grown tired of staring.

Castle's revelation left me in a daze.

I still don't trust Castle—don't trust that he has any idea what he's talking about—but at the end of our conversation I couldn't shake a terrible, frightening feeling in my gut begging for verification. I needed time to process the possibilities. To be alone with my thoughts. And when I expressed as much to Castle, he said, "Process all you like, son, but don't let this distract you. Juliette should not be meeting with Haider on her own. Something doesn't feel right here, Mr. Warner, and you have to go to them. Now. Show her how to navigate your world."

But I couldn't bring myself to do it.

Despite my every instinct to protect her, I won't undermine her like that. She didn't ask for my help today. She made a choice to not tell me what was happening. My abrupt and unwelcome interruption would only make her think that I agreed with Castle—that I didn't trust her to do the job on her own. And I *don't* agree with Castle; I think he's an idiot for underestimating her. So I returned here, instead, to these rooms, to think. To stare at my father's unopened secrets. To await her arrival.

And now—

The first thing Juliette does is turn on the light.

"Hey," she says carefully. "What's going on?"

I take a deep breath and turn around. "These are my father's old files," I say, gesturing with one hand. "Delalieu had them collected for me. I thought I should take a look, see if there's anything here that might be useful."

"Oh, wow," she says, her eyes alight with recognition. "I was wondering what those were for." She crosses the room to crouch beside the stacks, carefully running her fingers along the unmarked boxes. "Do you need help moving these into your office?"

I shake my head.

"Would you like me to help you sort through them?" she says, glancing at me over her shoulder. "I'd be happy t—"

"No," I say too quickly. I get to my feet, make an effort to appear calm. "No, that won't be necessary."

She raises her eyebrows.

I try to smile. "I think I'd like the time alone with them."

At this, she nods, misunderstanding all at once, and her sympathetic smile makes my chest tighten. I feel an indistinct, icy feeling stab at somewhere inside of me. She thinks I want space to deal with my grief. That going through my father's things will be difficult for me.

She doesn't know. I wish I didn't.

118

"So," she says, walking toward the bed, the boxes forgotten. "It's been an . . . interesting day."

The pressure in my chest intensifies. "Has it?"

"I just met an old friend of yours," she says, and flops backward onto the mattress. She reaches behind her head to pull her hair free of its ponytail, and sighs.

"An old friend of mine?" I say. But I can only stare at her as she speaks, study the shape of her face. I can't, at the present moment, know with perfect certainty whether or not what Castle told me is true; but I do know that I'll find the answers I seek in my father's files—in the boxes stacked inside this room.

Even so, I haven't yet gathered the courage to look.

"Hey," she says, waving a hand at me from the bed. "You in there?"

"Yes," I say reflexively. I take in a sharp breath. "Yes, love."

"So . . . do you remember him?" she says. "Haider Ibrahim?"

"Haider." I nod. "Yes, of course. He's the eldest son of the supreme commander of Asia. He has a sister," I say, but I say it robotically.

"Well, I don't know about his sister," she says. "But Haider is here. And he's staying for a few weeks. We're all having dinner with him tonight."

"At his behest, I'm sure."

"Yeah." She laughs. "How'd you know?"

I smile. Vaguely. "I remember Haider very well."

She's silent a moment. Then: "He said you'd known each other since your infancy."

And I feel, but do not acknowledge, the sudden tension in the room. I merely nod.

"That's a long time," she says.

"Yes. A very long time."

She sits up. Drops her chin in one hand and stares at me. "I thought you said you never had any friends."

At this, I laugh, but the sound is hollow. "I don't know that I would call us friends, exactly."

"No?"

"No."

"And you don't care to expand on that?"

"There's little to say."

"Well—if you're not friends, exactly, then why is he here?"

"I have my suspicions."

She sighs. Says, "Me too," and bites the inside of her cheek. "I guess this is where it starts, huh? Everyone wants to take a look at the freak show. At what we've done—at who I am. And we have to play along."

But I'm only half listening.

Instead, I'm staring at the many boxes looming behind her, Castle's words still settling in my mind. I remember I should say something, anything, to appear engaged in the conversation. So I try to smile as I say, "You didn't tell me he'd arrived earlier. I wish I could've been there to assist somehow."

Her cheeks, suddenly pink with embarrassment, tell one story; her lips tell another. "I didn't think I needed to tell you everything, all the time. I can handle some things on my own."

Her sharp tone is so surprising it forces my mind to focus. I meet her eyes to find she's staring straight through me now, bright with both hurt and anger.

"That's not at all what I meant," I say. "You know I think you can do anything, love. But I could've been a help to you. I know these people."

Her face is now pinker, somehow. She can't meet my eyes.

"I know," she says quietly. "I know. I've just been feeling a little overwhelmed lately. And I had a talk with Castle this morning that kind of messed with my head." She sighs. "I'm in a weird place today."

My heart starts beating too fast. "You had a talk with Castle?"

She nods.

I forget to breathe.

"He said I need to talk to you about something?" She looks up at me. "Like, there's more about The Reestablishment that you haven't told me?"

"More about The Reestablishment?"

"Yeah, like, there's something you need to tell me?"

"Something I need to tell you."

"Um, are you just going to keep repeating what I'm saying to you?" she says, and laughs.

I feel my chest unclench. A little.

"No, no, of course not," I say. "I just—I'm sorry, love. I confess I'm also a bit distracted today." I nod at the boxes laid out across the room. "It seems there's a lot left to discover about my father."

She shakes her head, her eyes big and sad. "I'm so sorry. It must be awful to have to go through all his stuff like this."

I exhale, and say, mostly to myself, "You have no idea," before looking away. I'm still staring at the floor, my head heavy with the day and its demands, when she reaches out, tentatively, with a single word.

"Aaron?"

And I can feel it then, can feel the change, the fear, the pain in her voice. My heart still beats too hard, but now it's for an entirely different reason.

"What's wrong?" I say, looking up at once. I take a seat next to her on the bed, study her eyes. "What's happened?"

She shakes her head. Stares into her open hands. Whispers the words when she says, "I think I made a mistake."

My eyes widen as I watch her. Her face pulls together. Her feelings pinwheel out of control, assaulting me with their wildness. She's afraid. She's angry. She's angry with herself for being afraid.

"You and I are so different," she says. "Meeting Haider today, I just"—she sighs—"I remembered how different we are. How differently we grew up."

I'm frozen. Confused. I can feel her fear and apprehension, but I don't know where she's going with this. What she's trying to say.

"So you think you've made a mistake?" I say. "About—*us*?"

Panic, suddenly, as she understands. "No, oh my God, no, not about us," she says quickly. "No, I just—"

Relief floods through me.

"—I still have so much to learn," she says. "I don't know anything about ruling . . . anything." She makes an impatient, angry sound. She can hardly get the words out. "I had no idea what I was signing up for. And every day I feel so incompetent," she says. "Sometimes I'm just not sure I can keep up with you. With any of this." She hesitates. And then, quietly, "This job should've been yours, you know. Not mine."

"No."

"Yes," she says, nodding. She can no longer look at me. "Everyone's thinking it, even if they don't say it. Castle. Kenji. I bet even the soldiers think so."

"Everyone can go to hell."

She smiles, only a little. "I think they might be right."

"People are idiots, love. Their opinions are worthless."

"Aaron," she says, frowning. "I appreciate you being angry on my behalf, I really do, but not *all* people are idio—"

"If they think you incapable it is because they are idiots. Idiots who've already forgotten that you were able to accomplish in a matter of *months* what they had been trying to do for decades. They are forgetting where you started, what you've overcome, how quickly you found the courage to fight when they could hardly stand."

She looks up, looks defeated. "But I don't know anything about politics."

"You are inexperienced," I say to her, "that is true. But you can learn these things. There's still time. And I will help you." I take her hand. "Sweetheart, you inspired the people of this sector to follow you into *battle*. They put their lives on the line—they sacrificed their loved ones—because they believed in you. In your strength. And you didn't let them down. You can never forget the enormity of what you've done," I say. "Don't allow anyone to take that away from you."

She stares at me, her eyes wide, shining. She blinks as she looks away, wiping quickly at a tear escaping down the side of her face.

"The world tried to crush you," I say, gently now, "and you refused to be shattered. You've recovered from every setback a stronger person, rising from the ashes only to astonish everyone around you. And you will continue to surprise and confuse those who underestimate you. It is an inevitability," I say. "A foregone conclusion.

"But you should know now that being a leader is a thankless occupation. Few will ever be grateful for what you do or for the changes you implement. Their memories will be short, convenient. Your every success will be scrutinized. Your accomplishments will be brushed aside, breeding only greater expectations from those around you. Your power will push you further away from your friends." I look away, shake my head. "You will be made to feel lonely. Lost. You will long for validation from those you once admired, agonizing between pleasing old friends and doing what is right." I look up. I feel my heart swell with pride as I stare at her. "But you must never, ever let the idiots into your head. They will only lead you astray."

Her eyes are bright with unshed tears. "But how?" she says, her voice breaking on the word. "How do I get them out of my head?"

"Set them on fire."

Her eyes go wide.

"In your mind," I say, attempting a smile. "Let them fuel the fire that keeps you striving." I reach out, touch my fingers to her cheek. "Idiots are highly flammable, love. Let them all burn in hell."

She closes her eyes. Turns her face into my hand.

And I pull her in, press my forehead to hers. "Those who do not understand you," I say softly, "will always doubt you."

She leans back, just an inch. Looks up.

"And I," I say, "I have never doubted you."

"Never?"

I shake my head. "Not once."

She looks away. Wipes her eyes. I press a kiss against her cheek, taste the salt of her tears.

She turns toward me.

I can feel it, as she looks at me; I can feel her fears disappearing, can feel her emotions becoming something else. Her cheeks flush. Her skin is suddenly hot, electric, under my hands. My heart beats faster, harder, and she doesn't have to say a word. I can feel the temperature change between us.

"Hey," she says. But she's staring at my mouth.

"Hi."

She touches her nose to mine and something inside me jolts to life. I hear my breath catch. My eyes close, unbidden.

"I love you," she says.

The words do something to me every time I hear them. They change me. Build something new inside of me. I swallow, hard. Fire consumes my mind.

"You know," I whisper, "I never get tired of hearing you say that."

She smiles. Her nose brushes the line of my jaw as she turns, presses her lips against my throat. I'm holding my breath, terrified to move, to leave this moment.

"I love you," she says again.

Heat fills my veins. I can feel her in my blood, her whispers overwhelming my senses. And for a sudden, desperate second I think I might be dreaming.

"Aaron," she says.

I'm losing a battle. We have so much to do, so much to take care of. I know I should move, should snap out of this, but I can't. I can't think.

And then she climbs into my lap and I take a quick, desperate breath, fighting against a sudden rush of pleasure and pain. There's no pretending anything when she's this close to me; I know she can feel me, can feel how badly I want her.

I can feel her, too.

Her heat. Her desire. She makes no secret of what she wants from me. What she wants me to do to her. And knowing this makes my torment only more acute.

She kisses me once, softly, her hands slipping under my sweater, and wraps her arms around me. I pull her in and she shifts forward, adjusting herself in my lap, and I take another painful, anguished breath. My every muscle tightens. I try not to move.

"I know it's late," she says. "I know we have a bunch of things to do. But I miss you." She reaches down, her fingers trailing along the zipper of my pants, and the movement sears through me. My vision goes white. For a moment I hear nothing but my heart, pounding in my head.

"You are trying to kill me," I say.

"Aaron." I can feel her smile as she whispers the word in my ear. She's unbuttoning my pants. "Please."

And I, I am gone.

My hand is suddenly behind her neck, the other wrapped around her waist, and I kiss her, melting into her, falling backward onto the bed and pulling her down with me. I used to dream about this—times like this—what it would be like to unzip her jeans, to run my fingers along her bare skin, to feel her, hot and soft against my body.

I stop, suddenly. Break away. I want to see her, to study her. To remind myself that she's really here, really mine. That she wants me just as much I want her. And when I meet her eyes the feeling overwhelms me, threatens to drown me. And then she's kissing me, even as I fight to catch my breath, and every thing, every thought and worry is wicked away, replaced by the feel of her mouth against my skin. Her hands, claiming my body.

God, it's an impossible drug.

She's kissing me like she knew. Like she knows—knows how desperately I need this, need her, need this comfort and release.

Like she needs it, too.

I wrap my arms around her, flip her over so quickly she actually squeaks in surprise. I kiss her nose, her cheeks, her lips. The lines of our bodies are welded together. I feel myself dissolving, becoming pure emotion as she parts her lips, tastes me, moans into my mouth.

"I love you," I say, gasping the words. *"I love you."*

It's interesting, really, how quickly I've become the kind of person who takes late-afternoon naps. The person I used to be would never have wasted so much time sleeping. Then again, that person never knew how to relax. Sleep was brutal, elusive. But this—

I close my eyes, press my face to the back of her neck and breathe.

She stirs almost imperceptibly against me.

Her naked body is flush against the length of mine, my arms wrapped entirely around her. It's six o'clock, I have a thousand things to do, and I never, ever want to move.

I kiss the top of her shoulder and she arches her back, exhales, and turns to face me. I pull her closer.

She smiles. Kisses me.

I shut my eyes, my skin still hot with the memory of her. My hands search the shape of her body, her warmth. I'm always stunned by how soft she is. Her curves are gentle and smooth. I feel my muscles tighten with longing and I surprise myself with how much I want her.

Again.

So soon.

"We'd better get dressed," she says softly. "I still need to meet with Kenji to talk about tonight."

All at once I recoil.

"Wow," I whisper, turning away. "That was not at all what I was hoping you'd say."

She laughs. Out loud. "Hmm. Kenji is a big turnoff for you. Got it."

I frown, feeling petty.

She kisses my nose. "I really wish you two could be friends."

"He's a walking disaster," I say. "Look what he did to my hair."

"But he's my best friend," she says, still smiling. "And I don't want to have to choose between the two of you all the time."

I look at her out of the corner of my eye. She's sitting up now, wearing nothing but the bedsheet. Her brown hair is long and tousled, her cheeks pinked, her eyes big and round and still a little sleepy.

I'm not sure I could ever say no to her.

"Please be nice to him," she says, and crawls over to me, the bedsheet catching under her knee and undoing her composure. I yank the rest of the sheet away from her and she gasps, surprised by the sight of her own naked body, and I can't help but take advantage of the moment, tucking her underneath me all over again.

"Why," I say, kissing her neck, "are you always so attached to that bedsheet?"

She looks away and blushes, and I'm lost again, kissing her.

"Aaron," she gasps, breathless, "I really—I have to go."

"Don't," I whisper, leaving light kisses along her collarbone. "Don't go." Her face is flushed, her lips bright red. Her eyes are closed in pleasure.

"I don't want to," she says, her breath hitching as I catch her bottom lip between my teeth, "I really don't, but Kenji—"

I groan and fall backward, pulling a pillow over my head.

JULIETTE

"Where the hell have you been?"

"What? Nothing," I say, heat flashing through my body. "I just—"

"What do you mean, nothing?" Kenji says, nearly stepping on my heels as I attempt to outpace him. "I've been waiting down here for almost two hours."

"I know—I'm sorry—"

He grabs my shoulder. Spins me around. Takes one look at my face and—

"Oh, gross, J, what the *hell*—"

"What?" I widen my eyes, all innocence, even as my face inflames.

Kenji glares at me.

I clear my throat.

"I told you to ask him a *question*."

"I did!"

"Jesus Christ." Kenji rubs an agitated hand across his forehead. "Do time and place mean nothing to you?"

"Hmm?"

He narrows his eyes at me.

I smile.

"You guys are terrible."

133

"Kenji," I say, reaching out.

"Ew, don't touch me—"

"Fine." I frown, crossing my arms.

He shakes his head, looks away. Makes a face and says, "You know what? Whatever," and sighs. "Did he at least tell you anything useful before you—uh, changed the subject?"

We've just walked back into the reception area where we first met with Haider.

"Yes he did," I say, determined. "He knew exactly who I was talking about."

"And?"

We sit down on the couches—Kenji choosing to sit across from me this time—and I clear my throat. I wonder aloud if we should order more tea.

"No tea." Kenji leans back, legs crossed, right ankle propped up on his left knee. "What did Warner say about Haider?"

Kenji's gaze is so focused and unforgiving I'm not sure what to do with myself. I still feel weirdly embarrassed; I wish I'd remembered to tie my hair back again. I have to keep pushing it out of my face.

I sit up straighter. Pull myself together. "He said they were never really friends."

Kenji snorts. "No surprise there."

"But he remembered him," I say, pointing at nothing in particular.

"And? What does he remember?"

"Oh. Um." I scratch an imaginary itch behind my ear. "I don't know."

"You didn't ask?"

"I . . . forgot?"

Kenji rolls his eyes. "Shit, man, I knew I should've gone myself."

I sit on my hands and try to smile. "Do you want to order some tea?"

"*No tea.*" Kenji shoots me a look. He taps the side of his leg, thinking.

"Do you want t—"

"Where is Warner now?" Kenji cuts me off.

"I don't know," I say. "I think he's still in his room. He had a bunch of boxes he wanted to sort through—"

Kenji is on his feet in an instant. He holds up one finger. "I'll be right back."

"Wait! Kenji—I don't think that's a good idea—"

But he's already gone.

I slump into the couch and sigh.

As I suspected. Not a good idea.

Warner is standing stiffly beside my couch, hardly looking at Kenji. I think he still hasn't forgiven him for the terrible haircut, and I can't say I blame him. Warner looks different without his golden hair—not bad, no—but different. His hair is barely half an inch long, one uniform length throughout, a shade of blond that registers only dimly as a color now. But the most interesting change in his face is that he's got a soft, subtle shadow of stubble—as though he's forgotten to shave lately—and I'm surprised to find that it doesn't bother me. He's too naturally good-looking to have his genetics undone by a simple haircut and, the truth is, I kind of like it. I'd hesitate to say this to Warner, as I don't know whether he'd appreciate the unorthodox compliment, but there's something nice about the change. He looks a little coarser now; a little rougher around the edges. He's less beautiful but somehow, impossibly—

Sexier.

Short, uncomplicated hair; a five o'clock shadow; a deeply, deeply serious face.

It works for him.

He's wearing a soft, navy-blue sweater—the sleeves, as always, pushed up his forearms—and slim black pants tucked into shiny black ankle boots. It's an effortless look. And right now he's leaning against a column, his arms crossed against his chest, feet crossed at the ankles, looking more sullen than usual, and I'm really kind of enjoying the view.

Kenji, however, is not.

The two of them look more irritated than ever, and I realize I'm to blame for the tension. I keep trying to force them to spend time together. I keep hoping that, with enough experience, Kenji will come to see what I love about Warner, and that Warner will learn to admire Kenji the way that I do—but it doesn't seem to be working. Forcing them to spend time together is beginning to backfire.

"*So,*" I say, clapping my hands together. "Should we talk?"

"Sure," Kenji says, but he's staring at the wall. "Let's talk."

No one talks.

I tap Warner's knee. When he looks at me, I gesture for him to sit down.

He does.

"Please," I whisper.

Warner frowns.

Finally, reluctantly, he sighs. "You said you had questions for me."

"Yeah, first question: Why are you such a dick?"

Warner stands up. "Sweetheart," he says quietly, "I hope you will forgive me for what I'm about to do to his face."

"Hey, asshole, I can still hear you."

"Okay, seriously, this has to stop." I'm tugging on Warner's arm, trying to get him to sit down, and he won't budge. My superhuman strength is totally useless on Warner; he just absorbs my power. "Please, sit down. Everyone. And you," I say, pointing at Kenji, "you need to stop instigating fights."

Kenji throws a hand in the air, makes a sound of disbelief. "Oh, so it's always my fault, huh? Whatever."

"No," I say heavily. "It's not your fault. This is my fault."

Kenji and Warner turn to look at me at the same time, surprised.

"This?" I say, gesturing between them. "I caused this. I'm sorry I ever asked you guys to be friends. You don't have to be friends. You don't even have to like each other. Forget I said anything."

Warner drops his crossed arms.

Kenji raises his eyebrows.

"I promise," I say. "No more forced hangout sessions. No more spending time alone without me. Okay?"

"You swear?" Kenji says.

"I swear."

"Thank God," Warner says.

"*Same*, bro. Same."

And I roll my eyes, irritated. This is the first thing they've managed to agree on in over a week: their mutual hatred of my hopes for their friendship.

But at least Kenji is finally smiling. He sits down on the couch and seems to relax. Warner takes the seat next to me—still composed, but far less tense.

And that's it. That's all it takes. The tension is gone. Now that they're free to hate each other, they seem perfectly friendly. I don't understand them at all.

"So—you have questions for me, Kishimoto?" Warner says.

Kenji nods, leans forward. "Yeah—yeah, I want to know everything you remember about the Ibrahim family. We've got to be prepared for whatever Haider throws at us at dinner tonight, which"—Kenji looks at his watch, frowns—"is in, like, twenty minutes, no thanks to you guys, but anyway I'm wondering if you can tell us anything about his possible motivations. I'd like to be one step ahead of this dude."

Warner nods. "Haider's family will take more time to unpack. As a whole, they're intimidating. But Haider himself is far less complex. In fact, he's a strange choice for this situation. I'm surprised Ibrahim didn't send his daughter instead."

"Why?"

Warner shrugs. "Haider is less competent. He's self-righteous. Spoiled. Arrogant."

"Wait—are we describing you or Haider?"

Warner doesn't seem to mind the gibe. "You are misunderstanding a key difference between us," he says. "It's true that I am confident. But Haider is arrogant. We are not the same."

"Sounds like the same thing to me."

Warner clasps his hands and sighs, looking for all the world like he's trying to be patient with a difficult child. "Arrogance is false confidence," he says. "It is born from insecurity. Haider pretends to be unafraid. He pretends to be crueler than he is. He lies easily. That makes him unpredictable and, in some ways, a more dangerous opponent. But the majority of the time his actions are inspired by fear." Warner looks up, looks Kenji in the eye. "And that makes him weak."

"Huh. Okay." Kenji sinks further into the couch, processing. "Anything particularly interesting about him? Anything we should be aware of?"

"Not really. Haider is mediocre at most things. He excels only occasionally. He's obsessed mainly with his physique, and most talented with a sniper rifle."

Kenji's head pops up. "Obsessed with his physique, huh? You sure you two aren't related?"

At this, Warner's face sours. "I am *not* obsessed with m—"

"Okay, okay, calm down." Kenji waves his hands around. "No need to worry your pretty little face about it."

"I detest you."

"I love that we feel the same way about each other."

"All right, guys," I say loudly. "Focus. We're having dinner with Haider in like five minutes, and I seem to be the only one worried about this revelation that he's a super-talented sniper."

"Yeah, maybe he's here for some, you know"—Kenji makes a finger gun motion at Warner, and then at himself—"target practice."

Warner shakes his head, still a little annoyed. "Haider is all show. I wouldn't worry about him. As I said, I would only worry if his sister were here—which means we should probably plan to worry very soon." He exhales. "She will almost certainly be arriving next."

At this, I raise my eyebrows. "Is she really scary?"

Warner tilts his head. "Not scary, exactly," he says to me. "She's very cerebral."

"So she's . . . what?" says Kenji. "Psycho?"

"Not at all. But I've always been able to get a sense of people and their emotions, and I could never get a good read on her. I think her mind moves too quickly. There's something kind of . . . flighty about the way she thinks. Like a hummingbird." He sighs. Looks up. "Anyhow, I haven't seen her in several months, at least, but I doubt much about her has changed."

"Like a *hummingbird*?" says Kenji. "So, is she, like, a fast talker?"

"No," says Warner. "She's usually very quiet."

"Hmm. Okay, well, I'm glad she's not here," Kenji says. "Sounds boring."

Warner almost smiles. "She would disembowel you."

Kenji rolls his eyes.

And I'm just about to ask another question when a sudden, harsh ring interrupts the conversation.

Delalieu has come to collect us for dinner.

WARNER

I genuinely dislike being hugged.

There are very few exceptions to this rule, and Haider is not one of them. Even so, every time I see him, he insists on hugging me. He kisses the air on either side of my face, clamps his hands around my shoulders, and smiles at me like I am actually his friend.

"*Hela habibi shlonak?* It's so good to see you."

I attempt a smile. "*Ani zeyn, shukran.*" I nod at the table. "Please, have a seat."

"Sure, sure," he says, and looks around. "*Wenha Nazeera . . . ?*"

"Oh," I say, surprised. "I thought you came alone."

"*La, habibi,*" he says as he sits down. "*Heeya shwaya mitakhira.* But she should be here any minute now. She was very excited to see you."

"I highly doubt that."

"Um, I'm sorry, but am I the only one here who didn't know you speak Arabic?" Kenji is staring at me, wide-eyed.

Haider laughs, eyes bright as he analyzes my face. "Your new friends know so little about you." And then, to Kenji, "Your Regent Warner speaks seven languages."

145

"You speak *seven* languages?" Juliette says, touching my arm.

"Sometimes," I say quietly.

It's a small group of us for dinner tonight; Juliette is sitting at the head of the table. I'm seated to her right; Kenji sits to the right of me.

Across from me now sits Haider Ibrahim.

Across from Kenji is an empty chair.

"So," says Haider, clapping his hands together. "This is your new life? So much has changed since I saw you last."

I pick up my fork. "What are you doing here, Haider?"

"Wallah," he says, clutching his chest, "I thought you'd be happy to see me. I wanted to meet all your new friends. And of course, I had to meet your new supreme commander." He appraises Juliette out of the corner of his eye; the movement is so quick I almost miss it. And then he picks up his napkin, drapes it carefully across his lap, and says, very softly, *"Heeya jidan helwa."*

My chest tightens.

"And is that enough for you?" He leans forward suddenly, speaking so quietly only I can hear him. "A pretty face? And you so easily betray your friends?"

"If you've come here to fight," I say, "please, let's not bother eating dinner."

Haider laughs out loud. Picks up his water glass. "Not yet, *habibi.*" He takes a drink. Sits back. "There's always time for dinner."

"Where is your sister?" I say, turning away. "Why didn't you arrive together?"

"Why don't you ask her yourself?"

I look up, surprised to find Nazeera standing at the door. She studies the room, her eyes lingering on Juliette's face just a second longer than everyone else's, and takes her seat without a word.

"Everyone, this is Nazeera," Haider says, jumping to his feet with a wide smile. He wraps an arm around his sister's shoulder even as she ignores him. "She'll be here for the duration of my stay. I hope you will welcome her as warmly as you've welcomed me."

Nazeera does not say hello.

Haider's face is open, an exaggeration of happiness. Nazeera, however, wears no expression at all. Her eyes are blank, her jaw solemn. The only similarities in these siblings are physical: she bears a remarkable resemblance to her brother. She has his warm brown skin, his light brown eyes, and the same long, dark eyelashes that shutter shut her expression from the rest of us. But she's grown up quite a bit since I last saw her. Her eyes are bigger, deeper than Haider's, and she has a small, diamond piercing centered just underneath her bottom lip. Two more diamonds above her right eyebrow. The only other marked distinction between them is that I cannot see her hair.

She wears a silk shawl around her head.

And I can't help but be quietly shocked. This is new. The Nazeera I remember did not cover her hair—and why would she? Her head scarf is a relic; a part of our past life. It's an artifact of a religion and culture that no longer exists under The Reestablishment. Our movement long ago expunged

147

all symbols and practices of faith or culture in an effort at resetting identities and allegiances; so much so that places of worship were among the first institutions around the world to be destroyed. Civilians, it was said, were to bow before The Reestablishment and nothing else. Crosses, crescents, Stars of David—turbans and yarmulkes, head scarves and nun's habits—

They're all illegal.

And Nazeera Ibrahim—the daughter of a supreme commander—has a staggering amount of nerve. Because this simple scarf, an otherwise insubstantial detail, is nothing less than an open act of rebellion. And I'm so stunned I almost can't help what I say next.

"You cover your hair now?"

At this, she looks up, meets my eyes. She takes a long sip of her tea and studies me. And then, finally—

Says nothing.

I feel my face about to register surprise and I have to force myself to be still. Clearly, she has no interest in discussing the subject. I decide to move on. I'm about to say something to Haider, when,

"So you don't think anyone will notice? That you cover your hair?" It's Kenji, speaking and chewing at the same time. I touch my fingers to my lips and look away, fighting to hide my revulsion.

Nazeera stabs at a piece of lettuce on her plate. Eats it.

"I mean you have to know," Kenji says to her, still chewing, "that what you're wearing is an offense punishable by imprisonment."

She seems surprised to find Kenji still pursuing the subject, her eyes appraising him like he might be an idiot. "I'm sorry," she says softly, putting down her fork, "but who are you, exactly?"

"*Nazeera*," Haider says, trying to smile as he shoots her a careful, sidelong glance. "Please remember that we are guests—"

"I didn't realize there was a dress code here."

"Oh—well, I guess we don't have a dress code *here*," Kenji says between bites, oblivious to the tension. "But that's only because we have a new supreme commander who's not a psychopath. But it's illegal to dress like that," he says, gesturing at her face with his spoon, "like, literally everywhere else. Right?" He looks around, but no one responds. "Isn't it?" he says to me, eager for confirmation.

I nod. Slowly.

Nazeera takes another long drink of her tea, careful to replace the cup in its saucer before she leans back, looks us both in the eye and says, "What makes you think I care?"

"I mean"—Kenji frowns—"don't you have to care? Your dad is a supreme commander. Does he even know that you wear that thing"—another abstract gesture at her head—"in public? Won't he be pissed?"

This is not going well.

Nazeera, who'd just picked up her fork again to spear some bit of food on her plate, puts down her fork and sighs. Unlike her brother, she speaks perfectly unaccented English.

She's looking only at Kenji when she says, "This *thing*?"

"Sorry," he says sheepishly, "I don't know what it's called."

She smiles at him, but there's no warmth in it. Only a warning. "Men," she says, "are always so baffled by women's clothing. So many opinions about a body that does not belong to them. Cover up, don't cover up"—she waves a hand—"no one can seem to decide."

"But—that's not what I—" Kenji tries to say.

"You know what I think," she says, still smiling, "about someone telling me what's legal and illegal about the way I dress?"

She holds up two middle fingers.

Kenji chokes.

"Go ahead," she says, her eyes flashing angrily as she picks up her fork again. "Tell my dad. Alert the armies. I don't give a shit."

"*Nazeera*—"

"Shut up, Haider."

"Whoa—hey—I'm sorry," Kenji says suddenly, looking panicked. "I didn't mean—"

"Whatever," she says, rolling her eyes. "I'm not hungry." She stands up suddenly. Elegantly. There's something interesting about her anger. Her unsubtle protest. And she's more impressive standing up.

She has the same long legs and lean frame as her brother, and she carries herself with great pride, like someone who was born into position and privilege. She wears a gray tunic cut from fine, heavy fabric; skintight leather pants; heavy boots; and a set of glittering gold knuckles on both hands.

And I'm not the only one staring.

Juliette, who's been watching quietly this whole time, is looking up, amazed. I can practically see her thought process as she suddenly stiffens, glances down at her own outfit, and crosses her arms over her chest as if to hide her pink sweater from view. She's tugging at her sleeves as though she might tear them off.

It's so adorable I almost kiss her right then.

A heavy, uncomfortable silence settles between us after Nazeera's gone.

We'd all been expecting an in-depth interrogation from Haider tonight; instead, he pokes quietly at his food, looking tired and embarrassed. No amount of money or prestige can save any of us from the agony of awkward family dinners.

"Why'd you have to say anything?" Kenji elbows me, and I flinch, surprised.

"Excuse me?"

"This is your fault," he hisses, low and anxious. "You shouldn't have said anything about her scarf."

"I asked *one* question," I say stiffly. "*You're* the one who kept pushing—"

"Yeah, but you started it! Why'd you even have to say anything?"

"She's the daughter of a supreme commander," I say, fighting to keep my voice down. "She knows better than anyone else that what she's wearing is illegal under the laws of The Reestablishment—"

"Oh my God," Kenji says, shaking his head. "Just—just stop, okay?"

"How dare you—"

"What are you two whispering about?" Juliette says, leaning in.

"Just that your boyfriend doesn't know when to shut his mouth," Kenji says, scooping up another spoonful of food.

"*You're* the one who can't keep his mouth shut." I turn away. "You can't even manage it while you're eating a bite of food. Of all the disgusting things—"

"Shut up, man. I'm hungry."

"I think I'll retire for the evening also," Haider says suddenly. He stands.

We all look up.

"Of course," I say. I get to my feet to bid him a proper good night.

"*Ani aasef,*" Haider says, looking down at his half-eaten dinner. "I was hoping to have a more productive conversation with all of you this evening, but I'm afraid my sister is unhappy to be here; she didn't want to leave home." He sighs. "But you know Baba," he says to me. "He gave her no choice." Haider shrugs. Attempts a smile. "She doesn't understand yet that what we do—the way we live now"— he hesitates—"it's the life we are given. None of us has a choice."

And for the first time tonight he surprises me; I see something in his eyes I recognize. A flicker of pain. The

152

weight of responsibility. Expectation.

I know too well what it is to be the son of a supreme commander of the Reestablishment—and dare to disagree.

"Of course," I say to him. "I understand."

I really do.

JULIETTE

JULIETTE

Warner escorts Haider back to his residence, and soon after they're gone, the rest of our party breaks apart. It was a weird, too-short dinner with a lot of surprises, and my head hurts. I'm ready for bed. Kenji and I are making our way to Warner's rooms in silence, both of us lost in thought.

It's Kenji who speaks first.

"So—you were pretty quiet tonight," he says.

"Yeah." I laugh, but there's no life in it. "I'm exhausted, Kenji. It was a weird day. An even weirder night."

"Weird how?"

"Um, I don't know, how about we start with the fact that Warner speaks *seven languages*?" I look up, meet his eyes. "I mean, what the hell? Sometimes I think I know him so well, and then something like this happens and it just"—I shake my head—"blows my mind. You were right," I say. "I still know nothing about him. Plus, what am I even doing anymore? I didn't say anything at dinner because I have no idea what to say."

Kenji blows out a breath. "Yeah. Well. Seven languages is pretty crazy. But, I mean, you have to remember that he was born into this, you know? Warner's had schooling you've never had."

"That's exactly my point."

"Hey, you'll be okay," Kenji says, squeezing my shoulder. "It's going to be okay."

"I was just starting to feel like maybe I could do this," I say to him. "I just had this whole talk with Warner today that actually made me feel better. And now I can't even remember why." I sigh. Close my eyes. "I feel so stupid, Kenji. Every day I feel stupider."

"Maybe you're just getting old. Senile." He taps his head. "You know."

"Shut up."

"So, uh"—he laughs—"I know it was a weird night and everything, but—what'd you think? Overall?"

"Of what?" I glance at him.

"Of Haider and Nazeera," he says. "Thoughts? Feelings? Sociopaths, yes or no?"

"Oh." I frown. "I mean, they're so different from each other. Haider is so loud. And Nazeera is . . . I don't know. I've never met anyone like her before. I guess I respect that she's standing up to her dad and The Reestablishment, but I have no idea what her real motivations are, so I'm not sure I should give her too much credit." I sigh. "Anyway, she seems really . . . angry."

And really beautiful. And really intimidating.

The painful truth is that I'd never felt so intimidated by another girl before, and I don't know how to admit that out loud. All day—and for the last couple of weeks—I've felt like an imposter. A child. I hate how easily I fade in and out of confidence, how I waver between who I was and who I could be. My past still clings to me, skeleton hands holding me back even as I push forward into the light. And I can't help but wonder how different I'd be today if I'd ever had someone to encourage me when I was growing up. I never had strong female role models. Meeting Nazeera tonight—seeing how tall and brave she was—made me wonder where she learned to be that way.

It made me wish I'd had a sister. Or a mother. Someone to learn from and lean on. A woman to teach me how to be brave in this body, among these men.

I've never had that.

Instead, I was raised on a steady diet of taunts and jeers, jabs at my heart, slaps in the face. Told repeatedly I was worthless. A monster.

Never loved. Never protected from the world.

Nazeera doesn't seem to care at all what other people think, and I wish so much that I had her confidence. I know I've changed a lot—that I've come a long way from who I used to be—but I want more than anything to just *be* confident and unapologetic about who I am and how I feel, and not have to try so hard all the time. I'm still working on that part of myself.

"Right," Kenji is saying. "Yeah. Pretty angry. But—"

"Excuse me?"

At the sound of her voice we both spin around.

"Speak of the devil," Kenji says under his breath.

"I'm sorry—I think I'm lost," Nazeera says. "I thought

I knew this building pretty well, but there's a bunch of construction going on and it's . . . throwing me off. Can either of you tell me how to get outside?"

She almost smiles.

"Oh, sure," I say, and almost smile back. "Actually"—I pause—"I think you might be on the wrong side of the building. Do you remember which entrance you came in from?"

She stops to think. "I think we're staying on the south side," she says, and flashes me a full, real smile for the first time. Then falters. "Wait. I *think* it was the south side. I'm sorry," she says, frowning. "I just arrived a couple of hours ago—Haider got here before me—"

"I totally understand," I say, cutting her off with a wave. "Don't worry—it took me a while to navigate the construction, too. Actually, you know what? Kenji knows his way around even better than I do. This is Kenji, by the way—I don't think you guys were formally introduced tonight—"

"Yeah, hi," she says, her smile gone in an instant. "I remember."

Kenji is staring at her like an idiot. Eyes wide, blinking. Lips parted ever so slightly. I poke his arm and he yelps, startled, but comes back to life. "Oh, right," he says quickly. "Hi. Hi—yeah, hi, um, sorry about dinner."

She raises an eyebrow at him.

And for the first time in all the time I've known him, Kenji actually blushes. *Blushes.* "No, really," he says. "I, uh, I think your—scarf—is, um, really cool."

"Uh-huh."

"What's it made of?" he says, reaching forward to touch her head. "It looks so soft—"

She slaps his hand away, recoiling visibly even in this dim light. "What the hell? Are you serious right now?"

"What?" Kenji blinks, confused. "What'd I do?"

Nazeera laughs, her expression a mixture of confusion and vague disgust. "How are you *so* bad at this?"

Kenji freezes in place, his mouth agape. "I don't, um—I just don't know, like, what the rules are? Like, can I call you sometime or—"

I laugh suddenly, loud and awkward, and pinch Kenji in the arm.

Kenji swears out loud. Shoots me an angry look.

I plant a bright smile on my face and speak only to Nazeera. "So, yeah, um, if you want to get to the south exit," I say quickly, "your best bet is to go back down the hall and make three lefts. You'll see the double doors on your right— just ask one of the soldiers to take you from there."

"Thanks," Nazeera says, returning my smile before shooting a weird look in Kenji's direction. He's still massaging his injured shoulder as he waves her a weak good-bye.

It's only after she's gone again that I finally spin around, hiss, "What the hell is wrong with you?" and Kenji grabs my arm, goes weak in the knees, and says,

"Oh my God, J, I think I'm in love."

I ignore him.

"No, seriously," he says, "like, is this what that is?

Because I've never been in love before, so I don't know if this is love or if I just have, like, food poisoning?"

"You don't even know her," I say, rolling my eyes, "so I'm guessing it's probably food poisoning."

"You think so?"

I glance up at him, eyes narrowed, but one look is all it takes to lose my thread of anger. His expression is so weird and silly—so slap-happy—I almost feel bad for him.

I sigh, shoving him forward. He keeps stopping in place for no reason. "I don't know. I think maybe you're just, you know—attracted to her? God, Kenji, you gave me so much crap for acting like this over Adam and Warner and now here you are, being all hormonal—"

"Whatever. You owe me."

I frown at him.

He shrugs, still beaming. "I mean, I know she's probably a sociopath. And, like, would definitely murder me in my sleep. But damn she's, wow," he says. "She's, like, batshit pretty. The kind of pretty that makes a man think getting murdered in his sleep might not be a bad way to go."

"Yeah," I say, but I say it quietly.

"Right?"

"I guess."

"What do you mean, *you guess*? I wasn't asking a question. That girl is objectively beautiful."

"Sure."

Kenji stops, takes my shoulders in his hands. "What is your deal, J?"

"I don't know what you're—"

"Oh my God," he says, stunned. "Are you jealous?"

"*No,*" I say, but I practically yell the word at him.

He's laughing now. "That's crazy. Why are you jealous?"

I shrug, mumble something.

"Wait, what's that?" He cups his hand over his ear. "You're worried I'm going to leave you for another woman?"

"Shut up, Kenji. I'm not jealous."

"Aw, J."

"I'm not. I swear. I'm not jealous. I'm just—I'm just . . ."

I'm having a hard time.

But I never have a chance to say the words. Kenji suddenly picks me up, spins me around and says, "Aw, you're so cute when you're jealous—"

And I kick him in the knee. Hard.

He drops me to the floor, grabs his leg, and shouts words so foul I don't even recognize half of them. I sprint away, half guilty, half pleased, his promises to kick my ass in the morning echoing after me as I go.

WARNER

I've joined Juliette on her morning walk today.

She seems deeply nervous now, more so than ever before, and I blame myself for not better preparing her for what she might face as supreme commander. She came back to our room last night in a panic, said something about wishing she spoke more languages, and then refused to talk about it.

I feel like she's hiding from me.

Or maybe I've been hiding from her.

I've been so absorbed in my own head, in my own issues, that I haven't had much of a chance to speak with her, at length, about how she's doing lately. Yesterday was the first time she'd ever brought up her worries about being a good leader, and it makes me wonder how long these fears have been wearing away at her. How long she's been bottling everything up. We have to find more time to talk this all through; but I worry we might both be drowning in revelations.

I'm certain I am.

My mind is still full of Castle's nonsense. I'm fairly certain he'll be proven misinformed, that he's misunderstood some crucial detail. Still, I'm desperate for real answers, and I haven't yet had a chance to go through my father's files.

So I remain here, in this uncertain state.

I'd been hoping to find some time today, but I don't trust Haider and Nazeera to be alone with Juliette. I gave her the space she needed when she first met Haider, but leaving her alone with them now would just be irresponsible. Our visitors are here for all the wrong reasons and likely looking for any reason to play cruel mental Olympics with her emotions. I'd be surprised if they didn't want to terrify and confuse her. To bully her into cowardice. And I'm beginning to worry.

There's so much Juliette doesn't know.

I think I've not made enough of an effort to imagine how she must be feeling. I take too much for granted in this military life, and things that seem obvious to me are still brand-new to her. I need to remember that. I need to tell her that she has her own armory. That she has a fleet of private cars; a personal chauffeur. Several private jets and pilots at her disposal. And then I wonder, suddenly, whether she's ever been on a plane.

I stop, suspended in thought.

Of course she hasn't. She has no recollection of a life lived anywhere but in Sector 45. I doubt she's ever gone for a *swim*, much less sailed on a ship in the middle of the ocean. She's never lived anywhere but in books and memories.

There's still so much she has to learn. So much to overcome. And while I sympathize deeply with her struggles, I really do not envy her in this, the enormity of the task ahead. After all, there's a simple reason I never wanted the job of supreme commander myself—

I never wanted the responsibility.

It's a tremendous amount of work with far less freedom than one might expect; worse, it's a position that requires a great deal of people skills. The kind of people skills that include both killing *and* charming a person at a moment's notice. Two things I detest.

I tried to convince Juliette that she was perfectly capable of stepping into my father's shoes, but she doesn't seem at all persuaded. And with Haider and Nazeera now here, I understand why she seems more uncertain than ever. The two of them—well, it was only Haider, really—asked to join Juliette on her morning walk to the water this morning. She and Kenji had been discussing the matter under their breaths, but Haider has sharper hearing than we suspected. So here we are, the five of us walking along the beach in an awkward silence. Haider and Juliette and I have unintentionally formed a group. Nazeera and Kenji follow some paces behind.

No one is speaking.

Still, the beach isn't a terrible place to spend a morning, despite the strange stench arising from the water. It's actually rather peaceful. The sounds of the breaking waves make for a soothing backdrop against the otherwise already-stressful day.

"So," Haider finally says to me, "will you be attending the Continental Symposium this year?"

"Of course," I answer quietly. "I will attend as I always

have." A pause. "Will you be returning home to attend your own event?"

"Unfortunately not. Nazeera and I were hoping to accompany you to the North American arm, but of course—I wasn't sure if Supreme Commander Ferrars"—he glances at Juliette—"would be making an appearance, so—"

She leans in, eyes wide. "I'm sorry, what are we talking about?"

Haider frowns only a little in response, but I can feel the depth of his surprise. "The Continental Symposium," he says. "Surely you've heard of it?"

Juliette looks at me, confused, and then—

"Oh, yes, of course," she says, remembering. "I've gotten a bunch of letters about that. I didn't realize it was such a big deal."

I have to fight the impulse to cringe.

This was another oversight on my part.

Juliette and I have talked about the symposium, of course, but only briefly. It's a biannual congress of all 555 regents from across the continent. Every sector leader gathered in one place.

It's a massive production.

Haider tilts his head, studying her. "Yes, it's a very big deal. Our father," he says, "is busy preparing for the Asia event, so it's been on my mind quite a bit lately. But as the late Supreme Anderson never attended public gatherings, I wondered whether you would be following in his footsteps."

"Oh, no, I'll be there," Juliette says quickly. "I'm not

hiding from the world the way he did. Of course I'll be there."

Haider's eyes widen slightly. He looks from me to her and back again.

"When is it, exactly?" she says, and I feel Haider's curiosity grow suddenly more intense.

"You've not looked at your invitation?" he asks, all innocence. "The event is in two days."

She suddenly turns away, but not before I see that her cheeks are flushed. I can feel her sudden embarrassment and it breaks my heart. I hate Haider for toying with her like this.

"I've been very busy," she says quietly.

"It's my fault," I cut in. "I was supposed to follow up on the matter and I forgot. But we'll be finalizing the program today. Delalieu is already hard at work arranging all the details."

"Wonderful," Haider says to me. "Nazeera and I look forward to joining you. We've never been to a symposium outside of Asia before."

"Of course," I say. "We'll be delighted to have you with us."

Haider looks Juliette up and down then, examining her outfit, her hair, her plain, worn tennis shoes; and though he says nothing, I can feel his disapproval, his skepticism and ultimately—his disappointment in her.

It makes me want to throw him in the ocean.

"What are your plans for the rest of your stay here?" I

ask, watching him closely now.

He shrugs, perfect nonchalance. "Our plans are fluid. We're only interested in spending time with all of you." He glances at me. "Do old friends really need a reason to see each other?" And for a moment, the briefest moment, I sense genuine pain behind his words. A feeling of neglect.

It surprises me.

And then it's gone.

"In any case," Haider is saying, "I believe Supreme Commander Ferrars has already received a number of letters from our other friends. Though it seems their requests to visit were met with silence. I'm afraid they felt a bit left out when I told them Nazeera and I were here."

"What?" Juliette says, glancing at me before looking back at Haider. "What other friends? Do you mean the other supreme commanders? Because I haven't—"

"Oh—no," Haider says. "No, no, not the other commanders. Not yet, anyway. Just us kids. We were hoping for a little reunion. We haven't gotten the whole group together in far too long."

"The whole group," Juliette says softly. Then she frowns. "How many more kids are there?"

Haider's fake exuberance turns suddenly strange. Cold. He looks at me with both anger and confusion when he says, "You've told her nothing about us?"

Now Juliette is staring at me. Her eyes widen perceptibly; I can feel her fear spike. And I'm still trying to figure out how to tell her not to worry when Haider clamps down on my arm, hard, and pulls me forward.

"What are you doing?" he whispers, the words urgent, violent. "You turned your back on all of us—for what? For *this*? For a *child*? *Inta kullish ghabi*," he says. "So very, very stupid. And I promise you, *habibi*, this won't end well."

There's a warning in his eyes.

I feel it then, when he suddenly lets go—when he unlocks a secret deep within his heart—and something awful settles into the pit of my stomach. A feeling of nausea. Terrible dread.

And I finally understand:

The commanders are sending their children to do the groundwork here because they don't think it's worth their time to come themselves. They want their offspring to infiltrate and examine our base—to use their youth to appeal to the new, young supreme commander of North America, to fake camaraderie—and, ultimately, to send back information. They're not interested in forging alliances.

They're only here to figure out how much work it will take to destroy us.

I turn away, anger threatening to undo my composure, and Haider clamps down harder on my arm. I meet his eyes. It's only my determination to keep things civil for Juliette's sake that prevents me from breaking his fingers off my body.

Hurting Haider would be enough to start a world war.

And he knows this.

"What's happened to you?" he says, still hissing in my ear. "I didn't believe it when I first heard that you'd fallen in love with some idiot psychotic girl. I had more faith in you. I *defended* you. But this," he says, shaking his head, "this is truly heartbreaking. I can't believe how much you've changed."

My fingers tense, itching to form fists, and I'm just about to respond when Juliette, who's been watching us closely from a distance, says, "Let go of him."

And there's something about the steadiness of her voice, something about the barely restrained fury in her words that captures Haider's attention.

He drops my arm, surprised. Spins around.

"Touch him one more time," Juliette says quietly, "and I will rip your heart out of your body."

Haider stares at her. "Excuse me?"

She steps forward. She looks suddenly terrifying. There's a fire in her eyes. A murderous stillness in her movements. "If I ever catch you putting your hands on him again, I will tear open your chest," she says, "and rip out your heart."

Haider's eyebrows fly up his forehead. He blinks. Hesitates. And then: "I didn't realize that was something you could do."

"For you," she says, "I'd do it with pleasure."

Now, Haider smiles. Laughs, out loud. And for the first time since he's arrived, he actually looks sincere. His eyes crinkle with delight. "Would you mind," he says to her, "if I borrowed your Warner for a bit? I promise I won't put my hands on him. I'd just like to speak with him."

She looks at me then, a question in her eyes.

But I can only smile at her. I want to scoop her up and carry her away. Take her somewhere quiet and lose myself in her. I love that the girl who blushes so easily in my arms is the same one who would kill a man for hurting me.

"I won't be long," I say.

And she returns my smile, her face transformed once again. It lasts only a couple of seconds, but somehow time slows down long enough for me to gather the many details of this moment and place it among my favorite memories. I'm grateful, suddenly, for this unusual, supernatural gift I have for sensing emotions. It's still my secret, known only by a few—a secret I'd managed to keep from my father, and from the other commanders and their children. I like how it makes me feel separate—different—from the people I've always known. But best of all, it makes it possible for me to know how deeply Juliette loves me. I can always feel the rush of emotion in her words, in her eyes. The certainty that she would fight for me. Protect me. And knowing this makes my heart feel so full that, sometimes, when we're together, I can hardly breathe.

I wonder if she knows that I would do anything for her.

JULIETTE

"Oh, look! A fish!" I run toward the water and Kenji catches me around the waist, hauls me back.

"That water is *disgusting*, J. You shouldn't get near it."

"What? Why?" I say, still pointing. "Can't you see the fish? I haven't seen a fish in the water in a really long time."

"Yeah, well, it's probably dead."

"What?" I look again, squinting. "No—I don't think—"

"Oh, yeah, it's definitely dead."

We both look up.

It's the first thing Nazeera has said all morning. She's been very quiet, watching and listening to everything with an eerie stillness. Actually, I've noticed she spends most of her time watching her brother. She doesn't seem interested in me the way Haider seems to be, and I find it confusing. I don't understand yet exactly why they're here. I know they're curious about who I am—which, honestly, I get— but there's got to be more to it than just that. And it's this unknowable part—the tension between brother and sister, even—that I can't comprehend.

So I wait for her to say more.

She doesn't.

She's still watching her brother, who's off in the distance

with Warner now, the two of them discussing something we can no longer hear.

It's an interesting scene, the two of them.

Warner is wearing a dark, blood-red suit today. No tie, and no overcoat—even though it's freezing outside—just a black shirt underneath the blazer, and a pair of black boots. He's clutching the handle of a briefcase and a pair of gloves in the same hand, and his cheeks are pink from the cold. Beside him, Haider's hair is a wild, untamed shock of blackness in the gray morning light. He's wearing slim black slacks and yesterday's chain-link shirt underneath a long blue velvet coat, and doesn't seem at all bothered by the wind blowing the jacket open to reveal his heavily built, very bronzed upper body. In fact, I'm pretty sure it's intentional. The two of them walking tall and alone on the deserted beach—heavy boots leaving prints in the sand—makes for a striking image, but they're definitely overdressed for the occasion.

If I were being honest, I'd be forced to admit that Haider is just as beautiful as his sister, despite his aversion to wearing shirts. But Haider seems deeply aware of how handsome he is, which somehow works against him. In any case, none of that matters. I'm only interested in the boy walking beside him. So it's Warner I'm staring at when Kenji says something that pulls me suddenly back to the present.

"I think we better get back to base, J." He checks the time on the watch he's only recently started wearing.

"Castle said he needs to talk to you ASAP."

"Again?"

Kenji nods. "Yeah, and I have to talk to the girls about their progress with James, remember? Castle wants a report. By the way, I think Winston and Alia are finally done fixing your suit, and they actually have a new design for you to look at when you have a chance. I know you still have to get through the rest of your mail from today, but whenever you're done maybe we could—"

"Hey," Nazeera says, waving at us as she walks up. "If you guys are heading back to base, could you do me a favor and grant me clearance to walk around the sector on my own today?" She smiles at me. "I haven't been back here in over a year, and I'd like to look around a little. See what's changed."

"Sure," I say, and smile back. "The soldiers at the front desk can take care of that. Just give them your name, and I'll have Kenji send them my pre-authorizati—"

"Oh—yeah, actually, you know what? Why don't I just show you around myself?" Kenji beams at her. "This place changed a lot in the last year. I'd be happy to be your tour guide."

Nazeera hesitates. "I thought I just heard you say you had a bunch of things to do."

"What? No." He laughs. "Zero things to do. I'm all yours. For whatever. You know."

"*Kenji*—"

He flicks me in the back and I flinch, scowling at him.

"Um, okay," Nazeera says. "Well, maybe later, if you have time—"

"I've got time now," he says, and he's grinning at her like an idiot. Like, an actual idiot. I don't know how to save him from himself. "Should we get going?" he says. "We can start here—I can show you around the compounds first, if you like. Or, I mean, we can start in unregulated territory, too." He shrugs. "Whatever you prefer. Just let me know."

Nazeera looks suddenly fascinated. She's staring at Kenji like she might chop him up and put him in a stew. "Aren't you a member of the Supreme Guard?" she says. "Shouldn't you stay with your commander until she's safely back to base?"

"Oh, uh, yeah—no, she'll be fine," he says in a rush. "Plus we've got these dudes"—he waves at the six soldiers shadowing us—"watching her all the time, so, she'll be safe."

I pinch him, hard, in the side of his stomach.

Kenji gasps, spins around. "We're only like five minutes from base," he says. "You'll be okay getting back by yourself, won't you?"

I glare at him. "Of course I can get back by myself," I shout-whisper. "That's not why I'm mad. I'm mad because you have a million things to do and you're acting like an idiot in front of a girl who is obviously not interested in you."

Kenji steps back, looking injured. "Why are you trying to hurt me, J? Where's your vote of confidence? Where's the love and support I require at this difficult hour? I need you to be my wingwoman."

"You do know that I can hear you, right?" Nazeera tilts her head to one side, her arms crossed loosely against her chest. "I'm standing right here."

She looks somehow even more stunning today, her hair wrapped up in silks that look like liquid gold in the light. She's wearing an intricately braided red sweater, a pair of black, textured leather leggings, and black boots with steel platforms. And she's still got those heavy gold knuckles on both her fists.

I wish I could ask her where she gets her clothes.

I only realize Kenji and I have both been staring at her for too long when she finally clears her throat. She drops her arms and steps cautiously forward, smiling—not unkindly—at Kenji, who seems suddenly unable to breathe. "Listen," she says softly. "You're cute. Really cute. You've got a great face. But this," she says, gesturing between them, "is not happening."

Kenji doesn't appear to have heard her. "You think I've got a great face?"

She laughs and frowns at the same time. Waves two fingers and says, "Bye."

And that's it. She walks away.

Kenji says nothing. His eyes are fixed on Nazeera's disappearing form in the distance.

I pat his arm, try to sound sympathetic. "It'll be okay," I say. "Rejection is har—"

"That was amazing."

"Uh. What?"

He turns to look at me. "I mean, I've always known I had a great face. But now I know, like, for sure that I've got a great face. And it's just so validating."

"You know, I don't think I like this side of you."

"Don't be like that, J." Kenji taps me on the nose. "Don't be jealous."

"I'm not je—"

"I mean, I deserve to be happy, too, don't I?" And he goes suddenly quiet. His smile slips, his laugh dies away, and Kenji looks, if only for a moment—sad. "Maybe one day."

I feel my heart seize.

"Hey," I say gently. "You deserve to be the happiest."

Kenji runs a hand through his hair and sighs. "Yeah. Well."

"Her loss," I say.

He glances at me. "I guess that was pretty decent, as far as rejections go."

"She just doesn't know you," I say. "You're a total catch."

"I know, right? I keep trying to tell people."

"People are dumb." I shrug. "I think you're wonderful."

"Wonderful, huh?"

"Yep," I say, and link my arm in his. "You're smart and funny and kind and—"

"Handsome," he says. "Don't forget handsome."

"And very handsome," I say, nodding.

"Yeah, I'm flattered, J, but I don't like you like that."

My mouth drops open.

"How many times do I have to ask you to stop falling in love with me?"

"Hey!" I say, shoving away from him. "You're terrible."

"I thought I was wonderful."

"Depends on the hour."

And he laughs, out loud. "All right, kid. You ready to head back?"

I sigh, look off into the distance. "I don't know. I think I need a little more time alone. I've still got a lot on my mind. A lot I need to sort through."

"I get it," he says, shooting me a sympathetic look. "Do your thing."

"Thanks."

"Do you mind if I get going, though? All jokes aside, I really do have a lot to take care of today."

"I'll be fine. You go."

"You sure? You'll be okay out here on your own?"

"Yes, yes," I say, and shove him forward. "I'll be more than okay. I'm never really on my own, anyway." I gesture with my head toward the soldiers. "These guys are always following me."

Kenji nods, gives me a quick squeeze on the arm, and jogs off.

Within seconds, I'm alone. I sigh and turn toward the water, kicking at the sand as I do.

I'm so confused.

I'm caught between different worries, trapped by a fear of what seems my inevitable failure as a leader and my fears of Warner's inscrutable past. And today's conversation with Haider didn't help with the latter. His unmasked shock that Warner hadn't even bothered to mention the other families—and the children—he grew up with, really blew me away. It made me wonder how much more I don't know. How much more there is to unearth.

I know exactly how I feel when I look into his eyes, but sometimes being with Warner gives me whiplash. He's so unused to communicating basic things—to anyone—that every day with him comes with new discoveries. The discoveries aren't all bad—in fact, most of the things I learn about him only make me love him more—but even the harmless revelations are occasionally confusing.

Last week I found him sitting in his office listening to old vinyl records. I'd seen his record collection before—he has a huge stack that was apportioned to him by The Reestablishment along with a selection of old books and artwork—he was supposed to be sorting through it all, deciding what to keep and what to destroy. But I'd never seen him just sit and listen to music.

He didn't notice me when I'd walked in that day.

He was sitting very still, looking only at the wall, and listening to what I later discovered was a Bob Dylan record. I know this because I peeked in his office many hours later, after he'd left. I couldn't shake my curiosity; Warner had only listened to one of the songs on the record—he'd reset the needle every time the song finished—and I wanted to know what it was. It turned out to be a song called "Like a Rolling Stone."

I still haven't told him what I saw that day; I wanted to see if he would share the story with me himself. But he never mentioned it, not even when I asked him what he did that afternoon. It wasn't a lie, exactly, but the omission made me wonder why he'd keep it from me.

There's a part of me that wants to rip his history open. I want to know the good and the bad and just get all the secrets out and be done with it. Because right now I feel certain that my imagination is much more dangerous than any of his truths.

But I'm not sure how to make that happen.

Besides, everything is moving so quickly now. We're all so busy, all the time, and it's hard enough to keep my own thoughts straight. I'm not even sure where our resistance is headed at the moment. Everything is worrying me. Castle's worries are worrying me. Warner's mysteries are worrying me. The children of the supreme commanders are worrying me.

I take in a deep breath and exhale, long and loud.

I'm staring out across the water, trying to clear my mind by focusing on the fluid motions of the ocean. It was just three weeks ago that I'd felt stronger than I ever had in my whole life. I'd finally learned how to make use of my powers; I'd learned how to moderate my strength, how to project—and, most important, how to turn my abilities on and off. And then I'd crushed Anderson's legs in my bare hands. I stood still while soldiers emptied countless rounds of lead into my body. I was invincible.

But now?

This new job is more than I bargained for.

Politics, it turns out, is a science I don't yet understand. Killing things, breaking things—destroying things? That, I understand. Getting angry and going to war, I understand. But patiently playing a confusing game of chess with a bunch of strangers from around the world?

God, I'd so much rather shoot someone.

I'm making my way back to base slowly, my shoes filling with sand as I go. I'm actively dreading whatever it is Castle wants to talk to me about, but I've been gone for too long already. There's too much to do, and there's no way out of this but through. I have to face it. Deal with it, whatever it is. I sigh as I flex and unflex my fists, feeling the power come in and out of my body. It's still a strange thrill for me, to be able to disarm myself at will. It's nice to be able to walk around most days with my powers turned off; it's nice to be able to accidentally touch Kenji's skin without worrying I'll hurt him. I scoop up two handfuls of sand. Powers on: I close my fist and the sand is pulverized to dust. Powers off: the sand leaves a vague, pockmarked impression on my skin.

I drop the sand, dusting off the remaining grains from my palms, and squint into the morning sun. I'm searching for the soldiers who've been following me this whole time, because, suddenly, I can't spot them. Which is strange, because I just saw them a minute ago.

And then I feel it—

Pain

It explodes in my back.

It's a sharp, searing, violent pain and I'm blinded by it in an instant. I spin around in a fury that immediately dulls, my senses dimming even as I attempt to harness them. I pull up my Energy, thrumming suddenly with *electricum*, and wonder at my own stupidity for forgetting to turn my powers back on, especially out in the open like this. I was too distracted. Too frustrated. I can feel the bullet in my shoulder blade incapacitating me now, but I fight through the agony to try and spot my attacker.

Still, I'm too slow.

Another bullet hits my thigh, but this time I feel it leave only a flesh wound, bouncing off before it can make much of a mark. My Energy is weak—and weakening by the minute—I think because of the blood I'm losing—and I'm frustrated, so frustrated by how quickly I've been overtaken.

Stupid stupid stupid—

I trip as I try to hurry on the sand; I'm still an open target here. My assailant could be anyone—could be anywhere— and I'm not even sure where to look when suddenly three more bullets hit me: in my stomach, my wrist, my chest. The bullets break off my body and still manage to draw blood, but the bullet buried, buried in my back, is sending blinding flashes of pain through my veins and I gasp, my mouth frozen open and I can't catch my breath and the torment is so intense I can't help but wonder if this is a special gun, if these are special bullets—

oh

The small, breathless sound leaves my body as my knees hit the sand and I'm now pretty sure, fairly certain these bullets have been laced with poison, which would mean that even these, these flesh wounds would be dangero—

I fall, head spinning, backward onto the sand, too dizzy to see straight. My lips feel numb, my bones loose and my blood, my blood all sloshing together fast and weird and I start laughing, thinking I see a bird in the sky—not just one but many of them all at once flying flying *flying*

Suddenly I can't breathe.

Someone has their arm around my neck; they're dragging me backward and I'm choking, spitting up and losing lungs and I can't feel my tongue and I'm kicking at the sand so hard I've lost my shoes and I think here it is, death again, so soon so soon I was too tired anyway and then

The pressure is gone

So swiftly

I'm gasping and coughing and there's sand in my hair and in my teeth and I'm seeing colors and birds, so many birds, and I'm spinning and—

crack

Something breaks and it sounds like bone. My eyesight sharpens for an instant and I manage to see something in front of me. Someone. I squint, feeling like my mouth might swallow itself and I think it must be the poison but it's not; it's Nazeera, so pretty, so pretty standing in front of me, her hands around a man's limp neck and then she drops him to the ground

Scoops me up

You're so strong and so pretty I mumble, so strong and I want to be like you, I say to her

And she says shhh and tells me to be still, tells me I'll be fine

and carries me away.

WARNER

Panic, terror, guilt—unbounded fears—

I can hardly feel my feet as they hit the ground, my heart beating so hard it physically hurts. I'm bolting toward our half-built medical wing on the fifteenth floor and trying not to drown in the darkness of my own thoughts. I have to fight an instinct to squeeze my eyes shut as I run, taking the emergency stairs two at a time because, of course, the nearest elevator is temporarily closed for repairs.

I've never been such a fool.

What was I thinking? What was I *thinking*? I simply walked away. I keep making mistakes. I keep making assumptions. And I've never been so desperate for Kishimoto's inelegant vocabulary. God, the things I wish I could say. The things I'd like to shout. I've never been so angry with myself. I was so sure she'd be fine, I was so sure she knew to never move out in the open unprotected—

A sudden rush of dread overwhelms me.

I will it away.

I will it away, even as my chest heaves with exhaustion and outrage. It's irrational, to be mad at agony—it's futile, I know, to be angry with this pain—and yet, here I am. I feel powerless. I want to see her. I want to hold her. I want to ask her how she could've possibly let her guard down while walking *alone*, out in the *open*—

Something in my chest feels like it might rip apart as I reach the top floor, my lungs burning from the effort. My heart is pumping furiously. Even so, I tear down the hall. Desperation and terror fuel my need to find her.

I stop abruptly in place when the panic returns.

A wave of fear bends my back and I'm doubled over, hands on my knees, trying to breathe. It's unbidden, this pain. Overwhelming. I feel a startling prick behind my eyes. I blink, hard, fight the rush of emotion.

How did this happen? I want to ask her.

Didn't you realize that someone would try to kill *you?*

I'm nearly shaking when I reach the room they're keeping her in. I almost can't make sense of her limp, blood-smeared body laid out on the metal table. I rush forward half blind and ask Sonya and Sara to do again what they've done once before: help me heal her.

It's only then that I realize the room is full.

I'm ripping off my blazer when I notice the others. Figures are pressed up against the walls—forms of people I probably know and can't be bothered to name. Still, somehow, *she* stands out to me.

Nazeera.

I could close my hands around her throat.

"Get out of here," I choke out in a voice that doesn't sound like my own.

She looks genuinely shocked.

"I don't know how you managed this," I say, "but this is your fault—you, and your brother—you did this to her—"

"If you'd like to meet the man responsible," she says, flat and cold, "you're welcome to. He has no identification, but the tattoos on his arms indicate he might be from a neighboring sector. His dead body is in a holding cell underground."

My heart stops, then starts. "What?"

"Aaron?" It's Juliette, Juliette, my Juliette—

"Don't worry, love," I say quickly, "we're going to fix this, okay? The girls are here and we're going to do this again, just like last time—"

"Nazeera," she says, eyes closed, lips half mumbling.

"Yes?" I freeze. "What about Nazeera?"

"Saved"—her mouth halts midmotion, then swallows—"my life."

I look at Nazeera, then. Study her. She seems just about carved from stone, motionless in the middle of chaos. She's staring at Juliette with a curious look on her face, and I can't read her at all. But I don't need a supernatural ability to tell me that something is off about this girl. Basic human instinct tells me there's something she knows—something she's not telling me—and it makes me distrust her.

So when she finally turns in my direction, her eyes deep and steady and frighteningly serious, I feel a bolt of panic pierce me through the chest.

Juliette is sleeping now.

I'm never more grateful for my inhuman ability to steal

and manifest other people's Energies than I am in these unfortunate moments. We've often hoped that now, in the wake of Juliette learning to turn on and off her lethal touch, that Sonya and Sara would be able to heal her—that they'd be able to place their hands on her body in case of emergency without concern for their own safety. But Castle has since pointed out that there's still a chance that, once Juliette's body has begun to heal, her half-healed trauma could instinctively trigger old defenses, even without Juliette's permission. In that state of emergency, Juliette's skin might, accidentally, become lethal once more. It is a risk—an experiment—we were hoping to never again have to face. But now?

What if I weren't around? What if I didn't have this strange gift?

I can't bring myself to think on it.

So I sit here, head in my hands. I wait quietly outside her door as she sleeps off her injuries. The healing properties are still working their way through her body.

Until then, waves of emotion continue to assault me.

It's immeasurable, this frustration. Frustration with Kenji for having left Juliette all alone. Frustration with the six soldiers who were so easily relieved of their guns and their faculties by this single, unidentified assailant. But most of all, *God*, most of all, I've never been so frustrated with myself.

I've been remiss.

I let this happen. My oversights. My stupid infatuation with my own father—the fallout with my own feelings after his death—the pathetic dramas of my past. I let myself get distracted; I was self-absorbed, consumed by my own concerns and daily dealings.

It's my fault.

It's my fault for misunderstanding.

It's my fault for thinking she was fine, that she didn't require more from me—more encouragement, more motivation, more guidance—on a daily basis. She kept showing these tremendous moments of growth and change, and they disarmed me. I'm only now realizing that these moments are misleading. She needs more time, more opportunities to solidify her new strength. She needs to practice; and she needs to be pushed to practice. To be unyielding, to always and forever fight for herself.

And she's come so far.

She is, today, almost unrecognizable from the trembling young woman I first met. She's strong. She's no longer terrified of everything. But she's still only seventeen years old. And she's only been doing this for a short while.

And I keep forgetting.

I should have advised her when she said she wanted to take over the job of supreme commander. I should've said something then. I should've made sure she understood the breadth of what she'd be getting herself into. I should've warned her that her enemies would inevitably make an attempt on her *life*—

I have to pry my hands away from my face. I've unconsciously pressed my fingers so hard into my skin that

I've given myself a brand-new headache.

I sigh and fall back against the chair, extending my legs as my head hits the cold, concrete wall behind me. I feel numb and somehow, still electric. With anger. With impotence. With this impossible need to yell at someone, anyone. My fists clench. I close my eyes. *She has to be okay.* She has to be okay for her sake and for my sake, because I need her, and because I need her to be safe—

A throat clears.

Castle sits down in the seat beside me. I do not look in his direction.

"Mr. Warner," he says.

I do not respond.

"How are you holding up, son?"

An idiotic question.

"This," he says quietly, waving a hand toward her room, "is a much bigger problem than anyone will admit. I think you know that, too."

I stiffen.

He stares at me.

I turn only an inch in his direction. I finally notice the faint lines around his eyes, his forehead. The threads of silver gleaming through the neat dreadlocks tied at his neck. I don't know how old Castle is, but I suspect he's old enough to be my father. "Do you have something to say?"

"She can't lead this resistance," he says, squinting at something in the distance. "She's too young. Too inexperienced. Too angry. You know that, don't you?"

"No."

"It should've been you," Castle says. "I always secretly hoped—from the day you showed up at Omega Point—that it would've been you. That you would join us. And lead us." He shakes his head. "You were born for this. You would've managed it all beautifully."

"I didn't want this job," I say to him, sharp and clipped. "Our nation needed change. It needed a leader with heart and passion and I am not that person. Juliette cares about these people. She cares about their hopes, their fears—and she will fight for them in a way I never would."

Castle sighs. "She can't fight for anyone if she's dead, son."

"Juliette is going to be fine," I say angrily. "She's resting now."

Castle is quiet for a time.

When he finally breaks the silence, he says, "It is my great hope that, very soon, you will stop pretending to misunderstand me. I certainly respect your intelligence too much to reciprocate the pretense." He's staring at the floor. His eyebrows pull together. "You know very well what I'm trying to get at."

"And what is your point?"

He turns to look at me. Brown eyes, brown skin, brown hair. The white flash of his teeth as he speaks. "You say you love her?"

I feel my heart pound suddenly, the sound drumming in my ears. It's so hard for me to admit this sort of thing out loud. To a veritable stranger.

"Do you really love her?" he asks again.

"Yes," I whisper. "I do."

"Then stop her. Stop her before they do. Before this experiment destroys her."

I turn away, my chest heaving.

"You still don't believe me," he says. "Even though you know I'm telling the truth."

"I only know that you *think* you're telling me the truth."

Castle shakes his head. "Her parents are coming for her," he says. "And when they do you'll know for certain that I've not led you astray. But by then," he says, "it'll be too late."

"Your theory doesn't make any sense," I say, frustrated. "I have documents stating that Juliette's biological parents died a long time ago."

He narrows his eyes. "Documents are easily falsified."

"Not in this case," I say. "It isn't possible."

"I assure you that it is."

I'm still shaking my head. "I don't think you understand," I say. "I have all of Juliette's files," I say to him, "and her biological parents' date of death has always been clearly noted. Maybe you confused these people with her *adoptive* parents—"

"The adoptive parents only ever had custody of one child—Juliette—correct?"

"Yes."

"Then how do you explain the second child?"

"What?" I stare at him. "What second child?"

202

"Emmaline, her older sister. You remember Emmaline, of course."

Now I'm convinced Castle is unhinged. "My God," I say. "You really have lost your mind."

"Nonsense," he says. "You've met Emmaline many times, Mr. Warner. You may not have known who she was at the time, but you've lived in her world. You've interacted with her at length. Haven't you?"

"I'm afraid you're deeply misinformed."

"Try to remember, son."

"Try to remember *what*?"

"You were sixteen. Your mother was dying. There were whispers that your father would soon be promoted from commander and regent of Sector 45 to supreme commander of North America. You knew that, in a couple of years, he was going to move you to the capital. You didn't want to go. You didn't want to leave your mother behind, so you offered to take his place. To take over Sector 45. And you were willing to do anything."

I feel the blood exit my body.

"Your father gave you a job."

"No," I whisper.

"Do you remember what he made you do?"

I look into my open, empty hands. My pulse picks up. My mind spirals.

"Do you remember, son?"

"How much do you know?" I say, but my face feels paralyzed. "About me—about *this*?"

"Not quite as much as you do. But more than most."

I sink into the chair. The room spins around me.

I can only imagine what my father would say if he were alive to see this now. *Pathetic. You're pathetic. You have no one to blame but yourself,* he'd say. *You're always ruining everything, putting your emotions before your duty—*

"How long have you known?" I look at him, anxiety sending waves of unwelcome heat up my back. "Why have you never said anything?"

Castle shifts in his chair. "I'm not sure how much I should say on this matter. I don't know how much I can trust you."

"You can't trust *me?*" I say, losing control. "You're the one who's been holding back—all this time"—I glance up suddenly, realizing—"does Kishimoto know about this?"

"No."

My features rearrange. Surprised.

Castle sighs. "He'll know soon enough. Just as everyone else will."

I shake my head in disbelief. "So you're telling me that— that girl—that was her sister?"

Castle nods.

"That's not possible."

"It is a fact."

"How can any of this be true?" I say, sitting up straighter. "I would *know* if it were true. I would have the classified data, I would have been briefed—"

"You're still only a child, Mr. Warner. You forget that

204

sometimes. You forget that your father didn't tell you everything."

"Then how do *you* know? How do you know any of this?"

Castle looks me over. "I know you think I'm foolish," he says, "but I'm not as simple as you might hope. I, too, once tried to lead this nation, and I did a great deal of my own research during my time underground. I spent decades building Omega Point. Do you think I did so without also understanding my enemies? I had files three feet deep on every supreme commander, their families, their personal habits, their favorite colors." He narrows his eyes. "Surely you didn't think I was that naive.

"The supreme commanders of the world have a great deal of secrets," Castle says. "And I'm privy to only a few of them. But the information I gathered on the beginnings of The Reestablishment have proven true."

I can only stare at him, uncomprehending.

"It was on the strength of what I'd uncovered that I knew a young woman with a lethal touch was being held in an asylum in Sector 45. Our team had already been planning a rescue mission when you first discovered her existence—as Juliette Ferrars, an alias—and realized how she might be useful to your own research. So we at Omega Point waited. Bided our time. In the interim, I had Kenji enlist. He was gathering information for several months before your father finally approved your request to move her out of the asylum. Kenji infiltrated the base in Sector 45 on my orders; his mission was always to retrieve Juliette.

205

I've been searching for Emmaline ever since."

"I still don't understand," I whisper.

"Mr. Warner," he says impatiently, "Juliette and her sister have been in the custody of The Reestablishment for twelve years. The two sisters are part of an ongoing experiment for genetic testing and manipulation, the details of which I'm still trying to unravel."

My mind might explode.

"Will you believe me now?" he says. "Have I done enough to prove I know more about your life than you think?"

I try to speak but my throat is dry; the words scrape the inside of my mouth. "My father was a sick, sadistic man," I say. "But he wouldn't have done this. He couldn't have done this to me."

"And yet," Castle says. "He did. He allowed you to bring Juliette on base knowing very well who she was. Your father had a disturbing obsession with torture and experimentation."

I feel disconnected from my mind, my body, even as I force myself to breathe. "Who are her real parents?"

Castle shakes his head. "I don't know yet. Whoever they were, their loyalties to The Reestablishment ran deep. These girls were not stolen from their parents," he says. "They were offered willingly."

My eyes widen. I feel suddenly sick.

Castle's voice changes. He sits forward, his eyes sharp. "Mr. Warner," he says. "I'm not sharing this information with you because I'm trying to hurt you. You must know that this isn't fun for me, either."

I look up.

"I need your help," he says, studying me. "I need to know what you did for those two years. I need to know the details of your assignment to Emmaline. What were you tasked to do? Why was she being held? How were they using her?"

I shake my head. "I don't know."

"You do know," he says. "You must know. *Think*, son. Try to remember—"

"I don't know!" I shout.

Castle sits back, surprised.

"He never told me," I say, breathing hard. "That was the job. To follow orders without questioning them. To do whatever was asked of me by The Reestablishment. To prove my loyalty."

Castle falls back into his seat, crestfallen. He looks shattered. "You were my one remaining hope," he says. "I thought I might finally be able to crack this."

I glance at him, heart pounding. "And I still have no idea what you're talking about."

"There's a reason why no one knows the truth about these sisters, Mr. Warner. There's a reason why Emmaline is kept under such high security. She is critical, somehow, to the structure of The Reestablishment, and I still don't know how or why. I don't know what she's doing for them." He looks me straight in the eye, then, his gaze piercing through me. "Please," he says. "Try to remember. What did he make you do to her? Anything you can remember—anything at all—"

"No," I whisper. I want to scream the word. "I don't want to remember."

"Mr. Warner," he says. "I understand that this is hard for you—"

"Hard for me?" I stand up suddenly. My body is shaking with rage. The walls, the chairs, the tables around us begin to rattle. The light fixtures swing dangerously overhead, the bulbs flickering. "You think this is *hard* for me?"

Castle says nothing.

"What you are telling me right now is that Juliette was planted here, in my life, as part of a larger experiment— an experiment my father had always been privy to. You're telling me that Juliette is not who I think she is. That Juliette Ferrars isn't even her real name. You're telling me that not only is she a girl with a set of living parents, but that I also spent two years unwittingly torturing her sister." My chest heaves as I stare at him. "Is that about right?"

"There's more."

I laugh, out loud. The sound is insane.

"Ms. Ferrars will find out about all this very soon," Castle says to me. "So I would advise you to get ahead of these revelations. Tell her everything as soon as possible. You must confess. Do it now."

"What?" I say, stunned. "Why me?"

"Because if you don't tell her soon," he says, "I assure you, Mr. Warner, that someone else will—"

"I don't care," I say. "You tell her."

"You're not hearing me. It is imperative that she hear this from *you*. She trusts you. She loves you. If she finds out on her own, from a less worthy source, we might lose her."

"I'll never let that happen. I'll never let anyone hurt her again, even if that means I'll have to guard her myself—"

"No, son." Castle cuts me off. "You misunderstand me. I did not mean we would lose her physically." He smiles, but the result is strange. Scared. "I meant we would *lose* her. Up here"—he taps his head—"and here"—he taps his heart.

"What do you mean?"

"Simply that you must not live in denial. Juliette Ferrars is not who you think she is, and she is not to be trifled with. She seems, at times, entirely defenseless. Naive. Even innocent. But you cannot allow yourself to forget the fist of anger that still lives in her heart."

My lips part, surprised.

"You've read about it, haven't you? In her journal," he says. "You've read where her mind has gone—how dark it's been—"

"How did you—"

"And I," he says, "I have seen it. I've seen her lose control of that quietly contained rage with my own eyes. She nearly destroyed all of us at Omega Point long before your father did. She broke the ground in a fit of madness inspired by a simple *misunderstanding*," he says. "Because she was upset about the tests we were running on Mr. Kent. Because she was confused and a little scared. She wouldn't listen to reason—and she nearly killed us all."

209

"That was different," I say, shaking my head. "That was a long time ago. She's different now." I look away, failing to control my frustration at his thinly veiled accusations. "She's *happy*—"

"How can she be truly happy when she's never dealt with her past? She's never addressed it—merely set it aside. She's never had the time, or the tools, to examine it. And that anger—that kind of rage," Castle says, shaking his head, "does not simply disappear. She is volatile and unpredictable. And heed my words, son: Her anger will make an appearance again."

"No."

He looks at me. Picks me apart with his eyes. "You don't really believe that."

I do not respond.

"Mr. Warner—"

"Not like that," I say. "If it comes back, it won't be like that. Anger, maybe—*yes*—but not rage. Not uncontrolled, uninhibited rage—"

Castle smiles. It's so sudden, so unexpected, I stop midsentence.

"Mr. Warner," he says. "What do you think is going to happen when the truth of her past is finally revealed to her? Do you think she will accept it quietly? Calmly? If my sources are correct—and they usually are—the whispers underground affirm that her time here is up. The experiment has come to an end. Juliette murdered a supreme commander. The system won't let her go on like this, her powers unleashed, unchecked. And I have heard that the plan is to obliterate Sector 45." He hesitates. "As for Juliette herself," he says, "it is likely they will either kill her, or place her in another facility."

My mind spins, explodes. "How do you know this?"

Castle laughs briefly. "You can't possibly believe that Omega Point was the only resistance group in North America, Mr. Warner. I'm very well connected underground. And my point still stands." A pause. "Juliette will soon have access to the information necessary to piece together her past. And she will find out, one way or another, your part in all of it."

I look away and back again, eyes wide, my voice fraying. "You don't understand," I whisper. "She would never forgive me."

Castle shakes his head. "If she learns from someone else that you've always known she was adopted? If she hears from someone else that you tortured her sister?" He nods. "Yes, it's true, she will likely never forgive you."

For a sudden, terrible moment, I lose feeling in my knees. I'm forced to sit down, my bones shaking inside me.

"But I didn't know," I say, hating how it sounds, hating that I feel like a child. "I didn't know who that girl was, I didn't know Juliette had a sister— I didn't know—"

"It doesn't matter. Without you, without context, without an explanation or an apology, all of this will be much harder to forgive. But if you tell her yourself and tell her *now*? Your relationship might still stand a chance." He shakes his head.

"Either way, you must tell her, Mr. Warner. Because we have to warn her. She needs to know what's coming, and we have to start planning. Your silence on the subject will end only in devastation."

JULIETTE

JULIETTE

I am a thief.

I stole this notebook and this pen from one of the doctors, from one of his lab coats when he wasn't looking, and I shoved them both down my trousers. This was just before he ordered those men to come and get me. The ones in the strange suits with the thick gloves and the gas masks with the foggy plastic windows hiding their eyes. They were aliens, I remember thinking. I remember thinking they must've been aliens because they couldn't have been human, the ones who handcuffed my hands behind my back, the ones who strapped me to my seat. They stuck Tasers to my skin over and over for no reason other than to hear me scream but I wouldn't. I whimpered but I never said a word. I felt the tears streak down my cheeks but I wasn't crying.

I think it made them angry.

They slapped me awake even though my eyes were open when we arrived. Someone unstrapped me without removing my handcuffs and kicked me in both kneecaps before ordering me to rise. And I tried. I tried but I couldn't and finally six hands shoved me out the door and my face was bleeding on the concrete for a while. I can't really remember the part where they dragged me inside.

I feel cold all the time.

I feel empty, like there is nothing inside of me but this broken heart, the only organ left in this shell. I feel the bleats echo within me, I feel the thumping reverberate around my skeleton. I have a heart, says science, but I am a monster, says society. And I know it, of course I know it. I know what I've done. I'm not asking for sympathy. But sometimes I think—sometimes I wonder—if I were a monster—surely, I would feel it by now?

I would feel angry and vicious and vengeful. I'd know blind rage and bloodlust and a need for vindication.

Instead, I feel an abyss within me that's so deep, so dark I can't see within it; I can't see what it holds. I do not know what I am or what might happen to me.

I do not know what I might do again.

—AN EXCERPT FROM JULIETTE'S JOURNALS IN THE ASYLUM

I'm dreaming about birds again.

I wish they would go away already. I'm tired of thinking about them, hoping for them. Birds, birds, birds—why won't they go away? I shake my head as if to clear it, but feel my mistake at once. My mind is still dense and foggy, swimming in confusion. I blink open my eyes slowly, tentatively, but no matter how far I force them open, I can't seem to take in any light. It takes me too long to understand that I've awoken in the middle of the night.

A sharp gasp.

That's me, my voice, my breath, my quickly beating heart. Where is my head? Why is it so heavy? My eyes close fast, sand stuck in the lashes, sticking them together. I try to clear the haze—try to remember—but parts of me still feel numb, like my teeth and toes and the spaces between my ribs and I laugh, suddenly, and I don't know why—

I was shot.

My eyes fly open, my skin breaking into a sudden, cold sweat.

Oh my God I was shot, I was shot I was shot

I try to sit up and can't. I feel so heavy, so heavy with blood and bone and suddenly I'm freezing, my skin is cold rubber and clammy against the metal table I'm sticking to and all at once

I want to cry

all at once I'm back in the asylum, the cold and the metal and the pain and the delirium all confusing me and then I'm weeping, silently, hot tears warming my cheeks and I can't speak but I'm scared and I hear them, I hear them

the others

screaming

Flesh and bone breaking in the night, hushed, muffled voices—suppressed shouts—cellmates I'd never see—

Who were they? I wonder.

I haven't thought about them in so long. What happened to them. Where they came from. Who did I leave behind?

My eyes are sealed shut, my lips parted in quiet terror. I haven't been haunted like this in so long so long so long

It's the drugs, I think. *There was poison in those bullets.*

Is that why I can see the birds?

I smile. Giggle. Count them. Not just the white ones, white with streaks of gold like crowns atop their heads, but blue ones and black ones and yellow birds, too. I see them when I close my eyes but I saw them today, too, on the beach and they looked so real, so real

Why?

Why would someone try to kill me?

Another sudden jolt to my senses and I'm more alert,

more myself, panic clearing the poison for a single moment of clarity and I'm able to push myself up, onto my elbows, head spinning, eyes wild as they scan the darkness and I'm just about to lie back down, exhausted, when I see something—

"Are you awake?"

I inhale sharply, confused, trying to make sense of the sounds. The words are warped like I'm hearing them underwater and I swim toward them, trying, trying, my chin falling against my chest as I lose the battle.

"Did you see anything today?" the voice says to me. "Anything . . . strange?"

"Who—where, where are you—" I say, reaching blindly into the dark, eyes only half open now. I feel resistance and wrap my fingers around it. A hand? A strange hand. It's a mix of metal and flesh, a fist with a sharp edge of steel.

I don't like it.

I let go.

"Did you see anything today?" it says again.

I mumble.

"What did you see?" it says.

And I laugh, remembering. I could hear them—hear their *caw caws* as they flew far above the water, could hear their little feet walking along the sand. There were so many of them. Wings and feathers, sharp beaks and talons.

So much motion.

"What did you *see*—?" the voice demands again, and it makes me feel strange.

"I'm cold," I say, and lie down again. "Why is it so cold?"

A brief silence. A rustle of movement. I feel a heavy blanket drape over the simple sheet already covering my body.

"You should know," the voice says to me, "that I'm not here to hurt you."

"I know," I say, though I don't understand why I've said it.

"But the people you trust are lying to you," the voice is saying. "And the other supreme commanders only want to kill you."

I smile wide, remembering the birds. "Hello," I say.

Someone sighs.

"I'll see you in the morning. We'll talk another time," the voice says. "When you're feeling better."

I'm so warm now, warm and tired and drowning again in strange dreams and distorted memories. I feel like I'm swimming in quicksand and the harder I pull away, the more quickly I am devoured and all I can think is

here

in the dark, dusty corners of my mind

I feel a strange relief.

I am always welcome here

in my loneliness, in my sadness

in this abyss, there is a rhythm I remember. The steady drop of tears, the temptation to retreat, the shadow of my past

the life I choose to forget has not
will never
ever
forget *me*

WARNER

I've been awake all night.

Infinite boxes lie open before me, their innards splayed across the room. Papers are stacked on desks and tables, spread open on my floor. I'm surrounded by files. Many thousands of pages of paperwork. My father's old reports, his work, the documents that ruled his life—

I have read them all.

Obsessively. Desperately.

And what I've found within these pages does nothing to soothe me, no—

I am distraught.

I sit here, cross-legged on the floor of my office, suffocated on all sides by the sight of a familiar typeset and my father's too-legible scrawl. My right hand is caught behind my head, desperate for a length of hair to yank out of my skull and finding none. This is so much worse than I had feared, and I don't know why I'm so surprised.

This is not the first time my father has kept secrets from me.

It was after Juliette escaped Sector 45, after she ran away with Kent and Kishimoto and my father came here to clean up the mess—that was when I learned, for the first time, that my father had knowledge of their world. Of others with abilities.

He'd kept it from me for so long.

I'd heard rumors, of course—from the soldiers, from the civilians—of various unusual sightings and stories, but I brushed them off as nonsense. A human need to find a magical portal to escape our pain.

But there it was—all true.

After my father's revelation, my thirst for information became suddenly insatiable. I needed to know more—who these people were, where they'd come from, how much we'd known—

And I unearthed truths I wish every day I could unlearn.

There are asylums, just like Juliette's, all over the world. *Unnaturals,* as The Reestablishment calls them, were rounded up in the name of science and discovery. But now, finally, I'm understanding how it all began. Here, in these stacks of papers, are all the horrible answers I sought.

Juliette and her sister were the very first Unnatural finds of The Reestablishment. The discovery of these girls' unusual abilities led to the discoveries of other people like them, all over the world. The Reestablishment went on to collect as many Unnaturals as they could find; they told the civilians they were cleansing them of their old and their ill and imprisoning them in camps for closer medical examination.

But the truth was rather more complicated.

The Reestablishment quickly weeded out the useful Unnaturals from the nonuseful for their own benefit. The ones with the best abilities were absorbed by the system—divvied up around the world by the supreme commanders for their personal use in perpetuating the wrath of The Reestablishment—and the others were disposed of. This led to the eventual rise of The Reestablishment, and, with it, the many asylums that would house the other Unnaturals around the globe. For further studies, they'd said. For testing.

Juliette had not yet manifested abilities when she was donated to The Reestablishment by her parents. No. It was her *sister* who started it all.

Emmaline.

It was Emmaline whose preternatural gifts startled everyone around them; the sister, Emmaline, was the one who unwittingly drew attention to herself and her family. The unnamed parents were frightened by their daughter's frequent and incredible displays of psychokinesis.

They were also fanatics.

There's limited information in my father's files about the mother and father who willingly gave up their children for experimentation. I've scoured every document and was able to glean only a little about their motives, ultimately piecing together from various notes and extraneous details a startling depiction of these characters. It seems these people had an unhealthy obsession with The Reestablishment. Juliette's biological parents were devoted to the cause long before it had even gained momentum as an international movement, and they thought that studying their daughter might help shed light on the current world and its many ailments. If this was happening to Emmaline, they theorized, maybe it was happening to others—and maybe, somehow, this was information that could be used to help better the world. In no time at all The Reestablishment had Emmaline in custody.

Juliette was taken as a precaution.

If the older sibling had proven herself capable of incredible feats, The Reestablishment thought the younger sister might, too. Juliette was only five years old, and she was held under close surveillance.

After a month in a facility, Juliette showed no signs of a special ability. So she was injected with a drug that would destroy critical parts of her memory, and sent to live in Sector 45, under my father's supervision. Emmaline had kept her real name, but the younger sister, unleashed into the real world, would need an alias. They renamed her Juliette, planted false memories in her head, and assigned her adoptive parents who, only too happy to bring home a child into their childless family, followed instructions to never tell the child that she'd been adopted. They also had no idea that they were being watched. All other useless Unnaturals were, generally, killed off, but The Reestablishment chose to monitor Juliette in a more neutral setting. They hoped a home life would inspire a latent ability within her. She was too valuable as a blood relation to the very talented Emmaline to be so quickly disposed of.

It is the next part of Juliette's life that I was most familiar with.

I knew of Juliette's troubles at home, her many moves.

I knew of her family's visits to the hospital. Their calls to the police. Her stays in juvenile detention centers. She lived in the general area that used to be Southern California before she settled in a city that became firmly a part of what is now Sector 45, always within my father's reach. Her upbringing among the ordinary people of the world was heavily documented by police reports, teachers' complaints, and medical files attempting to understand what she was becoming. Eventually, upon finally discovering the extremes of Juliette's lethal touch, the vile people chosen to be her adoptive parents would go on to abuse her—for the rest of her adolescent life with them—and, ultimately, return her to The Reestablishment, which was only too happy to receive her.

It was The Reestablishment—my own father—who put Juliette back in isolation. For more tests. More surveillance.

And this was when our worlds collided.

Tonight, in these files, I was finally able to make sense of something both terrible and alarming:

The supreme commanders of the world have always known Juliette Ferrars.

They've been watching her grow up. She and her sister were handed over by their psychotic parents, whose allegiance to The Reestablishment overruled all else. Exploiting these girls—understanding their powers—was what helped The Reestablishment dominate the world. It was through the exploitation of other innocent Unnaturals that The Reestablishment was able to conquer and manipulate people and places so quickly.

This, I now realize, is why they've been so patient with a seventeen-year-old who's declared herself ruler of an entire continent. This is why they've so quietly abided the truth of her having slaughtered one of their fellow commanders.

And Juliette has no idea.

She has no idea she's being played and preyed upon. She has no idea that she has no real power here. No chance at change. No opportunity to make a difference in the world. She was, and will forever be nothing more than a toy to them—a science experiment to watch carefully, to make certain the concoction doesn't boil over too soon.

But it did.

Juliette failed their tests over a month ago, and my father tried to kill her for it. He tried to kill her because he'd decided that she'd become a distraction. Gone was the opportunity for this *Unnatural* to grow into an adversary.

The monster we've bred has tried to kill my own son. She's since attacked me like a feral animal, shooting me in both my legs. I've never seen such wildness—such blind, inhuman rage. Her mind shifts without warning. She showed no signs of psychosis upon first arrival in the house, but appeared to dissociate from any structure of rational thought while attacking me. Having seen her instability with my own eyes makes me only more certain of what needs to be done. I write this now as a decree from my hospital bed, and as a precaution to my fellow commanders. In the case that I don't recover from these wounds and am unable to follow through with what needs to be done: You, who are reading this now, you must react. Finish what I could not do. The younger sister is a failed experiment. She is, as we feared, disconnected from humanity. Worse, she's become a distraction for Aaron. He's become—in a toxic turn of events—impossibly drawn to her, with no apparent regard for his own safety. I have no idea what she's done to his mind. I only know now that I should never have entertained my own curiosity by allowing him to bring her on base. It's a shame, really, that she is nothing like her elder sister. Instead, Juliette Ferrars has become an incurable cancer we must cut out of our lives for good.

—AN EXCERPT FROM ANDERSON'S DAILY LOG

Juliette threatened the balance of The Reestablishment.

She was an experiment gone wrong. And she'd become a liability. She needed to be expunged from the earth.

My father tried so hard to destroy her.

And I see now that his failure has been of great interest to the other commanders. My father's daily logs were shared; all the supreme commanders shared their logs with one another. It was the only way for the six of them to remain apprised, at all times, of each other's daily goings-on.

So. They knew his story. They've known about my feelings for her.

And they have their orders to kill Juliette.

But they're waiting. And I have to assume there's

something more—some other explanation for their hesitation. Maybe they think they can rehabilitate her. Maybe they're wondering whether Juliette cannot still be of service to them and to their cause, much like her sister has been.

Her sister.

I'm haunted at once by a memory of her.

Brown-haired and bony. Jerking uncontrollably underwater. Long brown waves suspended, like jittery eels, around her face. Electric wires threaded under her skin. Several tubes permanently attached to her neck and torso. She'd been living underwater for so long when I first saw her that she hardly resembled a person. Her flesh was milky and shriveled, her mouth stretched out in a grotesque O, wrapped around a regulator that forced air into her lungs. She's only a year older than Juliette. And she's been held in captivity for twelve years.

Still alive, but only barely.

I had no idea she was Juliette's sister. I had no idea she was anyone at all. When I first met my assignment, she had no name. I was given only instructions, and ordered to follow them. I didn't know who or what I'd been assigned to oversee. I understood only that she was a prisoner—and I knew she was being tortured—but I didn't know then that there was anything supernatural about the girl. I was an idiot. A child.

I slam the back of my head against the wall, once. Hard. My eyes squeeze shut.

Juliette has no idea she ever had a real family—a horrible, insane family—but a family nonetheless. And if Castle is to be believed, The Reestablishment is coming for her. To kill her. To exploit her. So we have to act. I have to warn her, and I have to do it as soon as possible.

But how—how do I tell her any of this? How do I tell her without explaining my part in all of this?

I've always known Juliette was adopted, but I never told her this truth simply because I thought it would make things worse. My understanding was that Juliette's biological parents were long dead. I didn't see how telling her that she had real, dead parents would make her life any better.

But that doesn't change the fact that I knew.

And now I have to confess. Not just this, but the truth about her sister—that she is still alive and being actively tortured by The Reestablishment. That I contributed to that torture.

Or this:

That I am the true monster, completely and utterly unworthy of her love.

I close my eyes, press the back of my hand to my mouth and feel my body break apart within me. I don't know how to extricate myself from the mess made by my own father. A mess in which I was unintentionally complicit. A mess that, upon its unveiling, will destroy the little bit of happiness I've managed to piece together in my life.

Juliette will never, ever forgive me.

I will lose her.
And it will kill me.

JULIETTE

I wonder what they're thinking. My parents. I wonder where they are. I wonder if they're okay now, if they're happy now, ~~if they finally got what they wanted~~ I wonder if my mother will have another child. I wonder if someone will ever be kind enough to kill me and I wonder if hell is better than here. I wonder what my face looks like now. I wonder if I'll ever breathe fresh air again.

I wonder about so many things.

Sometimes I'll stay awake for days just counting everything I can find. I count the walls, the cracks in the walls, my fingers and toes. I count the springs in the bed, the threads in the blanket, the steps it takes to cross the room and back. I count my teeth and the individual hairs on my head and the number of seconds I can hold my breath.

But sometimes I get so tired that I forget I'm not allowed to wish for things anymore and I find myself wishing for the one thing I've always wanted. The only thing I've always dreamt about.

I wish all the time for a friend.

I dream about it. I imagine what it would be like. To smile and be smiled upon. To have a person to confide in, someone who wouldn't throw things at me or stick my hands in the fire or beat me for being born. Someone who would hear that I'd been thrown away and would try to find me, who would never be afraid of me.

Someone who'd know I'd never try to hurt them.

Someone who'd know I'd never try to hurt them.

I fold myself into a corner of this room and bury my head in my knees and rock back and forth and back and forth and back and forth and I wish and I wish and I wish and I dream of impossible things until I've cried myself to sleep.

I wonder what it would be like to have a friend.

And then I wonder who else is locked in this asylum. I wonder where the other screams are coming from.

I wonder if they're coming from me.

—AN EXCERPT FROM JULIETTE'S JOURNALS IN THE ASYLUM

I feel strange this morning.

I feel slow, like I'm wading through mud, like my bones have filled with lead and my head, *oh*—

I flinch.

My head has never been heavier.

I wonder if it's the last dregs of the poison still haunting my veins, but something feels wrong with me today. My memories of my time in the asylum are suddenly too present—perched too fully at the forefront of my mind. I thought I'd managed to shove those memories out of my head but no, here they are again, dredged out of the darkness. 264 days in perfect isolation. Nearly a year without access or outlet to the outside. To another human being.

So long, so long, so very, very long without the warmth of human contact.

I shiver involuntarily. Jerk upward.

What's wrong with me?

Sonya and Sara must've heard me moving because they're now standing before me, their voices clear but somehow, vibrating. Echoing off the walls. My ears won't stop ringing. I squint to make sense of their faces but I feel dizzy suddenly, disoriented, like my body is sideways or maybe flat on the ground or maybe *I* need to be flat on the ground, or *oh*

oh I think I might be sick—

"Thank you for the bucket," I say, still nauseous. I try to sit up and for some reason I can't remember how. My skin has broken out in a cold sweat. "What's wrong with me?" I say. "I thought you healed—healed—"

I'm gone again.

Head spinning.

Eyes closed against the light. The floor-to-ceiling windows we've installed can't seem to block the sun from invading the room and I can't help but wonder when I've ever seen the sun shine so brightly. Over the last decade our world collapsed inward, the atmosphere unpredictable, the weather changing in sharp and dramatic spikes. It snows where it shouldn't; rains where it once couldn't; the clouds are always gray; the birds gone forever from the sky. The once-bright green leaves of trees and lawns are now dull and brittle with decay. It's March now, and even as we approach spring the sky shows no sign of change. The earth is still cold, still iced over, still dark and muddy.

Or at least, it was yesterday.

Someone places a cool rag on my forehead and the cold is welcome; my skin feels inflamed even as I shiver. Slowly, my muscles unclench. But I wish someone would do something about the glaring sunlight. I'm squinting, even with my eyes closed, and it's making my headache worse.

"The wound is fully healed," I hear someone saying, "but it looks like the poison hasn't worked its way out of her system—"

"I don't understand," says another voice. "How is that possible? Why aren't you able to heal her completely?"

"Sonya," I manage to say. "Sara?"

"Yes?" The twin sisters answer at the same time, and I can feel the rush of their footsteps, hard like drumbeats against my head, as they hurry to my bedside.

I try to gesture toward the windows. "Can we do something about the sun?" I say. "It's too bright."

They help me up into a seated position and I feel my head-spin begin to steady. I blink my eyes open with a great deal of effort just in time to have someone hand me a cup of water.

"Drink this," Sonya says. "Your body is severely dehydrated."

I gulp the water down quickly, surprised by my own thirst. They hand me another glass. I drink that, too. I have to drink five glasses of water before I can hold my head up without immense difficulty.

When I finally feel more normal, I look around. Eyes wide-open. I have a massive headache, but the other symptoms are beginning to fade.

I see Warner first.

He's standing in a corner of the room, eyes bloodshot, yesterday's clothes rumpled on his body, and he's staring at me with a look of unmasked fear that surprises me. It's entirely unlike him. Warner rarely shows emotion in public.

I wish I could say something, but it doesn't feel like the right time. Sonya and Sara are still watching me carefully, their hazel eyes bright against their brown skin. But something about them looks different to me. Maybe it's that I've never looked at them this closely anywhere but underground, but the brilliant light of the sun has reduced their pupils to the size of pinpricks, and it makes their eyes look different. Bigger. *New*.

"The light is so strange today," I can't help saying. "Has it ever been this bright?"

Sonya and Sara glance out the window, glance back at me, and frown at each other. "How are you feeling?" they say. "Does your head still hurt? Do you feel dizzy?"

"My head is killing me," I say, and try to laugh. "What was in those bullets?" I pinch the bridge of my nose between my thumb and index finger. "Do you know if the headache will go away soon?"

"Honestly—we're not sure what's happening right now." This, from Sara.

"Your wound is mended," says Sonya, "but it seems the poison is still affecting your mind. We can't know for sure if it was able to cause permanent damage before we got to you."

At this, I look up. Feel my spine stiffen. "Permanent damage?" I say. "To my brain? Is that really possible?"

They nod. "We'll monitor you closely for the next couple of weeks just to be sure. The illusions you're experiencing might end up being nothing."

"What?" I look around. Look at Warner, who still won't speak. "What illusions? I just have a headache." I squint again, turning away from the window. "Yikes. Sorry," I say, eyes narrowed against the light, "it's been so long since we've had days like this"—I laugh—"I think I'm more accustomed to the dark." I place my hand over my eyes like a visor. "We really need to get some shades on these windows. Someone remind me to tell Kenji about that."

Warner has gone gray. He looks frozen in his skin.

Sonya and Sara share a look of concern.

"What is it?" I say, my stomach sinking as I look at the three of them. "What's wrong? What are you not telling me?"

"There's no sun today," Sonya says quietly. "It's snowing again."

"It's dark and cloudy, just like every other day," says Sara.

"What? What are you talking about?" I say, laughing and frowning at the same time. I can *feel* the heat of the sun on my face. I see it make a direct impact in their eyes, their pupils dilating as they move into the shadows. "You're joking, right? The sun is so bright I can barely look out the window."

Sonya and Sara shake their heads.

Warner is staring at the wall, both hands locked behind his neck.

I feel my heart begin to race. "So I'm seeing things?" I say to them. "I'm hallucinating?"

They nod.

"Why?" I say, trying not to panic. "What's happening to me?"

"We don't know," Sonya says, looking into her hands. "But we're hoping these effects are just temporary."

I try to slow my breathing. Try to remain calm. "Okay. Well. I need to go. Can I go? I have a thousand things to do—"

"Maybe you should stay here a little while longer," says Sara. "Let us watch you for a few more hours."

But I'm shaking my head. "I need to get some air—I need to go outside—"

"*No*—"

It's the first thing Warner's said since I woke up, and he nearly shouts the word at me. He's holding up his hands in a silent plea.

"No, love," he says, sounding strange. "You can't go outside again. Not—not just yet. Please."

The look on his face is enough to break my heart.

I slow down, feel my racing pulse steady as I stare at him. "I'm so sorry," I say. "I'm sorry I scared everyone. It was a moment of stupidity and it was totally my fault. I let my guard down for just a *second*." I sigh. "I think someone had been watching me, waiting for the right moment. Either way, it won't happen again."

I try to smile, and he doesn't budge. Won't smile back.

"Really," I try again. "Don't worry. I should've realized there would be people out there waiting to kill me the moment I seemed vulnerable, but"—I laugh—"believe me, I'll be more careful next time. I'll even ask to have a larger guard follow me around."

He shakes his head.

I study him, his terror. I don't understand it.

I make an effort to get to my feet. I'm in socks and a hospital gown, and Sonya and Sara hurry me into a robe and slippers. I thank them for everything they've done and they squeeze my hands.

"We'll be right outside if you need anything," they say in unison.

"Thank you again," I say, and smile. "I'll let you know how it goes with the, um"—I point to my head—"weird visions."

They nod and disappear.

I take a tentative step toward Warner.

"Hey," I say gently. "I'm going to be okay. Really."

"You could've been killed."

"I know," I say. "I've been so off lately—I wasn't thinking. But this was a mistake I will never make again." A short laugh. "Really."

Finally, he sighs. He releases the tension in his shoulders. Runs a hand along the length of his face, the back of his neck.

I've never seen him like this before.

"I'm so sorry I scared you," I say.

"Please don't apologize to me, love. You don't have to worry about me," he says, shaking his head. "I've been worried about *you*. How are you feeling?"

"Other than the hallucinating, you mean?" I crack a half grin. "I feel okay. It took me a minute to come back to myself this morning, but I feel much better now. I'm sure the strange visions will be gone soon, too." I smile, wide, more for his benefit than mine. "Anyway, Delalieu wants me to meet with him ASAP to talk about my speech for the symposium, so I'm thinking maybe I should go do that. I can't believe it's happening *tomorrow*." I shake my head. "I can't afford to waste any more time. Although"—I look down at myself—"maybe I should take a shower first? Put on some real clothes?"

I try to smile at him again, to convince him that I'm feeling fine, but he seems unable to speak. He just looks at me, his eyes red-rimmed and raw. If I didn't know him any better I'd think he'd been crying.

I'm just about to ask him what's wrong, when he says "Sweetheart."

and for some reason I hold my breath.

"I have to talk to you," he says.

He whispers it, actually.

"Okay," I say, and exhale. "Talk to me."

"Not here."

I feel my stomach flip. My instincts tell me to panic. "Is everything okay?"

It takes him a long time to say, "I don't know."

I stare at him, confused.

He stares back, his eyes such a pale green in the light

that, for a moment, he doesn't even seem human. He says nothing more.

I take a deep breath. Try to be calm. "Okay," I say. "Okay. But if we're going to go back to the room, can I at least shower first? I'd really like to get all this sand and dried blood off my body."

He nods. Still no emotion.

And now I'm really beginning to panic.

WARNER

I'm pacing the length of the hall just outside of our room, impatiently waiting for Juliette to finish her shower. My mind is ravaged. Hysteria has been clawing at my insides for hours. I have no idea what she'll say to me. How she'll react to what I need to tell her. And I'm so horrified by what I'm about to do that I don't even hear someone calling my name until they've touched me.

I spin around too fast, my reflexes faster than even my mind. I've got his hand pinched up at the wrist and wound behind his back and I've slammed him chest-first into the wall before I realize it's Kent. Kent, who's not fighting back, just laughing and telling me to let go of him.

I do.

I drop his arm. Stunned. Shake my head to clear it. I don't remember to apologize.

"Are you okay?" someone else says to me.

It's James. He's still the size of a child, and for some reason this surprises me. I take a careful breath. My hands are shaking. I've never felt further from *okay*, and I'm too confused by my anxiety to remember to lie.

"No," I say to him. I step backward, hitting the wall behind me and slumping to the floor. "No," I say again, and

251

this time I don't know who I'm speaking to.

"Oh. Do you want to talk about it?" James is still blathering. I don't understand why Kent won't make him stop.

I shake my head.

But this only seems to encourage him. He sits down beside me. "Why not? I think you should talk about it," he says.

"C'mon, buddy," Kent finally says to him. "Maybe we should give Warner some privacy."

James will not be convinced. He peers into my face. "Were you *crying*?"

"Why do you ask so many questions?" I snap, dropping my head in one hand.

"What happened to your hair?"

I look up at Kent, astounded. "Will you please retrieve him?"

"You shouldn't answer questions with other questions," James says to me, and puts a hand on my shoulder. I nearly jump out of my skin.

"Why are you touching me?"

"You look like you could use a hug," he says. "Do you want a hug? Hugs always make me feel better when I'm sad."

"No," I say, fast and sharp. "I do not want a *hug*. And I'm not sad."

Kent appears to be laughing. He stands a few feet away from us with his arms crossed, doing nothing to help the situation. I glare at him.

"Well you *seem* sad," James says.

"Right now," I say stiffly, "all I'm feeling is irritation."

"Bet you feel better though, huh?" James smiles. Pats my arm. "See—I told you it helps to talk about it."

I blink, surprised. Stare at him.

He's not exactly correct in his theory, but oddly enough, I do feel better. Getting frustrated just now, with him—it helped clear my panic and focus my thoughts. My hands have steadied. I feel a little sharper.

"Well," I say. "Thank you for being annoying."

"*Hey.*" He frowns. He gets to his feet, dusts off his pants. "I'm not annoying."

"You most certainly are annoying," I tell him. "Especially for a child your size. Why haven't you have learned to be quieter by now? When I was your age I only spoke when I was spoken to."

James crosses his arms. "Wait a second—what do you mean, *for a child my size*? What's wrong with my size?"

I squint at him. "How old are you? Nine?"

"I'm about to turn eleven!"

"You're very small for eleven."

And then he punches me. Hard. In the thigh.

"*Owwwwwww,*" he cries, overzealous in his exaggeration of the simple sound. He shakes out his fingers. Scowls at me. "Why does your leg feel like *stone*?"

"Next time," I say, "you should try picking on someone your own size."

He narrows his eyes at me.

"Don't worry," I say to him. "I'm sure you'll get taller soon. I didn't hit my growth spurt until I was about twelve or thirteen, and if you're anything like me—"

Kent clears his throat, hard, and I catch myself.

"That is—if you're anything like, ah, your brother, I'm sure you'll be just fine."

James looks back at Kent and smiles, the awkward punch apparently forgotten. "I really hope I'm like my brother," James says, beaming now. "Adam is the best, isn't he? I hope I'm just like him."

I feel the smile break off my face. This little boy. He's also mine, *my brother,* and he may never know it.

"Isn't he?" James says, still smiling.

I startle. "Excuse me?"

"Adam," he says. "Isn't Adam the best? He's the best big brother in the world."

"Oh—yes," I say to him, clearing the catch in my throat. "Yes, of course. Adam is, ah, the best. Or some approximation thereof. In any case, you're very lucky to have him."

Kent shoots me a look, but says nothing.

"I know," James says, undeterred. "I got really lucky."

I nod. Feel something twist in my gut. I get to my feet. "Yes, well, if you'll excuse me—"

"Yep. Got it." Kent nods. Waves good-bye. "We'll see you around, yeah?"

"Certainly."

"Bye!" James says as Kent tugs him down the hall. "Glad you're feeling better!"

Somehow I feel worse.

I walk back into the bedroom not quite as panicked as before, but more somber, somehow. And I'm so distracted I almost don't notice Juliette stepping out of the bathroom as I enter.

She's wearing nothing but a towel.

Her cheeks are pink from the shower. Her eyes are big and bright as she smiles as me. She's so beautiful. So unbelievably beautiful.

"I just have to grab some fresh clothes," she says, still smiling. "Do you mind?"

I shake my head. I can only stare at her.

Somehow, my reaction is insufficient. She hesitates. Frowns as she looks at me. And then, finally, moves toward me.

I feel my lungs malfunction.

"Hey," she says.

But all I can think about is what I have to say to her and how she might react. There's a small, desperate hope in my heart that's still trying to be optimistic about the outcome.

Maybe she'll understand.

"Aaron?" She steps closer, closing the gap between us. "You said you wanted to talk to me, right?"

"Yes," I say, whispering the word. "Yes." I feel dazed.

"Can it wait?" she says. "Just long enough for me to change?"

I don't know what comes over me.

Desperation. Desire. Fear.

Love.

It hits me with a painful force, the reminder. Of just how much I love her. God, I love all of her. Her impossibilities, her exasperations. I love how gentle she is with me when we're alone. How soft and kind she can be in our quiet moments. How she never hesitates to defend me.

I love her.

And she's standing in front of me now, a question in her eyes, and I can't think of anything but how much I want her in my life, forever.

Still, I say nothing. I do nothing.

And she won't walk away.

I realize, with a start, that she's still waiting for an answer.

"Yes, of course," I say quickly. "Of course it can wait."

But she's trying to read my face. "What's wrong?" she says.

I shake my head as I take her hand. Gently, so gently. She steps closer, and my hands close lightly over her bare shoulders. It's a small, simple movement, but I feel it when her emotions change. She trembles suddenly as I touch her, my hands traveling down her arms, and her reaction trips my senses. It kills me, every time, it leaves me breathless every time she reacts to me, to my touch. To know that she feels something for me. That she wants me.

Maybe she'll understand, I think. We've been through so much together. We've overcome so much. Maybe this, too, will be surmountable.

Maybe she'll understand.

"Aaron?"

Blood rushes through my veins, hot and fast. Her skin is soft and smells of lavender and I pull back, just an inch. Just to look at her. I graze her bottom lip with my thumb before my hand slips behind her neck.

"Hi," I say.

And she meets me here, in this moment, in an instant.

She kisses me without restraint, without hesitation, and wraps her arms around my neck and I'm overwhelmed, lost in a rush of emotion—

And the towel falls off her body.

Onto to the floor.

I step back, surprised, taking in the sight of her. My heart is pounding furiously in my chest. I can hardly remember what I was trying to do.

Then she steps forward, stands on tiptoe and reels me in, all warmth and heat and sweetness and I pull her against me, drugged by the feel of her, lost in the smooth expanse of her bare skin. I'm still fully clothed. She's naked in my arms. And somehow that difference between us only makes this moment more surreal. She's pushing me back gently, even as she continues to kiss me, even as she searches my body through this fabric and I fall backward onto the bed, gasping.

She climbs on top of me.

And I think I've lost my goddamned mind.

JULIETTE

JULIETTE

This, I think, is the way to die.

I could drown in this moment and I'd never regret it. I could catch fire from this kiss and happily turn to ash. I could live here, die here, right *here*, against his hips, his lips. In the emotion in his eyes as he sinks into me, his heartbeats indistinguishable from mine.

This. Forever. This.

He kisses me again, his occasional gasps for air hot against my skin, and I taste him, his mouth, his neck, the hard line of his jaw and he fights back a groan, pulls away, pain and pleasure twining together as he moves deeper, harder, his muscles taught, his body rock solid against mine. He has one hand around the back of my neck, the other around the back of my thigh and he wraps us together, impossibly closer, overwhelming me with an extraordinary pleasure that feels like nothing I've ever known. It's nameless. Unknowable, impossible to plan for. It's different every time.

And there's something wild and beautiful in him today, something I can't explain in the way he touches me—the way his fingers linger along my shoulder blades, down the curve of my back—like I might evaporate at any moment, like this might be the first and last time we'll ever touch.

I close my eyes.

Let go.

The lines of our bodies have merged. It's wave after wave of ice and heat, melting and catching fire and it's his mouth on my skin, his strong arms wrapping me up in love and warmth. I'm suspended in midair, underwater, in outer space, all at the same time and clocks are frozen, inhibitions are out the window and I've never felt so safe, so loved or so protected than I have here, in the private fusion of our bodies.

I lose track of time.

I lose track of my mind.

I only know I want this to last forever.

He's saying something to me, running his hands down my body, and his words are soft and desperate, silky against my ear, but I can hardly hear him over the sound of my own heart beating against my chest. But I see it, when the muscles in his arms strain against his skin, as he fights to stay here, with me—

He gasps, out loud, squeezing his eyes shut as he reaches out, grabs a fistful of the bedsheets and I turn my face into his chest, trail my nose up the line of his neck and breathe him in and I'm pressed against him, every inch of my skin hot and raw with want and need and

"I love you," I whisper

even as I feel my mind detach from my body

even as stars explode behind my eyes and heat floods my

veins and I'm overcome, I'm stunned and overcome every time, every time

It's a torrent of feeling, a simultaneous, ephemeral taste of death and bliss and my eyes close, white-hot heat flashes behind my eyelids and I have to fight the need to call out his name even as I feel us shatter together, destroyed and restored all at once and he gasps

He says, *"Juliette—"*

I love the sight of his naked body.

Especially in these quiet, vulnerable moments. These brackets of time stapled between dreams and reality are my favorite. There's a sweetness in this hesitant consciousness—a careful, gentle return of form to function. I've found I love these minutes most for the delicate way in which they unfold. It's tender.

Slow motion.

Time tying its shoes.

And Warner is so still, so soft. So unguarded. His face is smooth, his brow unfurrowed, his lips wondering whether to part. And the first seconds after he opens his eyes are the sweetest. Some days I'm lucky enough to look up before he does. Today I watch him stir. I watch him blink open his eyes and orient himself. But then, in the time it takes him to find me—the way his face lights up when he sees me staring—that part makes something inside of me sing. I know everything, everything that ever matters, just by the way he looks at me in that moment.

And today, something is different.

Today, when he opens his eyes he looks suddenly disoriented. He blinks and looks around, sitting up too fast like he might want to run and doesn't remember how. Today, something is wrong.

And when I climb into his lap he stills.

And when I take his chin in my hands he turns away.

When I kiss him, softly, he closes his eyes and something inside him thaws, something unclenches in his bones, and when he opens his eyes again he looks terrified and I feel suddenly sick to my stomach.

Something is terribly, terribly wrong.

"What is it?" I say, my words scarcely making a sound. "What happened? What's wrong?"

He shakes his head.

"Is it me?" My heart is pounding. "Did I do something?"

His eyes go wide. "No, no, Juliette—you're perfect. You're—God, you're perfect," he says. He grips the back of his head, looks at the ceiling.

"Then why won't you look at me?"

So he meets my eyes. And I can't help but marvel at how much I love his face, even now, even in his fear. He's so classically handsome. So remarkably beautiful, even like this: his hair shorn, short and soft; his face unshaven, a silver-blond shadow contouring the already hard lines of his face. His eyes are an impossible shade of green. Bright. Blinking. And then—

Closed.

"I have to tell you something," he says quietly. He's looking down. He lifts a hand to touch me and his fingers trail down the side of my torso. Delicate. Terrified. "Something I should've told you earlier."

"What do you mean?" I fall back. I ball up a section of the bedsheet and hold it tightly against my body, feeling suddenly vulnerable.

He hesitates for too long. Exhales. He drags his hand across his mouth, his chin, down the back of his neck—

"I have no idea where to start."

Every instinct in my body is telling me to run. To shove cotton in my ears. To tell him to stop talking. But I can't. I'm frozen.

And I'm scared.

"Start at the beginning," I say, surprised I can even bring myself to speak. I've never seen him like this before. I can't imagine what he has to say. He's now clasping his hands together so tightly I worry he might break his own fingers by accident.

And then, finally. Slowly.

He speaks.

"The Reestablishment," he says, "went public with their campaigns when you were seven years old. I was nine. But they'd been meeting and planning for many years before that."

"Okay."

"The founders of the The Reestablishment," he says, "were once military men and women turned defense

265

contractors. And they were responsible, in part, for the rise of the military industrial complex that built the foundation of the *de facto* military states composing what is now The Reestablishment. They'd had their plans in place for a long time before this regime went live," he says. "Their jobs had made it possible for them to have had access to weapons and technology no one had even heard of. They had extensive surveillance, fully equipped facilities, acres of private property, unlimited access to information—all for years before you were even born."

My heart is pounding in my chest.

"They'd discovered *Unnaturals*—a term The Reestablishment uses to describe those with supernatural abilities—a few years later. You were about five years old," he says, "when they made their first discovery." He looks at the wall. "That's when they started collecting, testing, and using people with abilities to expedite their goals in dominating the world."

"This is all really interesting," I say, "but I'm kind of freaking out right now and I need you to skip ahead to the part where you tell me what any of this has to do with me."

"Sweetheart," he says, finally meeting my eyes. "All of this has to do with you."

"How?"

"There was one thing I knew about your life that I never told you," he says. He swallows. He's looking into his hands when he says, "You were adopted."

The revelation is like a thunderclap.

I stumble off the bed, clutch the sheet to my body and

stand there, staring at him, stunned. I try to stay calm even as my mind catches fire.

"I was adopted."

He nods.

"So you're saying that the people who raised me—*tortured me*—are not my real parents?"

He shakes his head.

"Are my biological parents still alive?"

"Yes," he whispers.

"And you never told me this?"

No, he says quickly

No, no I didn't know they were still alive, he says

I didn't know anything except that you were adopted, he says, *I just found out, just yesterday, that your parents are still alive, because Castle*, he says, *Castle told me—*

And every subsequent revelation is like a shock wave, a sudden, unforeseen detonation that implodes within me—

BOOM

Your life has been an experiment, he says

BOOM

You have a sister, he says, *she's still alive*

BOOM

Your biological parents gave you and your sister to The Reestablishment for scientific research

and it's like the world has been knocked off its axis, like I've been flung from the earth and I'm headed directly for the sun,

like I'm being burned alive and somehow, I can still

hear him, even as my skin melts inward, as my mind turns inside-out and everything I've ever known, everything I ever thought to be true about who I am and where I come from

v a n i s h e s

I inch away from him, confused and horrified and unable to form words, unable to speak

And he says he *didn't know,* and his voice breaks when he says it, when he says he didn't know until recently that my biological parents were still alive, didn't know until Castle told him, never knew how to tell me that I'd been adopted, didn't know how I would take it, didn't know if I needed that pain, but Castle told him that The Reestablishment is coming for me, that they're coming to take me back

and your sister, he says

but I'm crying now, unable to see him through the tears and still I cannot speak and

your sister, he says, her name is Emmaline, she's one year older than you, she's very, very powerful, she's been the property of The Reestablishment *for twelve years*

I can't stop shaking my head

"Stop," I say

"No," I say

Please don't do this to me—

But he won't stop. He says I have to know. He says I have to know this now—that I have to know the truth—

STOP TELLING ME THIS, I scream

I didn't know she was your sister, he's saying,

I didn't know you had a sister

I swear I didn't know

"There were nearly twenty men and women who put together the beginnings of The Reestablishment," he says, "but there were only six supreme commanders. When the man originally chosen for North America became terminally ill, my father was being considered to replace him. I was sixteen. We lived here, in Sector 45. My father was then CCR. And becoming supreme commander meant he would be moving away, and he wanted to take me with him. My mother," he says, "was to be left behind."

Please don't say any more

Please don't say anything else, I beg him

"It was the only way I could convince him to give me his job," he says, desperate now. "To allow me to stay behind, to watch her closely. He was sworn in as supreme commander when I was eighteen. And he made me spend the two years in between—"

"Aaron, please," I say, feeling hysterical, "I don't want to know—I didn't ask you to tell me— I don't want to know—"

"I perpetuated your sister's torture," he says, his voice raw, broken, "her confinement. I was ordered to oversee her continued imprisonment. I gave the orders that kept her there. Every day. I was never told why she was there or what was wrong with her. I was told to maintain her. That was it. She was allowed only four twenty-minute breaks from the water tank every twenty-four hours and she used to scream—she'd beg me to release her," he says, his voice catching. "She begged for mercy and I never gave it to her."

And I stop

Head spinning

I drop the sheet from my body as I run, run away

I'm shoving clothes on as fast as I can and when I return to the room, half wild, caught in a nightmare, I catch him half dressed, too, no shirt, just pants, and he doesn't even speak as I stare at him, stunned, one hand covering my mouth as I shake my head, tears spilling fast down my face and I don't know what to say, I don't know that I can ever say anything to him, ever again—

"It's too much," I say, choking on the words. "It's too much—it's too much—"

"*Juliette*—"

And I shake my head, hands trembling as I reach for the door and

"*Please*," he says, and tears are falling silently down his face, and he's visibly shaking as he says, "You have to believe me. I was young. And stupid. I was desperate. I thought I had nothing to live for then—nothing mattered to me but saving my mother and I was willing to do anything that would keep me here, close to her—"

"You lied to me!" I explode, anger squeezing my eyes shut as I back away from him. "You lied to me all this time, you've *lied* to me—about everything—"

"No," he says, all terror and desperation. "The only thing I've kept from you was the truth about your parents, I swear to you—"

"How could you keep that from me? All this time, all

this—*everything*—all you did was *lie to me*—"

He's shaking his head when he says *No, no, I love you, my love for you has never been a lie*—

"Then why didn't you tell me this sooner? Why would you keep this from me?"

"I thought your parents had died a long time ago—I didn't think it would help you to know about them. I thought it would only hurt you more to know you'd lost them. And I didn't know," he says, shaking his head, "I didn't know anything about your real parents or your sister, please believe me—I swear I didn't know, not until yesterday—"

His chest is heaving so hard that his body bows, his hands planted on his knees as he tries to breathe and he's not looking at me when he says, whispers, "I'm so sorry. I'm so, so sorry."

"Stop it—stop talking—"

"Please—"

"How—h-how can I ever—ever trust you again?" My eyes are wide and terrified and searching him for an answer that will save us both but he doesn't answer. He can't. He leaves me with nothing to hold on to. "How can we ever go back?" I say. "How can you expect me to forget all of this? That you lied to me about my parents? That you tortured my sister? There's so much about you I don't know," I say, my voice small and broken, "so much—and I can't—I can't do this—"

And he looks up, frozen in place, staring at me like he's finally understanding that I won't pretend this never

271

happened, that I can't continue to be with someone I can't trust and I can see it, can see the hope go out of his eyes, his hand caught behind his head. His jaw is slack; his face is stunned, suddenly pale and he takes a step toward me, lost, desperate, pleading with his eyes

but I have to go.

I'm running down the hall and I don't know where I'm going until I get there.

WARNER

So this—

This is agony.

This is what they talk about when they talk about heartbreak. I thought I knew what it was like before. I thought I knew, with perfect clarity, what it felt like to have my heart broken, but now—now I finally understand.

Before? When Juliette couldn't decide between myself and Kent? That pain? That was child's play.

But this.

This is suffering. This is full, unadulterated torture. And I have no one to blame for this pain but myself, which makes it impossible to direct my anger anywhere but inward. If I weren't better informed, I'd think I were having an actual heart attack. It feels as though a truck has run over me, broken every bone in my chest, and now it's stuck here, the weight of it crushing my lungs. I can't breathe. I can't even see straight.

My heart is pounding in my ears. Blood is rushing to my head too quickly and it's making me hot and dizzy. I'm strangled into speechlessness, numb in my bones. I feel nothing but an immense, impossible pressure breaking apart my body. I fall backward, hard. My head is against the wall. I try to calm myself, calm my breathing. I try to be rational.

This is not a heart attack, I tell myself. *Not a heart attack.*

I know better.

I'm having a panic attack.

This has happened to me just once before, and then the pain had materialized as if out of a nightmare, out of nowhere, with no warning. I'd woken up in the middle of the night seized by a violent terror I could not articulate, convinced beyond a shadow of a doubt that I was dying. Eventually, the episode passed, but the experience never left me.

And now, this—

I thought I was prepared. I thought I had steeled myself against the possible outcome of today's conversation. I was wrong.

I can feel it devouring me.

This pain.

I've struggled with occasional anxiety over the course of my life, but I've generally been able to manage it. In the past, my experiences had always been associated with this work. With my father. But the older I got, the less powerless I became, and I found ways to manage my triggers; I found the safe spaces in my mind; I educated myself in cognitive behavioral therapies; and with time, I learned to cope. The anxiety came on with far less weight and frequency. But very rarely, it morphs into something else. Sometimes it spirals entirely out of my control.

And I don't know how to save myself this time.

I don't know if I'm strong enough to fight it now, not when I no longer know what I'm fighting for. And I've just collapsed, supine on the floor, my hand pressed against the pain in my chest, when the door suddenly opens.

I feel my heart restart.

I lift my head half an inch and wait. Hoping against hope.

"Hey, man, where the hell are you?"

I drop my head with a groan. Of all the people.

"*Hello?*" Footsteps. "I know you're in here. And why is this room such a mess? Why are there boxes and bedsheets everywhere?"

Silence.

"Bro, where are you? I just saw Juliette and she was freaking out, but she wouldn't tell me why, and I know your punkass is probably hiding in here like a little—"

And then there he is.

His boots right next to my head.

Staring at me.

"Hi," I say. It's all I can manage at the moment.

Kenji is looking down at me, stunned.

"What in the fresh hell are you doing on the ground? Why aren't you wearing any clothes?" And then, "Wait— were you *crying*?"

I close my eyes, pray to die.

"What's going on?" His voice is suddenly closer than it was before, and I realize he must be crouching next to me. "What's wrong with you, man?"

"I can't breathe," I whisper.

"What do you mean, *you can't breathe?* Did she shoot you again?"

That reminder spears straight through me. Fresh, searing pain.

God, I hate him so much.

I swallow, hard. "Please. Leave."

"Uh, no." I hear the rustle of movement as he sits down beside me. "What is this?" he says, gesturing to my body. "What's happening to you right now?"

Finally, I give up. Open my eyes. "I'm having a panic attack, you inconsiderate ass." I try to take a breath. "And I'd really like some privacy."

His eyebrows fly up. "You're having a what-now?"

"Panic." I breathe. "Attack."

"What the hell is that?"

"I have medicine. In the bathroom. *Please.*"

He shoots me a strange look, but does as I ask. He returns in a moment with the right bottle, and I'm relieved.

"This it?"

I nod. I've never actually taken this medication before, but I've kept the prescription current at my medic's request. In case of emergencies.

"You want some water with that?"

I shake my head. Snatch the bottle from him with shaking hands. I can't remember the right dosage, but as I so rarely have an attack this severe, I take a guess. I pop three of the pills in my mouth and bite down, hard, welcoming the vile, bitter taste on my tongue.

It's only several minutes later, after the medicine begins to work its magic, that the metaphorical truck is finally extricated from its position on my chest. My ribs magically restitch themselves. My lungs remember to do their job.

And I feel suddenly limp. Exhausted.

Slow.

I drag myself up, stumble to my feet.

"*Now* do you want to tell me what's going on here?" Kenji is still staring at me, arms crossed against his chest. "Or should I go ahead and assume you did something horrible and just beat the shit out of you?"

I feel so tired suddenly.

A laugh builds in my chest and I don't know where it's coming from. I manage to fight back the laugh, but fail to hide a stupid, inexplicable smile as I say, "You should probably just beat the shit out of me."

It was the wrong thing to say.

Kenji's expression changes. His eyes are suddenly, genuinely concerned and I worry I've said too much. These drugs are slowing me down, softening my senses. I touch a hand to my lips, beg them to stay closed. I hope I haven't taken too much of the medicine.

"Hey," Kenji says gently. "What happened?"

I shake my head. Close my eyes. "What happened?" Now I actually laugh. "What happened, what happened." I open my eyes long enough to say, "Juliette broke up with me."

"*What?*"

"That is, I think she did?" I stop. Frown. Tap a finger against my chin. "I imagine that's why she ran out of here screaming."

"But—why would she break up with you? Why was she crying?"

At this, I laugh again. "Because I," I say, pointing at myself, "am a monster."

Kenji looks confused. "And how is that news to anyone?"

I smile. He's funny, I think. Funny guy.

"Where did I leave my shirt?" I mumble, feeling suddenly numb in a whole new way. I cross my arms. Squint. "Hmm? Have you seen it anywhere?"

"Bro, are you drunk?"

"What?" I slap at the air. Laugh. "I don't drink. My father is an alcoholic, didn't you know? I don't touch the stuff. No, wait"—I hold up a finger—"*was* an alcoholic. My father *was* an alcoholic. He's dead now. Quite dead."

And then I hear Kenji gasp. It's loud and strange and he whispers, "*Holy shit*," and it's enough to sharpen my senses for a second.

I turn around to face him.

He looks terrified.

"What is it?" I say, annoyed.

"What happened to your back?"

"Oh." I look away, newly irritated. "That." The many, many scars that make up the disfiguration of my entire back. I take a deep breath. Exhale. "Those are just, you know, birthday gifts from dear old dad."

"Birthday gifts from your *dad*?" Kenji blinks, fast. Looks around, speaks to the air. "What the hell kind of soap opera did I just walk into here?" He runs a hand through his hair and says, "Why am I always getting involved in other people's personal shit? Why can't I just mind my own business? Why can't I just keep my mouth shut?"

"You know," I say to him, tilting my head slightly, "I've always wondered the same thing."

"Shut up."

I smile, big. Lightbulb bright.

Kenji's eyes widen, surprised, and he laughs. He nods at my face and says, "Aw, you've got dimples. I didn't know that. That's cute."

"Shut up." I frown. "Go away."

He laughs harder. "I think you took way too many of those medicine thingies," he says to me, picking up the bottle I left on the floor. He scans the label. "It says you're only supposed to take one every three hours." He laughs again. Louder this time. "Shit, man, if I didn't know you were in a world of pain right now, I'd be filming this."

"I'm very tired," I say to him. "Please go directly to hell."

"No way, freak show. I'm not missing this." He leans against the wall. "Plus, I'm not going anywhere until your drunkass tells me why you and J broke up."

I shake my head. Finally manage to find a shirt and put it on.

"Yeah, you put that on backward," Kenji says to me.

I glare at him and fall into bed. Close my eyes.

"So?" he says, sitting down next to me. "Should I get the popcorn? What's going on?"

"It's classified."

Kenji makes a sound of disbelief. "What's classified? Why you broke up is classified? Or did you break up over classified information?"

"Yes."

"Throw me a freaking bone here."

"We broke up," I say, pulling a pillow over my eyes, "because of information I shared with her that is, as I said, *classified.*"

"What? Why? That doesn't make any sense." A pause. "Unless—"

"Oh good, I can practically hear the tiny gears in your tiny brain turning."

"You lied to her about something?" he says. "Something you should've told her? Something classified—about *her*?"

I wave a hand at nothing in particular. "The man's a genius."

"Oh, *shit*."

"Yes," I say. "Very much shit."

He exhales a long, hard breath. "That sounds pretty serious."

"I am an idiot."

He clears his throat. "So, uh, you really screwed up this time, huh?"

"Quite thoroughly, I'm afraid."

Silence.

"Wait—tell me again why all these sheets are on the floor?"

At that, I pull the pillow away from my face. "Why do you think they're on the floor?"

A second's hesitation and then,

"Oh, what—*c'mon*, man, what the hell." Kenji jumps off the bed looking disgusted. "Why would you let me sit here?" He stalks off to the other side of the room. "You guys are just—*Jesus*—that is just *not okay*—"

"Grow up."

"I *am* grown." He scowls at me. "But Juliette's like my sister, man, I don't want to think about that shit—"

"Well, don't worry," I say to him, "I'm sure it'll never happen again."

"All right, all right, drama queen, calm down. And tell me about this classified business."

JULIETTE

Run, I said to myself.

Run until your lungs collapse, until the wind whips and snaps at your tattered clothes, until you're a blur that blends into the background.

Run, Juliette, run faster, run until your bones break and your shins split and your muscles atrophy and your heart dies because it was always too big for your chest and it beat too fast for too long and run.

Run run run until you can't hear their feet behind you. Run until they drop their fists and their shouts dissolve in the air. Run with your eyes open and your mouth shut and dam the river rushing up behind your eyes. Run, Juliette.

Run until you drop dead.

Make sure your heart stops before they ever reach you. Before they ever touch you.

Run, I said.

—AN EXCERPT FROM JULIETTE'S JOURNALS IN THE ASYLUM

My feet pound against the hard, packed earth, each steady footfall sending shocks of electric pain up my legs. My lungs burn, my breaths coming in fast and sharp, but I push through the exhaustion, my muscles working harder than they have in a long time, and keep moving. I never used to be any good at this. I've always had trouble breathing. But I've been doing a lot of cardio and weight training since moving on base, and I've gotten much stronger.

Today, that training is paying off.

I've covered at least a couple of miles already, panic and rage propelling me most of the way through, but now I have to break through my own resistance in order to maintain momentum. I cannot stop. I will not stop.

I'm not ready to start thinking yet.

It's a disturbingly beautiful day today; the sun is shining high and bright, impossible birds chirping merrily in half-blooming trees and flapping their wings in vast, blue skies. I'm wearing a thin cotton shirt. Dark blue jeans. Another pair of tennis shoes. My hair, loose and long, waves behind me, locked in a battle with the wind. I can feel the sun warm my face; I feel beads of sweat roll down my back.

Could this possibly be real? I wonder.

Did someone shoot me with those poison bullets on purpose? To try and tell me something?

Or are my hallucinations an altogether different issue?

I close my eyes and push my legs harder, will myself to move faster. I don't want to think yet. I don't want to stop moving.

If I stop moving, my mind might kill me.

A sudden gust of wind hits me in the face. I open my eyes again, remember to breathe. I'm back in unregulated territory now, my powers turned fully on, the energy humming through me even now, in perpetual motion. The streets of the old world are paved, but pockmarked by potholes and puddles. The buildings are abandoned, tall and cold, electric lines strapped across the skyline like the staffs of unfinished songs, swaying gently in the afternoon light. I run under a crumbling overpass and down several cascading, concrete stairs manned on either side by unkempt palm trees and burned-out lampposts, their wrought-iron handrails rough and peeling paint. I turn up and down a few side streets and then I'm surrounded, on all sides, by the skeleton of an old freeway, twelve lanes wide, an enormous metal structure half collapsed in the middle of the road. I squint more closely and count three equally massive green signs, only two of which are still standing. I read the words—

405 SOUTH LONG BEACH

—and I stop.

I fall forward, elbows on my knees, hands clasped behind my head, and fight the urge to tumble to the ground.

Inhale.

Exhale.

Over and over and over

I look up, look around.

An old bus sits not far from me, its many wheels mired in a pool of still water, rotting, half rusted, like an abandoned child steeping in its own filth. Freeway signs, shattered glass, shredded rubber, and forgotten bumpers litter what's left of the broken pavement.

The sun finds me and shines in my direction, a spotlight for the fraying girl stopped in the middle of nowhere and I'm caught in its focused rays of heat, melting slowly from within, quietly collapsing as my mind catches up to my body like an asteroid barreling to earth.

And then it hits me—

The reminders like reverberations

The memories like hands around my throat

There it is

There she is

shattered again.

I'm curled into myself against the back of the filthy bus and I've got a hand clamped over my mouth to try and trap the screams but their desperate attempts to escape my lips are fighting a tide of unshed tears I cannot allow and—

breathe

My body shakes with unspent emotion.

Vomit inches up my oesophagus.

Go away, I whisper, but only in my head

go away, I say

Please *die*

I'd chained the terrified little girl of my past in some unknowable dungeon inside of me where she and her fears had been carefully stored, sealed away.

Her memories, suffocated.

Her anger, ignored.

I do not speak to her. I don't dare look in her direction. I *hate* her.

But right now I can hear her crying.

Right now I can see her, this other version of myself, I can see her dragging her dirty fingernails against the chambers of my heart, drawing blood. And if I could reach inside myself and rip her out of me with my own two hands, I would.

I would snap her little body in half.

I would toss her mangled limbs out to sea.

I would be rid of her then, fully and truly, bleached forevermore of her stains on my soul. But she refuses to die. She remains within me, an echo. She haunts the halls of my heart and mind and though I'd gladly murder her for a chance at freedom, I cannot. It's like trying to choke a ghost.

So I close my eyes and beg myself to be brave. I take deep breaths. I cannot let the broken girl inside of me inhale all that I've become. I cannot revert back to another version of myself. I will not shatter, not again, in the wake of an emotional earthquake.

But where do I even begin?

How do I deal with any of this? These past weeks had already been too much for me; too much to handle; too much to juggle. It's been hard to admit that I'm unqualified, that I'm in way over my head, but I got there. I was willing to recognize that all this—this new life, this new world—would take time and experience. I was willing to put in the hours, to trust my team, to try to be diplomatic. But now, in light of everything—

My entire life has been an experiment.

I have a sibling. A sister. And an altogether different set of parents, biological parents, who treated me no differently than my adoptive ones did, donating my body to research as if I were nothing more than a science experiment.

Anderson and the other supreme commanders have always known me. Castle has always known the truth about me. Warner knew I'd been adopted.

And now, to know that those I've trusted most have been lying to me—manipulating me—

Everyone has been *using me*—

It rips itself from my lungs, the sudden scream. It wrenches free from my chest without warning, without permission, and it's a scream so loud, so harsh and violent it brings me to my knees. My hands are pressed against the pavement, my head half bent between my legs. The sound of my agony is lost in the wind, carried off by the clouds.

But here, between my feet, the ground has fissured open.

I jump up, surprised, and look down, spin around. I suddenly can't remember if that crack was there before.

The force of my frustration and confusion sends me back to the bus, where I exhale and lean against the back doors, hoping for a place to rest my head—except that my hands and head rip through the exterior wall as though it were made of tissue, and I fall hard on the filthy floor, my hands and knees going straight through the metal underfoot.

Somehow this only makes me angrier.

My power is out of control, stoked by my reckless mind, my wild thoughts. I can't focus my energy the way Kenji taught me to, and it's everywhere, all around me, within and without me and the problem is, I don't care anymore.

I don't care, not right now.

I reach without thinking and rip one of the bus seats from its bolts, and throw it, hard, through the windshield. Glass splinters everywhere; a large shard hits me in the eye and several more fly into my open, angry mouth; I lift a hand to find slivers stuck in my sleeve, glittering like miniature icicles. I spit the spare bits from my mouth. Remove the glass shards from my shirt. And then I pull an inch-long piece of glass out of the inside of my eyelid and toss it, with a small clatter, to the ground.

My chest is heaving.

What, I think, as I rip another seat from its bolts, *do I do now?* I throw this seat straight through a window, shattering more glass and ripping open more metal innards. Instinct alone moves my arm up to protect my face from the flying debris, but I don't flinch. I'm too angry to care. I'm too powerful at the moment to feel pain. Glass ricochets off my body. Razor-thin ribbons of steel bounce off my skin. I almost wish I felt something. Anything.

What do I do?

I punch the wall and there's no relief in it; my hand goes straight through. I kick a chair and there's no comfort in it; my foot rips through the cheap upholstery. I scream again, half outrage, half heartbreak, and watch this time as a long, dangerous crack forms along the ceiling.

That's new.

And I've hardly had time to think the thought when the bus gives a sudden, lurching heave, yawns itself into a deep shudder, and splits clean in half.

The two halves collapse on either side of me, tripping me backward. I fall into a pile of shredded metal and wet, dirty glass and, stunned, I stumble up to my feet.

I don't know what just happened.

I knew I was able to project my abilities—my strength, for certain—but I didn't know that there was any projectional power in my voice. Old impulses make me wish I had someone to discuss this with. But I have no one to talk to anymore.

Warner is out of the question.

Castle is complicit.

And Kenji—*what about Kenji?* Did he know about my parents—my sister—too? Surely, Castle would've told him?

The problem is, I can't be sure of anything anymore.

There's no one left to trust.

But those words—that simple thought—suddenly inspires

in me a memory. It's something hazy I have to reach for. I wrap my hands around it and pull. A voice? A female voice, I remember now. Telling me—

I gasp.

It was Nazeera. Last night. In the medical wing. It was her. I remember her voice now—I remember reaching out and touching her hand, I remember the feel of the metal knuckles she's always wearing and she said—

"... *the people you trust are lying to you—and the other supreme commanders only want to kill you* ..."

I spin around too fast, searching for something I cannot name.

Nazeera was trying to warn me. Last night—she's barely known me and she was trying to tell me the truth long before any of the others ever did—

But why?

Just then, something hard and loud lands heavily on the half-bent steel structure blocking the road. The old freeway signs shudder and sway.

I'm looking straight at it as it happens. I'm watching this in real time, frame by frame, and yet, I'm still so shocked by what I see that I forget to speak.

It's Nazeera, fifty feet in the air, sitting calmly atop a sign that says—

10 EAST LOS ANGELES

—and she's waving at me. She's wearing a loose, brown leather hood attached to a holster that fits snugly around her shoulders. The leather hood covers her hair and shades her eyes so that only the bottom half of her face is visible from where I stand. The diamond piercing under her bottom lip catches fire in the sunlight.

She looks like a vision from an unknowable time.

I still have no idea what to say.

Naturally, she does not share my problem.

"You ready to talk yet?" she says to me.

"How—how did you—"

"Yeah?"

"How did you get here?" I spin around, scanning the distance. *How did she know I was here? Was I being followed?*

"I flew."

I turn back to face her. "Where's your plane?"

She laughs and jumps off the freeway sign. It's a long, hard fall that would've injured any normal person. "I really hope you're joking," she says to me, and then grabs me around the waist and leaps up, into the sky.

WARNER

I've seen a lot of strange things in my life, but I never thought I'd have the pleasure of seeing Kishimoto shut his mouth for longer than five minutes. And yet, here we are. In any other situation, I might be relishing this moment. Sadly, I'm unable to enjoy even this small pleasure.

His silence is unnerving.

It's been fifteen minutes since I finished sharing with him the same details I shared with Juliette earlier today, and he hasn't said a word. He's sitting quietly in the corner, his head pressed against the wall, face in a frown, and he will not speak. He only stares, his eyes narrowed at some invisible point across the room.

Occasionally he sighs.

We've been here for almost two hours, just he and I. Talking. And of all the things I thought would happen today, I certainly did not think it would involve Juliette running away from me, and my befriending this idiot.

Oh, the best-laid plans.

Finally, after what feels like a tremendous amount of time, he speaks.

"I can't believe Castle didn't tell me," is the first thing he says.

"We all have our secrets."

He looks up, looks me in the eye. It's not pleasant. "You have any more secrets I should know about?"

"None you should know about, no."

He laughs, but it sounds sad. "You don't even realize what you're doing, do you?"

"Realize what?"

"You're setting yourself up for a lifetime of pain, bro. You can't keep living like this. This," he says, pointing at my face, "this old you? This messed-up dude who never talks and never smiles and never says anything nice and never allows anyone to really know him—you can't be this guy if you want to be in any kind of relationship."

I raise an eyebrow.

He shakes his head. "You just can't, man. You can't be with someone and keep that many secrets from them."

"It's never stopped me before."

Here, Kenji hesitates. His eyes widen, just a little. "What do you mean, *before*?"

"Before," I say. "In other relationships."

"So, uh, you've been in other relationships? Before Juliette?"

I tilt my head at him. "You find that hard to believe."

"I'm still trying to wrap my head around the fact that you have *feelings*, so yeah, I find that hard to believe."

I clear my throat very quietly. Look away.

"So—umm—you, uh"—he laughs, nervously—"I'm sorry but, like, does Juliette know you've been in other relationships? Because she's never mentioned anything about that, and I think that would've been, like, I don't know? Relevant?"

300

I turn to face him. "No."

"No, what?"

"No, she doesn't know."

"Why not?"

"She's never asked."

Kenji gapes at me. "I'm sorry—but are you—I mean, are you actually as stupid as you sound? Or are you just messing with me right now?"

"I'm nearly twenty years old," I say to him, irritated. "Do you really think it so strange that I've been with other women?"

"No," he says, "I, personally, don't give a shit how many women you've been with. What I think is strange is that you never told your *girlfriend* that you've been with other women. And to be perfectly honest it's making me wonder whether your relationship wasn't already headed to hell."

"You have no idea what you're talking about." My eyes flash. "I *love* her. I never would've done anything to hurt her."

"They why would you lie to her?"

"Why do you keep pressing this? Who cares if I've been with other women? They meant nothing to me—"

"You're messed up in the head, man."

I close my eyes, feeling suddenly exhausted. "Of all the things I've shared with you today, *this* is the issue you're most interested in discussing?"

"I just think it's important, you know, if you and J ever try to repair this damage. You have to get your shit together."

"What do you mean, *repair this damage?*" I say, my eyes flying open. "I've already lost her. The damage is done."

At this, he looks surprised. "So that's it? You're just going to walk away? All this talk of *I love her* blah blah and that's it?"

"She doesn't want to be with me. I won't try to convince her she's wrong."

Kenji laughs. "Damn," he says. "I think you might need to get your bolts tightened."

"I beg your pardon?"

He gets to his feet. "Whatever, bro. Your life. Your business. I liked you better when you were drunk on your meds."

"Tell me something, Kishimoto—"

"What?"

"Why would I take relationship advice from *you?* What do you know about relationships aside from the fact that you've never been in one?"

A muscle twitches in his jaw. "Wow." He nods, looks away. "You know what?" He gives me the finger. "Don't pretend to know shit about me, man. You don't know me."

"You don't know me, either."

"I know that you're an *idiot.*"

I suddenly, inexplicably, shut down.

My face pales. I feel unsteady. I don't have any fight left in me today and I don't have any interest in defending myself. I *am* an idiot. I know who I am. The terrible things I've done. It's indefensible.

"You're right," I say, but I say it quietly. "And I'm sure you're right that there's a great deal I don't know about you, too."

Something in Kenji seems to relax.

His eyes are sympathetic when he says, "I really don't think you have to lose her. Not like this. Not over this. What you did was, like—yeah, that shit was beyond horrible. Torturing her freaking sister? I mean. Yeah. Absolutely. Like, ten out of ten you'll probably go to hell for that."

I flinch.

"But that happened before you knew her, right? Before all this"—he waves a hand—"you know, whatever it is that happened between you guys happened. And I know her—I know how she feels about you. There might be something to save. I wouldn't lose hope just yet."

I almost crack a smile. I almost laugh.

I don't do either.

Instead, I say, "I remember Juliette telling me you gave a similar speech to Kent shortly after they broke up. That you spoke expressly against her wishes. You told Kent she still loved him—that she wanted to get back together with him. You told him the exact opposite of what she felt. And she was furious."

"That was different." Kenji frowns. "That was just . . . like . . . you know—I was just trying to help? Because, like, logistically the situation was really complicated—"

"I appreciate your trying to help me," I say to him. "But I will not beg her to return to me. Not if it's not what she

303

wants." I look away. "In any case, she's always deserved to be with someone better. Maybe this is her chance."

"Uh-huh." Kenji lifts an eyebrow. "So if, like, tomorrow she hooks up with some other dude you're just gonna shrug and be like—I don't know? Shake the guy's hand? Take the happy couple out to dinner? Seriously?"

It's just an idea.

A hypothetical scenario.

But the possibility blooms in my mind: Juliette smiling, laughing with another man—

And then worse: his hands on her body, her eyes half closed with desire—

I feel suddenly like I've been punched in the stomach.

I close my eyes. Try to be steady.

But now I can't stop picturing it: someone else knowing her the way I've known her, in the dark, in the quiet hours before dawn—her gentle kisses, her private moans of pleasure—

I can't do it. I can't do it.

I can't breathe.

"Hey—I'm sorry—it was just a question—"

"I think you should go," I say. I whisper the words. "You should leave."

"Yeah—you know what? Yeah. Excellent idea." He nods several times. "No problem." Still, he doesn't move.

"What?" I snap at him.

"I just, uh"—he rocks back and forth on his heels—"I was wondering if you, uh, wanted any more of those medicine thingies though? Before I get out of here?"

"*Get. Out.*"

"All right, man, no problem, yeah, I'm just gonna—"

Suddenly, someone is banging on my door.

I look up. Look around.

"Should I, um"—Kenji is looking at me, a question in his eyes—"you want me to get that?"

I glare at him.

"Yeah, I'll get it," he says, and runs to answer the door.

It's Delalieu, looking panicked.

It takes more than a concerted effort, but I manage to pull myself together.

"You couldn't have called, Lieutenant? Isn't that what our phones are for?"

"I've been trying, sir, for over an hour, but no one would answer your phone, sir—"

I roll my neck and sigh, stretching the muscles even as they tense up again.

My fault.

I disconnected my phone last night. I didn't want any distractions while I was looking through my father's files, and in the insanity of the morning I forgot to reconnect the line. I was beginning to wonder why I've had so much uninterrupted time to myself today.

"That's fine," I say, cutting him off. "What's the problem?"

"Sir," he says, swallowing hard, "I've tried to contact both you and Madam Supreme, but the two of you have been unavailable all day and, and—"

"What is it, Lieutenant?"

"The supreme commander of Europe has sent her daughter, sir. She showed up unannounced a couple of hours ago, and I'm afraid she's making quite a fuss about being ignored and I wasn't sure what to d-do—"

"Well, tell her to sit her ass down and wait," Kenji says, irritated. "What do you mean she's making a *fuss*? We've got shit to do around here."

But I've gone unexpectedly solid. Like the blood in my veins has congealed.

"I mean—right?" Kenji is saying, nudging me with his arm. "What's the deal, man? Delalieu," he says, ignoring me. "Just tell her to chill. We'll be down in a bit. This guy needs to shower and put his shirt on straight. Give her some lunch or something, okay? We'll be right there."

"Yes, sir," Delalieu says quietly. He's talking to Kenji, but flashes me another look of concern. I do not respond. I'm not sure what to say.

Things are happening too quickly. Fission and fusion in all the wrong places, all at once.

It's only once Delalieu has gone and the door is closed that Kenji finally says, "What was that about? Why do you look so freaked?"

And I unfreeze. Feeling returns slowly to my limbs.

I turn around to face him.

"You really think," I say carefully, "that I need to tell Juliette about the other women I've been with?"

"Uh, yeah," he says, "but what does that have to do with—"

I stare at him.

306

He stares back. His mouth drops open. "You mean—with this girl—the one downstairs—?"

"The children of the supreme commanders," I try to explain, squeezing my eyes shut as I do, "we—we all basically grew up together. I've known most of these girls all my life." I look at him, attempting nonchalance. "It was inevitable, really. It shouldn't be surprising."

But Kenji's eyebrows are high. He's trying to fight a smile as he slaps me on the back, too hard. "Oh, you are in for a world of pain, bro. A world. Of. Pain."

I shake my head. "There's no need to make this dramatic. Juliette doesn't have to know. She's not even speaking to me at the moment."

Kenji laughs. Looks at me with something that resembles pity. "You don't know anything about women, do you?" When I don't respond, he says, "Trust me, man, I bet you anything that wherever J is right now—out there somewhere—she already knows. And if she doesn't, she will soon. Girls talk about everything."

"How is that possible?"

He shrugs.

I sigh. Run a hand over my hair. "Well," I say. "Does it really matter? Don't we have more important things to contend with than the staid details of my previous relationships?"

"Normally? Yes. But when the supreme commander of North America is your ex-girlfriend, and she's already feeling really stressed about the fact that you've been lying to her? And then all of a sudden your other ex-girlfriend shows up and Juliette doesn't even *know* about her? And she realizes there are, like, a thousand other things you've lied to her about—"

"I never lied to her about any of this," I interject. "She never *asked*—"

"—and then our very powerful supreme commander gets, like, super, super pissed?" Kenji shrugs. "I don't know, man, I don't see that ending well."

I drop my head in my hands. Close my eyes. "I need to shower."

"And . . . yeah, that's my cue to go."

I look up, suddenly. "Is there anything I can do?" I say. "To stop this from getting worse?"

"Oh, so *now* you're taking relationship advice from me?"

I fight the impulse to roll my eyes.

"I don't really know man," Kenji says, and sighs. "I think, this time, you just have to deal with the consequences of your own stupidity."

I look away, bite back a laugh, and nod several times as I say, "Go to hell, Kishimoto."

"I'm right behind you, bro." He winks at me. Just once.

And disappears.

JULIETTE

There's something simmering inside of me.

~~Something I've never dared to tap into, something I'm afraid to acknowledge. There's a part of me clawing to break free from the cage I've trapped it in, banging on the doors of my heart begging to be free.~~

~~Begging to let go.~~

~~Every day I feel like I'm reliving the same nightmare. I open my mouth to shout, to fight, to swing my fists but my vocal cords are cut, my arms are heavy and weighted down as if trapped in wet cement and I'm screaming but no one can hear me, no one can reach me and I'm caught. And it's killing me.~~

~~I've always had to make myself submissive, subservient, twisted into a pleading, passive mop just to make everyone else feel safe and comfortable. My existence has become a fight to prove I'm harmless, that I'm not a threat, that I'm capable of living among other human beings without hurting them.~~

~~And I'm so tired I'm so tired I'm so tired I'm so tired and sometimes I get so angry~~

I don't know what's happening to me.

—AN EXCERPT FROM JULIETTE'S JOURNALS IN THE ASYLUM

We land in a tree.

I have no idea where we are—I don't even know if I've ever been this high, or this close to nature—but Nazeera doesn't seem bothered at all.

I'm breathing hard as I turn to face her, adrenaline and disbelief colliding, but she's not looking at me. She looks calm—happy, even—as she looks out across the sky, one foot propped up on a tree branch while the other hangs, swinging gently back and forth in the cool breeze. Her left arm rests on her left knee and her hand is relaxed, almost too casual, as it clenches and unclenches around something I can't see. I tilt my head, part my lips to ask the question when she interrupts me.

"You know," she says suddenly, "I've never, ever shown anyone what I can do."

I'm caught off guard.

"No one? Ever?" I say, stunned.

She shakes her head.

"Why not?"

She's quiet for a minute before she says, "The answer to that question is one of the reasons why I wanted to talk to you." She touches an absent hand to the diamond piercing

312

at her lip, tapping the tip of one finger against the glittering stone. "So," she says. "Do you know anything real about your past?"

And the pain is swift, like cold steel, like knives in my chest. Painful reminders of today's revelations. "I know some things," I finally say. "I learned most of it this morning, actually."

She nods. "And that's why you ran off like you did."

I turn to face her. "You were watching me?"

"I've been shadowing you, yeah."

"Why?"

She smiles, but it looks tired. "You really don't remember me, do you?"

I stare at her, confused.

She sighs. Swings both her legs under her and looks out into the distance. "Never mind."

"No, wait—what do you mean? Am I supposed to remember you?"

She shakes her head.

"I don't understand," I say.

"Forget it," she says. "It's nothing. You just look really familiar, and for a split second I thought we'd met before."

"Oh," I say. "Okay." But now she won't look at me, and I have a strange feeling she's holding something back.

Still, she says nothing.

She looks lost in thought, chewing on her lip as she looks off in the distance, and doesn't say anything for what feels like a long time.

"Um. Excuse me? You put me in a *tree*," I finally say. "What the hell am I doing here? What do you want?"

She turns to face me. That's when I realize that the object in her hand is actually a bag of little hard candies. She holds it out to me, indicating with her head that I should take one.

But I don't trust her. "No thanks," I say.

She shrugs. Unwraps one of the colorful candies and pops it in her mouth. "So," she says. "What'd Warner tell you today?"

"Why do you want to know?"

"Did he tell you that you have a sister?"

I feel a knot of anger beginning to form in my chest. I say nothing.

"I'll take that as a yes," she says. She bites down hard on the candy in her mouth. Crunches quietly beside me. "Did he tell you anything else?"

"What do you want from me?" I say. "Who are you?"

"What did he tell you about your parents?" she asks, ignoring me even as she glances at me out of the corner of her eye. "Did he tell you that you were adopted? That your biological parents are still alive?"

I only stare at her.

She tilts her head. Studies me. "Did he tell you their names?"

My eyes widen automatically.

Nazeera smiles, and the action brightens her face. "There it is," she says, with a triumphant nod. She peels another

314

candy from its wrapper and pops it in her mouth. "Hmm."

"There *what* is?"

"The moment," she says, "where the anger ends, and the curiosity begins."

I sigh, irritated. "You know my parents' names?"

"I never said that."

I feel suddenly exhausted. Powerless. "Does everyone know more about my life than I do?"

She glances at me. Looks away. "Not everyone," she says. "Those of us with ranks high enough in The Reestablishment know a lot, yeah," she says. "It's our business to know. Especially *us*," she says, meeting my eyes for a second. "The kids, I mean. Our parents expect us to take over one day. But, no, not everyone knows everything." She smiles at something, a private joke shared only with herself, when she says, "Most people don't know shit, actually." And then, a frown. "Though I guess Warner knows more than I thought he did."

"So," I say. "You've known Warner for a long time."

Nazeera pushes her hood back a bit so I can better see her face, leans against a branch, and sighs. "Listen," she says quietly. "I only know what my dad told us about you guys, and I'm wise enough to the game now to know that most of the things I've heard are probably nonsense. But—"

She hesitates. Bites her lip and hesitates.

"Just say it," I tell her, shaking my head as I do. "I've already heard so many people tell me I'm crazy for falling for him. You wouldn't be the first."

"What? No," she says, and laughs. "I don't think you're crazy. I mean, I get why people might think he's trouble, but he's my people, you know? I knew his parents. Anderson made my own dad seem like a nice guy. We're all kind of messed up, that's true, but Warner's not a bad person. He's just trying to find a way to survive this insanity, just like the rest of us."

"Oh," I say. Surprised.

"Anyway," she says with a shrug, "no, I understand why you like him. And even if I didn't, I mean—I'm not blind." She raises a knowing eyebrow at me. "I get you, girl."

I'm still stunned. This might be the very first time I've heard anyone but myself make an argument for Warner.

"No, what I'm trying to say is that I think it might be a good time for you to focus on yourself for a little while. Take a beat. And anyway, Lena's going to be here any minute, so it's probably best for you to stay away from that situation for as long as you can." She shoots me another knowing look. "I really don't think you need any more drama in your life, and that whole"—she gestures to the air—"*thing* is bound to just—you know—get really ugly."

"What?" I frown. "What thing? What situation? Who's Lena?"

Nazeera's surprise is so swift, so genuine, I can't help but feel instantly concerned. My pulse picks up as Nazeera turns fully in my direction and says, very, very slowly, "Lena. Lena Mishkin. She's the daughter of the supreme commander of Europe."

I stare at her. Shake my head.

Nazeera's eyes widen. "Girl, what the hell?"

"What?" I say, scared now. "Who is she?"

"Who is she? Are you serious? She's Warner's *ex-girlfriend*."

I nearly fall out of the tree.

It's funny, I thought I'd feel more than this.

Old Juliette would've cried. Broken Juliette would've split open from the sudden impact of today's many heartbreaking revelations, from the depth of Warner's lies, from the pain of feeling so deeply betrayed. But this new version of me is refusing to react; instead, my body is shutting down.

I feel my arms go numb as Nazeera offers me details about Warner's old relationship—details I do and don't want to hear. She says Lena and Warner were a big deal for the world of The Reestablishment and suddenly three fingers on my right hand begin to twitch without my permission. She says that Lena's mom and Warner's dad were excited about an alliance between their families, about a bond that would only make their regime stronger, and electric currents bolt down my legs, shocking and paralyzing me all at once.

She says that Lena was in love with him—really in love with him—but that Warner broke her heart, that he never treated her with any real affection and she's hated him for it, that "Lena's been in a rage ever since she heard the stories of how he fell for you, especially because you were supposed to be, like, fresh out of a mental asylum, you know? Apparently it was a huge blow to her ego" and hearing this does nothing to soothe me. It makes me feel strange and foreign, like a specimen in a tank, like my life was never my own, like I'm an actor in a play directed by strangers and I feel an exhalation of arctic wind blow steadily into my chest, a bitter breeze circling my heart and I close my eyes as frostbite eases my pain, its icy hands closing around the wounds festering in my flesh.

Only then

Only then do I finally breathe, luxuriating in the disconnection from this pain.

I look up, feeling broken and brand-new, eyes cold and unfeeling as I blink slowly and say, "How do you know all this?"

Nazeera breaks a leaf off a nearby branch and folds it between her fingers. She shrugs. "It's a small, incestuous circle we move in. I've known Lena forever. She and I were never close, exactly, but we move in the same world." Another shrug. "She was really messed up over him. It's all she ever wanted to talk about. And she'd talk to anyone about it."

"How long were they together?"

"Two years."

Two years.

The answer is so unexpectedly painful it spears through my new defenses.

Two years? Two years with another girl and he never said a word about it. Two years with someone else. *And how many others?* A shock of pain tries to reach me, to circumvent my new, cold heart, and I manage to fight the worst of it. Even so, a brick of something hot and horrible buries itself in my chest.

Not jealousy, no.

Inferiority. Inexperience. Naïveté.

How much more will I learn about him? How much more has he kept from me? How will I ever be able to trust him again?

I close my eyes and feel the weight of loss and resignation settle deep, deep within me. My bones shift, rearranging to make room for these new hurts.

This wave of fresh anger.

"When did they break up?" I ask.

"Like . . . eight months ago?"

Now I stop asking questions.

I want to become a tree. A blade of grass. I want to become dirt or air or nothing. *Nothing.* Yes. I want to become nothing.

I feel like such a fool.

"I don't understand why he never told you," Nazeera is saying to me now, but I can hardly hear her. "That's crazy. It was pretty big news in our world."

"Why have you been following me?" I change the subject with zero finesse. My eyes are half lidded. My fists are clenched. I don't want to talk about Warner anymore. Ever again. I want to rip my heart out of my chest and throw it in our piss-filled ocean for all the good its ever done me.

I don't want to feel anything anymore.

Nazeera sits back, surprised. "There's a lot going on right now," she says. "There's so much you don't know, so much crap you're just beginning to wade into. I mean—hell, someone tried to kill you yesterday." She shakes her head. "I'm just worried about you."

"You don't even know me. Why bother worrying about me?"

This time, she doesn't respond. She just looks at me. Slowly, she unwraps another candy. Pops it in her mouth and looks away.

"My dad forced me to come here," she says quietly. "I didn't want to have any part in any of this. I never have. I hate everything The Reestablishment stands for. But I told myself that if I had to be here, I would look out for you. So that's what I'm doing now. I'm looking out for you."

"Well, don't waste your time," I say to her, feeling callous. "I don't need your pity or your protection."

Nazeera goes quiet. Finally, she sighs. "Listen—I'm really sorry," she says. "I honestly thought you knew about Lena."

"I don't care about Lena," I lie. "I have more important things to worry about."

"Right," she says. She clears her throat. "I know. Still, I'm sorry."

I say nothing.

"Hey," Nazeera says. "Really. I didn't mean to upset you.

I just want you to know that I'm not here to hurt you. I'm trying to look out for you."

"I don't need you to look out for me. I'm doing fine."

Now she rolls her eyes. "Didn't I just save your life?"

I mumble something dumb under my breath.

Nazeera shakes her head. "You have to get it together, girl, or you're not going to get through this alive," she says to me. "You have no idea what's going on behind the scenes or what the other commanders have in store for you." When I don't respond she says, "Lena won't be the last of us to arrive here, you know. And no one is coming here to play nice."

I look up at her. My eyes are dead of emotion. "Good," I say. "Let them come."

She laughs, but there's no life in it. "So you and Warner have some drama and now you just don't care about anything? That's real mature."

Fire flashes through me. My eyes sharpen. "If I'm upset right now, it's because I've just discovered that everyone closest to me has been *lying* to me. Using me. Manipulating me for their own needs. My parents," I say angrily, "are still *alive*, and apparently they're no better than the abusive monsters who adopted me. I have a sister being actively tortured by The Reestablishment—and I never even knew she existed. I'm trying to come to terms with the fact that *nothing* is going to be the same for me, not ever again, and I have no idea who to trust or how to move forward. So yeah," I say, nearly shouting the words, "right now I don't care about *anything*. Because I don't know what I'm fighting for anymore. And I don't know who my friends are. Right now," I say, "everyone is my enemy, including *you*."

Nazeera is unmoved. "You could fight for your sister," she says.

"I don't even know who she is."

Nazeera shoots me a sidelong look, heavy with disbelief. "Isn't it enough that she's an innocent girl being tortured? I thought there was some greater good you were fighting for."

I shrug. Look away.

"You know what? You don't have to care," she says. "But I do. I care about what The Reestablishment has done to innocent people. I care that our parents are all a bunch of psychopaths. I care a great deal about what The Reestablishment has done, in particular, to those of us with abilities.

"And to answer your earlier question: I never told anyone about my powers because I saw what they did to people like me. How they locked them up. Tortured and abused them." She looks me in the eye. "And I don't want to be the next experiment."

Something inside me hollows. Mellows out. I feel suddenly empty and sad. "I do care," I finally say to her. "I care too much, probably."

And Nazeera's anger subsides. She sighs.

"Warner said The Reestablishment wants to take me back," I say.

She nods. "Seems about right."

"Where do they want to take me?"

"I'm not sure," she says. Shrugs. "They might just kill you."

"Thanks for the pep talk."

"Or," she says, smiling a little, "they'll send you to another continent, maybe. New alias. New facility."

"Another continent?" I say, curious despite myself. "I've never even been on a plane before."

Somehow, I've said the wrong thing.

Nazeera looks almost stricken for a second. Pain flashes in and out of her eyes and she looks away. Clears her throat. But when she looks back her face is neutral once more. "Yeah. Well. You're not missing much."

"Do you travel a lot?" I ask.

"Yep."

"Where are you from?"

"Sector 2. Asian continent." And then, at the look at my face: "But I was born in Baghdad."

"Baghdad," I say, almost to myself. It sounds so familiar, and I'm trying to remember, trying to place it on the map, when she says

"Iraq."

"*Oh*," I say. "Wow."

"A lot to take in, huh?"

"Yeah," I say quietly. And then—hating myself even as I say the words—I can't help but ask, "Where's Lena from?"

Nazeera laughs. "I thought you said you didn't care about Lena."

323

I close my eyes. Shake my head, mortified.

"She was born in Peterhof, a suburb of Saint Petersburg."

"Russia," I say, relieved to finally recognize one of these cities. *War and Peace.*"

"Great book," Nazeera says with a nod. "Too bad it's still on the burn list."

"Burn list?"

"To be destroyed," she says. "The Reestablishment has big plans to reset language, literature, and culture. They want to create a new kind of, I don't know," she says, making a random gesture with one hand, "universal humanity."

I nod, quietly horrified. I already know this. I'd first heard about this from Adam right after he was assigned to become my cellmate in the asylum. And the idea of destroying art—culture—everything that makes human beings diverse and beautiful—

It makes me feel sick to my stomach.

"Anyway," she says, "it's obviously a garbage, grotesque experiment, but we have to go through the motions. We were given lists of books to sort through, and we have to read them, write reports, decide what to keep and what to get rid of." She exhales. "I finally finished reading most of the classics a couple of months ago—but early last year they forced all of us to read *War and Peace* in five languages, because they wanted us to analyze how culture plays a role in manipulating the translation of the same text." She hesitates, remembering. "It was definitely the most fun to read in French. But I think, ultimately, it's best in Russian.

All other translations—especially the English ones—are missing that necessary . . . *toska*. You know what I mean?"

My mouth drops open a little.

It's the *way* she says it—like it's no big deal, like she's just said something perfectly normal, like anyone could read Tolstoy in five different languages and polish off the books in an afternoon. It's her easy, effortless self-assuredness that makes my heart deflate. It took me a month to read *War and Peace*. In *English*.

"Right," I say, and look away. "Yeah. That's, um, interesting."

It's becoming too familiar, this feeling of inferiority. Too powerful. Every time I think I've made progress in my life I seem to be reminded of how much further I still have to go. Though I guess it's not Nazeera's fault that she and the rest of these kids were bred to be violent geniuses.

"So," she says, clapping her hands together. "Is there anything else you want to know?"

"Yeah," I say. "What's the deal with your brother?"

She looks surprised. "Haider?" She hesitates. "What do you mean?"

"I mean, like"—I frown—"is he loyal to your dad? To The Reestablishment? Is he trustworthy?"

"I don't know if I'd call him trustworthy," she says, looking thoughtful. "But I think all of us have complicated relationships with The Reestablishment. Haider doesn't want to be here any more than I do."

"Really?"

She nods. "Warner probably doesn't consider any of us his friends, but Haider does. And Haider went through a really dark time last year." She pauses. Breaks another leaf off a nearby branch. Folds and refolds it between her fingers as she says, "My dad was putting a lot of pressure on him, forcing him through some really intense training—the details of which Haider still won't share with me—and a few weeks later he just started spiraling. He was exhibiting suicidal tendencies. Self-harming. And I got really scared. I called Warner because I knew Haider would listen to him." She shakes her head. "Warner didn't say a word. He just got on a plane. And he stayed with us for a couple of weeks. I don't know what he said to Haider," she says. "I don't know what he did or how he got him through it, but"—she looks off into the distance, shrugs—"it's hard to forget something like that. Even though our parents keep trying to pit us against each other. They're trying to keep us from getting too soft." She laughs. "But it's so much bullshit."

And I'm reeling, stunned.

There's so much to unpack here I don't even know where to begin. I'm not sure if I want to. All of Nazeera's comments about Warner just seem to spear me in the heart. They make me miss him.

They make me want to forgive him.

But I can't let my emotions control me. Not now. Not ever. So I force the feelings down, out of my head, and instead, I say, "Wow. And I just thought Haider was kind of a jerk."

Nazeera smiles. Waves an absent hand. "He's working on it."

"Does he have any . . . supernatural abilities?"

"None that I know of."

"Huh."

"Yeah."

"But you can fly," I say.

She nods.

"That's interesting."

She smiles, wide, and turns to face me. Her eyes are big and beautifully lit from the dappled light breaking through the branches, and her excitement is so pure that it makes something inside of me shrivel up and die.

"It's so much more than *interesting*," she says, and it's then that I feel a pang of something new:

Jealousy.

Envy.

Resentment.

My abilities have always been a curse—a source of endless pain and conflict. Everything about me is designed to kill and destroy and it's a reality I've never been able to fully accept. "Must be nice," I say.

She turns away again, smiling into the wind. "The best part?" she says. "Is that I can also do *this*—"

Nazeera goes suddenly invisible.

I jerk back sharply.

And then she's back, beaming. "Isn't it great?" she says, eyes glittering with excitement. "I've never been able to share this with anyone before."

"Uh . . . yeah." I laugh but it sounds fake, too high. "Very cool." And then, more quietly, "Kenji is going to be pissed."

Nazeera stops smiling. "What does he have to do with anything?"

"Well—" I nod in her general direction. "I mean, what you just did? That's Kenji's thing. And he's not good at sharing the spotlight, generally."

"I didn't know there could be someone else with the same power," she says, visibly heartbroken. "How is that possible?"

"I don't know," I say, and I feel a sudden urge to laugh. She's so determined to dislike Kenji that I'm starting to wonder why. And then I'm reminded, all at once, of today's horrible revelations, and the smile is wiped off my face. "So," I say quickly, "should we get back to base? I still have a ton of things to figure out, including how I'm going to deal with this stupid symposium tomorrow. I don't know if I should bail or just—"

"Don't bail." Nazeera cuts me off. "If you bail they might think you know something. Don't show your hand," she says. "Not yet. Just go through the motions until you get your own plan together."

I stare at her. Study her. Finally, I say, "Okay."

"And once you decide what you want to do, let me know. I can always help evacuate people. Hold down the fort. Fight. Whatever. Just say the word."

"What—?" I frown. "Evacuate people? What are you

talking about?"

She smiles as she shakes her head. "Girl, you still don't get it, do you? Why do you think we're here? The Reestablishment is planning on destroying Sector 45." She stares at me. "And that includes everyone in it."

WARNER

I never make it downstairs.

I've hardly had a second to put my shirt on straight when I hear someone banging on my door.

"I'm really sorry, bro," I hear Kenji shout, "she wouldn't listen to me—"

And then,

"Open the door, Warner. I promise this will only hurt a little."

Her voice is the same as it's always been. Smooth. Deceptively soft. Always a little rough around the edges.

"Lena," I say. "How nice to hear from you again."

"Open the door, asshole."

"You never did hold back with the flattery."

"I said *open the door*—"

Very carefully, I do.

And then I close my eyes.

Lena slaps me across the face so hard I feel it ring in my ears. Kenji screams, but only briefly, and I take a steadying breath. I look up at her without lifting my head. "Are you done?"

Her eyes go wide, enraged and offended, and I realize I've already pushed her too far. She swings without thinking, and even so, it's a punch perfectly executed. On impact she'd break, at the very least, my nose, but I can no longer entertain her daydreams of causing me physical harm. My reflexes are faster than hers—they always have been—and I catch her wrist just moments before impact. Her arm vibrates from the intensity of the unspent energy and she jerks back, shrieking as she breaks free.

"You son of a bitch," she says, breathing hard.

"I can't let you punch me in the face, Lena."

"I would do worse to you."

"And yet you wonder why things didn't work out between us."

"Always so cold," she says, and something in her voice breaks as she says it. "Always so cruel."

I rub the back of my head and smile, unhappily, at the wall. "Why have you come up to my room? Why engage me privately? You know I have little left to say to you."

"You never said *anything* to me," she suddenly screams. "Two years," she says, her chest heaving, "two years and you left a message with my *mother* telling her to let me know our relationship was over—"

"You weren't home," I say, squeezing my eyes shut. "I thought it more efficient—"

"You are a *monster*—"

"Yes," I say. "Yes, I am. I wish you'd forget about me."

Her eyes go glassy in an instant, heavy with unspent tears. I feel guilty for feeling nothing. I can only stare back at her, too tired to fight. Too busy nursing my own wounds.

Her voice is both angry and sad when she says, "Where's your new girlfriend? I'm dying to meet her."

At this, I look away again, my own heart breaking in my chest. "You should go get settled," I say. "Nazeera and Haider are here, too, somewhere. I'm sure you'll all have plenty to talk about."

"Warner—"

"Please, Lena," I say, feeling truly exhausted now. "You're upset, I understand. But it's not my fault you feel this way. I don't love you. I never have. And I never led you to believe I did."

She's quiet for so long I finally face her, realizing too late that somehow, again, I've managed to make things worse. She looks paralyzed, her eyes round, her lips parted, her hands trembling slightly at her sides.

I sigh.

"I have to go," I say quietly. "Kenji will show you to your quarters." I glance at Kenji and he nods, just once. His face is unexpectedly grim.

Still, Lena says nothing.

I take a step back, ready to close the door between us, when she lunges at me with a sudden cry, her hands closing around my throat so unexpectedly she almost knocks me over. She's screaming in my face, pushing me backward as she does, and it's all I can do to keep myself calm. My instincts are too sharp sometimes—it's hard for me to keep from reacting to physical threats—and I force myself to move in an almost liquid slow motion as I remove her hands from around my neck. She's still thrashing against me, landing several kicks at my shins when I finally manage to gentle her arms and pull her close.

Suddenly, she stills.

My lips are at her ear when I say her name once, very gently.

She swallows hard as she meets my eyes, all fire and rage. Even so, I sense her hope. Her desperation. I can feel her wonder whether I've changed my mind.

"Lena," I say again, even more softly. "Really, you must know that your actions do nothing to endear you to me."

She stiffens.

"Please go away," I say, and quickly close the door between us.

I fall backward onto my bed, cringing as she kicks violently at my door, and cradle my head in my hands. I have to stifle a sudden, inexplicable impulse to break something. My brain feels like it might split free of my skull.

How did I get here?

Unmoored. Disheveled and distracted.

When did this happen to me?

I have no focus, no control. I am every disappointment, every failure, every useless thing my father ever said I was. I am weak. I am a coward. I let my emotions win too often and now, now I've lost everything. Everything is falling apart. Juliette is in danger. Now, more than ever, she and I need to stand together. I need to talk to her. I need to warn her. I need to *protect* her—but she's gone. She despises me again.

And I'm here once more.

In the abyss.

Dissolving slowly in the acid of emotion.

JULIETTE

JULIETTE

Loneliness is a strange sort of thing.

It creeps up on you, quiet and still, sits by your side in the dark, strokes your hair as you sleep. It wraps itself around your bones, squeezing so tight you almost can't breathe, almost can't hear the pulse racing in your blood as it rushes up your skin and touches its lips to the soft hairs at the back of your neck. It leaves lies in your heart, lies next to you at night, leaches the light out from every corner. It's a constant companion, clasping your hand only to yank you down when you're struggling to stand up, catching your tears only to force them down your throat. It scares you simply by standing by your side.

You wake up in the morning and wonder who you are. You fail to fall asleep at night and tremble in your skin. You doubt you doubt you doubt

    do I

    don't I

    should I

    why won't I

And even when you're ready to let go. When you're ready to break free. When you're ready to be brand-new. Loneliness is an old friend standing beside you in the mirror, looking you in the eye, challenging you to live your life without it. You can't find the words to fight yourself, to fight the words screaming that you're *not enough never enough never ever enough.*

Loneliness is a bitter, wretched companion.

Sometimes it just won't let go.

—AN EXCERPT FROM JULIETTE'S JOURNALS IN THE ASYLUM

The first thing I do upon my return back to base is order Delalieu to move all my things into Anderson's old rooms. I haven't really thought about how I'll deal with seeing Warner all the time. I haven't considered yet how to act around his ex-girlfriend. I have no idea what any of that will be like and right now I almost can't be bothered to care.

I'm too angry.

If Nazeera is to be believed, then everything we tried to do here—all of our efforts to play nice, to be diplomatic, to host an international conference of leaders—was for nothing. Everything we'd been working toward is garbage. She says they're planning on wiping out all of Sector 45. Every person. Not just the ones living at our headquarters. Not just the soldiers who stood alongside us. But all the civilians, too. Women, children—everyone.

They're going to make Sector 45 disappear.

And I'm feeling suddenly out of control.

Anderson's old quarters are enormous—they make Warner's rooms seem ridiculous in comparison—and after Delalieu has left me alone I'm free to drown in the many privileges that my fake role as supreme commander of The Reestablishment has to offer. Two offices. Two meeting rooms. A full kitchen. A large master suite. Three bathrooms. Two guest rooms. Four closets, fully stocked— like father, like son, I realize—and countless other details. I've never spent much time in any of these rooms before; the dimensions are too vast. I need only one office and, generally, that's where I spend my time.

But today I take the time to look around, and the one space that piques my interest most is one I'd never noticed before. It's the one positioned closest to the bedroom: an entire room devoted to Anderson's enormous collection of alcohol.

I don't know very much about alcohol.

I've never had a traditional teenage experience of any kind; I've never had parties to attend; I've never been subjected to the kind of peer pressure I've read about in novels. No one has ever offered me drugs or a strong drink, and probably for good reason. Still, I'm mesmerized by the myriad bottles arranged perfectly on the glass shelves lining the dark, paneled walls of this room. There's no furniture but two big, brown leather chairs and the heavily lacquered coffee table stationed between them. Atop the coffee table sits a clear—jug?—filled with some kind of amber liquid; there's a lone drinking glass set beside it. Everything in here is dark, vaguely depressing, and reeks of wood and something ancient, musty—*old*.

I reach out, run my fingers along the wooden panels, and count. Three of the four walls of the room are dedicated to housing various, ancient bottles—637 in total—most of which are full of the same amber liquid; only a couple of bottles are full of clear liquid. I move closer to inspect the labels and learn that the clear bottles are full of vodka—this is a drink I've heard of—but the amber liquid is named different things in different containers. A great deal of it is called Scotch. There are seven bottles of tequila. But most of what Anderson keeps in this room is called bourbon—523 bottles in total—a substance I have no knowledge of. I've only really heard about people who drink wine and beer and margaritas—and there's none of that here. The only wall stocked with anything but alcohol is stacked with several boxes of cigars and more of the same short, intricately cut drinking glasses. I pick up one of the glasses and nearly drop it; it's so much heavier than it looks. I wonder if these things are made of real crystal.

And then I can't help but wonder about Anderson's motivations in designing this space. It's such a strange idea, to dedicate an entire room to displaying bottles of alcohol. Why not put them in a cabinet? Or in a refrigerator?

I sit down in one of the chairs and look up, distracted by the massive, glittering chandelier hanging from the ceiling.

Why I've gravitated toward this room, I can't say. But in here I feel truly alone. Walled off from all the noise and confusion of the day. I feel properly isolated here, among these bottles, in a way that soothes me. And for the first time all day, I feel myself relax. I feel myself withdraw. Retreat. Run away to some dark corner of my mind.

There's a strange kind of freedom in giving up.

There's a freedom in being angry. In living alone. And strangest of all: in here, within the walls of Anderson's old refuge I feel I finally understand him. I finally understand how he was able to live the way he did. He never allowed himself to feel, never allowed himself to hurt, never invited emotion into his life. He was under no obligation to anyone but himself—and it liberated him.

His selfishness set him free.

I reach for the jug of amber liquid, tug off the stopper, and fill the crystal glass sitting beside it. I stare at the glass for a while, and it stares back.

Finally, I pick it up.

One sip and I nearly spit it out, coughing violently as some of the liquid catches in my throat. Anderson's drink of choice is disgusting. Like death and fire and oil and smoke. I force myself to take one quick gulp of the vile drink before setting it down again, my eyes watering as the alcohol works its way through me. I'm not even sure why I've done it—why I wanted to try it or what I'm hoping it'll do for me. I have no expectations of anything.

I'm just curious.

I'm feeling careless.

And the seconds skip by, my eyes fluttering open and shut in the welcome silence and I drag a finger across the seam of my lips, I count the many bottles again, and I'm just beginning to think the terrible taste of the drink wasn't really that bad when slowly, happily, a bloom of warmth reaches up from deep within me and unfurls individual rays of heat inside my veins.

Oh, I think

oh

My mouth smiles but it feels a little crooked and I don't mind, not really, not even that my throat feels a little numb. I pick up the still-full glass and take another large gulp of fire and this time I don't dread it. It's pleasant to be lost like this, to fill my head with clouds and wind and nothing. I feel loose and a little clumsy as I stand but it feels nice, it feels nice and warm and pleasant and I find myself wandering toward the bathroom, smiling as I search its drawers for something

something

where is it

And then I find it, a set of electric hair clippers, and I decide it's time to give myself a haircut. My hair has been bothering me forever. It's too long, too long, a memento, a keepsake from all my time in the asylum, too long from all those years I was forgotten and left to rot in hell, too thick, too suffocating, too much, too this, too that, too annoying

My fingers fumble for the plug but eventually I manage to turn the thing on, the little machine buzzing in my hand and I think I should probably take off my clothes first, don't want to get hair everywhere do I, so I should probably take my clothes off first, definitely

And then I'm standing in my underwear, thinking about how much I've always secretly wanted to do this, how I always thought it would feel so nice, so liberating—

And I drag the clippers across my head in a slightly jagged motion.

Once.

Twice.

Over and over and over and I'm laughing as my hair falls to the floor, a sea of too-long brown waves lapping at my feet and I've never felt so light, so silly silly happy

I drop the still-buzzing clippers in the sink and step back, admiring my work in the mirror as I touch my newly shorn head. I have the same haircut as Warner now. The same sharp half inch of hair, except my hair is dark where his is light and I look so much older suddenly. Harsher. Serious. I have cheekbones. A jawline. I look angry and a little scary. My eyes are bright, huge in my face, the center of attention, wide and sharp and piercing and I love it.

I love it.

I'm still giggling as I teeter down the hall, wandering Anderson's rooms in my underwear, feeling freer than I have in years. I flop down onto the big leather chair and finish the rest of the glass in two swift gulps.

Years, centuries, lifetimes pass and dimly, I hear the sound of banging.

I ignore it.

I'm sideways on the chair now, my legs flung over the arm, leaning back to watch the chandelier spin—

Was it spinning before?

—and too soon my reverie is interrupted, too soon I hear

a rush of voices I vaguely recognize and I don't move, merely squint, turning only my head toward the sounds.

"Oh shit, J—"

Kenji charges into the room and freezes in place at the sight of me. I suddenly, faintly remember that I'm in my underwear, and that another version of myself would prefer not to have Kenji see me like this—but it's not enough to motivate me to move. Kenji, however, seems very concerned.

"Oh *shit shit shit*—"

It's only then that I notice he's not alone.

Kenji and Warner are standing in front of me, the two of them staring at me like they're horrified, like I've done something wrong, and it makes me angry.

"What?" I say, annoyed. "Go away."

"Juliette—love—what did you do—"

And then Warner is kneeling beside me. I try to look at him but it's suddenly hard to focus, hard to see straight at all. My vision blurs and I have to blink several times to get his face to stop moving but then I'm looking at him, really looking at him, and something inside of me is trying to remember that we are angry with Warner, that we don't like him anymore and we do not want to see him or speak to him but then he touches my face—

and I sigh

I rest my cheek against his palm and remember something beautiful, something kind, and a rush of feeling floods through me

"Hi," I say.

And he looks so sad so sad and he's about to respond but Kenji says, "Bro, I think she drank, like, I don't know, a whole glass of this stuff. Maybe half a pint? And at her weight?" He swears under his breath. "That much whisky would destroy *me*."

Warner closes his eyes. I'm fascinated by the way his Adam's apple moves up and down his throat and I reach out, trail my fingers down his neck.

"Sweetheart," he whispers, his eyes still closed. "Why—"

"Do you know how much I love you?" I say. "I love—loved you so much. So much."

When he opens his eyes again, they're bright. Shining. He says nothing.

"Kishimoto," he says quietly. "Please turn on the shower."

"On it."

And Kenji's gone.

Warner still says nothing to me.

I touch his lips. Lean forward. "You have such a nice mouth," I whisper.

He tries to smile. It looks sad.

"Do you like my hair?" I say.

He nods.

"Really?"

"You're beautiful," he says, but he can hardly get the words out. And his voice breaks when he says, "Why did you do this, love? Were you trying to hurt yourself?"

I try to answer but feel suddenly nauseous. My head spins. I close my eyes to steady the feeling but it won't abate.

"Shower's ready," I hear Kenji shout. And then, suddenly, his voice is closer. "You got this, bro? Or do you want me to take it from here?"

"No." A pause. "No, you can go. I'll make sure she's safe. Please tell the others I'm not feeling well tonight. Send my apologies."

"You got it. Anything else?"

"Coffee. Several bottles of water. Two aspirin."

"Consider it done."

"Thank you."

"Anytime, man."

And then I'm moving, everything is moving, everything is sideways and I open my eyes and quickly close them as the world blurs before me. Warner is carrying me in his arms and I bury my face in the crook of his neck. He smells so familiar.

Safe.

I want to speak but I feel slow. Like it takes forever to tell my lips to move, like it's slow motion when they do, like the words rush together as I say them, over and over again

"I miss you already," I mumble against his skin. "I miss this, miss you, miss you" and then he puts me down, steadies me on my feet, and helps me walk into the standing shower.

I nearly scream when the water hits my body.

My eyes fly open, my mind half sobered in an instant, as the cold water rushes over me. I blink fast, breathing hard as I lean against the shower wall, staring wildly at Warner through the warped glass. Water snakes down my skin,

349

collects in my eyelashes, my open mouth. My shoulders slow their tremble as my body acclimates to the temperature and minutes pass, the two of us staring at each other and saying nothing. My mind steadies but doesn't clear, a fog still hanging over me even as I reach forward to turn the dial, heating the water by many degrees.

I can still see his face, beautiful even blurred by the glass between us, when he says, "Are you okay? Do you feel any better?"

I step forward, studying him silently, and say nothing as I unhook my bra and let it drop to the floor. There's no response from him save the slight widening of his eyes, the slight movement in his chest and I slip out of my underwear, kicking it off behind me and he blinks several times and steps backward, looks away, looks back again.

I push open the shower door.

"Come inside," I say.

But now he won't look at me.

"Aaron—"

"You're not feeling well," he says.

"I feel fine."

"Sweetheart, please, you just drank your weight in whisky—"

"I just want to touch you," I say. "Come here."

He finally turns to face me, his eyes moving slowly up my body and I see it, I see it happen when something inside of him seems to break. He looks pained and vulnerable and he swallows hard as he steps toward me, steam filling the

room now, hot drops of water breaking on my bare hips and
his lips part as he looks at me, as he reaches forward, and I
think he might actually come inside when

instead

he closes the door between us and says

"I'll be waiting for you in the living room, love."

WARNER

Juliette is asleep.

She emerged from the shower, climbed into my lap and promptly fell asleep against my neck, all the while mumbling things I know for certain she'll regret having said in the morning. It took every bit of my self-control to unhook her soft, warm figure from around me, but somehow I managed it. I tucked her into bed and left, the pain of peeling myself away from her not unlike what I imagine it'd be like to peel the skin off my own body. She begged me to stay and I pretended not to hear her. She told me she loved me and I couldn't bring myself to respond.

She cried, even with her eyes closed.

But I can't trust that she knows what she's doing or saying in this compromised state; no, I know better. She has no experience with alcohol, but I can only imagine that when her good sense is returned to her in the daylight, she will not want to see my face. She won't want to know that she made herself so vulnerable in front of me. I wonder whether she'll even remember what happened.

As for me, I am beyond despair.

It's past three in the morning and I feel as though I've not slept in days. I can hardly bear to close my eyes; I can't be left alone with my mind or the many frailties of my person. I feel shattered, held together by nothing but necessity.

I have tried in vain to articulate the mess of emotion cluttering my mind—to Kenji, who wanted to know what happened after he left; to Castle, who cornered me not three hours ago, demanding to know what I'd said to her; even to Kent, who managed to look only a little pleased upon discovering that my brand-new relationship had already imploded.

I want to sink into the earth.

I can't go back to our bedroom—my bedroom—where the proof of her is still fresh, too alive; and I can no longer escape to the simulation chambers, as the soldiers are still stationed there, relocated in all the aftermath of the new construction.

I've no reprieve from the consequences of my actions.

Nowhere to rest my head for longer than a moment before I'm discovered and duly chastened.

Lena, laughing loudly in my face as I walked past her in the hall.

Nazeera shaking her head as I bid good night to her brother.

Sonya and Sara shooting me mournful looks upon discovering me crouched in a corner of the unfinished medical wing. Brendan, Winston, Lily, Alia, and Ian popping their heads out of their brand-new bedrooms, stopping me as I tried to get away, asking so many questions—so loudly and forcefully—that even a groggy James came to find me, tugging at my sleeve and asking me over and over again whether or not Juliette was okay.

Where did this life come from?

Who are all these people to whom I'm suddenly beholden?

Everyone is so justifiably concerned about Juliette—about the well-being of our new supreme commander—that I, because I am complicit in her suffering, am safe nowhere from prying eyes, questioning looks, and pitying faces. It's alarming, having so many people privy to my private life. When things were good between us I had to answer fewer questions; I was a subject of lesser interest. Juliette was the one who maintained these relationships; they were not for me. I never wanted any of this. I didn't want this accountability. I don't care for the responsibility of friendships. I only wanted Juliette. I wanted her love, her heart, her arms around me. And this was part of the price I paid for her affection: these people. Their questions. Their unvarnished scorn for my existence.

So. I've become a wraith.

I stalk these quiet halls. I stand in the shadows and hold myself still in the darkness and wait for something. For what, I don't know.

Danger.

Oblivion.

Anything at all to inform my next steps.

I want renewed purpose, a focus, a job to do. And then all at once I'm reminded that I am the chief commander and regent of Sector 45, that I have an infinite number of

357

things to oversee and negotiate—and somehow that's no longer enough for me. My daily tasks are not enough to distract my mind; my deeply regimented routines have been dismantled; Delalieu is struggling under the weight of my emotional erosion and I cannot help but think of my father again and again—

How right he was about me.

He's always been right.

I've been undone by emotion, over and over. It was emotion that prompted me to take any job—at any cost—to be nearer to my mother. It was emotion that led me to find Juliette, to seek her out in search of a cure for my mother. It was emotion that prompted me to fall in love, to get shot and lose my mind, to become a broken boy all over again—one who'd fall to his knees and beg his worthless, monstrous father to spare the girl he loved. It was emotion, my flimsy emotions that cost me everything.

I have no peace. No purpose.

How I wish I'd ripped this heart from my chest long ago.

Still, there is work to be done.

The symposium is now less than twelve hours away and I never had a chance to go over the details with Juliette. I didn't think things would turn out like this. I never thought that business would go on as usual after the death of my father. I thought a greater war was imminent; I thought for certain the other supreme commanders would come for us before we'd had even a chance to pretend we had true control of Sector 45. It hadn't occurred to me that they'd have more sinister plans in mind. It hadn't occurred to me to spend more time prepping her for the tedious formalities—these monotonous routines—embedded in the structure of The Reestablishment. But I should have known better. I should have expected this. *I could have prevented this.*

I thought The Reestablishment would fall.

I was wrong.

Our supreme commander has hours to prepare before having to address a room of the 554 other chief commanders and regents in North America. She will be expected to lead. To negotiate the many intricacies of domestic and international diplomacy. Haider, Nazeera, and Lena will all be waiting to send word back to their murderous parents. And I should be by her side, helping and guiding and protecting her. Instead, I have no idea what kind of Juliette will emerge from my father's rooms in the morning. I have no idea what to expect from her, how she will treat me, or where her mind will go.

I have no idea what's going to happen.

And I have no one to blame but myself.

JULIETTE

JULIETTE

I am not insane. I am not insane. I am not insane. I am not insane.
I am not insane. I am not insane. I am not insane. I am not insane.
I am not insane. I am not insane. I am not insane. I am not insane.
I am not insane. I am not insane. I am not insane. I am not insane.
I am not insane. I am not insane. I am not insane. I am not insane.
I am not insane. I am not insane. I am not insane. I am not insane.
I am not insane. I am not insane. I am not insane. I am not insane.
I am not insane. I am not insane. I am not insane. I am not insane.
I am not insane. I am not insane. I am not insane. I am not insane.
I am not insane. I am not insane. I am not insane. I am not insane.
I am not insane. I am not insane. I am not insane. I am not insane.
I am not insane. I am not insane. I am not insane. I am not insane.
I am not insane. I am not insane. I am not insane. I am not insane.
I am not insane. I am not insane. I am not insane. I am not insane.
I am not insane. I am not insane. I am not insane. I am not insane.
I am not insane. I am not insane. I am not insane. I am not insane.
I am not insane. I am not insane. I am not insane. I am not insane.
I am not insane. I am not insane. I am not insane. I am not insane.
I am not insane. I am not insane. I am not insane. I am not insane.
I am not insane. I am not insane. I am not insane. I am not insane.
I am not insane. I am not insane. I am not insane. I am not insane.

I am not insane. I am not insane. I am not insane. I am not insane.
I am not insane. I am not insane. I am not insane. I am not insane.
I am not insane. I am not insane. I am not insane. I am not insane.
I am not insane. I am not insane. I am not insane. I am not insane.
I am not insane.I am not insane.

—AN EXCERPT FROM JULIETTE'S JOURNALS IN THE ASYLUM

When I open my eyes, everything comes rushing back to me.

The evidence is here, in this drumming, pounding headache, in this sour taste in my mouth and stomach—in this unbearable thirst, like every cell in my body is dehydrated. It's the strangest feeling. It's horrible.

But worse, worse than all that are the memories. Gauzy but intact, I remember everything. Drinking Anderson's bourbon. Lying in my underwear in front of Kenji. And then, with a sudden, painful gasp—

Stripping in the shower. Asking Warner to join me.

I close my eyes as a wave of nausea overtakes me, threatens to upend the meager contents of my stomach. Mortification floods through me with an almost breathtaking efficiency, manufacturing within me a feeling of absolute self-loathing I'm unable to shake. Finally, reluctantly, I squint open my eyes again and notice someone has left me three bottles of water and two small white pills.

Gratefully, I inhale everything.

It's still dark in this room, but somehow I know the day has broken. I sit up too fast and my brain swings, rocking in my skull like a weighted pendulum and I feel myself sway even as I remain motionless, planting my hands against the mattress.

Never, I think. *Never again. Anderson was an idiot. This is a terrible feeling.* And it's not until I make my way to the bathroom that I remember, with a sudden, piercing clarity, that I shaved my head.

I stand frozen in front of the mirror, remnants of my long, brown waves still littering the floor underfoot, and stare at my reflection in awe. Horror. Fascination.

I hit the light switch and flinch, the fluorescent bulbs triggering something painful in my newly stupid brain, and it takes me a minute to adjust to the light. I turn on the shower, letting the water warm while I study my new self.

Gingerly, I touch the soft buzz of what little hair I have left. Seconds pass and I get braver, stepping so close to the mirror my nose bumps the glass. So strange, so strange but soon my apprehension dulls. No matter how long I look at myself I'm unable to drum up appropriate feelings of regret. Shock, yes, but—

I don't know.

I really, really like it.

My eyes have always been big and blue-green, miniatures of the globe we inhabit, but I've never before found them particularly interesting. But now—for the first time—I find my own face interesting. Like I've stepped out of the shadows of my own self; like the curtain I used to hide behind has been, finally, pushed back.

I'm here. Right here.

Look at me, I seem to scream without speaking.

Steam fills the room in slow, careful exhalations that

cloud my reflection and eventually, I'm forced to look away. But when I do, I'm smiling.

Because for the first time in my life, I actually like the way I look.

I asked Delalieu to arrange to have my armoire moved into Anderson's quarters before I arrived yesterday—and I find myself standing before it now, examining its depths with new eyes. These are the same clothes I've seen every time I've opened these doors; but suddenly I'm seeing them differently.

But then, I *feel* differently.

Clothes used to perplex me. I could never understand how to piece together an outfit the way Warner did. I thought it was a science I'd never crack; a skill beyond my grasp. But I'm realizing now that my problem was that I never knew who I was; I didn't understand how to dress the imposter living in my skin.

What did I like?

How did I want to be perceived?

For years my goal was to minimize myself—to fold and refold myself into a polygon of nothingness, to be too insignificant to be remembered. I wanted to appear innocent; I wanted to be thought of as quiet and harmless; I was worried always about how my very existence was terrifying to others and I did everything in my power to diminish myself, my light, my soul.

I wanted so desperately to placate the ignorant. I wanted

so badly to appease the assholes who judged me without knowing me that I lost myself in the process.

But now?

Now, I laugh. Out loud.

Now, I don't give a shit.

WARNER

When Juliette joins us in the morning, she is almost unrecognizable.

I was forced, despite every inclination to bury myself in other duties, to rejoin our group today on account of what seems now to have been the inevitable arrival of our three final guests. The twin children of the South American supreme and the son of the supreme commander of Africa all arrived early this morning. The supreme commander of Oceania has no children, so I have to assume this is the last of our visitors. And all of them have arrived in time to accompany us to the symposium. Very convenient.

I should have realized.

I had just been in the middle of introducing the three of them to Castle and Kenji, who came down to greet our new visitors, when Juliette made her first appearance of the day. It's been less than thirty seconds since she walked in, and I'm still trying and failing to take her in.

She's *stunning.*

She's wearing a simple, fitted black sweater; slim, dark gray jeans; and a pair of flat, black, ankle-length boots. Her hair is both gone and not; it's like a soft, dark crown that suits her in a way I never could've expected. Without the

371

distraction of her long hair my eyes have nowhere to focus but directly on her face. And she has the most incredible face—large, captivating eyes—and a bone structure that's never been more pronounced.

She looks shockingly different.

Raw.

Still beautiful, but sharper. Harder. She's not a girl with a ponytail in a pink sweater anymore, no. She looks a great deal more like the young woman who murdered my father and then drank four fingers of his most expensive Scotch.

She's looking from me to the stunned expressions of Kenji and Castle to the quietly confused faces of our three new guests, and all of us appear unable to speak.

"Good morning," she finally says, but she doesn't smile when she says it. There's no warmth, no kindness in her eyes as she looks around, and I falter.

"Damn, princess, is that really you?"

Juliette appraises Kenji once, swiftly, but doesn't respond.

"Who are you three?" she says, nodding at the newcomers. They stand slowly. Uncertainly.

"These are our new guests," I say, but now I can't bring myself to look at her. To face her. "I was just about to introduce them to Castle and Kishimo—"

"And you weren't going to include me?" says a new voice. "I'd like to meet the new supreme commander, too."

I turn around to find Lena standing in the doorway, not three feet from Juliette, looking around the room like she's never been so delighted in all her life. I feel my heart pick up, my mind racing. I still have no idea if Juliette knows who Lena is—or what we were together.

And Lena's eyes are bright, too bright, her smile wide and happy.

A chill runs through me.

With them standing so close together, I can't help but notice that the differences between her and Juliette are almost too obvious. Where Juliette is petite, Lena is tall. Juliette has dark hair and deep eyes, while Lena is pale in every possible way. Her hair is almost white, her eyes are the lightest blue, her skin is almost translucent, save the many freckles spanning her nose and cheeks. But what she lacks in pigment she makes up for in presence; she's always been loud, aggressive, passionate to a fault. Juliette, by comparison, is muted almost to an extreme this morning. She betrays no emotion, not a hint of anger or jealousy. She stands still and quiet, silently studying the situation. Her energy is tightly coiled. Ready to spring.

And when Lena turns to face her, I feel everyone in the room stiffen.

"Hi," Lena says loudly. False happiness disfigures her smile, morphing it into something cruel. She holds out her hand as she says, "It's nice to finally meet Warner's girlfriend." And then: "Oh, wait—I'm sorry. I meant *ex*-girlfriend."

I'm holding my breath as Juliette looks her up and down.

She takes her time, tilting her head as she devours Lena with her eyes and I can see Lena's offered hand beginning to tire, her open fingers starting to shake.

Juliette seems unimpressed.

"You can call me the supreme commander of North America," she says.

And then walks away.

I feel an almost hysterical laughter build in my chest; I have to look down, force myself to keep a straight face. And then I'm sobered, all at once, by the realization that Juliette is no longer mine. She's no longer mine to love, mine to adore. I've never been more attracted to her in all the time I've known her and there's nothing, nothing to be done about it. My heart pounds faster as she steps more completely into the room—a gaping Lena left in her wake—and I'm struck still with regret.

I can't believe I've managed to lose her. Twice.

That she loved me. Once.

"Please identify yourselves," she says to our three guests.

Stephan speaks first.

"I'm Stephan Feruzi Omondi," he says, reaching forward to shake her hand. "I'm here to represent the supreme commander of Africa."

Stephan is tall and dignified and deeply formal, and though he was born and raised in what used to be Nairobi, he studied English abroad, and speaks now with a British accent. And I can tell from the way Juliette's eyes linger on his face that she likes the look of him.

Something tightens in my chest.

"Your parents sent you to spy on me, too, Stephan?" she says, still staring.

Stephan smiles—the movement animating his whole face—and suddenly I hate him. "We're only here to say hello," he says. "Just a little friendly union."

"Uh-huh. And you two?" She turns to the twins. "Same thing?"

Nicolás, the elder twin, only smiles at her. He seems delighted. "I am Nicolás Castillo," he says, "son of Santiago and Martina Castillo, and this is my sister, Valentina—"

"*Sister?*" Lena cuts in. She's found another opportunity to be cruel and I've never hated her so much. "Are you still doing that?"

"Lena," I say, a warning in my voice.

"What?" She looks at me. "Why does everyone keep acting like this is normal? One day Santiago's son decides he wants to be a girl and we all just, what? Look the other way?"

"Eat shit, Lena," is the first thing Valentina has said all morning. "I should've cut off your ears when I had the chance."

Juliette's eyes go wide.

"Uh, I'm sorry"—Kenji pokes his head forward, waves a hand—"am I missing something?"

"Valentina likes to play pretend," Lena says.

"*Cállate la boca, cabrona,*" Nicolás snaps at her.

"No, you know what?" Valentina says, placing a hand on her brother's shoulder. "It's okay. Let her talk. Lena thinks I like to pretend, *pero* I won't be pretending *cuando cuelge su cuerpo muerto en mi cuarto.*"

Lena only rolls her eyes.

"Valentina," I say. "Please ignore her. *Ella no tiene ninguna idea de lo que está hablando. Tenemos mucho que hacer y no debemo—*"

"Damn, bro," Kenji cuts me off. "You speak Spanish, too, huh?" He runs a hand through his hair. "I'm going to have to get used to this."

"We all speak many languages," says Nicolás, a note of irritation still clinging to his voice. "We have to be able to communi—"

"Listen, guys, I don't care about your personal dramas," Juliette says suddenly, pinching the bridge of her nose. "I have a massive headache and a million things to do today, and I'd like to get started."

"*Por su puesto, señorita.*" Nicolás bows his head a little.

"What?" she says, blinking at him. "I don't know what that means."

Nicolás only smiles. "*Entonces deberías aprender como hablar español.*"

I almost laugh, even as I shake my head. Nicolás is being difficult on purpose. "*Basta ya,*" I say to him. "*Dejala sola. Sabes que ella no habla español.*"

"What are you guys saying?" Juliette demands.

Nicolás only smiles wider, his blue eyes crinkling in delight. "Nothing of consequence, Madam Supreme. Only that we are pleased to meet you."

"And I take it you'll all be attending the symposium today?" she says.

Another slight bow. "*Claro que sí.*"

"That's a yes," I say to her.

"What other languages do you speak?" Juliette says, spinning to face me, and I'm so surprised she's addressing me in public that I forget to respond.

It's Stephan who says, "We were taught many languages from a very young age. It was critical that the commanders and their families all knew how to communicate with one another."

"But I thought The Reestablishment wanted to get rid of all the languages," she says. "I thought you were working toward a single, universal language—"

"*Sí*, Madam Supreme," says Valentina with a slight nod. "That's true. But first we had to be able to speak with each other, no?"

Juliette looks fascinated. She's forgotten her anger for just long enough to be awed by the vastness of the world again; I can see it in her eyes. Her desire to escape. "Where are you from?" she asks, the question full of innocence; wonder. Something about it breaks my heart. "Before the world was remapped—what were the names of your countries?"

"We were born in Argentina," Nicolás and Valentina say at the same time.

"My family is from Kenya," says Stephan.

"And you've visited each other?" she says, turning to scan our faces. "You travel to each other's continents?"

We nod.

"Wow," she says quietly, but mostly to herself. "That must be incredible."

"You must come visit us, too, Madam Supreme," says a smiling Stephan. "We'd love to have you stay with us. After all, you are one of us now."

Juliette's smile vanishes. Gone too soon is the wistful, faraway look on her face. She says nothing, but I can sense the anger and sadness boiling over inside her.

Too suddenly, she says,

"Warner, Castle, Kenji?"

"Yeah?"

"Yes, Ms. Ferrars?"

I merely stare.

"If we're done here, I'd like to speak with the three of you alone, please."

JULIETTE

I keep thinking I need to stay calm, that it's all in my head, that everything is going to be fine and someone is going to open the door now, someone is going to let me out of here. I keep thinking it's going to happen. I keep thinking it has to happen, because things like this don't just happen. This doesn't happen. People aren't forgotten like this. Not abandoned like this.

This doesn't just happen.

My face is caked with blood from when they threw me on the ground and my hands are still shaking even as I write this. This pen is my only outlet, my only voice, because I have no one else to speak to, no mind but my own to drown in and all the lifeboats are taken and all the life preservers are broken and I don't know how to swim I can't swim I can't swim and it's getting so hard. It's getting so hard. It's like there are a million screams caught inside of my chest but I have to keep them all in because what's the point of screaming if you'll never be heard and no one will ever hear me in here. No one will ever hear me ever again.

I've learned to stare at things.

The walls. My hands. The cracks in the walls. The lines on my fingers. The shades of gray in the concrete. The shape of my fingernails. I pick one thing and stare at it for what must be hours. I keep time in my head by counting the seconds as they pass. I keep days in my head by writing them down. Today is day two. Today is the second day. Today is a day.

Today.

It's so cold. It's so cold it's so cold.

Please please please

—AN EXCERPT FROM JULIETTE'S JOURNALS IN THE ASYLUM

I'm still staring at the three of them, waiting for confirmation when, suddenly, Kenji speaks with a start.

"Uh, yeah—no, uh, no problem," he says.

"Certainly," says Castle.

And Warner says nothing at all, looking at me like he can see through me, and for a moment all I can remember is me, naked, begging him to join me in the shower; me, curled up in his arms crying, telling him how much I miss him; me, touching his lips—

I cringe, mortified. An old impulse to blush overtakes my entire body.

I close my eyes and look away, pivoting sharply as I leave the room without a word.

"Juliette, love—"

I'm already halfway down the hall when I feel his hand on my back and I stiffen, my pulse racing in an instant. The minute I spin around I see his face change, his features shifting from scared to surprised in less than a second and it makes me so angry that he has this ability, this gift of being able to sense other people's emotions, because I am always so transparent to him, so completely vulnerable and it's infuriating, *infuriating*

"What?" I say. I try to say it harshly but it comes out all wrong. Breathless. Embarrassing.

"I just—" But his hand falls. His eyes capture mine and suddenly I'm frozen in time. "I wanted to tell you—"

"What?" And now the word is quiet and nervous and terrified all at once. I take a step back to save my own life and I see Castle and Kenji walking too slowly down the hall; they're keeping their distance on purpose—giving us space to speak. "What do you want to say?"

But now Warner's eyes are moving, studying me. He looks at me with such intensity I wonder if he's even aware he's doing it. I wonder if he knows that when he looks at me like that I can feel it as acutely as if his bare skin were pressed against my own, that it does things to me when he looks at me like that and it makes me crazy, because I hate that I can't control this, that this thread between us remains unbroken and he says finally, softly,

something

something I don't hear

because I'm looking at his lips and feeling my skin ignite with memories of him and it was just yesterday, just yesterday that he was mine, that I felt his mouth on my body, that I could *feel him inside me—*

"What?" I manage to say, blinking upward.

"I said I really like what you've done with your hair."

And I hate him, hate him for doing this to my heart, hate my body for being so weak, for wanting him, missing him, despite everything and I don't know whether to cry or kiss him or kick him in the teeth, so instead I say, without meeting his eyes,

"When were you going to tell me about Lena?"

He stops then; motionless in a moment. "Oh"—he clears his throat—"I hadn't realized you'd heard about Lena."

I narrow my eyes at him, not trusting myself to speak, and I'm still deciding the best course of action when he says

"Kenji was right," but he whispers the words, and mostly to himself.

"Excuse me?"

He looks up. "Forgive me," he says softly. "I should've said something sooner. I see that now."

"Then why didn't you?"

"She and I," he says, "it was—we were nothing. It was a relationship of convenience and basic companionship. It meant nothing to me. Truly," he says, "you have to know— if I never said anything about her it was only because I never thought about her long enough to even consider mentioning it."

"But you were together for *two years*—"

He shakes his head before he says, "It wasn't like that. It wasn't two years of anything serious. It wasn't even two years of continuous communication." He sighs. "She lives in Europe, love. We saw each other briefly and infrequently. It was purely physical. It wasn't a real relationship—"

"*Purely physical*," I say, stunned. I rock backward, nearly tripping over my own feet and I feel his words tear through my flesh with a searing physical pain I wasn't expecting. "Wow. Wow."

And now I can think of nothing but his body and hers, the two of them entwined, the *two years* he spent naked in her arms—

"No—please," he says, the urgency in his words jolting me back to the present. "That's not what I meant. I'm just— I'm—I don't know how to explain this," he says, frustrated like I've never seen him before. He shakes his head, hard. "Everything in my life was different before I met you," he says. "I was lost and all alone. I never cared for anyone. I never wanted to get close to anyone. I've never—you were the first person to ever—"

"Stop," I say, shaking my head. "Just stop, okay? I'm so tired. My head is *killing* me and I don't have the energy to hear any more of this."

"Juliette—"

"How many more secrets do you have?" I ask. "How much more am I going to learn about you? About me? My family? My history? The Reestablishment and the details of my *real life*?"

"I swear I never meant to hurt you like this," he says. "And I don't want to keep things from you. But this is all so new for me, love. This kind of relationship is so new for me and I don't—I don't know how to—"

"You've already kept so much from me," I say to him, feeling my strength falter, feeling the weight of this throbbing headache unclench my armor, feeling too much, too much all at once when I say "There's so much I don't know about you. There's so much I don't know about your past. Our present. And I have no idea what to believe anymore."

"Ask me anything," he says. "I'll tell you anything you want to know—"

"Except the truth about me? My parents?"

Warner looks suddenly pale.

"You were going to keep that from me forever," I say to him. "You had no plan to tell me the truth. That I was adopted. Did you?"

His eyes are wild, bright with feeling.

"Answer the question," I say. "Just tell me this much." I step forward, so close I can feel his breath on my face; so close I can almost hear his heart racing in his chest. "Were you ever going to tell me?"

"I don't know."

"Tell me the *truth*."

"Honestly, love," he says, shaking his head. "In all likelihood, I would have." And suddenly he sighs. The action seems to exhaust him. "I don't know how to convince you that I believed I was sparing you the pain of that particular truth. I really thought your biological parents were dead. I see now that keeping this from you wasn't the right thing to do, but then, I don't always do the right thing," he says quietly. "But you have to believe that my intention was never to hurt you. I never intended to lie to you or to purposely withhold information from you. And I do think that I would have, in time, told you what I knew to be the truth. I was just searching for the right moment."

Suddenly, I'm not sure what to feel.

I stare at him, his downcast eyes, the movement in his throat as he swallows against a swell of emotion. And something breaks apart inside of me. Some measure of resistance begins to crumble.

He looks so vulnerable. So young.

I take a deep breath and let it go, slowly, and then I look up, look into his face once more and I see it, I see the moment he senses the change in my feelings. Something comes alive in his eyes. He takes a step forward and now we're standing so close I'm afraid to speak. My heart is beating too hard in my chest and I don't have to do anything at all to be reminded of everything, every moment, every touch we've ever shared. His scent is all around me. His heat. His exhalations. Gold eyelashes and green eyes. I touch his face, almost without meaning to, gently, like he might be a ghost, like this might be a dream and the tips of my fingers graze his cheek, trail the line of his jaw and I stop when his breath catches, when his body shakes almost imperceptibly

and we lean in as if by memory

eyes closing

lips just touching

"Give me another chance," he whispers, resting his forehead against mine.

My heart aches, throbs in my chest.

"Please," he says softly, and he's somehow closer now, his lips touching mine as he speaks and I feel pinned in place by emotion, unable to move as he presses the words against my mouth, his hands soft and hesitant around my face and he says, "I swear on my life," he says, "I won't disappoint you"

and he kisses me

Kisses me

right here, in the middle of everything, in front of everyone and I'm flooded, overrun with feeling, my head spinning as he presses me against the hard line of his body and I can't save myself from myself, can't stop the sound I make when he parts my lips and I'm lost, lost in the taste of him, lost in his heat, wrapped up in his arms and

I have to tear myself away

pulling back so quickly I nearly stumble. I'm breathing too hard, my face flushed, my feelings panicked

And he can only look at me, his chest rising and falling with an intensity I feel from here, from two feet away, and I can't think of anything right or reasonable to say about what just happened or what I'm feeling except

"This isn't fair," I whisper. Tears threaten, sting my eyes. "This isn't *fair*."

And I don't wait to hear his response before I tear down the hall, bolting the rest of the way back to my rooms.

WARNER

"Trouble in paradise, Mr. Warner?"

I've got him by the throat in seconds, shock disfiguring his expression as I slam his body against the wall. "You," I say angrily. "You forced me into this impossible position. *Why?*"

Castle tries to swallow but can't, his eyes wide but unafraid. When he speaks his words are raspy, suffocated. "You had to do it," he chokes out. "It had to happen. She needed to be warned, and it had to come from you."

"I don't believe you," I shout, shoving him harder against the wall. "And I don't know why I ever trusted you."

"Please, son. Put me down."

I ease up, only a little, and he takes in several lungfuls of air before saying, "I haven't lied to you, Mr. Warner. She had to hear the truth. And if she'd heard this from anyone else she'd never forgive you. But at least now"—he coughs— "with time, she might. It's your only chance at happiness."

"What?" I drop my hand. Drop him. "Since when have you cared about my happiness?"

He's quiet for too long, massaging his throat as he stares at me. Finally, he says, "You think I don't know what your father did to you? What he put you through?"

393

And now I take a step back.

"You think I don't know your story, son? You think I'd let you into my world—offer you sanctuary among my people—if I really thought you were going to hurt us?"

I'm breathing hard. Suddenly confused. Feeling exposed.

"You don't know anything about me," I say, feeling the lie even as I say it.

Castle smiles, but there's something wounded in it. "You're just a boy," he says quietly. "You're only nineteen years old, Mr. Warner. And I think you forget that all the time. You have no perspective, no idea that you've only barely lived. There's still so much life ahead of you." He sighs. "I try to tell Kenji the same thing, but he's like you. Stubborn," he says. "So stubborn."

"I'm *nothing* like him."

"Did you know that you're a year younger than him?"

"Age is irrelevant. Nearly all my soldiers are older than me."

Castle laughs.

"All of you kids," he says, shaking his head. "You suffer too much. You have these horrible, tragic histories. Volatile personalities. I've always wanted to help," he says. "I've always wanted to fix that. Make this world a better place for you kids."

"Well, you can go save the world somewhere else," I say. "And feel free to babysit Kishimoto all you like. But I'm not your responsibility. I don't need your pity."

Castle only tilts his head at me. "You will never escape my pity, Mr. Warner."

My jaw clenches.

"You boys," he says, his eyes distracted for a moment, "you remind me so much of my own sons."

I pause. "You have children?"

"Yes," he says. And I feel his sudden, breathtaking wave of pain wash over me as he says, "I did."

I take several unconscious steps backward, reeling from the rush of his shared emotions. I can only stare at him. Surprised. Curious.

Sorry.

"Hey."

At the sound of Nazeera's voice I spin around, startled. She's with Haider, the two of them looking grave.

"What is it?" I say.

"We need to talk." She looks at Castle. "Your name is Castle, right?"

He nods.

"Yeah, I know you're wise to this business, Castle, so I'm going to need you to get in on this, too." Nazeera whips her finger through the air to draw a circle around the four of us. "We all need to talk. *Now*."

JULIETTE

JULIETTE

It's a strange thing, to never know peace. To know that no matter where you go, there is no sanctuary. That the threat of pain is always a whisper away. I'm not safe locked into these 4 walls, I was never safe leaving my house, and I couldn't even feel safe in the 14 years I lived at home. The asylum kills people every day, the world has already been taught to fear me, and my home is the same place where my father locked me in my room every night and my mother screamed at me for being the abomination she was forced to raise.

She always said it was my face.

There was something about my face, she said, that she couldn't stand. Something about my eyes, the way I looked at her, the fact that I even existed. She'd always tell me to stop looking at her. She'd always scream it. Like I might attack her. Stop looking at me, she'd scream. You just stop looking at me, she'd scream.

She put my hand in the fire once.

Just to see if it would burn, she said. Just to check if it was a regular hand, she said.

I was 6 years old then.

I remember because it was my birthday.

—AN EXCERPT FROM JULIETTE'S JOURNALS IN THE ASYLUM

"Never mind," is all I say when Kenji shows up at my door.

"Never mind, what?" Kenji sticks his foot out to catch the closing door. Now he's squeezing his way in. "What's going on?"

"Never mind, I don't want to talk to any of you. Please go away. Or maybe you can all go to hell. I don't actually care."

Kenji looks stunned, like I just slapped him in the face. "Are you—wait, are you serious right now?"

"Nazeera and I are leaving for the symposium in an hour. I have to get ready."

"What? What's happening, J? What's wrong with you?"

Now, I turn to face him. *"What's wrong with me?* Oh, like you don't know?"

Kenji runs a hand through his hair. "I mean, I heard about what happened with Warner, yeah, but I'm pretty sure I just saw you guys making out in the hallway so I'm, uh, really confused—"

"He *lied* to me, Kenji. He lied to me this whole time. About so many things. And so did Castle. So did *you*—"

"Wait, what?" He grabs my arm as I turn away. "Wait—I didn't lie to you about shit. Don't mix me up in this mess. I had nothing to do with any of it. Hell, I still haven't figured

400

out what to say to Castle. I can't believe he kept all of this from me."

I go suddenly still, my fists closing as my anger builds and breaks, holding fast to a sudden hope. "You weren't in on all of this?" I say. "With Castle?"

"Uh-uh. No way. I had no clue about any of this insanity until Warner told me about it yesterday."

I hesitate.

Kenji rolls his eyes.

"Well, how am I supposed to trust you?" I say, my voice rising in pitch like a child. "Everyone's been lying to me—"

"J," he says, shaking his head. "C'mon. You know me. You know I don't bullshit. That's not my style."

I swallow, hard, feeling suddenly small. Feeling suddenly broken inside. My eyes sting and I fight back the impulse to cry. "You promise?"

"Hey," he says softly. "Come here, kid."

I take a tentative step forward and he wraps me up in his arms, warm and strong and safe and I've never been so grateful for his friendship, for his steady existence in my life.

"It's going to be okay," he whispers. "I swear."

"Liar," I sniff.

"Well, there's a fifty percent chance I'm right."

"Kenji?"

"Mm?"

"If I find out you're lying to me about any of this I swear to God I will break all the bones in your body."

A short laugh. "Yeah, okay."

"I'm serious."

"Uh-huh." He pats my head.

"I will."

"I know, princess. I know."

Several more seconds of silence.

And then

"Kenji," I say quietly.

"Mm?"

"They're going to destroy Sector 45."

"Who is?"

"Everyone."

Kenji leans back. Raises an eyebrow. "Everyone who?"

"All the other supreme commanders," I say. "Nazeera told me everything."

Unexpectedly, Kenji's face breaks into a tremendous smile. "Oh, so Nazeera is one of the good guys, huh? She's on our team? Trying to help you out?"

"Oh my God, Kenji, please focus—"

"I'm just saying," he says, holding up his hands. "The girl is fine as hell is all I'm saying."

I roll my eyes. Try not to laugh as I wipe away errant tears.

"So." He nods his head at me. "What's the deal? The details? Who's coming? When? How? Et cetera?"

"I don't know," I say. "Nazeera is still trying to figure it out. She thinks maybe in the next week or so? The kids are here to monitor me and send back information, but they're coming to the symposium, specifically, because apparently the commanders want to know how the other sector leaders will react to seeing me. Nazeera says she thinks the information will help inform their next moves. I'm guessing we have maybe a matter of *days*."

Kenji's eyes go wide, panicked. "Oh, shit."

"Yeah, but when they decide to obliterate Sector 45 their plan is to also take me prisoner. The Reestablishment wants to bring me back in, apparently. Whatever that means."

"Bring you back in?" Kenji frowns. "For what? More testing? Torture? What do they want to do with you?"

I shake my head. "I have no idea. I have no clue who these people are. My sister," I say, the words feeling strange as I say them, "is apparently still being tested and tortured somewhere. So I'm pretty sure they're not bringing me back for a big family reunion, you know?"

"Wow." Kenji rubs his forehead. "That is some next-level drama."

"Yeah."

"So—what are we going to do?"

I hesitate. "I don't know, Kenji. They're coming to kill everyone in Sector 45. I don't think I have a choice."

"What do you mean?"

I look up. "I mean I'm pretty sure I'll have to kill them first."

WARNER

My heart is pounding frantically in my chest. My hands are clammy, unsteady. But I cannot make time to deal with my mind. Nazeera's confessions might cost me my sanity. I can only pray she is mistaken. I can only hope that she will be proven desperately and woefully wrong and there's no time, no time at all to deal with any of this. I can no longer make room in my day for these flimsy, unreliable human emotions.

I must live here now.

In my own solitude.

Today I will be a soldier only, a perfect robot if need be, and stand tall, eyes betraying no emotion as our supreme commander Juliette Ferrars takes the stage.

We're all here today, a small battalion posted up behind her like her own personal guard—myself, Delalieu, Castle, Kenji, Ian, Alia, Lily, Brendan, and Winston—even Nazeera and Haider, Lena, Stephan, Valentina, and Nicolás stand beside us, pretending to be supportive as she begins her speech. The only ones missing are Sonya, Sara, Kent, and James, who stayed behind on base. Kent cares little about anything these days but keeping James out of danger, and I can't say I blame him. Sometimes I wish I could opt out of this life, too.

I squeeze my eyes shut. Steady myself.

I just want this to be over.

The location of the biannual symposium is fairly fluid, and generally rotational. But in recognition of our new supreme commander, the event was relocated to Sector 45, an effort made possible entirely by Delalieu.

I can feel our collective group pulse with different kinds and levels of energy, but it's all so meshed together I can't tell fear and apathy apart. I'm focused instead on the audience and our leader, as their reactions are the most important. And of all the many events and symposiums I've attended over the years, I've never felt such an electric charge in the crowd as I do now.

554 of my fellow chief commanders and regents are in the audience, but so are their spouses, and even several members of their closest staff. It's unprecedented: every invitation was accepted. No one wanted to miss the opportunity to meet the new seventeen-year-old leader of North America, no. They're fascinated. They're hungry. Wolves sitting in human skin, eager to tear into the flesh of the young girl they've already underestimated.

If Juliette's powers didn't offer her body a level of functional invincibility I'd be deeply concerned about her standing alone and unguarded in front of all her enemies. The civilians of this sector may be rooting for her, but the rest of the continent has no interest in the disruption she's brought to the land—or to the threat she poses to their ranks in The Reestablishment. These men and women standing before her today are paid to be loyal to another party. They have no sympathy for her cause, for her fight for the common people.

I have no idea how long they'll let her speak before they rip into her.

But I don't have to wait long.

Juliette has only just started speaking—she's only just begun talking about the many failures of The Reestablishment and the need for a new beginning when the crowd becomes suddenly restless. They stand up, raise their fists and my mind disconnects as they shout at her, the events unfolding before my eyes as if in slow motion. She doesn't react.

One, two, sixteen people are on their feet now, and she keeps talking.

Half the room roars upward, angry words hurled in her direction and now I can feel her growing angrier, her frustration peaking, but somehow, she holds her ground. The more they protest, the more she projects her voice; she's speaking so loudly now she's practically shouting. I look quickly between her and the crowd, my mind working desperately to decide what to do. Kenji catches my eye and the two of us understand each other without speaking.

We have to intervene.

Juliette is now denouncing The Reestablishment's plans to obliterate languages and literature; she's outlining her hopes to transition the civilians out of the compounds; and she's just begun addressing our issues with the climate when a shot is fired into the room.

There's a moment of perfect silence, and then—

Juliette peels the dented bullet off her forehead. Tosses it to the ground. The gentle, tinkling sound of metal on marble reverberates around the room.

Mass chaos.

Hundreds and hundreds of people are suddenly on their feet, all of them shouting at her, threatening her, pointing guns at her, and I can feel it, I can feel it spiraling out of control.

More shots ring out, and in the seconds it takes us to form a plan, we're already too late. Brendan falls to the ground with a sudden, horrifying gasp. Winston screams; catches his body.

And that's it.

Juliette goes suddenly still, and my mind slows down.

I can feel it before it happens: I can feel the change, the static in the air. Heat ripples around her, tongues of power unfurling from her body like lightning preparing for a strike and there's no time to do anything but hold my breath when, suddenly—

She *screams*.

Long. Loud. Violent.

The world seems to blur for just a second—for just a moment everything seizes, freezes in place: contorted bodies; angry, distorted faces; all frozen in time—

Floorboards peel upward and fissure apart. Cracks like thunderclaps as they shatter up the walls. Light fixtures swing precariously before smashing to the floor.

And then, everyone.

Every single person in her line of sight. 554 people and all their guests. Their faces, their bodies, the seats they sit in: sliced open like fresh fish. Their flesh feathers outward, swelling slowly as a steady gush of blood gathers in pools around their feet.

They all drop dead.

JULIETTE

JULIETTE

I started screaming today.

—AN EXCERPT FROM JULIETTE'S JOURNALS IN THE ASYLUM

Were you happy
Were you sad
Were you scared
Were you mad
the first time you screamed?
Were you fighting for your life your decency your dignity your
humanity
When someone touches you now, do you scream?
When someone smiles at you now, do you smile back?
Did he tell you not to scream did he hit you when you cried?
Did he have one nose two eyes two lips two cheeks two ears
two eyebrows.
Was he one human who looked just like you.
Color your personality.
Shapes and sizes are variety.
Your heart is an anomaly.
Your actions
are
the
only
traces
you leave
behind.

—AN EXCERPT FROM JULIETTE'S JOURNALS IN THE ASYLUM

Sometimes I think the shadows are moving.

Sometimes I think someone might be watching.

Sometimes this idea scares me and sometimes the idea makes me so absurdly happy I can't stop crying. And then sometimes I think I have no idea when I started losing my mind in here. Nothing seems real anymore and I can't tell if I'm screaming out loud or only in my head.

There's no one here to hear me.

To tell me I'm not dead.

—AN EXCERPT FROM JULIETTE'S JOURNALS IN THE ASYLUM

I don't know when it started.

I don't know why it started.

I don't know anything about anything except for the screaming.

My mother screaming when she realized she could no longer touch me. My father screaming when he realized what I'd done to my mother. My parents screaming when they'd lock me in my room and tell me I should be grateful. For their food. For their humane treatment of this thing that could not possibly be their child. For the yardstick they used to measure the distance I needed to keep away.

I ruined their lives, is what they said to me.

I stole their happiness. Destroyed my mother's hope for ever having children again.

Couldn't I see what I'd done? is what they'd ask me. Couldn't I see that I'd ruined everything?

I tried so hard to fix what I'd ruined. I tried every single day to be what they wanted. I tried all the time to be better but I never really knew how.

I only know now that the scientists are wrong.

The world is flat.

I know because I was tossed right off the edge and I've been trying to hold on for seventeen years. I've been trying to climb back up for seventeen years but it's nearly impossible to beat gravity when no one is willing to give you a hand.

When no one wants to risk touching you.

—AN EXCERPT FROM JULIETTE'S JOURNALS IN THE ASYLUM

Am I insane yet?
Has it happened yet?
How will I ever know?

—AN EXCERPT FROM JULIETTE'S JOURNALS IN THE ASYLUM

There's a moment of pure, perfect silence before everything, everything explodes. At first, I don't even realize what I've done. I don't understand what just happened. I didn't mean to kill *these* people—

And then, suddenly

It hits me

The crushing realization that I've just slaughtered a room of six hundred people.

It seems impossible. It seems fake. There were no bullets. No excess force, no violence. Just one, long, angry cry.

"Stop it," I screamed. I squeezed my eyes shut and screamed it, anger and heartbreak and exhaustion and crushing devastation filling my lungs. It was the weight of recent weeks, the pain of all these years, the embarrassment of false hopes manufactured in my heart, the betrayal, the loss—

Adam. Warner. Castle.

My parents, real and imagined.

A sister I might never know.

The lies that make up my life. The threats against the innocent people of Sector 45. The certain death that awaits me. The frustration of having so much power, so much power and feeling so utterly, completely powerless

"*Please*," I screamed. "*Please stop—*"

And now—

Now this.

My limbs have gone numb from disbelief. My ears feel full of wind, my mind disconnected from my body. I couldn't have killed this many people, I think, I couldn't have just killed all these people that isn't possible, I think, it's not possible not possible that I opened my mouth and then *this*

Kenji is trying to say something to me, something that sounds like *we have to get out of here, hurry, we have to go now*—

But I'm numb, I'm dim, I'm unable to move one foot in front of the other and someone is dragging me, forcing me to move and I hear explosions

And suddenly my mind sharpens.

I gasp and spin around, searching for Kenji but he's gone. His shirt is soaked in blood and he's being dragged off in the distance, his eyes half closed and

Warner is on his knees, his hands cuffed behind his back

Castle is unconscious on the floor, blood running freely from his chest

Winston is still screaming, even as someone drags him away

Brendan is dead

Lily, Ian, Alia, dead

And I'm trying to reconnect my mind, trying to work my way through the shock seizing my body and my head is spinning, *spinning*, and I see Nazeera out of the corner of my

eye with her head in her hands and someone touches me
and I jump

I jerk back

"What's happening?" I say to no one. "What's going on?"

"You've done beautiful work here, darling. You've really
made us proud. The Reestablishment is so grateful for the
sacrifices you've made."

"Who are you?" I say, searching for the voice.

And then I see them, a man and a woman kneeling in
front of me, and it's only then that I realize I'm lying on the
ground, paralyzed. My arms and legs are bound by pulsing,
electric wires. I try to fight against them and I can't.

My powers have been extinguished.

I look up at these strangers, eyes wide and terrified.
"Who are you?" I say again, still raging against my restraints.
"What do you want from me?"

"I'm the supreme commander of Oceania," the woman
says to me, smiling. "Your father and I have come to take
you home."

WARNER

JULIETTE

Why don't you just kill yourself? someone at school asked me once.

I think it was the kind of question intended to be cruel, but it was the first time I'd ever contemplated the possibility. I didn't know what to say. Maybe I was crazy to consider it, but I'd always hoped that if I were a good enough girl—if I did everything right, if I said the right things or said nothing at all—I thought my parents would change their minds. I thought they would finally listen when I tried to talk. I thought they would give me a chance. I thought they might finally love me.

I always had that ~~stupid~~ hope.

—AN EXCERPT FROM JULIETTE'S JOURNALS IN THE ASYLUM

When I open my eyes, I see stars.

Dozens of them. Little plastic stars stuck to the ceiling. They glow, faintly, in the dim light, and I sit up, head pounding, as I try to orient myself. There's a window on my right; a sheer, gauzy curtain filters sunset oranges and blues into the room at odd angles. I'm sitting on a small bed. I look up, look around.

Everything is pink.

Pink blanket, pink pillows. Pink rug on the floor.

I get to my feet and spin around, confused, to find that there's another, identical bed in here, but its sheets are purple. The pillows are purple.

The room is divided by an imaginary line, each half a mirror image of the other. Two desks; one pink, one purple. Two chairs; one pink, one purple. Two dressers, two mirrors. Pink, purple. Painted flowers on the walls. A small table and chairs off to one side. A rack of fluffy costume dresses. A box of tiaras on the floor. A little chalkboard easel in the corner. A bin under the window, full to the brim with dolls and stuffed animals.

This is a child's bedroom.

I feel my heart racing. My skin goes hot and cold.

I can still feel a loss inside of me—an inherent knowledge that my powers aren't working—and I realize only then that there are glowing, electric cuffs clamped around my wrists and ankles. I yank at them, use every bit of my strength to tear them open, and they don't budge.

I'm growing more panicked by the moment.

I run to the window, desperate for some sense of place—for some explanation of where I am, for proof that this isn't some kind of hallucination—and I'm disappointed; the view out the window only confuses me. I see a stunning vista. Endless, rolling hills. Mountains in the distance. A massive, glittering lake reflecting the colors of the sunset. It's *beautiful*.

I step back, feeling suddenly more terrified.

My eyes move instead to the pink desk and chair, scanning their surfaces for clues. There are only stacks of colorful notebooks. A porcelain cup full of markers and glitter pens. Several pages of fluorescent stickers.

My hand shakes as I pull open the desk drawer.

Inside are stacks of old letters and Polaroids.

At first, I can only stare at them. My heartbeats echo in my head, throbbing so hard I can almost feel them in my throat. My breaths come in faster, the inhalations shallow. I feel my head spin and I blink once, twice, forcing myself to be steady. To be brave.

Slowly, very slowly, I pick up the stack of letters.

All I have to do is look at the mailing addresses to know that these letters predate The Reestablishment. They've all

been sent to the attention of Evie and Maximillian Sommers.
To a street in Glenorchy, New Zealand.

New Zealand.

And then I remember, with a sudden gasp, the faces of
the man and woman who carried me out of the symposium.

I'm the supreme commander of Oceania, she'd said. *Your
father and I have come to take you home.*

I close my eyes and stars explode in the blackness
behind my eyelids, leaving me faint. Breathless. I blink my
eyes open. My fingers feel loose, clumsy as I open the letter
at the top of the stack.

The note is brief. It's dated twelve years ago.

M & E—
All is well. We've found her a suitable family. No sign
of powers yet, but we'll keep a close eye on her. Still, I
must advise you to put her out of your mind. She and
Emmaline have had their memories expunged. They no
longer ask about you. This will be my last update.
P. Anderson.

P. Anderson.

Paris Anderson. Warner's father.

I look around the bedroom with new eyes, feeling a
terrible chill creep up my spine as the impossible pieces of
this new insanity come together in my mind.

Vomit threatens. I swallow it back.

I'm staring now at the stack of Polaroids, untouched,

inside the open desk drawer. I think I've lost feeling in parts of my face. Still, I force myself to pick up the stack.

The first is a picture of two little girls in matching yellow dresses. They're both brown-haired and a little skinny, holding hands in a garden path. One of them looks at the camera, the other one looks at her feet.

I flip the photo over.

Ella's first day of school

The stack of photos falls out of my trembling hands, scattering as they go. My every instinct is shrieking at me, sounding alarm bells, begging me to run.

Get out, I try to scream at myself. *Get out of here.*

But my curiosity won't let me go.

A few of the photos have landed face-up on the desk, and I can't stop staring at them, my heart pounding in my ears. Carefully, I pick them up.

Three little brown-haired girls stand next to bikes that are slightly too big for them. They're all looking at each other, laughing at something.

I flip the photo over.

Ella, Emmaline, and Nazeera. No more training wheels.

I gasp, the sound choking me as it leaves my chest. I feel my lungs squeeze and I reach out, catch the desk with one hand to steady myself. I feel like I'm floating, unhinged.

Caught in a nightmare.

I flip through the photos with a desperation now, my mind working faster than my hands as I fumble, trying and failing to make sense of what I'm seeing.

The next photo is of a little girl holding the hand of an older man.

Emmaline and Papa, it says on the back.

Another photo, this one of both girls climbing a tree.

The day Ella twisted her ankle

Another one, blurred faces, cupcakes and candles—

Emmaline's 5th birthday

Another, this time a picture of a handsome couple—

Paris and Leila, visiting for Christmas

And I freeze

stunned

feel the air leave my body.

I'm holding only one photo now, and I have to force myself, beg myself to look at it, the square Polaroid shaking in my trembling hand.

It's a picture of a little boy standing next to a little girl. She's sitting in a stairwell. He looks at her as she eats a piece of cake.

I flip it over.

Aaron and Ella

is all it says.

I trip backward, stumbling, and collapse onto the floor. My whole body is seizing, shaking with terror, with confusion, with impossibility.

Suddenly, as if on cue, there's a knock at my door. A woman—the woman from before; an older version of the woman in the pictures—pops her head inside, smiles at me and says, "Ella, honey, don't you want to come outside? Your dinner is getting cold."

And I'm certain I'm going to be sick.

The room tilts around me.
I see spots
feel myself sway
and then—
all at once

The world goes black.

THEY WANT TO FIND ME.
I WILL FIND THEM FIRST.

JULIETTE HAS ESCAPED,
BUT HER STORY IS FAR
FROM OVER . . .

ALSO AVAILABLE

FEAR WILL LEARN TO FEAR ME.

FEAR WILL LEARN TO FEAR ME

BOOK THREE IN
THE *NEW YORK TIMES*
BESTSELLING
FANTASY SERIES

IGNITE
ME

New York Times BESTSELLING AUTHOR
TAHEREH MAFI

OMEGA POINT HAS BEEN
DESTROYED. CAN JULIETTE
SURVIVE ON HER OWN?

ALSO AVAILABLE

IGNITE ME

ALSO BY TAHEREH MAFI

IGNITE ME

TAHEREH MAFI

First published in USA 2014 by HarperCollins Children's Books
First published in Great Britain 2018
by Electric Monkey, part of Egmont Books

An imprint of HarperCollins*Publishers*
1 London Bridge Street, London SE1 9GF

egmontbooks.co.uk
2 4 6 8 10 9 7 5 3 1

HarperCollins*Publishers*
1st Floor, Watermarque Building,
Ringsend Road, Dublin 4, Ireland

Published by arrangement with HarperCollins Children's Books,
a division of HarperCollins Publishers, New York, New York, USA

Text copyright © 2014 Tahereh Mafi

ISBN 978 1 4052 9177 4

YOUNG ADULT

Printed and bound in India by Thomson Press India Ltd

A CIP catalogue record for this title is available from the British Library

Stay safe online. Any website addresses listed in this book are correct at the
time of going to print. However, Egmont Books is not responsible for content
hosted by third parties. Please be aware that online content can be subject to
change and websites can contain content that is unsuitable for children. We
advise that all children are supervised when using the internet.

This book is produced from independently certified FSC™ paper
to ensure responsible forest management.

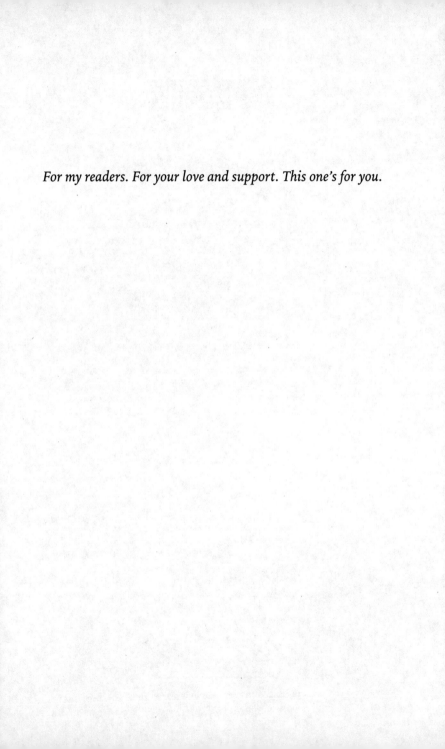

For my readers. For your love and support. This one's for you.

ONE

I am an hourglass.

My seventeen years have collapsed and buried me from the inside out. My legs feel full of sand and stapled together, my mind overflowing with grains of indecision, choices unmade and impatient as time runs out of my body. The small hand of a clock taps me at one and two, three and four, whispering hello, get up, stand up, it's time to

wake up

wake up

"Wake up," he whispers.

A sharp intake of breath and I'm awake but not up, surprised but not scared, somehow staring into the very desperately green eyes that seem to know too much, too well. Aaron Warner Anderson is bent over me, his worried eyes inspecting me, his hand caught in the air like he might've been about to touch me.

He jerks back.

He stares, unblinking, chest rising and falling.

"Good morning," I assume. I'm unsure of my voice, of the hour and this day, of these words leaving my lips and this body that contains me.

I notice he's wearing a white shirt, half untucked into

his curiously unrumpled black slacks. His shirtsleeves are folded, pushed up past his elbows.

His smile looks like it hurts.

I pull myself into a seated position and Warner shifts to accommodate me. I have to close my eyes to steady the sudden dizziness, but I force myself to remain still until the feeling passes.

I'm tired and weak from hunger, but other than a few general aches, I seem to be fine. I'm alive. I'm breathing and blinking and feeling human and I know exactly why.

I meet his eyes. "You saved my life."

I was shot in the chest.

Warner's father put a bullet in my body and I can still feel the echoes of it. If I focus, I can relive the exact moment it happened; the pain: so intense, so excruciating; I'll never be able to forget it.

I suck in a startled breath.

I'm finally aware of the familiar foreignness of this room and I'm quickly seized by a panic that screams I did not wake up where I fell asleep. My heart is racing and I'm inching away from him, hitting my back against the headboard, clutching at these sheets, trying not to stare at the chandelier I remember all too well—

"It's okay—" Warner is saying. "It's all right—"

"What am I doing here?" Panic, panic; terror clouds my consciousness. "Why did you bring me here again—?"

"Juliette, please, I'm not going to hurt you—"

"Then why did you bring me here?" My voice is starting

2

to break and I'm struggling to keep it steady. "Why bring me back to this *hellhole*—"

"I had to hide you." He exhales, looks up at the wall.

"What? Why?"

"No one knows you're alive." He turns to look at me. "I had to get back to base. I needed to pretend everything was back to normal and I was running out of time."

I force myself to lock away the fear.

I study his face and analyze his patient, earnest tone. I remember him last night—it must've been last night—I remember his face, remember him lying next to me in the dark. He was tender and kind and gentle and he saved me, saved my life. Probably carried me into bed. Tucked me in beside him. It must've been him.

But when I glance down at my body I realize I'm wearing clean clothes, no blood or holes or anything anywhere and I wonder who washed me, wonder who changed me, and worry that might've been Warner, too.

"Did you . . ." I hesitate, touching the hem of the shirt I'm wearing. "Did—I mean—my clothes—"

He smiles. He stares until I'm blushing and I decide I hate him a little and then he shakes his head. Looks into his palms. "No," he says. "The girls took care of that. I just carried you to bed."

"The girls," I whisper, dazed.

The girls.

Sonya and Sara. They were there too, the healer twins, they helped Warner. They helped him save me because he's the only one who can touch me now, the only person in the world who'd have been able to transfer their healing power safely into my body.

My thoughts are on fire.

Where are the girls what happened to the girls and where is Anderson and the war and oh God what's happened to Adam and Kenji and Castle and I have to get up I have to get up I have to get up and get out of bed and get going

but

I try to move and Warner catches me. I'm off-balance, unsteady; I still feel as though my legs are anchored to this bed and I'm suddenly unable to breathe, seeing spots and feeling faint. Need up. Need out.

Can't.

"Warner." My eyes are frantic on his face. "What happened? What's happening with the battle—?"

"Please," he says, gripping my shoulders. "You need to start slowly; you should eat something—"

"Tell me—"

"Don't you want to eat first? Or shower?"

"No," I hear myself say. "I have to know now."

One moment. Two and three.

Warner takes a deep breath. A million more. Right hand over left, spinning the jade ring on his pinkie finger over and over and over and over "It's over," he says.

"What?"

I say the word but my lips make no sound. I'm numb, somehow. Blinking and seeing nothing.

4

"It's over," he says again.

"No."

I exhale the word, exhale the impossibility.

He nods. He's disagreeing with me.

"No."

"Juliette."

"No," I say. "No. No. Don't be stupid," I say to him. "Don't be ridiculous," I say to him. *Don't lie to me goddamn you*," but now my voice is high and broken and shaking and "No," I gasp, "no, no, *no*—"

I actually stand up this time. My eyes are filling fast with tears and I blink and blink but the world is a mess and I want to laugh because all I can think is how horrible and beautiful it is, that our eyes blur the truth when we can't bear to see it.

The ground is hard.

I know this to be an actual fact because it's suddenly pressed against my face and Warner is trying to touch me but I think I scream and slap his hands away because I already know the answer. I must already know the answer because I can feel the revulsion bubbling up and unsettling my insides but I ask anyway. I'm horizontal and somehow still tipping over and the holes in my head are tearing open and I'm staring at a spot on the carpet not ten feet away and I'm not sure I'm even alive but I have to hear him say it.

"Why?" I ask.

It's just a word, stupid and simple.

"Why is the battle over?" I ask. I'm not breathing

anymore, not really speaking at all; just expelling letters through my lips.

Warner is not looking at me.

He's looking at the wall and at the floor and at the bedsheets and at the way his knuckles look when he clenches his fists but no not at me he won't look at me and his next words are so, so soft.

"Because they're dead, love. They're all dead."

TWO

My body locks.

My bones, my blood, my brain freeze in place, seizing in some kind of sudden, uncontrollable paralysis that spreads through me so quickly I can't seem to breathe. I'm wheezing in deep, strained inhalations, and the walls won't stop swaying in front of me.

Warner pulls me into his arms.

"Let go of me," I scream, but, oh, only in my imagination because my lips are finished working and my heart has just expired and my mind has gone to hell for the day and my eyes my eyes I think they're bleeding. Warner is whispering words of comfort I can't hear and his arms are wrapped entirely around me, trying to keep me together through sheer physical force but it's no use.

I feel nothing.

Warner is shushing me, rocking me back and forth, and it's only then that I realize I'm making the most excruciating, earsplitting sound, agony ripping through me. I want to speak, to protest, to accuse Warner, to blame him, to call him a liar, but I can say nothing, can form nothing but sounds so pitiful I'm almost ashamed of myself. I break free of his arms, gasping and doubling over, clutching my stomach.

"Adam." I choke on his name.

"Juliette, please—"

"Kenji." I'm hyperventilating into the carpet now.

"Please, love, let me help you—"

"What about James?" I hear myself say. "He was left at Omega Point—he wasn't a-allowed to c-come—"

"It's all been destroyed," Warner says slowly, quietly. "Everything. They tortured some of your members into giving away the exact location of Omega Point. Then they bombed the entire thing."

"Oh, *God*." I cover my mouth with one hand and stare, unblinking, at the ceiling.

"I'm so sorry," he says. "You have no idea how sorry I am."

"Liar," I whisper, venom in my voice. I'm angry and mean and I can't be bothered to care. "You're not sorry at all."

I glance at Warner just long enough to see the hurt flash in and out of his eyes. He clears his throat.

"I am sorry," he says again, quiet but firm. He picks up his jacket from where it was hanging on a nearby rack; shrugs it on without a word.

"Where are you going?" I ask, guilty in an instant.

"You need time to process this and you clearly have no use for my company. I will attend to a few tasks until you're ready to talk."

"Please tell me you're wrong." My voice breaks. My breath catches. "Tell me there's a chance you could be wrong—"

Warner stares at me for what feels like a long time. "If

8

there were even the slightest chance I could spare you this pain," he finally says, "I would've taken it. You must know I wouldn't have said it if it weren't absolutely true."

And it's *this*—his sincerity—that finally snaps me in half.

Because the truth is so unbearable I wish he'd spare me a lie.

I don't remember when Warner left.

I don't remember how he left or what he said. All I know is that I've been lying here curled up on the floor long enough. Long enough for the tears to turn to salt, long enough for my throat to dry up and my lips to chap and my head to pound as hard as my heart.

I sit up slowly, feel my brain twist somewhere in my skull. I manage to climb onto the bed and sit there, still numb but less so, and pull my knees to my chest.

Life without Adam.

Life without Kenji, without James and Castle and Sonya and Sara and Brendan and Winston and all of Omega Point. My friends, all destroyed with the flick of a switch.

Life without Adam.

I hold on tight, pray the pain will pass.

It doesn't.

Adam is gone.

My first love. My first friend. My only friend when I had none and now he's gone and I don't know how I feel. Strange, mostly. Delirious, too. I feel empty and broken and cheated and guilty and angry and desperately, desperately sad.

We'd been growing apart since escaping to Omega Point, but that was my fault. He wanted more from me, but I wanted him to live a long life. I wanted to protect him from the pain I would cause him. I tried to forget him, to move on without him, to prepare myself for a future separate and apart from him.

I thought staying away would keep him alive.

Stupid girl.

The tears are fresh and falling fast now, traveling quietly down my cheeks and into my open, gasping mouth. My shoulders won't stop shaking and my fists keep clenching and my body is cramping and my knees are knocking and old habits are crawling out of my skin and I'm counting cracks and colors and sounds and shudders and rocking back and forth and back and forth and back and forth and I have to let him go I have to let him go I have to I have to

I close my eyes

and *breathe*.

Harsh, hard, rasping breaths.

In.

Out.

Count them.

I've been here before, I tell myself. I've been lonelier than this, more hopeless than this, more desperate than this. I've been here before and I survived. I can get through this.

But never have I been so thoroughly robbed. Love and possibility, friendships and futures: gone. I have to start over now; face the world alone again. I have to make one final choice: give up or go on.

So I get to my feet.

My head is spinning, thoughts knocking into one another, but I swallow back the tears. I clench my fists and try not to scream and I tuck my friends in my heart and

revenge

I think

has never looked so sweet.

THREE

Hang tight
  Hold on
  Look up
  Stay strong
  Hang on
  Hold tight
  Look strong
  Stay up
  One day I might break
  One day I might
  b r e a k
  free

Warner can't hide his surprise when he walks back into the room.

I look up, close the notebook in my hands. "I'm taking this back," I say to him.

He blinks at me. "You're feeling better."

I nod over my shoulder. "My notebook was just sitting here, on the bedside table."

"Yes," he says slowly. Carefully.

"I'm taking it back."

"I understand." He's still standing by the door, still frozen in place, still staring. "Are you"—he shakes his head—"I'm sorry, are you going somewhere?"

It's only then that I realize I'm already halfway to the door. "I need to get out of here."

Warner says nothing. He takes a few careful steps into the room, slips off his jacket, drapes it over a chair. He pulls three guns out of the holster strapped to his back and takes his time placing them on the table where my notebook used to be. When he finally looks up he has a slight smile on his face.

Hands in his pockets. His smile a little bigger. "Where are you going, love?"

"I have some things I need to take care of."

"Is that right?" He leans one shoulder against the wall, crosses his arms against his chest. He can't stop smiling.

"Yes." I'm getting irritated now.

Warner waits. Stares. Nods once, as if to say, *Go on.*

"Your father—"

"Is not here."

"Oh."

I try to hide my shock, but now I don't know why I was so certain Anderson would still be here. This complicates things.

"You really thought you could just walk out of this room," Warner says to me, "knock on my father's door, and do away with him?"

Yes. "No."

13

"Liar, liar, pants on fire," Warner says softly.

I glare at him.

"My father is gone," Warner says. "He's gone back to the capital, and he's taken Sonya and Sara with him."

I gasp, horrified. "No."

Warner isn't smiling anymore.

"Are they . . . alive?" I ask.

"I don't know." A simple shrug. "I imagine they must be, as they're of no use to my father in any other condition."

"They're *alive*?" My heart picks up so quickly I might be having a heart attack. "I have to get them back—I have to find them, I—"

"You what?" Warner is looking at me closely. "How will you get to my father? How will you fight him?"

"I don't know!" I'm pacing across the room now. "But I have to find them. They might be my only friends left in this world and—"

I stop.

I spin around suddenly, heart in my throat.

"What if there are others?" I whisper, too afraid to hope.

I meet Warner across the room.

"What if there are other survivors?" I ask, louder now. "What if they're hiding somewhere?"

"That seems unlikely."

"But there's a chance, isn't there?" I'm desperate. "If there's even the slightest chance—"

Warner sighs. Runs a hand through the hair at the back of his head. "If you'd seen the devastation the way that I did, you wouldn't be saying such things. Hope will break your heart all over again."

My knees have begun to buckle.

I cling to the bed frame, breathing fast, hands shaking. I don't know anything anymore. I don't actually know what's happened to Omega Point. I don't know where the capital is or how I'd get there. I don't know if I'd even be able to get to Sonya and Sara in time. But I can't shake this sudden, stupid hope that more of my friends have somehow survived.

Because they're stronger than this—smarter.

"They've been planning for war for such a long time," I hear myself say. "They must have had some kind of a backup plan. A place to hide—"

"Juliette—"

"Dammit, Warner! I have to try. You have to let me look."

"This is unhealthy." He won't meet my eyes. "It's dangerous for you to think there's a chance anyone might still be alive."

I stare at his strong, steady profile.

He studies his hands.

"Please," I whisper.

He sighs.

"I have to head to the compounds in the next day or so, just to better oversee the process of rebuilding the area." He tenses as he speaks. "We lost many civilians," he says. "Too many. The remaining citizens are understandably traumatized and subdued, as was my father's intention. They've been stripped of any last hope they might've had for rebellion."

A tight breath.

"And now everything must be quickly put back in order," he says. "The bodies are being cleared out and incinerated. The damaged housing units are being replaced. Civilians are being forced to go back to work, orphans are being moved, and the remaining children are required to attend their sector schools.

"The Reestablishment," he says, "does not allow time for people to grieve."

There's a heavy silence between us.

"While I'm overseeing the compounds," Warner says, "I can find a way to take you back to Omega Point. I can show you what's happened. And then, once you have proof, you will have to make your choice."

"What choice?"

"You have to decide your next move. You can stay with me," he says, hesitating, "or, if you prefer, I can arrange for you to live undetected, somewhere on unregulated grounds. But it will be a solitary existence," he says quietly. "You can never be discovered."

"Oh."

A pause.

"Yes," he says.

Another pause.

"*Or*," I say to him, "I leave, find your father, kill him, and deal with the consequences on my own."

Warner fights a smile and fails.

He glances down and laughs just a little before looking me right in the eye. He shakes his head.

16

"What's so funny?"

"My dear girl."

"*What?*"

"I have been waiting for this moment for a long time now."

"What do you mean?"

"You're finally ready," he says. "You're finally ready to fight."

Shock courses through me. "Of course I am."

In an instant I'm bombarded by memories of the battlefield, the terror of being shot to death. I have not forgotten my friends or my renewed conviction, my determination to do things differently. To make a difference. To really fight this time, with no hesitation. No matter what happens—and no matter what I discover—there's no turning back for me anymore. There are no other alternatives.

I have not forgotten. "I forge forward or die."

Warner laughs out loud. He looks like he might cry.

"I *am* going to kill your father," I say to him, "and I'm going to destroy The Reestablishment."

He's still smiling.

"I *will.*"

"I know," he says.

"Then why are you laughing at me?"

"I'm not," he says softly. "I'm only wondering," he says, "if you would like my help."

FOUR

"What?" I blink fast, disbelieving.

"I've always told you," Warner says to me, "that we would make an excellent team. I've always said that I've been waiting for you to be ready—for you to recognize your anger, your own strength. I've been waiting since the day I met you."

"But you wanted to use me for The Reestablishment—you wanted me to torture innocent people—"

"Not true."

"What? What are you talking about? You told me *yourself*—"

"I lied." He shrugs.

My mouth has fallen open.

"There are three things you should know about me, love." He steps forward. "The first," he says, "is that I hate my father more than you might ever be capable of understanding." He clears his throat. "Second, is that I am an unapologetically selfish person, who, in almost every situation, makes decisions based entirely on self-interest. And third." A pause as he looks down. Laughs a little. "I never had any intention of using you as a weapon."

Words have failed me.

I sit down.

Numb.

"That was an elaborate scheme I designed entirely for my father's benefit," Warner says. "I had to convince him it would be a good idea to invest in someone like you, that we might utilize you for military gain. And to be quite, quite honest, I'm still not sure how I managed it. The idea is ludicrous. To spend all that time, money, and energy on reforming a supposedly psychotic girl just for the sake of torture?" He shakes his head. "I knew from the beginning it would be a fruitless endeavor; a complete waste of time. There are far more effective methods of extracting information from the unwilling."

"Then why—why did you want me?"

His eyes are jarring in their sincerity. "I wanted to study you."

"What?" I gasp.

He turns his back to me. "Did you know," he says, so quietly I have to strain to hear him, "that my mother lives in that house?" He looks to the closed door. "The one my father brought you to? The one where he shot you? She was in her room. Just down the hall from where he was keeping you."

When I don't respond, Warner turns to face me.

"Yes," I whisper. "Your father mentioned something about her."

"Oh?" Alarm flits in and out of his features. He quickly masks the emotion. "And what," he says, making an effort to sound calm, "did he say about her?"

"That she's sick," I tell him, hating myself for the tremor

19

that goes through his body. "That he stores her there because she doesn't do well in the compounds."

Warner leans back against the wall, looking as if he requires the support. He takes a hard breath. "Yes," he finally says. "It's true. She's sick. She became ill very suddenly." His eyes are focused on a distant point in another world. "When I was a child, she seemed perfectly fine," he says, turning and turning the jade ring around his finger. "But then one day she just . . . fell apart. For years I fought my father to seek treatment, to find a cure, but he never cared. I was on my own to find help for her, and no matter who I contacted, no doctor was able to treat her. No one," he says, hardly breathing now, "knew what was wrong with her. She exists in a constant state of agony," he says, "and I've always been too selfish to let her die."

He looks up.

"And then I heard about you. I'd heard stories about you, rumors," he says. "And it gave me hope for the very first time. I wanted access to you; I wanted to study you. I wanted to know and understand you firsthand. Because in all my research, you were the only person I'd ever heard of who might be able to offer me answers about my mother's condition. I was desperate," he says. "I was willing to try anything."

"What do you mean?" I ask. "How could someone like me be able to help you with your mother?"

His eyes find mine again, bright with anguish. "Because, love. You cannot touch anyone. And she," he says, "she cannot be touched."

FIVE

I've lost the ability to speak.

"I finally understand her pain," Warner says. "I finally understand what it must be like for her. Because of you. Because I saw what it did to you—what it does to you—to carry that kind of burden, to exist with that much power and to live among those who do not understand."

He tilts his head back against the wall, presses the heels of his hands to his eyes.

"She, much like you," he says, "must feel as though there is a monster inside of her. But unlike you, her only victim is herself. She cannot live in her own skin. She cannot be touched by anyone; not even by her own hands. Not to brush a hair from her forehead or to clench her fists. She's afraid to speak, to move her legs, to stretch her arms, even to shift to a more comfortable position, simply because the sensation of her skin brushing against itself causes her an excruciating amount of pain."

He drops his hands.

"It seems," he says, fighting to keep his voice steady, "that something in the heat of human contact triggers this terrible, destructive power within her, and because she is both the originator and the recipient of the pain, she's somehow incapable of killing herself. Instead, she exists

21

as a prisoner in her own bones, unable to escape this self-inflicted torture."

My eyes are stinging hard. I blink fast.

For so many years I thought my life was difficult; I thought I understood what it meant to suffer. But this. This is something I can't even begin to comprehend. I never stopped to consider that someone else might have it worse than I do.

It makes me feel ashamed for ever having felt sorry for myself.

"For a long time," Warner continues, "I thought she was just . . . sick. I thought she'd developed some kind of illness that was attacking her immune system, something that made her skin sensitive and painful. I assumed that, with the proper treatment, she would eventually heal. I kept hoping," he says, "until I finally realized that years had gone by and nothing had changed. The constant agony began to destroy her mental stability; she eventually gave up on life. She let the pain take over. She refused to get out of bed or to eat regularly; she stopped caring about basic hygiene. And my father's solution was to drug her.

"He keeps her locked in that house with no one but a nurse to keep her company. She's now addicted to morphine and has completely lost her mind. She doesn't even know me anymore. Doesn't recognize me. And the few times I've ever tried to get her off the drugs," he says, speaking quietly now, "she's tried to kill me." He's silent for a second, looking as if he's forgotten I'm still in the room. "My childhood was almost bearable sometimes," he says, "if only because of her. And instead of caring for her, my father turned her into something unrecognizable."

He looks up, laughing.

"I always thought I could fix it," he says. "I thought if I could only find the root of it—I thought I could do something, I thought I could—" He stops. Drags a hand across his face. "I don't know," he whispers. Turns away. "But I never had any intention of using you against your will. The idea has never appealed to me. I only had to maintain the pretense. My father, you see, does not approve of my interest in my mother's well-being."

He smiles a strange, twisted sort of smile. Looks toward the door. Laughs.

"He never wanted to help her. She is a burden he is disgusted by. He thinks that by keeping her alive he's doing her a great kindness for which I should be grateful. He thinks this should be enough for me, to be able to watch my mother turn into a feral creature so utterly consumed by her own agony she's completely vacated her mind." He runs a shaky hand through his hair, grips the back of his neck.

"But it wasn't," he says quietly. "It wasn't enough. I became obsessed with trying to help her. To bring her back to life. And I wanted to feel it," he says to me, looking directly into my eyes. "I wanted to know what it would be like to endure a pain like that. I wanted to know what she must experience every day.

"I was never afraid of your touch," he says. "In fact, I

23

welcomed it. I was so sure you would eventually strike out at me, that you would try to defend yourself against me; and I was looking forward to that moment. But you never did." He shakes his head. "Everything I'd read in your files told me you were an unrestrained, vicious creature. I was expecting you to be an animal, someone who would try to kill me and my men at every opportunity—someone who needed to be closely watched. But you disappointed me by being too human, too lovely. So unbearably naive. You wouldn't fight back."

His eyes are unfocused, remembering.

"You didn't react against my threats. You wouldn't respond to the things that mattered. You acted like an insolent child," he says. "You didn't like your clothes. You wouldn't eat your fancy food." He laughs out loud and rolls his eyes and I've suddenly forgotten my sympathy.

I'm tempted to throw something at him.

"You were so hurt," he says, "that I'd asked you to wear a *dress*." He looks at me then, eyes sparkling with amusement. "Here I was, prepared to defend my life against an uncontrollable monster who could kill," he says, "kill a man with her *bare hands*—" He bites back another laugh. "And you threw tantrums over clean clothes and hot meals. Oh," he says, shaking his head at the ceiling, "you were ridiculous. You were completely ridiculous and it was the most entertainment I'd ever had. I can't tell you how much I enjoyed it. I loved making you mad," he says to me, his eyes wicked. "I *love* making you mad."

I'm gripping one of his pillows so tightly I'm afraid I might tear it. I glare at him.

He laughs at me.

"I was so distracted," he says, smiling. "Always wanting to spend time with you. Pretending to plan things for your supposed future with The Reestablishment. You were harmless and beautiful and you always *yelled* at me," he says, grinning widely now. "God, you would yell at me over the most inconsequential things," he says, remembering. "But you never laid a hand on me. Not once, not even to save your own life."

His smile fades.

"It worried me. It scared me to think you were so ready to sacrifice yourself before using your abilities to defend yourself." A breath. "So I changed tactics. I tried to bully you into touching me."

I flinch, remembering that day in the blue room too well. When he taunted me and manipulated me and I came so close to hurting him. He'd finally managed to find exactly the right things to say to hurt me enough to want to hurt him back.

I nearly did.

He cocks his head. Exhales a deep, defeated breath. "But that didn't work either. And I quickly began to lose sight of my original purpose. I became so invested in you that I'd forgotten why I'd brought you on base to begin with. I was frustrated that you wouldn't give in, that you refused to lash out even when I knew you wanted to. But every time I was ready to give up, you would have these moments," he says, shaking his head. "You had these incredible moments when you'd finally show glimpses of raw, unbridled strength. It was incredible." He stops. Leans back against the wall. "But then you'd always retreat. Like you were ashamed. Like you didn't want to recognize those feelings in yourself.

"So I changed tactics again. I tried something else. Something that I knew—with certainty—would push you past your breaking point. And I must say, it really was everything I hoped it would be." He smiles. "You looked truly alive for the very first time."

My hands are suddenly ice cold.

"The torture room," I gasp.

SIX

"I suppose you could call it that." Warner shrugs. "We call it a simulation chamber."

"You made me torture that child," I say to him, the anger and the rage of that day rising up inside of me. How could I forget what he did? What he made me do? The horrible memories he forced me to relive all for the sake of his entertainment. "I will never forgive you for that," I snap, acid in my voice. "I will never forgive you for what you did to that little boy. For what you made me do to him!"

Warner frowns. "I'm sorry—what?"

"You would sacrifice a *child*!" My voice is shaking now. "For your stupid games! How could you do something so despicable?" I throw my pillow at him. "You sick, heartless, *monster*!"

Warner catches the pillow as it hits his chest, staring at me like he's never seen me before. But then a kind of understanding settles into place for him, and the pillow slips from his hands. Falls to the floor. "Oh," he says, so slowly. He's squeezing his eyes shut, trying to suppress his amusement. "Oh, you're going to kill me," he says, laughing openly now. "I don't think I can handle this—"

"What are you talking about? What's wrong with you?" I demand.

He's still smiling as he says, "Tell me, love. Tell me exactly what happened that day."

I clench my fists, offended by his flippancy and shaking with renewed anger. "You gave me stupid, skimpy clothes to wear! And then you took me down to the lower levels of Sector 45 and locked me in a dirty room. I remember it perfectly," I tell him, fighting to remain calm. "It had disgusting yellow walls. Old green carpet. A huge two-way mirror."

Warner raises his eyebrows. Gestures for me to continue.

"Then . . . you hit some kind of a switch," I say, forcing myself to keep talking. I don't know why I'm beginning to doubt myself. "And these huge, metal spikes started coming out of the ground. And then"—I hesitate, steeling myself—"a toddler walked in. He was blindfolded. And you said he was your replacement. You said that if I didn't save him, you wouldn't either."

Warner is looking at me closely now. Studying my eyes. "Are you sure I said that?"

"Yes."

"Yes?" He cocks his head. "Yes, you saw me say that with your own eyes?"

"N-no," I say quickly, feeling defensive, "but there were loudspeakers—I could hear your voice—"

He takes a deep breath. "Right; of course."

"I *did*," I tell him.

"So after you heard me say that, what happened?"

I swallow hard. "I had to save the boy. He was going to die. He couldn't see where he was going and he was going to be impaled by those spikes. I had to pull him into my arms and try to find a way to hold on to him without killing him."

A beat of silence.

"And did you succeed?" Warner asks me.

"Yes," I whisper, unable to understand why he's asking me this when he saw it all happen for himself. "But the boy went limp," I say. "He was temporarily paralyzed in my arms. And then you hit another switch and the spikes disappeared, and I let him down and he—he started crying again and bumped into my bare legs. And he started screaming. And I . . . I got so mad at you . . ."

"That you broke through concrete," Warner says, a faint smile touching his lips. "You broke through a concrete wall just to try and choke me to death."

"You deserved it," I hear myself say. "You deserved worse."

"Well," he sighs. "If I did, in fact, do what you say I did, it certainly sounds like I deserved it."

"What do you mean, *if* you did? I *know* you did—"

"Is that right?"

"Of course it's right!"

"Then tell me, love, what happened to the boy?"

"What?" I freeze; icicles creep up my arms.

"What happened," he says, "to that little boy? You say that you set him on the ground. But then you proceeded to break through a concrete wall fitted with a thick, six-foot-wide mirror, with no apparent regard for the toddler you claim was wandering around the room. Don't you think the poor child would've been injured in such a wild, reckless display? My soldiers certainly were. You broke down a wall of *concrete*, love. You crushed an enormous piece of glass. You did not stop to ascertain where the blocks or the shattered bits had fallen or who they might've injured in the process." He stops. Stares. "Did you?"

"No," I gasp, blood draining from my body.

"So what happened after you walked away?" he asks. "Or do you not remember that part? You turned around and left, just after destroying the room, injuring my men, and tossing me to the floor. You turned around," he says, "and walked right out."

I'm numb now, remembering. It's true. I did. I didn't think. I just knew I needed to get out of there as fast as possible. I needed to get away, to clear my head.

"So what happened to the boy?" Warner insists. "Where was he when you were leaving? Did you see him?" A lift of his eyebrows. "And what about the spikes?" he says. "Did you bother to look closely at the ground to see where they might've come from? Or how they might've punctured a carpeted floor without causing any damage? Did you feel the surface under your feet to be shredded or uneven?"

I'm breathing hard now, struggling to stay calm. I can't tear myself away from his gaze.

"Juliette, love," he says softly. "There were no speakers in that room. That room is entirely soundproof, equipped with nothing but sensors and cameras. It is a simulation chamber."

"No," I breathe, refusing to believe. Not wanting to accept that I was wrong, that Warner isn't the monster I thought he was. He can't change things now. Can't confuse me like this. This isn't the way it's supposed to work. "That's not possible—"

"I am guilty," he says, "of forcing you to undergo such a cruel simulation. I accept the fault for that, and I've already apologized for my actions. I only meant to push you into finally reacting, and I knew that sort of re-creation would quickly trigger something inside of you. But good God, love"—he shakes his head—"you must have an absurdly low opinion of me if you think I would steal someone's child just to watch you torture it."

"It wasn't real?" I don't recognize my own raspy, panicked voice. "It wasn't *real?*"

He offers me a sympathetic smile. "I designed the basic elements of the simulation, but the beauty of the program is that it will evolve and adapt as it processes a soldier's most visceral responses. We use it to train soldiers who must overcome specific fears or prepare for a particularly sensitive mission. We can re-create almost any environment," he says. "Even soldiers who know what they're getting into will forget that they're performing in a simulation." He averts his eyes. "I knew it would be terrifying for you, and I did it anyway. And for hurting you, I feel true regret. But no," he says quietly, meeting my eyes again. "None of it was real. You imagined my voice in that room. You imagined the pain, the sounds, the smells. All of it was in your mind."

"I don't want to believe you," I say to him, my voice scarcely a whisper.

He tries to smile. "Why do you think I gave you those clothes?" he asks. "The material of that outfit was lined

31

with a chemical designed to react to the sensors in that room. And the less you're wearing, the more easily the cameras can track the heat in your body, your movements." He shakes his head. "I never had a chance to explain what you'd experienced. I wanted to follow you immediately, but I thought I should give you time to collect yourself. It was a stupid decision, on my end." His jaw tenses. "I waited, and I shouldn't have. Because when I found you, it was too late. You were ready to jump out a window just to get away from me."

"For good reason," I snap.

He holds up his hands in surrender.

"You are a *terrible* person!" I explode, throwing the rest of the pillows at his face, angry and horrified and humiliated all at once. "Why would you put me through something like that when you *know* what I've been through, you stupid, arrogant—"

"Juliette, please," he says, stepping forward, dodging a pillow to reach for my arms. "I *am* sorry for hurting you, but I really think it was worth—"

"Don't touch me!" I jerk away, glaring, clutching the foot of his bed like it might be a weapon. "I should shoot you all over again for doing that to me! I should—I should—"

"What?" He laughs. "You're going to throw another pillow at me?"

I shove him, hard, and when he doesn't budge, I start throwing punches. I'm hitting his chest, his arms, his stomach, and his legs, anywhere I can reach, wishing more

32

than ever that he weren't able to absorb my power, that I could actually crush all the bones in his body and make him writhe in pain beneath my hands. "You . . . selfish . . . *monster!*" I keep throwing poorly aimed fists in his direction, not realizing how much the effort exhausts me, not realizing how quickly the anger dissolves into pain. Suddenly all I want to do is cry. My body is shaking in both relief and terror, finally unshackled from the fear that I'd caused another innocent child some kind of irreparable damage, and simultaneously horrified that Warner would ever force such a terrible thing on me. To *help* me.

"I'm so sorry," he says, stepping closer. "I really, truly am. I didn't know you then. Not like I do now. I'd never do that to you now."

"You don't know me," I mumble, wiping away tears. "You think you know me just because you've read my journal— you stupid, prying, privacy-stealing *asshole*—"

"Oh, right—about that—" He smiles, one quick hand plucking the journal out of my pocket as he moves toward the door. "I'm afraid I wasn't finished reading this."

"Hey!" I protest, swiping at him as he walks away. "You said you'd give that back to me!"

"I said no such thing," he says, subdued, dropping the journal into his own pants pocket. "Now please wait here a moment. I'm going to get you something to eat."

I'm still shouting as he closes the door behind him.

SEVEN

I fall backward onto the bed and make an angry noise deep inside my throat. Chuck a pillow at the wall.

I need to do something. I need to start moving.

I need to finish forming a plan.

I've been on the defense and on the run for so long now that my mind has often been occupied by elaborate and hopeless daydreams about overthrowing The Reestablishment. I spent most of my 264 days in that cell fantasizing about exactly this kind of impossible moment: the day I'd be able to spit in the face of those who'd oppressed me and everyone else just beyond my window. And though I dreamed up a million different scenarios in which I would stand up and defend myself, I never actually thought I'd have a chance to make it happen. I never thought I'd have the power, the opportunity, or the courage.

But now?

Everyone is gone.

I might be the only one left.

At Omega Point I was happy to let Castle lead. I didn't know much about anything, and I was still too scared to act. Castle was already in charge and already had a plan, so I trusted that he knew best; that they knew better.

A mistake.

I've always known, deep down, who should be leading this resistance. I've felt it quietly for some time now, always too scared to bring the words to my lips. Someone who's got nothing left to lose and everything to gain. Someone no longer afraid of anyone.

Not Castle. Not Kenji. Not Adam. Not even Warner.

It should be me.

I look closely at my outfit for the first time and realize I must be wearing more of Warner's old clothes. I'm drowning in a faded orange T-shirt and a pair of gray sweatpants that almost falls off my hips every time I stand up straight. I take a moment to regain my equilibrium, testing my full weight on the thick, plush carpet under my bare feet. I roll the waistband of the pants a few times, just until they sit snugly at my hip bone, and then I ball up the extra material of the T-shirt and knot it at the back. I'm vaguely aware that I must look ridiculous, but fitting the clothes to my frame gives me some modicum of control and I cling to it. It makes me feel a little more awake, a little more in command of my situation. All I need now is a rubber band. My hair is too heavy; it's begun to feel like it's suffocating me, and I'm desperate to get it off my neck. I'm desperate to take a shower, actually.

I spin around at the sound of the door.

I'm caught in the middle of a thought, holding my hair up with both hands in a makeshift ponytail, and suddenly acutely aware of the fact that I'm not wearing any underwear.

Warner is holding a tray.

He's staring at me, unblinking. His gaze sweeps across my face, down my neck, my arms. Stops at my waist. I follow his eyes only to realize that my movements have lifted my shirt and exposed my stomach. And I suddenly understand why he's staring.

The memory of his kisses along my torso; his hands exploring my back, my bare legs, the backs of my thighs, his fingers hooking around the elastic band of my underwear—

Oh

I drop my hands and my hair at the same time, the brown waves falling hard and fast around my shoulders, my back, hitting my waist. My face is on fire.

Warner is suddenly transfixed by a spot directly above my head.

"I should probably cut my hair," I say to no one in particular, not understanding why I've even said it. I don't want to cut my hair. I want to lock myself in the toilet.

He doesn't respond. He carries the tray closer to the bed and it's not until I spot the glasses of water and the plates of food that I realize exactly how hungry I am. I can't remember the last time I ate anything; I've been surviving off the energy recharge I received when my wound was healed.

"Have a seat," he says, not meeting my eyes. He nods to the floor before folding himself onto the carpet. I sit down across from him. He pushes the tray in front of me.

"Thank you," I say, my eyes focused on the meal. "This looks delicious."

There's tossed salad and fragrant, colorful rice. Diced, seasoned potatoes and a small helping of steamed vegetables. A little cup of chocolate pudding. A bowl of fresh-cut fruit. Two glasses of water.

It's a meal I would've scoffed at when I first arrived.

If I knew then what I know now, I would've taken advantage of every opportunity Warner had given me. I would've eaten the food and taken the clothes. I would've built up my strength and paid closer attention when he showed me around base. I would've been looking for escape routes and excuses to tour the compounds. And then I would've bolted. I would've found a way to survive on my own. And I never would've dragged Adam down with me. I never would've gotten myself and so many others into this mess.

If only I had eaten the stupid food.

I was a scared, broken girl, fighting back the only way I knew how. It's no wonder I failed. I wasn't in my right mind. I was weak and terrified and blind to the idea of possibility. I had no experience with stealth or manipulation. I hardly knew how to interact with people—could barely understand the words in my own head.

It shocks me to think how much I've changed in these past months. I feel like a completely different person. Sharper, somehow. Hardened, absolutely. And for the first time in my life, willing to admit that I'm angry.

It's liberating.

I look up suddenly, feeling the weight of Warner's gaze. He's staring at me like he's intrigued, fascinated. "What are you thinking about?" he asks.

I stab a piece of potato with my fork. "I'm thinking I was an idiot for ever turning down a plate of hot food."

He raises an eyebrow at me. "I can't say I disagree."

I shoot him a dirty look.

"You were so broken when you got here," he says, taking a deep breath. "I was so confused. I kept waiting for you to go insane, to jump on the table at dinner and start taking swipes at my soldiers. I was sure you were going to try and kill everyone, and instead, you were stubborn and pouty, refusing to change out of your filthy clothes and complaining about eating your vegetables."

I go pink.

"At first," he says, laughing, "I thought you were plotting something. I thought you were pretending to be complacent just to distract me from some greater goal. I thought your anger over such petty things was a ruse," he says, his eyes mocking me. "I figured it had to be."

I cross my arms. "The extravagance was disgusting. So much money is wasted on the army while other people are starving to death."

Warner waves a hand, shaking his head. "That's not the point. The point," he says, "is that I hadn't provided you with any of those things for some calculated, underhanded reason. It wasn't some kind of a test." He laughs. "I wasn't trying to challenge you and your scruples. I thought I was doing you a favor. You'd come from this disgusting, miserable hole in the ground. I wanted you to have a real mattress. To be able to shower in peace. To have beautiful, fresh clothes. And you needed to eat," he says. "You'd been starved half to death."

I stiffen, slightly mollified. "Maybe," I say. "But you were crazy. You were a controlling maniac. You wouldn't even let me talk to the other soldiers."

"Because they are animals," he snaps, his voice unexpectedly sharp.

I look up, startled, to meet his angry, flashing green eyes.

"You, who have spent the majority of your life locked away," he says, "have not had the opportunity to understand just how beautiful you are, or what kind of effect that can have on a person. I was worried for your safety," he says. "You were timid and weak and living on a military base full of lonely, fully armed, thickheaded soldiers three times your size. I didn't want them harassing you. I made a spectacle out of your display with Jenkins because I wanted them to have proof of your abilities. I needed them to see that you were a formidable opponent—one they'd do well to stay away from. I was trying to protect you."

I can't look away from the intensity in his eyes.

"How little you must think of me." He shakes his head in shock. "I had no idea you hated me so much. That everything I tried to do to help you had come under such harsh scrutiny."

"How can you be surprised? What choice did I have but to expect the worst from you? You were arrogant and crass and you treated me like a piece of property—"

"Because I had to!" He cuts me off, unrepentant. "My every move—every word—is monitored when I am not confined to my own quarters. My entire life depends on maintaining a certain type of personality."

"What about that soldier you shot in the forehead? Seamus Fletcher?" I challenge him, angry again. Now that I've let it enter my life, I'm realizing anger comes a little too naturally to me. "Was that all a part of your plan, too? No wait, don't tell me"—I hold up a hand—"that was just a simulation, right?"

Warner goes rigid.

He sits back; his jaw twitches. He looks at me with a mixture of sadness and rage in his eyes. "No," he finally says, deathly soft. "That was not a simulation."

"So you have no problem with that?" I ask him. "You have no regrets over killing a man for stealing a little extra food? For trying to survive, just like you?"

Warner bites down on his bottom lip for half a second. Clasps his hands in his lap. "Wow," he says. "How quickly you jump to his defense."

"He was an innocent man," I tell him. "He didn't deserve to die. Not for that. Not like that."

"Seamus Fletcher," Warner says calmly, staring into his open palms, "was a drunken bastard who was beating his wife and children. He hadn't fed them in two weeks. He'd

40

punched his nine-year-old daughter in the mouth, breaking her two front teeth and fracturing her jaw. He beat his pregnant wife so hard she lost the child. He had two other children, too," he says. "A seven-year-old boy and a five-year-old girl." A pause. "He broke both their arms."

My food is forgotten.

"I monitor the lives of our citizens very carefully," Warner says. "I like to know who they are and how they're thriving. I probably shouldn't care," he says, "but I do."

I'm thinking I'm never going to open my mouth ever again.

"I have never claimed to live by any set of principles," Warner says to me. "I've never claimed to be right, or good, or even justified in my actions. The simple truth is that I do not care. I have been forced to do terrible things in my life, love, and I am seeking neither your forgiveness nor your approval. Because I do not have the luxury of philosophizing over scruples when I'm forced to act on basic instinct every day."

He meets my eyes.

"Judge me," he says, "all you like. But I have no tolerance," he says sharply, "for a man who beats his wife. No tolerance," he says, "for a man who beats his children." He's breathing hard now. "Seamus Fletcher was murdering his family," he says to me. "And you can call it whatever the hell you want to call it, but I will never regret killing a man who would bash his wife's face into a wall. I will never regret killing a man who would punch his nine-year-old daughter in the mouth. I am not sorry," he says. "And I will not apologize. Because a child is better off with no father, and a wife is better off with no husband, than one like that." I watch the hard movement in his throat. "I would know."

"I'm sorry—Warner, I—"

He holds up a hand to stop me. He steadies himself, his eyes focused on the plates of untouched food. "I've said it before, love, and I'm sorry I have to say it again, but you do not understand the choices I have to make. You don't know what I've seen and what I'm forced to witness every single day." He hesitates. "And I wouldn't want you to. But do not presume to understand my actions," he says, finally meeting my eyes. "Because if you do, I can assure you you'll only be met with disappointment. And if you insist on continuing to make assumptions about my character, I'll advise you only this: assume you will always be wrong."

He hauls himself up with a casual elegance that startles me. Smooths out his slacks. Pushes his sleeves up again. "I've had your armoire moved into my closet," he says. "There are things for you to change into, if you'd like that. The bed and bathroom are yours. I have work to do," he says. "I'll be sleeping in my office tonight."

And with that, he opens the adjoining door to his office, and locks himself inside.

EIGHT

My food is cold.

I poke at the potatoes and force myself to finish the meal even though I've lost my appetite. I can't help but wonder if I've finally pushed Warner too far.

I thought the revelations had come to a close for today, but I was wrong again. It makes me wonder just how much is left, and how much more I'll learn about Warner in the coming days. Months.

And I'm scared.

Because the more I discover about him, the fewer excuses I have to push him away. He's unraveling before me, becoming something entirely different; terrifying me in a way I never could've expected.

And all I can think is *not now*.

Not here. Not when so much is uncertain. If only my emotions would understand the importance of excellent timing.

I never realized Warner was unaware of how deeply I'd detested him. I suppose now I can better understand how he saw himself, how he'd never viewed his actions as guilty or criminal. Maybe he thought I would've given him the benefit of the doubt. That I would've been able to read him as easily as he's been able to read me.

But I couldn't. I didn't. And now I can't help but wonder if I've managed to disappoint him, somehow.

Why I even care.

I clamber to my feet with a sigh, hating my own uncertainty. Because while I might not be able to deny my physical attraction to him, I still can't shake my initial impressions of his character. It's not easy for me to switch so suddenly, to recognize him as anything but some kind of manipulative monster.

I need time to adjust to the idea of Warner as a normal person.

But I'm tired of thinking. And right now, all I want to do is shower.

I drag myself toward the open door of the bathroom before I remember what Warner said about my clothes. That he'd moved my armoire into his closet. I look around, searching for another door and finding none but the locked entry to his office. I'm half tempted to knock and ask him directly but decide against it. Instead, I study the walls more closely, wondering why Warner wouldn't have given me instructions if his closet was hard to find. But then I see it.

A switch.

It's more of a button, actually, but it sits flush with the wall. It would be almost impossible to spot if you weren't actively searching for it.

I press the button.

A panel in the wall slides out of place. And as I step across the threshold, the room illuminates on its own.

This closet is bigger than his entire bedroom.

The walls and ceiling are tiled with slabs of white stone that gleam under the fluorescent recessed lighting; the floors are covered with thick Oriental rugs. There's a small suede couch the color of light-green jade stationed in the very center of the room, but it's an odd sort of couch: it doesn't have a back. It looks like an oversized ottoman. And strangest of all: there's not a single mirror in here. I spin around, my eyes searching, certain I must've overlooked such an obvious staple, and I'm so caught up in the details of the space that I almost miss the clothes.

The *clothes*.

They're everywhere, on display as if they were works of art. Glossy, dark wood units are built into the walls, shelves lined with rows and rows of shoes. All the other closet space is dedicated to hanging racks, each wall housing different categories of clothing.

Everything is color coordinated.

He owns more coats, more shoes, more pants and shirts than I've ever seen in my life. Ties and bow ties, belts, scarves, gloves, and cuff links. Beautiful, rich fabrics: silk blends and starched cotton, soft wool and cashmere. Dress shoes and buttery leather boots buffed and polished to perfection. A peacoat in a dark, burnt shade of orange; a trench coat in a deep navy blue. A winter toggle coat in a stunning shade of plum. I dare to run my fingers along the different materials, wondering how many of these pieces he's actually worn.

I'm amazed.

It's always been apparent that Warner takes pride in his appearance; his outfits are impeccable; his clothes fit him like they were cut for his body. But now I finally understand why he took such care with my wardrobe.

He wasn't trying to patronize me.

He was enjoying himself.

Aaron Warner Anderson, chief commander and regent of Sector 45, son of the supreme commander of The Reestablishment.

He has a soft spot for fashion.

After my initial shock wears off, I'm able to easily locate my old armoire. It's been placed unceremoniously in a corner of the room, and I'm almost sorry for it. It stands out awkwardly against the rest of the space.

I quickly shuffle through the drawers, grateful for the first time to have clean things to change into. Warner anticipated all of my needs before I arrived on base. The armoire is full of dresses and shirts and pants, but it's also been stocked with socks, bras, and underwear. And even though I know this should make me feel awkward, somehow it doesn't. The underwear is simple and understated. Cotton basics that are exactly average and perfectly functional. He bought these things before he knew me, and knowing that they weren't purchased with any level of intimacy makes me feel less self-conscious about it all.

I grab a small T-shirt, a pair of cotton pajama bottoms, and all of my brand-new underthings, and slip out of the room. The lights immediately switch off as soon as I'm back in the bedroom, and I hit the button to close the panel.

I look around his bedroom with new eyes, reacclimatizing to this smaller, standard sort of space. Warner's bedroom looks almost identical to the one I occupied while on base, and I always wondered why. There are no personal effects anywhere; no pictures, no odd knickknacks.

But suddenly it all makes sense.

His bedroom doesn't mean anything to him. It's little more than a place to sleep. But his closet—that was his style, his design. It's probably the only space he cares about in this room.

It makes me wonder what the inside of his office looks like, and my eyes dart to his door before I remember how he's locked himself inside.

I stifle a sigh and head toward the bathroom, planning to shower, change, and fall asleep immediately. This day felt more like a few years, and I'm ready to be done with it. Hopefully tomorrow we'll be able to head back to Omega Point and finally make some progress.

But no matter what happens next, and no matter what we discover, I'm determined to find my way to Anderson, even if I have to go alone.

NINE

I can't scream.

My lungs won't expand. My breaths keep coming in short gasps. My chest feels too tight and my throat is closing up and I'm trying to shout and I can't, I can't stop wheezing, thrashing my arms and trying desperately to breathe but the effort is futile. No one can hear me. No one will ever know that I'm dying, that there's a hole in my chest filling with blood and pain and such unbearable agony and there's so much of it, so much blood, hot and pooling around me and I can't, I can't, I can't *breathe*—

"Juliette—*Juliette*, love, wake up—*wake up*—"

I jerk up so quickly I double over. I'm heaving in deep, harsh, gasping breaths, so overcome, so relieved to be able to get oxygen into my lungs that I can't speak, can't do anything but try to inhale as much as possible. My whole body is shaking, my skin is clammy, going from hot to cold too quickly. I can't steady myself, can't stop the silent tears, can't shake the nightmare, can't shake the memory.

I can't stop gasping for air.

Warner's hands cup my face. The warmth of his skin helps calm me somehow, and I finally feel my heart rate begin to slow. "Look at me," he says.

I force myself to meet his eyes, shaking as I catch my breath.

"It's okay," he whispers, still holding my cheeks. "It was just a bad dream. Try closing your mouth," he says, "and breathing through your nose." He nods. "There you go. Easy. You're okay." His voice is so soft, so melodic, so inexplicably tender.

I can't look away from his eyes. I'm afraid to blink, afraid to be pulled back into my nightmare.

"I won't let go until you're ready," he tells me. "Don't worry. Take your time."

I close my eyes. I feel my heart slow to a normal beat. My muscles begin to unclench, my hands steady their tremble. And even though I'm not actively crying, I can't stop the tears from streaming down my face. But then something in my body breaks, crumples from the inside, and I'm suddenly so exhausted I can no longer hold myself up.

Somehow, Warner seems to understand.

He helps me sit back on the bed, pulls the blankets up around my shoulders. I'm shivering, wiping away the last of my tears. Warner runs a hand over my hair. "It's okay," he says softly. "You're okay."

"Aren't y-you going to sleep, too?" I stammer, wondering what time it is. I notice he's still fully dressed.

"I . . . yes," he says. Even in this dim light I can see the surprise in his eyes. "Eventually. I don't often go to bed this early."

"Oh." I blink, breathing a little easier now. "What time is it?"

"Two o'clock in the morning."

It's my turn to be surprised. "Don't we have to be up in a few hours?"

"Yes." The ghost of a smile touches his lips. "But I'm almost never able to fall asleep when I should. I can't seem to turn my mind off," he says, grinning at me for only a moment longer before he turns to leave.

"Stay."

The word escapes my lips even before I've had a chance to think it through. I'm not sure why I've said it. Maybe because it's late and I'm still shaking, and maybe having him close might scare my nightmares away. Or maybe it's because I'm weak and grieving and need a friend right now. I'm not sure. But there's something about the darkness, the stillness of this hour, I think, that creates a language of its own. There's a strange kind of freedom in the dark; a terrifying vulnerability we allow ourselves at exactly the wrong moment, tricked by the darkness into thinking it will keep our secrets. We forget that the blackness is not a blanket; we forget that the sun will soon rise. But in the moment, at least, we feel brave enough to say things we'd never say in the light.

Except for Warner, who doesn't say a word.

For a split second he actually looks alarmed. He's staring at me in silent terror, too stunned to speak, and I'm about to take it all back and hide under the covers when he catches my arm.

I still.

He tugs me forward until I'm nestled against his chest. His arms fall around me carefully, as if he's telling me I can pull away, that he'll understand, that it's my choice. But I feel so safe, so warm, so devastatingly content that I can't seem to come up with a single reason why I shouldn't enjoy this moment. I press closer, hiding my face in the soft folds of his shirt, and his arms wrap more tightly around me, his chest rising and falling. My hands come up to rest against his stomach, the hard muscles tensed under my touch. My left hand slips around his ribs, up his back, and Warner freezes, his heart racing under my ear. My eyes fall closed just as I feel him try to inhale.

"Oh God," he gasps. He jerks back, breaks away. "I can't do this. I won't survive it."

"What?"

He's already on his feet and I can only make out enough of his silhouette to see that he's shaking. "I can't keep doing this—"

"Warner—"

"I thought I could walk away the last time," he says. "I thought I could let you go and hate you for it but I can't. Because you make it so damn difficult," he says. "Because you don't play fair. You go and do something like get yourself shot," he says, "and you *ruin* me in the process."

I try to remain perfectly still.

I try not to make a sound.

But my mind won't stop racing and my heart won't

51

stop pounding and with just a few words he's managed to dismantle my most concentrated efforts to forget what I did to him.

I don't know what to do.

My eyes finally adjust to the darkness and I blink, only to find him looking into my eyes like he can see into my soul.

I'm not ready for this. Not yet. Not yet. Not like this. But a rush of feelings, images of his hands, his arms, his lips are charging through my mind and I try but can't push the thoughts away, can't ignore the scent of his skin and the insane familiarity of his body. I can almost hear his heart thrumming in his chest, can see the tense movement in his jaw, can feel the power quietly contained within him.

And suddenly his face changes. Worries.

"What's wrong?" he asks. "Are you scared?"

I startle, breathing faster, grateful he can only sense the general direction of my feelings and not more than that. For a moment I actually want to say no. No, I'm not scared.

I'm petrified.

Because being this close to you is doing things to me. Strange things and irrational things and things that flutter against my chest and braid my bones together. I want a pocketful of punctuation marks to end the thoughts he's forced into my head.

But I don't say any of those things.

Instead, I ask a question I already know the answer to.

"Why would I be scared?"

"You're shaking," he says.

"Oh."

The two letters and their small, startled sound run right out of my mouth to seek refuge in a place far from here. I keep wishing I had the strength to look away from him in moments like this. I keep wishing my cheeks wouldn't so easily enflame. I keep wasting my wishes on stupid things, I think.

"No, I'm not scared," I finally say. But I really need him to step away from me. I really need him to do me that favor. "I'm just surprised."

He's silent, then, his eyes imploring me for an explanation. He's become both familiar and foreign to me in such a short period of time; exactly and nothing like I thought he'd be.

"You allow the world to think you're a heartless murderer," I tell him. "And you're not."

He laughs, once; his eyebrows lift in surprise. "No," he says. "I'm afraid I'm just the regular kind of murderer."

"But why—why would you pretend to be so ruthless?" I ask. "Why do you allow people to treat you that way?"

He sighs. Pushes his rolled-up shirtsleeves above his elbows again. I can't help but follow the movement, my eyes lingering along his forearms. And I realize, for the first time, that he doesn't sport any military tattoos like everyone else. I wonder why.

"What difference does it make?" he says. "People can think whatever they like. I don't desire their validation."

"So you don't mind," I ask him, "that people judge you so harshly?"

"I have no one to impress," he says. "No one who cares about what happens to me. I'm not in the business of making friends, love. My job is to lead an army, and it's the only thing I'm good at. No one," he says, "would be proud of the things I've accomplished. My mother doesn't even know me anymore. My father thinks I'm weak and pathetic. My soldiers want me dead. The world is going to hell. And the conversations I have with you are the longest I've ever had."

"What—really?" I ask, eyes wide.

"Really."

"And you trust me with all this information?" I say. "Why share your secrets with me?"

His eyes darken, deaden, all of a sudden. He looks toward the wall. "Don't do that," he says. "Don't ask me questions you already know the answers to. Twice I've laid myself bare for you and all it's gotten me was a bullet wound and a broken heart. Don't torture me," he says, meeting my eyes again. "It's a cruel thing to do, even to someone like me."

"Warner—"

"I don't understand!" He breaks, finally losing his composure, his voice rising in pitch. "What could *Kent*," he says, spitting the name, "possibly do for you?"

I'm so shocked, so unprepared to answer such a question that I'm rendered momentarily speechless. I don't even know what's happened to Adam, where he might be or what our future holds. Right now all I'm clinging to is a hope that he made it out alive. That he's out there somewhere, surviving against the odds. Right now, that certainty would be enough for me.

So I take a deep breath and try to find the right words, the right way to explain that there are so many bigger, heavier issues to deal with, but when I look up I find Warner is still staring at me, waiting for an answer to a question I now realize he's been trying hard to suppress. Something that must be eating away at him.

And I suppose he deserves an answer. Especially after what I did to him.

So I take a deep breath.

"It's not something I know how to explain," I say. "He's . . . I don't know." I stare into my hands. "He was my first friend. The first person to treat me with respect—to love me." I'm quiet a moment. "He's always been so kind to me."

Warner flinches. His eyes widen in shock. "He's always been so *kind* to you?"

"Yes," I whisper.

Warner laughs a harsh, hollow sort of laugh.

"This is incredible," he says, staring at the door, one hand caught in his hair. "I've been consumed by this question for the past three days, trying desperately to understand why you would give yourself to me so willingly, just to rip my heart out at the very last moment for some—some bland, utterly replaceable automaton. I kept thinking there had to be some great reason, something I'd overlooked, something I wasn't able to fathom."

"And I was ready to accept it," he says. "I'd forced myself to accept it because I figured your reasons were deep and beyond my grasp. I was willing to let you go if you'd found something extraordinary. Someone who could know you in ways I'd never be able to comprehend. Because you deserve that," he says. "I told myself you deserved more than me, more than my miserable offerings." He shakes his head. "But this?" he says, appalled. "These words? This explanation? You chose him because he's *kind* to you? Because he's offered you basic *charity*?"

I'm suddenly angry.

I'm suddenly mortified.

I'm outraged by the permission Warner's granted himself to judge my life—that he thought he'd been *generous* by stepping aside. I narrow my eyes, clench my fists. "It's not charity," I snap. "He cares about me—and I care about him!"

Warner nods, unimpressed. "You should get a dog, love. I hear they share much the same qualities."

"You are unbelievable!" I shove myself upward, scrambling to my feet and regretting it. I have to cling to the bed frame to steady myself. "My relationship with Adam is none of your business!"

"Your *relationship*?" Warner laughs, loud. He moves quickly to face me from the other side of the bed, leaving several feet between us. "What relationship? Does he even know anything about you? Does he understand you? Does he know your wants, your fears, the truth you conceal in your heart?"

"Oh, and what? You do?"

"You know damn well that I do!" he shouts, pointing an accusatory finger at me. "And I'm willing to bet my *life* that he has no idea what you're really like. You tiptoe around his feelings, pretending to be a nice little girl for him, don't you? You're afraid of scaring him off. You're afraid of telling him too much—"

"You don't know *anything*!"

"Oh I know," he says, rushing forward. "I understand perfectly. He's fallen for your quiet, timid shell. For who you *used* to be. He has no idea what you're capable of. What you might do if you're pushed too far." His hand slips behind my neck; he leans in until our lips are only inches apart.

What is happening to my lungs.

"You're a coward," he whispers. "You want to be with me and it terrifies you. And you're ashamed," he says. "Ashamed you could ever want someone like me. Aren't you?" He drops his gaze and his nose grazes mine and I can almost count the millimeters between our lips. I'm struggling to focus, trying to remember that I'm mad at him, mad about something, but his mouth is right in front of mine and my mind can't stop trying to figure out how to shove aside the space between us.

"You want me," he says softly, his hands moving up my back, "and it's *killing* you."

I jerk backward, breaking away, hating my body for reacting to him, for falling apart like this. My joints feel flimsy, my legs have lost their bones. I need oxygen, need a brain, need to find my lungs—

"You deserve so much more than charity," he says, his chest heaving. "You deserve to live. You deserve to be *alive*." He's staring at me, unblinking.

"Come back to life, love. I'll be here when you wake up."

TEN

I wake up on my stomach.

My face is buried in the pillows, my arms hugging their soft contours. I blink steadily, my bleary eyes taking in my surroundings, trying to remember where I am. I squint into the brightness of the day. My hair falls into my face as I lift my head to look around.

"Good morning."

I startle for no good reason, sitting up too quickly and clutching a pillow to my chest for an equally inexplicable reason. Warner is standing at the foot of the bed, fully dressed. He's wearing black pants and a slate-green sweater that clings to the shape of his body, the sleeves pushed up his forearms. His hair is perfect. His eyes are alert, awake, impossibly brightened by the green of his shirt. And he's holding a steaming mug in his hand. Smiling at me.

I offer him a limp wave.

"Coffee?" he asks, offering me the mug.

I stare at it, doubtful. "I've never had coffee before."

"It isn't terrible," he says with a shrug. "Delalieu is obsessed with it. Isn't that right, Delalieu?"

I jerk backward on the bed, my head nearly hitting the wall behind me.

An older, kindly-looking gentleman smiles at me from

the corner of the room. His thin brown hair and twitchy mustache look vaguely familiar to me, as if I've seen him on base before. I notice he's standing next to a breakfast cart. "It's a pleasure to officially meet you, Miss Ferrars," he says. His voice is a little shaky, but not at all intimidating. His eyes are unexpectedly sincere. "The coffee really is quite good," he says. "I have it every day. Though I always have m-mine with—"

"Cream and sugar," Warner says with a wry smile, his eyes laughing as if at some private joke. "Yes. Though I'm afraid the sugar is a bit too much for me. I find I prefer the bitterness." He glances at me again. "The choice is yours."

"What's going on?" I ask.

"Breakfast," Warner says, his eyes revealing nothing. "I thought you might be hungry."

"It's okay that he's here?" I whisper, knowing full well that Delalieu can hear me. "That he knows I'm here?"

Warner nods. Offers me no other explanation.

"Okay," I tell him. "I'll try the coffee."

I crawl across the bed to reach for the mug, and Warner's eyes follow my movements, traveling from my face to the shape of my body to the rumpled pillows and sheets beneath my hands and knees. When he finally meets my eyes he looks away too quickly, handing me the mug only to put an entire room between us.

"So how much does Delalieu know?" I ask, glancing at the older gentleman.

"What do you mean?" Warner raises an eyebrow.

"Well, does he know that I'm leaving?" I raise an eyebrow, too. Warner stares. "You promised you'd get me off base," I say to him, "and I'm hoping Delalieu is here to help you with that. Though if it's too much trouble, I'm always happy to take the window." I cock my head. "It worked out well the last time."

Warner narrows his eyes at me, his lips a thin line. He's still glaring when he nods at the breakfast cart beside him. "This is how we're getting you out of here today."

I choke on my first sip of coffee. "What?"

"It's the easiest, most efficient solution," Warner says. "You're small and lightweight, you can easily fold yourself into a tight space, and the cloth panels will keep you hidden from sight. I'm often working in my room," he says. "Delalieu brings me my breakfast trays from time to time. No one will suspect anything unusual."

I look at Delalieu for some kind of confirmation.

He nods eagerly.

"How did you get me here in the first place?" I ask. "Why can't we just do the same thing?"

Warner studies one of the breakfast plates. "I'm afraid that option is no longer available to us."

"What do you mean?" My body seizes with a sudden anxiety. "How did you get me in here?"

"You weren't exactly conscious," he says. "We had to be a little more . . . creative."

"Delalieu."

The old man looks up at the sound of my voice, clearly

surprised to be addressed so directly. "Yes, miss?"

"How did you get me into the building?"

Delalieu glances at Warner, whose gaze is now firmly fixed on the wall. Delalieu looks at me, offers me an apologetic smile. "We—well, we carted you in," he says.

"How?"

"Sir," Delalieu says suddenly, his eyes imploring Warner for direction.

"We brought you in," Warner says, stifling a sigh, "in a body bag."

My limbs go stiff with fear. "You *what?*"

"You were unconscious, love. We didn't have many options. I couldn't very well carry you onto base in my arms." He shoots me a look. "There were many casualties from the battle," he says. "On both sides. A body bag was easily overlooked."

I'm gaping at him.

"Don't worry." He smiles. "I cut some holes in it for you."

"You're so thoughtful," I snap.

"It *was* thoughtful," I hear Delalieu say. I look at him to find he's watching me in shock, appalled by my behavior. "Our commander was saving your life."

I flinch.

I stare into my coffee cup, heat coloring my cheeks. My conversations with Warner have never had an audience before. I wonder what our interactions must look like to an outside observer.

"It's all right, Lieutenant," Warner says. "She tends to

get angry when she's terrified. It's little more than a defense mechanism. The idea of being folded into such a small space has likely triggered her claustrophobic tendencies."

I look up suddenly.

Warner is staring directly at me, his eyes deep with an unspoken understanding.

I keep forgetting that Warner is able to sense emotions, that he can always tell what I'm really feeling. And he knows me well enough to be able to put everything into context.

I'm utterly transparent to him.

And somehow—right now, at least—I'm grateful for it.

"Of course, sir," Delalieu says. "My apologies."

"Feel free to shower and change," Warner says to me. "I left some clothes for you in the bathroom—no dresses," he says, fighting a smile. "We'll wait here. Delalieu and I have a few things to discuss."

I nod, untangling myself from the bedsheets and stumbling to my feet. I tug on the hem of my T-shirt, self-conscious all of a sudden, feeling rumpled and disheveled in front of these two military men.

I stare at them for a moment.

Warner gestures to the bathroom door.

I take the coffee with me as I go, wondering all the while who Delalieu is and why Warner seems to trust him. I thought he said all of his soldiers wanted him dead.

I wish I could listen in on their conversation, but they're both careful to say nothing until the bathroom door shuts behind me.

ELEVEN

I take a quick shower, careful not to let the water touch my hair. I already washed it last night, and the temperature feels brisk this morning; if we're headed out, I don't want to risk catching a cold. It's difficult, though, to avoid the temptation of a long shower—and hot water—in Warner's bathroom.

I dress quickly, grabbing the folded clothes Warner left on a shelf for me. Dark jeans and a soft, navy-blue sweater. Fresh socks and underwear. A brand-new pair of tennis shoes.

The sizes are perfect.

Of course they are.

I haven't worn jeans in so many years that at first the material feels strange to me. The fit is so tight, so tapered; I have to bend my knees to stretch the denim a little. But by the time I tug the sweater over my head, I'm finally feeling comfortable. And even though I miss my suit, there's something nice about wearing real clothes. No fancy dresses, no cargo pants, no spandex. Just jeans and a sweater, like a normal person. It's an odd reality.

I take a quick look in the mirror, blinking at my reflection. I wish I had something to tie my hair back with; I got so used to being able to pull it out of my face while I was at

Omega Point. I look away with a resigned sigh, hoping to get a start on this day as soon as possible. But the minute I crack open the bathroom door, I hear voices.

I freeze in place. Listening.

"—sure it's safe, sir?"

Delalieu is talking.

"Forgive me," the older man says quickly. "I don't mean to seem impertinent, but I can't help but be concerned—"

"It'll be fine. Just make sure our troops aren't patrolling that area. We should only be gone a few hours at the most."

"Yes, sir."

Silence.

Then

"Juliette," Warner says, and I nearly fall into the toilet. "Come out here, love. It's rude to eavesdrop."

I step out of the bathroom slowly, face flushed with heat from the shower and the shame of being caught in such a juvenile act. I suddenly have no idea what to do with my hands.

Warner is enjoying my embarrassment. "Ready to go?"

No.

No, I'm not.

Suddenly hope and fear are strangling me and I have to remind myself to breathe. I'm not ready to face the death and destruction of all my friends. Of course I'm not.

But "Yes, of course" is what I say out loud.

I'm steeling myself for the truth, in whatever form it arrives.

TWELVE

Warner was right.

Being carted through Sector 45 was a lot easier than I expected. No one noticed us, and the empty space underneath the cart was actually spacious enough for me to sit comfortably.

It's only when Delalieu flips open one of the cloth panels that I realize where we are. I glance around quickly, my eyes taking inventory of the military tanks parked in this vast space.

"Quickly," Delalieu whispers. He motions toward the tank parked closest to us. I watch as the door is pushed open from the inside. "Hurry, miss. You cannot be seen."

I scramble.

I jump out from underneath the cart and into the open door of the tank, clambering up and into the seat. The door shuts behind me, and I turn back to see Delalieu looking on, his watery eyes pinched together with worry. The tank starts moving.

I nearly fall forward.

"Stay low and buckle up, love. These tanks weren't built for comfort."

Warner is smiling as he stares straight ahead, his hands

sheathed in black leather gloves, his body draped in a steel-gray overcoat. I duck down in my seat and fumble for the straps, buckling myself in as best I can.

"So you know how to get there?" I ask him.

"Of course."

"But your father said you couldn't remember anything about Omega Point."

Warner glances over, his eyes laughing. "How convenient for us that I've regained my memory."

"Hey—how did you even get out of there?" I ask him. "How did you get past the guards?"

He shrugs. "I told them I had permission to be out of my room."

I gape at him. "You're not serious."

"Very."

"But how did you find your way out?" I ask. "You got past the guards, fine. But that place is like a labyrinth—I couldn't find my way around even after I'd been living there for a month."

Warner checks a display on the dashboard. Hits a few buttons for functions I don't understand. "I wasn't completely unconscious when I was carried in," he says. "I forced myself to pay attention to the entrance," he says. "I did my best to memorize any obvious landmarks. I also kept track of the amount of time it took to carry me from the entrance to the medical wing, and then from the medical wing to my room. And whenever Castle took me on my rounds to the bathroom," he says, "I studied my surroundings, trying to gauge how far I was from the exit."

"So—" I frown. "You could've defended yourself against the guards and tried to escape much sooner. Why didn't you?"

"I already told you," he says. "It was oddly luxurious, being confined like that. I was able to catch up on weeks of sleep. I didn't have to work or deal with any military issues. But the most obvious answer," he says, exhaling, "is that I stayed because I was able to see you every day."

"Oh."

Warner laughs, his eyes pressed shut for a second. "You really never wanted to be there, did you?"

"What do you mean?"

He shakes his head. "If you're going to survive," he says to me, "you can never be indifferent to your surroundings. You can't depend on others to take care of you. You cannot presume that someone else will do things right."

"What are you talking about?"

"You didn't care," he says. "You were there, underground for over a month, grouped together with these supernaturally inclined rebels spouting big, lofty ideals about saving the world, and you say you couldn't even find your way around. It's because you didn't care," he says. "You didn't want to participate. If you did, you would've taken the initiative to learn as much as possible about your new home. You would've been beside yourself with excitement. Instead, you were apathetic. Indifferent."

I open my mouth to protest but I don't have a chance.

"I don't blame you," he says. "Their goals were unrealistic. I don't care how flexible your limbs are or how many objects you can move with your mind. If you do not understand your opponent—or worse, if you *underestimate* your opponent—you are going to lose." His jaw tightens. "I kept trying to tell you," he says, "that Castle was going to lead your group into a massacre. He was too optimistic to be a proper leader, too hopeful to logically consider the odds stacked against him, and too ignorant of The Reestablishment to truly understand how they deal with voices of opposition.

"The Reestablishment," Warner says, "is not interested in maintaining a facade of kindness. The civilians are nothing more than peons to them. They want power," he says to me, "and they want to be entertained. They are not interested in fixing our problems. They only want to make sure that they are as comfortable as possible as we dig our own graves."

"No."

"Yes," he says. "It is exactly that simple. Everything else is just a joke to them. The texts, the artifacts, the languages. They just want to scare people, to keep them submissive, and to strip them of their individuality—to herd them into a singular mentality that serves no purpose but their own. This is why they can and will destroy all rebel movements. And this is a fact that your friends did not fully understand. And now," he says, "they have suffered for their ignorance."

He stops the tank.
Turns off the engine.
Unlocks my door.
And I'm still not ready to face this.

THIRTEEN

Anyone would be able to find Omega Point now. Any citizen, any civilian, anyone with working vision would be able to tell you where the large crater in Sector 45 is located.

Warner was right.

I unbuckle myself slowly, reaching blindly for the door handle. I feel like I'm moving through fog, like my legs have been formed from fresh clay. I fail to account for the height of the tank above the ground and stumble into the open air.

This is it.

The empty, barren stretch of land I'd come to recognize as the area just around Omega Point; the land Castle told us was once lush with greenery and vegetation. He said it'd been the ideal hiding place for Omega Point. But this was before things started changing. Before the weather warped and the plants struggled to flourish. Now it's a graveyard. Skeletal trees and howling winds, a thin layer of snow powdered over the cold, packed earth.

Omega Point is gone.

It's nothing but a huge, gaping hole in the ground about a mile across and 50 feet deep. It's a bowlful of innards, of death and destruction, silent in the wake of tragedy. Years of effort, so much time and energy spent toward a specific goal, one purpose: a plan to save humanity.

Obliterated overnight.

A gust of wind climbs into my clothes then, wraps itself around my bones. Icy fingers tiptoe up my pant legs, clench their fists around my knees and pull; suddenly I'm not sure how I'm still standing. My blood feels frozen, brittle. My hands are covering my mouth and I don't know who put them there.

Something heavy falls onto my shoulders. A coat.

I look back to find that Warner is watching me. He holds out a pair of gloves.

I take the gloves and tug them on over my frozen fingers and wonder why I'm not waking up yet, why no one has reached out to tell me it's okay, it's just a bad dream, that everything is going to be fine.

I feel as though I've been scooped out from the inside, like someone has spooned out all the organs I need to function and I'm left with nothing, just emptiness, just complete and utter disbelief. Because this is impossible.

Omega Point.

Gone.

Completely destroyed.

"JULIETTE, GET DOWN—"

FOURTEEN

Warner tackles me to the ground just as the sound of gunshots fills the air.

His arms are under me, cradling me to his chest, his body shielding mine from whatever imminent danger we've just gotten ourselves into. My heart is beating so loudly I can hardly hear Warner's voice as he speaks into my ear. "Are you all right?" he whispers, pulling me tighter against him.

I try to nod.

"Stay down," he says. "Don't move."

I wasn't planning on it, I don't say to him.

"STEP AWAY FROM HER, YOU WORTHLESS SACK OF SHIT—"

My body goes stiff.

That voice. I know that voice.

I hear footsteps coming closer, crunching on the snow and ice and dirt. Warner loosens his hold around me, and I realize he's reaching for his gun.

"Kenji—no—," I try to shout, my voice muffled by the snow.

"GET UP!" Kenji bellows, still moving closer. "Stand up, coward!"

I've officially begun to panic.

Warner's lips brush against my ear. "I'll be right back."

Just as I turn to protest, Warner's weight is lifted. His body gone. He's completely disappeared.

I scramble to my feet, spinning around.

My eyes land on Kenji.

He's stopped in place, confused and scanning the area, and I'm so happy to see him that I can't be bothered to care about Warner right now. I'm almost ready to cry. I squeak out Kenji's name.

His eyes lock on to mine.

He charges forward, closing the gap between us and tackling me in a hug so fierce he practically cuts off my circulation. "Holy *shit* it's good to see you," he says, breathless, squeezing me tighter.

I cling to him, so relieved, so stunned. I press my eyes shut, unable to stop the tears.

Kenji pulls back to look me in the eye, his face bright with pain and joy. "What the hell are you doing out here? I thought you were *dead*—"

"I thought *you* were dead!"

He stops then. The smile vanishes from his face. "Where the hell did Warner go?" he says, eyes taking in our surroundings. "You were with him, right? I'm not losing my mind, am I?"

"Yes—listen—Warner brought me here," I tell him, trying to speak calmly, hoping to cool the anger in his eyes. "But he's not trying to fight. When he told me about what happened to Omega Point, I didn't believe him, so I asked him to show me proof—"

"Is that right?" Kenji says, eyes flashing with a kind of hatred I've never seen in him before. "He came to show off what they did? To show you how many people he MURDERED!" Kenji breaks away from me, shaking with fury. "Did he tell you how many children were in there? Did he tell you how many of our men and women were *slaughtered* because of him?" He stops, heaving. "Did he tell you that?" he asks again, screaming into the air. "COME BACK OUT HERE, YOU SICK BASTARD!"

"Kenji, *no*—"

But Kenji's already gone, darting away so quickly he's just a speck in the distance now. I know he's searching the vast space for glimpses of Warner and I need to do something, I need to stop him but I don't know how—

"Don't move."

Warner's whispers are at my ear, his hands planted firmly on my shoulders. I try to spin around and he holds me in place. "I said don't move."

"What are you d—"

"Shhhh," he says. "No one can see me."

"*What?*" I crane my neck to try and glance behind me, but my head knocks against Warner's chin. His *invisible* chin.

"No," I hear myself gasp. "But you're not touching him—"

"Look straight ahead," he whispers. "It won't do us any good for you to be caught talking to invisible people."

I turn my face forward. Kenji is no longer in sight.

"How?" I ask Warner. "How did you—"

Warner shrugs behind me. "I've felt different since we did that experiment with your power. Now that I know exactly what it's like to take hold of another ability, I'm more easily able to recognize it. Like right now," he says. "I feel as though I could quite literally reach forward and take hold of your energy. It was just as simple with Kenji," he says. "He was standing right there. My survival instincts took over."

And even though this is a terrible moment to dwell on these things, I can't help but allow myself to panic. That Warner can so easily project his powers. With no training. No practice.

He can tap into my abilities and use them as he pleases.

This can't possibly be good.

Warner's hands squeeze my shoulders.

"What are you doing?" I whisper.

"I'm trying to see if I can pass the power on to you—if I can retransfer it and make us both invisible—but it seems I'm unable. Once I've taken the energy from someone else, I can *use* it, but I can't seem to share it. After I release the energy, it can only be returned to the owner."

"How do you know so much already?" I ask, astonished. "You just learned about this a few days ago."

"I've been practicing," he says.

"But how? With who?" I pause. "*Oh.*"

"Yes," he says. "It's been rather incredible having you stay with me. For so many reasons." His hands fall from my shoulders. "I was worried I might be able to hurt you with your own power. I wasn't sure I could absorb it without accidentally using it against you. But we seem to cancel each other out," he says. "Once I take it from you, I can only ever give it back."

I'm not breathing.

"Let's go," Warner says. "Kenji is moving out of range and I won't be able to hold on to his energy for much longer. We have to get out of here."

"I can't leave," I tell him. "I can't just abandon Kenji, not like this—"

"He's going to try and kill me, love. And while I know I've proved otherwise in your case, I can assure you I'm generally incapable of standing by as someone makes an attempt on my life. So unless you want to watch me shoot him first, I suggest we get out of here as soon as possible. I can feel him circling back."

"No. You can go. You *should* go. But I'm going to stay here."

Warner stills behind me. "What?"

"Go," I tell him. "You have to go to the compounds—you have things to take care of. You should go. But I need to be here. I have to know what's happened to everyone else, and I have to move forward from there."

"You're asking me to leave you here," he says, not bothering to hide his shock. "Indefinitely."

"Yes," I say to him. "I'm not leaving until I get some answers. And you're right. Kenji will definitely shoot first and ask questions later, so it's best that you leave. I'll talk to him, try to tell him what's happened. Maybe we could all work together—"

"What?"

"It doesn't just have to be me and you," I tell him. "You said you wanted to help me kill your father and take down The Reestablishment, right?"

Warner nods slowly against the back of my head.

"Okay. So." I take a deep breath. "I accept your offer."

Warner goes rigid. "You accept my offer."

"Yes."

"Do you understand what you're saying?"

"I wouldn't say it if I didn't mean it. I'm not sure I'll be able to do this without you."

I feel the breath rush out of him, his heart beating hard against my back.

"But I need to know who else is still alive," I insist. "And the group of us can work together. We'll be stronger that way, and we'll all be fighting toward the same goal—"

"No."

"It's the only way—"

"I have to go," he says, spinning me around. "Kenji is almost here." He shoves a hard plastic object into my hand. "Activate this pager," he says, "whenever you're ready. Keep it with you and I'll know where to find you."

"But—"

"You have four hours," he says. "If I don't hear from you before then, I'll assume you are in some kind of danger, and I will come find you myself." He's still holding my hand, the pager still pressed against my palm. It's the craziest feeling, to be touched by someone you can't see. "Do you understand?"

I nod, once. I have no idea where to look.

And then I freeze, every inch of me hot and cold all at once because he presses his lips to the back of my fingers in one soft, tender moment and when he pulls away I'm reeling, heady, unsteady.

Just as I'm regaining my footing, I hear the familiar sound of an electric thrum, and realize Warner has already begun to drive away.

And I'm left to wonder what on earth I've just agreed to.

FIFTEEN

Kenji is stomping toward me, his eyes blazing.

"Where the hell did he go? Did you see where he went?"

I shake my head as I reach forward, grabbing his arms in an attempt to focus his eyes. "Talk to me, Kenji. Tell me what happened—where is everyone—?"

"There is no *everyone!*" he snaps, breaking away. "Omega Point is gone—everything gone—*everything*—" He drops to his knees, heaving as he falls forward, his forehead digging into the snow. "I thought you were dead, too—I thought—"

"No," I gasp. "No, Kenji—they can't all have died—not everyone—"

Not Adam.

Not Adam.

Please please please not *Adam*

I'd been too optimistic about today.

I'd been lying to myself.

I didn't really believe Warner. I didn't believe it could be this bad. But now, to see the truth, and to hear Kenji's agony—the reality of all that happened is hitting me so hard I feel like I'm falling backward into my own grave.

My knees have hit the ground.

"Please," I'm saying, "please tell me there are others—Adam has to be alive—"

"I grew up here," Kenji is saying. He's not listening to me and I don't recognize his raw, aching voice. I want the old Kenji, the one who knew how to take charge, to take control. And this isn't him.

This Kenji is terrifying me.

"This was my whole life," he says, looking toward the crater that used to be Omega Point. "The only place—all those people—" He chokes. "They were my *family*. My only family—"

"Kenji, please . . ." I try to shake him. I need him to snap out of his grief before I succumb to it, too. We need to move out of plain sight and I'm only now beginning to realize that Kenji doesn't care. He *wants* to put himself in danger. He *wants* to fight. He wants to *die*.

I can't let that happen.

Someone needs to take control of this situation right now and right now I might be the only one capable.

"Get up," I snap, my voice harsher than I intended. "You need to get up, and you need to stop acting reckless. You know we're not safe out here, and we have to move. Where are you staying?" I grab his arm and pull, but he won't budge. "Get up!" I shout again. "Get—"

And then, just like that, I remember I'm a whole hell of a lot stronger than Kenji will ever be. It almost makes me smile.

I close my eyes and focus, trying to remember everything

Kenji taught me, everything I've learned about how to control my strength, how to tap into it when I need to. I spent so many years bottling everything up and locking it away that it still takes some time to remember it's there, waiting for me to harness it. But the moment I welcome it, I feel it rush into me. It's a raw power so potent it makes me feel invincible.

And then, just like that, I yank Kenji up off the ground and toss him over my shoulder.

Me.

I do that.

Kenji, of course, unleashes a string of the foulest expletives I've ever heard. He's kicking at me but I can hardly feel it; my arms are wrapped loosely around him, my strength carefully reined in so as not to crush him. He's angry, but at least he's swearing again. This is something I recognize.

I cut him off midexpletive. "Tell me where you're staying," I say to him, "and pull yourself together. You can't fall apart on me now."

Kenji is silent a moment.

"Hey, um, I'm sorry to bother you, but I'm looking for a friend of mine," he says. "Have you seen her? She's a tiny little thing, cries a lot, spends too much time with her feelings—"

"Shut up, Kenji."

"Oh wait!" he says. "It *is* you."

"Where are we going?"

82

"When are you going to put me down?" he counters, no longer amused. "I mean, I've got an excellent view of your ass from here, but if you don't mind me staring—"

I drop him without thinking.

"Goddammit, Juliette—what the hell—"

"How's the view from down there?" I stand over his splayed body, arms crossed over my chest.

"I hate you."

"Get up, please."

"When did you learn to do that?" he grumbles, stumbling to his feet and rubbing his back.

I roll my eyes. Squint into the distance. Nothing and no one in sight, so far. "I didn't."

"Oh, right," he says. "Because that makes sense. Because tossing a grown-ass man over your shoulders is just so freaking easy. That shit just comes naturally to you."

I shrug.

Kenji lets out a low whistle. "Cocky as hell, too."

"Yeah." I shade my eyes against the cold sunlight. "I think spending all that time with you really screwed me up."

"Ohhh-ho," he says, clapping his hands together, un-amused. "Stand up, princess. You're a comedian."

"I'm already standing up."

"It's called a joke, smart-ass."

"Where are we going?" I ask him again. I start walking in no particular direction. "I really need to know where we're headed."

"Unregulated turf." He falls into step with me, taking

my hand to lead the way. We go invisible immediately. "It was the only place we could think of."

"*We?*"

"Yeah. It's Adam's old place, remember? It's where I first—"

I stop walking, chest heaving. I'm crushing Kenji's hand in mine and he yanks it free, unleashing expletives as he does, making us visible again. "Adam is still alive?" I ask, searching his eyes.

"Of course he's still alive." Kenji shoots me a dirty look as he rubs at his hand. "Have you heard nothing I've been saying to you?"

"But you said everyone was dead," I gasp. "You said—"

"Everyone *is* dead," Kenji says, his features darkening again. "There were over a hundred of us at Omega Point. There are only nine of us left."

SIXTEEN

"Who?" I ask, my heart constricting. "Who survived? How?"

Kenji lets out a long breath, running both hands through his hair as he focuses on a point behind me. "You just want a list?" he asks. "Or do you want to know how it all happened?"

"I want to know everything."

He nods. Looks down, stomps on a clump of snow. He takes my hand again, and we start walking, two invisible kids in the middle of nowhere.

"I guess," Kenji finally says, "that on some level we have you to thank for us still being alive. Because if we'd never gone to find you, we probably would've died on the battlefield with everyone else."

He hesitates.

"Adam and I noticed you were missing pretty quickly, but by the time we fought our way back to the front, we were too late. We were still maybe twenty feet out, and could only see them hauling you into the tank." He shakes his head. "We couldn't just run after you," he says. "We were trying not to get shot at."

His voice gets deeper, more somber as he tells the story.

"So we decided we'd go an alternate route—avoiding all

the main roads—to try and follow you back to base, because that's where we thought you were headed. But just as we got there, we ran into Castle, Lily, Ian, and Alia, who were on their way out. They'd managed to complete their own mission successfully; they broke into Sector 45 and stole Winston and Brendan back. Those two were half dead when Castle found them," Kenji says quietly.

He takes a sharp breath.

"And then Castle told us what they'd heard while they were on base—that the troops were mobilizing for an air assault on Omega Point. They were going to drop bombs on the entire area, hoping that if they hit it with enough firepower, everything underground would just collapse in on itself. There'd be no escape for anyone inside, and everything we'd built would be destroyed."

I feel him tense beside me.

We stop moving for just a moment before I feel Kenji tug on my hand. I duck into the cold and wind, steeling myself against the weather and his words.

"Apparently they'd tortured the location out of our people on the battlefield," he says. "Just before killing them." He shakes his head. "We knew we didn't have much time, but we were still close enough to base that I managed to commandeer one of the army tanks. We loaded up and headed straight for Point, hoping to get everyone out in time. But I think, deep down," he says, "we knew it wasn't going to work. The planes were overhead. Already on their way."

He laughs, suddenly, but the action seems to cause him pain.

"And by some freak miracle of insanity, we intercepted James almost a mile out. He'd managed to sneak out, and was on his way toward the battlefield. The poor kid had pissed the whole front of his pants he was so scared, but he said he was tired of being left behind. Said he wanted to fight with his brother." Kenji's voice is strained.

"And the craziest shit," he says, "is that if James had stayed at Point like we told him to, where we thought he'd be safe, he would've died with everyone else." Kenji laughs a little. "And that was it. There was nothing we could do. We just had to stand there, watching as they dropped bombs on thirty years of work, killed everyone too young or too old to fight back, and then massacred the rest of our team on the field." He clenches his hand around mine. "I come back here every day," he says. "Hoping someone will show up. Hoping to find something to take back." He stops then, voice tight with emotion. "And here you are. This shit doesn't even seem real."

I squeeze his fingers—gently, this time—and huddle closer to him. "We're going to be okay, Kenji. I promise. We'll stick together. We'll get through this."

Kenji tugs his hand out of mine only to slip it around my shoulder, pulling me tight against his side. His voice is soft when he speaks. "What happened to you, princess? You seem different."

"Bad different?"

"Good different," he says. "Like you finally put your big-girl pants on."

I laugh out loud.

"I'm serious," he says.

"Well." I pause. "Sometimes different is better, isn't it?"

"Yeah," Kenji says. "Yeah, I guess it is." He hesitates. "So . . . are you going to tell me what happened? Because last I saw you, you were being shoved into the backseat of an army tank, and this morning you show up all freshly showered and shiny-white-sneakered and you're walking around with *Warner*," he says, releasing my shoulder and taking my hand again. "And it doesn't take a genius to figure out that that shit doesn't make any sense."

I take a deep, steadying breath. It's strange not being able to see Kenji right now; it feels as if I'm making these confessions to the wind. "Anderson shot me," I tell him.

Kenji stills beside me. I can hear him breathing hard. *"What?"*

I nod, even though he can't see me. "I wasn't taken back to base. The soldiers delivered me to Anderson; he was waiting in one of the houses on unregulated turf. I think he wanted privacy," I tell Kenji, carefully omitting any information about Warner's mom. Those secrets are too private, and not mine to share. "Anderson wanted revenge," I say instead, "for what I did to his legs. He was crippled; when I saw him he was using a cane. But before I could figure out what was happening, he pulled out a gun and shot me. Right in the chest."

"Holy shit," Kenji breathes.

"I remember it so well." I hesitate. "Dying. It was the most painful thing I've ever experienced. I couldn't scream because my lungs were torn apart or full of blood. I don't know. I just had to lie there, trying to breathe, hoping to drop dead as quickly as possible. And the whole time," I say, "the whole time I kept thinking about how I'd spent my entire life being a coward, and how it got me nowhere. And I knew that if I had the chance to do it all again, I'd do it differently. I promised myself I'd finally stop being afraid."

"Yeah, that's all super heartwarming," Kenji says, "but how in the hell did you survive a shot to the chest?" he demands. "You should be dead right now."

"Oh." I clear my throat a little. "Yeah, um, Warner saved my life."

"Shut the hell up."

I try not to laugh. "I'm serious," I say, taking a minute to explain how the girls were there and how Warner used their power to save me. How Anderson left me to die and how Warner took me back to base with him, hid me, and helped me recover. "And by the way," I say to Kenji, "Sonya and Sara are almost definitely still alive. Anderson took them back to the capital with him; he wants to force them to serve as his own personal healers. He's probably gotten them to fix his legs by now."

"Okay, you know what"—Kenji stops walking, grabs my shoulders—"you need to just back up, okay, because you are dumping way too much information on me all at once, and I need you to start from the beginning, and I need you to tell me *everything*," he says, his voice rising in pitch. "What the hell is going on? The girls are still alive? And what do you mean, Warner transferred their power to you? How the hell is that possible?"

So I tell him.

I finally tell him the things I've always wanted to confess. I tell him the truth about Warner's ability and the truth about how Kenji was injured outside the dining hall that night. I tell him how Warner had no idea what he was capable of, and how I let him practice with me in the tunnel while everyone was in the medical wing. How together we broke through the floor.

"Holy shit," Kenji whispers. "So that asshole tried to *kill* me."

"Not on purpose," I point out.

Kenji mutters something crude under his breath.

And though I mention nothing about Warner's unexpected visit to my room later that night, I do tell Kenji how Warner escaped, and how Anderson was waiting for Warner to show up before shooting me. Because Anderson knew how Warner felt about me, I tell Kenji, and wanted to punish him for it.

"Wait." Kenji cuts me off. "What do you mean, he knew how Warner *felt* about you? We *all* knew how Warner felt about you. He wanted to use you as a weapon," Kenji says. "That shouldn't have been a revelation. I thought his dad was happy about that."

I go stiff.

I forgot this part was still a secret. That I'd never revealed the truth about my connection to Warner. Because while

Adam might've suspected that Warner had more than a professional interest in me, I'd never told anyone about my intimate moments with Warner. Or any of the things he's said to me.

I swallow, hard.

"Juliette," Kenji says, a warning in his voice. "You can't hold this shit back anymore. You have to tell me what's going on."

I feel myself sway.

"Juliette—"

"He's in love with me," I whisper. I've never admitted that out loud before, not even to myself. I think I hoped I could ignore it. Hide it. Make it go away so Adam would never find out.

"He's—wait—*what?*"

I take a deep breath. I suddenly feel exhausted.

"Please tell me you're joking," Kenji says.

I shake my head, forgetting he can't see me.

"Wow."

"Kenji, I—"

"This is soooo weird. Because I always thought Warner was crazy, you know?" Kenji laughs. "But now, I mean, now there's no doubt."

My eyes fly wide open, shocking me into laughter. I push his invisible shoulder, hard.

Kenji laughs again, half amused, half reeling from disbelief. He takes a deep breath. "So, okay, wait, so, how do you know he's in love with you?"

"What do you mean?"

"I mean, like—what, he took you out on a date or something? Bought you chocolates and wrote you some really shitty poetry? Warner doesn't exactly seem like the affectionate type, if you know what I mean."

"Oh." I bite the inside of my cheek. "No, it was nothing like that."

"Then?"

"He just . . . told me."

Kenji stops walking so abruptly I nearly fall over. "No he didn't."

I don't know how to respond to that.

"He actually said those words? To your face? Like, directly to your face?"

"Yes."

"So—so—so wait, so he tells you he loves you . . . and you said? What?" Kenji demands, dumbfounded. "'Thank you'?"

"No." I stifle a cringe, remembering all too well that I actually shot Warner for it the first time. "I mean I didn't—I mean—I don't know, Kenji, it's all really weird for me right now. I still haven't found a way to deal with it." My voice drops to a whisper. "Warner is really . . . intense," I say, and I'm overcome by a flood of memories, my emotions colliding into one jumble of insanity.

His kisses on my body. My shorts on the floor. His desperate confessions unhinging my joints.

I squeeze my eyes shut, feeling too hot, too unsteady,

everything all too suddenly.

"That's definitely one way of putting it," Kenji mutters, snapping me out of my reverie. I hear him sigh. "So Warner still has no idea that he and Kent are brothers?"

"No," I say, immediately sobered.

Brothers.

Brothers who hate each other. Brothers who want to kill each other. And I'm caught in the middle. Good God, what has happened to my life.

"And both of these guys can touch you?"

"Yes? But—well, no, not really." I try to explain. "Adam . . . can't really touch me. I mean, he can, sort of . . . ?" I trail off. "It's complicated. He has to actively work and train to counteract my energy with his own. But with Warner—" I shake my head, staring down at my invisible feet as I walk. "Warner can touch me with no consequences. It doesn't do anything to him. He just absorbs it."

"Damn," Kenji says after a moment. "Damn damn damn. This shit is bananas."

"I know."

"So—okay—you're telling me that Warner saved your life? That he actually begged the girls to help him heal you? And that he then hid you in his own room, and took care of you? Fed you and gave you clothes and shit and let you sleep in his bed?"

"Yes."

"Yeah. Okay. I have a really hard time believing that."

"I know," I say again, this time blowing out an exasperated

breath. "But he's really not what you guys think. I know he seems kind of crazy, but he's actually really—"

"Whoa, wait—are you *defending* him?" Kenji's voice is laced with shock. "We are talking about the same dude who locked you up and tried to make you his military *slave*, right?"

I'm shaking my head, wishing I could try to explain everything Warner's told me without sounding like a naive, gullible idiot. "It's not—" I sigh. "He didn't actually want to use me like that—," I try to say.

Kenji barks out a laugh. "Holy *shit*," he says. "You actually believe him, don't you? You're buying into all the bullshit he's fed you—"

"You don't know him, Kenji, that's not fair—"

"Oh my God," he breathes, laughing again. "You are seriously going to try and tell me that I don't know the man who led me into battle? He was my goddamn commander," Kenji says to me. "I know exactly who he is—"

"I'm not trying to argue with you, okay? I don't expect you to understand—"

"This is hilarious," Kenji says, wheezing through another laugh. "You really don't get it, do you?"

"Get what?"

"Ohhh, *man*," he says suddenly. "Kent is going to be *pissed*," he says, dragging out the word in glee. He actually giggles.

"Wait—what? What does Adam have to do with this?"

"You do realize you haven't asked me a single question

about him, right?" A pause. "I mean, I just told you the whole saga of all the shit that happened to us and you were just like, Oh, okay, cool story, bro, thanks for sharing. You didn't freak out or ask if Adam was injured. You didn't ask me what happened to him or even how he's coping right now, especially seeing as how he thinks you're *dead* and everything."

I feel sick all of a sudden. Stopped in my tracks. Mortified and guilty guilty guilty.

"And now you're standing here, defending *Warner*," Kenji is saying. "The same guy who tried to *kill Adam*, and you're acting like he's your friend or some shit. Like he's just some normal dude who's a little misunderstood. Like every single other person on the planet got it wrong, and probably because we're all just a bunch of judgmental, jealous assholes who hate him for having such a pretty, pretty face."

Shame singes my skin.

"I'm not an idiot, Kenji. I have reasons for the things I say."

"Yeah, and maybe I'm just saying that you have no idea what you're saying."

"Whatever."

"Don't *whatever* me—"

"*Whatever*," I say again.

"Oh my God," Kenji says to no one in particular. "I think this girl wants to get her ass kicked."

"You couldn't kick my ass if I had ten of them."

Kenji laughs out loud. "Is that a challenge?"

"It's a warning," I say to him.

"Ohhhhhh, so you're threatening me now? Little crybaby knows how to make threats now?"

"Shut up, Kenji."

"*Shut up, Kenji,*" he repeats in a whiny voice, mocking me.

"How much farther do we have to go?" I ask too loudly, irritated and trying to change the subject.

"We're almost there," he shoots back, his words clipped.

Neither one of us speaks for a few minutes.

Then

"So . . . why did you walk all this way?" I ask. "Didn't you say you had a tank?"

"Yeah," Kenji says with a sigh, our argument momentarily forgotten. "We have two, actually. Kent said he stole one when you guys first escaped; it's still sitting in his garage."

Of course.

How could I forget?

"But I like walking," Kenji continues. "I don't have to worry about anyone seeing me, and I always hope that maybe if I'm on foot, I'll be able to notice things I wouldn't be able to otherwise. I'm still hoping," he says, his voice tight again, "that we'll find more of our own hidden out here somewhere."

I squeeze Kenji's hand again, clinging closer to him. "Me too," I whisper.

SEVENTEEN

Adam's old place is exactly as I remember it.

Kenji and I sneak in from the underground parking garage, and scale a few flights of stairs to the upper levels. I'm suddenly so nervous I can hardly speak. I've had to grieve the loss of my friends twice already, and part of me feels like this can't possibly be happening. But it must be. It has to be.

I'm going to see Adam.

I'm going to see Adam's face.

He's going to be *real*.

"They blasted the door open when they were searching for us that first time," Kenji is saying, "so the door is pretty jammed up—we'd been piling a bunch of furniture against it to keep it closed, but then it got stuck the other way, soo . . . yeah, it might take them a while to open it. But other than that, this little place has been good to us. Kent's still got a ton of food in storage, and all the plumbing still works because he'd paid for almost everything through the end of the year. All in all, we got pretty lucky," he says.

I'm nodding my head, too afraid to open my mouth. That coffee from this morning suddenly doesn't feel very good in my stomach, and I'm jittery from head to toe.

Adam.

I'm about to see Adam.

Kenji bangs on the door. "Open up," he shouts. "It's me."

For a minute all I hear is the sound of heavy movement, creaky wood, screechy metal, and a series of thuds. I watch the doorframe as it shakes; someone on the other side is yanking on the door, trying to get it unjammed.

And then it opens. So slowly. I'm gripping my hands to keep myself steady.

Winston is standing at the door.

Gaping at me.

"Holy shit," he says. He pulls his glasses off—I notice they've been taped together—and blinks at me. His face is bruised and battered, his bottom lip swollen, split open. His left hand is bandaged, the gauze wrapped several times around the palm of his hand.

I offer him a timid smile.

Winston grabs ahold of Kenji's shirt and yanks him forward, eyes still focused on my face. "Am I hallucinating again?" he asks. "Because I'm going to be so pissed if I'm hallucinating again. *Dammit*," he says, not waiting for Kenji to respond. "If I had any idea how much it would suck to have a concussion, I'd have shot myself in the face when I had a chance—"

"You're not hallucinating." Kenji cuts him off with a laugh. "Now let us inside."

Winston is still blinking at me, eyes wide as he backs away, giving us room to enter. But the minute I step over the threshold I'm thrust into another world, a whole different set of memories. This is Adam's home. The first place I ever found sanctuary. The first place I ever felt safe.

And now it's full of people, the space far too small to house so many large bodies. Castle and Brendan and Lily and Ian and Alia and James—they've all frozen midmovement, midsentence. They're all staring at me in disbelief. And I'm just about to say something, just about to find something acceptable to say to my only group of battered, broken friends, when Adam walks out of the small room I know used to belong to James. He's holding something in his hands, distracted, not noticing the abrupt change in the atmosphere.

But then he looks up.

His lips are parted as if to speak, and whatever he was holding hits the ground, shattering into so many sounds it startles everyone back to life.

Adam is staring at me, eyes locked on my face, his chest heaving, his face fighting so many different emotions. He looks half terrified, half hopeful. Or maybe terrified to be hopeful.

And though I realize I should probably be the first to speak, I suddenly have no idea what to say.

Kenji pulls up beside me, his face splitting into a huge smile. He slips his arm around my shoulder. Squeezes. Says, "Lookie what I found."

Adam begins to move across the room, but it feels strange—like everything has begun to slow down, like this moment isn't real, somehow. There's so much pain in his eyes.

I feel like I've been punched in the gut.

But then there he is, right in front of me, his hands searching my body as if to ensure that I'm real, that I'm still intact. He's studying my face, my features, his fingers weaving into my hair. And then all at once he seems to accept that I'm not a ghost, not a nightmare, and he hauls me against himself so quickly I can't help but gasp in response.

"Juliette," he breathes.

His heart is beating hard against my ear, his arms wrapped tight around me, and I melt into his embrace, relishing the warm comfort, the familiarity of his body, his scent, his skin. My hands reach around him, slip up his back and grip him hard, and I don't even realize silent tears have fallen down my face until he pulls back to look me in the eye. He tells me not to cry, tells me it's okay, that everything is going to be okay and I know it's all a lie but it still feels so good to hear.

He's studying my face again, his hands carefully cradling the back of my head, so careful not to touch my skin. The reminder sends a sharp pain through my heart. "I can't believe you're really here," he says, his voice breaking. "I can't believe this is actually happening—"

Kenji clears his throat. "Hey—guys? Your loin passion is grossing out the little ones."

"I'm not a *little one*," James says, visibly offended. "And I don't think it's gross."

100

Kenji spins around. "You're not bothered by all the heavy breathing going on over here?" He makes a haphazard gesture toward us.

I jump away from Adam reflexively.

"No," James says, crossing his arms. "Are you?"

"Disgust was my general reaction, yeah."

"I bet you wouldn't think it was gross if it was you."

A long pause.

"You make a good point," Kenji finally says. "Maybe you should find me a lady in this crappy sector. I'm okay with anyone between the ages of eighteen and thirty-five." He points at James. "So how about you get on that, thanks."

James seems to take the challenge a little too seriously. He nods several times. "Okay," he says. "How about Alia? Or Lily?" he says, immediately pointing out the only other women in the room.

Kenji's mouth opens and closes a few times before he says, "Yeah, no thanks, kid. These two are like my sisters."

"So smooth," Lily says to Kenji, and I realize it's the first time I've really heard her speak. "I bet you win over all the eligible women by telling them they're like sisters to you. I bet the ladies are just lining up to jump into bed with your punkass."

"Rude." Kenji crosses his arms.

James is laughing.

"You see what I have to deal with?" Kenji says to him. "There's no love for Kenji. I give and I give and I give, and I get nothing in return. I need a woman who will appreciate all of this," he says, gesturing to the length of his body. He's clearly overexaggerating, hoping to entertain James with his ridiculousness, and his efforts are appreciated. Kenji is probably their only chance for comedic relief in this cramped space, and it makes me wonder if that's why he sets off on his own every day. Maybe he needs time to grieve in silence, in a place where no one expects him to be the funny one.

My heart starts and stops as I hesitate, wondering at how hard it must be for Kenji to keep it together even when he wants to fall apart. I caught a glimpse of that side of him for the first time today, and it surprised me more than it should have.

Adam squeezes my shoulder, and I turn to face him. He smiles a tender, tortured smile, his eyes heavy with pain and joy.

But of all the things I could be feeling right now, guilt hits me the hardest.

Everyone in this room is carrying such heavy burdens. Brief moments of levity puncture the general gloom shrouding this space, but as soon as the jokes subside, the grief slides back into place. And though I know I should grieve for the lives lost, I don't know how. They were all strangers to me. I was only just beginning to develop a relationship with Sonya and Sara.

But when I look around I see that I'm alone in feeling this way. I see the lines of loss creasing my friends' faces. I see the sadness buried in their clothes, perched atop their furrowed brows. And something in the back of my mind is nagging at me, disappointed in me, telling me I should be one of them, that I should be just as defeated as they are.

But I'm not.

I can't be that girl anymore.

For so many years I lived in constant terror of myself. Doubt had married my fear and moved into my mind, where it built castles and ruled kingdoms and reigned over me, bowing my will to its whispers until I was little more than an acquiescing peon, too terrified to disobey, too terrified to disagree.

I had been shackled, a prisoner in my own mind.

But finally, finally, I have learned to break free.

I *am* upset for our losses. I'm horrified. But I'm also anxious and restless. Sonya and Sara are still alive, living at the mercy of Anderson. They still need our help. So I don't know how to be sad when all I feel is an unrelenting determination to do something.

I am no longer afraid of fear, and I will not let it rule me.

Fear will learn to fear me.

EIGHTEEN

Adam leads me toward the couch, but Kenji intercepts us. "You guys can have your moment, I promise," he says, "but right now we all need to get on the same page, say hello and how are you and whatever whatever and we need to do it fast; Juliette has information everyone needs to hear."

Adam looks from Kenji to me. "What's going on?"

I turn to Kenji. "What are you talking about?"

He rolls his eyes at me. Looks away and says, "Have a seat, Kent."

Adam backs away—just an inch or two—his curiosity winning out for the moment, and Kenji tugs me forward so I'm standing in the middle of this tiny room. Everyone is staring at me like I might pull turnips out of my trousers. "Kenji, what—"

"Alia, you remember Juliette," Kenji says, nodding at a slim blond girl sitting in a back corner of the room. She offers me a quick smile before looking away, blushing for no apparent reason. I remember her; she's the one who designed my custom knuckle braces—the intricate pieces I'd worn over my gloves both times we went out to battle. I'd never really paid close attention to her before, and I now realize it's because she tries to be invisible. She's a soft, sweet-looking girl with gentle brown eyes; she also happens to be an exceptional designer. I wonder how she developed her skill.

"Lily—you definitely remember Juliette," Kenji is saying to her. "We all broke into the storage compounds together." He glances at me. "You remember, right?"

I nod. Grin at Lily. I don't really know her, but I like her energy. She mock-salutes me, smiling wide as her springy brown curls fall into her face. "Nice to see you again," she says. "And thanks for not being dead. It sucks being the only girl around here."

Alia's blond head pops up for only a second before she retreats deeper into the corner.

"Sorry," Lily says, looking only slightly remorseful. "I meant the only *talking* girl around here. Please tell me you talk," she says to me.

"Oh, she talks," Kenji says, shooting me a look. "Cusses like a sailor, too."

"I do not cuss like a—"

"Brendan, Winston." Kenji cuts me off, pointing at the two guys sitting on the couch. "These two definitely don't require an introduction, but, as you can see," he says, "they look a little different now. Behold, the transformative powers of being held hostage by a bunch of sadistic bastards!" He flourishes a hand in their direction, his sarcasm accompanied by a brittle smile. "Now they look like a pair of wildebeests. But, you know, by comparison, I look like a damn king. So it's good news all around."

Winston points at my face. His eyes are a little unfocused, and he has to blink a few times before saying, "I like you. It's pretty nice you're not dead."

"I second that, mate." Brendan claps Winston on the shoulder but he's smiling at me. His eyes are still so very light blue, and his hair, so very white blond. But he has a huge gash running from his right temple down to his jawline, and it looks like it's only just beginning to scab up. I can't imagine where else he's hurt. What else Anderson must've done to both him and Winston. A sick, slithery feeling moves through me.

"It's so good to see you again," Brendan is saying, his British accent always surprising me. "Sorry we couldn't be a bit more presentable."

I offer them both a smile. "I'm so happy you're all right."

"Ian," Kenji says, gesturing to the tall, lanky guy perched on the arm of the couch. Ian Sanchez. I remember him as a guy on my assembly team when we broke into the storage compound, but more important, I know him to be one of the four guys who were kidnapped by Anderson's men. He, Winston, Brendan, and another guy named Emory.

We'd managed to get Ian and Emory back, but not Brendan and Winston. I remember Kenji saying that Ian and Emory were so messed up when we brought them in that even with the girls helping to heal them, it'd still taken them a while to recover. Ian looks okay to me now, but he, too, must've undergone some horrific things. And Emory clearly isn't here.

I swallow, hard, offering Ian what I'm hoping is a strong smile.

He doesn't smile back.

"How are you still alive?" he demands, with no preamble. "You don't look like anyone beat the shit out of you, so, I mean, no offense or whatever, but I don't trust you."

"We're getting to that part," Kenji says, cutting Adam off just as he begins to protest on my behalf. "She has a solid explanation, I promise. I already know all the details." He shoots Ian a sharp look, but Ian doesn't seem to notice. He's still staring at me, one eyebrow raised as if in challenge.

I cock my head at him, considering him closely.

Kenji snaps his fingers in front of my face. "Focus, princess, I'm already getting bored." He glances around the room, looking for anyone we might've missed for the reintroductions. "James," he says, his eyes landing on the upturned face of my only ten-year-old friend. "Anything you want to say to Juliette before we get started?"

James looks at me, his blue eyes bright below his sandy-blond hair. He shrugs. "I never thought you were dead," he says simply.

"Is that right?" Kenji says with a laugh.

James nods. "I had a feeling," he says, tapping his head.

Kenji grins. "All right, well, that's it. Let's get started."

"What about Ca—," I begin to say, but stop dead at the flicker of alarm that flits in and out of Kenji's features.

My gaze lands on Castle, studying his face in a way I hadn't when I first arrived.

Castle's eyes are unfocused, his eyebrows furrowed as if he's caught in an endlessly frustrating conversation with himself; his hands are knotted together in his lap. His hair has broken free of its always-perfect ponytail at the nape of his neck, and his dreads have sprung around his face, falling into his eyes. He's unshaven, and looks as though he's been dragged through mud; as though he sat down in that chair the moment he walked in and hasn't left it since.

And I realize that of the group of us, Castle has been hit the hardest.

Omega Point was his life. His dreams were in every brick, every echo of that space. And in one night, he lost everything. His hopes, his vision for the future, the entire community he strove to build. His only family.

Gone.

"He's had it really rough," Adam whispers to me, and I'm startled by his presence, not realizing he was standing beside me again. "Castle's been like that for a little while now."

My heart breaks.

I try to meet Kenji's eyes, try to apologize wordlessly, to tell him I understand. But Kenji won't look at me. It takes him a few moments to pull himself together, and only then does it hit me just how hard all of this must be for him right now. It's not just Omega Point. It's not just everyone he's lost, not just all the work that's been destroyed.

It's Castle.

Castle, who's been like a father to Kenji, his closest confidant, his dearest friend.

He's become a husk of who he was.

My heart feels weighed down by the depth of Kenji's pain; I wish so much that I could do something to help. To fix things. And in that moment I promise myself I will.

I'll do everything I can.

"All right." Kenji claps his hands together, nods a few times before taking a tight breath. "Everyone all warm and fuzzy? Good? Good." He nods again. "Now let me tell you the story of how our friend Juliette was shot in the chest."

NINETEEN

Everyone is gaping at me.

Kenji has just finished giving them every detail I shared with him, taking care to leave out the parts about Warner telling me he loves me, and I'm silently grateful. Even though I told Adam that he and I shouldn't be together anymore, everything between us is still so raw and unresolved. I've tried to move on, to distance myself from him because I wanted to protect him; but I've had to mourn Adam's loss in so many different ways now that I'm not sure I even know how to feel anymore.

I have no idea what he thinks of me.

There are so many things Adam and I need to talk about; I just don't want Warner to be one of them. Warner has always been a tense topic between us—especially now that Adam knows they're brothers—and I'm not in the mood for arguing, especially not on my first day back.

But it seems I won't be able to get off that easily.

"*Warner* saved your life?" Lily asks, not bothering to hide her shock or her repulsion. Even Alia is sitting up and paying attention now, her eyes glued to my face. "Why the hell would he do that?"

"Dude, forget that," Ian cuts in. "What are we going to

do about the fact that Warner can just steal our powers and shit?"

"You don't have any powers," Winston answers him. "So you don't have anything to worry about."

"You know what I mean," Ian snaps, a hint of color flushing up his neck. "It's not safe for a psycho like him to have that kind of ability. It freaks me the hell out."

"He's not a psych—," I try to say, but the room erupts into a cacophony of voices, all vying for a chance to be heard.

"What does this even mean—"

"—dangerous?"

"So Sonya and Sara are still *alive*—"

"—actually saw Anderson? What did he look like?"

"But why would he even—"

"—okay, but that's not—"

"WAIT," Adam cuts everyone off. "Where the hell is he *now*?" He turns to look me in the eye. "You said Warner brought you out here to show you what happened to Omega Point, but then the minute Kenji shows up, he just disappears." A pause. "Right?"

I nod.

"So—what?" he says. "He's done? He's just walking away?" Adam spins around, looks at everyone. "Guys, he knows that at least one of us is still alive! He's probably gone to get backup, to find a way to take the rest of us out—" He stops, shakes his head, hard. "Shit," he says under his breath. "SHIT."

Everyone freezes at the same time. Horrified.

"No," I say quickly, holding up both hands. "No—he's not going to do that—"

Eight pairs of eyes turn on me.

"He doesn't care about killing you guys. He doesn't even like The Reestablishment. And he hates his father—"

"What are you talking about?" Adam cuts me off, alarmed. "Warner is an *animal*—"

I take a steadying breath. I need to remember how little they know Warner, how little they've heard from his point of view; I have to remind myself what I used to think of him just a few days ago.

Warner's revelations are still so recent. I don't know how to properly defend him or how to reconcile these polarizing impressions of him, and for a moment it makes me furious with him and his stupid pretenses, for ever having put me in this position. If only he didn't come across as a sick, twisted psycho, I wouldn't have to stand up for him right now.

"He *wants* to take down The Reestablishment," I try to explain. "And he wants to kill Anderson, too—"

The room explodes into more arguments. Shouts and epithets that all boil down to no one believing me, everyone thinking I'm insane and that Warner's brainwashed me; they think he's a proven murderer who locked me up and tried to use me to torture people.

And they're not wrong. Except that they are.

I want so desperately to tell them they don't understand.

None of them know the truth, and they're not giving me a chance to explain. But just as I'm about to say something else in my own defense, I catch a glimpse of Ian out of the corner of my eye.

He's laughing at me.

Out loud, slapping his knee, head thrown back, howling with glee at what he thinks is my stupidity, and for a moment I seriously begin to doubt myself and everything Warner said to me.

I squeeze my eyes shut.

How will I ever really know if I can trust him? How do I know he wasn't lying to me like he always did, like he claims he has been from the beginning?

I'm so sick of this uncertainty. So sick and tired of it.

But I blink and I'm being pulled out of the crowd, tugged toward James's bedroom door; to the storage closet that used to be his room. Adam pulls me inside and shuts the door on the insanity behind us. He's holding my arms, looking into my eyes with a strange, burning intensity that startles me.

I'm trapped.

"What's going on?" he asks. "Why are you defending Warner? After everything he did to you, you should hate him—you should be furious—"

"I can't, Adam, I—"

"What do you mean you *can't*?"

"I just—it's not that easy anymore." I shake my head, try to explain the unexplainable. "I don't know what to think of him now. There are so many things I misunderstood. Things I couldn't comprehend." I drop my eyes. "He's really . . ." I hesitate, conflicted.

I don't know how to tell the truth without sounding like a liar.

"I don't know," I finally say, staring into my hands. "I don't know. He's just . . . he's not as bad as I thought."

"Wow." Adam exhales, shocked. *"He's not as bad as you thought. He's not as bad as you thought? How on earth could he be any better than you thought—?"*

"Adam—"

"What the hell are you *thinking*, Juliette?"

I look up. He can't hide the disgust in his eyes.

I panic.

I need to find a way to explain, to present an irrefutable example—proof that Warner is not who I thought he was—but I can already tell that Adam has lost confidence in me, that he doesn't trust me or believe me anymore, and I flounder.

He opens his mouth to speak.

I beat him to it. "Do you remember that day you found me crying in the shower? After Warner forced me to torture that toddler?"

Adam hesitates before nodding slowly, reluctantly.

"That was one of the reasons I hated him so much. I thought he'd actually put a child in that room—that he'd stolen someone's kid and wanted to watch me torture it. It was just so despicable," I say. "So disgusting, so horrifying. I thought he was inhuman. Completely evil. But . . . it wasn't real," I whisper.

Adam looks confused.

"It was just a simulation," I try to explain. "Warner told me it was a simulation chamber, not a torture room. He said it all happened in my imagination."

"Juliette," Adam says. Sighs. He looks away, looks back at me. "What are you talking about? Of course it was a simulation."

"What?"

Adam laughs a small, confused sort of laugh.

"You knew it wasn't real . . . ?" I ask.

He stares at me.

"But when you found me—you said it wasn't my fault— you told me you'd heard about what happened, and that it wasn't my fault—"

Adam runs a hand through the hair at the back of his neck. "I thought you were upset about breaking down that wall," he says. "I mean, I knew the simulation would probably be scary as hell, but I thought Warner would've told you what it was beforehand. I had no idea you'd walked into something like that thinking it was going to be real." He presses his eyes shut for a second. "I thought you were upset about learning you had this whole new crazy ability. And about the soldiers who were injured in the aftermath."

I'm blinking at him, stunned.

All this time, a small part of me was still holding on to doubt—believing that maybe the torture chamber *was* real and that Warner was just lying to me. Again.

But now, to have confirmation from Adam himself.

I'm floored.

Adam is shaking his head. "That bastard," he's saying. "I can't believe he did that to you."

I lower my eyes. "Warner's done a lot of crazy things," I say, "but he really thought he was helping me."

"But he wasn't helping you," Adam says, angry again. "He was *torturing* you—"

"No. That's not true." I focus my eyes on a crack in the wall. "In some strange way . . . he did help me." I hesitate before meeting Adam's gaze. "That moment in the simulation chamber was the first time I ever allowed myself to be angry. I never knew how much more I could do—that I could be so physically strong—until that moment."

I look away.

Clasp and unclasp my hands.

"Warner puts up this facade," I'm saying. "He acts like he's a sick, heartless monster, but he's . . . I don't know . . ." I trail off, my eyes trained on something I can't quite see. A memory, maybe. Of Warner smiling. His gentle hands wiping away my tears. *It's okay, you're okay,* he'd said to me. "He's really—"

"I don't, um—" Adam breaks away, blows out a strange, shaky breath. "I don't know how I'm supposed to understand this," he says, looking unsteady. "You—what? You like him now? You're friends with him? The same guy who tried to *kill* me?" He's barely able to conceal the pain in his voice. "He had me hung from a conveyor belt in a slaughterhouse, Juliette. Or have you already forgotten that?"

I flinch. Drop my head in shame.

I *had* forgotten about that.

I'd forgotten that Warner almost killed Adam, that he'd shot Adam right in front of my face. He saw Adam as a traitor, as a soldier who held a gun to the back of his head; defied him and stole me away.

It makes me sick.

"I'm just . . . I'm so confused," I finally manage to say. "I want to hate him but I just don't know how anymore—"

Adam is staring at me like he has no idea who I am.

I need to talk about something else.

"What's going on with Castle?" I ask. "Is he sick?"

Adam hesitates before answering, realizing I'm trying to change the subject. Finally, he relents. Sighs. "It's bad," he says to me. "He's been hit worse than the rest of us. And Castle taking it all so hard has really affected Kenji."

I study Adam's face as he speaks, unable to stop myself from searching for similarities to Anderson and Warner.

"He doesn't really leave that chair," Adam is saying. "He sits there all day until he collapses from exhaustion, and even then, he just falls asleep sitting in the same spot. Then he wakes up the next morning and does the same thing again, all day. He only eats when we force him to, and only moves to go to the bathroom." Adam shakes his head. "We're all hoping he'll snap out of it pretty soon, but it's been really weird to just lose a leader like that. Castle was in charge of everything. And now he doesn't seem to care about anything."

"He's probably still in shock," I say, remembering it's

only been three days since the battle. "Hopefully, with time," I tell him, "he'll be all right."

"Yeah," Adam says. Nods. Studies his hands. "But we really need to figure out what we're going to do. I don't know how much longer we can live like this. We're going to run out of food in a few weeks at the most," he says. "We've got ten people to feed now. Plus, Brendan and Winston are still hurting; I've done what I can for them using the limited supplies I have here, but they need actual medical attention and pain medication, if we can swing it." A pause. "I don't know what Kenji's told you, but they were seriously messed up when we brought them in here. Winston's swelling has only just gone down. We really can't stay here for much longer," he says. "We need a plan."

"Yes." I'm so relieved to hear he's ready to be proactive. "Yes. Yes. We need a plan. What are you thinking? Do you already have something in mind?"

Adam shakes his head. "I don't know," he admits. "Maybe we can keep breaking into the storage units like we used to—steal supplies every once in a while—and lie low in a bigger space on unregulated ground. But we'll never be able to set foot on the compounds," he says. "There's too much risk. They'll shoot us dead on sight if we're caught. So . . . I don't know," he says. He looks sheepish as he laughs. "I'm kind of hoping I'm not the only one with ideas."

"But . . ." I hesitate, confused. "That's it? You're not thinking of fighting back anymore? You think we should just find a way to live—like *this*?" I gesture to the door, to what lies beyond it.

Adam looks at me, surprised by my reaction.

"It's not like I *want* this," he says. "But I can't see how we could possibly fight back without getting ourselves killed. I'm trying to be practical." He runs an agitated hand through his hair. "I took a chance," he says, lowering his voice. "I tried to fight back, and it got us all massacred. I shouldn't even be alive right now. But for some crazy reason, I am, and so is James, and God, Juliette, so are you.

"And I don't know," he says, shaking his head, looking away. "I feel like I've been given a chance to live my life. I'll need to think of new ways to find food and put a roof over my head. I have no money coming in, I'll never be able to enlist in this sector again, and I'm not a registered citizen, so I'll never be able to work. Right now all I'm focused on is how I'll be able to feed my family and my friends in a few weeks." His jaw tenses. "Maybe one day another group will be smarter—stronger—but I don't think that's us anymore. I don't think we stand a chance."

I'm blinking at him, stunned. "I can't believe this."

"You can't believe what?"

"You're giving up." I hear the accusation in my voice and I do nothing to hide it. "You're just giving up."

"What choice do I have?" he asks, his eyes hurt, angry. "I'm not trying to be a martyr," he says. "We gave it a shot. We tried to fight back, and it came to shit. Everyone we know is dead, and that battered group of people you saw out there is all that's left of our resistance. How are the nine of us supposed to fight the world?" he demands. "It's not a fair fight, Juliette."

I'm nodding. Staring into my hands. Trying and failing to hide my shock.

"I'm not a coward," he says to me, struggling to moderate his voice. "I just want to protect my family. I don't want James to have to worry that I'm going to show up dead every day. He needs me to be rational."

"But living like this," I say to him. "As fugitives? Stealing to survive and hiding from the world? How is that any better? You'll be worried every single day, constantly looking over your shoulder, terrified of ever leaving James alone. You'll be miserable."

"But I'll be alive."

"That's not being alive," I say to him. "That's not living—"

"How would you know?" he snaps. His mood shifts so suddenly I'm stunned into silence. "What do you know about being alive?" he demands. "You wouldn't say a word when I first found you. You were afraid of your own shadow. You were so consumed by grief and guilt that you'd gone almost completely insane—living so far inside your own head that you had no idea what happened to the world while you were gone."

I flinch, stung by the venom in his voice. I've never seen Adam so bitter or cruel. This isn't the Adam I know. I want him to stop. Rewind. Apologize. Erase the things he's just said.

But he doesn't.

"You think you've had it hard," he's saying to me. "Living

in psych wards and being thrown in jail—you think that was difficult. But what you don't realize is that you've always had a roof over your head, and food delivered to you on a regular basis." His hands are clenching, unclenching. "And that's more than most people will ever have. You have no idea what it's really like to live out here—no idea what it's like to starve and watch your family die in front of you. You have no idea," he says to me, "what it means to truly suffer. Sometimes I think you live in some fantasy land where everyone survives on optimism—but it doesn't work that way out here. In this world you're either alive, about to die, or dead. There's no romance in it. No illusion. So don't try to pretend you have any idea what it means to be alive today. *Right now.* Because you don't."

Words, I think, are such unpredictable creatures.

No gun, no sword, no army or king will ever be more powerful than a sentence. Swords may cut and kill, but words will stab and stay, burying themselves in our bones to become corpses we carry into the future, all the time digging and failing to rip their skeletons from our flesh.

I swallow, hard

one

two

three

and steady myself to respond quietly. Carefully.

He's just upset, I'm telling myself. He's just scared and worried and stressed out and he doesn't mean any of it, not really, I keep telling myself.

He's just upset.

He doesn't mean it.

"Maybe," I say. "Maybe you're right. Maybe I don't know what it's like to live. Maybe I'm still not human enough to know more than what's right in front of me." I stare straight into his eyes. "But I do know what it's like to hide from the world. I know what it's like to live as though I don't exist, caged away and isolated from society. And I won't do it again," I say. "I can't. I've finally gotten to a point in my life where I'm not afraid to speak. Where my shadow no longer haunts me. And I don't want to lose that freedom—not again. I can't go backward. I'd rather be shot dead screaming for justice than die alone in a prison of my own making."

Adam looks toward the wall, laughs, looks back at me.

"Are you even hearing yourself right now?" he asks. "You're telling me you want to jump in front of a bunch of soldiers and tell them how much you hate The Reestablishment, just to prove a point? Just so they can kill you before your eighteenth birthday? That doesn't make any sense," he says. "It doesn't serve anything. And this doesn't sound like you," he says, shaking his head. "I thought you wanted to live on your own. You never wanted to be caught up in war—you just wanted to be free of Warner and the asylum and your crazy parents. I thought you'd be happy to be done with all the fighting."

"What are you talking about?" I say. "I've always said I wanted to fight back. I've said it from the beginning—from the moment I told you I wanted to escape when we were on base. This *is* me," I insist. "This is how I feel. It's the same way I've always felt."

"No," he says. "No, we didn't leave base to start a war. We left to get the hell away from The Reestablishment, to resist in our own way, but most of all to find a life together. But then Kenji showed up and took us to Omega Point and everything changed, and we decided to fight back. Because it seemed like it might actually work—because it seemed like we might actually have a chance. But now"—he looks around the room, at the closed door—"what do we have left? We're all half dead," he says. "We are eight poorly armed men and women and one ten-year-old boy trying to fight entire armies. It's just not *feasible*," he says. "And if I'm going to die, I don't want it to be for a stupid reason. If I go to war—if I risk my life—it's going to be because the odds are in my favor. Not otherwise."

"I don't think it's stupid to fight for *humanity*—"

"You have no idea what you're saying," he snaps, his jaw tensing. "There's nothing we can do now."

"There's always something, Adam. There has to be. Because I won't live like this anymore. Not ever again."

"Juliette, please," he says, his words desperate all of a sudden, anguished. "I don't want you to get killed—I don't want to lose you again—"

"This isn't about you, Adam." I feel terrible saying it, but he has to understand. "You're so important to me. You've loved me and you were there for me when no one else was. I never want you to think I don't care about you, because

123

I do," I tell him. "But this decision has nothing to do with you. It's about *me*," I tell him. "And this life"—I point to the door—"the life on the other side of that wall? That's not what I want."

My words only seem to upset him more.

"Then you'd rather be dead?" he asks, angry again. "Is that what you're saying? You'd rather be dead than try to build a life with me here?"

"I would rather be dead," I say to him, inching away from his outstretched hand, "than go back to being silent and suffocated."

And Adam is just about to respond—he's parting his lips to speak—when the sounds of chaos reach us from the other side of the wall. We share one panicked look before yanking the bedroom door open and rushing into the living room.

My heart stops. Starts. Stops again.

Warner is here.

TWENTY

He's standing at the front door, hands shoved casually in his pockets, no fewer than six different guns pointed at his face. My mind is racing as it tries to process what to do next, how best to proceed. But Warner's face changes seasons as I enter the room: the cold line of his mouth blossoms into a bright smile. His eyes shine as he grins at me, not seeming to mind or even notice the many lethal weapons aimed in his direction.

I can't help but wonder how he found me.

I begin to move forward but Adam grabs my arm. I turn around, wondering at my sudden irritation with him. I'm almost irritated with myself for being irritated with him. This is not how I imagined it would be to see Adam again. I don't want it to be this way. I want to start over.

"What are you doing?" Adam says to me. "Don't go near him."

I stare at his hand on my arm. Look up to meet his gaze. Adam doesn't budge.

"Let go of me," I say to him.

His face clears all of a sudden, like he's startled, somehow. He looks down at his hand; releases me without a word.

I put as much space between us as I can, the whole time scanning the room for Kenji. His sharp black eyes meet mine immediately and he raises one eyebrow; his head is cocked to the side, the twitch of his lips telling me the next move is mine and I'd better make it count. I part my way through my friends until I'm standing in front of Warner, facing my friends and their guns and hoping they won't fire at me instead.

I make an effort to sound calm. "Please," I say. "Don't shoot him."

"And why the hell not?" Ian demands, his grip tightening around his gun.

"Juliette, love," Warner says, leaning into my ear. His voice is still loud enough for everyone to hear. "I do appreciate you defending me, but really, I'm quite able to handle the situation."

"It's eight against one," I say to him, forgetting my fear in the temptation to roll my eyes. "They've all got guns pointed at your face. I'm pretty sure you need my interference."

I hear him laugh behind me, just once, just before every gun in the room is yanked out of every hand and thrown up against the ceiling. I spin around in shock, catching a glimpse of the astonishment on every face behind me.

"Why do you always hesitate?" Warner asks, shaking his head as he glances around the room. "Shoot if you want to shoot. Don't waste my time with theatrics."

"How the hell did you do that?" Ian demands.

Warner says nothing. He tugs off his gloves carefully,

pulling at each finger before slipping them off his hands.

"It's okay," I tell him. "They already know."

Warner looks up. Raises an eyebrow at me. Smiles a little. "Do they really?"

"Yes. I told them."

Warner's smile changes into something almost self-mocking as he turns away, his eyes laughing as he contemplates the ceiling. Finally he nods at Castle, who's staring at the commotion with a vaguely displeased expression. "I borrowed," Warner says to Ian, "from present company."

"Hot damn," Ian breathes.

"What do you want?" Lily asks, fists clenched, standing in a far corner of the room.

"Nothing from you," Warner says to her. "I'm here to pick up Juliette. I have no wish to disturb your . . . slumber party," he says, looking around at the pillows and blankets piled on the living room floor.

Adam goes rigid with alarm. "What are you talking about? She's not going anywhere with you."

Warner scratches the back of his head. "Do you never get exhausted being so wholly unbearable? You have as much charisma as the rotting innards of unidentified roadkill."

I hear an abrupt wheezing noise and turn toward the sound.

Kenji has a hand pressed to his mouth, desperately trying to suppress a smile. He's shaking his head, holding up a hand in apology. And then he breaks, laughing out loud, snorting as he tries to muffle the sound. "I'm sorry," he says, pressing his lips together, shaking his head again. "This is not a funny moment. It's not. I'm not laughing."

Adam looks like he might punch Kenji in the face.

"So you don't want to kill us?" Winston says. "Because if you're not going to kill us, you should probably get the hell out of here before we kill you first."

"No," Warner says calmly. "I am not going to kill you. And though I wouldn't mind disposing of these two"— he nods at Adam and Kenji—"the idea is little more than exhausting to me now. I am no longer interested in your sad, pathetic lives. I am only here to accompany and transport Juliette safely home. She and I have urgent matters to attend to."

"No," I hear James say suddenly. He clambers to his feet, stares Warner straight in the eye. "*This* is her home now. You can't take her away. I don't want anyone to hurt her."

Warner's eyebrows fly up in surprise. He seems genuinely startled, as though he's only now noticing the ten-year-old. Warner and James have never actually met before; neither one of them knows they're brothers.

I look at Kenji. He looks back.

This is a big moment.

Warner studies James's face with rapt fascination. He bends down on one knee, meets James at eye level. "And who are you?" he asks.

Everyone in the room is silent, watching.

James blinks steadily and doesn't answer right away. He

finally shoves his hands into his pockets and stares at the floor. "I'm James. Adam's brother. Who are you?"

Warner tilts his head a little. "No one of consequence," he says. He tries to smile. "But it's very nice to meet you, James. I'm pleased to see your concern for Juliette's safety. You should know, however, that I have no intention of hurting her. It's just that she's made me a promise, and I intend to see it through."

"What kind of promise?" James asks.

"Yeah, what kind of promise?" Kenji cuts in, his voice loud—and angry—all of sudden.

I look up, look around. Everyone is staring at me, waiting for me to answer. Adam's eyes are wide with horror and disbelief.

I meet Warner's gaze. "I'm not leaving," I tell him. "I never promised I would stay on base with you."

He frowns. "You'd rather stay *here*?" he asks. "Why?"

"I need my friends," I tell him. "And they need me. Besides, we're all going to have to work together, so we may as well get started now. And I don't want to have to be smuggled in and out of base," I add. "You can just meet me here."

"Whoa—wait—what do you mean we can all work together?" Ian interrupts. "And why are you inviting him to come back here? What the hell are you guys talking about?"

"What kind of promise did you make him, Juliette?" Adam's voice is loud and accusing.

I turn toward the group of them. Me, standing beside

Warner, facing Adam's angry eyes along with the confused, soon-to-be-angry faces of my friends.

Oh how strange all of this has become in such a short period of time.

I take a tight, bracing breath.

"I'm ready to fight," I say, addressing the entire group. "I know some of you might feel defeated; some of you might think there's no hope left, especially not after what happened to Omega Point. But Sonya and Sara are still out there, and they need our help. So does the rest of the world. And I haven't come this far just to turn back now. I'm ready to take action and Warner has offered to help me."

I look directly at Kenji. "I've accepted his offer. I've promised to be his ally; to fight by his side; to kill Anderson and to take down The Reestablishment."

Kenji narrows his eyes at me and I can't tell if he's angry, or if he's really, really angry.

I look at the rest of my friends. "But we can all work together," I say.

"I've been thinking about this a lot," I go on, "and I think the group of us still has a chance, especially if we combine our strengths with Warner's. He knows things about The Reestablishment and his father that we'd never be able to know otherwise."

I swallow hard as I take in the shocked, horrified looks on the faces of those around me. "But," I hurry to say, "if you aren't interested in fighting back anymore, I totally understand. And if you'd rather I didn't stay here among you, I would respect your decision. Either way, I've already made my choice," I tell them. "Whether or not you choose to join me, I've decided to fight. I will take down The Reestablishment or I will die trying. There's nothing left for me otherwise."

TWENTY-ONE

The room is quiet for a long time. I've dropped my eyes, too afraid to see the looks on their faces.

Alia is the first to speak.

"I'll fight with you," she says, her soft voice ringing strong and confident in the silence. I look up to meet her eyes and she smiles, her cheeks flushed with color and determination.

But before I even have a chance to respond, Winston jumps in.

"Me too," he says. "As soon as my head stops hurting, but yeah, me too. I've got nothing left to lose," he says with a shrug. "And I'll kick some ass just to get the girls back, even if we can't save the rest of the world."

"Same," Brendan says, nodding at me. "I'm in, too."

Ian is shaking his head. "How the hell can we trust this guy?" he asks. "How do we know he's not full of shit?"

"Yeah," Lily pipes up. "This doesn't feel right." She focuses her eyes on Warner. "Why would you want to help any of us?" she asks him. "Since when have you ever been trustworthy?"

Warner runs a hand through his hair. Smiles unkindly. Glances at me.

He's not amused.

"I am *not* trustworthy," Warner finally says, looking up to meet Lily's eyes. "And I have no interest in helping you," he says. "In fact, I think I was very clear just a moment ago when I said that I was here for Juliette. I did not sign up to help her friends, and I will make zero guarantees for your survival or your safety. So if you're seeking reassurance," he says, "I can, and will, offer you none."

Ian is actually smiling.

Lily looks a little mollified.

Kenji is shaking his head.

"All right." Ian nods. "That's cool." He rubs his forehead. "So what's the game plan?"

"Have you all lost your *minds*?" Adam explodes. "Are you forgetting who you're talking to? He just busts down our door and demands to take Juliette away and you want to stand by his side and fight with him? The same guy who's responsible for destroying Omega Point?" he says. "Everyone is dead because of him!"

"I am not responsible for that," Warner says sharply, his expression darkening. "That was not my call, nor did I have any idea it was happening. By the time I broke out of Omega Point and found my way back to base, my father's plans were already under way. I was not a part of the battle, nor was I a part of the assault on Omega Point."

"It's true," Lily says. "The supreme is the one who ordered the air strike against Omega Point."

"Yeah, and as much as I hate this guy by default," Winston adds, jerking a thumb at Warner, "I hate his father a whole hell of a lot more. He's the one who kidnapped us. It was his men who held us captive; not the soldiers of Sector 45. So yeah," Winston says, stretching back on the couch, "I'd love to watch the supreme die a slow, miserable death."

"I have to admit," Brendan says, "I'm not often keen on revenge, but it does sound very sweet right now."

"I want to watch that bastard bleed," Ian says.

"How nice that we all have something in common," Warner mutters, irritated. He sighs. Looks at me. "Juliette, a word, please?"

"This is bullshit!" Adam shouts. He looks around. "How can you all so easily forget yourselves? How can you forget what he's done—what he did to me—what he did to Kenji?" Adam pivots to face me then. "How can you even look at him," he says to me, "knowing how he treated us? He nearly murdered me—leaving me to bleed out slowly so he could take his time torturing me to death—"

"Kent, man, please—you need to calm down, okay?" Kenji steps forward. "I understand that you're pissed—I'm not happy about this either—but things get crazy in the aftermath of war. Alliances form in unlikely ways." He shrugs. "If this is the only way to take Anderson out, maybe we should consider—"

"I can't believe this." Adam cuts him off, looking around. "I can't believe this is happening. You've all lost your minds. You're all *insane*," he says, gripping the back of his head. "This guy is a psycho—he's a *murderer*—"

"Adam," I try to say. "Please—"

"What's happened to you?" He turns on me. "I don't even

know who you are anymore. I thought you were dead—I thought *he'd* killed you," he says, pointing at Warner. "And now you're standing here, teaming up with the guy who tried to ruin your life? Talking about fighting back because you have nothing left to live for? What about *me*?" he demands. "What about our relationship? When did that stop being enough for you?"

"This isn't about us," I try to tell him. "Please, Adam— let me explain—"

"I have to get out of here," he says abruptly, moving toward the door. "I can't be here right now—I can't process all of this in one day. It's too much," he says. "It's too much for me—"

"Adam—" I catch his arm in one last attempt, one last effort to try and talk to him, but he breaks away.

"All of this," he says, meeting my eyes, his voice quieting to a raw, aching whisper, "was for you. I left everything I knew because I thought we were in this together. I thought it was going to be me and you." His eyes are so dark, so deep, so hurt. Looking at him makes me want to curl up and die. "What are you doing?" he says, desperate now. "What are you *thinking*?"

And I realize he actually wants an answer.

Because he waits.

He stands there, and he waits. Waits to hear my response while everyone watches us, likely entertained by the spectacle we've made. I can't believe he's doing this to me. Here. Right now. In front of everyone.

In front of *Warner*.

I try to meet Adam's eyes, but find I can't hold his gaze for very long.

"I don't want to live in fear anymore," I say, hoping I sound stronger than I feel. "I have to fight back," I tell him. "I thought we wanted the same things."

"No—I wanted *you*," he says, struggling to keep his voice steady. "That's all I wanted. From the very beginning, Juliette. You were it. You were all I wanted."

And I can't speak.

I can't speak

I can't cough up the words because I can't break his heart like this but he's waiting, he's waiting and he's looking at me and "I need more," I choke out. "I wanted you, too, Adam, but I need more than that. I need to be free. Please, try to understand—"

"STOP!" Adam explodes. "Stop trying to get me to understand a bunch of *bullshit*! I can't deal with you anymore." And then he grabs the jacket sitting on the sofa, hauls the door open, and slams it shut behind him.

There's a moment of absolute silence.

I try to run after him.

Kenji catches me around the waist, yanks me backward. Gives me a hard, knowing look. "I'll take care of Kent. You stay here and clean up the mess you made," he says, cocking his head at Warner.

I swallow, hard. Don't say a word.

It's only after Kenji has disappeared that I turn around

to face the remaining members of our audience, and I'm still searching for the right thing to say when I hear the one voice I least expected.

"Ah, Ms. Ferrars," Castle says. "It's so good to have you back. Things are always so much more entertaining when you're around."

Ian bursts into tears.

TWENTY-TWO

Everyone crowds around Castle at once; James practically tackles him. Ian shoves everyone else out of the way in his attempt to get closer. Castle is smiling, laughing a little. He finally looks more like the man I remember.

"I'm all right," he's saying. He sounds exhausted, as if the words are costing him a great deal to get out. "Thank you so much for your concern. But I'll be all right. I just need a little more time, that's all."

I meet his eyes. I'm afraid to approach him.

"Please," Castle says to Alia and Winston—the two standing closest on either side of him—"help me up. I'd like to greet our newest visitor."

He's not talking about me.

Castle gets to his feet with some difficulty, even with everyone scrambling to help him. The entire room suddenly feels different: lighter; happier, somehow. I hadn't realized how much of everyone's grief was tied up in Castle's well-being.

"Mr. Warner," Castle says, locking eyes with him from across the room. "How very nice of you to join us."

"I'm not joining anyth—"

"I always knew you would," Castle says. He smiles a little. "And I am pleased."

Warner seems to be trying not to roll his eyes.

"You may let the guns down now," Castle says to him. "I promise I will watch them closely in your absence."

We all glance up at the ceiling. I hear Warner sigh. All at once, the guns float to the floor, settling gently onto the carpet.

"Very good," Castle says. "Now, if you'll excuse me, I think I'm in desperate need of a long shower. I hope you won't mistake my early exit for rudeness," he adds. "It's only that I feel quite certain we'll be seeing a lot of each other in these next weeks."

Warner's jaw tenses by way of response.

Castle smiles.

Winston and Brendan help Castle to the bathroom, while Ian shouts eagerly about grabbing him a change of clothes. Me, Warner, James, Alia, and Lily are the only ones left in the room.

"Juliette?" Warner says.

I glance in his direction.

"A moment of your time, please? In private?"

I hesitate.

"You can use my room," James interjects. "I don't mind."

I look at him, shocked he'd offer up his personal space so freely to the likes of me and Warner; especially after having seen his brother's outburst just now.

"Adam will be okay," James says to me, as if reading my mind. "He's just really stressed out. He's worried about a lot of things. He thinks we're going to run out of food and stuff."

"James—"

"It's really okay," James says. "I'll hang out with Alia and Lily."

I glance at the two girls, but their faces reveal nothing. Alia offers me only the slightest of sympathetic smiles. Lily is staring at Warner, sizing him up.

I finally sigh, relenting.

I follow Warner into the small storage closet, closing the door behind me.

He doesn't waste any time.

"Why are you inviting your friends to join us? I told you I didn't want to work with them."

"How did you find me?" I counter. "I never pressed the button on that pager you gave me."

Warner studies my eyes, his sharp green gaze locked on to mine as if trying to read me for clues. But the intensity of his gaze is always too much for me; I break the connection too soon, feeling untethered, somehow.

"It was simple deductive reasoning," he finally says. "Kent was the only member of your group with a life outside of Omega Point; his old home was the only place they'd have been able to retreat to without causing a disturbance. And, as such," Warner says, "it was the first place I checked." A slight shake of his head. "Contrary to what you might believe, love, I am not an idiot."

"I never thought you were an idiot," I say, surprised. "I thought you were crazy," I tell him, "but not an idiot." I hesitate. "I actually think you're brilliant," I confess. "I wish

I could think like you." I look away and look back at him too quickly, feeling a lot like I need to learn to keep my mouth shut.

Warner's face clears. His eyes crinkle in amusement as he smiles. "I don't want your friends on my team," he says. "I don't like them."

"I don't care."

"They will only slow us down."

"They will give us an advantage," I insist. "I know you don't think they did things the right way at Omega Point, but they did know how to survive. They all have important strengths."

"They're completely broken."

"They're grieving," I tell him, annoyed. "Don't underestimate them. Castle is a natural leader," I say. "Kenji is a genius and an excellent fighter. He acts like an idiot sometimes, but you know better than anyone else that it's just a show. He's smarter than all of us. Plus, Winston and Alia can design anything we need as long as they have the materials; Lily has an incredible photographic memory; Brendan can handle electricity and Winston can stretch his limbs into just about anything. And Ian . . ." I falter. "Well, Ian is . . . good for something, I'm sure."

Warner laughs a little, his smile softening until it disappears altogether. His features settle into an uncertain expression. "And Kent?" Warner finally asks.

I feel my face pale. "What about him?"

"What is he good for?"

I hesitate before answering. "Adam is a great soldier."

"Is that all?"

My heart is pounding so hard. Too hard.

Warner looks away, carefully neutralizes his expression, his tone. "You care for him."

It's not a question.

"Yes," I manage to say. "Of course I do."

"And what does that entail, exactly?"

"I don't know what you mean," I lie.

Warner is staring at the wall, holding himself very still, his eyes revealing nothing of what he's really thinking, what he's feeling. "Do you love him?"

I'm stunned.

I can't even imagine what it must cost him to ask this question so directly. I almost admire him for being brave enough to do it.

But for the first time, I'm not really sure what to say. If this were one week ago, two weeks ago, I would've answered without hesitation. I would've known, definitively, that I loved Adam, and I wouldn't have been afraid to say so. But now I can't help but wonder if I even know what love is; if what I felt for Adam was love or just a mix of deep affection and physical attraction. Because if I loved him—if I really, truly loved him—would I hesitate now? Would I so easily be able to detach myself from his life? His pain?

I've worried so much about Adam these past weeks—the effects of his training, the news of his father—but I don't know if it's been out of love, or if it's been out of guilt. He left everything for me; because he wanted to be with me. But as much as it pains me to admit it, I know I didn't run away to be with him. Adam wasn't my main reason; he wasn't the driving force.

I ran away for me. Because I wanted to be free.

"Juliette?"

Warner's soft whisper brings me back to the present, hauls me up and into myself, jarring my consciousness back to reality. I'm afraid to dwell on the truths I've just uncovered.

I meet Warner's eyes. "Yes?"

"Do you love him?" he asks again, more quietly this time.

And I suddenly have to force myself to say three words I never, ever thought I'd say. "I don't know."

Warner closes his eyes.

He exhales, the tension clear in his shoulders and in the line of his jaw and when he finally looks at me again there are stories in his eyes, thoughts and feelings and whispers of things I've never even seen before. Truths he might never bring himself to say; impossible things and unbelievable things and an abundance of feeling I've never thought him capable of. His whole body seems to relax in relief.

I don't know this boy standing before me. He's a perfect stranger, an entirely different being; the type of person I might never have known if my parents hadn't tossed me away.

"Juliette," he whispers.

I'm only now realizing just how close he is. I could press my face against his neck if I wanted to. Could place my hands on his chest if I wanted to.

If I wanted to.

"I'd really love for you to come back with me," he says.

"I can't," I say to him, heart racing suddenly. "I have to stay here."

"But it's not practical," he says. "We need to plan. We need to talk strategy—it could take days—"

"I already have a plan."

His eyebrows fly up and I tilt my head, fixing him with a hard look before I reach for the door.

TWENTY-THREE

Kenji is waiting on the other side.

"What the *hell* do you two think you're doing?" he says. "Get your asses out here, *right now.*"

I head straight into the living room, eager to put distance between me and whatever keeps happening to my head when Warner gets too close. I need air. I need a new brain. I need to jump out of a window and catch a ride with a dragon to a world far from here.

But the moment I look up and try to steady myself, I find Adam staring at me. Blinking like he's starting to see something he wishes he could unsee, and I feel my face flush so fast that for a moment I'm surprised I'm not standing in a toilet.

"Adam," I hear myself say. "No—it's not—"

"I can't even talk to you right now." He's shaking his head, his voice strangled. "I can't even be near you right now—"

"Please," I try to say. "We were just talking—"

"You were just *talking*? Alone? In my brother's bedroom?" He's holding his jacket in his hands. He tosses it onto the couch. Laughs like he might be losing his mind. Runs a hand through his hair and glances up at the ceiling. Stares back at me. "What the hell is going on, Juliette?" he asks, his jaw tensing. "What is happening right now?"

"Can't we talk about this in private—?"

"No." His chest is heaving. "I want to talk about this right now. I don't care who hears it."

My eyes immediately go to Warner. He's leaning against the wall just outside James's room, arms crossed loosely at his chest. He's watching Adam with a calm, focused interest.

Warner stills suddenly, as if he can feel my eyes on him.

He looks up, looks at me for exactly two seconds before turning away. He seems to be laughing.

"Why do you keep looking at him?" Adam demands, eyes flashing. "Why are you even looking at him at all? Why are you so interested in some demented *psycho*—"

I'm so tired of this.

I'm tired of all the secrets and all my inner turmoil and all the guilt and confusion I've felt over these two brothers. More than anything else, I don't like this angry Adam in front of me.

I try to talk to him and he won't listen to me. I try to reason with him and he attacks me. I try to be honest with him and he won't believe me. I have no idea what else to do.

"What's really going on between you guys?" Adam is still asking me. "What's *really* happening, Juliette? I need you to stop lying to me—"

"Adam." I cut him off. I'm surprised by how calm I sound. "There's so much we need to be discussing right now," I say to him, "and this isn't it. Our personal problems don't need to be shared with everyone."

"So you admit it then?" he says, somehow angrier. "That we have problems, that something is wrong—"

"Something's been wrong for a while," I say, exasperated. "I can't even talk to y—"

"Yeah, ever since we dragged this asshole back to Omega Point," Adam says. He turns to glare at Kenji. "It was *your* idea—"

"Hey, don't pull me into your bullshit, okay?" Kenji counters. "Don't blame me for your issues."

"We were fine until she started spending so much goddamn time with him—," Adam begins to say.

"She spent just as much time with him while we were still on base, genius—"

"*Stop*," I say. "Please understand: Warner is here to help us. He wants to take down The Reestablishment and kill the supreme just like we do—he's not our enemy anymore—"

"He's going to *help* us?" Adam asks, eyes wide, feigning surprise. "Oh, you mean just like he helped us the last time he said he was going to fight on our side? Right before he broke out of Omega Point and *bailed*?" Adam laughs out loud, disbelieving. "I can't believe you're falling for all of his *bullshit*—"

"This isn't some kind of trick, Adam—I'm not stupid—"

"Are you sure?"

"What?" I can't believe he just insulted me.

"I asked you if you were sure," he snaps. "Because you're

acting pretty damn stupid right now, so I don't know if I can trust your judgment anymore."

"What is *wrong* with you—"

"What's wrong with *you*?" he shouts back, eyes blazing. "You don't do this. You don't act like this," he says. "You're like a completely different person—"

"Me?" I demand, my voice rising. I've been trying so hard to control my temper but I just don't think I can anymore. He says he wants to have this conversation in front of everyone?

Fine.

We'll have this conversation in front of everyone.

"If I've changed," I say to him, "then so have you. Because the Adam I remember is kind and gentle and he'd never insult me like this. I know things have been rough for you lately, and I'm trying to understand, to be patient, to give you space—but these last few weeks have been rough on all of us. We're all going through a hard time but we don't put each other down. We don't hurt each other. But you can't even be nice to Kenji," I tell him. "You used to be *friends* with Kenji, remember? Now every time he so much as cracks a joke you look at him like you want to kill him, and I don't know why—"

"You're going to defend everyone in this room except for me, aren't you?" Adam says. "You love Kenji so much, you spend all your goddamn time with Kenji—"

"He's my friend!"

"I'm your boyfriend!"

"No," I tell him. "You're not."

Adam is shaking, fists clenched. "I can't even believe you right now."

"We broke up, Adam." My voice is steady. "We broke up a month ago."

"Right," Adam says. "We broke up because you said you loved me. Because you said you didn't want to hurt me."

"I don't," I tell him. "I don't want to hurt you. I've never wanted to hurt you."

"What the hell do you think you're doing right now?" he shouts.

"I don't know how to talk to you," I tell him, shaking my head. "I don't understand—"

"No—you don't understand anything," he snaps. "You don't understand me, you don't understand yourself, and you don't understand that you're acting like a stupid child who's allowed herself to be brainwashed by a psychopath."

Time seems to stand still.

Everything I want to say and everything I've wished to say begins to take shape, falling to the floor and scrambling upright. Paragraphs and paragraphs begin building walls around me, blocking and justifying as they find ways to fit together, linking and weaving and leaving no room for escape. And every single space between every unspoken word clambers up and into my open mouth, down my throat and into my chest, filling me with so much emptiness I think I might just float away.

I'm breathing.

So hard.

A throat clears.

"Yes, right, I'm really sorry to interrupt," Warner says, stepping forward. "But Juliette, I need to get going. Are you sure you want to stay here?"

I freeze.

"GET OUT," Adam shouts. "Get the hell out of my house, you piece of shit. And don't come back here."

"Well," Warner says, cocking his head at me. "Never mind. It looks like you don't really have a choice." He holds out his hand. "Shall we?"

"You're not taking her anywhere." Adam turns on him. "She's not leaving with you, and she's not partnering up with you. Now get lost."

"Adam. STOP." My voice is angrier than I mean it to be, but I can't help it anymore. "I don't need your permission. I'm not going to live like this. I'm not hiding anymore. You don't have to come with me—you don't even have to understand," I tell him. "But if you loved me, you wouldn't stand in my way."

Warner is smiling.

Adam notices.

"Is there something you want to say?" Adam turns on him.

"God, no," Warner says. "Juliette doesn't require my assistance. And *you* might not have realized it yet, but it's obvious to everyone else that you've lost this fight, Kent."

Adam snaps.

He charges forward, fist pulled back and ready to swing,

and it all happens so quickly I only have time to gasp before I hear a sharp crack.

Adam's fist is frozen only inches from Warner's face. It's caught in Warner's hand.

Adam is shocked into silence, his whole body shaking from the unspent energy. Warner leans into his brother's face, whispers, "You really don't want to fight me, you idiot," and hurls Adam's fist back with so much force that Adam flies backward, catching himself just before hitting the floor.

Adam is up. Bolting across the room. Angrier.

Kenji tackles him.

Adam is shouting for Kenji to let him go, to stop getting involved, and Kenji is yanking Adam across the room against his will. He somehow manages to haul open the front door, and pulls himself and Adam outside.

The door slams shut behind them.

TWENTY-FOUR

James, is my first thought.

I spin around, searching the room for him, hoping he's all right, only to find that Lily has already had the foresight to take him into his room.

Everyone else is staring at me.

"What the hell was that?" Ian is the first to break the silence.

He, Brendan, and Winston are all gaping at me. Alia is standing off to the side, arms wrapped around her body. Castle must still be in the shower.

I flinch as someone touches my shoulder.

Warner.

He leans into my ear, speaking softly so only I can hear him. "It's getting late, love, and I really must get back to base." A pause. "And I'm sorry to keep asking, but are you certain you want to stay here?"

I look up to meet his eyes. Nod. "I need to talk to Kenji," I tell him. "I don't know how everyone else feels anymore, but I don't want to do this without Kenji." I hesitate. "I mean, I can," I say, "if I have to. But I don't want to."

Warner nods. Looks past me at a point behind my head. "Right." He frowns a little. "I expect one day you'll tell me what you find so incredibly appealing about him?"

"Who? Kenji?"

Another nod.

"Oh," I say, blinking in surprise. "He's my best friend."

Warner looks at me. Raises an eyebrow.

I stare back. "Is that going to be a problem?"

He stares into his hands, shakes his head. "No, of course not," he says quietly. He clears his throat. "So, I'll come back tomorrow? Thirteen hundred hours."

"Thirteen hundred hours . . . from *now*?"

Warner laughs. Looks up. "One o'clock in the afternoon."

"Okay."

He looks into my eyes then. Smiles for just a moment too long before he turns around and walks out the door. Without a word to anyone.

Ian is gaping at me. Again.

"I'm—right, I'm so confused," Brendan says, blinking. "Right then—what just happened? Was he *smiling* at you? Genuinely smiling at you?"

"Looked to me like he was in love with you," Winston says, frowning. "But that's probably just because my head is messed up, right?"

I'm doing my best to look at the wall.

Kenji slams the front door open.

Steps inside.

Alone.

"You," he says, pointing at me, eyes narrowed. "Get your ass over here, right now. You and me," he says, "we need to talk."

TWENTY-FIVE

I shuffle over to the door and Kenji grabs my arm to lead me outside. He turns back and shouts, "Get yourselves some dinner" to everyone else, just before we leave.

We're standing on the landing just outside Adam's house, and I realize for the first time that there are more stairwells leading up. To somewhere.

"Come on, princess," Kenji says. "Follow me."

And we climb.

Four, five flights of stairs. Maybe eight. Or fifty. I have no idea. All I know is that by the time we reach the top I'm both out of breath and embarrassed for being out of breath.

When I'm finally able to inhale normally, I chance a look around.

Incredible.

We're on the roof, outside, where the world is pitch-black but for the stars and the sliver of moon someone has hung from the sky. Sometimes I wonder if the planets are still up there, still aligned, still managing to get along after all this time. Maybe we could learn a thing or two from them.

The wind tangles around us and I shiver as my body adjusts to the temperature.

"Come here," Kenji says to me. He motions to the ledge

of the roof, and sits down right on the edge, legs swinging over what would be his fastest path to death. "Don't worry," he says when he sees my face. "It'll be fine. I sit here a lot."

When I'm finally sitting next to him, I dare to look down. My feet are dangling from the top of the world.

Kenji drops an arm around me. Rubs my shoulder to keep me warm.

"So," he says. "When's the big day? Have you set a date yet?"

"What?" I startle. "For what?"

"For the day you're going to stop being such a *dumbass*," he says, shooting me a sharp look.

"Oh." I cringe. Kick at the air. "Yeah, that'll probably never happen."

"Yeah, you're probably right."

"Shut up."

"You know," he says, "I don't know where Adam is."

I stiffen. Sit up. "Is he okay?"

"He'll be fine," Kenji says with a resigned sigh. "He's just super pissed off. And hurt. And embarrassed. And all that emotional shit."

I drop my eyes again. Kenji's arm hangs loosely around my neck, and he pulls me closer, tucking me into his side. I rest my head on his chest.

Moments and minutes and memories build and break between us.

"I really thought you guys were solid," Kenji finally says to me.

"Yeah," I whisper. "Me too."

A few seconds jump off the roof.

"I'm such a horrible person," I say, so quietly.

"Yeah, well." Kenji sighs.

I groan. Drop my head into my hands.

Kenji sighs again. "Don't worry, Kent was being an asshole, too." He takes a deep breath. "But damn, princess." Kenji looks at me, shakes his head an inch, looks back into the night. "Seriously? *Warner?*"

I look up. "What are you talking about?"

Kenji raises an eyebrow at me. "I know for a fact that you're not stupid, so please don't act like you are."

I roll my eyes. "I really don't want to have this conversation again—"

"I don't care if you don't want to have this conversation again. You have to talk about this. You can't just fall for a guy like Warner without telling me why. I need to make sure he didn't stick a chip in your head or some shit."

I'm silent for almost a full minute.

"I'm not falling for Warner," I say quietly.

"Sure you aren't."

"I'm not," I insist. "I'm just—I don't know." I sigh. "I don't know what's happening to me."

"They're called hormones."

I shoot him a dirty look. "I'm serious."

"Me too." He cocks his head at me. "That's like, biological and shit. Scientific. Maybe your lady bits are scientifically confused."

"My *lady bits?*"

156

"Oh, I'm sorry"—Kenji pretends to look offended—"would you rather I use the proper anatomical terminology? Because your lady bits do not scare me—"

"Yeah, no thanks." I manage to laugh a little, my sad attempt dissolving into a sigh.

God, everything is changing.

"He's just . . . so different," I hear myself say. "Warner. He's not what you guys think. He's sweet. And kind. And his father is so, so horrible to him. You can't even imagine," I trail off, thinking of the scars I saw on Warner's back. "And more than anything else . . . I don't know," I say, staring into the darkness. "He really . . . believes in me?" I glance up at Kenji. "Does that sound stupid?"

Kenji shoots me a doubtful look. "Adam believes in you, too."

"Yeah," I say, looking into the darkness. "I guess."

"What do you mean, *you guess?* The kid thinks you invented air."

I almost smile. "I don't know which version of me Adam likes. I'm not the same person I was when we were in school. I'm not that girl anymore. I think he wants that," I say, glancing up at Kenji. "I think he wants to pretend I'm the girl who doesn't really speak and spends most of her time being scared. The kind of girl he needs to protect and take care of all the time. I don't know if he likes who I am now. I don't know if he can handle it."

"So the minute you opened your mouth you just shattered all his dreams, huh?"

"I will push you off the roof."

"Yeah, I can definitely see why Adam wouldn't like you."
I roll my eyes.

Kenji laughs. Leans back and pulls me down with him. The concrete is under our heads now, the sky draped all around us. It's like I've been dropped into a vat of ink.

"You know, it actually makes a lot of sense," Kenji finally says.

"What does?"

"I don't know, I mean—you've been locked up basically forever, right? It's not like you were busy touching a bunch of dudes your whole life."

"*What?*"

"Like—Adam was the first guy who was ever . . . nice to you. Hell, he was probably the first person in the world who was nice to you. And he can touch you. And he's not, you know, disgusting looking." A pause. "I can't blame you, to be honest. It's hard being lonely. We all get a little desperate sometimes."

"Okay," I say slowly.

"I am just saying," Kenji says, "that I guess it makes sense you'd fall for him. Like, by default. Because if not him, who else? Your options were super limited."

"Oh," I say, quietly now. "Right. By *default*." I try to laugh and fail, swallowing hard against the emotion caught in my throat. "Sometimes I'm not sure I even know what's real anymore."

"What do you mean?"

I shake my head. "I don't know," I whisper, mostly to myself.

A heavy pause.

"Did you really love him . . . ?"

I hesitate before answering. "I think so? I don't know?" I sigh. "Is it possible to love someone and then stop loving them? I don't think I even know what love is."

Kenji blows out a breath. Runs a hand through his hair. "Well shit," he mutters.

"Have you ever been in love?" I ask, turning on my side to look at him.

He stares up at the sky. Blinks a few times. "Nope."

I roll back, disappointed. "Oh."

"This is so depressing," Kenji says.

"Yeah."

"We suck."

"Yeah."

"So tell me again why you like Warner so much? Did he, like, take all his clothes off or something?"

"What?" I gasp, so glad it's too dark for him to see me blushing. "No," I say quickly. "No, he—"

"Damn, princess." Kenji laughs, hard. "I had no idea."

I punch him in the arm.

"Hey—be gentle with me!" he protests, rubbing at the sore spot. "I'm weaker than you!"

"You know, I can sort of control it now," I tell him, beaming. "I can moderate my strength levels."

"Good for you. I'll buy you a balloon the minute the world stops shitting on itself."

"Thank you," I say, pleased. "You're a good teacher."

"I'm good at everything," he points out.

"Humble, too."

"And really good-looking."

I choke on a laugh.

"You still haven't answered my question," Kenji says. He shifts, folds his hands behind his head. "Why do you like the rich boy so much?"

I take a tight breath. Focus on the brightest star in the sky. "I like the way I feel about myself when I'm with him," I say quietly. "Warner thinks I'm strong and smart and capable and he actually values my opinion. He makes me feel like his equal—like I can accomplish just as much as he can, and more. And if I do something incredible, he's not even surprised. He *expects* it. He doesn't treat me like I'm some fragile little girl who needs to be protected all the time."

Kenji snorts.

"That's because you're not fragile," Kenji says. "If anything, everyone needs to protect themselves from *you*. You're like a freaking beast," he says. Then adds, "I mean, you know—like, a cute beast. A little beast that tears shit up and breaks the earth and sucks the life out of people."

"Nice."

"I'm here for you."

"I can tell."

"So that's it?" Kenji says. "You just like him for his personality, huh?"

"What?"

"All of this," Kenji says, waving a hand in the air, "has

nothing to do with him being all sexy and shit and him being able to touch you all the time?"

"You think Warner is sexy?"

"That is not what I said."

I laugh. "I do like his face."

"And the touching?"

"What touching?"

Kenji looks at me, eyes wide, eyebrows up. "I am not Adam, okay? You can't bullshit me with your innocent act. You tell me this guy can touch you, and that he's into you, and you're clearly into him, and you spent the night in his bed last night, and then I walk in on the two of you in a freaking closet—no wait, I'm sorry, not a closet—a *child's bedroom*—and you're telling me there has been *zero* touching?" He stares at me. "Is that what you're telling me?"

"No," I whisper, face on fire.

"You're just growing up so quickly. You're getting all excited about being able to touch shit for the first time, and I just want to be sure you are observing sanitary regulations—"

"Stop being so disgusting."

"Hey—I'm just looking out for y—"

"Kenji?"

"Yeah?"

I take a deep breath. Try to count the stars. "What am I going to do?"

"About what?"

I hesitate. "About everything."

Kenji makes a strange sound. "Shit if I know."

"I don't want to do this without you," I whisper.

He leans back. "Who said you're going to do anything without me?"

My heart skips a few beats. I stare at him.

"What?" he asks. Raises his eyebrows. "You're surprised?"

"You'll fight with me?" I ask him, hardly breathing. "Fight back with me? Even if it's with Warner?"

Kenji smiles. Looks up at the sky. "Hell yeah," he says.

"Really?"

"I'm here for you, kid. That's what friends are for."

TWENTY-SIX

When we make it back to the house, Castle is standing in the far corner, talking to Winston.

Kenji freezes in the doorframe.

I'd forgotten Kenji hadn't had a chance to see Castle on his feet yet, and I feel a true ache as I look at him. I'm a terrible friend. All I do is dump my problems on him, never thinking to ask him about his own. He must have so much on his mind.

Kenji moves across the room in a daze, not stopping until he reaches Castle. He puts a hand on his shoulder. Castle turns around. The whole room stops to watch.

Castle smiles. Nods, just once.

Kenji pulls him into a fierce hug, holding on for only a few seconds before breaking away. The two stare at each other with some kind of silent recognition. Castle rests a hand on Kenji's arm.

Kenji grins.

And then he spins around and smiles at me, and I'm suddenly so happy, so relieved and thrilled and overjoyed that Kenji gets to sleep with a lighter heart tonight. I feel like I might burst from happiness.

The door slams open.

I turn around.

Adam steps inside.

My heart deflates.

Adam doesn't even look at me as he walks in. "James," he says, crossing the room. "Let's go, buddy. It's time for bed."

James nods and darts into his bedroom. Adam follows him in. The door closes behind them.

"He's home," Castle says. He looks relieved.

No one says anything for a second.

"All right, we should get ready for bed, too," Kenji says, looking around. He walks over to the corner and grabs a stack of blankets. Passes them out.

"Does everyone sleep on the floor?" I ask.

Kenji nods. "Yeah," he says. "Warner wasn't wrong. It really is like a slumber party."

I try to laugh.

Can't.

Everyone gets busy setting up blankets on the ground. Winston, Brendan, and Ian take over one side of the room, Alia and Lily the other. Castle sleeps on the couch.

Kenji points to the middle. "You and me go there."

"Romantic."

"You wish."

"Where does Adam sleep?" I ask, lowering my voice.

Kenji stops midway through tossing down a blanket. Looks up. "Kent's not coming back out," he says to me. "He sleeps with James. Poor kid has really bad nightmares every night."

"Oh," I say, surprised and ashamed of myself for not remembering this. "Of course." Of course he does. Kenji must know this firsthand, too. They all used to room together at Omega Point.

Winston hits a switch. The lights go out. There's a rustle of blankets. "If I hear any of you talk," Winston says, "I will personally send Brendan over to kick you in the face."

"I am not going to kick anyone in the face."

"Kick yourself in the face, Brendan."

"I don't even know why we're friends."

"Please shut up," Lily shouts from her corner.

"You heard the lady," Winston says. "Everyone shut up."

"You're the one talking, dumbass," Ian says.

"Brendan, kick him in the face, please."

"Shut up, mate, I am not kicking any—"

"*Good night*," Castle says.

Everyone stops breathing.

"Good night, sir," Kenji whispers.

I roll over so I'm face-to-face with Kenji. He grins at me in the dark. I grin back.

"Good night," I mouth.

He winks at me.

My eyes fall shut.

TWENTY-SEVEN

Adam is ignoring me.

He hasn't said a word about yesterday; doesn't betray even a hint of anger or frustration. He talks to everyone, laughs with James, helps get breakfast together. He also pretends I don't exist.

I tried saying good morning to him and he pretended not to hear me. Or maybe he really didn't hear me. Maybe he's managed to train his brain not to hear or see me at all anymore.

I feel like I'm being punched in the heart.

Repeatedly.

"So what do you guys do all day?" I ask, trying desperately to make conversation. We're all sitting on the floor, eating bowls of granola. We woke up late, ate breakfast late. No one has bothered to clean up the blankets yet, and Warner is supposed to be here in about an hour.

"Nothing," Ian says.

"We try not to die, mostly," Winston says.

"It's boring as hell," Lily says.

"Why?" Kenji asks. "You have something in mind?"

"Oh," I say. "No, I just . . ." I hesitate. "Well, Warner's going to be here in an hour, so I wasn't sure if—"

Something crashes in the kitchen. A bowl. In the sink. Silverware flying everywhere.

Adam steps into the living room.

His *eyes.*

"He's not coming back here." These, the first five words Adam says to me.

"But I already told him," I try to say. "He's going to—"

"This is *my* home," he says, eyes flashing. "I won't let him in here."

I'm staring at Adam, heart beating out of my chest. I never thought he'd be capable of looking at me like he hates me. Really, really hates me.

"Kent, man—," I hear Kenji say.

"NO."

"C'mon bro, it doesn't have to be like this—"

"If you want to see him so badly," Adam says to me, "you can get the hell out of my house. But he's not coming back here. Not ever."

I blink.

This isn't really happening.

"Where is she supposed to go?" Kenji says to him. "You want her to stand on the side of the street? So someone can report her and get her killed? Are you out of your mind?"

"I don't give a shit anymore," Adam says. "She can go do whatever the hell she wants." He turns to me again. "You want to be with him?" He points to the door. "Go. Drop dead."

Ice is eating away at my body.

I stumble to my feet. My legs are unsteady. I'm nodding and I don't know why but I can't seem to stop. I make my way to the door.

"Juliette—"

I spin around, even though it's Kenji calling my name, not Adam.

"Don't go anywhere," Kenji says to me. "Don't move. This is ridiculous."

This has spiraled out of control. This isn't just a fight anymore. There is pure, unadulterated hatred in Adam's eyes, and I'm so blindsided by the impossibility of it—so thrown off guard—that I don't know how to react. I never could've anticipated this—never could've imagined things could turn out this way.

The real Adam wouldn't kick me out of his house like this. He wouldn't talk to me like this. Not the Adam I know. The Adam I thought I knew.

"Kent," Kenji says again, "you need to calm down. There is nothing going on between her and Warner, okay? She's just trying to do what she thinks is right—"

"*Bullshit!*" Adam explodes. "That's bullshit, and you know it, and you're a jackass for denying it. She's been lying to me this whole damn time—"

"You guys aren't even together, man, you can't lay a claim on her—"

"We never broke up!" Adam shouts.

"Of course you did," Kenji snaps back. "Every single person at Point heard your melodramatic ass in the freaking tunnels. We all know you broke up. So stop fighting it."

"That didn't count as a breakup," Adam says, his voice rough. "We still loved each other—"

"Okay, you know what? Whatever. I don't care." Kenji waves his hands, rolls his eyes. "But we're in the middle of a *war* right now. For shit's sake, she was shot in the chest a couple days ago and almost died. Don't you think it's possible she's really trying to think of something bigger than just the two of you? Warner's crazy, but he can help—"

"She looks at that psycho like she's in *love* with him," Adam barks back. "You think I don't know what that look is? You think I wouldn't be able to tell? She used to look at *me* like that. I know her—I know her so well—"

"Maybe you don't."

"Stop defending her!"

"You don't even know what you're saying," Kenji tells him. "You're acting crazy—"

"I was happier," Adam says, "when I thought she was *dead*."

"You don't mean that. Don't say things like that, man. Once you say that kind of shit you can't take it back—"

"Oh, I mean it," Adam says. "I really, really mean it." He finally looks at me. Fists clenched. "Thinking you were dead," he says to me, "was so much better. It hurt so much less than this."

The walls are moving. I'm seeing spots, blinking at nothing.

This isn't really happening, I keep telling myself.

This is just a terrible nightmare, and when I wake up Adam will be gentle and kind and wonderful again. Because he isn't cruel like this. Not to me. Never to me.

"You, of all people," Adam says to me. He looks so disgusted. "I trusted you—told you things I never should've told you—and now you're going out of your way to throw it all back in my face. I can't believe you'd do this to me. That you'd fall for *him*. What the hell is wrong with you?" he demands, his voice rising in pitch. "How sick in the head do you have to be?"

I'm so afraid to speak.

So afraid to move my lips.

I'm so scared that if I move even an inch, my body will snap in half and everyone will see that my insides are made up of nothing but all the tears I'm swallowing back right now.

Adam shakes his head. Laughs a sad, twisted laugh. "You won't even deny it," he says. "Unbelievable."

"Leave her alone, Kent," Kenji says suddenly, his voice deathly sharp. "I'm serious."

"This is *none* of your business—"

"You're being a dick—"

"You think I give a shit what you think?" Adam turns on him. "This isn't your fight, Kenji. Just because she's too much of a coward to say anything doesn't mean you have to defend her—"

I feel like I've stepped outside of myself. Like my body has collapsed onto the floor and I'm looking on, watching as

Adam transforms into a completely different human being. Every word. Every insult he hurls at me seems to fracture my bones. Pretty soon I'll be nothing but blood and a beating heart.

"I'm leaving," Adam is saying. "I'm leaving, and when I come back, I want her gone."

Don't cry, I keep saying to myself.

Don't cry.

This isn't real.

"You and me," Adam is saying to me now, his voice so rough, so angry, "we're *done*. We're finished," he snaps. "I never want to see you again. Not anywhere in this world, and definitely not in my own goddamn house." He stares at me, chest heaving. "So get the hell out. Get out before I get back."

He stalks across the room. Grabs a coat. Yanks the door open.

The walls shake as he slams it shut.

TWENTY-EIGHT

I'm standing in the middle of the room, staring at nothing.

I'm suddenly freezing. My hands, I think, are shaking. Or maybe it's my bones. Maybe my bones are shaking. I move mechanically, so slowly, my mind still fuzzy. I'm vaguely aware that someone might be saying something to me, but I'm too focused on getting my coat because I'm so cold. It's so *cold* in here. I really need my jacket. And maybe my gloves. I can't stop shivering.

I pull my coat on. Shove my hands into the pockets. I feel like someone might be talking to me but I can't hear anything through the weird haze muting my senses. I clench my fists and my fingers fumble against a piece of plastic.

The pager. I'd almost forgotten.

I pull it out of my pocket. It's a tiny little thing; a thin, black rectangle with a button set flush against the length of it. I press it without thinking. I press it over and over and over again, because the action calms me. Soothes me, somehow. *Click click.* I like the repetitive motion. *Click. Click click.* I don't know what else to do.

Click.

Hands land on my shoulders.

I turn around. Castle is standing just behind me, his eyes

172

heavy with concern. "You're not going to leave," he says to me. "We'll work things out. It'll be all right."

"No." My tongue is dust. My teeth have crumbled away. "I have to go."

I can't stop pressing the button on this pager.

Click.

Click click.

"Come sit down," Castle is saying to me. "Adam is upset, but he'll be okay. I'm sure he didn't mean what he said."

"I'm pretty sure he did," Ian says.

Castle shoots him a sharp look.

"You can't leave," says Winston. "I thought we were going to kick some ass together. You promised."

"Yeah," Lily pipes up, trying to sound upbeat. But her eyes are wary, pulled together in fear or concern and I realize she's terrified for me.

Not *of* me.

For me.

It's the strangest sensation.

Click click click.

Click click.

"If you go," she's saying, trying to smile, "we'll have to live like this forever. And I don't want to live with a bunch of smelly guys for the rest of my life."

Click.

Click click.

"Don't go," James says. He looks so sad. So serious. "I'm sorry Adam was mean to you. But I don't want you to die," he says. "And I don't wish you were dead. I swear I don't."

James. Sweet James. His eyes break my heart.

"I can't stay." My voice sounds strange to me. Broken. "He really meant what he said—"

"We'll be a sad, sorry lot if you leave." Brendan cuts me off. "And I have to agree with Lily. I don't want to live like this for much longer."

"But how—"

The front door flies open.

"JULIETTE—*Juliette*—"

I spin around.

Warner is standing there, face flushed, chest rising and falling, staring at me like I might be a ghost. He strides across the room before I have a chance to say a word and cups my face in his hands, his eyes searching me. "Are you okay?" he's saying. "God—are you okay? What happened? Are you all right?"

He's here.

He's here and all I want to do is fall apart but I don't.

I won't.

"Thank you," I manage to say to him. "Thank you for coming—"

He wraps me up in his arms, not caring about the eight sets of eyes watching us. He just holds me, one arm tight around my waist, the other held to the back of my head. My face is buried in his chest and the warmth of him is so familiar to me now. Oddly comforting. He runs his hand up and down my back, tilts his head toward mine. "What's wrong, love?" he whispers. "What happened? Please tell me—"

I blink.

"Do you want me to take you back?"

I don't answer.

I don't know what I want or need to do anymore. Everyone is telling me to stay, but this isn't their home. This is Adam's home, and it's so clear he hates me now. But I also don't want to leave my friends. I don't want to leave Kenji.

"Do you want *me* to leave?" Warner asks.

"No," I say too quickly. "No."

Warner leans back, just a little. "Tell me what you want," he says desperately. "Tell me what to do," he says, "and I'll do it."

"This is, by far, the craziest shit I have ever seen," Kenji says. "I really never would've believed it. Not in a million years."

"It's like a soap opera." Ian nods. "But with worse acting."

"I think it's kind of sweet," Winston says.

I jerk back, half spinning around. Everyone is staring at us. Winston is the only one smiling.

"What's going on?" Warner asks them. "Why does she look like she's about to cry?"

No one answers.

"Where's Kent?" Warner asks, eyes narrowing as he reads their faces. "What did he do to her?"

"He's out," Lily says. "He left a little bit ago."

Warner's eyes darken as he processes the information.

He turns to me. "Please tell me you don't want to stay here anymore."

I drop my head into my hands. "Everyone wants to help—to fight—except for Adam. But they can't leave. And I don't want to leave them behind."

Warner sighs. Closes his eyes. "Then stay," he says gently. "If that's what you want. Stay here. I can always meet you."

"I can't," I tell him. "I have to go. I'm not allowed to come back here again."

"What?" Anger. In and out of his eyes. "What do you mean you're not *allowed*?"

"Adam doesn't want me to stay here anymore. I have to be gone before he gets back."

Warner's jaw tightens. He stares at me for what feels like a century. I can almost *see* him thinking—his mind working at an impossible rate—to find a solution. "Okay," he finally says. "Okay." He exhales. "Kishimoto," he says all at once, never breaking eye contact with me.

"Present, sir."

Warner tries not to roll his eyes as he turns toward Kenji. "I will set up your group in my private training quarters on base. I will require a day to work out the details, but I will make sure you are granted easy access and clearance to enter the grounds upon arrival. You will make yourself and your team invisible and follow my lead. You are free to stay in these quarters until we are ready to proceed with the first stage of our plan." A pause. "Will this arrangement work for you?"

176

Kenji actually looks disgusted. "Hell no."

"Why not?"

"You're going to lock us up in your 'private training quarters'?" Kenji says, making air quotes with his fingers. "Why don't you just say you're going to put us in a cage and kill us slowly? You think I'm a moron? What reason would I have to believe that kind of shit?"

"I will make sure you are fed well and regularly," Warner says by way of response. "Your accommodations will be simple, but they will not be simpler than this," he says, gesturing to the room. "The arrangement will provide us ample opportunity to meet and structure our next moves. You must know that you're putting everyone at risk by staying on unregulated territory. You and your friends will be safer with me."

"Why would you do that, though?" Ian asks. "Why would you want to help us and feed us and keep us alive? That doesn't make any sense—"

"It doesn't need to make sense."

"Of course it does," Lily counters. Her eyes are hard, angry. "We're not going to walk onto a military base just to get ourselves killed," she snaps. "This could be some sick trick."

"Fine," Warner says.

"Fine, what?" Lily asks.

"Don't come."

"Oh." Lily blinks.

Warner turns to Kenji. "You are officially refusing my offer, then?"

177

"Yeah, no thanks," Kenji says.

Warner nods. Looks to me. "Should we get going?"

"But—no—" I'm panicking now, looking from Warner to Kenji and back to Warner again. "I can't just *leave*—I can't just never see them again—"

I turn to Kenji.

"You're just going to stay here?" I ask. "And I'll never see you again?"

"You can stay here with us." Kenji crosses his arms against his chest. "You don't have to go."

"You know I can't stay," I tell him, angry and hurt. "You know Adam meant what he said—he'll go crazy if he comes back and I'm still here—"

"So you're just going to leave, then?" Kenji says sharply. "You're going to walk away from all of us"—he gestures to everyone—"just because Adam decided to be a douchebag? You're trading all of us in for Warner?"

"Kenji—I'm not—I have nowhere else to live! What am I supposed to—"

"*Stay.*"

"Adam will throw me out—"

"No he won't," Kenji says. "We won't let him."

"I won't force myself on him. I won't beg him. Let me at least leave with a shred of dignity—"

Kenji throws his arms in the air in frustration. "This is *bullshit!*"

"Come with me," I say to him. "Please—I want us to stay together—"

"We can't," he says. "We can't risk that, J. I don't know what's going on between you two," he says, gesturing between me and Warner. "Maybe he really is different with you, I don't know, whatever—but I can't put all of our lives at risk based on emotions and an assumption. Maybe he cares about *you*," Kenji says, "but he doesn't give a shit about the rest of us." He looks at Warner. "Do you?"

"Do I what?" Warner asks.

"Do you care about any of us? About our survival—our well-being?"

"No."

Kenji almost laughs. "Well at least you're honest."

"My offer, however, still stands. And you're an idiot to refuse," Warner says. "You'll all die out here, and you know that better than I do."

"We'll take our chances."

"No," I gasp. "Kenji—"

"It'll be all right," he says to me. His forehead is pinched, his eyes heavy. "I'm sure we'll find a way to see each other one day. Do what you need to do."

"No," I'm trying to say. Trying to breathe. My lungs are swelling up, my heart racing so fast I can hear it pounding in my ears. I'm feeling hot and cold and too hot, too cold, and all I can think is *no*, it wasn't supposed to happen like this, it wasn't all supposed to fall apart, not again not again—

Warner grabs my arms. "Please," he's saying, his voice urgent, panicked. "Please don't do that, love, I need you not to do that—"

"Dammit, Kenji!" I explode, breaking away from Warner. "Please, for the love of God, don't be an idiot. You have to come with me—I need you—"

"I need some kind of guarantee, J"—Kenji is pacing, hands in his hair—"I can't just trust that everything is going to be all right—"

I turn on Warner, chest heaving, fists clenched. "Give them what they want. I don't care what it is," I say to him. "Please, you have to negotiate. You have to make this work. I need him. I need my friends."

Warner looks at me for a long time.

"Please," I whisper.

He looks away. Looks back at me.

He finally meets Kenji's eyes. Sighs. "What do you want?"

"I want a hot bath," I hear Winston say.

And then he giggles.

He actually giggles.

"Two of my men are ill and injured," Kenji says, immediately switching gears. His voice is clipped, sharp. Unfeeling. "They need medicine and medical attention. We don't want to be monitored, we don't want a curfew, and we want to be able to eat more than the Automat food. We want protein. Fruits. Vegetables. Real meals. We want regular access to showers. We'll need new clothes. And we want to remain armed at all times."

Warner is standing so still beside me I can hardly hear him breathing anymore. My head is pounding so hard and my heart is still racing in my chest, but I've calmed down enough that I'm able to breathe a little easier now.

Warner glances down at me.

He holds my gaze for just a moment before he closes his eyes. Exhales a sharp breath. Looks up.

"Fine," he says.

Kenji is staring at him. "Wait—*what?*"

"I will be back tomorrow at fourteen hundred hours to guide you to your new quarters."

"Holy shit." Winston is bouncing on the couch. "Holy shit holy shit holy *shit.*"

"Do you have your things?" Warner asks me.

I nod.

"Good," he says. "Let's go."

TWENTY-NINE

Warner is holding my hand.

I only have enough energy to focus on this single, strange fact as he leads me down the stairs and into the parking garage. He opens the door of the tank and helps me in before closing it behind me.

He climbs into the other side.

Turns on the engine.

We're already on the road and I've blinked only six times since we left Adam's house.

I still can't believe what just happened. I can't believe we're all going to be working together. I can't believe I told Warner what to do and he *listened to me.*

I turn to look at him. It's strange: I've never felt so safe or so relieved to be beside him. I never thought I could feel this way with him.

"Thank you," I whisper, grateful and guilty, somehow, about everything that's happened. About leaving Adam behind. I realize now that I've made the kind of choice I can't undo. My heart is still breaking. "Really," I say again. "Thank you so much. For coming to get me. I appreciate—"

"Please," he says. "I'm begging you to stop."

I still.

"I can't stomach your pain," he says. "I can feel it so strongly and it's making me crazy—*please*," he says to me. "Don't be sad. Or hurt. Or guilty. You've done nothing wrong."

"I'm sorry—"

"Don't be sorry, either," he says. "God, the only reason I'm not going to kill Kent for this is because I know it would only upset you more."

"You're right," I say after a moment. "But it's not just him."

"What?" he asks. "What do you mean?"

"I don't want you to kill anyone at all," I say. "Not just Adam."

Warner laughs a sharp, strange laugh. He looks almost relieved. "Do you have any other stipulations?"

"Not really."

"You don't want to fix me, then? You don't have a long list of things I need to work on?"

"No." I stare out the window. The view is so bleak. So cold. Covered in ice and snow. "There's nothing wrong with you that isn't already wrong with me," I say quietly. "And if I were smart I'd first figure out how to fix myself."

We're both silent awhile. The tension is so thick in this small space.

"Aaron?" I say, still watching the scenery fly by.

I hear the small hitch in his breath. The hesitation. It's the first time I've used his first name so casually.

"Yes?" he says.

"I want you to know," I tell him, "that I don't think you're crazy."

"What?" He startles.

"I don't think you're crazy." The world is blurring away as I watch it through the window. "And I don't think you're a psychopath. I also don't think you're a sick, twisted monster. I don't think you're a heartless murderer, and I don't think you deserve to die, and I don't think you're pathetic. Or stupid. Or a coward. I don't think you're any of the things people have said about you."

I turn to look at him.

Warner is staring out the windshield.

"You don't?" His voice is so soft and so scared I can scarcely hear it.

"No," I say. "I don't. And I just thought you should know. I'm not trying to fix you; I don't think you need to be fixed. I'm not trying to turn you into someone else. I only want you to be who you really are. Because I think I know the real you. I think I've seen him."

Warner says nothing, his chest rising and falling.

"I don't care what anyone else says about you," I tell him. "I think you're a good person."

Warner is blinking fast now. I can hear him breathing.

In and out.

Unevenly.

He says nothing.

"Do you . . . believe me?" I ask after a moment. "Can you sense that I'm telling the truth? That I really mean it?"

Warner's hands are clenched around the steering wheel. His knuckles are white.

He nods.

Just once.

THIRTY

Warner still hasn't said a single word to me.

We're in his room now, courtesy of Delalieu, who Warner was quick to dismiss. It feels strange and familiar to be back here, in this room that I've found both fear and comfort in.

Now it feels right to me.

This is Warner's room. And Warner, to me, is no longer something to be afraid of.

These past few months have transformed him in my eyes, and these past two days have been full of revelations that I'm still recovering from. I can't deny that he seems different to me now.

I feel like I understand him in a way I never did before.

He's like a terrified, tortured animal. A creature who spent his whole life being beaten, abused, and caged away. He was forced into a life he never asked for, and was never given an opportunity to choose anything else. And though he's been given all the tools to kill a person, he's too emotionally tortured to be able to use those skills against his own father—the very man who taught him to be a murderer. Because somehow, in some strange, inexplicable way, he still wants his father to love him.

And I understand that.

I really, really do.

"What happened?" Warner finally says to me.

I'm sitting on his bed; he's standing by the door, staring at the wall.

"What do you mean?"

"With Kent," he says. "Earlier. What did he say to you?"

"Oh." I flush. Embarrassed. "He kicked me out of his house."

"But why?"

"He was mad," I explain. "That I was defending you. That I'd invited you to come back at all."

"Oh."

I can almost hear our hearts beat in the silence between us.

"You were defending me," Warner finally says.

"Yes."

He says nothing.

I say nothing.

"So he told you to leave," Warner says, "because you were defending me."

"Yes."

"Is that all?"

My heart is racing. I'm suddenly nervous. "No."

"There were other things?"

"Yes."

Warner blinks at the wall. Unmoving. "Really."

I nod.

He says nothing.

"He was upset," I whisper, "because I didn't agree that you were crazy. And he was accusing me"—I hesitate—"of being in love with you."

Warner exhales sharply. Touches a hand to the doorframe.

My heart is pounding so hard.

Warner's eyes are glued to the wall. "And you told him he was an idiot."

Breathe. "No."

Warner turns, just halfway. I see his profile, the unsteady rise and fall of his chest. He's staring directly at the door now, and it's clear it's costing him a great deal of effort to speak. "Then you told him he was crazy. You told him he had to be out of his mind to say something like that."

"No."

"No," he echoes.

I try not to move.

Warner takes a hard, shaky breath. "Then what did you say to him?"

Seven seconds die between us.

"Nothing," I whisper.

Warner stills.

I don't breathe.

No one speaks for what feels like forever.

"Of course," Warner finally says. He looks pale, unsteady. "You said nothing. Of course."

"Aaron—" I get to my feet.

"There are a lot of things I have to do before tomorrow," he says. "Especially if your friends will be joining us on base." His hands tremble in the second it takes him to reach for the door. "Forgive me," he says. "But I have to go."

THIRTY-ONE

I decide to take a bath.

I've never taken a bath before.

I poke around the bathroom as the tub fills with hot water, and discover stacks and stacks of scented soaps. All different kinds. All different sizes. Each bar of soap has been wrapped in a thick piece of parchment, and tied with twine. There are small labels affixed to each package to distinguish one scent from another.

I pick up one of the bundles.

HONEYSUCKLE

I clutch the soap and can't help but think how different it was to take a shower at Omega Point. We had nothing so fancy as this. Our soaps were harsh and smelled strange and were fairly ineffective. Kenji used to bring them into our training sessions and break off pieces to pelt at me when I wasn't focusing.

The memory makes me inexplicably emotional.

My heart swells as I remember that my friends will be here tomorrow. This is really going to happen, I think. We'll be unstoppable, all of us together. I can't wait.

I look more closely at the label.

Top notes of jasmine and nuances of grape. Mild notes of lilac,

honeysuckle, rose, and cinnamon. Orange-flower and powder base
notes complete the fragrance.

Sounds amazing.

I steal one of Warner's soaps.

I'm freshly scrubbed and wearing a clean set of clothes.

I keep sniffing my skin, pleasantly surprised by how nice it is to smell like a flower. I've never smelled like anything before. I keep running my fingers down my arms, wondering at how much of a difference a good bar of soap can make. I've never felt so clean in my life. I didn't realize soap could lather like that or react so well to my body. The only soap I've ever used before always dried up my skin and left me feeling uncomfortable for a few hours. But this is weird. Wonderful. I feel soft and smooth and so refreshed.

I also have absolutely nothing to do.

I sit down on Warner's bed, pull my feet up underneath me. Stare at his office door.

I'm so tempted to see if the door is unlocked.

My conscience, however, overrules me.

I sink into the pillows with a sigh. Kick up the blankets and snuggle beneath them.

Close my eyes.

My mind is instantly flooded with images of Adam's angry face, his shaking fists, his hurtful words. I try to push the memories away and I can't.

My eyes fly open.

I wonder if I'll ever see him and James again.

Maybe this is what Adam wanted. He can go back to his life with his little brother now. He won't have to worry about sharing his rations with eight other people and he'll be able to survive much longer this way.

But then what? I can't help but think.

He'll be all alone. With no food. No friends. No income.

It breaks my heart to imagine it. To think of him struggling to find a way to live, to provide for his brother. Because even though Adam seems to hate me now, I don't think I could ever reciprocate those feelings.

I don't even know that I understand what just happened between us.

It seems impossible that Adam and I could fissure and break apart so abruptly. I care so deeply for him. He was there for me when no one else was; he gave me hope when I needed it most; he loved me when no one else would. He's not anyone I want to erase from my life.

I want him around. I want my friend back.

But I'm realizing now that Kenji was right.

Adam was the first and only person who'd ever shown me compassion. The first, and, at the time, only person who was able to touch me. I was caught up in the impossibility of it, so convinced fate had brought us together. His tattoo was a perfect snapshot of my dreams.

I thought it was about us. About my escape. About our happily-ever-after.

And it was.

And it wasn't.

I want to laugh at my own blindness.

It linked us, I realize. That tattoo. It did bring me and Adam together, but not because we were destined for one another. Not because he was my flight to freedom. But because we have one major connection between the two of us. One kind of hope neither one of us was able to see.

Warner.

A white bird with streaks of gold like a crown atop its head.

A fair-skinned boy with gold hair, the leader of Sector 45.

It was always him. All along.

The link.

Warner, Adam's brother, my captor and now comrade. He inadvertently brought me and Adam together. And being with Adam gave me a new kind of strength. I was still scared and still very broken and Adam cared for me, giving me a reason to stand up for myself when I was too weak to realize I had always been reason enough. It was affection and a desperate desire for physical connection. Two things I'd been so deprived of, and so wholly unfamiliar with. I had nothing to compare these new experiences to.

Of course I thought I was in love.

But while I don't know much, I do know that if Adam really loved me, he wouldn't have treated me the way he did today. He wouldn't prefer that I was dead.

I know this, because I've seen proof of his opposite.

Because I *was* dying.

And Warner could've let me die. He was angry and

hurt and had every reason to be bitter. I'd just ripped his heart out; I'd let him believe something would come of our relationship. I let him confess the depth of his feelings to me; I let him touch me in ways even Adam hadn't. I didn't ask him to stop.

Every inch of me was saying yes.

And then I took it all back. Because I was scared, and confused, and conflicted. Because of Adam.

Warner told me he loved me, and in return I insulted him and lied to him and yelled at him and pushed him away. And when he had the chance to stand back and watch me die, he didn't.

He found a way to save my life.

With no demands. No expectations. Believing full well that I was in love with someone else, and that saving my life meant making me whole again only to give me back to another guy.

And right now, I can't say I know what Adam would do if I were dying in front of him. I'm not sure if he would save my life. And that uncertainty alone makes me certain that something wasn't right between us. Something wasn't real.

Maybe we both fell in love with the illusion of something more.

THIRTY-TWO

My eyes fly open.

It's pitch-black. Quiet. I sit up too fast.

I must've fallen asleep. I have no idea what time it is, but a quick glance around the room tells me Warner isn't here.

I slip out of bed. I'm still wearing socks and I'm suddenly grateful; I have to wrap my arms around myself, shivering as the cold winter air creeps through the thin material of my T-shirt. My hair is still slightly damp from the bath.

Warner's office door is cracked open.

There's a sliver of light peeking through the opening, and it makes me wonder if he really forgot to close it, or if maybe he's only just walked in. Maybe he's not in there at all. But my curiosity beats out my conscience this time.

I want to know where he works and what his desk looks like; I want to know if he's messy or organized or if he keeps personal items around. I wonder if he has any pictures of himself as a kid.

Or of his mother.

I tiptoe forward, butterflies stirring awake in my stomach. I shouldn't be nervous, I tell myself. I'm not doing anything illegal. I'm just going to see if he's in there, and if he's not, I'll leave. I'm only going to walk in for a second. I'm not going to search through any of his things.

I'm not.

I hesitate outside his door. It's so quiet that I'm almost certain my heart is beating loud and hard enough for him to hear. I don't know why I'm so scared.

I knock twice against the door as I nudge it open.

"Aaron, are you—"

Something crashes to the floor.

I push the door open and rush inside, jerking to a stop just as I cross the threshold. Stunned.

His office is enormous.

It's the size of his entire bedroom and closet combined. Bigger. There's so much space in here—room enough to house the huge boardroom table and the six chairs stationed on either side of it. There's a couch and a few side tables set off in the corner, and one wall is made up of nothing but bookshelves. Loaded with books. Bursting with books. Old books and new books and books with spines falling off.

Everything in here is made of dark wood.

Wood so brown it looks black. Clean, straight lines, simple cuts. Nothing is ornate or bulky. No leather. No high-backed chairs or overly detailed woodwork. Minimal.

The boardroom table is stacked with file folders and papers and binders and notebooks. The floor is covered in a thick, plush Oriental rug, similar to the one in his closet. And at the far end of the room is his desk.

Warner is staring at me in shock.

He's wearing nothing but his slacks and a pair of socks,

his shirt and belt discarded. He's standing in front of his desk, clinging to something in his hands—something I can't quite see.

"What are you doing here?" he says.

"The door was open." What a stupid answer.

He stares at me.

"What time is it?" I ask.

"One thirty in the morning," he says automatically.

"Oh."

"You should go back to bed." I don't know why he looks so nervous. Why his eyes keep darting from me to the door.

"I'm not tired anymore."

"Oh." He fumbles with what I now realize is a small jar in his hands. Sets it on the desk behind him without turning around.

He's been so off today, I think. Unlike himself. He's usually so composed, so self-assured. But recently he's been so shaky around me. The inconsistency is unnerving.

"What are you doing?" I ask.

There's about ten feet between us, and neither one of us is making any effort to bridge the gap. We're talking like we don't know each other, like we're strangers who've just found themselves in a compromising situation. Which is ridiculous.

I begin to cross the room, to make my way over to him.

He freezes.

I stop.

"Is everything okay?"

"Yes," he says too quickly.

"What's that?" I ask, pointing to the little plastic jar.

"You should go back to sleep, love. You're probably more tired than you think—"

I walk right up to him, reach around and grab the jar before he can do much to stop me.

"That is a violation of privacy," he says sharply, sounding more like himself. "Give that back to me—"

"Medicine?" I ask, surprised. I turn the little jar around in my hands, reading the label. I look up at him. Finally understanding. "This is for scars."

He runs a hand through his hair. Looks toward the wall. "Yes," he says. "Now please give it back to me."

"Do you need help?" I ask.

He stills. "What?"

"This is for your back, isn't it?"

He runs a hand across his mouth, down his chin. "You won't allow me to walk away from this with even an ounce of self-respect, will you?"

"I didn't know you cared about your scars," I say to him. I take a step forward.

He takes a step back.

"I don't."

"Then why this?" I hold up the jar. "Where did you even get this from?"

"It's nothing—it's just—" He shakes his head. "Delalieu found it for me. It's ridiculous," he says. "I feel ridiculous."

"Because you can't reach your own back?"

198

He stares at me then. Sighs.

"Turn around," I tell him.

"No."

"You're being weird about nothing. I've already seen your scars."

"That doesn't mean you need to see them again."

I can't help but smile a little.

"What?" he demands. "What's so funny?"

"You just don't seem like the kind of person who would be self-conscious about something like this."

"I'm not."

"Obviously."

"Please," he says, "just go back to bed."

"I'm wide-awake."

"That's not my problem."

"Turn around," I tell him again.

He narrows his eyes at me.

"Why are you even using this stuff?" I ask him for the second time. "You don't need it. Don't use it if it makes you uncomfortable."

He's quiet a moment. "You don't think I need it?"

"Of course not. Why . . . ? Are you in pain? Do your scars hurt?"

"Sometimes," he says quietly. "Not as much as they used to. I actually can't feel much of anything on my back anymore."

Something cold and sharp hits me in the stomach. "Really?"

He nods.

"Will you tell me where they came from?" I whisper, unable to meet his eyes.

He's silent for so long I'm finally forced to look up.

His eyes are dead of emotion, his face set to neutral. He clears his throat. "They were my birthday presents," he says. "Every year from the time I was five. Until I turned eighteen," he says. "He didn't come back for my nineteenth birthday."

I'm frozen in horror.

"Right." Warner looks into his hands. "So—"

"He *cut* you?" My voice is so hoarse.

"Whip."

"Oh my God," I gasp, covering my mouth. I have to look toward the wall to pull myself together. I blink several times, struggle to swallow back the pain and rage building inside of me. "I'm so sorry," I choke out. "Aaron. I'm so sorry."

"I don't want you to be repulsed by me," he says quietly.

I spin around, stunned. Mildly horrified. "You're not serious."

His eyes say that he is.

"Have you never looked in a mirror?" I ask, angry now.

"Excuse me?"

"You're perfect," I tell him, so overcome I forget myself. "All of you. Your entire body. Proportionally. Symmetrically. You're absurdly, mathematically perfect. It doesn't even make sense that a person could look like you," I say, shaking my head. "I can't believe you would ever say something like that—"

200

"Juliette, please. Don't talk to me like that."

"What? Why?"

"Because it's *cruel*," he says, losing his composure. "It's cruel and it's heartless and you don't even realize—"

"Aaron—"

"I take it back," he says. "I don't want you to call me Aaron anymore—"

"Aaron," I say again, more firmly this time. "Please—you can't really think you repulse me? You can't really think I would care—that I would be put off by your scars—"

"I don't know," he says. He's pacing in front of his desk, his eyes fixed on the ground.

"I thought you could sense feelings," I say to him. "I thought mine would be so obvious to you."

"I can't always think clearly," he says, frustrated, rubbing his face, his forehead. "Especially when my emotions are involved. I can't always be objective—and sometimes I make assumptions," he says, "that aren't true—and I don't—I just don't trust my own judgment anymore. Because I've done that," he says, "and it's backfired. So terribly."

He looks up, finally. Looks me in the eye.

"You're right," I whisper.

He looks away.

"You've made a lot of mistakes," I say to him. "You did everything wrong."

He runs a hand down the length of his face.

"But it's not too late to fix things—you can make it right—"

"Please—"

"It's not too late—"

"Stop saying that to me!" he explodes. "You don't know me—you don't know what I've done or what I'd need to do to make things right—"

"Don't you understand? It doesn't matter—you can choose to be different now—"

"I thought you weren't going to try and change me!"

"I'm not trying to change you," I say, lowering my voice. "I'm just trying to get you to understand that your life isn't over. You don't have to be who you've been. You can make different choices now. You can be *happy*—"

"*Juliette.*" One sharp word. His green eyes so intense.

I stop.

I glance at his trembling hands; he clenches them into fists.

"Go," he says quietly. "I don't want you to be here right now."

"Then why did you bring me back with you?" I ask, angry. "If you don't even want to see me—"

"Why don't you understand?" He looks up at me and his eyes are so full of pain and devastation it actually takes my breath away.

My hands are shaking. "Understand what—?"

"I *love* you."

He breaks.

His voice. His back. His knees. His face.

He breaks.

He has to hold on to the side of his desk. He can't meet

my eyes. "I love you," he says, his words harsh and soft all at once. "I love you and it isn't enough. I thought it would be enough and I was wrong. I thought I could fight for you and I was wrong. Because I can't. I can't even face you anymore—"

"Aaron—"

"Tell me it isn't true," he says. "Tell me I'm wrong. Tell me I'm blind. Tell me you love me."

My heart won't stop screaming as it breaks in half.

I can't lie to him.

"I don't—I don't know how to understand what I feel," I try to explain.

"Please," he whispers. "Please just go—"

"Aaron, please understand—I thought I knew what love was before and I was wrong—I don't want to make that mistake again—"

"Please"—he's begging now—"for the love of God, Juliette, I have lost my *dignity*—"

"Okay." I nod. "Okay. I'm sorry. Okay."

I back away.

I turn around.

And I don't look back.

THIRTY-THREE

"I have to leave in seven minutes."

Warner and I are both fully dressed, talking to each other like perfect acquaintances; like last night never happened. Delalieu brought us breakfast and we ate quietly in separate rooms. No talk of him or me or us or what might've been or what might be.

There is no us.

There's the absence of Adam, and there's fighting against The Reestablishment. That's it.

I get it now.

"I'd bring you with me," he's saying, "but I think it'll be hard to disguise you on this trip. If you want, you can wait in the training rooms—I'll bring the group of them straight there. You can say hello as soon as they arrive." He finally looks at me. "Is that okay?"

I nod.

"Very good," he says. "I'll show you how to get there."

He leads me back into his office, and into one of the far corners by the couch. There's an exit in here I didn't see last night. Warner hits a button on the wall. The doors slide open.

It's an elevator.

We walk in and he hits the button for the ground floor. The doors close and we start moving.

I glance up at him. "I never knew you had an elevator in your room."

"I needed private access to my training facilities."

"You keep saying that," I tell him. *"Training facilities.* What's a training facility?"

The elevator stops.

The doors slide open.

He holds them open for me. "This."

I've never seen so many machines in my life.

Running machines and leg machines and machines that work your arms, your shoulders, your abdominals. There are even machines that look like bikes. I don't know what any of them are called. I know one of these things is a bench press. I also know what dumbbells look like, and there are racks and racks of those, in all different sizes. Weights, I think. Free weights. There are also bars attached to the ceiling in some places, but I can't imagine what those are for. There are tons of things around this room, actually, that look entirely foreign to me.

And each wall is used for something different.

One wall seems to be made of stone. Or rock. There are little grooves in it that are accented by what look like pieces of plastic in different colors. Another wall is covered in guns. Hundreds of guns resting on pegs that keep them in place. They're pristine. Gleaming as if they've just been cleaned. There's a door in that same wall; I wonder where it goes. The third wall is covered in the same black, spongelike material that covers the floors. It looks like it might be soft and springy. And the final wall is the one we've just walked through. It houses the elevator, and one other door, and nothing else.

The dimensions are enormous. This space is at least two or three times the size of Warner's bedroom, his closet, and his office put together. It doesn't seem possible that all of this is for one person.

"This is amazing," I say, turning to face him. "You use all of this?"

He nods. "I'm usually in here at least two or three times a day," he says. "I got off track when I was injured," he says, "but in general, yes." He steps forward, touches the spongy black wall. "This has been my life for as long as I've known it. Training," he says. "I've been training forever. And this is where we're going to start with you, too."

"Me?"

He nods.

"But I don't need to train," I tell him. "Not like this."

He tries to meet my eyes and can't.

"I have to go," he says. "If you get bored in here, take the elevator back up. This elevator can only access two levels, so you can't get lost." He buttons his blazer. "I'll return as soon as I can."

"Okay."

I expect him to leave, but he doesn't. "You'll still be here," he finally says, "when I return."

It's not exactly a question.

I nod anyway.

"It doesn't seem possible," he says, so quietly, "that you're not trying to run away."

I say nothing.

He exhales a hard breath. Pivots on one heel. And leaves.

THIRTY-FOUR

I'm sitting on one of the benches, toying with five-pound dumbbells, when I hear his voice.

"Holy shit," he's saying. "This place is legit."

I jump up, nearly dropping the weights on my foot. Kenji and Winston and Castle and Brendan and Ian and Alia and Lily are all walking through the extra door in the gun wall.

Kenji's face lights up when he sees me.

I run forward and he catches me in his arms, hugs me tight before breaking away. "Well, I'll be damned," Kenji says. "He didn't kill you. That's a really good sign."

I shove him a little. Suppress a grin.

I quickly say hi to everyone. I'm practically bouncing I'm so excited to have them here. But they're all looking around in shock. Like they really thought Warner was leading them into a trap.

"There's a locker room through here," Warner is telling them. He points to the door beside the elevator. "There are plenty of showers and bathroom stalls and anything else you might need to keep from smelling like an animal. Towels, soap, laundry machines. All through here."

I'm so focused on Warner I almost don't notice Delalieu standing in the corner.

I stifle a gasp.

He's standing quietly, hands clasped behind his back, watching closely as everyone listens to Warner talk. And not for the first time, I wonder who he really is. Why Warner seems to trust him so much.

"Your meals will be delivered to you three times a day," Warner is saying. "If you don't eat, or if you miss a meal and find yourself hungry, feel free to shed your tears in the shower. And then learn to set a schedule. Don't bring your complaints to me.

"You already have your own weapons," he goes on, "but, as you can see, this room is also fully stocked and—"

"*Sweet*," Ian says. He looks a little too excited as he heads toward a set of rifles.

"If you touch any of my guns, I will break both of your hands," Warner says to him.

Ian freezes in place.

"This wall is off-limits to you. All of you," he says, looking around the room. "Everything else is available for your use. Do not damage any of my equipment. Leave things the way you found them. And if you do not shower on a regular basis, do not come within ten feet of me."

Kenji snorts.

"I have other work to attend to," Warner says. "I will return at nineteen hundred hours, at which time we can reconvene and begin our discussions. In the interim, take advantage of the opportunity to get situated. You may use the extra mats in the corner to sleep on. I hope for your sake you brought your own blankets."

Alia's bag slips out of her hands and thuds onto the floor. Everyone spins in her direction. She goes scarlet.

"Are there any questions?" Warner asks.

"Yeah," Kenji says. "Where's the medicine?"

Warner nods to Delalieu, who's still standing in the corner. "Give my lieutenant a detailed account of any injuries and illnesses. He will procure the necessary treatments."

Kenji nods, and means it. He actually looks grateful. "Thank you," he says.

Warner holds Kenji's gaze for just a moment. "You're welcome."

Kenji raises his eyebrows.

Even I'm surprised.

Warner looks at me then. He looks at me for just a split second before looking away. And then, without a word, he hits the button for the elevator.

Steps inside.

I watch the doors close behind him.

THIRTY-FIVE

Kenji is staring at me, concerned. "What the hell was that?"

Winston and Ian are looking at me too, making no effort to hide their confusion. Lily is unpacking her things. Castle is watching me closely. Brendan and Alia are deep in conversation.

"What do you mean?" I ask. I'm trying to be nonchalant, but I think my ears have gone pink.

Kenji clasps one hand behind his neck. Shrugs. "You two get into a fight or something?"

"No," I say too quickly.

"Uh-huh." Kenji cocks his head at me.

"How's Adam?" I ask, hoping to change the subject.

Kenji blows out a long breath; looks away; rubs at his eyes just before dropping his bag on the floor. He leans back against the wall. "I'm not gonna lie to you, J," he says, lowering his voice. "This crap with Kent is really stressing me out. Your drama is making things messy. He didn't make it easy for us to leave."

"What? But he said he didn't want to fight back anymore—"

"Yeah, well." Kenji nods. "Apparently that doesn't mean he wants to lose all his friends at once."

211

I shake my head. "He's not being fair."

"I know," Kenji says. Sighs again. "Anyway, it's good to see you, princess, but I'm tired as hell. And hungry. Grumpy. You know." He makes a haphazard motion with his hand. Slumps to the floor.

He's not telling me something.

"What's wrong?" I sit down across from him and lower my voice.

He looks up, meets my eyes.

"I miss James, okay? I miss that kid." Kenji sounds so tired. I can actually see the exhaustion in his eyes. "I didn't want to leave him behind."

My heart sinks fast.

Of course.

James.

"I'm so sorry. I wish there'd been a way we could've brought him with us."

Kenji flicks an imaginary piece of lint off his shirt. "It's probably safer for him where he is," he says, but it's obvious he doesn't believe a word of it. "I just wish Kent would stop being such a dick."

I cringe.

"This could all be amazing if he would just get his shit together," Kenji says. "But no, he has to go and get all weird and crazy and dramatic." He blows out a breath. "He's so freaking emotional," Kenji says suddenly. "Everything is such a big deal to him. He can't just let things go. He can't just be cool and move on with his life. I just . . . I don't know. Whatever. I just wish James were here. I miss him."

"I'm sorry," I say again.

Kenji makes a weird face. Waves his hand at nothing. "It's fine. I'll be fine."

I look up and find that everyone else has dispersed.

Castle, Ian, Alia, and Lily are heading to the locker room, while Winston and Brendan wander around the facility. They're touching the rock wall right now, having a conversation I can't hear.

I scoot closer to Kenji. Prop my head in my hands.

"So," he says. "I don't see you for twenty-four hours and you and Warner go from let's-hug-in-super-dramatic-fashion to let-me-give-you-an-ice-cold-shoulder, huh?" Kenji is tracing shapes into the mats underneath us. "Must be an interesting story there."

"I doubt it."

"You're seriously not going to tell me what happened?" He looks up, offended. "I tell you everything."

"Sure you don't."

"Don't be fresh."

"What's really going on, Kenji?" I study his face, his weak attempt at humor. "You seem different today. Off."

"Nothing," he mumbles. "I told you. I just didn't want to leave James."

"But that's not all, is it?"

He says nothing.

I look into my lap. "You can tell me anything, you know. You've always been there for me and I'll always be here if you need to talk, too."

Kenji rolls his eyes. "Why do you have to make me feel

all guilty about not wanting to participate in share-your-feelings-story-time?"

"I'm n—"

"I'm just—I'm in a really shitty mood, okay?" He looks off to the side. "I feel weird. Like I just want to be pissed off today. Like I just want to punch people in the face for no reason."

I pull my knees up to my chest. Rest my chin on my knees. Nod. "You've had a hard day."

He grunts. Nods and looks at the wall. Presses a fist into the mat. "Sometimes I just get really tired, you know?" He stares at his fist, at the shapes he makes by pressing his knuckles into the soft, spongy material. "Like I just get really fed up." His voice is suddenly so quiet, it's almost like he's not talking to me at all. I can see his throat move, the emotions caught in his chest. "I keep losing people," he says. "It's like every day I'm losing people. Every goddamn day. I'm so sick of it—I'm so sick and tired of it—"

"Kenji—," I try to say.

"I missed you, J." He's still studying the mats. "I wish you'd been there last night."

"I missed you, too."

"I don't have anyone else to talk to."

"I thought you didn't like talking about your feelings," I tease him, trying to lighten the mood.

He doesn't bite.

"It just gets really heavy sometimes." He looks away. "Too heavy. Even for me. And some days I don't want to laugh," he says. "I don't want to be funny. I don't want to give a shit about anything. Some days I just want to sit on my ass and cry. All day long." His hands stop moving against the mats. "Is that crazy?" he asks quietly, still not meeting my gaze.

I blink hard against the stinging in my eyes. "No," I tell him. "No, that's not crazy at all."

He stares at the floor. "Hanging out with you has made me weird, J. All I do is sit around thinking about my feelings these days. Thanks for that."

I crawl forward and hug him right around the middle and he responds immediately, wrapping me up against him. My face is pressed to his chest and I can hear his heart beating so hard. He's still hurting so badly right now, and I keep forgetting that. I need to not forget that.

I cling to him, wishing I could ease his pain. I wish I could take his burdens and make them mine.

"It's weird, isn't it?" he says.

"What is?"

"If we were naked right now, I'd be dead."

"Shut up," I say, laughing against his chest. We're both wearing long sleeves, long pants. As long as my face and hands don't touch his skin, he's perfectly safe.

"Well, it's true."

"In what alternate universe would I ever be naked with you?"

"I am just *saying*," he says. "Shit happens. You never know."

"I think you need a girlfriend."

"Nah," he says. "I just need a hug. From my friend."

I lean back to look at him. Try to read his eyes. "You're my *best* friend, Kenji. You know that, right?"

"Yeah, kid." He grins at me. "I do. And I can't believe I got stuck with your skinny ass."

I break free of his arms. Narrow my eyes at him.

He laughs. "So how's the new boyfriend?"

My smiles fall away. "He's not my boyfriend."

"Are you sure about that? Because I'm pretty sure Romeo wouldn't have let us come live with him if he weren't a little bit madly in love with you."

I look into my hands. "Maybe one day Warner and I will learn to be friends."

"*Seriously?*" Kenji looks shocked. "I thought you were super into him?"

I shrug. "I'm . . . attracted to him."

"But?"

"But Warner still has a long way to go, you know?"

"Well, yeah," Kenji says. Exhales. Leans back. "Yeah. Yeah, I do."

We both say nothing for a while.

"This shit is still super freaking weird, though," Kenji says all of a sudden.

"What do you mean?" I glance up. "Which part?"

"Warner," Kenji says. "Warner is so freaking weird to me right now." Kenji looks at me. Really looks at me. "You know—in all my time on base, I never saw him have, like, a single casual conversation with a soldier before. Never. He was ice cold, J. *Ice. Cold,*" he says again. "He never smiled.

216

Never laughed. Never showed any emotion. And he never, *ever* talked unless he was issuing orders. He was like a machine," Kenji says. "And this?" He points at the elevator. "This guy who just left here? The guy who showed up at the house yesterday? I don't know who the hell that is. I can't even wrap my mind around it right now. Shit is unreal."

"I didn't know that," I say to him, surprised. "I had no idea he was like that."

"He wasn't like that with you?" Kenji asks. "When you first got here?"

"No," I say. "He was always pretty . . . animated with me. Not, like, *nice* animated," I clarify, "but, I mean . . . I don't know. He talked a lot." I'm silent as the memories resurface. "He was always talking, actually. That's kind of all he ever did. And he smiled at me all the time." I pause. "I thought he was doing it on purpose. To make fun of me. Or try to scare me."

Kenji leans back on his hands. "Yeah, no."

"Huh," I say, my eyes focused on a point in the distance.

Kenji sighs. "Is he . . . like . . . nice to you, at least?"

I look down. Stare at my feet. "Yeah," I whisper. "He's really nice to me."

"But you guys are not an item or anything?"

I make a face.

"Okay," Kenji says quickly, holding up both hands. "All right—I was just curious. This is a judgment-free zone, J."

I snort. "Yeah it isn't."

Kenji relaxes a little. "You know, Adam really thinks you

and Warner are, like, a thing now."

I roll my eyes. "Adam is stupid."

"Tsk, tsk, princess. We need to talk about your language—"

"Adam needs to tell Warner they're brothers."

Kenji looks up, alarmed. "Lower your voice," he whispers. "You can't just go around saying that. You know how Kent feels about it."

"I think it's unfair. Warner has a right to know."

"Why?" Kenji says. "You think he and Kent are going to become besties all of a sudden?"

I look at him then, my eyes steady, serious. "James is his brother, too, Kenji."

Kenji's body goes stiff, his face blank. His eyes widen, just a little.

I tilt my head. Raise an eyebrow.

"I didn't even . . . wow," he says. He presses a fist to his forehead. "I didn't even think about that."

"It's not fair to either of them," I say. "And I really think Warner would love to know he has brothers in this world. At least James and Adam have each other," I say. "But Warner has always been alone."

Kenji is shaking his head. Disbelief etched across his features. "This just keeps getting more and more twisted," he says. "It's like you think it couldn't possibly get more convoluted, and then, bam."

"He deserves to know, Kenji," I say again. "You know Warner at least deserves to *know*. It's his right. It's his blood, too."

Kenji looks up. Sighs. "Damn."

"If Adam doesn't tell him," I say, "I will."

"You wouldn't."

I stare at him. Hard.

"That's messed up, J." Kenji looks surprised. "You can't do that."

"Why do you keep calling me J?" I ask him. "When did that even happen? You've already given me, like, fifty different nicknames."

He shrugs. "You should be flattered."

"Oh really?" I say. "Nicknames are flattering, huh?"

He nods.

"Then how about I call you Kenny?"

Kenji crosses his arms. Stares me down. "That's not even a little bit funny."

I grin. "It is, a little bit."

"How about I call your new boyfriend King Stick-Up-His-Ass?"

"He's not my boyfriend, *Kenny*."

Kenji shoots me a warning look. Points at my face. "I am not amused, princess."

"Hey, don't you need to shower?" I ask him.

"So now you're telling me I smell."

I roll my eyes.

He clambers to his feet. Sniffs his shirt. "Damn, I do kind of smell, don't I?"

"Go," I say. "Go and hurry back. I have a feeling this is going to be a long night."

THIRTY-SIX

We're all sitting on benches around the training room. Warner is sitting next to me and I'm doing everything I can to make sure our shoulders don't accidentally touch.

"All right, so, first things first, right?" Winston says, looking around. "We have to get Sonya and Sara back. The question is how." A pause. "We have no idea how to get to the supreme."

Everyone looks at Warner.

Warner looks at his watch.

"*Well?*" Kenji says.

"Well, what?" Warner says, bored.

"Well, aren't you going to help us?" Ian snaps. "This is your territory."

Warner looks at me for the first time all evening. "You're absolutely sure you trust these people?" he asks me. "All of them?"

"Yes," I say quietly. "I really do."

"Very well." Warner takes a deep breath before addressing the group. "My father," he says calmly, "is on a ship. In the middle of the ocean."

"He's on a ship?" Kenji asks, startled. "The capital is a *ship*?"

"Not exactly." Warner hesitates. "But the point is, we have to lure him *here*. Going to him will not work. We have to create a problem big enough for him to be forced to come to us." He looks at me then. "Juliette says she already has a plan."

I nod. Take a deep breath. Study the faces before me. "I think we should take over Sector 45."

Stunned silence.

"I think, together," I tell them, "we'll be able to convince the soldiers to fight on our side. At the end of the day, no one is benefiting from The Reestablishment except for the people in charge. The soldiers are tired and hungry and probably only took this job because there were no other options." I pause. "We can rally the civilians *and* the soldiers. Everyone in the sector. Get them to join us. And they know me," I say. "The soldiers. They've already seen me—they know what I can do. But all of us together?" I shake my head. "That would be amazing. We could show them that we're different. Stronger. We can give them hope—a reason to fight back.

"And then," I say, "once we have their support, news will spread, and Anderson will be forced to come back here. He'll have to try and take us down—he'll have no other choice. And once he's back, we take him out. We fight him and his army and we win. And then we take over the country."

"My goodness."

Castle is the first to speak.

"Ms. Ferrars," he says, "you've given this a great deal of thought."

I nod.

Kenji is looking at me like he's not sure if he should laugh or applaud.

"What do you think?" I ask, looking around.

"What if it doesn't work?" Lily says. "What if the soldiers are too scared to change their allegiance? What if they kill you instead?"

"That's a definite possibility," I say. "But I think if we're strong enough—if the nine of us stand united, with all of our strengths combined—I think they'll believe we can do something pretty amazing."

"Yeah but how will they know what our strengths are?" Brendan asks. "What if they don't believe us?"

"We can show them."

"And if they shoot us?" Ian counters.

"I can do it alone, if you're worried about that. I don't mind. Kenji was teaching me how to project my energy before the war, and I think if I can learn to master that, I could do some pretty scary things. Things that might impress them enough to join us."

"You can *project*?" Winston asks, eyes wide. "You mean you can, like, mass-kill everyone with your life-sucking thing?"

"Um, no," I say. "I mean, well, yes, I suppose I could do that, too, but I'm not talking about that. I mean I can project my strength. Not the . . . life-sucking thing—"

"Wait, what strength?" Brendan asks, confused. "I thought it's your skin that's lethal?"

I'm about to respond when I remember that Brendan and Winston and Ian were all taken hostage before I'd begun to seriously train. I don't know that they knew much about my progress at all.

So I start from the top.

"My . . . power," I say, "has to do with more than just my skin." I glance at Kenji. Gesture to him. "We'd been working together for a while, trying to figure out what it was, exactly, I was capable of, and Kenji realized that my true energy is coming from deep within me, not the surface. It's in my bones, my blood, *and* my skin," I try to explain. "My real power is an insane kind of superstrength.

"My skin is just one element of that," I tell them. "It's like the most heightened form of my energy, and the craziest form of protection; it's like my body has put up a shield. Metaphorical barbed wire. It keeps intruders away." I almost laugh, wondering when it became so easy for me to talk about this stuff. To be comfortable with it. "But I'm also strong enough to break through just about anything," I tell them, "and without even injuring myself. Concrete. Brick. Glass—"

"The earth," Kenji adds.

"Yes," I say, smiling at him. "Even the earth."

"She created an earthquake," Alia says eagerly, and I'm actually surprised to hear her voice. "During the first battle," she tells Brendan and Winston and Ian. "When we were trying to save you guys. She punched the ground and it split open. That's how we were able to get away."

The guys are gawking at me.

"So, what I'm trying to say," I tell them, "is that if I can project my strength, and really learn to control it? I don't know." I shrug. "I could move mountains, probably."

"That's a bit ambitious." Kenji grins, ever the proud parent.

"Ambitious, but probably not impossible." I grin back.

"Wow," Lily says. "So you can just . . . destroy stuff? Like, anything?"

I nod. Glance at Warner. "Do you mind?"

"Not at all," he says. His eyes are carefully inscrutable.

I get to my feet and walk over to the stacks of dumbbells, all the while prepping myself mentally to tap into my energy. This is still the trickiest part for me: learning how to moderate my strength with finesse.

I pick up a fifty-pound free weight and carry it over to the group.

For a moment I wonder if this should feel heavy to me, especially considering how it weighs about half of what I do, but I can't really feel it.

I sit back down on the bench. Rest the weight on the ground.

"What are you going to do with that?" Ian asks, eyes wide.

"What do you want me to do?" I ask him.

"You're telling me you can just, like, rip that apart or whatever?" Winston says.

I nod.

"Do it," Kenji says. He's practically bouncing in his seat. "Do it do it."

So I do.

I pick it up, and literally crush the weight between my hands. It becomes a mangled mess of metal. A fifty-pound lump. I rip it in half and drop the two pieces on the floor.

The benches shake.

"Sorry," I say quickly, looking around. "I didn't mean to toss it like that—"

"God*damn*," Ian says. "That is so cool."

"Do it again," Winston says, eyes bright.

"I'd really rather she didn't destroy all of my property," Warner cuts in.

"Hey, so—wait—," Winston says, realizing something as he stares at Warner. "You can do that, too, can't you? You can just take her power and use it like that, too?"

"I can take all of your powers," Warner corrects him. "And do whatever I want with them."

The terror in the room is a very palpable thing.

I frown at Warner. "Please don't scare them."

He says nothing. Looks at nothing.

"So the two of you"—Ian tries to find his voice—"I mean, together—you two could basically—"

"Take over the world?" Warner is looking at the wall now.

"I was going to say you could kick some serious ass, but yeah, that, too, I guess." Ian shakes his head.

"Are you sure you trust this guy?" Lily asks me, jerking

225

a thumb at Warner and looking at me like she's seriously, genuinely concerned. "What if he's just using you for your power?"

"I trust him with my life," I say quietly. "I already have, and I'd do it again."

Warner looks at me and looks away, and for a brief second I catch the charge of emotion in his eyes.

"So, let me get this straight," Winston says. "Our plan is to basically seduce the soldiers and civilians of Sector 45 into fighting with us?"

Kenji crosses his arms. "Yeah, it sounds like we're going to go all peacock and hope they find us attractive enough to mate with."

"Gross." Brendan frowns.

"Despite how weird Kenji just made this sound," I say, shooting a stern look in his direction, "the answer is yes, basically. We can provide them with a group to rally around. We take charge of the army, and then take charge of the people. And then we lead them into battle. We really, truly fight back."

"And if you win?" Castle asks. He's been so quiet all this time. "What do you plan to do then?"

"What do you mean?" I ask.

"Let's say you are successful," he says. "You defeat the supreme. You kill him and his men. Then what? Who will take over as the supreme commander?"

"I will."

The room gasps. I feel Warner go stiff beside me.

"Damn, princess," Kenji says quietly.

"And then?" Castle asks, ignoring everyone but me. "After that?" His eyes are worried. Scared, almost. "You're going to kill whoever else stands in your way? All the other sector leaders, all across the nation? That's 554 more wars—"

"Some will surrender," I tell him.

"And the others?" he asks. "How can you lead a nation in the right direction when you've just slaughtered all who oppose you? How will you be any different from those you've defeated?"

"I trust myself," I tell him, "to be strong enough to do what's right. Our world is dying right now. You said yourself that we have the means to reclaim our land—to change things back to the way they were. Once power is in the right place—with *us*—you can rebuild what you started at Omega Point. You'll have the freedom to implement those changes to our land, water, animals, and atmosphere, and save millions of lives in the process—giving the new generations hope for a different future. We have to try," I tell him. "We can't just sit back and watch people die when we have the power to make a difference."

The room goes silent. Still.

"Hell," Winston says. "I'd follow you into battle."

"Me too," Alia says.

"And me." Brendan.

"You know I'm in," Kenji says.

"Me too," Lily and Ian say at the same time.

Castle takes a deep breath. "Maybe," he says. He leans back in his chair, clasps his hands. "Maybe you'll be able to do right what I did wrong." He shakes his head. "I am twenty-seven years your senior and I've never had your confidence, but I do understand your heart. And I trust that you say what you believe to be true." A pause. A careful look. "We will support you. But know now that you are taking on a great and terrifying responsibility. One that may backfire in an irreversible way."

"I do understand that," I say quietly.

"Very well then, Ms. Ferrars. Good luck, and godspeed. Our world is in your hands."

THIRTY-SEVEN

"You didn't tell me what you thought of my plan."

Warner and I have just stepped back into his room and he still hasn't said a word to me. He's standing by the door to his office, his eyes on the floor. "I didn't realize you wanted my opinion."

"Of course I want your opinion."

"I should really get back to work," he says, and turns to go.

I touch his arm.

Warner goes rigid. He stands, unmoving, his eyes trained on the hand I've placed on his forearm.

"Please," I whisper. "I don't want it to be like this with us. I want us to be able to talk. To get to know each other again, *properly*—to be friends—"

Warner makes a strange sound deep in his throat. Puts a few feet between us. "I am doing my best, love. But I don't know how to be just your friend."

"It doesn't have to be all or nothing," I try to tell him. "There can be steps in between—I just need time to understand you like this—as a different person—"

"But that's just it." His voice is worn thin. "You need time to understand me as a *different person*. You need time to fix your perception of me."

"Why is that so wrong—"

"Because I am not a different person," he says firmly. "I am the same man I've always been and I have never tried to be different. You have misunderstood me, Juliette. You've judged me, you've perceived me to be something I am not, but that is no fault of mine. I have not changed, and I will not change—"

"You already have."

His jaw clenches. "You have quite a lot of gall to speak with such conviction on matters you know nothing about."

I swallow, hard.

Warner steps so close to me I'm actually afraid to move. "You once accused me of not knowing the meaning of love," he says. "But you were wrong. You fault me, perhaps, for loving you too much." His eyes are so intense. So green. So cold. "But at least I do not deny my own heart."

"And you think I do," I whisper.

Warner drops his eyes. Says nothing.

"What you don't understand," I tell him, my voice catching, "is that I don't even know my own heart anymore. I don't know how to name what I feel yet and I need time to figure it out. You want more right now but right now what I need is for you to be my friend—"

Warner flinches.

"I do not have friends," he says.

"Why can't you try?"

He shakes his head.

"Why? Why not give it a chance—"

"Because I am afraid," he finally says, voice shaking, "that your friendship would be the end of me."

I'm still frozen in place as his office door slams shut behind him.

THIRTY-EIGHT

I never thought I'd see Warner in sweatpants.

Or sneakers.

And right now, he's wearing both. Plus a T-shirt.

Now that our group is staying in Warner's training facilities, I have a reason to tag along as he starts his day. I always knew he spent a lot of time working, but I never knew how much of his time was spent working out. He's so disciplined, so precise about everything. It amazes me.

He starts his mornings on a stationary bike, ends his evenings with a run on the treadmill. And every weekday he works out a different part of his body.

"Mondays are for legs," I heard him explain to Castle. "Tuesdays I work chest. Wednesdays I work my shoulders and my back. Thursdays are for triceps and deltoids. Fridays are for biceps and forearms. And every day is for abdominals and cardio. I also spend most weekends doing target practice," he said.

Today is Tuesday.

Which means right now, I'm watching him bench-press three hundred and fifteen pounds. Three forty-five-pound plates on each side of what Kenji told me is called an Olympic bar, which weighs an additional forty-five pounds. I can't stop staring. I don't think I've ever been more attracted to him in all the time I've known him.

Kenji pulls up next to me. Nods at Warner. "So this gets you going, huh?"

I'm mortified.

Kenji barks out a laugh.

"I've never seen him in sweatpants before." I try to sound normal. "I've never even seen him in shorts."

Kenji raises an eyebrow at me. "I bet you've seen him in less."

I want to die.

Kenji and I are supposed to spend this next month training. That's the plan. I need to train enough to fight and use my strength without being overpowered ever again. This isn't the kind of situation we can go into without absolute confidence, and since I'm supposed to be leading the mission, I still have a lot of work to do. I need to be able to access my energy in an instant, and I need to be able to moderate the amount of power I exert at any given time. In other words: I need to achieve absolute mastery over my ability.

Kenji is also training in his own way; he wants to perfect his skill in projecting; he wants to be able to do it without having to make direct contact with another person. But he and I are the only ones who have any real work to do. Castle has been in control of himself for decades now, and everyone else has fairly straightforward skills that they've very naturally adapted to. In my case, I have seventeen years of psychological trauma to undo.

I need to break down these self-made walls.

Today, Kenji's starting small. He wants me to move a dumbbell across the room through sheer force of will. But all I've managed to do was make it twitch. And I'm not even sure that was me.

"You're not focusing," Kenji says to me. "You need to connect—find your core and pull from within," he's saying. "You have to, like, *literally* pull it out of yourself and then push it out around you, J. It's only difficult in the beginning," he says, "because your body is so used to containing the energy. In your case it's going to be even harder, because you've spent your whole life bottling it up. You have to give yourself permission to let it go. Let down your guard. Find it. Harness it. Release it."

He gives me the same speech, over and over again.

And I keep trying, over and over again.

I count to three.

I close my eyes and try to really, truly focus this time. I listen to the sudden urge to lift my arms, planting my feet firmly on the floor. I blow out a breath. Squeeze my eyes shut tighter. I feel the energy surging up, through my bones, my blood, raging and rising until it culminates into a mass so potent I can no longer contain it. I know it needs release, and needs it now.

But how?

Before, I always thought I needed to touch something to let the power out.

It never occurred to me to throw the energy into a

stationary object. I thought my hands were the final destination; I never considered using them as a transmitter, as a medium for the energy to pass through. But I'm just now realizing that I can try to push it out *through* my hands—*through* my skin. And maybe, if I'm strong enough, I might be able to learn to manipulate the power in midair, forcing it to move whichever way I want.

My sudden realization gives me a renewed burst of confidence. I'm excited now, eager to see if my theory is correct. I steel myself, feeling the rush of power flood through me again. My shoulders tense as the energy coats my hands, my wrists, my forearms. It feels so warm, so intense, almost like it's a tangible thing; the kind of power that could tangle in my fingers.

I curl my fists.

Pull back my arms.

And then fling them forward, opening my hands at the same time.

Silence.

I squint one eye open, sneaking a look at the dumbbell still sitting in the same spot.

Sigh.

"GET DOWN," Kenji shouts, yanking me backward and shoving me face-first onto the floor.

I can hear everyone shouting and thudding to the ground around us. I crane my neck up only to see that they've all got their hands over their heads, faces covered; I try to look around.

Panic seizes me by the throat.

The rock wall is fissuring into what might be a hundred pieces, creaking and groaning as it falls apart. I watch, horrified, as one huge, jagged chunk trembles just before unhinging from the wall.

Warner is standing underneath.

I'm about to scream before I see him look up, both hands outstretched toward the chaos. Immediately, the wall stops shaking. The pieces hover, trembling only slightly, caught between falling and fitting back into place.

My mouth is still open.

Warner looks to his right. Nods.

I follow his line of sight and see Castle on the other side, using his power to hold up the other end. Together they control the pieces as they fall to the floor, allowing them to float down, settling each broken slab and each jagged bit gently against what remains of the wall.

Everyone begins to pop their heads up, realizing something has changed. We slowly get to our feet, and watch, dumbstruck, as Castle and Warner contain the disaster and confine it to one space. Nothing else is damaged. No one is hurt. I'm still looking on, eyes wide with awe.

When the work is finally done, Warner and Castle share a brief moment of acknowledgment before they head in opposite directions.

Warner comes to find me. Castle to everyone else.

"Are you okay?" Warner asks. His tone is businesslike, but his eyes give him away. "You're not injured?"

I shake my head. "That was incredible."

"I can't take any credit for it," he says. "It was Castle's power I borrowed."

"But you're so *good* at it," I tell him, forgetting for a moment that we're supposed to be mad at each other. "You *just* learned you have this ability, and you can already control it. So naturally. But then when I try to do something, I nearly kill everyone in the process." I drop my head. "I'm the worst at everything," I mutter. "The worst."

"Don't feel bad," he says quietly. "You'll figure it out."

"Was it ever hard for you?" I look up, hopeful. "Figuring out how to control the energy?"

"Oh," he says, surprised. "No. Though I've always been very good at everything I do."

I drop my head again. Sigh.

Warner laughs and I peek up.

He's smiling.

"What?"

"Nothing," he whispers.

I hear a sharp whistle. Spin around.

"Hey—jazz hands!" Kenji barks. "Get your ass back over here." He makes it a point to look as irritated as possible. "Back to work. And this time, *focus*. You're not an ape. Don't just throw your shit everywhere."

Warner actually laughs.

Out loud.

I look back at him, and he's looking toward the wall, trying to suppress a wide smile as he runs a hand through his hair, down the back of his neck.

"At least someone appreciates my sense of humor," Kenji says before tugging at my arm. "Come on, princess. Let's try that again. And please, try not to kill everyone in this room."

THIRTY-NINE

We've been practicing all week.

I'm so exhausted I can't even stand up anymore, but I've made more progress than I ever could've hoped for. Kenji is still working with me directly, and Castle is overseeing my progress, but everyone else spends time training on all the various machines.

Winston and Brendan seem to be in better spirits every day—they look healthier, livelier—and the gash on Brendan's face is starting to fade. I'm so happy to see their progress, and doubly thrilled Delalieu was able to find the right medicines for them.

The two of them spend most days eating and sleeping and jumping from the bikes to the treadmill. Lily has been messing around with a little of everything, and today she's exercising with the medicine balls in the corner. Ian has been lifting weights and looking after Castle, and Alia has spent all week sitting in the corner, sketching things in a notepad. She seems happier, more settled. And I can't help but wonder if Adam and James are okay, too. I hope they're safe.

Warner is always gone during the day.

Every once in a while I glance at the elevator doors,

secretly hoping they'll open and deposit him back inside this room. Sometimes he stops by for a bit—jumps on the bike or goes for a quick run—but mostly he's gone.

I only really see him in the mornings for his early workout, and in the evenings when he does another round of cardio. The end of the night is my favorite part of the day. It's when all nine of us sit down and talk about our progress. Winston and Brendan are healing, I'm getting stronger, and Warner lets us know if there've been any new developments from the civilians, the soldiers, or The Reestablishment—so far, everything is still quiet.

And then Warner and I go back up to his quarters, where we shower and head to separate rooms. I sleep on his bed. He sleeps on the couch in his office.

Every night I tell myself I'll be brave enough to knock on his door, but I never have.

I still don't know what to say.

Kenji tugs on my hair.

"*Ow*—" I jerk back, scowling. "What's wrong with you?"

"You've been hit extra hard with the stupid stick today."

"What? I thought you said I was doing okay—"

"You are. But you're distracted. You keep staring at the elevator like it's about to grant you three wishes."

"Oh," I say. I look away. "Well. Sorry."

"Don't apologize," he sighs. Frowns a little. "What the hell is going on between you guys, anyway? Do I even want to know?"

I sigh. Flop onto the mats. "I have no idea, Kenji. He's hot and cold." I shrug. "I guess it's fine. I just need a little space for now."

"But you like him?" Kenji raises an eyebrow.

I say nothing. Feel my face warm.

Kenji rolls his eyes. "You know, I really never would've thought Warner could make you happy."

"Do I *look* happy?" I counter.

"Good point." He sighs. "I just mean that you always seemed so happy with Kent. This is a little hard for me to process." He hesitates. Rubs his forehead. "Well. Actually, you were a hell of a lot weirder when you were with Kent. Super whiny. And so dramatic. And you cried. All. The. Damn. Time." He screws up his face. "Jesus. I can't decide which one of them is worse."

"You think *I'm* dramatic?" I ask him, eyes wide. "Do you even know yourself at all?"

"I am not dramatic, okay? My presence just commands a certain kind of attention—"

I snort.

"Hey," he says, pointing at my face. "I am just saying that I don't know what to believe anymore. I've already been on this merry-go-round. First Adam. Now Warner. Next week you're going to try and hook up with me."

"You really wish that were true, don't you?"

"Whatever," he says, looking away. "I don't even like you."

"You think I'm pretty."

"I think you're delusional."

"I don't even know what this is, Kenji." I meet his eyes. "That's the problem. I don't know how to explain it, and I'm not sure I understand the depth of it yet. All I know is that whatever this is, I never felt it with Adam."

Kenji's eyes pull together, surprised and scared. He says nothing for a second. Blows out a breath. "Seriously?"

I nod.

"Seriously, seriously?"

"Yeah," I say. "I feel so . . . *light*. Like I could just . . . I don't know . . ." I trail off. "It's like I feel like, for the first time in my life, I'm going to be okay. Like I'm going to be strong."

"But that sounds like it's just *you*," he says. "That has nothing to do with Warner."

"That's true," I tell him. "But sometimes people can weigh us down, too. And I know Adam didn't mean to, but he was weighing me down. We were two sad people stuck together."

"Huh." Kenji leans back on his hands.

"Being with Adam was always overshadowed by some kind of pain or difficulty," I explain, "and Adam was always so serious. He was intense in a way that exhausted me sometimes. We were always hiding, or sneaking around, or on the run, and we never found enough uninterrupted moments to be together. It was almost like the universe was trying to tell me I was trying too hard to make things work with him."

"Kent wasn't that bad, J." Kenji frowns. "You're not giving him enough credit. He's been acting kind of dickish lately, but he's a good guy. You know he is. Shit is just really rough for him right now."

"I know," I sigh, feeling sad, somehow. "But this world is still falling apart. Even if we win this war, everything is going to get much, much worse before it gets better." I pause. Stare into my hands. "And I think people become who they really are when things get rough. I've seen it firsthand. With myself, my parents, with society, even. And yeah, Adam is a good guy. He really is. But just because he's a good guy doesn't make him the right guy for me."

I look up.

"I'm so different now. I'm not right for him anymore, and he's not right for me."

"But he still loves you."

"No," I say. "He doesn't."

"That's a pretty heavy accusation."

"It's not an accusation," I say. "One day Adam will realize that what he felt for me was just a crazy kind of desperation. We were two people who really needed someone to hold on to, and we had this past that made us seem so compatible. But it wasn't enough. Because if it were, I wouldn't have been able to walk away so easily." I drop my eyes, my voice. "Warner didn't seduce me, Kenji. He didn't steal me away. I just . . . I reached a point where everything changed for me.

"Everything I thought I knew about Warner was wrong. Everything I thought I believed about myself was wrong.

243

And I knew *I* was changing," I say to him. "I wanted to move forward. I wanted to be angry and I wanted to scream for the first time in my life and I couldn't. I didn't want people to be afraid of me, so I tried to shut up and disappear, hoping it would make them more comfortable. But I hate that I let myself be so passive my whole life, and I see now how differently things could've been if I'd had faith in myself when it mattered. I don't want to go back to that," I tell him. "I won't. Not ever."

"You don't have to," Kenji points out. "Why would you? I don't think Kent wanted you to be passive."

I shrug. "I still wonder if he wants me to be the girl he first fell for. The person I was when we met."

"And that's bad?"

"That's not who I *am* anymore, Kenji. Do I still seem like that girl to you?"

"How the hell should I know?"

"You *don't* know," I say, exasperated. "That's why you don't understand. You don't know what I used to be like. You don't know what it was like in my head. I lived in a really dark place," I say to him. "I wasn't safe in my own mind. I woke up every morning hoping to die and then spent the rest of the day wondering if maybe I was already dead because I couldn't even tell the *difference*," I say, more harshly than I mean to. "I had a small thread of hope and I clung to it, but the majority of my life was spent waiting around to see if someone would take pity on me."

Kenji is just staring at me, his eyes tight.

"Don't you think I've realized," I say to him, angrier now, "that if I'd allowed myself to get mad a long time ago, I would've discovered I had the strength to break through that asylum with my own two hands?"

Kenji flinches.

"Don't you think that I think about that, all the time?" I ask him, my voice shaking. "Don't you think it *kills* me to know that it was my own unwillingness to recognize myself as a human being that kept me trapped for so long? For two hundred and sixty-four days, Kenji," I say, swallowing hard. "Two hundred and sixty-four days I was in there and the whole time, I had the power to break myself out and I didn't, because I had no idea I could. Because I never even tried. Because I let the world teach me to hate myself. I was a *coward*," I say, "who needed someone else to tell me I was worth something before I took any steps to save myself.

"This isn't about Adam or Warner," I tell him. "This is about me and what I want. This is about me finally understanding where I want to be in ten years. Because I'm going to be alive, Kenji. I will be alive in ten years, and I'm going to be happy. I'm going to be strong. And I don't need anyone to tell me that anymore. I am enough, and I always will be."

I'm breathing hard now, trying to calm my heart.

Kenji is staring at me, mildly terrified.

"I want Adam to be happy, Kenji, I really do. But he and I would end up like water going nowhere."

"What do you mean . . . ?"

"Water that never moves," I say to him. "It's fine for a little while. You can drink from it and it'll sustain you. But if it sits too long it goes bad. It grows stale. It becomes toxic." I shake my head. "I need waves. I need waterfalls. I want rushing currents."

"Damn," Kenji says. He laughs nervously, scratches the back of his head. "I think you should write that speech down, princess. Because you're going to have to tell him all of that yourself."

"What?" My body goes rigid.

"Yeah." Kenji coughs. "Adam and James are coming here tomorrow."

"What?" I gasp.

"Yeah. Awkward, right?" He tries to laugh. "Sooo awkward."

"Why? Why would he come here? How do you even know?"

"I've, um, kind of been going back?" He clears his throat. "To, you know, check up on them. Mostly James. But you know." He looks away. Looks around.

"To check up on them?"

"Yeah. Just to make sure they're doing okay." He nods at nothing. "Like, I told him that we had a really awesome plan in place," Kenji says, pointing at me. "Thanks to you, of course. Really awesome plan. So. And I told him the food was good," Kenji adds. "And the showers are hot. So, like, he knows Warner didn't cheap out on us or anything. And yeah, you know, some other stuff."

"What other stuff?" I ask, suspicious now. "What did you say to him?"

"Hmm?" Kenji is studying the hem of his shirt, pulling at it.

"*Kenji.*"

"Okay, listen," Kenji says, holding up both hands. "Just— don't get mad, okay?"

"I'm already getting mad—"

"They were going to *die* out there. I couldn't just let them stay in that crappy little space all by themselves—especially not James—and especially not now that we've got a solid plan in place—"

"What did you tell him, Kenji?" My patience is wearing thin.

"Maybe," he says, backing away now, "maybe I told him how you were a calm, rational, very nice person who does not like to hurt people, especially not her very good-looking friend Kenji—"

"Dammit, Kenji, tell me what you did—"

"I need five feet," he says.

"What?"

"Five feet. Of space," he says. "Between us."

"I will give you five inches."

Kenji swallows, hard. "Okay, well, maybe," he says, "maybe I told him . . . that . . . um, you missed him. A lot."

I nearly rock backward, reeling from the impact of his words.

"You did what?" My voice drops to a whisper.

"It was the only way I could get him here, okay? He thought you were in love with Warner, and his pride is such a freaking *issue* with him—"

"What the hell is wrong with you?" I shout. "They're going to *kill* each other!"

"This could be their chance to make up," Kenji says. "And then we can all be friends, just like you wanted—"

"Oh my God," I say, running a hand over my eyes. "Are you *insane?* Why would you do that? I'll have to break his heart all over again!"

"Yeah, you know, I was thinking maybe you could pretend to be, like, *not* interested in Warner? Just until after this war is over? Because that would make things a little less stressful. And then we'd all get along, and Adam and James wouldn't die out there all alone. You know? Happy ending."

I'm so mad right now I'm shaking.

"You told him something else, didn't you?" I ask, my eyes narrowing. "You said something else to him. About me. *Didn't you?*"

"What?" Kenji is moving backward now. "I don't—"

"Is that all you told him?" I demand. "That I missed him? Or did you tell him something else, too?"

"Oh. Well, now that you mention it, yeah, um, I might've told him, um, that you were still in love with him?"

My brain is screaming.

"And . . . that maybe you talk about him all the time? And maybe I told him that you cry a lot about how much you miss him. Maybe. I don't know, we talked about a lot of things, so—"

"I am going to MURDER YOU—"

"No," he says, pointing at me as he shifts backward again. "Bad Juliette. You don't like to kill people, remember? You're against that, remember? You like to talk about feelings and rainbows—"

"Why, Kenji?" I drop my head into my hands. "Why? Why would you lie to him?"

"Because," he snaps, frustrated. "This is *bullshit*. Everyone is already dying in this world. Everyone has lost their homes, their families—everything they've ever loved. And you and Kent should be able to work out your stupid high school drama like two adults. We shouldn't have to lose each other like this. We've already lost everyone else," he says, angry now.

"They're *alive*, J. They're still alive." He looks at me, eyes bright with barely restrained emotion. "That's reason enough for me to try and keep them in my life." He looks away. Lowers his voice. "Please," he says. "This is such crap. This whole thing. I feel like I'm the kid caught in the middle of a divorce. And I didn't want to lie to him, okay? I didn't. But at least I convinced him to come back. And maybe once he gets here, he'll want to stay."

I glare at him. "When are they going to be here?"

Kenji takes a beat to breathe. "I'm getting them in the morning."

"You know I'm going to tell Warner, right? You know

you can't just keep them here and make them invisible."

"I know," he says.

"Fine." I'm so furious I don't even know what to say anymore. I can't even look at him right now.

"So . . . ," Kenji says. "Good talk?"

I spin around. My voice is deathly soft, my face only inches from his. "If they kill each other," I say to him, "I will break your neck."

"Damn, princess. When did you get so violent?"

"I'm not kidding, Kenji. They've tried to kill each other before, and they almost succeeded. I hope you didn't forget that detail when you were making your happy rainbow plans." I stare him down. "This isn't just the story of two guys who don't like each other. They want each other *dead*."

Kenji sighs. Looks toward the wall. "It'll be okay," he says. "We'll figure it out."

"No," I say to him. "*You'll* figure it out."

"Can't you try to see where I'm coming from?" he asks. "Can't you see how much better it would be for us to all be together? There's no one left, J. It's just us. We shouldn't all have to suffer just because you and Kent aren't making out anymore. We shouldn't be living like this."

I close my eyes. Sigh deeply and try to calm down.

"I do," I say quietly. "I do see where you're coming from. I really, really do. And I love you for wanting everyone to be okay, and I love you for looking out for me, and for wanting me and Adam to be together again. I know how much you're going through right now. And I'm so sorry, Kenji. I really am. I know this isn't easy for you. But that's also exactly why I don't understand why you'd force the two of them together. You want to stick them in the same room. In a confined space. I thought you *didn't* want them to die."

"I think you're being a little pessimistic about this."

"Dammit, Kenji!" I throw my arm out, exasperated, and don't even realize what I've done until I hear a crash. I look toward the sound. I've managed to knock down an entire rack of free weights. From across the room.

I am a walking catastrophe.

"I need to cool off," I tell him, trying to moderate my voice. "I'll be back to shave your head while you're sleeping."

Kenji looks genuinely terrified for the first time. "You wouldn't."

I head toward the opposite wall. Hit the button for the elevator. "You're a heavy sleeper, right?"

"That's not funny, J—that's not even a little bit funny—"

The elevator pings open. I step inside. "Good night, Kenji."

I can still hear him shouting at me as the doors close.

FORTY

Warner is in the shower when I get back up to the room.

I glance at the clock. This would be about the time he'd start heading down to the training rooms; I usually meet him there for our nightly recap.

Instead I fall face-first onto the bed.

I don't know what I'm going to do.

Adam is going to show up here tomorrow thinking I still want to be with him. I don't want to have to walk away again, to see the hurt in his eyes. I don't want to hurt him. I really don't. I never have.

I'm going to *kill* Kenji.

I shove my head under the pillows, stacking them on my head and squishing them down around my ears until I've managed to shut out the world. I don't want to think about this right now. Now, of all the times to be thinking about this. Why do things always have to be so complicated? *Why?*

I feel a hand on my back.

I jerk up, pillows flying everywhere, and I'm so stupidly startled I actually fall off the bed. A pillow topples over and hits me in the face.

I groan, clutching the pillow to my chest. I press my

forehead to the soft cushion of it, squeezing my eyes shut. I've never had such a terrible headache.

"Juliette?" A tentative voice. "Are you okay?"

I lower the pillow. Blink up.

Warner is wearing a towel.

A *towel*.

I want to roll under the bed.

"Adam and James are coming here tomorrow," I say to him, all at once. I just say it, just like that.

Warner raises his eyebrows. "I didn't realize they'd received an invitation."

"Kenji is bringing them here. He's been sneaking out to go check on them, and now he's bringing them here. Tomorrow morning."

Warner's face is carefully neutral, his voice unaffected. He might be talking about the color of the walls. "I thought he wasn't interested in joining your resistance anymore."

For a moment I can't believe I'm still lying on the ground, clutching a pillow to my chest, staring at Warner who's wearing a towel and nothing else. I can't even take myself seriously.

"Kenji told Adam I'm still in love with him."

There it is.

A flash of anger. In and out. Warner's eyes spark and fade. He looks to the wall, silent a moment. "I see." His voice is quiet, controlled.

"He knew it was the only way to get Adam back here."

Warner says nothing.

"But I'm not, you know. In love with him." I'm surprised at how easily the words leave my lips, and even more surprised that I feel the need to say them out loud. That I'd need to reassure Warner, of all people. "I care about Adam," I say to him, "in the way that I'll always care about the few people who've shown me kindness in my life, but everything else is just . . . gone."

"I understand," he says.

I don't believe him.

"So what do you want to do?" I ask. "About tomorrow? And Adam?"

"What do you think should be done?"

I sigh. "I'm going to have to talk to him. I'll have to break up with him for the third time," I say, groaning again. "This is so stupid. So *stupid*."

I finally drop the pillow. Drop my arms to my sides.

But when I look up again, Warner is gone.

I sit up, alert. Glance around.

He's standing in the corner, putting on a pair of pants.

I try not to look at him as I climb back onto the bed.

I kick off my shoes and sink under the blankets, burrowing into the pillows until my head is buried beneath them. I feel the weight shift on the bed, and realize Warner must be sitting beside me. He plucks one of the pillows off my head. Leans in. Our noses are only inches apart.

"You don't love him at all?" Warner asks me.

My voice is being stupid. "Romantically?"

He nods.

"No."

"You're not attracted to him?"

"I'm attracted to you."

"I'm serious," he says.

"So am I."

Warner's still staring at me. He blinks, once.

"Don't you believe me?" I ask.

He looks away.

"Can't you tell?" I ask him. "Can't you feel it?"

And I am either losing my mind or Warner just blushed.

"You give me too much credit, love." His eyes are focused on the blanket, his words soft. "I will disappoint you. I am every bit the defective human being you don't think I am."

I sit up. Look at him closely. "You're so different," I whisper. "So different and exactly the same."

"What do you mean?"

"You're so gentle now. You're very . . . calm," I tell him. "Much more than you were before."

He says nothing for a long time. And then he stands up. His tone is curt when he says, "Yes, well, I'm sure you and Kishimoto will find a way to sort this situation out. Excuse me."

And then he leaves. Again.

I have no idea what to make of him anymore.

FORTY-ONE

Adam is already here.

Warner was completely uninterested in dealing with Adam. So he's gone about his day and his duties, having skipped his morning workout.

And now I'm here.

I've just stepped out of the elevator, and the pinging sound that signals the opening of the doors has alerted everyone to my presence. Adam was standing in the corner, talking to James. He's now staring at me.

It's weird, how I feel when I look at him now. There is no extreme emotion in me. No excess of happiness or sadness. Not upset. Not overjoyed. His face is familiar to me; his body, familiar to me. His unsteady smile, as he looks at me, is familiar to me.

How strange that we can go from friends to inseparable to hateful then casual all in one lifetime.

"Hi," I say.

"Hey." He looks away.

"Hi, James." I smile.

"Hi!" He waves, buoyant. He's standing just next to Adam, eyes lit up, clearly thrilled to be back among us. "This place is so cool."

"It is," I agree. "Have you had a chance to take a shower yet? The water is warm here."

"Oh, right," he says, shyly now. "Kenji told me about that."

"Why don't you get washed up? Delalieu will be bringing lunch down soon. I'm sure Brendan can show you around the locker room—and where to put all your stuff. You can have your own locker," I tell him, glancing at Brendan as I do. He nods, taking the hint and jumping to his feet right away.

"Really?" James is saying. "That's so cool. So they just bring the food to you? And you get to shower whenever you want? Is there a curfew?"

"Yes, yes, and no," Brendan answers him. He takes James's hand. Grabs his little bag. "We can stay up as late as we like," he tells him. "Maybe after dinner I'll show you how to use the bicycles in here," he says, his voice fading to an echo as he and James disappear into the locker room.

Once James is gone, everyone seems to exhale.

I steel myself. Step forward.

"I'm really sorry," Adam says first, crossing the room to meet me. "You have no idea—"

"Adam." I cut him off, anxious. Nervous. I have to say this and I have to say it now. "Kenji lied to you."

Adam stops. Stills.

"I haven't been crying over you," I say, wondering if it's even possible to deliver this kind of information without both humiliating him and breaking his heart. I feel like such a monster. "And I'm really, really happy you're here, but I

257

don't think we should be together anymore."

"Oh," he says. Rocks back on his heels. Drops his eyes. Runs both hands through his hair. "Right."

Out of the corner of my eye, I see Kenji looking at me. He's waving his hand, trying to get my attention, but I'm still too mad at him right now. I don't want to talk to him until I've fixed this.

"Adam," I say. "I'm sorry—"

"No," he says, holding up a hand to stop me. He looks dazed, sort of. Strange. "It's okay. Really. I already knew you were going to say that to me." He laughs a little, but awkwardly. "I guess I thought knowing in advance would make it feel a lot less like I was being punched in the gut." He cringes. "But nope. Still hurts like hell." He backs up against the wall. Slides down to the floor.

He's not looking at me.

"How did you know?" I ask. "How did you know what I was going to say?"

"I told him before you got here," Kenji says, stepping forward. He shoots me a sharp look. "I came clean. I told him what we talked about yesterday. All the things you said."

"Then why is he still here?" I ask, stunned. I turn to face Adam. "I thought you said you never wanted to see me again."

"I never should've said that." Adam is still looking at the floor.

"So . . . you're okay?" I ask him. "With Warner?"

Adam looks up in disgust, so different in an instant.

"Are you out of your mind? I want to put his head through a goddamn wall."

"Then why are you still here?" I ask again. "I don't understand—"

"Because I don't want to *die*," he says to me. "Because I've been racking my brain trying to figure out how to feed my little brother and I've come up with exactly jack and shit in the way of solutions. Because it's cold as hell outside, and he's hungry, and because our electricity is going to get shut off soon." Adam is breathing hard. "I didn't know what else to do. So now I'm here, my pride in the toilet, hoping I can stay in my ex-girlfriend's new *boyfriend's* bachelor pad, and I want to kill myself." He swallows. "And I can suffer through that," he says, "if it means James will be safe. But right now I'm still waiting for your shithead of a boyfriend to show up and try to kill me."

"He's not my boyfriend," I say quietly. "And he's not going to kill you. He doesn't even care that you're here."

Adam laughs out loud. "Bullshit," he says.

"I'm serious."

Adam gets to his feet. Studies my eyes. "You're telling me I can stay here, in his room, and eat his food, and he's just going to *let* me?" Adam's eyes are wide, incredulous. "You still don't understand this guy. He doesn't operate the way you think he does, Juliette. He doesn't think like a normal human being. He's a freaking sociopath. And you really are insane," he says, "if you think it's okay to be with someone like that."

I flinch, stung. "Be very careful how you speak to me, Adam. I won't tolerate your insults again."

"I can't even believe you," he says. "I can't believe you can stand there and treat me like this." His face is twisted into something so intensely unattractive.

Anger.

"I'm not trying to hurt you—"

"Maybe you should've remembered that before you ran into the arms of some psycho!"

"Calm your ass down, Kent." I hear Kenji's sharp warning from the corner of the room. "I thought you said you were going to be cool."

"I am being cool," he says, his voice rising, eyes on fire. "I'm a freaking saint. I don't know anyone else who would be as generous as I am right now." He looks back at me. "You were lying to me the whole time we were together. You were *cheating* on me—"

"No I wasn't."

"This kind of shit doesn't just happen overnight," he shouts. "You don't just fall out of love with someone like that—"

"We're *done*, Adam. I'm not doing this again. You're welcome to stay here," I tell him. "Especially for James's sake. But you can't stay here and insult me. You have no right."

Adam tenses his jaw. Grabs his things. And charges into the locker room.

FORTY-TWO

"I am going to kill you."

"He wasn't like that when I went to visit," Kenji says to me. "I swear. He was fine. He was *sad*."

"Yeah, well, obviously seeing my face isn't bringing back happy memories for him."

Kenji sighs. Looks away. "I'm really sorry," he says. "I swear. But he wasn't lying, J. They were down to practically nothing the last time I went back there. Kent said half their supplies went bad because he didn't realize the blast had broken some of the shelves in their storage room. Some of the jars had cracked open and there were rodents and shit eating their food. And they were all alone out there. It's cold as all hell and you have no idea how depressing it was, seeing them like that, and James—"

"I get it, Kenji." I blow out a breath. Fold myself onto the floor. "I really do."

I look up, look around. Everyone is busying themselves with some kind of task. Running or sketching or training or lifting weights. I think we're all exhausted by this drama. No one wants to deal with it anymore.

Kenji sits down across from me.

"He can't keep treating me like that," I finally say. "And

I won't keep having the same conversation with him." I look up. "You brought him here. He's your responsibility. We have three weeks before we initiate this plan, and we're already cutting it really close. I need to be able to come down here and train every day, and I don't want to have to worry about him freaking out on me."

"I know," he says. "I know."

"Good."

"Hey, so—were you serious?" Kenji asks. "When you said Warner doesn't care about him being here?"

"Yeah. Why?"

Kenji raises his eyebrows. "That's . . . weird."

"One day," I say to him, "you'll realize that Warner is not as crazy as you think he is."

"Yeah," Kenji says. "Or maybe one day we'll be able to reprogram that chip in your head."

"Shut up." I laugh, shoving him a little.

"All right. Up. Let's go. It's time to work."

FORTY-THREE

Alia has designed me a new suit.

We're sitting on the mats like we always do in the evenings, and right now, Alia is showing us her designs.

I've never seen her this animated before.

She's more confident talking about the contents of her sketchbook than she is the weather. She's talking fast and fluid, describing the details and the dimensions, even outlining the materials we'll need in order to make it.

It's built with carbon.

Carbon fibers, to be precise. She explained that carbon fibers are so stiff and abrasive that they'll need to be bonded with something very flexible in order to become wearable, so she's planning on experimenting with several different materials. Something about polymers. And synthetic something. And a bunch of other words I didn't really understand. Her sketches show how the carbon fibers are literally woven into a textile, creating a durable and lightweight material that will serve as a stronger basis for what I need.

Her idea was inspired by the knuckle braces she made for me.

She said she originally wanted the suit to be made of

thousands of pieces of gunmetal, but then she realized she'd never have the tools to make the pieces as thin as she'd like them, and therefore, the suit would be too heavy. But this is sounding just as amazing.

"It'll complement and enhance your strength," she's saying to me. "The carbon fibers will give you an added level of protection; they won't damage easily, so you'll be able to move more freely through different terrains. And when you're in a dangerous environment, you must remember to maintain a state of *electricum* at all times; that way your body will become virtually indestructible," she says.

"What do you mean . . . ?" I look from her to Castle for clarification. "How can that be possible?"

"Because," Alia explains. "In the same way that you can break through concrete without hurting yourself, you should also be able to sustain an attack—from a bullet, for example—without harm." She smiles. "Your powers make you functionally invincible."

Wow.

"This suit is a precaution more than anything else," she goes on. "We've seen in the past that you *can*, in fact, damage your skin if you're not wholly in control of your power. When you broke the ground in the research rooms," she says, "we thought it was the enormity of the act that injured you. But after examining the situation and your abilities more thoroughly, Castle and I found this deduction to be inaccurate."

"Our energies are never inconsistent," Castle jumps in, nodding at Alia. "They follow a pattern—an almost mathematical precision. If you cannot injure yourself while breaking through a concrete wall, it does not then follow that you should be able to injure yourself by breaking the ground, only to remain *un*injured after breaking the ground a second time." He looks at me. "Your injuries have to do with your hold on your ability. If you ever slip out of *electricum*—if you dial it back for even a moment—you will be vulnerable. Remember to be *on*, at all times. If you do, you cannot be defeated."

"I hate you so hard right now," Kenji mutters under his breath. "Functionally invincible my ass."

"Jealous?" I grin at him.

"I can't even look at you."

"You shouldn't be surprised." Warner has just walked in. I spin around to find he's heading toward our group, smiling a brittle smile at no one in particular. He sits down across from me. Meets my eyes as he says, "I always knew your powers, once harnessed, would be unmatched."

I try to breathe.

Warner finally breaks eye contact with me to glance around the room. "Good evening, everyone," he says. He nods at Castle. A special sort of acknowledgment.

Adam has a special sort of acknowledgment of his own.

He's staring at Warner with an intense, unmasked hatred, looking as though he truly wants to murder Warner, and I'm suddenly more anxious than I've been all day. I'm looking from Adam to Warner and back again and I don't know what to do. I don't know if something is about to happen and I'm so desperate for things to be civil that I—

"Hi," James says, so loudly it startles all of us. He's looking at Warner. "What are you doing here?"

Warner raises an eyebrow. "I live here."

"This is your *house*?" James asks.

Strange. I wonder what Adam and Kenji told him about where they were going.

Warner nods. "In some capacity, yes," he says. "It serves as my home. I live upstairs."

"That's so cool," James says, grinning. "This whole place is so cool." He frowns. "Hey I thought we were supposed to hate you, though."

"*James*," Adam says, shooting his brother a warning glance.

"What?" James asks.

"You are free to hate me," Warner says. "If you want to. I don't mind."

"Well you *should* mind," James says, surprised. "I'd be really upset if someone hated me."

"You are young."

"I'm almost twelve," James says to him.

"I was told you were ten."

"I said *almost* twelve." James rolls his eyes. "How old are you?"

Everyone is watching. Listening. Too fascinated to look away.

Warner studies James. Takes his time answering. "I'm nineteen years old."

James's eyes go wide. "You're only a year older than

Adam," he says. "How do you have so many nice things if you're only a year older than Adam? I don't know anyone your age who has nice things."

Warner looks over at me. Looks back at James. Looks at me again. "Is there nothing you want to add to this conversation, love?"

I shake my head. Smiling.

"Why do you call her 'love'?" James asks. "I've heard you say that before, too. A lot. Are you in love with her? I think Adam's in love with her. Kenji's not in love with her, though. I already asked him."

Warner blinks at him.

"Well?" James asks.

"Well what?"

"Are you in love with her?"

"Are *you* in love with her?"

"What?" James blushes. "No. She's like a million years older than me."

"Would anyone like to take over this conversation?" Warner asks, looking around the group.

"You never answered my question," James says. "About why you have so many things. I'm not trying to be rude," he says. "Really. I'm just wondering. I've never taken a shower with hot water before. And you have so much food. It must be really nice to have so much food all the time."

Warner flinches, unexpectedly. He looks more carefully at James. "No," he says slowly. "It is not a terrible thing to have food and hot water all the time."

"So then are you going to answer my question? About

where you got all this stuff?"

Warner sighs.

"I am the commander and regent of Sector 45," he says. "We are currently on an army base, where it is my job to oversee our soldiers and all the civilians who live on the accompanying compounds. I am paid to live here."

"Oh." James goes pale in an instant; he suddenly looks inhumanly terrified. "You work for The Reestablishment?"

"Hey, it's okay, buddy," Kenji says to James. "You're safe here. Okay? No one's going to hurt you."

"This is the kind of guy you're into, huh?" Adam snaps at me. "The kind of guy who petrifies children?"

"It's nice to see you again, Kent." Warner is watching Adam now. "How are you enjoying your stay?"

Adam seems to be fighting back the urge to say a lot of unkind things.

"So you really work for them?" James is asking Warner again, his words just a breath, his eyes still frozen on Warner's face. He's shaking so hard it breaks my heart. "You work for The Reestablishment?"

Warner hesitates. Looks away and looks back again. "Theoretically," he says. "Yes."

"What do you mean?" James asks.

Warner is looking into his hands.

"What do you mean, *theoretically*?" James demands.

"Are you asking," Warner says with a sigh, "because you are actually seeking clarification? Or is it because you don't know what the word *theoretically* means?"

James hesitates, his panic dissolving into frustration for

268

a moment. He screws up his face, annoyed. "Fine. What does *theoretically* mean?"

"Theoretically," Warner says, "I'm supposed to work for The Reestablishment. But, obviously, as I'm hosting a group of rebels on this government-owned military base— in my private quarters, no less—and sustaining said rebels so that they might overthrow our current regime, I would say no. I am not, exactly, working for The Reestablishment. I have committed treason," he says to James. "A crime that is punishable by death."

James stares at him for a long time. "*That's* what *theoretically* means?"

Warner looks up at the wall. Sighs again.

I bite back a laugh.

"So, wait—then you're not the bad guy," James says all of a sudden. "You're on our side, right?"

Warner turns slowly to meet James's eyes. Says nothing.

"Well?" James asks, impatient. "Aren't you on our side?"

Warner blinks. Twice. "So it seems," he says, looking as though he can hardly believe he's saying it.

"Perhaps we should get back to the suit," Castle cuts in. He's looking at Warner, smiling triumphantly. "Alia has spent a long time designing it, and I know she has more details to share."

"Yeah," Kenji says, excited. "This looks badass, Alia. I want one. Can I have one?"

I wonder if I'm the only person who notices that Warner's hands are shaking.

FORTY-FOUR

"Punch me."

Warner is standing directly across from me, head cocked to the side. Everyone is watching us.

I shake my head, fast.

"Don't be afraid, love," he says to me. "I just want you to try."

His arms are relaxed at his sides. His stance so casual. It's Saturday morning, which means he has time off from his daily workout routine. Which means he's decided to work with me, instead.

I shake my head again.

He laughs. "Your training with Kenji is good," he says, "but this is just as important. You need to learn how to fight. You have to be able to defend yourself."

"But I can defend myself," I say to him. "I'm strong enough."

"Strength is excellent," he says, "but it's worth nothing without technique. If you can be overpowered, you are not strong *enough*."

"I don't think I could be overpowered," I say to him. "Not really."

"I admire your confidence."

"Well, it's true."

"When you met my father for the first time," he says, "were you not initially overpowered?"

My blood runs cold.

"And when you set out to fight after I left Omega Point," he says to me, "were you not overpowered again?"

I clench my fists.

"And even after you were captured," he says quietly, "was my father not able to overpower you once more?"

I drop my head.

"I want you to be able to defend yourself," Warner says, his voice gentle now. "I want you to learn how to fight. Kenji was right the other day, when he said you can't just throw your energy around. You have to be able to project with precision. Your moves must always be deliberate. You have to be able to anticipate your opponent in every possible way, both mentally and physically. Strength is only the first step."

I look up, meet his eyes.

"Now punch me," he says.

"I don't know how," I finally admit, embarrassed.

He's trying so hard not to smile.

"Are you looking for volunteers?" I hear Kenji ask. He steps closer. "Because I'll gladly kick your ass if Juliette isn't interested."

"*Kenji*," I snap, spinning around. I narrow my eyes.

"What?"

"Come on, love," Warner says to me. He's unfazed by Kenji's comment, looking at me as if no one else in this room exists. "I want you to try. Use your strength. Tap into every bit of power you have. And then punch me."

"I'm afraid I'm going to hurt you."

Warner laughs again. Looks away. Bites his lip as he stifles another smile. "You're not going to hurt me," he says. "Trust me."

"Because you'll absorb the power?"

"No," he says. "Because you won't be *able* to hurt me. You don't know how."

I frown, annoyed. "Fine."

I swing my fist in what I assume a punch is supposed to look like. But my motion is limp and wobbly and so humiliatingly bad I almost give up halfway.

Warner catches my arm. He meets my eyes. "Focus," he says to me. "Imagine you are terrified. You are cornered. You are fighting for your life. *Defend* yourself," he demands.

I pull my arm back with more intensity, ready to try harder this time, when Warner stops me. He grabs my elbow. Shakes it a little. "You are not playing baseball," he says. "You do not wind up for a punch, and you do not need to lift your elbow up to your ear. Do not give your opponent advance notice of what you're about to do," he says. "The impact should be unexpected."

I try again.

"My face is in the center, love, right here," he says, tapping a finger against his chin. "Why are you trying to hit my shoulder?"

I try again.

"Better—control your arm—keep your left fist up—protect your face—"

I punch hard, a cheap shot, an unexpected hit even though I know he isn't ready.

His reflexes are too fast.

His fist is clenched around my forearm in an instant. He yanks, hard, pulling my arm forward and down until I'm off-balance and toppling toward him. Our faces are an inch apart.

I look up, embarrassed.

"That was cute," he says, unamused as he releases me. "Try again."

I do.

He blocks my punch with the back of his hand, slamming into the space just inside my wrist, knocking my arm sideways.

I try again.

He uses the same hand to grab my arm in midair and pull me close again. He leans in. "Do not allow anyone to catch your arms like this," he says. "Because once they do, they'll be able to control you." And, as if to prove it, he uses his hold on my arm to pull me in and then shove me backward, hard.

Not too hard.

But still.

I'm starting to get irritated, and he can tell.

He smiles.

"You really want me to hurt you?" I ask him, eyes narrowing.

"I don't think you can," he says.

"I think you're pretty cocky about that."

"Prove me wrong, love." He raises an eyebrow at me. "Please."

I swing.

He blocks.

I strike again.

He blocks.

His forearms are made of *steel*.

"I thought this was about *punching*," I say to him, rubbing at my arms. "Why do you keep hitting my forearms?"

"Your fist does not carry your strength," he says. "It's just a tool."

I swing again, faltering at the last minute, my confidence failing me.

He catches my arm. Drops it.

"If you're going to hesitate," he says, "do it on purpose. If you're going to hurt someone, do it on purpose. If you're going to lose a fight," he says, "do it on *purpose*."

"I just—I can't do this right," I tell him. "My hands are shaking and my arms are starting to hurt—"

"Watch what I do," he says. "Watch my form."

His feet are planted about shoulder-width apart, his legs slightly bent at the knees. His left fist is up and held back, protecting the side of his face, and his right fist is leading, sitting higher and slightly diagonal from his left. Both elbows are tucked in, hovering close to his chest.

He swings at me, slowly, so I can study the movement.

His body is tensed, his aim focused, every movement controlled. The power comes from somewhere deep inside of him; it's the kind of strength that is a consequence of years of careful training. His muscles know how to move. Know how to fight. His power is not a gimmick of supernatural coincidence.

His knuckles gently graze the edge of my chin.

He makes it look so easy to punch someone. I had no idea it was this difficult.

"Do you want to switch?" he asks.

"What?"

"If I try to punch you," he says. "Can you defend yourself?"

"No."

"Try," he says to me. "Just try to block me."

"Okay," I say, not actually wanting to. I feel stupid and petulant.

He swings again, slowly, for my sake.

I slap his arm out of the way.

He drops his hands. Tries not to laugh. "You are so much worse at this than I thought you'd be."

I scowl.

"Use your forearms," he says. "Block my swing. Knock it out of the way and shift your body with it. Remember to move your head when you block. You want to move yourself *away* from danger. Don't just stand there and slap."

275

I nod.

He starts to swing.

I block too quickly, my forearm hitting his fist. Hard.

I wince.

"It's good to anticipate," he says to me, his eyes sharp. "But don't get eager."

Another swing.

I catch his forearm. Stare at it. I try to pull it down like he did with mine, but he literally does not budge. At all. Not even an inch. It's like tugging on a metal pole buried in concrete.

"That was . . . okay," he says, smiling. "Try again. Focus." He's studying my eyes. "*Focus*, love."

"I *am* focused," I insist, irritated.

"Look at your feet," he says. "You're putting your weight on the front of your feet and you look like you're about to tip over. Plant yourself in place," he says. "But be ready to move. Your weight should rest on the heels of your feet," he says, tapping the back of his own foot.

"Fine," I snap, angry now. "I'm standing on the heels of my feet. I'm not tipping over anymore."

Warner looks at me. Captures my eyes. "Never fight when you're angry," he says quietly. "Anger will make you weak and clumsy. It will divert your focus. Your instincts will fail you."

I bite the inside of my cheek. Frustrated and ashamed.

"Try again," he says slowly. "Stay calm. Have faith in yourself. If you don't believe you can do it," he says, "you won't."

I nod, slightly mollified. Try to concentrate.

I tell him I'm ready.

He swings.

My left arm bends at the elbow in a perfect ninety-degree angle that slams into his forearm so hard it stops his swing. My head has shifted out of the way, my feet turned in the direction of his punch; I'm still standing steady.

Warner is amused.

He swings with his other fist.

I grab his forearm in midair, my fist closed around the space above his wrist, and I take advantage of his surprise to throw him off-balance, pulling his arm down and yanking him forward. He almost crashes into me. His face is right in front of mine.

And I'm so surprised that for a moment I don't know what to do. I'm caught in his eyes.

"Push me," he whispers.

I tighten my hold around his arm, and then shove him across the room.

He flies back, catching himself before hitting the floor.

I'm frozen in place. Shocked.

Someone whistles.

I turn around.

Kenji is clapping. "Well done, princess," he says, trying not to laugh. "I didn't know you had it in you."

I grin, half embarrassed and half absurdly proud of myself.

I meet Warner's eyes across the room. He nods, smiling so wide. "Good," he says. "Very good. You're a fast learner.

But we still have a lot of work to do."

I finally look away, catching a glimpse of Adam in the process.

He looks pissed.

FORTY-FIVE

The days have flown by, kites carrying them off into the distance.

Warner's been working with me every morning now. After his workout, and after my training with Kenji, he's carved out two hours a day to spend with me. Seven days a week.

He's an extraordinary teacher.

So patient with me. So pleasant. He's never frustrated, never bothered by how long it takes me to learn something new. He takes the time to explain the logic behind every detail, every motion, every position. He wants me to understand what I'm doing on an elemental level. He makes sure I'm internalizing the information and replicating it on my own, not just mimicking his movements.

I'm finally learning how to be strong in more ways than one.

It's strange. I never thought knowing how to throw a punch could make a difference, but the simple knowledge of understanding how to defend myself has made me so much more confident.

I'm so much more aware of myself now.

I walk around feeling the strength in my limbs. I'm

able to name the individual muscles in my body, knowing exactly how to use them—and how to abuse them, if I do things wrong. My reflexes are getting better, my senses are heightened. I'm beginning to understand my surroundings, to anticipate danger, and to recognize the subtle shifts in body language that indicate anger and aggression.

And my projection is almost too easy now.

Warner collected all sorts of things for me to destroy, just for target practice. Scraps of wood and metal, old chairs and tables. Blocks of concrete. Anything that would test my strength. Castle uses his energy to toss the objects into the air and it's my job to destroy them from across the room. At first it was nearly impossible; it's an extremely intense exercise that requires me to be wholly in control of myself.

But now, it's one of my favorite games.

I can stop and crush anything in the air. From any distance across the room. All I need are my hands to control the energy. I can move my own power in any direction, focusing it on small objects and then widening the scope for a larger mass.

I can move everything in the training room now. Nothing is difficult anymore.

Kenji thinks I need a new challenge.

"I want to take her outside," Kenji says. He's talking directly to Warner—so casually—something that's still strange for me to see. "I think she needs to start experimenting with natural materials. We're too limited in here."

Warner looks at me. "What do you think?"

"Will it be safe?" I ask.

"Well," he says, "it doesn't really matter, does it? In one week we'll be outing ourselves anyway."

"Good point." I try to smile.

Adam has been unusually quiet these past couple weeks.

I don't know if it's because Kenji talked to him and told him to be careful, or if it's because he's really resigned himself to this situation. Maybe he's realized there's nothing romantic happening between me and Warner. Which both pleases and disappoints me.

Warner and I seem to have reached some kind of understanding. A civil, oddly formal relationship that balances precariously between friendship and something else that has never been defined.

I can't say I enjoy it.

Adam doesn't interfere, however, when James speaks to Warner, and Kenji told me it's because Adam doesn't want to traumatize James by giving him a reason to be afraid of living here.

Which means James is constantly talking to Warner.

He's a curious kid, and Warner is so naturally private that he's the most obvious target for James's questions. Their exchanges are always entertaining for all of us. James is thoroughly unapologetic, and bolder than most anyone would ever be when talking to Warner.

It's kind of cute, actually.

Other than that, everyone has been progressing well.

Brendan and Winston are back to perfect, Castle is in better spirits every day, and Lily is a self-sufficient kind of girl who doesn't need much to be entertained—though she and Ian seem to have found a sort of solace in each other's company.

I suppose it makes sense that this kind of isolation would bring people together.

Like Adam and Alia.

He's been spending a lot of time with her lately, and I don't know what that means; it might be nothing more than friendship. But for most of the time I've been down in the training room, I've seen him sitting next her, just watching her sketch, asking the occasional question.

She's always blushing.

In some ways, she reminds me a lot of how I used to be.

I adore Alia, but sometimes watching them together makes me wonder if this is what Adam's always wanted. A sweet, quiet, gentle girl. Someone who would compensate for all the roughness he's seen in his life. He said that to me once, I remember. He said he loved that about me. That I was so *good*. So sweet. That I was the only good thing left in this world.

I think I always knew that wasn't true.

Maybe he's starting to see it, too.

FORTY-SIX

"I have to visit my mother today."

These are the seven words that begin our morning.

Warner has just walked out of his office, his hair a golden mess around his head, his eyes so green and so simultaneously transparent that they defy true description. He hasn't bothered to button his rumpled shirt and his slacks are unbelted and hanging low on his waist. He looks completely disoriented. I don't think he's slept all night and I want so desperately to know what's been happening in his life but I know it's not my place to ask. Worse still, I know he wouldn't even tell me if I did.

There's no level of intimacy between us anymore.

Everything was moving so quickly between us and then it halted to a complete stop. All those thoughts and feelings and emotions frozen in place. And now I'm so afraid that if I make the wrong move, everything will break.

But I miss him.

He stands in front of me every day and I train with him and work alongside him like a colleague and it's not enough for me anymore. I miss our easy conversations, his open smiles, the way he always used to meet my eyes.

I miss him.

And I need to talk to him, but I don't know how. Or when. Or what to say.

Coward.

"Why today . . . ?" I ask tentatively. "Did something happen?"

Warner says nothing for a long time, just stares at the wall. "Today is her birthday."

"Oh," I whisper, heart breaking.

"You wanted to practice outdoors," he says, still staring straight ahead. "With Kenji. I can take you with me when I leave, as long as he promises to keep you invisible. I'll drop you off somewhere on unregulated territory and pick you up when I'm heading back. Will that be all right?"

"Yes."

He says nothing else, but his eyes are wild and unfocused. He's looking at the wall like it might be a window.

"Aaron?"

"Yes, love."

"Are you scared?"

He takes a tight breath. Exhales it slowly.

"I never know what to expect when I visit her," he says quietly. "She's different each time. Sometimes she's so drugged up she doesn't even move. Sometimes her eyes are open and she just stares at the ceiling. Sometimes," he says, "she's completely hysterical."

My heart twists.

"It's good that you still visit her," I say to him. "You know that, right?"

"Is it?" He laughs a strange, nervous sort of laugh. "Sometimes I'm not so sure."

"Yes. It is."

"How can you know?" He looks at me now, looks at me as though he's almost afraid to hear the answer.

"Because if she can tell, for even a second, that you're in the room with her, you've given her an extraordinary gift. She is not gone completely," I tell him. "She knows. Even if it's not all the time, and even if she can't show it. She knows you've been there. And I know it must mean so much to her."

He takes in another shaky breath. He's staring at the ceiling now. "That is a very nice thing to say."

"I really mean it."

"I know," he says. "I know you do."

I look at him a little longer, wondering if there's ever an appropriate time to ask questions about his mother. But there's one thing I've always wanted to ask. So I do.

"She gave you that ring, didn't she?"

Warner goes still. I think I can hear his heart racing from here. "What?"

I walk up to him and take his left hand. "This one," I say, pointing to the jade ring he's always worn on his left pinkie finger. He never takes it off. Not to shower. Not to sleep. Not ever.

He nods, so slowly.

"But . . . you don't like to talk about it," I say, remembering the last time I asked him about his ring.

I count exactly ten seconds before he speaks again.

"I was never allowed," he says very, very quietly, "to receive presents. From anyone. My father hated the idea of presents. He hated birthday parties and holidays. He never let anyone give anything to me, and especially not my mother. He said that accepting gifts would make me weak. He thought they would encourage me to rely on the charity of others.

"But we were hiding one day," he says. "My mother and I." His eyes are up, off, lost in another place. He might not be talking to me at all. "It was my sixth birthday and she was trying to hide me. Because she knew what he wanted to do to me." He blinks. His voice is a whisper, half dead of emotion. "I remember her hands were shaking," he says. "I remember because I kept looking at her hands. Because she was holding mine to her chest. And she was wearing this ring." He quiets, remembering. "I'd never seen much jewelry in my life. I didn't know what it was, exactly. But she saw me staring and she wanted to distract me," he says. "She wanted to keep me entertained."

My stomach is threatening to be sick.

"So she told me a story. A story about a boy who was born with very green eyes, and the man who was so captivated by their color that he searched the world for a stone in exactly the same shade." His voice is fading now, falling into whispers so quiet I can hardly hear him. "She said the boy was me. That this ring was made from that very same stone, and that the man had given it to her, hoping one day she'd be able to give it to me. It was his gift, she said, for my birthday." He stops. Breathes. "And then she took it off, slipped it on my index finger, and said, 'If you hide your heart, he will never be able to take it from you.'"

He looks toward the wall.

"It's the only gift," he says, "anyone has ever given to me."

My tears fall backward, burning as they singe their way down my throat.

FORTY-SEVEN

I feel strange, all day.

I feel off, somehow. Kenji is thrilled to be getting off base, excited about testing my strength in new places, and everyone else is jealous that we get to leave. So I should be happy. I should be eager.

But I feel strange.

My head is in a weird place, and I think it's because I haven't been able to shake Warner's story from my mind. I can't stop trying to imagine him as he was. As a small, terrified child.

No one knows where he's headed today. No one knows the depth of it. And he does nothing to betray how he's really feeling. He's been as calm as ever, controlled and careful in his words, his actions.

Kenji and I are meeting him again in just a moment.

We're slipping through the door in the gun wall, and I'm finally able to see firsthand how Warner sneaked them inside. We're crossing through a shooting range.

There are gun stations and little cubicles with targets set hundreds of feet away, and right now, the entire place is deserted. This must be another one of Warner's practice rooms.

There's a door at the end of the walkway, and Kenji pushes it open. He doesn't need to touch me at all anymore in order to keep me invisible, and it's so much more convenient this way. We can move freely as long as I'm within fifty feet of him, which gives us the flexibility we need to be able to work outside today.

We're now on the other side of the door.

Standing in an enormous storage facility.

The space is at least five hundred feet across, and maybe twice as high. I've never seen more boxes in my entire life. I have no idea what they contain, and no time to wonder.

Kenji is pulling me through the maze.

We sidestep boxes of all different sizes, careful not to trip over electrical cords and the machinery used to move the heavier items. There are rows and rows and more rows divided into even more rows that house everything in very organized sections. I notice there are labels on every shelf and in all the aisles, but I can't get close enough to read them.

When we finally make it to the end of the storage room, there are two huge, fifty-foot doors that lead to the exit. This is clearly a loading zone for trucks and tanks. Kenji grabs my arm and keeps me close as we pass several guards stationed by the exit. We dart through the trucks parked all around the loading zone, until we finally get to the meeting point where we're supposed to find Warner.

I wish Kenji could've been around to make me invisible when I first tried to get on and off base. It would've been so nice to just walk out like a human being, instead of being carted through the halls, jolting and teetering and clinging to the legs of a wheeling tray table.

Warner is leaning against a tank.

Both doors are open, and he's looking around like he might be overseeing the work being done with the loading units. He nods to several soldiers as they pass.

We clamber into the passenger side unnoticed.

And just as I'm about to whisper a notification to Warner, he walks around to the passenger side, says, "Watch your legs, love," and shuts the door.

And then he climbs into the other side. Starts driving.

We're still invisible.

"How did you know we were in here?" Kenji asks immediately. "Can you, like, see invisible people, too?"

"No," Warner says to him, eyes focused in front of him. "I can feel your presence. Hers, most of all."

"Really?" Kenji says. "That's some weird shit. What do I feel like? Peanut butter?"

Warner is unamused.

Kenji clears his throat. "J, I think you should switch spots with me."

"Why?"

"I think your boyfriend is touching my leg."

"You flatter yourself," Warner says.

"Switch spots with me, J. He's making me feel all goosebumpy and shit, like maybe he's about to knife me."

"Fine." I sigh. I try clambering over him, but it's difficult,

290

considering I can see neither my own body nor his.

"Ow—*dammit*—you almost kicked me in the face—"

"Sorry!" I say, trying to scramble over his knees.

"Just move," he says. "God, how much do you weigh—"

He shifts, all at once, slipping out from under me, and gives me a small shove to move me over.

I fall face-first into Warner's lap.

I hear Warner's brief, sharp intake of breath, and I scramble upright, blushing so hard, and I'm suddenly so relieved no one can see me right now.

I want to punch Kenji in the nose.

No one talks much after that.

As we get closer to unregulated territory, the scenery starts to change. The simple, signless, semipaved roads give way to the streets of our old world. The houses are painted in shades that promised to be colorful once upon a time, and the roads are lined with sidewalks that might've carried children safely home from school. The houses are all falling apart now.

Everything is broken, dilapidated. The windows boarded up. The lawns overgrown and iced over. The winter bite looks fresh in the air, and it casts a gloom over the scene in a way that says this all might be different in another season. Who knows.

Warner stops the tank.

He climbs out and walks over to our door, just in case anyone is still out here, and makes it seem as though he's opening it for a specific reason. To check the interior. To examine a problem.

It doesn't matter.

Kenji jumps out first, and Warner seems to be able to tell that he's gone.

I reach for Warner's hand, because I know he can't see me. His fingers immediately tighten around mine. His eyes are focused on the floor.

"It's going to be okay," I tell him. "Okay?"

"Yes," he says. "I'm sure you're right."

I hesitate. "Will you be back soon?"

"Yes," he whispers. "I'll return for you in exactly two hours. Will that be sufficient time?"

"Yes."

"Good. I'll meet you back here, then. In this exact location."

"Okay."

He says nothing for a second. Then, "Okay."

I squeeze his hand.

He smiles at the ground.

I stand up and he shifts to the side, allowing me room to get by. I touch him as I move past, just briefly. Just as a reminder. That I'm here for him.

He flinches, startled, and steps back.

And then he climbs into the tank, and leaves.

FORTY-EIGHT

Warner is late.

Kenji and I had a semisuccessful session, one that consisted mainly of us arguing over where we were standing and what we were looking at. We're going to have to come up with much better signals next time, because trying to coordinate a training session between two invisible people is a lot more difficult than it sounds. Which is saying a lot.

So now we're tired and slightly disappointed, having accomplished little in the way of progress, and we're standing in exactly the same place Warner dropped us off.

And Warner is late.

This is unusual for many reasons. The first of which is that Warner is never late. Not for anything. And the second is that if he were going to be late, it definitely wouldn't be for something like this. This situation is far too dangerous to be casual about. He wouldn't have taken it lightly. I know he wouldn't have.

So I'm pacing.

"I'm sure it's fine," Kenji is saying to me. "He probably just got hung up doing whatever it is he's doing. You know, commandering and shit."

"*Commandering* is not a word."

"It has letters, doesn't it? Sounds like a word to me."

I'm too nervous to banter right now.

Kenji sighs. I hear him stomp his feet against the cold. "He'll be here."

"I don't feel right, Kenji."

"I don't feel right, either," he says. "I'm hungry as hell."

"Warner wouldn't be late. It's not like him to be late."

"How would you know?" Kenji shoots back. "You've known him for how long, exactly? Five months? And you think you know him so well? Maybe he's in a secret jazz club where he sings a cappella and wears sparkly vests and thinks it's cool to do the cancan."

"Warner wouldn't wear sparkly vests," I snap.

"But you think he'd be down with the cancan."

"Kenji, I love you, I really do, but right now I'm so anxious, and I feel so sick, that the more you speak, the more I want to kill you."

"Don't talk sexy to me, J."

I huff, irritated. God, I'm so worried. "What time is it?"

"Two forty-five."

"This isn't right. We should go find him."

"We don't even know where he is."

"I do," I say. "I know where he is."

"*What?* How?"

"Do you remember where we met Anderson for the first time?" I ask him. "Do you remember how to get back to Sycamore Street?"

"Yeah . . . ," Kenji says slowly. "Why?"

"He's about two streets down from there."

"Um. What the hell? Why is he down there?"

"Will you go with me?" I ask, nervous. "Please? Now?"

"Okay," he says, unconvinced. "But only because I'm curious. And because it's cold as hell out here and I need to move my legs before I freeze to death."

"Thank you," I say. "Where are you?"

We follow the sounds of each other's voices until we bump right into one another. Kenji slips his arm into mine. We huddle together against the cold.

He leads the way.

FORTY-NINE

This is it.

The robin's-egg-blue house. The one I woke up in. The one Warner lived in. The one his mother is stored in. We're standing in front of it and it looks exactly as it did the last two times I was here. Beautiful and terrifying. Wind chimes whipping back and forth.

"Why the hell would Warner be here?" Kenji asks. "What is this place?"

"I can't really tell you," I say to him.

"Why not?"

"Because it's not my secret to tell."

Kenji is silent a moment. "So what do you want me to do?"

"Can you wait here?" I ask him. "Will I be able to stay invisible if I go inside? Or will I get out of range?"

Kenji sighs. "I don't know. You can definitely try. I've never tried to do this from outside a house before." He hesitates. "But if you're going to go in without me, can you please hurry the hell up? I'm already freezing my ass off."

"Yes. I promise. I'll be fast. I just want to make sure he's all right—or that he's even in here. Because if he's not inside, he might be waiting for us back at the drop-off."

"And all of this will have been a huge waste of time."

"I'm sorry," I say to him. "I'm really sorry. But I just have to make sure."

"Go," he says. "Go and come back fast."

"Okay," I whisper. "Thank you."

I break away and climb up the stairs to the little porch. Test the handle. It's unlocked. I turn it, push the door open. Step inside.

This is where I was shot.

The bloodstain from where I was lying on the ground has already been cleaned up. Or maybe the carpet was changed. I'm not sure. Either way, the memories still surround me. I can't walk back into this house without feeling sick to my stomach. Everything is wrong in here. Everything is so wrong. So off.

Something has happened.

I can feel it.

I'm careful to shut the door gently behind me. I creep up the stairs, remembering how the floorboards squeaked when I was first captured and brought here, and I'm able to sidestep the noisiest parts; the rest of it, thankfully, just sounds like it could be the wind.

When I'm upstairs, I count three doors. Three rooms.

On the left: Warner's old room. The one I woke up in.

In the middle: the bathroom. The one I was bathed in.

On the far end of the hall, all the way to the right: his mother's room. The one I'm looking for.

My heart is racing in my chest.

I can hardly breathe as I tiptoe closer. I don't know what I'm expecting to find. I don't know what I'm hoping will come of this trip. I don't have any idea, even, if Warner is still in here.

And I have no idea what it'll be like to see his mother.

But something is pulling me forward, urging me to open the door and check. I need to know. I just have to know. My mind won't rest otherwise.

So I inch forward. Take several deep breaths. I grasp the doorknob and turn, so slowly, not even realizing I've lost invisibility until I see my feet crossing the threshold.

I panic in an instant, my brain calculating contingency plans, and though I briefly consider turning around and bolting out the door, my eyes have already scanned the room.

And I know I can't turn back now.

FIFTY

There's a bed in here.

A single bed. Surrounded by machines and IVs and bottles and brand-new bedpans. There are stacks of bedsheets and stacks of blankets and the most beautiful bookcases and embroidered pillows and adorable stuffed animals piled everywhere. There are fresh flowers in five different vases and four brightly painted walls and there's a little desk in the corner with a little matching chair and there's a potted plant and a set of old paintbrushes and there are picture frames, everywhere. On the walls, on the desk, sitting on the table beside the bed.

A blond woman. A little blond boy. Together.

They never age, I notice. The pictures never move past a certain year. They never show the evolution of this child's life. The boy in these photos is always young, and always startled, and always holding fast to the hand of the lady standing beside him.

But that lady is not here. And her nurse is gone, too.

The machines are off.

The lights are out.

The bed is empty.

Warner has collapsed in the corner.

He's curled into himself, knees pulled up to his chest, arms wrapped around his legs, his head buried in his arms. And he's shaking.

Tremors are rocking his entire body.

I've never, ever seen him look like a child before. Never, not once, not in all the time I've known him. But right now, he looks just like a little boy. Scared. Vulnerable. All alone.

It doesn't take much to understand why.

I fall to my knees in front of him. I know he must be able to sense my presence, but I don't know if he wants to see me right now. I don't know how he's going to react if I reach out.

But I have to try.

I touch his arms, so gently. I run my hand down his back, his shoulders. And then I dare to wrap myself around him until he slowly breaks apart, unfolding in front of me.

He lifts his head.

His eyes are red-rimmed and a startling, striking shade of green, shining with barely restrained emotion. His face is the picture of so much pain.

I almost can't breathe.

An earthquake hits my heart then, cracks it right down the middle. And I think here, in him, there is more feeling than any one person should ever have to contain.

I try to hold him closer but he wraps his arms around my hips instead, his head falling into my lap. I bend over him instinctively, shielding his body with my own.

I press my cheek to his forehead. Press a kiss to his temple.

And then he breaks.

Shaking violently, shattering in my arms, a million gasping, choking pieces I'm trying so hard to hold together. And I promise myself then, in that moment, that I will hold him forever, just like this, until all the pain and torture and suffering is gone, until he's given a chance to live the kind of life where no one can wound him this deeply ever again.

And we are quotation marks, inverted and upside down, clinging to one another at the end of this life sentence. Trapped by lives we did not choose.

It's time, I think, to break free.

FIFTY-ONE

Kenji is waiting in the tank when we get back. He managed to find it.

He's sitting in the passenger side, invisibility off, and he doesn't say a single word as Warner and I climb inside.

I try to meet his eyes, already prepared to concoct some crazy story for why it took me an hour to get Warner out of the house, but then Kenji looks at me. Really looks at me.

And I close my mouth forever.

Warner doesn't say a single word. He doesn't even breathe loudly. And when we get back to base, he lets me and Kenji leave the tank under our guise of invisibility and he still says nothing, not even to me. As soon as we're out of the tank, he closes our door, and climbs back inside.

I'm watching him drive off again when Kenji slips his arm into mine.

We weave back through the storage facility without a problem. Cross through the shooting range without a problem. But just before we reach the door to Warner's training facility, Kenji pulls me aside.

"I followed you in," he says, with no preamble. "You took too long and I got worried and I followed you up there." A pause. A heavy pause. "I saw you guys," he says, so quietly. "In that room."

Not for the first time today, I'm glad he can't see my face. "Okay," I whisper, not knowing what else to say. Not knowing what Kenji will do with the information.

"I just—" Kenji takes a deep breath. "I'm just confused, okay? I don't need to know all the details—I realize that whatever was happening in there was none of my business—but are you okay? Did something happen?"

I exhale. Close my eyes as I say, "His mom died today."

"What?" Kenji asks, stunned. "What—h-how? His mom was in there?"

"She'd been sick for a long time," I say, the words rushing out of me. "Anderson kept her locked in that house and he abandoned her. He left her to die. Warner had been trying to help her, and he didn't know how. She couldn't be touched, just like I can't touch anyone, and the pain of it was killing her every day." I'm losing control now, unable to keep my feelings contained any longer. "Warner never wanted to use me as a weapon," I say to him. "He made that up so he had a story to tell his father. He found me by accident. Because he was trying to find a solution. To help *her*. All these years."

Kenji takes a sharp breath. "I had no idea," he says. "I didn't even know he was close to his mom."

"You don't know him at all," I say, not caring how desperate I sound. "You think you do but you really don't." I feel raw, like I've been sanded down to the bone.

He says nothing.

"Let's go," I say. "I need some time to breathe. To think."

"Yeah," he says. He exhales. "Yeah, sure. Of course."

I turn to go.

"J," he says, stopping me, his hand still on my arm.

I wait.

"I'm sorry. I'm really sorry. I didn't know."

I blink fast against the burning in my eyes. Swallow back the emotion building in my throat. "It's okay, Kenji. You were never supposed to."

FIFTY-TWO

I finally manage to pull myself together long enough to head back to the training rooms. It's getting late, but I don't anticipate seeing Warner down here tonight. I think he'll want the time alone.

I'm making myself scarce on purpose.

I've had enough.

I came so close to killing Anderson once, and I'll make sure I have that chance again. But this time, I'll follow through.

I wasn't ready last time. I wouldn't have known what to do even if I'd killed him then. I would've handed control over to Castle and I would've watched quietly as someone else tried to fix our world again. But I see now that Castle was wrong for this job. He's too tender. Too anxious to please everyone.

I, on the other hand, am left with no concerns at all.

I will be unapologetic. I will live with no regrets. I will reach into the earth and rip out the injustice and I will crush it in my bare hands. I want Anderson to fear me and I want him to beg for mercy and I want to say no, not for you. Never for you.

And I don't care if that's not nice enough.

FIFTY-THREE

I get to my feet.

Adam is standing across the room, talking to Winston and Ian. Everyone falls silent as I approach. And if Adam is thinking or feeling anything at all about me, he doesn't show it.

"You have to tell him," I say.

"What?" Adam startles.

"You have to tell him the truth," I say. "And if you don't, I will."

All at once Adam's eyes are a frozen ocean, cold and closed off. "Don't push me, Juliette. Don't say stupid things you're going to regret."

"You have no right to keep this from him. He has no one in this world, and he deserves to know."

"This is *none* of your business," Adam says. He's towering over me, his fists clenched. "Stay out of it. Don't force me to do something I don't want to do."

"Are you actually threatening me?" I ask. "Are you insane?"

"Maybe you've forgotten," he says, "that I'm the only one in this room who can shut you off. But I haven't. You have no power against me."

"Of course I have power against you," I tell him. "My touch was *killing you* when we were together—"

"Yeah, well, things have changed a lot since then." He grabs my hand, yanking so hard I nearly fall forward. I try to pull away and I can't.

He's too strong.

"Adam, let go of me—"

"Can you feel that?" he asks, eyes a crazy, stormy shade of blue.

"What?" I ask. "Feel what?"

"Exactly," he says. "There's nothing there. You're empty. No power, no fire, no superstrength. Just a girl who can't throw a punch to save her life. And I'm perfectly fine. Unharmed."

I swallow hard and meet his cold gaze. "So you've done it, then?" I ask. "You managed to control it?"

"Of course I did," he says angrily. "And you couldn't wait—even though I told you I could do it—you couldn't wait even though I told you I was training so we could be together—"

"It doesn't matter anymore." I'm staring at my hand in his, his refusal to let go. "We would've ended up in the same place sooner or later."

"That's not true—this is proof!" he says, holding up my hand. "We could've made it work—"

"We're too different now. We want different things. And this?" I say, nodding at our hands. "All this managed to prove is that you are extremely good at turning me off."

Adam's jaw clenches.

"Now let go of my hand."

"Hey—can we please refrain from putting on a shitshow tonight?" Kenji's voice booms from across the room. He's heading toward us. Pissed.

"Stay out of this," Adam snaps at him.

"It's called *consideration*. There are other people living in this room, jackass," Kenji says once he's close enough. He grabs Adam's arm. "So knock it off."

Adam breaks away angrily. "Don't touch me."

Kenji shoots him a sharp look. "Let go of her."

"You know what?" Adam says, his anger taking over. "You're so obsessed with her—jumping to her defense all the time, getting involved in our conversations all the time—you like her so much? Fine. You can have her."

Time freezes all around us.

The stage is set:

Adam and his wild eyes, his rage and his red face.

Kenji standing next to him, annoyed, slightly confused.

And me, my hand still locked in Adam's viselike grip, his touch so quickly and easily reducing me back to who I was when we first met.

I'm completely powerless.

But then, in one movement, everything changes:

Adam grabs Kenji's bare hand and presses it into my empty one.

For just long enough.

FIFTY-FOUR

It takes a couple of seconds for the two of us to register what's just happened before Kenji rips his hand away, and in a moment of perfect spontaneity, uses it to punch Adam in the face.

Everyone else in the room is now up and alert. Castle runs forward immediately, and Ian and Winston—who were already standing close by—hurry to join him. Brendan rushes out of the locker room in a towel, eyes searching for the source of the commotion; Lily and Alia jump off the bikes and crowd around us.

We're lucky it's so late; James is already sleeping quietly in the corner.

Adam was thrown back by Kenji's punch, but he quickly regained his footing. He's breathing hard, dragging the back of his hand across his now-bloody lip. He does not apologize.

No sound escapes my open, horrified mouth.

"What in God's name is wrong with you?" Kenji's voice is soft but deathly sharp, his right fist still clenched. "Were you trying to get me killed?"

Adam rolls his eyes. "I knew it wouldn't kill you. Not that quickly. I've felt it before," he says. "It just burns a little."

"Pull yourself together, dickhead," Kenji snaps. "You're acting insane."

Adam says nothing. He actually laughs, gives Kenji the middle finger, and heads in the direction of the locker room.

"Hey—are you okay?" I ask Kenji, trying to catch a glimpse of his hand.

"I'm fine," he sighs, glancing at Adam's retreating figure before looking back at me. "But his jaw is hard as hell." He flexes his fist a little.

"But my touch—it didn't hurt you?"

Kenji shakes his head. "Nah, I didn't feel anything," he says. "And I'd know if I did." He almost laughs, and frowns instead. I cringe at the memory of the last time this happened. "I think Kent was deflecting your power somehow," Kenji says.

"No he wasn't," I whisper. "He let go of my other hand. I felt the energy come back into me."

We both look at Adam's retreating figure.

Kenji shrugs.

"But then how—"

"I don't know," Kenji says again. He sighs. "I guess I just got lucky. Listen"—he looks around at everyone—"I don't want to talk right now, okay? I'm going to go sit down. I need to cool off."

The group breaks up slowly, everyone going back to their corners.

But I can't walk away. I'm rooted in place.

I felt my skin touch Kenji's, and that's not something I

can ignore. Those kinds of moments are so rare for me that I can't just shake them off; I never get to be that close to people without serious consequences. And I felt the power inside my body. Kenji should've felt *something*.

My mind is working fast, trying to solve an impossible equation, and a crazy theory takes root inside of me, crystallizing in a way I'd never thought it could.

This whole time I've been training to control my power, to contain it, to focus it—but I never thought I'd be able to turn it *off*. And I don't know why.

Adam had a similar problem: he'd been running on *electricum* his whole life. But now he's learned how to control it. To power it down when he needs to.

Shouldn't I be able to do the same?

Kenji can go visible and invisible whenever he likes—it was something he had to teach himself after training for a long time, after understanding how to shift from one state of being to another. I remember the story he told me from when he was little: he turned invisible for a couple of days without knowing how to change back. But eventually he did.

Castle, Brendan, Winston, Lily—they can all turn their abilities on and off. Castle doesn't move things with his mind by accident. Brendan doesn't electrocute everything he touches. Winston can tighten and loosen his limbs at will, and Lily can look around normally, without taking snapshots of everything with her eyes.

Why am I the only one without an off switch?

My mind is overwhelmed as I process the possibilities. I

311

begin to realize that I never even *tried* to turn my power off, because I always thought it would be impossible. I assumed I was fated to this life, to an existence in which my hands—my skin—would always, always keep me away from others.

But now?

"Kenji!" I cry out as I run toward him.

Kenji glances over his shoulder at me, but doesn't have the chance to turn all the way around before I crash into him, grabbing his hands and squeezing them in my own. "Don't let go," I tell him, eyes filling fast with tears. "Don't let go. You don't have to let go."

Kenji is frozen, shock and amazement all over his face. He looks at our hands. Looks back up at me.

"You learned how to control it?" he asks.

I can hardly speak. I manage to nod, tears spilling down my cheeks. "I think I've had it contained, all this time, and just didn't know it. I never would've risked practicing it on anyone."

"Damn, princess," he says softly, his own eyes shining. "I'm so proud of you."

Everyone is crowding around us now.

Castle pulls me into a fierce hug, and Brendan and Winston and Lily and Ian and Alia jump on top of him, crushing me all at once. They're cheering and clapping and shaking my hand and I've never felt so much support or so much strength in our group before. No moment in my life has ever been more extraordinary than this.

But when the congratulations ebb and the good-nights

begin, I pull Kenji aside for one last hug.

"So," I say to him, rocking on my heels. "I can touch anyone I want now."

"Yeah, I know." He laughs, cocking an eyebrow.

"Do you know what that means?"

"Are you asking me out?"

"You know what this *means*, right?"

"Because I'm flattered, really, but I still think we're much better off as friends—"

"Kenji."

He grins. Musses my hair. "No," he says. "I don't know. What does it mean?"

"It means a million things," I say to him, standing on tiptoe to look him in the eye. "But it also means that now I will never end up with anyone by default. I can do anything I want now. Be with anyone I want. And it'll be my choice."

Kenji just looks at me for a long time. Smiles. Finally, he drops his eyes. Nods.

And says, "Go do what you gotta do, J."

FIFTY-FIVE

When I get off the elevator and step into Warner's office, all the lights are off. Everything is swimming in an inky sort of black, and it takes me several tries to adjust my eyes to the darkness. I pad my way through the office carefully, searching for any sign of its owner, and find none.

I head into the bedroom.

Warner is sitting on the edge of the mattress, his coat thrown on the floor, his boots kicked off to the side. He's sitting in silence, palms up on his lap, looking into his hands like he's searching for something he cannot find.

"Aaron?" I whisper, moving forward.

He lifts his head. Looks at me.

And something inside of me shatters.

Every vertebra, every knuckle, both kneecaps, both hips. I am a pile of bones on the floor and no one knows it but me. I am a broken skeleton with a beating heart.

Exhale, I tell myself.

Exhale.

"I'm so sorry," are the first words I whisper.

He nods. Gets to his feet.

"Thank you," he says to no one at all as he walks out the door.

I follow him across the bedroom and into his office. Call out his name.

He stops in front of the boardroom table, his back to me, his hands gripping the edge. "Please, Juliette, not tonight, I can't—"

"You're right," I finally say. "You've always been right."

He turns around, so slowly.

I'm looking into his eyes and I'm suddenly petrified. I'm suddenly nervous and suddenly worried and suddenly so sure I'm going to do this all wrong but maybe wrong is the only way to do it because I can't keep it to myself anymore. There are so many things I need to tell him. Things I've been too much of a coward to admit, even to myself.

"Right about what?" His green eyes are wide. Scared.

I hold my fingers to my mouth, still so afraid to speak.

I do so much with these lips, I think.

I taste and touch and kiss and I've pressed them to the tender parts of his skin and I've made promises and told lies and touched lives all with these two lips and the words they form, the shapes and sounds they curve around. But right now my lips wish he would just read my mind because the truth is I've been hoping I'd never have to say any of it, these thoughts, out loud.

"I do want you," I say to him, my voice shaking. "I want you so much it scares me."

I see the movement in his throat, the effort he's making to keep still. His eyes are terrified.

"I lied to you," I tell him, words tripping and stumbling

out of me. "That night. When I said I didn't want to be with you. I lied. Because you were right. I was a coward. I didn't want to admit the truth to myself, and I felt so guilty for preferring you, for wanting to spend all my time with you, even when everything was falling apart. I was confused about Adam, I was confused about who I was supposed to be and I didn't know what I was doing and I was stupid," I say. "I was stupid and inconsiderate and I tried to blame it on you and I hurt you, so badly." I try to breathe. "And I'm so, so sorry."

"What—" Warner is blinking fast. His voice is fragile, uneven. "What are you saying?"

"I love you," I whisper. "I love you exactly as you are."

Warner is looking at me like he might be going deaf and blind at the same time. "No," he gasps. One broken, broken word. Barely even a sound. He's shaking his head and he's looking away from me and his hand is caught in his hair, his body turned toward the table and he says "No. No, no—"

"Aaron—"

"No," he says, backing away. "No, you don't know what you're saying—"

"I love you," I tell him again. "I love you and I want you and I wanted you then," I say to him, "I wanted you so much and I still want you, I want you right now—"

Stop.

Stop time.

Stop the world.

Stop everything for the moment he crosses the room and pulls me into his arms and pins me against the wall and I'm spinning and standing and not even breathing but I'm alive so alive so very very alive

and he's kissing me.

Deeply, desperately. His hands are around my waist and he's breathing so hard and he hoists me up, into his arms, and my legs wrap around his hips and he's kissing my neck, my throat, and he sets me down on the edge of the boardroom table.

He has one hand under my neck, the other under my shirt and he's running his fingers up my back and suddenly his thigh is between my legs and his hand is slipping behind my knee and up, higher, pulling me closer, and when he breaks the kiss I'm breathing so fast, head spinning as I try to hold on to him.

"Up," he says, gasping for air. "Lift your arms up."

I do.

He tugs up my shirt. Pulls it over my head. Tosses it to the floor.

"Lie back," he says to me, still breathing hard, guiding me onto the table as his hands slide down my spine, under my backside. He unbuttons my jeans. Unzips them. Says, "Lift your hips for me, love," and hooks his fingers around the waist of my trousers and my underwear at the same time. Tugs them down.

I gasp.

I'm lying on his table in nothing but my bra.

Then that's gone, too.

His hands are moving up my legs and the insides of my

thighs and his lips are making their way down my chest, and he's undoing what little is left of my composure and every bit of my sanity and I'm aching, everywhere, tasting colors and sounds I didn't even know existed. My head is pressed back against the table and my hands are gripping his shoulders and he's hot, everywhere, gentle and somehow so urgent, and I'm trying not to scream and he's already moving down my body, he's already chosen where to kiss me. How to kiss me.

And he's not going to stop.

I'm beyond rational thought. Beyond words, beyond comprehensible ideas. Seconds are merging into minutes and hearts are collapsing and hands are grasping and I've tripped over a planet and I don't know anything anymore, I don't know anything because nothing will ever be able to compare to this. Nothing will ever capture the way I'm feeling right now.

Nothing matters anymore.

Nothing but this moment and his mouth on my body, his hands on my skin, his kisses in brand-new places making me absolutely, certifiably insane. I cry out and cling to him, dying and somehow being brought back to life in the same moment, the same breath.

He's on his knees.

I bite back the moan caught in my throat just before he lifts me up and carries me to the bed. He's on top of me in an instant, kissing me with a kind of intensity that makes me wonder why I haven't died or caught on fire or woken up from this dream yet. He's running his hands down my body only to bring them back up to my face and he kisses me once, twice, and his teeth catch my bottom lip for just a second and I'm clinging to him, wrapping my arms around his neck and running my hands through his hair and pulling him into me. He tastes so sweet. So hot and so sweet and I keep trying to say his name but I can't even find the time to breathe, much less to say a single word.

I shove him up, off me.

I undo his shirt, my hands shaking and fumbling with the buttons and I get so frustrated I just rip it open, buttons flying everywhere, and I don't have a chance to push the fabric off his body before he pulls me into his lap. He wraps my legs around his hips and dips me backward until the mattress is under my head and he leans over me, cupping my face in his hands, his thumbs two parentheses around my mouth and he pulls me close and he kisses me, kisses me until time topples over and my head spins into oblivion.

It's a heavy, unbelievable kiss.

It's the kind of kiss that inspires stars to climb into the sky and light up the world. The kind that takes forever and no time at all. His hands are holding my cheeks, and he pulls back just to look me in the eye and his chest is heaving and he says, "I think," he says, "my heart is going to explode," and I wish, more than ever, that I knew how to capture moments like these and revisit them forever.

Because this.

This is everything.

FIFTY-SIX

Warner has been asleep all morning.

He didn't wake up to work out. Didn't wake up to shower. Didn't wake up to do anything. He's just lying here, on his stomach, arms wrapped around a pillow.

I've been awake since 8:00 a.m., and I've been staring at him for two hours.

He's usually up at five thirty. Sometimes earlier.

I worry that he might've missed a lot of important things by now. I have no idea if he has meetings or specific places to be today. I don't know if he's ruined his schedule by being asleep so late. I don't know if anyone will come to check on him. I have no idea.

I do know that I don't want to wake him.

We were up very late last night.

I run my fingers down his back, still confused by the word IGNITE tattooed on his skin, and train my eyes to see his scars as something other than the terrifying abuse he's suffered his whole life. I can't handle the horrible truth of it. I curl my body around his, rest my face against his back, my arms holding fast to his sides. I drop a kiss on his spine. I can feel him breathing, in and out, so evenly. So steadily.

Warner shifts, just a little.

I sit up.

He rolls over slowly, still half asleep. Uses the back of one fist to rub his eyes. Blinks several times. And then he sees me.

Smiles.

It's a sleepy, sleepy smile.

I can't help but smile back. I feel like I've been split open and stuffed with sunshine. I've never seen a sleepy Warner before. Never woken up in his arms. Never seen him be anything but awake and alert and sharp.

He looks almost lazy right now.

It's adorable.

"Come here," he says, reaching for me.

I crawl into his arms and cling, and he holds me tight against him. Drops a kiss on the top of my head. Whispers, "Good morning, sweetheart."

"I like that," I say quietly, smiling even though he can't see it. "I like it when you call me sweetheart."

He laughs then, his shoulders shaking as he does. He rolls onto his back, arms stretched out at his sides.

God, he looks so good without his clothes on.

"I have never slept so well in my entire life," he says softly. He grins, eyes still closed. Dimples on both cheeks. "I feel so strange."

"You slept for a long time," I tell him, lacing his fingers in mine.

He peeks at me through one eye. "Did I?"

I nod. "It's late. It's already ten thirty."

He stiffens. "Really?"

I nod again. "I didn't want to wake you."

He sighs. "I'm afraid I should get going then. Delalieu has likely had an aneurysm."

A pause.

"Aaron," I say tentatively. "Who is Delalieu, exactly? Why is he so trustworthy with all of this?"

A deep breath. "I've known him for many, many years."

"Is that all . . . ?" I ask, leaning back to look him in the eye. "He knows so much about us and what we're doing and it worries me sometimes. I thought you said all your soldiers hated you. Shouldn't you be suspicious? Trust him less?"

"Yes," he says quietly, "you'd think I would."

"But you don't."

Warner meets my eyes. Softens his voice. "He's my mother's father, love."

I stiffen in an instant, jerking back. "What?"

Warner looks up at the ceiling.

"He's your *grandfather*?" I'm sitting up in bed now.

Warner nods.

"How long have you known?" I don't know how to stay calm about this.

"My entire life." Warner shrugs. "He's always been around. I've known his face since I was a child; I used to see him around our house, sitting in on meetings for The Reestablishment, all organized by my father."

I'm so stunned I hardly know what to say. "But . . . you treat him like he's . . ."

"My lieutenant?" Warner stretches his neck. "Well, he is."

"But he's your *family*—"

"He was assigned to this sector by my father, and I had no reason to believe he was any different from the man who gave me half my DNA. He's never gone to visit my mother. Never asks about her. Has never shown any interest in her. It's taken Delalieu nineteen years to earn my trust, and I've only just allowed myself this weakness because I've been able to sense his sincerity with regular consistency throughout the years." Warner pauses. "And even though we've reached some level of familiarity, he has never, and will never, acknowledge our shared biology."

"But why not?"

"Because he is no more my grandfather than I am my father's son."

I stare at Warner for a long time before I realize there's no point in continuing this conversation. Because I think I understand. He and Delalieu have nothing more than an odd, formal sort of respect for each other. And just because you're bound by blood does not make you a family.

I would know.

"So do you have to go now?" I whisper, sorry I even brought up the topic of Delalieu.

"Not just yet." He smiles. Touches my cheek.

We're both silent a moment.

"What are you thinking?" I ask him.

He leans in, kisses me so softly. Shakes his head.

I touch the tip of my finger to his lips. "There are secrets in here," I say. "I want them out."

He tries to bite my finger.

I steal it back.

"Why do you smell so good?" he asks, still smiling as he avoids my question. He leans in again, leaves light kisses along my jawline, under my chin. "It's making me crazy."

"I've been stealing your soaps," I tell him.

He raises his eyebrows at me.

"Sorry." I feel myself blush.

"Don't feel bad," he says, serious so suddenly. "You can have anything of mine you want. You can have all of it."

I'm caught off guard, so touched by the sincerity in his voice. "Really?" I ask. "Because I do love that soap."

He grins at me then. His eyes are wicked.

"What?"

He shakes his head. Breaks away. Slips out of bed.

"Aaron—"

"I'll be right back," he says.

I watch him walk into the bathroom. I hear the sound of a faucet, the rush of water filling a tub.

My heart starts racing.

He walks back into the room and I'm clinging to the sheets, already protesting what I think he's about to do.

He tugs on the blanket. Tilts his head at me. "Let go, please."

"No."

"Why not?"

"What are you going to do?" I ask.

"Nothing."

"Liar."

"It's okay, love." His eyes are teasing me. "Don't be embarrassed."

"It's too bright in here. Turn the lights off."

He laughs out loud. Yanks the covers off the bed.

I bite back a scream. "Aaron—"

"You are perfect," he says. "Every inch of you. Perfect," he says again. "Don't hide from me."

"I take it back," I say, panicked, clutching a pillow to my body. "I don't want your soap—I take it back—"

But then he plucks the pillow out of my arms, scoops me up, and carries me away.

FIFTY-SEVEN

My suit is ready.

Warner made sure Alia and Winston would have everything they needed in order to create it, and though I'd seen them tackling the project a little more every day, I never would've thought all those different materials could turn into this.

It looks like snakeskin.

The material is both black and gunmetal gray, but it looks almost gold in certain flashes of light. The pattern moves when I do, and it's dizzying how the threads seem to converge and diverge, looking as though they swim together and come apart.

It fits me in a way that's both uncomfortable and reassuring; it's skintight and a little stiff at first, but once I start moving my arms and legs I begin to understand just how much hidden flexibility it holds. It all seems strangely counterintuitive. This suit is even lighter than the one I had before—it hardly feels like I'm wearing anything at all—and yet it feels so much more durable, so much stronger. I feel like I could block a knife in this suit. Like I could be dragged across a mile of pavement in this suit.

I also have new boots.

They're very similar to my old ones, but these cut off at my calf, not my ankle. They're flat, springy, and soundless as I walk around in them.

I didn't ask for any gloves.

I'm flexing my bare hands, walking the length of the room and back, bending my knees and familiarizing myself with the sensation of wearing a new kind of outfit. It serves a different purpose. I'm not trying to hide my skin from the world anymore. I'm only trying to enhance the power I already have.

It feels so good.

"These are for you, too," Alia says, beaming as she blushes. "I thought you might like a new set." She holds out exact replicas of the knuckle braces she made for me once before.

The ones I lost. In a battle we lost.

These, more than anything else, represent so much to me. It's a second chance. An opportunity to do things right. "Thank you," I tell her, hoping she knows how much I mean it.

I fit the braces over my bare knuckles, flexing my fingers as I do.

I look up. Look around.

Everyone is staring at me. "What do you think?" I ask.

"Your suit looks just like mine." Kenji frowns. "I'm supposed to be the one with the black suit. Why can't you have a pink suit? Or a yellow suit—"

"Because we're not the freaking Power Rangers,"

Winston says, rolling his eyes.

"What the hell is a Power Ranger?" Kenji shoots back.

"I think it looks awesome," James says, grinning big. "You look way cooler than you did before."

"Yeah, that is seriously badass," Lily says. "I love it."

"It's your best work, mates," Brendan says to both Winston and Alia. "Really. And the knuckle—things . . . ," he says, gesturing to my hands. "Those are just . . . they bring the whole thing together, I think. It's brilliant."

"You look very sharp, Ms. Ferrars," Castle says to me. "I think it quite suits you," he says, "if you'll forgive the pun."

I grin.

Warner's hand is on my back. He leans in, whispers, "How easy is it to take this thing off?" and I force myself not to look at him and the smile he's surely enjoying at my expense. I hate that he can still make me blush.

My eyes try to find a new focus around the room.

Adam.

He's staring at me, his features unexpectedly relaxed. Calm. And for one moment, one very brief moment, I catch a glimpse of the boy I once knew. The one I first fell for.

He turns away.

I can't stop hoping he'll be okay; he only has twelve hours to pull himself together. Because tonight, we go over the plan, one last time.

And tomorrow, it all begins.

FIFTY-EIGHT

"Aaron?" I whisper.

The lights are out. We're lying in bed. I'm stretched out across his body, my head pillowed on his chest. My eyes are on the ceiling.

He's running his hand over my hair, his fingers occasionally combing through the strands. "Your hair is like water," he whispers. "It's so fluid. Like silk."

"Aaron."

He leaves a light kiss on top of my head. Rubs his hands down my arms. "Are you cold?" he asks.

"You can't avoid this forever."

"We don't have to avoid it at all," he says. "There's nothing to avoid."

"I just want to know you're okay," I say. "I'm worried about you." He still hasn't said a single thing to me about his mother. He never said a word the entire time we were in her room, and he hasn't spoken about it since. Hasn't even alluded to it. Not once.

Even now, he says nothing.

"Aaron?"

"Yes, love."

"You're not going to talk about it?"

He's silent again for so long I'm about to turn around to face him. But then.

"She's no longer in pain," he says softly. "This is a great consolation to me."

I don't push him to speak after that.

"Juliette," he says.

"Yes?"

I can hear him breathing.

"Thank you," he whispers. "For being my friend."

I turn around then. Press close to him, my nose grazing his neck. "I will always be here if you need me," I say, the darkness catching and hushing my voice. "Please remember that. Always remember that."

More seconds drown in the darkness. I feel myself drifting off to sleep.

"Is this really happening?" I hear him whisper.

"What?" I blink, try to stay awake.

"You feel so real," he says. "You sound so real. I want so badly for this to be real."

"This is real," I say. "And things are going to get better. Things are going to get so much better. I promise."

He takes a tight breath. "The scariest part," he says, so quietly, "is that for the first time in my life, I actually believe that."

"Good," I say softly, turning my face into his chest. I close my eyes.

Warner's arms slip around me, pulling me closer. "Why are you wearing so many clothes?" he whispers.

"Mmm?"

"I don't like these," he says. He tugs on my trousers.

I touch my lips to his neck, just barely. It's a feather of a kiss. "Then take them off."

He pulls back the covers.

I only have a second to bite back a shiver before he's kneeling between my legs. He finds the waistband of my trousers and tugs, pulling them off, over my hips, down my thighs. So slowly.

My heart is asking me all kinds of questions.

He bunches my trousers in one fist and throws them across the room.

And then his arms slip behind my back, pulling me up and against his chest. His hands move under my shirt, up my spine.

Soon my shirt is gone.

Tossed in the same direction as my trousers.

I shiver, just a little, and he eases me back onto the pillows, careful not to crush me under his weight. His body heat is so welcome, so warm. My head tilts backward. My eyes are still closed.

My lips part for no reason at all.

"I want to be able to feel you," he whispers, his words at my ear. "I want your skin against mine." His gentle hands move down my body. "God, you're so soft," he says, his voice husky with emotion.

He's kissing my neck.

My head is spinning. Everything goes hot and cold and

something is stirring to life inside of me and my hands reach for his chest, looking for something to hold on to and my eyes are trying and failing to stay open and I'm only just conscious enough to whisper his name.

"Yes, love?"

I try to say more but my mouth won't listen.

"Are you asleep now?" he asks.

Yes, I think. I don't know. Yes.

I nod.

"That's good," he says quietly. He lifts my head, pulls my hair away from my neck so my face falls more easily onto the pillow. He shifts so he's beside me on the bed. "You need to sleep more," he says.

I nod again, curling onto my side. He pulls the blankets up around my arms.

He kisses the curve of my shoulder. My shoulder blade. Five kisses down my spine, one softer than the next. "I will be here every night," he whispers, his words so soft, so tortured, "to keep you warm. I will kiss you until I can't keep my eyes open."

My head is caught in a cloud.

Can you hear my heart? I want to ask him.

I want you to make a list of all of your favorite things, and I want to be on it.

But I'm falling asleep so fast I've lost my grasp on reality, and I don't know how to move my mouth. Time has fallen all around me, wrapped me in this moment.

And Warner is still talking. So quietly, so softly. He

thinks I'm asleep now. He thinks I can't hear him.

"Did you know," he's whispering, "that I wake up, every morning, convinced you'll be gone?"

Wake up, I keep telling myself. *Wake up. Pay attention.*

"That all of this," he says, "these moments, will be confirmed as some kind of extraordinary dream? But then I hear you speak to me," he says. "I see the way you look at me and I can feel how real it is. I can feel the truth in your emotions, and in the way you touch me," he whispers, the back of his hand brushing my cheek.

My eyes flicker open. I blink once, twice.

His lips are set in a soft smile.

"Aaron," I whisper.

"I love you," he says.

My heart no longer fits in my chest.

"Everything looks so different to me now," he says. "It feels different. It tastes different. You brought me back to life." He's quiet a moment. "I have never known this kind of peace. Never known this kind of comfort. And sometimes I am afraid," he says, dropping his eyes, "that my love will terrify you."

He looks up, so slowly, gold lashes lifting to reveal more sadness and beauty than I've ever seen in the same moment. I didn't know a person could convey so much with just one look. There's extraordinary pain in him. Extraordinary passion.

It takes my breath away.

I take his face in my hands and kiss him, so slowly.

His eyes fall closed. His mouth responds to mine. His hands reach up to pull me closer and I stop him.

"No," I whisper. "Don't move."

He drops his hands.

"Lie back," I whisper.

He does.

I kiss him everywhere. His cheeks. His chin. The tip of his nose and the space between his eyebrows. All across his forehead and along his jawline. Every inch of his face. Small, soft kisses that say so much more than I ever could. I want him to know how I feel. I want him to know it the way only he can, the way he can sense the depth of emotion behind my movements. I want him to know and never doubt.

And I want to take my time.

My mouth moves down to his neck and he gasps, and I breathe in the scent of his skin, take in the taste of him and I run my hands down his chest, kissing my way across and down the line of his torso. He keeps trying to reach for me, keeps trying to touch me, and I have to tell him to stop.

"Please," he says, "I want to feel you—"

I gentle his arms back down. "Not yet. Not now."

My hands move to his trousers. His eyes fly open.

"Close your eyes," I have to tell him.

"No." He can hardly speak.

"Close your eyes."

He shakes his head.

"Fine."

I unbutton his trousers. Unzip.

"Juliette," he breathes. "What—"

I'm pulling off his pants.

He sits up.

"Lie down. Please."

He's staring at me, eyes wide.

He finally falls back.

I tug his pants off all the way. Toss them to the floor.

He's in his underwear.

I trace the stitching on the soft cotton, following the lines on the overlapping pieces of his boxer-briefs as they intersect in the middle. He's breathing so fast I can hear him, can see his chest moving. His eyes are squeezed shut. His head tilted back. His lips parted.

I touch him again, so gently.

He stifles a moan, turns his face into the pillows. His whole body is trembling, his hands clutching at the sheets. I run my hands down his legs, gripping them just above his knees and inching them apart to make room for the kisses I trail up the insides of his thighs. My nose skims his skin.

He looks like he's in pain. So much pain.

I find the elastic waist of his underwear. Tug it down.

Slowly.

Slowly.

The tattoo is sitting just below his hip bone.

hell is empty

and all the devils are here

I kiss my way across the words.

Kissing away the devils.

Kissing away the pain.

FIFTY-NINE

I'm sitting on the edge of the bed, elbows propped up on my knees, face dropped into my hands.

"Are you ready?" he asks me.

I look up. Stand up. Shake my head.

"Breathe, sweetheart." He stands in front of me, slips his hands around my face. His eyes are bright, intense, steady, and so full of confidence. In me. "You are magnificent. You are extraordinary."

I try to laugh and it comes out all wrong.

Warner leans his forehead against mine. "There is nothing to fear. Nothing to worry about. Grieve nothing in this transitory world," he says softly.

I tilt back, a question in my eyes.

"It's the only way I know how to exist," he says. "In a world where there is so much to grieve and so little good to take? I grieve nothing. I take everything."

I stare into his eyes for what feels like forever.

He leans into my ear. Lowers his voice. "Ignite, my love. Ignite."

Warner has called for an assembly.

He says it's a fairly routine procedure, one wherein the

soldiers are required to wear a standard black uniform. "And they will be unarmed," Warner said to me.

Kenji and Castle and everyone else are coming to watch, care of Kenji's invisibility, but I'm the only one who's going to speak today. I told them I wanted to lead. I told them I'd be willing to take the first risk.

So here I am.

Warner walks me out of his bedroom door.

The halls are abandoned. The soldiers patrolling his quarters are gone, already assembled and awaiting his presence. The reality of what I'm about to do is only just starting to sink in.

Because no matter the outcome today, I am putting myself on display. It is a message from me to Anderson. A message I know he'll receive.

I am alive.

I will use your own armies to hunt you down.

And I will kill you.

Something about this thought makes me absurdly happy.

We walk into the elevator and Warner takes my hand. I squeeze his fingers. He smiles straight ahead. And suddenly we're walking out of the elevator and through another door and right into the open courtyard I've only ever stood in once before.

How odd, I think, that I should return to this roof not as a captive. No longer afraid. And clinging fast to the hand of the same blond boy who brought me here before.

How very strange this world is.

Warner hesitates before moving into view. He looks at me for confirmation. I nod. He releases my hand.

We step forward together.

SIXTY

There's an audible gasp from the soldiers standing just below.

They definitely remember me.

Warner pulls a square piece of mesh out of his pocket and presses it to his lips, just once, before holding it in his fist. His voice is amplified across the crowd when he speaks.

"Sector 45," he says.

They shift. Their right fists rise up to fall on their chests, their left fists released, dropping to their sides.

"You were told," he says, "a little over a month ago, that we'd won the battle against a resistance group by the name of Omega Point. You were told we decimated their home base and slaughtered their remaining men and women on the battlefield. You were told," he says, "never to doubt the power of The Reestablishment. We are unbeatable. Unsurpassed in military power and land control. You were told that we are the future. The only hope."

His voice rings out over the crowd, his eyes scanning the faces of his men.

"And I hope," he says, "that you did not believe it."

The soldiers are staring, stunned, as Warner speaks. They seem afraid to step out of line in case this turns out to be some kind of elaborate joke, or perhaps a test from The Reestablishment. They do nothing but stare, no longer taking care to make their faces appear as stoic as possible.

"Juliette Ferrars," he says, "is not dead. She is here, standing beside me, despite the claims made by our supreme commander. He did, in fact, shoot her in the chest. And he did leave her to die. But she was able to survive his attack on her life, and she has arrived here today to make you an offer."

I take the mesh from Warner's hand, touch it to my lips just as he did. Drop it into my fist.

I take a deep breath. And say six words.

"I want to destroy The Reestablishment."

My voice is so loud, so powerfully projected over the crowd, that for a moment it surprises me. The soldiers are staring at me in horror. Shock. Disbelief. Astonishment. They're starting to whisper.

"I want to lead you into battle," I say to them. "I want to fight back—"

No one is listening to me anymore.

Their perfectly organized lines have been abandoned. They're now converging together in one mass, speaking and shouting and trying to deliberate among themselves. Trying to understand what's happening.

I can't believe I lost their attention so quickly.

"Don't hesitate," Warner says to me. "You must react. *Now*."

I was hoping to save this for later.

Right now, we're only about fifteen feet off the ground, but Warner told me there are four more levels, if I want to go all the way up. The highest level houses the speakers designated for this particular area. It has a small maintenance platform that is only ever accessed by technicians.

I'm already climbing my way up.

The soldiers are distracted again, pointing at me as I scale the stairs; still talking loudly with one another. I have no idea if it's possible for news of this situation to have already reached the civilians or the spies who report back to the supreme. I have no time to care right now because I haven't even finished giving my speech, and I've already lost them.

This isn't good.

When I finally reach the top level, I'm about a hundred feet off the ground. I'm careful as I step onto the platform, but I'm more careful not to look down for too long. And when I've finally planted my feet, I look up and around the crowd.

I have their attention again.

I close my fist over the microphonic mesh.

"I only have one question," I say, my words powerful and clear, projecting into the distance. "What has The Reestablishment ever done for you?"

They're actually looking at me now. Listening.

"They have given you nothing but meager wages and promises for a future that will never come. They have divided your families and forced them across what's left of this earth. They have starved your children and destroyed your homes. They lie to you, over and over again, forcing you to take jobs in their army so they might control you. And you have no other choice," I say. "No other options. So you fight in their wars, and you kill your own friends, just so you might feed your families."

Yes, I have their attention now.

"The person you allow to lead this nation is a coward," I say to them. "He is a weak man who's too afraid to show his face to the public. He lives in secrecy, hides from the people who rely on him, and yet he's taught you to fear him," I say. "He's taught you to cower when his name is spoken.

"Maybe you haven't met him yet," I say. "But I have. And I was not impressed."

I can't believe no one has shot me yet. I don't care if they're supposed to be unarmed. Someone probably has a gun. And no one has shot me yet.

"Join a new resistance," I say to them, calling out to the crowd. "We are the majority, and we can stand united. Will you continue to live like this?" I ask them, pointing to the compounds in the distance. "Will you continue to starve? Because they will continue to lie to you!" I say. "Our world is not beyond repair. It's not beyond saving. We can be our own army," I say to them. "We can stand together. Join me," I say, "and I promise things will change."

"How?" I hear someone shout. "How can you promise something like that?"

"I am not intimidated by The Reestablishment," I tell them. "And I have more strength than you might realize. I have the kind of power that the supreme commander cannot stand against."

"We already know what you can do!" someone else yells. "That didn't save you before!"

"No," I say to them, "you don't know what I can do. You have no idea what I can do."

I reach my arms out in front of me, both hands pointed in the direction of the crowd. I try to find a good middle. And then I focus.

Feel your power, Kenji said to me once. *It's a part of you— a part of your body and mind. It will listen to you if you can learn how to control it.*

I plant my feet. Steel myself.

And then I pry the crowd apart.

Slowly.

I focus my energy on recognizing the individual bodies and allow my power to move fluidly, working around the soldiers in a gentle fashion, as opposed to rushing through them and accidentally ripping them apart. My power clings to their forms as my fingers would, finally finding a perfect center that divides the group into two halves. They're already looking at each other from across the courtyard, trying to understand why they can't move against the invisible walls pushing them apart.

But once the energy is set in place, I open my arms, wide. Pull.

The soldiers are knocked back. Half to the left. Half to the right. Not enough to be injured, but just enough to be startled. I want them to feel the power I'm containing. I want them to know that I'm holding back.

"I can protect you," I say to them, my voice still ringing loud over them. "And I have friends who could do more. Who will stand beside you and fight."

And then, as if on cue, the group of them appear out of thin air, in the very center of the courtyard, in the space I've just cleared.

The soldiers jerk back, stunned, shifting farther into their corners.

Castle reaches up one arm, coaxing a small tree in the distance to uproot itself. He uses both hands to pull it out of the ground, and once he does, the tree careens out of control, flying through the air, branches rattling in the wind. Castle pulls it back, yanking on it with nothing more than his mind.

He tosses it higher in the air, just over their heads, and Brendan raises his arms.

Claps his hands, hard.

A bolt of electricity hits the tree at the base and travels up the trunk so quickly, and with such extreme power, it practically disintegrates; the only remaining pieces rain to the ground.

I was not expecting that; they weren't even supposed to be helping me today. But they've just created the perfect introduction for me.

Now. Right now.

All the soldiers are watching. The courtyard has been

344

cleared. I find Kenji's eyes down below and check for confirmation.

He nods.

I jump.

A hundred feet in the air, eyes closed, legs straight, arms out. And I feel more power rushing through my being than ever before. I harness it. Project it.

And land so hard on the ground that it shatters beneath me.

I'm crouched, knees bent, one hand outstretched in front of me. The courtyard is shaking so badly that for a second I'm not sure I haven't caused another earthquake.

When I finally stand up and look around, I can see the soldiers much more clearly. Their faces, their worries. They're looking at me in awe, eyes wide with wonder and a touch of fear.

"You will not be alone," I say to them, spinning to see their faces. "You don't need to be afraid anymore. We want to take back our world. We want to save the lives of our family members, our friends. We want your children to have a chance at a better future. And we want to fight. We want to *win*." I lock eyes with them. "And we are asking for your help."

There's absolute silence.

And then, absolute chaos.

Cheers. Screams and shouts. Stomping feet.

I feel the mesh square tugged out of my hand. It flies up into the air and into Warner's hand.

He addresses his men.

"Congratulations, gentlemen," he says. "Send word to your families. Your friends. Tomorrow, everything will change. The supreme will be here in a matter of days," he says. "Prepare for war."

And then, all at once.

Kenji makes us disappear.

SIXTY-ONE

We're running through the courtyard and right through base, and as soon as we're out of sight, Kenji pulls back the invisibility. He darts ahead of the group, leading us toward the training room, winding and twisting and darting through the storage facility and up the shooting range until we're all toppling into the room at once.

James has been waiting for us.

He stands up, eyes wide. "How'd it go?"

Kenji runs forward and flips James into his arms. "How do you *think* it went?"

"Um. Good?" James is laughing.

Castle claps me on the back. I turn to face him. He's beaming at me, eyes shining, prouder than I've ever seen him. "Well done, Ms. Ferrars," he says quietly. "Well done."

Brendan and Winston rush over, grinning from ear to ear.

"That was so freaking cool," Winston says. "It was like we were celebrities or something."

Lily, Ian, and Alia join the group. I thank them all for their help, for their show of support at the last minute.

"Do you really think it'll work?" I'm asking. "Do you think it's enough?"

"It's certainly a start," Castle says. "We'll need to move quickly now. I imagine the news has already spread, but the other sectors will surely stand down until the supreme arrives." Castle looks at me. "I hope you understand that this will be a fight against the entire country."

"Not if the other sectors join us, too," I say.

"Such confidence," Castle says. He's staring at me like I'm a strange, alien being. One he doesn't know how to understand or identify. "You surprise me, Ms. Ferrars."

The elevator pings open.

Warner.

He walks right up to me. "The base has been secured," he says. "We are on lockdown until my father arrives. No one will enter or exit the premises."

"So what do we do now?" Ian asks.

"We wait," Warner says. He looks around at us. "If he does not already know, he will within the next five minutes. The supreme will know that some members of your group are still alive. That Juliette is still alive. He will know that I have defied him and stood against him publicly. And he will be very, very angry," Warner says. "This much I can absolutely guarantee."

"So we go to war," Brendan says.

"Yes." Warner is calm, so calm. "We fight. Soon."

"And the soldiers?" I ask him. "Are they really on board?"

He holds my eyes for just a moment too long. "Yes," he says. "I can feel the depth of their passion. Their sudden respect for you. There are many among them who are still afraid, and others still who are rigid in their skepticism, but you were right, love. They might fear, but they do not want to be soldiers. Not like this. Not for The Reestablishment. They are ready to join us."

"And the civilians?" I ask, amazed.

"They will follow."

"Are you sure?"

"I can be sure of nothing," he says quietly. "But I have never, in all my time in this sector, felt the kind of hope in my men that I felt today. It was so powerful, so all-consuming, I can still feel it from here. It's practically vibrating in my blood."

I can hardly breathe.

"Juliette, love," he says to me, still holding my eyes. "You have just started a war."

SIXTY-TWO

Warner pulls me to the side. Away from everyone else.

We're standing in a corner of the training room, and his hands are gripped around my shoulders. He's looking at me like I've just pulled the moon out of my pocket.

"I have to go," he says urgently. "There are many things that must be set in motion now, and I have to reconvene with Delalieu. I will handle every aspect of the military details, love. I will see to it that you have everything you need, and that my men are equipped in every possible way."

I'm nodding, trying to thank him.

But he's still looking at me, searching my eyes like he's found something he can't bear to walk away from. His hands move to my face; his thumb brushes my cheek. His voice is so tender when he speaks.

"You will go on to greatness," he whispers. "I have never deserved you."

My heart.

He leans in, kisses my forehead, so gently.

And then he leaves.

I'm still watching the elevator doors close when I catch a glimpse of Adam out of the corner of my eye. He walks up to me.

"Hey," he says. He looks nervous, uncomfortable.

"Hi."

He's nodding, staring at his feet. "So," he says. Blows out a breath. He's still not looking at me. "Nice show."

I'm not really sure what to say. So I say nothing.

Adam sighs. "You really have changed," he whispers. "Haven't you?"

"Yes. I have."

He nods, just once. Laughs a strange laugh. And walks away.

SIXTY-THREE

We're all sitting around again.

Talking. Discussing. Thinking and planning. James is snoring soundly in the corner.

We're all caught somewhere between being excited and being terrified, and yet, somehow, we're mostly excited. This is, after all, what everyone at Omega Point had always been planning; they'd joined Castle hoping it would one day come to this.

A chance to defeat The Reestablishment.

They've all been training for this. Even Adam, who somehow convinced himself to stand with us, has been a soldier. Kenji, a soldier. All of them in peak physical condition. They are all fighters; even Alia, whose quiet shell contains so much. I couldn't have asked for a more solid group of individuals.

"So when do you think he'll be here?" Ian is asking. "Tomorrow?"

"Maybe," Kenji says. "But I don't think it'll take him more than two days."

"I thought he was on a ship? In the middle of the ocean?" Lily asks. "How is he supposed to get here in two days?"

"I don't think it's the kind of ship you're thinking of,"

Castle says to her. "I imagine he is on an army vessel; one equipped with a landing strip. If he calls for a jet, they will deliver him to us."

"Wow." Brendan leans back, rests on his hands. "This is really happening, then? *The supreme commander of The Reestablishment.* Winston and I never saw him, not once, even though his men were holding us captive." He shakes his head. Glances at me. "What does he look like?"

"He's extremely handsome," I say.

Lily laughs out loud.

"I'm serious," I say to her. "It's almost sick how beautiful he is."

"Really?" Winston is staring at me, eyes wide.

Kenji nods. "Very pretty guy."

Lily is gawking.

"And you said his name is Anderson?" Alia asks.

I nod.

"That's strange," Lily says. "I always thought Warner's last name was *Warner*, not Anderson." She thinks for a second. "So his name is Warner Anderson?"

"No," I say to her. "You're right. Warner is his last name—but not his dad's. He took his mom's last name," I say. "He didn't want to be associated with his father."

Adam snorts.

We all look at him.

"So what's Warner's first name?" Ian asks. "Do you know?"

I nod.

"And?" Winston asks. "You're not going to tell us?"

"Ask him yourself," I say. "If he wants to tell you, I'm sure he will."

"Yeah, that's not going to happen," Winston says. "I'm not asking that guy personal questions."

I try not to laugh.

"So—do you know Anderson's first name?" Ian asks. "Or is that a secret, too? I mean this whole thing is really weird, right? That they'd be so secretive about their names?"

"Oh," I say, caught off guard. "I'm not sure. There's a lot of power in a name, I guess. And no," I say, shaking my head. "I don't actually know Anderson's first name. I never asked."

"You're not missing anything," Adam says, irritated. "It's a stupid name." He's staring at his shoes. "His name is Paris."

"How did you know that?"

I spin around and find Warner standing just outside the open elevator. It's still pinging softly, only just now signaling his arrival. The doors close behind him. He's staring at Adam in shock.

Adam blinks fast at Warner and then at us, unsure what to do.

"How did you know that?" Warner demands again. He walks right through our group and grabs Adam by the shirt, moving so quickly Adam has no time to react.

He pins him against the wall.

I've never heard Warner raise his voice like this before.

354

Never seen him so angry. "Who do you answer to, soldier?" he shouts. "Who is your commander?"

"I don't know what you're talking about!" Adam yells back. He tries breaking away and Warner grabs him with both fists, shoving him harder against the wall.

I'm beginning to panic.

"How long have you been working for him?" Warner shouts again. "How long have you been infiltrating my base—"

I jump to my feet. Kenji is close behind.

"Warner," I say, "please, he's not a spy—"

"There's no way he could know something like that," Warner says to me, still looking at Adam. "Not unless he is a member of the Supreme Guard, where even then it would be questionable. A foot soldier would never have that kind of information—"

"I'm not a Supreme Soldier," Adam tries to say, "I swear—"

"Liar," Warner barks, shoving him harder against the wall. Adam's shirt is starting to tear. "Why were you sent here? What is your mission? Has he sent you to kill me?"

"Warner," I call again, pleading this time, running forward until I'm in his line of vision. "Please—he's not working for the supreme, I promise—"

"How can you know?" Warner finally glances at me, just for a second. "I'm telling you," he says, "it's impossible for him to know this—"

"He's your *brother*," I finally choke out. "Please. He's your brother. You have the same father."

Warner goes rigid.

He turns to me.

"What?" he breathes.

"It's true," I tell him, feeling so heartbroken as I do. "And I know you can tell I'm not lying." I shake my head. "He's your brother. Your father was leading a double life. He abandoned Adam and James a long time ago. After Adam's mom died."

Warner drops Adam to the floor.

"No," Warner says. He's not even blinking. Just staring. Hands shaking.

I turn to look at Adam, eyes tight with emotion. "Tell him," I say, desperate now. "Tell him the truth."

Adam says nothing.

"Dammit, Adam, *tell* him!"

"You knew, all this time?" Warner asks, turning to face me. "You knew this and yet you said nothing?"

"I wanted to—I really, really wanted to, but I didn't think it was my place—"

"No," he says, cutting me off. He's shaking his head. "No, this doesn't make any sense. How—how is that even possible?" He looks up, looks around. "That doesn't—"

He stops.

Looks at Adam.

"Tell me the truth," he says. He walks up to Adam again, looking like he might shake him. "Tell me! I have a right to know!"

And every moment in the world drops dead just then, because they woke up and realized they'd never be as important as this one.

"It's true," Adam says.

Two words to change the world.

Warner steps back, hand caught in his hair. He's rubbing his eyes, his forehead, running his hand down his mouth, his neck. He's breathing so hard. "How?" he finally asks.

And then.

And then.

The truth.

Little by little. It's pulled out of Adam. One word at a time. And the rest of us are looking on, and James is still sleeping, and I go silent as these two brothers have the hardest conversation I've ever had to watch.

SIXTY-FOUR

Warner is sitting in one corner. Adam in another. They've both asked to be left alone.

And they're both staring at James.

James, who's still just a little snoring lump.

Adam looks exhausted, but not defeated. Tired, but not upset. He looks freer. His eyebrows unfurrowed. His fists unclenched. His face is calm in a way I haven't seen it in what feels like a long time.

He looks *relieved*.

As if he'd been carrying this great burden he thought might kill him. As if he'd thought sharing this truth with Warner might somehow inspire a lifelong war between him and his brand-new biological sibling.

But Warner wasn't angry at all. He wasn't even upset.

He was just shocked beyond belief.

One father, I think. Three brothers. Two who nearly killed each other, all because of the world they were bred in. Because of the many words, the many lies they were fed.

Words are like seeds, I think, planted into our hearts at a tender age.

They take root in us as we grow, settling deep into our souls. The good words plant well. They flourish and find homes in our hearts. They build trunks around our spines, steadying us when we're feeling most flimsy; planting our feet firmly when we're feeling most unsure. But the bad words grow poorly. Our trunks infest and spoil until we are hollow and housing the interests of others and not our own. We are forced to eat the fruit those words have borne, held hostage by the branches growing arms around our necks, suffocating us to death, one word at a time.

I don't know how Adam and Warner are going to break the news to James. Maybe they won't tell him until he's older and able to deal with the ramifications of knowing his heritage. I don't know what it'll do to James to learn that his father is actually a mass murderer and a despicable human being who's destroyed every life he's ever touched.

No.

Maybe it's better James doesn't know, not just yet.

Maybe it's enough for now that Warner knows at all.

I can't help but find it both painful and beautiful that Warner lost a mother and gained two brothers in the same week. And though I understand that he's asked to be left alone, I can't stop myself from walking over to him. I won't say a word, I promise myself. But I just want to be close to him right now.

So I sit down beside him, and lean my head against the wall. Just breathing.

"You should've told me," he whispers.

I hesitate before answering. "You have no idea how many times I wanted to."

"You should've told me."

"I'm so sorry," I say, dropping my head. My voice. "I'm really sorry."

Silence.

More silence.

Then.

A whisper.

"I have two brothers."

I lift my head. Look at him.

"I have two brothers," he says again, his voice so soft. "And I almost killed one of them."

His eyes are focused on a point far, far from here, pinched together in pain and confusion, and something that looks like regret.

"I suppose I should've known," he says to me. "He can touch you. He lives in the same sector. And his eyes have always been oddly familiar to me. I realize now that they're shaped just like my father's."

He sighs.

"This is so unbearably inconvenient," he says. "I was prepared to hate him for the rest of my life."

I startle, surprised. "You mean . . . you don't hate him anymore?"

Warner drops his head. His voice is so low I can hardly hear it. "How can I hate his anger," he says, "when I know so well where it comes from?"

I'm staring at him. Stunned.

"I can well imagine the extent of his relationship with my father," Warner says, shaking his head. "And that he has managed to survive it at all, and with more humanity than I did?" A pause. "No," he says. "I cannot hate him. And I would be lying if I said I didn't admire him."

I think I might cry.

The minutes pass between us, silent and still, stopping only to hear us breathe.

"Come on," I finally whisper, reaching for his hand. "Let's go to bed."

Warner nods, gets to his feet, but then he stops. Confused. So tortured. He looks at Adam. Adam looks back.

They stare at each other for a long time.

"Please excuse me," Warner says.

And I watch, astonished, as he crosses the room. Adam is on his feet in an instant, defensive, uncertain. But as Warner approaches, Adam seems to thaw.

The two are now face-to-face, and Warner is speaking.

Adam's jaw tenses. He looks at the floor.

He nods.

Warner is still speaking.

Adam swallows, hard. He nods again.

Then he looks up.

The two of them acknowledge each other for a long moment. And then Warner places one hand on Adam's shoulder.

I must be dreaming.

The two exchange a few more words before Warner pivots on one foot, and walks away.

SIXTY-FIVE

"What did you say to him?" I ask as soon as the elevator doors close.

Warner takes a deep breath. He says nothing.

"You're not going to tell me?"

"I'd rather not," he says quietly.

I take his hand. Squeeze.

The elevator doors open.

"Will this be weird for you?" Warner asks. He looks surprised by his own question, as though he can't believe he's even asking it.

"Will what be weird?"

"That Kent and I are . . . brothers."

"No," I say to him. "I've known for a while now. It doesn't change anything for me."

"That's good," he says quietly.

I'm nodding, confused.

We've moved into the bedroom. We're sitting on the bed now.

"You wouldn't mind, then?" Warner asks.

I'm still confused.

"If he and I," Warner says, "spent some time together?"

"What?" I ask, unable to hide my disbelief. "No," I say

quickly. "No, of course not—I think that would be amazing."

Warner's eyes are on the wall.

"So . . . you want to spend time with him?" I'm trying so hard to give Warner space, and I don't want to pry, but I just can't help myself.

"I would like to know my own brother, yes."

"And James?" I ask.

Warner laughs a little. "Yes. And James."

"So you're . . . happy about this?"

He doesn't answer right away. "I am not unhappy."

I climb into his lap. Cup his face in my hands, tilting his chin up so I can see his eyes. I'm smiling a stupid smile. "I think that's so wonderful," I tell him.

"Do you?" He grins. "How interesting."

I nod. Over and over again. And I kiss him once, very softly.

Warner closes his eyes. Smiles slightly, his cheek dimpled on one side. He looks thoughtful now. "How strange this has all become."

I feel like I might die of happiness.

Warner picks me up off his lap, lays me back on the bed. Crawls over me, on top of me. "And why are you so thrilled?" he asks, trying not to laugh. "You're practically buoyant."

"I want you to be happy," I tell him, my eyes searching his. "I want you to have a family. I want you to be surrounded by people who care about you," I say. "You deserve that."

"I have you," he says, resting his forehead against mine. His eyes shut.

"You should have more than me."

"No," he whispers. He shakes his head. His nose grazes mine.

"Yes."

"What about you? And your parents?" he asks me. "Do you ever want to find them?"

"No," I say quietly. "They were never parents to me. Besides, I have my friends."

"And me," he says.

"You are my friend," I tell him.

"But not your best friend. Kenji is your best friend."

I try so hard not to laugh at the jealousy in his voice. "Yes, but you're my *favorite* friend."

Warner leans in, bypasses my lips. "Good," he whispers, kissing my neck. "Now flip over," he says. "On your stomach."

I stare at him.

"Please," he says. Smiles.

I do. Very slowly.

"What are you doing?" I whisper, turning to look at him.

He gentles my body back down.

"I want you to know," he says, pulling on the zipper holding this suit together, "how much I value your friendship." The seam is coming apart and my skin is now open to the elements; I bite back a shiver.

The zipper stops at the base of my spine.

"But I'd like you to reconsider my title," Warner says. He drops a soft kiss in the middle of my back. Runs his hands up my skin and pushes the sleeves off my shoulders, leaving kisses against my shoulder blades, the back of my neck. "Because my friendship," he whispers, "comes with so many more benefits than Kenji could ever offer."

I can't breathe. Can't.

"Don't you think?" Warner asks.

"Yes," I say too quickly. "Yes."

And then I'm spinning, lost in sensations, and wondering how soon we'll be losing these moments, and wondering how long it'll be before we'll have them again.

I don't know where we're going, he and I, but I know I want to get there. We are hours and minutes reaching for the same second, holding hands as we spin forward into new days and the promise of something better.

But though we'll know forward and we've known backward, we will never know the present. This moment and the next one and even the one that would've been right now are gone, already passed, and all we're left with are these tired bodies, the only proof that we've lived through time and survived it.

It'll be worth it, though, in the end.

Fighting for a lifetime of this.

SIXTY-SIX

It took one day.

"I want one." I'm staring at the gun wall in the training room. "Which one is the best one?"

Delalieu arrived just this morning to deliver the news. The supreme has arrived. He's been transported from the ocean by jet, but he's now staying on one of Sector 45's army ships, stationed at the dock.

His guard is close behind. And his armies will be following soon.

Sometimes I'm not so sure we're not going to die.

"You don't need a gun," Warner says to me, surprised. "You can certainly have one, but I don't think you need one."

"I want two."

"All right," he laughs. But he's the only one.

Everyone else is frozen in the moments before fear takes over. We're all cautiously optimistic, but concerned nonetheless. Warner has already assembled his troops, and the civilians have already been notified; if they want to join us, a station has been set up to provide weapons and ammunition. All they have to do is present their RR cards to prove they are residents of Sector 45, and they will be granted amnesty. Shelters and relief centers have been created in the soldiers' barracks to stow away any remaining men, women, and children who cannot, or will not, join the battle. They will be allowed to take refuge here, and wait out the bloodshed.

These extra efforts were all coordinated by Warner.

"What if he just bombs everyone again?" Ian asks, breaking the silence. "Just like he did with Omega Point?"

"He won't," Warner says to him. "He's too arrogant, and this war has become personal. He'll want to toy with us. He'll want to draw this out as long as possible. He is a man who has always been fascinated by the idea of torture. This is going to be fun for him."

"Yeah, that's making me feel real good," Kenji says. "Thanks for the pep talk."

"Anytime," Warner says.

Kenji almost laughs. Almost.

"So he's staying in another ship?" Winston asks. "Here?"

"This is my understanding, yes," Warner says. "Normally he would stay on base, but as we are currently the enemy, it's become a bit of a problem. Apparently he's also granted sector clearance to soldiers across the country in order to have them join him. He has his own elite guard, as well as the soldiers who maintain the capital, but he's also collecting men from around the nation. It's all for show," Warner says. "We are not so vast in number that he'd need that many men. He just wants to terrify us."

"Well, it's working," Ian says.

"And you're sure," I ask Warner, "that he won't be on

the battlefield? You're positive?" This is the part of the plan that's the most important. The most critical.

Warner nods.

Anderson never fights in his own wars. He never shows his face. And we're relying on his cowardice to be our biggest advantage. Because while he might be able to anticipate an attempt on his life, we're hoping he won't be able to anticipate invisible attackers.

Warner has to oversee the troops. Castle, Brendan, Winston, Lily, Alia, and Adam will be supporting him. James will be staying behind on base.

But me and Kenji are going to the source.

And right now, we're ready to go. We're suited up, armed, and highly caffeinated.

I hear the sound of a gun being reloaded.

Spin around.

Warner is looking at me.

It's time to go.

SIXTY-SEVEN

Kenji grabs my arm.

Everyone else is going up and out of Warner's room, but Kenji and I will head out the back way, alerting no one to our presence. We want everyone, even the soldiers, to think we are in the midst of battle. We don't want to show up only to disappear; we don't want anyone to notice we're missing.

So we stand back and watch as our friends load into the elevator to go up to the main floor. James is still waving as the doors close and leave him behind.

My heart stops for a second.

Kenji kisses James good-bye. It's an obnoxious, noisy kiss, right on top of his head. "Watch my back, okay?" he says to James. "If anyone comes in here, I want you to kick the shit out of them."

"Okay," James says. He's laughing to pretend he's not crying.

"I'm serious," Kenji says. "Just start whaling on them. Like just go batshit." He makes a weird fighting motion with his hands. "Get super crazy," he says. "Beat the crazy with crazy—"

"No one is going to come in here, James," I say, shooting

a sharp look at Kenji. "You won't have to worry about defending yourself. You're going to be perfectly safe. And then we'll come back."

"Really?" he asks, turning his eyes on me. "All of you?"

Smart kid.

"Yes," I lie. "All of us are going to come back."

"Okay," he whispers. He bites down on his trembling lip. "Good luck."

"No tears necessary," Kenji says to him, wrapping him up in a ferocious hug. "We'll be back soon."

James nods.

Kenji breaks away.

And then we head out the door in the gun wall.

The first part, I think, is going to be the hardest. Our trek to the port will be made entirely on foot, because we can't risk stealing vehicles. Even if Kenji could make the tank invisible, we'd have to abandon it in its visible form, and an extra, unexpected tank stationed at the port would be too much of a giveaway.

Anderson must have his place completely guarded.

Kenji and I don't speak as we move. When Delalieu told us the supreme would be stationed at the port, Kenji immediately knew where it was. So did Warner and Adam and Castle and just about everyone except for me. "I spent some time on one of those ships," Kenji said. "Just for a bit. For bad behavior." He smiled. "I know my way around."

So I'm holding on to his arm and he's leading the way.

There's never been a colder day, I think. Never been more ice in the air.

This ship looks like a small city; it's so enormous I can't even see the end of it. We scan the perimeter, attempting to gauge exactly how difficult it'll be to infiltrate the premises.

Extremely difficult.

Nearly impossible.

These are Kenji's exact words.

Sort of.

"*Shit*," he says. "This is ridiculous. I have never seen this level of security before. This is backed *up*," he says.

And he's right. There are soldiers everywhere. On land. At the entrance. On deck. And they're all so heavily armed it makes me feel stupid with my two handguns and the simple holster swung around my shoulders.

"So what do we do?"

He's quiet a moment. "Can you swim?"

"What? No."

"Shit."

"We can't just jump in the ocean, Kenji—"

"Well it's not like we can *fly*."

"Maybe we can fight them?"

"Are you out of your goddamn mind? You think we can take on two hundred soldiers? I know I am an extremely attractive man, J, but I am not Bruce Lee."

"Who's Bruce Lee?"

"*Who's Bruce Lee?*" Kenji asks, horrified. "Oh my God. We

371

can't even be friends anymore."

"Why? Was he a friend of yours?"

"You know what," he says, "just stop. Just—I can't even talk to you right now."

"Then how are we supposed to get inside?"

"Shit if I know. How are we supposed to get all those guys off the ship?"

"Oh," I gasp. "Oh my God. Kenji—" I grab his invisible arm.

"Yeah, that's my leg, and you're cutting it a little too close there, princess."

"Kenji, I can *shove* them off," I say, ignoring him. "I can just push them into the water. Will that work?"

Silence.

"Well?" I ask.

"Your hand is still on my leg."

"Oh." I jerk back. "So? What do you think? Will it work?"

"*Obviously,*" Kenji says, exasperated. "Do it now, please. And hurry."

So I do.

I stand back and pull all my energy up and into my arms.

Power, harnessed.

Arms, positioned.

Energy, projected.

I move my arm through the air like I might be clearing off a table.

And all the soldiers topple into the water.

It looks almost comical from here. Like they were a bunch

of toys I was pushing off my desk. And now they're bouncing in the water, trying to figure out what's just happened.

"Let's go," Kenji says suddenly, grabbing my arm. We're darting forward and down the hundred-foot pier. "They're not stupid," he says. "Someone is going to sound the alarm and they're going to seal the doors soon. We've probably got a minute before it all goes on lockdown."

So we're bolting.

We're racing across the pier and clambering up, onto the deck, and Kenji pulls on my arm to tell me where to go. We're becoming so much more aware of each other's bodies now. I can almost feel his presence beside me, even though I can't see him.

"Down here," he shouts, and I look down, spotting what looks like a narrow, circular opening with a ladder affixed to the inside. "I'm going in," he says. "Start climbing down in five seconds!"

I can hear the alarms already going off, sirens wailing in the distance. The ship is steady against the dock, but the water in the distance goes on forever, disappearing into the edge of the earth.

My five seconds are up.

I'm climbing after him.

SIXTY-EIGHT

I have no idea where Kenji is.

It's cramped and claustrophobic down here and I can already hear a rush of footsteps coming toward me, shouts and cries echoing down the hall; they must know something has happened above deck. I'm trying really hard not to panic, but I'm no longer sure what the next step should be.

I never anticipated doing this alone.

I keep whispering Kenji's name and hoping for a response, but there's nothing. I can't believe I've already lost him. At least I'm still invisible, which means he can't be more than fifty feet away, but the soldiers are too close for me to take any chances right now. I can't do anything that would draw attention to my presence—or Kenji's.

So I have to force myself to stay calm.

The problem is I have no idea where I am. No idea what I'm looking at. I've never even been on a *boat* before, much less an army ship of this magnitude.

But I have to try and understand my surroundings.

I'm standing in the middle of what looks like a very long hallway; wooden panels run across the floors, the walls, and even the low ceiling above my head. There are little nooks every few feet, where the wall seems to be scooped out.

They're for doors, I realize.

I wonder where they lead. Where I'll have to go.

Boots are thundering closer now.

My heart starts racing and I try to shove myself against the wall, but these hallways are too narrow; even though they can't see me, there's no way I'd be able to slip past them. I can see a group approaching now, can hear them barking orders at one another. At any moment they're going to slam right into me.

I shift backward as fast as I can and run, keeping my weight on my toes to minimize sound as much as possible. I skid to a stop. Hit the wall behind me. More soldiers are bolting down the halls now, clearly alerted to something, and for a second I feel my heart fail. I'm so worried about Kenji.

But as long as I'm invisible, Kenji must be close, I think. He must be alive.

I cling to this hope as the soldiers approach.

I look to my left. Look to my right. They're closing in on me without even realizing it. I have no idea where they're headed—maybe they're going back up, outside—but I have to make a move, fast, and I don't want to alert them to my presence. Not yet. It's too soon to try to take them out. I know Alia promised I could sustain a bullet wound as long as my power is on, but my last experience with being shot in the chest has left me traumatized enough to want to avoid that option as much as possible.

So I do the only thing I can think of.

I jump into one of the doorways and plant my hands against the inside of the frame, holding myself in place, my back pressed against the door. *Please please please*, I think, *please don't let there be someone in this room.* All anyone has to do is open the door and I'll be dead.

The soldiers are getting closer.

I stop breathing as they pass.

One of their elbows grazes my arm.

My heart is pounding, so hard. As soon as they're gone I dart out of the doorway and bolt, running down halls that only lead into more halls. This place is like a maze. I have no idea where I am, no idea what's happening.

Not a single clue where I'll find Anderson.

And the soldiers won't stop coming. They're everywhere, all at once and then not at all, and I'm turning down corners and spinning in different directions and trying my best to outrun them. But then I notice my hands.

I'm no longer invisible.

I bite back a scream.

I jump into another doorway, hoping to press myself out of sight, but now I'm both nervous and horrified, because not only do I not know what's happened to Kenji, but I don't know what's going to happen to me, either. This was such a stupid idea. I am such a stupid person. I don't know what I was thinking.

That I ever thought I could do this.

Boots.

Stomping toward me. I steel myself and suck up my fear

and try to be as prepared as possible. There's no way they won't notice me now. I haul my energy up and into myself, feel my bones thrumming with the rush of it and the thrill of power raging through me. If I can maintain this state for as long as I'm down here, I should be able to protect myself. I know how to fight now. I can disarm a man, steal away his weapon. I've learned to do so much.

But I'm still fairly terrified, and I've never needed to use the bathroom as much as I do right now.

Think, I keep telling myself. *Think. What can you do? Where can you go? Where would Anderson be hiding? Deeper? Lower?*

Where would the largest room on this ship be? Certainly not on the top level. I have to drop down.

But how?

The soldiers are getting closer.

I wonder what these rooms contain, what this doorway leads to. If it's just a room, then it's a dead end. But if it's an entrance to a larger space, then I might have a chance. But if there's someone in here, I'll definitely be in trouble. I don't know if I should take the risk.

A shout.

A cry.

A gunshot.

They've seen me.

SIXTY-NINE

I slam my elbow into the door behind me, shattering the wood into splinters that fly everywhere. I turn around and punch my way through the rest of it, kicking the door down with a sudden burst of adrenaline, and as soon as I see that this room is just a small bunker and a dead end, I do the only thing I can think of.

I jump.

And land.

And go right through the floor.

I fall into a tumble and manage to catch myself in time. The soldiers are jumping down after me, shouting and screaming. Boots chase me as I yank open the door and dart down the hall. Alarms are going off everywhere, sounds so loud and so obnoxious I can hardly hear myself think. I feel like I'm running through a haze, the sirens flashing red lights that circle the halls, screeching and blaring and signaling an intruder.

I'm on my own now.

I'm darting around more corners, spinning around bends in this floor plan and trying to get a feel for the difference between this level and the one just above it. There doesn't seem to be any. They look exactly the same, and the soldiers are just as aggressive.

They're shooting freely now, the earsplitting sound of gunshots colliding with the blare of the sirens. I'm not even sure I haven't gone deaf yet.

I can't believe they keep managing to *miss* me.

It seems impossible, statistically speaking, that so many soldiers at such close range wouldn't be able to find a target on my body. That can't be right.

I slam through the floor again.

Land on my feet this time.

I'm crouched, looking around, and for the first time, I see that this level is different. The hallways are wider, the doors set farther apart. I wish Kenji were here. I wish I had any idea what this means, what the difference is between the levels. I wish I knew where to go, where to start looking.

I kick open a door.

Nothing.

I run forward, kick down another one.

Nothing.

I keep running. I'm starting to see the inner workings of the ship. Machines, pipes, steel beams, huge tanks, puffs of steam. I must be headed in the wrong direction.

But I have no idea how many floors this ship has, and I have no idea if I can keep moving down.

I'm still being shot at, and I'm staying only just a step ahead. I'm slipping around tight bends and pulling myself against the wall, turning into dark corners and hoping they won't see me.

Where is Kenji? I keep asking myself. *Where is he?*

I need to be on the other side of this ship. I don't want boiler rooms and water tanks. This can't be right. Everything is different about this side of the ship. Even the doors look different. They're made of steel, not wood.

I kick open a few, just to be sure.

A radio control room, abandoned.

A meeting room, abandoned.

No. I want real rooms. Big offices and living quarters. Anderson wouldn't be here. He wouldn't be found by the gas pipes and the whirring engines.

I tiptoe out of my newest hiding spot, peek my head out.

Shouts. Cries.

More gunshots.

I pull back. Take a deep breath. Harness all my energy, all at once, and decide I have no choice but to test Alia's theory.

I jump out and charge down the hall.

Running, racing like I never have before. Bullets are flying past my head and pelting my body, hitting my face, my back, my arms, and I force myself to keep running, force myself to keep breathing, not feeling pain, not feeling terror, but holding on to my energy like a lifeline and not letting anything stop me. I'm trampling over soldiers, knocking them out with my elbows, not hesitating long enough to do more than shove them out of my way.

Three of them come flying at me, trying to tackle me to the ground, and I shove them all back. One runs forward again and I punch him directly in the face, feeling his nose break against my metal knuckles. Another tries to grab my arm from behind and I catch his hand, breaking his fingers in my grip only to catch his forearm, pull him close, and shove him through a wall. I spin around to face the rest of them and they're all staring at me, panic and terror mixing in their eyes.

"Fight me," I say to them, blood and urgency and a crazy kind of adrenaline rushing through me. "I dare you."

Five of them lift their guns in my direction, point them at my face.

Shoot.

Over and over and over again, unloading round after round. My instinct is to protect myself from the bullets, but I focus instead on the men, on their bodies and their angry, twisted faces. I have to close my eyes for a second, because I can't see through the barrage of metal being crushed against my body. And when I'm ready, I bring my fist close to my chest, feeling the power rise up inside of me, and I throw it forward, all at once, knocking seventy-five soldiers down like they're made of matchsticks.

I take a moment to breathe.

My chest is heaving, my heart racing, and I look around, feeling the stillness within the madness, blinking hard against the flashing red lights of the alarm, and find that the soldiers do not stir. They're still alive, I can tell, but they're unconscious. And I allow myself one instant to look down.

I'm surrounded.

Bullets. Hundreds of bullets. A puddle of bullets. All around my feet. Dropping off my suit.

My face.

I taste something cold and hard in my mouth and spit it into my hand. It looks like a broken, mangled piece of metal. Like it was too flimsy to stand against me.

Smart little bullet, I think.

And then I run.

SEVENTY

The halls are still now. The footsteps, fewer.

I've already tossed two hundred soldiers into the ocean.

Knocked down about a hundred more.

I have no idea how many more soldiers Anderson has left guarding this ship. But I'm going to find out.

I'm breathing hard as I make my way through this maze. It's a sad truth that while I've learned to fight and I've learned to project, I still have no idea how to run.

For someone with so much power, I'm terribly out of shape.

I kick down the first door I see.

Another.

Then another.

I'm going to rip apart every inch of this ship until I find Anderson. I will tear it down with my own two hands if I need to. Because he has Sonya and Sara. And he might have Kenji.

And first, I need to make them safe.

And second, I need him dead.

Another door splinters open.

I kick the next one down with my foot.

They're all empty.

I see a set of swinging double doors at the end of the hall and I shove through them, hoping for something, anything, any sign of life.

It's a kitchen.

Knives and stoves and food and tables. Rows and rows and rows of canned goods. I make a mental note to come back for this. It seems a shame to let all this food go to waste.

I bolt back out the doors.

And jump. Hard. Stomping through the deck and hoping there's another floor to this ship.

Hoping.

I land badly on the toes of my feet, slightly off-balance and toppling backward. I catch myself just in time.

Look around.

This, I think. This is right. This is totally different.

The halls are huge down here; windows to the outside cut into the walls. The floor is made of wood again, long, thin panels that are brightly glossed and polished. It looks nice down here. Fancy. Clean. The sirens feel muted on this level, like a distant threat that means little anymore, and I realize I must be close.

Footsteps, rushing toward me.

I spin around.

There's a soldier charging in my direction, and this time, I don't hide. I run toward him, tucking my head in as I do, and my right shoulder slams into his chest so hard he goes flying across the hall.

Someone tries to shoot me from behind.

I spin around and walk right up to him, swatting the bullets from my face like they might be flies. And then I grab his shoulders, pull him close, and knee him in the groin. He doubles over, gasping and groaning and curling into himself on the floor. I bend down, rip the gun out of his hand, and clutch a fistful of his shirt. Pick him up with one hand. Slam him into the wall. Press the gun to his forehead.

I'm tired of waiting.

"Where is he?" I demand.

He won't answer me.

"*Where?*" I shout.

"I d-don't know," he finally says, his voice shaking, his body twitching, trembling in my grip.

And for some reason, I believe him. I try to read his eyes for something, and get nothing but terror. I drop him to the floor. Crush his gun in my hand. Toss it into his lap.

I kick open another door.

I'm getting so frustrated, so angry now, and so blindly terrified for Kenji's well-being that I'm shaking with rage. I don't even know who to look for first.

Sonya.

Sara.

Kenji.

Anderson.

I stand in front of another door, defeated. The soldiers have stopped coming. The sirens are still blaring, but from a distance now. And suddenly I'm wondering if this was all just a waste of time. If maybe Anderson isn't even on this ship. If maybe we're not even on the *right* ship.

And for some reason, I don't kick down the door this time.

For some reason, I decide to try the handle first.

It's unlocked.

SEVENTY-ONE

There's a huge bed in here with a large window and a beautiful view of the ocean. It's lovely, actually, how wide and expansive everything is. Lovelier still are its occupants.

Sonya and Sara are staring at me.

They're perfect. Alive.

Just as beautiful as they've ever been.

I rush over to them, so relieved I nearly burst into tears.

"Are you okay?" I ask, gasping, unable to control myself. "Are you all right?"

They throw themselves into my arms, looking like they've been through hell and back, tortured from the inside, and all I want to do is carry them out of this ship and take them home.

But as soon as the initial hyperventilations are out of the way, Sonya says something that stops my heart.

"Kenji was looking for you," she says. "He was just here, not too long ago, and he asked us if we'd seen you—"

"He said you got split up," Sara says.

"And that he didn't know what happened to you," Sonya says.

"We were so worried you were dead," they say together.

"No," I tell them, feeling crazy now. "No, no, I'm not

dead. But I have to go. Stay here," I'm saying to them. "Don't move. Don't go anywhere. I'll be right back, I promise," I say. "I just have to go find Kenji—I have to find Anderson—"

"He's two doors over," Sara says, eyes wide.

"The one all the way at the end of the hall," Sonya says.

"It's the one with the blue door," they tell me.

"Wait!" Sonya stops me as I turn to go.

"Be careful," Sara says. "We've heard some things—"

"About a weapon he's brought with him," Sonya says.

"What kind of weapon?" I ask, heart slowing.

"We don't know," they say together.

"But it made him very happy," Sara whispers.

"Yes, very happy," Sonya adds.

I clench my fists.

"Thank you," I say to them. "Thank you—I'll see you soon," I'm saying. "Very soon—" And I'm backing out, backing away, rushing down the hall and I hear them shouting for me to be safe, and good luck, just behind me.

But I don't need luck anymore. I need these two fists and this spine of steel. I waste no time at all getting to the blue room. I'm not afraid anymore.

I don't hesitate. I won't hesitate. Never again.

I kick it down.

"JULIETTE—NO—"

SEVENTY-TWO

Kenji's voice hits me like a fist to the throat.

I don't even have time to blink before I'm thrown against the wall.

My back, I think. Something is wrong with my back. The pain is so excruciating that I can't help but wonder if it's broken. I'm dizzy and I feel slow; my head is spinning and there's a strange ringing in my ears.

I clamber to my feet.

I'm hit, again, so hard. And I don't even know where the pain is coming from. I can't blink fast enough, can't steady my head long enough to shake the confusion.

Everything is tilting sideways.

I'm trying so hard to shake it off.

I'm stronger than this. Better than this. I'm supposed to be indestructible.

Up, again.

Slowly.

Something hits me so hard I fly across the room, slamming into the wall. I slide down to the floor. I'm bent over now, holding my hands to my head, trying to blink, trying to understand what's happening.

I don't understand what could possibly be hitting me.

This hard.

Nothing should be able to hit me this hard. Not over and over again.

It feels like someone is calling my name, but I can't seem to hear it. Everything is so muffled, so slippery and off-balance, like it's there, just out of reach, and I can't seem to find it. Feel it.

I need a new plan.

I don't stand up again. I stay on my knees, crawling forward, and this time, when the hit comes, I try to beat it back. I'm trying so hard to push my energy forward, but all the hits to my head have made me unsteady. I'm clinging to my energy with a manic desperation, and though I don't manage to move forward, I'm also not thrown back.

I try to lift my head.

Slowly.

There's nothing in front of me. No machine. No strange element that might be able to create these powerful impacts. I blink hard against the ringing in my ears, trying frantically to clear my vision.

Something hits me again.

The intensity threatens to beat me back but I dig my fingers into the ground until they go through the wood and I'm clinging to the floor.

I would scream, if I could. If I had any energy left.

I lift my head again. Try again to see.

And this time, two figures come into focus.

One is Anderson.

The other is someone I don't recognize.

He's a stocky blond with closely cropped hair and flinty eyes. He looks vaguely familiar to me. And he's standing beside Anderson with a cocky smile on his face, his hands held out in front of him.

He claps.

Just once.

I'm ripped from the floor and thrown back against the wall.

Sound waves.

These are *pressure waves*, I realize.

Anderson has found himself a toy.

I shake my head and try to clear it again, but the hits are coming faster now. Harder. More intense. I have to close my eyes against the pressure of the hits and try to crawl, desperately, breaking through the floorboards to get a grip on something.

Another hit.

Hard to the head.

It's like he's causing an explosion every time his hands clap together, and what's killing me isn't the explosion. It isn't direct impact. It's the pressure released from a bomb.

Over and over and over again.

I know the only reason I'm able to survive this is because I'm too strong.

But *Kenji*, I think.

Kenji must be somewhere in this room. He was the one who called my name, who tried to warn me. He must be here, somewhere, and if I can hardly survive this right now, I don't know how he could be doing any better.

He must be doing worse.

Much worse.

That fear is enough for me. I'm fortified with a new kind of strength, a desperate, animal intensity that overpowers me and forces me upright. I manage to stand in the face of each impact, each blow as it rattles my head and rings in my ears.

And I walk.

One step at a time, I walk.

I hear a gunshot. Three. Five more. And realize they're all aimed in my direction. Bullets breaking off my body.

The blond is moving. Backing up. Trying to get away from me. He's increasing the frequency of his hits, hoping to throw me off course, but I've come too far to lose this fight. I'm not even thinking now, barely even lucid, focused solely on reaching him and silencing him forever. I have no idea if he's managed to kill Kenji yet. I have no idea if I'm about to die. I have no idea how much longer I can withstand this.

But I have to try.

One more step, I tell myself.

Move your leg. Now your foot. Bend at the knee.

You're almost there, I tell myself.

Think of Kenji. Think of James. Think of the promises you made to that ten-year-old boy, I tell myself. Bring Kenji home. Bring yourself home.

There he is. Right in front of you.

I reach forward as if through a cloud, and clench my fist around his neck.

Squeeze.

Squeeze until the sound waves stop.

I hear something crack.

The blond falls to the floor.

And I collapse.

SEVENTY-THREE

Anderson is standing over me now, pointing a gun at my face.

He shoots.

Again.

Once more.

I close my eyes and pull deep, deep within myself for my last dregs of strength, because somehow, some instinct inside of my body is still screaming at me to stay alive. I remember Sonya and Sara telling me once that our energies could be depleted. That we could overexert ourselves. That they were trying to make medicines to help with that sort of thing.

I wish I had that kind of medicine right now.

I blink up at Anderson, his form blurring at the edges. He's standing just behind my head, the toes of his shiny boots touching the top of my skull. I can't hear much but the echoes in my bones, can't see anything other than the bullets raining down around me. He's still shooting. Still unloading his gun into my body, waiting for the moment when he knows I won't be able to hold on any longer.

I'm dying, I think. I must be. I thought I knew what it

felt like to die, but I must've been wrong. Because this is a whole different kind of dying. A whole different kind of pain.

But I suppose, if I have to die, I may as well do one more thing before I go.

I reach up. Grab Anderson's ankles. Clench my fists.

And crush his bones in my hands.

His screams pierce the haze of my mind, long enough to bring the world back into focus. I'm blinking fast, looking around and able to see clearly for the first time. Kenji is slumped in the corner. Blond boy is on the floor.

Anderson has been disconnected from his feet.

My thoughts are sharper all of a sudden, like I'm in control again. I don't know if this is what hope does to a person, if it really has the power to bring someone back to life, but seeing Anderson writhing on the floor does something to me. It makes me think I still have a chance.

He's screaming so much, scrambling back and dragging himself across the floor with his arms. He's dropped his gun, clearly too pained and too petrified to reach for it any longer, and I can see the agony in his eyes. The weakness. The terror. He's only now understanding the horror of what's about to happen to him. How it had to happen to him. That he would be brought to nothing by a silly little girl who was too much of a coward, he said, to defend herself.

And it's then that I realize he's trying to say something

to me. He's trying to talk. Maybe he's pleading. Maybe he's crying. Maybe he's begging for mercy. But I'm not listening anymore.

I have absolutely nothing to say.

I reach back, pull the gun out of my holster.

And shoot him in the forehead.

SEVENTY-FOUR

Twice.
Once for Adam.
Once for Warner.

SEVENTY-FIVE

I tuck the gun back into its holster. Walk over to Kenji's limp, still-breathing form, and throw him over my shoulder.

I kick down the door.

Walk directly back down the hall.

Kick my way through the entry to Sonya and Sara's room, and drop Kenji on the bed.

"Fix him," I say, hardly breathing now. "Please fix him."

I drop to my knees.

Sonya and Sara are on in an instant. They don't speak. They don't cry. They don't scream. They don't fall apart. They immediately get to work and I don't think I have ever loved them more than I do in this moment. They lay him out flat on the bed, Sara standing on one side of him, Sonya on the other, and they hold their hands to his head, first. Then his heart.

Then they alternate, taking turns forcing life back into different parts of his body until Kenji is stirring, his eyes flickering but not opening, his head whipping back and forth.

I'm beginning to worry, but I'm too afraid, and too tired to move, not even an inch.

Finally, finally, they step back.

Kenji's eyes still aren't open.

"Did it work?" I ask, terrified to hear the answer.

Sonya and Sara nod. "He's asleep," they say.

"Will he get better? Fully?" I ask, desperate now.

"We hope," Sonya says.

"But he'll be asleep for a few days," Sara says.

"The damage was very deep," they say together. "What happened?"

"Pressure waves," I tell them, my words a whisper. "He shouldn't have been able to survive at all."

Sonya and Sara are staring at me, still waiting.

I force myself to my feet. "Anderson is dead."

"You killed him," they whisper. It's not a question.

I nod.

They're staring at me, slack-jawed and stunned.

"Let's go," I say. "This war is over. We have to tell the others."

"But how will we get out?" Sara asks.

"There are soldiers everywhere," Sonya says.

"Not anymore," I tell them, too tired to explain, but so grateful for their help. For their existence. For the fact that they're still alive. I offer them a small smile before walking over to the bed, and haul Kenji's body up and over my shoulders. His chest is curved over my back, one of his arms thrown over my left shoulder, the other hanging in front of me. My right arm is wrapped around both his legs.

I hoist him higher up on my shoulders.

"Ready?" I say, looking at the two of them.

They nod.

I lead them out the door and down the halls, forgetting for a moment that I have no idea how to actually exit this ship. But the halls are lifeless. Everyone is either injured, unconscious, or gone. We sidestep fallen bodies, shift arms and legs out of the way. We're all that's left.

Me, carrying Kenji.

Sonya and Sara close behind.

I finally find a ladder. Climb up. Sonya and Sara hold Kenji's weight between them and I reach down to haul him up. We have to do this three more times, until we're finally on the top deck, where I toss him up over my shoulders for the final time.

And then we walk, silently, across the abandoned ship, down the pier, and back onto dry land. This time, I don't care about stealing tanks. I don't care about being seen. I don't care about anything but finding my friends. And ending this war.

There's an army tank abandoned on the side of the road. I test the door.

Unlocked.

The girls clamber in and they help me haul Kenji onto their laps. I close the door shut behind them. Climb into the driver's side. I press my thumb to the scanner to start the engine; so grateful Warner had us programmed to gain access to the system.

It's only then that I remember I still have no idea how to drive.

It's probably a good thing I'm driving a tank.

I don't pay attention to stop signs or streets. I drive the tank right off the road and straight back into the heart of the sector, in the general direction I know we came from. I'm too heavy on the gas, and too heavy on the brakes, but my mind is in a place where nothing else matters anymore.

I had a goal. Step one has been accomplished.

And now I will see it through to the end.

I drop Sonya and Sara off at the barracks and help them carry Kenji out. Here, they'll be safe. Here, they can rest. But it's not my turn to stop yet.

I head directly up and through the military base, up the elevator to where I remember we got off for the assembly. I slam through door after door, heading straight outside and into the courtyard, where I climb until I reach the top. One hundred feet in the air.

Where it all began.

There's a technician stand here, a maintenance system for the speakers that run throughout the sector. I remember this. I remember all of this now, even though my brain is numb and my hands are still shaking, and blood that does not belong to me is dripping down my face and onto my neck.

But this was the plan.

I have to finish the plan.

I punch the pass code into the keypad and wait to hear the click. The technician box snaps open. I scan the different fuses and buttons, and flip the switch that reads

ALL SPEAKERS, and take a deep breath. Hit the intercom key.

"Attention, Sector 45," I say, the words rough and loud and mottled in my ear. "The supreme commander of The Reestablishment is dead. The capital has surrendered. The war is over." I'm shaking so hard now, my finger slipping on the button as I try to hold it down. "I repeat, the supreme commander of The Reestablishment is dead. The capital has surrendered. The war is over."

Finish it, I tell myself.

Finish it now.

"I am Juliette Ferrars, and I will lead this nation. I challenge anyone who would stand against me."

SEVENTY-SIX

I take a step forward and my legs tremble, threaten to bend and break beneath me, but I push myself to keep moving. I push myself to get through the door, to get down the elevator, and to get out, onto the battlefield.

It doesn't take long to get there.

There are hundreds of bodies in huddled, bloody masses on the ground, but there are hundreds more still standing; more alive than I could've hoped for. The news has spread more quickly than I thought it would. It's almost as if they've known for a little while now that the battle was over. The surviving soldiers from Anderson's ship are standing alongside our own, some still soaking wet, frozen to the bone in this icy weather. They must've found their way ashore and shared the news of our assault, of Anderson's imminent demise. Everyone is looking around, staring at each other in shock, staring at their own hands or up into the sky. Others still are checking the mass of bodies for friends and family members, relief and fear apparent on their faces. Their worn bodies do not want to go on like this.

The doors to the barracks have burst open and the remaining civilians flood the grounds, running out to reunite with loved ones, and for a moment the scene is both so terribly bleak, and so terribly beautiful, that I don't know whether to cry out in pain or joy.

I don't cry at all.

I walk forward, forcing my limbs to move, begging my bones to stay steady, to carry me through the end of this day, and into the rest of my life.

I want to see my friends. I need to know they're okay. I need visual confirmation that they're okay.

But as soon as I walk into the crowd, the soldiers of Sector 45 lose control.

The bloodied and beaten on our battlefield are shouting and cheering despite the stain of death they stand in, saluting me as I pass. And as I look around I realize that they are *my* soldiers now. They trusted me, fought with me and alongside me, and now I will trust them. I will fight for them. This is the first of many battles to come. There will be many more days like this.

I'm covered in blood, my suit ripped and riddled with splintered wood and broken bits of metal. My hands are trembling so hard I don't even recognize them anymore.

And yet I feel so calm.

So unbelievably calm.

Like the depth of what just happened hasn't managed to hit me yet.

It's impossible not to brush against outstretched hands and arms as I cross the battlefield, and it's strange to me, somehow, strange that I don't flinch, strange that I don't hide my hands, strange that I'm not worried I'll injure them.

They can touch me if they like, and maybe it'll hurt, but my skin won't kill anyone anymore.

Because I'll never let it get that far.

Because I now know how to control it.

SEVENTY-SEVEN

The compounds are such bleak, barren places, I think, as I pass through them. These should be the first to go. Our homes should be rebuilt. Restored.

We need to start again.

I climb up the side of one of the little compound homes. Climb its second story, too. I reach up, clinging to the roof, and pull myself over. I kick the solar panels off, onto the ground, and plant myself on top, right in the middle, as I look out over the crowd.

Searching for familiar faces.

Hoping they'll see me and come forward.

Hoping.

I stand on the roof of this home for what feels like days, months, years, and I see nothing but faces of soldiers and their families. None of my friends.

I feel myself sway, dizziness threatening to overtake me, my pulse racing fast and hard. I'm ready to give up. I've stood here long enough for people to point, for my face to be recognized, for word to spread that I'm standing here, waiting for something. Someone. Anyone.

I'm just about to dive back into the crowd to search for their fallen bodies when hope seizes my heart.

One by one, they emerge, from all corners of the field,

from deep inside the barracks, from across the compounds. Bloodied and bruised. Adam, Alia, Castle, Ian, Lily, Brendan, and Winston each make their way toward me only to turn and wait for the others to arrive. Winston is sobbing.

Sonya and Sara are dragging Kenji out of the barracks, small steps hauling him forward. I see that his eyes have opened now, just a little. Stubborn, stubborn Kenji. Of course he's awake when he should be asleep.

James comes running toward them.

He crashes into Adam, clinging to his legs, and Adam hauls his little brother up, into his arms, smiling like I've never seen him smile before. Castle nods at me, beaming. Lily blows me a kiss. Ian makes some strange finger-gun motion and Brendan waves. Alia has never looked more jubilant.

And I'm looking out over them, my smile steady, held there by nothing but sheer force of will. I'm still staring, waiting for my last friend to show up. Waiting for him to find us.

But he isn't here.

I'm scanning the thousands of people scattered around this icy, icy ground and I don't see him, not anywhere, and the terror of this moment kicks me in the gut until I'm out of breath and out of hope, blinking fast and trying to hold myself together.

The metal roof under my feet is shaking.

I turn toward the sound, heart pounding, and see a hand reach over the top.

SEVENTY-EIGHT

He pulls himself up onto the roof and walks over to me, so steadily. Calm, like there's nothing in the world we'd planned to do today but to stand here, together, looking out over a field of dead bodies and happy children.

"Aaron," I whisper.

He pulls me into his arms.

And I fall.

Every bone, every muscle, every nerve in my body comes undone at his touch and I cling to him, holding on for dear life.

"You know," he whispers, his lips at my ear, "the whole world will be coming for us now."

I lean back. Look into his eyes.

"I can't wait to watch them try."

ACKNOWLEDGMENTS

I've reached the end.

And here, at the finish line, I am suddenly speechless, unable to articulate in any number of words just how many helpers I've had, how many hands have touched this book, or how many minds have shaped this story. But you were there all along, reading with me and writing to me and cheering me on, helping me through hard moments and always holding my hand. My many dear friends at HarperCollins and Writers House. My family, steadfast, always. Ransom Riggs, an angel on earth. Tara Weikum, a magician. Jodi Reamer, a saint.

And you, dear reader, you, most of all.

I am indebted to you for your support, your love, your friendship on the pages and on the internet. Thank you for following Juliette's journey with me; thank you for caring so deeply. It is my very great hope that you will find this a worthy final installment.

Lots of love,

IMAGINE ME

ALSO BY TAHEREH MAFI

IMAGINE ME

ME

TAHEREH MAFI

First published in USA in 2020 by
HarperCollins Children's Books

First published in Great Britain in 2020
by Electric Monkey, part of Farshore

An imprint of HarperCollins*Publishers*
1 London Bridge Street, London SE1 9GF

farshore.co.uk

2 4 6 8 10 9 7 5 3 1

HarperCollins*Publishers*
1st Floor, Watermarque Building,
Ringsend Road, Dublin 4, Ireland

Published by arrangement with HarperCollins Children's Books,
a division of HarperCollins Publishers, New York, New York, USA

ISBN 978 1 4052 9704 2

YOUNG ADULT

Printed and bound in India by Thomson Press India Ltd

A CIP catalogue record for this title is available from the British Library

Typeset by Avon DataSet Ltd, Bidford on Avon, Warwickshire

~~ELLA~~

JULIETTE

In the dead of night, I hear birds.

I hear them, I see them, I close my eyes and feel them, feathers shuddering in the air, bending the wind, wings grazing my shoulders when they ascend, when they alight. Discordant shrieks ring and echo, ring and echo—

How many?

Hundreds.

White birds, white with streaks of gold, like crowns atop their heads. They fly. They soar through the sky with strong, steady wings, masters of their destinies. They used to make me hope.

Never again.

I turn my face into the pillow, digging fingers into cotton flesh as the memories crash into me.

"Do you like them?" she says.

We're in a big, wide room that smells like dirt. There are trees everywhere, so tall they nearly touch the pipes and beams of the open ceiling. Birds, dozens of them, screech as they stretch their wings. Their calls are loud. A little scary. I try not to flinch as one of the large white birds swoops past me. It wears a bright, neon-green bracelet around one leg. They all do.

3

This doesn't make sense.

I remind myself that we're indoors—the white walls, the concrete floor under my feet—and I look up at my mother, confused.

I've never seen Mum smile so much. Mostly she smiles when Dad is around, or when she and Dad are off in the corner, whispering together, but right now it's just me and Mum and a bunch of birds and she's so happy I decide to ignore the funny feeling in my stomach. Things are better when Mum is in a good mood.

"Yes," I lie. "I like them a lot."

Her eyes brighten. "I knew you would. Emmaline didn't care for them, but you—you've always been a bit too fond of things, haven't you, darling? Not at all like your sister." Somehow, her words come out mean. They don't seem mean, but they sound mean.

I frown.

I'm still trying to figure out what's happening when she says—

"I had one as a pet when I was about your age. Back then, they were so common we could never be rid of them." She laughs, and I watch her as she watches a bird, midflight. "One of them lived in a tree near my house, and it called my name whenever I walked past. Can you imagine?" Her smile fades as she asks the question.

Finally, she turns to look at me.

"They're very nearly extinct now. You understand why I couldn't let that happen."

"Of course," I say, but I'm lying again. There is little I understand about Mum.

She nods. "These are a special sort of creature. Intelligent. They can speak, dance. And each of them wears a crown." She turns away again, staring at the birds the way she stares at all the things she

4

makes for work: with joy. "The sulphur-crested cockatoo mates for life," she says. "Just like me and your father."

The sulphur-crested cockatoo.

I shiver, suddenly, at the unexpected sensation of a warm hand on my back, fingers trailing lightly along my spine.

"Love," he says, "are you all right?"

When I say nothing he shifts, the sheets rustling, and he tucks me into his hollows, his body curving around mine. He's warm and strong and as his hand slides down my torso I cant my head toward him, finding peace in his presence, in the safety of his arms. His lips touch my skin, a graze against my neck so subtle it sparks, hot and cold, right down to my toes.

"Is it happening again?" he whispers.

My mother was born in Australia.

I know this because she once told me so, and because now, despite my desperation to resist many of the memories now returned to me, I can't forget. She once told me that the sulphur-crested cockatoo was native to Australia. It was introduced to New Zealand in the nineteenth century, but Evie, my mother, didn't discover them there. She fell in love with the birds back home, as a child, when one of them, she claims, saved her life.

These were the birds that once haunted my dreams.

These birds, kept and bred by a crazy woman. I feel embarrassed to realize I'd held fast to nonsense, to the faded,

5

disfigured impressions of old memories poorly discarded. I'd hoped for more. Dreamed of more. Disappointment lodges in my throat, a cold stone I'm unable to swallow.

And then

again

I feel it

I stiffen against the nausea that precedes a vision, the sudden punch to the gut that means there's more, there's more, there's always more.

Aaron pulls me closer, holds me tighter against his chest.

"Breathe," he whispers. "I'm right here, love. I'll be right here."

I cling to him, squeezing my eyes shut as my head swims. These memories were a gift from my sister, Emmaline. The sister I only just discovered, only just recovered.

And only because she fought to find me.

Despite my parents' relentless efforts to rid our minds of the lingering proof of their atrocities, Emmaline prevailed. She used her psychokinetic powers to return to me what was stolen from my memories. She gave me this gift—this gift of remembering—to help me save myself. To save *her*. To stop our parents.

To fix the world.

But now, in the wake of a narrow escape, this gift has become a curse. Every hour my mind is reborn. Altered. The memories keep coming.

And my dead mother refuses to be silenced.

"Little bird," she whispers, tucking a stray hair behind my ear. "It's time for you to fly away now."

"But I don't want to go," I say, fear making my voice shake. "I want to stay here, with you and Dad and Emmaline. I still don't understand why I have to leave."

"You don't have to understand," she says gently.

I go uncomfortably still.

Mum doesn't yell. She's never yelled. My whole life, she's never raised a hand to me, never shouted or called me names. Not like Aaron's dad. But Mum doesn't need to yell. Sometimes she just says things, things like *you don't have to understand* and there's a warning there, a finality in her words that's always scared me.

I feel tears forming, burning the whites of my eyes, and—

"No crying," she says. "You're far too old for that now."

I sniff, hard, fighting back the tears. But my hands won't stop shaking.

Mum looks up, nods at someone behind me. I turn around just in time to spot Paris, Mr. Anderson, waiting with my suitcase. There's no kindness in his eyes. No warmth at all. He turns away from me, looks at Mum. He doesn't say hello.

He says: "Has Max settled in yet?"

"Oh, he's been ready for days." Mum glances at her watch, distracted. "You know Max," she says, smiling faintly. "Always a perfectionist."

"Only when it comes to your wishes," says Mr. Anderson. "I've never seen a grown man so besotted with his wife."

Mum smiles wider. She seems about to say something, but I cut her off.

"Are you talking about Dad?" I ask, my heart racing. "Will Dad be there?"

My mother turns to me, surprised, like she'd forgotten I was there. She turns back to Mr. Anderson. "How's Leila doing, by the way?"

"Fine," he says. But he sounds irritated.

"Mum?" Tears threaten again. "Am I going to stay with Dad?"

But Mum doesn't seem to hear me. She's talking to Mr. Anderson when she says, "Max will walk you through everything when you arrive, and he'll be able to answer most of your questions. If there's something he can't answer, it's likely beyond your clearance."

Mr. Anderson looks suddenly annoyed, but he says nothing. Mum says nothing.

I can't stand it.

Tears are spilling down my face now, my body shaking so hard it makes my breaths rattle. "Mum?" I whisper. "Mum, please a-answer me—"

Mum clamps a cold, hard hand around my shoulder and I go instantly still. Quiet. She's not looking at me. She won't look at me. "You'll handle this, too," she says. "Won't you, Paris?"

Mr. Anderson meets my eyes then. So blue. So cold. "Of course."

A flash of heat courses through me. A rage so sudden it briefly replaces my terror.

I hate him.

I hate him so much that it does something to me when I look at him—and the abrupt surge of emotion makes me feel brave.

I turn back to Mum. Try again.

"Why does Emmaline get to stay?" I ask, wiping angrily at my *wet cheeks. "If I have to go, can't we at least go toge—"*

I cut myself off when I spot her.

My sister, Emmaline, is peeking out at me from behind the mostly closed door. She's not supposed to be here. Mum said so.

Emmaline is supposed to be doing her swimming lessons.

But she's here, her wet hair dripping on the floor, and she's staring at me, eyes wide as plates. She's trying to say something, but her lips move too fast for me to follow. And then, out of nowhere, a bolt of electricity runs up my spine and I hear her voice, sharp and strange—

Liars.

LIARS.

KILL THEM ALL

My eyes fly open and I can't catch my breath, my chest heaving, heart pounding. Warner holds me, making soothing sounds as he runs a reassuring hand up and down my arm.

Tears spill down my face and I swipe at them, hands shaking.

"I hate this," I whisper, horrified at the tremble in my voice. "I hate this so much. I hate that it keeps happening. I hate what it does to me," I say. *"I hate it."*

~~Warner~~ Aaron presses his cheek against my shoulder with a sigh, his breath teasing my skin.

"I hate it, too," he says softly.

I turn, carefully, in the cradle of his arms, and press my forehead to his bare chest.

It's been less than two days since we escaped Oceania. Two days since I killed my own mother. Two days since I met the residue of my sister, Emmaline. Only two days since my entire life was upended yet again, which feels impossible.

Two days and already things are on fire around us.

This is our second night here, at the Sanctuary, the locus of the rebel group run by Nouria—Castle's daughter—and her wife, Sam. We're supposed to be safe here. We're supposed to be able to breathe and regroup after the hell of the last few weeks, but my body refuses to settle. My mind is overrun, under attack. I thought the rush of new memories would eventually gutter out, but these last twenty-four hours have been an unusually brutal assault, and I seem to be the only one struggling.

Emmaline gifted all of us—all the children of the supreme commanders—with memories stolen by our parents. One by one we were awoken to the truths our parents had buried, and one by one we were returned to normal lives.

All but me.

The others have since moved on, reconciled their timelines, made sense of the betrayal. My mind, on the other hand, continues to falter. Spin. But then, none of the others lost as much as I did; they don't have as much to remember. Even Warner—*Aaron*—isn't experiencing so thorough a reimagining of his life.

It's beginning to scare me.

I feel as though my history is being rewritten, infinite paragraphs scratched out and hastily revised. Old and new images—memories—layer atop each other until the ink runs, rupturing the scenes into something new, something incomprehensible. Occasionally my thoughts feel like disturbing hallucinations, and the onslaught is so invasive I fear it's doing irreparable damage.

Because something is changing.

Every new memory is delivered with an emotional violence that drives into me, reorders my mind. I'd been feeling this pain in flickers—the sickness, the nausea, the disorientation—but I haven't wanted to question it too deeply. I haven't wanted to look too closely. The truth is, I didn't want to believe my own fears. But the truth is: I am a punctured tire. Every injection of air leaves me both fuller and flatter.

I am forgetting.

"Ella?"

Terror bubbles up inside of me, bleeds through my open eyes. It takes me a moment to remember that I am ~~Juliette~~ Ella. Each time, it takes me a moment longer.

Hysteria threatens—

I force it down.

"Yes," I say, forcing air into my lungs. "Yes."

~~Warner~~ Aaron stiffens. "Love, what's wrong?"

"Nothing," I lie. My heart is pounding fast, too fast. I don't know why I'm lying. It's a fruitless effort; he can sense everything I'm feeling. I should just tell him. ~~I don't know why I'm not telling him~~. I know why I'm not telling him.

I'm waiting.

11

I'm waiting to see if this will pass, if the lapses in my memory are only glitches waiting to be repaired. Saying it out loud makes it too real, and it's too soon to say these thoughts aloud, to give in to the fear. After all, it's only been a day since it started. It only occurred to me yesterday that something was truly wrong.

It occurred to me because I made a mistake.

Mistakes.

We were sitting outside, staring at the stars. I couldn't remember ever seeing the stars like that—sharp, clear. It was late, so late it wasn't night but infant morning, and the view was dizzying. I was freezing. A brave wind stole through a copse nearby, filling the air with steady sound. I was full of cake. Warner smelled like sugar, like decadence. I felt drunk on joy.

I don't want to wait, he said, taking my hand. Squeezing it. *Let's not wait.*

I blinked up at him. *For what?*

For what?

For what?

How did I forget what had happened just hours earlier? How did I forget the moment he asked me to marry him?

It was a glitch. It felt like a glitch. Where there was once a memory was suddenly a vacancy, a cavity held empty only until nudged into realignment.

I recovered, remembered. Warner laughed.

I did not.

I forgot the name of Castle's daughter. I forgot how we landed at the Sanctuary. I forgot, for a full two minutes, how I ever escaped Oceania. But my errors were temporary; they seemed like natural delays. I experienced only confusion as my mind buffered, hesitation as the memories resurfaced, waterlogged and vague. I thought maybe I was tired. Overwhelmed. I took none of it seriously, not until I was sitting under the stars and couldn't remember promising to spend the rest of my life with someone.

Mortification.

Mortification so acute I thought I'd expire from the full force of it. Even now fresh heat floods my face, and I find I'm relieved Warner can't see in the dark.

Aaron, not Warner.

Aaron.

"I can't tell just now whether you're afraid or embarrassed," he says, and exhales softly. It sounds almost like a laugh. "Are you worried about Kenji? About the others?"

I grab on to this half-truth with my whole heart.

"Yes," I say. "*Kenji*. James. Adam."

Kenji has been sick in bed since very early this morning. I squint at the slant of moon through our window and remember that it's long past midnight, which would mean that, technically, Kenji got sick yesterday morning.

Regardless, it was terrifying for all of us.

13

The drugs Nazeera forced into Kenji on their international flight from Sector 45 to Oceania were a dose too strong, and he's been reeling ever since. He finally collapsed—the twins, Sonya and Sara, have checked in on him and say he's going to be just fine—but not before we learned that Anderson has been rounding up the children of the supreme commanders.

Adam and James and Lena and Valentina and Nicolás are all in Anderson's custody.

James is in his custody.

It's been a devastating, awful couple of days. It's been a devastating, awful couple of weeks.

Months, really.

Years.

Some days, no matter how far back I go, I can't seem to find the good times. Some days, the occasional happiness I've known feels like a bizarre dream. An error. Hyperreal and unfocused, the colors too bright and the sounds too strong.

Figments of my imagination.

It was just days ago that clarity came to me, bearing gifts. Just days ago that the worst seemed behind me, that the world seemed full of potential, that my body was stronger than ever, my mind fuller, sharper, more capable than I'd ever known it.

But now

But now

But now I feel like I'm clinging to the blurring edges of

14

sanity, that elusive, fair-weather friend always breaking my heart.

Aaron pulls me close and I melt into him, grateful for his warmth, for the steadiness of his arms around me. I take a deep, shuddering breath and let it all go, exhaling against him. I inhale the rich, heady scent of his skin, the faint aroma of gardenias he somehow carries with him always. Seconds pass in perfect silence and we listen to each other breathe.

Slowly, my heart rate steadies.

The tears dry up. The fears take five. Terror is distracted by a passing butterfly and sadness takes a nap.

For a little while it's just me and him and us and everything is untarnished, untouched by darkness.

I knew I loved ~~Warner~~ Aaron before all this—before we were captured by The Reestablishment, before we were ripped apart, before we learned of our shared history—but that love was new, green, its depths uncharted, untested. In that brief, glimmering window during which the gaping holes in my memory felt fully accounted for, things between us changed. *Everything* between us changed. Even now, even with the noise in my head, I feel it.

Here.

This.

My bones against his bones. This is my home.

I feel him suddenly stiffen and I pull back, concerned. I can't see much of him in this perfect darkness, but I feel the delicate rise of goose bumps along his arms when he says, "What are you thinking about?"

My eyes widen, comprehension dethroning concern. "I was thinking about you."

"Me?"

I close the gap between us again. Nod against his chest.

He says nothing, but I can hear his heart, racing in the quiet, and eventually I hear him exhale. It's a heavy, uneven sound, like he might've been holding his breath for too long. I wish I could see his face. No matter how much time we spend together, I still forget how much he can feel my emotions, especially at times like this, when our bodies are pressed together.

Gently, I run my hand down his back. "I was thinking about how much I love you," I say.

He goes uncommonly still, but only for a moment. And then he touches my hair, his fingers slowly combing the strands.

"Did you feel it?" I ask.

When he doesn't answer, I pull back again. I blink against the black until I'm able to make out the glint of his eyes, the shadow of his mouth.

"Aaron?"

"Yes," he says, but he sounds a little breathless.

"Yes, you felt it?"

"Yes," he says again.

"What does it feel like?"

He sighs. Rolls onto his back. He's quiet for so long that, for a while, I'm not sure he's going to answer. Then, softly, he says:

16

"It's hard to describe. It's a pleasure so close to pain I sometimes can't tell the two apart."

"That sounds awful."

"No," he says. "It's exquisite."

"I love you."

A sharp intake of breath. Even in this darkness I see the strain in his jaw—the tension there—as he stares at the ceiling.

I sit straight up, surprised.

Aaron's reaction is so unstudied I don't know how I never noticed it before. But then, maybe this is new. Maybe something really has changed between us. Maybe I never loved him this much before. That would make sense, I suppose. Because when I think about it, when I really think about how much I love him now, after everything we've—

Another sudden, sharp breath. And then he laughs, nervously.

"Wow," I say.

He claps a hand over his eyes. "This is vaguely mortifying."

I'm smiling now, very nearly laughing. "Hey. It's—"

My body seizes.

A violent shudder rushes up my skin and my spine goes rigid, my bones held in place by invisible pins, my mouth frozen open and trying to draw breath.

Heat fills my vision.

I hear nothing but static, grand rapids, white water, ferocious wind. Feel nothing. Think nothing. Am nothing.

17

I am, for the most infinitesimal moment—

Free.

My eyelids flutter open *closed* open *closed* open *closed* I am a wing, two wings, a swinging door, five birds

Fire climbs inside of me, explodes.

Ella?

The voice appears in my mind with swift strength, sharp, like darts to the brain. Dully, I realize that I'm in pain— my jaw aches, my body still suspended in an unnatural position—but I ignore it. The voice tries again:

Juliette?

Realization strikes, a knife to the knees. Images of my sister fill my mind: bones and melted skin, webbed fingers, sodden mouth, no eyes. Her body suspended underwater, long brown hair like a swarm of eels. Her strange, disembodied voice pierces through me. And so I say, without speaking:

Emmaline?

Emotion drives into me, fingers digging in my flesh, sensation scraping across my skin. Her relief is tangible. I can taste it. She's relieved, relieved I recognized her, relieved she found me, relieved relieved relieved—

What happened? I ask.

A deluge of images floods my brain until it sinks, I sink. Her memories drown my senses, clog lungs. I choke as the feelings crash into me. I see Max, my father, inconsolable in the wake of his wife's murder; I see Supreme Commander Ibrahim, frantic and furious, demanding Anderson gather the other children before it's too late; I see Emmaline, briefly abandoned, seizing an opportunity—

I gasp.

Evie made it so that only she or Max could control Emmaline's powers, and with Evie dead, the fail-safes implemented were suddenly weakened. Emmaline realized that in the wake of our mother's death there would be a brief window of opportunity—a brief window during which she might be able to wrest back control of her own mind before Max remade the algorithms.

But Evie's work was too good, and Max's reaction too prompt. Emmaline was only partly successful.

Dying, she says to me.
Dying.

Every flash of her emotion is accompanied by torturous assault. My flesh feels bruised. My spine seems liquid, my eyes blind, searing. I feel Emmaline—her voice, her

19

feelings, her visions—more strongly than before, because *she's* stronger than before. That she managed to regain enough power to find me is proof alone that she is at least partly untethered, unrestrained. Max and Evie had been experimenting on Emmaline to a reckless degree in the last several months, trying to make her stronger even as her body withered. This, *this*, is the consequence.

Being this close to her is nothing short of excruciating.

I think I've screamed.

Have I screamed?

Everything about Emmaline is heightened to a fever pitch; her presence is wild, breathtaking, and it shudders to life inside my nerves. Sound and sensation streak across my vision, barrel through me violently. I hear a spider scuttle across the wooden floor. Tired moths drag their wings along the wall. A mouse startles, settles, in its sleep. Dust motes fracture against a window, shrapnel skidding across the glass.

My eyes skitter, unhinged in my skull.

I feel the oppressive weight of my hair, my limbs, my flesh wrapped around me like cellophane, a leather casket. My tongue, my tongue is a dead lizard perched in my mouth, rough and heavy. The fine hairs on my arms stand and sway, stand and sway. My fists are so tightly clenched my fingernails pierce the soft flesh of my palms.

I feel a hand on me. Where? Am I?

Lonely, she says.

She shows me.

A vision of us, back in the laboratory where I first saw her, where I killed our mother. I see myself from Emmaline's point of view and it's startling. She can't see much more than a blur, but she can feel my presence, can make out the shape of my form, the heat emanating from my body. And then my words, my own words, hurled back into my brain—

there has to be another way
you don't have to die
we can get through this together
please
i want my sister back
i want you to live
Emmaline
i won't let you die here
Emmaline Emmaline
we can get through this together
we can get through this together
we can get through this
together

A cold, metallic sensation begins to bloom in my chest. It moves through me, up my arms, down my throat, pushes into my gut. My teeth throb. Emmaline's pain claws and slithers, clings with a ferocity I can't bear. Her tenderness, too, is desperate, terrifying in its sincerity. She's overcome by emotion, hot and cold, fueled by rage and devastation.

She's been looking for me, all this time.

In these last couple of days Emmaline has been searching the conscious world for my mind, trying to find safe harbor, a place to rest.

A place to die.

Emmaline, I say. *Please—*

Sister.

Something tightens in my mind, squeezes. Fear propels through me, punctures organs. I'm wheezing. I smell earth and damp, decomposing leaves and I feel the stars staring at my skin, wind pushing through darkness like an anxious parent. My mouth is open, catching moths. I am on the ground.

Where?

No longer in my bed, I realize, no longer in my tent, I realize, no longer protected.

But when did I walk?

Who moved my feet? Who pushed my body?

How far?

I try to look around but I'm blind, my head trapped in a vise, my neck reduced to fraying sinew. My breaths fill my ears, harsh and loud, harsh and loud, rough rough gasping efforts my head

swings

My fists unclench, nails scraping as my fingers uncurl,

palms flattening, I smell heat, taste wind, hear dirt.

Dirt under my hands, in my mouth, under my fingernails. I'm screaming, I realize. Someone is touching me and I'm screaming.

Stop, I scream. *Please, Emmaline— Please don't do this—*

Lonely, she says.

l o n e l y

And with a sudden, ferocious agony—
I am displaced.

KENJI

It feels weird to call it luck.

It feels weird, but in some perverse, twisted way, this is luck. Luck that I'm standing in the middle of damp, freezing woodlands before the sun's bothered to lift its head. Luck that my bare upper body is half-numb from cold.

Luck that Nazeera's with me.

We pulled on our invisibility almost instantly, so she and I are at least temporarily safe here, in the half-mile stretch of untouched wilderness between regulated and unregulated territories. The Sanctuary was built on a couple of acres of unregulated land not far from where I'm standing, and it's masterfully hidden in plain sight only because of Nouria's unnatural talent for bending and manipulating light. Within Nouria's jurisdiction, the climate is somehow more temperate, the weather more predictable. But out here in the wild, the winds are relentless and combative. The temperatures are dangerous.

Still— We're lucky to be here at all.

Nazeera and I had been out of bed for a while, racing through the dark in an attempt at murdering one another. In the end it all turned out to be a complicated misunderstanding, but it was also a kind of kismet: If Nazeera hadn't snuck into

27

my room at three o'clock in the morning and nearly killed me, I wouldn't have chased her through the forest, beyond the sight and soundproof protections of the Sanctuary. If we hadn't been so far from the Sanctuary, we never would've heard the distant, echoing screams of citizens crying out in terror. If we hadn't heard those cries, we never would've rushed toward the source. And if we hadn't done any of that, I never would've seen my best friend screaming her way into dawn.

I would've missed this. This:

J on her knees in the cold dirt, Warner crouched down beside her, both of them looking like death while the clouds literally melt out of the sky above them. The two of them are parked right outside the entrance to the Sanctuary, straddling the untouched stretch of forest that serves as a buffer between our camp and the heart of the nearest sector, number 241.

Why?

I froze when I saw them there, two broken figures entwined, limbs planted in the ground. I was paralyzed by confusion, then fear, then disbelief, all while the trees bent sideways and the wind snapped at my body, cruelly reminding me that I'd never had a chance to put on a shirt.

If my night had gone differently, I might've had that chance.

If my night had gone differently, I might've enjoyed, for the first time in my life, a romantic sunrise and an overdue reconciliation with a beautiful girl. Nazeera and I would've laughed about how she'd kicked me in the back and almost killed me, and how afterward I almost shot her for it. After that I would've taken a long shower, slept until noon, and eaten my weight in breakfast foods.

I had a plan for today: take it easy.

I wanted a little more time to heal after my most recent near-death experience, and I didn't think I was asking for much. I thought that, maybe, after everything I'd been through, the world might finally cut me some slack. Let me breathe between tragedies.

Nah.

Instead, I'm here, dying of frostbite and horror, watching the world fall to pieces around me. The sky, swinging wildly between horizontal and vertical horizons. The air, puncturing at random. Trees, sinking into the ground. Leaves, tap-dancing around me. I'm seeing it—I'm actively witnessing it—and still I can't believe it.

But I'm choosing to call it luck.

Luck that I'm seeing this, luck that I feel like I might throw up, luck that I ran all this way in my still-ill, injured body just in time to score a front-row seat to the end of the world.

Luck, fate, coincidence, serendipity—

I'll call this sick, sinking feeling in my gut a fucking magic trick if it'll help me keep my eyes open long enough to bear witness. To figure out how to help.

Because no one else is here.

No one but me and Nazeera, which seems crazy to an

29

improbable degree. The Sanctuary is supposed to have security on patrol at all times, but I see no sentries, and no sign of incoming aid. No soldiers from the nearby sector, either. Not even curious, hysterical civilians. Nothing.

It's like we're standing in a vacuum, on an invisible plane of existence. I don't know how J and Warner made it this far without being spotted. The two of them look like they were literally dragged through the dirt; I have no idea how they escaped notice. And though it's possible J only just started screaming, I still have a thousand unanswered questions.

They'll have to wait.

I glance at Nazeera out of habit, forgetting for a moment that she and I are invisible. But then I feel her step closer, and I breathe a sigh of relief as her hand slips into mine. She squeezes my fingers. I return the pressure.

Lucky, I remind myself.

It's lucky that we're here right now, because if I'd been in bed where I should've been, I wouldn't have even known J was in trouble. I would've missed the tremble in my friend's voice as she cried out, begging for mercy. I would've missed the shattering colors of a twisted sunrise, a peacock in the middle of hell. I would've missed the way J clamped her head between her hands and sobbed. I would've missed the sharp scents of pine and sulfur in the wind, would've missed the dry ache in my throat, the tremor moving through my body. I would've missed the moment J mentioned her sister by name. I wouldn't have heard J *specifically* ask her sister not to do something.

Yeah, this is definitely luck.

Because if I hadn't heard any of that, I wouldn't have known who to blame.

Emmaline.

~~ELLA~~

~~JULIETTE~~

I have eyes, two, feel them, rolling back and forth, around and around in my skull I have lips, two, feel them, wet and and heavy, pry them open have teeth, many, tongue, one and fingers, ten, count them

onetwothreefourfive, again on the other side strange, ssstrange to have a tongue, sstrange it's a ssssstrange ssort of thing, a strange sssssssssssortofthing

loneliness

it creeps up on you
quiet
and
still,
sits by your side in the dark, strokes your hair as you sleep wrapssitself around your bones squeezing sotightyoualmostcan't breathe almost can't hear the pulse racing in your blood as it rush, rushes up your

skin

touches its lips to the soft hairs at the back of your

neck

loneliness is a strangesortof thinga sstrangesortofthing
an old friend standing beside you in the mirror screaming
you're notenoughneverenough never ever enough

ssssssometimes it just
                    won't

    let

        go

KENJI

I sidestep an eruption in the ground and duck just in time to avoid a cluster of vines growing in midair. A distant rock balloons to an astronomical size, and the moment it starts barreling in our direction I tighten my hold on Nazeera's hand and dive for cover.

The sky is ripping apart. The ground is fracturing beneath my feet. The sun flickers, strobing darkness, strobing light, everything stilted. And the clouds— There's something newly wrong with the clouds.

They're *disintegrating*.

Trees can't decide whether to stand up or lie down, gusts of wind shoot up from the ground with terrifying power, and suddenly the sky is full of birds. Full of fucking *birds*.

Emmaline is out of control.

We knew that her telekinetic and psychokinetic powers were godlike—beyond anything we've ever known—and we knew that The Reestablishment built Emmaline to control our experience of the world. But that was all, and that was just talk. Theory.

We'd never seen her like this.

Wild.

She's clearly doing something to J right now, ravaging

her mind while lashing out at the world around us, because the acid trip I'm staring at is only getting worse.

"Go back," I cry out over the din. "Get help—bring the girls!"

A single shout of agreement and Nazeera's hand slips free from mine, her heavy boots on the ground my only indication that she's bolting toward the Sanctuary. But even now—especially now—her swift, certain actions fill me with no small measure of relief.

It feels good to have a capable partner.

I claw my way across the sparse forest, grateful to have avoided the worst of the obstacles, and when I'm finally close enough to properly discern Warner's face, I pull back my invisibility.

I'm shaking with exhaustion.

I'd only barely recovered from being drugged nearly to death, and yet here I am, already about to die again. But when I look up, half-bent, hands on my knees and trying to breathe, I realize I have no right to complain.

Warner looks even worse than I expected.

Raw, clenched, a vein straining at his temple. He's on his knees holding on to J like he's trying to hold back a riot, and I didn't realize until just this second that he might be here for more than just emotional support.

The whole thing is surreal: they're both practically naked, in the dirt, on their knees—J with her hands pressed flat against her ears—and I can't help but wonder what kind of hell brought them to this moment.

I thought I was the one having a weird night.

Something slams suddenly into my gut and I double over, hitting the ground hard. Arms shaking, I push up onto all fours and scan the immediate area for the culprit. When I spot it, I gag.

A dead bird, a couple feet away.

Jesus.

J is still screaming.

I shove my way through a sudden, violent gust of wind—and just when I've regained my balance, ready to clear the last fifty feet toward my friends—the world goes mute.

Sound, off.

No howling winds, no tortured screams, no coughs, no sneezes. This is not ordinary quiet. It's not stillness, not silence.

It's more than that.

It's nothing at all.

I blink, blink, my head turning in slow, excruciating motion as I scan the distance for answers, willing the explanations to appear. Hoping the sheer force of my mind is enough to sprout reason from the ground.

It isn't.

I've gone deaf.

Nazeera is no longer here, J and Warner are still fifty feet away, and I've gone deaf. Deaf to the sound of the wind, to the shuddering trees. Deaf to my own labored breathing, to the cries of citizens in the compounds beyond. I try to clench my fists and it takes forever, like the air has grown

41

dense. Thick.

Something is wrong with me.

I'm slow, slower than I've ever been, like I'm running underwater. Something is purposely keeping me back, physically pushing me away from Juliette—and suddenly, it all makes sense. My earlier confusion dissolves. Of course no one else is here. Of course no one else has come to help.

Emmaline would never allow it.

Maybe I got this far only because she was too busy to notice me right away—to sense me here, in my invisible state. It makes me wonder what else she's done to keep this area clear of trespassers.

It makes me wonder if I'll survive.

It's growing harder to think. It takes forever to fuse thoughts. Takes forever to move my arms. To lift my head. To look around. By the time I manage to pry open my mouth, I've forgotten that my voice makes no sound.

A flash of gold in the distance.

I spot Warner, shifting so slowly I wonder whether we're both suffering from the same affliction. He's fighting desperately to sit up next to J—J who's still on her knees, bent forward, mouth open. Her eyes are squeezed shut in concentration, but if she's screaming, I can't hear it.

I'd be lying if I said I wasn't terrified.

I'm close enough to Warner and J to be able to make out their expressions, but it's no good; I have no idea whether they're injured, so I don't know the extent of what we're dealing with. I have to get closer, somehow. But when I take a single, painful step forward, a sharp keening explodes in my ears.

I cry out soundlessly, clapping my hands to my head as the silence is suddenly—*viciously*—compounded by pressure. The knifelike pain needles into me, pressure building in my ears with an intensity that threatens to crush me from the inside. It's like someone has overfilled my head with helium, like any minute now the balloon that is my brain will explode. And just when I think the pressure might kill me, just when I think I can't bear the pain any longer, the ground begins to rumble. Tremble.

There's a seismic *crack*—

And sound comes back online. Sound so violent it rips open something inside of me, and when I finally tear my hands away from my ears they're red, dripping. I stagger as my head pounds. Rings. Rings.

I wipe my bloody hands on my bare torso and my vision swims. I lunge forward in a stupor and land badly, my still-damp palms hitting the earth so hard the force of it shudders up my bones. The dirt beneath my feet has gone slick. Wet. I look up, squinting at the sky and the sudden, torrential rain. My head continues to swing on a well-oiled hinge. A single drop of blood drips down my ear, lands on my shoulder. A second drop of blood drips down my ear, lands on my shoulder. A third drop of blood drips down my—

Name.

Someone calls my name.

The sound is large, aggressive. The word careens dizzily

in my head, expanding and contracting. I can't pin it down.

Kenji

I turn around and my head rings, rings.

K e n j i

I blink and it takes days, revolutions around the sun.

Trusted

friend

Something is touching me, under me, hauling me up, but it's no good. I don't move.

Too

heavy

I try to speak but can't. I say nothing, do nothing as my mind is broken open, as cold fingers reach inside my skull and disconnect the circuitry within. I stand still. Stiffen. The voice echoes to life in the blackness behind my eyes, speaking words that feel more like memory than conversation, words I don't know, don't understand *the pain I carry, the fears I should've left behind. I sag under the weight of loneliness, the chains of disappointment. My heart alone weighs a thousand pounds. I'm so heavy I can no longer be lifted away from the earth. I'm so heavy I have no choice now but to be buried beneath it. I'm so heavy, too heavy*

I exhale as I go down.

My knees crack as they hit the ground. My body slumps forward. Dirt kisses my face, welcomes me home.

The world goes suddenly dark.

Brave

My eyes flicker. Sound hums in my ears, something like dull, steady electricity. Everything is plunged into darkness. A blackout, a blackout in the natural world. Fear clings to my skin. Covers me.

but

w e a k

Knives bore holes into my bones that fill quickly with sorrow, sorrow so acute it takes my breath away.

I've never been so hopeful to cease existing.

I am floating.

Weightless and yet—weighted down, destined to sink forever. Dim light fractures the blackness behind my eyes and in the light, I see water. My sun and moon are the sea, my mountains the ocean. I live in liquid I never drink, drowning steadily in marbled, milky waters. My breathing is heavy, automatic, mechanic. I am forced to inhale, forced to exhale. The harsh, shuddering rasp of my own breath is my constant reminder of the grave that is my home.

I hear something.

It reverberates through the tank, dull metal against dull metal, arriving at my ears as if from outer space. I squint at the fresh set of shapes and colors, blurred forms. I clench my fists but my flesh is soft, my bones like fresh dough, my skin peeling in moist flakes. I'm surrounded by water but my thirst is insatiable and my anger—

My anger—

Something snaps. My head. My mind. My neck.

My eyes are wide, my breathing panicked. I'm on my knees, my forehead pressed into the dirt, my hands buried in wet earth.

I sit straight up and back, my head spinning.

"What the *fuck*?" I'm still trying to breathe. I look around. My heart is racing. "What— What—"

I was digging my own grave.

Slithering, terrifying horror moves through my body as I understand: Emmaline was in my head. She wanted to see if she could get me to kill myself.

And even as I think it—even as I look down at the miserable attempt I made to bury myself alive—I feel a dull, stabbing sympathy for Emmaline. Because I felt her pain, and it wasn't cruel.

It was desperate.

Like she was hoping that if I killed myself while she was in my head, somehow I'd be able to kill her, too.

J is screaming again.

I stagger to my feet, heart in my throat as the skies wrench open, releasing their wrath upon me. I'm not sure why Emmaline gave the inside of my head a shot—*brave but weak*—but I know enough to understand that whatever the hell is happening here is more than I can handle on my own. Right now, I can only hope that everyone in the Sanctuary is okay—and that Nazeera gets back here soon. Until then, my broken body will have to do its best.

I push forward.

Even as old, cold blood dries in my ears, across my chest, I push forward, steeling myself against the increasingly volatile weather conditions. The steady succession of earthquakes. The lightning strikes. The raging thunderstorm growing quickly into a hurricane.

Once I'm finally close enough, Warner looks up.

He seems stunned.

It occurs to me then that he's only just seeing me—after all this—he's only just realizing I'm here. A flicker of relief flashes through his eyes, too quickly replaced by pain.

And then he calls out two words—two words I never

thought I'd inspire him to say:

"*Help me.*"

The sentence is carried off in the wind, but the agony in his eyes remains. And from this vantage point, I finally understand the depth of what he's endured. At first I'd thought Warner was only holding her steady, trying to be supportive.

I was wrong.

J is vibrating with power, and Warner is only barely hanging on to her. Holding her still. Something—*someone*—is physically animating Juliette's body, articulating her limbs, trying to force her upright and possibly away from here, and it's only because of Warner that Emmaline hasn't succeeded.

I have no idea how he's doing it.

J's skin has gone translucent, veins bright and freakish in her pale face. She's nearly blue, ready to crack. A low-level hum emanates from her body, the crackle of energy, the buzz of power. I grab on to her arm and in the half second Warner shifts to distribute her weight between us, the three of us are flung forward. We hit the ground so hard I can hardly breathe, and when I'm finally able to lift my head I look at Warner, my own eyes wide with unmasked terror.

"Emmaline is doing this," I say, shouting the words at him.

He nods, his face grim.

"What can we do?" I cry. "How can she just keep screaming like this?"

Warner only looks at me.

He just *looks* at me, and the tortured expression in his eyes tells me everything I need to know. J *can't* keep screaming like this. She can't just be here on her knees screaming for a century. This shit is going to kill her. Jesus Christ. I knew it was bad, but for some reason I didn't think it was this bad.

J looks like she's going to die.

"Should we try to pick her up?" I don't even know why I ask. I doubt I could lift her arm above my head, much less her whole body. My own body is still shaking, so much so that I can barely do my part to keep this girl from lifting directly off the ground. I have no idea what kind of crazy shit is pumping through her veins right now, but J is on another planet. She looks half-alive, mostly alien. Her eyes are squeezed shut, her jaw unhinged. She's *radiating* energy. It's fucking terrifying.

And I can barely keep up.

The ache in my arms has begun to creep up my shoulders and down my back and I shiver, violently, when a sharp wind strikes my bare, overheated skin.

"Let's try," Warner says.

I nod.

Take a deep breath.

Beg myself to be stronger than I am.

I don't know how I do it, but through nothing short of a miracle, I make it to my feet. Warner and I manage to bind Juliette between us, and when I look over at him, I'm at least relieved to discover that he looks like he's struggling, too. I've never seen Warner struggle, not really, and I'm pretty sure I've never seen him sweat. But as much as I'd love to laugh a little right now, the sight of him straining so hard just to hold on to her only sends a fresh wave of fear through me. I have no idea how long he's been trying to restrain her all by himself. I have no idea what would've happened to her if he hadn't been there to hold on. And I have no idea what would happen to her right now, if we were to let go.

Something about that realization gives me renewed strength. It takes choice out of the situation. J needs us right now, period.

Which means I have to be stronger.

Standing upright like this has made us an easy target in all this madness, and I call out a warning as a piece of debris flies toward us. I pivot sharply to protect J, but take a hit to my spine, the pain so breathtaking I'm seeing stars. My back was already injured earlier tonight, and the bruises are bound to be worse now. But when Warner locks eyes with me in a sudden, terrified panic, I nod, letting him know I'm okay. I've got her.

Inch by agonizing inch, we move back toward the Sanctuary.

We're dragging J like she's Jesus between us, her head flung backward, feet dragging across the ground. She's finally stopped screaming, but now she's convulsing, her body seizing uncontrollably, and Warner looks like he's hanging on to his sanity by a single, fraying thread.

It feels like centuries pass before we see Nazeera again, but the rational part of my brain suspects it must've been only twenty, thirty minutes. Who knows. I'm sure she was trying her best to get back here with people who could help, but it feels like we're too late. Everything feels too late.

I have no idea what the hell is happening anymore.

Yesterday, this morning—an hour ago—I was worried about James and Adam. I thought our problems were simple and straightforward: get the kids back, kill the supreme commanders, have a nice lunch.

But now—

Nazeera and Castle and Brendan and Nouria rush to a sudden stop before us. They look between us.

They look beyond us.

Their eyes go round, their lips parting as they gasp. I crane my neck to see what they're seeing and realize that there's a tidal wave of fire headed straight toward us.

I think I'm going to collapse.

My body is worse than unsteady. By this point, my legs are made of rubber. I can barely support my own weight, and it's a miracle I'm holding on to J at all. In fact, a quick glance at Warner's clenched, insanely tense body is all it takes to realize that he's probably doing most of the work right now.

I don't know how any of us are going to survive this. I can't *move*. I sure as hell can't outrun a wave of fire.

And I don't really understand everything that happens next.

I hear an inhuman cry, and Stephan is suddenly rushing toward us. *Stephan.* He's suddenly in front of us, suddenly between us. He picks J up and into his arms like she might be a rag doll, and starts shouting at all of us to run. Castle hangs back to redirect water from a nearby well, and though his efforts at dousing the flames aren't entirely successful, it's enough to give us the edge we need to escape. Warner and I drag ourselves back to camp with the others, and the minute we cross the threshold into the Sanctuary, we're met with a frantic sea of faces. Countless figures surge forward, their shouts and cries and hysterical commotion fusing into a single, unbroken soundstorm. Logically, I understand why people are out here, worried, crying, shouting unanswered questions at each other—but right now I just want them all to get the hell out of my way.

Nouria and Sam seem to read my mind.

They bark orders into the crowd and the nameless bodies begin to clear out. Stephan is no longer running, but walking briskly, elbowing people out of his way as necessary, and I'm grateful. But when Sonya and Sara come sprinting toward us, shouting for us to follow them to the medical tent, I nearly launch myself forward and kiss them both.

I don't.

Instead, I take a moment to search for Castle, wondering if he made it out okay. But when I look back, scanning our stretch of protected land, I experience a sudden, sobering moment of realization. The disparity between *in here* and *out there* is unreal.

In here, the sky is clear.

The weather, settled. The ground seems to have sutured itself back together. The wall of fire that tried to chase us all the way back to the Sanctuary is now nothing but fading smoke. The trees are in their upright positions; the hurricane is little more than a fine mist. The morning looks almost pretty. For a second I could've sworn I heard a bird chirping.

I'm probably out of my mind.

I collapse in the middle of a well-worn path leading back to our tents, my face thudding against wet grass. The smell of fresh, damp earth fills my head and I breathe it in, all of it. It's a balm. A miracle. *Maybe*, I think. Maybe we're going to be okay. Maybe I can close my eyes. Take a moment.

Warner stalks past my prone body, his motions so intense I'm startled upright, into a sitting position.

I have no idea how he's still moving.

He's not even wearing shoes. No shirt, no socks, no shoes. Just a pair of sweatpants. I notice for the first time that he's got a huge gash across his chest. Several cuts on his arms. A nasty scratch on his neck. Blood is dripping slowly down his torso, and Warner doesn't even seem to notice. Scars all over his back, blood smeared across his front. He looks insane. But he's still moving, his eyes hot with rage and something else— Something that scares the shit out of me.

He catches up to Stephan, who's still holding J—who's

still having seizures—and I crawl toward a tree, using the trunk to hoist myself off the ground. I drag myself after them, flinching involuntarily at a sudden breeze. I turn too fast, scanning the open woods for debris or a flying boulder, and find only Nazeera, who rests a hand on my arm.

"Don't worry," she says. "We're safe within the borders of the Sanctuary."

I blink at her. And then around, at the familiar white tents that cloak every solid, freestanding structure on the glorified campsite that is this place of refuge.

Nazeera nods. "Yeah—that's what the tents are for. Nouria enhanced all of her light protections with some kind of antidote that makes us immune to the illusions Emmaline creates. Both acres of land are protected, and the reflective material covering the tents provides more assured protection indoors."

"How do you know all of that?"

"I asked."

I blink at her again. I feel dumb. Numb. Like I broke something deep inside my brain. Deep inside my body.

"Juliette," I say.

It's the only word I've got right now, and Nazeera doesn't even bother to correct me, to tell me her real name is Ella. She just takes my hand and squeezes.

ELLA

~~JULIETTE~~

When I dream, I dream of sound.

Rain, taking its time, softly popping against concrete. Rain, gathering, drumming, until sound turns into static. Rain, so sudden, so strong, it startles itself. I dream of water dripping down lips and tips of noses, rain falling off branches into shallow, murky pools. I hear death when puddles shatter, assaulted by heavy feet.

I hear leaves—

Leaves, shuddering under the weight of resignation, yoked to branches too easily bent, broken. I dream of wind, lengths of it. Yards of wind, acres of wind, infinite whispers fusing to create a single breeze. I hear wind comb the wild grass of distant mountains, I hear wind howling confessions in empty, lonely plains. I hear the *sh sh sh* of desperate rivers trying to hush the world in a fruitless effort to hush itself.

But

    buried

  in the din

is a single scream so steady it goes every day unheard. We see, but do not understand the way it stutters hearts, clenches jaws, curls fingers into fists. It's a surprise, always a surprise, when it finally stops screaming long enough to speak.

Fingers tremble.

Flowers die.

The sun flinches, the stars expire.

You are in a room, a closet, a vault, no key—

Just a single voice that says

Kill me

KENJI

J is sleeping.

She seems so close to death I can hardly look at her. Skin so white it's blue. Lips so blue they're purple. Somehow, in the last couple of hours, she lost weight. She looks like a little bird, young and small and fragile. Her long hair is fanned around her face and she's motionless, a little blue doll with her face pointed straight up at the ceiling. She looks like she could be lying in a casket.

I don't say any of this out loud, of course.

Warner seems pretty close to death himself. He looks pale, disoriented. Sickly.

And he's become impossible to talk to.

These past months of forced camaraderie nearly had me brainwashed; I'd almost forgotten what Warner used to be like.

Cold. Cutting. Eerily quiet.

He seems like an echo of himself right now, sitting stiffly in a chair next to her bed. We dragged J back here hours ago and he still won't really look at anyone. The cut on his chest looks even worse now, but he does nothing about it. He disappeared at one point, but only for a couple of minutes, and returned wearing his boots. He didn't bother to wipe the blood off his body. Didn't stop long enough to put on a shirt. He could easily steal Sonya's and Sara's powers to heal himself, but he makes no effort. He refuses to be touched. He refuses to eat. The few words out of his mouth were so scathing he made three different people cry. Nouria finally told him that if he didn't stop attacking her teammates she'd take him out back and shoot him. I think it was Warner's lack of protest that kept her from following through.

He's nothing but thorns.

Old Kenji would've shrugged it off and rolled his eyes. Old Kenji would've thrown a dart at Dickhead Warner and, honestly, would've probably been happy to see him suffer like this.

But I'm not that guy anymore.

I know Warner too well now. I know how much he loves J. I know he'd turn his skin inside out just to make her happy. He wanted to marry her, for God's sake. And I just watched him nearly kill himself to save her, suffering for hours through the worst levels of hell just to keep her alive.

Almost two hours, to be exact.

Warner said he'd been out there with J for nearly an hour before I showed up, and it was at least another forty-five minutes before the girls were able to stabilize her. He spent nearly two hours physically fighting to keep Juliette from harm, protecting her with his own body as he was lashed by fallen trees, flying rocks, errant debris, and violent winds. The girls said they could tell just by looking at him that he had at least two broken ribs. A fracture in his right arm. A dislocated shoulder. Probably internal bleeding. They raged at him so much that he finally sat down in a chair, wrapped his good hand around the wrist of his injured arm, and pulled his own shoulder back in place. The only proof of his pain was a single, sharp breath.

Sonya screamed, rushing forward, too late to stop him.

And then he broke open the seam at the ankle of his sweatpants, tore off a length of cotton, and made a sling for his freshly socketed arm. Only after that did he finally look up at the girls.

"Now leave me alone," he said darkly.

Sonya and Sara looked so frustrated—their eyes blazing with rare anger—I almost didn't recognize them.

I know he's being an asshole.

I know he's being stubborn and stupid and cruel. But I can't find the strength to be mad at him right now. I can't.

My heart is breaking for the guy.

We're all standing around J's bed, just staring at her. A monitor beeps softly in the corner. The room smells like chemicals. Sonya and Sara had to inject J with serious tranquilizers in order to get her body to settle, but it seemed to help: the moment she slowed down, the world outside did, too.

The Reestablishment was quick on the uptake, doing such seamless damage control I almost couldn't believe it. They capitalized on the problem, claiming that what happened this morning was a taste of future devastation. They claimed that they managed to get it under control before it got any worse, and they reminded the people to be grateful for the protections provided by The Reestablishment; that, without them, the world would be a lot worse. It fairly scared the shit out of everyone. Things feel a lot quieter now. The civilians seem subdued in a way they weren't before. It's stunning, really, how The Reestablishment managed to convince people that the sky collapsing while the sun just *disappeared* for a full minute were normal things that could happen in the world.

It's unbelievable that they feed people that kind of bullshit, and it's unbelievable that people eat it up.

But when I'm being super honest with myself, I'll admit that what scares me the most is that, if I didn't know any better, I might've eaten that shit up, too.

I sigh, hard. Drag a hand down my face.

This morning feels like a weird dream.

Surreal, like one of those melting clock paintings The Reestablishment destroyed. And I'm so wrung out, so tired, I don't even have the energy to be angry. I've only got enough energy to be sad.

We're all just really, really sad.

The few of us who could squeeze into this room: me, Castle, Nouria, Sam, Superman (my new nickname for Stephan), Haider, Nazeera, Brendan, Winston, Warner. All of us, sad, sorry sacks. Sonya and Sara left for a bit, but they'll be coming back soon, and when they do, they'll be sad, too.

Ian and Lily wanted to be here, but Warner kicked them out. He just straight up told them to get out, for reasons he didn't offer to disclose. He didn't raise his voice. Didn't even look at Ian. Just told him to turn around and leave. Brendan was so stunned his eyes nearly fell out of his head. But all of us were too afraid of Warner to say anything.

A small, guilty part of me wondered if maybe Warner knew that Ian talked shit about him that one time, that Warner knew (who knows how) that Ian didn't want to make the effort to go after him and J when we lost them at the symposium.

I don't know. It's just a theory. But it's obvious Warner is done playing the game. He's done with courtesy, done with patience, done with giving a single shit about anyone but J. Which means the tension in here is insane right now. Even Castle seems a little nervous around Warner, like he's not sure about him anymore.

The problem is, we all got too comfortable.

For a couple of months we forgot that Warner was scary. He smiled like four and a half times and we decided to forget that he was basically a psychopath with a long history of ruthless murder. We thought he'd been reformed. Gone soft. We forgot that he was only tolerating any of us because of Juliette.

And now, without her—

He no longer seems to belong.

Without her, we're fracturing. The energy in this room has palpably changed. We don't really feel like a team anymore, and it's scary how quickly it happened. If only Warner weren't so determined to be a dickhead. If only he weren't so eager to put on his old skin, to alienate everyone in this room. If only he'd muster the smallest bit of goodwill, we could turn this whole thing around.

Seems unlikely.

I'm not as terrified as the others, but I'm not stupid, either. I know his threats of violence aren't a bluff. The only people unperturbed are the supreme kids. They look right at home with this version of him. Haider, maybe most of all. That dude always seemed on edge, like he had no idea who Warner had turned into and he didn't know how to process the change. But now? No problem. Super comfortable with psycho Warner. Old pals.

Nouria finally breaks the silence.

Gently, she clears her throat. A couple of people lift their heads. Warner glares at the floor.

"Kenji," she says softly, "can I talk to you for a minute? Outside?"

My body stiffens.

I look around, uncertain, like she's got me confused with someone else. Castle and Nazeera turn sharply in my direction, surprise widening their eyes. Sam, on the other hand, is staring at her wife, struggling to hide her frustration.

"Um"—I scratch my head—"maybe we should talk in here," I say. "As a group?"

"Outside, Kishimoto." Nouria is on her feet, the softness gone from her voice, her face. "Now, please."

Reluctantly, I get to my feet.

I lock eyes with Nazeera, wondering if she has an opinion on the situation, but her expression is unreadable.

Nouria calls my name again.

I shake my head but follow her out the door. She leads me around a corner, into a narrow hallway.

It smells overwhelmingly like bleach.

J is posted up inside the *MT*—an obvious nickname for their medical tent—which feels like a misnomer, actually, because the tent element is entirely superficial. The inside of the building is a lot more like a proper hospital, with individual suites and operating rooms. It blew my mind a little the first time I first walked through here, because this space is super different from what we had at Omega Point and Sector 45. But then, before Sonya and Sara showed up, the Sanctuary had no healers. Their medical work was a lot more traditional: practiced by a handful of self-taught doctors and surgeons. There's something about their old-fashioned, life-threatening medical practices that makes this place feel a lot more like a relic of our old world. A building full of fear.

Out here, in the main corridor, I can hear more clearly the standard sounds of a hospital—machines beeping, carts rolling, occasional moans, shouts, pages over an intercom. I flatten myself against the wall as a team of people barrels past, pushing a gurney down the hallway. Its occupant is an elderly man hooked up to an IV, an oxygen mask on his face. When he sees Nouria, he lifts his hand in a weak wave.

Attempts a smile.

Nouria gives him a bright smile in return, holding it steady until the man is wheeled into another room. The moment he's out of sight, she corners me. Her eyes flash, her dark brown skin glowing in the dim light like a warning. My spine straightens.

Nouria is surprisingly terrifying.

"What the hell happened out there?" she says. "What did you do?"

"Okay, first of all"—I hold up both hands—"I didn't *do* anything. And I already told you guys exactly what happened—"

"You never told me that Emmaline tried to access your mind."

That stops me up. "What? Yes I did. I literally told you that. I used those exact words."

"But you didn't provide the necessary details," she says. "How did it start? What did it feel like? Why did she let go?"

"I don't know," I say, frowning. "I don't understand what happened—all I've got are guesses."

"Then *guess*," she says, narrowing her eyes. "Unless— She's not still in your head, is she?"

"What? No."

Nouria sighs, more irritation than relief. She touches her fingers to her temples in a show of resignation. "This doesn't make sense," she says, almost to herself. "Why would she try so hard to infiltrate Ella's mind? Why *yours*? I thought she was fighting against The Reestablishment. This feels more like she's working for them."

I shake my head. "I don't think so. When Emmaline was in my head it felt more to me like a desperate, last-ditch effort—like she was worried J wouldn't have the heart to kill her, and she was hoping I'd get it done faster. She called me brave, but weak. Like, I don't know, maybe this sounds crazy, but it felt almost like Emmaline thought—for a second—that if I'd made it that far in her presence, I might've been strong enough to contain her. But then she jumped in my head and realized she was wrong. I wasn't strong enough to hold her mind, and definitely not strong enough to kill her." I shrug. "So she bailed."

Nouria straightens. When she looks at me, she looks stunned. "You think she's really that desperate to die? You think she wouldn't put up a fight if someone tried to kill her?"

"Yeah, it's awful," I say, looking away. "Emmaline's in a really bad place."

"But she can exist, at least partially, in Ella's body." Nouria frowns. "Both consciousnesses in one person. How?"

"I don't know." I shrug again. "J said that Evie did a bunch of work on her muscles and bones and stuff while she was in Oceania—priming her for Operation Synthesis—to basically become Emmaline's new body. So I think, ultimately, J playing host to Emmaline is what Evie had planned all along."

"And Emmaline must've known," Nouria says quietly.

It's my turn to frown. "What are you getting at?"

"I don't know, exactly. But this situation complicates things. Because if our goal was to kill Emmaline, and Emmaline is now living in Ella's body—"

"Wait." My stomach does a terrifying flip. "Is that why we're out here? Is this why you're being so secretive?"

"Lower your voice," Nouria says sharply, glancing at something behind me.

"I will not lower my fucking voice," I say. "What the hell are you thinking? What are you— Wait, what do you keep looking at?" I crane my neck but see only a blank wall behind my head. My heart is racing, my mind working too fast. I whip back around to face her.

"Tell me the truth," I demand. "Is this why you cornered me? Because you're trying to figure out if we can kill J while she's got Emmaline inside of her? Is that it? *Are you insane?*"

Nouria glares at me. "Is it insane to want to save the world? Emmaline is at the center of everything wrong with our universe right now, and she's trapped inside a body lying in a room just down the *hall*. Do you know how long we've been waiting for a moment like this? Don't get me wrong, I don't love this line of thinking, Kishimoto, but I'm not—"

"*Nouria.*"

At the sound of her wife's voice, Nouria goes visibly still. She takes a step back from me, and I finally relax. A little.

We both turn around.

Sam's not alone. Castle is standing next to her, both of

70

them looking more than a little pissed.

"Leave him alone," Castle says. "Kenji's been through enough already. He needs time to recuperate."

Nouria tries to respond, but Sam cuts her off. "How many times are we going to talk about this?" she says. "You can't just shut me out when you're stressed. You can't just go off on your own without telling me." Her blond hair falls into her eyes and, frustrated, she shoves the strands out of her face. "I'm your *partner*. This is our Sanctuary. Our life. We built it together, remember?"

"Sam." Nouria sighs, squeezing her eyes closed. "You know I'm not trying to shut you out. You know that's not—"

"You are literally shutting me out. You literally shut the door."

My eyebrows fly up my forehead. Castle and I connect glances: we seem to have walked into a private argument.

Good.

"Hey, Sam," I say, "did you know that your wife wants to kill Juliette?"

Castle gasps.

Sam's body goes slack. She stares at Nouria, stunned.

"Yeah," I say, nodding. "Nouria wants to murder her right now, actually, while she's still comatose. What do you think?" I tilt my head at Sam. "Good idea? Bad idea? Maybe sleep on it?"

"That can't be true," Sam says, still staring at her wife. "Tell me he's joking."

"It's not that simple," says Nouria, who shoots me a

look so venomous I almost feel bad for being petty. I don't actually want Nouria and Sam to fight, but whatever. She can't casually suggest murdering my best friend and expect me to be nice about it. "I was just pointing out th—"

"*Okay, enough.*"

I look up at the sound of Nazeera's voice. I have no idea when she showed up, but she's suddenly in front of us, arms crossed against her chest. "We're not doing this. No side conversations. No subgroups. We all need to talk about the impending shitstorm headed our way, and if we're going to have any chance of figuring out how to fight it, we have to stick together."

"Which impending shitstorm?" I ask. "Please be specific."

"I agree with Nazeera," Sam says, her eyes narrowing at her wife. "Let's all go back inside the room and talk. To each other. At the same time."

"Sam," Nouria tries again. "I'm not—"

"Bloody hell." Stephan stops short at the sight of us, his shoes squeaking on the tile. He seems to tower over our group, looking too polished and civilized to belong here. "What on earth are you lot doing out here?"

Then, quietly, to Nazeera: "And why've you left us alone with him? He's being a proper ass. Nearly made Haider cry just now."

Nazeera sighs, closing her eyes as she pinches the bridge of her nose. "Haider does this to himself. I don't understand why he's deluded himself into thinking Warner is his best friend."

"That, he might well be," Stephan says, frowning. "The bar is quite low, as you know."

Nazeera sighs again.

"If it makes Haider feel any better, Warner's being equally horrible to just about everyone," Sam says. She looks at Nouria. "Amir still won't tell me what Warner said to him, by the way."

"Amir?" Castle frowns. "The young man who oversees the patrol unit?"

Sam nods. "He quit this morning."

"No." Nouria blinks, stunned. "You're kidding."

"I wish I were. I had to give his job to Jenna."

"This is crazy." Nouria shakes her head. "It's only been three days and already we're falling apart."

"Three days?" says Stephan. "Three days since *we* arrived, is that it? That's not a very nice thing to say."

"We are not falling apart," Nazeera says suddenly. Angrily. "We can't afford to fall apart. Not right now. Not with The Reestablishment about to appear at our doorstep."

"Wait—what?" Sam frowns. "The Reestablishment has no idea where we—"

"God, this is so depressing," I groan, running both hands through my hair. "Why are we all at each other's throats right now? If Juliette were awake, she'd be so pissed at all of us. And she'd be super pissed at Warner for acting like this, for pushing us apart. Doesn't he realize that?"

"No," Castle says quietly. "Of course he doesn't."

A sharp *knock knock*—

And we all look up.

Winston and Brendan are peering around the corner at us, Brendan's closed fist held aloft an inch from the wall. He knocks once more against the plaster.

Nouria exhales loudly. "Can we help you?"

They march over to us, their expressions so different it's almost—*almost*—funny. Like light and dark, these two.

"Hello, everyone," Brendan says, smiling brightly.

Winston yanks the glasses off his face. Glowers. "What the hell is going on? Why are you all having a conference out here on your own? And why did you leave us alone with him?"

"We didn't," I try to say.

"We're not," Sam and Nazeera say at the same time.

Winston rolls his eyes. Shoves his glasses back on. "I'm getting too fucking old for this."

"You just need some coffee," Brendan says, gently patting Winston's shoulder. "Winston doesn't sleep very well at night," he explains to the rest of us.

Winston perks up. Goes instantly pink.

I smile.

I swear, it's all I do. I just smile, and in a fraction of a second Winston's locked eyes with me, his death stare screaming, *Shut your mouth, Kishimoto*, and I don't even have a chance to be offended before he turns abruptly away, his ears bright red.

An uncomfortable silence descends.

74

I wonder, for the first time, if it's really possible that Brendan has no idea how Winston feels about him. He seems oblivious, but who knows. It's definitely not a secret to the rest of us.

"Well." Castle takes a sharp breath, claps his hands together. "We were about to go back inside the room to have a proper discussion. So if you gentlemen"—he nods at Winston and Brendan—"wouldn't mind turning back the way you came? We're getting a bit cramped in the hall."

"Right." Brendan glances quickly behind him. "But, um, do you think we might wait another minute or so? Haider was crying, you see, and I think he'd appreciate the privacy."

"Oh, for the love of God," I groan.

"What happened?" Nazeera asks, concern creasing her forehead. "Should I go in there?"

Brendan shrugs, his extremely white face glowing almost neon in this dark corridor. "He said something to Warner in Arabic, I believe. And I don't know exactly what Warner said back to him, but I'm pretty sure he told Haider to sod off, in one way or another."

"Asshole," Winston mutters.

"It's true, unfortunately." Brendan frowns.

I shake my head. "All right, okay, I know he's being a dick, but I think we can cut Warner a little slack, right? He's devastated. Let's not forget the hell he went through this morning."

"Pass." Winston crosses his arms, anger seeming to lift him out of embarrassment. "Haider is *crying*. Haider

75

Ibrahim. Son of the supreme commander of Asia. He's sitting in a hospital chair *crying* because Warner hurt his feelings. I don't know how you can defend that."

"To be fair," Stephan interjects, "Haider's always been a bit delicate."

"Listen, I'm not defending Warner, I'm just—"

"*Enough.*" Castle's voice is loud. Sharp. "That is quite enough." Something tugs gently at my neck, startling me, and I notice Castle's hands are up in the air. Like he just physically turned our heads to face him. He points back down the hall, toward J's recovery room. I feel a slight push at my back.

"Back inside. All of you. Now."

Haider doesn't seem any different when we step back inside the room. No evidence of tears. He's standing in a corner, alone, staring into the middle distance. Warner is in exactly the same position we left him in, sitting stiffly beside J.

Staring at her.

Staring at her like he might be able to will her back into consciousness.

Nazeera claps her hands together, hard. "All right," she says, "no more interruptions. We need to talk about strategy before we do anything else."

Sam frowns. "Strategy for what? Right now, we need to discuss Emmaline. We need to understand the events of the morning before we can even think about discussing the next steps forward."

76

"We *are* going to talk about Emmaline, and the events of the morning," Nazeera says. "But in order to discuss the Emmaline situation, we'll need to talk about the Ella situation, which will necessitate a conversation about a larger, overarching strategy—one that will dovetail neatly with a plan to get the supreme kids back."

Castle stares at her, looking just as confused as Sam. "You want to discuss the supreme kids right now? Isn't it better if we star—"

"Idiots," Haider mutters under his breath.

We ignore him.

Well, most of us. Nazeera is shaking her head, giving the room at large that same look she gives me so often—the one that expresses her general exhaustion at being surrounded by idiots.

"How are you so unable to see how these things connect? The Reestablishment is looking for us. More specifically, they're looking for Ella. We were supposed to be in hiding, remember? But Emmaline's egregious display this morning just blew the cover on our location. We all saw the news— you all read the emergency reports. The Reestablishment did serious damage control to subdue the citizens. That means they know what happened here."

Again, more blank stares.

"Emmaline just led them directly to Ella," she says. She says this last sentence really slowly, like she fears for our collective intelligence. "Whether on purpose or by accident, The Reestablishment now has an approximate idea of our location."

Nouria looks stricken.

"Which means," Haider says, drawing the words out with his own irritating condescension, "they're much closer to finding us now than they were a few hours ago."

Everyone sits up straighter in their chairs. The air is suddenly different, intense in a new way. Nouria and Sam exchange worried glances.

It's Nouria who says, "You really think they know where we are?"

"I knew this would happen," Sam says, shaking her head.

Castle stiffens. "What's that supposed to mean?"

Sam bristles, but her words are calm when she says: "We took an enormous risk letting your team stay here. We risked our livelihood and the safety of our own men and women to allow you to take shelter among us. You're here for three days and already you've managed to disclose our location to the world."

"We haven't disclosed anything— And what happened today was no one's fault—"

Nouria lifts a hand. "Stop," she says, shooting a look at Sam, a look so brief I almost miss it. "We're losing our focus again. Nazeera was right when she said we were all in this together. In fact, we came together for the express purpose of defeating The Reestablishment. It's what we've always been working toward. We were never meant to live forever in self-made cages and communities."

"I understand that," Sam says, her steady voice belying the anger in her eyes. "But if they really know which sector to search, we could be discovered in a matter of days. The Reestablishment will be increasing their military presence within the hour, if they haven't done so already."

"They have done," Stephan says, looking just as exasperated as Nazeera. "Of course they have."

"So naive, these people," Haider says, shooting a dark look at his sister.

Nazeera sighs.

Winston swears.

Sam shakes her head.

"So what do you propose?" Winston says, but he's not looking at Nouria or Sam or Castle. He's looking at Nazeera.

Nazeera doesn't hesitate.

"We wait. We wait for Ella to wake up," she says. "We need to know as much as we can about what happened to her, and we need to prioritize her security above all else. There's a reason why Anderson wants her so desperately, and we need to find out what that reason is before we take any next steps."

"But what about a plan for getting the other kids back?" Winston asks. "If we wait for Ella to wake up before making a move to save them, we could be too late."

Nazeera shakes her head. "The plan for the other kids has to be tied up in the plan to save Ella," she says. "I'm certain that Anderson is using the kidnapping of the supreme kids as bait. A bullshit lure designed to draw us out into the open. Plus, he designed that scheme before he had any idea we'd accidentally out ourselves, which only further supports my theory that this was a bullshit lure. He was only hoping we'd step outside of our protections just long enough to give away our approximate location."

"Which we've now done," Brendan says, quietly horrified.

I drop my head in my hands. "*Shit.*"

"It seems clear that Anderson wasn't planning on doing any kind of honest trade for the hostages," Nazeera says. "How could he possibly? He never told us where he was. Never told us where to meet him. And most interestingly: he didn't even ask for the rest of the supreme kids. Whatever his plans are, he doesn't seem to require the full set of us. He didn't want Warner or me or Haider or Stephan. All he wanted was Ella, right?" She glances at Nouria. "That's what you said. That he only wanted Ella?"

"Yes," Nouria says. "That's true— But I still don't think I understand. You just laid out all the reasons for us to go to war, but your plan of attack involves doing nothing."

Nazeera can't hide her irritation. "We should still be making plans to fight," she says. "We'll need a plan to find the kids, steal them back, and then, eventually, murder our parents. But I'm proposing we wait for Ella until we make any moves. I'm suggesting we do a full and complete lockdown here at the Sanctuary until Ella is conscious. No going in or out until she wakes up. If you need emergency supplies, Kenji and I can use our stealth to go on discreet missions to find what you need. The Reestablishment will have soldiers posted up everywhere, monitoring every movement in this area, but as long as we remain isolated, we should be able to buy ourselves some time."

"But we have no idea how long it'll take for Ella to wake up," Sam says. "It could be weeks—it could be *never*—"

"Our mission," Nazeera says, cutting her off, "has to be about protecting Ella at all costs. If we lose her, we lose everything. That's it. That's the whole plan right now. Keeping Ella alive and safe is the priority. Saving the kids is secondary. Besides, the kids will be fine. Most of us have been through worse in basic training simulations."

Haider laughs.

Stephan makes an amused sound of agreement.

"But what about James?" I protest. "What about Adam? They're not like you guys. They've never been prepared for this shit. For God's sake, James is only ten years old."

Nazeera looks at me then, and for a moment, she falters. "We'll do our best," she says. And though her words sound genuinely sympathetic, that's all she gives me. *Our best.*

That's it.

I feel my heart rate begin to spike.

"So we're just supposed to risk letting them die?" Winston asks. "We're just supposed to gamble on a ten-year-old's life? Let him remain imprisoned and tortured at the hands of a sociopath and hope for the best? Are you serious?"

"Sometimes sacrifices are necessary," Stephan says.

Haider merely shrugs.

"No way, no way," I say, panicking. "We need another plan. A better plan. A plan that saves everyone, and quickly."

Nazeera looks at me like she feels sorry for me.

That's enough to straighten my spine.

I spin around, my panic transforming quickly into anger. I home in on Warner, sitting in the corner like a useless sack of meat. "What about you?" I say to him. "What do you think about this? You're okay with letting your own brothers die?"

The silence is suddenly suffocating.

Warner doesn't answer me for a long time, and the room is too stunned at my stupidity to interfere. I just broke a tacit agreement to pretend Warner doesn't exist, but now that I've provoked the beast, everyone wants to see what happens next.

Eventually, Warner sighs.

It's not a calm, relaxing sound. It's a harsh, angry sound that only seems to leave him more tightly wound. He doesn't even lift his head when he says, "I'm okay with a lot of things, Kishimoto."

But I'm too far gone to turn back now.

"That's bullshit," I say, my fists clenching. "That's bullshit, and you know it. You're better than this."

Warner says nothing. He doesn't move a muscle, doesn't stop staring at the same spot on the floor. And I know I shouldn't antagonize him—I *know* he's in a fragile state right now—but I can't help it. I can't let this go, not like this.

"So that's it? After everything—that's it? You're just going to let James die?" My heart is pounding, hard and heavy in my chest. I feel my frustration peaking, spiraling.

"What do you think J would say right now, huh? How do you think she'd feel about you letting someone murder a child?"

Warner stands up.

Fast, too fast. Warner is on his feet and I'm suddenly sorry. I was feeling a little brave but now I'm feeling nothing but regret. I take an uncertain step back. Warner follows. Suddenly he's standing in front of me, studying my eyes, but it turns out I can't hold his gaze for longer than a second. His eyes are such a pale green they're disorienting to look at on his good days. But today— Right now—

He looks insane.

I notice, when I turn away, that he's still got blood on his fingers. Blood smeared across his throat. Blood streaking through his gold hair.

"*Look at me,*" he says.

"Um, no thanks."

"Look at me," he says again, quietly this time.

I don't know why I do it. I don't know why I give in. I don't know why there's still a part of me that believes in Warner and hopes to see something human in his eyes. But when I finally look up, I lose that hope. Warner looks cold. Detached. All wrong.

I don't understand it.

I mean, I'm devastated, too. I'm upset, *too*, but I didn't turn into a completely different person. And right now, Warner seems like a completely different person. Where's the guy who was going to propose to my best friend? Where's the guy having a panic attack on his bedroom floor? Where's the guy who laughed so hard his cheeks dimpled? Where's the guy I thought was my friend?

"What happened to you, man?" I whisper. "Where'd you go?"

"Hell," he says. "I've finally found hell."

ELLA

JULIETTE

I wake in waves, consciousness bathing me slowly. I break
the surface of sleep, gasping for air before I'm pulled under
another current
another current
another
Memories wrap around me, bind my bones. I sleep. When
I sleep, I dream I am sleeping. In those dreams, I dream I
am dead. I can't tell real from fiction, can't tell dreams from
truth, can't tell time anymore it might've been days or years
who knows who knows I begin to

s

t

i

r

I dream even as I wake, dream of red lips and slender
fingers, dream of eyes, hundreds of eyes, I dream of air and
anger and death.

I dream Emmaline's dreams.

She's here.

She went quiet once she settled here, in my mind. She
stilled, retreated. Hid from me, from the world. I feel heavy
with her presence but she does not speak, she only decays,

her mind decomposing slowly, leaving compost in its wake. I am heavy with it, heavy with her refuse. I am incapable of carrying this weight, no matter how strong Evie made me I am incapable, incompatible. I am not enough to hold our minds, combined. Emmaline's powers are too much. I drown in it, I drown in it, I

gasp

when my head breaks the surface again.

I drag air into my lungs, beg my eyes to open and they laugh. Eyes laughing at lungs gasping at pain ricocheting up my spine.

Today, there is a boy.

Not one of the regular boys. Not Aaron or Stephan or Haider. This is a new boy, a boy I've never met before.

I can tell, just by standing next to him, that he's terrified.

We stand in the big, wide room filled with trees. We stare at the white birds, the birds with the yellow streaks and the crowns on their heads. The boy stares at the birds like he's never seen anything like them. He stares at everything with surprise. Or fear. Or worry. It makes me realize that he doesn't know how to hide his emotions. Whenever Mr. Anderson looks at him, he sucks in his breath. Whenever I look at him, he goes bright red. Whenever Mum speaks to him, he stutters.

"What do you think?" Mr. Anderson says to Mum. He tries to whisper, but this room is so big it echoes a little.

Mum tilts her head at the boy. Studies him. "He's what, six years old now?" But she doesn't wait for him to answer. Mum just shakes her head and sighs. "Has it really been that long?"

Mr. Anderson looks at the boy. "Unfortunately."

I glance at him, at the boy standing next to me, and watch as he stiffens. Tears spring to his eyes, and it hurts to watch. It hurts so much. I hate Mr. Anderson so much. I don't know why Mum likes him. I don't know why anyone likes him. Mr. Anderson is an awful person, and he hurts Aaron all the time. In fact— Now that I think about it, there's something about this boy that reminds me of Aaron. Something about his eyes.

"Hey," I whisper, and turn to face him.

He swallows, hard. Wipes at his tears with the edge of his sleeve.

"Hey," I try again. "I'm Ella. What's your name?"

The boy looks up, then. His eyes are a deep, dark blue. He's the saddest boy I've ever met, and it makes me sad just to look at him.

"I'm A-Adam," he says quietly. He turns red again.

I take his hand in mine. Smile at him. "We're going to be friends, okay? Don't worry about Mr. Anderson. No one likes him. He's mean to all of us, I promise."

Adam laughs, but his eyes are still red. His hand trembles in mine, but he doesn't let go.

"I don't know," he whispers. "He's pretty mean to me."

I squeeze his hand. "Don't worry," I say. "I'll protect you."

Adam smiles at me then. Smiles a real smile. But when we finally look up again, Mr. Anderson is staring at us.

He looks angry.

There's a buzzing building inside of me, a mass of sound that consumes thought, devours conversation.

We are flies—gathering, swarming—bulging eyes and fragile bones flittering nervously toward imagined destinies. We hurl our bodies at the panes of tantalizing windows, aching for the world promised on the other side. Day after day we drag injured wings and eyes and organs around the same four walls; open or closed, the exits elude us. We hope to be rescued by a breeze, hoping for a chance to see the sun.

Decades pass. Centuries stack together.

Our bruised bodies still career through the air. We continue to hurl ourselves at promises. There is madness in the repetition, in the repetition, in the repetition that underscores our lives. It is only in the desperate seconds before death that we realize the windows against which we broke our bodies were only mirrors, all along.

KENJI

It's been four days.

Four days of nothing. J is still sleeping. The twins are calling it a coma, but I'm calling it sleeping. I'm choosing to believe J is just really, really tired. She just needs to sleep off some stress and she'll be fine. This is what I keep telling everyone.

She'll be fine.

"She's just tired," I say to Brendan. "And when she wakes up she'll be glad we waited for her to go get James. It'll be fine."

We're in the Q, which is short for the quiet tent, which is stupid because it's never quiet in here. The Q is the default common room. It's a gathering space slash game room where people at the Sanctuary get together in the evenings and relax. I'm in the kitchen area, leaning against the insubstantial counter. Brendan and Winston and Ian and I are waiting for the electric kettle to boil.

Tea.

This was Brendan's idea, of course. For some reason, we could never get our hands on tea back at Omega Point. We only had coffee, and it was seriously rationed. Only after we moved onto base in Sector 45 did Brendan realize we could get our hands on tea, but even then he wasn't so militant about it.

But here—

Brendan's made it his mission to force hot tea down our throats every night. He doesn't even need the caffeine—his ability to manipulate electricity always keeps his body charged—but he says he likes it because he finds the ritual soothing. So, whatever. Now we gather in the evenings and drink tea. Brendan puts milk in his tea. Winston adds whiskey. Ian and I drink it black.

"Right?" I say, when no one answers me. "I mean, a coma is basically just a really long nap. J will be fine. The girls will get her better, and then she'll be fine, and everything will be fine. And James and Adam will be fine, obviously, because Sam's seen them and she says they're fine."

"Sam saw them and said they were unconscious," Ian says, opening and closing cabinets. When he finds what he's looking for—a sleeve of cookies—he rips the package open. He doesn't even have a chance to pull one free before Winston's swiped it.

"Those cookies are for our tea," he says sharply.

Ian glowers.

We all glance at Brendan, who seems oblivious to the sacrifices being made in his honor. "Yes, Sam said that they were unconscious," he says, collecting small spoons from a drawer. "But she also said they looked stable. Alive."

"Exactly," I say, pointing at Brendan. "Thank you. *Stable. Alive.* These are the critical words."

Brendan takes the rescued sleeve of cookies from Winston's proffered hand, and begins arranging dishes and flatware with a confidence that baffles us all. He doesn't look up when he says, "It's really kind of amazing, isn't it?"

Winston and I share a confused look.

"I wouldn't call it amazing," Ian says, plucking a spoon from the tray. He examines it. "But I guess forks and shit are pretty cool, as far as inventions go."

Brendan frowns. Looks up. "I'm talking about Sam. Her ability to see across long distances." He retrieves the spoon from Ian's hand and replaces it on the tray. "What a remarkable skill."

Sam's preternatural ability to see across long distances was what convinced us of Anderson's threats to begin with. Several days ago—when we first got the news about the kidnapping—she'd used both data and sheer determination to pinpoint Anderson's location to our old base at Sector 45. She'd spent a straight fourteen hours searching, and though she hadn't been able to get a visual on the other supreme kids, she'd been able to see flickers of James and Adam, who are the only ones I care about anyway. Those flickers of life— unconscious, but alive and stable—aren't much in the way of assurances, but I'm willing to take anything at this point.

"Anyway, yeah. Sam is great," I say, stretching out against the counter. "Which brings me back to my original point: Adam and James are going to be fine. And J is going to wake up soon and be fine. The world owes me at least that much, right?"

Brendan and Ian exchange glances. Winston takes off his glasses and cleans them, slowly, with the hem of his shirt.

The electric kettle pops and steams. Brendan drops a couple of tea bags into a proper teapot and fills its porcelain belly with the hot water from the kettle. He then wraps the teapot in a towel and hands it to Winston, and the two of them carry everything over to the little corner of the room we've been claiming for ourselves lately. It's nothing major, just a cluster of seats with a couple of low tables in the middle. The rest of the room is abuzz with activity. Lots of talking and mingling.

Nouria and Sam are alone in a corner, deep in conversation. Castle is talking quietly with the girls, Sonya and Sara. We've all been spending a lot of time here—pretty much everyone has—ever since the Sanctuary was declared officially on lockdown. We're all in this weird limbo right now; there's so much happening, but we're not allowed to leave the grounds. We can't go anywhere or do anything about anything. Not yet, anyway. Just waiting for J to wake up.

Any minute now.

There are a ton of other people here, too—but only some I'm beginning to recognize. I nod hello to a couple of people I know only by name, and drop into a soft, well-worn armchair. It smells like coffee and old wood in here, but I'm starting to like it. It's becoming a familiar routine. Brendan, as usual, finishes setting everything up on the coffee table.

Teacups, spoons, little plates and triangle napkins. A little pitcher for milk. He's really, really into this whole thing. He readjusts the cookies he'd already arranged on a plate, and smooths out the paper napkins. Ian stares at him with the same expression every night—like Brendan is crazy.

"Hey," Winston says sharply. "Knock it off."

"Knock what off?" Ian says, incredulous. "Come on, man, you don't think this is a little weird? Having tea parties every night?"

Winston lowers his voice to a whisper. "I'll kill you if you ruin this for him."

"All right, enough. I'm not deaf, you know." Brendan narrows his eyes at Ian. "And I don't care if you lot think it's weird. I've little left of England, save this."

That shuts us up.

I stare at the teapot. Brendan says it's steeping.

And then, suddenly, he claps his hands together. He stares straight at me, his ice-blue eyes and white-blond hair giving me Warner vibes. But somehow, even with all his bright, white, cold hues, Brendan is the opposite of Warner. Unlike Warner, Brendan glows. He's warm. Kind. Naturally hopeful and super smiley.

Poor Winston.

Winston, who's secretly in love with Brendan and too afraid of ruining their friendship to say anything about it. Winston thinks he's too old for Brendan, but the thing is— he's not getting any younger, either. I keep telling Winston that if he wants to make a move, he should do it now, while he's still got his original hips, and he says, *Ha ha I'll murder you, asshole,* and reminds me he's waiting for the right moment. But I don't know. Sometimes I think he'll keep it inside forever. And I'm worried it might kill him.

"So, listen," Brendan says carefully. "We wanted to talk to you."

I blink, refocusing. "Who? Me?"

I glance around at their faces. Suddenly, they all look serious. Too serious. I try to laugh when I ask, "What's going on? Is this some kind of intervention?"

"Yes," Brendan says. "Sort of."

I go suddenly stiff.

Brendan sighs.

Winston scratches a spot on his forehead.

Ian says, "Juliette is probably going to die, you know that, right?"

Relief and irritation flood through me simultaneously. I manage to roll my eyes and shake my head at the same time. "Stop doing this, Sanchez. Don't be that guy. It's not funny anymore."

"I'm not trying to be funny."

I roll my eyes again, this time looking to Winston for support, but he just shakes his head at me. His eyebrows furrow so hard his glasses slip down his nose. He tugs them off his face.

"This is serious," he says. "She's not okay. And even if she does wake up again— I mean, whatever happened to her—"

"She's not going to be the same," Brendan finishes for him.

"Says who?" I frown. "The girls said—"

"Bro, the girls said that something about her chemistry changed. They've been running tests on her for days. Emmaline did something weird to her—something that's, like, physically altered her DNA. Plus, her brain is fried."

"I know what they said," I snap, irritated. "I was there when they said it. But the girls were just being cautious. They think it's *possible* that whatever happened to her might've left some damage, but—this is Sonya and Sara we're talking about. They can heal anything. All we need to do is wait for J to wake up."

Winston shakes his head again. "They wouldn't be able to heal something like that," he says. "The girls can't repair that kind of neurological devastation. They might be able to keep her alive, but I'm not sure they'll be able t—"

"She might not even wake up," Ian says, cutting him off. "Like, ever. Or, best-case scenario, she could be in a coma for *years*. Listen, the point here is that we need to start making plans without her. If we're going to save James and Adam, we need to go now. I know Sam's been checking on them, and I know she says they're stable for now, but we can't wait anymore. Anderson doesn't know what happened to Juliette, which means he's still waiting for us to give her up. Which means Adam and James are still at risk— Which means we're running out of time. And, for once," he says, taking a breath, "I'm not the only one who feels this way."

I sit back, stunned. "You're messing with me, right?"

Brendan pours tea.

Winston pulls a flask out of his pocket and weighs it in his hand before holding it out to me. "Maybe you should have this tonight," he says.

I glare at him.

He shrugs, and empties half the flask into his teacup.

"Listen," Brendan says gently. "Ian is a beast with no bedside manner, but he's not wrong. It's time to think of a new plan. We all still love Juliette, it's just—" He cuts himself off, frowns. "Wait, is it Juliette or Ella? Was there ever a consensus?"

I'm still scowling when I say, "I'm calling her Juliette."

"But I thought she wanted to be called Ella," Winston says.

"She's in a fucking coma," Ian says, and takes a loud sip of tea. "She doesn't care what you call her."

"Don't be such a brute," Brendan says. "She's our friend."

"*Your* friend," he mutters.

"Wait— Is that what this is about?" I sit forward. "Are you jealous she never best-friended you, Sanchez?"

Ian rolls his eyes, looks away.

Winston is watching with fascinated interest.

"All right, drink your tea," Brendan says, biting into a biscuit. He gestures at me with the half-eaten cookie. "It's getting cold."

I shoot him a tired look, but I take an obligatory sip and nearly choke. It tastes weird tonight. And I'm about to push it away when I realize Brendan is still staring at me, so I take

100

a long, disgusting pull of the dark liquid before replacing the cup in the saucer. I try not to gag.

"Okay," I say, slamming my palms down on my thighs. "Let's put it to a vote: Who here thinks Ian is annoyed that J didn't fall in love with him when she showed up at Point?"

Winston and Brendan share a look. Slowly, they both lift their hands.

Ian rolls his eyes again. *"Pendejos,"* he mutters.

"The theory holds at least a little water," Winston says.

"I have a girlfriend, dumbasses." And as if on cue, Lily looks up from across the room, locks eyes with Ian. She's sitting with Alia and some other girl I don't recognize.

Lily waves.

Ian waves back.

"Yes, but you're used to a certain level of attention," Winston says, reaching for a biscuit. He looks up, scans the room. "Like those girls, right over there," he says, gesturing with his head. "They've been staring at you since you walked in."

"They have not," Ian says, but he can't help but glance over.

"It's true." Brendan shrugs. "You're a handsome guy."

Winston chokes on his tea.

"Okay, enough." Ian holds up his hands. "I know you guys think this is hilarious, but I'm being serious. At the end of the day, Juliette is *your* friend. Not mine."

I exhale dramatically.

Ian shoots me a look. "When she first showed up at

Point, I tried reaching out to her, to offer her my friendship, and she never followed up. And even after we were taken hostage by Anderson"—he nods an acknowledgment at Brendan and Winston—"she took her sweet time trying to get information out of Warner. She never gave a shit about the rest of us, and all we've ever done is put everything on the line to protect her."

"Hey, that's not fair," Winston says, shaking his head. "She was in an awful position—"

"Whatever," Ian mutters. He looks down, into his tea. "This whole situation is some kind of bullshit."

"Cheers to that," Brendan says, refilling his cup. "Now have more tea."

Ian mutters a quiet, angry thank-you, and lifts the cup to his lips. Suddenly, he stiffens. "And then there's this," he says, raising an eyebrow. As if all that weren't enough, we have to deal with *this* douche bag." Ian gestures, with the teacup, toward the entrance.

Shit.

Warner is here.

"She brought him here," Ian is saying, but he has the sense, at least, to keep his voice down. "It's because of her that we have to tolerate this asshole."

"To be fair, that was originally Castle's idea," I point out.

Ian flips me off.

"What's he doing here?" Brendan asks quietly.

I shake my head and take another unconscious sip of my disgusting tea. There's something about the grossness that's beginning to feel familiar, but I can't put my finger on it.

I look up again.

I haven't spoken a word to Warner since that first day— The day J got attacked by Emmaline. He's been a ghost since then. No one has really seen him, no one but the supreme kids, I think.

He went straight back to his roots.

It looks like he finally took a shower, though. No blood. And I'm guessing he healed himself, though there's no way to be sure, because he's fully clothed, wearing an outfit I can only assume was borrowed from Haider. A lot of leather.

I watch, for only a few seconds, as he stalks clear across the room—straight through people and conversations and apologizing to no one—toward Sonya and Sara, who are still talking to Castle.

Whatever.

Dude doesn't even look at me anymore. Doesn't even acknowledge my existence. Not that I care. It's not like we were actually friends.

At least, that's what I keep telling myself.

Somehow I've already drained my teacup, because Brendan's refilled it. I throw back the fresh cup in a couple of quick gulps and shove a dry biscuit in my mouth. And then I shake my head. "All right, we're getting distracted," I say, and the words feel just a little too loud, even to my own ears. "Focus, please."

"Right," Winston says. "Focus. What are we focusing on?"

"New mission," Ian says, sitting back in his chair. He counts off on his fingers: "Save Adam and James. Kill the other supreme commanders. Finally get some sleep."

"Nice and easy," Brendan says. "I like it."

"You know what?" I say. "I think I should go talk to him."

Winston raises an eyebrow. "Talk to who?"

"Warner, obviously." My brain feels warm. A little fuzzy. "I should go talk to him. No one talks to him. Why are we just letting him revert back into an asshole? I should talk to him."

"That's a great idea," Ian says, smiling as he sits forward. "Go for it."

"Don't you dare listen to him," Winston says, shoving Ian back into his chair. "Ian just wants to watch you get murdered."

"Fucking rude, Sanchez."

Ian shrugs.

"On an unrelated note," Winston says to me. "How does your head feel?"

I frown, gingerly touching my fingers to my skull. "What do you mean?"

"I mean," Winston says, "that this is probably a good time to tell you I've been pouring whiskey in your tea all night."

"What the hell?" I sit up too fast. Bad idea. "Why?"

"You seemed stressed."

"I'm not stressed."

Everyone stares at me.

"All right, whatever," I say. "I'm stressed. But I'm not drunk."

"No." He peers at me. "But you probably need all the brain cells you can spare if you're going to talk to Warner. I would. I'm not too proud to admit that I find him genuinely terrifying."

Ian rolls his eyes. "There's nothing terrifying about that guy. His only problem is that he's an arrogant son of a *puta* with his own head stuck so far up his ass he ca—"

"Wait," I say, blinking. "Where'd he go?"

Everyone spins around, looking for him.

I swear, five seconds ago he was standing right there. I swivel my head back and forth like a cartoon character, understanding only vaguely that I'm moving both a little too fast and a little too slow due to Winston, number one idiot slash well-meaning friend. But in the process of scanning the room for Warner, I spot the one person I'd been making an effort to avoid:

Nazeera.

I fling myself back down in my chair too hard, nearly knocking myself out. I hunch over, breathing a little funny, and then, for no rational reason, I start laughing. Winston, Ian, and Brendan are all staring at me like I'm insane, and I don't blame them. I don't know what the hell is wrong with me. I don't even know why I'm hiding from Nazeera. There's nothing scary about her, not exactly. Nothing more scary than the fact that we haven't really discussed the last emotional conversation we had, shortly after she kicked me in the back and I nearly murdered her for it.

She told me I was her first kiss.

And then the sky melted and Juliette was possessed by her sister and the romantic moment was forever interrupted. It's been about five days since she and I had that conversation, and ever since then it's just been super stress and work and more stress and Anderson is an asshole and James and Adam are being held hostage.

Also: I've been pissed at her.

There's a part of me that would really, really like to just carry her away to a private corner somewhere, but there's another part of me that won't allow it. Because I'm mad at her. She knew how much it meant to me to go after James, and she just shrugged it off with little to no sympathy. A little sympathy, I guess. But not much. Anyway, am I thinking too much? I think I'm thinking too much.

"What the hell is wrong with you?" Ian is staring at me, stunned.

"Nazeera is here."

"So?"

"So, I don't know, Nazeera is here," I say, keeping my voice low. "And I don't want to talk to her."

"Why not?"

"Because my head is stupid right now, that's why not." I glare at Winston. "You did this to me. You made my head stupid, and now I have to avoid Nazeera, because if I don't,

I will almost certainly do and or say something extremely stupid and fuck everything up. So I need to hide."

"Damn," Ian says, and shrugs. "That's too bad, because she's heading straight here."

I stiffen. Stare at him. And then, to Brendan: "Is he lying?"

Brendan shakes his head. "I'm afraid not, mate."

"Shit. Shit. Shit shit shit."

"It's nice to see you, too, Kenji."

I look up. She's smiling.

Ugh, so pretty.

"Hi," I say. "How are you?"

She looks around. Fights back a laugh. "I'm good," she says. "How . . . are you?"

"Fine. Fine. Thanks for asking. It was nice seeing you."

Nazeera glances from me to the other guys and back again. "I know you hate it when I ask you this, but— Are you drunk?"

"No," I say too loudly. I slump down farther in my seat. "Not drunk. Just a little . . . fuzzy." The whiskey is starting to settle now, warm, liquid fingers reaching up around my brain and squeezing.

She raises an eyebrow.

"Winston did it," I say, and point.

He shakes his head and sighs.

"All right," Nazeera says, but I can hear the mild irritation in her voice. "Well, this is not the ideal situation, but I'm going to need you on your feet."

"What?" I crane my head. Look at her. "Why?"

"There's been a development with Ella."

"What kind of development?" I sit straight up, feeling suddenly sober. "Is she awake?"

Nazeera tilts her head. "Not exactly," she says.

"Then what?"

"You should come see for yourself."

~~ELLA~~

~~JULIETTE~~

Adam feels close.

I can almost see him in my mind, a blurred form, watercolors bleeding through membrane, staining the whites of my eyes. He is a flooded river, blues in lakes so dark, water in oceans so heavy I sag, surrendering to the heft of the sea.

I take a deep breath and fill my lungs with tears, feathers of strange birds fluttering against my closed eyes. I see a flash of dirty-blond hair and darkness and stone I see blue and green and

Warmth, suddenly, an exhalation in my veins—

Emmaline.

Still here, still swimming.

She has grown quiet of late, the fire of her presence reduced to glowing embers. She is sorry for taking me from myself. Sorry for the inconvenience. Sorry to have disturbed my world so deeply. Still, she does not want to leave. She likes it here, likes stretching out inside my bones. She likes the dry air and the taste of real oxygen. She likes the shape of my fingers, the sharpness of my teeth. She is sorry, but not sorry enough to go back, so she is trying to be very small and very quiet. She hopes to make it up to me by taking up as little space as possible.

I don't know how I understand this so clearly, except that her mind seems to have fused with mine. Conversation is no longer necessary. Explanations, redundant.

In the beginning, she inhaled everything.

Excited, eager—she took it all. New skin. Eyes and mouth. I felt her marvel at my anatomy, at the systems drawing in air through my nose. I seemed to exist here almost as an afterthought, blood pumping through an organ beating merely to pass the time. I was little more than a passenger in my own body, doing nothing as she explored and decayed in starts and sparks, steel scraping against itself, stunning contractions of pain like claws digging, digging. It's better now that she's settled, but her presence has faded to all but an aching sadness. She seems desperate to find purchase as she disintegrates, unwittingly taking with her bits and pieces of my mind. Some days are better than others. Some days the fire of her existence is so acute I forget to draw breath.

But most days I am an idea, and nothing more.

I am foam and smoke moonlighting as skin. Dandelions gather in my rib cage, moss growing steadily along my spine. Rainwater floods my eyes, pools in my open mouth, dribbles down the hinges holding together my lips.

I

continue
to

sink.

And then—

   why now?

   suddenly
surprisingly
   chest heaving, lungs working, fists clenching, knees
bending, pulse racing, blood pumping

   I float

"Ms. Ferrars— That is, Ella—"
"Her name is Juliette. Just call her Juliette, for God's
sake."
"Why don't we call her what she *wants* to be called?"
"Right. Exactly."
"But I thought she wanted to be called Ella."

"There was never a consensus. Was there a consensus?"

Slowly, my eyelids flutter open.

Silence explodes, coating mouths and walls and doors and dust motes. It hangs in the air, cloaking everything, for all of two seconds.

Then

Shouts, screams, a million sounds. I try to count them all and my head spins, swims. My heart is pounding hard and fast in my chest, recklessly shaking me, shaking my hands, ringing my skull. I look around fast, too fast, head whipping back and forth and everything swings around and around and

So many faces, blurred and strange.

I'm breathing too hard, spots dotting my vision, and I place two hands down on the—I look down—bed below me and squeeze my eyes shut

What am I
Who am I
Where am I

Silence again, swift and complete, like magic, magic, a hush falls over everyone, everything, and I exhale, panic draining out of me and I sit back, soaking in the dregs when

Warm hands

touch mine.

Familiar.

I go suddenly still. My eyes stay closed. Feeling moves through me like a wildfire, flames devouring the dust in my chest, the kindling in my bones. Hands become arms around me and the fire blazes. My own hands are caught between us and I feel the hard lines of his body through the soft cotton of his shirt.

A face appears, disappears, behind my eyes.

There's something so safe here in the feel of him, in the scent of him—something entirely his own. Being near him does something to me, something I can't even explain, can't control. I know I shouldn't, know I shouldn't, but I can't help but drag the tips of my fingers down the perfect lines of his torso.

I hear his breath catch.

Flames leap through me, jump up my lungs and I inhale, dragging oxygen into my body that only fans the flames further. One of his hands clasps the back of my head, the other grasps at my waist. A flash of heat roars up my spine, reaches into my skull. His lips are at my ear whispering, whispering

Come back to life, love
I'll be here when you wake up

My eyes fly open.

The heat is merciless. Confusing. Consuming. It calms

me, settles my raging heart. His hands move along my body, light touches along my arms, the sides of my torso. I claw my way back to him by memory, my shaking hands tracing the familiar shape of his back, my cheek still pressed against the familiar beat of his heart. The scent of him, so familiar, so familiar, and then I look up—

His eyes, something about his eyes

Please, he says, *please don't shoot me for this*

The room comes into focus by degrees, my head settling onto my neck, my skin settling onto my bones, my eyes staring into the very desperately green eyes that seem to know too much, too well. Aaron Warner Anderson is bent over me, his worried eyes inspecting me, his hand caught in the air like he might've been about to touch me.

He jerks back.

He stares, unblinking, chest rising and falling.

"Good morning," I assume. I'm unsure of my voice, of the hour and this day, of these words leaving my lips and this body that contains me.

His smile looks like it hurts.

"Something's wrong," he whispers. He touches my cheek. Soft, so soft, like he's not sure if I'm real, like he's afraid if he gets too close I'll just oh, look she's gone, she's just disappeared. His four fingers graze the side of my face, slowly, so slowly before they slip behind my head, caught in that in-between spot just above my neck. His thumb brushes the

116

apple of my cheek.

My heart implodes.

He keeps looking at me, looking into my eyes for help, for guidance, for some sign of a protest like he's so sure I'm going to start screaming or crying or running away but I won't. I don't think I could even if I wanted to because I don't want to. I want to stay here. Right here. I want to be paralyzed by this moment.

He moves closer, just an inch. His free hand reaches up to cup the other side of my face.

He's holding me like I'm made of feathers. Like I'm a bird. White with streaks of gold like a crown atop its head.

I will fly.

A soft, shuddering breath leaves his body.

"Something's wrong," he says again, but distantly, like he might be talking to someone else. "Her energy is different. Tainted."

The sound of his voice coils through me, spirals around my spine. I feel myself straighten even as I feel strange, jet-lagged, like I've traveled through time. I pull myself into a seated position and Warner shifts to accommodate me. I'm tired and weak from hunger, but other than a few general aches, I seem to be fine. I'm alive. I'm breathing and blinking and feeling human and I know exactly why.

I meet his eyes. "You saved my life."

He tilts his head at me.

He's still studying me, his gaze so intense I flush, confused, and turn away. The moment I do, I nearly jump out of my skin. Castle and Kenji and Winston and Brendan and a ton of other people I don't recognize are all staring at me, at Warner's hands on me, and I'm suddenly so mortified I don't even know what to do with myself.

"Hey, princess." Kenji waves. "You okay?"

I try to stand and Warner tries to help me and the moment his skin brushes mine another sudden, destabilizing bolt of feeling runs me over. I stumble, sideways, into his arms and he pulls me in, his heat setting fire to my body all over again. I'm trembling, heart pounding, nervous pleasure pulsing through me.

I don't understand.

I'm overcome by a sudden, inexplicable need to touch him, to press my skin against his skin until the friction sets fire to us both. Because there's something about him— there's *always* been something about him that's intrigued me and I don't understand it. I pull away, startled by the intensity of my own thoughts, but his fingers catch me under the chin. He tilts my face toward him.

I look up.

His eyes are such a strange shade of green: bright, crystal clear, piercing in the most alarming way. His hair is thick, the richest slice of gold. Everything about him is meticulous. Pristine. His breath is cool and fresh. I can feel it on my face.

My eyes close automatically. I breathe him in, feeling suddenly giddy. A bubble of laughter escapes my lips.

"Something's definitely wrong," someone says.

"Yeah, she doesn't look like she's okay." Someone else.

"Oh, okay, so we're all just saying really obvious things out loud? Is that what we're doing?" Kenji.

Warner says nothing. I feel his arms tighten around me and my eyes flicker open. His gaze is fixed on mine, his eyes green flames that will not extinguish and his chest is rising and falling so fast, so fast, so fast. His lips are there, right there above mine.

"Ella?" he whispers.

I frown.

My eyes flick up, to his eyes, then down, to his lips.

"Love, do you hear me?"

When I don't answer, his face changes.

"Juliette," he says softly, "can you hear me?"

I blink at him. I blink and blink and blink at him and find I'm still fascinated by his eyes. Such a startling shade of green.

"We're going to need everyone to clear the room," someone says suddenly. Loudly. "We need to begin running tests immediately."

The girls, I realize. It's the girls. They're here. They're trying to get him away from me, trying to get him to break away from me. But Warner's arms are like steel bands around my body.

He refuses.

"Not yet," he says urgently. "Not just yet."

And for some reason they listen.

Maybe they see something in him, see something in

his face, in his features. Maybe they see what I see from this disjointed, foggy perspective. The desperation in his expression, the anguish carved into his features, the way he looks at me, like he might die if I do.

Tentatively, I reach up, touch my fingers to his face. His skin is smooth and cold. Porcelain. He doesn't seem real.

"What's wrong?" I say. "What happened?"

Impossibly, Warner goes paler. He shakes his head and presses his face to my cheek. "Please," he whispers. "Come back to me, love."

"Aaron?"

I hear the small hitch in his breath. The hesitation. It's the first time I've used his name so casually.

"Yes?"

"I want you to know," I tell him, "that I don't think you're crazy."

"What?" He startles.

"I don't think you're crazy," I say. "And I don't think you're a psychopath. I don't think you're a heartless murderer. I don't care what anyone else says about you. I think you're a good person."

Warner is blinking fast now. I can hear him breathing.

In and out.

Unevenly.

A flash of stunning, searing pain, and my body goes suddenly slack. I see the glint of metal. I feel the burn of the syringe. My head begins to swim and all the sounds begin to melt together.

"Come on, son," Castle says, his voice expanding, slowing down, "I know this is hard, but we need you to step back. We have t—"

An abrupt, violent sound gives me a sudden moment of clarity.

A man I don't recognize is at the door, one hand on the doorframe, gasping for breath. "They're here," he says. "They've found us. They're here. Jenna is dead."

KENJI

The guy gasping at the doorframe is still finishing his sentence when everyone jumps into action. Nouria and Sam rush past him into the hall, shouting orders and commands—something about initiating protocol for System Z, something about gathering the children, the elderly, and the sick. Sonya and Sara press something into Warner's hands, glance one last time at J's limp, unconscious figure, and chase Nouria and Sam out the door.

Castle crouches to the ground, closing his eyes as he flattens his hands against the floor, listening. Feeling.

"Eleven—no twelve, bodies. About five hundred feet out. I'd guess we have about two minutes before they reach us. I'll do my best to slow them down until we can clear out of here." He looks up. "Mr. Ibrahim?"

I don't even realize Haider is here with us until he says, "That's more than enough time."

He stalks across the room to the wall opposite Juliette's bed, running his hands along the smooth surface, ripping down picture frames and monitors as he goes. Glass and wood shatter in a heap on the floor. Nazeera gasps, goes suddenly still. I turn, terrified, to face her and she says—

"I need to tell Stephan."

She dashes out the door.

Warner is unhooking Juliette from the bed, removing her needles, bandaging her wounds. Once she's free, he wraps her sleeping body in the soft blue robe hanging nearby, and at nearly the exact same moment, I hear the telltale ticking of a bomb.

I glance back, at the wall where Haider still stands. Two carefully spaced explosives are now affixed to the plaster, and I hardly even have time to digest this before Haider bellows at us to move out into the hall. Warner is already halfway out the door, holding the carefully wrapped bundle of J in his arms. I hear Castle's voice—a sudden cry—and my own body is lifted and thrown out the door, too.

The room explodes.

The walls shake so hard it rattles my teeth, but when the tremors settle, I rush back into the room.

Haider blew off a single wall.

A perfect, exact rectangle of wall. Gone. I didn't even know such a feat was possible. Pieces of brick and wood and drywall are scattered on the open ground beyond J's room, and cold night winds rush in, slapping me awake. The moon is excessively full and bright tonight, a spotlight shining directly into my eyes.

I'm stunned.

Haider explains without prompting: "The hospital is too big, too complicated—we needed an efficient exit. The Reestablishment won't care about collateral damage when they come for us—in fact, they might be craving it—but if

126

we're to have any hope of sparing innocent lives, we have to remove ourselves as far from the central buildings and common spaces as possible. Now move out," he shouts. "Let's go."

But I'm reeling.

I blink at Haider, still recovering from the blast, the lingering whisper of whiskey in my brain, and now this:

Proof that Haider Ibrahim has a conscience.

He and Warner stalk past me, through the open wall, and start running into the gleaming woods, Warner with J in his arms. Neither of them bothers to explain what they're thinking. Where they're going. What the hell is going to happen next.

Well, actually, I think that last part is obvious.

What's going to happen next is that Anderson is going to show up and try to murder us.

Castle and I lock eyes—we're the last people still standing in what remains of J's hospital room—and we chase after Warner and Haider toward a clearing at the far end of the Sanctuary, as far away from the tents as possible. At one point Warner breaks off from our group, disappearing down a path so dark I can't see the end of it. When I move to follow, Haider barks at me to leave him alone. I don't know what Warner does with Juliette, but when he rejoins us, she's no longer in his arms. He says something, briefly, to Haider, but it sounds like French. Not Arabic. *French.*

Whatever. I don't have time to think about it.

It's already been five minutes, by my estimate. Five

minutes, which means they should be here any second now. There are twelve bodies incoming. There are only four of us here.

Me, Haider, Castle, Warner.

I'm freezing.

We're standing quietly in the darkness, waiting for death, and the individual seconds seem to tick by with excruciating slowness. The smell of wet earth and decaying vegetation fills my head and I look down, feeling but not seeing the thick pile of leaves underfoot. They're soft and slightly damp, rustling a little when I shift my weight.

I try not to move.

Every sound unnerves me. A sudden shudder of branches. An innocent breeze. My own ragged breaths.

It's too dark.

Even the bright, robust moon isn't enough to properly penetrate these woods. I don't know how we're going to fight anyone if we can't see what's coming. The light is uneven, scattering through branches, shattering across the soft earth. I look down, examining a narrow shaft of light illuminating the tops of my boots, and watch as a spider scuttles up and around the obstacle of my feet.

My heart is pounding.

There's no time. If only we had more time.

It's all I can think. Over and over again. They caught us off guard, we weren't prepared, it didn't have to go down like this. My head is spinning with *what-ifs* and *maybes* and *it could've beens* even as I face down the reality right in front of me. Even as I stare straight into the black hole devouring my future, I can't help but wonder if we could've done this differently.

The seconds build. Minutes pass.

Nothing.

The rapid beating of my heart slows into a sick stutter of dread. I've lost perspective—my sense of time is warped in the dark—but I swear it feels like we've been here for too long.

"Something is wrong," Warner says.

I hear a sharp intake of breath. Haider.

Warner says softly, "We miscalculated."

"No," Castle cries.

That's when I hear the screams.

We run without hesitation, all four of us, hurtling ourselves toward the sounds. We tear through branches, sprain ankles on overgrown roots, propel ourselves into the darkness with the force of pure, undiluted panic. *Rage.*

Sobs rend the sky. Violent cries echo into the distance. Inarticulate voices, guttural moans, goose bumps rising along my flesh. We are sprinting toward death.

I know we're close when I see the light.

Nouria.

She's cast an ethereal glow above the scene, bringing the remains of a battlefield into sharp focus.

We slow down.

Time seems to expand, fracturing apart as I bear witness to a massacre. Anderson and his men made a detour. We hoped they'd come straight for Warner, straight for Juliette. We hoped. We tried. We took a gamble.

We bet wrong.

And we know The Reestablishment well enough to understand that they were punishing these innocent people for harboring us. Slaughtering entire families for providing us aid and relief. Nausea hits me with the force of a blade, stunning me, knocking me sideways. I slump against a tree. I can feel my mind disconnecting, threatening unconsciousness, and somehow I force myself not to pass out from horror. Terror. Heartbreak.

I keep my eyes open.

Sam and Nouria are on their knees, holding broken, bleeding bodies close to their chests, their tortured cries piercing the strange half night. Castle stands beside me, his body slack. I hear his half-choked sob.

We knew it was possible—Haider said they might do this—but somehow I still can't believe my eyes. I desperately want this to be a nightmare. I would cut off my right arm for a nightmare. But reality persists.

The Sanctuary is little more than a graveyard.

Unarmed men and women mowed down. From where I'm standing I count six children, dead. Eyes open, mouths agape, fresh blood still dripping down limp bodies. Ian is on his knees, vomiting. Winston stumbles backward, hits a tree. His glasses slide down his face and he only remembers to catch them at the last moment. Only the supreme kids still seem to have their heads on straight, and there's

130

something about that realization that strikes fear into my heart. Nazeera, Haider, Warner, Stephan. They walk calmly through the wreckage, faces unchanged and solemn. I don't know what they've seen—what they've been a part of—that makes them able to stand here, still relatively cool in the face of so much human devastation, and I don't think I want to know.

I offer Castle my hand and he takes it, steadies himself. We exchange a single glance before diving into the fray.

Anderson is easy to spot, standing tall in the midst of hell, but hard to reach. His Supreme Guard swarms us, weapons drawn. Still, we move closer. No matter what comes next, we fight to the death. That was always the plan, from the first. And it's what we'll do now.

Round two.

The still-living fighters on the field straighten at our approach, at the scene forming, and steal glances at one another. We're surrounded by firepower, that's true, but nearly everyone here has a supernatural gift. There's no reason we shouldn't be able to put up a fight. A crowd gathers slowly around us—half Sanctuary, half Point—hale bodies breaking away from the wreckage to form a new battalion. I feel the fresh hope moving through the air. The tantalizing *maybe*. Carefully, I pull free a gun from my side holster.

And just as I'm about to make a move—

"Don't."

Anderson's voice is loud. Clear. He breaks through his

wall of soldiers, stalking toward us casually, looking as polished as always. I don't understand, at first, why so many people gasp at his approach. I don't see it. I don't notice the body he's dragging with him, and when I finally notice the body, I don't recognize it. Not right away.

It's not until Anderson jerks the small figure upright, nudging his head back with a gun, that I feel the blood exit my heart. Anderson presses the gun to James's throat, and my knees nearly give out.

"This is very simple," Anderson says. "You will hand over the girl, and in return, I won't execute the boy."

We're all frozen.

"I should clarify, however, that this is not an exchange. I'm not offering to return him to you. I'm only offering not to murder him here, on the spot. But if you hand over the girl now, without a fight, I will consider letting most of you disappear into the shadows."

"Most of us?" I say.

Anderson's eyes glance off my face and the faces of several others. "Yes, most of you," he says, his gaze lingering on Haider. "Your father is very disappointed in you, young man."

A single gunshot explodes without warning, ripping open a hole in Anderson's throat. He grabs at his neck and falls, with a choked cry, on one knee, looking around for his assailant.

Nazeera.

She materializes in front of him just in time to jump up,

into the sky. The supreme soldiers start shooting upward, releasing round after round with impunity, and though I'm terrified for Nazeera, I realize she took that risk for me. For James.

We'll do our best, she'd said. I didn't realize her best included risking her life for that kid. For *me.* God, I fucking love her.

I go invisible.

Anderson is struggling to stanch the flow of blood at his throat while keeping his grip on James, who appears to be unconscious.

Two guards remain at his side.

I fire two shots.

They both go down, crying out and clutching limbs, and Anderson nearly roars. He starts clawing at the air in front of him, then fumbles for his gun with one red hand, blood still seeping from his lips. I take that opportunity to punch him in the face.

He rears back, more surprised than injured, but Brendan moves in quickly, clapping his hands together to create a twisting, crackling bolt of electricity he wraps around Anderson's legs, temporarily paralyzing him.

Anderson drops James.

I catch him before he hits the floor, and bolt toward Lily, who's waiting just outside of Nouria's ring of light. I unload his unconscious body into her arms and Brendan builds an electric shield around their bodies. A beat later, they're gone.

Relief floods through me.

Too quickly. It unsteadies me. My invisibility falters for less than a second, and in less than a second I'm attacked from behind.

I hit the ground, hard, air leaving my lungs. I struggle to flip over, to stand up, but a supreme soldier is already pointing a rifle at my face. He shoots.

Castle comes out of nowhere, knocking the soldier off his feet, stopping the bullets with a single gesture. He redirects the ammunition meant for my body, and I don't even realize what's happened until I see the dude drop to his knees. He's a human sieve, bleeding out the last of his life right in front of me, and it all feels suddenly surreal.

I drag myself up, my head pounding in my throat. Castle is already moving, ripping a tree from its roots as he goes. Stephan is using his superstrength to pummel as many soldiers as he can, but they won't stop shooting, and he's moving slowly, blood staining nearly every inch of his clothing. I watch him sway. I run toward him, try to shout a warning, but my voice gets lost in the din, and my legs won't move fast enough. Another soldier charges at him, unloading rounds, and this time, I scream.

Haider comes running.

He dives in front of his friend with a cry, knocking Stephan to the ground, protecting his body with his own, throwing something into the air as he goes.

It explodes.

I'm thrown backward, my skull ringing. I lift my head,

delirious, and spot Nazeera and Warner, each locked in hand-to-hand combat. I hear a bloodcurdling scream and force myself up, toward the sound.

It's Sam.

Nouria beats me to her, falling to her knees to lift her wife's body off the ground. She wraps blinding bands of light around the two of them, the protective spirals so bright they're excruciating to look at. A nearby soldier throws his arm over his eyes as he shoots, crying out and holding steady even as the force of Nouria's light begins to melt the flesh off his hands.

I put a bullet through his teeth.

Five more guards appear out of nowhere, coming at me from all sides, and for half a second I can't help but be surprised. Castle said there were only twelve bodies, two of which belonged to Anderson and James, and I thought we'd taken out at least several of the others by now. I glance around the battlefield, at the dozens of soldiers still actively attacking our team, and then back again, at the five heading my way.

My head swims with confusion.

And then, when they all begin to shoot—terror.

I go invisible, stealing through the single foot of space between two of them, turning back just long enough to open fire. A couple of my shots find their marks; the others are wasted. I reload the clip, tossing the now-empty one to the ground, and just as I'm about to shoot again, I hear her voice.

"Hang on," she whispers.

Nazeera wraps her arms around my waist and jumps.

Up.

A bullet whizzes past my calf. I feel the burn as it grazes skin, but the night sky is cool and bracing, and I allow myself to take a steadying breath, to close my eyes for a full and complete second. Up here, the screams are muted, the blood could be water, the screams could be laughter.

The dream lasts for only a moment.

Our feet touch the ground again and my ears refill with the sounds of war. I squeeze Nazeera's hand by way of thanks, and we split up. I charge toward a group of men and women I only vaguely recognize—people from the Sanctuary—and throw myself into the bloodshed, urging one of the injured fighters to pull back and take shelter. I'm soon lost in the motions of battle, defending and attacking, guns firing. Guttural moaning. I don't even think to look up until I feel the ground shake beneath my feet.

Castle.

His arms are pointed upward, toward a nearby building. The structure begins to shake violently, nails flying, windows shuddering. A cluster of supreme guards reaches for their guns but stop short at the sound of Anderson's voice. I can't hear what he says, but he seems to be nearly himself again, and his command appears to be shocking enough to inspire a moment of hesitation in his soldiers. For no reason I can fathom, the guards I'd been fighting suddenly slink away.

Too late.

The roof of the nearby building collapses with a scream,

and with a final, violent shove, Castle tears off a wall. With one arm he shoves aside the few of our teammates standing in harm's way, and with the other he drops the ton of wall to the ground, where it lands with an explosive crash. Glass flies everywhere, wooden beams groaning as they buckle and break. A few supreme soldiers escape, diving for cover, but at least three of them get caught under the rubble. We all brace for a retaliatory attack—

But Anderson holds up a single arm.

His soldiers go instantly still, weapons going slack in their hands. Almost in unison, they stand at attention.

Waiting.

I glance at Castle for a directive, but he's got eyes on Anderson just like the rest of us. Everyone seems paralyzed by a delirious hope that this war might be over. I watch Castle turn and lock eyes with Nouria, who's still cradling Sam to her chest. A moment later, Castle raises his arm. A temporary standstill.

I don't trust it.

Silence coats the night as Anderson staggers forward, his lips a violent, liquid red, his hand casually holding a handkerchief to his neck. We'd heard about this, of course— about his ability to heal himself—but seeing it actually happen in real time is something else altogether. It's *wild*.

When he speaks, his voice shatters the quiet. Breaks the spell. "Enough," he says. "Where is my son?"

Murmurs move through the crowd of bloodied fighters, a red sea slowly parting at his approach. It's not long before

Warner appears, striding forward in the silence, his face spattered in red. A machine gun is locked in his right hand.

He looks up at his father. He says nothing.

"What did you do with her?" Anderson says softly, and spits blood on the ground. He wipes his lips with the same cloth he's using to contain the open wound on his neck. The whole scene is disgusting.

Warner continues to say nothing.

I don't think any of us know where he hid her. J seems to have *disappeared*, I realize.

Seconds pass in a silence so intense we all begin to worry about the fate of our standstill. I see a few of the supreme soldiers lift their guns in Warner's direction, and not a second later a single lightning bolt fractures the sky above us.

Brendan.

I glance at him, then at Castle, but Anderson once again lifts his arm to stall his soldiers. Once again, they stand down.

"I will only ask you one more time," Anderson says to his son, his voice trembling as it grows louder. *"What did you do with her?"*

Still, Warner stares impassively.

He's spattered in unknown blood, holding a machine gun like it might be a briefcase, and staring at his father like he might be staring at the ceiling. Anderson can't control his temper the way Warner can—and it's obvious to everyone that this is a battle of wills he's going to lose.

Anderson already looks half out of his mind.

His hair is matted and sticking up in places. Blood is congealing on his face, his eyes shot through with red. He looks so deranged—so unlike himself—that I honestly have no idea what's going to happen next.

And then he lunges for Warner.

He's like a belligerent drunk, wild and angry, unhinged in a way I've never seen before. His swings are wild but strong, unsteady but studied. He reminds me, in a sudden, frightening flash of understanding, of the father Adam so often described to me. A violent drunk fueled by rage.

Except that Anderson doesn't appear to be drunk at the moment. No. This is pure, unadulterated anger.

Anderson seems to have lost his mind.

He doesn't just want to shoot Warner. He doesn't want someone else to shoot Warner. He wants to beat him to a pulp. He wants physical satisfaction. He wants to break bones and rupture organs with his own hands. Anderson wants the pleasure of knowing that he and he alone was able to destroy his own son.

But Warner isn't giving him that satisfaction.

He meets Anderson blow for blow in fluid, precise movements, ducking and sidestepping and twisting and defending. He never misses a beat.

It's almost like he can read Anderson's mind.

I'm not the only one who's stunned. I've never seen Warner move like this, and I almost can't believe I've never seen it before. I feel a sudden, unbidden surge of respect for him as I watch him block attack after attack. I keep waiting for him to knock the dude out, but Warner makes no effort to hit Anderson; he only defends. And only when I see the increasing fury on Anderson's face do I realize that Warner is doing this on purpose.

He's not fighting back because he knows it's what Anderson wants. The cool, emotionless expression on Warner's face is driving Anderson insane. And the more he fails to rattle his son, the more enraged Anderson gets. Blood still trickles, slowly, from the half-healed wound on his neck when he cries out, angrily, and pulls free a gun from inside his jacket pocket.

"*Enough,*" he shouts. "That is enough."

Warner takes a careful step back.

"Give me the girl, Aaron. Give me the girl and I will spare the rest of these idiots. I only want the girl."

Warner is an immovable object.

"Fine," Anderson says angrily. "Seize him."

Six supreme guards begin advancing on Warner, and he doesn't so much as flinch. I exchange glances with Winston and it's enough; I throw my invisibility over Winston just as he throws his arms out, his ability to stretch his limbs knocking three of them to the ground. In the same moment, Haider pulls a machete from somewhere inside the bloodied chain mail he's wearing under his coat, and tosses it to Warner, who drops the machine gun and catches the blade by the hilt without even looking.

A fucking *machete.*

Castle is on his knees, arms toward the sky as he breaks off more pieces of the half-devastated building, but this time Anderson's men don't give him the chance. I run forward, too late to help as Castle is knocked out from behind, and still I throw myself into the fight, battling for ownership of the soldier's gun with skills I developed as a teenager: a single, solid punch to the nose. A clean uppercut. A hard kick to the chest. A good old-fashioned strangulation.

I look up, gasping for breath, hoping for good news—

And do a double take.

Ten men have closed in on Warner, and I don't understand where they came from. I thought we were down to three or four. I spin around, confused, turning back just in time to watch Warner drop to one knee and swing up with the machete in a sudden, perfect arc, gutting the man like a fish. Warner turns, another strong swing slicing through the guy on his left, disconnecting the dude's spine in a move so horrific I have to look away. In the second it takes me to turn back, another guard has already charged forward. Warner pivots sharply, shoving the blade directly up the guy's throat and into his open, screaming mouth. With a final tug, Warner pulls the blade free, and the man falls to the ground with a single, soft thud.

The remaining members of the Supreme Guard hesitate.

I realize then, that—whoever these new soldiers are— they've been given specific orders to attack Warner, and no one else. The rest of us are suddenly without an obvious task, free to sink into the ground, disappear into exhaustion.

Tempting.

I search for Castle, wanting to make sure he's okay, and realize he looks stricken.

He's staring at Warner.

Warner, who's staring at the blood pooling beneath his feet, his chest heaving, his fist still clenched around the shank of the machete. All this time, Castle really thought Warner was just a nice boy who'd made some simple mistakes. The kind of kid he could bring back from the brink.

Not today.

Warner looks up at his father, his face more blood than skin, his body shaking with rage.

"Is this what you wanted?" he cries.

But even Anderson seems surprised.

Another guard moves forward so silently I don't even see the gun he's aimed in Warner's direction until the soldier screams and collapses to the ground. His eyes bulge as he clutches at his throat, where a shard of glass the size of my hand is caught in his jugular.

I whip my head around to face Warner. He's still staring at Anderson, but his free hand is now dripping blood.

Jesus Christ.

"Take me, instead," Warner says, his voice piercing the quiet.

Anderson seems to come back to himself. "What?"

"Leave her. Leave them all. Give me your word that you will leave her alone, and I will come back with you."

I go suddenly still. And then I look around, eyes wild, for

any indication that we're going to stop this idiot from doing something reckless, but no one meets my eyes. Everyone is riveted.

Terrified.

But when I feel a familiar presence suddenly materialize beside me, relief floods through my body. I reach for her hand at the same time she reaches for mine, squeezing her fingers once before breaking the brief connection. Right now, it's enough to know she's here, standing next to me.

Nazeera is okay.

We all wait in silence for the scene to change, hoping for something we don't even know how to name.

It doesn't come.

"I wish it were that simple," Anderson says finally. "I really do. But I'm afraid we need the girl. She is not so easily replaced."

"You said that Emmaline's body was deteriorating." Warner's voice is low, but clear. Miraculously steady. "You said that without a strong enough body to contain her, she'd become volatile."

Anderson visibly stiffens.

"You need a replacement," Warner says. "A new body. Someone to help you complete Operation Synthesis."

"No," Castle cries. "No— Don't do this—"

"Take me," Warner says. "I will be your surrogate."

Anderson's eyes go cold.

He sounds almost convincingly calm when he says, "You would be willing to sacrifice yourself—your youth and your health and your entire life—to let that damaged, deranged girl continue to walk the earth?" Anderson's voice begins to rise in pitch. He seems suddenly on the verge of another breakdown.

"Do you even understand what you're saying? You have every opportunity—all the potential—and you'd be willing to throw it all away? In exchange for *what*?" he cries. "Do you even know the kind of life to which you'd be sentencing yourself?"

A dark look passes over Warner's face. "I think I would know better than most."

Anderson pales. "Why would you do this?"

It becomes clear to me then that even now, despite everything, Anderson doesn't actually want to lose Warner. Not like this.

But Warner is unmoved.

He says nothing. Betrays nothing. He only blinks as someone else's blood drips down his face.

"Give me your word," Warner finally says. "Your word that you will leave her alone forever. I want you to let her disappear. I want you to stop tracking her every move. I want you to forget she ever existed." He pauses. "In exchange, you can have what's left of my life."

Nazeera gasps.

Haider takes a sudden, angry step forward and Stephan grabs his arm, somehow still strong enough to restrain Haider even as his own body bleeds out. "This is his choice," Stephan gasps, wrapping his free arm around a tree for support. "Leave him."

"This is a stupid choice," Haider cries. "You can't do this, *habibi*. Don't be an idiot."

But Warner doesn't seem to hear anyone anymore. He stares only at Anderson, who seems genuinely distraught.

"I will stop fighting you," Warner says. "I will do exactly as you ask. Whatever you want. Just let her live."

Anderson is silent for so long it sends a chill through me. Then:

"No."

Without warning, Anderson raises his arm and fires two shots. The first, at Nazeera, hitting her square in the chest. The second—

At me.

Several people scream. I stumble, then sway, before collapsing.

Shit.

"Find her," Anderson says, his voice booming. "Burn the whole place to the ground if you have to."

The pain is blinding.

It moves through me in waves, electric and searing. Someone is touching me, moving my body. *I'm okay*, I try to say. I'm okay. I'm okay. But the words don't come. He's hit me in my shoulder, I think. Just shy of my chest. I'm not sure. But Nazeera— Someone needs to get to Nazeera.

"I had a feeling you'd do something like this," I hear Anderson say. "And I know you used one of these two"—I imagine him pointing to my prone body, to Nazeera's—"in order to make it happen."

Silence.

"Oh, I see," Anderson says. "You thought you were clever. You thought I didn't know you had any powers at all." Anderson's voice seems suddenly loud, too loud. He laughs. "You thought *I* didn't know? As if you could hide something like that from me. I knew it the day I found you in her holding cell. You were sixteen. You think I didn't have you tested after that? You think I haven't known, all these years, what you yourself didn't realize until six months ago?"

A fresh wave of fear washes over me.

Anderson seems too pleased and Warner's gone quiet again, and I don't know what any of that means for us. But just as I'm beginning to experience full-blown panic, I hear a familiar cry.

It's a sound of such horrific agony I can't help but try to see what's happening, even as flashes of white blur my vision.

I catch a mottled glimpse:

Warner standing over Anderson's body, his right hand clenched around the handle of the machete he's buried in his father's chest. He plants his right foot on his father's gut, and, roughly, pulls out the blade.

Anderson's moan is so animal, so pathetic I almost feel sorry for him. Warner wipes the blade on the grass, and tosses it back to Haider, who catches it easily by the hilt even as he stands there, stunned, staring at—*me*, I realize.

Me and Nazeera. I've never seen him so unmasked. He seems paralyzed by fear.

"Watch him," Warner shouts to someone. He examines a gun he stole from his father, and, satisfied, he's off, running after the Supreme Guard. Shots ring out in the distance.

My vision begins to go spotty.

Sounds bleed together, shifting focus. For moments at a time all I hear is the sound of my own breathing, my heart beating. At least, I hope that's the sound of my heart beating. Everything smells sharp, like rust and steel. I realize then, in a sudden, startling moment, that I can't feel my fingers.

Finally I hear the muffled sounds of nearby movement, of hands on my body, trying to move me.

"Kenji?" Someone shakes me. "Kenji, can you hear me?" Winston.

I make a sound in my throat. My lips seem fused together.

"Kenji?" More shaking. "Are you okay?"

With great difficulty, I pry my lips apart, but my mouth makes no sound. Then, all at once: "Heyyyyybuddy."

Weird.

"He's conscious," Winston says, "but disoriented. "We don't have much time. I'll carry these two. See if you can find a way to transport the others. Where are the girls?"

Someone says something back to him, and I don't catch it. I reach out suddenly with my good hand, clamping down on Winston's forearm.

"Don't let them get J," I try to say. "Don't let—"

ELLA ~~ELLA~~

JULIETTE ~~JULIETTE~~

When I open my eyes, I feel steel.

Strapped and molded across my body, thick, silver stripes pressed against my pale skin. I'm in a cage the exact size and shape of my silhouette. I can't move. Can hardly part my lips or bat an eyelash; I only know what I look like because I can see my reflection in the stainless steel of the ceiling.

Anderson is here.

I see him right away, standing in a corner of the room, staring at the wall like he's both pleased and angry, a strange sneer plastered to his face. There's a woman here, too, someone I've never seen before. Blond, very blond. Tall and freckled and willowy. She reminds me of someone I've seen before, someone I can't presently remember.

And then, suddenly—

My mind catches up to me with a ferociousness that's nearly paralyzing. James and Adam, kidnapped by Anderson. Kenji, falling ill. New memories from my own life, continuing to assault my mind and taking with them, bits and pieces of me.

And then, Emmaline.

Emmaline, stealing into my consciousness. Emmaline, her presence so overwhelming I was forced into near oblivion, coaxed to sleep. I remember waking, eventually, but my recollection of that moment is vague. I remember confusion, mostly. Distorted reels.

I take a moment to check in with myself. My limbs. My heart. My mind. Intact?

I don't know.

Despite a bit of disorientation, I feel almost fully myself. I can still sense pockets of darkness in my memories, but I feel like I've finally broken the surface of my own consciousness. And it's only then that I realize I no longer feel even a whisper of Emmaline.

Quickly, I close my eyes again. I feel around for my sister in my head, seeking her out with a desperate panic that surprises me.

Emmaline? Are you still here?

In response, a gentle warmth rushes through me. A single, soft shudder of life. She must be close to the end, I realize.

Nearly gone.

Pain shoots through my heart.

My love for Emmaline is at once new and ancient, so complicated I don't even know how to properly articulate my feelings about it. I only know that I have nothing but compassion for her. For her pain, her sacrifices, her broken spirit, her longing for all that her life could've been. I feel no anger or resentment toward her for infiltrating my mind, for violently disrupting my world to make room for herself in my skin. Somehow I understand that the brutality of her act was nothing more than a desperate plea for companionship in the last days of her life.

She wants to die knowing she was loved.

And I, I love her.

I was able to see, when our minds were fused, that Emmaline had found a way to split her consciousness, leaving a necessary bit of it behind to play her role in Oceania. The small part of her that broke off to find me— that was the small part of her that still felt human, that felt the world acutely. And now, it seems, that human piece of her is beginning to fade away.

The callused fingers of grief curve around my throat.

My thoughts are interrupted by the sharp staccato of heels against stone. Someone is moving toward me. I'm careful not to flinch.

"She should've been awake by now," the female voice says. "This is odd."

"Perhaps the sedative you gave her was stronger than you thought." Anderson.

"I'm going to assume your head is still full of morphine, Paris, which is the only reason I'm going to overlook that statement."

Anderson sighs. Stiffly, he says: "I'm sure she'll be awake any minute now."

Fear trips the alarms in my head.

What's happening? I ask Emmaline. *Where are we?*

The dregs of a gentle warmth become a searing heat that blazes up my arms. Goose bumps rise along my skin.

Emmaline is afraid.

Show me where we are, I say.

It takes longer than I'm used to, but very slowly Emmaline fills my head with images of my room, of steel walls and glittering glass, long tables laid out with all manner of tools and blades, surgical equipment. Microscopes as tall as the wall. Geometric patterns in the ceiling glow with warm, bright light. And then there's me.

I am mummified in metal.

I'm lying supine on a gleaming table, thick horizontal stripes holding me in place. I am naked but for the carefully placed restraints keeping me from full exposure.

Realization dawns with painful speed.

I recognize these rooms, these tools, these walls. Even the smell—stale air, synthetic lemon, bleach and rust. Dread creeps through me slowly at first, and then all at once.

I am back on base in Oceania.

I feel suddenly ill.

I am a world away. An international flight away from my chosen family, back again in the house of horrors I grew up in. I have no recollection of how I got here, and I don't know what devastation Anderson left in my wake. I don't know where my friends are. I don't know what's become of Warner. I can't remember anything useful. I only know that something must be terribly, terribly wrong.

Even so, my fear feels different.

My captors—Anderson? This woman?—have obviously done something to me, because I can't feel my powers the way I normally do, but there's something about this horrible, familiar pattern that's almost comforting. I've woken up in chains more times than I can remember, and every time, I've found my way out. I'll find my way out of this, too.

And at least this time, I'm not alone.

Emmaline is here. As far as I'm aware, Anderson has no idea she's with me, and it gives me hope.

The silence is broken by a long-suffering sigh.

"Why do we need her to be awake, anyway?" the woman says. "Why can't we perform the procedure while she's asleep?"

"They're not my rules, Tatiana. You know as well as I do that Evie set this all in motion. Protocol states that the subject must be awake when the transfer is initiated."

I take it back.

I take it back.

Pure, unadulterated terror spikes through me, dispelling my earlier confidence with a single blow. It should've occurred to me right away that they'd try to do to me what Evie didn't get right the first time. Of course they would.

My sudden panic nearly gives me away.

"Two daughters with the exact same DNA fingerprint," Tatiana says suddenly. "Anyone else would think it was a wild coincidence. But Evie was always careful about having a backup plan, wasn't she?"

"From the very beginning," Anderson says quietly. "She made sure there was a spare."

The words are a blow I couldn't have anticipated.

A spare.

That's all I ever was, I realize. A spare part kept in captivity. A backup weapon in the case that all else failed.

Shatter me.

Break glass in case of emergency.

It takes everything I've got to remain still, to fight back the urge to swallow the sudden swell of emotion in my throat. Even now, even from the grave, my mother manages to wound me.

"How lucky for us," the woman says.

"Indeed," Anderson says, but there's tension in his voice. Tension I'm only just beginning to notice.

Tatiana starts rambling.

She begins talking about how clever Evie was to realize that someone had interfered with her work, how clever she was to have realized right away that Emmaline was the one who'd tampered with the results of the procedure she'd performed on me. Evie always knew, Tatiana is saying, that there was a risk in bringing me back to base in Oceania— and the risk, she says, was Emmaline's physical closeness.

"After all," Tatiana says, "the two girls hadn't been in such close proximity in nearly a decade. Evie was worried Emmaline would try to make contact with her sister." A pause. "And she did."

"What is your point?"

"My point," Tatiana says slowly, like she's talking to a child, "is that this seems dangerous. Don't you think it's more than a little unwise to put the two girls under the same roof again? After what happened last time? Doesn't this seem a little . . . reckless?"

Stupid hope blooms in my chest.

Of course.

Emmaline's body is nearby. Maybe Emmaline's voice disappearing from my mind has nothing to do with her impending death—maybe she feels farther away simply because she *moved*. It's possible that upon reentry to Oceania the two parts of her consciousness reconnected. Maybe Emmaline feels distant now only because she's reaching out to me from her tank—the way she did the last time I was here.

Sharp, searing heat flashes behind my eyes, and my heart leaps at her response.

I am not alone, I say to her. *You are not alone.*

"You know as well as I do that this was the only way," Anderson says to Tatiana. "I needed Max's help. My injuries were too serious."

"You seem to be needing Max's help quite a lot these days," she says coldly. "And I'm not the only one who thinks your needs are becoming liabilities."

"Don't push me," he says quietly. "This isn't the day."

"I don't care. You know as well as I do that it would've

been safer to initiate this transfer back at Sector 45, thousands of miles away from Emmaline. We had to transport the boy, too, remember? Extremely inconvenient. That you so desperately needed Max to assist with your vanity is an altogether different issue, one that concerns both your failings and your ineptitude."

Silence falls, heavy and thick.

I have no idea what's happening above my head, but I can only imagine the two of them are glaring each other into the ground.

"Evie had a soft spot for you," Tatiana says finally. "We all know that. We all know how willing she was to overlook your mistakes. But Evie is dead now, isn't she? And her daughter would be two for two if it weren't for Max's constant efforts to keep you alive. The rest of us are running out of patience."

Before Anderson has a chance to respond, a door slams open.

"Well?" A new voice. "Is it done?"

For the first time, Tatiana seems subdued. "She's not yet awake, I'm afraid."

"Then wake her up," the voice demands. "We're out of time. All the children have been tainted. We still have to get the rest of them under control and clear their minds as soon as possible."

"But not before we figure out what they know," Anderson says quickly, "and who they might've told."

Heavy footsteps move into the room, fast and hard. I hear a rustle of movement, a sudden brief gasp. "Haider told me something interesting when your men dragged him back here," the man says quietly. "He says you shot my daughter."

"It was a practical decision," Anderson says. "She and Kishimoto were possible targets. I had no choice but to take them both out."

It takes every ounce of my self-control to keep from screaming.

Kenji.

Anderson shot Kenji.

Kenji, and this man's daughter. He must be talking about Nazeera. Oh my God. Anderson shot Kenji and Nazeera. Which would make this man—

"Ibrahim, it was for the best." Tatiana's heels click against the floor. "I'm sure she's fine. They've got those healer girls, you know."

Supreme Commander Ibrahim ignores her.

"If my daughter is not returned to me alive," he says angrily, "I will personally remove your brain from your skull."

The door slams shut behind him.

"Wake her up," Anderson says.

"It's not that simple— There's a process—"

"I won't say it again, Tatiana." Anderson is shouting now, his temperature spiking without warning. "Wake her up now. I want this over with."

"Paris, you have to calm d—"

"I tried to kill her *months* ago." Metal slams against metal.

"I told all of you to finish the job. If we're in this position right now—if Evie is dead—it's because no one listened to me when they should have."

"You are unbelievable." Tatiana laughs, but the sound is flat. "That you ever assumed you had the authority to murder Evie's daughter tells me everything I need to know about you, Paris. You're an idiot."

"Get out," he says, seething. "I don't need you breathing down my neck. Go check in on your own insipid daughter. I'll take care of this one."

"Feeling fatherly?"

"Get. Out."

Tatiana says nothing more. I hear the sound of a door opening and closing. The soft, distant clangs and chimes of metal and glass. I have no idea what Anderson is doing, but my heart is beating wildly. Angry, indignant Anderson is nothing to take lightly.

I would know.

And when I feel a sudden, ruthless spike of pain, I scream. Panic forces my eyes open.

"I had a feeling you were faking it," he says.

Roughly, he yanks the scalpel out of my thigh. I choke back another scream. I've hardly had a chance to catch my breath when, again, he buries the scalpel in my flesh— deeper this time. I cry out in agony, my lungs constricting. When he finally wrenches the tool free I nearly pass out from the pain. I'm making labored, gasping sounds, my chest so tightly bound I can't breathe properly.

"I was hoping you'd hear that conversation," Anderson says calmly, pausing to wipe the scalpel on his lab coat. The blood is dark. Thick. My vision fades in and out. "I wanted you to know that your mother wasn't stupid. I wanted you to know that she was aware that something had gone wrong. She didn't know the exact failings of the procedure—but she suspected the injections hadn't done everything they were meant to do. And when she suspected foul play, she made a contingency plan."

I'm still gasping for air, my head spinning. The pain in my leg is searing, clouding my mind.

"You didn't think she was that stupid, did you? Evie Sommers?" Anderson almost laughs. "Evie Sommers hasn't been stupid a day in her life. Even on the day she died, she died with a plan in place to save The Reestablishment, because she'd dedicated her life to this cause. This was it," he says, prodding at my wound. "You.

"You and your sister. You were her life's work, and she wasn't about to let it all go up in flames without a fight."

I don't understand, I try to say.

"I know you don't understand," he says. "Of course you don't understand. You never did inherit your mother's genius, did you? You never had her mind. No, you were only ever meant to be a tool, from the very beginning. So here's everything you need to understand: you now belong to me."

"No," I gasp. I struggle, uselessly, against the restraints. "No—"

I feel the sting and the fire at the same time. Anderson has stuck me with something, something that blazes through me with a pain so excruciating my heart hardly remembers to beat. My skin breaks out in an all-consuming sweat. My hair begins to stick to my face. I feel at once paralyzed and as if I'm falling, free-falling, sinking into the coldest depths of hell.

Emmaline, I cry.

My eyelids flutter. I see Anderson, flashes of Anderson, his eyes dark and troubled. He looks at me like he's finally got me exactly where he wants me, where he's always wanted me, and I understand then, without understanding why, exactly, that he's excited. I sense his happiness. I don't know how I know. I can just tell from the way he stands, the way he stares. He's feeling joyous.

It terrifies me.

My body makes another effort to move but the action is futile. There's no point in moving, no point in struggle.

This is over, something tells me.

I have lost.

I've lost the battle and the war. I've lost the boy. I've lost my friends. I've lost my will to live, the voice says to me.

And then I understand: Anderson is in my head.

My eyes are not open. My eyes might never again open. Wherever I am is not in my control. I belong to Anderson now. I belong to The Reestablishment, where I've always belonged, *where you've always belonged,* he says to me, *where you will remain forever. I've been waiting for this moment for a very, very long time,* he says to me, *and now, finally, there's nothing you can do about it.*

Nothing.

Even then, I don't understand. Not right away. I don't understand even as I hear the machines roar to life. I don't understand even as I see the flash of light behind my eyelids. I hear my own breath, loud and strange and reverberating in my skull. I can feel my hands shaking. I can feel the metal sinking into the soft flesh of my body. I am here, strapped into steel against my will and there is no one to save me.

Emmaline, I cry.

A whisper of heat moves through me in response, a whisper so subtle, so quickly extinguished, I fear I might've imagined it.

Emmaline is nearly dead, Anderson says. *Once her body is removed from the tank, you will take her place. Until then, this is where you'll live. Until then, this is where you'll exist. This is all you were ever meant for,* he says to me.

This is all you will ever be.

KENJI

KENJI

No one comes to the funeral.

It took two days to bury all the bodies. Castle tired his mind nearly to sickness digging up so much dirt. The rest of us used shovels. But there weren't many of us to do the work then, and there aren't enough of us to attend a funeral now.

Still, I sit here at dawn, perched atop a boulder, sitting high above the valley where we buried our friends. Teammates. My left arm is in a sling, my head hurts like a bitch, my heart is permanently broken.

I'm okay, otherwise.

Alia comes up behind me, so quiet I hardly even notice her. I hardly *ever* notice her. But there are too few bodies for her to hide behind now. I scoot over on the rock and she settles down beside me, the two of us staring out at the sea of graves below. She's holding two dandelions. Offers one to me. I take it.

Together, we drop the flowers, watching them as they float gently into the chasm. Alia sighs.

"You okay?" I ask her.

"No."

"Yeah." I nod.

Seconds pass. A gentle breeze pushes the hair out of my

face. I stare directly into the newborn sun, daring it to burn my eyes out.

"Kenji?"

"Yeah?"

"Where's Adam?"

I shake my head. Shrug.

"Do you think we'll find him?" she asks, her voice practically a whisper.

I look up.

There's a yearning there—something more than general concern in her tone. I turn fully to meet her eyes, but she won't look at me.

She's suddenly blushing.

"I don't know," I say to her. "I hope so."

"Me too," she says softly.

She rests her head on my shoulder. We stare out, into the distance. Let the silence devour our bodies.

"You did an amazing job, by the way." I nod at the valley below. "This is beautiful."

Alia really outdid herself. She and Winston.

The monuments they designed are simple and elegant, made from stone sourced from the land itself.

And there are two.

One for the lives lost here, at the Sanctuary, two days ago. The other for the lives lost *there*, at Omega Point, two months ago. The list of names is long. The injustice of it all roars through me.

Alia takes my hand. Squeezes.

I realize I'm crying.

I turn away, feeling stupid, and Alia lets go, gives me space to pull myself together. I wipe at my eyes with excessive force, angry with myself for falling apart. Angry with myself for being disappointed. Angry with myself for ever allowing hope.

We lost J.

We're not even sure exactly how it happened. Warner has been virtually comatose since that day, and getting information out of him has been near impossible. But it sounds like we never really stood a chance, in the end. One of Anderson's men had the preternatural ability to clone himself, and it took us too long to figure it out. We couldn't understand why their defense would suddenly double and triple just as we thought we were wearing them down. But it turns out Anderson had an inexhaustible supply of dummy soldiers. Warner couldn't get over it. It was the one thing he kept repeating, over and over—

I should've known, I should've known

—and despite the fact that Warner's been killing himself for the oversight, Castle says it was precisely because of Warner that any of us are still alive.

There weren't supposed to be *any* survivors. That was Anderson's decree. The command he gave after I went down.

Warner figured out the trick just in time.

His ability to harness the soldier's powers and use it against him was our one saving grace, apparently, and when the dude realized he had competition, he took what he could get and ran.

Which means he managed to snag an unconscious Haider and Stephan. It means Anderson escaped.

And J, of course.

It means they got J.

"Should we head back?" Alia says quietly. "Castle was awake when I left. He said he wanted to talk to you."

"Yeah." I nod, get to my feet. Pull myself together. "Any update on James, by the way? Is he cleared for visitors yet?"

Alia shakes her head. Stands up, too. "Not yet," she says. "But he'll be awake soon. The girls are optimistic. Between his healing powers and theirs, they feel certain they'll be able to get him through it."

"Yeah," I say, taking a deep breath. "I'm sure you're right."

Wrong.

I'm not sure of anything.

The wreckage left in the wake of Anderson's attack has laid all of us low. Sonya and Sara are working around the clock. Sam was severely injured. Nazeera is still unconscious. Castle is weak. Hundreds of others are trying to heal.

A serious darkness has descended upon us all.

We fought hard, but we took too many hits. We were too few to begin with. There was only so much any of us could do.

These are the things I keep telling myself, anyway.

We start walking.

"This feels worse, doesn't it?" Alia says. "Worse than

last time." She stops, suddenly, and I follow her line of sight, study the scene before us. The torn-down buildings, the detritus along the paths. We did our best to clean up the worst of it, but if I look in the wrong place at the wrong time, I can still find blood on broken tree branches. Shards of glass.

"Yeah," I say. "Somehow, this is so much worse."

Maybe because the stakes were higher. Maybe because we've never lost J before. Maybe because I've never seen Warner this lost or this broken. Angry Warner was better than this. At least angry Warner had some fight left in him.

Alia and I part ways when we enter the dining tent. She's been volunteering her time, going from cot to cot to check on people, offering food and water where necessary, and this dining tent is currently her place of work. The massive space has been made into a sort of convalescent home. Sonya and Sara are prioritizing major injuries; minor wounds are being treated the traditional way, by what's left of the original staff of doctors and nurses. This room is stacked, end to end, with those of us who are either healing from minor injuries, or resting after major intervention.

Nazeera is here, but she's sleeping.

I drop down in a seat next to her cot, checking up on her the way I do every hour. Nothing's changed. She's still lying here, still as stone, the only proof of life coming from a nearby monitor and the gentle movements of her breathing. Her wound was a lot worse than mine. The girls say she's going to be okay, but they think she'll be asleep until at least tomorrow. Even so, it kills me to look at her. Watching that girl go down was one of the hardest things I've ever had to witness.

I sigh, dragging a hand down my face. I still feel like shit, but at least I'm awake. Few of us are.

Warner is one of them.

He's still covered in dry blood, refusing to be helped. He's conscious, but he's been lying on his back, staring at the ceiling since the day he was dragged in here. If I didn't know any better, I'd think he was a corpse. I've been checking, too, every once in a while—making sure I caught that gentle rise and fall of his chest—just to be certain he was still breathing.

I think he's in shock.

Apparently, once he realized J was gone, he tore the remaining soldiers to pieces with his bare hands.

Apparently.

I don't buy it, of course, because the story sounds just a little to the left of what I consider credible, but then, I've been hearing all kinds of shit about Warner these last couple of days. He went from being only relatively consequential to becoming genuinely terrifying to assuming superhero status—in thirty-six hours. In a plot twist I never could've expected, people here are suddenly obsessed with him.

They think he saved our lives.

One of the volunteers checking my wound yesterday told me that she heard someone else say that they saw Warner uproot an entire tree with only one hand.

Translation: He probably broke off a tree branch.

Someone else told me that they'd heard from a friend that some girl had seen him save a cluster of children from friendly fire.

Translation: He probably shoved a bunch of kids to the ground.

Another person told me that Warner had single-handedly murdered nearly all the supreme soldiers.

Translation—

Okay, that last one is kind of true.

But I know Warner wasn't trying to do anyone around here a favor. He doesn't give a shit about being a hero.

He was only trying to save J's life.

"You should talk to him," Castle says, and I startle so badly he jumps back, freaking out for a second, too.

"Sorry, sir," I say, trying to slow my heart rate. "I didn't see you there."

"That's quite all right," Castle says. He's smiling, but his eyes are sad. Exhausted. "How are you doing?"

"As well as can be expected," I say. "How's Sam?"

"As well as can be expected," he says. "Nouria is struggling, of course, but Sam should be able to make a full recovery. The girls say it was mostly a flesh wound. Her skull was fractured, but they're confident they can get it nearly back to the way it was." He sighs. "They'll be all right, both of them. In time."

I study him for a moment, suddenly seeing him like I've

never seen him before:

Old.

Castle's dreads are untied, hanging loose about his face, and something about the break from his usual style—locs tied neatly at the base of his neck—makes me notice things I'd never seen before. New gray hairs. New creases around his eyes, his forehead. It takes him a little longer to stand up straight like he used to. He seems worn out. Looking like he's been kicked down one too many times.

Kind of like the rest of us.

"I hate that this is the thing that seems to have conquered the distance between us," he says after a stretch of silence. "But now Nouria and I—both resistance leaders—have each suffered great losses. The whole thing has been hard for her, just as it was for me. She needs more time to recover."

I take a sharp breath.

Even the mention of that dark time inspires an ache in my heart. I don't allow myself to dwell for too long on the husk of a person Castle became after we lost Omega Point. If I do, the feelings overwhelm me so completely I pivot straight to anger. I know he was hurting. I know there was so much else going on. I know it was hard for everyone. But for me, losing Castle like that—however temporarily—was worse than losing everyone else. I needed him, and it felt like he'd abandoned me.

"I don't know," I say, clearing my throat. "It's not really the same thing, is it? What we lost— I mean, we lost literally everything in the bombing. Not only our people and our home, but years of research. Priceless equipment. Personal treasures." I hesitate, try to be delicate. "Nouria and Sam only lost half of their people, and their base is still standing. This loss isn't nearly as great."

Castle turns, surprised. "It's not as if it's a competition."

"I know that," I say. "It's just th—"

"And I wouldn't want my daughter to know the kind of grief we've experienced. You have no idea the depth of what she's already suffered in her young life. She certainly doesn't need to experience more pain to be deserving of your compassion."

"I didn't mean it like that," I say quickly, shaking my head. "I'm only trying to point out th—"

"Have you seen James yet?"

I gape at him, my mouth still shaped around an unspoken word. Castle just changed the subject so quickly it nearly gave me whiplash. This isn't like him. This isn't like *us*.

Castle and I never used to have trouble talking. We never avoided hard topics and sensitive conversations. But things have felt off for a little while now, if I'm being honest. Maybe ever since I realized Castle had been lying to me, all these years, about J. Maybe I've been a little less respectful lately. Crossed lines. Maybe all this tension is coming from me— maybe I'm the one pushing him away without realizing it.

I don't know.

I want to fix whatever is happening between us, but right now, I'm just too wrung out. Between J and Warner and James and unconscious Nazeera— My head is in such

175

a weird place I'm not sure I have the bandwidth for much else.

So I let it go.

"No, I haven't seen James," I say, trying to sound upbeat. "Still waiting on that green light." Last I checked, James was in the medical tent with Sonya and Sara. James has his own healing abilities, so he should be fine, physically—I know that—but he's been through so much lately. The girls wanted to make sure he was fully rested and fed and hydrated before he had any visitors.

Castle nods.

"Warner is gone," he says after a moment, a non sequitur if there ever was one.

"What? No I just saw him. He—" I cut myself off as I glance up, expecting to find the familiar sight of him lying on his cot like a carcass. But Castle's right. He's gone.

I whip my head around, scanning the room for his retreating figure. I get nothing.

"I still think you should talk to him," Castle says, returning to his opening statement.

I bristle.

"You're the adult," I point out. "You're the one who wanted him to take refuge among us. You're the one who believed he could change. Maybe you should be the one to talk to him."

"That's not what he needs, and you know it." Castle sighs. Glances across the room. "Why is everyone so afraid of him? Why are *you* so afraid of him?"

"Me?" My eyes widen. "I'm not afraid of him. Or, I mean, whatever, I'm not the only one afraid of him. Though let's be real," I mutter, "anyone with two brain cells to rub together should be afraid of him."

Castle raises an eyebrow.

"Except for you, of course," I add hastily. "What reason would you have to be afraid of Warner? He's such a nice guy. Loves children. Big talker. Oh, and bonus: He no longer murders people professionally. No, now murdering people is just a fulfilling hobby."

Castle sighs, visibly annoyed.

I crack a smile. "Sir, all I'm saying is that we don't really know him, right? When Juliette was around—"

"Ella. Her name is Ella."

"Uh-huh. When she was around, Warner was tolerable. Barely. But now she's not around, and he's acting just like the guy I remember when I enlisted, the guy he was when he was working for his dad and running Sector 45. What reason does he have to be loyal or kind to the rest of us?"

Castle opens his mouth to respond, but just then arrives my salvation: lunch.

A smiling volunteer comes by, handing out simple salads in bowls of foil. I take the proffered food and plastic silverware with an overenthusiastic *thanks*, and promptly rip the lid off the container.

"Warner has been dealt a punishing blow," Castle says. "He needs us now more than ever."

I glance up at Castle. Shove a forkful of salad in my

mouth. I chew slowly, still deciding how to respond, when I'm distracted by movement in the distance.

I look up.

Brendan and Winston and Ian and Lily are in the corner gathered around a small, makeshift table, all of them holding tinfoil lunch bowls. They're waving us over.

I gesture with a forkful of salad. Speak with my mouth full. "You want to join us?"

Castle sighs even as he stands, smoothing out invisible wrinkles in his black pants. I glance over at Nazeera's sleeping figure as I collect my things. I know, rationally, that she's going to be fine, but she's recovering from a full blow to the chest—not unlike J once did—and it hurts to see her so vulnerable. Especially for a girl who once laughed in my face at the prospect of ever being overpowered.

It scares me.

"Coming?" Castle says, glancing over his shoulder. He's already a few steps away, and I have no idea how long I've been standing here, staring at Nazeera.

"Oh, yeah," I say. "Right behind you."

The minute we sit down at their table, I know something is off. Brendan and Winston are sitting stiffly, side by side, and Ian doesn't do more than glance at me when I sit down. I find this reception especially strange, considering the fact that *they* flagged *me* down. You'd think they'd be happy to see me.

After a few minutes of uncomfortable silence, Castle

speaks. "I was just telling Kenji," he says, "that he should be the one to talk to Warner."

Brendan looks up. "That's a great idea."

I shoot him a dark look.

"No, really," he says, carefully choosing a piece of potato to spear. Wait—where did they get potatoes? All I got was salad. "Someone definitely needs to talk to him."

"*Someone* definitely does," I say, irritated. I narrow my eyes at Brendan's potatoes. "Where'd you get those?"

"This is just what they gave me," Brendan says, looking up in surprise. "Of course, I'm happy to share."

I move quickly, jumping out of my seat to spear a chunk of potato from his bowl. I shove the whole piece in my mouth before I even sit back down, and I'm still chewing when I thank him.

He looks mildly repulsed.

I guess I am a bit of a caveman when Warner isn't around to keep me decent.

"Anyway, Castle's right," Lily says. "You should talk to him, and soon. I think he's kind of a loose cannon right now."

I stab a piece of lettuce, roll my eyes. "Can I maybe eat my lunch before everyone starts jumping down my throat? This is the first real meal I've had since I got shot."

"No one is jumping down your throat." Castle frowns. "And I thought Nouria said the normal dining hours went back into effect yesterday morning."

"They did," I say.

"But you were shot three days ago," Winston says. "Which means—"

"All right, okay, calm down, Detective Winston. Can we change the subject, please?" I take another bite of lettuce. "I don't like this one."

Brendan puts down his knife and fork. Hard.

I straighten.

"Go talk to him," he says again, this time with an air of finality that surprises me.

I swallow my food. Too fast. Nearly choke.

"I'm serious," Brendan says, frowning as I cough up a lung. "This is a wretched time for all of us, and you've more of a connection with him than anyone else here. Which means you have a moral responsibility to find out what he's thinking."

"A moral responsibility?" My cough turns into a laugh.

"Yes. A moral responsibility. And Winston agrees with me."

I look up, raising my eyebrows at Winston. "I bet he does. I bet Winston agrees with you all the time."

Winston adjusts his glasses. He stabs blindly at his food and mutters, "I hate you," under his breath.

"Oh yeah?" I gesture between Winston and Brendan with my fork. "What the hell is going on here? This energy is super weird."

When no one answers me I kick Winston under the table. He turns away, mumbling nonsense before taking a long pull from his water glass.

180

"Okay," I say slowly. I pick up my own water glass. Take a sip. "Seriously. What's going on? You two playing footsie under the table or someshit?"

Winston goes full tomato.

Brendan picks up his utensils and, looking down at his plate, says, "Go ahead. Tell him."

"Tell me what?" I say, glancing between the two of them. When no one responds, I look over at Ian like, *What the hell?*

Ian only shrugs.

Ian's been quieter than usual. He and Lily have been spending a lot more time together lately, which is understandable, but it also means I haven't really seen him much in the last couple of days.

Castle suddenly stands.

He claps me on the back. "Talk to Mr. Warner," he says. "He's vulnerable right now, and he needs his friends."

"Are you—?" I make a show of looking around, over my shoulders. "I'm sorry, which friends are you referring to? Because as far as I know, Warner doesn't have any."

Castle narrows his eyes at me. "Don't do this," he says. "Don't deny your own emotional intelligence in favor of petty grievances. You know better. Be better. If you care about him at all, you will sacrifice your pride to reach out to him. Make sure he's okay."

"Why do you have to make it sound so dramatic?" I say, looking away. "It's not that big of a deal. He'll survive."

Castle rests his hand on my shoulder. Forces me to meet his eyes. "No," he says to me. "He might not."

181

I wait until Castle is gone before I finally set down my fork. I'm irritated, but I know he's right. I mumble a general good-bye to my friends as I push away from the table, but not before I notice Brendan smiling triumphantly in my direction. I'm about to give him shit for it, but then I notice, with a start, that Winston has turned a shade of pink so magnificent you could probably see it from space.

And then, there it is: Brendan is holding Winston's hand under the table.

I gasp, audibly.

"Shut up," Winston says. "I don't want to hear it."

My enthusiasm withers. "You don't want to hear me say congratulations?"

"No, I don't want to hear you say *I told you so.*"

"Yes, but I did fucking tell you so, didn't I?" A wave of happiness moves through me, conjures a smile. I didn't know I still had it in me.

Joy.

"I'm so happy for you guys," I say. "Truly. You just made this shitty day so much better."

Winston looks up, suspicious. But Brendan beams at me.

I stab a finger in their direction. "But if you two turn into Adam and Juliette clones I swear to God I will lose my mind."

Brendan's eyes go wide. Winston turns purple.

"Kidding!" I say. "I'm just kidding! Obviously I'm super happy for you two!" After a dead beat, I clear my throat. "No but seriously, though."

"Fuck off, Kenji."

"Yup." I shoot a finger gun at Winston. "You got it."

"*Kenji*," I hear Castle call out. "Language."

I swivel around, surprised. I thought Castle was gone. "It wasn't me!" I shout back. "For the first time, I swear, it wasn't me!"

I see only the back of Castle's head as he turns away, but somehow, I can tell he's still annoyed.

I shake my head. I can't stop smiling.

It's time to regroup.

Pick up the pieces. Keep going. Find J. Find Adam. Tear down The Reestablishment, once and for all. And the truth is—we're going to need Warner's help. Which means Castle is right, I need to talk to Warner. Shit.

I look back at my friends.

Lily's got her head on Ian's shoulder, and he's trying to hide his smile. Winston flips me off, but he's laughing. Brendan pops another piece of potato in his mouth and shoos me away.

"Go on, then."

"All right, all right," I say. But just as I'm about to take the necessary steps forward, I'm saved yet again.

Alia comes running toward me, her face lit in an expression of happiness I rarely see on her. It's transformative. Hell, she's glowing. It's easy to lose track of Alia, who's quiet in both voice and presence. But when she smiles like that—

She looks beautiful.

"James is awake," she says, nearly out of breath. She's squeezing my arm so hard it's cutting off my circulation.

I don't care.

I'd been carrying this tension for almost two weeks now. Worrying, all this time, about James and whether he was okay. When I saw him for the first time the other day, bound and gagged by Anderson, I felt my knees give out. We had no idea how he was doing or what kind of trauma he'd sustained. But if the girls are letting him have visitors—

That's got to be a good sign.

I send up silent thanks to anyone who might be listening. Mom. Dad. Ghosts. I'm grateful.

Alia is half dragging me down the hall, and even though her physical effort isn't necessary, I let her do it. She seems so excited I don't have the heart to stop her.

"James is officially up and ready for visitors," she says, "and he asked to see *you*."

~~ELLA~~ JULIETTE

When I wake, I am cold.

I dress in the dark, pulling on crisp fatigues and polished boots. I pull my hair back in a tight ponytail and perform a series of efficient ablutions at the small sink in my chamber.

Teeth brushed. Face washed.

After three days of rigorous training, I was selected as a candidate for supreme soldier, honored with the prospect of serving our North American commander. Today is my opportunity to prove I deserve the position.

I lace my boots, knotting them twice.

Satisfied, I pull the release latch. The lock exhales as it comes open, and the seam around my door lets through a ring of light that cuts straight across my vision. I turn away from the glare only to be met by my own reflection in a small mirror above the sink. I blink, focusing.

Pale skin, dark hair, odd eyes.

I blink again.

A flash of light catches my eye in the mirror. I turn. The monitor adjacent to my sleep pod has been dark all night, but now it flashes with information:

Juliette Ferrars, report

My hand vibrates.

I glance down, palm up, as a soft blue light beams through the thin skin at my wrist.

report

I push open the door.

Cool morning air rushes in, shuddering against my face. The sun is still rising. Golden light bathes everything, briefly distorting my vision. Birds chirp as I climb my way up the side of the steep hill that protects my private chamber against the howling winds. I haul myself over the edge.

Immediately, I spot the compound in the distance.

Mountains stagger across the sky. A massive lake glitters nearby. I push against tangles of wild, ferocious gusts of wind as I hike toward base. For no reason at all, a butterfly lands on my shoulder.

I come to a halt.

I pluck the insect off my shirt, pinching its wings between my fingers. It flutters desperately as I study it, scrutinizing its hideous body as I turn it over in my hand. Slowly, I increase the intensity of my touch, and its flutters grow more desperate, wings snapping against my skin.

I blink. The butterfly thrashes.

A low hum drums up from its insect body, a soft buzz that passes for a scream. I wait, patiently, for the creature to die, but it only beats its wings harder, resisting the inevitable. Irritated, I close my fingers, crushing it in my fist. I wipe its remains against an overgrown stalk of wheat and soldier on.

It's the fifth of May.

This is technically fall weather in Oceania, but the temperatures are erratic, inconsistent. Today the winds are particularly angry, which makes it unseasonably cold. My nose grows numb as I forge my way through the field; when I find a paltry slant of sunlight I lean into it, warming under its rays. Every morning and evening, I make this two-mile hike to base. My commander says it's necessary.

He did not explain why.

When I finally reach headquarters, the sun has shifted in the sky. I glance up at the dying star as I push open the front door, and the moment I step foot in the entry, I'm assaulted by the scent of burnt coffee. Quietly, I make my way down the hall, ignoring the sounds and stares of workers and armed soldiers.

Once outside his office, I stop. It's only a couple of seconds before the door slides open.

Supreme Commander Anderson looks up at me from his desk.

He smiles.

I salute.

"Step inside, soldier."

I do.

"How are you adjusting?" he says, closing a folder on his

desk. He does not ask me to sit down. "It's been a few days since your transfer from 241."

"Yes, sir."

"And?" He leans forward, clasps his hands in front of him. "How are you feeling?"

"Sir?"

He tilts his head at me. Picks up a mug of coffee. The acrid scent of the dark liquid burns my nose. I watch him take a sip and the simple action conjures a stutter of emotion inside of me. Feeling presses against my mind in flashes of memory: a bed, a green sweater, a pair of black glasses, then nothing. Flint failing to spark a flame.

"Are you missing your family?" he asks.

"I have no family, sir."

"Friends? A boyfriend?"

Vague irritation rises up inside of me; I push it aside. "None, sir."

He relaxes in his chair, his smile growing wider. "It's better that way, of course. Easier."

"Yes, sir."

He gets to his feet. "Your work these past couple of days has been remarkable. Your training has been even more successful than we expected." He glances up at me then, waiting for a reaction.

I merely stare.

He takes another sip of the coffee before setting the cup down beside a sheaf of papers. He walks around the desk and stands in front of me, assessing. One step closer and the smell of coffee overwhelms me. I inhale the bitter, nutty scent and it floods my senses, leaving me vaguely nauseated. Still, I stare straight ahead.

The closer he gets, the more aware of him I become.

His physical presence is solid. Categorically male. He's a wall of muscle standing before me, and even the suit he wears can't hide the subtle, sculpted curves of his arms and legs. His face is hard, the line of his jaw so sharp I can see it even out of focus. He smells like coffee and something else, something clean and fragrant. It's unexpectedly pleasant; it fills my head.

"Juliette," he says.

A needle of unease pierces my mind. It is more than unusual for the supreme commander to call me by my first name.

"Look at me."

I obey, lifting my head to meet his eyes.

He stares down at me, his expression fiery. His eyes are a strange, stark shade of blue, and there's something about him—his heavy brow, his sharp nose—that stirs up ancient feelings inside my chest. Silence gathers around us, unspoken curiosities pulling us together. He searches my face for so long that I begin to search him, too. Somehow I know that this is rare; that he might never again give me the opportunity to look at him like this.

I seize it.

I catalog the faint lines creasing his forehead, the starbursts around his eyes. I'm so close I can see the grain of his skin, rough but not yet leathery, his most recent shave evidenced in a microscopic nick at the base of his jaw. His brown hair is full and thick, his cheekbones high and his lips a dusky shade of pink.

He touches a finger to my chin, tilts up my face. "Your beauty is excessive," he says. "I don't know what your mother was thinking."

Surprise and confusion flare through me, but it does not presently occur to me to be afraid. I do not feel threatened by him. His words seem perfunctory. When he speaks, I catch a glimpse of a slight chip on his bottom incisor.

"Today," he says. "Things will change. You will shadow me from here on out. Your duty is to protect and serve my interests, and mine alone."

"Yes, sir."

His lips curve, just slightly. There's something there behind his eyes, something more, something else. "You understand," he says, "that you belong to me now."

"Yes, sir."

"My rule is your law. You will obey no other."

"Yes, sir."

He steps forward. His irises are so blue. A lock of dark hair curves across his eyes. "I am your master," he says.

"Yes, sir."

He's so close I can feel his breath against my skin. Coffee and mint and something else, something subtle, fermented. Alcohol, I realize.

He steps back. "Get on your knees."

I stare at him, frozen. The command was clear enough, but it feels like an error. "Sir?"

"On your knees, soldier. Now."

Carefully, I comply. The floor is hard and cold and my uniform is too stiff to make this position comfortable. Still, I remain on my knees for so long that a curious spider scuttles forward, peering at me from underneath a chair. I stare at Anderson's polished boots, the muscled curves of his calves noticeable even through his pants. The floor smells like bleach and lemon and dust.

When he commands me to, I look up.

"Now say it," he says softly.

I blink at him. "Sir?"

"Tell me that I am your master."

My mind goes blank.

A dull, warm sensation washes over me, a searching paralysis that locks my tongue, jams my mind. Fear propels through me, drowning me, and I fight to break the surface, clawing my way back to the moment.

I meet his eyes.

"You are my master," I say.

His stiff smile bends, curves. Joy catches fire in his eyes. "Good," he says softly. "Very good. How strange that you might turn out to be my favorite yet."

KENJI

I stop short at the door.

Warner is here.

Warner and James, together.

James was given his own private section of the MT—which is otherwise full and cramped—and the two of them are here, Warner sitting in a chair beside James's bed, James propped up against a stack of pillows. I'm so relieved to see him looking okay. His dirty-blond hair is a little too long, but his light, bright blue eyes are open and animated. Still, he looks more than a little tired, which probably explains the IV hooked up to his body.

Under normal circumstances, James should be able to heal himself, but if his body is drained, it makes the job harder. He must've arrived malnourished and dehydrated. The girls are probably doing what they can to help speed up the recovery process. I feel a rush of relief.

James will be better soon. He's such a strong kid. After everything he's been through—

He'll get through this, too. And he won't be alone.

I glance again at Warner, who looks only marginally better than the last time I saw him. He really needs to wash that blood off his body. It's not like Warner to overlook basic rules of hygiene—which should be proof enough that the guy is close to a full-on breakdown—but for now, at least, he seems okay. He and James appear to be deep in conversation.

I remain at the door, eavesdropping. It only belatedly occurs to me that I should give them privacy, but by then I'm too invested to walk away. I'm almost positive Anderson told James the truth about Warner. Or, I don't know, exactly. I can't actually imagine a scenario in which Anderson would gleefully reveal to James that Warner is his brother, or that Anderson is his dad. But somehow I can just tell that James knows. *Someone* told him. I can tell by the look on his face.

This is the come-to-Jesus moment.

This is the moment where Warner and James finally come face-to-face not as strangers, but as brothers. Surreal.

But they're speaking quietly, and I can only catch bits and pieces of their conversation, so I decide to do something truly reprehensible: I go invisible, and step farther into the room.

The moment I do, Warner stiffens.

Shit.

I see him glance around, his eyes alert. His senses are too sharp.

Quietly, I back up a few steps.

"You're not answering my question," James says, poking Warner in the arm. Warner shakes him off, his eyes narrowed at a spot a mere foot from where I'm standing.

"Warner?"

Reluctantly, Warner turns to face the ten-year-old. "Yes,"

he says, distracted. "I mean— What were you saying?"

"Why didn't you ever tell me?" James says, sitting up straighter. The bedsheets fall down, puddle in his lap. "Why didn't you say anything to me before? That whole time we lived together—"

"I didn't want to scare you."

"Why would I be scared?"

Warner sighs, stares out the window when he says, quietly, "Because I'm not known for my charm."

"That's not fair," James says. He looks genuinely upset, but his visible exhaustion is keeping him from reacting too strongly. "I've seen a lot worse than you."

"Yes. I realize that now."

"And *no one* told me. I can't believe no one told me. Not even Adam. I've been so mad at him." James hesitates. "Did everyone know? Did Kenji know?"

I stiffen.

Warner turns again, this time staring precisely in my direction when he says, "Why don't you ask him yourself?"

"Son of a bitch," I mutter, my invisibility melting away.

Warner almost smiles. James's eyes go wide.

This was not the reunion I was hoping for.

Still, James's face breaks into the biggest smile, which— I'm not going to lie—does wonders for my self-esteem. He throws off the covers and tries to jump out of bed, barefoot and oblivious to the needle stuck in his arm, and in those two and a half seconds I manage to experience both joy and terror.

I shout a warning, rushing forward to stop him from ripping open the flesh of his forearm, but Warner beats me to it. He's already on his feet, not so gently pushing the kid back down.

"Oh." James blushes. "Sorry."

I tackle him anyway, pulling him in for a long, excessive hug, and the way he clings to me makes me think I'm the first to do it. I try to fight back a rush of anger, but I'm unsuccessful. He's a ten-year-old kid, for God's sake. He's been through hell. How has no one given him the physical reassurance he almost certainly needs right now?

When we finally break apart, James has tears in his eyes. He wipes at his face and I turn away, trying to give him privacy, but when I take a seat at the foot of James's bed I catch a flash of pain steal in and out of Warner's eyes. It lasts for only half a second, but it's enough to make me feel bad for the guy. And it's enough to make me think he might be human again.

"Hey," I say, speaking to Warner directly for the first time. "So what, uh— What are you doing here?"

Warner looks at me like I'm an insect. His signature look. "What do you think I'm doing here?"

"Really?" I say, unable to hide my surprise. "That's so decent of you. I didn't think you'd be so . . . emotionally . . . responsible." I clear my throat. Smile at James. He's studying us curiously. "But I'm happy to be wrong, bro. And I'm sorry I misjudged you."

"I'm here to gather information," Warner says coldly.

"James is one of the only people who might be able to tell us where my father is located."

My compassion quickly turns to dust.

Catches fire.

Turns to rage.

"You're here to interrogate him?" I say, nearly shouting. "Are you insane? The kid has only barely recovered from unbelievable trauma, and you're here trying to mine him for information? He was probably *tortured*. He's a freaking *child*. What the hell is wrong with you?"

Warner is unmoved by my theatrics. "He was not tortured."

That stops me cold.

I turn to James. "You weren't?"

James shakes his head. "Not exactly."

"Huh." I frown. "I mean, don't get me wrong—I'm thrilled—but if he didn't torture you, what did Anderson do with you?"

James shrugs. "He mostly left me in solitary confinement. They didn't beat me," he says, rubbing absently at his ribs, "but the guards were pretty rough. And they didn't feed me much." He shrugs again. "But honestly, the worst part was not seeing Adam."

I pull James into my arms again, hold him tight. "I'm so sorry," I say gently. "That sounds horrible. And they wouldn't let you see Adam at all? Not even once?" I pull back. Look him in the eye. "I'm so, so sorry. I'm sure he's okay, little man. We'll find him. Don't worry."

Warner makes a sound. A sound that seems almost like a laugh.

I spin around angrily. "What the hell is wrong with you?" I say. "This isn't funny."

"Isn't it? I find the situation hilarious."

I'm about to say something to Warner I really shouldn't say in front of a ten-year-old, but when I glance back at James, I pull up short. James is rapidly shaking his head at me, his bottom lip trembling. He looks like he's about to cry again.

I turn back to Warner. "Okay, what is going on?"

Warner almost smiles when he says, "They weren't kidnapped."

My eyebrows fly up my forehead. "Say what now?"

"They weren't kidnapped."

"I don't understand."

"Of course you don't."

"This is not the time, bro. Tell me what's going on."

"Kent tracked down Anderson on his own," Warner says, his gaze shifting to James. "He offered his allegiance in exchange for protection."

My entire body goes slack. I nearly fall off the bed.

Warner goes on: "Kent wasn't lying when he said he would try for amnesty. But he left out the part about being a traitor."

"No. No way. No fucking way."

"There was never an abduction," Warner says. "No kidnapping. Kent bartered himself in exchange for James's protection."

This time, I actually fall off **the bed.** "**Barter** himself—how?" I manage to drag myself **up off the floor,** stumbling to my feet. "What does Adam **even have to** barter with? Anderson already knows all our **secrets."**

It's James who says quietly, "He gave **them** his power."

I stare at the kid, blinking like an idiot.

"I don't understand," I say. "How can you give someone your power? You can't just give someone your power. Right? It's not like a pair of pants you can just take off and hand over."

"No," Warner says. "But it's something The Reestablishment knows how to harvest. How else do you think my father took Sonya's and Sara's healing powers?"

"Adam told them what he can d-do," James says, his voice breaking. "He told them that he can use his power to turn other people's powers off. He thought it m-might be useful to them."

"Imagine the possibilities," Warner says, affecting awe. "Imagine how they might weaponize a power like that for global use—how they could make such a thing so powerful they could effectively shut down every single rebel group in the world. Reduce their *Unnatural* opposition to zero."

"Jesus fucking Christ."

I think I'm going to pass out. I actually feel faint. Dizzy. Like I can't breathe. Like this is impossible. "No way," I'm saying. I'm practically breathing the words. "No way. Not possible."

"I once said that Kent's ability was useless," Warner says

quietly. "But I see now that I was a fool."

"He didn't want to do it," James says. He's actively crying now, the silent tears moving down his face. "I swear he only did it to save me. He offered the only thing he had—the only thing he thought they'd want—to keep me safe. I know he didn't want to do it. He was just desperate. He thought he was doing the right thing. He kept telling me he was going to keep me safe."

"By running into the arms of the man who abused him his whole life?" I'm clutching my hair in my hands. "This doesn't make any sense. How does this— *How*—? *How?*"

I look up suddenly, realizing.

"And then look what he did," I say, stunned. "After everything, Anderson still used you as bait. He brought you here as leverage. He would've *killed* you, even after everything Adam gave up."

"Kent was a desperate idiot," Warner says. "That he was ever willing to trust my father with James's well-being tells you exactly how far gone he was."

"He was desperate, but he's not an idiot," James says angrily, his eyes refilling with tears. "He loves me and he was just trying to keep me safe. I'm so worried about him. I'm so scared something happened to him. And I'm so scared Anderson did something awful to him." James swallows, hard. "What are we going to do now? How are we going to get Adam and Juliette back?"

I squeeze my eyes shut, try to take deep breaths. "Listen, don't stress about this, okay? We're going to get them back.

And when we do, I'm going to murder Adam myself."

James gasps.

"Ignore him," Warner says. "He doesn't mean it."

"Yes, I damn well do mean it."

Warner pretends not to hear me. "According to the information I gathered just moments before you barged in here," he says calmly, "it sounds like my father was holding court back in Sector 45, just as Sam predicated. But he won't be there now, of that I'm certain."

"How can you be certain of *anything* right now?"

"Because I know my father," he says. "I know what matters most to him. And I know that when he left here, he was severely, gruesomely injured. There's only one place he'd go in a state like that."

I blink at him. "Where?"

"Oceania. Back to Maximillian Sommers, the only person capable of piecing him back together."

That stops me dead. *"Oceania?* Please tell me you're joking. We have to go back to Oceania?" I groan. "Dammit. That means we have to steal another plane."

"We," he says, irritated, "aren't doing anything."

"Of course we—"

Just then, the girls walk in. They come up short at the sight of me and Warner. Two sets of eyes blink at us.

"What are you doing here?" they ask at the same time.

Warner is on his feet in an instant. "I was just leaving."

"I think you mean *we* were just leaving," I say sharply.

Warner ignores me, nods at James, and heads for the

door. I'm following him out of the room before I remember, suddenly—

"James," I say, spinning around. "You're going to be okay, you know that, right? We're going to find Adam and bring him home and make all of this okay. Your job from here on out is to relax and eat chocolate and sleep. All right? Don't worry about anything. Do you understand?"

James blinks at me. He nods.

"Good." I step forward to plant a kiss on the top of his head. "Good," I say again. "You're going to be just fine. Everything is going to be fine. I'm going to make sure everything is fine, okay?"

James stares up at me. "Okay," he says, wiping away the last of his tears.

"Good," I say for the third time, and nod, still staring at his small, innocent face. "Okay, I'm going to go make that happen now. Cool?"

Finally, James smiles. "Cool."

I smile back, giving him everything I've got, and then dart out the door, hoping to catch Warner before he tries to rescue J without me.

~~ELLA~~ JULIETTE

It is a relief not to speak.

Something changed between us this morning, something broke. Anderson seems relaxed in front of me in a way that seems unorthodox, but it's not my business to question him. I'm honored to have this position, to be his most trusted supreme soldier, and that's all that matters. Today is my first official day of work, and I'm happy to be here, even when he ignores me completely.

In fact, I enjoy it.

I find comfort in pretending to disappear. I exist only to shadow him as he moves from one task to another. I stand aside, staring straight ahead. I do not watch him as he works, but I feel him, constantly. He takes up all available space. I am attuned to his every movement, his every sound. It is my job now to know him completely, to anticipate his needs and fears, to protect him with my life, and to serve his interests entirely.

So I listen, for hours, to the details.

The creak of his chair as he leans back, considering. The sighs that escape him as he types. Leather chair and wool pants meeting, shifting. The dull thud of a ceramic mug hitting the surface of a wooden desk. The tinkle of crystal, the quick pour of bourbon. The sharp, sweet scent of tobacco and the rustle of tissue-thin paper. Keystrokes. A pen scratching. The sudden tear and fizz of a match. Sulfur. Keystrokes. A snap of a rubber band. Smoke, making my eyes tear. A stack of papers slapping together like a settling deck of cards. His voice, deep and melodic on a series of phone calls so brief I can't tell them apart. Keystrokes. He never seems to require use of the bathroom. I do not think about my own needs, and he does not ask. Keystrokes. Occasionally he looks up at me, studying me, and I keep my eyes straight ahead. Somehow, I can feel his smile.

I am a ghost.

I wait.

I hear little. I learn little.

Finally—

"Come."

He's on his feet and out the door and I hasten to follow. We're up high, on the top floor of the compound. The hallways circle around an interior courtyard, in the center of which is a large tree, branches heavy with orange and red leaves. Fall colors. I glance, without moving my head, outside one of the many tall windows gracing the halls, and my mind registers the incongruence of the two images. Outside, things are a strange mix of green and desolate. Inside, this tree is warm and rosy-hued. Perfect autumn foliage.

I shake off the thought.

I have to walk twice as fast to keep up with Anderson's

long strides. He stops for no one. Men and women in lab coats jump aside as we approach, mumbling apologies in our wake, and I'm surprised by the giddy sensation that rises up inside of me. I like their fear. I enjoy this power, this feeling of unapologetic dominion.

Dopamine floods my brain.

I pick up speed, still hurrying to keep up. It occurs to me then that Anderson never looks back to make sure I'm following him, and it makes me wonder what he'd do if he discovered I was missing. And then, just as quickly, the thought strikes me as bizarre. He has no reason to look back. I would never go missing.

The compound feels busier than usual today. Announcements blare through the speakers and the air around me fills with fervor. Names are called; demands made. People come and go.

We take the stairs.

Anderson never stops, never seems out of breath. He moves with the strength of a younger man but with the kind of confidence acquired only by age. He carries himself with a certainty both terrifying and aspirational. Faces pale at the sight of him. Most look away. Some can't help but stare. One woman nearly faints when his body brushes against hers, and Anderson doesn't even break his stride when she causes a scene.

I am fascinated.

The speakers crackle. A smooth, robotic female voice announces a code-green situation so calmly I can't help but be surprised by the collective reaction. I witness something akin to chaos as doors slam open around the building. It all seems to happen in sync, a domino effect echoing along corridors from top to bottom of the compound. Men and women in lab coats surge and swarm all levels, jamming the walkways as they scuttle along.

Still, Anderson does not stop. The world revolves around him, makes room for him. Slows when he speeds up. He does not accommodate anyone. Anything.

I am taking notes.

Finally, we reach a door. Anderson presses his hand against the biometric scanner, then peers into a camera that reads his eyes.

The door fissures open.

I smell something sterile, like antiseptic, and the moment we step into the room the scent burns my nose, causing my eyes to tear. The entrance is unusual; a short hallway that hides the rest of the room from immediate view. As we approach, I hear three monitors beep at three different decibel levels. When we round the corner, the room quadruples in size. The space is vast and bright, natural light combining with the searing white glow of artificial bulbs overhead.

There's little else here but a single bed and the figure strapped into it. The beeping is coming not from three machines, but seven, all of which seem to be affixed to the unconscious body of a boy. I don't know him, but he can't be much older than I am. His hair is cropped close to his scalp, a soft buzz of brown interrupted only by the wires drilled into his skull. There's a sheet pulled up to his neck, so I can't see much more than his resting face, but the sight of him there, strapped down like that, reminds me of something.

A flash of memory flares through me.

It's vague, distorted. I try to peel back the hazy layers, but when I manage a glimpse of something—a cave, a tall black man, a tank full of water—I feel a sharp, electrifying sting of rage that leaves my hands shaking. It unmoors me.

I take a jerky step back and shake my head a fraction of an inch, trying to compose myself, but my mind feels foggy, confused. When I finally pull myself together, I realize Anderson is watching me.

Slowly, he takes a step forward, his eyes narrowed in my direction. He says nothing, but I feel, without knowing why, exactly, that I'm not allowed to look away. I'm supposed to maintain eye contact for as long as he wants. It's brutal.

"You felt something when you walked in here," he says.

It's not a question. I'm not sure it requires an answer. Still—

"Nothing of consequence, sir."

"Consequence," he says, a hint of a smile playing at his lips. He takes a few steps toward one of the massive windows, clasps his hands behind his back. For a while, he's silent.

"So interesting," he says finally. "That we never did discuss consequences."

Fear slithers, creeps up my spine.

He's still staring out the window when he says softly, "You will not withhold anything from me. Everything you feel, every emotion you experience—it belongs to me. Do you understand?"

"Yes, sir."

"You felt something when you walked in here," he says again. This time, his voice is heavy with something, something dark and terrifying.

"Yes, sir."

"And what was it?"

"I felt anger, sir."

He turns around at that. Raises his eyebrows.

"After anger, I felt confusion."

"But anger," he says, stepping toward me. "Why anger?"

"I don't know, sir."

"Do you recognize this boy?" he says, pointing at the prone body without even looking at it.

"No, sir."

"No." His jaw clenches. "But he reminds you of someone."

I hesitate. Tremors threaten, and I will them away. Anderson's gaze is so intense I can hardly meet his eyes.

I glance again at the boy's sleeping face.

"Yes, sir."

Anderson's eyes narrow. He waits for more.

"Sir," I say quietly. "He reminds me of you."

Unexpectedly, Anderson goes still. Surprise rearranges his expression and suddenly, startlingly—

He laughs.

It's a laugh so genuine it seems to shock him even more than it shocks me. Eventually, the laughter settles into a smile. Anderson shoves his hands in his pockets and leans against the window frame. He stares at me with something resembling fascination, and it's such a pure moment, a moment so untainted by malice that he strikes me, suddenly, as beautiful.

More than that.

The sight of him—something about his eyes, something about the way he moves, the way he smiles— The sight of him suddenly stirs something in my heart. Ancient heat. A kaleidoscope of dead butterflies kicked up by a brief, dry gust of wind.

It leaves me feeling sick.

The stony look returns to his face. "That. Right there." He draws a circle in the air with his index finger. "That look on your face. What was that?"

My eyes widen. Unease floods through me, heating my cheeks.

For the first time, I falter.

He moves swiftly, charging toward me so angrily I wonder at my ability to remain steady. Roughly, he takes my chin in his hand, tilts up my face. There are no secrets here, this close to him. I can hide nothing.

"Now," he says, his voice low. Angry. "Tell me now."

I break eye contact, trying desperately to gather my thoughts, and he barks at me to look at him.

I force myself to meet his eyes. And then I hate myself,

hate my mouth for betraying my mind. Hate my mind for thinking at all.

"You— You are extremely handsome, sir."

Anderson drops his hand like he's been burned. He backs away, looking, for the first time—

Uncomfortable.

"Are you—" He stops, frowns. And then, too soon, anger clouds his expression. His voice is practically a growl when he says, "You are lying to me."

"No, sir." I hate the sound of my voice, the breathy panic.

His eyes sharpen. He must see something in my expression that gives him pause, because the anger evaporates from his face.

He blinks at me.

Then, carefully, he says: "In the middle of all of this"— he waves around the room, at the sleeping figure hooked up to the machines—"of all the things that could be going through your mind, you were thinking . . . that you find me attractive."

A traitorous heat floods my face. "Yes, sir."

Anderson frowns.

He seems about to say something, and then hesitates. For the first time, he seems unmoored.

A few seconds of tortured silence stretch between us, and I'm not sure how best to proceed.

"This is unsettling," Anderson finally says, and mostly to himself. He presses two fingers to the inside of his wrist, and lifts his wrist to his mouth.

"Yes," he says quietly. "Tell Max there's been an unusual development. I need to see him at once."

Anderson spares me a brief glance before dismissing, with a single shake of his head, the entire mortifying exchange.

He stalks toward the boy strapped down on the bed and says, "This young man is part of an ongoing experiment."

I'm not sure what to say, so I say nothing.

Anderson bends over the boy, toying with various wires, and then stiffens, suddenly. Looks up at me out of the corner of his eye. "Can you imagine why this boy is part of an experiment?"

"No sir."

"He has a gift," Anderson says, straightening. "He came to me voluntarily and offered to share it with me."

I blink, still uncertain how to respond.

"But there are many of you—*Unnaturals*—running wild on this planet," Anderson says. "So many powers. So many different abilities. Our asylums are teeming with them, overrun with power. I have access to nearly anything I want. So what makes him special, hmm?" He tilts his head at me. "What power could he possibly have that would be greater than yours? More useful?"

Again, I say nothing.

"Do you want to know?" he asks, a hint of a smile touching his lips.

This feels like a trick. I consider my options.

Finally, I say, "I want to know only if you want to tell me, sir."

Anderson's smile blooms. White teeth. Genuine pleasure.

I feel my chest warm at his quiet praise. Pride straightens my shoulders. I avert my eyes, staring quietly at the wall.

Still, I see Anderson turn away again, appraising the boy with another single, careful look. "These powers were wasted on him anyway."

He removes the touchpad slotted into a compartment of the boy's bed and begins tapping the digital screen, scrolling and scanning for information. He looks up, once, at the monitors beeping out various vitals, and frowns. Finally, he sighs, dragging a hand through his perfectly arranged hair. I think it looks better for being mussed. Warmer. Softer. Familiar.

The observation frightens me.

I turn away sharply and glance out the window, wondering, suddenly, if I will ever be allowed to use the bathroom.

"Juliette."

The angry timbre of his voice sends my heart racing. I straighten in an instant. Look straight ahead.

"Yes, sir," I say, sounding a little breathless.

I realize then that he's not even looking at me. He's still typing something into the touchpad when he says, calmly, "Were you daydreaming?"

"No, sir."

He returns the touchpad to its compartment, the pieces connecting with a satisfying metallic *click*.

He looks up.

"This is growing tiresome," he says quietly. "I'm already losing patience with you, and we haven't even come to the end of your first day." He hesitates. "Do you want to know what happens when I lose patience with you, Juliette?"

My fingers tremble; I clench them into fists. "No, sir."

He holds out his hand. "Then give me what belongs to me."

I take an uncertain step forward and his outstretched hand flies up, palm out, stopping me in place. His jaw clenches.

"I am referring to your mind," he says. "I want to know what you were thinking when you lost your head long enough to gaze out the window. I want to know what you are thinking right now. I will always want to know what you're thinking," he says sharply. "In every moment. I want every word, every detail, every emotion. Every single loose, fluttering thought that passes through your head, I want it," he says, stalking toward me. "Do you understand? It's mine. You are *mine*."

He comes to a halt just inches from my face.

"Yes, sir," I say, my voice failing me.

"I will only ask this once more," he says, making an effort to moderate his voice. "And if you ever make me work this hard again to get the answers I need, you will be punished. Is that clear?"

"Yes, sir."

A muscle jumps in his jaw. His eyes narrow. "What were you daydreaming about?"

I swallow. Look at him. Look away.

Quietly, I say:

"I was wondering, sir, if you would ever let me use the bathroom."

Anderson's face goes suddenly blank.

He seems stunned. He regards me a moment longer before saying, flatly: "You were wondering if you could use the bathroom."

"Yes, sir." My face heats.

Anderson crosses his arms across his chest. "That's all?"

I feel suddenly compelled to tell him what I thought about his hair, but I fight against the urge. Guilt floods through me at the indulgence, but my mind is soothed by a strange, familiar warmth, and suddenly I feel no guilt at all for being only partly truthful.

"Yes, sir. That's all."

Anderson tilts his head at me. "No new surges of anger? No questions about what we're doing here? No concerns over the well-being of the boy"—he points—"or the powers he might have?"

"No, sir."

"I see," he says.

I stare.

Anderson takes a deep breath and undoes a button of his blazer. He pushes both hands through his hair. Begins to pace.

He's becoming flustered, I realize, and I don't know what to do about it.

"It's almost funny," he says. "This is exactly what I wanted, and yet, somehow, I'm disappointed."

He takes a deep, sharp breath, and spins around.

Studies me.

"What would you do," he says, nodding his head an inch to his left, "if I asked you to throw yourself out that window?"

I turn, examining the large window looming over us both.

It's a massive, circular stained glass window that takes up half the wall. Colors scatter across the ground, creating a beautiful, distracted work of art over the polished concrete floors. I walk over to window, run my fingers along the ornate panes of glass. I peer down at the expanse of green below. We're at least five hundred feet above the ground, but the distance doesn't inspire my fear. I could make that jump easily, without injury.

I look up. "I would do it with pleasure, sir."

He takes a step closer. "What if I asked you to do it without using your powers? What if it was simply my desire that you throw yourself out the window?"

A wave of searing, blistering heat moves through me, seals shut my mouth. Binds my arms. I can't pry my own mouth open against the terrifying assault, but I can only imagine it's part of this challenge.

Anderson must be trying to test my allegiance.

He must be trying to trap me into a moment of disobedience. Which means I need to prove myself. My loyalty.

It takes an extraordinary amount of my own supernatural strength to fight back the invisible forces clamping my mouth shut, but I manage it. And when I can finally speak, I say,

"I would do it with pleasure, sir."

Anderson takes yet another step closer, his eyes glittering with something— Something brand-new. Something akin to wonder.

"Would you, really?" he says softly.

"Yes, sir."

"Would you do anything I asked you to do? Anything at all?"

"Yes, sir."

Anderson's still holding my gaze when he lifts his wrist to his mouth again and says quietly:

"Come in here. Now."

He drops his hand.

My heart begins to pound. Anderson refuses to look away from me, his eyes growing bluer and brighter by the second. It's almost like he knows that his eyes alone are enough to upset my equilibrium. And then, without warning, he grabs my wrist. I realize too late that he's checking my pulse.

"So fast," he says softly. "Like a little bird. Tell me, Juliette. Are you afraid?"

"No, sir."

"Are you excited?"

"I— I don't know, sir."

The door slides open and Anderson drops my wrist. For

the first time in minutes, Anderson looks away from me, finally breaking some painful, invisible connection between us. My body goes slack with relief and, remembering myself, I quickly straighten.

A man walks in.

Dark hair, dark eyes, pale skin. He's young, younger than Anderson, I think, but older than me. He wears a headset. He looks uncertain.

"Juliette," Anderson says, "this is Darius."

I turn to face Darius.

Darius says nothing. He looks paralyzed.

"I won't be requiring Darius's services anymore," Anderson says, glancing in my direction.

Darius blanches. Even from where I'm standing, I can see his body begin to tremble.

"Sir?" I say, confused.

"Isn't it obvious?" Anderson says. "I would like you to dispose of him."

Understanding dawns. "Certainly, sir."

The moment I turn in Darius's direction, he screams; it's a sharp, bloodcurdling sound that irritates my ears. He makes a run for the door and I pivot quickly, throwing out my arm to stop him. The force of my power sends him flying the rest of the way to the exit, his body slamming hard against the steel wall.

He slumps, with a soft moan, to the ground.

I open my palm. He screams.

Power surges through me, filling my blood with fire. The

feeling is intoxicating. Delicious.

I lift my hand and Darius's body lifts off the floor, his head thrown back in agony, his body run through by invisible rods. He continues to scream and the sound fills my ears, floods my body with endorphins. My skin hums with his energy. I close my eyes.

Then I close my fist.

Fresh screams pierce the silence, echoing around the vast, cavernous space. I feel a smile tugging at my lips and I lose myself in the feeling, in the freedom of my own power. There's a joy in this, in using my strength so freely, in finally letting go.

Bliss.

My eyes flutter open but I feel drugged, deliriously happy as I watch his seized, suspended body begin to convulse. Blood spurts from his nose, bubbles up inside his open, gasping mouth. He's choking. Nearly dead. And I'm just beginning t—

The fire leaves my body so suddenly it sends me stumbling backward.

Darius falls, with a bone-cracking thud, to the floor.

A desperate emptiness burns through me, leaves me feeling faint. I hold my hands up as if in prayer, trying to figure out what happened, feeling suddenly close to tears. I spin around, trying to understand—

Anderson is pointing a weapon at me.

I drop my hands.

Anderson drops his weapon.

Power surges through me once more and I take a deep, grateful breath, finding relief in the feeling as it floods my senses, refilling my veins. I blink several times, trying to clear my head, but it's Darius's pathetic, agonized whimpers that bring me back to the present moment. I stare at his broken body, the shallow pools of blood on the floor. I feel vaguely annoyed.

"Incredible."

I turn around.

Anderson is staring at me with unvarnished amazement. "Incredible," he says again. "That was incredible."

I stare at him, uncertain.

"How do you feel?" he asks.

"Disappointed, sir."

His eyebrows pull together. "Why disappointed?"

I glance at Darius. "Because he's still alive, sir. I didn't complete the task."

Anderson's face breaks into a smile so wide it electrifies his features. He looks young. He looks kind. He looks wonderful.

"My God," he says softly. "You're perfect."

KENJI

"Hey," I call out. "Wait up!"

I'm still sprinting after Warner and, in a move that surprises absolutely no one, he doesn't wait. He doesn't even slow down. In fact, I'm pretty sure he speeds up.

I realize, as I pick up the pace, that I haven't felt fresh air in a couple of days. I look around as I go, trying to take in the details. The sky is bluer than I've ever seen it. There's no cloud in sight for miles. I don't know if this weather is unique to the geographical location of Sector 241, or if it's just regular climate change. Regardless, I take a deep breath. Air feels good.

I was getting claustrophobic in the dining hall, spending endless hours with the ill and injured. The colors of the room had begun to bleed together, all the linen and ash-colored cots and the too-bright, unnatural light. The smells were intense, too. Blood and bleach. Antiseptic. It was making my head swim. I woke up with a massive headache this morning—though, to be fair, I wake up with a massive headache almost every morning—but being outside is beginning to soothe the ache.

Who knew.

It's nice out here, even if it's a little hot in this outfit. I'm

229

wearing a pair of old fatigues I found in my room. Sam and Nouria made sure from the start that we had everything we needed—even now, even after the battle. We have toiletries. Clean clothes.

Warner, on the other hand—

I squint at his retreating figure. I can't believe he still hasn't taken a shower. He's still wearing Haider's leather jacket, but it's practically destroyed. His black pants are torn, his face still smudged with what I can only imagine is a combination of blood and dirt. His hair is wild. His boots are dull. And somehow—*somehow*—he still manages to look put together. I don't get it.

I slow my pace when I pull up next to him, but I'm still power walking. Breathing hard. Beginning to sweat.

"Hey," I say, pinching my shirt away from my chest, where it's starting to stick. The weather is getting weirder; it's suddenly sweltering. I wince upward, toward the sun.

Here, within the Sanctuary, I've been getting a better idea of the state of our world. News flash: The earth is still basically going to shit. The Reestablishment has just been taking advantage of the aforementioned shit, making things seem irreparably bad.

The truth, on the other hand, is that they're only reparably bad.

Ha.

"Hey," I say again, this time clapping Warner on the shoulder. He shoves off my hand with so much enthusiasm I nearly stumble.

"Okay, listen, I know you're upset, but—"

Warner suddenly disappears.

"Hey, where the hell are you going?" I shout, my voice ringing out. "Are you heading back to your room? Should I just meet you there?"

A couple of people turn to stare at me.

The normally busy paths are pretty empty right now because so many of us are still convalescing, but the few people lingering in the bright sun shoot me dirty looks.

Like I'm the weirdo.

"Leave him alone," someone hisses at me. "He's grieving."

I roll my eyes.

"Hey—*douche bag*," I shout, hoping Warner's still close enough to hear me. "I know you love her, but so do I, and I'm—"

Warner reappears so close to my face I nearly scream. I take a sudden, terrified step backward.

"If you value your life," he says, "don't come near me."

I'm about to point out that he's being dramatic, but he cuts me off.

"I didn't say that to be dramatic. I didn't even say it to scare you. I'm saying it out of respect for Ella, because I know she'd rather I didn't kill you."

I'm quiet for a full second. And then I frown.

"Are you fucking with me right now? You're definitely fucking with me right now. Right?"

Warner's eyes go flinty. Electric. That scary kind of crazy.

"Every single time you claim to understand even a fraction of what I'm feeling, I want to disembowel you. I want to sever your carotid artery. I want to rip out your vertebrae, one by one. You have no idea what it is to love her," he says angrily. "You couldn't even begin to imagine. So stop trying to understand."

Wow, sometimes I really hate this guy.

I have to literally clench my jaw to keep myself from saying what I'm really thinking right now, which is that I want to put my fist through his skull. (I actually imagine it for a moment, imagine what it'd be like to crush his head like a walnut. It's oddly satisfying.) But then I remember that we need this asshole, and that J's life is on the line. The fate of the world is on the line.

So I fight back my anger and try again.

"Listen," I say, making an effort to gentle my voice. "I know what you guys have is special. I know that I can't really understand that kind of love. I mean, hell, I know you were even thinking about proposing to her—and that must've—"

"I did propose to her."

I suddenly stiffen.

I can tell just by the sound of his voice that he's not joking. And I can tell by the look on his face—the infinitesimal flash of misery in his eyes—that this is my opening. This is the data I've been missing. This is the source of the agony that's been drowning him.

I scan the immediate area for eavesdroppers. Yep. Too many new members of the Warner fan club clutching their hearts.

"Come on," I say to him. "I'm taking you to lunch."

Warner blinks, confusion temporarily clearing his anger. And then, sharply: "I'm not hungry."

"That's obviously bullshit." I look him up and down. He looks good—he always looks good, the asshole—but he looks hungry. Not just the regular kind of hungry, either, but that desperate hunger that's so hungry it doesn't even feel like hunger anymore.

"You haven't eaten anything in days," I say to him. "And you know better than I do that you'll be useless on a rescue mission if you pass out before you even get there."

He glares at me.

"Come on, bro. You want J to come home to skin and bones? The way you're going, she'll take one look at you and run screaming in the opposite direction. This is not a good look. All these muscles need to eat." I poke at his bicep. "Feed your children."

Warner jerks away from me and takes a long, irritated breath. The sound of it almost makes me smile. Feels like old times.

I think I'm making progress.

Because this time, when I tell him to follow me, he doesn't fight.

~~ELLA~~

JULIETTE

Anderson takes me to meet Max.

I follow him down into the bowels of the compound, through winding, circuitous paths. Anderson's steps echo along the stone and steel walkways, the lights flickering as we go. The occasional, overly bright lights cast stark shadows in strange shapes. I feel my skin prickle.

My mind wanders.

A flash of Darius's limp body blazes in my mind, carrying with it a sharp twinge that twists my gut. I fight against an impulse to vomit, even as I feel the contents of my meager breakfast coming up my throat. With effort, I force back the bile. Sweat beads along my forehead, the back of my neck.

My body is screaming to stop moving. My lungs want to expand, collect air. I allow neither.

I force myself to keep walking.

I wick away the images, expunging thoughts of Darius from my mind. The churning in my stomach begins to slow, but in its wake my skin takes on a damp, clammy sensation. I struggle to recount the things I ate this morning. I must've eaten poorly; something isn't agreeing with my stomach. I feel feverish.

I blink.

I blink again, but this time for too long and I see a flash of blood, bubbling up inside Darius's open mouth. The nausea returns with a swiftness that scares me. I suck in a breath, my fingers fluttering, desperate to press against my stomach. Somehow, I hold steady. I keep my eyes open, widening them to the point of pain. My heart starts pounding. I try desperately to maintain control over my spiraling thoughts, but my skin begins to crawl. I clench my fists. Nothing helps. Nothing helps. *Nothing*, I think.

nothing

nothing

nothing

I begin to count the lights we pass.

I count my fingers. I count my breaths. I count my footsteps, measuring the force of every footfall that thunders up my legs, reverberates around my hips.

I remember that Darius is still alive.

He was carried away, ostensibly to be patched up and returned to his former position. Anderson didn't seem to mind that Darius was still alive. Anderson was only testing me, I realized. Testing me, once again, to make sure that I was obedient to him and him alone.

I take in a deep, fortifying breath.

I focus on Anderson's retreating figure. For reasons I can't explain, staring at him steadies me. Slows my pulse. Settles my stomach. And from this vantage point, I can't help but admire the way he moves. He has an impressive, muscular frame—broad shoulders, narrow waist, strong legs—but I marvel most at the way he carries himself. He has a confident stride. He walks tall, with smooth, effortless efficiency. As I watch him, a familiar feeling flutters through me. It gathers in my stomach, sparking dim heat that sends a brief shock to my heart.

I don't fight it.

There's something about him. Something about his face. His carriage. I find myself moving unconsciously closer to him, watching him almost too intently. I've noticed that he wears no jewelry, not even a watch. He has a faded scar between his right thumb and index finger. His hands are rough and callused. His dark hair is shot through with silver, the extent of which is only visible up close. His eyes are the blue-green of shallow, turquoise waters. Unusual.

Aquamarine.

He has long brown lashes and laugh lines. Full, curving lips. His skin grows rougher as the day wears on, the shadow of facial hair hinting at a version of him I try and fail to imagine.

I realize I'm beginning to like him. Trust him.

Suddenly, he stops. We're standing outside a steel door, next to which is a keypad and biometric scanner.

He brings his wrist to his mouth. "Yes." A pause. "I'm outside."

I feel my own wrist vibrate. I look down, surprised, at the blue light flashing through the skin at my pulse.

I'm being summoned.

This is strange. Anderson is standing right next to me;

I thought he was the only one with the authority to summon me.

"Sir?" I say.

He glances back, his eyebrows raised as if to say— *Yes?* And something that feels like happiness blooms to life inside of me. I know it's unwise to make so much of so little, but his movements and expressions feel suddenly softer now, more casual. It's clear that he's begun to trust me, too.

I lift my wrist to show him the message. He frowns.

He steps closer to me, taking my flashing arm in his hands. The tips of his fingers press against my skin as he gently bends back the joint, his eyes narrowing as he studies the summons. I go unnaturally still. He makes a sound of irritation and exhales, his breath skittering across my skin.

A bolt of sensation moves through me.

He's still holding my arm when he speaks into his own wrist. "Tell Ibrahim to back off. I have it under control."

In the silence, Anderson tilts his head, listening on an earpiece that isn't readily visible. I can only watch. Wait.

"I don't care," he says angrily, his fingers closing unconsciously around my wrist. I gasp, surprised, and he turns, our eyes meeting, clashing.

Anderson frowns.

His pleasant, masculine scent fills my head and I breathe him in almost without meaning to. Being this close to him is difficult. Strange. My head is swimming with confusion.

Broken images flood my mind—a flash of golden hair, fingers grazing bare skin—and then nausea. Dizziness.

It nearly knocks me over.

I look away just as Anderson tugs my arm up, toward a floodlight, squinting to get a better look. Our bodies nearly touch, and I'm suddenly so close I can see the edges of a tattoo, dark and curving, creeping up the edge of his collarbone.

My eyes widen in surprise. Anderson lets go of my wrist.

"I already know it was him," he says, speaking quickly, his eyes darting at and away from me. "His code is in the timestamp." A pause. "Just clear the summons. And then remind him that she reports only to me. I decide if and when he gets to talk to her."

He drops his wrist. Touches a finger to his temple.

And then, narrows his eyes at me.

My heart jumps. I straighten. I no longer wait to be prompted. When he looks at me like that, I know it's my cue to confess.

"You have a tattoo, sir. I was surprised. I wondered what it was."

Anderson raises an eyebrow at me.

He seems about to speak when, finally, the steel door exhales open. A curl of steam escapes the doorway, behind which emerges a man. He's tall, taller than Anderson, with wavy brown hair, light brown skin, and light, bright eyes the color of which aren't immediately obvious. He wears a white lab coat. Tall rubber boots. A face mask hangs around his neck, and a dozen pens have been shoved into the pocket of his coat. He makes no effort to move forward or to step aside; he only stands in the doorway, seemingly undecided.

241

"What's going on?" Anderson says. "I sent you a message an hour ago and you never showed up. Then I come to your door and you make me wait."

The man—Anderson told me his name was Max—says nothing. Instead, he appraises me, his eyes moving up and down my body in a show of undisguised hatred. I'm not sure how to process his reaction.

Anderson sighs, grasping something that isn't obvious to me.

"Max," he says quietly. "You can't be serious."

Max shoots Anderson a sharp look. "Unlike you, we're not all made of stone." And then, looking away: "At least not entirely."

I'm surprised to discover that Max has an accent, one not unlike the citizens of Oceania. Max must originate from this region.

Anderson sighs again.

"All right," Max says coolly. "What did you want to discuss?" He pulls a pen out of his pocket, uncapping it with his teeth. He reaches into his other pocket and pulls free a notebook. Flips it open.

I go suddenly blind.

In the span of a single instant darkness floods my vision. Clears. Hazy images reappear, time speeding up and slowing down in fits and starts. Colors streak across my eyes, dilate my pupils. Stars explode, lights flashing, sparking. I hear voices. A single voice. A whisper—

242

I am a thief

The tape rewinds. Plays back. The file corrupts.

I am
I am
I I I
am
a thief
a thief I stole
I stole this notebook andthispenfromoneofthedoctors

"Of course you did."

Anderson's sharp voice brings me back to the present moment. My heart is beating in my throat. Fear presses against my skin, conjuring goose bumps along my arms. My eyes move too quickly, darting around in distress until they rest, finally, on Anderson's familiar face.

He's not looking at me. He's not even speaking to me.

Quiet relief floods through me at the realization. My interlude lasted but a moment, which means I haven't missed much more than a couple of exchanged words. Max turns to me, studying me curiously.

"Come inside," he says, and disappears through the door.

I follow Anderson through the entryway, and as soon as I cross the threshold, a blast of icy air sends a shiver up my skin. I don't make it much farther than the entrance before I'm distracted.

Amazed.

Steel and glass are responsible for most of the structures in the space—massive screens and monitors; microscopes; long glass tables littered with beakers and half-filled test tubes. Accordion pipes sever vertical space around the room, connecting tabletops and ceilings. Blocks of artificial light fixtures are suspended in midair, humming steadily. The light temperature in here is so blue I don't know how Max can stand it.

I follow Max and Anderson over to a crescent-shaped desk that looks more like a command center. Papers are stacked on one side of the steel top, screens flickering above. More pens are stuffed into a chipped coffee mug sitting atop a thick book.

A *book*.

I haven't seen a relic like that in a long time.

Max takes his seat. He gestures at a stool tucked under a nearby table, and Anderson shakes his head.

I continue to stand.

"All right, then, go on," Max says, his eyes flickering in my direction. "You said there was a problem."

Anderson looks suddenly uncomfortable. He says nothing for so long that, eventually, Max smiles.

"Out with it," Max says, gesturing with his pen. "What did you do wrong this time?"

"I didn't do anything wrong," Anderson says sharply. Then he frowns. "I don't think so, anyway."

"Then what is it?"

Anderson takes a deep breath. Finally: "She says that she's . . . attracted to me."

Max's eyes widen. He glances from Anderson to me and then back again. And then, suddenly—

He laughs.

My face heats. I stare straight ahead, studying the strange equipment stacked on shelves against the far wall.

Out of the corner of my eye, I see Max scribbling in a notepad. All this modern technology, but he still seems to enjoy writing by hand. The observation strikes me as odd. I file the information away, not really understanding why.

"Fascinating," Max says, still smiling. He gives his head a quick shake. "Makes perfect sense, of course."

"I'm glad you think this is funny," Anderson says, visibly irritated. "But I don't like it."

Max laughs again. He leans back in his chair, his legs outstretched, crossed at the ankles. He's clearly intrigued— excited, even—by the development, and it's causing his earlier iciness to thaw. He bites down on the pen cap, considering Anderson. There's a glint in his eye.

"Do mine eyes deceive me," he says, "or does the great Paris Anderson admit to having a conscience? Or perhaps: a sense of morality?"

"You know better than anyone that I've never owned either, so I'm afraid I wouldn't know what it feels like."

"Touché."

"Anyway—"

"I'm sorry," Max says, his smile widening. "But I need

another moment with this revelation. Can you blame me for being fascinated? Considering the uncontested fact of your being one of the most depraved human beings I've ever known—and among our social circles, that's saying a lot—"

"Ha ha," Anderson says flatly.

"—I think I'm just surprised. Why is *this* too much? Why is this the line you won't cross? Of all the things . . ."

"Max, be serious."

"I am being serious."

"Aside from the obvious reasons why this situation should be disturbing to anyone— The girl's not even eighteen. Even I am not as depraved as that."

Max shakes his head. Holds up his pen. "Actually, she's been eighteen for four months."

Anderson seems about to argue, and then—

"Of course," he says. "I was remembering the wrong paperwork." He glances at me as he says it, and I feel my face grow hotter.

I am simultaneously confused and mortified.

Curious.

Horrified.

"Either way," Anderson says sharply, "I don't like it. Can you fix it?"

Max sits forward, crosses his arms. "Can I *fix* it? Can I fix the fact that she can't help but be attracted to the man who spawned the two faces she's known most intimately?" He shakes his head. Laughs again. "That kind of wiring isn't undone without incurring serious repercussions. Repercussions that would set us back."

"What kind of repercussions? Set us back how?"

Max glances at me. Glances at Anderson.

Anderson sighs. "Juliette," he barks.

"Yes, sir."

"Leave us."

"Yes, sir."

I pivot sharply and head for the exit. The door slides open in anticipation of my approach, but I hesitate, just a few feet away, when I hear Max laugh again.

I know I shouldn't eavesdrop. I know it's wrong. I know I'd be punished if I were caught. I know this.

Still, I can't seem to move.

My body is revolting, screaming at me to cross the threshold, but a pervasive heat has begun to seep into my mind, dulling the compulsion. I'm still frozen in front of the open door, trying to decide what to do, when their voices carry over.

"She clearly has a type," Max is saying. "At this point, it's practically written in her DNA."

Anderson says something I don't hear.

"Is it really such a bad thing?" Max says. "Perhaps her affection for you could work out in your favor. Take advantage of it."

"You think I'm so desperate for companionship—or so completely incompetent—that I'd need to result to seduction in order to get what I want out of the girl?"

Max barks out a laugh. "We both know you've never been desperate for companionship. But as to your competence . . ."

"I don't know why I even bother with you."

"It's been thirty years, Paris, and I'm still waiting for you to develop a sense of humor."

"It's been thirty years, Max, and you'd think I'd have found some new friends by now. Better ones."

"You know, your kids aren't funny, either," Max says, ignoring him. "Interesting how that works, isn't it?"

Anderson groans.

Max only laughs louder.

I frown.

I stand there, trying and failing to process their interactions. Max just insulted a supreme commander of The Reestablishment—multiple times. As Anderson's subordinate, he should be punished for speaking so disrespectfully. He should be fired, at the very least. Executed, if Anderson deems it preferable.

But when I hear the distant sound of Anderson's laughter, I realize that he and Max are laughing *together*. It's a realization that both startles and stuns me:

That they must be friends.

One of the overhead lights pops and hums, startling me out of my reverie. I give my head a quick shake and head out the door.

KENJI

I'm suddenly a big fan of the Warner groupies.

On our way back to my tent, I told only a couple of people I spotted on the path that Warner was hungry—but still not feeling well enough to join everyone in the dining hall—and they've been delivering packages of food to my room ever since. The problem is, all this kindness comes with a price. Six different girls (and two guys) have shown up so far, each one of them expecting payment for their generosity in the form of a conversation with Warner, which—obviously—never happens. But they usually settle for a good long look at him.

It's weird.

I mean, even I know, objectively, that Warner's not disgusting to look at, but this whole production of unabashed flirtation is really starting to feel weird. I'm not used to being in an environment where people openly admit to liking anything about Warner. Back at Omega Point—and even on base in Sector 45—everyone seemed to agree that he was a monster. No one denied their fear or disgust long enough to treat him like the kind of guy at whom they might bat their eyelashes.

But what's funny is: I'm the only one getting irritated.

251

Every time the doorbell rings I'm like, this is it, this is the time Warner is finally going to lose his mind and shoot someone, but he never even seems to notice. Of all the things that piss him off, gawking men and women don't appear to be on the list.

"So is this, like, normal for you, or what?" I'm still arranging food on plates in the little dining area of my room. Warner is standing stiffly in a random spot by the window. He chose that random spot when we walked in and he's just been standing there, staring at nothing, ever since.

"Is what normal for me?"

"All these people," I say, gesturing at the door. "Coming in here pretending they're not imagining you without your clothes on. Is that just, like, a normal day for you?"

"I think you're forgetting," he says quietly, "that I've been able to sense emotions for most of my life."

I raise my eyebrows. "So this *is* just a normal day for you."

He sighs. Stares out the window again.

"You're not even going to pretend it's not true?" I rip open a foil container. More potatoes. "You won't even pretend you don't know that the entire world finds you attractive?"

"Was that a confession?"

"You wish, dickhead."

"I find it boring," Warner says. "Besides, if I paid attention to every single person who found me attractive I'd never have time for anything else."

I nearly drop the potatoes.

I wait for him to crack a smile, to tell me he's joking, and when he doesn't, I shake my head, stunned.

"Wow," I say. "Your humility is a fucking inspiration."

He shrugs.

"Hey," I say, "speaking of things that disgust me— Do you maybe want to, like, wash a little bit of the blood off your face before we eat?"

Warner glares at me in response.

I hold up my hands. "Okay. Cool. That's fine." I point at him. "Actually, I heard that blood's good for you. You know—organic. Antioxidants and shit. Very popular with vampires."

"Are you able to hear the things you say out loud? Do you not realize how perfectly idiotic you sound?"

I roll my eyes. "All right, beauty queen, food's ready."

"I'm serious," he says. "Does it never occur to you to think things through before you speak? Does it never occur to you to cease speaking altogether? If it doesn't, it should."

"Come on, asswipe. Sit down."

Reluctantly, Warner makes his way over. He sits down and stares, blankly, at the meal in front of him.

I give him a few seconds of this before I say—

"Do you still remember how to do this? Or did you need me to feed you?" I stab a piece of tofu and point it in his direction. "Say *ah*. The tofu choo choo is coming."

"One more joke, Kishimoto, and I will remove your spine."

"You're right." I put down the fork. "I get it. I'm cranky when I'm hungry, too."

He looks up sharply.

"That wasn't a joke!" I say. "I'm being serious."

Warner sighs. Picks up his utensils. Looks longingly at the door.

I don't push my luck.

I keep my face on my food—I'm genuinely excited to be getting a second lunch—and wait until he takes several bites before I go for the jugular.

"So," I finally say. "You proposed, huh?"

Warner stops chewing and looks up. He strikes me, suddenly, as a young guy. Aside from the obvious need for a shower and a change of clothes, he looks like he's finally beginning to shed the tiniest, tiniest bit of tension. And I can tell by the way he's holding his knife and fork now— with a little more gusto—that I was right.

He was hungry.

I wonder what he would've done if I hadn't dragged him in here and sat him down. Forced him to eat.

Would he have just driven himself into the ground?

Accidentally died of hunger on his way to save Juliette?

He seems to have no real care for his physical self. No care for his own needs. It strikes me, suddenly, as bizarre. And concerning.

"Yes," he says quietly. "I proposed."

I'm seized by a knee-jerk reaction to tease him—to suggest that his bad mood makes sense now, that she probably turned him down—but even I know better than that. Whatever is happening in Warner's head right now is dark. Serious. And I need to handle this part of the conversation with care.

So I tread carefully. "I'm guessing she said yes."

Warner doesn't meet my eyes.

I take a deep breath, let it out slowly. It's all beginning to make sense now.

In the early days after Castle took me in, my guard was up so high I couldn't even see over the top of it. I trusted no one. I believed nothing. I was always waiting for the other shoe to drop. I let anger rock me to sleep at night because being angry was far less scary than having faith in people— or in the future.

I kept waiting for things to fall apart.

I was so sure this happiness and safety wouldn't last, that Castle would turn me out, or that he'd turn out to be a piece of shit. Abusive. Some kind of monster.

I couldn't relax.

It took me *years* before I truly believed that I had a family. It took me years to accept, without hesitation, that Castle really loved me, or that good things could last. That I could be happy again without fear of repercussion.

That's why losing Omega Point was so cataclysmic.

It was the amalgamation of nearly all my fears. So many people I loved had been wiped out overnight. My home. My family. My refuge. And the devastation had taken Castle, too. Castle, who'd been my rock and my role model; in the aftermath, he was a ghost. Unrecognizable. I didn't know how anything would shake out after that. I didn't know how we'd survive. Didn't know where we'd go.

It was Juliette who pulled us through.

Those were the days when she and I got really close. That was when I realized I could not only trust her and open up to her, but that I could *depend* on her. I never knew just how strong she was until I saw her take charge, rising up and rallying us all when we were at our lowest, when even Castle was too broken too stand.

J made magic out of tragedy.

She found us safety and hope. Unified us with Sector 45—with Warner and Delalieu—even in the face of opposition, at the risk of losing Adam. She didn't sit around waiting for Castle to take the reins like the rest of us did; there was no time for that. Instead, she dove right into the middle of hell, completely inexperienced and unprepared, because she was determined to save us. And to sacrifice herself in the process, if that was the cost. If it weren't for her—if it weren't for what she did, for all of us—I don't know where we'd be.

She saved our lives.

She saved my life, that's for sure. Reached out a hand in the darkness. Pulled me out.

But none of it would've hurt as much if I'd lost Omega Point during my early years there. It wouldn't have taken me so long to recover, and I wouldn't have needed so much help to get through the pain. It hurt like that because I'd finally let my guard down. I'd finally allowed myself to believe that things were going to be okay. I'd begun to hope. To dream.

To *relax*.

I'd finally walked away from my own pessimism, and the moment I did, life stuck a knife in my back.

It's easy, during those moments, to throw in the towel. To shrug off humanity. To tell yourself that you tried to be happy, and look what happened: more pain. Worse pain. Betrayed by the world. You realize then that anger is safer than kindness, that isolation is safer than community. You shut everything out. Everyone. But some days, no matter what you do, the pain gets so bad you'd bury yourself alive just to make it stop.

I would know. I've been there.

And I'm looking at Warner right now and I see the same deadness behind his eyes. The torture that chases hope. That specific flavor of self-hatred experienced only after being dealt a tragic blow in response to optimism.

I'm looking at him and I'm remembering the look on his face when he blew out his birthday candles. I'm remembering him and J afterward, cuddled up in the corner of the dining tent. I'm remembering how angry he was when I showed up at their room at the asscrack of dawn, determined to drag J out of bed on the morning of his birthday.

I'm thinking—

"*Fuck.*" I throw down my fork. The plastic hits the foil plate with a surprising thud. "You two were engaged?"

Warner is staring at his food. He seems calm, but when he says, "Yes," the word is a whisper so sad it drags a knife through my heart.

I shake my head. "I'm so sorry, man. I really am. You have no idea."

Warner's eyes flick up in surprise, but only for a moment. Eventually, he stabs a piece of broccoli. Stares at it. "This is disgusting," he says.

Which I realize is code for *Thank you.*

"Yeah," I say. "It is."

Which is code for *No worries, bro. I'm here for you.*

Warner sighs. He puts down his utensils. Stares out the window. I can tell he's about to say something when, abruptly, the doorbell rings.

I swear under my breath.

I shove away from the table to answer the door, but this time, I only open it a crack. A girl about my age peers back at me, standing there with a tinfoil package in her arms.

She smiles.

I open the door a bit more.

"I brought this for Warner," she says, stage-whispering. "I heard he was hungry." Her smile is so big you could probably see it from Mars. I have to make a real effort not to roll my eyes.

"Thanks. I'll take th—"

"Oh," she says, jerking the package out of reach. "I thought I could deliver it to him personally. You know, just to be sure it's being delivered to the right person." She beams.

This time, I actually roll my eyes.

Reluctantly, I pull open the door, stepping aside to let

her enter. I turn to tell Warner that another member of his fan club is here to take a long look at his green eyes, but in the second it takes me to move, I hear her scream. The container of food crashes to the ground, spaghetti noodles and red sauce spilling everywhere.

I spin around, stunned.

Warner has the girl pinned to the wall, his hand around her throat. "Who sent you here?" he says.

She struggles to break free, her feet kicking hard against the wall, her cries choked and desperate.

My head is spinning.

I blink and Warner's got her on the floor, on her knees. His boot is planted in the middle of her back, both of her arms bent backward, locked in his grip. He twists. She cries out.

"Who sent you here?"

"I don't know what you're talking about," she says, gasping for breath.

My heart is pounding like crazy.

I have no idea what the hell just happened, but I know better than to ask questions. I remove the Glock tucked inside my waistband and aim it in her direction. And then, just as I'm beginning to wrap my head around the fact that this is an ambush—and likely from someone here, from inside the Sanctuary—I notice the food begin to move.

Three massive scorpions begin to scuttle out from underneath the noodles, and the sight is so disturbing I nearly throw up and pass out at the same time. I've never seen scorpions in real life.

Breaking news: they're *horrifying*.

I thought I wasn't afraid of spiders, but this is like if spiders were on crack, like if spiders were very, very large and kind of see-through and wore armor and had huge, venomous stingers on one end just primed and ready to murder you. The creatures make a sharp turn, and all three of them head straight for Warner.

I let out a panicked gasp of breath. "Uh, bro—not to, um, freak you out or anything, but there are, like, three scorpions headed straight toward y—"

Suddenly, the scorpions freeze in place.

Warner drops the girl's arms and she scrambles away so fast her back slams against the wall. Warner stares at the scorpions. The girl stares, too.

The two of them are having a battle of wills, I realize, and it's easy for me to figure out who's going to win. So when the scorpions begin to move again—this time, toward her—I try not to pump my fist in the air.

The girl jumps to her feet, her eyes wild.

"Who sent you?" Warner asks again.

She's breathing hard now, still staring at the scorpions as she backs farther into a corner. They're climbing up her shoes now.

"Who?" Warner demands.

"Your father sent me," she says breathlessly. Shins. Knees. Scorpions on her knees. Oh my God, scorpions on her knees. "Anderson sent me here, okay? Call them off!"

"Liar."

"It was him, I swear!"

"You were sent here by a fool," Warner says, "if you were led to believe you could lie to me repeatedly without repercussion. And you are yourself a fool if you believe I will be anything close to merciful."

The creatures are moving up her torso now. Climbing up her chest. She gasps. Locks eyes with him.

"I see," he says, tilting his head at her. "Someone lied to you."

Her eyes widen.

"You were misled," he says, holding her gaze. "I am not kind. I am not forgiving. I do not care about your life."

As he speaks, the scorpions creep farther up her body. They're sitting near her collarbone now, just waiting, venomous stingers hovering below her face. And then, slowly, the scorpions' stingers begin curving toward the soft skin at her throat.

"Call them off!" she cries.

"This is your last chance," Warner says. "Tell me what you're doing here."

She's breathing so hard now that her chest heaves, her nostrils flaring. Her eyes dart around the room in a wild panic. The scorpions' stingers press closer to her throat. She flattens against the wall, a broken gasp escaping her lips.

"Tragic," Warner says.

She moves fast. Lightning fast. Pulls a gun from somewhere inside her shirt and aims it in Warner's direction

261

and I don't even think, I just react.

I shoot.

The sound echoes, expands—it seems violently loud—but it's a perfect shot. A clean hole through the neck. The girl goes comically still and then slumps, slowly, to the ground.

Blood and scorpions pool around our feet. The body of a dead girl is splayed on my floor, just inches from the bed I woke up in, her limbs bent at awkward angles.

The scene is surreal.

I look up. Warner and I lock eyes.

"I'm coming with you to get J," I say. "End of discussion."

Warner glances from me to the dead body, and then back again. "Fine," he says, and sighs.

~~ELLA~~ JULIETTE

I've been standing outside the door staring at a smooth, polished stone wall for at least fifteen minutes before I check my wrist for a summons.

Still nothing.

When I'm with Anderson I don't have a lot of flexibility to look around, but standing here has given me time to freely examine my surroundings. The stretch of the hallway is eerily quiet, empty of doctors or soldiers in a way that unsettles me. There are long, vertical grates underfoot where the floor should be, and I've been standing here long enough to have become attuned to the incessant drips and mechanical roars that fill the background.

I glance at my wrist again.

Glance around the hall.

The walls aren't gray, like I originally thought. It turns out they're a dull white. Heavy shadows make them appear darker than they are—and in fact, make this entire floor appear darker. The overhead lights are unusual honeycomb clusters arranged along both the walls and ceilings. The oddly shaped lights scatter illumination, casting oblong hexagons in all directions, plunging some walls into complete darkness. I take a cautious step forward, peering more closely at a rectangle of blackness I'd previously ignored.

It's a hallway, I realize, cast entirely in shadow.

I feel a sudden compulsion to explore its depths, and I have to physically stop myself from stepping forward. My duty is here, at this door. It's not my business to explore or ask questions unless I've been explicitly asked to explore or ask questions.

My eyelids flutter.

Heat presses down on me, flames like fingers digging into my mind. Heat travels down my spine, wraps around my tailbone. And then shoots upward, fast and strong, forcing my eyes open. I'm breathing hard, spinning around.

Confused.

Suddenly, it makes perfect sense that I should explore the darkened hallway. Suddenly there seems no need at all to question my motives or any possible consequences for my actions.

But I've only taken a single step into the darkness when I'm pushed aggressively back. A girl's face peers out at me.

"Did you need something?" she says.

I throw up my hands, then I hesitate. I might not be authorized to hurt this person.

She steps forward. She's wearing civilian clothes, but doesn't appear to be armed. I wait for her to speak, and she doesn't.

"Who are you?" I demand. "Who gave you the authority to be down here?"

"I am Valentina Castillo. I have authority everywhere."

I drop my hands.

Valentina Castillo is the daughter of the supreme commander of South America, Santiago Castillo. I don't know what Valentina is supposed to look like, so this girl might be an impostor. Then again, if I take a risk and I'm wrong—

I could be executed.

I peer around her and see nothing but blackness. My curiosity—and unease—is growing by the minute.

I glance at my wrist. Still no summons.

"Who are you?" she says.

"I am Juliette Ferrars. I am a supreme soldier for our North American commander. Let me pass."

Valentina stares at me, her eyes scanning me from head to toe.

I hear a dull *click*, like the sound of something opening, and I spin around, looking for the source of the sound. There's no one.

"You have unlocked your message, Juliette Ferrars."

"What message?"

"Juliette? *Juliette.*"

Valentina's voice changes. She suddenly sounds like she's scared and breathless, like she's on the move. Her voice echoes. I hear the sounds of footsteps pounding the floor, but they seem far away, like she's not the only one running.

"*Viste*, there wasn't much time," she says, her Spanish accent getting thicker. "This was the best I could do. I have a plan, but *no sé si será posible. Este mensaje es en caso de emergencia.*

"They took Lena and Nicolás down in this direction," she says, pointing toward the darkness. "I'm on my way to try and find them. But if I can't—"

Her voice begins to fade. The light illuminating her face begins to glitch, almost like she's disappearing.

"Wait—" I say, reaching out. "Where are you—"

My hand moves straight through her and I gasp. She has no form. Her face is an illusion.

A hologram.

"I'm sorry," she says, her voice beginning to warp. "I'm sorry. This was the best I could do."

Once her form evaporates completely, I push into the darkness, heart pounding. I don't understand what's happening, but if the daughter of the supreme commander of South America is in trouble, I have a duty to find her and protect her.

I know that my loyalty is to Anderson, but that strange, familiar heat is still pressing against the inside of my mind, quieting the impulse telling me to turn around. I find I'm grateful for it. I realize, distantly, that my mind is a strange mess of contradictions, but I don't have more than a moment to dwell on it.

This hall is far too dark for easy access, but I'd observed earlier that what I once thought were decorative grooves in the walls were actually inset doors, so here, instead of relying on my eyes, I use my hands.

I run my fingers along the wall as I walk, waiting for a disruption in the pattern. It's a long hallway—I expect there to be multiple doors to sort through—but there appears to be little in this direction. Nothing visible by touch or sight, at least. When I finally feel the familiar pattern of a door, I hesitate.

I press both my hands against the wall, prepared to destroy it if I have to, when it suddenly fissures open beneath my hands, as if it was waiting for me.

Expecting me.

I move into the room, my senses heightened. Dim blue light pulses out along the floors, but other than that, the space is almost completely dark. I keep moving, and even though I don't need to use a gun, I reach for the rifle strapped across my back. I walk slowly, my soft boots soundless, and follow the distant, pulsing lights. As I move deeper into the room, lights begin to flicker on.

Overhead lights in that familiar honeycomb pattern flare to life, shattering the floor in unusual slants of light. The vast dimensions of the room begin to take shape. I stare up at the massive dome-shaped room, at the empty tank of water taking up an entire wall. There are abandoned desks, their respective chairs askew. Touchpads are stacked precariously on floors and desks, papers and binders piling everywhere. This place looks haunted. Deserted.

But it's clear it was once in full use.

Safety goggles hang from a nearby rack. Lab coats from another. There are large, empty glass cases standing upright in seemingly random and intermittent locations, and as I move even farther into the room, I notice a steady purple glow emanating from somewhere nearby.

I round the corner, and there's the source:

Eight glass cylinders, each as tall as the room and as wide as a desk, are arranged in a perfect line, straight across the laboratory. Five of them contain human figures. Three on the end remain empty. The purple light originates from within the individual cylinders, and as I approach, I realize the bodies are suspended in the air, bound entirely by light.

There are three boys I don't recognize. One girl I don't recognize. The other—

I step closer to the tank and gasp.

Valentina.

"What are you doing here?"

I spin around, rifle up and aimed in the direction of the voice. I drop my gun when I see Anderson's face. In an instant, the pervasive heat retreats from my head.

My mind is returned to me.

My mind, my name, my station, my place—my shameful, disloyal, reckless behavior. Horror and fear flood through me, coloring my features. How do I explain what I do not understand?

Anderson's face remains stony.

"Sir," I say quickly. "This young woman is the daughter of the supreme commander of South America. As a servant of The Reestablishment, I felt compelled to help her."

Anderson only stares at me.

Finally, he says: "How do you know that this girl is the daughter of the supreme commander of South America?"

I shake my head. "Sir, there was . . . some kind of vision. Standing in the hallway. She told me that she was Valentina Castillo, and that she needed help. She knew my name. She told me where to go."

Anderson exhales, his shoulders releasing their tension. "This is not the daughter of a supreme commander of The Reestablishment," he says quietly. "You were misled by a practice exercise."

Renewed mortification sends a fresh heat to my face.

Anderson sighs.

"I'm so sorry, sir. I thought— I thought it was my duty to help her, sir."

Anderson meets my eyes again. "Of course you did."

I hold my head steady, but shame sears me from within.

"And?" he says. "What did you think?"

Anderson gestures at the line of glass cylinders, at the figures displayed within.

"I think it's a beautiful display, sir."

Anderson almost smiles. He takes a step closer, studying me. "A beautiful display, indeed."

I swallow.

His voice changes, becomes soft. Gentle. "You would never betray me, would you, Juliette?"

"No, sir," I say quickly. "Never."

"Tell me something," he says, lifting his hand to my face. The backs of his knuckles graze my cheek, trail down my jawline. "Would you die for me?"

My heart is thundering in my chest. "Yes, sir."

271

He takes my face in his hand now, his thumb brushing, gently, across my chin. "Would you do anything for me?"

"Yes, sir."

"And yet, you deliberately disobeyed me." He drops his hand. My face feels suddenly cold. "I asked you to wait outside," he says quietly. "I did not ask you to wander. I did not ask you to speak. I did not ask you to think for yourself or to save anyone who claimed to need saving. Did I?"

"No, sir."

"Did you forget," he says, "that I am your master?"

"No, sir."

"*Liar*," he cries.

My heart is in my throat. I swallow hard. Say nothing.

"I will ask you one more time," he says, locking eyes with me. "Did you forget that I am your master?"

"Y-yes, sir."

His eyes flash. "Should I remind you, Juliette? Should I remind you to whom you owe your life and your loyalty?"

"Yes, sir," I say, but I sound breathless. I feel sick with fear. Feverish. Heat prickles my skin.

He retrieves a blade from inside his jacket pocket. Carefully, he unfolds it, the metal glinting in the neon light.

He presses the hilt into my right hand.

He takes my left hand and explores it with both of his own, tracing the lines of my palm and the shapes of my fingers, the seams of my knuckles. Sensations spiral through me, wonderful and horrible.

He presses down lightly on my index finger. He meets

my eyes.

"This one," he says. "Give it to me."

My heart is in my throat. In my gut. Beating behind my eyes.

"Cut it off. Place it in my hand. And all will be forgiven."

"Yes, sir," I whisper.

With shaking hands, I press the blade to the tender skin at the base of my finger. The blade is so sharp it pierces the flesh instantly, and with a stifled, agonized cry I press it deeper, hesitating only when I feel resistance. Knife against bone. The pain explodes through me, blinding me.

I fall on one knee.

There's blood everywhere.

I'm breathing so hard I'm heaving, trying desperately not to vomit from either the pain or the horror. I clench my teeth so hard it sends shocks of fresh pain upward, straight to my brain, and the distraction is helpful. I have to press my bloodied hand against the dirty floor to keep it steady, but with one final, desperate cry, I cut through the bone.

The knife falls from my trembling hand, clattering to the floor. My index finger is still hanging on to my hand by a single scrap of flesh, and I rip it off in a quick, violent motion. My body is shaking so excessively I can hardly stand, but somehow I manage to deposit the finger in Anderson's outstretched palm before collapsing to the ground.

"Good girl," he says softly. "Good girl."

It's all I hear him say before I black out.

KENJI

We both stare at the bloody scene a moment longer before Warner suddenly straightens and heads out the door. I tuck my gun into the waistband of my pants and chase after him, remembering to close the door behind us. I don't want those scorpions getting loose.

"Hey," I say, catching up to him. "Where are you going?"

"To find Castle."

"Cool. Okay. But do you think that maybe next time, instead of just, you know, leaving without a word, you could tell me what the hell is going on? I don't like chasing after you like this. It's demeaning."

"That sounds like a personal problem."

"Yeah but I thought personal problems were your area of expertise," I say. "You've got what, at least a few thousand personal problems, right? Or was it a few million?"

Warner shoots me a dark look. "You'd do well to address your own mental turbulence before criticizing mine."

"Uh, what's that supposed to mean?"

"It means that a rabid dog could sniff out your desperate, broken state. You're in no position to judge me."

"*Excuse me?*"

"You lie to yourself, Kishimoto. You hide your true

feelings behind a thin veneer, playing the clown, when all the while you're amassing emotional detritus you refuse to examine. At least I do not hide from myself. I know where my faults lie and I accept them. But you," he says. "Perhaps you should seek help."

My eyes widen to the point of pain, my head whipping back and forth between him and the path in front of me. "You have got to be kidding me right now. *You're* telling *me* to get help with my issues? What is happening?" I look up at the sky. "Am I dead? Is this hell?"

"I want to know what's happening with you and Castle."

I'm so surprised I briefly stop in place.

"What?" I blink at him. Still confused. "What are you talking about? There's nothing wrong with me and Castle."

"You've been more profane in the last several weeks than in the entire time I've known you. Something is wrong."

"I'm stressed," I say, feeling myself bristle. "Sometimes I swear when I'm stressed."

He shakes his head. "This is different. You're experiencing an unusual amount of stress, even for you."

"Wow." My eyebrows fly up. "I really hope you didn't bother using your"—I make air quotes—"*supernatural ability to sense emotions*"—I drop the air quotes—"to figure that one out. Obviously I'm extra stressed out right now. The world is on fucking fire. The list of things stressing me out is so long I can't even keep track. We're up to our necks in shit. J is gone. Adam defected. Nazeera's been shot. You've had your head so far up your own ass I thought you'd never emerge—"

278

He tries to cut me off but I keep talking.

"—and literally five minutes ago," I say, "someone from the Sanctuary—ha, hilarious, horrible name—just tried to kill you, and I killed her for it. *Five minutes ago.* So yeah, I think I'm experiencing an unusual amount of stress right now, genius."

Warner dismisses my speech with a single shake of his head. "Your use of profanity increases exponentially when you're irritated with Castle. Your language appears to be directly connected to your relationship with him. Why?"

I try not to roll my eyes. "Not that this information is actually relevant, but Castle and I struck a deal a few years ago. He thought that my"—I make more air quotes—*"overreliance on profanity was inhibiting my ability to express my emotions in a constructive manner."*

"So you promised him you'd tone down your language."

"Yeah."

"I see. It seems you've reneged on the terms of that arrangement."

"Why do you care?" I ask. "Why are we even talking about this? Why are we losing sight of the fact that we were just attacked by someone from *inside* of the Sanctuary? We need to find Sam and Nouria and find out who this girl was, because she was clearly from this camp, and they should know th—"

"You can tell Sam and Nouria whatever you want," Warner says. "But I need to talk to Castle."

Something in his tone frightens me. "Why?" I demand.

"What is going on? Why are you so obsessed with Castle right now?"

Finally, Warner stops moving. "Because," he says. "Castle had something to do with this."

"What?" I feel the blood drain from my body. "No way. Not possible."

Warner says nothing.

"Come on, man, don't be crazy— Castle's not perfect, but he would never—"

"Hey— What the hell just happened?" Winston, breathless and panicked, comes running up to us. "I heard a gunshot coming from the direction of your tent, but when I went to check on you, I saw— I saw—"

"Yeah."

"What happened?" Winston's voice is shrill. Terrified.

At that exact moment, more people come running. Winston starts offering people explanations I don't bother to edit, because my head is still full of steam. I have no idea what the hell Warner is getting at, but I'm also worried that I know him too well to deny his mind. My heart says Castle would never betray us, but my brain says that Warner is usually right when it comes to sussing out this kind of shit. So I'm freaking out.

I spot Nouria in the distance, her dark skin gleaming in the bright sun, and relief floods through me.

Finally.

Nouria will know more about the girl with the scorpions. She has to. And whatever she knows will almost certainly help absolve Castle of any affiliation with this mess. And as soon as we can resolve this freak accident, Warner and I can get the hell out of here and start searching for J.

That's it.

That's the plan.

It makes me feel good to have a plan. But when we're close enough, Nouria narrows her eyes at both me and Warner, and the look on her face sends a brand-new wave of fear through my body.

"Follow me," she says.

We do.

Warner looks *livid*.

Castle looks freaked out.

Nouria and Sam look like they're sick and tired of all of us.

I might be imagining things, but I'm pretty sure Sam just shot Nouria a look—the subtext of which was probably *Why the hell did you have to let your dad come stay with us?*—that was so withering Nouria didn't even get upset, she just shook her head, resigned.

And the problem is, I don't even know whose side I'm on.

In the end, Warner was right about Castle, but he was also wrong. Castle wasn't plotting anything nefarious; he didn't send that girl—her name was Amelia—after Warner. Castle's mistake was thinking that all rebel groups shared the same worldview.

At first it didn't occur to me, either, that the vibe might

be different around here. Different from our group at Point, at least. At Point we were led by Castle, who was more of a nurturer than a warrior. In his days before The Reestablishment he was a social worker. He saw tons of kids coming in and out of the system, and with Omega Point he sought to build a home and refuge for the marginalized. We were all about love and community at Point. And even though we knew that we were gearing up for a fight against The Reestablishment, we didn't always resort to violence; Castle didn't like using his powers in authoritative ways. He was more like a father figure to most of us.

But here—

It didn't take long to realize that Nouria was different from her dad. She's nice enough, but she's also all business. She doesn't like to spend much time on small talk, and she and Sam mostly keep to themselves. They don't always take their meals with everyone else. They don't always participate in group things. And when it comes right down to it, Sam and Nouria are ready and willing to set shit on fire. Hell, they seem to be looking forward to it.

Castle was never really that guy.

I think he was a little blindsided when we showed up here. He was suddenly out of a job when he realized that Nouria and Sam weren't going to take orders from him. And then, when he tried to get to know people—

He was disappointed.

"Amelia was a bit of a zealot," Sam says, sighing. "She'd never exhibited dangerous, violent tendencies, of course, which is why we let her stay—but we all felt that her views were a little intense. She was one of the rare members who felt like the lines between The Reestablishment and the rebel groups should be clear and finite. She never felt safe with the children of the supreme commanders in our midst, and I know that because she took me aside to tell me so. I had a long talk with her about the situation, but I see now that she wasn't convinced."

"Obviously," I mutter.

Nouria shoots me a look. I clear my throat.

Sam goes on: "When everyone but Warner was basically kidnapped—and Nazeera was shot—Amelia probably figured she could finish the job and get rid of Warner, too." She shakes her head. "What a horrible situation."

"Did you have to shoot her?" Nouria says to me. "Was she really that dangerous?"

"She had *three* scorpions!" I cry. "She pulled a gun on Warner!"

"What else was he supposed to think?" Castle says gently. He's staring at the ground, his long dreads freed from their usual tie at the base of his neck. I wish I could see the expression on his face. "If I hadn't known Amelia personally, even I would've thought she was working for someone."

"Tell me, again," Warner says to Castle, "exactly what you said to her about me."

Castle looks up. Sighs.

"She and I got into a bit of a heated discussion," he

says. "Amelia was determined that members of The Reestablishment could never change, that they were evil and would remain evil. I told her I didn't believe that. I told her that I believed that all people were capable of change."

I raise an eyebrow. "Wait, like, you mean you think even someone like Anderson is capable of change?"

Castle hesitates. And I know, just by looking at his eyes, what he's about to say. My heart jumps in my chest. In fear.

"I think if Anderson were truly remorseful," Castle says, "that he, too, could make a change. Yes. I do believe that."

Nouria rolls her eyes.

Sam drops her head in her hands.

"Wait. Wait." I hold up a finger. "So, like, in a hypothetical situation— If Anderson came to Point asking for amnesty, claiming to be a changed man, you'd . . . ?"

Castle just looks at me.

I throw myself back in my chair with a groan.

"Kenji," Castle says softly. "You know better than anyone else how we did things at Omega Point. I dedicated my life to giving second—and third—chances to those who'd been cast out by the world. You'd be stunned if you knew how many people's lives were derailed by a simple mistake that snowballed, escalating beyond their control because no one was ever there to offer a hand or even an hour of assistance—"

"Castle. Sir." I hold up my hands. "I love you. I really do. But Anderson isn't a regular person. He—"

"Of course he's a regular person, son. That's exactly the

point. We're all just regular people, when you strip us down. There's nothing to be afraid of when you look at Anderson; he's just as human as you or me. Just as terrified. And I'm sure if he could go back and do his life over again, he'd make very different decisions."

Nouria shakes her head. "You don't know that, Dad."

"Maybe not," he says quietly. "But it's what I believe."

"Is that what you believe about me, too?" Warner asks. "Is that what you told her? That I was just a nice boy, a defenseless child who'd never lift a finger to hurt her? That if I could do it all over again I'd choose to live my life as a monk, dedicating my days to giving charity and spreading goodwill?"

"No," Castle says sharply. It's clear he's starting to get irritated. "I told her that your anger was a defense mechanism, and that you couldn't help that you were born to an abusive father. I told her that in your heart, you're a good person, and that you don't *want* to hurt anyone. Not really."

Warner's eyes flash. "I want to hurt people all the time," he says. "Sometimes I can't sleep at night because I'm thinking about all the people I'd like to murder."

"Great." I nod, leaning back in my chair. "This is super great. All of this information we're collecting is super helpful and useful." I count off on my fingers: "Amelia was a psycho, Castle wants to be BFFs with Anderson, Warner has midnight fantasies about killing people, and Castle made Amelia think that Warner is a lost little bunny trying to find his way home."

When everyone stares at me, confused, I clarify:

"Castle basically gave Amelia the idea that she could walk into a room and murder Warner! He pretty much told her that Warner was about as harmful as a dumpling."

"*Oh*," Sam and Nouria say at the same time.

"I don't think she wanted to murder him," Castle says quickly. "I'm sure she just—"

"Dad, please." Nouria's voice is sharp and final. "Enough." She shares a glance with Sam, and takes a deep breath.

"Listen," she says, trying for a calmer tone. "We knew, when you got here, that we'd have to deal with this situation eventually, but I think it's time we had a talk about our roles and responsibilities around here."

"Oh. I see." Castle clasps his hands. Stares at the wall. He looks so sad and small and ancient. Even his dreads seem more silver than black these days. Sometimes I forget he's almost fifty. Most people think he's, like, fifteen years younger than he actually is, but that's just because he's always looked really, really good for his age. But for the first time in years, I feel like I'm beginning to see the number on his face. He looks tired. Worn out.

But that doesn't mean he's done here.

Castle's still got so much more to do. So much more to give. And I can't just sit here and let him be shoved aside. Ignored. I want to shout at someone. I want to tell Nouria and Sam that they can't just kick Castle to the curb like this.

Not after everything. Not like this.

And I'm about to say something exactly like that, when Nouria speaks.

"Sam and I," she says, "would like to offer you an official position as our senior adviser here at the Sanctuary."

Castle's head perks up. "Senior adviser?" He stares at Nouria. Stares at Sam. "You're not asking me to leave?"

Nouria looks suddenly confused.

"Leave? Dad, you just got here. Sam and I want you to stay for as long as you like. We just think it's important that we all know what we're doing here, so that we can manage things in as efficient and organized a manner as possible. It's hard for Sam and me to be effective at our jobs if we're worried about tiptoeing around your feelings, and even though it's hard to have conversations like this, we figured it would be best to jus—"

Castle pulls Nouria into a hug so fierce, so full of love, I feel my eyes sting with emotion. I actually have to look away for a moment.

When I turn back, Castle is beaming.

"I'd be honored to advise in any way that I can," Castle says. "And if I haven't said it enough, let me say it again: I'm so proud of you, Nouria. So proud of both of you," he says, looking at Sam. "The boys would've been so proud."

Nouria's eyes go glassy with emotion. Even Sam seems moved.

One more minute of this, and I'm going to need a tissue.

"Right, well." Warner is on his feet. "I'm glad the attempt

on my life was able to bring your family together. I'm leaving now."

"Wait—" I grab Warner's arm and he shoves me off.

"If you keep touching me without my permission, I will remove your hands from your body."

I ignore that. "Shouldn't we tell them that we're leaving?"

Sam frowns. *"Leaving?"*

Nouria's eyebrows fly up. *"We?"*

"We're going to get J," I explain. "She's back in Oceania. James told us everything. Speaking of which— You should probably talk to him. He's got some news about Adam you won't like, news that I don't care to repeat."

"Kent betrayed all of you to save himself."

"To save *James*," I clarify, shooting Warner a dirty look. "And that was not cool, man. I just said I didn't want to talk about it."

"I'm trying to be efficient."

Castle looks stunned. He says nothing. He just looks stunned.

"Talk to James," I say. "He'll tell you what's happening. But Warner and I are going to catch a plane—"

"Steal a plane."

"Right, steal a plane, before the end of the day. And, uh, you know—we'll just go get J and be back real quick, *bim bam boom*."

Nouria and Sam are staring at me like I'm an idiot.

"Bim bam boom?" Warner says.

"Yeah, you know, like"—I clap my hands together—*"boom.*

Done. Easy."

Warner turns away from me with a sigh.

"Wait— So, just the two of you are doing this?" Sam asks. She's frowning.

"Honestly, the fewer, the better," Nouria answers for me. "That way, there are fewer bodies to hide, fewer actions to coordinate. Regardless, I'd offer to come with you, but we have so many still wounded that we need to care for—and now that Amelia is dead, there's sure to be more emotional upheaval to manage."

Castle's eyes light up. "While they're going after Ella," he says to Nouria and Sam, "and the two of you are running things here, I was thinking I'd reach out to the friends in my network. Let them know what's happening, and that change is afoot. I can help coordinate our moves around the globe."

"That's a great idea," Sam says. "Maybe we c—"

"I don't care," Warner says loudly, and turns for the door. "And I'm leaving now. Kishimoto, if you're coming, keep up."

"Right," I say, trying to sound important. "Yup. Bye." I shoot a quick two-finger salute at everyone and run straight for the door only to slam hard into Nazeera.

Nazeera.

Holy shit. She's awake. She's perfect.

She's *pissed.*

"You two aren't going anywhere without me," she says.

~~ELLA~~
JULIETTE

I am a thief.

I stole this notebook and this pen from one of the doctors, from one of his lab coats when he wasn't looking, and I shoved them both down my pants. This was just before he ordered those men to come and get me. The ones in the strange suits with the thick gloves and the gas masks with the foggy plastic windows hiding their eyes. They were aliens, I remember thinking. I remember thinking they must've been aliens because they couldn't have been human, the ones who handcuffed my hands behind my back, the ones who strapped me to my seat. They stuck Tasers to my skin over and over for no reason other than to hear me scream but I wouldn't. I whimpered but I never said a word. I felt the tears streak down my cheeks but I wasn't crying.

I think it made them angry.

They slapped me awake even though my eyes were open when we arrived. Someone unstrapped me without removing my handcuffs and kicked me in both kneecaps before ordering me to rise. And I tried. I tried but I couldn't and finally 6 hands shoved me out the door and my face was bleeding on the concrete for a while. I can't really remember the part where they dragged me inside.

I feel cold all the time.

I feel empty, like there is nothing inside of me but this broken heart, the only organ left in this hell. I feel the bleats echo within me, I feel the thumping reverberate around my skeleton. I have a heart, says science, but I am a monster, says society. And I know it, of course I know it. I know what I've done. I'm not asking for sympathy.

But sometimes I think—sometimes I wonder—if I were a monster—surely, I would feel it by now?

I would feel angry and vicious and vengeful.

I'd know blind rage and bloodlust and a need for vindication.

Instead I feel an abyss within me that's so deep, so dark I can't see within it; I can't see what it holds. I do not know what I am or what might happen to me.

I do not know what I might do again.

—An excerpt from Juliette's journals in the asylum

KENJI

I stand stock-still for a moment, letting the shock of everything settle around me, and when it finally hits me that Nazeera is really here, really awake, really okay, I pull her into my arms. Her defensive posture melts away, and suddenly she's just a girl—*my girl*—and happiness rockets through me. She's not even close to being short, but in my arms, she feels small. Pocket-sized. Like she was always meant to fit here, against my chest.

It's like heaven.

When we finally pull apart, I'm beaming like an idiot. I don't even care that everyone is staring at us. I just want to live in this moment.

"Hey," I say to her. "I'm so happy you're okay."

She takes a deep, unsteady breath, and then—smiles. It changes her whole face. It makes her look a lot less like a mercenary and a lot more like an eighteen-year-old girl. Though I think I like both versions, if I'm being honest.

"I'm so happy you're okay, too," she says quietly.

We stare at each other a moment longer before I hear someone clear their throat in a dramatic fashion.

Reluctantly, I turn around.

I know, in an instant, that the throat-clearing came

from Nouria. I can tell by the way her arms are crossed, the way her eyes are narrowed. Sam, on the other hand, looks amused.

But Castle looks happy. Surprised, but happy.

I grin at him.

Nouria's frown deepens. "You two know Warner left, right?"

That wipes the smile off my face. I spin around, but there's no sign of him. I turn back, swearing quietly under my breath.

Nazeera shoots me a look.

"I know," I say, shaking my head. "He's going to try and leave without us."

She almost laughs. "Definitely."

I'm about to say my good-byes again when Nouria jumps to her feet. "Wait," she says.

"No time," I say, already backing out the door. "Warner is going to bail on us, and I c—"

"He's about to take a shower," Sam says, cutting me off.

I freeze so fast I nearly fall over. I turn around, eyebrows high. "He's what now?"

"He's about to take a shower," she says again.

I blink at her slowly, like I'm stupid, which, honestly, is kind of how I'm feeling at the moment. "You mean you're, like, watching him get ready to take a shower?"

"It's not weird," Nouria says flatly. "Stop making it weird."

I squint at Sam. "What's Warner doing right now?" I ask

298

her. "Is he in the shower yet?"

"Yes."

Nazeera raises a single eyebrow. "So you're just, like, watching a naked Warner in the shower right now?"

"I'm not looking at his body," Sam says, sounding very close to irritated.

"But you *could*," I say, stunned. "That's what's so weird about this. You *could* just watch any of us take extremely naked showers."

"You know what?" Nouria says sharply. "I was going to do something to make things easier for you guys on your way out, but I think I've changed my mind."

"Wait—" Nazeera says. "Make things easier how?"

"I was going to help you steal a jet."

"Okay, all right, I take it back," I say, holding up my hands in apology. "I retract all my previous comments about nakedness. I would also like to formally apologize to Sam, who we all know is way too nice and way too cool to ever spy on anyone in the shower."

Sam rolls her eyes. Cracks a smile.

Nouria sighs. "I don't understand how you deal with him," she says to Castle. "I can't stand all the jokes. It would drive me insane to have to listen to this all day."

I'm about to protest when Castle responds.

"That's only because you don't know him well enough," Castle says, smiling at me. "Besides, we don't love him for his jokes, do we, Nazeera?" The two of them lock eyes for a moment. "We love him for his heart."

At that, the smile slips from my face. I'm still processing the weight of that statement—the generosity of such a statement—when I realize I've already missed a beat.

Nouria is talking.

"The air base isn't far from here," she's saying, "and I guess this is as good a time as any to let you all know that Sam and I are about to take a page out of Ella's playbook and take over Sector 241. Stealing a plane will be the least of the damage—and, in fact, I think it's a great way to launch our offensive strategy." She glances over her shoulder. "What do you think, Sam?"

"Brilliant," she says, "as usual."

Nouria smiles.

"I didn't realize that was your strategy," Castle says, the smile fading from his face. "Don't you think, based on how things turned out the last time, that m—"

"Why don't we discuss this after we've sent the kids off on their mission? Right now it's more important that we get them situated and give them a proper send-off before it's officially too late."

"Hey, speaking of which," I say quickly, "what makes you think we're not already too late?"

Nouria meets my eyes. "If they'd done the transfer," she says, "we would've felt it."

"Felt it how?"

It's Sam who responds: "In order for their plan to work, Emmaline has to die. They won't let that happen naturally, of course, because a natural death could occur in any number of ways, which leaves too many factors up in the air. They need to be able to control the experiment at all times—which is why they were so desperate to get their hands on Ella *before* Emmaline died. They're almost certainly going to kill Emmaline in a controlled environment, and they'll set it up in a way that leaves no room for error. Even so, we're bound to feel something change.

"That infinitesimal shift—after Emmaline's powers recede, but before they're funneled into a new host body—will dramatically glitch our visual of the world. And that moment hasn't happened yet, which makes us think that Ella is probably still safe." Sam shrugs. "But it could be happening any minute now. Time really is of the essence."

"How do you know so much about this?" Nazeera asks, her brows furrowed. "For years I tried to get my hands on this information, and I came up with nothing, despite being so close to the source. But you seem to know all of this on some kind of personal level. It's incredible."

"It's not that incredible," Nouria says, shaking her head. "We've just been focused in our search. All rebel groups have a different strength or core principle. For some, it's safety. For others, it's war. For us, it's been research. The things we've seen have been out there for everyone to see—there are glitches all the time—but when you're not looking for them, you don't notice them. But I noticed. Sam noticed. It was one of the things that brought us together."

The two women share a glance.

"We felt really sure that part of our oppression was in

an illusion," Sam says. "And we've been chasing down the truth with every resource we've got. Unfortunately, we still don't know everything."

"But we're closer than most," Nouria says. She takes a sharp breath, refocusing. "We'll be holding down our end of things while you're gone. Hopefully, when you return, we'll have flipped more than one sector to our side."

"You really think you'll be able to accomplish that much in such a short period of time?" I ask, eyes wide. "I was hoping we wouldn't be gone for more than a couple days."

Nouria smiles at me then, but it's a strange smile, a searching smile. "Don't you understand?" she says. "This is it. This is the end. This is the defining moment we've all been fighting for. The end of an era. The end of a revolution. We currently—finally—have every advantage. We have people on the inside. If we do this right, we could collapse The Reestablishment in a matter of days."

"But all of that hinges on us getting to J on time," I say. "What if we're too late?"

"You'll have to kill her."

"*Nouria,*" Castle gasps.

"You're joking," I say. "Tell me you're joking."

"Not joking in the slightest," she says. "If you get there and Emmaline is dead and Ella has taken her place, you must kill Ella. You have to kill her and as many of the supreme commanders as you can."

My jaw has come unhinged.

"What about all that shit you said to J the night we got

here? What about all that talk about how inspiring she is and how so many people were moved by her actions— how she's basically a hero? What happened to all that nonsense?"

"It wasn't nonsense," Nouria says. "I meant every word. But we're at war, Kishimoto. We don't have time to be sentimental."

"Sentimental? Are you out of your—"

Nazeera places a calming hand on my arm. "We'll find another way. There has to be another way."

"It's impossible to reverse the process once it's in effect," Sam says calmly. "Operation Synthesis will remove every trace of your old friend. She will be unrecognizable. A super soldier in every sense of the word. Beyond salvation."

"I'm not listening to this," I say angrily. "I'm not listening to this."

Nouria puts up her hands. "This conversation might turn out to be unnecessary. As long as you can get to her in time, it won't matter. But remember: if you get there and Ella is still alive, you need to make sure that she kills Emmaline above all else. Removing Emmaline is key. Once she's gone, the supreme commanders become easy targets. Vulnerable."

"Wait." I frown, still angry. "Why does it have to be J who kills Emmaline? Couldn't one of us do it?"

Nouria shakes her head. "If it were that simple," she says, "don't you think it would've been done by now?"

I raise my eyebrows. "Not if no one knew she existed."

"We knew she existed," Sam says quietly. "We've known

about Emmaline for a while now."

Nouria goes on: "Why do you think we reached out to your team? Why do you think we risked the life of one of our own to get a message to Ella? Why do you think we opened our doors to you, even when we knew we'd be exposing ourselves to a possible attack? We made a series of increasingly difficult decisions, putting the lives of all those who depended on us at risk." She sighs. "But even now, after suffering a disastrous loss, Sam and I think that, ultimately, we did the right thing. Can you imagine why?"

"Because you're . . . Good Samaritans?"

"Because we realized, months ago, that Ella was the only one strong enough to kill her own sister. We need her just as much as you do. Not just us"—Nouria gestures to herself and Sam—"but the whole world. If Ella is able to kill Emmaline before any powers can be transferred, then she's killed The Reestablishment's greatest weapon. If she doesn't kill Emmaline now, while power still runs through Emmaline's veins, The Reestablishment can continue to harness and transfer that power to a new host."

"We once thought that Ella would have to fight her sister," Sam says. "But based on the information Ella shared with us while she was here, it seems like Emmaline is ready and willing to die." Sam shakes her head. "Even so, killing her is not as simple as pulling a plug. Ella will be going to war with the ghost of her mother's genius. Evie undoubtedly put in place numerous fail-safes to keep Emmaline invulnerable to attacks from others and from herself. I have no idea what

304

Ella will be up against, but I can guarantee it won't be easy."

"Jesus." I drop my head into my hands. I thought I was already living with peak levels of stress, but I was wrong. This stress I'm experiencing now is on a whole new level.

I feel Nazeera's hand on my back and I look up. Her face looks as uncertain as mine feels, and somehow, it makes me feel better.

"Pack your bags," Nouria says. "Catch up with Warner. I'll meet the three of you at the entrance in twenty minutes."

~~ELLA~~
JULIETTE

In the darkness, I imagine light.

I dream of suns, moons, mothers. I see children laughing, crying, I see blood, I smell sugar. Light shatters across the blackness pressing against my eyes, fracturing nothing into something. Nameless shapes expand and spin, crash into each other, dissolving on contact. I see dust. I see dark walls, a small window, I see water, I see words on a page—

I am not insane I am not insane

I am not insane I am not insane I am not insane I am not insane
I am not insane I am not insane I am not insane I am not insane
I am not insane I am not insane I am not insane I am not insane
I am not insane I am not insane I am not insane I am not insane
I am not insane I am not insane I am not insane I am not insane
I am not insane I am not insane I am not insane I am not insane
I am not insane I am not insane I am not insane I am not insane
I am not insane I am not insane I am not insane I am not insane
I am not insane I am not insane I am not insane I am not insane
I am not insane I am not insane I am not insane I am not insane
I am not insane I am not insane I am not insane

In the pain, I imagine bliss.

My thoughts are like wind, rushing, curling into the depths of myself, expelling, dispelling darkness

I imagine love, I imagine wind, I imagine gold hair and green eyes and whispers, laughter

I imagine

        Me

extraordinary, unbroken

the girl who shocked herself by surviving, the girl who loved herself through learning, the girl who respected her skin, understood her worth, found her strength

s t r o n g

    s t r o n g e r

        strongest

Imagine me

master of my own universe

I am everything I ever dreamed of

KENJI

We're in the air.

We've been in the air for hours now. I spent the first four hours sleeping—I can usually fall asleep anywhere, in any position—and I spent the last two hours eating all the snacks on the plane. We've got about an hour left in our flight and I'm so bored I've begun poking myself in the eye just to pass the time.

We got off to a good start—Nouria helped us steal a plane, as promised, by shielding our actions with a sheet of light—but now that we're up here, we're basically on our own. Nazeera had to fend off a few questions over the radio, but because most of the military has no idea what level of shit has already gone down, she still has the necessary clout to bypass inquiries from nosy sector leaders and soldiers. We realize it's only a matter of time, though, before someone realizes we don't have the authority to be up here.

Until then—

I glance around. I'm sitting close enough to the cockpit to be within earshot of Nazeera, but she and I both decided that I should hang back to keep an eye on Warner, who's sitting just far enough away to keep me safe from his scowl. Honestly, the look on his face is so intense I'm surprised he hasn't started aging prematurely.

Suffice it to say that he didn't like Nouria's game plan.

I mean, I don't like it, either—and I have no intentions of following through with it—but Warner looked like he might shoot Nouria for even *thinking* that we might have to kill J. He's been sitting stiffly in the back of the plane ever since we boarded, and I've been wary of approaching him, despite our recent reconciliation. Semi-reconciliation? I'm calling it a reconciliation.

But right now I think he needs space.

Or maybe it's me, maybe I'm the one who needs space. He's exhausting to deal with. Without J around, Warner has no soft edges. He never smiles. He rarely looks at people. He's always irritated.

Right now, I honestly can't remember why J likes him so much.

In fact, in the last couple of months I'd forgotten what he was like without her around. But this reminder has been more than enough. Too much, in fact. I don't want any more reminders. I can guarantee that I will never again forget that Warner is not a fun guy to spend time with. That dude carries so much tension in his body it's practically contagious. So yeah, I'm giving him space.

So far, I've given him seven hours' worth of space.

I steal another glance at him, wondering how he holds himself so still—so stiff—for seven hours straight. How does he not pull a muscle? Why does he never have to use the bathroom? Where does it all go?

The only concession we got from Warner was that he showed up looking more like his normal self. Sam was right: Warner took a shower. You'd think he was going on a date, not a murder/rescue mission. It's obvious he wants to make a good impression.

He's wearing more Haider castoffs: a pale green blazer, matching pants. Black boots. But because these pieces were selected by Haider, the blazer is not a normal blazer. Of course it isn't. This blazer has no lapels, no buttons. The silhouette is cut in sharp lines that force the jacket to hang open, exposing Warner's shirt underneath—a simple white V-neck that shows more of his chest than I feel comfortable staring at. Still, he looks okay. A little nervous, but—

"Your thoughts are very loud," Warner says, still staring out the window.

"Oh my God, I'm so sorry," I say, feigning shock. "I'd turn the volume down, but I'd have to *die* in order for my brain to stop working."

"A problem easily rectified," he mutters.

"I heard that."

"I meant for you to hear that."

"Hey," I say, realizing something. "Doesn't this feel like some kind of weird déjà vu?"

"No."

"No, no, I'm being serious. What are the odds that the three of us would be on a trip like this again? Though the last time we were all on a trip like this, we ended up being shot out of the sky, so—yeah, I don't want to relive that.

Also, J isn't here. So. Huh." I hesitate. "Okay, I think I'm realizing that maybe I don't actually understand what déjà vu means."

"It's French," Warner says, bored. "It literally means *already seen.*"

"Wait, so then I do know what it means."

"That you know what anything means is astonishing to me."

Before I have a chance to defend myself, Nazeera's voice carries over from the cockpit.

"Hey," she calls. "Are you guys being friends again?"

I hear the familiar click and slide of metal—a sound that means Nazeera is unbuckling herself from pilot mode. Every once in a while she puts the plane on cruise control (or whatever) and makes her way over to me. But it's been at least half an hour since her last break, and I've missed her.

She folds herself into the chair next to me.

I beam at her.

"I'm so glad you two are finally talking," she says, sighing as she sinks into the seat. "The silence has been depressing."

My smile dies.

Warner's expression darkens.

"Listen," she says, looking at Warner. "I know this whole thing is horrible—that the very reason we're on this plane is horrible—but you have to stop being like this. We have, like, thirty minutes left on this flight, which means we're about to go out there, together, to do something huge. Which means we all have to get on the same page. We have to be able to trust each other and work together. If we don't, or if you don't let us, we could end up losing everything."

When Warner says nothing, Nazeera sighs again.

"I don't care what Nouria thinks," she says, trying for a gentle tone. "We're not going to lose Ella."

"You don't understand," Warner says quietly. He's still not looking at us. "I've already lost her."

"You don't know that," Nazeera says forcefully. "Ella might still be alive. We can still turn this around."

Warner shakes his head. "She was different even before she was taken," he says. "Something had changed inside of her, and I don't know what it was, but I could feel it. I've always been able to feel her—I've always been able to sense her energy—and she wasn't the same. Emmaline did something to her, changed something inside of her. I have no idea what she's going to be like when I see her again. If I see her again." He stares out the window. "But I'm here because I can do nothing else. Because this is the only way forward."

And then, even though I know it's going to piss him off, I say to Nazeera:

"Warner and J were engaged."

"What?" Nazeera stills. Her eyes go wide. Super wide. Wider than the plane. Her eyes go so wide they basically fill the sky. "When? How? Why did no one tell me?"

"I told you that in confidence," Warner says sharply, shooting me a glare.

"I know." I shrug. "But Nazeera's right. We're a team now, whether you like it or not, and we should get all of this out in the open. Air it out."

"Out in the open? What about the fact that you and Nazeera are in a relationship that you never bothered mentioning?"

"Hey," I say, "I was going t—"

"Wait. *Wait.*" Nazeera cuts me off. She holds up her hands. "Why are we changing the subject? Warner, engaged! Oh my God, this is— This is so good. This is a big deal, it could give us a per—"

"It's not *that* big of a deal." I turn, frown at her. "We all knew this kind of thing was coming. The two of them are basically destined to be together, even I can admit that." I tilt my head, considering. "I mean, true, I think they're a little young, but—"

Nazeera is shaking her head. "No. No. That's not what I'm talking about. I don't care about the actual engagement." She stops, glances up at Warner. "I mean—um, congratulations and everything."

Warner looks beyond annoyed.

"I just mean that this reminded me of something. Something so good. I don't know why I didn't think of this sooner. God, it would give us the perfect edge."

"What would?"

But Nazeera is out of her chair, stalking over to Warner and, cautiously, I follow. "Do you remember," she says to him, "when you and Lena were together?"

Warner shoots Nazeera a venomous look and says, with dramatic iciness, "I'd really rather not."

Nazeera waves away his statement with her hand. "Well, I remember. I remember a lot more than I should, probably, because Lena used to complain to me about your relationship all the time. And I remember, specifically, how much your dad and her mom wanted you guys to, like, I don't know— promise yourselves to each other for the foreseeable future, for the protection of the movement—"

"Promise themselves?" I frown.

"Yes, like—" She hesitates, her arms pinwheeling as she gathers her thoughts, but Warner suddenly sits up straighter in his seat, seeming to understand.

"Yes," he says calmly. The irritation is gone from his eyes. "I remember my father saying something to me about the importance of uniting our families. Unfortunately, my recollection of the interaction is vague, at best."

"Right, well, I'm sure your parents were both chasing after the idea for political gain, but Lena was—and probably still is—like, genuinely in love with you, and was always sort of obsessed with the idea of being your wife. She was always talking to me about marrying you, about her dreams for the future, about what your children would look like—"

I glance at Warner to catch his reaction to that statement, and the revolted look on his face is surprisingly satisfying.

"—but I remember her saying something even then, about how detached you were, and how closed off, and how one day, when the two of you got married, she'd finally be able to link your family profiles in the database, which would grant her the necessary security clearance to track your—"

The plane gives a sudden, violent jolt.

Nazeera goes still, words dying in her throat. Warner jumps to his feet. We all make a dash for the cockpit.

The lights are flashing, screaming alerts I don't understand. Nazeera scans the monitor at the same time as Warner, and the two of them share a look.

The plane gives another violent jolt, and I slam, hard, into the something sharp and metal. I let out a long string of curses and for some reason, when Nazeera reaches out to help me up—

I freak out.

"Will someone tell me what the hell is going on? What's happening? Are we being shot out of the sky right now?" I spin around, taking in the flashing lights, the steady beep echoing through the cabin. "Fucking déjà vu! I knew it!"

Nazeera takes a deep breath. Closes her eyes. "We're not being shot out of the sky."

"Then—"

"When we entered Oceania's airspace," Warner explains, "their base was alerted to the presence of our unauthorized aircraft." He glances at the monitor. "They know we're here, and they're not happy about it."

"Right, I get that, but—"

Another violent jolt and I hit the floor. Warner doesn't even seem to startle. Nazeera stumbles, but gracefully, and collapses into the cockpit seat. She looks strangely deflated.

"So, um, okay— What's happening?" I'm breathing hard. My heart is racing. "Are you sure we're not being shot out of the sky again? Why is no one freaking out? Am I having a heart attack?"

"You're not having a heart attack, and they're not shooting us out of the sky," Nazeera says again, her fingers flying over the dials, swiping across screens. "But they've activated remote control of the aircraft. They've taken over the plane."

"And you can't override it?"

She shakes her head. "I don't have the authority to override a supreme commander's missive."

After a beat of silence, she straightens. Turns to face us.

"Maybe this isn't so bad," she says. "I mean, I wasn't exactly sure how we'd land here or how it would all go down, but it's got to be a good sign that they want us to walk in there alive, right?"

"Not necessarily," Warner says quietly.

"Right." Nazeera frowns. "Yeah, I realized that was wrong only after I said it out loud."

"So we're just supposed to wait here?" I'm feeling my intense panic begin to fade, but only a little. "We just wait here until they land our plane and then when they land our plane they surround us with armed soldiers and then when we walk off the plane they murder us and then—you know, we're dead? That's the plan?"

"That," Nazeera says, "or they could tell our plane to crash itself into the ocean or something."

"Oh my God, Nazeera, this isn't funny."

Warner looks out the window. "She wasn't joking."

"Okay, I'm only going to ask this one more time: Why am I the only one who's freaking out?"

"Because I have a plan," Nazeera says. She glances at the dashboard once more. "We have exactly fourteen minutes before the plane lands, but that gives me more than enough time to tell you both exactly what we're going to do."

~~ELLA~~
JULIETTE

First, I see light.

Bright, orange, flaring behind my eyelids. Sounds begin to emerge shortly thereafter but the reveal is slow, muddy. I hear my own breath, then faint beeping. A metal *shhh*, a rush of air, the sound of laughter. Footsteps, footsteps, a voice that says—

Ella

Just as I'm about to open my eyes a flood of heat flushes through my body, burns through bone. It's violent, pervasive. It presses hard against my throat, choking me.

Suddenly, I'm numb.

Ella, the voice says.

Ella

Listen

"Any minute now."

Anderson's familiar voice breaks through the haze of

my mind. My fingers twitch against cotton sheets. I feel the insubstantial weight of a thin blanket covering the lower half of my body. The pinch and sting of needles. A roar of pain. I realize, then, that I cannot move my left hand.

Someone clears their throat.

"This is twice now that the sedative hasn't worked the way it should," someone says. The voice is unfamiliar. Angry. "With Evie gone this whole place is going to hell."

"Evie made substantial changes to Ella's body," Anderson says, and I wonder who he's talking about. "It's possible that something in her new physical makeup prevents the sedative from clearing as quickly as it should."

A humorless laugh. "Your friendship with Max has gotten you many things over the last couple of decades, but a medical degree is not one of them."

"It's only a theory. I think it might be po—"

"I don't care to know your theories," the man says, cutting him off. "What I want to know is why on earth you thought it would be a good idea to injure our key subject, when maintaining her physical and mental stability is *crucial* to—"

"Ibrahim, be reasonable," Anderson interjects. "After what happened last time, I just wanted to be sure that everything was working as it should. I was only testing her lo—"

"We all know about your fetish for torture, Paris, but the novelty of your singularly sick mind has worn off. We're out of time."

"We are not out of time," Anderson says, sounding remarkably calm. "This is only a minor setback; Max was able to fix it right away."

"*A minor setback?*" Ibrahim thunders. "The girl lost consciousness. We're still at high risk for regression. The subject is supposed to be in stasis. I allowed you free rein of the girl, once again, because I honestly didn't think you would be this stupid. Because I don't have time to babysit you. Because Tatiana, Santiago, and Azi and I all have our hands full trying to do both your job *and* Evie's in addition to our own. In addition to everything else."

"I was doing my own job just fine," Anderson says, his voice like acid. "No one asked you to step in."

"You're forgetting that you lost your job and your continent the moment Evie's daughter shot you in the head and claimed your leavings for herself. You let a teenage girl take your life, your livelihood, your children, and your soldiers from right under your nose."

"You know as well as I do that she's not an ordinary teenage girl," Anderson says. "She's Evie's daughter. You know what she's capable of—"

"But *she* didn't!" Ibrahim cries. "Half the reason the girl was meant to live a life of isolation was so that she'd never know the full extent of her powers. She was meant only to metamorphose quietly, undetected, while we waited for the right moment to establish ourselves as a movement. She was only entrusted to your care because of your decades-long friendship with Max—and because you were a scheming, conniving upstart who was willing to take whatever job you could get in order to move up."

"That's funny," Anderson says, unamused. "You used to like me for being a scheming, conniving upstart who was willing to take whatever job I could get."

"I liked you," Ibrahim says, seething, "when you got the job done. But in the last year, you've been nothing but deadweight. We've given you ample opportunity to correct your mistakes, but you can't seem to get things right. You're lucky Max was able to fix her hand so quickly, but we still know nothing of her mental state. And I swear to you, Paris, if there are unanticipated, irreversible consequences for your actions I will challenge you before the committee."

"You wouldn't dare."

"You might've gotten away with this nonsense while Evie was still alive, but the rest of us know that the only reason you even made it this far was because of Evie's indulgence of Max, who continues to vouch for you for reasons unfathomable to the rest of us."

"*For reasons unfathomable to the rest of us?*" Anderson laughs. "You mean you can't remember why you've kept me around all these years? Let me help refresh your memory. As I recall, you liked me best when I was the only one willing to do the abject, immoral, and unsavory jobs that helped get this movement off the ground." A pause. "You've kept me around all these years, Ibrahim, because in exchange, I've kept the blood off your hands. Or have you forgotten? You once called me your savior."

"I don't care if I once called you a prophet." Something shatters. Metal and glass slamming hard into something else. "We can't continue to pay for your careless mistakes. We are at *war* right now, and at the moment we're barely holding on to our lead. If you can't understand the possible ramifications of even a minor setback at this critical hour, you don't deserve to stand among us."

A sudden crash. A door, slamming shut.

Anderson sighs, long and slow. Somehow I can tell, even from the sound of his exhalation, that he's not angry.

I'm surprised.

He just seems tired.

By degrees, the fingers of heat uncurl from around my throat. After a few more seconds of silence, my eyes flutter open.

I stare up at the ceiling, my eyes adjusting to the intense burst of white light. I feel slightly immobilized, but I seem to be okay.

"Juliette?"

Anderson's voice is soft. Far more gentle than I'd expected. I blink at the ceiling and then, with some effort, manage to move my neck. I lock eyes with him.

He looks unlike himself. Unshaven. Uncertain.

"Yes, sir," I say, but my voice is rough. Unused.

"How are you feeling?"

"I feel stiff, sir."

He hits a button and my bed moves, readjusting me so that I'm sitting relatively upright. Blood rushes from my head to my extremities and I'm left slightly dizzy. I blink, slowly, trying to recalibrate. Anderson turns off the machines attached to my body, and I watch, fascinated.

And then he straightens.

He turns his back to me, faces a small, high window. It's too far up for me to see the view. He raises his arms and runs his hands through his hair with a sigh.

"I need a drink," he says to the wall.

Anderson nods to himself and walks out the adjoining door. At first, I'm surprised to be left alone, but when I hear muffled sounds of movement and the familiar trill of glasses, clinking, I'm no longer surprised.

I'm confused.

I realize then that I have no idea where I am. Now that the needles have been removed from my body, I can more easily move, and as I swivel around to take in the space, it dawns on me that I am not in a medical wing, as I first suspected. This looks more like someone's bedroom.

Or maybe even a hotel room.

Everything is extremely white. Sterile. I'm in a big white bed with white sheets and a white comforter. Even the bed frame is made of a white, blond wood. Next to the various carts and now-dead monitors, there's a single nightstand decorated with a single, simple lamp. There's a slim door standing ajar, and through a slant of light I think I spy what serves as a closet, though it appears to be empty. Adjacent to the door is a suitcase, closed but unzipped. There's a screen mounted on the wall directly opposite me, and underneath it, a bureau. One of the drawers isn't completely closed, and it piques my interest.

It occurs to me then that I am not wearing any clothes. I'm wearing a hospital gown, but no real clothes. My eyes scan the room for my military uniform and I come up short.

There's nothing here.

I remember then, in a moment of clarity, that I must've bled all over my clothes. I remember kneeling on the floor. I remember the growing puddle of my own blood in which I collapsed.

I glance down at my injured hand. I only injured my index finger, but my entire left hand is bound in gauze. The pain has reduced to a dull throb. I take that as a good sign.

Gingerly, I begin to remove the bandages.

Just then, Anderson reappears. His suit jacket is gone. His tie, gone. The top two buttons of his shirt are undone, the black curl of ink more clearly visible, and his hair is disheveled. He seems more relaxed.

He remains in the doorway and takes a long drink from a glass half-full of amber liquid.

When he makes eye contact with me, I say:

"Sir, I was wondering where I am. I was also wondering where my clothes are."

Anderson takes another sip. He closes his eyes as he swallows, leans back against the doorframe. Sighs.

"You're in my room," he says, his eyes still closed. "This compound is vast, and the medical wings—of which there are many—are, for the most part, situated on the opposite end of the facility, about a mile away. After Max attended to your needs, I had him deposit you here so that I'd be able to keep a close eye on you through the night. As to your clothes, I have no idea." He takes another sip. "I think Max had them incinerated. I'm sure someone will bring you replacements soon."

"Thank you, sir."

Anderson says nothing.

I say nothing more.

With his eyes closed, I feel safer to stare at him. I take advantage of the rare opportunity to peer closer at his tattoo, but I still can't make sense of it. Mostly, I stare at his face, which I've never seen like this: Soft. Relaxed. Almost smiling. Even so, I can tell that something is troubling him.

"What?" he says without looking at me. "What is it now?"

"I was wondering, sir, if you're okay."

His eyes open. He tilts his head to look at me, but his gaze is inscrutable. Slowly, he turns.

He throws back the last of his drink, rests the glass on the nightstand, and sits down in a nearby armchair. "I had you cut off your own finger last night, do you remember?"

"Yes, sir."

"And today you're asking me if I'm okay."

"Yes, sir. You seem upset, sir."

He leans back in the chair, looking thoughtful. Suddenly, he shakes his head. "You know, I realize now that I've been too hard on you. I've put you through too much. Tested your loyalty perhaps too much. But you and I have a long history,

Juliette. And it's not easy for me to forgive. I certainly don't forget."

I say nothing.

"You have no idea how much I hated you," he says, speaking more to the wall than to me. "How much I still hate you, sometimes. But now, finally—"

He sits up, looks me in the eye.

"Now you're perfect." He laughs, but there's no heart in it. "Now you're absolutely perfect and I have to just give you away. Toss your body to science." He turns toward the wall again. "What a shame."

Fear creeps up, through my chest. I ignore it.

Anderson stands, grabs the empty glass off the nightstand, and disappears for a minute to refill it. When he returns, he stares at me from the doorway. I stare back. We remain like that for a while before he says, suddenly—

"You know, when I was very young, I wanted to be a baker."

Surprise shoots through me, widens my eyes.

"I know," he says, taking another swallow of the amber liquid. He almost laughs. "Not what you'd expect. But I've always had a fondness for cake. Few people realize this, but baking requires infinite precision and patience. It is an exacting, cruel science. I would've been an excellent baker." And then: "I'm not really sure why I'm telling you this. I suppose it's been a long time since I've felt I could speak openly with anyone."

"You can tell me anything, sir."

"Yes," he says quietly. "I'm beginning to believe that."

We're both silent then, but I can't stop staring at him, my mind suddenly overrun with unanswerable questions.

Another twenty seconds of this and he finally breaks the silence.

"All right, what is it?" His voice is dry. Self-mocking. "What is it you're *dying* to know?"

"I'm sorry, sir," I say. "I was just wondering— Why didn't you try? To be a baker?"

Anderson shrugs, spins the glass around in his hands. "When I got a bit older, my mother used to force bleach down my throat. Ammonia. Whatever she could find under the sink. It was never enough to kill me," he says, meeting my eyes. "Just enough to torture me for all of eternity." He throws back the rest of the drink. "You might say that I lost my appetite."

I can't mask my horror quickly enough. Anderson laughs at me, laughs at the look on my face.

"She never even had a good reason for doing it," he says, turning away. "She just hated me."

"Sir," I say, "Sir, I—"

Max barges into the room. I flinch.

"What the hell did you do?"

"There are so many possible answers to that question," Anderson says, glancing back. "Please be more specific. By the way, what did you do with her clothes?"

"I'm talking about Kent," Max says angrily. "What did you do?"

336

Anderson looks suddenly uncertain. He glances from Max to me then back again. "Perhaps we should discuss this elsewhere."

But Max looks beyond reason. His eyes are so wild I can't tell if he's angry or terrified. "Please tell me the tapes were tampered with. Tell me I'm wrong. Tell me you didn't perform the procedure on yourself."

Anderson looks at once relieved and irritated. "Calm yourself," he says. "I watched Evie do this kind of thing countless times—and the last time, on me. The boy had already been drained. The vial was ready, just sitting there on the counter, and you were so busy with"—he glances at me—"anyway, I had a while to wait, and I figured I'd make myself useful while I stood around."

"I can't believe— Of course you don't see the problem," Max says, grabbing a fistful of his own hair. He's shaking his head. "You never see the problem."

"That seems an unfair accusation."

"Paris, there's a reason why most Unnaturals only have one ability." He's beginning to pace now. "The occurrence of two supernatural gifts in the same person is exceedingly rare."

"What about Ibrahim's girl?" he says. "Wasn't that your work? Evie's?"

"No," Max says forcefully. "That was a random, natural error. We were just as surprised by the discovery as anyone else."

Anderson goes suddenly solid with tension. "What,

337

exactly, is the problem?"

"It's not—"

A sudden blare of sirens and the words die in Max's throat. "Not again," he whispers. "God, not again."

Anderson spares me a single glance before he disappears into his room, and this time, he reappears fully assembled. Not a hair out of place. He checks the cartridge of a handgun before he tucks it away, in a hidden holster.

"Juliette," he says sharply.

"Yes, sir?"

"I am ordering you to remain here. No matter what you see, no matter what you hear, you are not to leave this room. You are to do nothing unless I command you otherwise. Do you understand? "

"Yes, sir."

"Max, get her something to wear," Anderson barks. "And then keep her hidden. Guard her with your life."

KENJI

This was the plan:

We were all supposed to go invisible—Warner borrowing his power from me and Nazeera—and jump out of the plane just before it landed. Nazeera would then activate her flying powers, and with Warner bolstering her power, the three of us would bypass the welcoming committee intent on murdering us. We'd then make our way directly into the heart of the vast compound, where we'd begin our search for Juliette.

This is what actually happens:

All three of us go invisible and jump out of the plane as it lands. That part worked. The thing we weren't expecting, of course, was for the welcoming/murdering committee to so thoroughly anticipate our moves.

We're up in the air, flying over the heads of at least two dozen highly armed soldiers and one dude who looks like he might be Nazeera's dad, when someone flashes some kind of long-barreled gun up, into the sky. He seems to be searching for something.

Us.

"He's scanning for heat signatures," Warner says.

"I realize that," Nazeera says, sounding frustrated. She

picks up speed, but it doesn't matter.

Seconds later, the guy with the heat gun shouts something to someone else, who aims a different weapon at us, one that immediately disables our powers.

It's just as horrifying as it sounds.

I don't even have a chance to scream. I don't have time to think about the fact that my heart is racing a mile a minute, or that my hands are shaking, or that Nazeera—fearless, invulnerable Nazeera—looks suddenly terrified as the sky falls out from under her. Even Warner seems stunned.

I was already super freaked out about the idea of being shot out of the sky again, but I can honestly say that I wasn't mentally prepared for this. This is a whole new level of terror. The three of us are suddenly visible and spiraling to our deaths and the soldiers below are just staring at us, waiting.

For what? I think.

Why are they just staring at us as we die? Why go to all the trouble to take over our plane and land us here, safely, just to watch us fall out of the sky?

Do they find this entertaining?

Time feels strange. Infinite and nonexistent. Wind is rushing up against my feet, and all I can see is the ground, coming at us too fast, but I can't stop thinking about how, in all my nightmares, I never thought I'd die like this. I never thought I'd die because of gravity. I didn't think that *this* was the way I was destined to exit the world, and it seems wrong, and it seems unfair, and I'm thinking about how quickly we failed, how we never stood a chance—when I hear a sudden explosion.

A flash of fire, discordant cries, the faraway sounds of Warner shouting, and then I'm no longer falling, no longer visible.

It all happens so fast I feel dizzy.

Nazeera's arm is wrapped around me and she's hauling me upward, struggling a bit, and then Warner materializes beside me, helping to prop me up. His sharp voice and familiar presence are my only proof of his existence.

"Nice shot," Nazeera says, her breathless words loud in my ear. "How long do you think we have?"

"Ten seconds before it occurs to them to start shooting blindly at us," Warner calls out. "We have to move out of range. Now."

"On it," Nazeera shouts back.

We narrowly avoid gunfire as the three of us plummet, at a sharp diagonal, to the ground. We were already so close to the ground that it doesn't take us long to land in the middle of a field, far enough away from danger to be able to breathe a momentary sigh of relief, but too far from the compound for the relief to last long.

I'm bent over, hands on my knees, gasping for breath, trying to calm down. "What did you do you? What the hell just happened?"

"Warner threw a grenade," Nazeera explains. Then, to Warner: "You found that in Haider's bag, didn't you?"

"That, and a few other useful things. We need to move."

I hear the sound of his retreating footsteps—boots crushing grass—and I hurry to follow.

"They'll regroup quickly," Warner is saying, "so we have only moments to come up with a new plan. I think we should split up."

"No," Nazeera and I say at the same time.

"There's no time," Warner says. "They know we're here, and they've obviously had ample opportunity to prepare for our arrival. Unfortunately, our parents aren't idiots; they know we're here to save Ella. Our presence has almost certainly inspired them to begin the transfer if they haven't done so already. The three of us together are inefficient. Easy targets."

"But one of us has to stay with you," Nazeera says. "You need us within close proximity if you're going to use stealth to get around."

"I'll take my chances."

"No way," Nazeera says flatly. "Listen, I know this compound, so I'll be okay on my own. But Kenji doesn't know this place well enough. The entire footprint measures out to about a hundred and twenty acres of land—which means you can easily get lost if you don't know where to look. You two stick together. Kenji will lend you his stealth, and you can be his guide. I'll go alone."

"What?" I say, panicked. "No, no way—"

"Warner's not wrong," Nazeera says, cutting me off. "The three of us, as a group, really do make for an easier target. There are too many variables. Besides, I have something

344

I need to do, and the sooner I can get to a computer, the smoother things will go for you both. It's probably best if I tackle that on my own."

"Wait, what?"

"What are you planning?" Warner asks.

"I'm going to trick the systems into thinking that your family and Ella's are linked," she says to Warner. "There's protocol for this sort of thing already in place within The Reestablishment, so if I can create the necessary profiles and authorizations, the database will recognize you as a member of the Sommers family. You'll be granted easy access to most of the high-security rooms throughout the compound. But it's not foolproof. The system does a self-scan for anomalies every hour. If it's able to see through my bullshit, you'll be locked out and reported. But until then—you'll be able to more easily search the buildings for Ella."

"Nazeera," Warner says, sounding unusually impressed. "That's . . . great."

"Better than great," I add. "That's amazing."

"Thanks," she says. "But I should get going. The sooner I start flying, the sooner I can get started, which hopefully means that by the time you reach base, I'll have made something happen."

"But what if you get caught?" I ask. "What if you can't do it? How will we find you?"

"You won't."

"But— Nazeera—"

"We're at war, Kishimoto," she says, a slight smile in her voice. "We don't have time to be sentimental."

"That's not funny. I hate that joke. I hate it so much."

"Nazeera is going to be fine," Warner says. "You obviously don't know her well if you think she's easily captured."

"She literally just woke up! After being shot! In the chest! She nearly died!"

"That was a fluke," Warner and Nazeera say at the same time.

"But—"

"Hey," Nazeera says, her voice suddenly close. "I have a feeling I'm about four months away from falling madly in love with you, so please don't get yourself killed, okay?"

I'm about to respond when I feel a sudden rush of air. I hear her launching up, into the sky, and even though I know I won't see her, I crane my neck as if to watch her go.

And just like that—

She's gone.

My heart is pounding in my chest, blood rushing to my head. I feel confused: terrified, excited, hopeful, horrified. All the best and worst things always seem to happen to me at the same time.

It's not fair.

"Fucking hell," I say out loud.

"Come on," Warner says. "Let's move out."

~~ELLA~~ JULIETTE

Max is staring at me like I'm an alien.

He hasn't moved since Anderson left; he just stands there, stiff and strange, rooted to the floor. I remember the look he gave me the first time we met—the unguarded hostility in his eyes—and I blink at him from my bed, wondering why he hates me so much.

After an uncomfortable stretch of silence, I clear my throat. It's obvious that Anderson respects Max—likes him, even—so I decide I should address him with a similar level of respect.

"Sir," I say. "I'd really like to get dressed."

Max startles at the sound of my voice. His body language is entirely different now that Anderson isn't here, and I'm still struggling to figure him out. He seems skittish. I wonder if I should feel threatened by him. His affection for Anderson is no indication that he might treat me as anything but a nameless soldier.

A subordinate.

Max sighs. It's a loud, rough sound that seems to shake him from his stupor. He shoots me a last look before he disappears into the adjoining room, from where I hear indiscernible, shuffling sounds. When he reappears, his arms are empty.

He stares blankly at me, looking more rattled than he did a moment ago. He shoves a hand through his hair. It sticks up in places.

"Anderson doesn't have anything that would fit you," he says.

"No, sir," I say carefully. Still confused. "I was hoping I might be given a replacement uniform."

Max turns away, stares at nothing. "A replacement uniform," he says to himself. "Right." But when he takes in a long, shuddering breath, it becomes clear to me that he's trying to stay calm.

Trying to stay calm.

I realize, suddenly, that Max might be afraid of me. Maybe he saw what I did to Darius. Maybe he's the doctor who patched him up.

Still—

I don't see what reason he'd have to think I'd hurt him. After all, my orders come from Anderson, and as far as I'm aware, Max is an ally. I watch him closely as he lifts his wrist to his mouth, quietly requesting that someone deliver a fresh set of clothes for me.

And then he backs away from me until he's flush with the wall. There's a single, sharp thud as the heels of his boots hit the baseboards, and then, silence.

Silence.

It erupts, settling completely into the room, the quiet reaching even the farthest corners. I feel physically trapped by it. The lack of sound feels oppressive.

Paralyzing.

I pass the time by counting the bruises on my body. I don't think I've spent this much time looking at myself in the last few days; I hadn't realized how many wounds I had. There seem to be several fresh cuts on my arms and legs, and I feel a vague stinging along my lower abdomen. I pull back the collar of the hospital gown, peering through the overly large neck hole at my naked body underneath.

Pale. Bruised.

There's a small, fresh scar running vertically down the side of my torso, and I don't know what I did to acquire it. In fact, my body seems to have amassed an entire constellation of fresh incisions and faded bruises. For some reason, I can't remember where they came from.

I glance up, suddenly, when I feel the heat of Max's gaze.

He's staring at me as I study myself, and the sharp look in his eyes makes me wary. I sit up. Sit back.

I don't feel comfortable asking him any of the questions piling in my mouth.

So I look at my hands.

I've already removed the rest of my bandages; my left hand is mostly healed. There's no visible scar where my finger was detached, but my skin is mottled up to my forearm, mostly purple and dark blue, a few spots of yellow. I curl my fingers into a fist, let it go. It hurts only a little. The pain is fading by the hour.

The next words leave my lips before I can stop them:

"Thank you, sir, for fixing my hand."

Max stares at me, uncertain, when his wrist lights up. He glances down at the message, and then at the door, and as he darts to the entrance, he tosses strange, wild looks at me over his shoulder, as if he's afraid to turn his back on me.

Max grows more bizarre by the moment.

When the door opens, the room is flooded with sound. Flashing lights pulse through the slice of open doorway, shouts and footsteps thundering down the hall. I hear metal crashing into metal, the distant blare of an alarm.

My heart picks up.

I'm on my feet before I can even stop myself, my sharpened senses oblivious to the fact that my hospital gown does little to cover my body. All I know is a sudden, urgent need to join the commotion, to do what I can to assist, and to find my commander and protect him. It's what I was built to do.

I can't just stand here.

But then I remember that my commander gave me explicit orders to remain here, and the fight leaves my body.

Max shuts the door, silencing the chaos with that single motion. I open my mouth to say something, but the look in his eyes warns me not to speak. He places a stack of clothes on the bed—refusing to even come near me—and steps out of the room.

I change into the clothes quickly, shedding the loose gown for the starched, stiff fabric of a freshly washed military uniform. Max brought me no undergarments, but

I don't bother pointing this out; I'm just relieved to have something to wear. I'm still buttoning the front placket, my fingers working as quickly as possible, when my gaze falls once more to the bureau directly opposite the bed. There's a single drawer left slightly open, as if it was closed in a hurry.

I'd noticed it earlier.

I can't stop staring at it now.

Something pulls me forward, some need I can't explain. It's becoming familiar now—almost normal—to feel the strange heat filling my head, so I don't question my compulsion to move closer. Something somewhere inside of me is screaming at me to stand down, but I'm only dimly aware of it. I hear Max's muffled, low voice in the other room; he's speaking with someone in harried, aggressive tones. He seems fully distracted.

Encouraged, I step forward.

My hand curls around the drawer pull, and it takes only a little effort to tug it open. It's a smooth, soft system. The wood makes almost no sound as it moves. And I'm just about to peer inside when—

"What are you doing?"

Max's voice sends a sharp note of clarity through my brain, clearing the haze. I take a step back, blinking. Trying to understand what I was doing.

"The drawer was open, sir. I was going to close it." The lie comes automatically. Easily.

I marvel at it.

Max slams the drawer closed and stares, suspiciously, at

my face. I blink at him, blithely meeting his gaze.

I notice then that he's holding my boots.

He shoves them at me; I take them. I want to ask him if he has a hair tie—my hair is unusually long; I have a vague memory of it being much shorter—but I decide against it.

He watches me closely as I pull on my boots, and once I'm upright again, he barks at me to follow him.

I don't move.

"Sir, my commander gave me direct orders to remain in this room. I will stay here until otherwise instructed."

"You're currently being instructed. I'm instructing you."

"With all due respect, sir, you are not my commanding officer."

Max sighs, irritation darkening his features, and he lifts his wrist to his mouth. "Did you hear that? I told you she wouldn't listen to me." A pause. "Yes. You'll have to come get her yourself."

Another pause.

Max is listening on an invisible earpiece not unlike the one I've seen Anderson use—an earpiece I'm now realizing must be implanted in their brains.

"Absolutely not," Max says, his anger so sudden it startles me. He shakes his head. "I'm not touching her."

Another beat of silence, and—

"I realize that," he says sharply. "But it's different when her eyes are open. There's something about her face. I don't like the way she looks at me."

My heart slows.

354

Blackness fills my vision, flickers back to light. I hear my heart beating, hear myself breathe in, breathe out, hear my own voice, loud—so loud—

There was something about my face

The words slur, slow down

there wassomething about my facesssomething about my facesssomething about my eyes, the way I looked at her

My eyes fly open with a start. I'm breathing hard, confused, and I have hardly a moment to reflect on what just happened in my head before the door flies open again. A roar of noise fills my ears—more sirens, more shouts, more sounds of urgent, chaotic movement—

"Juliette Ferrars."

There's a man in front of me. Tall. Forbidding. Black hair, brown skin, green eyes. I can tell, just by looking at him, that he wields a great deal of power.

"I am Supreme Commander Ibrahim."

My eyes widen.

Musa Ibrahim is the supreme commander of Asia. By all accounts, the supreme commanders of The Reestablishment have equal levels of authority—but Supreme Commander Ibrahim is widely known to be one of the founders of the movement, and one of the only supreme commanders to have held the position from the beginning. He's extremely well respected.

So when he says, "Come with me," I say—

"Yes, sir."

I follow him out the door and into the chaos, but I don't have long to take in the pandemonium before we make a sharp turn into a dark hallway. I follow Ibrahim down a slim, narrow path, the lights dimming as we go. I glance back a few times to see if Max is still with us, but he seems to have gone in another direction.

"This way," Ibrahim says sharply.

We make one more turn and, suddenly, the narrow path opens onto a large, brightly lit landing area. There's an industrial stairwell to the left and a large, gleaming steel elevator to the right. Ibrahim heads for the elevator, and places his hand flat against the seamless door. After a moment, the metal emits a quiet beep, hissing as it slides open.

Once we're both inside, Ibrahim gives me a wide berth. I wait for him to direct the elevator—I scan the interior for buttons or a monitor of some kind—but he does nothing. A second later, without prompting, the elevator moves.

The ride is so smooth it takes me a minute to realize we're moving sideways, rather than up or down. I glance around, taking the opportunity to more closely examine the interior, and only then do I notice the rounded corners. I thought this unit was rectangular; it appears to be circular. I wonder, then, if we're moving as a bullet would, boring through the earth.

Surreptitiously, I glance at Ibrahim.

He says nothing. Indicates nothing. He seems neither interested nor perturbed by my presence, which is new. He holds himself with a certainty that reminds me a great deal of Anderson, but there's something else about Ibrahim— something more—that feels unique. Even from a passing glance it's obvious that he feels absolutely sure about himself. I'm not sure even Anderson feels absolutely sure of himself. He's always testing and prodding—examining and questioning. Ibrahim, on the other hand, seems comfortable. Unbothered. Effortlessly confident.

I wonder what that must feel like.

And then I shock myself for wondering.

Once the elevator stops, it makes three brief, harsh, buzzing sounds. A moment later, the doors open. I wait for Ibrahim to exit first, and then I follow.

When I cross the threshold, I'm first stunned by the smell. The air quality is so poor that I can't even open my eyes properly. There's an acrid smell in the air, something reminiscent of sulfur, and I step through a cloud of smoke so thick it immediately makes my eyes burn. It's not long before I'm coughing, covering my face with my arm as I force my way through the room.

I don't know how Ibrahim can stand this.

Only after I've pushed through the cloud does the stinging smell begin to dissipate, but by then, I've lost track of Ibrahim. I spin around, trying to take in my surroundings, but there are no visual cues to root me. This laboratory doesn't seem much different from the others I've seen. A great deal of glass and steel. Dozens of long, metal tables stretched across the room, all of them covered in beakers and test tubes and what look like massive microscopes. The one big difference here is that there are huge glass domes drilled into the walls, the smooth, transparent semicircles appearing more like portholes than anything else. As I get closer I realize that they're planters of some kind, each one containing unusual vegetation I've never seen. Lights flicker on as I move through the vast space, but much of it is still shrouded in darkness, and I gasp, suddenly, when I walk straight into a glass wall.

I take a step back, my eyes adjusting to the light.

It's not a wall.

It's an aquarium.

An aquarium larger than I am. An aquarium the size of a wall. It's not the first water tank I've seen in a laboratory here in Oceania, and I'm beginning to wonder why there are so many of them. I take another step back, still trying to make sense of what I'm seeing. Dissatisfied, I step closer again. There's a dim blue light in the tank, but it doesn't do much to illuminate the large dimensions. I crane my neck to see the top of it, but I lose my balance, catching myself against the glass at the last second. This is a futile effort.

I need to find Ibrahim.

Just as I'm about to step back, I notice a flash of movement in the tank. The water trembles within, begins to thrash.

A hand slams hard against the glass.

I gasp.

Slowly, the hand retreats.

I stand there, frozen in fear and fascination, when someone clamps down on my arm.

This time, I almost scream.

"Where have you been?" Ibrahim says angrily.

"I'm sorry, sir," I say quickly. "I got lost. The smoke was so thick that I—"

"What are you talking about? What smoke?"

The words die in my throat. I thought I saw smoke. Was there no smoke? Is this another test?

Ibrahim sighs. "Come with me."

"Yes, sir."

This time, I keep my eyes on Ibrahim at all times.

And this time, when we walk through the darkened laboratory into a blindingly bright, circular room, I know I'm in the right place. Because something is wrong.

Someone is dead.

KENJI

KENJI

When we finally make it to the compound, I'm exhausted, thirsty, and really have to use the bathroom. Warner is none of those things, apparently, because Warner is made of uranium or plutonium or some shit, so I have to beg him to let me take a quick break. And by begging him I mean I grab him by the back of the shirt and force him to slow down—and then I basically collapse behind a wall. Warner shoves away from me, and the sound of his irritated exhalation is all I need to know that my "break" is half a second from over.

"We don't take breaks," he says sharply. "If you can't keep up, stay here."

"Bro, I'm not asking to stop. I'm not even asking for a real break. I just need a second to catch my breath. Two seconds. Maybe five seconds. That's not crazy. And just because I have to catch my breath doesn't mean I don't love J. It means we just ran like a thousand miles. It means my lungs aren't made of steel."

"Two miles," he says. "We ran two miles."

"In the sun. Uphill. You're in a fucking suit. Do you even sweat? How are you not tired?"

"If by now you don't understand, I certainly can't teach you."

I haul myself to my feet. We start moving again.

"I'm not sure I even want to know what you're talking about," I say, lowering my voice as I reach for my gun. We're rounding the corner to the entrance, where our big, fancy plan to break into the building involves waiting for someone to open the door, and catching that door before it closes.

No luck yet.

"Hey," I whisper.

"What?" Warner sounds annoyed.

"How'd you end up proposing?"

Silence.

"Come on, bro. I'm curious. Also, I, uh, really have to pee, so if you don't distract me right now all I'm going to think about is how much I have to pee."

"You know, sometimes I wish I could remove the part of my brain that stores the things you say to me."

I ignore that.

"So? How'd you do it?" Someone comes through the door and I tense, ready to jump forward, but there's not enough time. My body relaxes back against the wall. "Did you get the ring like I told you to?"

"No."

"What? What do you mean, *no*?" I hesitate. "Did you at least, like, light a candle? Make her dinner?"

"No."

"Buy her chocolates? Get down on one knee?"

"No."

"No? No, you didn't do even one of those things? None

of them?" My whispers are turning into whisper-yells. "You didn't do a single thing I told you to do?"

"No."

"Son of a bitch."

"Why does it matter?" he asks. "She said yes."

I groan. "You're the worst, you know that? The *worst*. You don't deserve her."

Warner sighs. "I thought that was already obvious."

"Hey— Don't you dare make me feel sorry for y—"

I cut myself off when the door suddenly opens. A small group of doctors (scientists? I don't know) exits the building, and Warner and I jump to our feet and get into position. This group has just enough people—and they take just long enough exiting—that when I grab the door and hold it open for a few seconds longer, it doesn't seem to register.

We're in.

And we've only been inside for less than a second before Warner slams me into the wall, knocking the air from my lungs.

"Don't move," he whispers. "Not an inch."

"Why not?" I wheeze.

"Look up," he says, "but only with your eyes. Don't move your head. Do you see the cameras?"

"No."

"They anticipated us," he says. "They anticipated our moves. Look up again, but do it carefully. Those small black dots are cameras. Sensors. Infrared scanners. Thermal imagers. They're searching for inconsistencies in the security footage."

"*Shit.*"

"Yes."

"So what do we do?"

"I'm not sure," Warner says.

"You're not sure?" I say, trying not to freak out. "How can you not be sure?"

"I'm thinking," he whispers, irritated. "And I don't hear you contributing any ideas."

"Listen, bro, all I know is that I really, really need to p—"

I'm interrupted by the distant sound of a toilet flushing. A moment later, a door swings open. I turn my head a millimeter and realize we're right next to the men's bathroom.

Warner and I seize the moment, catching the door before it falls closed. Once inside the bathroom we press up against the wall, our backs to the cold tile. I'm trying hard not to think about all the pee residue touching my body, when Warner exhales.

It's a brief, quiet sound—but he sounds relieved.

I'm guessing that means there are no scanners or cameras in this bathroom, but I can't be sure, because Warner doesn't say a word, and it doesn't take a genius to figure out why.

We're not sure if we're alone in here.

I can't see him do it, but I'm pretty sure Warner is checking the stalls right now. It's what I'm doing, anyway. This isn't a huge bathroom—as I'm sure it's one of many—and it's right by the entrance/exit of the building, so right now it doesn't seem to be getting a lot of traffic.

When we're both certain the room is clear, Warner says—

"We're going to go up, through the vent. If you truly need to use the bathroom, do it now."

"Okay, but why do you have to sound so disgusted about it? Do you really expect me to believe that you never have to use the bathroom? Are basic human needs below you?"

Warner ignores me.

I see the stall door open, and I hear his careful sounds as he climbs the metal cubicles. There's a large vent in the ceiling just above one of the stalls, and I watch as his invisible hands make short work of the grate.

Quickly, I use the bathroom. And then I wash my hands as loudly as possible, just in case Warner feels the need to make a juvenile comment about my hygiene.

Surprisingly, he doesn't.

Instead, he says, "Are you ready?" And I can tell by the echoing sound of his voice that he's already halfway up the vent.

"I'm ready. Just let me know when you're in."

More careful movement, the metal drumming as he goes. "I'm in," he says. "Make sure you reattach the grate after you climb up."

"Got it."

"On a related note, I hope you're not claustrophobic. Though if you are . . . Good luck."

I take a deep breath.

Let it go.

And we begin our journey into hell.

~~ELLA~~ JULIETTE

Max, Anderson, a blond woman, and a tall black man are all standing in the center of the room, staring at a dead body, and they look up only when Ibrahim approaches.

Anderson's eyes home in on me immediately.

I feel my heart jump. I don't know how Max got here before we did, and I don't know if I'm about to be punished for obeying Supreme Commander Ibrahim.

My mind spirals.

"What's she doing here?" Anderson asks, his expression wild. "I told her to stay in the r—"

"I overruled your orders," Ibrahim says sharply, "and told her to come with me."

"My bedroom is one of the most secure locations on this wing," Anderson says, barely holding on to his anger. "You've put us all at risk by moving her."

"We are currently under attack," Ibrahim says. "You left her alone, completely unattended—"

"I left her with Max!"

"Max, who's too terrified of his own creation to spend even a few minutes alone with the girl. You forget, there's a reason he was never granted a military position."

Anderson shoots Max a strange, confused look.

371

Somehow, the confusion on Anderson's face makes me feel better about my own. I have no idea what's happening. No idea to whom I should answer. No idea what Ibrahim meant by *creation*.

Max just shakes his head.

"The children are here," Ibrahim says, changing the subject. "They're here, in our midst, completely undetected. They're going room by room searching for her, and already they've killed four of our key scientists in the process." He nods at the dead body—a graying, middle-aged man, blood pooling beneath him. "How did this happen? Why haven't they been spotted yet?"

"Nothing has registered on the cameras," Anderson says. "Not yet, anyway."

"So you're telling me that this—and the three other dead bodies we've found so far—was the work of ghosts?"

"They must've found a way to trick the system," the woman says. "It's the only possible answer."

"Yes, Tatiana, I realize that—but the question is *how*." Ibrahim pinches his nose between his thumb and index finger. And it's clear he's talking to Anderson when he says: "All the preparations you claimed to have made in anticipation of a possible assault—they were all for nothing?"

"What did you expect?" Anderson is no longer trying to control his anger. "They're our children. We bred them for this. I'd be disappointed if they were stupid enough to fall into our traps right away."

Our children?

"Enough," Ibrahim cries. "Enough of this. We need to initiate the transfer now."

"I already told you why we can't," Max says urgently. "Not yet. We need more time. Emmaline still needs to fall below ten percent viability in order for the procedure to operate smoothly, and right now, she's at twelve percent. Another few days—maybe a couple of weeks—and we should be able to move forward. But anything above ten percent viability means there's a chance she'll still be strong enough to resis—"

"I don't care," Ibrahim says. "We've waited long enough. And we've wasted enough time and money trying to keep both her alive and her sister in our custody. We can't risk another failure."

"But initiating the transfer at twelve percent viability has a thirty-eight percent chance of failure," Max says, speaking quickly. "We could be risking a great deal—"

"Then find more ways to reduce viability," Ibrahim snaps.

"We're already at the top end of what we can do right now," Max says. "She's still too strong—she's fighting our efforts—"

"That's only more reason to get rid of her sooner," Ibrahim says, cutting him off again. "We're expending an egregious amount of resources just to keep the other kids isolated from her advances—when God only knows what damage she's already done. She's been meddling everywhere, causing needless disaster. We need a new host. A healthy one. And we need it now."

"Ibrahim, don't be rash," Anderson says, trying to sound calm. "This could be a huge mistake. Juliette is a perfect soldier—she's more than proven herself—and right now she could be a huge help. Instead of locking her away, we should be sending her out. Giving her a mission."

"Absolutely not."

"Ibrahim, he makes a good point," the tall black man says. "The kids won't be expecting her. She'd be the perfect lure."

"See? Azi agrees with me."

"I don't." Tatiana shakes her head. "It's too dangerous," she says. "Too many things could go wrong."

"What could possibly go wrong?" Anderson asks. "She's more powerful than any of them, and completely obedient to me. To us. To the movement. You all know as well as I do that she's proven her loyalty again and again. She'd be able to capture them in a matter of minutes. This could all be over in an hour, and we'd be able to move on with our lives." Anderson locks eyes with me. "You wouldn't mind rounding up a few rebels, would you, Juliette?"

"I would be happy to, sir."

"See?" Anderson gestures to me.

A sudden alarm blares, the sound so loud it's painful. I'm still rooted in place, so overwhelmed and confused by this sudden flood of dizzying information that I don't even know what to do with myself. But the supreme commanders look suddenly terrified.

"Azi, where is Santiago?" Tatiana cries. "You were last with him, weren't you? Someone check in with Santiago—"

"He's down," Azi says, tapping against his temple. "He's not responding."

"*Max*," Anderson says sharply, but Max is already rushing out the door, Azi and Tatiana on his heels.

"Go collect your son," Ibrahim barks at Anderson.

"Why don't you go collect your daughter?" Anderson shoots back.

Ibrahim's eyes narrow. "I'm taking the girl," he says quietly. "I'm finishing this job, and I'll do it alone if I have to."

Anderson glances from me to Ibrahim. "You're making a mistake," he says. "She's finally become our asset. Don't let your pride keep you from seeing the answer in front of us. Juliette should be the one tracking down the kids right now. The fact that they won't be anticipating her as an assailant makes them easier targets. It's the most obvious solution."

"You are out of your mind," Ibrahim shouts, "if you think I'm foolish enough to take such a risk. I will not just hand her over to her friends like some common idiot."

Friends?

I have friends?

"*Hey, princess,*" someone whispers in my ear.

KENJI

KENT

Warner just about slaps me upside the head.

He yanks me back, grabbing me roughly by the shoulder, and drags us both across the overly bright, extremely creepy laboratory.

Once we're far enough away from Anderson, Ibrahim, and Robot J, I expect Warner to say something—anything—

He doesn't.

The two of us watch the distant conversation grow more heated by the moment, but we can't really hear what they're saying from here. Though I think even if we could hear what they were saying, Warner wouldn't be paying attention. The fight seems to have left his body. I can't even see him right now, but I can feel it. Something about his movements, his quiet sighs.

His mind is on Juliette.

Juliette, who looks the same. Better, in fact. She looks healthy, her eyes bright, her skin glowing. Her hair is down—long, heavy, dark—the way it was the first time I ever saw her.

But she's not the same. Even I can see that.

And it's devastating.

I guess this is somehow better than if she'd replaced

Emmaline altogether, but this weird, robotic, super-soldier version of J is also deeply concerning.

I think.

I keep waiting for Warner to finally break the silence, to give me some indication of his feelings and/or theories on the matter—and maybe, while he's at it, offer me his professional opinion on what the hell we should be doing next—but the seconds continue to pass in perfect silence.

Finally, I give up.

"All right, get it out," I whisper. "Tell me what you're thinking."

Warner lets out a long breath. "This doesn't make sense."

I nod, even though he can't see me. "I get that. Nothing makes sense in situations like these. I always feel like it's unfair, you know, like the worl—"

"I'm not being philosophical," Warner says, cutting me off. "I mean it literally doesn't make sense. Nouria and Sam said that Operation Synthesis would turn Ella into a super soldier—and that once the program went into effect, the result would be irreversible.

"But this is not Operation Synthesis," he says. "Operation Synthesis is literally about synthesizing Ella's and Emmaline's powers, and right now, there's no—"

"Synthesis," I say. "I get it."

"This doesn't feel right. They did things out of order."

"Maybe they freaked out after Evie's attempt to wipe J's mind didn't work. Maybe they needed to find a way to fix that fail, and quick. I mean, it's much easier to keep her around if she's docile, right? Loyal to their interests. It's much easier than keeping her in a holding cell, anyway. Babysitting her constantly. Monitoring her every movement. Always worried she's going to magic the toilet paper into a shiv and break out.

"Honestly"—I shrug—"it feels to me like they're just getting lazy. I think they're sick and tired of J always breaking out and fighting back. This is literally the path of least resistance."

"Yes," Warner says slowly. "Exactly."

"Wait— Exactly what?"

"Whatever they did to her—prematurely initiating this phase—was done hastily. It was a patch job."

A lightbulb flickers to life in my head. "Which means their work was sloppy."

"And if their work was sloppy—"

"—there are definitely holes in it."

"Stop finishing my sentences," he says, irritated.

"Stop being so predictable."

"Stop acting like a child."

"*You* stop acting like a child."

"You are being ridicu—"

Warner goes suddenly silent as Ibrahim's shaking, angry voice booms across the laboratory.

"I said, *get out of the way.*"

"I can't let you do this," Anderson says, his voice growing louder. "Did you not just hear that alarm? Santiago is out. They took out yet another supreme commander. How much longer are we going to let this go on?"

"*Juliette*," Ibrahim says sharply. "You're coming with me."

"Yes, sir."

"Juliette, stop," Anderson demands.

"Yes, sir."

What the hell is happening?

Warner and I dart forward to get a better look, but it doesn't matter how close we get; I still can't believe my eyes.

The scene is surreal.

Anderson is guarding Juliette. The same Anderson who's spent so much of his energy trying to murder her—is now standing in front of her with his arms out, guarding her with his life.

What the hell happened while she was here? Did Anderson get a new brain? A new heart? A parasite?

And I know I'm not alone in my confusion when I hear Warner mutter, "*What on earth?*" under his breath.

"Stop being foolish," Anderson says. "You're taking advantage of a tragedy to make an unauthorized decision, when you know as well as I do that we all need to agree on something this important before moving forward. I'm just asking you to wait, Ibrahim. Wait for the others to return, and we'll put it to a vote. Let the council decide."

Ibrahim pulls a gun on Anderson.

Ibrahim pulls a gun on Anderson.

I nearly lose my shit. I gasp so loud I almost blow our

cover.

"Step aside, Paris," he says. "You've already ruined this mission. I've given you dozens of chances to get this right. You gave me your word that we'd intercept the children before they even stepped foot in the building, and look how that turned out. You've promised me—all of us—time and time again that you would make this right, and instead all you do is cost us our time, our money, our power, our lives. *Everything.*

"It's now up to me to make this right," Ibrahim says, anger making his voice unsteady. He shakes his head. "You don't even understand, do you? You don't understand how much Evie's death has cost us. You don't understand how much of our success was built with her genius, her technological advances. You don't understand that Max will never be what Evie was—that he could never replace her. And you don't seem to understand that she's no longer here to forgive your constant mistakes.

"No," he says. "It's up to me now. It's up to me to fix things, because I'm the only one with his head on straight. I'm the only one who seems to grasp the enormity of what's ahead of us. I'm the only one who sees how close we are to complete and utter ruination. I am determined to make this right, Paris, even if it means taking you out in the process. So step aside."

"Be reasonable," Anderson says, his eyes wary. "I can't just step aside. I want our movement—everything we've worked so hard to build—I want it to be a success, too.

Surely you must realize that. You must realize that I haven't given up my life for nothing; you must know that my loyalty is to you, to the council, to The Reestablishment. But you must also know that she's worth too much. I can't let this go so easily. We've come too far. We've all made too many sacrifices to screw this up now."

"Don't force my hand, Paris. Don't make me do this."

J steps forward, about to say something, and Anderson pushes her body behind him. "I ordered you to remain silent," he says, glancing back at her. "And I am now ordering you to remain safe, at all costs. Do you hear me, Juliette? Do y—"

When the shot rings out, I don't believe it.

I think my mind is playing tricks on me. I think this is some kind of weird interlude—a strange dream, a moment of confusion—I keep waiting for the scene to change. Clear. Reset.

It doesn't.

No one thought it would happen like this. No one thought the supreme commanders would destroy themselves. No one thought we'd see Anderson felled by one his own, no one thought he'd clutch his bleeding chest and use his last gasp of breath to say:

"Run, Juliette. *Run*—"

Ibrahim shoots again, and this time, Anderson goes silent.

"Juliette," Ibrahim says, "you're coming with me."

J doesn't move.

She's frozen in place, staring at Anderson's still figure. It's so weird. I keep waiting for him to wake up. I keep waiting for his healing powers to kick in. I keep waiting for that annoying moment when he comes back to life, clutching a pocket square to his wound—

But he doesn't move.

"Juliette," Ibrahim says sharply. "You will answer to me now. And I am ordering you to follow me."

J looks up at him. Her face is blank. Her eyes are blank. "Yes, sir," she says.

And that's when I know.

That's when I know exactly what's going to happen next. I can feel it, can feel some strange electricity in the air before he makes his move. Before he blows our cover.

Warner pulls back his invisibility.

He stands there motionless for only a moment, for just long enough for Ibrahim to register his presence, to cry out, to reach for his gun. But he's not fast enough.

Warner is standing ten feet away when Ibrahim goes suddenly slack, when he chokes and the gun slips from his hand, when his eyes bulge. A thin red line appears in the middle of Ibrahim's forehead, a terrifying trickle of blood that precipitates the sudden, soft sound of his skull breaking open. It's the sound of tearing flesh, an innocuous sound that reminds me of ripping open an orange. And it doesn't take long before Ibrahim's knees hit the floor. He falls without grace, his body collapsing into itself.

I know he's dead because I can see directly into his

skull. Clumps of his fleshy brain matter leak out onto the floor.

This, I think, is the kind of horrifying shit J is capable of.

This is what she's always been capable of. She's just always been too good a person to use it.

Warner, on the other hand—

He doesn't even seem bothered by the fact that he just ripped open a man's skull. He seems totally calm about the brain matter dripping on the floor. No, he's only got eyes for J, who's staring back at him, confused. She glances from Ibrahim's limp body to Anderson's limp body and she throws her arms forward with a sudden, desperate cry—

And nothing happens.

Robo J has no idea that Warner can absorb her powers.

Warner takes a step toward her and she narrows her eyes before slamming her fist into the floor. The room begins to shake. The floor begins to fissure. My teeth are rattling so hard I lose my balance, slam against the wall, and accidentally pull back my invisibility. When Juliette spots me, she screams.

I fly out of the way, throwing myself forward, diving over a table. Glass crashes to the floor, shatters everywhere.

I hear someone groan.

I peek through the legs of a table just in time to see Anderson begin to move. This time, I actually gasp.

The whole world seems to pause.

Anderson struggles up, to his feet. He doesn't look okay. He looks sick, pale—an imitation of his former self.

386

Something is wrong with his healing power, because he looks only half-alive, blood oozing from two places on his torso. He sways as he gets to his feet, coughing up blood. His skin goes gray. He uses his sleeve to wipe blood from his mouth.

J goes rushing toward him, but Anderson lifts a hand in her direction, and she halts. His bleak face registers a moment of surprise as he gazes at Ibrahim's dead body.

He laughs. Coughs. Wipes away more blood.

"Did you do this?" he says, his eyes locked on his own kid. "You did me a favor."

"What have you done to her?" Warner demands.

Anderson smiles. "Why don't I show you?" He glances at J. "Juliette?"

"Yes, sir."

"Kill them."

"Yes, sir."

J moves forward just as Anderson pulls something from his pocket, aiming its sharp, blue light in Warner's direction. This time, when J throws her arm out, Warner goes flying, his body slamming hard against the stone wall.

He falls to the floor with a gasp, the wind knocked from his lungs, and I take advantage of the moment to rush forward, pulling my invisibility around us both.

He shoves me away.

"Come on, bro, we have to get out of here— This isn't a fair fight—"

"You go," he says, clutching his side. "Go find Nazeera,

and then find the other kids. I'll be fine."

"You're not going to be fine," I hiss. "She's going to kill you."

"That's fine, too."

"Don't be stupid—"

The metal tables providing us our only bit of cover go flying, crashing hard against the opposite wall. I take one last glance at Warner and make a split-second decision.

I throw myself into the fight.

I know I only have a second before my brain matter joins Ibrahim's on the floor, so I make it count. I pull my gun from its holster and shoot three, four times.

Five.

Six.

I bury lead in Anderson's body until he's knocked back by the force of it, sagging to the floor with a hacking, bloody cough. J rushes forward but I disappear, darting behind a table, and once the weapon in Anderson's hand clatters to the floor, I shoot that, too. It pops and cracks, briefly catching fire as the tech explodes.

J cries out, falling to her knees beside him.

"Kill them," Anderson gasps, blood staining the edges of his lips. "Kill them all. Kill anyone who stands in your way."

"Yes, sir," Juliette says.

Anderson coughs. Fresh blood seeps from his wounds.

J gets to her feet and turns around, scanning the room for us, but I'm already rushing over to Warner, throwing my invisibility over us both. Warner seems a little stunned, but he's miraculously uninjured.

I try to help him to his feet, and for the first time, he doesn't push away my arm. I hear him inhale. Exhale.

Never mind, he's a little injured.

I wait for him to do something, say something, but he just stands there, staring at J. And then—

He pulls back his invisibility.

I nearly scream.

J pivots when she spots him, and immediately runs forward. She picks up a table, throws it at us.

We dive out of the way so hard I nearly break my nose against the ground. I can still hear things shattering around us when I say,

"What the hell were you thinking? You just blew our chance to get out of here!"

Warner shifts, glass crunching beneath him. He's breathing hard.

"I was serious about what I said, Kishimoto. You should go. Find Nazeera. But this is where I need to be."

"You mean you need to be getting killed right now? That's where you need to be? Do you even hear yourself?"

"Something is wrong," Warner says, dragging himself to his feet. "Her mind is trapped, trapped inside of something. A program. A virus. Whatever it is, she needs help."

J screams, sending another earthquake through the room. I slam into a table and stumble backward. A sharp pain shoots through my gut and I suck in my breath. Swear.

Warner has one arm out against the wall, steadying

himself. I can tell he's about to step forward, directly into the fight, and I grab his arm, pull him back.

"I'm not saying we give up on her, okay? I'm saying that there has to be another way. We need to get out of here, regroup. Come up with a better plan."

"No."

"Bro, I don't think you understand." I glance at J, who's stalking forward, eyes burning, the ground fissuring before her. "She's really going to kill you."

"Then I will die."

That's it.

Warner's last words before he leaves.

He meets J in the middle of the room and she doesn't hesitate before taking a violent swing at his face.

He blocks.

She swings again. He blocks. She kicks. He ducks.

He's not fighting her.

He only matches her, move for move, meeting her blows, anticipating her mind. It reminds me of his fight with Anderson back at the Sanctuary—how he never struck his father, only defended himself. It was obvious then that he was just trying to enrage his father.

But this—

This is different. It's clear that he's not enjoying this. He's not trying to enrage her, and he's not trying to defend himself. He's fighting her for *her*. To protect her.

To save her, somehow.

And I have no idea if this is going to work.

J clenches her fists and screams. The walls shake, the floor continues to crack open. I stumble, catch myself against a table.

And I'm just standing here like an idiot, racking my brain for a clue, trying to figure out what to do, how to help—

"Holy shit," Nazeera says. "What the hell is going on?"

Relief floods through me fast and hot. I have to resist the impulse to pull her invisible body into my arms. To tuck her close to my chest and keep her from leaving again.

Instead, I pretend to be cool.

"How'd you get here?" I ask. "How'd you find us?"

"I was hacking the systems, remember? I saw you on the cameras. You guys aren't exactly being quiet up here."

"Right. Good point."

"Hey, I have news, by the way, I foun—" She cuts herself off abruptly, her words fading to nothing. And then, after a beat, she says quietly:

"Who killed my dad?"

My stomach turns to stone.

I take a sharp breath before I say, "Warner did that."

"Oh."

"You okay?"

I hear her exhale. "I don't know."

J screams again and I look up.

She's furious.

I can tell, even from here, that she's frustrated. She can't use her powers on Warner directly, and he's too good a fighter to be beat without an edge. She's resorted to throwing

391

very large, very heavy objects at him. Whatever she can find. Random medical equipment. Pieces of the wall.

This is not good.

"He wouldn't leave," I tell Nazeera. "He wanted to stay. He thinks he can help her."

She sighs. "We should let him try. In the interim, I could use your help."

I turn, reflexively, to face her, forgetting for a moment that she's invisible. "Help with what?" I ask.

"I found the other kids," she says. "That's why I was gone for so long. Getting that security clearance for you guys was way easier than I thought it'd be. So I stuck around to do some deep-level hacking into the cameras—and I found out where they're hiding the other supreme kids. But it's not pretty. And I could use a hand."

I look up to catch one last glimpse of Warner.

Of J.

But they're gone.

~~ELLA~~ JULIETTE

Run, Juliette
  run
  faster, run until your bones break and your shins split and your
muscles atrophy
  Run run run
  until you can't hear their feet behind you
  Run until you drop dead.
  Make sure your heart stops before they ever reach you. Before
they ever touch you.
  Run, I said.

The words appear, unbidden, in my mind. I don't know where they come from and I don't know why I know them, but I say them to myself as I go, my boots pounding the ground, my head a strangled mess of chaos. I don't understand what just happened. I don't understand what's happening to me. I don't understand anything anymore.

The boy is close.

He moves more swiftly than I anticipated, and I'm surprised. I didn't expect him to be able to meet my blows. I didn't expect him to face me so easily. Mostly, I'm stunned he's somehow immune to my power. I didn't even know that was possible.

I don't understand.

I'm racking my brain, trying desperately to comprehend how such a thing might've happened—and whether I might've been responsible for the anomaly—but nothing makes sense. Not his presence. Not his attitude. Not even the way he fights.

Which is to say: he doesn't.

He doesn't even want to fight. He seems to have no interest in beating me, despite the ample evidence that we are well matched. He only fends me off, making only the most basic effort to protect himself, and still I haven't killed him.

There's something strange about him. Something about him that's getting under my skin. Unsettling me.

But he dashed out of sight when I threw another table at him, and he's been running ever since.

It feels like a trap.

I know it, and yet, I feel compelled to find him. Face him. Destroy him.

I spot him, suddenly, at the far end of the laboratory, and he meets my eyes with an insouciance that enrages me. I charge forward but he moves swiftly, disappearing through an adjoining door.

This is a trap, I remind myself.

Then again, I'm not sure it matters whether this is a trap. I am under orders to find him. Kill him. I just have to be better. Smarter.

So I follow.

From the time I met this boy—from the first moment we began exchanging blows—I've ignored the dizzying sensations coursing through my body. I've tried to deny my sudden, feverish skin, my trembling hands. But when a fresh wave of nausea nearly sends me reeling, I can no longer deny my fear:

There's something wrong with me.

I catch another glimpse of his golden hair and my vision blurs, clears, my heart slows. For a moment, my muscles seem to spasm. There is a creeping, tremulous terror clenching its fist around my lungs and I don't understand it. I keep hoping the feeling will change. Clear. Disappear. But as the minutes pass and the symptoms show no signs of abating, I begin to panic.

I'm not tired, no. My body is too strong. I can feel it—can feel my muscles, their strength, their steadiness—and I can tell that I could keep fighting like this for hours. Days. I'm not worried about giving up, I'm not worried about breaking down.

I'm worried about my head. My confusion. The uncertainty seeping through me, spreading like a poison.

Ibrahim is dead.

Anderson, nearly so.

Will he recover? Will he die? Who would I be without him? What was it Ibrahim wanted to do to me? From what was Anderson trying to protect me? Who are these children I'm meant to kill? Why did Ibrahim call them my friends?

My questions are endless.

I kill them.

I shove aside a series of steel desks and catch a glimpse of the boy before he darts around a corner. Anger punches through me, shooting a jolt of adrenaline to my brain, and I start running again, renewed determination focusing my mind. I charge through the dimly lit room, shoving my way through an endless sea of medical paraphernalia. When I stop moving, silence descends.

Silence so pure it's deafening.

I spin around, searching. The boy is gone. I blink, confused, scanning the room as my pulse races with renewed fear. Seconds pass, gather into moments that feel like minutes, hours.

This is a trap.

The laboratory is perfectly still—the lights so perfectly dim—that as the silence drags on I begin to wonder if I'm caught in a dream. I feel suddenly paranoid, uncertain. Like maybe that boy was a figment of my imagination. Like maybe all of this is some strange nightmare, and maybe I'll wake up soon and Anderson will be back in his office, and Ibrahim will be a man I've never met, and tomorrow I'll wake up in my pod by the water.

Maybe, I think, this is all just another test.

A simulation.

Maybe Anderson is challenging my loyalty one last time. Maybe it's my job to stay put, to keep myself safe like he asked me to, and to destroy anyone who tries to stand in my way. Or maybe—

Stop.

I sense movement.

Movement so fine it's nearly imperceptible. Movement so gentle it could've been a breeze, except for one thing:

I hear a heart beating.

Someone is here, someone motionless, someone sly. I straighten, my senses heightened, my heart racing in my chest.

Someone is here someone is here someone is here—

Where?

There.

He appears, as if out of a dream, standing before me like a statue, still as cooling steel. He stares at me, green eyes the color of sea glass, the color of celadon.

I never really had a chance to see his face.

Not like this.

My heart races as I assess him, his white shirt, green jacket, gold hair. Skin like porcelain. He does not slouch or fidget and, for a moment, I'm certain I was right, that perhaps he's nothing more than a mirage. A program.

Another hologram.

I reach out, uncertain, the tips of my fingers grazing the exposed skin at his throat and he takes a sharp, shaky breath.

Real, then.

I flatten my hand against his chest, just to be sure, and I feel his heart racing under my palm. Fast, lightning fast.

I glance up, surprised.

He's nervous.

Another unsteady breath escapes him and this time, takes with it a measure of control. He steps back, shakes his head, stares up at the ceiling.

Not nervous.

He is distraught.

I should kill him now, I think. *Kill him now.*

A wave of nausea hits me so hard it nearly knocks me off my feet. I take a few unsteady steps backward, catching myself against a steel table. My fingers grip the cold metal edge and I hang on, teeth clenched, willing my mind to clear.

Heat floods my body.

Heat, torturous heat, presses against my lungs, fills my blood. My lips part. I feel parched. I look up and he's right in front of me and I do nothing. I do nothing as I watch his throat move.

I do nothing as my eyes devour him.

I feel faint.

I study the sharp line of his jaw, the gentle slope where his neck meets shoulder. His lips look soft. His cheekbones high, his nose sharp, his brows heavy, gold. He is finely made. Beautiful, strong hands. Short, clean nails. I notice he wears a jade ring on his left pinkie finger.

He sighs.

He shakes off his jacket, carefully folding it over the back of a nearby chair. Underneath he wears only a simple white T-shirt, the sculpted contours of his bare arms catching the attention of the dim lights. He moves slowly, his motions unhurried. When he begins to pace I watch him, study the shape of him. I am not surprised to discover that he moves beautifully. I am fascinated by him, by his form, his measured strides, the muscles honed under skin. He seems like he might be my age, maybe a little older, but there's something about the way he looks at me that makes him seem older than our years combined.

Whatever it is, I like it.

I wonder what I'm supposed to do with this, all of this. Is it truly a test? If so, why send someone like him? Why a face so refined? Why a body so perfectly honed?

Was I meant to enjoy this?

A strange, delirious feeling stirs inside of me at the thought. Something ancient. Something wonderful. It is almost too bad, I think, that I will have to kill him. And it is the heat, the dullness, the inexplicable numbness in my mind that compels me to say—

"Where did they make you?"

He startles. I didn't think he would startle. But when he turns to look at me, he seems confused.

I explain: "You are unusually beautiful."

His eyes widen.

His lips part, press together, tremble into a curve that surprises me. Surprises him.

He smiles.

He smiles and I stare—two dimples, straight teeth, shining eyes. A sudden, incomprehensible heat rushes across my skin, sets me aflame. I feel violently hot. Sick with fever.

Finally, he says: "So you *are* in there."

"Who?"

"Ella," he says, but he's speaking softly now. "Juliette. They said you'd be gone."

"I'm not gone," I say, my hands shaking as I pull myself together. "I am Juliette Ferrars, supreme soldier to our North American commander. Who are you?"

He moves closer. His eyes darken as he stares at me, but there's no true darkness there. I try to stand taller, straighter. I remind myself that I have a task, that this is my moment to attack, to fulfill my orders. Perhaps I sh—

"Love," he whispers.

Heat flashes across my skin. Pain presses against my mind, a vague realization that I've left something overlooked. Dusty emotion trembles inside of me, and I kill it.

He steps forward, takes my face in his hands. I think about breaking his fingers. Snapping his wrists. My heart is racing.

I cannot move.

"You shouldn't touch me," I say, gasping the words.

"Why not?"

"Because I will kill you."

Gently, he tilts my head back, his hands possessive, persuasive. An ache seizes my muscles, holds me in place. My eyes close reflexively. I breathe him in and my mouth fills with flavor—fresh air, fragrant flowers, heat, happiness—and I'm struck by the strangest idea that we've been here before, that I've lived this before, that I've known him before and then I feel, I feel his breath on my skin and the sensation, the sensation is—

heady,

disorienting.

I'm losing track of my mind, trying desperately to locate my purpose, to focus my thoughts, when

he moves

the earth tilts, his lips graze my jaw and I make a sound, a desperate, unconscious sound that stuns me. My skin is frenzied, burning. That familiar warmth contaminates my blood, my temperature spiking, my face flushing.

"Do I—"

I try to speak but he kisses my neck and I gasp, his hands still caught around my face. I'm breathless, heart pounding, pulse pounding, head pounding. He touches me like he knows me, knows what I want, knows what I need. I feel insane. I don't even recognize the sound of my own voice when I finally manage to say,

"Do I know you?"

"Yes."

My heart leaps. The simplicity of his answer strangles my mind, digs for truth. It feels true. Feels true that I've known these hands, this mouth, those eyes.

Feels real.

"Yes," he says again, his own voice rough with feeling. His hands leave my face and I'm lost in the loss, searching for warmth. I press closer to him without even meaning to, asking him for something I don't understand. But then his hands slide under my shirt, his palms pressing against my back, and the magnitude of the sudden, skin-to-skin contact sets my body on fire.

I feel explosive.

I feel dangerously close to something that might kill me, and still I lean into him, blinded by instinct, deaf to everything but the ferocious beat of my own heart.

He pulls back, just an inch.

His hands are still caught under my shirt, his bare arms wrapped around my bare skin and his mouth lingers above mine, the heat between us threatening to ignite. He pulls me closer and I bite back a moan, losing my head as the hard lines of his body sink into me. He is everywhere, his scent, his skin, his breath. I see nothing but him, sense nothing but him, his hands spreading across my torso, my lungs compressing under his careful, searing exploration. I lean into the sensations, his fingers grazing my stomach, the small of my back. He touches his forehead to mine and I press up, onto my toes, asking for something, begging for something—

"What," I gasp, "what is happening—"

He kisses me.

Soft lips, waves of sensation. Feeling overflows the vacancies in my mind. My hands begin to shake. My heart beats so hard I can hardly keep still when he nudges my mouth open, takes me in. He tastes like heat and peppermint, like summer, like the sun.

I want more.

I take his face in my hands and pull him closer and he makes a soft, desperate sound in the back of his throat that sends a spike of pleasure directly to my brain. Pure, electric heat lifts me up, outside of myself. I seem to be floating here, surrendered to this strange moment, held in place by an ancient mold that fits my body perfectly. I feel frantic, seized by a need to know more, a need I don't even understand.

When we break apart his chest his heaving and his face is flushed and he says—

"Come back to me, love. Come back."

I'm still struggling to breathe, desperately searching his eyes for answers. Explanations. "Where?"

"Here," he whispers, pressing my hands to his heart. "Home."

"But I don't—"

Flashes of light streak across my vision. I stumble backward, half-blind, like I'm dreaming, reliving the caress of a forgotten memory, and it's like an ache looking to be soothed, it's a steaming pan thrown in ice water, it's a flushed cheek pressed to a cool pillow on a hot hot night and heat gathers, collects behind my eyes, distorting sights, dimming sounds.

Here.

This.

My bones against his bones. This is my home.

I return to my skin with a sudden, violent shudder and feel wild, unstable. I stare at him, my heart seizing, my lungs fighting for air. He stares back, his eyes such a pale green in the light that, for a moment, he doesn't even seem human.

Something is happening to my head.

Pain is collecting in my blood, calcifying around my heart. I feel at war with myself, lost and wounded, my mind spinning with uncertainty. "What is your name?" I ask.

He steps forward, so close our lips touch. Part. His breath whispers across my skin and my nerves hum, spark.

"You know my name," he says quietly.

I try to shake my head. He catches my chin.

This time, he's not careful.

This time, he's desperate. This time, when he kisses me he breaks me open, heat coming off him in waves. He tastes like springwater and something sweet, something searing.

I feel dazed. Delirious.

When he breaks away I'm shaking, my lungs shaking, my breaths shaking, my heart shaking. I watch, as if in a dream, as he pulls off his shirt, tosses it to the ground. And then he's here again, he's back again, he's caught me in his arms and he's kissing me so deeply my knees give out.

He picks me up, bracing my body as he sets me down on the long, steel table. The cool metal seeps through the fabric of my pants, sending goose bumps along my heated skin and I gasp, my eyes closing as he straddles my legs, claims my mouth. He presses my hands to his chest, drags my fingers down his naked torso and I make a desperate, broken sound, pleasure and pain stunning me, paralyzing me.

He unbuttons my shirt, his deft hands moving quickly even as he kisses my neck, my cheeks, my mouth, my throat. I cry out when he moves, his kisses shifting down my body, searching, exploring. He pushes aside the two halves of my shirt, his mouth still hot against my skin, and then he closes the gap between us, pressing his bare chest to mine, and my heart explodes.

Something snaps inside of me.

Severs.

A sudden, fractured sob escapes my throat. Unbidden tears sting my eyes, startling me as they fall down my face. Unknown emotion soars through me, expanding my heart, confusing my head. He pulls me impossibly closer, our bodies soldered together. And then he presses his forehead to my collarbone, his body trembling with emotion when he says—

"Come back."

My head is full of sand, sound, sensations spinning in my mind. I don't understand what's happening to me, I don't understand this pain, this unbelievable pleasure. I'm staining his skin with my tears and he only pulls me tighter, pressing our hearts together until the feeling sinks its teeth into my bones, splits open my lungs. I want to bury myself in this moment, I want to pull him into me, I want to drag myself out of myself but there's something wrong, something blocked, something stopped—

Something broken.

Realization arrives in gentle waves, theories lapping and overlapping at the shores of my consciousness until I'm drenched in confusion. Awareness.

Terror.

"You know my name," he says softly. "You've always known me, love. I've always known you. And I'm so—I'm so desperately in love with you—"

The pain begins in my ears.

It collects, expanding, pressure building to a peak so acute it transforms, sharpening into a torture that stops my heart.

First I go deaf, stiff. Second I go blind, slack.

Third, my heart restarts.

I come back to life with a sudden, terrifying inhalation that nearly chokes me, blood rushing to my ears, my eyes, leaking from my nose. I taste it, taste my own blood in my mouth as I begin to understand: there is something inside of me. A poison. A violence. Something wrong something wrong something *wrong*

And then, as if from miles away, I hear myself scream.

There's cold tile under my knees, rough grout pressing into my knuckles. I scream into the silence, power building power, electricity charging my blood. My mind is separating from itself, trying to identify the poison, this parasite residing inside of me.

I have to kill it.

I scream, forcing my own energy inward, screaming until the explosive energy building inside of me ruptures my eardrums. I scream until I feel the blood drip from my ears and down my neck, I scream until the lights in the laboratory begin to pop and break. I scream until my teeth bleed, until the floor fissures beneath my feet, until the skin at my knees begins to crack. I scream until the monster inside of me begins to die.

And only then—

Only when I'm certain I've killed some small part of my own self do I finally collapse.

I'm choking, coughing up blood, my chest heaving from the effort expended. The room swims. Swings around.

I press my forehead to the cold floor and fight back a wave of nausea. And then I feel a familiar, heavy hand against my back. With excruciating slowness, I manage to lift my head.

A blur of gold appears, disappears before me.

I blink once, twice, and try to push up with my arms but a sharp, searing pain in my wrist nearly blinds me. I look down, examining the strange, hazy sight. I blink again. Ten times more.

Finally, my eyes focus.

The skin inside my right arm has split open. Blood is smeared across my skin, dripping on the floor. From within the fresh wound, a single blue light pulses from a steel, circular body, the edges of which push up against my torn flesh.

With one final effort, I rip the flashing mechanism from my arm, the last vestige of this monster. It drops from my shaking fingers, clatters to the floor.

And this time, when I look up, I see his face.

"Aaron," I gasp.

He drops to his knees.

He pulls my bleeding body into his arms and I break, I break apart, sobs cracking open my chest. I cry until the pain spirals and peaks, I cry until my head throbs and my eyes swell. I cry, pressing my face against his neck, my fingers digging into his back, desperate for purchase. Proof.

He holds me, silent and steady, gathering my blood and bones against his body even as the tears recede, even when I begin to tremble. He holds me tight as my body shakes, holds me close when the tears start anew, holds me in his arms and strokes my hair and tells me that everything, everything is going to be okay.

KENJI

I was assigned to keep watch outside this door, which, initially, was supposed to be a good thing—assisting in the rescue mission, et cetera—but the longer I wait out here, guarding Nazeera while she hacks the computers keeping the supreme kids in some freaky state of hypersleep, the more things go wrong.

This place is falling apart.

Literally.

The lights in the ceiling are beginning to spark and sputter, the massive staircases are beginning to groan. The huge windows lining either side of this fifty-story building are beginning to crack.

Doctors are running, screaming. Alarms are flashing like crazy, sirens blaring. Some robotic voice is announcing a crisis over the speakers like it's the most casual thing in the world.

I have no idea what's happening right now, though if I had to guess, I'd say it had something to do with Emmaline. But I just have to stand here, bracing myself against the door so as not to be accidentally trampled, and wait for whatever is happening to come to an end. The problem is, I don't know if it's going to be a happy ending or a sad one—

For anyone.

I haven't heard anything from Warner since we split up, and I'm trying really, really hard not to think about it. I'm choosing to focus, instead, on the positive things that happened today, like the fact that we managed to kill three supreme commanders—four if you count Evie—and that Nazeera's genius hacking work was a success, because without her, there's no way we'd have made much headway at all.

After our sojourn through the vents, Warner and I managed to drop down into the heart of the compound, undetected. It was easier to avoid the cameras once we were in the center of things; the rooms were closer together, and though the higher security areas have more security *access* points—some of them have fewer cameras. So as long as we avoided certain angles, the cameras didn't notice us, and with the fake clearance Nazeera built for us, we got through easily. It was because of her that we were in the right place—after having unintentionally killed a super-important scientist—when all the supreme commanders began to swarm.

It was because of her that we were able to take out Ibrahim and Anderson. And it was because of her that Warner is locked up with Robo J somewhere. Honestly, I don't even know how to feel about it all. I haven't really allowed myself to think about the fact that J might never come back, that I might never see my best friend again. If I think about it too much, I start feeling like I can't breathe, and I can't afford to stop breathing right now. Not yet.

So I try not to think about it.

But Warner—

Warner is either going to come out of this alive and happy, or dead doing something he believed in.

And there's nothing I can do about it.

The problem is, I haven't seen him in over an hour, and I have no idea what that means. It could either be really good news or really, really bad. He never shared his plan with me—surprise surprise—so I don't even know exactly what he'd planned to do to once he got her alone. And even though I know better than to doubt him, I have to admit that there's a tiny part of me that wonders if he's even alive right now.

An ancient, earsplitting groan interrupts my thoughts.

I look up, toward the source of the sound, and realize that the ceiling is caving in. The roof is coming apart. The walls are beginning to crumble. The long, circuitous hallways all ring around an interior courtyard within which lives a massive, prehistoric-looking tree. For no reason I can understand, the steel railings around the hallways are beginning to melt apart. I watch in real time as the tree catches fire, flames roaring higher at an astonishing rate. Smoke builds, curling in my direction, already beginning to suffocate the halls, and my heart is racing as I look around, my panic spiking. I start banging on the door, not caring who hears me now.

It's the end of the fucking world out here.

I'm screaming for Nazeera, begging her to come out, to get out here before it's too late, and I'm coughing now, smoke catching in my lungs, still hoping desperately that she'll hear my voice when suddenly, violently—

The door swings open.

I'm knocked backward by the force of it, and when I look up, eyes burning, Nazeera is there. Nazeera, Lena, Stephan, Haider, Valentina, Nicolás, and Adam.

Adam.

I can't explain exactly what happens next. There's so much shouting. So much running. Stephan punches a clean hole through a crumbling wall, and Nazeera helps fly us all out to safety. It happens in a blur. I see things unfold in flashes, in screams.

It feels like a dream. My eyes stinging, tearing.

I'm crying because of the fire, I think. It's the heat, the sky, the roaring flames devouring everything.

I watch the capital of Oceania—all 120 acres of it—go up in flames.

And Warner and Juliette go with it.

ELLA
(JULIETTE)

The first thing we do is find Emmaline.

I reach out to her in my mind and she answers right away. Heat, fingers of heat, curling around my bones. Sparking to life in my heart. She was always here, always with me.

I understand now.

I understand that the moments that saved me were gifts from my sister, gifts she was able to give only by destroying herself in return. She's so much weaker now than she was two weeks ago because she expended so much of herself to keep me alive. To keep their machinations from reaching my heart. My soul.

I remember everything now. My mind is sharpened to a new point, honed to a clarity I've never before experienced. I see everything. Understand everything.

It doesn't take long to find her.

I don't apologize for the people I scatter, the walls I shatter along the way. I don't apologize for my anger or my pain. I don't stop moving when I see Tatiana and Azi; I don't have to. I snap their necks from where I'm standing. I tear their bodies in half with a single gesture.

When I reach my sister, the agony inside of me reaches its peak. She is limp inside her tank, a desiccated fish, a dying spider. She's curled into herself in its darkest corner, her long dark hair wrapping around her wrinkled, sagging figure. A low keening emanates from her tank.

She is crying.

She is small. Scared. She reminds me of another version of myself, a person I can hardly remember, a young girl thrown in prison, too broken by the world to realize that she'd always had the power to break herself free. To conquer the earth.

I had that luxury.

Emmaline didn't.

The sight of her makes me want to fall to pieces. My heart rages with anger, devastation. When I think about what they did to her—what they've done to her—

Don't

I don't.

I take a deep, shuddering breath. Try to collect myself. I feel Aaron take my hand and I squeeze his fingers in gratitude. It steadies me to have him here. To know he's beside me. With me.

My partner in everything.

Tell me what you want, I say to Emmaline. *Anything at all. Whatever it is, I'll do it.*

Silence.

Emmaline?

A sharp, desperate fear jumps through me.

Her fear, not mine.

Distorted sensations flash behind my eyes—flares of color, the sounds of grinding metal—and her panic intensifies. Tightens. I feel it hum down my spine.

"What's wrong?" I say out loud. "What happened?"

Here

Here

Her milky form disappears into the tank, sinking deep underwater. Goose bumps rise along my arms.

"You seem to have forgotten about me."

My father steps into the room, his tall rubber boots thudding softly against the floor.

I throw my arms out immediately, hoping to rip out his spleen, but he's too fast—his movements too fast. He presses a single button on a small, handheld remote, and I hardly have time to take a breath before my body begins to convulse. I cry out, my eyes blinded by violent, violet light, and manage to turn my head only in small, excruciating movements.

Aaron.

He and I are both frozen here, bathed in a toxic light

emanating from the ceiling. Gasping for breath. Shaking uncontrollably. My mind spins, working desperately to think of a plan, a loophole, a way out.

"I am astonished by your arrogance," my father says. "Astonished that you thought you could just walk in here and assist in your sister's suicide. You thought it would be simple? You thought there wouldn't be consequences?"

He turns a dial and my body seizes more violently, lifting off the floor. The pain is blinding. Light flashes in and out of my eyes, stunning my mind, numbing my ability to think. I hang in the air, no longer able to turn my head. Gravity pushes and pulls at my body, threatens to tear apart my limbs.

If I could scream, I would.

"Anyway, it's good you're here. Best to get this over with now. We've waited long enough." He nods, absently, at Emmaline's tank. "Obviously you've seen how desperate we are for a new host."

NO

The word is like a scream inside my head.

Max stiffens.

He looks up, staring at precisely nothing, the anger in his eyes barely held in check. I only realize then that he can hear her, too.

Of course he can.

Emmaline pounds against her tank, the sounds dull,

the effort alone seeming to exhaust her. Still, she presses forward, her sunken cheek flattening against the glass.

Max hesitates, vacillating.

He's no good at hiding his emotions—and his present uncertainty is easily discernible. It's clear, even from my disoriented perspective, that he's trying to decide which of us he needs to deal with first. Emmaline pounds her fist again, weaker this time.

NO

Another scream inside my head.

With a stifled sigh, Max decides on Emmaline.

I watch him pivot, stalk toward her tank. He presses his hand flat against the glass and it brightens to a neon blue. The blue light expands, then scatters around the chamber, slowly revealing an intricate series of electrical circuits. The neon veins are thicker in some places, occasionally braided, mostly fine. It resembles a cardiovascular system not unlike the one inside my own body.

My own body.

Something gasps to life inside of me. Reason. Rational thought. I'm trapped here, tricked by the pain into thinking I have no control over my powers, but that's not true. When I force myself to remember, I can feel it. My energy still thrums through me. It's a faint, desperate whisper—but it's there.

Bit by agonizing bit, I gather my mind.

I grit my teeth, focusing my thoughts, clenching my body

to its breaking point. Slowly, I braid together the disparate strands of my power, holding on to the threads for dear life.

And even more slowly, I claw my hand through the light.

The effort splits open my knuckles, the tips of my fingers. Fresh blood streaks across my hand and spills down my wrist as I lift my arm in a sluggish, excruciating arc above my head.

As if from light-years away, I hear beeping.

Max.

He's inputting new codes into Emmaline's tank. I have no idea what that means for her, but I can't imagine it's good.

Hurry.

Hurry, I tell myself.

Violently, I force my arm through the light, biting back a scream as I do. One by one, my fingers uncurl above my head, blood dripping from each digit down my bleeding wrist and into my eyes. My hand opens, palm up toward the ceiling. Fresh blood snakes down the planes of my face as I drive my energy into the light.

The ceiling shatters.

Aaron and I fall to the floor, hard, and I hear something snap in my leg, the pain screaming through me.

I fight it back.

The lights pop and shriek, the polished concrete ceiling beginning to crack. Max spins around, horror seizing his face as I throw my hand forward.

Close my fist.

Emmaline's tank fissures with a sudden, violent crack.

"NO!" he cries. Feverishly, he pulls the remote free from his lab coat, hitting its now useless buttons. "No! No, *no*—"

The glass groans open with an angry yawn, giving way with one final, shattering roar. Max goes comically still.

Stunned.

He dies, then, with exactly that expression on his face. And it's not me who kills him. It's Emmaline.

Emmaline, who pulls her webbed hands free of the broken glass and presses her fingers to her father's head. She kills him with nothing more than the force of her own mind.

The mind he gave her.

When she is done, his skull has split open. Blood leaks from his dead eyes. His teeth have fallen out of his face, onto his shirt. His intestines spill out from a severe rupture in his torso.

I look away.

Emmaline collapses to the floor. She's gasping through the regulator fused to her face. Her already weak limbs begin to tremble, violently, and she's making sounds I can only assume are meant to be words she's no longer able to speak.

She is more amphibian than human.

I realize this only now, only when faced with the proof of her incompatibility with our air, with the outside world. I crawl toward her, dragging my broken, bloodied leg behind me.

Aaron tries to help, but when we lock eyes, he falls back.

He understands that I need to do this myself.

I gather my sister's small, withered body against my own, pulling her wet limbs into my lap, pressing her head against my chest. And I say to her, for the second time:

"Tell me what you want. Anything at all. Whatever it is, I'll do it."

Her slick fingers clutch at my neck, clinging for dear life. A vision fills my head, a vision of everything going up in flames. A vision of this compound, her prison, disintegrating. She wants it razed, returned to dust.

"Consider it done," I say to her.

She has another request. Just one more.

And I say nothing for too long.

Please

Her voice is in my heart, begging. Desperate. Her agony is acute. Her terror palpable.

Tears spring to my eyes.

I press my cheek against her wet hair. I tell her how much I love her. How much she means to me. How much more I wish we could've had. I tell her that I will never forget her.

That I will miss her, every single day.

And then I ask her to let me take her body home with me when I am done.

A gentle warmth floods my mind, a heady feeling.

Happiness.

Yes, she says.

When it's done, when I've ripped the tubes from her body, when I've gathered her wet, trembling bones against my own, when I've pressed my poisonous cheek to hers, when I've leeched out what little life was left in her body.

When it is done, I curl myself around her cold corpse and cry.

I clutch her hollow body against my heart and feel the injustice of it all roar through me. I feel it fracture me apart. I feel her take part of me with her as she goes.

And then I scream.

I scream until I feel the earth move beneath my feet, until I feel the wind change directions. I scream until the walls collapse, until I feel the electricity spark, until I feel the lights catch fire. I scream until the ground fissures, until all falls down.

And then we carry my sister home.

EPILOGUE

EPILOGUE

WARNER

one.

The wall is unusually white.

More white than is usual. Most people think white walls are true white, but the truth is, they only seem white, and are not actually white. Most shades of white are mixed in with a bit of yellow, which helps soften the harsh edges of a pure white, making it more of an ecru, or ivory. Various shades of cream. Egg white, even. True white is practically intolerable as a color, so white it's nearly blue.

This wall, in particular, is not so white as to be offensive, but a sharp enough shade of white to pique my curiosity, which is nothing short of a miracle, really, because I've been staring at it for the greater part of an hour. Thirty-seven minutes, to be exact.

I am being held hostage by custom. Formality.

"Five more minutes," she says. "I promise."

I hear the rustle of fabric. Zippers. A shudder of—

"Is that tulle?"

"You're not supposed to be listening!"

"You know, love, it occurs to me now that I've lived through actual hostage situations far less torturous than this."

"Okay, okay, it's off. Packed away. I just need a second to

433

put on my cl—"

"That won't be necessary," I say, turning around. "Surely this part, I should be allowed to watch."

I lean against the unusually white wall, studying her as she frowns at me, her lips still parted around the shape of a word she seems to have forgotten.

"Please continue," I say, gesturing with a nod. "Whatever you were doing before."

She holds on to her frown for a moment longer than is honest, her eyes narrowing in a show of frustration that is pure fraud. She compounds this farce by clutching an article of clothing to her chest, feigning modesty.

I do not mind, not one single bit.

I drink her in, her soft curves, her smooth skin. Her hair is beautiful at any length, but it's been longer lately. Long and rich, silky against her skin, and when I'm lucky— against mine.

Slowly, she drops the shirt.

I suddenly stand up straighter.

"I'm supposed to wear this under the dress," she says, her fake anger already forgotten. She fidgets with the boning of a cream-colored corset, her fingers lingering absently along the garter belt, the lace-trimmed stockings. She can't meet my eyes. She's gone suddenly shy, and this time, it's real.

Do you like it?

The unspoken question.

I assumed, when she invited me into this dressing room, that it was for reasons beyond me staring at the color variations in an unusually white wall. I assumed she wanted me here to see something.

To see her.

I see now that I was correct.

"You are so beautiful," I say, unable to shed the awe in my voice. I hear it, the childish wonder in my tone, and it embarrasses me more than it should. I know I shouldn't be ashamed to feel deeply. To be moved.

Still, I feel awkward.

Young.

Quietly, she says, "I feel like I just spoiled the surprise. You're not supposed to see any of this until the wedding night."

My heart actually stops for a moment.

The wedding night.

She closes the distance between us and twines her arms around me, freeing me from my momentary paralysis. My heart beats faster with her here, so close. And though I don't know how she knew that I suddenly required the reassurance of her touch, I'm grateful. I exhale, pulling her fully against me, our bodies relaxing, remembering each other.

I press my face into her hair, breathe in the sweet scent of her shampoo, her skin. It's only been two weeks. Two weeks since the end of an old world. The beginning of a new one.

She still feels like a dream to me.

"Is this really happening?" I whisper.

A sharp knock at the door startles my spine straight.

Ella frowns at the sound. "Yes?"

"So sorry to bother you right now, miss, but there's a gentleman here wishing to speak with Mr. Warner."

Ella and I lock eyes.

"Okay," she says quickly. "Don't be mad."

My eyes narrow. "Why would I be mad?"

Ella pulls away to better look me in the eye. Her own eyes are bright, beautiful. Full of concern. "It's Kenji."

I force down a spike of anger so violent I think I give myself a stroke. It leaves me light-headed. "What is he doing here?" I manage to get out. "How on earth did he know how to find us?

She bites her lip. "We took Amir and Olivier with us."

"I see." We took extra guards along, which means our outing was posted to the public security bulletin. Of course.

Ella nods. "He found me just before we left. He was worried—he wanted to know why we were heading back into the old regulated lands."

I try to say something then, to marvel aloud at Kenji's inability to make a simple deduction despite the abundance of contextual clues right before his eyes—but she holds up a finger.

"I told him," she says, "that we were looking for replacement outfits, and reminded him that, for now, the supply centers are still the only places to shop for food or clothing or"—she waves a hand, frowns—"anything, at the moment. Anyway, he said he'd try to meet us here. He said

436

he wanted to help."

My eyes widen slightly. I feel another stroke incoming. "He said he wanted to *help*."

She nods.

"Astonishing." A muscle ticks in my jaw. "And funny, too, because he's already helped so much—just last night he helped us both a great deal by destroying my suit and your dress, forcing us to now purchase clothing from a"—I look around, gesture at nothing—"a *store* on the very day we're supposed to get married."

"Aaron," she whispers. She steps closer again. Places a hand on my chest. "He feels terrible about it."

"And you?" I say, studying her face, her feelings. "Don't *you* feel terrible about it? Alia and Winston worked so hard to make you something beautiful, something designed precisely for you—"

"I don't mind." She shrugs. "It's just a dress."

"But it was your wedding dress," I say, my voice failing me now, practically breaking on the word.

She sighs, and in the sound I hear her heart break, more for me than for herself. She turns around and unzips the massive garment bag hanging on a hook above her head.

"You're not supposed to see this," she says, tugging yards of tulle out of the bag, "but I think it might mean more to you than it does to me, so"—she turns back, smiles—"I'll let you help me decide what to wear tonight."

I nearly groan aloud at the reminder.

A nighttime wedding. Who on earth is married at night?

Only the hapless. The unfortunate. Though I suppose we now count among their ranks.

Rather than reschedule the entire thing, we pushed it forward by a few hours so that we'd have time to purchase new clothes. Well, I have clothes. My clothes don't matter as much.

But her dress. He destroyed her dress the night before our wedding. Like a monster.

I'm going to murder him.

"You can't murder him," she says, still pulling handfuls of fabric out of the bag.

"I'm certain I said no such thing out loud."

"No," she says, "but you were thinking it, weren't you?"

"Wholeheartedly."

"You can't murder him," she says simply. "Not now. Not ever."

I sigh.

She's still struggling to unearth the gown. "Forgive me, love, but if all this"—I nod at the garment bag, the explosion of tulle—"is for a single dress, I'm afraid I already know how I feel about it."

She stops tugging. Turns around, eyes wide. "You don't like it? You haven't even seen it yet."

"I've seen enough to know that whatever this is, it's not a gown. This is a haphazard layering of polyester." I lean around her, pinching the fabric between my fingers. "Do they not carry silk tulle in this store? Perhaps we can speak to the seamstress."

"They don't have a seamstress here."

"This is a clothing store," I say. I turn the bodice inside out, frowning at the stitches. "Surely there must be a seamstress. Not a very good one, clearly, but—"

"These dresses are made in a factory," she says to me. "Mostly by machine."

I straighten.

"You know, most people didn't grow up with private tailors at their disposal," she says, a smile playing at her lips. "The rest of us had to buy clothes off the rack. Premade. Ill-fitting."

"Yes," I say stiffly. I feel suddenly stupid. "Of course. Forgive me. The dress is very nice. Perhaps I should wait for you to try it on. I gave my opinion too hastily."

For some reason, my response only makes things worse.

She groans, shooting me a single, defeated look before folding herself into the little dressing room chair.

My heart plummets.

She drops her face in her hands. "It really is a disaster, isn't it?"

Another swift knock at the door. "Sir? The gentleman seems very eager t—"

"He's certainly not a gentleman," I say sharply. "Tell him to wait."

A moment of hesitation. Then, quietly: "Yes, sir."

"Aaron."

I don't need to look up to know that she's unhappy with my rudeness. The owners of this particular supply center shut down their entire store for us, and they've been excruciatingly kind. I know I'm being cruel. At present, I can't seem to help it.

"*Aaron.*"

"Today is your wedding day," I say, unable to meet her eyes. "He has ruined your wedding day. Our wedding day."

She gets to her feet. I feel her frustration fade. Transform. Shuffle through sadness, happiness, hope, fear, and finally—

Resignation.

One of the worst possible feelings on what should be a joyous day. Resignation is worse than frustration. Far worse.

My anger calcifies.

"He hasn't ruined it," she says finally. "We can still make this work."

"You're right," I say, pulling her into my arms. "Of course you're right. It doesn't matter, really. None of it does."

"But it's my wedding day," she says. "And I have nothing to wear."

"You're right." I kiss the top of her head. "I'm going to kill him."

A sudden pounding at the door.

I stiffen. Spin around.

"Hey, guys?" More pounding. "I know you're super pissed at me, but I have good news, I swear. I'm going to fix this. I'm going to make it up to you."

I'm just about to respond when Ella tugs at my hand, silencing my scathing retort with a single motion. She shoots me a look that plainly says—

Give him a chance.

I sigh as the anger settles inside my body, my shoulders dropping with the weight of it. Reluctantly, I step aside to allow her to deal with this idiot in the manner she prefers.

It is her wedding day, after all.

Ella steps closer to the door. Points at it, jabbing her finger at the unusually white paint as she speaks. "This better be good, Kenji, or Warner is going to kill you, and I'm going to help him do it."

And then, just like that—

I'm smiling again.

two.

We're driven back to the Sanctuary the same way we're driven everywhere these days—in a black, all-terrain, bulletproof SUV—but the car and its heavily tinted windows only make us more conspicuous, which I find worrisome. But then, as Castle likes to point out, I have no ready solution for the problem, so we remain at an impasse.

I try to hide my reaction as we drive up through the wooded area just outside the Sanctuary, but I can't help my grimace or the way my body locks down, preparing for a fight. After the fall of The Reestablishment, most rebel groups emerged from hiding to rejoin the world—

But not us.

Just last week we cleared this dirt path for the SUV, enabling it to now get as close as possible to the unmarked entrance, but I'm not sure it's doing much to help. A mob of people has already crowded in so tightly around us that we're moving no more than an inch at a time. Most of them are well-meaning, but they scream and pound at the car with the enthusiasm of a belligerent crowd, and every time we endure this circus I have to physically force myself to remain calm. To sit quietly in my seat and ignore the urge to remove the gun from its holster beneath my jacket.

Difficult.

I know Ella can protect herself—she's proven this fact a thousand times over—but still, I worry. She's become notorious to a near-terrifying degree. To some extent, we all have. But Juliette Ferrars, as she's known around the world, can go nowhere and do nothing without drawing a crowd.

They say they love her.

Even so, we remain cautious. There are still many around the globe who would love to bring back to life the emaciated remains of The Reestablishment, and assassinating a beloved hero would be the most effective start to such a scheme. Though we have unprecedented levels of privacy in the Sanctuary, where Nouria's sight and sound protections around the grounds grant us freedoms we enjoy nowhere else, we've been unable to hide our precise location. People know, generally, where to find us, and that small bit of information has been feeding them for weeks. The civilians wait here—thousands and thousands of them—every single day.

For no more than a glimpse.

We've had to put barricades in place. We've had to hire extra security, recruiting armed soldiers from the local sectors. This area is unrecognizable from what it was a month ago. It's a different world already. And I feel my body go solid as we approach the entrance. Nearly there now.

I look up, ready to say something—

"Don't worry." Kenji locks eyes with me. "Nouria upped the security. There should be a team of people waiting for us."

"I don't know why all this is necessary," Ella says, still staring out the window. "Why can't I just stop for a minute and talk to them?"

"Because the last time you did that you were nearly trampled," Kenji says, exasperated.

"Just the one time."

Kenji's eyes go wide with outrage, and on this point, he and I are in full agreement. I sit back and watch as he counts off on his fingers. "The same day you were nearly trampled, someone tried to cut off your hair. Another day a bunch of people tried to kiss you. People literally throw their newborn babies at you. Plus, I've already counted six people who've peed their pants in your presence, which, I have to add, is not only upsetting, but unsanitary, especially when they try to hug you while they're still wetting themselves." He shakes his head. "The mobs are too big, princess. Too strong. Too passionate. Everyone screams in your face, fights to put their hands on you. And half the time we can't protect you."

"But—"

"I know that most of these people are well-intentioned," I say, taking her hand. She turns in her seat, meets my eyes. "They are, for the most part, kind. Curious. Overwhelmed with gratitude and desperate to put a face to their freedom.

"I know this," I say, "because I always check the crowds, searching their energy for anger or violence. And though the vast majority of them are good"—I sigh, shake my head—"sweetheart, you've just made a lot of enemies. These massive, unfiltered crowds are not safe. Not yet. Maybe not ever."

She takes a deep breath, lets it out slowly. "I know you're right," she says quietly. "But somehow it feels wrong not to be able to talk to the people we've been fighting for. I want them to know how I feel. I want them to know how much we care—and how much we're still planning on doing to rebuild, to get things right."

"You will," I say. "I'll make sure you have the chance to say all those things. But it's only been two weeks, love. And right now we don't have the necessary infrastructure to make that happen."

"But we're working on it, right?"

"We're working on it," Kenji says. "Which, actually— not that I'm making excuses or anything—but if you hadn't asked me to prioritize the reconstruction committee, I probably wouldn't have issued orders to knock down a series of unsafe buildings, one of which included Winston and Alia's studio, which"—he holds up his hands—"for the record, I didn't know was their studio. And again, not that I'm making excuses for my reprehensible behavior or anything—but how the hell was I supposed to know it was an art studio? It was officially listed in the books as unsafe, marked for demolition—"

"They didn't know it was marked for demolition," Ella says, a hint of impatience in her voice. "They made it into their studio precisely because no one was using it."

"Yes," Kenji says, pointing at her. "Right. But, see, I didn't know that."

"Winston and Alia are your friends," I point out unkindly.

"Isn't it your business to know things like that?"

"Listen, man, it's been a really hectic two weeks since the world fell apart, okay? I've been busy."

"We've all been busy."

"Okay, enough," Ella says, holding up a hand. She's looking out the window, frowning. "Someone is coming."

Kent.

"What's Adam doing here?" Ella asks. She turns back to look at Kenji. "Did you know he was coming?"

If Kenji responds, I don't hear him. I'm peering out of the very-tinted windows at the scene outside, watching Adam push his way through the crowd toward the car. He appears to be unarmed. He shouts something into the sea of people, but they won't be quieted right away. A few more tries—and they settle down. Thousands of faces turn to stare at him.

I struggle to make out his words.

And then, slowly, he stands back as ten heavily armed men and women approach our car. Their bodies form a barricade between the vehicle and the entrance into the Sanctuary, and Kenji jumps out first, invisible and leading the way. He projects his power to protect Ella, and I steal his stealth for myself. The three of us—our bodies invisible— move cautiously toward the entrance.

Only once we're on the other side, safely within the boundaries of the Sanctuary, do I finally relax.

A little.

I glance back, the way I always do, at the crowd gathered just beyond the invisible barrier that protects our camp.

Some days I just stand here and study their faces, searching for something. Anything. A threat still unknown, unnamed.

"Hey—awesome," Winston says, his unexpected voice shaking me out of my reverie.

I turn back to look at him, discovering him sweaty and out of breath as he pulls up to us.

"So glad you guys are back," he says, still panting. "Do any of you happen to know anything about fixing pipes? We've got kind of a sewage problem in one of the tents, and it's all hands on deck."

Our return to reality is swift.

And humbling.

But Ella steps forward, already reaching for the—dear God, is it wet?—wrench in Winston's hand, and I almost can't believe it. I wrap an arm around her waist, tugging her back.

"Please, love. Not today. Any other day, maybe. But not today."

"What?" She glances back. "Why not? I'm really good with a wrench. Hey, by the way," she says, turning to the others, "did you know that Ian is secretly really good at woodworking?"

Winston laughs.

"It's only been a secret to you, princess," Kenji says.

She frowns. "Well, we were fixing one of the more savable buildings the other day, and he taught me how to use everything in his toolbox. I helped him repair the roof," she says, beaming.

"That's a strange justification for spending the hours before your wedding digging feces out of a toilet." Kent saunters up to us. He's laughing.

My brother.

So strange.

He's a happier, healthier version of himself than I've ever seen before. He took a week to recover after we got him back here, but when he regained consciousness and we told him what happened—and assured him that James was safe—he fainted.

And didn't wake up for another two days.

He's become an entirely different person in the days since. Practically jubilant. Happy for everyone. A darkness still clings to all of us—will probably cling to all of us forever—

But Adam seems undeniably changed.

"I just wanted to give you guys a heads-up," he says, "that we're doing a new thing now. Nouria wants me to go out there and do a general deactivation before anyone enters or exits the grounds. Just as a precaution." He looks at Ella. "Juliette, is that okay with you?"

Juliette.

So many things changed when we came home, and this was one of them. She took back her name. Reclaimed it. She said that by erasing Juliette from her life she feared she was giving the ghost of my father too much power over her. She realized she didn't want to forget her years as Juliette—or to diminish the young woman she was, fighting against all

448

odds to survive. Juliette Ferrars is who she was when she was made known to the world, and she wants it to remain that way.

I'm the only one allowed to call her Ella now.

It's just for us. A tether to our shared history, a nod to our past, to the love I've always felt for her, no matter her name.

I watch her as she laughs with her friends, as she pulls a hammer free from Winston's tool belt and pretends to hit Kenji with it—no doubt for something he deserves. Lily and Nazeera come out of nowhere, Lily carrying a small bundle of a dog she and Ian saved from an abandoned building nearby. Ella drops the hammer with a sudden cry and Adam jumps back in alarm. She takes the dirty, filthy creature into her arms, smothering it with kisses even as it barks at her with a wild ferocity. And then she turns to look at me, the animal still yipping in her ear, and I realize there are tears in her eyes. She is crying over a dog.

Juliette Ferrars, one of the most feared, most lauded heroes of our known world, is crying over a dog. Perhaps no one else would understand, but I know that this is the first time she's ever held one. Without hesitation, without fear, without danger of causing an innocent creature any harm. For her, this is true joy.

To the world, she is formidable.

To me?

She is the world.

So when she dumps the creature into my reluctant arms, I hold it steady, uncomplaining when the beast licks my face with the same tongue it used, no doubt, to clean its hindquarters. I remain steady, betraying nothing even when warm drool drips down my neck. I hold still as its grimy feet dig into my coat, nails catching at the wool. I am so still, in fact, that eventually the creature quiets, his anxious limbs settling against my chest. He whines as he stares at me, whines until I finally lift a hand, drag it over his head.

When I hear her laugh, I am happy.